GOLDEN
LOTUS

GOLDEN LOTUS

A Saga of Ambition, Murder and Lust in Medieval China

Translated by **CLEMENT EGERTON** & **SHU QINGCHUN**
Introduction by **ROBERT E. HEGEL**

TUTTLE Publishing

Tokyo | Rutland, Vermont | Singapore

Published by Tuttle Publishing, an imprint of Periplus Editions (HK) Ltd.

www.tuttlepublishing.com

Copyright © 2023 by Periplus Editions (HK) Ltd.

Based on the edition first published in 1939 by Routledge & Kegan Paul Ltd. Pinyinized and corrected for this first Tuttle edition.

Library of Congress Cataloging-in-Publication Data

ISBN 978-0-8048-5672-0

Distributed by

North America, Latin America & Europe
Tuttle Publishing
364 Innovation Drive
North Clarendon,
VT 05759 9436, USA
Tel: 1(802) 773 8930
Fax: 1(802) 773 6993
info@tuttlepublishing.com

www.tuttlepublishing.com
Asia Pacific
Berkeley Books Pte Ltd
3 Kallang Sector #04-01
Singapore 349278
Tel: (65) 6741 2178
Fax: (65) 6741 2179
inquiries@periplus.com.sg
www.tuttlepublishing.com

First Tuttle edition
27 26 25 24 23
10 9 8 7 6 5 4 3 2 1   2303VP
Printed in Malaysia

TUTTLE PUBLISHING® is a registered trademark of Tuttle Publishing, a division of Periplus Editions (HK) Ltd.

Contents

General Introduction
by Robert Hegel

For centuries now, the novel in your hands has been denigrated as a "dirty book" (*yinshu*), one that describes, and might encourage the reader's own, illicit behavior. Consequently it has frequently been proscribed, and many editions are expurgated. Yet even before it was completed, perhaps around 1590, leading Chinese writers of the time shared the manuscript among themselves, avidly poring over it, marveling at its rich and nuanced representations of daily life and individual social interactions. They also commented on its intricate structure and its biting indictment of the immorality and cruelty of its age, especially on the part of the leaders of the state. *Golden Lotus* was without precedent in China and was not to be equaled in sophistication in any of these areas for another two centuries.

In contrast to more "sprawling" sagas in other languages and all previous Chinese-language novels, *Golden Lotus* is tightly focused on one household, and for much of its length on two individuals. One is the prominent merchant Ximen Qing, a handsome, well-placed, and fortunate young man; his connections in the imperial government lead to his appointment in the local judicial administration. But unlike the other Chinese novels of the time that narrate great military campaigns and the far-ranging adventures of outlaws, this text focuses on Ximen's private life: his parents are dead, leaving him with a substantial inheritance and no one to rein in his excessive self-indulgence. Much of the novel takes place within his extensive household, at the center of which is his beautiful fifth wife, Pan Jinlian (literally, "Golden Lotus"). Initially, she had been the helpless plaything of older men. But after her seduction by Ximen Qing she becomes insatiable in her desire to exert control over her husband and, through him, the entire household. Jinlian's primary weapon in this struggle is simply sex: she employs any and all activities to monopolize his desire. *Golden Lotus* reveals the inner politics of this wealthy family, particularly the machinations of Jinlian and others as she claws her way to a position of dominance. The intertwined lives of these two central characters bring out their brutality in their incessant concern for momentary pleasure; both are heedlessly self-destructive, and that tendency brings about the ultimate collapse of the entire household. Throughout this process, parallels between events within the Ximen household and the attitudes and activities of the emperors of the time suggest a scathing condemnation of petty self-indulgence on the part of Ming imperial house.

Approaches to the Novel

Jin Ping Mei cihua, its original title, combines elements from the names of three female protagonists: Pan *Jin*lian ("Golden Lotus"), Li *Ping*'er ("Vase"), and Hua Chun*mei* ("Spring Plum"), to read "The Plum in the Golden Vase, a ballad tale." The title provides rich clues to its meaning. Although its final element celebrates the inclusion of large numbers of poems and songs, the novel is primarily about characters, not just these three but dozens of others as well, and about their complex interactions as each makes his or her way through life always on the lookout for personal advantage. From the perspective of the seventeenth-century critic Zhang Zhupo (1670–1698), placing beautiful "flowers" (women) in elegant surroundings allows them to be appreciated properly by the refined reader. Yet the title would seem to refer to an anonymous earlier poem suggesting that when these most beautiful flowers are placed in an elegant vase, the aesthetic elements clash with each other, and the combined effect cheapens both the blossoms and their receptacle. From its very title, the novel suggests ambiguity and calls for the reader's engagement in interpreting its various meanings, ranging from the elegant to the decidedly vulgar.[1] Thus from the outset the perceptive reader is warned to be aware of multiple levels of signification.

The novel is justly famous for two very conspicuous elements: its detailed characterization and its frequent narrations of sexual encounters. The denizens of the Ximen house and his contacts outside are realized primarily through extensive dialogue; the novelist creates a multiplicity of voices, dialects, and social registers to suggest the texture of contemporary society. Pan Jinlian seems to mimic the language of popular romantic songs, even though their plaintive lyrics contrast sharply with her often cold-blooded plots against her rivals. Ximen Qing adopts the language of official documents when communicating with his prospective patrons.[2] Efforts to identify the native place of the author through these voices and that of the narrator have been unconvincing; the novelist was simply a

---

1. Roy, *Plum*, Vol. 1, p. xvii. The conventional epithet for the tiny bound foot, *sancun jinlian*, "three inch golden lotus," makes Jinlian's name itself into an erotic image; "vase," too, appears in erotic descriptions.
2. Shang, "*Jin Ping Mei* and Late Ming Print Culture," pp. 201–02.

master of many voices.[3]

Chinese editions regularly delete portions of the novel's numerous scenes of sexual activity, considering these frank descriptions a liability appropriately kept away from the delicate eyes of a susceptible reading audience. Few editions preserve the entire text as it was first printed in 1618. The present translation, its first complete rendition in English, deletes much of the original poetry and yet it retains all of these problematic scenes. However, they were put under wraps. Even though many are comprised of flowery phrases in the original, the translator initially (1939) rendered selected terms and phrases into Latin. A subsequent edition (1972) translated the Latin passages into an English that is often more anatomically correct than the original, as they appear in this version. Yet when one counts up the passages Egerton found offensive, or those deleted from even the most heavily bowdlerized Chinese editions, we find the novel to have been only slightly diminished: for all its notoriety, only a very small portion of this complex narrative—some fraction of one percent of the total text—is devoted to describing sex. Instead, the bulk records the speech and recounts the more mundane daily activities of its many characters. This does not make the narrative any less troubling to read, however; its view of humanity is generally far from positive.

As early readers clearly perceived, the text is structured with mathematical precision. The novel is a hundred chapters in length, with a pivotal scene in Chapter 49. Up until that point, and apparently slightly thereafter, Ximen Qing's fortunes are on the rise: he grows in wealth, prominence, and power. The novel's second half narrates his decline: he is overextended financially and socially and physically depleted. The first twenty chapters introduce the novel's main characters; they are mirrored by Chapters 80 to 100 in which they scatter after Ximen Qing's death in Chapter 79. Scenes set in cold places are balanced by those set in hot locales; frigid comments occur in hot places, and heated encounters happen where it is cool. In terms of their narrative flow, chapters occur in groups of ten throughout the work: decades generally reach an emotional peak in the fifth chapter with a narrative twist in the seventh, while a dramatic climax is reached in the ninth. This is a major reason the novel was so celebrated: close reading reveals that it was meticulously constructed by a highly self-conscious—and remarkably innovative—author.[4]

The Golden Lotus is considered the first single-authored novel in the Chinese tradition. To a great extent, this is true. However, a substantial

3. Roy, *Plum*, Vol. 1, pp. xxiii, 451n30.
4. See Roy, *Plum*, vol. 1, pp. xxxiii, xxxv; Plaks, *Four Masterworks*, pp. 72-82.

portion of the early chapters was borrowed from an earlier novel, a short story and other prose texts; likewise, hundreds of popular songs, common sayings, and current jokes have been adapted here. Yet each earlier text is woven into the fabric of the novel so skillfully that they do not necessarily stand out to later readers. Recognizing popular stories and songs that would have delighted the novel's original readers is a pleasure now lost to us; only a few of these adapted texts are visible in this translation. Critics from the seventeenth century onward have complained that readers tend to overlook what was an ongoing and very complicated literary game successfully crafted to impress and enthrall the author's highly educated contemporaries—with whom the critics identify. The novelist's endless sampling of texts from contemporary culture does contribute a degree of choppiness in his style, as translators and some critics have noted. Even so, generations of readers have found the novel gripping, its characters mesmerizing in their tragic vulnerability even as they treat others with callous lack of concern or even cruelty.

At the most obvious level, the novelist demands that his readers understand his essential message: the inevitable consequences of self-indulgence, particularly in the four vices of drunkenness, lust, greed, and anger, are suffering and ultimate destruction. In this he offers the "counsel" that Walter Benjamin saw in all stories.[5] The novel offers glimmers of hope of release through Buddhist salvation, but even these are compromised by contradictory versions of the role of Ximen's posthumous son in his father's ultimate salvation, for example. Some critics consider such indeterminate interpretations to be evidence of sloppy editing on the part of the novelist;[6] I see them as his means of throwing into question any quick and easy escape from the consequences of one's actions or the pervasive venality of his age.

The historical setting of the novel is itself ominous. As the first chapter tells us, the fictitious Ximen Qing lived during the reign of the Emperor Huizong (r. 1101–1126) of the Song Empire (968–1279). This monarch was an accomplished painter and calligrapher; his work can be found in major museum collections around the world. But he was a far better artist than he was administrator; during his reign bandits pillaged widely, in numbers far beyond the ability of his imperial armies to control. Moreover, growing tensions along the northern frontier erupted into a fullscale invasion by the Jurchens, a nomadic people who had established

---

5. Walter Benjamin, "The Storyteller," in *Illuminations,* ed. Hannah Arendt, Harry Zohn trans (New York: Schocken Books, 1969), p. 86.
6. See Hsia, *Classic Chinese Novel*, pp. 164–202, esp. 170–73.

a sedentary empire of their own in 1114, the Jin. Song imperial guards were no match for their disciplined and dedicated forces. Huizong and his successor, the Song emperor Qinzong, were taken captive in 1127 and eventually died of exposure and disease after long periods of detention in the north by the Jin. As a consequence of that military disaster, the Song Empire hastily moved its capital south to the modern city of Hangzhou; there the Southern Song persisted until the Mongol conquest brought the dynasty to an end in 1279.

The novel regularly refers to six major villains at the imperial court; these are historical ministers who garnered great wealth and power for themselves at the expense of their talented but ineffective liege. Ximen Qing wins his position in the local judiciary by currying favor with their ringleader, Cai Jing (1046–1126): he uses major portions of the wealth brought by his marriage to sixth wife, Li Ping'er, to secure lavish birthday presents for Cai—who was later impeached by the censor Yuwen Xu-zhong, (1079–1146). By setting the novel at this particular juncture, the novelist casts a pall over the heedless merriment of Ximen and his fellows, rendering all his activities even more frivolous in the face of the looming cataclysm. Not surprisingly, the novel was produced at a time (ca. 1590) when central power in the Ming Empire (1368–1644) was at the mercy of similar strongmen in the position of central ministers; late Ming rulers were among the least competent in Chinese history. The novel was first printed during the decades when the throne was in thrall of the ruthless eunuch Wei Zhongxian (1568–1627) and the gang of bureaucrats at his bidding. Its unmistakable resonances between the fall of the Northern Song and contemporary events imbue the novel with an air of prophecy— about the potential in the author's own time for another disaster similar to what befell the Song. That did come to pass before long, of course. Banditry rose and spread during the last decades of the Ming, to become so powerful that one of the major rebels captured Beijing in 1644, driving the last Ming emperor to kill his wife and daughters and then to hang himself on the hill just north of the Forbidden City, the present Imperial Palace Museum. This act provided the necessary rationalization for the Manchus—who saw themselves as successors of the Jin—to invade and overrun the Ming in order to restore social order. They rapidly succeeded; their empire, the Qing ("Pure"), lasted until 1911.[7]

---

7. For a succinct history of the period during which the novel was produced and initially circulat-ed, see Mote, *Imperial China*. David Roy discusses these historical references very persuasively in his introduction to *Plum*, vol. 1, pp. xxix–xxxvi. For biographical sketches of the Jiajing and Wanli Emperors of the Ming, see *Dictionary of Ming Biography*, pp. 315, 325.

The Literary Context for the Novel

The Golden Lotus appeared toward the end of the century that witnessed the birth of both the novel and the short story in vernacular Chinese. Before then, and indeed until the twentieth century, Chinese narratives had generally been written in the classical literary style. Ultimately derived from a written version of the language spoken during the time of the great philosophers Confucius (Kong Zhongni, 551–479 BCE) and Mencius (Meng Ke, 371–289? BCE), the succinct ancient style was the vehicle for philosophy, history, and especially poetry—the major form in the Chinese literary tradition. Despite its generally didactic function, narrative was often considered more utilitarian than artistic, and could be written with less formality as a consequence—in contrast to refined classical prose essays that often incorporated the arts of the poet. Writing in the vernacular, especially when it imitated the verbal art of the professional storyteller, seemingly took this educational function seriously as it focused on the mistakes and crimes committed by people at all levels of society. However, the vernacular literature of late imperial China demonstrates the authors' uses of these new forms to develop the art of writing.

The earliest novel in Chinese was *Sanguo zhi tongsu yanyi,* "A Popular Elaboration on *The Chronicles of the Three Kingdoms,*" commonly referred to in English as *The Romance of the Three Kingdoms.* Its first imprint was dated 1522, although one preface bears the date 1494, suggesting that it was completed two decades earlier. By tradition it has been attributed to a fourteenth-century playwright named Luo Guanzhong, but there is no evidence to suggest that the text is anywhere that old. Starting around 1550 there appeared a virtually unbroken series of fictionalized histories of the individual empires that occupied portions of the Chinese landmass of today; most of these texts were dreary adaptations and rewordings of historical chronicles demonstrating little sense of how to develop a good story. By contrast, a second novel, the *Shuihu zhuan* (known in English as The Water Margin or, more recently, *Outlaws of the Marsh*) relates the adventures of 108 bandits whose individual exploits and misadventures draw them together as an ever-growing rebel band in a Shandong mountain fastness called Liangshan. The product of many hands, this novel circulated in versions of dissimilar lengths; it was "finalized" to a degree by the seventeenth-century editor Jin Shengtan (1608–1661) whose annotated seventy-chapter version has been the standard ever since. Late in the sixteenth century two other major novels appeared, The *Golden Lotus* and *Xiyou ji* (Journey to the West). *Journey* relates the adventures of a timid cleric based on the historical monk Xuanzang (600–661) who traveled from Chang'an, the capital of the Tang Empire, through various

Central Asian kingdoms to India to obtain Buddhist scriptures. On this fictional pilgrimage he rides a horse that is really a transformed dragon and is guarded by a pig monster, a man-eating ogre known as Sand, and the Monkey King. For his wit and mischief, along with his physical and mental prowess, the Monkey becomes the novel's central character. Together these works have been termed the "Four Masterworks," *si da qishu*, in the Ming novel form. All are now available in fine English translations.

Due to their heavy debts to earlier texts, the other three novels should be considered compilations and adaptations, rather than the creative writing of single authors. *Three Kingdoms* makes this clear from its title: it refers to the earliest survey of the turbulent third century compiled by historian Chen Shou around the year 280. Its proximate source was one of the proto-novels known as *pinghua* ("plain tales") printed in the 1320s. By contrast, *Outlaws of the Marsh* drew upon a fertile tradition of oral and theatrical narratives about this heroic bandit troupe who ultimately come together to struggle against the evil ministers at court who are misleading their ruler—Emperor Huizong of the Song. They nominally retain their loyalty to the throne nonetheless. *Journey to the West* rewrites a broad range of plays, shorter vernacular tales, and historical accounts about the great Tang pilgrim to create a original composition that ultimately imitates the narrative structure of an esoteric Buddhist scripture. All three are essentially collective works that have been edited by one or more writers into their present forms. Although its multifaceted reliance on earlier texts is unmistakable, *Golden Lotus* represents a major step in the direction of originality.[8]

The best known textual source for *Golden Lotus* is, of course, *Outlaws of the Marsh*. There Wu Song is a stalwart hero, known, as are many of the others, for righting wrongs on behalf of the powerless. One is his misshapen brother, a dwarf whose attractive wife Pan Jinlian falls for the rake Ximen Qing and kills her husband to get him out of their way. Virtually all Chinese readers would have been familiar with the earlier novel and this episode in particular because of its long and detailed seduction scene—and for the equally detailed scene in which Wu Song kills a tiger with his bare hands. By building on that tale, *Golden Lotus* draws attention to the stark contrast between Ximen Qing's urban world of sex and commerce and the marginal realm of "rivers and lakes" (*jianghu*) inhabited by Wu Song and the other heroic outlaws; the adapted material merely sets the stage for a new location and far more developed characterization in *Golden Lotus*. Wu Song's revenge for his brother's murder comes swiftly in the parent novel;

---

8. For brief surveys of the history of the Chinese novel, see Hegel, "Chinese Novel," and Idema and Haft, *Guide to Chinese Literature*, pp. 198–211, 219–30. An extensive study of these four major novels as a group is Plaks, *Four Masterworks*.

by contrast, in *Golden Lotus* he is exiled for most of the text, returning only at the end to wreak bloody vengeance on Jinlian after Ximen's death.[9]

While the other early vernacular novels regularly narrate the violence of individual combat but avoid all explicit descriptions of sexual activity, *Golden Lotus* draws on a then-current fashion for erotic novellas in the classical language for many of its scenes. Of the fewer than twenty of these medium-length compositions still extant, all deal with the sexual exploits of one young scholar and many, many women. One has thirty wives by the end of the tale; others have fewer formal wives but more wide-ranging conquests among the other women their tireless heroes meet. Most detail sexual activity in the flowery language found in this novel as well.[10] By adapting this tradition of mindless titillation into serious vernacular fiction, the novelist has in effect harshly parodied a fashionable trend in reading of his day.

Golden Lotus appeared just as the vernacular short story in Chinese was developing. Around 1550 the eminent Hangzhou publisher Hong Pian edited a collection of sixty of these tales. They circulated in six collections of ten stories each; only twenty-seven of the total survive today, having been driven off the market by the success in the 1620s of more refined stories edited by Feng Menglong, a scholar who produced three collections of forty stories each before finally becoming a local administrator. Some of these were his original adaptations of earlier tales; many reflect older turns of phrase and thematic concerns. A number dating from around the middle of the Ming narrate the misadventures of merchants. Patrick Hanan has aptly described this theme as "folly and consequences." Here, again, our anonymous novelist developed this fairly commonplace idea from the short story form into the central motif of his novel.[11] In essence, *Golden Lotus* narrates the terrible consequences of excessive desire in its multiple forms.

Adaptation in *Golden Lotus* involves the use of earlier narrative material in new and original ways. Instead of simply copying both the text and the thematic content of pre-existing fiction, songs, jokes, and the like, our unidentified novelist carefully fitted each piece into his own overarching theme, adapting every one to suit his larger narrative project. He signaled this practice by following the conventions of presentation in the printed versions of these materials.[12] It is tempting to imagine that the novelist

---

9. See Hanan, "Sources of the *Chin P'ing Mei*." For a translation of *Shuihu zhuan*, see Sidney Shapiro, trans., *Outlaws of the Marsh* (Beijing: Foreign Languages Press, 1981), where the Wu Song-Pan Jinlian episode takes up chapters 23–27.

10. The first detailed study of this genre in English is R. G. Wang's *Genre, Consumption, and Religiosity*.

11. See Hanan, *Chinese Short Story*, pp. 133–51; see also his *Chinese Vernacular Story*, pp. 54–74.

12. See Shang, "*Jin Ping Mei* and Late Ming Print Culture."

simply wrote out of his own personal collection of popular literature. Although large private libraries were not uncommon among the learned who could afford them, to have a large collection of these ephemera was only possible because of the rapid development of printing during the Ming period: a broad range of printed texts would have been available at that time for a relatively modest investment.[13]

About the Edition Translated Here

Golden Lotus apparently was written during the early years of the Wanli era (1573–1620) of the Ming Empire, late in the sixteenth century. Several prominent scholars of the day commented on it as it circulated in manuscript around 1605;[14] its earliest extant printed edition, entitled *Jin Ping Mei cihua* ("Ballad Tale of ..."), is dated 1618. A second version, impoverished in style by some critical estimates, was produced somewhat later, during the Chongzhen reign period (1628–1644); it deletes a number of the poems from the older edition and other wording throughout to shorten the text somewhat. The Chongzhen edition was the only one available for centuries; this is the version translated here.[15] The earlier *cihua* edition was considered lost until 1932, when a copy was discovered in Shanxi and was purchased by the Beijing National Library. The Chongzhen edition also formed the basis for the most heavily annotated version, produced early in the Qing period by Zhang Zhupo (1670–1698); Zhang also wrote extensive prefatory notes pointing out the novel's artistic features. His preface is dated 1695.[16] Until David Roy began his monumental five-volume complete translation of *Jin Ping Mei cihua*, there were only Japanese and French renditions of the older and fuller version. The versions also vary in what comes first: the Chongzhen edition begins with Ximen Qing's oaths of brotherhood with his party-loving cronies, laying the emphasis from its first page on the protagonist's excessive indulgence. The older *cihua* edition first traces Wu Song's rise to prominence by kill-

---

13. A number of important studies of the developing print culture in late imperial China have appeared in recent years; for a review, see Brokaw, "On the History of the Book."

14. They include poet and critic Yuan Hongdao (1568–1610) and his brother Yuan Zhongdao (1570–1624), dramatist Tang Xianzu (1550–1617), and painter Dong Qichang (1555–1636). Tang has been identified as one possible author for *Golden Lotus*; see Roy, *Plum*, vol. 1, pp. xliii.

15. Egerton omitted most of the remaining poems, translating the few remaining into a generally very wordy style of English. The Chongzhen and later versions omit *cihua* from the title; presumably that term referred to the large number of popular songs incorporated into the original text but deleted subsequently.

16. See Roy, *Plum in the Golden Vase*, Vol. 1, pp. xvii–xlviii, esp. pp. xx–xxi. The first major study of these questions in English is Hanan, "Text of the *Chin P'ing Mei*." For a translation of Zhang's lengthy critical introduction to his edition, see Chang, "How to Read," pp. 196–243.

ing a tiger with his bare hands; this episode leads, elliptically, to an intro-duction of his stunted brother, the latter's wife Pan Jinlian, her affair with Ximen Qing, and then to life in the merchant house. Chapters 53–57 in both versions seem to have been written by yet another author, perhaps because that portion of the manuscript had been lost while being circu-lated among the small circle of its initial readers before it was completed.[17]

About the Author

As with the three other "masterworks" of the Ming novel, *Golden Lotus* was produced anonymously, using an untraceable pseudonym. In fact, the idea of individual authorship of vernacular fiction in Chinese only developed during the seventeenth century. Before then (and afterward as well) writers freely adapted and improved on earlier texts with no apparent concern for either originality or proprietary control over what they had written—even of the loose sort writers held for their poetry and essays. That is, writing lines parallel to, alluding to, or even quoting from earlier texts was not only acceptable, it was a common practice. By doing so a poet demonstrated his ability to appreciate an earlier writer by locating himself emotionally and intellectually in the same place as his predecessor; this practice was intended to expand the scope and significance of his own composition by generalizing, even universalizing, an individual's personal experience and insights.

Earlier novels, even the "masterworks," recast older material from the oral, theatrical, or print traditions, quoting or paraphrasing while writing new portions to create a unique compilation. Most authors did not derive income from publishing their novels directly, as far as can be known; most texts circulated in manuscript among limited circles of the elite, often the novelist's friends and acquaintances. In addition to the segment adapted from *Shuihu zhuan* which every reader would immediately recognize, this novelist incorporated dozens of songs, jokes, stories, and anecdotes then in circulation, and innumerable passing references to other narratives. Shang Wei has argued successfully that the novel could only have been written by a man who had access to hundreds of written texts, perhaps a collector of ephemera as suggested above.[18] But all *Golden Lotus* sources were sub-stantially modified to fit one overriding vision of the decline and fall of virtually all of his characters.[19]

---

17. Hanan, "Text of the *Chin P'ing Mei*." Given the time required to copy a lengthy text by hand, there were generally only one or two manuscript copies of an unprinted or unfinished novel available at any given time, making the loss of pages or even whole chapters not uncommon.
18. Shang, "*Jin Ping Mei* and Late Ming Print Culture."
19. See Hanan, "Sources of *Chin P'ing Mei*."

For that reason, *Golden Lotus* is the first substantially single-authored novel in Chinese, despite its reliance on other sources: the artistic vision is clear, consistent, individual, and unprecedented in its focus. Whoever he was, this novelist possessed keen insights into human weaknesses, had a broad knowledge of society, and felt considerable political outrage. He is usually identified with the prefacer of the first edition, "Lanling Xiaoxiao sheng," the "Scoffing Scholar of Lanling." Lanling is the old name for a place in Shandong province, as is the supposed setting for the novel, Qinghe County. And yet attempts to find Shandong dialectal expressions in the novel have not been particularly successful. American scholar David Roy uses these facts to bolster his argument that the novelist based his social critique on the teachings of the pessimistic Confucian philosopher Xun Qing (312?–240? BCE)—who held office in a place called Lanling and was later buried there. Roy argues that the philosopher's argument about human nature—that it is basically selfish and needs the discipline provided by proper ritual behavior in order to reform it—is amply exemplified in *Golden Lotus*.[20] Moreover, Master Xun's contention that leaders must serve as strong moral exemplars lies behind the novel's castigation of Ximen Qing, of the Song Emperor Huizong, and, by implication, the Ming Jiajing and Wanli emperors as well. Chinese scholar Wu Xiaoling also demonstrates that the nominal setting for the novel, the city called Qinghe ("Clear River," in practice an epithet of praise for the emperor's sagacity), has many features unique to the Ming imperial capital, Beijing.[21] Here again as with so many elements in the novel, the Shandong location is an ironic reference to the novelist's here and now, by implication the capital of a realm doomed by moral weaknesses to suffer a disastrous end.

About the Translator

Frederick Clement Christie Egerton was born around 1890, the son of an English country pastor. In 1910 he published a book of church music and the following year was consecrated as a bishop of the Anglican Church, an *episcopus vagans* of the Matthew Succession, a highly controversial move at that time. This heresy led a church scholar to remark that Egerton subsequently was "reconciled with the Holy See, became a soldier and performed no ministerial functions."[22]

---

20. See Roy, *Plum*, vol. 1, pp. xxiii–vii, xxix–xxxii, for his argument about the novel's moralistic perspective.

21. Wu Xiaoling, "*Jing Ping Mei cihua* li de Qinghe ji yi Jiajing shiqi de Beijing wei moxing chutan," *Zhongwai wenxue* 18.2 (1989), 107–22; cited in Roy, *Plum*, vol. 1," pp. xxxvi, 453n64.

22. Henry R. T. Brandreth, *Episcopi Vagantes and the Anglican Church* (London: Society for Promoting Christian Knowledge, 1947), pp. 16, 22n8.

During the Great War Egerton served in the British Army, where he rose to the rank of Lieutenant Colonel. After a divorce from his first wife—with whom he had run away when she was quite young and with whom he had four children—in 1923 he married Katherine Aspinwall Hodge (b. 1896) from New York; later she would work as a secretary at the American Consulate in London.[23] The couple had no children. During the 1920s he visited Japan and later commented on the beauty of Mount Fuji. Apparently he began his study of Chinese soon after returning from East Asia.

After the war Egerton's profession was listed as "editor." He was a skilled and prolific writer of broad experience and interests. From his early dedication to religion, Egerton turned to education, and then two decades later he published his translation of *Golden Lotus*. About the same time his highly detailed travelogue appeared, *African Majesty: A Record of Refuge at the Court of the King of Bangangté in the French Cameroons* (1938). This was followed by a short political treatise, *Reaction, Revolution, or Rebirth,* and in the 1940s by his biography of the right-wing Catholic prime minister of Portugal, António de Oliveira Salazar. He published two more books on Angola in the 1950s, presumably in favor of Salazar's policies toward Portugal's African colonies; Egerton had been highly favorable of the French colonial administration of the Cameroons in the 1930s.

In *African Majesty* Egerton described himself in his forties as "a fattish, bespectacled, middle-aged, would-be slightly cynical publisher" (p. xvii) who was largely bald (p. 189) and who resided on Lime Street in London, presumably near the Leadenhall Market. He had taken part in seminars offered at the London University School of Economics by the widely influential pioneer in that field, the Polish anthropologist Bronislaw Malinowski (1884–1942) (p. 4). He was also "very fond" of reading travel books, and yet he had little patience for "travelers" who seldom left their comfortable carriages to engage with the people they purported to be describing. His travel diaries demonstrate far more contact with local people.

Egerton's anthropological interests in learning more about the differences among human cultures is what drew him to West Africa (xvii) and to other subsequent adventures. It may also have informed his tackling *Golden Lotus* as a novel of social behavior. Although he was a prolific photographer who took innumerable still photos and even motion pictures while on his journeys, he admitted that he lacked the technical skills to keep his cameras functioning (p. 260). Egerton likewise acknowledged about his first African expedition,

---

23. Class of 1879 Hartford Public High School (http://www.ctgenweb.org/county/cohartford/files/misc/hphs.txt), accessed July 10, 2010.

I was very eager to find out, so far as I could, the attitude of the Ban-gangté people to what we call the problem of sex. We, ourselves, seem to have gone more wrong on sex than on anything else, and that is saying a great deal. It absorbs our energies out of all measure. It permeates every department of our lives. It arouses the bitterest controversies. It is the most popular form of amusement. It saturates our art and literature. It fills our gaols; it lurks in the background of most of our murders and suicides. Even the advertisers who try to sell us motor-cars or cigarettes endeavor to do so by appealing to our sex interest. When all other top-ics of conversation fail, there is always sex to fall back upon. And, most amazingly, we conventionally behave like ostriches and keep up a polite pretence that sex is not really important or, if it is important, it is too disgusting to be mentioned in decent society. With all this atmosphere behind me, I cannot pretend to be uninterested, or even purely scien-tifically interested, in the matter of sex. (p. 296)

From this perspective, a consuming interest in *Golden Lous* would seem perfectly natural for Clement Egerton.[24]

Egerton's work on the novel began soon after his second marriage. Short on cash and dependent on his new wife's meager income, Egerton suggested sharing an apartment with a friend he had made at London University, the man he referred to as C. C. Shu (Shu Qingchun, 1899–1966)—who was soon to become famous among Chinese readers as the Beijing novelist Lao She. At that time Shu was a lecturer in Chinese at the School of Oriental Studies, where he taught from 1924 to 1929; they agreed that he should pay the rent while Egerton and his wife provided food for the three of them. He and Egerton also exchanged language les-sons for their mutual benefit.

Although in his 1936 essay "My Several Landlords" ("Wode jige fang-dong") Lao She says that they lived together for three years, 1924 to 1926, he never mentioned their collaborative work on *Golden Lotus,* although he did admit that he read fiction avidly as a means to develop his own En-glish reading skills. Undoubtedly he encouraged Egerton to do the same for Chinese.[25] Shu was extremely productive himself, however; in addition

---

24. For a photograph of Egerton in the mid 1930s, see his *African Majesty*, Plate 121, "Saying Good-bye" to King N'jiké (facing p. 329); Egerton is wearing a pith helmet along with tie, white shirt, sweater, jacket, and glasses; his face is in profile.

25. Lao She, "Wode jige fangdong," http://www.eduzhai.net/wenxue/xdmj/laoshe/zw14/048.htm. For a photograph of Lao She during those years, perhaps taken in the apartment shared with the Egertons, see: http://baike.baidu.com/image/718e25c7a0f8959dd0006023 (both sites accessed August 16, 2010). For Shu's references to reading English fiction as language learning material, see Zhang Guixing, ed., *Lao She nianpu* (Shanghai: Shanghai Wenyi, 1997), vol. 1, p. 43.

to his teaching duties, during those years he completed two Dickensian novels in Chinese, *Old Zhang's Philosophy* (*Lao Zhang de zhexue*, 1926), and *Master Zhao Says* (*Zhao zi yue*, published 1928), and then his humorous and sensitive study of cultural differences, *Ma and Son* (*Er Ma*, also published 1928).

Many decades later and without citing his sources, martial arts film maker King Hu (Hu Jinquan) commented that the *Golden Lotus* translation was the product of close collaboration between the two men, and surely it must have been.[26] Egerton had begun to study Chinese in London not long before he and Lao She met. Lao She notes that Egerton finally landed a job just as he was moving out in 1926; whether Egerton continued his study of Chinese thereafter is not clear. Given the complexity of the various voices and the innumerable contemporary references in *Jin Ping Mei*, it is highly unlikely that a foreigner could translate the text after only a few years of language study, even for a gifted language learner (Egerton reportedly was able to read Latin, Greek, German, and French). It seems much more likely that as his Chinese tutor Shu might have provided a rough translation, which Egerton then spent years polishing into its present form. Ironically, Egerton complains that the novel's style was "telegraphese," more likely a characteristic of Lao She's imperfect English than an attribute of the Ming novelist writing in his own language.[27] But Egerton had a fine sense of English style, which is clearly visible in the resultant translation. For his part, even though he praised *Jin Ping Mei* as "one of the greatest Chinese works of fiction" and considered its author "very serious" in his intent, Lao She never acknowledged his role in this translation project. Perhaps he was embarrassed—not by its morally objectionable content as many have claimed, but by the linguistic mistakes he may have inadvertently introduced there.[28] Lao She need not have worried; generations of readers have found very few problems in this

26. Hu Jinquan, *Lao She he ta de zuopin* (Hong Kong: Wenhua Shenghuo, 1977), pp. 32–36, translated as "Lao She in England," pp. 46–47. In his 1939 preface to *The Golden Lotus*, Egerton notes that he had begun the translation fifteen years before and that he had spent many years polishing it with advice from various scholars, apparently after Lao She was no longer working on the project. I am grateful to Dr. Rüdiger Breuer for his unstinting assistance in locating sources of information about Lao She's activities in England.

27. This supposition seems to be confirmed by a comment made by Lionel Giles in his 1940 review of *Golden Lotus*. There he finds Egerton mistranslating *zhuli* as "bamboo fans" when instead it means literally "bamboo fence" (introductory poem to Chapter 79). The characters for "fans" (*shan*) and "fence" (*li*) look nothing alike, but a Chinese learner of English might well pronounce the two similarly.

28. See Hu, "Lao She in England." For Lao She's comments on the novel: *Zhongguo xiandai wenxue yanjiu congkan* 1986, no. 3, quoted in Li Zhenjie, *Lao She zai Lundun* (Beijing: Guoji wenhua, 1992), p. 13.

Golden Lotus translation. His efforts have surely contributed to a far more widespread appreciation of the Chinese novel of the late imperial period.

Egerton's translation of *Jin Ping Mei* has undergone 25 editions since its first appearance in 1939. The first major alteration came in 1972 when Routledge published an edition in which Egerton's Latin passages (inadvertently except one) had been rendered into English (that overlooked line has been translated from the Chinese for this edition); recently an abridgement has appeared (Rockville, MD: Silk Pagoda Press, 2008). *Golden Lotus* has been published in London, New York, Singapore, Tokyo, and, in 2008, by Renmin wenxue (People's Literature Press) in Beijing. The online bibliographical source *WorldCat* lists 366 separate printings to be found in participating libraries around the globe. It is my hope that this updated edition extends its life to reach yet another generation or two of readers.

About This Edition

Until around 1980, the dominant scheme for representing the standard pronunciation of Chinese was the Wade-Giles Romanization system, named after a missionary and a scholar, both British, of the late nineteenth century. But with the death of Mao and China's reemergence on the world stage, the Romanization system authorized by the People's Republic government and adopted by the United Nations has become the standard for Chinese language textbooks and, increasingly, for scholarly writings in Western languages. This edition has been reset in this international system, designated Hanyu pinyin, to make it easier for new generations of readers to equate the names given here with what they have read in other sources. Most of the secondary works in the bibliography that follows still use the Wade-Giles system, rendering the novel's original title as Chin P'ing Mei tz'u-hua.

Through the nineteenth and the first half of the twentieth century, English translators of Chinese fiction regularly Romanized the names of male characters while translating the names of all women and girls, ostensibly to make identification easier for readers unfamiliar with Chinese transliterations. Egerton followed this practice in his 1939 edition. But literal translations often produced odd or confusing renditions; two different names in Chinese could well turn out looking very similar in English. To avoid such confusion (and to avoid the sexist overtones of treating male names differently from women's names), this edition renders all names in the modern standard *pinyin* and provides a character finding list, as did Egerton's original, in the hope that this facilitates following each of them through the various chapters in which they appear. The work of Romanizing all names was ably carried out by Dr. Rumyana Cholakova. I am extremely grateful for her care and thoroughness in editing; through this process she also discovered and corrected occasional misidentifications of minor characters in Egerton's translation. I have corrected several other small errors here, including those pointed out by Lionel Giles in his 1940 review of the first edition.

Useful Sources in English

Brokaw, Cynthia. "On the History of the Book in China." In *Printing and Book Culture in Late Imperial China*, ed. Cynthia J. Brokaw and Kai-wing Chow (Berkeley: University of California Press, 2005), pp. 3–54.

Carlitz, Katherine. *The Rhetoric of Chin P'ing Mei*. Bloomington: Indiana University Press, 1986.

Chang Chu-p'o [Zhang Zhupo]. "How to Read the *Chin P'ing Mei*." Trans. David T. Roy, in David L. Rolston, ed., *How to Read the Chinese Novel* (Princeton, NJ: Princeton University Press, 1990), Chapter 4, pp. 196–243.

Dictionary of Ming Biography. Ed. L. Carrington Goodrich and Chaoying Fang. 2 vols. New York: Columbia University Press, 1976.

Egerton, Clement C. *African Majesty: A Record of Refuge at the court of the King of Bangangté in the French Cameroons*. London: G. Routledge & Sons, 1938.

Egerton, Clement C., trans. *The Golden Lotus: A Translation, from the Chinese Original, of the Novel, Chin P'ing Mei*. 4 vols. London: G. Routledge, 1939.

Giles, Lionel. Review of: *Golden Lotus*. In *Journal of the Royal Asiatic Society of Great Britain and Ireland* 3 (1940), 368–71.

Hanan, Patrick D. *The Chinese Short Story: Studies in Dating, Authorship, and Composition*. Cambridge, Mass.: Harvard University Press, 1974.

_____. *The Chinese Vernacular Story*. Cambridge, Mass.: Harvard University Press, 1981.

_____. "Sources of the *Chin P'ing Mei*." *Asia Major*, n. s. 10.1 (1963), 23–67.

_____. "The Text of the *Chin P'ing Mei*." *Asia Major*, n. s. 9.1 (1962), 1–57.

Hegel, Robert E. "The Chinese Novel: Beginnings to Twentieth Century." In *Encyclopedia of the Novel*, ed. Paul Schellinger (Chicago: Fitzroy Dearborn, 1998), Vol. 1, pp. 205–11.

Hsia, C. T. *The Classic Chinese Novel: A Critical Introduction*. New York: Columbia University Press, 1968. Esp. Chapter 5, pp. 165–202.

Hu, Jinquan [King Hu]. "Lao She in England." Trans. Cecilia Y.L. Tsim, *Renditions* 10 (1978), 46–51.

Idema, Wilt L., and Lloyd Haft. *A Guide to Chinese Literature*. Ann Arbor: University of Michigan Center for Chinese Studies, 1997.

Martinson, Paul V. "The *Chin P'ing Mei* as Wisdom Literature: A Methodological Essay." *Ming Studies* 5 (1977), 44–56.

Mote, F. W. *Imperial China 900–1800*. Cambridge and London: Harvard University Press, 1999. Esp. Chapter 29, "The Lively Society of the Late Ming," pp. 743–75.

Plaks, Andrew H. *The Four Masterworks of the Ming Novel: Ssu ta ch'i-shu*. Princeton: Princeton University Press, 1987. Esp. Chapter 2, pp. 55–180.

Roy, David Tod, trans. *The Plum in the Golden Vase or, Chin P'ing Mei*. 5 vols. Princeton: Princeton University Press, 1993–.

Shang Wei. "*Jin Ping Mei* and Late Ming Print Culture." In *Writing and Materiality in China: Essays in Honor of Patrick Hanan*, ed. Judith T. Zeitlin and Lydia H. Liu (Cambridge, Mass.: Harvard University Asia Center, 2003), pp. 187–219.

Shapiro, Sidney, trans. *Outlaws of the Marsh*. 2 vols. Beijing: Foreign Languages Press, 1981.

Wang, Richard G. *Genre, Consumption, and Religiosity: The Ming Erotic Novel in Cultural Practice*. Hong Kong: Chinese University Press, 2011.

Translator's Introduction

It is now fifteen years since I set to work on this translation of the *Jin Ping Mei,* and nearly ten since it was, as I imagined, almost ready for press. I did not flatter myself that it was a perfect translation—it would have needed the research of many years to clear up a number of difficult points —but I thought a few months' work would make possible a fairly adequate rendering of what I had come to regard as a very great novel. Now, looking at the proofs, I wish I had another ten years to spend on it. I have made no attempt to produce a "scholarly" translation, but it is not easy, from the staccato brevity of the original, to make a smooth English version and, at the same time, to preserve the spirit of the Chinese. It would, doubtless, have been possible to escape some of the difficulties by omitting the passages in which they occur, but I could not bring myself to do this or even to cut down occasional passages that seem to me a little dull. I made the best I could of them. The position was not quite the same with the poems. Nobody would, I think, claim that they are masterpieces of Chinese poetry, and some of them, turned into English, seemed very much like gibberish. I have allowed myself much more liberty with them and have omitted a great many. After all, they are merely conventional trimmings to the story, and I have no qualms of conscience about them. But for the rest, I confess that I have not even read the proofs. My long-suffering publishers knew that I was so anxious to go on polishing the translation that they thought the book would be indefinitely delayed if I was allowed to handle the proofs. They have been corrected by Mr. A. S. B. Glover.

There was one other problem that I must mention. I have already said that I could see no excuse for tampering with the author's text. He set out, coldly and objectively, to relate the rise to fortune and the later ruin of a typical household at a time when Chinese officialdom was exceedingly corrupt. He omitted no detail of this corruption, whether in public or in private life. Such detail he obviously considered essential to his story. If he had been an English writer, he would have avoided some subjects completely, skated over thin ice, and wrapped up certain episodes in a mist of words. This he does not do. He allows himself no reticences. Whatever he has to say, he says in the plainest of language. This, of course, frequently is acutely embarrassing for the translator. Again I felt that, if the book was to be produced at all, it must be produced in its entirety. But it could not all go into English, and the reader will therefore be exasperated to find occasional long passages in Latin. I am sorry about these, but there was nothing else to do.[1]

Perhaps I may be allowed to say how I came to translate the book. Some time after the Great War I became interested in the social applications of a certain modern school of psychology. I thought I should like to study these applications in the case of a developed civilization other than our own. So I began to learn Chinese and to search about for documentary material. The novel was the obvious field to be investigated.

The Chinese have never regarded novel writing as anything more than a rather doubtful diversion for a literary man. Literature, to them, was almost a sacred art, hedged about by conventions. It had a language of its own, and this language must not be profaned. For this reason, though there is a mass of novel "Literature" in Chinese, it has never been accepted as such, and novels were written in the colloquial language of the period and not in the literary language. It is only within the present generation that scholars like Hu Shi have come to appreciate the value and the interest of the Chinese novel.

This depreciatory attitude to the novel of the learned class in China is, perhaps, responsible for the absence of any true development of style. The *Jin Ping Mei* is written in a sort of telegraphese. There are no flowers of language. And when the author goes beyond plain narrative, his descriptions are bare and devoid of any very picturesque quality. But the narrative is so detailed and so ruthless in its searching delineation of character that there is little need for any attempt to convey atmosphere by deliberate means. It is this power of conveying the essential with the utmost economy in the use of literary devices that seems to me to make the *Jin Ping Mei* a great novel. It has something, surely, of the quality of a Greek tragedy in its very ruthlessness. It proceeds slowly and, apparently, unsuspectingly to its climax: and so suddenly, but inevitably, to its end.

In view of its limitations, the characterization of the book is very striking. There is a multitude of characters—Ximen Qing's wives, the women of the household, the singing girls with whom he associates, his disreputable *sponging friends,* the officials with whom he comes into contact—but there is no confusion among them. Each is a living character, clearly drawn and perfectly distinct. This distinctness comes, not from any deliberately

---

1 The passages formerly cloaked in Latin appear in English in thie edition. EDS.

drawn picture of each individual, but from his words and actions. I know no other book in any language in which such an effect has been produced by such means. It is partly for this reason—though my main reason was a very strong belief that a translator has no right to mutilate any author's book—that I felt it necessary not to cut out any of the details of behavior given by the author. I am convinced that such details were included in the original not for the purpose of titillating the reader's palate for the salacious, but because they, too, indicate shades of character that, given the author's stylistic limitations, could not be indicated by any other means.

It was more or less accident that made me choose the *Jin Ping Mei* as a suitable novel for my original purpose. I first came across it in Cordier's *Bibliotheca Sinica*. He says of it there, "In it there is set before us a whole company of men and women in all the different relationships that arise in social life, and we see them pass successively through all the situations through which civilized human beings can pass. The translation of such a book would render superfluous any other book upon the manners of the Chinese."

Grube, in his *Geschichte der chinesischen Literatur,* says that "the author of this book ... displays a power of observation and description so far above the average that all the remaining novel literature of China put together has nothing to compare with it."

Finally, Laufer in his *Skizze der manjurischen Literatur* declares that "As an artistic production, this work belongs . . . among the highest of its class. . . . That the novel is unmoral must be flatly denied: it is as little unmoral as any work of Zola or Ibsen, and like them a work of art from the hand of a master, who well understands his fellow men; who depicts them with their passions, as they are and not as . . . they ought to be."

In view of such opinions as these, it was clear that the *Jin Ping Mei* must be a mine of psychological and cultural material. I began its translation. And it is such a mine and it is unique. But, as the work of translation progressed, I found that I was becoming more and more absorbed by the book as a work of art, and, I am afraid, its value as a psychological document soon faded into the background. I have no doubt that a deliberately strictly literal translation, with an elaborate apparatus of notes and explanations, would be extremely valuable, but my interest in the book as a masterpiece of novel writing has made me try to render it in such a form that the reader may gain the same impression from it that I did myself. He will need patience occasionally, but his patience will be rewarded.

There is not much that I can say about the history of the book. Since novels were not "Literature," its authorship and history were not recorded with the care and solemnity that Chinese bibliographical study gives to canonized works. It deals with life in the Song Dynasty, in the reign of Huizong (1101–26 CE), but it was written towards the end of the Ming Dynasty. The identity of its author is not absolutely certain, but most writers attribute it to Wang Shizhen, who died in 1593. A popular tradition says that he poisoned the pages of his manuscript and then offered it to his enemy, the Prime Minister, Yan Shifan, in the hope that he would become engrossed in the reading of it and absorb the poison as he turned over the pages. The book existed in manuscript only for many years and, when it was first printed nearly a hundred years after its assumed author's death, the fifty-third and fifty-seventh chapters had been lost and were supplied by another unknown hand. The first edition was promptly placed on the list of prohibited books by the famous Emperor Kangxi, though his own brother made a translation of it into Manchu, which is one of the few literary masterpieces in that language.

Translator's Note

Without the untiring and generously given help of Mr. C. C. Shu, who, when I made the first draft of this translation, was Lecturer in Chinese at the School of Oriental Studies, I should never have dared to undertake such a task. I shall always be grateful to him.

I have to thank also Dr. Walter Simon, formerly Professor of Chinese in Berlin University, and now Reader at the School of Oriental Studies, for most valuable assistance in clearing up certain doubtful points that I have submitted to him. He has always taken the greatest interest in this translation.

Further, my thanks are due to Mr. A. S. B. Glover, who has had the objectionable and difficult task of going through the proofs, and to Mr. L. M. Chefdeville, who checked the Chinese names throughout.

Finally, Mr. Cecil Franklin deserves special thanks for the trouble he has taken in coordinating the labors of such a miscellaneous host of proofreaders and correctors. His was a most exasperating occupation, fulfilled with his accustomed imperturbable serenity.

List of Principal Characters

ing girl, niece of Ximen's Second Lady, sister of Li Guiqing

LI JIAO'ER (picture of Grace), Ximen's Second Lady; later wife of Zhang the Second

LI MING, a young musician, brother of Li Guijie

LI PING'ER (Lady of the Vase), wife of Hua Zixu, later Sixth Lady of Ximen

LIN, LADY, a lady of quality, mother of Wang the Third, and mistress of Ximen

LIU, "Old Woman," a procuress

MENG YULOU (Tower of Jade) or YULOU, Third Lady of Ximen; later, wife of Li Gongbi

PING'AN, boy of Ximen

PAN JINLIAN (Golden Lotus) or JINLIAN, originally a singing girl, later wife of Wu Da, and afterwards Fifth Lady of Ximen

PAN, "Old Woman," mother of Jinlian

PANG CHUNMEI (Plum Blosson) or CHUNMEI, maid to Wu Yueniang and later to Pan Jinlian; afterwards wife of Major Zhou

QITONG, boy of Ximen

QINTONG, boy of Meng Yulou; later lover of Pan Jinlian

QIUJU (Chrysanthemum), kitchen maid of Pan Jinlian

RUYI'ER (Heart's Delight), or Zhang the Fourth, nurse of Guan'ge

SHUTONG, Zhang Song, secretary to Ximen.

SONG HUILIAN (Wistaria), wife of Laiwang and mistress of Ximen

SUN GUAZUI or SUN TIANHUA, or Crooked-headed Sun, associate of Ximen and member of his brotherhood

SUN XUE'E (Beauty of the Snow) or XUE'E, originally a maid in Ximen's household; afterwards Ximen's fourth wife; also known as the Kitchen Lady

WANG, a Buddhist nun

WANG, "Old Woman," a procuress

WANG CAI (Wang the Third), a young nobleman; son of Lady Lin

WANG JING, brother of Wang Liu'er, later servant of Ximen

WANG LIU'ER (Porphyry), wife of Han Daoguo and mistress of Ximen

WEN BIGU, a dissolute scholar, secretary of Ximen

WEN, "Old Woman," a procuress

WU "The Immortal," a fortune-teller

WU, "Uncle," or Wu the Elder, brother of Wu Yueniang

WU DA, brother of Wu Song and first husband of Jinlian

WU DIAN'EN, friend of Ximen and member of his brotherhood

WU SONG, brother of Wu Da, and avenger of his murder

WU YIN'ER (Silver Maid), mistress of Hua Zixu, adopted as ward by Li Ping'er

WU YUENIANG (Moon Lady), or the Great Lady, Ximen's principal wife

WU ZONGJIA, abbot of the Temple of the Jade Emperor

XIA YANLING, a magistrate, friend of Ximen

XIAOGE, posthumous son of Ximen

by Wu Yueniang

XIAOYU (Tiny Jade), maid of Wu Yueniang; later, wife of Daian

XIE XIDA, friend of Ximen and member of his brotherhood

XIMEN QING, the central figure of this book, originally the owner of a considerable estate at Qinghe, later a magistrate

XIMEN DAJIE (Orchid), daughter of Ximen and wife of Chen Jingji

XIUCHUN (Hibiscus), maid to Li Ping'er and later to the Second Lady

XUE, a eunuch of the Imperial Household, friend of Ximen

XUE, "Old Woman," a procuress

YANG GUANGYAN, also Yang the Elder or Iron Fingernails, manager of one of Ximen's shops

YING BAO, eldest son of Ying Bojue

YING BOJUE, friend of Ximen and member of his brotherhood; known as Beggar Ying

YINGCHUN (Welcome Spring), maid of the Sixth Lady, later of Wu Yueniang

YING'ER (Jasmine), daughter of Wu Da by his first wife and stepdaughter of Pan Jinlian

YUN LISHOU, friend of Ximen and member of his brotherhood

YUXIAO (Autumn), maid of Wu Yueniang.

ZHANGJIE, Qiao Zhangjie, infant daughter of Madam Qiao, betrothed to Guan'ge

ZHANG SHENG, servant of Major Zhou

ZHENG AIXIANG (Perfume) or AIXIANG, a singing girl, sister of Zheng Feng and Zheng Aiyue

ZHENG AIYUE (Moonbeam) or AIYUE, a singing girl

ZHENG FENG, a young actor

ZHONGQIU, maid of Wu Yueniang

ZHOU, Major, later General Zhou, neighbor of Ximen

ZHU SHINIAN, friend of Ximen and member of his brotherhood; called Pockmarked Zhu

The Golden Lotus

The Golden Lotus

When wealth has taken wing, the streets seem desolate.
The strains of flute and stringed zither are heard no more.
The brave long sword has lost its terror; its splendor is tarnished.
The precious lute is broken, faded its golden star.

The marble stairs are deserted; only the autumn dew visits them
 now.
The moon shines lonely where once were dancing feet and merry
 songs.
The dancers are departed: the singers have gone elsewhere.
They return no more.
Today they are but ashes in the Western Tombs.

Beautiful is this maiden; her tender form gives promise of sweet
 womanhood,
But a two-edged sword lurks between her thighs, whereby destruc-
 tion comes to foolish men.
No head falls to that sword: its work is done in secret,
Yet it drains the very marrow from men's bones.

This poem was written by one Lū Yan [Lū Dongbin], an immortal
whose name in religion was Master Chunyang. He lived in the dynasty of Tang and spent his days in the pursuit of virtue and the mortifi-
cation of the flesh. So he attained to paradise, leaving this mortal world,
and there was given to him a seat in the Purple Palace. The gift of immortality was bestowed upon him, and he was made the Governor of the
Eight Caverns that are above, whence he brings succor to them in trouble
and adversity.

   It seems, unfortunately, too true that they who live in this world can
never wholly free themselves from their bondage to the Seven Feelings
and the Six Desires. There is no escape from the fatal circle of Wine and
Women, Wealth and Rage. Sooner or later the end comes to every man,
and he must give up his hold upon all of these, for, after death, they will
avail him nothing. Experience would seem to show that of these four
evils, women and wealth most surely bring disaster. Let us for a moment

consider the case of one who falls upon evil times, so that he finds himself in sore need, suffering misfortunes whereof he never dreamed. At night he searches diligently for a grain of rice, and finds the morrow must be foodless. In the morning he rises and looks around the kitchen, but cannot discover even the makings of a fire. His family is hungry and cold; his wife and children are starving, and he knows not where to turn for food. Where shall he find the money to buy wine? Worse even than this, his relatives and friends turn aside their eyes, and show him nothing but coldness and contempt. There may have been a time when the poor wretch had ambitions; now they must perish, for he is in no position to enter into rivalry with others.

Then there is the man who squanders his wealth to purchase the delights of love. It matters not how great that wealth may be, in one adventure he may cast away ten thousand golden pieces. Should he crave for wine, he will find it precious indeed, precious as molten jade, for to the outpouring of amber cups there is no end. Should it be rank he seeks, his wealth may conjure up spirits; a gesture may bring servants running to serve him, and a nod may summon his attendants. Men will flock to his presence and press forward to curry favor with him. They will hasten to abase themselves before his majesty, even to lick his sores and set their tongues where tongue should not be set. Only so long as he maintains his power will this continue: when once his influence is gone, they will shrug their shoulders and wait on him no more. No trial is more hard to bear than this change from hot to cold. Are not both the upstart and they who fawn upon him sufferers from the plague of wealth?

Then there is the danger that is to be had from women. Look around the world, I pray you. Liuxia Hui, though a fair lady seated herself upon his knee, remained unmoved. Where in these days shall we find conduct such as his? And he of Lu, who when a maid would have come to him, made fast his door and would not let her enter; where shall we find one like him? Or to Guan Yunchang who, with a lighted candle, kept chaste watch until the dawn? How many such heroes can history make known to us? What shall we say of those who, though they have four wives already, daily go forth to spend their substance on unlawful loves, unceasingly craving amorous delights? For the moment we will leave them, for there is that kind of lustful beast who cannot see a woman of even ordinary comeliness, without devising a hundred or a thousand plots to seduce her. He ensnares the woman, craving the pleasure of a moment, and for this neglects the affection of his friends, and takes no heed for the governance of his own household. To attain this paltry end, he pours forth countless wealth and casts immeasurable treasure to the dogs. His wantonness exceeds all bounds, and then come disputes, bloodshed, and all manner of evil. He is doomed. His wife and children are forever ruined and his business brought to the dust.

Such a man was Shi Jilun who, for love of his mistress Lu Zhu, died wretchedly in prison, though, at one time, the masses of his wealth were high enough to touch the skies. Another was Bawang [Xiang Yu] of Chu, whose heroism might have uprooted mountains. Because of his madness for Yu Ji [Concubine Yu], his head hung in Gaixia. The gate of Love may be the gate of Life, but just as surely is it the gate of Death. Time and time again our common sense reminds us of this fact; and yet our hearts still carry us away. So do men fall victims to the plague of love.

It is easy to talk thus of women and of wealth, yet there is none who is forever free of these plagues. If, in all the world, there be one who appreciates the truth, he will tell us that all our piles of gold and silver, all the jade we treasure, can never follow us beyond the grave. They are but refuse, no more worth than dust and slime. Our wealth may be so great that nothing can contain it, our rice so plentiful that it may rot because we cannot consume it: to our dead bodies it will be of no avail; all will become corruption and decay. Our lofty palaces and spacious halls will bring no joy to us when we are in the grave. Our silken gowns and our embroidered skirts, our robes of fur and wraps of sable, what are they but worthless rags, for all the pride our bones will take in them?

Those charming dainty maidens who serve our lusts so well, whose skill in self-adornment is so exquisite: when once the veil is torn aside, what shall we find in them but falseness? Are they not like a general who, when the signal is given for battle, can only manifest his valor by the noise he makes?

Those scarlet lips, those white and glistening teeth, that flashing of eyes and dallying with the sleeve: if true understanding were vouchsafed us, we should know them for the loathsome grimaces of the powers of Hell within the palace of the Prince of Hades.

The silken hose, the tiny feet are like the pick and shovel that dig our graves. Soft dalliance upon the pillow, the sport of love upon the bed, are but the forerunners of an eternity wherein, within the Fifth Abode of Hades, we shall be boiled in boiling oil.

Well does the *Diamond Sutra* speak of this foolish life "as dream and as illusion; as lightning and as dew." For though at the end of life all things are vain, during life men cannot bear the loss even of a trifle. We may be so strong that, unaided, we can lift a cauldron or tow a ship, but, when the end draws near, our bones will lose their strength and our sinews their power. Though our wealth may give us mountains of bronze and valleys of gold, they will melt like snow when the last moment comes. Though our beauty outshine the moon, and the flowers dare not raise their heads to look on us, the day will come when we shall be nothing but corruption, and men will hold their noses as they pass us by. Though we have the cunning of Lu Jia and Sui He, it will avail us nothing when our lips are cold, and no word may issue from our mouths.

Let us then purify our senses, and put upon us the garment of repentance, that so, contemplating the emptiness and illusion of this world, we may free ourselves from the gate of birth and death, and, falling not into the straits of adversity, advance towards perfection. Thus only may we enjoy leisure and good living and still escape the fires of Hell.

I am brought to these reflections upon the true significance of wine and women, wealth and rage, remembering a family that, once flourishing, sank at length into a state of deepest misery. Then neither worldly wisdom nor ingenuity could save it, and not a single relative or friend would put forth a hand to help. For a few brief years the master of this household enjoyed his wealth, and then he died, leaving behind a reputation that none would envy. There were many in that household who always sought to flatter, to do well for themselves, to join in amorous pleasures, to stir up strife, and to turn their influence to their own profit. At first it seemed that all was well with them, yet it was not long before their corpses lay in the shadow, and their blood stained the deserted chamber.

CHAPTER 1
The Brotherhood of Rascals

IN the mighty dynasty of Song, when Huizong was Emperor, and in the Zhenghe period of his reign [1111–1119], there lived at Qinghe, a city of the prefecture of Dongping in Shandong, a dissolute young man whose name was Ximen Qing. He was about twenty-seven years old, and the master of a fine estate. A gay, good-looking fellow, he was, unfortunately, flighty and unstable. His father, Ximen Da, had once traveled through Sichuan and Guangdong dealing in raw medicines, and later he opened a shop near the Town Hall of Qinghe. He lived in a splendid house that had a frontage of five rooms upon the street, and wings that went back even farther. He had a host of servants, and a very considerable number of horses and mules. Though, perhaps, he was not quite a millionaire, he was certainly one of the richest men in the whole district.

Ximen Da and his wife showered affection upon their only child, and allowed him to do exactly as he pleased. While he was still comparatively young, they died. The boy paid scant attention to his studies, idled about, and finally gave himself up entirely to dissipation. Indeed, after his parents' death, he was seldom to be found at home, but spent all his time in the pursuit of forbidden pleasures. He learned to box, to wield the quarterstaff, and to play a good game of chess. He gambled a great deal, and became so skilled in the game of *pai* that he could distinguish the different pieces by simply touching them. In fact, so far as such accomplishments were concerned, there was very little he did not know.

His friends and acquaintances were wastrels and spongers who spent all their lives in amusing themselves at other people's expense. The chief among them was Ying Bojue, the son of a silk merchant. He had squandered the wealth his father had left him, and had sunk so low that he spent all his time waiting about the Town Hall, ready to go with anyone to the bawdy house, or to dine with the first-comer who would pay for a meal. People nicknamed him Beggar Ying. He was an expert at kickball, backgammon, chess and all sorts of other games.

Then there was Xie Xida. This man's grandfather had been a minor official at Qinghe, and his parents had died while he was still a youth. He wasted his time, and paid no attention to his duties, so he lost his position, and now led a life of leisure. He played the lute.

These two and Ximen Qing were as thick as thieves, and there were several more, of varying degrees of disreputability. One was Zhu Shinian; another Sun Tianhua, also known as Greedy Chops. Then there was Wu Dian'en, who had once been Master of the Yin Yang for the district. He had been dismissed, and now was always to be found hanging about the Town Hall in the hope of finding a job as witness for the officials in their money-lending transactions. In this way he made the acquaintance of Ximen Qing.

Other friends were Yun Lishou, a younger brother of Colonel Yun; Chang Zhijie; Bu Zhidao; and Bai Laiguang, who was also known as Guangtang. When people remarked that this was a strange name, he would become very indignant and enter upon a long explanation, which, by reference to the *Book of History*, was supposed to show that his tutor, when he had conferred that name upon him, had made an admirable choice. "If there had been anything objectionable about it," he used to say, "I should have changed it long ago, but, obviously, it has important historical associations, and I shall most certainly retain it."

There were, perhaps, ten of them in all, and, when they discovered that Ximen Qing was not only a very rich man, but ready to throw his money about, they led him on to gamble, drink and run after women.

The House of Ximen had fallen upon evil days. It had given to the world an unworthy son, who chose his friends from among those destitute of every virtue. It was inevitably doomed to impoverishment.

Ximen Qing was reckless, but when he took it into his head to bestir himself, he was capable of showing that he was no fool. He lent money to the officials and even had dealings with the four corrupt ministers, Gao, Yang, Tong and Cai. So he came to be mixed up in all kinds of official matters, acting as intervener for people at law, arbitrating in cases of dispute, and, sometimes, acting as stakeholder. The people of Qinghe stood in awe of him and spoke of him as "His Lordship Ximen." His first wife, a Miss Chen, died young, leaving him with a little daughter, and this daughter was now betrothed to Chen Jingji, a relative of Marshal Yang, the Commander of the Imperial Guard at the Eastern Capital.

After the death of his wife, Ximen found himself without a housekeeper, and married the daughter of a certain Captain Wu. This lady was about twenty-five years old. As she was born on the fifteenth day of the eighth month, her parents called her Yueniang ["Moon Lady"], and she was still known by that name after her marriage to Ximen Qing. She was gentle and quiet, a good wife, and faultlessly obedient to her husband. She had three or four maids and serving women to wait upon her, and Ximen

Qing had taken his pleasure with all of them.

As a second wife, he married a girl from the bawdy house, called Li Jiao'er, and as his third, a young woman from South Street, who had been his mistress. She was not very strong, and suffered from so many different illnesses that Ximen Qing again went off to "fly with the wind and sport with the moon!"

One day, when Ximen Qing was at home with nothing to do, he said to his wife:

"It is the twenty-fifth day of the ninth month, and on the third of next month, I am supposed to be meeting my friends. I think I will entertain them here, and engage a couple of singing girls, so that we can have our amusement at home without needing to go elsewhere. Will you make the necessary arrangements?"

"I wish you wouldn't mention those horrible creatures to me," Wu Yueniang said. "There isn't a decent fellow among them. Day after day, they come here, like messengers of Hell, putting ideas into your silly mind and making an absolute fool of you. Never, since you've known them, have you spent a whole day in your own house. The Third Lady is anything but well, and I think you might give up these drinking parties, for a while at least."

"Generally," Ximen Qing said, "I find your conversation delightful, but today your remarks are a little wearying. To hear you talk, all my friends might be beyond the pale. I don't mind so much what you say about the others, but surely Brother Ying is an honest, entertaining fellow. If we ask him to do anything for us, he never raises any objection, and what he does, he does well. Then Xie Xida is clever as well as conscientious. But there is this much to be said. So long as our meetings are irregular and uncertain, we can never develop our friendship on the proper lines. The next time we all come together, the best thing we can do will be to form a brotherhood, and ever afterwards we shall be able to count upon receiving assistance, if we need any."

"I have nothing against this brotherhood idea," Yueniang said, "though I have no doubt whatever that the others will get more assistance out of you than you are ever likely to get out of them. They will be as much use to you as dancing dolls, and not half so lively."

Ximen Qing laughed. "If I find, by experience, that they are to be trusted, why shouldn't I trust them? As a matter of fact, I'm expecting Brother Ying any moment. When he comes, I'll see what he thinks of the idea."

At that moment an intelligent-looking boy with delicate eyebrows and charming eyes came in. This was Daian, Ximen Qing's body servant.

"Uncle Ying and Uncle Xie are outside," he said. "They would like to speak to you."

"I was just talking about them," Ximen said. He hastened to the hall. Ying Bojue was dressed in a new black hat and a shabby blue silk gown. He was sitting in the place of honor with Xie Xida opposite. When Ximen Qing came in, they both jumped up and saluted him with great deference. "We are glad to find you at home, Brother," they said. "We have not seen you for some time." Ximen asked them to sit down, and called for tea.

"You are a nice pair," he told them. "I have had a very anxious time lately. I could not leave the house, but I haven't seen even so much as your shadows."

"What did I say?" Bojue cried. "I knew our brother would be annoyed!" Then he turned to Ximen Qing. "I am not surprised that you are angry with us, but, really, I have been so busy that I haven't known what to do. It is all very well for you to give your orders, but it is not so easy for me to carry them out."

"Where have you been, these last few days?" Ximen asked them.

"Yesterday, I went to the Li's to see a young lady called Li Guijie. She is Li Guiqing's younger sister, a niece of your Second Lady. I hadn't seen her for some time, and I must say she has become a very pretty girl. There's no telling what she will be like in the future. Her mother urged me to find a handsome young man to make a woman of her. Really, you yourself would not find her too bad."

"If she is so attractive," Ximen said, "I must go and have a look at her."

"Brother," said Xie Xida, "if you don't trust him, you can at least take my word for it."

"Well," said Ximen, "that accounts for yesterday, but what about the day before?"

"A little time ago, our friend Bu Zhidao died, and I have had to spend several days at his house in connection with the funeral arrangements. His wife asked me to tell you how grateful she is for the incense and things you sent her. Her place is so small and the only entertainment she can offer so unworthy, that she did not venture to invite you to the funeral."

"Alas!" Ximen Qing said, "it seems only a few days since I first heard he was ill. I never thought he would die so soon. He once made me a present of a gilded fan, and I was thinking of giving him something in return. Then I heard of his death."

Xie Xida sighed. "Once there were ten of us, now one has gone. By the way, the third of next month is the day for our meeting. We shall be troubling His Lordship to spend some small sum on the day's amusement."

"I have just been telling my wife," Ximen said, "that these meetings, at which we do nothing but eat and drink, do not represent the essential element in our friendship. We ought to decide upon some temple, have an appropriate document drawn up, and band ourselves into a definite brotherhood. Then we shall be pledged to help one another ever afterwards. When the day comes, I will buy the three offerings needed for the sacrifice. I presume you will all be ready to give something towards the expenses, each according to his means. I do not insist on this, but it seems to me that, since we are forming a brotherhood, it will be much more satisfactory if every brother makes some little contribution."

"Certainly, Brother," Ying Bojue said hastily. "A man who never says his own prayers cannot expect to get credit for the incense his wife burns. We must all do something to show that we are in earnest, but I'm afraid we're rather like the warts on a rat's tail, there is not much to be got out of us."

"Oh, you funny dog," Ximen said, laughing. "Nobody expects you to give very much."

"If the brotherhood is to be complete," Xie Xida said, "there should be ten of us. Brother Bu Zhidao is dead. Whom can we find to take his place?"

Ximen Qing thought for a while. Then he said: "My neighbor, Brother Hua, the nephew of Eunuch Hua, is the very man. He spends his money without stint, and goes regularly to the bawdy house. He lives next door, and we are very good friends. I will send a boy to invite him to join us."

Bojue clapped his hands. "Do you mean Hua Zixu, who keeps a girl called Wu Yin'er?"

"That is the man," Ximen Qing said.

"Ask him by all means," Bojue said. "If I can only make friends with him, it will mean another house of call for me."

"You silly rascal," Ximen said, laughing. "To hear you talk about eating, one would imagine you were always on the point of starvation."

They all laughed. After a while, Ximen called Daian, and sent him to Hua's house. "Tell him that we are going to form a brotherhood on the third of next month, and that I shall be honored if he will join us. When you have heard what he says, come back and tell me."

"Shall we come here, or go to a temple?" Bojue asked.

"There are only two temples to go to," Xie Xida said. "One is the Buddhist temple of Eternal Felicity, and the other, the Daoist temple of the Jade Emperor. Either of them would do."

"Not at all," Ximen said. "This forming of a brotherhood is not a Buddhist practice, and, in any case, I don't know the priests of that temple very well. We must go to the Temple of the Jade Emperor. The abbot, Wu, is a good friend of mine; it is quiet there and we shall have room enough."

"You are right, Brother," Bojue said. "He only suggested the temple of Eternal Felicity because the monks there are on such good terms with his wife."

"You old villain," Xie Xida said, laughing. "Here we are, discussing a most serious matter, and you think it a suitable occasion to fart."

They were laughing and talking when Daian came back. "Master Hua was not at home," he said, "but I gave the message to his lady. She was very pleased. 'If Uncle Ximen is so kind as to invite my husband,' she said, 'I am sure he will not fail to come. He shall have the message as soon as he comes in, and when the day for the meeting comes, I will remind him.' She gave me two cakes for myself, and told me to give you her respects."

"Brother Hua's wife," Ximen said, "is not only a very pretty woman, but she has intelligence."

They drank another cup of tea, and the two men rose to go. "We will tell the other brothers," they said, "and collect their share of the expenses. Will you make the arrangements with Abbot Wu?"

"Yes," Ximen Qing said, "I'll see to that. Don't let me keep you any longer." He took them to the gate. Before they had gone very far, Ying Bojue turned. "Don't you think it would be fun if we had some singing girls?"

"Yes, indeed," Ximen said, "it will be more amusing if the brothers have someone to laugh and joke with." Bojue made a reverence and went away with Xie Xida.

It was soon the first day of the tenth month. Ximen Qing rose early and was sitting in Yueniang's room when there came a serving boy whose hair had been dressed in grown-up style. He brought with him a gilded and polished card case. First he made a reverence to Ximen Qing; then he came forward and said: "My master, Hua Zixu, sends his compliments. Some time ago you sent your servant with an invitation, but he was out on business and did not personally receive the message. He was told that you are arranging a party on the third of the month, and has sent this small gift, which he trusts you will use as you think fit. Afterwards he hopes you will tell him what his proper share of the expenses amounts to, and he will make up what is lacking."

Ximen Qing took the packet, examined the label upon it, and wrote a receipt for one tael of silver. "This is more than enough," he said; "your master must certainly not send any more. Remind him to keep the day free. He will have to get up very early so as to be ready to go to the temple with the rest of us."

When the boy was going away, Yueniang asked him to wait a moment. She told Yuxiao, the elder of her two maids, to give him two pieces of fruitcake. "This is instead of tea," she said to him. "When you get home, give my kind regards to your mistress, and tell her that one of these days I am going to ask her to come and have a talk with me." The boy took the cakes, made another reverence, and went out.

A few moments later, Ying Bao, Ying Bojue's boy, came. He, too, was carrying a visiting case. Daian introduced him. "My father has collected these presents from the others," he said, "and hopes you will accept them." Ximen Qing looked at the packets, saw that there were eight in all, and handed them to his wife without opening them. "Use them," he said to her, "to buy something for our visit to the temple." He dismissed Ying Bao.

Soon afterwards he got up and went to see his third wife, who was ill, but he had only just reached her room and sat down when Yuxiao came to tell him that her mistress would like to speak to him again. "Why didn't she say all she had to say before?" Ximen Qing said. He got up and went back to her, finding her with all the packets opened and spread out before her.

"Look here!" she said, laughing. "Ying sends a *qian* and two *fen* of bad silver, and the rest, three or five *fen* apiece. Judging by the color, some red, some yellow, it might be gold. Certainly, I've never seen anything like it in this house before. If you accept it, our reputation will be gone forever. You must send it back at once."

"What a fuss about nothing!" Ximen said. "This is all right. Don't let me hear any more about it." He went out.

The next day, he weighed four taels of silver and told his servant Laixing to buy a pig, a sheep, five or six jars of Jinhua wine, some chickens and ducks, candles and paper offerings. He put five *qian* in an envelope and told his man Laibao to take it and the other things, and go with Daian and Laixing to the temple of the Jade Emperor. They were to say to the abbot: "Tomorrow, our master proposes to form a solemn brotherhood, and he takes the liberty of asking you to compose an address suitable to the occasion. He would like to take dinner at your temple in the evening, and would be very grateful if you would make the necessary preparations. He will arrive in the morning."

Daian soon returned. He said that he had given the message, and that the abbot agreed.

The day soon passed. The next morning, Ximen Qing washed and dressed, and told Daian to go and ask Hua Zixu to come for breakfast before they joined the others on the expedition to the temple. Soon afterwards, Ying Bojue and the others arrived. They came in, and forming a circle, made reverence together.

"It is time to start," Bojue cried.

"No, breakfast first," Ximen Qing said. He called for tea and refreshments. Afterwards, he changed his clothes for brighter and more handsome attire, and they all set out together for the temple of the Jade Emperor.

Before they had gone very far, they could see the temple gateway. It was lofty and imposing, but the sanctuary, with walls reaching almost to the skies, was more commanding still. It was approached by a gate in the shape of the character *ba,* covered with a red wash. Within the precincts were three paths, like the character *chuan.* The buildings were of marble with wave-like markings. The sanctuary, its lofty eaves glittering in green and gold, was in the center. Images of the Three Pure Holy Ones stood in due order in the middle, and at the far end was Laozi, the Old Lord of the Most High, riding upon his black ox.

They entered the second sanctuary, went around, and passing through a side door, came to the abbot's quarters. On either hand grew grasses as green as jasper and flowers as red as coral. There were pine trees and bamboos. On either side of the door hung scrolls. One bore the inscription: "In Paradise, unending are the months, the years," and the other, "In the Vessel of Heaven there lies another world." On the north was a hall the size of three rooms, where the abbot officiated every day at morning and evening prayer.

The temple had been specially decorated for the occasion. In the middle of the north wall hung a picture of the Jade Emperor in the Golden Palace of Paradise, and on both sides were the nobles of the Purple Palace. The four generals, Ma, Zhao, Wen and Guan were there too.

Abbot Wu was standing outside the Hall of the Sacred Scriptures. He welcomed them with a priestly reverence, and Ximen Qing and his friends went in. After taking tea, they all got up and began to look at the pictures. Bai Laiguang took Chang Zhijie by the hand, and they examined the portrait of General Ma. He looked very brave and fierce, but he had three eyes. "I don't understand this," Bai Laiguang said. "We mortals find that with only two eyes it is well to keep one closed. Can he need an extra eye to keep a watch on us and on our misdeeds?"

Ying Bojue overheard him and went over to them. "You silly fellow," he said. "It is on your account alone that he needs an eye more than anybody else."

Everybody laughed, and Chang Zhijie pointed to the picture of General Wen. "Now here," he said, "there really is something out of the ordinary. He is blue from top to toe. I suppose he must be one of Lu Qi's ancestors."

Bojue burst out laughing. "Come over here, Father Abbot," he cried, "and I'll tell you a story.

"Once upon a time, a priest died and came before the Prince of Hades. The Prince bade him give an account of himself. 'I am a priest,' he said quite simply. Then the Prince ordered one of his officers to search the records and find out what was known of the man. They discovered that he was indeed a priest and a man of excellent character. So the Prince of Hades reprieved him and sent him back to earth.

"When he was once more in the land of the living, he met a man he knew, who worked at a dye works. 'However did you succeed in getting back, Father?' this man said to him. 'I only said I was a priest and they sent me back again,' his friend answered. The man remembered this, and when his time came to go before the Prince of Hades, he too declared that he was a priest. The Prince told his officials to examine the man's body. When they came to his hands, they found them both bright blue. 'What does this mean?' he was asked. 'That comes from the work I have done on General Wen's thing.'"

They laughed. Then they went to the other side to look at the pictures of red-faced Guan and Zhao. Zhao was a black-faced warrior, with a great tiger standing beside him. Bai Laiguang pointed to the tiger, and cried: "Look at that tiger! He must be one of the kind that don't eat meat, or he wouldn't be going about with a man so amiably."

"What!" said Ying Bojue. "Don't you know the tiger is his most trusted servant?"

Xie Xida, who had been listening, said, "If I had a servant like that, a quarter of an hour of his company would be quite enough. I should always be afraid he might take it into his head to eat me."

Bojue laughed: "That's a nice thing to say," he said to Ximen Qing.

"What's that?" said Ximen.

"Well," Bojue said, "Xie here says he would be afraid a trusted comrade might eat him. You certainly ought to go in fear of your life, for there are seven or eight of us, all trusted comrades, and all ready to feed at your expense at any time."

At that moment the abbot came back to the hall. "Do I hear you speaking of tigers, Gentlemen?" he said. "In this very district of Qinghe, one has recently caused very serious trouble. Scores of travelers, and more than a dozen hunters, have found that to their cost."

"Really?" Ximen Qing cried.

"Yes," said the priest. "I am surprised you gentlemen have not heard about it. I should not have known myself, but a little while ago, one of my young novices went to ask alms at Master Cai's house in Cangzhou, and he had to stay there several days before it was safe to return. Between Qinghe and Cangzhou there is a ridge called Jingyang, and it seems that a dragon-eyed, white-headed tiger has recently been making raids from there in search of human prey. Travelers have been afraid to pass the hill, and have had to form parties when they went that way. The local authorities are now offering a reward of fifty taels to anyone who kills the tiger, but so far, though several attempts have been made, they have all come to nothing. Indeed the hunters have been most unfortunate: they have had nothing but maulings for their pains."

Bai Laiguang jumped up. "We are too busy today, since we have this brotherhood to form, but tomorrow we will go and catch the tiger. It will be one way of putting a little money in our pockets."

"Evidently you don't value your life very highly," Ximen Qing said. The other laughed. "Let me get hold of something to spend, and I don't care what happens."

"That reminds me of another funny story," Ying Bojue said. "Once a man fell into a tiger's clutches, and his son, who wished to rescue him, took a knife and went to kill the beast. But the man, though the tiger had him actually in his jaws, cried out anxiously: 'Son, mind where you stick that knife. For goodness' sake, don't spoil the tiger's skin.'"

Abbot Wu was now preparing the offerings for sacrifice. When everything was ready, he came forward and said: "Gentlemen, it is time to burn the sacred papers." Then he produced a document. "I have already written the address," he said, "but I should be glad if you would tell me which of you is the elder brother and in what order I am to put the others. If you will kindly arrange yourselves in your due rank, I shall find it easier to write down your honorable names."

At this there was a chorus: "His Lordship comes first, of course," but Ximen Qing held back. "We should rank according to our age," he said. "Brother Ying is older than I am, and it is for him to take the first place." This was not at all what Ying Bojue wished. "Oh, no, Father!" he cried, I should be ruined. In these days, a man is judged by his wealth or by his position, and since there is no getting away from that, there is no point in taking age into consideration. Besides, there are others older than myself. And there are many other reasons why I should not be made elder brother. Both in dignity and moral standing, I do not rank so high as his Lordship. He is a paragon to the whole world. Then again, I have always been called Ying the Second, and if I were made elder brother I should have to be called Ying the Elder. If I met two acquaintances, and one addressed me as Ying the Elder and the other as Ying the Second, I shouldn't know which of them I ought to answer."

Ximen Qing laughed. "You talk such nonsense, anybody might die of laughing," he said. Xie Xida urged him not to decline, but Ximen continued modestly to prefer the others. Finally, after further pressure from Hua, Ying and the rest, he could hold out no longer and took the place

of honor. He was followed by Ying Bojue and Xie Xida, and Hua, out of
respect for his wealth, was allotted the fourth place. The others arranged
themselves in the lower positions. The abbot then filled up the document,
lighted candles, and, with all the men standing shoulder to shoulder in
their due order, the address was solemnly unfolded and read aloud.

IN THE EMPIRE OF THE GREAT SONG, THE PROVINCE OF SHANDONG, PREFECTURE OF DONGPING AND DISTRICT OF QINGHE

The faithful, Ximen Qing, Ying Bojue, Xie Xida, Hua Zixu, Sun Tianhua,
Zhu Shinian, Yun Lishou, Wu Dian'en, Chang Zhijie and Bai Laiguang,
here assembled, do wash their hands and burn incense to ask a blessing.

The oath of fidelity sworn within the Peach Orchard is the model of
all loyalty; with humble hearts we seek to take it as our example, and
strive to emulate the spirit that inspired it.

The love of Bao and Guan was as the depth of the ocean, and an-
imated by the same spirit, we hope to imitate their solemn purpose.

The peoples of the four oceans may yet be as brethren and they of
different names as of the same blood.

Therefore

In this period of Zhenghe—Year—Month—Day, devoutly offering
meat offerings of pig and sheep before the phoenix chariot, we humbly
bow before this holy altar and make our supplications.

We make our obeisance unto the Highest Heaven, where in a golden
palace dwell the Jade Emperor, the Guardian Angels of the Five Directions, the Tutelaries of City and Village, and all the spirits who come
and go.

We beseech them to accept the incense of our sincerity. May they
deign to protect us in all our doings.

We, Qing, etc. . . . , though born each at a different hour, pray that
death may find us united. May the bond between us remain ever unbroken. Our pleasures will we take together, and in time of need will
we succor one another. The memory of our friendship shall be ever
green, and in our wealth will we remember the unfortunate. Thus, at
the last, shall our confidence be confirmed: thus, coming with the sun
and going with the moon, shall our fellowship be established as high as
the heavens and as firm as the earth.

Henceforth, from this our solemn act of friendship, may our love be
eternal and our peace unending. May each of us enjoy length of days,
and his household unceasing felicity.

In Heaven alone do we place our trust, until our lives' end.

In token whereof, we diligently set this down.

REIGN PERIOD OF ZHENGHE.
YEAR.
MONTH.
DAY.

When the abbot had finished the reading of this declaration, the men worshipped, bowing together eight times before the shrine. One last time they bowed, and when the paper money had been consumed, the sacred utensils were removed. The abbot told his acolytes to remove the sacrificial animals and cut them up. Chicken, fish and fruits of every kind were set out in profusion upon two tables. Ximen Qing took the seat of honor, and the rest seated themselves in accordance with their rank. The abbot presided over the feast. Soon the wine had been passed around several times, and the men began to amuse themselves telling riddles and guessing fingers, making the hall ring with noisy laughter.

> They saw the sun rise in the distant east
> They watched it set behind the mountains.
> Deep have they drunk, and now unsteadily go forth
> While o'er the trees there hangs the tiny crescent moon.

In the midst of their enjoyment, Daian suddenly came in. He whispered to Ximen Qing, "Mother has sent me to take you home. She says the Third Lady has had a fainting fit, and you must not be late." Ximen rose at once.

"I don't wish to disturb the party, or to be the cause of its breaking up," he said, "but my third wife is ill, and I am afraid I must leave you."

"I go the same way as Brother Ximen," said Hua Zixu. "We will go together."

"If you two rich men both go away," Ying Bojue cried, "how can we stay? Brother Hua, you really must not go."

"There is no man in his house," Ximen said. "We must go back together and set his wife's mind at rest."

"Just as I was coming away," Daian said, "Mistress Hua was telling Tian Fu to saddle a horse and come here."

At that moment the boy arrived. He went to Hua and said, "Your horse is here, and Mother would like you to return."

Before leaving, they thanked Abbot Wu for his kindness, and saluted Ying Bojue and the others. "We are compelled to go now," they said, "but you must stay and have a good time." They went out, jumped on their horses, and rode away. Those who remained were indeed so ravenous that they would have devoured Taishan without leaving a particle of earth. They lingered in the temple and drank deep, and there we may leave them.

When Ximen Qing reached home, he said good-bye to Hua Zixu, and went at once to ask Yueniang how his third wife was.

"I only said she was ill," said Yueniang, "to get you away from those fellows. That is why I made Daian tell you that story. But in truth she has been steadily getting worse, and you ought to stay at home and devote a little of your time to her."

Ximen went to the other side of the house to visit his third wife, and for a few days continued to pay her some attention. On the tenth day of the tenth month, when Ximen Qing had just dispatched a boy to summon the doctor, he was still in the hall when Ying Bojue came in, smiling. Ximen greeted him, and asked him to sit down.

"How is my sister-in-law?" Bojue asked.

"I'm afraid she will never get any better," Ximen said, "it is very doubtful indeed whether anything can be done for her. What time did the party break up the other day?"

"Abbot Wu kept urging us to stay, and it was nearly the second watch before we left. I was very drunk. It was a good thing for you that you came home so early."

"Have you had dinner yet?" Ximen Qing said.

Ying Bojue could not make up his mind whether to say "Yes" or "No," so he asked Ximen to guess.

"I should say you have."

Ying politely put his hand before his mouth, laughed, and said, "You silly man, you've guessed wrong."

"Well, if you haven't, why didn't you say so, you greedy beast?" Ximen said, laughing. "I can't imagine what makes you such a donkey." He told a servant to prepare a meal for Bojue and himself.

"I should have dined," Bojue said, "but I have just heard a most extra-ordinary piece of news, and I had to come and tell you all about it. We can go and see for ourselves."

"What is this marvelous piece of news?" said Ximen.

"You remember the abbot telling us about the tiger of Jingyang Ridge?" Bojue said. "Well, yesterday a man killed that tiger with his bare fists."

"Don't talk such nonsense," Ximen said. "I don't believe a word of it."

"You say you don't believe me, but wait till I've told you all about it," Bojue went on, waving his arms and stamping his feet in his excitement. "The hero is a certain Wu Song, who some time ago got into trouble at Master Chai's house, and had to run away. He fell ill, and, when he recovered, thought he would like to come and see his brother again. On the way here, he had to pass Jingyang Ridge. There he came upon the tiger and killed it with no weapons but his hands and feet." Ying Bojue told this story in such minute detail that he might himself have been an eyewitness. Ximen Qing shook his head.

"In that case," he said, "as soon as we have finished dinner, I'll go with you and see what the tiger looks like."

"Don't let's wait for dinner, or we may be too late," said Bojue. "Let's go to the High Street, and spend an hour or two in the tavern there."

Laixing was setting the table, but his master told him not to trouble about the meal, and to ask Yueniang to have some clothes set out for him to wear. In a few moments he had changed, and set off arm in arm with Bojue. In the street they ran into Xie Xida. "Hullo, Brothers," he said, laughing, "are you coming to see the man who killed the tiger?"

"We are," said Ximen.

Xie Xida told them that the crowd was so great as to make the roadway almost impassable, and they went to a tavern overlooking the street. They had not long been there when they heard the sound of drums and gongs. The people were all craning their necks to see. Hunters, marching two by two, carrying their tasseled spears, went before the tiger's body. It was so huge that four men could hardly carry it, and it looked like a great embroidered sack. Then, riding upon a splendid white charger, came the bold fellow who had killed it. Ximen Qing gazed at him, bit his nails, and said, "Just look at that man. He must have the strength of a hippopotamus, or he could never have vanquished that great beast." They drank their wine and discussed the heroic deed.

> Full seven feet tall is this majestic figure
> A hero striking terror into all beholders
> With stern and rugged face, and sparkling eyes that blaze like glittering stars
> Clenched fists like sledgehammers.
> If he but raise his foot, the tigers in their mountain lair feel their courage wane
> One blow with that fist, and the great bear trembles in his lonely valley.
> He wears a magic cap with silver flowers
> And his long-sleeved gown is soaked with his victim's blood.

This was the man of whom Ying Bojue had spoken. His home was in the district of Yanggu, and it was only because he had taken a sudden fancy to pay a visit to his elder brother that the opportunity of killing the tiger had come to him.

The magistrate had summoned the hero to his presence, and a host of people were waiting to see him arrive at the Town Hall. As Wu Song dismounted, the magistrate took his place in the Hall of Audience, and the people carried the great beast to the front of the Hall. His Honor was greatly impressed by the hero's bearing, and reflected that a man must be strong indeed to kill such a tiger. He called Wu Song forward.

The hero paid his respects, and then told the story of his prowess so vividly that the officials were half paralyzed by fright. Then, in the Hall of Audience, the magistrate solemnly offered him three cups of wine, and from the public treasure that was stored there took fifty taels of silver.

"By your Honor's leave," said Wu Song, "I owe my victory over the tiger more to good fortune than to ability. I have no right to this reward. The hunters here have incurred your Honor's displeasure on account of this same brute, and I shall be grateful if you will give them the silver rather than myself."

"I will do so if you wish it," said the magistrate, and the money was distributed among the hunters. Seeing that Wu Song was generous-hearted and honest as well as a hero, he thought it would be a good idea to offer him a position. "You are a native of Yanggu," he said; "but that is not a great distance from here. I should like to offer you the appointment of captain of my police, and entrust to you the task of sweeping out the brigands that infest the neighborhood. What do you say?"

Wu Song knelt down. "I shall be eternally grateful to your Honor." The magistrate called his secretary, told him to prepare the necessary papers, and they were sent forward the same day. The notabilities of the district all came to offer their congratulations, and there was feasting for several days.

So Wu Song, who had only thought of his desire to see his elder brother, secured the appointment of police captain in Qinghe. He was delighted with the way things had turned out, and in all the prefecture of Dongping there was none who did not know the name of Wu Song.

> A hero this! A mighty hunter
> Who climbed the Jingyang Ridge with eager tread.
> With strong wine firing his veins he slew the terror of the mountain
> And now his fame is spread to every corner of the earth.

One day, as Wu Song was strolling along the street, he heard a voice behind him, crying: "Brother, Brother! Are you too proud to know me, now that you have become captain of the police?" He turned, and to his surprise, recognized the speaker. It was his brother Wu Da, the very man he had been hoping so long to meet. During a period of severe famine the brothers had been compelled to separate. Wu Da had moved to Qinghe and taken a house in Amethyst Street. He was a simple-minded man, not impressive in appearance. In fact people called him sometimes Tom Thumb and sometimes Old Scraggy Bark. (This was because his body was deformed and his face pinched.) The poor man was neither very strong nor very intelligent, so he became a constant butt for the wits of the neighborhood.

Wu Da had no established business, but scraped together a living by hawking baskets of cakes. His wife had died, leaving him with a little daughter, Ying'er, who was now about twelve years old. They lived alone together for some months, and then Wu Da fell into low water and removed to the house of a rich man named Zhang who lived in the High Street. Here he obtained a lodging of a single room. Zhang's people found him a very honest fellow, and they did their best for him, and started him off selling cakes. When they had time to spare, they used to go to his little place, and he was very attentive to them. They all liked him and spoke well of him to their master, and he, in consequence, did not worry Wu Da for his rent.

This rich man Zhang was more than sixty years old. He was wealthy and prosperous, but he had no children. His wife, a daughter of Master Yu, managed his household with a rod of iron, and he had no pretty maids to amuse him. He was always beating his breast, sighing and lamenting: "Here I am, aged and childless, and though perhaps I am not exactly poor, what use is all my wealth to me?"

"If you feel like that about it," his wife said one day, "I will tell the go-between to buy a couple of girls for you. They can study, morning and night, and learn how to play and sing for your entertainment, and then perhaps you will feel better."

At this, the rich man was delighted, and thanked his wife again and again. Before long, she redeemed her promise, sent for the go-between, and the two girls were bought. One, surnamed Pan, was called Jinlian, and the other, whose surname was Bai, was called Yulian. Yulian was about sixteen years old, and had been born in a bawdy house. She was fair, clear-skinned, dainty, and intelligent. Jinlian was the daughter of a certain Pan Cai who lived outside the South Gate. She was his sixth child, and had been given her name because she was very beautiful even as a child. Her tightly bound feet were particularly charming. When her father died, her mother had been entirely without resources, and when she was only nine years old, she was sold to General Wang. In his house, she learned to play and sing, and, in her spare time, to read and write also. She was clever and industrious, and before she was twelve years old acquired a host of accomplishments. She learned, for example, how to darken her eyes, powder her face, and rouge her lips, and she could play more than one musical instrument. Her needlework had not been neglected and she could read the characters in books. With her hair dressed in a braid, and wearing a simple gown, she made a very pretty picture.

When Jinlian was fifteen years old, General Wang died, and her mother sold her to Master Zhang for thirty taels of silver. She and Yulian were both given music lessons, but since she had had some previous experience, she did not find them very difficult. It was decided that she should play the lute and Yulian the zither. They shared the same room.

When the two girls first came to the house, their mistress was very kind and gave them gold and silver ornaments to make them look pretty. Then Yulian died, and Jinlian was left alone. By this time she was eighteen years old and as beautiful as a peach flower. Her eyebrows were arched like the crescent moon. Many times Master Zhang hungered for a closer acquaintance, but, under the austere eye of his wife, no opportunity was forthcoming. One day, however, when the mistress of the house had gone to take wine with one of her neighbors, the rich man secretly summoned her to his room, and had his way with her.

Unhappily, after he had thus disported himself with Jinlian, all sorts of troubles came upon him. His nose ran, tears streamed from his eyes, and he could not hear. He had severe pains in the loins, and difficulty in making water. He had not long suffered from these complaints before his lady got to know his secret. She upbraided him for several days, and devised all manner of punishment for Jinlian. Master Zhang, though he knew he was doing something he ought not, secretly provided the girl with a trousseau, and looked about for a suitable man to whom to marry her. Everybody said, "Wu Da is a widower and a very honest fellow," and it occurred to him that no one could be more desirable, for Wu Da lived in the same house, and there would be no need for him to lose sight of the young lady. So he married the girl to Wu Da without asking for anything in return. The marriage once celebrated, Zhang heaped kindnesses upon the bridegroom. If he needed money for the ingredients with which to make his buns, the rich man provided it, and when Wu Da went out with his baskets, the rich man, after making sure that there was no one about, would go to console Jinlian in her loneliness.

Wu Da could not help seeing that Zhang treated his wife as though she belonged to him, but he was not in a position to object. Master Zhang came in the morning and stayed until evening, until one day he was overcome by exhaustion and died on the spot. His wife had not been blind to all that was going on, and now, in a rage, she told her servants to turn Wu Da and his wife into the street. The poor man went to Amethyst Street, and there rented a couple of rooms in a nobleman's house, and continued to sell his cakes.

It did not take Jinlian very long to discover that her husband was not much of a man. He was by no means a model of manly vigor, and she came to hate him with an intense hatred. Never a day passed but she found some quarrel to pick with him, and she even cursed Master Zhang. "There is no lack of men in the world," said she. "Why should he have married me to a thing like this? It is always the same. Drive him as hard as I will, he never does a stroke of work, and if I try to push him forward, he only goes backward. No matter how busy the day, he malingers and will not touch his tools. I must have been a great sinner in my last existence to have been doomed to marry such a creature as this. My life is wretched indeed." And when she was quite alone, she sang this song :

> This was an ill-made match.
> A man I thought him; now I know that he is no true man.
> I would not boast, but it is plain
> The crow can ne'er be mated with the phoenix.
> I am as gold deep buried in the ground
> And he a lump of common brass
> Who may not hope to stand beside my golden glory.
> He is nothing but stupid clay.
> Shall my jade body, lying in his arms, thrill him with ecstasy
> As from a dunghill the dainty sesame springs?
> How can I pass my days with him forever?
> How can I suffer him so long as life shall last?
> I, that am purest gold, can never rest upon a bed so vile.

Women, my dear readers, are all very much the same. If a girl is pretty and intelligent, all goes well so long as she marries a fine specimen of a man. But if her husband turns out a simple-minded sort of fellow like Wu Da, it does not matter how virtuous she may be, some degree of hatred will sooner or later affect her attitude to him. And we must remember that seldom do beautiful maidens succeed in finding handsome husbands. The man who has gold to sell never seems to meet the man who wishes to buy.

Every day, Wu Da took his baskets and went out to sell his cakes, returning only at sunset, and when the woman had rid herself of him, she used to sit beneath the blind, chewing melon seeds and pushing forward her tiny feet in the hope of attracting the attention of some young ne'er-do-well. And, indeed, there was a constant stream of courtiers before the gate, who spoke in riddles and called out such remarks as:

"What a pity that such a tasty piece of lamb should fall into a dog's mouth!" They poured out smooth words like oil, till Wu Da came to the conclusion that Amethyst Street was no place to live, and decided to remove elsewhere. But when he talked to his wife about the matter, she cried, "You low creature, you are nothing but a fool. You take a wretched little place like this, and of course dishonorable fellows come and say whatever they think fit. The best thing you can do is to scrape together a few taels, find a decent house, and take a couple of rooms in it. Then perhaps we can live more respectably, and people will cease to treat us like dirt."

"Where am I to get the money from to take a house?" Wu Da said.

"You are not a baby, you lump of mud! Why can't you? Are you going to allow your wife to be continually insulted in this way? If you have no money, take my hair ornaments and sell them, then buy a house with the proceeds. We can buy them back again sometime if we wish to."

Wu Da succeeded in getting together ten taels of silver, and took a place not very far from the Town Hall. It had four rooms on two floors, and there were two small courtyards. The whole place was very clean. When they had taken up their abode in West Street, he still continued to make a living by selling cakes.

Now, unexpectedly, he had come across his younger brother, and their hearts overflowed with joy. Wu Da at once invited his brother to go home with him, and took him upstairs to sit down. Then he called Jinlian to come and see Wu Song. "You remember," he said, "the man who killed the tiger on Jingyang hill. He is none other than your brother, the son of the same mother as myself. He has just been appointed captain of police."

Jinlian made a reverence to her brother-in-law, and Wu Song knelt down to return her greeting. She would not allow this, and made him stand up, saying that such condescension on his part would embarrass her beyond measure. Wu Song, however, persisted, and for some time they carried on a polite dispute, until at last they both knelt and kowtowed down to one another. Soon afterwards, the little Ying'er brought tea for the two men. Wu Song, realizing the seductive charm of his sister-in-law, modestly refrained from looking at her. Wu Da, who was anxious to offer his brother some entertainment, went downstairs to buy some wine and refreshments, and left his wife alone with Wu Song in the upper room.

Jinlian admired his manly qualities and the nobility of his bearing, remembering how he had killed the tiger, and thinking what immeasurable vigor he must have. She said to herself: "These two men are both the sons of one mother; why should my husband's body be so ill-shapen that he seems more like a ghost than a man? In which of my former lives did I so misbehave that I should be doomed to marry an object like him? Wu Song is strong and lusty. Why should I not invite him to make his home with us? He seems the very man for me." She smiled sweetly, and said, "Where are you living, Uncle? Who looks after you?"

"I have just been appointed captain of the police," Wu Song said, "and, as I have to be ready for duty at all times, I live near the Town Hall. Two soldiers wait upon me and cook for me."

"Why not come and live here?" the woman said. "It would be much pleasanter for you than living near the Town Hall with only those nasty dirty soldiers to look after you. If you come and live with us, you will find it much more convenient and, any time you want any little thing to eat or drink, I shall be only too glad to prepare it for you myself and it will be perfectly clean."

"It is very good of you to suggest it," said Wu Song.

"Perhaps your wife is living somewhere in the neighborhood," Jinlian said delicately. "I hope you will ask me to call on her."

"I have never married," said Wu Song.

Then Jinlian inquired politely how old he was, and when he told her he was twenty-eight, she remarked that he was three years older than herself. Finally, she asked where he had been living.

"I have been at Cangzhou for more than a year. I didn't know my brother had moved here, but thought he still lived at the old place."

"Ah," Jinlian said, "that is a long story. We had to come here because, ever since I married your brother, people have taken advantage of his excessive meekness and never ceased to insult us. If only he were as strong as you, Uncle, no one would dare to answer him back."

"My brother has always been a good steady fellow," said Wu Song, "not a good-for-nothing like me."

"Don't be so absurd," the woman said, smiling. "There is an old saying that a man who has no spunk cannot long maintain his independence. I have some spirit myself, and I don't care for the sort of man who lets you hit him without turning a hair, and spins round and round like a top the more you strike him."

"If my brother does not make trouble," Wu Song said, "it is because he wishes to spare you unhappiness."

They were still talking in the upper room when Wu Da came back with a host of things to eat, and set them down in the kitchen. He came to the foot of the stairs and called, "Wife, Wife, come down!"

"Where are your manners?" Jinlian cried. "Why do you call me down? There is no one except myself to entertain your brother."

"Please do not trouble about me," Wu Song said.

"Why don't you go next door," the woman said, "and ask old woman Wang to come and get the dinner ready? That's what you ought to do."

Wu Da went off and asked the old woman to come. She busied herself, and when all was ready, took the food upstairs and set it on the table—fish, meat, fruit and cakes. The wine was heated, and Wu Da, having asked his wife to take the host's place, himself sat at the side and put his brother in the seat of honor. When they were all in their places, the wine was poured out. Wu Da himself heated it and served the other two. "Uncle," Jinlian said, as she took her cup, "please excuse our having made no special preparations for you. I am afraid this is very inferior wine."

"Please don't say that," said Wu Song. "It is most kind of you to trouble about me at all."

While Wu Da busied himself with the heating of the wine, Jinlian, all smiles, and with the word "Uncle" continually upon her lips, kept saying, "Will you not have something tasty?" and, taking the choicest parts from different dishes, herself offered them to her brother-in-law.

Wu Song was a simple-hearted fellow and treated her like a sister, not knowing the sort of woman she was. Cleverly enough, she assumed a modest air, and it never occurred to him that she was deliberately trying to seduce him. They sat together and drank several cups of wine, but she could not keep her eyes away from him, and this finally embarrassed him so much that he turned his head away. By this time, he had drunk much wine and, as he began to feel a little tipsy, he decided it was time to go and stood up to take his leave.

"What is your hurry?" Wu Da cried. "Stay and have a little more to drink. You have nothing to do now."

"Thank you," said Wu Song politely, "but I shall see you both some other time."

They went downstairs with him, and as he was going out of the door, Jinlian cried, "Don't forget to make arrangements to come here to live. If you don't, the neighbors will have a very poor opinion of our hospitality. Brothers are not strangers, and your company will be a pleasure to us."

"It is very kind of you," Wu Song said. "I will bring my things here this very evening."

"We shall be waiting for you," the woman said.

CHAPTER 2
Pan Jinlian

Wu Song went to the inn near the Town Hall, packed his baggage and his bedclothes, and told a soldier to carry them to his brother's house. When Pan Jinlian saw him coming, she was as delighted as if she had discovered a hidden treasure. She bustled about preparing a room for her brother-in-law and setting everything to rights. Wu Song sent back the orderly, and stayed the night at his brother's home. The next day, he rose very early, and Jinlian hastened to heat water for him. He washed, combed and tied his hair, and then made ready to go to the office to sign the roll.

"Uncle," Jinlian said, "when you have signed the roll, be sure to come home for lunch. You mustn't think of taking your meals anywhere but here."

After signing the roll, Wu Song waited all the morning in attendance at the office, and finally went home. Jinlian had taken the greatest pains over the cooking, and the three sat down together to lunch. Taking a cup of tea in both hands, the woman offered it to Wu Song.

"You take so much trouble on my account," he said, "that it makes me quite embarrassed. Tomorrow I will arrange for a soldier to come and wait on us."

"Please do no such thing," Jinlian cried anxiously. "We are the same flesh and blood, and this house is home to us all. I am not waiting upon a stranger. Certainly this little Ying'er is not much use, and I can't rely upon her. She always seems to do the wrong thing. But if we get a soldier to help about the house, I shall find him in the way in the kitchen, and it will fidget me to watch him."

"In that case," Wu Song said, "I can only accept your kindness gratefully."

Not long after Wu Song had taken up his abode in his brother's house, he gave Wu Da some money and asked him to make arrangements to give a party for the neighbors. They came with presents to pay their respects to Wu Song, and a little later Wu Da gave another party in return. Wu Song presented his sister with a length of colored silk to make dresses.

"Oh, Uncle," she cried delightedly, "I can't possibly accept such a magnificent present," but she hastened to add: "Since you have already bought it, I suppose I must not refuse." She made a reverence, and took the silk. From that time, Wu Song was definitely established as a member of his brother's household. Wu Da, as before, went to the street every day to sell his cakes, and Wu Song went to the Town Hall to perform his official duties. Whether he returned early or late, Jinlian always had something ready for him, and seemed delighted to wait upon him. He noticed this, but thought no more about it. Nonetheless, the woman was forever trying to lead him on by pretty speeches, though she found it no easy task, for he was really incorruptible. If he had anything of importance to say, he would stay long enough to say it, but if not, he went straight about his business.

A month soon passed. It was the eleventh month, and they began to experience seasonable weather. The north wind blew violently for several days and black clouds gathered on every hand. Then the snow began to fall, and soon it filled the skies.

> For miles and miles the skies were filled with thick dark clouds.
> Snowflakes, dancing past the window ledge, in midair formed a
>   screen like tiny flowers of jade.
> Zi Yu's boat, on the Yan River, was held and forced to tarry.
> Soon was a mantle laid on the high palaces
> River and mountain bound with a chain of silver
> The skies filled with winged salt and driving, powdery dust.
> That day, Lū Meng, in his little hut, sighed
> For all his wretchedness.

The snow continued without ceasing until the first night watch; the world was silver everywhere, and it seemed as though the earth had arrayed itself in a glorious garment of jade. Next morning, Wu Song went to the office and stayed till noon. Jinlian bade her husband go and sell his cakes and she went to ask her neighbor, old woman Wang, to go and buy some food and wine for her. Then she went to Wu Song's room, and made up the fire, thinking: "Today I will make sure of him. Beyond a doubt I can do something to wake him up." Afterwards, feeling quiet and lonely, she went and stood beneath the lattice and waited till she saw Wu Song trampling down the glistening snow as he hastened home.

She quickly raised the lattice for him and smiled. "You look frozen, Uncle." He answered her politely and came in, taking off his hat. Jinlian offered to take it, but he brushed the snow away himself and hung it on the wall. Then he unloosed his girdle, took off his outer gown of parrot green, and went into the living room.

"I have been expecting you all the morning," Jinlian said. "Why didn't you come back to lunch?"

"One of my friends asked me to lunch," Wu Song replied, "and just now I had another invitation, but I decided not to accept it, and came home instead."

"Is that so?" said the woman. "Won't you come a little nearer the fire?"

Wu Song thanked her and, taking off his oiled boots, changed his socks and put on a pair of slippers. Then he brought a bench and sat down by the fire. Jinlian told Ying'er to bolt the gate and shut the back door. She herself went to fetch some of the dishes she had cooked, and set them on the table before Wu Song.

"Where is my brother?" he said.

"He has not come back from business yet," the woman answered. "Let us drink a few cups of wine together."

"It is not late," Wu Song said. "We had better wait for him."

"Oh, why should we bother about him?" Jinlian cried.

At that moment Ying'er came in with the wine already warmed. Wu Song again apologized politely for causing so much trouble. Jinlian said nothing, but brought a bench to the fire and sat down. There were several dishes on the table, but she only took a cup of wine, looked at Wu Song, and invited him to drink it. This he did in one breath. She poured a second cup and handed that to him, saying, "It is so cold, you must drink this to keep the other company." This, too, Wu Song drank straight off. Then he filled a cup for her. She took the wine and sipped it delicately, then poured out still another cup and offered it to him. Her milk-white breast was partially uncovered, and her disordered hair was like a beautiful cloud. Desire had given color to her cheeks.

"People tell me you keep a singing girl over there by the Town Hall," she said slyly. "Is that true?"

"People always talk nonsense like that, but you shouldn't believe them, Sister," Wu Song said. "I never was that kind of man."

"I don't believe you," said Jinlian. "Your heart speaks one language and your tongue another."

"Ask my brother, if you don't believe me."

"What on earth is the use of bringing him into it?" Jinlian said. "His life is one long dream. Judging by the way he goes about, you might think he was always half tipsy. He would not have to spend all his days selling cakes if he had a particle of intelligence. But have another cup of wine."

She filled three or four cups one after the other, and Wu Song drank them all. She drank a few cups too, till the spur of desire pressed her more acutely and the passion within her blazed so that she lost all control of herself and could hardly speak. By this time, an inkling of the true state of affairs was beginning to dawn upon Wu Song, and he looked away from her. After a while she rose and went to heat some more wine. Wu Song, left alone in the room, took up the poker and began to poke the fire. Jinlian was soon back again with a jar of wine that she had warmed. In one hand she held the jar and with the other she gently pressed his shoulder. "Uncle," she said, "you must be cold with so few clothes." Wu Song was now beginning to feel thoroughly uncomfortable, and made no answer. Seeing him thus silent, she snatched the poker from his hand and cried, "You don't know how to poke. Let me do it for you. I want it as hot as a bowl of fire."

Wu Song felt even more uneasy, but he still said nothing. Jinlian was not in any way put out. She set down the poker and poured out another cup of wine. She drank a mouthful, looked meaningly at Wu Song, and said, "If you feel like it, drink what I have left."

This was too much. He snatched the cup from her hand and dashed the wine upon the floor, crying, "Don't be so shameless," and at the same time pushed her so violently that she almost fell. Then he gazed haughtily upon her.

"My feet are steadfast upon the earth and I aspire to reach the heavens. I am a man with teeth in my mouth and hair upon my head. I am a man, I say, not a swine or a cur, that I should pay no heed to the sacred laws of honor or flout the precepts of common decency. You must not behave in this shameless way. If I hear any whisper of your ever doing such a thing again, my eyes may tell me that you are my sister, but my fist will not recognize you."

This made Jinlian so confused and angry that her face became crimson. She called Ying'er to clear away the dishes, and muttered, "I was only joking. How could you think I was in earnest? You are not an honorable man." When the dishes had been removed, she went down to the kitchen.

So Jinlian came to realize that her blandishments were without effect, except that Wu Song had treated her roughly, while he, now sitting alone, grew angrier and angrier and thought very seriously about the matter.

It was still early, about the hour of the Monkey, when Wu Da came back, carrying his baskets over the snow. He opened the door, put down his burden, and going into the house at once saw that his wife's eyes were red with weeping. "With whom have you been quarreling now?" he said.

"If you were not such a mean-spirited creature," his wife cried, "things like this would not happen. But you never care whether outsiders insult me or not."

"Who has been insulting you?" Wu Da said.

"If you really wish to know, it was that scoundrel, your brother. When the snow was very heavy, I saw him coming back, and I was kindly getting something ready for him, when he saw there was nobody about, and tried to seduce me. It is perfectly true: Ying'er saw him."

"My brother is not that kind of man," her husband said. "He has always been high-principled and straightforward. Don't make so much noise, or the neighbors will hear you and laugh." He went to see Wu Song.

"You haven't eaten your cakes, Brother," he said. "I'll come and have some with you." But Wu Song did not answer him and, after brooding there a while, started to leave the house.

"Where are you going?" cried Wu Da, but his brother went off without replying. Wu Da went back to the room and said to his wife, "I called him, but he would not answer, and now he has gone down the road to the Town Hall. I'm sure I don't understand what all the bother is about."

"You thievish, stupid worm," Jinlian cried. "There is nothing to understand. The wretch is ashamed and dare not face you. That's why he has gone out. Probably he has not the audacity to inflict himself upon us any longer, and has gone to tell somebody to come and take his things away. I can't imagine why you bother about him."

"If he goes away," Wu Da said, "people will certainly laugh at us."

"You silly creature," Jinlian cried. "He is a shameless, immoral fellow, and he tried to seduce me. Is that a laughing matter? If you want him so much, go and live with him. I won't put up with it. Give me divorce papers if you like, and then the pair of you can live together."

After this, Wu Da did not dare to open his mouth again, and he had to suffer his wife's ill-temper for a long time. They were indeed still quarreling when Wu Song, with a soldier carrying a long pole, came back, packed up his luggage, and went off. Wu Da went after him, crying, "Why are you going away, Brother?"

"Ask no questions," Wu Song answered. "If I tell the truth, your good name will be ruined. Let me go."

Wu Da did not dare to question him any further, and was obliged to let him go with his luggage. Meanwhile his wife was scolding in her room: "That's better. Relations always prove a nuisance in the long run. People don't know the truth. Just because here is a young brother with a position at the Town Hall, they must needs conclude that he keeps his brother and sister. They never think that he is really eating us out of house and home. He is like a yellow quince, good to look at and rotten inside. I shall thank my lucky star if he takes himself off for good and all. Indeed there is nothing I hope more than that I may never set eyes on that piece of ill-fortune again."

Wu Da could not avoid hearing all his wife said, but still he could not make out what had really happened, and his heart was troubled. Now that his brother had gone back to live at the inn near the Town Hall, he still sold buns and cakes upon the street. He longed for an opportunity to go to the Town Hall and have a talk, but his wife gave him strict instructions that he must not dare to do anything of the sort, and he did not venture to disobey her. After Wu Song's departure, the snow suddenly stopped. Ten days passed.

The magistrate of Qinghe had been stationed there for more than two years and had amassed much gold and silver. Now he wanted a man of courage to take his treasure to the Eastern Capital, so that his relatives might take charge of it. In three years his term of office would expire, and knowing that he would then have to make his report to the Emperor, he thought it would be well to have this gold and silver in hand when he came to deal with officials more exalted than himself. But he felt the need of a stout fellow for the job, as thieves often beset the way. Then he thought of Wu Song. He was just the man. That very day he sent for Wu Song and said to him:

"I am thinking of sending an important present to one of my relatives at the Eastern Capital. I mean Zhu Mian, one of the Grand Marshal's officers. There may be some danger about the journey, but if you undertake it, I am sure all will be well. If you will do this for me, I will reward you handsomely when you get back."

"You have shown me so much kindness, Sir, that I should never think of refusing," Wu Song replied. "I will set off as soon as you give me your orders."

The magistrate was now perfectly satisfied. He gave Wu Song three cups of wine, and handed him ten taels of silver as journey money. After receiving his instructions, Wu Song went to the inn and, after getting his orderly to buy some food and a jar of wine at a shop in the street, went to his brother's house. When Wu Da returned, he found his brother waiting on the doorstep. He had told his servant to take the wine and food into the kitchen.

Jinlian had not abandoned all hope, and when she saw Wu Song coming with wine and other delicacies she said to herself: "He must still be thinking about me, or he would not have come back. I may get him yet." So she went upstairs to powder her face and arrange her hair, and when she had changed into a prettier dress, she came down to welcome him.

"I can't imagine what can have displeased you, Uncle," she said, as she made a reverence. "For several days you haven't been near us, and I have often wondered why. It is delightful to see you home again, but why did you trouble to bring wine and food?"

"I have something to say to my brother," Wu Song said. "That is why I have come."

Jinlian invited him to go upstairs, and they all three went to the upper room. Wu Da and his wife sat in the places of honor, and Wu Song sat down on a long bench. The orderly brought up the food and Wu Song invited his brother and sister to take some. From time to time, Jinlian glanced meaningly at her brother-in-law, but he paid no attention to anything but the wine he was drinking. When they had all drunk several cups, Wu Song asked Ying'er to bring a loving cup and, when the orderly had heated the wine, he took this cup in his hands and said to Wu Da:

"Honorable elder brother: today the magistrate has ordered me to go to the Eastern Capital for him. I am starting tomorrow, and it may easily be two or three months before I get back, though I hope it will be less. What I have come to say to you is this: you have always been a long-suffering kind of man, and I don't intend you to be imposed upon in my absence. Now, listen to me. You have been in the habit of selling ten trays of cakes, but in future you must only make five. Then you will be able to go out later and come home earlier. Don't let anyone persuade you to drink; pull down the shutters and bolt the door as soon as you get home. If you do this, you will be saved a great deal of unpleasantness, but if anything disagreeable should happen, don't let yourself be drawn into a quarrel. Wait till I come back, and I'll soon settle the matter. Now, my dear brother, if you agree, drink this cup of wine."

Wu Da took the cup and drained it. "I will do whatever you think fit," he said.

Wu Song filled up the cup again and spoke to Jinlian. "Sister, you are no fool, and I don't think I need say any more. My brother is so simple-hearted that the real management of the household is in your hands. You will remember the old saying that a proud appearance is not always the mirror of an honest heart. If you attend to your household duties as you should, my brother will have nothing to worry about. As our fathers used to say: 'When the fence is safe, dogs cannot get in.'"

Jinlian listened, and the crimson color spread across her face. She shook her finger at Wu Da, and addressed Wu Song through him. "You fool! What do you think you will gain by insulting me like this? I have to wear a woman's clothes, it is true, but I am as good as any man. I am always steady and reliable. A man might stand upon my fist or a horse ride over my arm. I am not a turtle to be wounded without bloodshed. Never, since I married Wu Da, has even an ant dared to sneak into my room. How dare you talk about dogs getting in if the fence is not safe? Tell the truth, not a pack of lies. I don't care in the slightest what you say."

Wu Song laughed. "Don't lose your temper, Sister. So long as your heart keeps company with your mouth, all will be well. But I shall remember what you have said. And now, won't you drink this cup?"

Jinlian dashed the cup aside and ran downstairs. Before she reached the bottom, she turned and cried, "You think you're very wise and clever, but how is it you don't seem to know that a brother's wife should be respected as a mother? When I first married Wu Da, nobody ever mentioned his having a brother. Where have you come from? Are you really a relative or are you not? One would think you were the master of the house. Oh, it makes me wild to have to put up with such nonsense." She went down the rest of the stairs, sobbing.

The brothers drank several more cups of wine together till they could stay no longer, while Jinlian affected many airs and graces. At last they both went downstairs, and took their leave of one another with tears streaming down their cheeks. "Brother," Wu Da said, "you must go, I suppose, but come back as soon as you can and let my eyes rejoice in you once more."

Wu Song said, "Wouldn't it be better if you stayed away from business altogether, and let me arrange with somebody to supply you with funds?" Finally, he cried, "Remember what I say, Brother, and keep a watch on your door." Wu Da promised.

So Wu Song parted from his brother. He went back to the inn, packed his luggage, and saw to his weapons. The next morning he took charge of the magistrate's presents, secured a horse, and set off for the Eastern Capital.

After his brother's departure Wu Da had to endure his wife's scoldings for several days, but he held himself in check, swallowed his wrath, and let her scold him. He did what his brother had told him, and made only half the number of cakes he had made before. Every day he returned before sunset and, setting down his baskets, pulled down the shutters and closed the outer gate before he came to sit down in the room. His wife saw this, and grew more and more resentful every day. "You horrible creature," she said at length, "one would think you couldn't tell the time. Even jailers don't bar the prison gate while the sun is still in the heavens. Our neighbors must be in fits of laughter and think we are afraid of ghosts. You are just like a newborn babe who has to do what his brother tells him. Aren't you ashamed to have everybody laughing at you?"

"Let them laugh," Wu Da said. "What my brother said is true enough, and may save us much trouble yet."

"Pah, you vile creature!" his wife shouted, and spat in his face. "You, a grown-up man, have no will of your own, but have to do whatever anybody tells you."

"Say what you like," Wu Da said with a gesture of weariness. "To me my brother's words are as gold and precious stones." He continued to go out late and return early, and he still shut the door as soon as he got home. This so infuriated his wife that she almost had a fit; she quarreled with him so incessantly that trouble seemed to have become a habit. About the time for his return, she would pull down the shutter and bolt the door, thinking that so she would annoy him, but instead of making him angry, this gave him considerable secret satisfaction and he thought: "If she takes things like this, so much the better for all concerned."

The sun's bright horses galloped past the window, and the sun and moon raced like a weaver's shuttles. It seemed but a moment since the winter solstice passed and it was the season when the plum trees blossom, yet now the weather was giving warning of spring's return. One day, in the third month, the sun shone so pleasantly that Jinlian decided to dress herself in her best clothes. Wu Da was out, and she was standing by the door beneath the lattice. Thinking it was nearly time for his return, she prepared to pull down the shutter and go back to the room to wait for him. But now the fates intervened. A man passed beneath the lattice.

In affairs of the heart we always find that Fate brings the lovers together, and a story would not be worth the telling if accidents never happened. Jinlian was holding the pole and preparing to pull down the shutter, when a gust of wind suddenly blew it out of her hand. She could not catch it, and it fell upon the man's head. She smiled her apologies, and stole a look at him. Upon his head he wore a tasseled hat, and golden filigree hairpins, with one of the signs of the zodiac edged with jade. Over slender hips he wore a green silk gown and on his feet a pair of fine but heavily soled shoes, with socks as white as the purest water. He was fanning himself with a gilt fan. He was indeed as handsome as Master Zhang, and worthy of comparison with Pan An.

Jinlian peeped at him from under the lattice. When first the pole struck him, he stopped and seemed on the point of an angry outburst, but, as he turned, he suddenly beheld an incredibly pretty woman.

Her hair was black as a raven's plumage; her eyebrows mobile as the kingfisher and as curved as the new moon. Her almond eyes were clear and cool, and her cherry lips most inviting. Her nose was noble and exquisitely modeled, and her dainty cheeks beautifully powdered. Her face had the delicate roundness of a silver bowl. As for her body, it was as light as a flower, and her fingers as slender as the tender shoots of a young onion. Her waist was as narrow as the willow, and her white belly yielding and plump. Her feet were small and tapering; her breasts soft and luscious. One other thing there was, black-fringed, grasping, dainty, and fresh, but the name of that I may not tell. Words fail to describe the charm of so beauteous a vision.

Her luxuriant coal-black hair was as thick as the clouds. On each side she wore small pins and, at the back, a pair of combs with a cleverly fashioned flower. Two peach flowers adorned her willow-leaf eyebrows. The jade pendants she wore were remarkable, but the glory of her uncovered bosom was that of jade beyond all price. She wore a blue gown bound with a long silk-embroidered sash, and in her cuff a tiny satchel of perfumes. Beneath her delicate throat, a many-buttoned corsage concealed her breast.

Her feet were graced by tiny shoes made like the mountain crow, with tips embroidered to look like the claws. Their high heels were of white silk, so that she seemed always to walk upon a fragrant dust. Her scarlet silken trousers were decorated with birds and flowers and, as she sat or when she rose, the wind would puff out her skirts and flowing undergarments. From her mouth there came a perfume as delicious as that of orchides and musk, while her cherry lips and beautiful cheeks had the glory of a flower. One glimpse of this vision, and the souls of men would flutter away and die. Many handsome young men might perish at the sight.

No sooner had the man set eyes upon all this beauty than he became almost beside himself with desire. His anger sped to Java and his face was quickly wreathed in smiles. Jinlian knew that she was to blame for the disaster, so she made a graceful reverence and said, "The wind suddenly blew the pole out of my hand, and I had the misfortune to strike you. Please do not be angry with me."

The man set his hat straight with one hand, and made a reverence so low that he almost swept the ground. "Lady," he said, "it was not of the slightest consequence. You may do with me what you will."

It so happened that the neighbor, old woman Wang, the tea seller, had seen everything that happened. She was greatly entertained. "Who may you be, Sir," she cried, "who pass by this house to be welcomed with blows upon the head?"

The man laughed. "It was all my fault. I should have been more careful. Please don't be vexed with me, Lady."

"Don't beat me," said the old woman Wang, still enjoying the joke. The man laughed again, and bowed most profoundly to express his regret. His roguish eyes, experienced in amorous adventure and well versed in the value of a woman's charms, could not look away from Jinlian. At last he went off, strutting and waving his fan, though not without turning around seven or eight times.

Jinlian had no sooner set eyes upon the man with his engaging manner and lively ways, no sooner heard him speak so winningly and brightly, than she fell head over heels in love with him. She had no idea who he was or where he lived, but she rightly concluded that he would not have turned his head so often unless he reciprocated her feelings in some measure. She stayed beneath the lattice until he was out of sight and then, pulling down the shutter, closed the door and went back to her room.

You may have guessed who this man was. None other than that chief of those who sought the pleasures of the couch, that captain of those who gather precious treasure and pursue unlawful fragrance, his Lordship Ximen. His third wife had just died and been given a solemn burial and, being distressed in mind, he was taking a stroll along the street intending to call upon Ying Bojue and thus secure a little distraction from his gloom. As he passed by Wu Da's house, he received, as we have seen, an unexpected blow on the head. But now that he had seen Jinlian under the lattice, Master Ximen went home again. "That was a splendid woman," he thought. "I wonder how I can get hold of her." He suddenly remembered old woman Wang, the neighbor who kept a tea shop. "She seems a clever old body," he said to himself, "and, if she can bring this affair to the conclusion I desire, she shall have a few taels of silver." He did not stay to eat anything, but hurried off to the street and dashed to old woman Wang's tea shop. He went in and took a seat, looking out beneath the awning.

"That was a very fine bow you made, Sir," said old woman Wang, laughing.

"Please come here, Stepmother," Ximen said. "That young neighbor of yours—er—that young woman—ahem— whose wife is she?"

"Oh," the old woman replied, "she is the sister of the King of Hell, the daughter of General Wu Dao. What makes you ask?"

"Don't treat the matter as a joke," Ximen said. "I am speaking seriously."

"Surely you know, Sir," said old woman Wang. "Her husband sells cakes outside the Town Hall."

"What! Xu the Third?" Ximen said.

The old woman shook her head. "No, if it were he, they would be something like a pair. Guess again, Sir."

"Perhaps it is Li the Third, then: he sells cakes."

The old woman shook her head again. "No, if he were the man, I should think they were perfectly matched."

"Well, then," Ximen cried, "it must be Liu Xiao. You know: the man they call Tattooed Arms."

Still the old woman laughed. "No," she said, "even if it were he, I should say they were a well-mated couple. Guess once more, Sir."

"I can't guess, Stepmother," Ximen said almost in despair, while the old woman roared with laughter.

"Well, I'll tell you. Her husband is that fellow Wu Da, who hawks his cakes about the streets."

When Ximen Qing heard this, he nearly jumped out of his chair. "You can't mean that Wu Da whom people call Tom Thumb or Old Scraggy Bark."

"That is the man," replied the old woman.

"Good Heavens," Ximen cried. "What a tasty piece of lamb to fall into a dog's mouth. However can it have happened?"

"It is always the same," old woman Wang replied. "You always find a beautiful horse ridden by some fool of a man, and a pretty girl sleeping with a husband who is not fit to be seen. The old Man in the Moon works things that way."

"How much do I owe you?" Ximen said.

"Nothing worth mentioning," the old woman replied. "We will leave it till another time."

"With whom is your son Wang Chao working now?" Ximen asked.

"He is away with a merchant, a native of Huai, but really he has been away so long that I don't know whether he's alive or dead."

"Why not let him come to me? He seems to be a smart lad."

"I am glad he meets with your approval."

"Very well," Ximen said, "when he comes back we must talk about the matter again." He thanked the old woman and went away. But in less than no time he was back again, sitting once more near the door that looked upon Wu Da's house.

"May I offer you some damson broth, Sir?" said old woman Wang, when she came out.

"I should like some very much," Ximen said, "but let it be a little sour, if you don't mind." The old woman made the broth, and offered it to him with both hands. When he had finished it, he put down the cup. "You make excellent damson broth, Stepmother," he said. "Have you got many damsons in your room there?"

"I have dealt in damsons all my life," the old woman said, "but I never keep them in my room."

"I was talking about damsons, not damsels," said Ximen. "You are getting a little mixed up."

"It was damsels you were thinking about, nonetheless," the old lady retorted.

"Well," said Ximen, "you admit you sell damsels. What about finding one for me? If you can let me have a nice tasty one, you won't lose by it."

"You are only teasing me," the old woman said. "If your wife heard about it, my old face would have a rough time."

"Not at all," Ximen said. "My wife is a most amiable woman, and I have several girls already, but none of them is exactly what I want. If you have a really good girl on your books, you must introduce her to me. I don't care whether she is somebody else's leavings or not, but she must be a woman who will satisfy me."

"Ah," the old woman said, "a few days ago I did hear of an excellent girl, but I'm afraid she wouldn't do for you."

"If she is the right stuff, just go ahead, and you shall be well paid for your pains."

"She is more than usually good-looking," said the old lady, "but rather old, perhaps."

"Well," said Ximen, "people have always said that a middle-aged woman has a charm all her own. It will not put me off if she happens to be a year or two older than I am. But how old is she?"

"She was born under the planet Mercury and her animal is the Pig, so as my reckoning goes, she will be ninety-three years old next New Year."

"You crazy old woman," Ximen cried. "Why do you screw up your silly old face and make fun all the time?" It was getting late and he decided to go away. The old woman had lighted her lamp and was going to fasten the gate, when Ximen Qing once again appeared. He sat down under the awning and gazed with longing eyes at Wu Da's house.

"Would you like a little allspice soup?" old woman Wang said.

"Yes, please," said Ximen, "but let it be sweet." The old woman hastily brought some soup, and he ate it all. He sat there till it was very late. At last he stood up. "Please make out my bill, old lady, and I will pay you next time I come."

"Don't worry about it," the old woman said; "we shall certainly have another opportunity of settling it." Ximen Qing laughed and went away.

At home, he could take no pleasure either eating or sleeping; his heart was consumed with desire for Jinlian. Wu Yueniang saw him in this sad state, but thought it was because of his third wife's death, and did not trouble him. Next morning, as soon as it was light and old woman Wang came out to unbolt her gate, Ximen Qing was already striding down the street.

"Ah," she thought, "new brooms sweep clean, and this one seems to be doing all its sweeping in this direction. I must keep the young man on tenterhooks for a while. In his dealings with the people here, he always manages to come off best, but if I get him into my clutches, I shall be surprised if I can't squeeze a little bawdy money out of him."

Old woman Wang's past history was none too creditable. She had been an efficient and busy go-between all her life, and occasionally dealt in children. She had also practiced midwifery, applying the requisite pressure to the mother and receiving the little ones on their arrival. In short, she was a thoroughly accomplished rogue.

The old woman had just opened her door to throw out the tea leaves when she saw Ximen Qing pacing up and down. Finally he came towards the tea shop and stood underneath the awning facing Wu Da's door. He was looking up at the lattice as though he could not take his eyes from it. The old woman pretended not to see him, and went on making a fire in her tea shop, until Ximen Qing, finding that she did not come out to offer him any tea, called to her to bring two cups.

"Ah," the old woman said, "is that you, my lord? Why have you allowed so long a time to pass without coming to see me? Please take a seat." In a few moments, she had made two cups of very strong tea and set them on the table.

"You'll take a cup with me, Stepmother, won't you?" Ximen said.

"I am not your shadow," the old woman said, laughing. "Why should I always drink tea with you?"

Ximen Qing laughed. "What do these neighbors of yours sell?"

"Roasted love darts; dried cuckoo's nests with parsley all around them; good fresh mincemeat; rolls all ready to be stuffed; oyster dumplings, and warm-heart pastries."

"You mad old woman," Ximen said, laughing. "I do wish you would talk sense."

"I am not mad by any means," said the old woman. "If you would rather go and ask the master of the house, you will find him at home."

"I am quite serious," Ximen said. "If they have good buns there, I should like to buy forty or fifty and take them home with me."

"There is no need to go to the house to buy them. The man will be going to the street in a minute or two, and you can get as many as you like."

"That is true," said Ximen. He drank his tea, lingered for a while, and at last went away. Old woman Wang watched him with her stony eyes, and saw him pacing to and fro, looking first to the right and then to the left. This he did seven or eight times. At last he came back to the tea shop.

"How do you do, Sir?" the old lady said. "I had almost forgotten what you look like."

Ximen Qing took a tael of silver from his sleeve and handed it to her. "This is for my tea," he said.

The old woman smiled. "Why do you give me so much?"

"I should take it if I were you," said Ximen, "and not trouble how much it is."

"Now," thought the old woman, "my chance has come. It is time this broom lost some of its bristles. I will take this today, and it will doubtless come in for my lodging tomorrow." She said aloud, "I see there is something you have set your heart upon."

"What makes you think that?" Ximen said.

"It is not very hard to see. There is an old saying, 'When a man enters your door, don't trouble to ask whether he is in luck or not. Look at his face.' I can assure you I've guessed things far more difficult than that."

"If you can guess what I am thinking about," said Ximen, "you shall have five taels of silver."

Old woman Wang laughed. "One guess will be enough. Let me whisper in your Lordship's ear. You have been haunting this neighborhood for two or three days, and it is quite clear that you have your eye on the lady next door. Am I right?"

Ximen Qing smiled. "Your intelligence, Stepmother, is worthy of Sui He, and you are even sharper than Lu Jia. I shall not attempt to hoodwink you. I don't know how it is, but ever since I saw her face under the lattice I seem to have lost both my heart and my head. Day and night I can think of nothing else. When I am at home, I can neither eat nor drink, and work is out of the question. I wonder if you can think of some way to help me."

"I shall not try to hoodwink you either," the old woman said. "People imagine that I keep a tea shop here, but to tell you the truth, a ghost playing the night watchman would fill the part as honestly as I do mine. One day, I certainly did sell some tea. It was three years ago, to be precise, when snow fell in the sixth month; but I've sold none since. No, sir, I make my living in quite another way."

"And what may that be?" Ximen asked.

"When I was thirty-six years old, my husband died. He left me with a young boy and not a penny to live on. So I took up the business of a go-between, and also made a little money by making clothes, acting the midwife, and introducing people to one another. Sometimes I let blood for people who are ill."

I had no idea your accomplishments were so many," Ximen said. "If you can arrange this matter to my satisfaction, I will give you ten taels of silver for your coffin. All you have to do is to get that woman to meet me."

"I was only joking," the old woman said. "Why did you take me seriously?"

CHAPTER 3
The Old Procuress

Ximen Qing was desperately anxious to possess Pan Jinlian. He gave the old woman no peace.

"Stepmother," he said, "if you bring this business to a happy end, I will give you ten taels of silver."

"Sir," said the old woman, "you may have heard, perhaps, of setting a love snare. The expression implies much that is difficult and is, indeed, what is more commonly known as wife stealing. Before a man can set about this wife-stealing business with any prospect of success, five things are essential. He must be as handsome as Pan An. His member must be at least as large as a donkey's. He must be as rich as Deng Tong, and reasonably young. Finally, he must have plenty of time on his hands, and almost endless patience. If you are possessed of all these qualifications, you may think of going in for this sort of entertainment."

"I think I may say I do possess them all," Ximen Qing said. "I would not venture to compare my handsome figure with that of Pan An, but it will serve. Ever since I was a boy, I have played in the lowest and most unsavory haunts, and I must say I have succeeded in keeping a very fat turtle well content. I may not have as much money as Deng Tong, but have a good deal put away, certainly sufficient to live upon. As for my patience, I should never think of retaliating though I received four hundred blows. Finally, if I had not plenty of time to waste, you would not be seeing me here so often. Stepmother, do this for me, and you shall not be disappointed with your reward."

"There is one thing more, Sir," the old woman said. "You tell me that you possess the five essential qualifications, but I fear this too is indispensable."

"What do you mean?" Ximen Qing cried.

"Forgive my speaking plainly," the old woman said, "but when a man would run off with somebody else's wife, there are very considerable difficulties in the way. A man may spend almost his last penny, and still fail. He must go to the absolute limit. I happen to know that you particularly dislike parting with your money, and that is the difficulty."

"It shall be no difficulty in this case," Ximen said, "for I will do anything you suggest."

"Very well," the old woman said, "if you are really prepared to spend a few taels, I have a plan that should enable you to secure the lady."

Ximen would have liked to hear it, but the old woman said, with a laugh, "It is too late today, and time you went home. Come back in six months, or perhaps three, and we will see what we can do."

"Stepmother," said Ximen, "don't joke about it. Only do this for me and you shall have a really handsome present." But the old woman laughed all the more.

"You certainly seem to be very keen," she said. "Nobody ever comes to say his prayers to me at the temple of Wu Cheng Wang, but my plan is as good and better than any that fellow Sun Wuzi could have made. He was able to turn girls into soldiers, but I could have captured eight out of ten of them. Let me tell you all I know about this woman. She comes of a poor family, but she is as clever as can be. She knows how to play and sing, her embroidery is excellent, and she is expert at many games. In fact, there is nothing she doesn't know. Her surname is Pan, and her personal name, Jinlian. Her father was Pan Cai, who used to live by the South Gate. Originally, she was sold to Master Zhang, and at his house she learned to sing and play. When Zhang was very old, he made a present of her to Wu Da. She does not go out very often and, when I am not busy, I go over to her place and get anything she happens to want. She always calls me Stepmother.

"These last few days, Wu Da has been going out early. If you wish to clinch the matter, you must buy some silk, one roll of blue, another of white, another of the finest white silk, and ten taels of good raw silk. Give them to me. I will go to her house to borrow a calendar, and ask her to tell me a day of good omen so that I can engage a dressmaker to come and make me some clothes. It may be that she will find a day for me, but not offer to come herself to make the clothes. In that case, there is nothing to be done. If she is very pleasant and says, 'Don't get a dressmaker. I will come and make the clothes for you,' that will be one to us. If I can persuade her to come here to sew, that will be another one to us. If she comes at noon, I will set out refreshments and invite her to have some. She may say, 'I am very sorry but I can't,' and go off home and, in that case, we shall have to give up. On the other hand, she may say nothing, but sit down and eat my lunch, and then we score again.

"You must not come tomorrow, but the day after. Put on your smartest clothes. Give a cough of warning, and then come to the door and call,

'How do you do, Stepmother? May I come in and have a cup of tea?' I will come out and ask you in. It is possible that, as soon as she sees you, she may want to go home, and, if she does, I cannot stop her. That will be the end. But if she stays where she is, we shall be four points to the good.

"When you sit down, I shall say to her, 'This is the gentleman who gave me the clothes. I can't tell you how grateful I am to him,' and I shall say all sorts of pretty things about your generosity. Then you will compliment her on her sewing. If she does not answer, we are done. If she does answer, and enters into conversation with you, our fifth point is gained.

"Then I shall say, 'Isn't this good lady kind to make my clothes for me?' and praise you both—you for giving me the money and her for making the clothes. I shall say, 'This lady is indeed good-hearted. I was lucky to be able to persuade her to come. Perhaps you would like to offer her some refreshment.' You will take some silver out of your pocket and ask me to go and buy something. If at that moment she decides to go, I can't hold her, and all is over. But, if she doesn't move, we shall have gained our sixth point.

"I shall take your silver and, as I go out, I shall say, 'I wonder if you would mind keeping this gentleman company?' She may jump up at that and, if she does so, I can't very well put my arms around her and hold her, but, if she doesn't, we shall have gained another point.

"When I come back with the things, I shall put them on the table and say, 'Lady, put the clothes aside for a while and let us drink a little wine. This gentleman has been good enough to spend his money on us.' If she will not join us, but takes her leave, the matter is ended. But if she says, 'Oh, really I can't stay,' but does not make any effort to go, the eighth point is ours.

"If she drinks her wine contentedly and begins to talk to you, I shall say, 'There is not enough wine,' and you will ask me to buy some more, and some fruits too, and give me silver for the purpose. Then I shall shut the door upon you both. If she is shy and tries to run away, we can do no more. But if she lets me fasten the door and does not get angry, we are within an ace of our goal. The last stage is the critical one. You, Sir, will stay in the room with the woman and talk prettily to her, but you must not be too rough when you begin to take liberties. If you touch her, and spoil the whole game, it will not be my fault. But it is possible that you might knock down a pair of chopsticks with your sleeve, and touch her foot when you pretend to pick them up. If this makes her angry, I shall come in and make peace between you, but all our chances will be gone and we can never hope to retrieve the position. If she says nothing, we gain our tenth point, and the game is ours. If I lead you to victory, what reward may I expect?"

Ximen Qing listened to all this, and was perfectly delighted. "Your plan may not come from the Ling Yan temple," he said, "but it is absolutely flawless."

"Don't forget those ten taels of silver," old woman Wang said.

"If I get but a single piece of orange peel," Ximen said, "I shall never forget the Dongting lake. But when do you propose to put this scheme into operation, Stepmother?"

"Come back this evening," the old woman said, "and you shall know. By this time Wu Da has gone out, and I will go over about the calendar and say my part. You send somebody with the silk as quickly as possible. Don't waste any time."

"I'll see to it at once," Ximen Qing cried. "You may count upon me absolutely." He went to the street to buy the three rolls of silk and the ten taels of raw silk, and told Daian to wrap them up and take them to the old woman. She received them with great satisfaction and sent the boy away.

When the silk had come, the old woman opened her back door and went across to Wu Da's house. Jinlian took her upstairs, and they sat down.

"Why have you not been to take tea in my poor house lately?" asked the old woman.

"I haven't been well these last few days," Jinlian replied, "and somehow I have not felt inclined to move."

"Have you a calendar in the house?" the old woman said. "I should like to see one. I wish to find a day favorable for making clothes."

"What clothes are you thinking of having made?"

"I am always suffering from something or another," the old woman said. "One of these days I shall find myself as high as the mountains and as deep as the ocean. And my son is not at home."

"Where has he been all this time?" Jinlian said.

"He went away with a stranger, and I have never had a word from him since. I worry about him all day long."

Jinlian asked how old the boy was, and when the old woman told her he was seventeen, she said, "Why don't you find him a wife? You would save yourself a great deal of work."

"You may well say that," the old woman said. "There never was a place so lonely as mine. I potter about, as best I can, and sometimes I do think I'll find a wife for him. When he comes home, I really must see about it. Day and night I have trouble with my breathing, and I cough till my body shakes as though it were being torn in pieces. And I can't sleep. I've come to the conclusion that it's time I was getting my funeral clothes together. Fortunately for me, there is a rich gentleman who often comes to have tea at my shop. When there is anybody ill at his place, he sends for me; I buy maids for him and see about marriages. He knows I am to be trusted;

that I never neglect any little point, however unimportant it may seem to others. He has given me the material for a full set of funeral clothes, and all the trimmings too. I have had this stuff put away for more than a year and have done nothing with it. But this year I have not felt at all well, and as there is an extra month in it, and I am not very busy, I have taken my chance and I am going to have it made up at last. Unfortunately, all the dressmakers say they are too busy to come and make my clothes. You've no idea how ill all this anxiety makes me."

Jinlian listened to this long story, and smiled. "I'm afraid I can't make the clothes as well as they should be made, but I have nothing particular to do, and, if you like, I'll see what I can do for you."

The old lady smiled delightedly. "With your precious hands to make the things, even if I die, my poor old body will rejoice. I have always heard what a good needlewoman you are, but I have never dared to come and trouble you."

"Why should I not make them?" Jinlian said. "Anyhow, I've promised now, and I must do them for you. Take the calendar, and get someone to find an auspicious day. Then I'll begin."

"Do you think I don't know that you can read all the characters in the poems and the hundred dramas? Why should I take the calendar to anybody else?"

"I have never had any education," Jinlian said, with a smile.

"Oh, thank you, thank you," the old woman cried, handing her the calendar. Jinlian examined it, then she said, "Tomorrow is no good, and the day after that is no good either. We shall have to wait."

The old woman took the calendar and hung it on the wall. "If you are willing to do the work you yourself are my lucky star. I need not bother whether the day is lucky or not. Others have looked at the calendar and told me that tomorrow is not a good day for the purpose, but that doesn't trouble me."

"Well," Jinlian said, "it may be that a day unlucky for other purposes is most suitable for the making of funeral clothes."

"If you don't mind, then come to my poor house tomorrow."

"Why not bring the material here?" said Jinlian.

"Because I should like to watch you sewing, and there is nobody to look after my house."

"Very well," Jinlian promised, "I will come to your house tomorrow after lunch."

"God bless you! God bless you!" the old lady cried. She went downstairs and away. That evening she told Ximen Qing the result of her efforts, and asked him to come two days later. The next morning the old woman swept out her room, prepared needles and thread, made some tea, and waited for Jinlian.

When Wu Da had eaten his breakfast, he went out with his baskets. His wife pulled up the lattice and ordered Ying'er to look after the house. Then she went by the back door to old woman Wang's house. The old lady, who was as pleased as could be, welcomed her and made her sit down. Then she made a cup of very strong tea, with walnuts and beech-nuts, and gave it to Jinlian. After wiping the table, she brought out the three rolls of silk. Jinlian measured them and cut all the garments out. Then she began to sew. The old woman watched her and poured forth a stream of compliments.

"What marvelous skill! I have lived nearly seventy years and never have I seen so swift a needle or such cunning fingers."

Jinlian sewed till noon. Then old woman Wang prepared lunch, and asked her to have some. Afterwards, Jinlian sewed till it was nearly dark; then she packed up the silk and went home. When Wu Da came in with his baskets, she closed the door and pulled down the blind. Wu Da saw that his wife's face was red, and asked her where she had been.

"I have been with our neighbor, Stepmother Wang," Jinlian said. "She asked me to make some funeral clothes for her and at lunchtime she set out some wine and cakes and insisted that I should have some."

"You ought not to eat her food," Wu Da said. "It is our place to invite her. She asked you to make these clothes, it is true, but you should take your meals at home and not trouble her. If you go tomorrow, take some money with you and buy some food and wine in your turn. The proverb says: 'Better a neighbor at hand than a relative far away.' Don't let us spoil the friendship between us. If she will not allow you to return her hospitality, you must bring the clothes here and make them."

Jinlian listened, but said nothing. The next day, after breakfast, Wu Da took his baskets and went out. Old woman Wang came over to invite Jinlian to go to her house, and soon they had brought the clothes out and were at work upon them again. Old woman Wang made a cup of tea for Jinlian, but at lunchtime Jinlian took three *fen* from her sleeve and gave them to the old woman.

"Stepmother," she said, "it is my turn to buy a cup of wine."

"Oh dear!" the old woman cried, "what can you be thinking about? It was I who asked you to come and make these clothes, and I can't possibly allow you to spend your money as well. Why, if I did, your wine and food would poison me."

"You must blame my foolish husband," Jinlian said, "but he said, if you did not take it kindly, I was to go home."

"If your husband feels like that about it," the old woman said, "I suppose I must keep it." She was very much afraid of doing anything that might interfere with her plans, so she put some of her own money to it and went out to buy better food and wine. Then she invited the woman to join her.

It would seem that in all the world there is not a single woman, no matter how intelligent she may be, who cannot be led astray by some trivial act of kindness. Nine women out of every ten are caught this way.

The old woman prepared some refreshments and enjoyed them with Jinlian. Afterwards they went on sewing and, when evening began to fall, the old woman thanked her very heartily, and she went home once more.

After breakfast on the third day, the old woman waited till Wu Da had gone out, then she went to the back door and called out: "Lady, may I make so bold . . ." Jinlian said she would come in a moment, and soon they were again in the old woman's room, sitting down to work upon the clothes. The old woman made tea as usual. About midday, Ximen Qing arrived.

He had waited anxiously for this day, and now he dressed himself very elegantly, put three or four taels of silver in his sleeve, and sauntered off to Amethyst Street, with a golden fan in his hand. When he came to the old woman's house, he coughed. Then he called, "Where are you, Stepmother Wang? I haven't seen you for ever so long."

"Who is that calling me?" the old woman cried.

"Ximen Qing."

"I could not imagine who it might be," the old woman said, hurrying to the door, "and here you are! You have just come at the right moment. Come in and see what I have to show you." She took him by the sleeve and led him to her room. "This is the very gentleman who gave me the silk," she said to Jinlian.

Ximen Qing opened his eyes wide and gazed at the woman. The masses of her piled-up hair seemed like clouds of the darkest hue. Her rosy cheeks had all the freshness of spring. She was wearing a white linen coat, a dark red skirt, and a blue stomacher. When Ximen came in, she was sewing, but she rose at once and made a reverence to him. He came forward and bowed profoundly. Then she put down the clothes and made a more profound reverence.

"I owe this gentleman a great deal," old woman Wang said. "It was he who gave me this material. I had it in the house a year before I could get anyone to make it up." Then she added, "I am greatly indebted to this lady too, for making the clothes for me. Her sewing is as fine as fine can be. Anything so good and fine is seldom seen in these days. Come and look at it, Sir."

Ximen Qing took up the clothes and examined them. "Indeed," he said, "the lady sews so exquisitely that only an angel could rival her."

Jinlian shyly looked at the ground, but she smiled. "Do not make fun of my poor efforts," she said.

"Stepmother,' Ximen Qing said, "I hardly dare to ask you, but who is this lady?"

"Guess," said the old woman.

"How can I guess?"

"Sit down then, and I will tell you. Do you remember passing by one day and getting a knock on the head?"

"Yes," Ximen said, "I know it is she who struck me that day, but I still don't know who she is."

Jinlian bowed her head more deeply and said with a smile, "It was very careless of your slave to strike you. Please don't be angry with me, my lord."

"How could I possibly be?" Ximen said hastily.

"This lady is the wife of my neighbor, Wu Da," the old woman said.

"Is that so?" Ximen said. "I am afraid I was forgetful of my good manners."

The old woman turned to Jinlian and asked if she knew the gentleman.

"I do not," the woman replied.

"He is one of the wealthiest men in our district and a very good friend of the magistrate. It is Master Ximen. He has thousands and thousands of strings of cash, and keeps a medicine shop near the Town Hall. The money in his house is piled so high that it touches the North Star and even his spoiled rice is enough to fill many barns. His gold is yellow and his silver white. His pearls are round and his precious stones brilliant. He has rhinoceros horns and elephants' tusks. It was I who arranged his first marriage. His wife is the daughter of Captain Wu, a very intelligent woman indeed." Then she turned to Ximen. "Why have you not been to have tea with me lately?"

"I have been very busy attending to my daughter's betrothal," Ximen said, "and that has left me very little leisure."

"Whom is your daughter going to marry?" the old woman said, "and why didn't you get me to arrange the marriage?"

"She is going to marry Chen Jingji, the son of that Chen who is related to General Yang, who commands the Imperial Guard. The young man is seventeen years old and still at his studies. I should have asked you to arrange this marriage, but a woman named Wen came from his family to ask for the betrothal papers, and Xue, the flower seller, acted for us. They arranged everything between them. But, Stepmother, we shall be giving a party very soon, and, if you care to come, I shall be delighted to have you join us."

"I was only joking," the old woman said. "The go-betweens in this city are all bitches. When they arranged the marriage, I had no finger in the pie, and, now that the dinner is cooked, they certainly won't wish me to have a bite. There is an old saying that there is never any love lost between those who follow the same profession. No, I will wait until the wedding is over and then I will come with a few humble presents, and I may pick up some of the leavings. That will be the best thing I can do. I can't allow myself to be left completely out of it." They chattered away in this strain, the old woman flattering him, and he muttering any nonsense in return. Meanwhile, Jinlian kept her head modestly bowed and went on with her needlework.

Ximen Qing glanced at her from time to time, and could see the passion within her growing stronger. This delighted him beyond measure, and he was more eager than ever to bring the matter to its consummation. The old woman made two cups of tea. She gave one to Ximen Qing and the other to Jinlian, and said: "Lady, won't you take a cup of tea with this gentleman?" She looked at Ximen, and stroked her cheek gently; it was a sign that five of their ten points were already gained. The power of tea to exhilarate, and the power of wine to bring people together, have always been acknowledged as the go-betweens of love.

"If you had not come here," old woman Wang said, "I should never have had the courage to go to your house and invite you. Good fortune brought you here, and good fortune, again, decided the moment of your coming. But there is an old saying: 'One guest never troubles two hosts.' You have given me money, and this kind lady has been good enough to work for me, and I don't know how I can express my gratitude to either of you. If the fates had not been kind, I should have found it hard to bring you two together. I suggest, Sir, that you take my place as host, and give me something to buy a little wine for the lady."

"I don't know whether I have any money with me," Ximen Qing said, feeling in his sleeve. He brought out a tael of silver, gave it to the old woman, and asked her to buy something with it.

"Not for me, please," Jinlian said, but she made no attempt to move. The old woman took the silver and, as she prepared to go out, said, "Lady, I wonder if you will be good enough to keep the gentleman company till I come back. I shall only be a few minutes."

"Stepmother, please don't trouble," Jinlian said, but still she remained in her place. The old woman went out, and left Ximen Qing and Pan Jinlian alone together.

Ximen's eyes seemed to devour the woman. She looked up at him coyly, then bowed her head again and went on with her sewing. Before long, the old woman was back again with cooked goose and roasted duck, meats of various kinds, and some luscious-looking fruits. She put them on dishes and set them on the table. Then she said to Jinlian: "Won't you put the clothes aside for a while, and take a cup of wine?"

"You drink with his Lordship," the woman said. "It is not for me to take such a liberty."

"You mustn't say that," the old woman cried, "it has all been arranged in your honor." She placed the dishes before them and, when they had taken their places, poured the wine.

"Stepmother," Ximen Qing said, "will you ask the lady to take wine with me?"

Jinlian thanked him. She dared not drink, she said, because a very little wine went to her head.

"Oh, you can hold a good deal," the old woman said, "I know that. Don't make a fuss about a cup or two." Jinlian took the wine and raised her glass to the others. Ximen Qing took up his chopsticks. "Stepmother," he said, "ask the lady to take something to eat." The old lady picked out some tidbits and passed them to the woman. The wine went around three times, and old woman Wang went out to warm some more.

"May I ask your age?" Ximen said.

"I am twenty-five," Jinlian said, bowing her head again.

"Then you and my wife are the same age. Her animal is the Dragon, and she was born on the fifteenth day of the eighth month."

"You are putting Earth and Heaven on the same plane," Jinlian said. "You pay me too great a compliment."

"This lady," old woman Wang said, "is as clever as can be, besides being such a good needlewoman. She knows all the philosophies of all the philosophers, not to speak of backgammon and chess. She can write very nicely too."

"Ah," Ximen said, with a sigh, "but where shall we find another like her?"

"I wouldn't say anything impertinent for the world," old woman Wang said, "but though you have many ladies in your house, I doubt whether there is one among them equal to this lady."

"That is true, I fear," Ximen said. "It is a long story. The fates have been unkind to me and I must own that none of them is really any use."

"Your first wife was good enough," the old woman said.

"Don't talk about her," Ximen cried. "If she had lived, things would have been very different, but now there is no real mistress in the house and the whole place is going to rack and ruin. There are three, five, nay seven people—all ready enough to eat my food, but not so ready to attend to their household duties."

"How long is it since your first wife died? I have forgotten."

"I hate to talk about it," Ximen said. "My first wife Chen came from a very poor family, but she was a clever woman and did all I needed. Unhappily, she died more than three years ago. I have married again, but my present wife is always ailing and the business of the household is too much for her. My domestic affairs are in complete disarray. Perhaps that is why I spend so much of my time away from home. If I didn't there would be trouble."

"You must excuse me, Sir," said the old woman, "but your late wife and your present wife together were not so skilled in needlework as this lady, or so attractive in appearance."

"My other wives also," said Ximen, "cannot compare with her."

"But what about the establishment in East Street?" the old woman said, laughing. "Why do you never ask me to tea there?"

"You are thinking of Zhang Xichun, the singing girl?" Ximen said. "I found she was a flighty creature and I have given her up."

"That may be," the old woman continued, "but what about Li Jiao'er, who used to be in the bawdy house? You have been on very good terms with her for a long time."

"Oh, I took her into my household some time ago and, if she proves satisfactory, I shall marry her."

"Then there was Miss Zhuo," the old woman suggested.

"Do not mention her name," Ximen said. "I made her my third wife, but a short time ago she fell ill and died."

"Dear me! Dear me!" cried the old woman. "Suppose I found a lady like this, one whom you really liked, and came to your house to talk over the matter? Don't you think it would cause a disturbance?"

"My parents are both dead, and I am my own master. Who would dare say a word to me?"

"However, I may try. Where can I find a lady so much to your liking as this one?"

"Oh, there may be one for all we know," Ximen said. "But I loathe the Fates who control my matrimonial affairs. If they had been more indulgent, I might have found such a woman."

They chatted in this way for some time. At last old woman Wang said, "Just when we are ready for a little more wine, it all seems to have gone. I am sorry to trouble you, Sir, but may I buy another jar?" Ximen Qing put his hand in his sleeve. There were still three or four taels there. He gave them all to the old lady, "Here you are," he said. "Any time we are short of wine, you need only go and get it."

The old woman thanked him, and got up. She glanced at Jinlian, who, after drinking three cups of wine, was already consumed with passion. The words that passed between them seemed only to add fuel to the fires that burned within. She bowed her head, but still she did not move.

CHAPTER 4
Ximen Qing Attains His End

The sun streams through the painted doorway into the bedchamber.
There stands a maiden whom no gold can buy.
She leans against the door
Her lovely eyes, like beams of sunshine, seek to pursue her lover
But he has gone so far, her tender feet may never hope to follow.

O ld woman Wang took the money and started for the door. Smiling, she said to Jinlian, "I must go to the street to buy a jar of wine; you will keep his Lordship company, won't you? If there is a drop left in the jar, warm two cups and drink them with him. The best wine is to be had in East Street. I shall have to go there for it, so I may be away some little time."

"Really I can't drink any more," Pan Jinlian cried. "Please don't go on my account."

"You and his Lordship are no longer strangers," said the old woman, "and you have nothing else to do. Drink a cup of wine with him. Why should you be afraid?"

With her lips Jinlian said she did not wish to drink, but her body told another story. The old woman shut the door and fastened it on the outside with a chain, imprisoning the two young people in her room. Then outside in the roadway, she sat down and began to roll some thread. Jinlian saw the old woman go, and pulled her chair to one side. As she settled down again, she glanced swiftly at Ximen Qing. He was sitting on the other side of the table, his eyes wide open, staring at her. At last he managed to speak.

"I forgot to ask your honorable name."

The woman bowed, and answered, smiling, "My unworthy name is Wu."

Ximen Qing pretended that he had not heard properly. "Did you say Du?" he said. Jinlian looked up, and said in a very soft voice, "I did not think you were deaf, Sir."

"I am sorry," Ximen said, "it was my mistake. You said 'Wu.' There are not many people called Wu in Qinghe. There is indeed one fellow who sells cakes outside the Town Hall, but he is no bigger than my thumb.

His name is Wu, Master Wu Da. Is he a relative of yours by any chance?"

Jinlian flushed. "He is my husband," she said, hanging her head.

Ximen Qing was silent for a long time, and seemed to be thinking very seriously. "How sad! How wrong!" he murmured at last. Jinlian smiled, and glanced at him.

"You have no reason to complain. Why should you say, 'How sad!'?"

"I was thinking how sad it must be for you," he said. He muttered many things, almost unintelligibly. Jinlian still looked down. She played with her skirt, nibbled at her sleeves, and bit her lips, sometimes talking, sometimes glancing slyly at him. Ximen pretended to find the heat trying, and took off his green silk coat.

"Would you mind putting my coat on the old lady's bed?" he said. Jinlian did not offer to take the coat. Keeping her head still turned away, she played with her sleeves and smiled. "Is there anything wrong with your own hands?" she said. "Why do you ask me to do things for you?" Ximen Qing laughed.

"So you won't do a little thing like that for me? Well, I suppose I must do it myself." He leaned over the table and put his coat on the bed. As he did so, he brushed the table with his sleeve and knocked down a chopstick. Luck favored him; the chopstick came to rest beneath the woman's skirt. Ximen, who had already drunk more wine than was good for him, invited her to join him. Then he wanted his chopsticks to help her to some of the dishes. He looked about. One of them was missing. Jinlian looked down, pushed the chopstick with her toe, and said, laughing, "Isn't this it?" Ximen Qing went to her, and bent down. "Ah, here it is!" he cried, but instead of picking up the chopstick, he took hold of her embroidered shoe.

Jinlian laughed. "I shall shout, if you are so naughty."

"Be kind to me, Lady," Ximen said, going down on his knees. As he spoke, he gently stroked her silken garments.

"It is horrid of you to pester me so," Jinlian cried. "I shall box your ears."

"Lady," he said, "if your blows should cause my death, it would be a happy end."

Without giving her time to object, he carried her to old woman Wang's bed, took off his clothes and, after unloosing her girdle, lay down with her. Their happiness reached its culmination.

In the days when Jinlian had performed the act of darkness with Zhang, that miserable old man had never been able to offer any substantial contribution to the proceedings, and not once had she been satisfied. Then she married Wu Da. You may imagine the prowess that might be expected from Master Tom Thumb. It could hardly be described as heroic. Now she met Ximen Qing, whose capacity in such matters was unlimited and whose skill was exceptionally refined and cunning.

> The mandarin ducks, with necks entwined, sport upon the water.
> The phoenix and his mate, their heads close pressed together, fly
>   among the blossoms.
> Joyful and tireless, the tree puts forth twin branches
> The girdle, tied in a lovers' knot, is full of sweetness.
> He, the red-lipped one, thirsts for a close embrace
> She, of the powdered cheeks, awaits it eagerly.
> The silken hose are raised on high
> And two new moons appear above his shoulders.
> The golden hairpins fall
> And on the pillow rests a bank of lowering clouds.
> They swear eternal oaths by ocean and by mountain
> Seeking a thousand new delights.
> The clouds are bashful and the rain is shy
> They play ten thousand naughty tricks.
> "Qia Qia," the oriole cries.
> Each sucks the nectar from the other's lips.
> The cherry lips breathe lightly, lightly.
> In those willowy hips the passion beats
> The mocking eyes are bright like stars
> Tiny drops of sweat are like a hundred fragrant pearls
> The sweet full breasts tremble
> The dew, like a gentle stream, reaches the heart of the peony
> They taste the joys of love in perfect harmony
> For stolen joys, in truth, are ever the most sweet.

Just when they had done and were putting on their clothes again, old woman Wang pushed open the door and came in, clapping her hands as though she had never been more surprised in her life.

"A fine state of affairs," she said. Ximen Qing and Jinlian were extremely embarrassed.

"Oh, splendid, splendid!" the old woman said to Jinlian. "I asked you to come here to make clothes, not to make love with someone else's husband. If your Wu Da found this out, he would blame me. I shall have to go and explain the matter to him at once." She turned, and started out. Jinlian caught her quickly by the skirt. She hid her blushing face and could only get out a single sentence: "Spare me, Stepmother."

"You must make me a promise, then," the old woman said. "From this day forward, you must deceive Wu Da and give his Lordship here whatever he desires. If I call you early, you must come early. If I call you late, you must come late. Then I will say no more about it. But, if there should be a day when you do not come, I shall tell Wu Da."

Jinlian was so abashed that she could find nothing to say. "Well," said the old woman, "what are you going to do about it? I must have an answer now." "I will come," the woman whispered. Old woman Wang turned to Ximen Qing. "I need say no more to you, Sir. This is a fine piece of work, and you owe it all to me. You must not forget your promise. You must keep your word. If you try to wriggle out of it, I shall be compelled to speak to Wu Da."

"Don't worry, Stepmother," Ximen said, "I shall not go back on my word."

"I haven't too much confidence in either of you," old woman Wang said. "Give me a pledge of some sort and then I'll believe you."

Ximen Qing took a golden pin from his head and set it in Jinlian's hair. She took it out again and put it in her sleeve, for she was afraid that if she went home wearing it, Wu Da would wish to know where it had come from. She hesitated to produce any pledge herself, but the old woman caught her by the sleeve and, finding a white silk handkerchief, handed it to Ximen Qing. Then they all drank several cups of wine. By this time it was getting dark and, saying that it was time for her to go home, Jinlian said good-bye to old woman Wang and Ximen Qing and went to her house by the back way. She pulled down the blind and, soon afterwards, Wu Da came in.

Old woman Wang looked at Ximen Qing.

"Did I play my cards well?" she said.

"No one could have done better," said Ximen.

"Were you satisfied?"

"Perfectly."

"She comes of singing girl stock," the old woman said, "and she must have had plenty of experience. I am very proud that I have been able to bring you two together, especially since I did it all by my own cleverness. Mind you give me what you promised."

"I will send you the silver as soon as I reach home."

"My eyes have seen the banner of victory and my ears have heard a sweet message," the old woman said, "but don't wait until my coffin is being carried out for burial, and then send money for the choirboys."

Ximen Qing laughed. He saw that the street was deserted, put on his eyeshades, and went home.

The next day he came again to the old woman's house. The old lady made tea for him and asked him to sit down. He took ten taels of silver from his sleeve and gave it to her. Money seems to produce an extraordinary effect upon people everywhere. As soon as the old woman's black eyes beheld this snow-white silver, she was as happy as could be. She took it, and twice made reverence to him. "I thank you, Sir," she said, "with all my heart."

"Wu Da is still at home," she continued, "but I will go over to his house and pretend I wish to borrow a gourd." She went by the back way to her neighbor's house. Jinlian was giving her husband his breakfast when she heard the knocking at the door, and told Ying'er to see who was there. It is Grandmother Wang," the girl said, "she has come to borrow a water gourd."

"I will lend you a water jug, Stepmother," Jinlian said, "but won't you come in and sit down a while?"

"There is nobody to look after my house," the old woman said, beckoning with her finger to Jinlian, thus giving her to understand that Ximen Qing had come. She took the gourd and went away, and Jinlian hustled her husband over his breakfast and packed him off with his baskets. She went upstairs and redressed herself, putting on beautiful new clothes, and told Ying'er to watch the house. "I am going to your Grandmother Wang's, but I shall be back in a moment. If your father comes home, let me know at once or it will be the worse for your little bottom." She went to the tea shop.

Jinlian came, and to Ximen Qing it seemed that she had come straight down from Heaven. Side by side, close pressed together, they sat. Old woman Wang gave them tea. "Did Wu Da ask you any questions when you got home yesterday?" she said.

"He asked me if I had finished your clothes, and I told him that the funeral shoes and socks had still to be made."

The old woman hastily set wine before them, and they drank together, very happily. Ximen Qing delighted in every detail of the woman's form. She seemed to him even more beautiful than when he had first seen her. The little wine she had taken brought roses to her pale face and, with her cloudlike hair, she might have been a fairy, more beautiful than Chang E.

Ximen Qing could not find words to express his admiration. He gathered her in his arms, and lifted her skirts that he might see her dainty feet. She was wearing shoes of raven-black silk, no broader than his two fingers. His heart was overflowing with delight. Mouth to mouth they drank together, and smiled. Jinlian asked how old he was. "I am twenty-seven. I was born on the twenty-eighth day of the seventh month." Then she said, "How many ladies are there in your household?" and he said, "Besides the mistress of my house, there are three or four, but with none of them am I really satisfied." Again she asked, "How many sons have you?" and he answered, "I have no sons, only one little girl who is shortly to be married." Then it was his turn to ask her questions.

He took from his sleeve a box, gilded on the outside and silver within. There were fragrant tea leaves in it and some small sweetmeats. Placing some of them on his tongue, he passed them to her mouth. They embraced and hugged one another; their cries and kissings made noise enough, but old woman Wang went in and out, carrying dishes and warming the wine, and paid not the slightest attention to them. They played their amorous games without any interference from her. Soon they had drunk as much as they desired, and a fit of passion swept over them. Ximen Qing's desire could no longer be restrained; he disclosed the treasure that sprang from his loins, and made the woman touch it with her delicate fingers. From his youth upwards he had constantly played with the maidens who live in places of ill-fame, and he was already wearing the silver clasp that had been washed with magic herbs. Upstanding, it was, and flushed with pride, the black hair strong and bristling. A mighty warrior in very truth.

> A warrior of stature not to be despised
> At times a hero and at times a coward.
> Who, when for battle disinclined,
> As though in drink sprawls to the east and west.
> But, when for combat he is ready,
> Like a mad monk he plunges back and forth
> And to the place from which he came returns.
> Such is his duty.
> His home is in the loins, beneath the navel.
> Heaven has given him two sons
> To go wherever he goes
> And, when he meets an enemy worthy of his steel,
> He will attack, and then attack again.

Then Jinlian took off her clothes. Ximen Qing fondled the fragrant blossom. No down concealed it; it had all the fragrance and tenderness of fresh-made pastry, the softness and the appearance of a new-made pie. It was a thing so exquisite that all the world would have desired it.

> Tender and clinging, with lips like lotus petals
> Yielding and gentle, worthy to be loved.
> When it is happy, it puts forth its tongue
> And welcomes with a smile.
> When it is weary, it is content
> To stay where Nature put it

> At home in Trouser Village
> Among the scanty herbage.
> But, when it meets a handsome gallant
> It strives with him and says no word.

After that day, Jinlian came regularly to the old woman's house to sport with Ximen Qing. Love bound them together as it were with glue; their minds and hearts were united as if with gum.

There is an old saying: "Good news never leaves the house, but ill news spreads a thousand miles." It was not long before all the neighbors knew what was going on. Only Wu Da remained ignorant.

In Qinghe there lived a boy called Qiao; he was about fifteen years old. As he had been born in Yunzhou, where his father was on military service, he was called Yun'ge. His father was now grown old, and they lived together alone. The boy was by no means without craft. He kept himself by selling fresh fruits in the different wineshops, and Ximen Qing often gave him small sums of money. One day he had filled his basket with snow-white pears and was carrying them about the streets, on the lookout for his patron. Somebody he chanced to meet said to him, "Yun'ge, I can tell you where to find him."

"Where can I find him, Uncle?" the boy said. "Tell me if you please."

"Ximen," the man said, "is carrying on with the wife of Wu Da, the cake seller. Every day he goes to old woman Wang's house in Amethyst Street. Most likely you will find him there now. There is nothing to prevent you going straight into the room."

Yun'ge thanked the man, and went along Amethyst Street with his basket till he came to old woman Wang's tea shop. The old woman was sitting on a small chair by the door, making thread. The boy put down his basket, looked at her, and said, "Greetings to you, Stepmother."

"What do you want, Yun'ge?" the old woman said.

"I have come to see his Lordship in the hope of getting thirty or fifty cash to help support my father," the boy told her.

"What 'Lordship' are you talking about?" asked the old woman.

"You know him."

"Well, I suppose every gentleman has some sort of a name," the old woman said.

"This gentleman's name has two characters in it."

"What two characters?"

"You are trying to fool me," Yun'ge said. "It is his Lordship Ximen to whom I am going to speak." He started to go into the house. The old woman caught him. "Where are you going, you little monkey? Don't you know the difference between the inside and the outside of people's houses?"

"I shall find him in the room," the boy said.

The old woman cursed him. "What makes you think you will find his Lordship in my house, you little rascal?"

"Stepmother, don't try to keep all the pickings for yourself. Leave a little gravy for me. I know all about it."

"What do you know?" the old woman cried. "You are a young scoundrel."

"And you are one of those people who would scrape a bowl clean with a knife. You don't mean to lose even a single drop of gravy. If I began to talk about this business, I shouldn't be surprised if my brother, the cake seller, had something to say about it."

This made the old woman furious. She was touched to the quick. "You little monkey," she screamed, "how dare you come to my house to let off your farts."

"Little monkey I may be," said Yun'ge, "but you're an old whoremonger, you old lump of dog meat."

The old woman caught him and boxed his ears twice.

"Why are you hitting me?" cried the boy.

"You son of a thief, you little monkey, make a noise like that and I'll thrash you out of the place."

"You knavish old scorpion," Yun'ge cried, "you have no right to beat me."

The old woman struck him again, and drove him out into the street, tossing his basket after him. The pears rolled all over the street, four here and five there. There was nothing the little monkey could do. He grumbled and cried as he picked them up. He shook his fist in the direction of the tea shop, and shouted, "Wait, you old worm! When I've told about this, you will be ruined, and then there will be nothing at all for you."

The young monkey picked up his basket and went off to the street to see if he could find Wu Da.

CHAPTER 5
The Murder of Wu Da

When deep in mystic contemplation
Sounding the shallows of this world's emptiness,
Even the marriage most blessed by Fate seems full of evil.
Men in their folly crave for love,
Yet, when in calm collectedness they study it,
Hateful it seems.

Leave the wild grasses
Gather not the idle flowers
So, thy truest self, the vigor of thy manhood,
Will know the peace of Nature.
A simple wife, young children, and plain fare
With these need no man suffer the pangs of love
Or lose his fortune.

Yun'ge could not contain his anger at the way old woman Wang had treated him. He took his basket and went to find Wu Da. He had gone through two streets before he met the man for whom he was looking. Wu Da, carrying his buns, was coming towards him. The boy stopped. "It is some time since I saw you last," he said, looking hard at the man. "How fat you have grown."

"Fat?" said Wu Da. "What do you mean? I am just the same as I always was."

"A few days ago," Yun'ge said, "I wanted some chicken food. I went for miles, but couldn't get any. Yet everybody tells me you have lots of it at your house."

"I keep neither geese nor ducks," Wu Da said. "Why should I have chicken food?"

"So you say," Yun'ge retorted, "but what makes you so much like a capon? Why! If you were held topsy-turvy, you would never turn a hair; you'd keep quite cool if you were being boiled in a cauldron."

"This is an insult, you young scoundrel," Wu Da cried. "My wife has not run off with anybody's husband. What makes you call me a capon?"

"Indeed?" the boy said. "So your wife has not run off with anybody's husband, hasn't she? Perhaps I should have said she has run off with *some-body's* husband."

"Who is the man?" Wu Da cried. "Tell me."

"You make me laugh. You can do what you like with me easily enough, but you won't find your wife's new friend so easy to dispose of."

"Good little brother, tell me who he is and I will give you ten cakes."

"Cakes won't do. I'd rather you were my host and gave me some wine. Three cups, and I'll tell you the whole story."

"If it's wine you want, come along," Wu Da said. He led the way to a little wineshop. Calling for a jar of wine and some meat, he took cakes from his basket and invited Yun'ge to join him. "Good little brother," he said, "you really must tell me."

"There is no hurry. Wait till I have finished my food. Then I'll tell you. You mustn't be impatient. I'll help you to catch them."

Wu Da waited till the young monkey had finished, and again asked him to explain himself.

"If you would like to know," the boy said, "put your hand on my head and feel the bumps."

"How did you get them?"

"I'll tell you. Today I have been carrying my pears about looking for his Lordship, Ximen. I walked and walked, but couldn't find him anywhere. Then somebody in the street told me he was at old woman Wang's tea shop, amusing himself with Mistress Wu; that he went there every day. I thought I might see him there, and get thirty or fifty cash from him, but the old sow Wang wouldn't let me in. She drove me away, and then I thought I'd come and see you. I was rather rude, but, if I hadn't made you wild, you wouldn't have asked me any questions."

"Is this the truth?"

"Don't you believe me?" the boy cried. "Didn't I say you were a white-livered fellow? Those two are making merry at this very moment. They wait till you have gone out, and then they go and meet at the old woman's house. You say, 'Is this the truth?' What reason have I for deceiving you?"

"Little brother, it is true. My wife goes every day to this old woman's house to make clothes and shoes, and when she comes back she has a red face. My first wife left me with a little daughter. This woman beats her every morning and scolds her every night. She gives her hardly anything to eat. Lately she certainly has been looking as if something was on her mind. She looked balefully at me, and I wondered whether anything was wrong. You have told the truth. I will put my baskets down and go and catch these evildoers in the act."

"You may be old as years go," Yun'ge said, "but for the little you know of the world, you might be a child. That old bitch Wang is not afraid of anybody. She would throw you out of the house. Besides, your wife and Ximen have a secret signal. If they knew you were coming, Ximen Qing would hide your wife. He is a very strong man and could dispose of twenty like you. You will never be able to touch him; much more likely you'll find his fist in your mouth. He is so rich and powerful that he would bring an accusation against you, and have you hauled to the courts. You have nobody to help you, and you'd come to an unhappy end."

"You are right, little brother, but what can I do to revenge myself?"

"I want revenge too," Yun'ge said, "for the old woman beat me. Listen to me. Go home today, show no sign of being angry, and don't say one word about the matter. Just behave as usual. Tomorrow, don't make more than a few cakes. Go out with them. I shall be waiting at the entrance to the lane. If Ximen Qing comes, I will give you a call, and you can take your baskets and wait for me somewhere near by. I will go first and plague the old bitch. She will certainly come out to hit me. I will throw my basket far into the street, and then you can run in. I will hold the old woman, and you can rush into the room, and tell them what you think about them. Don't you think that's a good plan?"

"I am greatly indebted to you," Wu Da said; "here are two strings of cash. Come early tomorrow and wait at the entrance to Amethyst Street."

Yun'ge took the money and some of the cakes, and went off. Wu Da paid the reckoning, picked up his baskets, and went back to the street to sell his cakes. A little later he went home.

His wife had never ceased to grumble at him and had found a hundred ways of making life unpleasant to him, but of late her conscience had smitten her and she showed signs of relenting. This evening, when Wu Da came home with his baskets and said nothing, as was usual, she asked him to have some wine. He refused, saying he had already taken wine with some merchants. She laid out his supper, but still he did not offer to speak, and next morning, after breakfast, he made only two or three trays of cakes, and put them in his baskets. Jinlian was so taken up with her thoughts of Ximen Qing that she did not notice how many cakes he made. She waited impatiently until he had gone out and then went to the tea shop to wait for her lover.

Wu Da took his baskets to the entrance to Amethyst Street. Yun'ge, also with a basket, was looking around.

"Well?" Wu Da said.

"It is too soon yet. Go and sell your cakes till he comes. Wait at the corner, and don't go far away."

Wu Da hurried away, but was soon back again. "The moment you see me throw down my basket," the boy said, "dash into the room." Wu Da put down his own basket and waited.

Yun'ge went to the tea shop. "You old pig," he said, in the most irritating tone he could command. "What did you mean by hitting me yesterday?"

Old woman Wang jumped up at once. "I have not done anything to you, you little monkey. Why have you come to insult me again?"

"For a very good reason, you old bitch, you old strumpet mistress. My ramrod to you!"

This made the old woman furious. She dashed at Yun'ge and tried to hit him. "Would you beat me?" he cried, and threw his basket as far as he could into the street. The old woman tried to hold him, but the little monkey cried, "Hit me if you can," put down his head, and butted her in the belly. She would have fallen if there had not been a wall behind her. The young monkey pushed as hard as he could and pinned her against the wall, while Wu Da pulled up his skirts and strode into the tea shop. The old woman saw him, and would have stopped him if she could, but the boy kept her close against the wall and she could not free herself.

"Wu Da is here," she cried.

Jinlian and Ximen Qing did not know what to do. Jinlian threw herself against the door, and Ximen Qing crawled under the bed. Wu Da tried to force open the door but failed. "This is a fine game you're playing," he cried. Jinlian was filled with confusion, but she succeeded in holding the door against him.

"You talk about the strength of your fists," she said to Ximen Qing, "and you are always boasting about your skill with the staff; why don't you come out and do something? Why, even a paper tiger is enough to frighten you." This she said to shame him into coming out, so that he might strike down Wu Da and make his escape. Ximen, in his hiding place under the bed, did grow bolder when he heard what she said. He crawled out nervously.

"I wasn't afraid," he said, "only a little taken by surprise." He threw open the door, and cried, "Stand back there!" Wu Da tried to close, but Ximen kicked out at him and, as the man was very small, the foot caught him in the ribs, and he fell backwards. Ximen Qing went out, and Yun'ge, seeing that matters had not turned out as he had hoped, released the old woman and ran away.

The neighbors knew Ximen Qing's power, and none of them dared to come and interfere. Old woman Wang lifted up Wu Da. His face was as yellow as a tallow candle, and he was spitting blood. She told Jinlian to bring a cup of water to revive him and then, each holding him by one arm, they took him home by the back way and put him to bed.

Next day Ximen did not hear any bad news, so he went as usual to the old woman's house to make merry with Jinlian. He hoped that Wu Da would die, and indeed for five days the poor man was very ill, and unable to leave his bed. He longed for food and could obtain none; he sighed for a drink and none was given him. Day after day he appealed to Jinlian, but she never answered. She went out, dressed in her best clothes, and came back with a flushed face. His daughter Ying'er had been forbidden to do anything for him. "If you dare to do anything for him and don't tell me," the woman had said, "you shall pay for it." After this the child did not venture to give her father a spoonful of soup or even a drop of water. Several times Wu Da fainted in his anger, but nobody paid the least attention to him. One day he cried to his wife, "You have done this because I found you out. You told that wicked man to kick me over the heart. And now I can neither die nor live. And the pair of you are as happy as can be. If I die, it is a small matter; you have nothing to fear from me. But don't forget Wu Song. Sooner or later he will come back, and he will have something to say about all this. Show me a little kindness and help me to get well as quickly as possible and I won't tell him anything. But if you still refuse to do anything for me, I shall have my reckoning with you on his return."

Jinlian listened, but made no answer. She went next door and told old woman Wang and Ximen Qing everything Wu Da had said. Ximen shivered as though a bucket of cold water had been poured over him. "This is most awkward," he said. "This brother is the Captain Wu who killed a tiger on Jingyang Hill. And now I have learned to love you. We get on together so perfectly. It is not conceivable that we should separate, but it means thinking out some way of dealing with the problem. Really, it is most unfortunate."

Old woman Wang laughed. "I've never seen such a man. You are at the helm and I am only at the oar, yet, while I see no difficulty, you seem to have no notion what to do."

"I am ashamed," Ximen said, "but I must admit I don't know what to do. Have you any plan for getting us out of the difficulty?"

"If you really wish for my help, I have a plan," the old woman said. "First, I must know whether you wish your relations to be permanent or temporary."

"What do you mean, Stepmother?"

"If you will be satisfied with a temporary arrangement, you must separate today. When Wu Da is well, you must ask his forgiveness. Then nobody will say anything to Wu Song about this affair. You will have to wait till some business takes him away again, and then you can meet once more. That is what I mean by 'temporary arrangement.' If you wish for something more permanent, I have an excellent idea, but it is one that I hesitate to tell you."

"Stepmother," Ximen said, "please do anything you can to keep us always together."

"There is one thing I need for this plan. It is not to be had everywhere, but I have no doubt you have some of it."

"If you want my eye, you shall have it," Ximen cried. "What is it you mean?"

"Wu Da is dangerously ill. Let us take the chance while we have it. Go to your shop, get some arsenic and give it to this lady. Then she can buy some medicine for Wu Da's sore chest and put the arsenic into it. So we shall rid ourselves of that little man. When he is dead, we will burn his body till not a trace remains. When Wu Song comes back, he can do nothing about it. A young man, when he takes a wife, marries to please his parents, but when he marries again he makes his own choice. What can a younger brother do? Six months or a year later, when the lady is out of mourning, there is nothing to prevent you marrying her. If you live together happily all your lives, won't that be permanent enough for you?"

"It is an admirable plan, Stepmother. As the proverb says: 'The treasure of a happy life can only be secured by desperate deeds.' Yes, one evil deed deserves another."

"So you think my scheme a good one!" the old woman said. "Well, there is nothing like pulling up the roots when we cut the grass. It never grows again. Go home, Sir, and bring the stuff to me. I'll show the lady what to do with it. But, when all is over, I shall expect a present worth having."

"Of course," Ximen said, "that goes without saying."

He went at once to his shop and soon returned with a packet of arsenic, which he gave to old woman Wang. She looked at Jinlian.

"Now, Lady, I am going to tell you how to use this. Wu Da has begged you to save him, and that gives you an opening. You must make a great show of affection. When he asks you for something to make him better, put this arsenic into some medicine to soothe his chest. When he complains of pain, pour it down his throat. As soon as the poison has got to work, his bowels will burst and he will cry out. So put the bedclothes over him, and press down the coverlet, and make sure that no one hears him. One thing you must do is to heat some water, and put a napkin into it. When the poison has taken effect, blood will stream from the seven openings of his body, and there will be marks on his lips. As soon as he is really dead, you must take off the bedclothes, and wipe away the blood. All that remains is to put him into a coffin and get him out of the way."

"I see," Jinlian said, "but my arms are weak. I shall not have strength enough."

"That doesn't matter. Knock on the wall, and I will come and help you."

"You must both be very careful," Ximen Qing said. "I will come tomorrow at the fifth watch to hear what news you have."

Old woman Wang powdered the arsenic and gave it to Jinlian, who went home. Wu Da was breathing so feebly that it seemed as though his soul had already left him. She sat on his bed, and pretended to cry.

"Why are you crying?" Wu Da said.

Jinlian dried her tears. "Because I allowed myself to be led astray by that Ximen Qing and, for a time, yielded to temptation. But I never meant him to kick you in the chest. Now, I have heard of some very good medicine, and I would go and buy some to make you well, if I were not afraid you would be suspicious. As it is, I don't dare go."

"If you will only save my life," Wu Da said, "I'll forgive you everything, and never hold this business against you. And I won't tell Wu Song anything about it, when he comes home. Go and buy the medicine, and save my life."

The woman took a few coins, and went to old woman Wang's, to make it appear as though she had asked her neighbor to go and buy it. When she came back, she showed the medicine to her husband. "This will soon cure you," she told him. "The doctor says you must drink it during the night, and cover yourself with one or two blankets to make you sweat. Then go to sleep, and tomorrow you will be able to get up."

"Splendid," Wu Da said. "I am very grateful to you. Don't go to sleep, but make up the medicine for me in the middle of the night."

"Go to sleep again," the woman said. "I will bring it to you without fail."

It was beginning to grow dark. Jinlian lighted the lamp. Then she went downstairs, put a great cauldron of water on the fire, and dipped a cloth into it. The watchman sounded the third night watch. She put the arsenic into a cup, filled it up with water, and took it upstairs.

"Brother, where is the medicine?"

"Here, underneath the mattress. Please make it for me at once."

Jinlian lifted the mattress, and took the medicine. She put it into a cup, then filled up the cup with the liquid she had brought, stirring it with a silver pin she took from her hair. With her left arm she supported her husband. Then she poured the medicine down his throat. Wu Da drank a mouthful.

"Sister," he said, "this medicine is very nasty."

"We are only trying to make you well. Don't be put off by the bitter taste."

Wu Da drank again, and the woman emptied the cup down his throat. She lowered him on to the bed again, herself got down from it. Wu Da groaned.

"Sister, I have taken the medicine, but the pain in my belly feels worse, worse. Oh, I can't bear it."

Jinlian took two coverlets from behind his head, and pulled them entirely over his head.

"I can't breathe," Wu Da cried.

"It is what the doctor told me to do. It will make you sweat, and you'll be better much sooner."

Wu Da again tried to speak, and Jinlian was afraid he might struggle. She leaped upon the bed and, riding astride his body, pressed down the bedclothes so that he could not move at all.

> His lungs were fried in boiling oil, his liver and bowels burned
>   with fire,
> His heart was pierced as by a butcher's knife, his belly stirred as by
>   a sword's sharp edge.
> Then froze his body to an icy cold, the seven openings all streamed
>   with blood.
> Through clenched teeth his three spirits sped to the city of ghosts.
> From his parched throat his seven souls fled to the watchtower of
>   Hell.
> Thus to the ghosts of all the poisoned deep in Hades
> Was joined another,
> And in the world of living none was left
> To hinder wantonness.

Wu Da groaned twice, and gasped for breath. Then his bowels burst, and he died.

Jinlian pulled down the bedclothes. Wu Da's teeth were tight clenched, and blood streamed from the seven openings. She was frightened and, getting down from the bed, knocked on the wall. When old woman Wang heard the knocking, she came to the back door and coughed. Jinlian went downstairs and opened the door.

"Is it all over?" the old woman asked.

"Over? Yes, it is over. My hands and feet fail me, and I can do no more."

"What is the matter with you?" the old woman said. "I'll help you." She rolled up her sleeves, took a tub of boiling water and put a napkin in it. Then she took them upstairs and gathered up all the bedclothes. She wiped Wu Da's lips, and cleaned away the blood from the seven openings. Then she piled the clothes on his body and, step by step, the pair of them carried him downstairs. There, they took an old door, and lifted the corpse onto it. They combed his hair and put a hat on his head, dressed him, and put shoes and socks upon his feet. They covered his face with a piece of white silk, and set clean bedclothes over him. Then they went upstairs again, and straightened the place. Old woman Wang went home, and Jinlian pretended to mourn for Wu Da, crying, "Husband! Husband!"

Readers, though there are many women in the world, they have but three ways of lamenting. Sometimes they weep and sob at the same time; sometimes they sob and do not weep; and sometimes they weep and do not sob. Jinlian sobbed for half the night, but not a tear accompanied her sobbing.

Next morning, just before dawn, Ximen Qing came to hear how the thing had gone. Old woman Wang told him all about it. He gave her some silver to pay for the coffin and the funeral expenses, and they called Jinlian to discuss the arrangements. When she came, she said to Ximen Qing:

"Wu Da is dead, and you are all I have in the world. All I have done, I have done for you. You must not, some day, cast me aside like a woman's hairnet that is no more needed."

"There is no fear of that."

"But what if ever you change your mind?"

"If I do, may I have the place that now is Wu Da's."

The old woman interrupted them. "There is one thing that must be attended to at once. We must have him put in his coffin without any delay. The coroner's officers might see that there is something wrong, especially He the Ninth, who is a smart man. He might even refuse to put Wu Da in his coffin."

"There will be no trouble from that quarter," Ximen said. "I will speak to He the Ninth. He will do anything I wish,"

"In that case," the old woman said, "you had better go and speak to him at once. Don't waste a moment." So Ximen Qing set out to find He the Ninth.

> The sun, the moon, the stars, all cast their shadows
> We cannot reach them.
> The multitude of happenings, which have no roots save in themselves,
> Comes into being.
>
> The herons are behind the clouds
> We see them only when they fly.
> The parrot is hidden in the willow tree.
> We hear him only when he speaks.

CHAPTER 6
The Funeral

When Ximen Qing left the old woman's house, it was broad daylight. Old woman Wang went out and bought a coffin, some paper offerings, incense, candles and paper money. When she came back, she lighted a lamp, and set it before Wu Da's body. The neighbors came to offer their condolences, and Pan Jinlian covered her lovely face and pretended to sob.

"How did the gentleman die?" the neighbors asked.

"There was something amiss with his heart, and, although we never expected anything like this, he got worse and worse and at last we saw that he could not get better. Last night, about the third watch, he died." Jinlian pretended to sob.

The neighbors thought that there was something mysterious about the manner of this man's death, but they did not venture to ask any more questions. They consoled Jinlian. "The dead are dead," they said, "but the living must live in peace. Do not grieve so much, Lady. It is too hot."

Jinlian thanked them, and they went away. Old woman Wang had the coffin brought, and went to see He the Ninth, the undertaker. She made all the arrangements, not only for the funeral, but for the household generally. She went to the Temple of Eternal Felicity and asked for two choirs of monks to come that night and sing a dirge for the departed.

He the Ninth sent some of his assistants in advance to set everything in order, and it was some time before he sauntered along himself. At the entrance to Amethyst Street, he met Ximen Qing.

"Where are you going, old Ninth?" Ximen said.

"I am just going to perform the last offices for Wu Da, the cake seller," said He the Ninth.

"Wait a moment, I want to speak to you." He the Ninth went with Ximen Qing till they came to a small wineshop at the corner of the street, and there they went into a small room.

"Take the upper seat, old Ninth," Ximen said.

"Who am I," said Ho, "that I should take the liberty of being seated in your presence?"

"Don't stand on ceremony, old Ninth; please sit down." They argued politely for a while, and then took their places. Ximen Qing ordered the waiter to bring a bottle of good wine. Refreshments were set out, and the wine warmed. He the Ninth wondered what was to come. "Ximen Qing has never taken wine with me before," he said to himself. "I wonder what he wants." They drank together for a long time. At last Ximen took from his sleeve a piece of pure silver, and put it down on the table before his companion.

"Old Ninth," he said, "do not think this too poor a present. I will express my thanks more worthily tomorrow."

"I have done nothing for you, Sir," He the Ninth said, making a reverence. "How can I take your silver? Any matter that you may care to entrust to me will naturally receive my most careful attention."

"Old Ninth," Ximen said, "don't behave as though you were a stranger. Please take it."

"Tell me what I can do for you," He the Ninth said.

"Only this. You are going to see about the disposal of Wu Da's body and, of course, his people will pay you for what you do there. But if in the course of your duties you should happen to notice anything, pay no attention, but cover him up with the bedclothes. That is all."

"I expected you to ask something really important," He the Ninth said, "and it is nothing more than this. It will be no trouble, and I couldn't think of taking your money."

"If you won't accept my money, I take it that you refuse to do this for me."

He the Ninth was aware of Ximen Qing's influence in official circles, and hesitated to offend him. He could not refuse to accept the money. They drank several more cups of wine, then Ximen Qing said to the waiter: "Put this down to my account, and come to my shop tomorrow for the money." They went downstairs and left the inn. As they took leave of one another, Ximen Qing said:

"Old Ninth, don't forget what I have told you, but not a word must be said about this. Later on, I will show my appreciation more tangibly." He walked away.

He the Ninth pocketed the silver. "I don't know what all this means, but it is evidently something to be kept quiet. Anyhow, here is the silver and if, as I expect, Wu Song has a few questions to ask when he comes back, I can produce it as evidence." A little later, he said to himself, "I need some money very badly just now, so I had better use this. When Wu Song comes back, I must think of something else." He came to Wu Da's house, where his men were all waiting for him at the door. Old woman Wang was also waiting anxiously.

"What did Wu Da die of?" He the Ninth said to his men.

"His wife says he suffered from pains at the heart, and died," his men said. He the Ninth pulled up the lattice and went in.

"We have been waiting a very long time for you," old woman Wang said, "and the Master of the Yin Yang has been here half a day. Why are you so late, old Ninth?"

"I had some business to attend to. That made me late."

Jinlian, wearing plain clothes, with a white covering on her head, sobbed as though her heart were breaking. "Do not grieve so, Lady," He the Ninth said. "Your husband is already on his way to Heaven."

"My sorrow is greater than I can bear," Jinlian said, drying her eyes. "My husband suffered from his heart and, after only a few days' illness, he died and left me inconsolable."

He the Ninth looked the woman up and down. "I have often heard people speak of Wu Da's wife," he said to himself, "but this is the first time I have seen her. So this is the lady Wu Da married. Ximen Qing is getting good value for his ten taels of silver."

He went to the bed and examined the body. By this time the Master of the Yin Yang had finished his ritual, so He the Ninth pulled aside the mortuary emblems and removed the white silk. He stared. Wu Da's fingers were green and his lips purple; his face was yellow, and his eyeballs protruded. The undertaker saw at once that a crime had been committed.

"Why is his face purple?" the two assistants asked. "What is the cause of these teeth marks and the blood on his lips?"

"Don't be silly," He the Ninth said. "It is very hot. How can you expect a corpse not to alter?" The men put the body into the coffin and nailed it up with two longevity nails. Old woman Wang asked He the Ninth to give his men a thousand cash between them.

"When is the funeral to be?" the undertaker asked. "The lady says," old woman Wang told him, "that we will take the body outside the city wall to be burned, three days hence." He the Ninth went away. That night, Jinlian prepared wine for the funeral supper, and the next day four monks came and read the funeral service. On the third day at the fifth watch the bearers came to carry the coffin, and some of the neighbors followed behind. Jinlian, dressed in mourning clothes, seated herself in a sedan chair and, all the way along the street, pretended to bemoan her husband. At last they came to an open place outside the city. Here the funeral pyre was, and word was given for the fires to be lighted and the coffin burned. Soon everything was consumed and the ashes thrown into a pond. All the fees at the temple were paid by Ximen Qing.

The woman returned home, and, in the upper room, set up a tablet with the words "In Memory of Wu Da, my beloved husband." Before it she placed a lamp, golden flags, paper money, and ingots of imitation gold and silver. That day, she sat with Ximen Qing and bade the old lady go home. So these two enjoyed each other's company without hindrance, not as before at the house of old woman Wang, where their pleasure had been as uncertain as that of a chicken thief. Now Wu Da was dead they were alone in the house. They were able to spend the whole night together without thought of consequences. At first, Ximen Qing was afraid the neighbors might discover what was going on, and he used to go to old woman Wang's house, wait there for a little while, and then go to Jinlian's back door. But afterwards they seemed to find it almost impossible to separate, and for three or five nights at a time he would not go home. His household was at sixes and sevens, and everybody was unhappy.

The days passed quickly, the sun and moon crossed and recrossed like a weaver's shuttles. It was now two months and more since Ximen Qing had first possessed the woman. It was the Dragon Boat Festival.

Ximen Qing was on his way back from the Temple of Yue and, calling at the old woman Wang's tea shop, he sat down there. The old woman quickly made him a cup of tea.

"Where have you been, Sir? Why haven't you been to see your lady?"

"I have just been to the Temple," said Ximen, "and as it is the Summer Festival, I thought of her and came to see her."

"Her mother, old woman Pan, has been here today," the old woman said. "I fancy she is still here, but I'll go and find out for you." She went to the back door and found Jinlian drinking wine with her mother. They asked her to sit down.

"Drink a welcoming cup," Jinlian said, smiling, "and have a lovely baby."

"But I have no husband," laughed the old woman. "Where shall I get a baby? You are still young. You're the one to have babies."

"The young tree bears no fruit; but the old tree bears well," Jinlian said, quoting an old saying.

"Do you hear your daughter making fun of me?" the old woman said, turning to Madam Pan. "She calls me old beggar, but she'll be glad enough of her 'old beggar' one of these days."

"She has always had a sharp tongue, Stepmother," old woman Pan said, "but you must not pay too much attention to it."

"Yes, indeed, your daughter is as clever as they make 'em. She is a good woman. Some lucky man will snap her up one of these days."

"You are a go-between, Stepmother," old woman Pan said, "and it rests with you." She set out a cup and chopsticks, and Jinlian poured out some wine. The old woman drank several glasses, and her face grew red. She was afraid that Ximen Qing would grow tired of waiting, so she gave a sly wink to Jinlian, said good-bye to them, and went back to her own place.

Jinlian understood that Ximen Qing had come and hurriedly sent her mother away. She tidied the room, burned some fine incense, took away what was left of her mother's food, and prepared some special dishes for Ximen Qing. Then she went down to the back door to meet him.

She took him into the room, made a reverence to him, and sat down. She had given up wearing mourning very soon after Wu Da's death, and had put his tablet aside with a sheet of white paper over it. She never dreamed of putting offerings of soup or food before it. Every day she painted her face, put on colored dresses, and looked very charming indeed. Ximen Qing had not been to see her for some days, and she scolded him.

"What a fickle rascal you are! Why have you run away from me? Have you another sweetheart hidden somewhere that you leave me in the cold?"

"I have been very busy these last few days," Ximen said, "but today I have been to the temple to buy you some ornaments, and some pearls and clothes."

This pleased her. Ximen called Daian and, unfastening the package, showed the things one by one to Jinlian. She thanked him and put them away. She no longer troubled to keep the matter secret from Ying'er, who was afraid of being punished, and told her to bring tea for Ximen Qing. She herself laid the table, and then sat down with him.

"You should not take so much trouble for me," he said. "I have given Stepmother some money to go and buy a few things. Now that the Summer Festival is here, the only thing I want is to sit here with you."

"It was for my mother originally," said Jinlian, "but this is quite fresh. If we wait for Stepmother to come back with her purchases, we shall have to wait a long time. Let's eat some of this." She pressed her cheek close against his, entwined her legs with his, and, side by side, they drank their wine.

The old woman had taken a basket and gone to the street to buy wine and meat. It was the beginning of the Fifth Month, and the rain was incessant. At one moment the sun was bright in the sky, the next it was hidden by black clouds, and there came down a torrent like the emptying of a washbasin.

> Lowering clouds gather from the four corners of the sky
> A chain of mist binds the far distances.
> *Xi-la-la*. The air is filled with flying drops that veil the sun.
> *Pit-pit*. They beat upon the plantain tree.
> The winds blow, and the old juniper tree is uplifted,
> Uplifted and overthrown.
> Once its topmost branches threatened the sky.

The crashing thunderclaps grow louder,
The mountains of Tai and Song are shaken as by an earthquake,
Yet now the sultry heat is washed away, its heaviness is banished.
The fields of young corn are fresh again
New water races down the four rivers.
The green bamboo and scarlet pomegranate
Are made clean once more.

The old woman had just bought a jar of wine and a basketful of green stuff and fruits, and was walking along the street when the downpour came. She ran under the balcony of a house and tied her kerchief over her head, but her clothes were wet through. She waited a while till the rain began to slacken, then rushed home like a flying cloud and set down her wine and meat in the kitchen. Ximen Qing and Jinlian were drinking wine.

"Yes, my Lord and Lady," cried she, laughingly, "you are drinking, but look at me! My clothes are drenched. I shall have to have a new dress."

"Oh, you old woman," Ximen said, "you are one of those spirits who always find somebody to throw the blame on."

"I am not a spirit at all," the old woman said, "but you will have to make me a present of a roll of the deepest indigo silk."

"Drink a cup of hot wine, Stepmother," Jinlian said.

The old lady drank three cups of wine with them and then said she must go to the kitchen to dry her clothes. When she had dried them, she made ready chicken, goose, and rice, carving and chopping till all was to her liking, set the other things on plates and dishes, and then took them into the room and warmed the wine. Ximen Qing and Jinlian again poured the wine and, close pressed together, drank from the same glass.

While Ximen was drinking, he saw a lute hanging on the wall. "A long time ago, I was told how well you play. You must play me a tune, and I shall enjoy my wine all the more."

"When I was a small child," Jinlian said, "I learned one or two bits of tunes, but none too well. Please do not make fun of me." Ximen took down the lute and made the woman sit on his knee. She placed the lute in her lap and, gently stretching her delicate fingers, slowly plucked the strings and sang in a low sweet voice:

I set no headdress on my brow; my idle hands refused to serve me.
Round and round I furled the silken tresses, black as night, the
    curls like clouds in shadow.
Golden pins, thrust crosswise, restrained the lowering masses.
"Oh, maiden, open wide the chests," I cried

And dressed in robes of whitest silk
I came forth from my tiring room, glorious as Xi Shi.
"Oh, maiden dear, throw back the lattice for me, come and burn a
   stick of evening incense."

This song sent Ximen Qing almost into ecstasy. He drew his loved one
to him and put his arms about her white neck.

"I never realized how clever you were," he said. "I have often wandered
through the haunts of singing girls, but never were their songs or music
so exquisite as yours."

"It is kind of you to praise me, my Lord. I am ready to do whatever
you wish. All I pray is that the time may never come when you forget me."

"How can I forget you?" Ximen cried, as he stroked her soft cheeks.
Then, lazily, they played the game of rain and clouds, joking with one another and making merry. Ximen took off one of her embroidered shoes,
poured a cup of wine into it, and drank.

"My feet are small enough," cried Jinlian. "Why should you make fun
of them?"

Soon they had taken their fill of wine and, shutting the door of the
room, they undressed and got onto the bed. Old woman Wang closed the
gate, and sat down in the kitchen with Ying'er. Jinlian and her lover turned
over and over, like the cock pheasant and his mate, and played as merrily
as the fishes in the water. Her skill in the arts of love was a hundred times
greater than that of any strumpet, and Ximen Qing himself was no mean
performer. They were at the age when a woman's beauty is at its loveliest
and a man's vigor at its highest. Youth was theirs.

Ximen Qing spent the whole day at his lover's house, and gave her several taels of silver for household expenses. At last she could not persuade
him to stay longer; he put on his eyeshades, and went home. Jinlian pulled
down the lattice and fastened the gate, then she and old woman Wang
drank wine together, and went their ways.

CHAPTER 7

Ximen Qing Meets Meng Yulou

One day there came to Ximen Qing's house an old woman called Xue. She was a seller of flowers made of kingfisher feathers, and was carrying a box of them. She could not find Ximen, but seeing Daian, asked him where his master was.

"My father," said the boy, "is in the shop, going through the accounts with Uncle Fu."

The old woman went straight to the shop door, pulled aside the lattice, and looked in. Ximen Qing was going through the books with his manager. With a movement of the head she signaled to him to come out. He left the shop at once, and they sought a quiet place in which to talk.

"What is your business with me?" Ximen Qing asked her.

"It is just an idea about a marriage that has come into my head," the old woman said. "The marriage I am thinking of should be satisfactory to you in every sense of the word, and it would fill the gap left in your household by the death of your Third Lady."

"Who is the lady?" Ximen asked.

"You probably know her. Her family name is Meng, and she is the widow of a cloth merchant, named Yang, who used to keep a shop outside the South Gate. She is by no means poor. She has a couple of Nanjing beds, and four or five chests so full of clothes for every season of the year that there isn't room to put a finger inside them. Her jewelry is beyond counting. She has about a thousand taels of ready money, and two or three hundred rolls of cloth woven with three shuttles. It is a year or more now since she became a widow, and she has no children of her own, only a younger brother of her husband, who is about ten years old. She is quite young, with no one to love, and her aunt thinks it is time she married again. She is about twenty-four years old this year, and very tall and beautiful. When she is dressed, she looks like a figure on a painted lantern. She is lively and charming, and just as intelligent as can be. She can govern a household, do needlework, and play backgammon and all kinds of games. There is nothing to hide. The lady's name is Meng, and she is the third of her family. She lives in Stinking Water Lane. I forgot to mention that she can play the moon guitar too. You will certainly fall in love with her the moment you see her."

Ximen was delighted when he heard that the girl could play the moon guitar. "When can I see her?" he cried.

"I don't anticipate any difficulty," the old woman said, "but one thing you must bear in mind. There is only one member of her family who counts for anything, and that is her aunt. There is indeed another relative, Zhang the Fourth, but he is like a mountain walnut, all shell. Many years ago this aunt married Crooked-Headed Sun, and they used to live in Master Xu's house on the north side of the High Street. But Sun has been dead these forty years. She has no children, and is entirely dependent upon her nephew and niece.

"She is the only person we have to consider. She cares about nothing but money, and she knows quite well that her nephew's widow has property. It is nothing to her whom her niece marries, so long as she gets a few taels of silver for herself. You have plenty of excellent silk. I suggest you take a roll of it, buy some presents, and call upon this old aunt. You might give her a little silver at the same time. If you do that, you will have disposed of her once and for all. Later, if anybody should venture to raise objections, the old lady will have her way and the objector will find himself powerless."

All this pleased Ximen Qing immensely. His face beamed with delight. They decided that the next day would suit their purpose, and that he should buy some presents and take them to the house of the young lady's aunt. Xue took up her box and went off, and Ximen Qing went back into the shop and continued to go through the books with Fu.

The next morning, Ximen rose early, and dressed himself in his finest clothes. He took a roll of silk and, buying four large dishes of beautiful fruits, had them put into carrying baskets and told a man to carry them. Then, on horseback, with Daian in attendance and old woman Xue leading the way, he set out to Aunt Yang's house. Xue went in to give the old lady warning.

"One of our neighbors," she said, "a very rich man, would like to have a word with you about your niece's marriage. I told him that you are the only person of any account in the family, and that he must come and see you before he goes to see the lady. I have brought him here today, and at this moment he is at the gate waiting your pleasure."

"Oh dear!" said the old lady. "Why didn't you tell me before?" She told a maid to prepare some fine tea, and gave orders that Ximen Qing should be asked to come in. Xue suggested that the presents should be sent in first, so that the empty baskets might be brought out again, and that then he should go and see the old lady.

He was wearing a large hat of woven palm and a pair of white-soled boots. When he came into the old lady's presence he made four reverences. Leaning on her stick, she hastily prepared to return them, but he would not allow this. "Please, Aunt," he said, "be so kind as to accept my greeting." They disputed amicably for some time, and the matter ended with half the required reverences. Then they sat down, hostess and guest in their proper places, and old woman Xue sat down beside them.

"May I know your honorable name, Sir?" said the old lady.

"This gentleman," answered Xue for him, "is the richest or the second richest man in Qinghe. He is Master Ximen, who keeps a medicine shop by the Town Hall. The money in his house reaches higher than the North Star, and his barns are filled with more spoiled rice than is to be found in the Imperial Storehouses. Now his household is without a mistress and, since he has heard that our lady is ready to marry, he has come expressly to talk to you about the marriage."

"Sir," the old lady said, "if you wanted my niece, you had only to come and tell me. Why have you spent your money upon a present for me? It has put me in the position that if I refuse it, I shall be impolite, and if I accept it, I shall feel ashamed."

"Most worthy Aunt," Ximen said, "this is not fit to be called a present." The old lady made two reverences as a sign of thanks and accepted the present. Tea was brought in and, as they were drinking it, the old lady said:

"You will think me lacking in intelligence if I fail to make myself quite clear. My nephew, when he was alive, was very rich, but unfortunately he is dead, and all his wealth has come into my niece's hands, probably no less than a thousand taels of silver. I am not in the least concerned whether you want her for the mistress of your household or as a second wife, but I should like to have a requiem sung for my nephew's soul—I am his own aunt—and a little money for my coffin. Of course, all this will cost you nothing. I would do anything to get the better of that old dog Zhang the Fourth, and I will see that this marriage is arranged. Perhaps, when you are married, you will allow her to come occasionally to see her poor old aunt, on my birthday and perhaps at the Summer Festival. I don't imagine you will find my poverty infectious."

Ximen Qing laughed. "Please make your mind quite at rest," he said. "I understand perfectly. If you arrange this matter for me, you may have a dozen coffins if you like."

He told Daian to bring his visiting box. From it he took six bars of the purest white official silver, worth thirty taels, and set them before her. "This is only a trifle, Lady, but I hope you will use it to buy a cup of tea. After the marriage, I will give you another seventy taels and two rolls of silk. That may suffice for your funeral. And at the four seasons and the eight festivals, I will certainly allow her to visit you."

When the cunning old woman set her black eyes on the thirty taels of shining white silver, her face became all smiles. "Honorable Sir," she said, "don't think that I am grasping, but it has always been considered the wisest plan to be quite definite at the very beginning. It avoids disputes later on."

"You are a very intelligent woman," old woman Xue said, "and, really, you need not have any fears. His Lordship is perfectly reliable. If he had not been, he would not have brought his box with him when he came to discuss the matter. Perhaps you are unaware that he is on friendly terms with the local officials. They know how open-handed he is. You need not be afraid of exhausting his resources."

The old lady was more and more delighted, and gave vent to her feelings in more ways than one. They drank two more cups of tea, and Ximen stood up to take his leave, though the old lady urged him to stay longer.

"Now that we have seen you," old woman Xue said, "we will go tomorrow to pay our respects to the young lady."

"His Lordship need not trouble to go and see my niece," the old lady said. "You go and tell her that I say if she won't marry a gentleman like this, I should like to know whom she will marry."

Ximen Qing prepared to leave.

"A poor old woman like me," the old lady said, "could never have dreamed that you, Sir, would condescend to come and see me, so I was taken unprepared. Please forgive my allowing you to go away empty-handed."

She took her stick and hobbled a few steps with him, till he begged her to return. As he was mounting his horse, Xue said, "Wasn't that a good idea? Go home now, I have a little more to say to the old lady. I will call for you early tomorrow morning."

Ximen Qing gave her a tael of silver to pay for the hire of a donkey, mounted his horse, and rode home. Xue went back again to the old lady, and they talked and drank together till the sun was setting. Then she went home.

The next morning Ximen Qing dressed himself exquisitely, put his purse in his sleeve, and rode on a white horse. His two boys, Daian and Ping'an, were in attendance, and old woman Xue rode on a donkey. They set off for the South Gate and soon reached the young lady's house.

The gatehouse was as large as an ordinary room and had a black-and-white screen. Xue asked Ximen Qing to dismount, and they went in together. They came to the inner door with another screen and a low fence of bamboo. There were flower pots with pomegranates in the courtyard and, on the steps, a row of blue jars and two long benches for beating cloth. The old woman pushed open the scarlet double doors and they went into a parlor, with seats arranged as for host and guests. The tables and chairs were new and brightly polished, and the curtains and blinds in excellent taste.

Old woman Xue told Ximen Qing to sit down, and she went to the courtyard. Very soon she returned and whispered, "The lady has not finished dressing yet. Do you mind waiting?" A boy brought in some Fujian tea and, while Ximen Qing was drinking it, the old woman with much gesticulation gave him what information she thought fit.

"Apart from the aunt, this young lady is the only person of consequence in the family. Her husband had a brother, but he is still very young and ignorant. When Master Yang was alive, they used to sell enough to fill two large baskets with coins, not to speak of silver, every day. He charged three *fen* a foot for the black cloth used for making shoes and twenty or thirty men were employed in the dye shop. This lady managed everything. She has two maids and a boy. The elder maid is fifteen, and has already had her hair dressed as a woman. That is Lanxiang. The little maid, Xiaoluan, is twelve. When she marries, they will go with her. If I bring off this marriage, I only ask one thing. I should like to be able to take a couple of rooms to live in."

"There will be no difficulty about that," Ximen said.

"But last year," the old woman said, "when you bought Chunmei, you promised me several rolls of silk. I have never had them. Perhaps you will remember that when you reward me on this occasion." A maid came to call her, and in a little while Ximen Qing heard the tinkling of ornaments and there came to him the fragrance of exquisite perfume. The old woman pulled up the lattice and Mistress Meng came in.

Ximen Qing was delighted with her the moment he saw her. She came into the room, modestly made a reverence, and sat down opposite him. He stared at her so fixedly that she bowed her head. "Lady," he said at last, "it is now a long time since my wife died, and I should like to take you to wife to govern my household. May I know your honorable wishes in this matter?"

The lady looked at him. He seemed a pleasant-looking fellow and she was well enough satisfied. She said to old woman Xue, "How old is this gentleman and how long is it since his lady died?"

"I have misspent twenty-eight years," Ximen Qing said, "and my wife unfortunately died more than a year ago. May I know how many fruitful springs you have seen?"

"I am thirty years old," the lady said.

"Then you are two years older than I am."

"When the wife is two years older than the husband," the old go-between said, "the yellow gold increases day by day; and when the wife is three years older, the yellow gold is piled up mountains high."

The little maid brought three cups of tea and some preserved golden oranges. Mistress Meng stood up, took one of the cups, and with her slender finger wiped the water from its rim, then offered it to Ximen Qing, at the same time making a reverence. Old woman Xue found an opportunity to lift the lady's skirt slightly, displaying her exquisite feet, three inches long and no wider than a thumb, very pointed and with high insteps. They were clad in a pair of scarlet shoes, embroidered in gold with a cloud design, with white silk high heels. Ximen Qing observed them with great satisfaction.

Mistress Meng gave a cup of tea to Xue, then took one herself and sat down. Ximen Qing told Daian to bring in the box of presents. In it were two silk handkerchiefs, a pair of jeweled pins, and six gold rings. Ximen took them out of the box and, putting them on a tray, presented them to the lady. The old woman prompted her to thank him. "When do you wish the ceremony to be performed?" she asked. "I shall have preparations to make."

"I take this as a pledge of your kind intention," Ximen Qing said. "On the twenty-fourth day of this month I will send my small gift, and I would suggest the second of next month for the wedding day."

"I must speak to my aunt about the matter," Mistress Meng said.

"His Lordship called upon your aunt yesterday, and discussed the matter," old woman Xue said.

"What did she say?" Mistress Meng asked.

"She was very pleased. Indeed, she said that if this gentleman was not good enough for you, she didn't know who would be. She will be very satisfied with you when she learns that you have agreed to marry his Lordship."

"If she really said that, all will be well."

"Ah, Lady," the old woman said, "you have to thank me for this good fortune."

Ximen Qing rose and said good-bye. Old woman Xue went with him as far as the entrance to the lane.

"Well," she said, "you have seen the lady. What do you think of her?"

"Sister," Ximen Qing said, "I thank you."

The old woman asked him to go home without her. She said that she had still something to say to Mistress Meng. Ximen mounted his horse and returned to the city, and the old woman went back to the room.

"You must feel satisfied, now that you have arranged to marry this gentleman," she said.

"But he may have a wife already for all I know," said Mistress Meng, "and I have no idea what his business is."

"My good lady," the old woman said, "supposing he is married, I can assure you that none of his ladies has any intelligence to speak of. When you marry him, you will find that I am telling the truth. As for his reputation, everybody knows that he is the famous medicine merchant, money lender to the officials, and the first or second richest man in the district. The magistrates, both of the prefecture and of the district, are on very intimate terms with him, and only recently he became a relation by marriage of Marshal Yang of the Eastern Capital. With a relative like that, who dare interfere with him?"

Mistress Meng prepared some refreshments. While they were eating, a boy came from Aunt Yang's house. He brought a box in which were four pieces of cake made of yellow rice and dates, two pieces of sweetmeat, and several dozen little pastries.

"My mistress would like to know whether you have accepted the man's proposal," the boy said. "She says if you don't accept him, she can't imagine whom you will have."

"Thank your mistress for her kind message," Mistress Meng said, "and tell her that I have accepted him."

"Now you have a proof that I was not lying to you," the old woman said. "Your aunt did know all about it."

Mistress Meng took the cakes out of the box, and gave it back filled with buns and cured meats. She gave the boy a handful of coins, and said, "Thank your mistress for me. Tell her that he is going to send his present on the twenty-fourth, and the wedding is to be on the second of next month." Then the boy went home.

"What did your aunt send you?" the old woman asked. "May I have some to take home to my children?" Mistress Meng gave her a piece of sweetmeat and a dozen pastries, and she went away.

Now, the lady's uncle, Zhang the Fourth, was very anxious to secure the guardianship of his nephew Yang Zongbao in order that he might get the woman's property into his own hands. He hoped that she would become the second wife of a certain Scholar Shang, who was the son of a local magistrate. Had it been any less important person, a few words would have settled the matter, but he knew that Ximen Qing was on good terms with the officials, and dared not oppose him openly. After thinking over every possible way of dealing with the situation, he decided that the best plan was to introduce some element of discord between them. So he came to see his niece.

"You mustn't think of accepting Ximen Qing's proposal," he said. "Shang is the man for you. He is a poet of distinction, owns several farms, and enjoys a very comfortable existence. He would be a much better match than that fellow Ximen, who has had too many dealings with the officials and is a truculent upstart and a ne'er-do-well. Ximen has one wife already. She was a Miss Wu. If you marry him, you won't be the mistress of his house; you'll be nothing but an underling. He has three or four other wives, and several young maids. No, if you marry him, with so many people already in the household, I'm afraid you'll have to put up with a great deal of unpleasantness."

Meng realized that Zhang the Fourth wished her to break off her engagement, and she decided to tease him. "There is an old saying," she said, "that though there are many ships upon the water, the traffic still goes on. I see no reason why we should not all get along very well. If he has a wife already, I will gladly revere her as an elder sister. If he has other wives, I will place absolute confidence in him. If I afford my husband pleasure, I don't mind how many wives he has; if not, even if I should be his only wife, life would be utterly miserable. In every rich family there are four or five ladies. My dear old uncle, don't trouble yourself any more about the matter. When I get there, I shall know how to look after myself. I don't anticipate any trouble on that score."

"But that is not all," Zhang the Fourth continued. "He is continually beating his women and ill using his wives. He makes a business of buying and selling young people, and if anyone in his establishment gives him the slightest cause for annoyance, he sends for the go-between and gets rid of her. Are you ready to put up with that sort of treatment?"

"No, Uncle, you are mistaken," his niece said. "Even a bad-tempered husband cannot punish a wife who does her duty and keeps her wits about her. If I marry him and perform my household duties properly, and if I know when to keep my mouth and other people's mouths shut, he will find no excuse for treating me badly."

"I am told," Zhang the Fourth persisted, "yes, I am told that he has a young unmarried daughter about fourteen years old, and I can't help thinking, if you marry him, that the girl will take every possible opportunity of annoying you."

"Why do you think that, Uncle? If I marry him, old is old and young is young. I treat children very kindly. I don't believe either that my husband will be dissatisfied with me, or that my daughter will be undutiful. If he had ten daughters, it wouldn't worry me."

"One more point," said Zhang the Fourth, "and perhaps this is the most serious of all. The fellow's behavior is atrocious. Strumpets and bawdy houses are the only interest he has in life. Moreover, he is a man of straw and frightfully in debt. What I fear most of all is that he will involve you in his downfall."

"Uncle, you are mistaken again. The man is young and occasionally he may philander away from home. There is nothing extraordinary about that, and there is no way in which wives can prevent their husbands from so amusing themselves. As for his financial position, you should remember the old saying: 'Money has no roots.' We have no means of telling whether a person will always be rich or always be poor. No, Uncle, marriages are made in Heaven, please don't distress yourself so much about this one."

Zhang the Fourth was forced to realize that there was nothing he could say to change his niece's purpose. She paid no heed to anything he advised. So he made a wry face, drank two cups of plain tea, stood up, and went home extremely crestfallen.

He talked over the matter with his wife, and they decided to wait until the wedding day, and then to use their nephew Yang Zongbao as an excuse for laying hands on Mistress Meng's belongings.

On the twenty-fourth Ximen Qing sent his marriage pledge. On the twenty-sixth twelve monks came to chant a dirge for the repose of the soul of the late Master Yang, and burn his tablet. Aunt Yang was definitely on Ximen's side, but, on the eve of the wedding, Zhang the Fourth asked a number of neighbors to accompany him and went to make a last attempt to dissuade his niece. Old woman Xue, with Ximen's servants and ten or twenty soldiers of the garrison, came to bring away the lady's bed, her curtains, and all her boxes. Zhang met them and stopped them. "Madam Go-between," he said, "please do not remove these things. I have a few words to say about the matter." Then he and all the neighbors went in to see Mistress Meng. They sat down and Zhang the Fourth addressed the company.

"Honorable neighbors all, please listen to what I have to say." Then he turned to his niece. "You are the mistress here, and I have nothing against that. But your husband Yang Zongxi and his younger brother Yang Zongbao were both nephews of mine. The elder of these two nephews is now dead and what he possessed has been inherited by others. That is right and fitting. But my second nephew Yang Zongbao is still a child, and the burden of this matter falls upon me. He was born of the same mother as your late husband, and has naturally a right to some share in the property. I call upon these honorable neighbors to witness. We will open all the boxes and everybody shall see what there is. Then we shall know whether there is much or nothing."

"Honorable neighbors," Mistress Meng said, beginning to cry, "now hear what I have to say." She turned to Zhang the Fourth. 'You are mistaken, old gentleman. I did not wickedly murder my husband, so that I might marry again to my dishonor. It is no secret that he had money. He laid by many taels of silver, and spent them on the building of this house. I am not taking this house away. I leave it for my young brother-in-law. I am not even taking away a single article of furniture. Three or four hundred taels of silver were due to me, but I handed over to you the contracts and documents, you collected the money, and I have used it to live upon. What else could I do?"

"Doubtless you have no money," Zhang said. "I am quite ready to agree. But in the presence of these good people, let the boxes be opened so that everyone can see for himself. Even if they turn out to be full of silver, you can take it away. I don't want it."

"Perhaps you would like to see my shoes too," Mistress Meng cried.

They were in the midst of this dispute when Aunt Yang came in, leaning on her stick. "Here comes the aunt," all the neighbors cried. They saluted her respectfully. She returned their greeting and sat down. Then she began.

"Honorable neighbors here present. I am her aunt, and it is natural that I should have something to say about all this. He who is dead was my nephew, and he who lives is just as much my nephew. If any one of our fingers is bitten, it is no less painful than any other. It has been stated that her husband was rich. Well, even if he had a hundred thousand taels, you should still treat her fairly. She has no children and she is young. What right have you to prevent her marrying again?"

"Quite right, quite right," said all the neighbors.

"Do you claim the things that came to her from her own family?" the old lady continued, addressing Zhang the Fourth. "She has had no secret understanding with me. All I want is justice." She turned again to the bystanders. "If my niece had not always been so good-hearted and sweet-natured, honorable neighbors, I should not be bothering my old bones about her. I hate to see her leave this place."

Zhang the Fourth glared at the old lady. "Oh," said he, "I know how full of fine ideas your mind is. I also know that the phoenix does not lay his head where there is no treasure."

This remark infuriated the old lady. Her face became purple. She shook her finger at Zhang the Fourth. "Don't talk such rubbish, Zhang the Fourth. I may not be the rightful representative of the Yang family, but as for you, old slippery tongue, what have you to do with the Yangs?"

"Even if I am not a Yang, these two nephews are my sister's sons. You biting old reptile, a woman ought to consider her husband's family. What is the use of lighting a fire with one hand and pouring water on it with the other?"

"You good-for-nothing old dog bone," the old lady cried. "She is a young and helpless woman. You wish to keep her in this house, but what is it you are really after? Either you have nasty lustful designs upon her yourself, or you are devising some scheme to grow fat upon her money."

"I don't want her money," Zhang the Fourth retorted, "but there will be nothing for Yang Zongbao when he grows up. I am not your sort, ripe for the slaughter, one who takes up with the rich and deceives the humble. You are like a yellow cat with a black tail."

"Zhang the Fourth, you offshoot of generations of beggars, you miserable old slave, you old mealy mouth, how dare you be such a humbug and talk like this? What utter nonsense! There will be no cords to tie your coffin when you die."

"You garrulous old whore, you want the money yourself to put a little warmth under your tail. No wonder you never had any children!"

The old lady became more and more wild.

"Zhang the Fourth, you son of a bawd. Pig! Dog! So I have no children, eh? Well, that's better than having an old woman who goes to the temple to sleep with the monks and carry on with the priests. You don't know what you're talking about."

By this time the pair were on the point of coming to blows. Fortunately, the neighbors stopped them. "Uncle, let the lady have her say," they said to Zhang the Fourth.

Old woman Xue, while the dispute was at its height, told Ximen's servants and the soldiers to hurry in. They carried out all the chests and beds, some on their shoulders and others on poles. It was like a whirlwind. Zhang the Fourth was furious, but he could only look on, speechless. The neighbors could not understand what the trouble was all about. They tried to make peace, and finally they went away.

On the second day of the sixth month Ximen Qing sent a large sedan chair, with four pairs of lanterns, for Mistress Meng. Yang Zongbao, his hair dressed in a knot, wearing green clothes, rode on a horse and acted as his sister-in-law's escort. Ximen Qing gave him a roll of silk and a piece of jade. Lanxiang and Xiaoluan, the two maids, went with her to be her chambermaids. Qintong, her boy, was now fifteen years old, and he too went to serve her. On the third day after the marriage Aunt Yang and Mistress Meng's sisters-in-law called to offer their congratulations. Ximen Qing gave Aunt Yang seventy taels of silver and two rolls of silk, and from that day forward their friendship was never broken. He prepared three rooms in the western wing for Mistress Meng, and established her there as his third wife, calling her "Yulou" [Tower of Jade] and giving orders to his household that she must be spoken of as the Third Lady. For two nights he slept in her room. The golden hangings seemed to indicate the coming of a new bride, but the story told by the scarlet silk coverlets was not new.

CHAPTER 8
The Magic Diagrams

Higher and yet higher the red dawn
Creeps slowly up the casement.
She wakes and throws her silken wrapper
Carelessly across one breast.
Is it not strange
This rising while the sun is not yet high?

Blown by the gentle breeze
The hastening flowers wander through the tower of jade.
She could not sleep
The image of her loved one lingered always with her.

Now that Ximen Qing had married Meng Yulou, their love was so deep that they could not bear to be away from one another even for a moment. One day old woman Wen came on behalf of the Chen family to propose that the marriage arranged between their son and Ximen's daughter should be celebrated on the twelfth day of the sixth month. Ximen Qing, in a great state of excitement, took one of his new wife's gilded Nanjing beds for his daughter. For more than a month he was so busy preparing for the ceremony that he could not find time to go and see Pan Jinlian. Day after day she leaned upon the door, and looked out for him till her eyes could see no longer. At last she asked old woman Wang to go to his house. The old woman went, but the servants knew whence she had come and paid no attention to her. Jinlian waited and waited, but still Ximen did not come and, after old woman Wang's fruitless visit, she told Ying'er to go to the street and see if she could see him. The girl did not venture to enter the great house, or even the courtyard, but stood in the gateway and peeped inside. But she too could see no sign of Ximen Qing and had to go back again. When she got home, Jinlian spat in her face, cursed and beat her, because, she said, she was no use. She made the child kneel down until midday, and would give her nothing to eat. Then, finding the hot weather very trying, she told Ying'er to heat some water that she might take a bath, and to cook some little meat pasties for Ximen Qing to eat if he should come.

Jinlian was wearing a thin gossamer shift, and she sat on her little bed. When her lover did not come, she cursed him for a fickle rogue. This made her only the more sad. With her slender fingers she took off her red embroidered shoes, and began to use them for working out the magic diagrams of love. There was no one she could talk to, and she used coins to try and find out what her absent lover was thinking of.

Jinlian played at the love diagrams for a long time. Then she tired of them and lay down to sleep. An hour later she awoke in a very bad temper. "Mother," Ying'er said, "the water is hot now; will you take your bath?"

"Are the pasties cooked?" Jinlian asked. "Bring them here and let me see." Ying'er hastily brought them, and Jinlian counted them with her dainty fingers. She had made a tray of thirty but, though she counted again and again, she could not find more than twenty-nine.

"Where is the other one?" she cried.

"I haven't seen it," Ying'er said; "you must have counted wrong."

"I have counted them twice. I want thirty for your father to eat. How dare you steal one? You are an impudent, whorish little slave. I suppose you were dying of starvation, and couldn't do without one of these particular pasties! A bowl of rice, whether large or small, is not good enough for you. Do you imagine I made them for you?"

Without giving the girl a chance to say a word, she stripped off her clothes and beat her twenty or thirty times with a whip, till she squealed like a pig being killed. "If I have to ask you again, and you still lie to me, I will most certainly beat you a hundred times."

The girl could bear no more. "Mother, don't beat me," she cried, "I was so hungry I had to take one."

"Why did you say I'd counted them wrongly, when you knew you'd stolen one? I knew it was you, you little whore, you thief. When that turtle was alive, you knew one or two things, and told him a great deal more than you really knew. Now he is not here. You play your tricks right in front of my eyes. I will break every bone in your whorish little body."

She beat the girl for some time longer, then made her put on her drawers, and told her to stand beside her and fan her. When the girl had fanned her for a long time, Jinlian cried, "Turn your face to me, you little strumpet, and I'll pinch it." Ying'er turned and the woman, with her long sharp nails, pinched it till the blood came. Then she let go. After a while, she went to the dressing table to dress again before going to stand at the door.

At last the Heavens relented. Daian on horseback, carrying a parcel, passed her door.

"Where are you going?" she cried.

The boy was by no means lacking in intelligence, and he had often come with his master to this house. Jinlian was in the habit of giving him little presents. He knew her quite well. He dismounted and said, "I have been with a present to one of the officers and now I'm going home."

"What is happening at your Father's?" Jinlian said. "Why hasn't he been here? It looks as though he had another sweetheart."

"He has no new sweetheart. But for the last few days everybody in the house has been very busy, and he couldn't get away."

"If he has been so busy, why didn't he send me word? I have been worried about him for ever so long. Tell me, what is he really doing?"

The boy smiled. He did not answer, and this made Jinlian think there must be something behind it all. Once again she asked him eagerly, "What has been happening?"

"Well, if there was anything," Daian said, smiling, "why should you want to know all about it?"

"If you don't tell me, little oily mouth, I will hate you all your life."

"If I tell you," the boy said, "you mustn't let my master know I did so."

Jinlian promised, and Daian told her how his master had married Meng Yulou. The woman could not prevent the tears from falling over her beautiful face. Daian was very much embarrassed. "Oh, Aunt," he said, "how easily upset you are. That is just why I didn't want to tell you." Jinlian leaned upon the door and sighed deeply.

"You don't understand," she said, "you don't know how fond of one another we used to be. And now he has cast me aside." Her tears fell faster and faster.

"You shouldn't let yourself be so distressed," Daian said. "Even our Great Lady can't keep him in order."

"Listen to me, Daian," said Jinlian. She sang a song to him about the fickleness of men.

Then she began to cry again. "Please don't cry," Daian said, "I'm sure he will come and see you very soon. Write him a short note and let me take it to him. He will certainly come when he gets it."

"I will, indeed," Jinlian said, "and, if you will be so kind, you shall have a fine pair of shoes for your pains. I should like him to come in time for me to congratulate him on his birthday, but whether he comes or not will depend absolutely on your little oily tongue."

She told Ying'er to put some of the pasties onto a dish, and asked Daian to have some tea. Meanwhile she went into her room, took a sheet of flowered paper, and wrote with a sheep's-hair brush in a jade holder. In a few minutes she had written this poem:

The words upon this flowered paper come from my heart.
I remember that our hair once mingled on the pillow.
How often I have leaned upon the door, under the lattice, filled
    with countless fears.
Now, if you are false to me, if you will not come
Give back to me my dainty handkerchief.

When she had written this, she folded the paper in a lover's knot and
gave it to Daian. "Tell him he must come on his birthday. I shall be waiting most anxiously for him."

When the boy had eaten the cakes and the pasties, Jinlian gave him a
handful of coins. As he was about to mount his horse, she said, "When you
get home and see your Father, tell him that I am very angry with him. Tell
him that if he does not come here, I shall get a sedan chair and come to him."

"Lady," the boy said, "you mustn't do anything of the sort. You would
be like a dumpling seller trying to do business with a fortune-teller. You
would never get a fair deal." He rode away.

Day after day, early and late, Jinlian waited for Ximen Qing, but he
did not come. It was the end of the seventh month and his birthday was
approaching. To Jinlian every day seemed like three autumns and every
night like half a summer. Still no word came from him. She clenched her
pearly teeth and rivers of tears flowed from her eyes. One evening she prepared a meal, and asked old woman Wang to come and see her. She took
a silver pin from her hair and gave it to the old woman, entreating her to
go to Ximen's house and ask him to come.

"This is no time to go," the old woman said, "he will certainly not be
able to come now. I will go and see him tomorrow morning."

"You must not forget, Stepmother."

"I am not unused to such business," the old woman said. "I'm not
likely to lose any time in a matter of this sort."

Old woman Wang never did anything without being paid. This time
the pin was her reward. She drank till her face was very red, and then
went home.

Jinlian burned incense to perfume the bedclothes, and lighted the silver lamp. Long and softly she sighed to express the inmost feelings of her
heart. All through the long night she played the lute, till the silence and
loneliness of the empty house made her feel that she could play no longer.
And as she played, she sang.

She tossed about all night, unable to sleep. As soon as it was light,
she sent Ying'er to see whether old woman Wang had gone to see Ximen
Qing. The little girl came back and told her that the old woman had gone.

It was still early when old woman Wang reached Ximen's gate. She asked the servants about him, but they all said they knew nothing. She waited a long time, standing by the wall opposite the gate, till Clerk Fu came out and opened the shop. She went over and greeted him respectfully. "Excuse me," she said politely, "but is his Lordship at home?"

"What do you want with him?" Fu said. "Yesterday his Lordship entertained a number of guests to celebrate his birthday and, after drinking all day here, they went to the bawdy house last night. He has not come back yet, and you will probably find him still there."

The old woman thanked him and set off down East Street to the lane in which the bawdy house was. There she met Ximen, on horseback, coming from the opposite direction, and two boys attending him. He was half drunk, nodding to and fro upon his horse, and his bleary eyes could hardly see. "You ought not to get as drunk as this, Sir," old woman Wang shouted. She took hold of his bridle.

"Hello, Stepmother Wang, is that you?" Ximen Qing drunkenly mumbled. "I suppose Sister Wu has sent you to look for me?"

The old woman whispered something. "My boy said something about it some time ago," Ximen said. "I hear she is very angry with me. I'll go and see her now." He chatted with the old woman as they went along. When they came to the door, old woman Wang went in first.

"Now you ought to be happy, Lady," she said. "In less than half an hour I've brought his Lordship to you."

Jinlian was so delighted that he seemed like a visitor from Heaven. She ran downstairs to meet him. Ximen Qing waved his fan airily and went in, still neither drunk nor sober. He gave the woman a nod, and in return she made a profound reverence.

"You are indeed a nobleman, my Lord, and not the sort of man who is to be gazed upon any day. Where have you been all this time? I suppose you have been so taken up with your new wife that you haven't had time for me?"

"My new wife!" Ximen said. "What do you mean? Surely you don't believe all the tittle-tattle you hear. I have not had time to come and see you. I have been busy making arrangements for my daughter's wedding."

"Still trying to deceive me, are you?" Jinlian cried. "Well, if this is not a case of off with the old love and on with the new, you must take oath upon your body."

"If I have forgotten you," Ximen Qing said, "may my body become the size of a bowl of rice and may I suffer for three years or more from yellow sickness. May a caterpillar as large as a carrying pole bite a hole in my pocket."

"You fickle rascal, what harm will it do you if a caterpillar as large as that does bite a hole in your pocket?" She went up to him and, snatching off his hat, threw it on the floor. Old woman Wang hastily picked it up and put it on the table.

"Lady," she cried, "you were angry with me because I didn't make his Worship come, and, when he does come, you treat him like this."

Jinlian pulled a pin from his hair, held it up, and looked at it. It was of gold, with two rows of characters engraved upon it.

> The horse, with golden bridle, neighs on the sweet turf.
> In the season of apricot blossoms, they who dwell in the jade tower
>   drink till they are merry.

This pin belonged to Yulou, but Jinlian thought some singing girl had given it to him. She thrust it into her sleeve. "Now will you say you haven't changed? Where is the pin I gave you?"

"The other day," Ximen said, "I was rather tipsy and fell off my horse. My hat blew away and my hair was all in a mess. I looked everywhere for the pin, but could not find it."

Jinlian snapped her fingers in his face. "Brother, you are so drunk you don't know what you're saying. A child of three would see through a story like that."

"Don't be so hard on his Lordship," old woman Wang said. "He is one of those men who can see a bee piddling forty miles away, but not an elephant outside their very own doors."

"When she is nearly done," Ximen Qing said, "you begin."

Jinlian saw a scarlet-trimmed finely gilded fan. She snatched it from him and took it to the light to look at. She was well skilled in the arts of love, and she was sure that certain marks upon it had been caused by teeth. She came to the conclusion that some girl must have given him the fan, and without a word tore it into pieces. Before Ximen Qing could stop her it was in shreds.

"My friend Bu Zhidao gave me that fan," he said, "and I've kept it put away for a long time. I've only been using it for two or three days, and now you've gone and spoiled it."

Jinlian plagued him a little longer, and then Ying'er brought in tea. The woman told her to put down the tray and kowtow to Ximen Qing.

"You two have been quarreling quite long enough," old woman Wang said. "Don't forget that you have more important business to attend to. I'll go into the kitchen and get something ready for you."

Jinlian told Ying'er to bring wine and refreshments in honor of Ximen's birthday. The girl obeyed and soon a meal was set upon the table.

Jinlian brought out her own present and, setting it on a tray, offered it to him. Besides a pair of black silk shoes, there was a pair of breeches made of purple silk, double sewn and embroidered with a design of pine, bamboo, and plum blossom, the three cold-weather friends. They were lined with green silk, scented with fragrant herbs, and the braces were again of purple. The stomacher was embroidered with roses. There was also a pin like the petals of the double lotus, on which was engraved a verse of four sentences, each sentence consisting of four characters:

> A double lotus, I,
> To dress your hair.
> Do not forget me
> Like a neglected ornament.

Ximen Qing was delighted with these presents. He caught Jinlian to him and kissed her. "I never knew you were so clever," he said.

Jinlian told Ying'er to bring the wine jar that she might offer Ximen a cup of wine. As she bowed four times in reverence before him, she seemed as graceful as a branch laden with blossoms, and each time she stood up as straight as a candle. Ximen Qing quickly lifted her up, and they sat together side by side. Old woman Wang drank several cups of wine with them and then went home, her face very red. Then they abandoned all restraint, and drank for a long time till darkness fell.

> Dark clouds have gathered over the mountains
> A chain of deepest mist stretches far into the distance.
> Stars come out to challenge the brightness of the moon
> And the green waters of the lake mirror the sky.
> The monks return to their ancient temples
> While, in the depths of the forest, the crows fly, crying
> Caw, caw, caw.
> People hasten back to the distant villages
> And in the tiny hamlets the dogs bark
> Bow, wow, wow.

Ximen Qing decided to stay the night with Jinlian, and ordered the boys to take his horse home. That night they spent their whole strength in the enjoyment of one another, and their passionate delight knew no bounds. Yet, as the proverb says, "When joy is at its height, there comes sad news." The time flew by.

❋   ❋   ❋

We must now return for a while to Wu Song. He had taken the magistrate's treasure to the palace of the Grand Marshal in the Eastern Capital. When he had safely handed over the letters and the chests, he stayed some time waiting for the return letter, and then ordered his men to start back to Shandong. When he had started, it was the third or fourth month; now it was already autumn. Rain fell incessantly, and they had to halt for a few days. He had already been away about three months, and somehow, on this journey homewards, he seemed unable to rid himself of a feeling of great uneasiness. At last he made up his mind to send one of the soldiers before him to carry a report to the magistrate and a letter to his brother, Wu Da. In this he said he would be home some time during the eighth month.

The soldier arrived and, after giving the letter to the magistrate, went off to find Wu Da. It so happened that old woman Wang was standing outside her door when the soldier was just about to knock at Wu Da's house. She went across and said to him, "What is it you want?"

"I have orders from Captain Wu," the soldier said, "to give this letter to his brother."

"Master Wu Da is not at home," the old woman said. "He has gone to visit his family tombs. Give me the letter and he shall have it as soon as he comes back. That is the best thing you can do."

The soldier saluted, took out the letter, and gave it to the old woman. Then he jumped on his horse and rode away. Old woman Wang immediately brought the letter to Jinlian's back door. She and Ximen Qing were not yet up; they had spent half the night in amorous combat.

"Get up, Master and Mistress," the old woman cried, "here is news for you. Wu Song has sent a soldier with a letter for his brother to say he is coming back shortly. I took the letter and sent the soldier about his business, but you will have to do something about it, and not waste any time."

Ximen Qing was feeling perfectly contented with life, but, when he heard this news, it seemed to him that the eight pieces of his skull had fallen apart and somebody was pouring a great jar of ice and snow through the opening. He and Jinlian quickly leapt out of bed, threw their clothes on, and asked the old woman to come in. She gave the letter to Ximen Qing to read. It only said that Wu Song would be back not later than the Autumn Day, but this was enough to make the lovers beside themselves with anxiety.

"What shall we do, Stepmother?" they cried. "If you can only think of some way out for us, we shall be so grateful that we shall find a splendid reward for you. We are so fond of one another that we cannot bear to be apart. But, if Wu Song comes back, we shall be obliged to separate, and life won't be worth living."

"Sir," said the old woman, "why all this to-do? I told you once before
that first marriages were arranged for people by their parents, but that
second marriages are the concern of no one but the parties themselves.
Nobody has ever suggested that a man and his brother's wife belong to the
same family. Wu Da has been dead a hundred days or so. Lady, you must
ask a few monks to come and burn his tablet before Wu Song comes back.
Then you, Sir, must send a sedan chair and take her into your establishment. When Wu Song does come back, I will have a word with him, and
what is there he can do? You will be able to spend all your lives together.
Isn't that good enough for you?"

"You are right, Stepmother," Ximen Qing said. He and Jinlian breakfasted together, and it was decided that on the sixth day of the eighth
month there should be a final requiem for Wu Da, when they would send
for monks and have the tablet burned. Two days later Ximen Qing would
take Jinlian into his own household. When all these arrangements had
been made, Daian came with a horse and Ximen went home.

Time sped like an arrow in flight. The sun and moon crossed and recrossed like a weaver's shuttles. It was the sixth day of the eighth month.
Ximen Qing brought several taels of silver to Wu Da's house, and told old
woman Wang to go to the Temple of Eternal Felicity and ask six monks
to come and sing a dirge for Wu Da and to burn his tablet the same evening. Before it was fully light the temple attendants came with their sacred
books and instruments. They set up a lectern and hung their pictures all
around, and old woman Wang in the kitchen helped the cooks to prepare
vegetarian food. Ximen Qing spent the whole day there. Soon the monks
arrived, tinkling their bells and beating their drums. They read their sacred
books and intoned their exorcisms.

Jinlian would perform none of the due purifications. She slept with
Ximen Qing till the sun was high in the heavens, and she would not have
risen then, had not the monks come to invite her to burn incense, sign the
documents, and make her reverence to Buddha. Finally she dressed herself
in white and went to worship Buddha.

As soon as the monks saw her, their Buddhist hearts were troubled and
their Buddhist natures stimulated to a furious degree, so that their passions
ran away with them, and they were in such a state that they did not know
what they were doing.

> The precentor lost his wits and, as he read the sacred books
> Knew not if they were upside down.
> The holy priests went mad and read their prayers
> By no means sure what line they read.

The thurifer upset the vases, and the acolyte seized the incense
   boat
Thinking it was his candle.
The lector should have read "The Mighty Empire of Song"
But called it "Tang" instead.
The exorcist, who should have chanted "Master Wu" cried "Mistress
   Wu."
The old monk's heart so wildly beat
He missed the drum and struck the young monk's hand.
The young monk's mind was so distraught
He used the drumstick on the old monk's head.
Long patient years of novicehood were all undone
And had ten thousand saints come down to earth
It would have been no better.

Jinlian burned incense before the image of Buddha, signed the papers, and made a reverence. Then she went back to her room and began again to play with Ximen Qing. She never even dreamed of abstaining from wine or any kind of food.

"If there should be anything that requires attention," Ximen said to old woman Wang, "you attend to it, and don't let anybody come to disturb the lady."

"You young people enjoy yourselves," the old woman said, laughing. "If there is anything to be done for these shaven-headed fellows, I'll do it."

Now that the monks had seen how beautiful Wu Da's widow was, they could not put her out of their minds. When they came back again from their temple after the evening meal, Jinlian was still drinking and making merry with Ximen Qing. There was only a wooden partition between her room and the temporary chapel. One of the monks had come back before the others and was washing his hands in a basin outside the window of her room when he heard soft whisperings and gentle murmurings that left him in little doubt about what was going on. He stopped washing his hands and stood still to listen. He heard Jinlian say, "Sweetheart, how long will you continue? The monks will be back soon and they may hear us. Do let me go. We must finish."

"Don't be in a hurry," Ximen's voice said. "I should like to 'set the cover on fire' just once more." It never occurred to them that there was a monk listening to every word they said.

Then all the monks came back, and they began to make music and intone their orisons. One told another, till there was none who did not know that Wu Da's widow was entertaining her lover in the house. They waved their arms and feet wildly without the slightest idea of what they

were doing. Thus were the Buddhist services performed, and thus, this
night, they sped Wu Da's spirit on its lonely journey.

Jinlian took off her mourning robes, dressed herself beautifully, and
came to stand with Ximen Qing behind the lattice. They watched the
monks preparing to burn the tablet and old woman Wang carrying water and fire. At last the tablet and the Buddhist pictures were completely
consumed.

Thievish shaven-heads peered with cold eyes through the lattice. A
man and a woman standing shoulder to shoulder could vaguely be seen.
This brought to their minds the remembrance of what had happened before, and they struck their instruments discordantly. An old monk's hat
was blown off by the wind and his bluish bald pate appeared. He did not
pick up his hat, but went on thumping his instrument and roaring with
laughter. Old woman Wang called, "Reverend Fathers, you have finished
your service. Why do you beat your instruments any longer?"

"We haven't set fire to the cover of a paper stove yet," one of the monks
cried. Ximen Qing heard this, and told the old woman to give them their
fee and send them packing, but the old monk insisted that they must see
the lady first and thank her.

"Please tell them that is quite unnecessary," Jinlian said, but the monks
answered with one voice, "Do let us go." Then, roaring with laughter, they
all went off.

CHAPTER 9

Wu Song Seeks to Avenge His Brother

So Ximen Qing and Pan Jinlian burned Wu Da's tablet. The next day they invited old woman Wang to a farewell party, and gave Ying'er into her charge.

"When Wu Song comes back," Ximen Qing said, "how am I to prevent his learning that I have married this lady?"

"I shall be here," the old woman said, smiling, "and no matter how inquisitive Wu Song may be, I shall have an answer ready for him. Don't worry about that."

Ximen Qing was only too glad to receive such a comforting reply, and gave the old woman three taels of silver. The same evening he took all Jinlian's belongings to his own house; the furniture and clothes were given to old woman Wang. The next day he sent a sedan chair with four lanterns, and Jinlian in her best clothes seated herself in it. Old woman Wang went with her as though she represented the bride's family, and Daian acted as escort. So Jinlian went to her new home. Everybody in the neighborhood knew what was happening, but people feared the rich and powerful Ximen Qing, and nobody dared to interfere. But someone composed a little poem in honor of the occasion.

Ximen Qing received his new bride, and had an apartment of three rooms set aside for her in the garden. There was a small gate in one of the corners of the courtyard, easily overlooked for it was hidden by flowers and flowerpots. Few people came that way. It was very secluded. One of the three rooms was furnished as a sitting room, and one as a bedroom. Ximen paid sixteen taels of silver for a bed of black lacquer and gilt with a crimson silk net. The chairs and tables were beautifully carved, and everything was arranged with excellent taste.

Wu Yueniang had two maids, Chunmei and Yuxiao. Ximen Qing directed that Chunmei should act as maid to his new wife, and paid five taels for a little girl called Xiaoyu to take her place with the Great Lady. For another six taels he bought a maid called Qiuju and gave her to Jinlian as a kitchen maid.

Ximen Qing's first wife, Chen, had brought with her a servant called Sun Xue'e. She was now about twenty years old, fairly tall and not bad-looking. Ximen had allowed her to assume the position of his fourth wife, so that Jinlian ranked as the fifth of his ladies.

Now that Jinlian was actually established in his own house, Ximen spent every night with her. They played together as merrily as fishes in water, and nothing could have surpassed their pleasure in each other. On the day after her arrival Jinlian put on her finest clothes and, when Chunmei had served her with tea, went to Wu Yueniang's room to make the acquaintance of the other members of the household. She took with her as a present a pair of shoes. Yueniang sat in her place as mistress of the house, and looked closely at the new bride. She was about twenty-five years old, and very beautiful.

Yueniang looked at her from her head to her feet; every inch of that exquisite body seemed endowed with the power of fascination. She looked at her from her feet to her head; this extraordinary charm seemed to issue from her as water from a fountain. She was like a translucent pearl lying on a crystal dish, like the early morning moon shining above the topmost branches of a pink apricot tree. Yueniang gazed at her without speaking, and she said to herself, "When the boys came home, they used to say, 'How strange that Wu Da should have so beautiful a wife.' I have never seen anyone so beautiful. No wonder that brave husband of mine fell in love with her."

Jinlian kowtowed to Yueniang, and offered her a present. When the Great Lady had acknowledged her reverence, she turned to Li Jiao'er, Meng Yulou, and Sun Xue'e, and greeted them as sisters. Then she stood till Yueniang bade a maid give her a chair and speak to her as the Fifth Lady.

Jinlian sat down and secretly considered her new sisters. Yueniang was about twenty-seven years old; her face was as beautiful as a bowl of silver and her eyes were like the kernel of an apricot. Her manner was gentle and her speech careful. Li Jiao'er, who had been a singing girl at the bawdy house, was inclined to be corpulent and not so attractive. Though she had been a famous strumpet, her skill in the arts of love was not to be compared with that of Jinlian. Yulou was about thirty years old. Her face was like the pear blossom, and her waist as slender as the willow. She was tall, and her oval face was marked by a few slight scars. But she was very beautiful, and it would have been difficult to say whether the tiny feet that peeped from beneath her skirt were larger or smaller than those of Jinlian herself. Xue'e had been a maid; she was not very tall and her manner was sharp. But there was no kind of soup she could not make and her skill with dishes and plates was almost miraculous.

In a very short time Jinlian had made herself acquainted with the characteristic features of her companions.

When the first three days were over, she rose early every morning and, as soon as she was dressed, went to Yueniang's room to sew and make shoes. She pretended to be very eager to do anything she could, moving things that did not need to be moved, calling Yueniang Great Lady, as all the maids did, and giving her little presents. This delighted Yueniang. She called Jinlian Sister, and gave her some clothes and ornaments of her own that she valued highly. They always took their meals together.

Li Jiao'er and the others became very jealous of the attentions that Yueniang paid Jinlian, and in secret had much to say about it. "We are wives of old standing," they said, "but the Great Lady cares not a whit about us. This woman has been here only a few days, and she is shown all these favors. Our eldest sister is not discreet."

Ximen Qing was now married to Jinlian, living in a splendid house and wearing the finest of clothes. So close was the attachment between this fascinating woman and her dissolute bridegroom that nothing could have separated them. Everything was as merry as could be, and Ximen Qing took advantage of the situation without ceasing.

It was the beginning of the eighth month when Wu Song reached Qinghe. First, he went to the Town Hall to give the magistrate the letters he had brought from the Eastern Capital. The magistrate was glad to know that his presents had been duly delivered. He gave Wu Song ten taels of silver and entertained him. After this, Wu Song went back to his own place, changed his clothes, put on a new hat, locked the door, and went straight to Amethyst Street. The neighbors saw that he was back and were tremendously excited, breaking into a perfect sweat. "Now the trouble will begin," they said. "This prince of the haughty spirit will not let this matter pass lightly."

Wu Song went to his brother's door and pulled up the shutter. Ying'er was sitting outside the room, making thread. He called, "Brother," but there was no reply. Then he cried, "Sister," but still there was no answer. He thought, "I must be getting deaf if I can't hear one or other of them." He spoke to Ying'er, but she was so terrified she could not utter a word.

"Where are your father and mother?" Wu Song said. Ying'er burst into tears.

Meanwhile old woman Wang had heard that he was back, and she was afraid that all would be discovered. She hurried over. When Wu Song saw her coming, he saluted.

"Where is my brother, and how is it my sister-in-law is not here?"

"Sit down, please," the old woman said, "and I will tell you. Some time during the fourth month, shortly after you had gone away, your brother was taken very ill, and died."

"When did he die? What did he die of? Who attended him?" Wu Song cried.

"About the twentieth of the fourth month your brother suddenly began to suffer from pains at the heart. After a week or so we went to make supplication to Heaven. We called in soothsayers, and got every medicine we could think of, but it was all no use. He died."

"My brother never suffered from anything of the sort before," Wu Song said. "It is a very curious thing that he should die of heart trouble so unexpectedly."

"Captain," the old woman said, "you should not say things like that. Heaven sends its storms upon us without warning, and, though we may take off our shoes and socks tonight, who can tell whether tomorrow morning we shall put them on again? Nobody can be certain that some sudden calamity will not befall him."

"When was my brother buried?" Wu Song asked.

"When your brother gave up the ghost," the old woman said, "he had not a halfpenny in the world. His wife was no better off than a crab without feet. She could never have bought a grave for him. Fortunately, one of our more wealthy neighbors, who happened to be a friend of your brother, provided a coffin, and, when Master Wu had been dead three days, we had the funeral ceremonies and cremated him."

"Where is my sister-in-law now?" Wu Song asked.

"She was a young and tender woman, with nothing to live on, so she wore her mourning for a hundred days, and then her mother persuaded her to marry some stranger who lives a long way from here. She left this troublesome little girl in my care, and said I was to give her to you when you came back. When I have done that, I shall have done all I was called upon to do."

Wu Song listened to this story, and pondered it for a while. Then he left old woman Wang. He went to his own rooms near the Town Hall and changed into white clothes. Then he told his servant to buy a hempen cord, a pair of cotton socks, and a mourning hat. He bought fruits, cakes, candles, and paper money. Returning to Wu Da's house, he prepared a new tablet, made ready soup and food, lighted the candles, set out the wine and food, and hung up all the paper offerings. By the time he had done this, it was already the first night watch.

Then Wu Song burned incense, and knelt down and said: "Brother, may your spirit draw near. When you were on earth, you were weak and feeble. Now you are dead, and I do not know the cause of your death. If you met your death at the hands of others, and your brooding spirit can find none to avenge it, send me a dream, and I will avenge you." He poured wine upon the ground, and burned all the paper money. Then he sobbed aloud. The neighbors heard him and were sorry for him, for they knew that Wu Song was brother to Wu Da.

When all was done, he gave the wine, food, and dishes to the soldiers. Then he brought two pallets, and told the soldiers to sleep in the outer room. Ying'er was asleep in the inner room, and he himself took a pallet and lay down before Wu Da's tablet. It was now midnight. He tossed over and over, unable to sleep. He could only sigh. The soldiers were sleeping as soundly as the dead. He rose, and it seemed that the lamp on the table was flickering, half light, half dark. He sat up on his pallet and said to himself, "My brother was very weak, and there is something very mysterious about his death. . . ." He had not finished this sentence when, over the table that supported his brother's tablet, there came an ice-cold wind.

> Formless and shadowless, neither mist nor smoke
> Round and round it moved,
> Like a spirit wind striking cold to the marrow,
> Gloomy and dark,
> Like the icy mist over a war-stricken land
> Chilling the flesh.
> The lamp before the tablet lost its brightness
> Sad and uncanny.
> The paper money hanging on the wall
> Whirled round and round.
> It seemed as if, within this mist, the souls of all the poisoned
>   marched,
> Their ghostly standards fluttering in the wind.

The cold wind made Wu Song's hair stand on end. He stared at the tablet and it seemed to him that there slowly emerged the form of a man who cried, "Oh, younger brother, I died in agony." Wu Song could not distinguish the figure very clearly and would have gone forward to question it, but, as he waited, the cold mist faded away and the figure vanished.

Wu Song sank down upon the pallet. "This is truly a strange thing," he thought, "a dream yet not a dream. My brother seemed to wish to tell me something, but the vigor of my body was too much for his frail spirit. Nevertheless, I am sure there is a mystery about his death." Then he heard the watchman striking the third watch. He went to look at the soldiers, but found them fast asleep. His soul was troubled. He watched till daybreak, when the cocks began to crow and the dawn broke in the eastern sky. Then the soldiers got up and heated some water for him, and he washed his face and cleansed his mouth. Calling Ying'er, he told her to look after the house, and went off with the soldiers.

As he passed down the street, he asked all the neighbors to tell him how his brother had died, and whom his sister-in-law had married. They knew all there was to be known, of course, but they were afraid of Ximen Qing and did not wish to get mixed up in the matter. "Captain," they said, "it is no use asking us. Old woman Wang is the nearest neighbor, go and ask her. Then you will learn the truth." One of the more talkative added: "Yun'ge, the pear seller, and He the Ninth know all about it, too."

Wu Song went down the street to find Yun'ge. At last he found that young monkey carrying a basket, coming back from buying some rice. He hailed him. When the boy saw that it was Wu Song who called him, he said, "Captain Wu, you have come back too late. You will not find it easy to get to the bottom of the matter and, if you take it to the courts, there will be no one to look after my poor old father."

"Come with me," Wu Song said. He took the boy to an eating house, and ordered two bowls of rice. "Brother," he said, "you are not very old, but I see that you pay proper respect to your father. That is as it should be." He took five taels of silver from his sleeve. "Take this for the present," he said, "and when I have attended to this matter, I will give you another ten taels to set you up in business. Now, I want you to tell me who it was who quarreled with my brother, who is responsible for his death, and who has married my sister-in-law. Tell me the whole story and don't hide anything."

Yun'ge took the silver. He decided that it would be enough to supply his father's needs for three or four months, and that he need no longer be anxious about going to the law courts. "Brother," he said, "listen, but do not be impatient." Then he told the whole story from beginning to end. Wu Song listened attentively. "Is this absolutely true?" he said. "Who took my sister-in-law away?"

"Ximen Qing took your sister to his place," the boy said. "She has given herself to him absolutely. Why do you ask whether I am telling the truth?"

"It is essential that you shall not tell any lies," Wu Song said.

"What I have told you is what I shall say at the law courts," the boy replied. Wu Song called for food and, when they had finished it, he paid the reckoning and they left the shop.

"Go home and give the silver to your father," Wu Song said, "and to-morrow morning come to the Town Hall to give your evidence. Tell me, where does He the Ninth live?"

"You won't find him," the boy said, "he disappeared three days ago, as soon as he heard you had come back."

Wu Song left Yun'ge and went to his own place. The next morning, he asked Master Chen to write an accusation for him, and went to the Town Hall. Yun'ge was already waiting for him. He went into the Hall of Audience, knelt down, and presented his accusation. The magistrate recognized Wu Song at once and asked what was the accusation he wished to make.

"My brother Wu Da has been murdered by that villain Ximen Qing, who was carrying on an intrigue with my sister-in-law. First, my brother was kicked in the chest; then old woman Wang devised a plan for murdering him. After his death the undertaker He the Ninth allowed his body to be cremated without properly examining it, and now Ximen Qing has carried off my sister-in-law to be one of his concubines. This boy, Yun'ge, is here to give evidence as to the facts, and I pray your Lordship to see that justice is done."

"Why is the undertaker He the Ninth not here?" the magistrate said.

"When he knew that the secret was out he ran away," Wu Song said. "Nobody knows where he is."

The magistrate examined Yun'ge and wrote down his evidence. Then he withdrew and called together his officials. The magistrate himself, his deputy, and all the other officers were very intimate with Ximen Qing, and the case was one they did not care to decide. The magistrate came back to Wu Song and said, "You are a captain in my district, and I am surprised to find that you don't seem to know the law. In cases of alleged adultery, it has always been customary to require that the guilty pair should be caught in the act; and, in cases of murder, to insist upon direct evidence. Your brother's body has been burned, and you did not, in fact, lay hold of the adulterers. It would not be right for me to give judgment in the case simply upon the evidence of this little fellow. Think over the matter for yourself, calmly."

"Sir," Wu Song replied, "what I have told you is the simple truth, not some fantastic tale of my own imagining. I beg you to order the arrest of Ximen Qing, the woman Pan, and old woman Wang. Let the law take its ordinary course with them, and the truth will come out. If I lie, I am ready to suffer the consequences."

"Well," the magistrate said, "I must think this over. If I decide that they ought to be arrested, I will arrest them." Wu Song rose and went out, leaving Yun'ge in the court.

By this time Ximen Qing had heard what was going on. He was greatly alarmed, and at once gave large sums of money to his trusted servants, Lai-bao and Laiwang, and sent them to bribe the officials. The next morning, when Wu Song went to the court in the hope of persuading the magistrate to have the criminals arrested, he found that all the officials had accepted Ximen's bribes and refused to have anything to do with his accusation.

"Wu Song," one said, "don't believe busybodies who simply wish to make trouble between you and Ximen Qing. There is really no evidence in this case, and it would be impossible to give a fair judgment upon it. A wise man says: 'Things I see with my own eyes, I can hardly credit; how shall I believe what others tell me?' You must not be so impetuous."

"You work in this office," another said, "and of course you understand the law. You know all that is to be known about murders and murderers. Now, before the case can be opened, five things are essential: the corpse, the wounds, the disease, the instruments by which the crime was committed, and the traces of the crime itself. Your brother's body has already disappeared. How can we decide this case?"

"If that is how you look at it," Wu Song cried, "my brother's murder will never be avenged. It is clear that the magistrate does not intend to deal with the matter, and I must do things my own way." He took away his accusation and went back to his place, sending Yun'ge home. Then he gazed towards the heavens and sighed deeply, gnashed his teeth, and cursed his sister-in-law's wantonness. Wu Song at that moment was ferocity itself! His anger was beyond control. He set off at once for Ximen Qing's shop, with his mind made up to engage Ximen in single combat. But only Fu the manager was there.

"Is your master at home?" Wu Song said.

Fu recognized Wu Song. "No," he said, "he is not at home. Is there anything I can tell him for you, Captain?"

"I must trouble you to come here," was the only reply. Fu did not dare refuse, and went with Wu Song to a secluded place. Suddenly, Wu Song turned and caught him by the throat, glaring wildly at him.

"Do you wish to live or to die?"

"Captain," Fu cried, "I have never done you any harm. Why are you so angry?"

"If you wish to die, say nothing. If you wish to live, tell me the truth. Now, where is that fellow Ximen? When did he marry my sister-in-law? Tell me everything, and I will let you go."

Fu was a poor-spirited creature, and Wu Song's rage made him panic-stricken. "Pleas don't be so angry, Captain," he stammered; "I work in his shop and he pays me two taels a month. My business is to look after the shop, nothing else, and I have no notion how he spends his time. Truly, my master is not at home now. He and his friends have gone to a wineshop in Lion Street. I would not dare to tell you a lie."

Wu Song released Fu, and rushed off to Lion Street as though possessed of wings. Fu was so terrified that he could not move for a long time. While Wu Song was striding towards the wineshop, Ximen Qing was drinking there with a man called Li the Merchant of Secrets. This man was one of the court runners and had a finger in the pie in all the matters that came up at the District Office. He used to find out everything that was to be found out and use the knowledge to his own advantage. If any dispute arose, he would suggest courses of action to both parties, and, if they thought of bribing the magistrate, he smoothed over any little difficulties. So he came to be called Merchant of Secrets. Today, after the magistrate had rejected Wu Song's accusation, he was reporting the matter to Ximen Qing. Ximen invited him to take wine and made him a present of five taels of silver.

They were contentedly drinking their wine when Ximen Qing happened to glance around to see what was going on in the street, and saw Wu Song, like an angry god, coming over the bridge towards the inn. He knew that Wu Song could have no peaceful intent, and was frightened out of his wits. He would have escaped, but could not get down the stairs in time, so he pretended he wished to change his clothes and hid himself somewhere at the back of the inn.

Wu Song came to the door and asked the waiter where Ximen was. "Master Ximen is taking wine with one of his friends upstairs." Wu Song pulled up his skirts and dashed upstairs. Ximen Qing had vanished. There was only a man sitting before a table, and a couple of singing girls on either side. Wu Song recognized the runner Li and knew that he must have been telling Ximen Qing what had happened. In a fury, he went forward and shook his fist at Li.

"You villain," he cried, "what have you done with Ximen Qing? Tell me at once or I'll give you a drubbing."

The very sight of Wu Song had terrified the runner, and, when he was spoken to so roughly, he could not get out a word in reply. Wu Song, finding that he received no answer, grew angrier and angrier, and kicked down the table. The cups and dishes were smashed. The two singing girls were so frightened that they swooned away. The runner realized that Wu Song meant him no good, and, though he did not find it easy, managed to pull himself to his feet and tried to shuffle downstairs. Wu Song pulled him back.

"I have asked you a question and you don't answer. Where do you think you're going? Be so kind as to eat one of my fists. I'll see whether you'll answer me or not." He struck Li a terrific blow in the face.

"Oh dear!" the man cried, finding his tongue at last, and agonized by the pain. "Ximen Qing has gone to the back to change his clothes. Please let me go, it has nothing to do with me."

Wu Song with both hands lifted the runner and hurled him out of the window. "If you wish to get out, there you are," he cried, and flung the merchant of secrets into the street.

Wu Song went to the back of the house to find Ximen Qing. Ximen had heard the disturbance and was in a terrible state of fright. Without giving a thought to the danger, he jumped out of the window, ran along the balcony, and found his way to somebody's courtyard. Wu Song could not find him and, thinking that Li had lied to him, he ran downstairs to where the runner was stretched out on the ground, half dead, though his eyes still moved. Wu Song kicked him twice in the guts, and he died.

"This is runner Li," the bystanders said. "What has he done to annoy you, Captain, that you should kill him like this?"

"It was Ximen Qing I was really after," Wu Song said, "and this ill-starred fellow happened to be with him. So he met his death at my hands."

The policeman saw that a man had been killed, but did not venture to take Wu Song by force. He went slowly towards him and tried to detain him by persuasion. A bond was put on the waiter and the two singing girls, and they were all taken together to the Town Hall. The news soon spread through the street and everybody was talking about it. They did not know that Ximen Qing had escaped, but thought Wu Song had killed him.

CHAPTER 10
The Exiling of Wu Song

Wu Song was taken by the watch to the city jail. Meanwhile Ximen Qing, who had jumped out of the wineshop window, found himself in a courtyard that belonged to old Doctor Hu. One of the maids had just gone to the privy and had lifted her skirts. Suddenly she saw a man crouching at the foot of the wall. As she could not run away, she called, "Thief! thief!" as loudly as she could, and Doctor Hu ran out to see what was the matter. He recognized Ximen Qing, and said:

"My Lord, I must congratulate you on your escape from Wu Song. He has killed a man, and they have taken him to the lockup. But you may go home now, Sir, I don't think there is likely to be any more trouble."

Ximen thanked the doctor, and went home with all the assurance in the world. He told Pan Jinlian what had happened, and they clapped their hands with delight to think that all their troubles were now over. Jinlian advised Ximen to send bribes to all the officials, so that they might make sure that Wu Song would be sentenced to death, for they by no means desired to set eyes on him again. Ximen Qing called his servant Laiwang, and told him to take the magistrate a set of gold and silver drinking cups, with fifty taels of silver, and sums of money for all the other officials, both great and small, and to ask that Wu Song should be punished with all the rigor of the law. The magistrate accepted the bribe and, the next morning, as soon as he entered the Hall of Audience, had Wu Song brought before him, with the waiter and the two singing girls. His manner had now completely changed.

"Wu Song," he said, "you are a desperate fellow and have brought accusations against perfectly innocent people. I have overlooked this more than once. Now you yourself have killed a man, without the slightest cause. Why don't you obey the laws?"

"My quarrel was really with Ximen Qing," Wu Song said, "but, as ill luck would have it, I met this man. He refused to tell me where Ximen Qing was, and I lost my temper and killed him. My Lord, I implore you to give me justice, and bring Ximen Qing to answer to the law for my brother's death. As for myself, I am ready to give my life for this dead man's."

"You are talking nonsense," the magistrate cried. "Do you mean to say you did not know he was an officer of this court? You must certainly have had some other reason for killing him. Why do you try to drag Ximen Qing into the matter? I can see that I shall never get the truth out of you without a beating."

He ordered his attendants to punish Wu Song. Three or four of them pulled him down and gave him twenty strokes of the rod, like drops of rain falling. Wu Song continued to insist that he was being unjustly dealt with. "I have done much for you," he cried, "and you should deal with me accordingly and not have me beaten so severely."

This only made the magistrate more angry. "You killed a man with your fist," he cried. "Now your boldness seems to have gone into your mouth." He ordered the thumbscrews to be put on, and Wu Song's fingers were pressed and his hands beaten fifty times, after which a cangue was put about his neck and he was returned to prison.

Some of the officers had been Wu Song's friends and knew that he was a man who had taken upon himself to avenge another's quarrel. They would have liked to clear him, but, as they had accepted Ximen Qing's bribes, their mouths were sealed and they were unable to do anything. As Wu Song persisted in demanding justice, the magistrate waited a few days and then drew up a dossier without hearing any evidence. All he did was to appoint an officer to go to Lion Street to examine Li's body and fill in the necessary particulars. Then the crime sheet was drawn up as follows:

> The accused Wu Song called to see Li, and there was a dispute with regard to the division of certain moneys. The parties became drunk and began to fight. The deceased was kicked and beaten and thrown from a high place. Green and red marks were found on his left side, his face, ribs, and groin.

After completing their examination, the officials went back to the office, and a document was drawn up to be sent with Wu Song to the Prefect of Dongping, where the matter would have to be further investigated and the final judgment made.

The Prefect of Dongping, His Excellency Chen Wenzhao, was a native of Henan and an official of exceptional probity. As soon as the documents were brought to him, he began the hearing of the case.

Chen Wenzhao went to his court and ordered everyone to be brought before him. He read through all the documents that had come from Qinghe and examined the depositions. The indictment said:

PREFECTURE OF DONGPING DISTRICT OF QINGHE
An Indictment

The accused Wu Song is twenty-eight years of age, formerly domiciled in the District of Yanggu. On account of his splendid physique he was appointed Captain of the Police in this District.

After returning to this District from a tour of duty, the accused visited his brother's tomb. He ascertained that his sister-in-law had not observed the required period of mourning, but had remarried. The same day he inquired from people in the streets concerning the matter, and ultimately proceeded to a wineshop in Lion Street, where he met Li Waichuan. Being drunk, he endeavored to recover the sum of three hundred cash that he alleged Li had previously borrowed from him, but Li refused to pay the money and the two men fought. Li was struck and kicked, and so severely injured that he died shortly afterwards.

In proof whereof the singing girls Niu and Bao are witnesses.

The watch arrested Wu Song, and officers deputed for that purpose proceeded to the place where Li's body lay and made a careful examination. We then heard Wu Song and prepared the accompanying depositions. We trust that upon further investigation you will find the particulars to be correct.

It is our submission that Wu Song fought with and killed the man, and that he should be executed in accordance with the law for the capital offense, not for fighting or the dispute over money. The waiter Wang, and the two girls Niu and Bao, appear to be guiltless in the matter, and we only await your permission to release them.

Dated this eighth day of the eighth month of the third year of Zhenghe:

> Li Dadian, *Magistrate*
> Luo He'an, *Deputy Magistrate*
> Hua Helu, *Keeper of the Archives*
> Xia Gongji, *Prosecutor*
> Qian Lao, *Chief Jailer*

When the Prefect had read this document, he asked Wu Song how he had come to kill Li Waichuan. Wu Song kowtowed.

"My Lord of the Blue Heavens," he said, "I trust that, in your court, justice may be done. If you will allow me to speak, I will tell the truth about the matter."

"Say on," the Prefect ordered.

Wu Song told him the whole story, not omitting a single detail, from Ximen Qing's seduction of Jinlian to the rejection of his accusation at the Qinghe court. He ended by saying: "I wished only to avenge my brother, and it was Ximen Qing of whom I was in search. Unhappily, I did kill this man, but the fault is not mine alone. Ximen Qing is very rich, and the officers did not dare to arrest him. I am not afraid of death. My sole desire is to avenge my murdered brother, whose remains lie in the tomb awaiting vengeance."

"I understand the case," the Prefect said. "That will do for the present." He called forward Qian Lao and ordered him to be given twenty strokes. "Your magistrate does not seem to know how to perform his duties. He should not allow himself to be moved by personal interest and sell justice in this way."

Again he questioned Wu Song, and amended the indictment that had come from Qinghe. Finally he said to his officers: "This fellow was anxious to avenge his brother and killed this man more or less accidentally. He seems a good man and he ought not to be treated like a common criminal." He gave orders that the cangue should be removed from Wu Song's neck and a lighter one put in its place, and that he should be detained in the prison. The rest of the party were sent back to Qinghe with instructions to the magistrate that Ximen Qing, Jinlian, old woman Wang, Yun'ge, and He the Ninth should be sent to the Prefect to be examined. When all this had been done, the Prefect said, he would send forward the documents to the Imperial Court.

Wu Song was still in prison, but the officials soon found what a good fellow he was, and sent him wine and food without taking anything in return. The news reached Qinghe and, when Ximen Qing heard it, he was greatly alarmed. He knew that Chen Wenzhao was incorruptible, and did not dare to try to bribe him, but he decided to send word to his relative Chen and ask for help. He told Laiwang to go to the Eastern Capital in all haste with a letter to Marshal Yang, the Provincial Commander-in-Chief, begging him to use all his influence with the Imperial Tutor Cai. When Cai heard of the matter he was afraid that the magistrate Li would suffer, so he secretly wrote to the Prefect of Dongping asking him not to proceed with the examination of Ximen Qing and Jinlian. Now Chen Wenzhao had been the chief magistrate of Dalisi before he had been appointed to the Prefecture of Dongping. He had been befriended by Cai, and knew that Marshal Yang was in high favor at court. He finally decided that the best thing he could do was to settle the matter without injury to either side.

He reprieved Wu Song, but ordered him to be given forty strokes, branded, and banished two thousand li. In Wu Da's case, it was declared that, as the body had been burned, the matter must be considered closed. The others were ordered to be sent home. This was all duly written down, and the documents sent, first to the Provincial Office, then to the Court.

They were returned by the higher authorities with orders that the Prefect's proposals should be put into execution. Chen Wenzhao took Wu Song from the jail, read over the papers in the case, gave him forty strokes, and set a cangue upon him. Two columns of characters were branded on his face, and he was ordered to leave for Mengzhou in the charge of two officials, who took the document with them. Then the other parties in the case were dismissed.

That day Wu Song, in the charge of two officers of the court, left the prefecture of Dongping for Qinghe. There, he sold all his furniture and gave the money to the officers, and asked one of his neighbors, named Yao, to look after Ying'er. "If His Majesty pardons me," he said, "I will pay you back. I can never forget your kindness."

Wu Song's neighbors knew well that he was a good man in misfortune, and they gave him, some silver, some a little wine; others offered food, money, and rice. He went once again to his own rooms and got a soldier to bring his personal belongings, and the next day they set off from Qinghe along the high road for Mengzhou.

When Ximen Qing heard that Wu Song had really started for Mengzhou, he felt secure at last. The canker that had ravaged his heart so long was now removed, and he felt completely at ease. He gave orders to Laiwang, Lai Po, and Laixing to make preparations in the garden. They set up folding screens and arranged embroidered hangings in the Hibiscus Arbor; a banquet was prepared, and a band of musicians engaged to sing and dance. Yueniang and the other ladies enjoyed the repast, and menservants, serving women, and maids waited upon them.

> Incense was burned in precious censers, and flowers set out in
>   golden vases
> Treasures from Xiangzhou in all their glory.
> When the lattice was raised, the shining pearls from He Pu gleamed.
> Flame-like dates and pears from Jiao heaped on crystal dishes
> Cups of green jade filled with a precious juice, a liquid jade.
> Of roasted dragon's liver, of fried phoenix giblets, one chopstick's
>   load was worth ten thousand pence.
> The palms of black bears, the hooves of purple camels
> Mingled their sweet savor with the wine's, filling the air.
> Then were ground the phoenix balls of tea,
> And a small clear wave rose in the white jade cups.
> As the precious liquid was outpoured, there came fragrance from
>   the golden jar.
> The lord Meng Chang was now outdone
> The wealth of Shi Chong rivaled.

Ximen Qing and Yueniang sat in the place of honor, and the other ladies arranged themselves according to their position in the household. As they passed the cups from one to the other, they seemed as full of grace as the flowers of a posy or the pattern upon a piece of brocade.

They were drinking when Daian brought in a boy and a young maid of great beauty, whose hair was dressed in a fringe upon her brows. She was carrying two boxes.

"Our neighbors the Huas," Daian said, "have sent some flowers for the ladies."

The maid came before Ximen and Yueniang, kowtowed to them, and said, "My mistress has sent me with this box of cakes and these flowers for you." Yueniang opened the boxes. One contained pastries, some of which were stuffed with fruit, and others with peppers. They were like those made in the Imperial palaces. The other box contained freshly picked lilies. She was greatly pleased, and told the little girl to thank her mistress. After giving them something to eat, she presented the girl with a handkerchief and the boy with a hundred coins.

"Tell your Mistress," she said, "that I am most grateful to her." She asked the little girl her name.

"I am called Yingchun, and this boy is Tian Fu." Then they both withdrew.

"Mistress Hua is really very kind," Yueniang said to Ximen Qing. "She is always sending her servants with something or other for us, and I have never made her any return."

"Brother Hua married the lady two years ago," Ximen said. "He himself told me what a sweet disposition she has, but that is clearly to be seen from the excellence of her maid."

"I saw her once," Yueniang said, "at her father-in-law's funeral. She is moderately tall and has a round face. She has two delicately arched eyebrows and a very clear skin. She certainly seems very gentle, and still quite young, not more than twenty-four or twenty-five, I should think."

"You may not know," Ximen said, "that before she married Hua, she was one of the second ladies of Minister Liang. She brought Hua a very good fortune."

"Well, she has sent us these two boxes," Yueniang said, "and we must not be less courteous than she is. I will send her something in return tomorrow."

The family name of Hua Zixu's wife was Li. She was born on the fifteenth day of the first month, and on that day somebody had sent the family a pair of fish-shaped vases. She was given the name of Li Ping'er. She had once been the concubine of Minister Liang of the Prefecture of

Daming, a son-in-law of the Imperial Tutor Cai. His wife was a very jealous woman, and had made an end of several maids and concubines, and buried their bodies in the garden. So Li Ping'er had to live hidden away in his study, with an old woman to wait on her.

On the fifteenth of the first month in the third year of Zhenghe, Minister Liang and his wife were in the Green Jade Pavilion, when the whole family except Li Ping'er and her servant were murdered by Li Kui. They succeeded in escaping, Li Ping'er taking with her a hundred large pearls and a pair of jewels as black as a raven's wings. They went to the Eastern Capital in the hope of finding some relatives there. At that time Eunuch Hua, one of the Imperial Chamberlains, had just been appointed to the Governorship of Guangnan. His nephew Hua Zixu was unmarried, so the eunuch secured the services of a go-between and arranged a marriage between his nephew and the woman. The eunuch went to Guangnan and they with him, but they had not been there very long before old Hua fell ill, had to resign his appointment, and go home again. His home was in the district of Qinghe. Then he died, and all his property came to his nephew. Every day this gentleman and his friends frequented the bawdy houses, and he had become a member of the brotherhood that Ximen Qing had founded.

With Ying Bojue, Xie Xida, and the rest, he amused himself with singing girls, and they were all most intimate. It was well known that he was a nephew of one of the Imperial Chamberlains and very free with his money, and his friends were always dragging him away to the bawdy house. Often he did not return for three or four nights at a time.

Ximen Qing and his ladies made merry in the Hibiscus Arbor. They drank till it was late, and then went to their own apartments. Ximen Qing went to Jinlian's room. He was already half drunk, and soon wished to enjoy the delights of love with his new lady. Jinlian hastily burned incense, and they took off their clothes and went to bed. But Ximen Qing would not allow her to go too fast. He knew that she played the flute exquisitely. He sat down behind the curtains of the bed, and set her before him. Then Jinlian daintily pushed back the golden bracelets from her wrists and stimulated his penis with her lips, while he leaned forward to enjoy the delight of her movements. She continued for a long time, and all the while his delight grew greater. He called Chunmei to bring in some tea. Jinlian was afraid that her maid would see her, and hastily pulled down the bed curtains.

"What are you afraid of?" Ximen said. "Our neighbor Hua has two excellent maids. One of them, the younger, brought us those flowers today, but there is another about as old as Chunmei. Brother Hua has already taken her virginity. Indeed wherever her mistress is, she is too. She is really very pretty, and of course no one can tell what a man like Brother Hua may do in the privacy of his own home."

Jinlian looked at him.

"You are a strange creature, but I will not scold you," she said. "If you wish to have this girl, have her and be done with it. Why go beating about the bush, pointing at a mountain when you really are thinking about something quite different. I know you would like to have somebody else to compare with me, but I am not jealous. She is not actually my maid. Tomorrow, I will go to the garden to rest for a while, and that will give you a chance. You can call her into this room and do what you like with her. Will that satisfy you?"

Ximen Qing was delighted. "You understand me so well!" he said. "How can I help loving you?" So these two agreed, and their delight in each other and in their love could not have been greater. After she had played the flute, they kissed each other, and went to sleep.

The next day Jinlian went to the apartments of Yulou, and Ximen Qing called Chunmei to his room, and had his pleasure of her.

From that day, Jinlian showered favors on this girl. She would not allow her to go and wait at the kitchen, but kept her to attend to her bedroom, and serve her with tea. She chose beautiful clothes and ornaments for her, and bound her feet very tightly.

Chunmei was a very different kind of girl from Qiuju. She was extremely intelligent and full of fun, and she had a pretty skill with her tongue, besides being very beautiful. Ximen Qing found her irresistible. Qiuju, on the other hand, was both simple and stupid: Jinlian was always punishing her.

CHAPTER 11
Li Guijie, the Singing Girl

Pan Jinlian, now settled in her new home and confident of Ximen's favor, grew more and more arrogant, and made so much trouble that the whole place was in a turmoil. She was suspicious too, and spent much time listening at doors and peeping through windows.

Chunmei was not a model of patience. One day she had been doing some trifling thing for her mistress, and Jinlian found fault with her about it. She could not vent her bad temper upon her own mistress, so she went to the kitchen and there began to thump the table and knock the chairs about. Sun Xue'e did not appreciate such behavior, so she said:

"You strange creature, if you are so anxious to find a husband, kindly try some other place. Why come here to display your nasty temper?"

Chunmei was already very angry, and this made her even more furious. "Who is the wretch who accuses me of wanting a man?" she cried.

It was quite clear that she was in a very bad temper, and Xue'e pretended not to hear her. Chunmei, however, continued in the same strain, and finally went to the front court where, with a few additions of her own, she related the story to Jinlian, to annoy her. "She says you asked his Lordship to have me so that we could try to keep him all to ourselves."

Jinlian was herself in the worst of moods. She had been obliged to get up very early to help Yueniang to dress for a funeral. She was tired, and decided to lie down for a while. When she awoke, she went to the arbor and there met Meng Yulou, who looked as charming as ever.

"Why are you looking so miserable, Sister?" Yulou said.

"Don't ask me," Jinlian said, "I had to get up very early, and I am tired. Where have you been?"

"I have just come from the kitchen."

"And what did you hear there?"

"I didn't hear anything."

Jinlian hated Xue'e, but she said nothing to Yulou. They sewed for a while in the arbor. Chunmei brought them tea and, after it, they wearied of their work and set out a chess table. Then Qintong came and told them that Ximen Qing had returned. Before they had time to clear their game away, he came through the garden gate.

The two women were wearing white silk hairnets, and their hair peeped out beneath. They had black jeweled earrings, and, in their white silk dresses, red bodices, embroidered skirts, and little red shoes, so tiny, arched, and tapering, they looked like figures carved in jade. Ximen Qing smiled at them.

"You are like a pair of singing girls," he said. "You must be worth a few hundred taels of silver."

"We are not singing girls," Jinlian said, "but if you want one you will find one in the back court."

Yulou was going to leave them, but Ximen Qing pulled her back. "Where are you going?" he said. "The moment I come in, you try to run away. Tell me, what do you do when I'm not here?"

"We were both feeling very miserable," Jinlian said, "so we came here to have a game. We don't play tricks behind your back, but we didn't expect you so early." She took his cloak. "The funeral was soon over," she said.

"There were many court officials at the temple, and it was so hot I couldn't stand it any longer. That is why I am home so early."

Yulou asked if Yueniang had come back, and Ximen said that he had come away before her, and had sent two boys to meet her. "I see you are playing chess," he said, sitting down. "What is the stake?"

"We are playing for love," Jinlian said. "Why should we have a stake?"

"I will play you both in turn," said Ximen, "and the loser shall spend a tael of silver, and treat us."

"We have no money," Jinlian said.

"Well, if you have no money, take one of your hairpins and pawn it with me. That will do."

The chessmen were set up, and Ximen Qing played against Jinlian. She was beaten, but, as soon as Ximen began to count the pieces, she jumbled them all together and ran away to a rock garden where there were many flowers, and pretended to be gathering them.

"Here, little oily mouth," Ximen Qing cried, and ran after her, "you lose, and then you run away." Jinlian laughed at him.

"You wonderful creature," she cried, "it was Yulou you beat, go and bother her instead of coming and plaguing me."

She had some flowers in her hand and, pulling them to pieces, she threw them at him. Ximen Qing went up to her and, taking her in his arms, set her down upon the rock garden, and gave her some sweets from his own mouth. They were amusing themselves in this way when Yulou came up. She told them that Yueniang had returned, and asked Jinlian to go with her to the back court that they might greet her. Jinlian left Ximen Qing, and, as she went, she called out, "Young man, I shall have something to tell you when I come back." She and Yulou then went to make their reverence before the mistress of the house.

"What are you laughing about?" Yueniang said.

"The Fifth Lady has been having a game of chess with Father," Yulou said. "She lost a tael of silver to him. Tomorrow, she is going to give a party. Of course, you must come."

Yueniang smiled. Jinlian stayed only a few moments, and then went back to the front court to Ximen Qing. She told Chunmei to burn incense in her room and to prepare the bath, that they might enjoy the pleasures of fishes in the water that evening.

Yueniang was the first wife, but she was always ill, and could not take her proper place in the management of all the household affairs. Engagements with friends and relatives and all the financial business of the household were attended to by Li Jiao'er. Xue'e acted as housekeeper and attended to the preparation of meals in the kitchen for the whole family. Wherever Ximen Qing happened to be spending the night, if he wished for anything, Xue'e would get it ready, and the maid of the lady with whom he was staying would go to the kitchen for it.

That night Ximen Qing slept in Jinlian's room. They drank wine, took a bath, and went to bed. The next morning it soon became apparent that trouble was brewing. Ximen Qing had promised Jinlian that he would go to the temple and buy a jeweled ornament for her hair. He got up very early and asked for some lotus cakes and soup. He told Chunmei to go to the kitchen for them, but Chunmei did not move.

"Just as well not tell her to go," Jinlian said. "Someone has said that I allow her liberties so that she and I may keep you all for ourselves. They called us all the nasty names they could think of. It will be much better not to send her."

"Who said such a thing? Tell me," Ximen Qing said.

"I shall not tell you," Jinlian said. "The basins and jars in this house have a way of hearing things. Just don't send her, that's all. Tell Qiuju to go."

Ximen Qing told Qiuju to go to the kitchen and tell Xue'e what he wanted. A very long time passed. Jinlian set the table, but there was no sign of food, and Ximen Qing grew more and more angry. Jinlian told Chunmei to go and find her fellow maid. "Go and see what that slave is doing. She doesn't seem to be coming; she must have taken root there." Chunmei went angrily to the kitchen and found Qiuju still waiting for the food.

"You thievish slave," she cried, "mother is going to take your trousers down. Why have you been all this time? Father is all ready to go to the temple, and he wants his cakes. He is in a terrible temper, and has sent me to fetch you."

Xue'e was greatly annoyed. "You marvelous little whore," she cried, "you behave like a Mohammedan Ma keeping a feast day. You think that if you want anything, you have only to run over here for it. I assure you the pans are made of iron, and things take time to cook. I made some gruel, and he won't eat it. Now he must have something new, cakes and soups and so on. I should like to know who is the worm at work in his belly."

This was too much for Chunmei. "Don't you begin any of your indecencies," she cried. "If Father hadn't sent me, I shouldn't be here. Are you going to get it ready or are you not? We will go and see what the master of the house has to say about it." She took Qiuju by the ear, and set off with her to the front court.

"Mistress and slave are far too insolent," Xue'e shouted after her, "but my time will come."

"Time or no time," Chunmei said, "we shall see what happens." She rushed off in a terrible temper.

Jinlian saw her pulling Qiuju along, and noticed that her face was very pale. She asked what was the matter.

"Ask her," Chunmei said. "When I got to the kitchen, she was acting the lady in there, waiting while they slowly stirred the flour. I just said a single sentence: 'Father is waiting, and Mother wants to know why you have not returned.' The one who lives in that little place cursed me in every way she could think of, as if I were a slave. She said Father is like some Mohammedan Ma, who thinks everyone's as devout as he is. She supposed Father had to ask permission from somebody or other before he could have anything to eat. She said they had made gruel for him, and then he has to have soup and cakes. She cursed everybody in the kitchen and would not do a thing."

"I told you so," Jinlian cried. "I told you not to make her go there, or somebody would make trouble with her, and say that we are always monopolizing you, and overwhelm us with insults."

Ximen Qing flew into a rage. He went to the kitchen and, without waiting to hear any explanation, kicked Xue'e several times.

"You crooked, thievish bone," he cried, "I told that maid to come here and ask for some cakes. What right had you to curse her? You called her a slave; but if you want to see a slave you'd better piddle and look at your own image in the pool you make."

Xue'e had to suffer Ximen's ill-usage. She was very angry, but dared not offer any excuses. When he had left the kitchen, she said to the Beanpole, Laizhao's wife:

"You see what bad luck I'm having today. You heard all that went on this morning. I didn't say anything very terrible, but in she came like a roaring demon and created all that disturbance. Then she dragged off the other maid, and went and told his Lordship, making a mountain out of a molehill, and he came here and made all this trouble. There's no rhyme or reason in it. But I will keep my eyes open and be on the watch for them. The mistress and the slave are both of them haughty, but one of these days they will take a false step."

Unfortunately for Xue'e, Ximen Qing heard everything she said. He went back, and struck her several blows with his fist. "You thievish slave, you strumpet," he cried, "you can't say now that you didn't insult her, for I have just heard you saying things about her." He continued to chastise the poor woman, causing her considerable pain. Then he went back to the front court. Xue'e shed many tears and sobbed loudly. Yueniang had just risen and was dressing herself. She said to Xiaoyu, "What is all that noise in the kitchen?"

"Father is going to the temple and he wished for some cakes before he left," Xiaoyu said, "but the Kitchen Lady was rude to Chunmei. Father heard about it. He kicked the Kitchen Lady several times and made her cry."

"I never heard of such a thing," Yueniang cried. "If he wants anything to eat, it is her business to make it for him as soon as she can, and be done with it. There is no reason for her to be rude to the maid."

She told Xiaoyu to go to the kitchen, stir up Xue'e and the maids, and order them to make some soup at once. They did so, and sent it to Ximen Qing. Then he set off to the temple.

Xue'e could not settle down. She went to Yueniang and told her all that had happened. While she was talking, Jinlian happened to come that way and stood outside the window to listen. She heard Xue'e say: "Why should she try to get our husband all for herself and make him do everything she wishes? It seems to me, Mother, you don't realize that this strumpet is more lustful than a woman who has half a dozen husbands. She can't bear to sleep alone even for a single night. Nobody else would ever have dreamed of making such a plot. She poisoned her husband, and now she wants to bury us alive. She has made our husband like a black-eyed chicken. He looks at us, but never gives us a thought."

"In my opinion, it is you who are in the wrong," Yueniang said. "He told the maid to come to you for some cakes, and, if you had given them to her, there would have been no trouble. There was no need for you to insult her."

"Well, I only brought more trouble upon myself," Xue'e said. "There was a time when that maid served in your part of the house. She was disobedient even in those days, and once I had to use the back of a knife upon her. You never said anything then, Mother. Why should she have become so high and mighty now that she belongs to the Fifth Lady?"

Then Xiaoyu came in and said, "The Fifth Lady is here," and a moment later Jinlian entered the room.

"Let us suppose I did murder my husband," she said, looking straight at Xue'e. "Why didn't you do something to prevent your husband from marrying me? There would have been no question then of my getting him all for myself and your nest being empty. Chunmei is not my maid. If you have anything against her, kindly tell the Great Lady, and let her return to her service. Then there will be no further trouble between you, and I shall be well out of the matter. As for the present state of affairs, there need be no difficulty about that. When he comes back, let him give me papers of divorce, and I will go away. Then, perhaps, you'll be satisfied."

"These squabbles are beyond me," Yueniang said, "you'd better both be quiet."

"Mother," Xue'e cried, "you must realize that her mouth is as the Huai River. There is not a person living who could get on with her. It is perfectly clear that she deceives our husband, but, even if she winks, she denies it the next moment. If you had your way," she added, turning to Jinlian, "you would have us all kicked out, except, perhaps, our mistress, so that you could be in sole possession."

Yueniang sat and said nothing, letting them bandy insults as they wished. Soon they began to curse each other. "You called me a slave," Xue'e cried, "but you are the genuine article and no doubt about it." At this, there was nearly a fight, but Yueniang would not allow things to go so far, and told Xiaoyu to take Xue'e to her room. Jinlian went to her own apartments, took off her beautiful dress, washed the powder from her cheeks, and pulled her dark hair about till she was hardly fit to be seen. She cried till her eyes had the color of peaches, and then lay down on the bed.

The sun was going down in the west when Ximen Qing came back from the temple with four taels of pearls. He went to Jinlian's room and asked what was the matter, but she sobbed louder than ever and demanded papers of divorce.

"From the very beginning," she cried, "I have cared nothing about your wealth. You were all I wanted. And in return you let everybody trample on me. They said I murdered my husband. If I had had no maid, there would have been no trouble. Why did you give me somebody else's maid, and then allow other people to insult her?"

Ximen Qing flew into a terrible rage. He rushed like a whirlwind to the back of the house, caught Xue'e by the hair, and thrashed her as hard as he could with a short stick until, fortunately, Yueniang came and stopped him.

"You should behave yourselves, all of you," she said. "Why do you make your master so angry?"

"You thievish, crooked bone," Ximen cried to Xue'e, "I heard you in the kitchen cursing them, yet you still try to blame other people. I don't care if I break every bone in your body."

If Jinlian had not carefully plotted the whole scheme beforehand, Ximen Qing would never have struck Xue'e that day. It was all her doing.

When he had done with Xue'e, Ximen Qing went back to Jinlian's room and gave her the pearls he had brought from the temple. Now that her husband had taken her side and vented her spite for her, there was no reason why she should remain upset, so for one loving overture on his part she repaid him tenfold. Their delight in each other grew unceasingly.

One day, it was Hua Zixu's turn to give a party in his house, next door to Ximen Qing's. There was a great feast, and all the brothers were present. Ximen Qing had another engagement, and did not arrive until the afternoon. They would not take their wine without him, and waited. When at last he came, they made reverences to one another and took their seats, with Ximen in the place of honor. Two singing girls played the lute, the cithern, and the flute.

Soon the wine had been passed three times, and the musicians had played twice. The singing girls put down their instruments, and came towards the guests. They had all the delicacy of a branch of flowers. When they had kowtowed, Ximen Qing told his servant to take two envelopes from his purse, each of which contained a small sum, and give it to them. They thanked him, and went back to their places. Then Ximen Qing said to his host, "These girls sing extraordinarily well. Who are they?" Hua said nothing, but Ying Bojue replied:

"My Lord, you have a very poor memory. Don't you remember them? The one who plays the cithern is Brother Hua's sweetheart, young Wu Yin'er. She lives in one of the back streets in the bawdy district. The one who plays the lute is the girl I told you about some time ago. Her name is Li Guijie, and she is the younger sister of Li Guiqing. One of your ladies is her aunt. It's no use pretending you don't know her."

Ximen Qing smiled. "Oh, that's who she is! I haven't seen her for about six years. I never thought of her as being grown up."

A little later the girls came to pour wine for them. Guijie pressed Ximen to drink a great deal, and murmured loving words in his ear.

"What are your mother and sister doing now?" Ximen said. "Why do they never come to see your aunt?"

"Since last year," Guijie said, "my mother has not been at all well. Even now she can hardly get about, and she has to have someone to lean upon if she wishes to walk. My sister Guiqing has taken up with a merchant from Anhui, and for some months she has been staying at the inn with him. He will not allow her to come home even for a few days, so there is no one at home but me. I have to support the household by going out day after day to sing at parties, and I'm very tired of it all. We are always thinking about coming to see Aunt, but really we never get an opportunity. Why have you not been to see us for so long, Father? It would be kind of you to send my aunt to see her sister one of these days."

Ximen Qing thought the girl very pleasant, and she talked intelligently. He soon found himself falling in love with her. "I think I shall invite one or two friends to help me take you home tonight," he said. "What do you say?"

"Don't make fun of me, Father," the girl said. "How can such noble feet as yours tread our unworthy ground?"

"I am not making fun of you," Ximen said. He took a handkerchief, a toothpick, arid a box of tea leaves from his sleeve, and gave them to her.

"When will you come?" Guijie asked. "I must tell the servant to go home, and give them a chance to get ready."

"We shall start as soon as the party is over."

Soon the wine was finished and it grew dark. Ximen Qing invited Ying Bojue and Xie Xida, and, without going home first, they went off together to Guijie's house in the bawdy district.

> A dark, deep pit is this for man's ensnarement
> Built like a prison pen, a cavern for the enticement of souls
> Like a butcher's yard, with corpses piled and laid in order.
> Here love brings death, and only money lives.
> The sign is written in great characters:
> "Here, golden brothers, would you purchase love, pray do not of-
>   fer silk for hairdresses.
> Before she yields her blossoms to you, Madam must have cash.
> In this house, sisters are to be had only for ready money."

Ximen Qing followed Guijie's sedan chair to her door. Guiqing opened it, and took them into the hall, and, after greeting them with due politeness, went to ask her mother to come and receive them. Soon the old procuress came, supporting herself on a stick, for she was almost paralyzed. As soon as she saw Ximen Qing, she cried, "Heavens, Sir, what wind has blown you here?"

Ximen Qing smiled. "Please forgive me, but I have been so busy, I couldn't come."

The old woman turned to Ying Bojue and Xie Xida. "Why haven't you two been here?"

"I have been busy too," Bojue said. "We have been to a party at Hua's house today, and we met Guijie there. Master Ximen and we have brought her home. But give us some wine as quickly as you like, and let us drink a cup or two and have some fun."

The old woman made the three sit down in the place of honor, and offered them tea. Meanwhile the table was laid, and wine and refreshments set out. Candles and lamps were lighted, and a plentiful repast was set before them. Guijie changed her clothes and came to sit beside them. The two sisters, their jade wrists keeping time together, filled the golden cups. They passed the wine and sang songs.

"I have been told," Ximen said to Guiqing, "that your sister can sing songs of the South. Here are these two gentlemen. Won't you ask her to sing a song in their honor?"

"Oh, I really could not trouble her," Bojue said. "I am only basking in your reflected glory, Sir, but I shall of course clean my ears the more respectfully to hear the exquisite melody."

Guijie sat and smiled, but did not get up. Ximen Qing really wished to make a woman of her, and that was why he asked her to sing. Her old mother was experienced in such matters and saw what was in the wind.

"My sister," Guiqing said, "has always been very independent. She won't let anybody hear her sing unless she thinks fit."

Ximen Qing told Daian to take five taels of silver from his purse, and set it on the table. "This is a mere trifle," he said, "but it may suffice to buy you some powder and rouge. I will send you some pretty clothes one of these days."

Guijie jumped up and thanked him, and, telling the maid to take the present away, she prepared to sing. Now, though she was very young, she was much more seductive and clever than many another. There was no flurry or haste about her. She gently touched her silken sleeves, and swung her dainty skirts. A handkerchief, tasseled and embroidered with a design of flowers and water, hung from her sleeve.

When she had ended her song, Ximen Qing was delighted beyond all measure. He told Daian to take the horse home, and spent the night with Guijie. He had been ready enough to make a woman of this girl, and, when Ying Bojue and Xie Xida urged him to do so, he yielded to their suggestions without raising any difficulties. The next day he sent a boy home for fifty taels of silver and four sets of clothes. These were to be the present customary on such occasions. When Li Jiao'er heard the news, she was delighted, for Guijie was her niece. She gave Daian a piece of silver, and he brought the clothes to the bawdy house. There a banquet was prepared, and there was singing, dancing, and wine for three days. They were all as merry as could be. Ying Bojue and Xie Xida brought along Sun Guazui, Zhu Shinian, and Chang Zhijie, and they all offered a few coins in token of congratulation. Ximen Qing provided the silken bedclothes, and every day there was wine and food without stint. They enjoyed themselves immensely.

CHAPTER 12
Pan Jinlian Narrowly
Escapes Disaster

The tree is pitiful that stands alone
Its branches fragile and its roots uncertain.
The dew may give it moisture, but the wind
Blows it to one side and the other.
There is none to raise the silken coverlet
I must sit and keep my watch from night to morning.
Sorrow has made me thin
No loving wish of yours has given me
This slender waist.

Ximen Qing was so delighted with Guijie's beauty that he stayed at the bawdy house for several days. Many times Wu Yueniang sent servants with horses to bring him back, but Guijie's family hid his hat and clothes, and would not let him go. The ladies of his own household were for once at a loss for something to do. Most of them were quite content, but Pan Jinlian was still not thirty years old, and her passions were by no means under control. Day after day, she made herself look as pretty as a jade carving, and stood at the main gate with gleaming teeth and scarlet lips, leaning upon the door and waiting for her husband to return. Not until evening did she go to her room, and there the pillow seemed deserted, and the curtains forlorn, and there was none to share the joys of her dressing table. Sleep would not come to her, and she went to the garden, walking delicately upon the flowers and moss and, when she saw the moon reflected in the water, she thought of the uncertainty of Ximen's nature, and as she watched the tortoiseshell cats enjoying each other's company, it brought only disturbance to her own sweet heart.

Qintong, the boy who had accompanied Meng Yulou when she married Ximen Qing, was now sixteen years old, and for the first time took his place in the household as a full-grown youth. He had finely arched eyebrows and eyes full of intelligence, and was indeed both clever and attractive. Ximen Qing had entrusted him with the care of the garden, and he slept every night in a small room there. Jinlian and Yulou sometimes sewed or played chess in an arbor in the garden, and at such times

Qintong waited upon them attentively, and, whenever Ximen Qing was about, would come and give them warning. Jinlian liked him and often summoned him to her room and gave him wine. So morning after morning, and evening after evening, they exchanged understanding glances, and were not entirely indifferent to one another.

It was now about the seventh month and Ximen's birthday was drawing near. Yueniang was well aware of her husband's doings, and once again told Daian to take a horse and go for him. Jinlian privately wrote a note, and told the boy to give it to Ximen Qing in secret. "Tell him," she said, "that I hope it will not be long before he comes back." Daian rode off to the bawdy house, and there found all Ximen's boon companions keeping company with him, kissing the girls, and being very merry.

"What has brought you here?" Ximen Qing said, when he saw Daian. "Is there anything wrong at home?" "No," said Daian. "Well, tell your uncle Fu to collect the money that is owing, and, when I come back, I'll settle up with him."

"He has been collecting some during the last few days," the boy said, "and he is only waiting for you to come home to go through the accounts."

"Did you bring the clothes for your Aunt Guijie?"

"Yes," the boy replied, "here they are." He took a red vest and a blue skirt from a parcel, and gave them to the girl. She made a reverence to him, and called for food and wine to be given him. When he had finished, he came over to Ximen and whispered in his ear: "The Fifth Lady has given me a note for you, asking you to go home soon."

Ximen Qing was just about to take the note when Guijie saw it. She thought it was a love letter from some other girl, and made a dash for it. When she opened it, she found a sheet of patterned paper, with several columns written in black ink, and handed it to Zhu Shinian, asking him to read it for her.

> I think of him as evening falls; I think of him when the sky is bright.
> I think about my lover till my thoughts overwhelm me, and I faint
>   Yet still he does not come.
> For him I am wounded; for him my spirit faints.
> Oh, it is sad.
> I lie alone under the figured coverlets; the flickering lamp is nearly
>   out.
> The world is sleeping, and the moonbeams creep across the window.
> That heart is unrelenting, like a wolf's
> How can I bear this agony another night?

Guijie listened to this, then left them and went to her room, where she threw herself face downwards on the bed. Ximen Qing saw that she was upset, tore the note to pieces, and kicked Daian. Twice he implored Guijie to come back, but she paid no heed. Finally, getting more and more excited, he went to her room and carried her out.

"Get on your horse and go home," he said to Daian. "As for the strumpet who told you to come, when I get home, I'll beat her till she comes to a disgusting end." Daian went home with tears in his eyes. "Please don't be so angry," Ximen said, "it is only from my fifth wife. She wants me to go home to talk about something or other. There is nothing else."

Zhu Shinian teased them. "Don't believe him, Guijie. He is deceiving you. Jinlian is his latest flame, a very pretty girl too. Don't let him go."

Ximen Qing slapped him. "You ruffian! You'll be the death of somebody with these silly jokes of yours. She is angry enough without your talking rubbish."

"Brother," Guiqing said, "you are not fair. If you were a good husband, you would not run about teaching singing girls the arts of love, you should stay at home. Then all would be well. Why, you've only been here a few hours, and now you're getting ready to go away again."

"That's quite true," Bojue said. "You had better take my advice, both of you. Your Lordship must stay here, and you, Guijie, must not lose your temper. The first person to leave will have to spend a couple of taels and treat the rest of us."

Ximen Qing took Guijie on his knee, and they drank together happily. Soon afterwards seven cups of the most delicious tea were brought and handed around.

"Now we'll have a song from everyone who can sing," Xie Xida said. "He who can't sing must tell a funny story, and we'll persuade Guijie to take a little more wine with us. I'll begin."

"Once, a bricklayer was doing some paving in a house, and the lady of the house treated him shabbily. So he quietly took a brick or two and stopped up the drain. Not very long afterwards it began to rain and, of course, the water flooded the whole place. The woman didn't know what on earth to do, and ran to find the bricklayer. This time she gave him a meal, and offered him some money, and got him to make the water flow again. When he had eaten his fill, he went to the gutter, took the bricks out, and the water flowed away at once. "What was the matter with it?" the lady of the house asked him. "Just what is the matter with you," the bricklayer replied. "If there is any money about, the water gate will open; but, if not, there will be no admission."

Guijie thought that this story was aimed at her, and she lost no time before retaliating.

"I should like to tell you a story," she said. "Once upon a time, Sun, the Immortal, thought he would give a banquet to his friends, and sent his tiger around to invite them. As ill luck would have it, the tiger gobbled them all up on the way. The Immortal waited until it was dark, but nobody came. At last the tiger came back. 'Where are my guests?' the Immortal said. 'Master,' said the tiger, 'I fear I am not a success at inviting people. Somehow I seem much better at eating them up.' "

This did not please the brothers at all. "Oh, indeed," Ying Bojue said, "so we are always sponging, are we?" He took a small silver pin from his hair. Xie Xida found in his hat a pair of gilt rings of no great value. Zhu Shinian took from his sleeve a tattered old handkerchief worth a pittance. Sun Guazui took a white apron from around his waist. Chang Zhijie had nothing, so he borrowed a small piece of silver from Ximen Qing. They handed all these things to Guiqing, and asked her to provide a feast in honor of Ximen Qing and Guijie. She turned them over to a servant to buy some pork and a chicken, but all the rest she had to pay for herself. Soon everything was brought in, and they sat down. The order was given: "Chopsticks into action." Our description must take time, but there was nothing slow about the movements we describe.

> Then every mouth was opened wide and every head was bent.
> No sun or sky was to be seen; it was like a cloud of locusts.
> They blinked their eyes, their shoulders heaved.
> Starvelings they might have been, from some dark dungeon.
> One quickly snatched a piece of leg, as though no food
> Had passed his lips for years.
> One waved his chopsticks thrice, it was as though for years and years
> He had not seen a meal.
> Sweat trickled down the cheeks of one, he carved a chicken bone
> As though inspired by hatred.
> Gravy adorned his comrade's lips. With copious drafts of spittle
> He gobbled down the pork, with hair and skin.
> They ate, and in a flash, the cups and plates were clean
> It might have been a den of wolves.
> They ate, and in a flash again, the flying chopsticks
> Crossed and recrossed the table.
> This is the marshal of the King of Gluttons
> This, the general of the Lickers-up.
> Though it has long been empty, from the wine jar
> They try to fill their cups.
> Though all the food has gone long since,
> They search and search again.

> The luscious meal, with all its hundred flavors
> Has vanished in a moment.
> To worship has it gone,
> To worship in the temple of the belly.

They cleared up everything till the plates and dishes looked like the head of a shining bald-pated Buddha. Ximen Qing and Guijie could get nothing but a cup of wine each. They did indeed pick out a few pieces of food, but the others snatched them away. Two of the chairs were broken. The boys, who were looking after the horses, could not get in to share in the repast, and contented themselves by pulling down the statue of the divinity of the place and piddling upon it. When the time came for them to go away, Sun Guazui took a gilded image of Buddha, which was venerated in an inner room, and slipped it inside his trousers. Ying Bojue pretended to kiss Guijie, and stole a gold pin from her hair. Xie Xida went off with Ximen's fan. Zhu Shinian went secretly to Guiqing's room and stole her mirror. As for Chang Zhijie, he did not hand over the money he had borrowed from Ximen Qing, but had the sum put down to his account. They were all in the highest spirits.

When Daian reached home, he found Yueniang, Yulou, and Jinlian sitting together. They asked him if his master was coming. "Father kicked me and cursed me," the boy said, his eyes still red. "He says that anyone who tries to get him away will find herself in trouble."

"What an outrageous fellow he is," Yueniang cried. "It is quite bad enough that he refuses to come, without ill-treating this poor boy."

"It was bad enough for him to kick the boy, but why should he threaten us?" Yulou said.

"The affection of a dozen of these strumpets wouldn't amount to anything," Jinlian said. "There is an old saying that a shipload of gold and silver would never satisfy people of their sort."

Li Jiao'er had seen Daian return, and, as Jinlian was speaking, she came to the window and listened. They could not see her. She heard Jinlian speak of her family as a host of strumpets. After that, she hated Jinlian from the bottom of her heart, and there was always enmity between them.

Jinlian, while Ximen was away, found that the days passed very slowly. When she realized that he did not mean to return, she waited till her two maids had gone to bed and then, making believe to go and walk in the garden, called Qintong to her room and made him drunk. Then she shut her door, undressed, and the pair made love together.

After this, she called the boy to her room every night and kept him there until daybreak. She gave him two or three of her golden pins, and put them in his hair. On another occasion she gave him a perfume box that she wore on her skirt. Unfortunately, the boy was not very discreet and, as he frequently went drinking and gambling with his fellow servants, it was not long before the affair became known. As the proverb says: "If you would have none to know your secret, you must do no evil." One day the rumor came to the ears of Xue'e and Li Jiao'er.

"That thievish strumpet has been high and mighty for a long time," they said, "but now we have her." They went and told Yueniang. She would not believe a word they said.

"You only wish to make things unpleasant for her," she said, "but you will annoy the Third Lady, and she will say you are slandering her boy." They said no more, and went away.

That evening Jinlian and the boy were amusing themselves. The woman had forgotten to shut the kitchen door. The maid Qiuju chanced to use that door on her way to the privy, and saw everything that was going on. The next morning, she told Xiaoyu, and Xiaoyu told Sun Xue'e.

Once again Xue'e and Li Jiao'er went to tell Yueniang. They gave her all the details, and added: "Her own maid told us about it; it is not something we have invented to get her into trouble. If you will not do anything in the matter, we will tell Father ourselves. If he can forgive a whore like this, he can forgive a scorpion."

It was the twenty-seventh day of the seventh month when Ximen Qing came back from the bawdy house to celebrate his birthday.

"He has just come back," Yueniang said to the two women, "and this should be a happy day for him. If you will not listen to me, and are still determined to tell him, I will not be responsible for the consequences."

They paid no attention to her, and, as soon as Ximen came in, they both ran up and told him that Jinlian was carrying on with one of the boys. Ximen Qing had been in an amiable mood, but at this he flew into a towering rage. He went to the front court, and called, "Qintong! Qintong!" over and over again. Jinlian had heard what was happening, and, with trembling hands and feet, she told Chunmei to call the boy to her room. She begged him not to say a word to his master, and took the pins out of his hair, but she was so excited that she forgot the perfume box.

Ximen Qing ordered the boy to the hall, and made him kneel down. Then he told some of the other servants to get a large bamboo and make it ready for use.

"You rascally slave," he cried, "do you confess your guilt?" Qintong made no reply.

"Take out his pins and let me see them," Ximen said to the boys. They looked, but could not find any.

"What have you done with the silver pin with a golden head?"

"I have no silver pin," Qintong said.

"Ah, you slave, you think you will deceive me, do you?" Ximen said, and ordered the boys to take down his trousers. Three or four of them stripped Qintong. On the jade-colored short trousers he was wearing the perfume box hung. As soon as Ximen caught sight of it, he made the boys show it to him, and recognized at once that it was the same one that used to hang on Jinlian's skirt.

"Where did you get this?" he cried in a fury. "Tell me the truth. Who gave it to you?"

The boy was so terrified that it was a long time before he could speak, but at last he said, "I was tidying the garden one day, and picked it up. Nobody gave it to me."

This reply made Ximen still more angry. He bit his lips, and told his servants to beat the boy with all their strength. Qintong was bound and given thirty terrible stripes till his flesh was torn and the blood ran down his legs. Then Ximen told Laibao to cut the boy's hair at the temples and turn him out, and on no account to allow him to return. Qintong kowtowed, wept, and went away.

Jinlian soon heard all that had happened and felt as though a stream of icy water had been poured over her. It was not long before Ximen Qing arrived. She was so frightened that she trembled, and the blood in her veins seemed to freeze. She went forward to take his clothes, but Ximen Qing boxed her ears so hard that he knocked her down. Then he told Chunmei to shut all the doors and keep everybody out. He took a small chair, went out, and sat in the courtyard in a shady place. Then he took a horse whip, and made the woman take off her clothes and kneel before him. She bowed her white face, but did not dare to make a sound.

"You rascally whore," Ximen cried, "don't pretend you are dreaming. I have questioned that slave and he has confessed everything. You had better tell me the truth. When I was away, how many times did you play your games with that boy?"

"Oh, Heavens! Heavens!" Jinlian said, sobbing, "somebody has been telling lies about me, and I shall die if you believe them. All these days you've been away, I have spent my whole time sewing with Yulou. As soon as it was dark, I locked my door and went to bed. Unless there was something very urgent, I never even ventured to go beyond the corner door. If you don't believe me, ask Chunmei. There was nothing I could do without her seeing." She called to Chunmei: "Sister, come here and tell your Father all about it."

"You rascally whore," Ximen said again, "I know you gave the boy two or three gold pins. Why don't you admit it?"

"These suspicions will be the death of me," Jinlian cried. "Some nasty-minded strumpet who will come to a foul end has been telling you lies. I suppose she was jealous because she saw you always coming to sleep in my room. You know how many pins there were, there is not one missing. Count them yourself, and see. How can you suspect me of being so base as to carry on with a slave? If he were a full-grown slave, they would probably tell the same story, but this short-haired lad is hardly out of his cradle. There is not a word of truth in the story. They have made up the whole chapter of scandal."

"We will leave the pins out of it," Ximen said, taking the perfume box from his sleeve. "This, I think, belongs to you. How do I come to find it on that boy's person? Now perhaps you will not have so much to say." And, with these words, Crash! fell the whip on her delicate white body. The pain was so great that she burst into tears.

"Oh, dear good Father," she cried, "you mustn't treat me like this. If you will only give me a chance, I can explain everything. If you won't give me the chance, but beat me to death, you'll make a very nasty mess here. As for that perfume box, one day when you were away Yulou and I were doing some needlework in the garden. It wasn't firmly attached, and it must have fallen down as I was going through the flower arbor. I looked everywhere for it, but the boy must have picked it up. I am sure I did not give it to him."

This certainly seemed to agree with what Qintong had said. Ximen looked again at the woman. Her flower-like body, unclothed, was kneeling as she uttered these softening words and wept so touchingly. His anger flew to Java, and he began to cool down. He called Chunmei and kissed her.

"Did she play heads and tails with that boy? If you tell me I ought to forgive the little strumpet, I will do so."

Chunmei sat on his knee, and made herself most charming and affectionate. "Father," she said, "you are making a fool of yourself. Mother and I never left one another the whole time. How can you possibly imagine that she would have anything to do with that slave? No, the whole thing is a plot made up by somebody, who is jealous. You must deal with the matter yourself, Father. If the story gets about, and you make yourself a laughingstock, that won't be very pleasant."

Ximen Qing could say no more. He told Jinlian to stand up and dress, and bade Qiuju prepare a meal. Jinlian poured out a full cup of wine and, offering it to him with both hands, knelt to wait for its return.

"This time I forgive you," Ximen said. "Whenever I am away, you must keep your mind pure and your ways clean. Shut your door early, and be on your guard against thoughts of evil. If I ever hear of anything of this sort again, there will be no more forgiveness."

"Your word is my law," Jinlian said meekly. She kowtowed four times, and sat down to drink with him.

So Jinlian, despite the high favor in which she was held by her husband, brought shame upon herself.

Ximen Qing was drinking wine in Jinlian's room when a boy knocked at the door and told him that Yueniang's two brothers, Fu, the manager of his shop, Ximen's daughter Ximen Dajie and her husband, and several other relatives had called to congratulate him on his birthday. He left Jinlian and went to receive his guests. Ying Bojue, Xie Xida, and the other brothers had also brought presents. Even Guijie had sent a servant with a gift. Ximen Qing was soon very busy receiving all his presents and sending out letters of invitation in return.

Meanwhile Meng Yulou, who had heard all about Jinlian's trouble, seized the opportunity while Ximen was not there, and went to see her without the others knowing anything about it. When she came, Jinlian was lying on the bed.

"Do tell me what it is all about, Sister," she said.

Jinlian cried bitterly. "That little strumpet has been telling tales about me. She made our husband so angry that he thrashed me. I hate those two whores with a hate as deep as the ocean."

"If you had to play tricks with the boy," Yulou said, "you might at least have made sure that I shouldn't lose him. But don't be unhappy. Our husband is bound to look at things from our point of view. If he comes to see me tomorrow, I shall tell him what I think about him."

"It is good of you to trouble about me," Jinlian said. She called Chunmei, and told her to serve tea. They chatted for a while, and Yulou went back to her own rooms. That night, Mistress Wu was staying with Yueniang and Ximen Qing went to sleep with Yulou.

"It was very wrong of you to distress Jinlian so unreasonably," Yulou said. "She did not do anything. This trouble has all come from her quarrel with Xue'e and Li Jiao'er. Without taking the trouble to make any inquiries, you had my boy beaten. You have certainly been most unjust, and it makes things very awkward for the poor woman. Do you imagine our mistress would not have told you, if there had been any truth in the story?"

"I did ask Chunmei," Ximen Qing said, "and she said exactly what you say."

"The Fifth Lady is very much upset," Yulou said. "Why don't you go and see her?"

"I will go and see her tomorrow," Ximen promised.

The next day was Ximen's birthday, and many visitors came to take wine with him, Major Zhou, the magistrate Xia, Captain Zhang, and Uncle Wu, Yueniang's brother. Ximen Qing sent a sedan chair for Guijie, and engaged two singing girls, who performed throughout the day.

As soon as her niece arrived, Li Jiao'er took her to visit Yueniang and the others, and she drank tea with them. They asked Jinlian to come and see her, and twice a maid went to her room to invite her, but she said she was not very well and refused to come. Later in the evening, when Guijie was about to go home, Yueniang gave her a silk handkerchief and some artificial flowers, and went with Li Jiao'er to see her off. Guijie was anxious to go to the garden and pay her respects to Jinlian, but as soon as Jinlian heard she was coming, she told Chunmei to bolt and bar the corner door. When Guijie got there, Chunmei said, "My Mistress's orders. I dare not open the door." Guijie had to go away, greatly abashed.

That evening Ximen Qing went to see Jinlian. Her beautiful tresses were all in disorder, and she seemed very weary and faded. But when he came, she took her clothes, served him with tea, and hot water to wash his feet, and showed him a hundred signs of affection. That night, as they played together, she did for him whatever he asked of her.

"Brother," she said, "who in all this household really cares about you? They are all just stale married women, nothing more. I am the only one who understands you, and you understand me. The others see that you show me favor and spend most of your time here; it makes them jealous, and they try to vent their spite on me. How could you be caught by such talk, and treat me so unkindly? There is an old saying: 'When a farmyard chicken is beaten, it turns round and round; a wild one flies away.' You may beat me to death, but I shall never run away. The other day, when you were at the bawdy house and kicked Daian, I never complained. The Great Lady and Yulou know that quite well. I said I was afraid the girls there would do you no good. I said singing girls in places like that care for nothing but money. What is true love to them? Is there a single one of them who really loves you? That is all I said. Somebody came slyly up and secretly listened, and then they plotted together to get me in disgrace. Fortunately, while people may injure others, they cannot kill them; it is only those whom Heaven wishes to destroy who die. In the future you will realize that I am speaking the truth, and you will know what to do if such a thing happens again."

Ximen Qing was completely won over, and his delight in her was greater than ever.

Some days afterwards he mounted his horse and went off to the bawdy

house, attended by Daian and Ping'an. Guijie had other visitors, but as
soon as she heard he was coming, she went to her room, washed off her
powder, removed her rings and ornaments, lay down on the bed, and
pulled the bedclothes over her. Ximen Qing came in. He waited for a long
time before the old woman appeared and made a reverence to him.

"Why is it so long since you were here?" the old lady said. She asked
him to take a seat.

"I was very busy on my birthday," Ximen Qing said, "and there is no
one at home who seems able to attend to things."

"I am afraid my daughter must have been a trouble to you," the old
lady said.

Ximen asked why Guiqing did not come to see him on his birthday.
The old woman told him that she had been away; a traveler had taken her
to stay with him at the inn, and she was still there. They talked for a while,
and the old woman offered him tea.

"Where is Guijie?" Ximen said at length. "Don't you know, Sir!" the
old woman said. "Ever since the child came back from your house, she
has been terribly overwrought. She is not at all well. I can't tell you what
is the matter with her, but she has stayed in bed all the time and refused
to leave her room. You must have a heart like a wolf's not to have been to
see her before."

"This is the first I have heard of it," Ximen said. "Where is she? I will
go and see her."

"She is lying down in her bedroom," the old lady said. She told a maid
to go and raise the lattice. Ximen Qing went into the room. Guijie, covered with the bedclothes, was sitting on the bed, her face turned to the
wall; her hair was in disorder and she seemed in a sad way. She did not
move when Ximen came in.

"Why have you been ill since you were at my place?" Ximen said. The
girl did not reply.

"What has made you so angry? Tell me." He questioned her for a long
time, and at last she said:

"It is all your Fifth Lady's doing. Since you have someone in your own
home who is as good as any strumpet, I can't imagine why you come here
and make love to a wicked girl like me. I may have been brought up in
this house, but I don't believe I'm any worse than some in other houses I
could mention. I did not go as a singing girl that day; I came to give you
a present. Your great lady was very kind and gave me flowers and clothes,
and when I heard you had a fifth lady, I asked to be allowed to pay my
respects to her. If I hadn't done so, she would have said that the girls from
the bawdy house are very ill-mannered, but I *did* ask, and she refused to

see me. When I was leaving your house, I asked once more, and she ordered her maid to shut the door in my face. Really she is lacking in the very elements of politeness."

"You mustn't blame her too much," Ximen Qing said. "She wasn't very well that day. If she had been, I'm sure she wouldn't have refused to come and see you. But I've often felt like giving that little strumpet a beating. She's always hurting somebody with that sharp tongue of hers."

Guijie slapped him lightly on the face. "Why haven't you beaten her, then, you shameless fellow?"

"You don't know how severe I can be," Ximen Qing said. "I have punished most unmercifully all the women and maids in my house, except, of course, my first wife. Sometimes I use a whip upon them twenty or thirty times or even more, and sometimes I cut their hair off."

"Oh," said Guijie, "I've met men before who talk about cutting the hair off their womenfolk, but never one who did more than brag about it. You may have bowed three times and made reverence twice to them for all anybody could prove. If you mean what you say, go home and cut off a single tress, bring it here, and show it to me. If you do that, I'll believe you are the greatest hero there is in this part of the world."

"Your hand upon it," Ximen cried.

"A hundred times, if it pleases you."

Ximen Qing spent the night with Guijie, and the next day, as he was mounting his horse to go home, she called after him: "If you don't bring it to me, don't dare to show your face here again."

This made Ximen very excited, especially as he was already half drunk. As soon as he got home, he went straight to Jinlian's room. She saw that he had had some wine, and was most careful in her attentions. She offered him something to eat, but he would have none of it. He told Chunmei to make the bed, then sent her away and shut the door. He sat on the bed and ordered the woman to take off his shoes. She took them off. Then he got on to the bed, but he would not go to sleep, and sat on a pillow. He bade Jinlian undress and kneel down. She was so terrified that the sweat rolled down her body. She had not the faintest notion what was amiss, and could only kneel down sobbing quietly.

"Father," she said, "tell me what is wrong, even if it kills me. I have been so careful all day, and still I don't seem to satisfy you. You are just sawing me asunder with a blunt knife. How can I bear it?"

"You rascally little whore," Ximen cried, "if you don't take your clothes off, I will show you no mercy." He called to Chunmei: "Bring me the whip that is hanging behind the door."

Chunmei would not go into the room, and he had to call for a long time before she slowly pushed the door open and went in. Jinlian was on her knees, and the lamp had fallen down beside the table. In spite of Ximen's orders, the maid did not obey him.

"Chunmei, Sister, please help me," Jinlian cried, "he is going to beat me again."

"Don't worry about her, little oily mouth," Ximen said. "Give me the whip. I am going to beat the strumpet."

"How can you be so shameless, Father?" Chunmei cried. "What has Mother done wrong? You seem to listen to anything any bad woman likes to tell you, making a storm in a teacup all the time. Mother is one heart and mind with you. What makes you so changeable? I shall not do what you say." She shut the door and went out. Ximen Qing could only burst out laughing.

"I won't beat you this time," he said to Jinlian. "Come here. I want you to give me something. Will you give it me or not?"

"My precious darling," Jinlian said, "I belong to you, heart and soul. Whatever you ask, it is yours. What do you want?"

"I want some of your hair," Ximen said.

"Heavens!" Jinlian cried, "if you had asked me to set myself on fire, I would have done it. But to cut off my hair . . . that is too much. You must wish to frighten me to death. From the day of my birth, twenty-six years until this very day, I have never done such a thing. And lately my hair has been falling out of its own accord. Do, please, spare me that indignity."

"You are always complaining about my bad tempers," Ximen Qing said, "yet you won't do a single thing I ask you."

"If I don't obey you, I don't obey anybody. But tell me, why do you want my hair?"

"I am thinking of having a hairnet made," Ximen said.

"If you want a net, I will make one for you, but you must not take my hair to that strumpet to lay a spell on me."

"I won't give it to anybody," Ximen said, "but I must have your hair to make the foundation for a net."

"Very well," Jinlian said, "in that case I will let you cut some off." She parted her hair. Ximen took a pair of scissors and cut a large tress from the crown of her head. He wrapped it in paper, and put it in his sleeve. Jinlian pressed close to him and wept quietly.

"I will do anything you wish," she said. "The only thing I ask is that you love me always. You may play with others as much as you please, but you must not forget me."

That night their joy in each other seemed more glorious than ever. The next morning, when Ximen Qing got up, she served him with tea; then he mounted his horse and rode to the bawdy house.

"Where is the hair you were going to cut off?" Guijie cried.

"Here you are," said Ximen. He took the hair from his sleeve, and handed it to her. She opened the packet. It contained a tress of beautiful hair, as black as the blackest coal. She put it into her sleeve.

"You have seen it now," Ximen said. "Give it back to me. She was terribly upset because I insisted on cutting off that hair, and, until I changed countenance and frightened her, she wouldn't hear of my cutting it off. I told her I wanted it to make a net. You see, I have brought it to you. Perhaps now you will believe that I always do what I say."

"I don't see why you should be so alarmed," Guijie said. "There is nothing so very extraordinary about it. I'll let you have it before you go. You shouldn't have taken it, if you are so frightened of her."

"What makes you think I'm afraid of her?" Ximen Qing said, laughing. "If I were, I shouldn't tell anybody."

Guijie asked her sister to take wine with Ximen Qing, and, going to a quiet place, put some of the hair into her shoe, that she might tread it underfoot every day. She kept Ximen a prisoner for several days and would not allow him to go home.

Jinlian was very unhappy for several days after her hair had been cut. She refused to leave her room and seemed too languid to take food or tea. Yueniang sent one of the boys to bring old woman Liu, an old favorite of hers, to see what was the matter.

"The lady is suffering from some secret grief," the old woman said, "and because the trouble is insistent and she can't free herself from it, she has headaches and gnawing pains at the heart, and does not feel inclined to take her food."

She opened her medicine box, and, taking out two black pills, told Jinlian to take them in the evening with some ginger water. "I will bring my husband tomorrow," she said. "He will tell your fortune for the coming year and see whether there is any bad luck in store."

"Can your husband really see what is in one's life?" Jinlian asked.

"He is blind," the old woman said, "but there are three things he can do. He can tell fortunes and read the Yin-Yang, and so save people from misadventure. He can bleed the sick, cauterize, and cure wens. The third thing is only to be mentioned with discretion, but, as a matter of fact, he can make philters to change people's hearts."

"What are these philters for?" Jinlian said.

"Well," old woman Liu said, "suppose father and son do not agree as well as they might, or there is a slight misunderstanding between brothers, or a quarrel between wives, if my husband is told the true state of affairs, he will make a spell and write a charm. This is put in water, and the people concerned are given it to drink. Three days after drinking this water, father and son will love one another again, brothers will reach a perfect understanding, and wives will live in harmony together.

"Again, when a man is unsuccessful in business, or his lands and family are not doing very well, my husband can produce the necessary money and increase profits. And when it comes to curing illnesses and making people immune, praying to the stars and invoking the planets, my husband is absolutely a master. People call him Liu the Master of the Stars. I remember the case of a household where there was a new wife who came from a family that was none too well off. She was inclined to be light-fingered, and was always stealing things from her mother-in-law to give to her own people. When her husband found her out, he beat her. My husband exercised his art on her behalf, made a charm, and when it had been burned to ashes, the ashes were put into the cistern. The whole family drank the water from this cistern, and afterwards, even if they actually saw her stealing, they didn't seem to realize what she was about. He also put another charm under her pillow, and when her husband had once slept on that pillow, his hands might have been tied, for he could not beat her any more."

Jinlian listened to this and stored it away in her mind. She told the maid to give the old woman some tea and cakes, and, when she was about to take her departure, she gave her not only three *qian* of silver for her fee, but five more to buy the materials needed for making a charm. She told her to bring the blind man early the next day so that he could burn the charm. The old woman went home, and next morning very early she brought the blind old rascal to the gate, and was about to go to the inner court. Ximen Qing was standing in the courtyard, and the gatekeeper asked the blind man what his business was.

"We have come to burn some papers for the Fifth Lady," the old woman said.

"Very well, in you go," the boy said, "but mind the dog doesn't bite you."

The old woman led her husband to Jinlian's apartments, and they waited some time for her. When she came, the blind man made a reverence to her; then they sat down, and Jinlian told him the eight characters of her destiny. The blind rascal reckoned for a while on his fingers, and said; "Lady, I will now interpret the eight characters of your destiny. They are *Gengchen* for the year, *Gengyin* for the month, *Yihai* for the day, and *Jichou* for the hour of your birth. The eighth of the month is the Spring Day, we must reckon your fate as from the first month. According to the admirable doctrine of Zi Ping, though your eight characters are indeed both clear and remarkable, you will never have the husband star in a favorable conjunction. The question of children, too, does not seem to be decided in your favor. The *Yi* tree grows in the first month and, though this would seem to show that you will enjoy good health, you must be careful lest you overdo things. *Geng* gold appears twice, and the *Yangren* star is unduly prominent, while the husband star is very troublesome. I should say that you will only reach contentment when you have outlived two husbands."

"I have already outlived one," Jinlian said.

"I beg you to excuse me, Lady," the blind rascal went on, "but though your life appears to be of the type known as *Shayin,* you are handicapped by the fact that there is the water of *Gui* in the *Hai* as well as in the *Chou.* This is decidedly a superabundance of water, and it rushes out of a single *Ji* earth. The stars *Guan* and *Sha* are confused. In the case of a man, if the influence of the *Sha* star is predominant, he will attain to dignity and prominence, but, in the case of a woman, such a state of affairs indicates that she will be dangerous to her husbands. The fact that you belong to this class shows that you know very well what you're about and that you attract men.

"With regard to your fortune for the present year, this year is *Jiachen* in the cycle, and this is a sign of coming calamity. The two stars *Xiaohao* and *Goujiao* are influencing you, and, though this does not indicate any real catastrophe, you will have trouble from friends and relations, and backbiters will prove a nuisance."

"It is kind of you to have gone so carefully into all this for me," Jinlian said, "and now I should like you to make a spell for me. Here is a tael of silver to spend on a cup of tea. All I want is that backbiters shall leave me in peace, and that my husband shall have a high esteem for me." She went to her room, found a couple of hair ornaments, and gave them to the blind man. He put them in his sleeve.

"If you would like me to make a spell," he said, "I shall take a piece of willow wood and fashion it into two figures, one male and the other female. On one I shall write your husband's eight characters and on the other your own. Then I shall bind them together with forty-nine red threads. I shall cover the man's eyes with a piece of red cloth and stuff him with the leaves of artemisia. I shall put a needle through his hands and stick the feet with gum. You must put the figures under his pillow, secretly. I shall also write a charm in red ink, and the ashes of this you must put into his tea. Then providing he sleeps on this pillow, you will see the result in three days at the utmost."

"What is the meaning of all this?" Jinlian said.

"I will explain," the old rogue replied. "The covering of the eyes with cloth will make you appear to him as beautiful as Xi Shi. Stuffing the figure with artemisia will make him love you. If I put a needle through the hands, that will ensure that, whatever your faults, he will not be able to raise his hand against you. Finally, the sticking of the feet with gum will prevent his wandering away from you."

Jinlian found this extremely satisfactory, and she wasted no time in getting candles and paper to burn the charms. The next day old woman Liu brought them, with water and the spell figures. Jinlian did with them as she had been told. She burned the charm to ashes, and prepared some of the best tea. When Ximen Qing came back, she told Chunmei to give him some of the tea. That night they slept on the same pillow. Two or three days passed, and their happiness was as great as that of fishes sporting in the water.

Readers, every household, no matter whether it be great or small, should make a rule that nuns, priests, nurses, and procuresses like these should always be kept at a distance.

CHAPTER 13
Li Ping'er

One day, when Ximen Qing went to Wu Yueniang's room, his wife told him that Master Hua had sent a boy to invite him to take wine that day. Ximen looked at the message. It said: "Come and talk with me this afternoon at Wu Yin'er's house. Call for me, and we will go together. I greet you heartily."

He dressed quickly and, summoning two boys to attend him, set off upon a fine horse to call on Master Hua. He was surprised to find that Hua was not at home, but Li Ping'er was standing on the steps that led to the inner part of the house. She wore a silken hairnet, with golden earrings set with amethysts, a coat with white trimmings, and an embroidered skirt, beneath which peeped forth a pair of dainty little feet. Ximen had entered hurriedly, and they bumped into one another.

Although he had seen her once before, in the country, he had not paid any particular attention to her, but she had made some impression upon him. Now they met face to face. She was pale and clear-skinned, rather short, with a face as oval as a melon seed, long, with two finely arched eyebrows. He was enraptured. Quickly he went forward and made a reverence to her, and she as quickly returned his greeting. Then she turned and went to the inner court. She sent to him a maid whose name was Xiuchun, a girl who had just grown out of childhood, and told her to ask Ximen to take a seat in the hall. She herself stood at the door of the courtyard, so that only half her charming face was visible.

"Pray sit down for a while, my lord," she said. "My husband has gone out, but he will be back in a few moments."

The maid brought Ximen a cup of tea.

"My husband has asked you to take wine with him today," Mistress Hua said, "but please, for my sake, persuade him to come home early. The two boys will be with him, and there will be nobody here but the two maids and myself."

"You have every right to speak as you do," Ximen Qing said. "The claims of a man's household should have his first attention. Since you wish it, we will not only go together, but come back together."

At that moment Hua Zixu returned, and his wife retired to her own room. The two men exchanged greetings.

"It was very good of you to come," Hua said. "I had to go out for a moment on business, and I hope you will forgive me for not being here to welcome you."

They sat down in the places appointed for host and guest, and Hua ordered a servant to bring tea. When they had drunk it, he said to the boy: "Ask your mistress to prepare some refreshments for us. I should like to drink some wine with Master Ximen before we go." He turned to Ximen and said, "It is Wu Yin'er's birthday today. That is why I asked you to come and have a little amusement."

"Why didn't you tell me earlier?" Ximen said. He told Daian to go home at once and bring five *qian* of silver. The servants were setting the table, but he said, "Don't let us stay any longer. We might as well take our wine at the bawdy house."

"I will keep you a very short time," Hua Zixu said, "but stay for a minute or two."

In a few moments refreshments were brought, and they drank a few cups of wine together. The cups were of silver with long stems like a sunflower. They ate some little buns, and gave what were left to the servant. When Daian had brought the silver, they went out and, mounting their horses, rode to Wu Yin'er's house to celebrate her birthday. There was singing, dancing, and music, and they were as happy as the flowers in a posy, drinking wine together till the first night watch. Ximen Qing deliberately made Hua very drunk, and then took him home, as Li Ping'er had asked him. The boys called for the gate to be opened, and they helped Master Hua to a chair in the hall. Li Ping'er and one of the maids brought a lamp, and took him to the inner part of the house.

Ximen Qing told her all that had happened, and was going away when she thanked him again.

"My foolish husband," she said, "has very little sense. He is too fond of wine, and I am afraid you must have found him a nuisance. It was out of kindness to me that you brought him back. Please, my lord, do not be too scornful of him."

"Not at all," Ximen said, bowing politely, "it was your desire. How could I do other than set your words in my heart and engrave them on my bones? If I had not brought him back, not only would you have been uneasy, but I should have shown myself no gentleman. My brother went to the bawdy house and they tried to keep him there, but I made him come home. When we were passing the Hall of the Joyful Star, he saw one of the girls standing outside. She was a very pretty girl and he would have liked to go in, but I would not let him. I told him that you were waiting anxiously for his return, and we came on together. If he had stayed there, he would not have come back tonight. Sister-in-law, it is not for me to say that my brother is a fool, but you are so young, and this is such a large house to be in. He ought not to leave you here alone at night. It is not right."

"No, indeed," Li Ping'er said. "He is always roaming about and making a fool of himself. I have reproached him till I have made myself quite ill. I do beg of you, my lord, if you meet him at the bawdy house, do, for my sake, persuade him to come home early. I shall always be grateful to you."

There never was a man more clever in the ways of women than Ximen Qing. He had spent many years pursuing them, and there was very little about such matters he did not know. It was perfectly clear to him that the woman was making overtures, and he appreciated the situation admirably. He smiled.

"Sister-in-law," he said, "there is really no need for you to say this. What are friends for? I cannot help feeling that my brother is very much to blame, but do not worry about it a moment longer."

Li Ping'er made a reverence to him, and told a maid to bring tea and fruits. Ximen drank the tea. "I must go home now," he said. "I hope you will see that all the doors are shut safely after me." Then he said good-night and went home.

From that day Ximen Qing racked his brains for a plan whereby he might make this woman his own. Several times he got Ying Bojue, Xie Xida, and the others to take Hua to the bawdy house to drink and pass the night, but he himself escaped from them and went home. He used to stand outside his own gate, and Li Ping'er, with her two maids, would stand outside hers. When he saw her, he would cough affectedly and walk up and down, or he would stand outside his gate and look towards her. When she saw him, Li Ping'er used to hide inside her gate, and put the door between them, but, as soon as he went away, she would put her head out to look after him. They longed for each other in their hearts, but showed their feelings only with their eyes.

One day Ximen Qing was standing outside the gate when Xiuchun brought him an invitation.

"Why does your lady invite me?" he said, pretending not to know. "Is your master at home?"

"Master is not at home," the maid said, "but my mistress would like to have a chat with you."

Ximen Qing did not wait for more, but set out at once. He went into the hall and sat down. After some time Li Ping'er came to him, made a reverence, and said: "I am extremely grateful for your kindness the other day. Indeed I have engraved it on my heart, for my gratitude is beyond expression. My husband has now been away two days. Perhaps you have seen him?"

"He was at the Zhengs' house yesterday, drinking with a few friends," said Ximen, "but I had some business to attend to and came away. Today I haven't been there, so I don't know whether he is still there or not. If I had been there, I should have considered myself in honor bound to persuade him to come home and not to make you so unhappy."

"He will not do a single thing I ask, and it is almost more than I can bear," Li Ping'er said. "He spends all his time playing with women of that sort and cares nothing at all about his home."

"If it were not for that one failing," Ximen said, "my brother's character would be beyond reproach."

The maid brought tea, but Ximen was afraid that Hua Zixu might return, and did not venture to stay very long. Li Ping'er said to him, "Whenever you do see my husband, please beg him to come home, and I shall be eternally grateful to you."

"We are such good friends," Ximen said, "that I should do so without your asking." He went home.

Next day Hua Zixu came back from the bawdy house. "All you care about," his wife said, "is strong wine and strange women. It is a good thing our neighbor, Master Ximen, has more than once taken some interest in our establishment. If you wish to keep his friendship, I should advise you to buy him a present to show your gratitude."

Hua wasted no time, but bought four boxes of presents and a jar of wine, and sent a servant with them to Ximen Qing. When he had accepted them and given the boy a present, Yueniang asked: "Why has Hua sent you these things?"

"Some time ago," Ximen said, "Brother Hua asked me to go with him to celebrate the Wu Yin'er's birthday. He got drunk, and I brought him home. Indeed, more than once I have urged him not to stay so late at the bawdy house, but to go home early. His lady seemed very grateful, and I imagine she must have told him to send me this present."

Yueniang folded her hands in an attitude of devotion. "I think you might begin by practicing a little self-control yourself. To me this seems a, case of a Buddha made of clay preaching to a Buddha made of mud. Why, there isn't a day when you don't go off to play with some woman or other, and here you are giving pious exhortations to other people's husbands. We can't accept this present without making some return. Whose name is written on the card? If it is Mistress Hua's, I must write and ask her to call. I'm sure she would like to come. If it is his name, you can invite him or not as you please. It is no concern of mine."

"It is Brother Hua's name," Ximen said; "I will ask him to come tomorrow." He sent an invitation to Hua Zixu to come and take wine with him.

"We must not be lacking in politeness," Mistress Hua said, when her husband returned. "We sent him a few small presents and in return he has asked you to take wine with him. Next time, you must get some wine and ask him."

The days passed quickly. It was the Feast of the Ancestral Tombs. Hua Zixu engaged two singing girls and sent to ask Ximen Qing to come and admire the chrysanthemums. He also sent invitations to Ying Bojue, Xie Xida, Zhu Shinian, and Sun Tianhua to come and play at passing the flower while the drums beat. So, in the best of good spirits, they drank their wine.

They drank till the lamps were brought. Then Ximen Qing left the table and went out to wash his hands. Li Ping'er was standing behind a screen peeping in at them. Ximen did not see her until he had almost run into her. She went to a door in the corner and told her maid Xiuchun to go over in the shadow to Ximen Qing and whisper, "My mistress asks you not to drink much wine, but to go home early. She has something to tell you tonight."

No message could have been more welcome to Ximen Qing, and though, after washing his hands, he went back to the table, he would not drink. The singing girls pressed wine upon him, but he pretended to be drunk and would have no more. It was about the first night watch. Li Ping'er paced up and down on the other side of the screen. She could see Ximen Qing lolling in his chair pretending to be half asleep. Ying Bojue and Xie Xida showed not the slightest intention of leaving, and sat there as if they were nailed to their chairs. Even when Zhu Shinian and Sun Guazui took their leave, the others still did not move, much to Mistress Hua's annoyance. Once Ximen Qing started to leave, but Hua Zixu stopped him. "It must be that I have not yet offered you becoming entertainment," he said.

"Really, I'm quite drunk already," Ximen said, "I can't possibly drink any more. He rolled about till Hua sent him home with two boys to assist him.

"I can't think what's wrong with him today," Ying Bojue said. "He won't drink. He has taken very little, yet he's drunk. You have been very kind, and so have these two good little sisters. May I have a large cup? We must drink ever so much more before we think of parting."

At this Li Ping'er, who was on the other side of the screen, secretly cursed them as a set of unprincipled ruffians, and told Tian Xi, one of the boys, to ask her husband to come out and speak to her.

"If you must drink with rascals like these," she said, "get off to the bawdy house at once. Don't stay here making yourselves a nuisance. It is midnight, and you have wasted fire and oil enough. This sort of behavior I will not have."

"You encourage me to go to the bawdy house as late as this?" said Hua Zixu. "Very well. If I can't get back, you mustn't blame me afterwards."

"Run along. I won't blame you."

Hua Zixu was only too pleased to receive such instructions. He went back to the others and said, "Now we will go to the bawdy house."

"Really?" cried Ying Bojue. "Don't try to be funny. You must see what your lady has to say about it first."

"I have spoken to her," Hua said, "and she says I may stay until to-morrow."

"Of course," put in Xie Xida, "Beggar Ying is too clever. Master Hua knows what he is about. Let us go without more ado." With the two singing girls they set off to the bawdy house. The two boys Tian Fu and Tian Xi went with them. It was about the second night watch.

Ximen Qing had gone home, pretending to be drunk. He went to Jinlian's room, but, as soon as he had changed his clothes, he went and sat down in the garden. There he waited for a summons from Li Ping'er. Some time passed; he heard the dog being driven out and the gate fastened next door. Then the maid Yingchun climbed up on the wall in a dark place, pretending to call the cat. Seeing Ximen Qing sitting in the arbor, she made a sign to him. He took a bench, mounted it, and got down a ladder that had been placed for him on the other side of the wall.

When Li Ping'er had made sure that her husband had gone, she took off her headdress and allowed the clouds of black hair to fall about her. Dressed simply, but still charming, she stood in an arbor. When Ximen came, she was delighted and quickly took him indoors. She had already prepared a table with wine, refreshments of various sorts, and fruit. The lamp was burning brightly. The wine jar was filled with a most fragrant wine, and, taking a jade cup in her hands, she offered it to Ximen Qing and made a most profound reverence.

"I have been anxious to show my gratitude to you for a long time," she said, "but you have given us present after present and put yourself out so much that I feel unbearably embarrassed. Today I have made ready this poor cup of wine and asked you to come so that I may at least give some expression to my feelings. Unfortunately those two shameless rogues stayed on and on, till I grew angry and packed them out of the house."

"I suppose Brother Hua will be coming back," Ximen said.

"He will not come back," the woman replied. "I told him to spend the night somewhere else. Both the boys have gone with him. There are only my two maids here, and old woman Feng who acts as doorkeeper. She is my old nurse and absolutely devoted to me. All the doors have been bolted."

This was all very pleasing to Ximen Qing. They sat as closely together as they could and drank each from the other's cup. Yingchun served the wine, and Xiuchun came in and out to take away the dishes. Under the silken net incense perfumed a coral bridal bed. When they had drunk together long enough, the two maids took away the jar and the dessert, and shut the door. The lovers went to bed to enjoy what pleasure they might.

The houses of wealthy families usually have double windows, the outer of which is called the window proper and the inner the casement. When Li Ping'er sent the maids away, she shut the casement so that, though there were lights in the room, they could not be overlooked from outside. But Yingchun was seventeen years old and not without experience. Realizing that her mistress and Ximen Qing were enjoying their unlawful loves, she quietly went between the windows and made a hole in the paper with a pin, so that she could see all that happened. The lovers accomplished their destiny, and all they did was seen by Yingchun as she stood outside the window.

"May I ask your age?" Ximen said.

"I am twenty-three," Li Ping'er said. "What is your lady's honorable age?"

"She is twenty-six."

"Three years older than I am. I should like to buy a present and call upon her, but perhaps she does not care to make friends."

"She is extremely good-natured."

"Does she know you come here?" Li Ping'er said. "What will you say if she asks you questions?"

"She lives well within the house," Ximen said. "My fifth wife, Jinlian, lives in the garden where she has a little house all to herself. But she dare not interfere."

"What is the honorable age of your Fifth Lady?" Li Ping'er said.

"She is the same age as my first wife."

"Good! Unless she considers my poor self too unworthy, I shall be happy to call her Sister. Tomorrow I will ask the size in shoes of your two ladies and make two pairs as a sign of affection." Then she took two golden pins and put them on Ximen's head. "Don't let Hua Zixu see them, if you go to the bawdy house."

Ximen Qing promised. Then they renewed their pleasures together as though they would never part. It was the fifth night watch. Outside the window a cock crew, and the light flooded the eastern sky. Ximen Qing was afraid lest Hua Zixu should take it into his head to come back, so he dressed and climbed back over the wall. Before he went they agreed upon a secret signal. When Hua Zixu was not at home, one of the maids should come to the wall and cough, or throw over a piece of brick, and, if there were nobody about on Ximen's side of the wall, she should climb up and he should get a ladder and come over. So this naughty couple made love over the wall, stealing hours of happiness together. Since they never went around by the gate, the neighbors could not possibly know what was going on.

> The moonbeams shine upon the flowers
> The water clock seems very slow.
> They meet. It seems like Gao Tang's dream.
> She takes the silver lamp to light them
> In the deep night.
> Fearful lest, through the crevices, the light should pass.

When Ximen Qing had climbed over the wall, he went to Jinlian's room. She was in bed.

"Where have you been?" she asked. "You have been away all night and you never told me where you were going."

"Brother Hua sent a boy," Ximen said, "and asked me to go with him to the bawdy house. We drank till the small hours of the morning, and then I was able to get away."

Jinlian suspected him, but she pretended to be satisfied. One day, however, when she and Yulou were sewing in the arbor after dinner, a piece of brick suddenly seemed to drop from the skies quite close to them. Yulou was bending down to fasten her shoe and did not see it, but Jinlian looked everywhere till at last she saw a pale face at the wall. She could not be certain whose it was. The face appeared once and vanished. Jinlian pulled Yulou by the sleeve.

"Look there! There's the elder of Hua's two maids. She must have been admiring our flowers, and jumped down as soon as she saw that we were here." They thought no more about it.

That evening when Ximen Qing came home from a party, he went to Jinlian's room. She took his clothes and asked if he would like anything to eat, but he said no. She offered him tea, but he would not drink it. He paced to and fro in the garden, and Jinlian watched him quietly. Soon the maid's face appeared again over the top of the wall. Ximen Qing took a ladder and climbed over to join Li Ping'er, who was waiting for him on the other side. Jinlian went to her room and tossed about on her bed. She did not sleep the whole night through. At daybreak Ximen Qing came back.

He opened the door, but Jinlian pretended to be asleep and did not speak. Ximen, somewhat embarrassed, went and sat on her bed. Jinlian jumped up and caught him by the ear.

"You fickle scamp!" she cried. "Where have you been? All night long I have been worried about you, but now things are so clear that I don't need to ask you for an explanation. The best thing you can do is to tell me the truth at once. What have you been doing with that strumpet who lives next door, and how many times did you do it? Tell me every little thing and I'll forgive you, but miss out a single word and tomorrow you shall march in front, and I'll march behind and I'll tell the whole world what you've been up to. You disgraceful rogue, I'll make you so dead you won't need to be buried. You have got a lot of fellows to keep her husband in the bawdy house, while you go and visit her. Very well, but I'll show you what's what. No wonder yesterday when Yulou and I were sewing, we saw that maid bobbing up and down over the wall, and in full daylight too. She is playing the part of the devil who runs after lost souls, and enticing you away to that whore. You don't think you can deceive me any longer. Only the day before yesterday that turtle of a fellow fetched you away in the middle of the night to go to the bawdy house. Why! his own house would have done as well."

This was extremely disturbing to Ximen Qing. He knelt down as though to make himself small.

"You funny little oily mouth," he said, smiling. "Don't speak so loud. I won't tell you any lies. She asked me how old you are, and one of these days she is going to find out your size in shoes and make you a pair. She would love to consider you her elder sister."

"I don't want a strumpet like her to consider me a sister, or a brother either for that matter. First she seduces another woman's husband, and then tries to offer some insignificant courtesy in return. I will not have dust thrown in my eyes. Why should I let people play such tricks on me?"

She pulled down Ximen's trousers and perceived that the warrior seemed anything but ready for the strife, though he still wore his silver armor.

"Tell me the truth," she cried, "how many times has this fellow returned to the attack?"

"That is an easy question to answer," Ximen said. "Once was enough for him."

"Will you swear that it was only once?" Jinlian said. "Why should he be so dejected, then? He seems half paralyzed. If he showed the slightest sign of courage, I might credit his master with some manly qualities at least." She stripped the warrior of his armor, and cursed him.

"You abandoned scoundrel. There cannot be another like you in all the world. You take this thing with you on the sly when you go to play with that wicked creature."

"You funny little strumpet," Ximen cried, "you are enough to drive a man crazy. She asked me several times to tell you that she is coming to kowtow to you, and she is going to make you a pair of shoes. Yesterday she sent a maid to find out what size Yueniang takes, and today she has given me this pair of pins, with the character *Shou* engraved upon them, for you." He removed his hat, took the pins from his hair, and gave them to Jinlian. She examined them. The lucky character was designed in gold upon an emerald ground. They were of very fine workmanship, for they had been made in a royal palace. She was delighted with them.

"Ah well," she said, "if that is how the land lies, I'll say no more about it. Indeed, when you go to call on her, I'll keep a lookout for you on this side, and the pair of you can enjoy yourselves in peace. Now what do you say?"

Ximen Qing was delighted. He took Jinlian in his arms. "You are a darling," he said. "The sort of baby I like is one who knows how to deal with a situation when it arises, as you do, not a miraculous creature who brings forth gold and silver when he performs his natural functions in the privy. Tomorrow I will show what I think about you by buying you a suit of fine embroidered clothes."

"I don't believe that honeyed tongue and that sugary mouth of yours," Jinlian said; "if you want me to help the pair of you, you must promise three things."

"I promise," said Ximen; "ask what you will."

"To begin with, I forbid you the bawdy house. Secondly, when I ask you to do anything, you must do it. And thirdly, every time you go to visit your sweetheart, I must know all that happens; you must not keep a single thing back."

"That will be easy," Ximen said. "I agree to all your conditions."

The next time Ximen Qing went to spend the night with Li Ping'er, he told Jinlian how white and flawless was the body of his lady love, as yielding as the softest down; how amorous her temperament; and how she loved wine. "We took a basket of fruits into the net with us," he said, "and played dominoes and drank wine, before we went to sleep." He took something from his sleeve and handed it to Jinlian.

"Her father-in-law brought this from the palace and, when we had lighted the lamp, we used it as a model of deportment."

Jinlian unfastened the roll of pictures and looked at it from end to end. Twenty-four subjects were painted upon it, and it was most exciting. She decided to keep it. She handed it to Chunmei and said, "Put this away in my chest. No doubt I shall find much to learn from it."

"You may have it for a few days," Ximen Qing said, "but I must have it back again. She thinks a great deal of it, and I only borrowed it to look at. I must return it to her."

"You shouldn't have given it to me, then," Jinlian said. "I didn't steal it from her. You will find it loves me so much it won't leave me."

"Little slave," Ximen cried, "don't be such a tease." He tried to take back the roll.

"If you try to snatch it," Jinlian said, "we will have a snatching match. I'll tear it into shreds and then it will be lost to all of us forever."

Ximen Qing laughed. "Have it your own way. I can't help myself, but I beg you to give it back to her when you've done with it. She has something else that is very interesting and, if you let her have this back, I'll ask her to let me show you the other."

"I wonder who trained you in artfulness, young man," Jinlian said. "You shall have this back when you bring me the other."

They talked for a long time, and that night Ximen stayed with Jinlian. She perfumed the bed and lighted the silver lamp. She dressed herself with all the skill at her command, performing her most intimate toilet, and they looked at the roll so that they might emulate the lovers who were painted upon it.

Readers, the wonders of witchcraft have been known to us since the most remote periods of antiquity. Very soon after the blind Liu had made a spell for Jinlian, her shame was turned to happiness and Ximen's displeasure to favor. He dared refuse her nothing. Though he had all the cunning of a ghost, he was compelled to drink the water in which she washed her feet.

CHAPTER 14

The Cuckold

One day, Wu Yueniang was not feeling well, and her brother's wife came to see her. Yueniang pressed her to stay a few days, and they were sitting together in her room when Ping'an came to announce his master's return. Mistress Wu went to Li Jiao'er's room.

Ximen Qing came in, took off his cloak, and sat down. Xiaoyu brought tea, but he did not drink it, and his wife noticed that he was very pale.

"Why have you come back so early?" she said.

"It was Brother Chang's turn today," he replied, "but his house is not very large, and he asked us to go to the Temple of Eternal Felicity outside the city. Brother Hua and Brother Ying—there were four or five of us in all—went to the Zhengs' bawdy house for some wine. We were enjoying ourselves when several constables appeared. Without a word they seized Hua and took him off with them. This scared us all. I went to Guijie's house, and hid there for a long time. I was so worried that I sent a man to find out what had happened. It seems that Hua's brothers have some grievance about the disposal of the family property. They made complaint at the Eastern Capital, and the courts have sent an order for Hua's arrest. When I had heard this, I didn't worry so much, and the rest of us came back."

"The best thing you could do," Yueniang said. "You have been going with those scamps day after day, gadding about and neglecting your home. Now, you see, there has been trouble. After this, I trust you will break with them completely. If you don't, you will find yourself involved in squabbles and disasters, and you will end by being beaten till you look like a rotten sheep's head. You will never believe what I tell you and stop this unbecoming manner of life, but the whores in the bawdy house can tell you any old story and you'll listen to them with your donkey's ears. You are the kind of man who lets the advice of his own people go in at one ear and out at the other, and treats everything outsiders tell him as if it were written in the golden characters of a sacred book."

"Who do you imagine would have courage enough to strike me?" Ximen said, laughing.

"Oh, you are a splendid braggart by your own fireside," Yueniang said.

Daian came in. "Our neighbor, Mistress Hua, has sent her boy to ask Father to go and talk to her."

Ximen Qing tried to escape as quietly as he could.

"Aren't you afraid people will talk about you?" Yueniang said.

"We are only neighbors. There's nothing in it. I must go and see what she has to say." He went to Hua's house.

Li Ping'er had given instructions that he was to be taken at once to the inner part of the house, and there Ximen Qing found her, wearing a silken gown. She looked disheveled and weary, and her face was as pale as wax. She came and knelt down before him.

"My lord," she said, "the priest may be nothing to you, but I pray you consider the glory of Buddha. There is an old maxim that when disaster overtakes a household, neighbors should do what they can to help. My husband has never paid any attention to me; he has never troubled in the least about domestic affairs, but has always gone elsewhere and played the fool. Now he has got into serious trouble and is in a difficulty, he sends one of the servants to say that I must get him out of it. I am a woman, and no more use than a crab without feet. How am I to find anybody who will take the trouble to do anything for him? When I realize how he has always refused to listen to me, I can't help thinking that it serves him right even if he is sent to the Eastern Capital and beaten till he rots. But my father-in-law's memory must be considered, and this would bring disgrace upon him. I feel bound to ask you to help me to persuade the officials not to send him there. Think of my poor face, and plead for him. I should not like him to suffer hardship."

Ximen Qing saw her kneeling before him and asked her to get up. "It can't be anything very serious," he said, "but so far I don't know what the trouble is."

"It will take some explanation," Li Ping'er said.

"My late father-in-law had four nephews. Ziyu was the eldest, Ziguang the third, and Zihua the fourth. My husband was the second. They are all blood relations. My father-in-law was very wealthy, but he knew that my husband was a fool and, when he came back from Guangnan, gave everything into my charge. The other three had all annoyed him in some way, and never dared to visit the old man. Last year, my father-in-law died. The other brothers divided between them a good deal of the furniture and some of the beds and curtains, but they got none of the money. I told my husband several times that he should give them something, but he would do nothing at all in the matter. Now, he has got himself into a hopeless situation, and the others have the whip hand." She burst into tears.

"Sister," Ximen Qing said, "don't distress yourself about it any more. I was under the impression that the matter was really serious, but it is only a family squabble. You have told me what you wish, and I will give my brother's business as much attention as if it were my own. Tell me what you wish me to do and I will do it."

"My lord," Li Ping'er said, "if you are really willing to undertake this, I could wish for nothing better. Tell me how much you will need for presents, and I will get it ready for you at once."

"Not very much," Ximen said. "I believe the Governor of Kaifengfu is a ward of the Imperial Tutor Cai. Both Cai and my relative, Marshal Yang, have a certain influence with his Majesty. If we send two presents and get those gentlemen to speak to Governor Yang, I don't think he will refuse anything they ask, no matter how serious the case may be. We must send a present to the Imperial Tutor, but, as Marshal Yang is a relative of mine, he can hardly accept a present from me."

Li Ping'er went to her room and took from a chest sixty large bars of silver each worth fifty taels. She gave them to Ximen Qing. The total value was three thousand taels of silver.

"Half of this will be enough," Ximen said. "Why do you give me so much?"

"Keep anything that is left for me," Li Ping'er said. "There are four chests behind my bed, full of the finest embroidered ceremonial clothes, jade girdles, and so on, without mentioning cap buttons, jewelry, and things of that sort. They are worth a great deal of money. Will you look after them for me and keep them in your house, so that when I want anything I can ask you for it? I feel very unsafe with all this stuff here. If anybody should come and take it away from me, I should be in a desperate fix."

"But what will you say when Brother Hua comes back and asks questions?" Ximen said.

"My father-in-law gave me all these things secretly," Li Ping'er said. "My husband knows nothing about them. You can take them without hesitation."

"I must go and see what my wife says," Ximen Qing said. "When I get home, I will send somebody for them." He went home to discuss the matter with Yueniang.

"We can tell the boys to take food boxes for the silver," she said, "but the chests and big things we must bring over the wall when it is dark. Then we shall be sure that the matter is kept secret; for, if we bring the stuff around by the gate, everybody in the neighborhood will know what is happening."

Ximen Qing thought this an excellent plan. He told Daian, Laiwang, Laixing and Ping'an to take two food boxes and bring the three thousand taels of silver. That evening, when the moon had risen, Li Ping'er and her two maids, Yingchun and Xiuchun, brought benches to the wall and lifted up the chests. On Ximen's side, Yueniang, Jinlian, and Chunmei set up a ladder and put a blanket on the top of the wall to receive the various articles one by one. Everything was taken to Yueniang's room.

In this manner Ximen Qing got into possession of many fine and delicate things, both gold and silver, while his neighbors had not the faintest inkling of what was afoot. He quickly prepared several loads of presents, and, after getting someone to write a letter to go with them, sent Laibao to the Eastern Capital. He was to ask Marshal Yang to send the presents to the Imperial Tutor, asking him to communicate with Governor Yang of Kaifengfu.

The Governor's name was Yang Shi, and he was also known as Guishan. Born at Hongnong in Shaanxi, he had obtained the third literary degree in the period of Guiwei. He had formerly been an official at Dalisi, and had been promoted to his present position at the Eastern Capital. He was an honest and fair-dealing official, but the Imperial Tutor had been his guardian, and Marshal Yang was in high favor at the palace, so he could not but fall in with their wishes.

When the presents arrived, the Governor went into his hall and, bringing Hua Zixu and the others from prison, questioned them about their property. Hua Zixu had received a message from Ximen Qing, so he knew how matters stood.

"When my worthy ancestor departed this life," he said to the Governor, "I spent what money there was upon his funeral expenses and the reading of the Buddhist sutras. There was nothing else beyond a parcel of land and a couple of houses. The furniture has already been distributed among the members of the family."

"It is never possible," the Governor said, "to be quite certain about the amount of a chamberlain's wealth. It comes easily, but it goes easily too. If you have spent all you had, I will send instructions to the magistrate at Qinghe to put up for sale your two houses and the parcel of land, and to share the proceeds between Ziyu and the others."

Hua Ziyu pleaded that his brother should be made to hand over to them all his property, but the request irritated the Governor. "You seem to be asking for trouble," he said. "When the chamberlain died, you made no complaint. Why are you trying to rake up matters that are over and done with?"

Hua Zixu escaped without the chastisement he had anticipated. The Governor sent a document to Qinghe, ordering the officials there to make a valuation of the houses and land, and dispose of them.

As soon as Laibao had heard the decision, he traveled posthaste to give the news to Ximen Qing, who was delighted to hear that Hua Zixu was free and on his way back. Li Ping'er sent for him to talk over the situation, and suggested that he should take some of her money and buy the house. "I shall be yours entirely then," she said. Ximen again went home to discuss the matter with Yueniang.

"I don't see how her husband can fail to have his suspicions," Yueniang said, "if he finds that you intend to buy his house. How do you propose to manage it?"

Ximen Qing considered what she said, but he did not answer.

In a few days Hua Zixu returned, and the magistrate of Qinghe appointed his deputy to make an inventory of the old chamberlain's estate. One house in the Street of Peace and Good Fortune was sold to the princely family of Wang for seven hundred taels, and the land by the South Gate to Major Zhou for six hundred and fifty-five taels. The house in which Hua Zixu had been living was valued at five hundred and forty taels, but nobody made an offer for it, because it was so near to Ximen Qing's house. More than once, Hua Zixu sent a messenger to ask Ximen to buy it, but he always said he had no money and didn't care to pass the transaction through his accounts. Meanwhile, seeing that the local authorities seemed anxious to get the matter over and done with, Li Ping'er grew more and more anxious, and secretly sent old woman Feng to Ximen to beg him to take five hundred and forty taels from the money that she had left in his care. Finally Ximen consented, and paid the money to the officials. Hua Zixu hurriedly signed all the documents, and his three brothers divided the eighteen hundred and ninety-five taels between them.

Hua Zixu was at last clear of the law, but he had not a penny to bless himself with, and both houses and land had been taken from him. The large bars of silver, amounting to three thousand taels, which he had had in his two chests, seemed to have completely vanished, a circumstance that he found exceedingly annoying and disturbing. He wished Li Ping'er to ask Ximen how much had been spent on his behalf and what was left, so that he could buy a house with the remainder, but the only reply he got from his wife was ill humor for several days.

"You idiot," she cried, "you have never paid the slightest attention to your own affairs; you have spent all your time chasing after women, and as a result you found yourself in a hole and were thrown into jail. You then condescended to ask me to find somebody to help you. I am not a woman given to gadding about. What do I know about matters of this sort? Whom do I know and where should I have found anybody to do anything for you? I am a creature of such insignificance that, if my body were made of iron, very few nails could be made out of me. All I could do was to go around like a baby, appealing for help, and, fortunately for you, Master Ximen remembered that you had once been his friend, and when things looked cold and bleak for you, sent his servant to the Eastern Capital to get everything settled for you. It was exceedingly kind and thoughtful of him. Now you are out of the mess and your feet are once more on dry land, you begin to think about money, though your life has only just been given back to you. As soon as your troubles are over, you forget all you have gone through, come back to rake up a business that has already been done with, and want to know whether there is any money left.

"Here is a letter from you, written in your own hand. Without this authority I should never have dared to spend your money on getting assistance for you. I am not so bold that I would steal your money and give it away."

"Although I said so in my letter," Hua Zixu said, "I did hope to keep a little something, sufficient, at least, to buy a house to live in."

"Pah, you dirty fool!" Li Ping'er cried, "you ought to have thought about that before. When you had money, you never gave it a thought; but it seems a very different matter now. You keep on saying that I have spent too much money. What was three thousand taels? Do you imagine that the Imperial Tutor Cai and Marshal Yang are so moderate in their desires? If I hadn't sent them a handsome present, do you think they would have attended to the matter so effectively that you never even felt the weight of a straw on your turtle's body, but got off scot-free? And you are proud of the fact! You have no influence with them. You are no relative of theirs that they should trouble to be kind to you. Unless it was for something worthwhile, why should they go tearing about to save your skin? Yet you come home, and instead of preparing a banquet and showing your gratitude by entertaining Ximen Qing, you brush everybody on one side and only think about reopening the whole business."

This was like a blow in the face to Hua Zixu. He said no more. Next day Ximen Qing sent Daian with a present to console him in his distress. In return he prepared wine, and invited Ximen Qing, hoping that he might get an opportunity to ask him about the money. As a matter of fact, Ximen would gladly have sent him a few hundred taels to buy a house with, but Li Ping'er would not hear of it. She sent old woman Feng to tell him not to come, and to send her husband a falsified account, making it appear that all the money had been spent.

Hua Zixu had not brains enough to see through the trick. He sent repeated invitations to Ximen Qing. But Ximen went off to the bawdy house, and told his servants to say that he was not at home whenever a message came for him. This so upset Hua Zixu that he almost fainted, yet he could do nothing but stamp his feet with impatience.

Readers, if a woman once ceases to love her husband and becomes unfaithful to him, he will never be able to find out her secrets, though he have strength enough to bite through iron. It is traditionally a man's duty to attend to matters outside the household and a woman's to govern within it, but over and over again a man's good repute has been brought to nothing by his wife. Why is this? It is because he has not treated his wife as the Sacred Principle requires. The relations between husband and wife should be based upon a generosity of spirit that gives rise to mutual understanding and brings their feelings into complete accord. When this is the case, the husband sets the tune and the wife follows; there is no reason to anticipate trouble. Hua Zixu lost his head and was blown hither and thither by every wind; he had no ideas at all about the management of a household. This being so, it could hardly be expected that he would exercise any control over his wife's doings.

Soon after this Hua Zixu succeeded in borrowing two hundred and fifty taels of silver and bought a house in Lion Street. But he was still smarting beneath a load of anger, and had not long been in his new house before he fell ill of a fever. At the beginning of the eleventh month he took to his bed, and never rose from it again. Early in his illness he was attended by a doctor, but he objected to the expense and allowed the illness to run its course till, on the twentieth, he breathed his last. He was only twenty-four. While he was ill, Tian Xi, one of his boys, stole five taels of silver and made off.

Hua Zixu was no sooner dead than his wife sent old woman Feng to ask Ximen Qing to come and talk to her. A coffin was bought, Hua was put into it, monks were engaged, and the coffin was sent to the tomb. The brothers Hua with their wives all came in deep mourning to assist at the funeral. Ximen Qing asked Yueniang to prepare a funeral offering of wine and food. Li Ping'er went to the funeral and returned in a sedan chair. She set up a tablet in her room, but, though it was a time when she should have respected her husband's memory, she could think of nobody but Ximen Qing.

While Hua Zixu was still alive, Ximen Qing had taken over the two maids, but after his death the two households were practically united. One day Li Ping'er heard that it was Pan Jinlian's birthday, and, though it was not five weeks after her husband's death, she bought some presents and went in a sedan chair to offer her congratulations. She wore a white silk gown and a blue skirt with gold embroidery, and upon her head was a white covering adorned with pearls. Old woman Feng attended her, and Tian Fu walked behind the sedan chair.

Li Ping'er kowtowed four times to Yueniang. "I am sorry," she said, "that at the graveside I had nothing better to offer you. It was kind of you to send such a handsome offering." After her reverence to Yueniang, she asked to see Li Jiao'er and Meng Yulou. Jinlian came in.

"Is this the Fifth Lady?" Li Ping'er said, preparing to kowtow to her. She repeatedly called her Elder Sister, and begged her to accept her reverence. But Jinlian would not do so, and, after disputing amicably for a long time, they ended by making equal reverences. Jinlian thanked her for her birthday present. After greeting Mistress Wu and Madam Pan, Li Ping'er asked after Ximen Qing.

"He has gone to make his devotions at the Temple of the Jade Emperor," Yueniang said. She asked Li Ping'er to sit down, and offered her tea. A little later Sun Xue'e came in. Li Ping'er saw that her attire was not so rich as that of the others, but she stood up. "Who is this lady?" she said, "I should have asked to be presented, had I known there was anyone else."

"She is one of my husband's ladies," Yueniang said. Li Ping'er would have made a reverence to Xue'e, but Yueniang would not allow her to do so. "Lady," she said, "you should make the reverence of an equal." So they greeted each other. Yueniang took Li Ping'er to her own room to change her clothes, and ordered the maids to set a table in the middle room. Charcoal was put into the brazier, and wine and food were brought. Mistress Wu, Madam Pan, and Li Ping'er sat in the place of honor; Yueniang and Li Jiao'er in the hostess's place, and Yulou and Jinlian sat at the side. Xue'e went to the kitchen to see to the serving of the meal, and it was some time before she took her own place.

Yueniang saw that Li Ping'er never refused any cup of wine that was offered. She herself poured wine for everyone, and told Li Jiao'er and the others that they must do so in their turn.

"Mistress Hua," she said, "since you have gone so far away, we do not see so much of one another, but I often think about you. It has been cruel of you not to come to see us."

"You would not have come today," Yulou said, "if it had not been the Fifth Lady's birthday."

"Good ladies," Li Ping'er said, "it is very good of you to say such kind words. I should have been only too glad to come, but I am still in deep mourning and there is nobody to leave at home. Even now it is only about five weeks since my husband died, and if I had not been afraid of incurring the Fifth Lady's displeasure, I should not have come today." She turned to Yueniang, and asked the date of her birthday.

"It is still a long way off," Yueniang said, but Jinlian contradicted her.

"Our Great Lady's birthday is the fifteenth day of the eighth month.

You must come and see us that day." Li Ping'er promised to come. Yulou suggested that she should spend the night with them.

I should enjoy the pleasure of your company very much indeed," Li Ping'er said, "but, as you know, I have only just removed to this new place and, since my husband died, there is not a soul in the house. The back of my house adjoins the garden of the princely family Qiao; it is very lonely and desolate. There are many nights when foxes come and throw bricks and tiles into my house, and it makes me very nervous. I used to have two serving boys, but the older of them has run away, and there is only young Tian Fu to attend to the front door and no one at all to keep watch at the back. Very fortunately for me, old woman Feng, an old friend, comes in frequently to do my washing."

"How old is Madam Feng?" Yueniang said. "She seems a very decent quiet old body."

"She is fifty-six this year," Li Ping'er replied. "She has no children, but lives upon her earnings as a go-between and what she makes by washing clothes for me. When my husband died, I asked her to come and live with me, and now she and the maid sleep in the same bed."

"Since there is old woman Feng to look after your house," Jinlian said, "there can be no possible reason why you should not spend the night here. In any case, Master Hua is dead, and you are not answerable to anybody but yourself."

"Do what I tell you," Yulou said, "and tell old woman Feng to send the sedan chair away. You don't go back today."

Li Ping'er laughed but said nothing.

The wine had now gone around several times. Old woman Pan was the first to rise, and she went to the front court with her daughter. Li Ping'er repeatedly declined to drink any more, but Li Jiao'er said, "Mistress Hua, you drank everything the other ladies offered you, yet you refuse me. That isn't fair." She took a large cup and filled it to the brim.

"My dear lady," Mistress Hua said, "I can't drink any more. I am not pretending."

"Just one cup more," Yueniang said, "and then we will let you off."

Li Ping'er took the cup, and put it down on the table. She went on talking to the ladies. Suddenly Yulou noticed Chunmei standing beside her.

"What is your mistress doing in the front court?" she said. "Go and tell her and old lady Pan to come back at once. The Great Lady wishes them to help to entertain Mistress Hua."

Chunmei went away, but was soon back again. "The old lady is not very well and has gone to bed," she said. "My mistress will be back in a moment. She is powdering her face."

"I never saw such a hostess," Yueniang said, "running away and leaving her guest like this. She is a good soul, but she behaves like a child at times."

When Jinlian came back, Yulou saw that she had dressed herself in her most beautiful clothes. She certainly looked very charming.

"Fifth Maid," Yulou said, jokingly, "my good woman, this is the feast of your donkey and horse, yet you ran away to your own room and left your guest behind. Do you call yourself a human being?"

Jinlian laughed, and slapped her playfully.

"You hussy of a fifth maid," Yulou cried, "come and pour out the wine."

"The Third Lady has given me too much wine already," Li Ping'er said, "I have had as much as I can take."

"What she gave you is her affair," Jinlian said, "but you must take a cup from me." She poured out a large cup for her guest. Li Ping'er took it, but did not drink it. Yueniang noticed that Jinlian was wearing in her hair a pin with the lucky character in gold. "Where did you buy your lucky character pins?" she said to Li Ping'er. "They are exactly like those the Fifth Lady is wearing. I must get a pair with the same design."

"If you would like some," Li Ping'er said, "I have several more pairs, and tomorrow I shall be delighted to offer a pair to each of you. They are some that my late father-in-law brought from the palace, and it is impossible to buy them outside the Court."

"You mustn't take me seriously," Yueniang said, there are too many of us. You can't possibly give us so many pins."

The ladies laughed and drank till the sun went down in the west. Old woman Feng had been drinking in the kitchen with Xue'e, and her face was very red. At last she went into the room and said to Li Ping'er, "Are you ready to go now? I must arrange about the chair."

"Don't go, Mistress Hua," Yueniang said. "Tell Madam Feng to send the chair away."

"There is no one at home," Li Ping'er persisted. "I will come and see you again some other day."

"You are very obstinate, Mistress Hua," Yulou said. "It looks as though you don't care in the least what we should like, since you won't send the chair away. If Father had been here, he would soon have persuaded you."

They finally persuaded her to give her key to old woman Feng. "These ladies have all urged me to stay," she said to the old woman, "and if I don't, it will be discourteous on my part. Send the sedan chair away and tell the men to call for me tomorrow. You take the boy home, and see that all the doors are shut." She added in a whisper: "Tell Yingchun to unlock the small box in my room. There is a little gilt case in it, and I want her to take four pairs of gold lucky-character pins out of it. Bring them to me tomorrow morning. I wish to make a present of them to these four ladies."

Old woman Feng made a reverence to Yueniang and went home. A little later, seeing that Li Ping'er would not drink any more, Yueniang asked her to go to the upper room and take tea with Mistress Wu.

Shortly afterwards Daian brought in the wrapper, and Ximen Qing came in. He pulled up the lattice and, as he entered the room, said, "Surely this is Mistress Hua!" Li Ping'er rose and made a reverence to him. Yueniang told Yuxiao to take his clothes.

"I have been outside the city to worship at the Temple of the Jade Emperor," Ximen Qing said. "I have to preside this year, and the Abbot and I had to go through the accounts in great detail. That is why I am so late. Are you staying the night, Mistress Hua?"

"Mistress Hua has made several attempts to get away," Yulou said, "but we succeeded in persuading her to stay."

"My only reason for wishing to go was that there is no one to look after my house," Li Ping'er said.

"That is nonsense," Ximen Qing said. "The constables have been very active lately, and there is nothing to be afraid of. If you should feel the least bit anxious, I would send my card to Major Zhou. He will do anything I ask him. But why do you sit there like a mouse, Lady Hua? Have you had any wine?"

"We have tried to persuade her to drink some, but she would not," Yulou said.

"You are none of you any good," Ximen cried. "Let me see what I can do. She can really drink quite a lot more."

Li Ping'er kept declaring that she could not drink another drop, but her objections were only half-hearted, and the maids once more set the table. Some dishes and dessert had been kept for Ximen Qing, and these were now brought out. Mistress Wu declined to drink any more, and went to Li Jiao'er's room. Li Ping'er now sat in the seat of honor, with Ximen Qing opposite to her, and Yueniang sat on the bed and warmed her feet at a small brazier. Yulou and Jinlian sat at the side. The wine was poured again, and they pledged each other in large cups. They drank so long that Mistress Hua's eyebrows grew heavy and her eyes could hardly see.

When Yueniang saw that both her husband and Li Ping'er had drunk more than was good for them, and were chattering nonsense to each other, she waited no longer but went to join her sister. The others stayed drinking till the third night watch, and then Li Ping'er could neither see straight nor stand upright. Jinlian helped her to the back court to wash her hands, and Ximen Qing, who was rolling in all directions, went to Yueniang's room.

"Where is she going to sleep?" he asked.

"In her hostess's room, I imagine," said his wife.

"Where shall I sleep, then?" Ximen said.

"Anywhere you like, though I expect you will go after her," Yueniang said.

"Nonsense," Ximen Qing said, laughing, "I'll stay here." He called Xiaoyu to help him undress.

'Don't be dirty," Yueniang said. "Where is my sister-in-law going to sleep if you stay here? Don't provoke me or I shall tell you what I think about you."

"All right! all right!" Ximen cried. "I'll go and sleep with Yulou." He went off to her room.

When Jinlian had shown her guest where to wash her hands, she took her to the front court and they slept with old woman Pan. Next morning Li Ping'er got up and dressed with the aid of Chunmei. She knew that the girl had passed through Ximen Qing's hands. She gave her a set of golden hair ornaments. Chunmei immediately went to tell Jinlian, and the Fifth Lady thanked her guest most effusively.

"I feel as though we were imposing on you, Mistress Hua," she said

"Not at all, Fifth Lady, you are fortunate to have so admirable a maid."

When they were dressed, Jinlian took her and old woman Pan into the garden, sending Chunmei to open the gate. Li Ping'er saw that a new gate had been made in the wall, and asked when Ximen was going to rebuild the house.

"The Master of the Yin Yang has been here," Jinlian said, "and he suggests our starting on the foundations in the middle of the second month. His Lordship proposes to make your old house and ours into one. In the front he is going to build an artificial mound, a pergola, and a large garden. At the back he will build a garden house of three rooms like mine."

Li Ping'er listened attentively. Then Yueniang sent Xiaoyu to invite them to take tea in the back court, and the three women went to her room. Yueniang, Li Jiao'er, Yulou, and Mistress Wu were waiting for them.

While they were having breakfast old woman Feng came in. She took an old handkerchief from her sleeve, in which were wrapped four pairs of gold pins, and gave the pins to her mistress. Li Ping'er gave them in turn to Yueniang, Li Jiao'er, Yulou, and Xue'e.

"I feel that I ought not to accept them," Yueniang said. "It is really too kind of you."

Li Ping'er smiled. "There is nothing very wonderful about them," she said, "I only offer them as playthings." Yueniang and the others thanked her, and put them in their hair.

"I believe the Feast of Lanterns is to be held near your house," Yueniang said. "It will be very lovely, and, when I go to see it, I will pay you a call. That is, unless you tell me you won't have me."

"I shall be only too glad to invite you all," Li Ping'er said.

"Perhaps you do not know, Sister," Jinlian said to Yueniang, "that it will be Mistress Hua's birthday on the fifteenth."

"In that case," Yueniang said, "we will make a definite arrangement now to come and offer our congratulations that day."

"My little room is no better than a snail's," Li Ping'er said, smiling, "but if you will condescend to come, I shall be only too happy."

They finished their breakfast, and wine was brought. It was now late in the morning, and the sedan chair came for Li Ping'er. She said good-bye to them all and, though they urged her to stay still longer, she prepared to go. As she was about to start, she asked for Ximen Qing, but Yueniang told her that he had gone early to say farewell to one of his friends who was going away. Li Ping'er got into her sedan chair and went home.

CHAPTER 15

The Feast of Lanterns

The days passed quickly. It was the birthday of Li Ping'er on the fifteenth of the eleventh month. The day before it Ximen Qing told Daian to get ready four courses of food, a large jar of wine, birthday cakes, and pastries. He himself added a suit of quilted silken clothes embroidered in gold. He wrote Wu Yueniang's name on a card, and sent everything as a birthday present from Yueniang to Li Ping'er.

Mistress Hua was dressing when Daian brought the present. She ordered the boy to be brought to her.

"It is only a few days," she said to him, "since your lady last troubled herself on my account. Now she has placed me in her debt again by sending this magnificent present."

"I was told to say that this is only a trifle, which you may well pass on to your maids."

Li Ping'er told Xiuchun to give Daian some cakes. As he was about to go, she gave him two *qian* and a colored handkerchief. "Tell your ladies," she said, "that I am going to send old woman Feng to ask them all to brighten my poor house by their presence."

Daian kowtowed and went away. Li Ping'er paid the porters, and sent old woman Feng with five cards of invitation to ask the ladies to come the following evening. Secretly she was to ask Ximen Qing to come later and take wine with her.

The next day Yueniang left Sun Xue'e to look after the house. She and the other ladies, all most charmingly dressed, got into their sedan chairs to go to Lion Street, where the Feast of Lanterns was being held. Laixing, Laian, Daian, and Huatong escorted them.

The house in which Li Ping'er now lived had three rooms at the front, and went back for the same distance. On the street it was two stores high, and, as one entered the gate, there were rooms on either side. Three formed a hall and one served as a passage to the third court, where there were three bedrooms and a kitchen. At the back of the house a wall separated the property of Li Ping'er from the garden belonging to the princely family of Qiao.

Yueniang and the others were coming specially to see the lanterns, and Li Ping'er set out screens, tables, and cushions, and hung up floral lanterns in the rooms that overlooked the street. When her guests arrived, she welcomed them and took them to the inner court for tea. They sat down, and two singing girls, Dong Jiao'er and Han Jinchuan, sang for them and served the wine. Afterwards refreshments were set out in the upper rooms, and she invited her guests to go upstairs and look at the lanterns. The windows had been decorated with bamboo shades, lanterns, and silken streamers.

Yueniang was dressed in a red-quilted cloak with an emerald green skirt, and she wore a mantle of leopard skin. Li Jiao'er, Meng Yulou, and Pan Jinlian were wearing white silk gowns and blue skirts. Li Jiao'er had a brown wrap embroidered in gold, Yulou a green one, and Jinlian a red one. They all wore masses of pearls and jade on their heads, and phoenix pins peeped out from their hair. They looked out of the window at the fair.

There were hosts of people at the fair, and it was a wonderful sight. Dozens of arches, with lanterns hanging all around them, had been set up in the street. There were all kinds of booths, surrounded by crowds of men and women admiring the lanterns, some red as roses, and some green as willows. Horses and carriages made a noise like thunder.

> Dragons flit through mountain peaks and sport in couples in the water.
> Lonely storks gaze at the skies, shining as the clouds themselves.
> Lanterns of the golden lotus; lanterns like towers of jade, glimmering like a mass of jewels.
> Lanterns of mimosa, lotus lanterns, shedding a thousand radiant hues.
> Lanterns of gossamer, light and dainty; sunflower lanterns, bobbing in the wind
> Student lanterns, bowing back and forth, attentive to the bidding of Confucius and Mencius.
> Wife lanterns, tender and obedient, picturing the virtues of Meng Jiang.
> Monkish lanterns, with Yue Ming and Liu Cui standing side by side.
> Lanterns of the Scribe of Hell, Zhong Kui and his sisters, sitting down together.
> Lanterns like witches with fluttering fans, conjuring up evil spirits.
> Lanterns of Liu Hai, with a golden frog, devouring precious treasure.
> Camel lanterns and green lion lanterns bearing gifts beyond price.
> Monkey lanterns and white elephant lanterns, with treasure worth the ransom of many cities.
> Crabs sporting with the incoming breakers, on their backs, all hands and feet.

Bull-headed fishes, with monstrous mouths and long beards, swal-
   lowing the river plants.
Silver moths, vying in beauty; snow-white willows, each more glo-
   rious than the last.
Fishes and dragons playing on the sands.
The seven immortals and the five ancients with their sacred books
The nine barbarians and the eight uncivilized coming to offer pre-
   cious gifts.

The drums at the fair beat sharply twice.
A hundred toys, each more cunning than its neighbor
The lanterns move round and round
The hanging lanterns bob up and down
There are glass vases painted with delicate maidens and exquisite
   flowers
There are screens of tortoiseshell, with Ying Zhou and Lang Yuan
   painted on them.

The young men gather at the rails where the ball is kicked as high
   as the eyes.
Hand in hand the maidens go to the upper floors that the beauty
   of their charms may be seen.
The booths of the palmists are like the clouds, and the tents of the
   readers of faces like the stars
They tell the fortunes of the coming year and read in the lives of
   men the joy and sadness that are to come.
They who sing the song of Yang Gong stand on the slopes.
Elsewhere, the wandering priests strike their cymbals and tell the
   story of San Cang.
There are sellers of Yuan Xiao, their pastries stuffed with fruits
And sellers of plum blossom with the dried branches cut away.
Hair ornaments sporting with the winds of spring; cold weather
   ornaments brightening the hair, their golden glory gleaming in
   the sun.
Round screens, painted with the gorgeous net of Shi Chong.
Lattices of mother of pearl, adorned with plum blossom and cres-
   cent moon, charming to the eyes.
We may not see all the beauties of Ao Shan
But before us is a year of happiness and joyful living.

Yueniang looked out upon the lanterns until the noise became too
great for her. Then she and Li Jiao'er went back to their places to drink for
a while. Jinlian, Yulou, and the two singing girls, stayed and still looked
out of the window at the fair.

Jinlian flaunted her silken sleeves and pointed with her fine fingers, showing off the gold rings on them. She leaned half out of the window, biting melon seeds and throwing the skins at the passersby. She and Yulou laughed all the time. She pointed to something in the street, and cried, "Great Sister, come and look at the two hydrangea-lanterns over at that house. They look so pretty, as the wind blows them to and fro." Then: "Second Sister, come and look at the great fish lanterns hanging over that door, and all the little fishes, crabs, and lobsters below. They are ever so funny." And again: "Third Sister, come and look at the old-man-and-woman lanterns."

Suddenly a gust of wind made a large hole in the lower part of the old-woman-lantern, and Jinlian laughed merrily. People standing below the window stared up at her, crowding till they almost trampled on each other. There were several dissolute young fellows among them. They pointed at the woman, and began to discuss her.

"She must have come from the palace of some duke or earl," one said.

"She is a concubine of one of the princely households, come to see the lanterns," another said. "She must be, or she would not be dressed in such splendid style."

"She is one of the little girls from the bawdy house, and some noble-man has engaged her to come here and sing," said a third.

Then another young man spoke. "You will never guess who they are. But I know. Those two women indeed belong to a distinguished family: they are the wives of the King of Hades, concubines of the General of the Five Directions. In other words, they belong to Master Ximen who keeps a medicine shop near the Town Hall and lends money to the officials. He is not at all the sort of man to fall out with. Probably they have come with the mistress of their household to see the lanterns. I don't know the one wearing the green wrapper, but the other, in red with the artificial flowers, looks like the wife of Wu Da the cake seller. Wu Da caught them misbe-having in old woman Wang's tea shop. His Lordship kicked Wu Da to death, and then took the woman to be one of his ladies. Her brother-in-law, Wu Song, went to the courts to bring an accusation, but, in mistake, killed the runner Li, and his Lordship had him punished. It is a year or two since I saw her last. She has certainly become very beautiful."

Yueniang saw that a crowd was collecting in the street, and told Jinlian and Yulou to come and sit down. They drank wine and the two singing girls sang the Lantern Song to them.

Yueniang was anxious to go home. "I have had as much wine as I can drink," she said, "and I and the Second Lady must leave you. But the others may stay and entertain you, Mistress Hua. My husband is not at home today, and there are only a few maids to look after things. I can't help being anxious."

Li Ping'er tried to persuade her to stay. "Good lady," she said, "if you go, it must be because I have entertained you so poorly. Today is a great holiday, and the lamps are not yet lighted or the food prepared. You mustn't think of going home. Even if Master Ximen is out, you have a number of maids. Why should you be uneasy? As soon as the moon rises, I will see you all home."

"Mistress Hua," Yueniang said, "I am afraid that is impossible. I never drink much wine. But I will leave the others here to take my place."

"Great Lady and Second Lady," Li Ping'er said. "Neither of you will drink with me. It is not fair. When I was at your house, your ladies would not let me off though I drank one cup after another. Today you have come to this poor place of mine, and though I can offer nothing worthy of you, I should like to do something to show my feelings."

She took a great silver cup, and asked Li Jiao'er to drink. Then she turned to Yueniang. "I dare not offer you so large a cup," she said, "but here is a small one." She poured out a cup of wine and offered it.

Yueniang gave each of the singing girls two *qian* of silver and, when Li Jiao'er had finished her wine, they prepared to leave. "We will go first," Yueniang said to Yulou and Jinlian, "and I will send the boys with lanterns to bring you home. You must not be too late, for there are not many of us at home." Li Ping'er took Yueniang and Li Jiao'er to the door, and saw them off in their sedan chairs. Then she came back to drink wine with Yulou and Jinlian. It was getting dark, and the lamps in the room were lighted. As they drank, they listened to the playing and singing of the two girls.

Ximen Qing dined at home with Ying Bojue and Xie Xida, and afterwards they set out to the Lantern Fair. When they reached the end of Lion Street, Ximen was afraid his companions might see the ladies drinking wine at Mistress Hua's house, so he turned aside into another street to look at the large lanterns. They went as far as one of the great booths and then came back. They met Sun Guazui and Zhu Shinian.

"It is a very long time since we saw you last," the newcomers said. "Our hearts were thirsting for the sight of you." They turned to Ying Bojue and Xie Xida. "You are a fine pair of rascals! You have been enjoying yourselves with our brother and never said a word to us about it."

"You are unfair to them," Ximen said. "I only met them in the street a moment ago."

"Well," Zhu Shinian said, "now that we've had enough of the lanterns, where shall we go?"

"Let us go to the wineshop and drink," Ximen Qing said. "I will not ask you to my place, because all my women have gone to a party."

"Why a wineshop?" Zhu Shinian said. "Why not call on Li Guijie? This is a great occasion. We will go and wish her a Happy New Year and enjoy ourselves at the same time. A few days ago we were at her place, and the very thought of you brought tears to her eyes. She told us she had been ill ever since the twelfth month, but not even your shadow had crossed her threshold. Brother, you have nothing else to do, and we shall be very glad to go with you."

Ximen Qing remembered that he had to go and see Li Ping'er that evening. He declined. "I have certain matters to attend to today," he said, "I'll go with you tomorrow." But they hustled him and dragged him till he found himself at the bawdy house in spite of himself.

When Ximen Qing and his companions reached the house, Guiqing, dressed very daintily, was standing outside the door. She brought them into the hall and made a reverence to each in turn.

"Come here at once, Mother," Zhu Shinian cried at the top of his voice. "We have been lucky enough to persuade his Lordship to come." The old procuress came, hobbling along with the help of her stick. She greeted Ximen Qing.

"I am a poor old body who has never done you any wrong," she said. "Why have you kept away from your sisters so long? Perhaps you have another girl somewhere."

"A good guess," Zhu Shinian said. "His Lordship has made the acquaintance of a very pretty girl, and he goes to see her every day. Now you know why he never bothers about Guijie any more. If we hadn't run into him at the Feast of Lanterns and dragged him along, he would not be here now. If you don't believe me, ask Sun." He pointed to Ying Bojue and Xie Xida. "Those unholy rascals belong to the same family of immortals as Master Ximen himself."

The old woman found this very amusing. "Good brother Ying," she said, "I have always treated you well. Why couldn't you speak for us to his Lordship? He is a busy man, and, of course, as the proverb says, a young man is never faithful to one girl. All the coins in the world are made with the same sort of hole. I don't mean to boast, but my daughter is a good-looking girl. Your own eyes, Sir, will tell you that much."

"Let me explain," Sun Guazui said. "His new girl does not live in any bawdy house. She is independent."

Ximen Qing ran after Sun Guazui and slapped him. "Don't believe this old oily mouth and all his crazy stories. His proper place is the slaughter-house."

Sun and the others roared with laughter. Ximen took three taels of

silver from his sleeve and offered it to Guiqing, saying that he would like
to give his friends a treat on this festival day. Guiqing would have nothing
to do with it; she passed it on to the old procuress.

"What does this mean?" the old woman cried. "Do you think that on
a festival day like this I cannot myself entertain your friends? If you offer
me this silver, it is quite clear you believe we never think of anything but
money."

Ying Bojue went to her. "Take my advice and accept the money," he
said, "and get us some wine at once."

"It is not right," the old woman mumbled, still pretending to refuse
the money, though she put it into her sleeve. Finally she thanked Ximen
Qing, and made a profound reverence to him.

"Wait a moment, Mother," Bojue cried. "I have a funny story to tell
you. There was once a young man who kept a girl at the bawdy house, and
one day, when he called to see her, he pretended to have been ruined. The
old woman saw how shabby his clothes were and would have nothing to
say to him. He sat for a long time, and she never even offered him a cup
of tea. 'May I have some rice, Mother?' the young man said at last. 'I am
very hungry.' 'My rice bin is empty,' the old woman replied. 'Where shall
I find rice for you?' 'If you have no rice,' said the young man, 'perhaps
you will give me a little water to wash my face?' But the old woman said,
'I can't afford to buy any water; we have had none for days.' But then the
young man produced a piece of silver, about ten taels in weight, and put
it on the table. Again he asked for rice and water. The old woman became
quite excited. 'Eat your face and wash your rice, Brother,' she cried, 'and
when you have washed your rice, eat your face.'"

They laughed. "You are trying to make fun of me," the old woman said.
"I have heard stories like that before, but I don't believe a word of them."

"Listen," Bojue said, "I'll tell you something. This girl his Lordship has
been courting is Brother Hua's girl, Wu Yin'er, who lives in the back lane.
He doesn't care for Guijie any more."

"I don't believe you," the old woman said, laughing. "I don't wish to
boast, but my daughter is certainly as good-looking as Wu Yin'er. Brother
is so wrapped up in us that not even the sharpest of knives could cut him
away from us. And he is not a fool either. He can tell real gold when he
sees it." With this, she went to see about the preparation of the feast.

In a short time Guijie came in. Her hair was dressed in the Hangzhou
style, with pins inlaid with gold, and green plum ornaments. She wore
a pearl headdress, a pair of golden earrings, a crimson silk skirt and a
white silk coat. She looked as beautiful as a carving in jade. When she had
greeted them all, she sat down by the side of her sister, and a little later tea

was brought in. Guijie handed the tea and kept a cup for herself. Then a maid came to clear away the tea things and set the table.

Suddenly several men, whose dress showed that they were of low degree, appeared before the lattice, and looked in on them. Then they came in and knelt down. They brought three or four measures of melon seeds.

"We bring you this present," their spokesman said, "in honor of the festival."

"Who are you?" Ximen asked. He only recognized the leader, Yu Chun.

"Nie Yue is outside," said Yu Chun. "He belongs to our party."

Nie Yue came in. When he saw Ying Bojue, he said, "So you are here, Master Ying." He kowtowed.

Ximen Qing took the melon seeds and threw a tael of silver to Yu Chun. Then the fellows thanked him politely and went away.

When Ximen Qing had got rid of them, he settled down to his wine. Guijie filled the golden cups, making great play with her crimson sleeves. The food was of the rarest and the dessert of seasonable fruits. The men reveled in the fragrance of the two girls, and the wine they drank only seemed to add to the charm. The cups were filled twice, then Guijie and her sister sang "The Sweetness of the Glorious Day," one playing the cithern and the other the lute. While they were singing, three members of the Ball Club came in, wearing dark clothes and bringing two roast geese and a couple of jars of wine. They made a profound reverence to Ximen Qing, and offered their gifts. Ximen knew them all. There were Bai Tuzi, little Zhang Xian, and Mohammedan Luo.

"Wait for us outside," he said, "and, as soon as we have finished our wine, we will come and have a game with you." He gave them four dishes of food, a large jar of wine, and some cakes. They got their ball ready and waited. When Ximen had drunk a little more wine, he went out to the courtyard to watch the ball game and asked Guijie to play with two of them, one to pitch and one to strike. She jumped about, kicked, elbowed, and struck the ball to the great admiration of those looking on. If sometimes she could not catch it, they hastily caught it for her. When the game was over, they went to Ximen Qing for money.

"Guijie's form has very greatly improved," one said. "When she elbows the ball, it takes us all our time to hold it. In a year or two, she may well be the finest ball player in all the bawdy houses. She is infinitely better than the Dong girls who live in the second lane."

By the time Guijie had played two games, dust covered her eyebrows and her cheeks were damp with sweat. Her limbs ached and she panted for breath. She took the fan from her sleeve and fanned herself, then held Ximen Qing's hand, while they watched Guiqing, Xie Xida, and Zhang Xian play a game. The others stood at the sides to pick the ball up for them.

Ximen Qing drank wine as he watched them. Then Daian came with a horse. "My mistress and the other ladies have now been gone some time," he whispered. "Mistress Hua hopes that you will come as soon as you can." Ximen told the boy to take the horse to the back and wait for him there. He refused to drink any more, but took Guijie to her room for a while, and then pretended to go out to wash his hands. Leaving her room, he opened the back door, mounted his horse, and was off like a flash. Ying Bojue saw him go and told a servant to detain him, but Ximen would not wait; he declared that he had business at home to attend to. He left Daian to give a tael and five *qian* to the ballplayers.

Thinking that Ximen had gone to Wu Yin'er's house, they sent a servant to follow him there. Bojue and the others drank till the second night watch, and then the party broke up.

CHAPTER 16
Li Ping'er Is Betrothed

Ximen Qing left the bawdy house. With Daian following, he went to see Li Ping'er at her house in Lion Street. When they found the gate closed, they knew that the guests had got into their sedan chairs and departed. Daian called to old woman Feng to open the door. She let Ximen Qing in. Li Ping'er, holding a candle, was waiting for him in the hall. She looked very charming in her pretty headdress and soft white clothes. She had been leaning on the framework of the lattice longing for him to come; and when he came, she ran downstairs to meet him, her lotus-like feet moving swiftly, her silken skirt fluttering.

"If you had been a little earlier," she said, smiling, "you would have found two of your ladies still here. They have only just gone. The Great Lady went away early, because she said you were not at home. If that is so, where have you been?"

"Brother Ying and Brother Xie asked me to go and see the lanterns with them," Ximen Qing said, "and we were passing your door when we met two other friends. They carried me off to the bawdy house, and I could not get away before this late hour. I thought you would be waiting for me, and, as soon as the boy came, I said I was going to wash my hands. I slipped away through the back door. If I hadn't done so, they would have kept me and I should never have been able to get away."

"Thank you very much for the splendid present you sent me," Li Ping'er said. "I could not prevail upon your ladies to stay. They said there was no one at home, but nonetheless I felt ashamed."

She heated some excellent wine and served food to him. The lanterns were lighted in the hall and the curtains drawn. Charcoal was put into the golden brazier and precious incense into the incense burner. She kowtowed before him and offered him a cup of wine.

"My foolish husband is dead now," she said, "and I have no other relatives. Today, my lord, I offer you this cup of wine and implore you to take me under your protection. Do not despise my lack of comeliness, for I wish nothing more than to be your slave and a sister to all your ladies. I have told you my wishes, but what you may think about it I do not know." As she said this, she shed tears.

Ximen took the wine and raised her up. "Do not kneel," he said, "I am grateful for your love. When your period of mourning is over, I shall know what course to take. You need worry no longer. This is your lucky day, and we can enjoy our wine without a care." He drank his own wine and poured a cup for Li Ping'er. Then they sat down and, in a little while, old woman Feng, who was in charge of the kitchen, brought them some dumplings.

"Who were the singing girls today?" Ximen Qing said.

"Dong Jiao'er and Han Jinchuan," Li Ping'er said. "They went after your ladies to get some flowers from them."

They sat on the bed and drank wine, exchanging cups. Xiuchun and Yingchun waited upon them. Daian came and kowtowed to Li Ping'er to congratulate her upon her birthday. She rose quickly and returned his greeting. She asked Yingchun to tell old woman Feng to give him some birthday dumplings, cakes, and a jar of wine in the kitchen.

"You may go home as soon as you have finished," Ximen told him.

"And when you get home," Li Ping'er said, "if any of the ladies ask where your master is, don't tell them he is here."

"I understand," the boy said. "I will tell them that Father is spending the night somewhere else. Tomorrow morning I will come back for him." Ximen nodded approval and Li Ping'er was very pleased. "What an intelligent boy he is," she cried. "You can see it in his eyes." She told Yingchun to give him two *qian* of silver with which to buy melon seeds. "Let me know what size you take," she said to him, "and I will make you a pair of shoes."

Daian kowtowed again, thanked her, and went away when he had had a meal in the kitchen. Old woman Feng bolted the gate. Ximen Qing and Li Ping'er guessed fingers, and then, taking a set of thirty-two ivory tablets, set a cloth upon the table and played dominoes as they drank their wine. Then they told Yingchun to light them with a candle to the bedroom. Now that Hua Zixu was dead, both Yingchun and Xiuchun had yielded to Ximen's desire. The lovers did as they pleased in the presence of these maids, and were quite at their ease. They called for the bed to be prepared and for fruit and wine to be placed within the purple silk net. Li Ping'er unveiled her white body and Ximen Qing sat beside her. They went on with their game of dominoes, and drank great cups of wine together.

"When are you going to begin the rebuilding of the house?" Li Ping'er asked suddenly.

"I shall get the work in hand at the middle of the second month," Ximen said. "I propose to make the two properties into one and let the gardens run together. At the front I am having an artificial mound and a shelter made, and at the back a garden pavilion of three rooms where we can go to enjoy the flowers."

"In some tea chests behind that bed," Li Ping'er said, "there are thirty or forty pounds of aloes, two hundred pounds of white wax, two jars of quicksilver, and eighty pounds of pepper. Take them all away and sell them; you can use the money to help pay the building expenses. If I find favor in your sight, when you get home tell the Great Lady that I hope to take a sister's place among your ladies. Give me any place you choose, but I cannot live without you." She began to sob again.

Ximen Qing took out his handkerchief and wiped away her tears. "I understand perfectly," he said, "but you must wait till the building is finished and your mourning is over. Until then there will be no place where you can live."

"If you really intend to marry me, you will build a little pavilion for me near that of your Fifth Lady. She is so nice, and I am very fond of her. The Third Lady too is very kind to me. One would never take them to be anything but sisters. The Great Lady is not quite so agreeable. Somehow those eyebrows of hers seem supercilious."

"My foolish wife is really one of the kindest of souls," Ximen Qing said, "or she would never have managed to keep such a large household in order. I will build a three-roomed pavilion with two little doors for you, as fine as the place in which you live now. What do you think of that?"

"Oh, Brother, what more could I wish for?" Li Ping'er said.

They played together unrestrainedly, as the male phoenix plays with his mate, and their delight was so great that it was the fourth night watch before they went to sleep. Then, close pressed in each other's arms, they slept until morning. Breakfast time came, but they did not rise, and Ying-chun brought them some rice porridge. They ate a little of it, and then called for wine. Li Ping'er liked to play at being a horse. She made Ximen Qing take up his position on a pillow, and she placed herself in the manner of a flower inverted. They were enjoying themselves like this when Daian, who had brought Ximen Qing's horse, came and knocked at the door. Ximen called him to the window and asked what he wanted.

"Three merchants from Sichuan and Guangdong have come to see you," the boy said. "They are waiting with a host of fine things. They have shown them to Uncle Fu. All they ask for them is a hundred taels of silver on the signing of the contract, and the rest in the eighth month. My mistress told me to ask you to come and see them."

"You didn't tell her I was here, did you?" Ximen Qing said.

"No," said the boy, "I told them you were spending the night at Gui-jie's house."

"They have no sense," Ximen said. "Your uncle Fu could have managed this perfectly well. Why send and bother me?"

"Uncle Fu has talked to them," Daian said, "but the strangers will not settle with him. They will not sign the contract unless you go yourself."

"Your family has sent the boy for you," Li Ping'er said. "Business must come first. You must go, or the Great Lady will be angry."

"You don't know these thievish barbarians," Ximen said. "They miss the proper season, can't get rid of their goods, and then come to me. If I show myself at all eager to accept their terms, they will very soon ask for more. In the whole of this district mine is the only wholesale house, and they must come to me, whatever I choose to offer."

"In business matters," Li Ping'er said, "you should take care not to turn friends into enemies. Please do as I tell you. Go home, and get rid of them. There are still as many days before us as there are leaves upon a willow tree."

Ximen agreed to do as she wished. He got out of bed in a leisurely manner, combed his hair, washed his face, and put on his hairnet and clothes. Li Ping'er served him with food. When he had eaten it, he put on his eyeshades and rode home.

Four or five merchants were waiting in the shop for him to check the goods and give them the money. When this had been done, they signed the contract and went away. Ximen Qing went to Jinlian's room.

"Where did you spend last night?" Jinlian cried. "Tell me the truth, or I will stir the dust with my complainings."

"You were all drinking wine with Mistress Hua," Ximen said, "so I went to the Lantern Fair with my friends. Afterwards we went to the bawdy house and spent the night there. This morning Daian came to bring me back, and here I am."

"I know the boy went to fetch you, but pray, in which of the bawdy houses does your particular ghost live? You fickle rogue, you are trying to deceive me. Last night that strumpet turned us out and invoked the aid of gods and devils alike to get you to go to her. When you have had enough, you come home. That thievish lump of knavery, Daian, is cunning enough to tell one story to his mistress, but it is quite another one he tells me. Last night when he came back, the Great Lady said, 'Why hasn't your Father come back? Where is he drinking?' and he said you and Uncle Fu had gone to see the lanterns, and that you had gone to Guijie's house to drink, and he was going to bring you back this morning. But afterwards, when I questioned him, he laughed and kept his mouth shut. When I pressed him, he admitted that you were spending the night with Mistress Hua in Lion Street. You villain, how does he know that I always let you do as you please? I suppose you told him."

"Indeed I did nothing of the sort," Ximen Qing said. He told her how Li Ping'er had asked him to take wine with her, how sorry she was that Jinlian had returned so early, how she cried and told him that she had no one to help her and was always terrified at night because her house was so lonely. "She begged me to marry her, and asked when I was going to rebuild the house. She has some incense and candles and all kinds of valuable stuff there, and she asked me to take it and use the money to pay the builder. She is very anxious that I should get the house finished quickly, so that she can come here and live with you as a sister. But it looks as though that won't suit you."

"One shadow more or less will not worry me," Jinlian said. "I shall be glad to have her, for, as things are, I'm very lonely, and, if she comes, she will keep me company. The fact that there are many ships on a river does not necessarily mean a block, and a road is not stopped because there are many carts upon it. There is no more reason why I should refuse to welcome her than others might have found when I came here myself. But I'm very much afraid you will not find everybody so amiably disposed as I am. You still have to see what our mistress thinks about it."

"Although I am talking about this matter now," Ximen said, "of course she is still in mourning."

Jinlian took Ximen's silken gown. Something dropped out of the sleeve, and fell tinkling to the ground. She picked it up and weighed it in her hand. It was like a little ball, but very heavy. She looked at it for a long time, but could not imagine what it was for. Jinlian stared at it.

"What is it?" she said, "and why does it seem so heavy?"

"Don't you know?" Ximen said, laughing. "They call it the Bell of Fecundity, and it comes from Burma, a country somewhere in the south. A good one is worth four or five taels of silver."

"Where do you put the thing?" the woman asked.

"First, you put it inside, then get on with what has to be done. The results are quite indescribable."

"Did you use it with Mistress Hua?" Jinlian asked.

Ximen Qing told her all that had passed during the night, and this so stirred up Jinlian's ardent mind that, though it was still day, these two disrobed themselves and behaved in a manner better befitting the night.

Ximen Qing went to see the valuers, taking with him the candles and wax and other things that belonged to Li Ping'er. They were all weighed up and sold for about three hundred and eighty taels of silver. Out of this Li Ping'er would take only one hundred and eighty taels, making Ximen Qing spend the rest on the house. He consulted the Master of the Yin

Yang, and work was begun on the eighth day of the second month. He gave five hundred taels to his servant Laizhao and his manager Ben the Fourth, to buy bricks, tiles, timber, and stone, and gave them instructions to superintend the work and keep account of the expenditure. Ben the Fourth was a dissipated young fellow, something of a windbag, but efficient and cunning. He began life as servant to a eunuch, but was sent away because of some irregularity. Then he lent himself to practices of doubtful morality and, still later, took employment as domestic in a family of position. But he seduced the nurse and ran off with her. For a while he acted as a tailor's tout. He could play the lute, the flute, and the double flute. Ximen Qing, who appreciated such accomplishments, gave Ben the Fourth help from time to time, and finally found a place for him in his shop, so that he could earn commission. In this way Ben the Fourth came to have a finger in the pie of all Ximen's enterprises.

Ben the Fourth and Laizhao supervised the workers during the building of the house. To begin with, the old rooms of Hua's house were demolished, then the walls were pulled down and new foundations laid. They constructed the shelter, the artificial mound, and all the arbors and apartments. This took a considerable time.

The days passed quickly. The sun and moon crossed and recrossed like the shuttles of a weaver. A little more than a month after Ximen's setting to work upon the gardens, it was a hundred days since Hua Zixu died. Li Ping'er asked Ximen to go and see her, to talk over the future. "I will have Hua's tablet burned," she said, "and you must decide whether you wish to have this house sold or not. You need only to give your orders, but you must marry me as soon as you can. Give me any position you like in your household. So long as I can be your chambermaid, I shall be quite happy." Her tears fell like rain.

"Don't cry," Ximen said. "I have told the Fifth Lady that, as soon as the house is finished and your mourning is over, I am going to marry you."

"If you really want me," Li Ping'er cried, "get my apartment finished first, and take me there. If I spend a single day in it and then die, I shall die content. Anything would be better than staying here, where each day seems like a year."

"I know," said Ximen.

"Why should I not go to live with the Fifth Lady for a few days, as soon as the tablet has been burned, and move into the new apartment as soon as it is finished? Go home and see what the Fifth Lady thinks of that, and I will wait. The hundredth day is the tenth of the third month, and I will arrange to have the dirge sung and the tablet burned."

Ximen Qing agreed, and spent the night with Li Ping'er. The next day he went home and told Jinlian all she had proposed.

"Very well," Jinlian said, "I am quite ready to clear a couple of rooms for her, but you must go and ask the Great Lady first. As for me, I am like the water in the river, there is no reason why I should not do my part in washing the boats."

Ximen Qing went at once to see Yueniang. She was dressing her hair, and Ximen told her the whole story.

"It is not at all a suitable arrangement," Yueniang said. "To begin with, she is still in mourning. Secondly, you were a very intimate friend of her husband. Thirdly, you have already had dealings with her, purchased her house, and stored many of her goods. The proverb says, If the loom is not speedy, the shuttle is. I understand that one member of her family, Hua the Elder, is a rogue. If he gets wind of this, I very much fear we shall find many fleas about our heads. What I have said is plain common sense. By Zhao, Qian, Sun and Li, think the matter over and see if you don't agree with me."

Ximen could think of no answer to make. He went and sat on a chair in the hall, and pondered the matter. He was by no means decided how he should answer Li Ping'er, but he could not make up his mind to give her up. The problem troubled him for a long time, and finally he went back to Jinlian's room.

"What did the Great Lady say?" Jinlian said. Ximen told her all that had passed.

"She is right," Jinlian said. "You did buy her house and you do wish to marry the widow of one of your most intimate friends. And, for that reason, you must forgo what otherwise you might have had. If you do not, your influential friends will look upon you with grave suspicion."

"That doesn't trouble me in the least," Ximen said, "but I am anxious about that fellow Hua the Elder. I don't want him to start interfering. If he hears what is going on, he will bring pressure to bear upon her before she is out of mourning. What can I do then? But I really don't know what to say to her."

"I see no difficulty at all," Jinlian said. "All you need do is to go and say to her, 'I have mentioned the matter to the Fifth Lady, but it appears that there is a great stock of merchandise stored on the upper floor of her apartments, and there is no room for your things. You must wait a few days more. My place is nearly finished, and I will hurry on the workmen and get the painting and decorating done as soon as possible. By that time your mourning will be over and I will marry you. That seems much the best plan, far better than your staying with the Fifth Lady, packed like herrings in a barrel, neither one thing nor another.' That ought to satisfy her."

Ximen Qing was delighted with this counsel, and went at once to see Li Ping'er. "The Fifth Lady says: Wait till the painting and decoration of your apartment are finished, and go straight there. At present there is a whole heap of things in her place, and there would be no room for your belongings. There is one thing more I must remind you of. May not your brother-in-law say that your period of mourning has not been duly fulfilled? What can we do about it?"

"He has no authority over me," Li Ping'er said. "We have already come to an arrangement about the property and we have signed a document in the courts to say that our relationship is at an end. We women certainly have our first marriages arranged for us, but for the rest we can surely please ourselves. There is a proverb that says: Brothers and sisters-in-law have no right to interfere in each other's affairs. My brother-in-law has not the slightest power to say a word in any matter that concerns myself alone. If I could not support myself, he would never raise a finger to help me. No, if that fellow dares to fart about, I shall tell him to die in his chair, and after that, he will not venture to die in his bed. Please don't let him worry you, my lord. He can do me no harm. When will the apartment be finished?"

"I have given orders for it to be painted and decorated before anything else. At the beginning of the fifth month it will certainly be ready."

"I will gladly wait till then, but you must do your best to hurry it on."

The maids brought wine, and they spent the night most pleasantly together. Thenceforth Ximen Qing went every few days to visit Li Ping'er.

It was not long before Ximen Qing had finished some of the side rooms and the three-roomed apartment. Only the arbor still remained to be done. It was the Summer Day, the fifth day of the fifth month.

Li Ping'er made preparations, and invited Ximen Qing to unfold the three-cornered dumplings, and also to talk over the arrangements for the wedding. She had decided to send for the monks to sing a dirge on the fifteenth day of the month, and then she proposed that Ximen should take her to his house.

"Are you going to invite the Hua brothers to the ceremony?" Ximen Qing said.

"I shall send each of them a card, and they may come or not as they please," Li Ping'er said. So the matter was settled.

On the fifteenth day of the fifth month, she asked twelve monks from the Temple of Eternal Felicity to sing a dirge at her house. The same day Ximen Qing took three *qian* of silver as a birthday present for Ying Bojue, and gave Daian five taels to spend in celebration of Li Ping'er's coming out of mourning. Just before noon Ximen mounted his horse and went to Ying Bojue's house. Ping'an and Shutong rode behind him. At Ying's house the ten brothers were already gathered, with Ben the Fourth, the latest accession to the band. Bojue had engaged two young actors to play and sing and serve them with wine. When everybody was seated, Ximen Qing called the actors to him. One of them, Wu Yin'er's brother, he knew already, but not the other, who knelt down and introduced himself as Zheng Feng, the brother of Zheng Aixiang.

Ximen Qing, who was sitting in the place of honor, gave each of the boys two *qian* of silver. They drank till it grew dark, and Daian appeared to escort his master home. The boy went to Ximen Qing and whispered, "Mistress Hua hopes you will not stay very late."

Ximen Qing winked at him and made to leave the table. Bojue cried, "You thievish bone of a dog! Come here and tell me what it is all about, or I will pull your little ears till they are both on the same side of your head. How many birthdays a year do you think I have? The sun is still high in the heavens, and you come here with a horse. Who told you to come? The ladies of your family, or someone else we know? If you don't tell me, I will never ask your father to find a wife for you, even if you live to be a hundred years old, you little bald-pated dog."

"Really," said Daian, "nobody told me. I thought it was going to be a rough night and that it would be better for Father to go home early, so I brought the horse and came to wait for him."

Ying Bojue questioned the boy for a long time, but Daian did not tell him the true story.

"So you won't tell me?" Ying Bojue cried. "Well, tomorrow I shall hear all about it, and then I'll settle with you, little oily mouth."

He gave Daian a cup of wine and half a dish of cakes, and told him to go away and eat them. Soon afterwards Ximen Qing came down to change his clothes. He called Daian to a quiet place.

"Who has been at the Huas' house today?" he asked.

"Hua the Third has gone to the country, and Hua the Fourth has something the matter with his eyes. Only Hua the Elder and his wife were at the funeral banquet. Master Hua went away first, and, before his wife followed him, Mistress Hua took her into her room and gave her ten taels of silver and two dresses. She kowtowed to Mistress Hua."

"Didn't she say anything?"

"Not a word, except that, when Mistress Hua was married, she would come to pay her respects on the third day."

"Did she really say that?" Ximen cried.

"I would not dare to lie to you," Daian said.

This was extremely satisfactory. Ximen asked if the service was over.

"The tablet has been burned and the monks have gone," said Daian.

"Mistress Hua says she hopes you will go as soon as you possibly can."

"Very well," said Ximen, "go and get the horse ready."

Daian was about to do so, when Ying Bojue, who had been listening in the passage, suddenly shouted and frightened him. "You thievish little dog bone," he cried, "you wouldn't tell me, but now I've heard everything. This is a nice little plot you and your father are hatching together."

"Don't make so much noise, you funny dog," Ximen Qing said.

"Talk nicely to me and I won't," Bojue answered.

They went back to the party, and Bojue told them all that had happened. Seizing Ximen Qing's hands, he cried, "Do you really call yourself a man, Brother? You have something like this on hand, and not a word of it do you mention to any of us. Why, if Hua the Elder had tried to say anything, all you had to do was to tell us, and we would have gone and dealt with him. One word from him, and we would have raised a fine big bump on him. There would have been no difficulty in getting his assent. We had no idea that this marriage was decided. Tell us all about it, or what use is there in calling ourselves a brotherhood? If we can serve you in any way, we will gladly go through fire and water. That is how we feel about you. Yet you keep your secrets from us."

"If you won't tell us," Xie Xida said, "we will tell Guijie and Wu Yin'er tomorrow. Then there will be trouble."

"Give me a chance to tell you," Ximen said, laughing. "The marriage has been definitely arranged."

"When is our new sister-in-law going to your house?" Xie Xida asked. "We must come and pay our respects, and you must engage four singing girls to serve us with wine. So we will celebrate your wedding."

"Of course," said Ximen, "I shall do myself the honor of sending you invitations."

"Far better drink the wedding cup now," Zhu Shinian said. Ying Bojue took the cup, Xie Xida the wine jar, Zhu Shinian held the dish, and the others knelt down. The two young actors also knelt and sang the thirteen melodies known as "Happy Is This Joyful Day." Ximen Qing swallowed three or four cups one after the other.

"If you invite us to take wine with you on the wedding day," Zhu Shinian said, "you must have these two boys at the house." Turning to the young actors, he said, "You must make a point of going that day." Zheng Feng replied, "We will most certainly attend the banquet."

After a while the wine was finished, and they all sat down to dinner. By this time it was dark, and Ximen Qing would stay no longer. He seized the first opportunity, and got up. Ying Bojue would have stopped him, but Xie Xida said, "Let him go, Brother Ying. Don't make him late when he

has such important business to attend to. Our sister-in-law will be angry."
So Ximen managed to escape, and went to Lion Street.

Li Ping'er had taken off her mourning clothes and changed into a dress
of bright colors. The fire and lamps were burning brightly in the hall. She
had prepared the finest of dishes and wine, and had set a single chair in
the place of honor. She asked Ximen Qing to take it. One of the maids
held the wine jar, and Li Ping'er poured out a cup of wine and kowtowed
four times.

"This day the tablet has been burned," she said. "I am most grateful
for the favor which will allow me to assist you at your dressing. The joys
of marriage with you will be joys indeed." She rose, and Ximen Qing rose
in his turn to offer her a cup of wine. Then they both sat down.

"Did Hua the Elder and his wife have anything to say?" Ximen said.

"I took them to my room after the banquet," said Li Ping'er, "and
told them about our marriage. Hua said that, three days after it, he would
tell his wife to come and see me. I gave them ten taels of silver and two
dresses. They both seemed quite satisfied. In fact, they thanked me again
and again."

"If they talk in that strain," Ximen said, "I shall have no objection to
their coming. We have nothing to be ashamed of. But if they begin to talk
any nonsense, I will never forgive them."

"If they dare to make a sound, I will never forgive them either," Li
Ping'er said.

Xiuchun poured the wine into inlaid silver cups and handed them to
her mistress. They drank many cups together. Though love may diminish
with age, wine improves more and more. It is a question of circumstances.
Li Ping'er rejoiced because her wedding day was drawing hear, and was
even more lively than usual.

"You were drinking at Ying's house," she said, smiling, "when Daian
went to ask you to come and see me. Do they know anything about this
matter?"

"Ying Bojue guessed," Ximen Qing said. "He tried to get the boy to
tell them, and they teased me for a long time. The Brothers insisted on
congratulating me. They asked me to give a dinner party and send for
singing girls. They tossed the wine down their throats, cup after cup.
When I thought I had a chance, I tried to get away, but they held me
back. I gave them pleasant words and unpleasant words, and at last they
were compelled to let me go."

"They know a thing or two, all the same," Li Ping'er said. "They let
you come away."

Ximen Qing saw that she was burning with desire, and he was by no means cold himself. He could refrain no longer. They passed fragrant sweetmeats from one to the other, and pressed their cheeks together. Li Ping'er kissed him.

"If you love me truly," she said, "you will make me your wife soon. I feel like a prisoner here. Do not leave me here alone by day or night." They turned again to the delights of love.

CHAPTER 17
The Amorous Doctor

The twentieth day of the fifth month was Major Zhou's birthday. Ximen Qing wrapped up five taels of silver and a pair of handkerchiefs, dressed himself in his best clothes, and, with four boys in waiting, set off to pay his respects, riding on a great white horse. Magistrate Xia, Captain Zhang, and other military gentlemen were there, and music and drama were performed for their entertainment. Daian took Ximen's cloak and went home with the horse. In the afternoon he came back to escort his master home. On his way through West Street, he met old woman Feng and asked where she was going.

"Silversmith Gu," the old woman said, "has finished my lady's headdress. He brought it today and she has sent me to ask your master to go and have a look at it. She wishes to have a talk with him."

"He is at a party at Major Zhou's house," the boy said, "and I am on my way to bring him back. Go home. I'll tell him what you say as soon as I see him."

"Tell him that my lady is expecting him."

Daian went on to Major Zhou's house. The gentlemen were still drinking together. He went to Ximen and said, "As I was bringing the horse for you, I met old woman Feng. She says the silversmith has finished Mistress Hua's headdress, and that her lady would like you to go and see it." This made Ximen anxious to get away, but Major Zhou urged him to stay and pressed him to drink another great cup of wine.

"I am most grateful for all your kindness," Ximen said, "but really I mustn't drink so much. I have a number of things to attend to, and I'm sorry I can't permit myself the pleasure I should wish."

He drank the wine, said farewell to Major Zhou, mounted his horse, and rode off to see Li Ping'er. She welcomed him, and Daian was told to take the horse away and come back the next morning. Li Ping'er bade her maid take the headdress from its box, and show it to Ximen Qing. It was indeed very bright and handsome. They put it away again. Then they arranged that the wedding gifts should be sent on the twenty-fourth day of that month, and the bride should leave for her new home on the fourth of the following month.

Li Ping'er was now perfectly content. She brought wine and drank it with her lover in great delight. She told the maids to prepare the summer bed. The lovers took off their clothes and sat side by side within the silken net on coverlets of the rarest silk, perfumed with orchids and musk. They laughed and played together till the flush of desire mounted to their brows and the passion in their hearts made them tremble. Then they performed the mystery of clouds and rain, and did whatever the wine inspired. Ximen sat on the bed and made Li Ping'er place herself upon the cushions and play the flute for him.

> Not from bamboo or stone, not played on strings,
> This is the song of an instrument that lives,
> That makes the emerald tassels quiver.
> Who shall say whether the mode is *Gong* or *Shang*
> Or *Jiao* or *Zheng?*
> The red lips open wide; the slender fingers
> Play their part daintily.
> Deep in, deep out. Their hearts are wild with passion.
> There are no words to tell the ecstasy that thrills their souls.

Ximen Qing was more than half drunk. "Did Hua Zixu enjoy himself with you like this?" he said.

"His life was one long dream," Li Ping'er said, "and he was still dreaming when he died. I had never any desire to act with him in this way. Day after day he went out and played the fool, and when he returned I would never allow him to come near me. In my father-in-law's lifetime I never shared my husband's room, and I cursed him till the dog's blood went to his head. I was always telling my father-in-law about him and getting him into trouble. No, I should have died of shame if anything of this sort had passed between us. But who could satisfy the cravings of my heart as you do? You act upon me just like a drug. I can think of nothing else by day or night."

They played some time longer, and once again performed the mystery. Yingchun brought in a small square box with all sorts of dainties, and a small golden jar of precious wine. From early evening till the first night watch they drank and sported together. Then, suddenly, they heard a loud knocking at the gate, and sent old woman Feng to see who was there. It was Daian.

"I told you to come for me tomorrow," Ximen Qing said. "Why have you come back tonight?" He told the boy to come in.

Daian, in a great flurry, ran first to the door of the room, but, when he found that his master and Li Ping'er were in bed, he did not venture to go in. Standing outside the lattice, he said, "Sister and Brother-in-law have just come home, and brought all their luggage with them. The Great Lady has sent me to ask you to come home at once."

Ximen wondered what could have brought them at this late hour, and decided to go home. He jumped out of bed, and Li Ping'er helped him to dress. She gave him a cup of hot wine. He mounted his horse, and rode away.

In the hall the lamps and candles were lighted. His daughter Ximen Dajie and her husband were there with trunks, hangings, and furniture, all piled up. This alarmed him. He asked why they had come. His son-in-law, Chen Jingji, kowtowed and said, weeping, "A few days ago, the Censor brought an accusation against our kinsman, Marshal Yang, and his Majesty has given orders that he shall be put in the Southern Prison to await his trial. All his relatives and dependents have been put in the cangue, and banished. Yesterday Yang's people brought word to my father, traveling day and night without resting. My father was much upset and bade my wife and myself bring these things here for you to keep, for the time being. He has gone to the Eastern Capital to try to find out from my aunt what has really happened. When the danger has passed, he will make you a handsome present, and he will remember your kindness so long as he lives."

"Did your father send me any letter?" Ximen asked.

"Here it is," Chen Jingji said. He took a letter from his sleeve and handed it to Ximen, who opened it.

Your kinsman Chen Hong [he read] kowtows and offers this to the most worthy Ximen. The matter of which I have to speak is most urgent. Some time ago the border garrison sent word of a surprise attack, as a result of which the enemy have already invaded Xiongzhou. Wang, the Minister of War, did not send the necessary troops, and the military situation has become disastrous. In consequence of this our kinsman Yang has been accused by the Censor in the most direct terms. His Majesty is extremely angry and has ordered Yang's arrest and his incarceration in the Southern Prison. He is to be tried by three justices. Orders have been given that all those under him and his relatives shall be banished to the frontier.

When this news reached us, we were all much distressed, for we have no possibility of escape. I am sending my son and your honorable daughter, with their belongings, to stay with you for a while. I myself am just about to leave for the Eastern Capital, to visit my brother-in-law, Zhang Shilian, to see if I can hear any news. We hope to return when the matter has been settled.

I shall be eternally grateful to you for your kindness. Even in your district there may be some little difficulty, so I am giving my son five hundred taels, which perhaps you will be good enough to expend on his account. I kowtow to express my gratitude, and so long as I have a tooth in my mouth I will remember your kindness.

Under the lamp, in haste, and without a proper expression of my affection.

Midsummer, the twentieth.

Your most obsequious kinsman Hong.

After reading this letter Ximen Qing was so perturbed that he did not know what to do with himself. He told Yueniang to give his daughter and her husband something to eat, and instructed the maids to make ready three rooms at one side of the hall for them to live in. The trunks and valuables were taken to Yueniang's room. Chen Jingji handed the five hundred taels to his father-in-law. Then Ximen gave one of his servants five taels, and sent him posthaste to the Town Hall to make a copy of the *Imperial Gazette* from the Eastern Capital. This is what it said:

THE PROCURATOR FOR MILITARY AFFAIRS, YUWEN XUZHONG
A Memorial

This is respectfully to implore Your Sacred Justice to punish the traitors in high places, that the morale of the army may be reconstituted and the disturbance at the frontier quelled.

I am not unaware that during every Dynasty there have been frontier attacks. In the Zhou dynasty this happened at Taiyuan; in the Han dynasty at Yinshan; and in the Tang dynasty at Hedong. During the period of the Five Kingdoms these attacks went on unceasingly. Since the great dynasty of Song has been established, our four frontiers have more than once been threatened. It is common knowledge that signs of decay without are an indication of the depredations of worms within. There is an old saying that when the bell booms in the hall, it is a sign of frost; and when the foundations are flooded, we may know that there has been rain. Good fortune and ill fortune alike have their proper causes. This is apparent in every case of sickness. When the heart and stomach suffer from disease, that disease has long been acquiring strength, and the patient's physique has been gradually sapped from within. Then, one day a cold wind blows, and the chill affects every part of his body. Even the physicians Lu and Bian can do nothing for that man and his days are numbered.

The condition of this Empire is precisely that of such an invalid, thin and wasted to a most precarious degree. Your Majesty is the head;

the Ministers are the stomach and heart; and the lesser officers the limbs. Your Majesty sits in sublime state above the Nine Degrees, and, if the officers whose duty it is to carry on the business of the Empire are loyal and dutiful in their less exalted stations, then the natural vigor of the Empire will be sound indeed; the armies will afford protection against attack from without; and the menace of these barbarians can remain unheeded.

Now, of those who are chiefly to be held responsible for the trouble between our soldiers and the barbarians, there is none more infamous than Cai Jing, the Minister of the Palace of Chong Zheng. His courses of action have been both dangerous and unpolitic, and he is, moreover, improvident and without shame. Since he but flatters your Majesty, he is unable to assist you and your ministers to maintain the Sacred Authority and to improve the condition of the people. He is unable to foster virtue and concord among the lower orders, thus promoting peace among the people. He maintains himself by selling profit and position, seeking only for favor and to make his own position secure. He has set up a faction of his own, and harbors evil designs. All this he has done in secret, deceiving your Sacred Majesty. He has done injury to all the well-affected, and faithful men have been alienated. There is in his household none who has not robed himself in red and purple garments of office. Lately, when there broke out disorder in He Huang, he suggested a declaration of war in the east, and lost three districts. The rebellion of Guo Yaoshi was the cause of the Jin country's denouncing its treaty with us; and we lost its friendship.

These are his greatest misdeeds, and they are due entirely to his disloyalty. Wang Fu is greedy for money and misconducts himself, behaving like an actor, but Cai Jing recommended him for appointment. Only a short time after securing this appointment, he led the army to disaster, and then, in the hope of saving his own skin, made a patched-up peace, without having any notion of further consequences. Now that Zhang Da has been defeated at Taiyuan, Wang Fu is terrified and all soldiers in a panic, so that by this time the invaders have already reached the interior, while he has escaped with his wife and children to the South. The guilt of such treasonable conduct deserves a punishment worse than death.

Yang Jian is nothing but a wealthy and ignorant young man, who relies upon the reputation of his ancestors and the favor of those in high official positions. He obtained a command but has succeeded very indifferently in this very vital position on the frontier. Though in reality he is a man of evil character, he poses as a devoted subject. His lack of determination is unrivaled.

These three officers have been in very intimate relations and, both within and without the Court, have been guilty of deceitful conduct. They are, as it were, the disease that has affected your Majesty's heart and stomach. For many years they have been the cause of troubles, and have brought upon us calamities that are sapping away the natural vigor of the body politic and undermining the State. Taxes have increased and the people have migrated in consequence. Bandits and thieves have shown unexampled boldness, and even bear arms against their lawful sovereign. The Imperial Treasury is exhausted and the laws of the Kingdom made of no effect. The crimes that these men have committed outnumber the hairs on their heads.

I accept responsibility for what I have said, but it is my duty to point out that which is in need of amendment, and if, when I perceive traitors meddling in the affairs of State, I fail to convey the fact to Your Majesty, I should be untrue to myself and unworthy the favor of a Lord and Father. I pray therefore that Your Exalted Justice will summon Jing and the others before the officers of the law that due chastisement may be awarded.

The penalties suggested are

> The Extreme Penalty
> The Cangue
> Banishment to a Far Country

Thus may the evil course be stayed and the favor of Heaven restored, while the desires of the common people will be satisfied. If the laws of this Empire are duly enforced, all disorders and troubles will come to an end of themselves. This would be indeed fortunate for our Empire, and for both officials and people.

Here follows the sentence of the Imperial Sage.

Cai Jing shall remain in office for the time being. Wang Fu and Yang Jian shall be sent before the Justices. Let them be tried with due care and the report sent to us.

TAKE HEED, TAKE HEED, AND OBEY.
The Findings of the Court

The traitors Wang Fu and Yang Jian are found guilty of negligence of duty as military commanders. They have permitted the soldiers of other nations to invade the interior, and many have lost their lives in consequence. Our armies have been defeated, many officers killed, and the territory of this Empire lost.

The Law decrees their execution.

Their households, secretaries, and underlings, Dong Sheng, Lu Hu, Yang Sheng, Bang Xuan, Han Zongren, Chen Hong, Huang Yu, Liu Sheng and Zhao Hongdao are all accessories in their crime, and, after wearing the cangue for one month, shall be banished to the frontiers as private soldiers.

When Ximen Qing had read this, his good humor vanished. He fell into a terrible state of agitation. At once he began to get ready gold, silver, and jewels, packed them with the greatest care, and, calling his two servants Laibao and Laiwang to his room, gave them secret instructions. They were to hire several beasts of burden, go to the Eastern Capital, traveling both night and day, and get all the information they could about the matter.

"It will be better for you not to go to Chen's house," Ximen said. "If the news you hear is bad, do what you can with these things, and come back and report to me." He gave them twenty taels of silver. Next morning, before it was light, they rose, hired drivers, and started for the Eastern Capital.

All that night Ximen Qing never closed his eyes. The next morning he ordered Laizhao and Ben the Fourth to cease work upon the garden and send all the workmen away. Every day he had the gate most carefully secured, and no one in his household was allowed to go out except on business of the utmost urgency. Ximen himself paced up and down his room like a centipede on hot earth, brooding over his sorrows and anticipating all manner of trouble. As for his marriage with Li Ping'er, all thoughts of that were banished to regions beyond the clouds. Yueniang saw how greatly his anxieties weighed upon her husband—his appearance showed that clearly—and tried to console him.

"You need not be so distressed over this misfortune of our kinsman Chen," she said. "Hatred and debt always pursue their proper object."

"Oh, woman! what do you know about it?" Ximen cried. "Chen is my kinsman, and so long as my daughter and her husband live with us, they will be a millstone about our necks. Nearly all our neighbors detest us, and as the old proverb says: Though the loom be slow, the shuttle is speedy, and Beat the sheep, and the young donkeys will stir up trouble. If there are any small-minded men among them who take it into their heads to uproot the tree to see what the roots are like, neither you nor I will be safe from them, to say nothing of the rest of the family. Even if we lie low here and keep our door shut, trouble will find its way through the roof."

Ximen Qing remained sadly at home.

Li Ping'er waited for him, one day, two days, but he did not come. She ordered old woman Feng to go to his house. The old woman went twice, but the gate was shut as closely as the iron cover of a well, and, though she waited a very long time, not a sign of life was to be seen and she could not find out what was amiss. The twenty-fourth day was drawing near, and again Li Ping'er told old woman Feng to take the headdresses to Ximen and ask him to come and talk to her. The old woman knocked at the door, but no answer was vouchsafed, so she took her stand beneath the eaves of a house opposite and waited. After a while Daian came out to water the horses, and saw her standing there.

"What are you doing here?" he asked.

"My mistress told me to bring these headdresses and find out why she has had no message from your master. She would like to see him."

"My master has been too busy to go out these last few days," Daian said. "Take the things back, old lady, and as soon as I have finished watering the horses I will tell him what you say."

"Take them in, good little brother," the old woman said, "and tell him that my lady is not at all pleased. I will wait here."

Daian tethered his horses, and went in. Some time later he came out again. "I have told my master, and he has taken the headdresses. He says you must ask your lady to wait a few days longer, and then he will come and see her."

The old woman went home and told her mistress all that had happened. For several days more she waited for him, till the fifth month had nearly come to an end. Morning and evening she longed for him to come, but there was not a word from him. Her dreams were dashed to the ground, her good fortune seemed to have come to an end.

Ximen Qing's absence made Li Ping'er lose her appetite. She became very languid. Night after night she slept alone, tossing about on her bed, the same ideas constantly re-echoing in her mind. Suddenly, she heard a knocking at the door. Ximen Qing had come at last. She opened the door for him and smiled, taking him by the hand to lead him within. She asked why he had so long delayed their marriage, and they spoke to each other the deepest thoughts of their hearts. They spent the whole night in the enjoyment of their love. When day broke and the cock crew, he rose and went away. It was a dream. The woman woke with a start, gave a great cry, and fainted away. Old woman Feng heard and quickly ran in.

"Master Ximen has just gone," Li Ping'er said. "Have you bolted the door?"

"Where is his Lordship?" the old woman said. "Your mind is wandering. Not even his shadow has been here."

From this time onward Li Ping'er dreamed many unseemly things and, night after night, foxes came, taking upon themselves human form, and sucked away her very life. By degrees her face grew pale and thin. She could neither eat nor drink, but lay all day upon her bed, unable to get up. With her permission, old woman Feng asked Doctor Jiang Zhushan of the High Street to come and see her. This Jiang was not more than thirty years of age, not very tall, and a very pleasant fellow. When he came in, Li Ping'er was lying on the bed with the bedclothes over her, her hair about her like a mist of cloud. The doctor could see that she was anything but well. After he had taken tea, a maid gave him a cushion, and he went to the bedside to feel his patient's pulse. This gave him an opportunity to find out how pretty she was.

"Lady," he said, "I think I know what is the matter with you. There is considerable irregularity in the pulse of the liver, which, above the wrist, appears to be too strong. As for that pulse which is peculiar to ladies, it is so weak above the wrist that it cannot be felt, but appears to have betaken itself to the hollow beneath the thumb. This is clearly due to the fact that the masculine and feminine principles are at war within you, thus interfering with the six passions and the seven emotions. So you sometimes feel hot and sometimes cold. Evidently you are suffering from repression of some sort. This produces a state of affairs rather like a fever, though it is not a fever, and makes you feel cold, though you are not cold. During the day it makes you weary, low-spirited, and anxious to lie down all the time; and at night you feel as though your spirit were on the point of departure, and dream that ghosts come and misconduct themselves with you. Unless something is done about it at once, the trouble will take a still more serious turn and you may even die. Oh, it is very serious, very."

"Doctor," Li Ping'er said, "please let me have some of your very best medicine, and when I am better you shall have a handsome fee."

"I will take the utmost care, Madam," Zhushan said, "and, when you take my medicine, you will soon be quite well again." He went away.

Old woman Feng took five taels of silver and went to the doctor's house for the medicine. The same evening Li Ping'er took it, and enjoyed an undisturbed night's rest. Gradually her appetite returned; she was able to get up and dress; and, in a very short time, was completely recovered.

One day she spent three taels, and sent old woman Feng to invite the doctor to dinner. As soon as Jiang Zhushan received the invitation, he dressed and went to the lady's house, for indeed, ever since he had first attended her, he had desired to possess her. Dressed in her most beautiful clothes, Li Ping'er received him in the hall. She made a reverence to him and offered him tea. Then she asked him to go into the inner room, where wine and dishes were set out and there was a delightful fragrance of orchids. Xiuchun came, holding a gilded tray upon which were three taels of white gold. Li Ping'er raised a jade cup high before her, and again made a reverence to the doctor.

"I was very ill," she said, "and I find it hard to express my gratitude to you for giving me such excellent medicine and curing me. Today, doctor, I have hastily prepared a poor cup of wine in token of my thankfulness, and now I beg you to accept it."

"It was no more than the business of a poor scholar like myself," Zhushan said. "It was my duty to come and attend you, and there was no occasion for you to give the matter a second thought." Then he saw the white gold. "I cannot possibly accept this," he said.

"It only represents a fraction of my gratitude," Li Ping'er said, "and is in no way what you deserve. But I hope, doctor, that you will condescend to accept it."

After much show of hesitation Zhushan finally accepted the present. Li Ping'er poured wine for him, and they sat down and drank together. Zhushan looked at her and realized how charming and attractive she was. He began to wonder what words he should choose to make an impression upon her.

"May I ask how old you are?" he said at last.

"I have lived twenty-four ill-spent years," she said.

"But that is a delightful age," Zhushan cried, "yet you live in such seclusion. You seem to be quite comfortably off and everything should be well with you. Why should you suffer so from depression?"

Li Ping'er smiled. "I will tell you, doctor," she said. "Since I lost my husband, things have been very lonely here. I live alone and worry. Does it surprise you that I should be ill?"

"When did your husband die?" the doctor said.

"It was the eleventh month of last year when he died of a fever. About eight months ago now."

"Ah," Zhushan exclaimed, "and whose medicine did he take?"

"Doctor Hu, who lives in the High Street, attended him."

"What? That foxy-mouthed Hu, who used to live in East Street in Eunuch Liu's house? He is not a member of the Royal Society of Medicine. He knows nothing about the pulse. What can have induced you to call him in?"

"The neighbors recommended him, and really I don't think it was his fault that my husband died so young."

"Have you any children?" Zhushan asked.

"None," said Li Ping'er.

"It is most unfortunate that you should have become a widow so young," Zhushan said, "especially since you have no children. Why do you not consider the desirability of another mode of life, something better than living by yourself like this and bringing sickness upon yourself?"

"As a matter of fact," Li Ping'er said, "I became engaged only a little while ago, and we are going to be married almost immediately."

"May I venture to ask to whom you are betrothed?"

"To Master Ximen, who keeps a medicine shop over by the Town Hall."

"Dear, dear!" Zhushan said. "Surely you haven't become engaged to him! I know him quite well. I often go to attend the members of his household when they are ill. He is the man who arranges things behind the scenes at the Town Hall and is mixed up in shady money-lending transactions. He makes quite a business of dealing in women. Apart from his maids, he must have at least half a dozen wives. He is always thrashing them. If one of his women upsets him in the slightest, he sends at once for the go-between and gets rid of her. In fact, he is a captain among wife beaters and a shining light among those who lead women astray.

"I am glad you have told me this, Lady, for otherwise you would have gone blindly to him, like a moth rushing headlong into a flame. If you do this, you will be in a hopeless position and it will be too late to repent. Moreover, only recently, one of his relatives has got into trouble. Ximen has had to hide away in his house and dares not go outside his own door. His new house is only half built, but all the work upon it has been stopped. An order has come from the Eastern Capital that he is to be arrested and his property confiscated to the State. How can you think of marrying him?"

Li Ping'er could think of no answer to make to this. She reflected that all her wealth was stored in Ximen's house, and her foot tapped nervously upon the floor. "Now I know why he has not been to see me though I have invited him more than once," she said to herself. "There is evidently something seriously wrong. Zhushan seems very agreeable and pleasant. If I married a man like him, I should not do so badly, but he may have a wife already for all I know."

"I am most grateful for your advice," she said aloud. "Thank you with all my heart. If you can think of anyone more suitable and will be kind enough to recommend him, I will take your advice."

Zhushan did not let this opportunity slip. "I have no idea what kind of man you would like," he said, "but I may be able to arrange matters for you, if you will speak quite frankly."

"Whether his family is of high or low degree is of no consequence to me," Li Ping'er said, "I should be quite satisfied with a man like you."

At this the doctor was so overjoyed he could hardly contain himself. He threw himself on his knees before her. "I have been long without a mistress in my house," he said, "and I am childless. Lady, if you will take compassion on me and link your destiny with mine, I can wish for nothing better. Even if you give me the work of a menial to do, I shall be eternally grateful."

Li Ping'er laughed and helped him to rise. "Please do not kneel," she said. "How long have you been a widower and under what star were you born? If you really wish to marry me, the Rites insist that you should send a go-between."

Zhushan kneeled down again. "I am now twenty-nine years old, and was born at the hour of the Hare on the twenty-seventh day of the first month. I grieve to say that my wife died last year. I am very poor, and, if you give me your promise, why should we trouble about a go-between?"

"If you cannot afford it," Li Ping'er said, smiling, "I have an old lady named Feng living with me, and we will make her our go-between. As for a betrothal present, don't worry about that. We will select an auspicious day, and you shall marry me and come and live here."

Zhushan bowed. "You are both father and mother to me, and have given me a new lease of life. Obviously our marriage was ordained several generations ago, and it is the greatest piece of luck I have had in any of my three lives."

They drank each other's health, and so this marriage was decided. Zhushan remained till nightfall. When he had gone away, Li Ping'er discussed the matter with old woman Feng.

"Ximen Qing," she said, "is now in a bad way. It is impossible to say whether his luck will ever turn. There is no one to bother about me, and I have been so ill I nearly died. The best thing I can do is to marry this doctor. There doesn't seem to be any reason why I should not."

The next day she sent old woman Feng with a letter to the doctor, saying that the eighteenth day of the sixth month appeared to be an auspicious day. He was to come then and live with her. Three days afterwards she gave Zhushan three hundred taels of silver, so that he could open a couple of rooms and decorate his surgery tastefully. Before this he had always gone on foot to visit his patients. Now he bought a donkey and rode up and down the street.

CHAPTER 18
Ximen Qing Bribes Officers
of the Court

Laibao and Laiwang set out to the Eastern Capital to try to put matters right there. They traveled at early dawn when the rising sun threw a purple haze over their path; they traveled in the evening when its setting cast a rosy light upon the dust. At last they came to their destination and entered the city through the Gate of Eternal Life. They found an inn and rested there. The next day they set out to pick up what news they could in the street. They heard people saying that Wang, the Minister for War, had been tried the previous day, and that the Emperor had ordered his execution in the coming autumn. Of Marshal Yang it was said that his case was not yet done with, for his household and his staff had not all been arrested.

Laibao and Laiwang took the treasures they had brought and went in haste to the palace of the Imperial Tutor. They had been there before and knew the way well, but, when they came to the Arch of Dragon Virtue, they waited for a time to see if they could learn anything more of interest. After a while a man wearing black robes came hurriedly from the palace and went eastwards. Laibao recognized him as one of the household of Marshal Yang. He would have liked to go and ask a few questions, but his master had told him to keep in the background, and he let the man pass. At last they went up to the palace gate, politely greeted the keeper of the gate, and asked if his Eminence was at home.

"His Eminence is still detained at the Court," the keeper of the gate said. "What is your business?"

"We should like to see Master Zhai the Comptroller of the Household," Laibao said. "Will you be good enough to ask him to see us?"

"His Lordship is not at home," the keeper of the gate said.

Laibao realized that the officer was not telling the truth and that something was expected of him. He took a tael of silver from his sleeve and gave it to the gatekeeper.

"Whom did you say you wished to see?" the man said. "His Eminence or his Excellency the Vice Chancellor? Zhai Qian is the great Comptroller of the Household and matters affecting the Imperial Tutor are referred to him. The lesser Comptroller Gao An deals with the Vice Chancellor's affairs. Their duties are quite distinct. The Imperial Tutor himself is not at home, but the Vice Chancellor is. What is the real nature of your business? Shall I ask Master Gao to come and see you? He will serve your purpose just as well."

"We are from Marshal Yang's palace," said Laibao, "and shall be very glad to see anyone."

The officer of the gate hastened into the palace, and, after a short delay, Gao An appeared. Laibao went forward and made a reverence, at the same time offering ten taels of silver. "I was to have come," he said, "with one of Marshal Yang's household. We hoped to see the Imperial Tutor to find out what is happening. But I had to stay for food, and so was late and missed the officer."

"Marshal Yang's courier has just gone," said Gao An, accepting the present, "but if you will wait a moment or two I will take you to see the Vice Chancellor." He took Laibao through the entrance hall, and passing through a side door they came to three large rooms on the north. Here was a green screen, with a scroll upon which the Emperor had written in his own hand 'The Music Chamber of the Vice Chancellor.' Cai Yu, the son of Cai Jing, was, like his father, a favorite at court. He was an Imperial Delegate at the Temple of the Great Monad and held high office at the Xiang He Palace and in the Board of Rites.

Laibao waited till Gao An, who had gone to announce him, came to summon him. Then he went in and knelt down. Cai Yu was dressed in his ordinary attire with a soft hat. He asked Laibao where he had come from.

"I am a servant of Chen Hong's household," said Laibao. "He is a kinsman of Marshal Yang. I was to have come with the Marshal's courier in the hope of seeing his Eminence and obtaining some information. Unfortunately, the courier got here before me." He took a paper from his sleeve and offered it to the minister. Cai Yu read on it the words "Five hundred measures of purest rice," and called Laibao nearer.

"His Eminence," he said, "has avoided becoming mixed up in this matter in view of the fact that his own name was mentioned to the Emperor in the Censor's report. Li, the Minister of the Right, dealt with the case yesterday. But so far as Marshal Yang is concerned, we heard from the Court that his Majesty is inclined to be merciful and will not deal severely with him, though his underlings, no doubt, will still have to be tried and sentenced. You must go and see Li."

Laibao kowtowed. "I am quite unknown at Li's palace," he said. "Pray have pity on me for Marshal Yang's sake."

"Go as far as the Bridge of the Heavenly River," said Cai Yu. "North of it you will see a very high building, and there you must ask for Li Bangyan, Minister of the Right. Everybody knows him. But I will send someone with you."

He called for official paper, set his seal upon it, and instructed Gao An to go with Laibao and introduce him. The two men left the hall together. They called to Laiwang to bring the presents, went down the Street of Dragon Virtue, and, passing the Bridge of the Heavenly River, came to the palace of Li Bangyan.

The minister, who had just returned from the Presence, was still wearing his robes of crimson silk and a girdle around his waist, fastened by a jade clasp. After bidding farewell to some man of rank, he had gone to his hall when the gatekeeper informed him that Vice Chancellor Cai had sent his Comptroller, Gao An, with a message. Gao An was then summoned, and, after he had exchanged a few words with the minister, Laibao and Laiwang were called forward. They went into the hall and knelt down. Gao An stood beside them and handed Cai Yu's note and the list of presents they had brought to the minister. Bangyan looked at it.

"You are connected with Marshal Yang," he said, "and Cai has been good enough to send you to me. How can I possibly accept presents from you? Besides, his Majesty is now quite well disposed to Marshal Yang: he will not be troubled further. But I fear the Censor has been so severe upon some of the Marshal's subordinates that they can hardly escape punishment." He called for the memorial that the Censor had laid before the Emperor the previous day.

"Wang Fu's archivist, Dong Sheng; his chamberlain, Wang Lian; Captain Huang Yu; Yang Jian's servant, the scrivener Lu Hu; Yang Sheng, his administrator; Fu Quan, his comptroller; Han Zongren; Zhao Hongdao; Captain Liu Sheng; Chen Hong; Ximen Qing; and Hu the Fourth. These are all men of utter unworthiness, scoundrelly fellows who, like foxes, invest themselves with the dignity of a tiger. We pray that justice may be done upon them. Some should be banished to the frontier that there may be an end to their deceits. Some should be put to death that the majesty of the law may be vindicated."

When Laibao heard this document read, he was greatly excited. Again and again he prostrated himself before the minister. "In truth, your Excellency," he cried, "I am Ximen Qing's servant. I implore you to be generous and spare my master's life." Gao An knelt down and added his prayers to those of Laibao. The minister allowed his glance to fall upon the gold and silver. There were, in all, five hundred taels, and it seemed to him that such a present might suffice to purchase the name of a single man. Why should he hesitate? He called for writing materials, took up a brush, and changed the name of Ximen Qing to Jia Lian. Then he accepted the presents and dismissed the men, sending a polite message to the Vice Chancellor Cai

Yu. To each of the three domestics he gave five taels of silver. Laibao and Laiwang took their leave of Gao An, returned to their inn, packed their luggage, paid their reckoning, and made haste back to Qinghe.

As soon as they reached home, they hurried to Ximen and told him all that had happened in the Eastern Capital. When he realized how narrowly he had escaped, he shivered as though he had been plunged into a bath of ice-cold water.

"If I had not bestirred myself at the right moment," he said to Yueniang, "I dare not think what would have happened. It would have been too late to do anything now."

A stone comfortably at rest upon the ground could not have felt more solidly established than Ximen Qing now. The gate was opened again; the work upon the garden restarted, and, in a little while, Ximen resumed his saunterings through the streets.

One day, Daian, riding down Lion Street, passed the house of Li Ping'er. He noticed that a large drug shop had been opened there, with a small red counter and a lacquer sign. It seemed to be prospering. When he reached home, he told Ximen Qing, but, as he knew nothing of the marriage between Li Ping'er and Jiang Zhushan, he said she had engaged a manager and opened a medicine shop. Ximen Qing did not pay much heed.

About the middle of the seventh month the autumn winds blew and the dew was cold and chill. Ximen Qing mounted his horse and set out for the main street. There he was hailed by Ying Bojue and Xie Xida, and got off his horse to greet them.

"Where have you been all this time, Brother?" they said. "We have been to your house several times, but the gate was fast shut and we did not venture to call. We could not imagine what was wrong. What have you been doing, keeping within doors like that? Have you married the lady? You never sent for us to take wine with you."

"It is not a very agreeable story," Ximen said, "but a near kinsman of mine, Chen, has been in trouble, and I have had to devote all my energies to getting him out of his difficulties. I had to put off my marriage."

"We knew nothing of any troubles," Bojue said. "Anyhow, now that we have run into you today, we shall not let you go. Come with us to see Wu Yin'er and drink some wine to drown your sorrows." They would take no refusal and rushed Ximen Qing to Wu Yin'er's house.

They drank all day, and not till night was falling and Ximen Qing was half drunk, would they let him go. On his way down East Street he saw old woman Feng hurrying along. "Where are you going?" he called, reining in his horse.

"My lady has sent me to the temple outside the city to burn paper offerings for my late master."

"How is your mistress?" Ximen said tipsily. "I'm going to come and have a chat with her one of these days."

"What is the use of asking after my mistress now?" the old woman said. "The rice was cooked, but you let someone else walk off with the pan."

Ximen was greatly agitated when he heard this. "You don't mean to say she's gone and married someone else?" he cried.

"My lady sent me to show you her wedding headdress, and I called at your house several times, but the gate was closed and I could not see you. I spoke to your boy and told him to ask you not to delay, but you paid no heed. It's no use complaining now if you find your place occupied by someone else."

"Who is the man?" Ximen cried.

Old woman Feng told him the whole story. She explained how Li Ping'er came to send for Jiang Zhushan, and finally married him, and how she gave him three hundred taels to set him up in a medicine shop.

"Terrible! Terrible!" Ximen cried. He flew into a furious rage and stamped his feet. "I wouldn't have minded so much if it had been anybody else, but that miserable little turtle! What use does she think he'll be to her?" He whipped up his horse and galloped home.

When he passed through the inner door, Wu Yueniang, Meng Yulou, Pan Jinlian, and Ximen Dajie were skipping in the courtyard. When Ximen came, they withdrew to the inner court. But Jinlian leaned against a pillar and began to tie her shoelaces.

"You little strumpet," Ximen cried, "have you nothing better to do than fool about like this?"

He kicked her twice and then went to the inner court, but, instead of going to change in Yueniang's room, he went to his own study in the wing and demanded bedclothes so that he could pass the night there. With unrelenting fury he beat the maids and cursed the boys, till all the women gathered together in terror, wondering what could be amiss. Yueniang blamed Jinlian. She said, "If you had got out of his way when you saw him in such a rage, all would have been well. Instead, you stayed there in front of him, laughing and playing with your shoelaces, and he cursed us like a host of grasshoppers, yes, and caterpillars too."

"It would not have mattered so much," Yulou said, "if he had only cursed us, but to abuse the Great Lady and call her a strumpet! Really, he is a most unmannerly fellow!"

"It was me he picked on," Jinlian cried. "You were all there, but I was the one to suffer. Why should I be selected to receive his special favors?"

This made Yueniang angry. "Why didn't you ask him to kick me?" she said. "You were treated neither worse nor better than anybody else. You don't know your place."

Jinlian saw that Yueniang was angry and she changed her tune. "Oh, Sister," she said, "I didn't mean that. He doesn't know what is the matter with him and he thought he would vent his spite on me. He set up a tremendous outcry and swore he would bring me to a doleful end."

"Nobody told you to make fun of him," Yueniang said. "He would have been all right if you had not given him cause to beat you."

"Great Sister," Yulou said, "let us send for the boy and find out where he was drinking this afternoon. He was in a perfectly good temper when he went out this morning. What has made him come back like this?"

Daian was summoned.

"You wicked young scoundrel," Yueniang said to him, "if you don't tell me the truth you shall have a thrashing. Ping'an too. You shall both have ten strokes of the rod."

"You need not beat me," Daian cried, "I will tell all there is to tell. Father spent the day drinking with Uncle Ying at Wu Yin'er's house. Afterwards, as he was going down East Street, he met old woman Feng and she told him that Mistress Hua had not waited, but had married the Doctor Jiang who used to live in the High Street. Father was fearfully angry, even in the street."

"So, just because that shameless hussy chooses another man, he must come home and take it out on us!" Yueniang said.

"That was not all," Daian said. "Mistress Hua has taken him to live with her and set him up in a fine medicine shop. I told Father so once before, but he wouldn't listen to me."

"It is only a few months ago since her husband died," Yulou said, "and she was not out of mourning. It is most unseemly."

"In these days," said Yueniang, "nobody stops to think whether things are unseemly or not. If she took a man before she was out of mourning, she was not the first one. Strumpets like her will drink or sleep with any man. How can one expect them to consider the virtuous estate of widowhood?"

This was a blow at Yulou and Jinlian. Both had married before their widowhood was over. Yueniang's remark made them feel so uncomfortable that they went to their own rooms and did not wait to hear what she would say next.

Ximen Qing spent the night in his study. The next day he sent his son-in-law, Chen Jingji, to the garden to superintend the work there and keep the accounts with Ben the Fourth. Laizhao, whose place he took, was given charge of the gate. Ximen's daughter, Ximen Dajie, took her meals in the inner court with Yueniang and the others, and only went to the front court to sleep. From morning till night Jingji labored in the garden. He never went into the other parts of the house unless he was invited, and, as all his meals were taken to him by the boys, the ladies of Ximen's household never set eyes on him.

One day, when Ximen Qing was at a farewell party for Captain He, Yueniang remembered that Jingji had to work very hard and that his services were poorly requited.

"If I do anything about it," she said to Yulou and Li Jiao'er, "his Lordship will say I meddle in things that don't concern me, but really I can't allow this sort of thing to go on. The boy is one of ourselves. He rises early and goes to bed late every single day, and all on our account. Nobody lifts a finger to make things more comfortable for him."

"Lady," Yulou said, "you are the mistress of the house, and if you do nothing, nobody else can."

Yueniang told a boy to lay a table for Jingji and ask him to join them. The young man at once handed over his work to Ben the Fourth and hurried to pay his respects to Yueniang. He made reverence to her and sat down. Xiaoyu brought tea and the table with refreshments was carried in.

"You work terribly hard," Yueniang said. "I should have asked you before to come and spend a few moments' leisure with us, but there has never been an opportunity. However, your father is away today and I am free. This is a poor sign of our appreciation of all you do for us."

"Mother," Jingji said, "you are too good to me. I have done nothing to deserve this."

They drank together, and Yueniang told a maid to invite his wife to come and join them. The maid told them that she was washing her hands and would be with them in a moment. Then they heard the clatter of dominoes in the next room, and Jingji asked who was playing there.

"It is your wife," Yueniang said, "playing with Yuxiao."

"She is most ill-mannered, not to come the moment you invite her."

Soon, however, she came, sat down, and drank with them. Yueniang asked her whether Jingji knew how to play. "He knows the difference between 'pleasant scent' and 'evil odor,'" Ximen Dajie said.

Yueniang believed that Jingji was all that could be desired as a son-in-law. She did not know that never was a rascal so well versed in poetry, backgammon, songs, and every other form of low amusement. "If you know how to play," she said, "why should we not go and take a hand?"

"Mother," Jingji said, "pray go and play with your daughter. It would be presumption on my part."

"Not at all," Yueniang said, "you are a close kinsman. Why shouldn't you join us?"

In the next room Yulou was playing, sitting on the bed on which a crimson coverlet had been laid. She rose when they came in and would have retired. "Our brother is no stranger," Yueniang said. "You must treat him as one of ourselves. This is the Third Lady," she said to Jingji.

The young man bowed, and Yulou returned his greeting. Then the three ladies began to play while Jingji stood and looked on. When Ximen Dajie was beaten, her husband took her place.

Jinlian came in. She was wearing a flower in her hair. "I wondered who was here," she said, laughing. "I see it is Brother Chen."

Chen Jingji turned quickly. When he saw Jinlian, his breath seemed to stop. It was as though, after five hundred years of separation, he met his loved one again.

"This is the Fifth Lady," Yueniang said, "you need only exchange simple greetings."

Chen Jingji rose to his feet and bowed low. Jinlian returned his greeting. Then Yueniang invited her to come and see how an old crow could be beaten by a greenhorn. Jinlian, with one hand resting on the bed and the other fluttering her fan, advised Yueniang how to set out her pieces, and they were all playing with great excitement when Daian came and told them that Ximen Qing had returned. Yueniang told Xiaoyu to take Jingji away by the corner door.

When Ximen had dismounted, he went to the outer court to see how the work in the garden was progressing. Then he went to Jinlian's room. She welcomed him and took his clothes. "You are back very early today," she said.

"Yes," said Ximen, "Captain He has just been promoted, and all the officials went out beyond the city gates to say good-bye to him. I was asked to join them, and I couldn't very well refuse."

Jinlian asked if he would like to drink, and told the maid to bring wine. Soon the table was laid. They sat together and enjoyed their food.

"We shall finish the work in the garden tomorrow," Ximen said; "I suppose some of our friends will be coming with presents and scrolls. We shall have to hire some extra cooks and have a banquet."

They talked for a while; then it began to grow dark. Chunmei went to her own room, and Ximen Qing and Jinlian went to bed. He had been up early and was very tired. A few cups of wine made him very sleepy. He was soon fast asleep and snoring like thunder.

It was the twentieth day of the seventh month, and the weather was very sultry. Jinlian could not sleep, the noisy buzzing of mosquitoes in the net annoyed her. Without putting on any clothes, she got up and with a candle in her hand searched all around the bed curtains for mosquitoes, burning each one in the flame as she caught them. Then she looked around. Ximen Qing was fast asleep. She shook him, but he would not wake. His weapon, with the clasp still upon it, seemed limp and heavy. The sight of it set her naughty mind in a whirl. She put down the candlestick and fondled it with her exquisite hands. After doing this for a short time, she bent her head and kissed it. Ximen woke and stormed at her. "You funny little strumpet. Your darling is sleepy, and you are a terrible nuisance." But he got up. Sitting on the bed, he told her to go on with what she was doing. He watched her, and found the sight particularly attractive. Here is a poem about the mosquito:

> I love that dainty body, its wondrous lightness,
> The beauty and softness of that tender waist.
> Music and song go where it goes.
> When evening comes, before the crimson doors are shut
> It steals within and seeks the silken net,
> Settles so lovingly on the fragrant flesh
> And lightly falls upon the jade-like form.
> Where those lips touch, there stays a rosy flush.
> It sings a hundred songs in people's ears
> Allowing none to sleep though it be midnight.

Jinlian continued for a long time, then Ximen Qing thought of a new plan. He called Chunmei to heat some wine and come and stand beside the bed to hold the wine jar. He set the candlestick beside the bed and told Jinlian to go down on all fours before him. When he saw her like this, he was quickly excited again, and gave himself once more to the delights of love, drinking wine as he did so.

"What a naughty fellow you are," Jinlian cried. "Where did you learn to carry on like this? A fine thing, to let the maid stand by and watch us in such unseemly circumstances."

"Li Ping'er and I used to do it," Ximen said. "She always told Yingchun to stand beside us and hold the wine jar. I think it is most amusing."

"I can't tell you what I think of you," Jinlian said. "And what do I care for that woman? Why do you bring her into it? I had to wait for what I wanted, but she couldn't wait; she had to go and find another man. I haven't forgotten how, when the three of us were skipping in the courtyard, you came home drunk. You vented your spite on me, kicked me, and got me into trouble with the others. I must be one of those who are fated to be ill-used."

"With whom did you have trouble?" Ximen asked.

"When you had gone into the house, she who lives in the upper room made a fine to-do. She accused me of deliberately raising my voice against hers and swore I did not know my place. She doesn't want anyone to like me."

"That day," Ximen said, "Brother Ying dragged me to the Wu Yin'er's house to drink. On the way back I met old woman Feng, and she told me what had happened. It was that which made me so furious. If she had married anybody else, I should not have cared, but Doctor Jiang, the wretched little turtle! What could she be thinking about to marry a man like that, take him to live with her, and give him the money to open a medicine shop right in front of me? And the business seems to be doing well!"

"It's all very well talking like that now," Jinlian said, "but what did I tell you? The one who is the first to cook the rice is always the first to eat it. You wouldn't listen to me; you went and asked what the Great Lady thought about it. I tell you: those who must always take the opinion of somebody else will never get what they want. You went the wrong way about things, and nobody is to blame but yourself."

Ximen Qing flew into a temper. "Let her say what she likes, the strumpet! I will never speak to her again."

Thenceforth Yueniang and Ximen Qing would have no dealings with each other. When they met, they would not speak. Yueniang paid no heed to Ximen's goings and comings, and never asked any questions. If he went to her rooms for anything, she told her maid to attend to him, but would do nothing for him herself. Their hearts were cold to one another.

After this quarrel Jinlian knew that she could do what she liked with her husband and she became more arrogant than ever. She flaunted herself about and made herself as pretty as she could, all to secure Ximen's favor and attentions for herself. When she met Chen Jingji, she was so impressed by that young man's smartness and liveliness that the idea of seducing him came into her head, but she was too afraid of Ximen Qing to attempt it. But when Ximen was out, she sent a maid to invite the young man to take tea in her room and they played chess together.

At last the work in the garden was completed, and relatives and friends came to present red scrolls of congratulation, some bringing boxes of fruits also. Ximen gave all the workmen food and money, and received his guests in the hall, where the celebrations were kept up until noon, when the party broke up. Ximen had been up so early that he decided to go to the inner court for a rest, and Jingji went to see Jinlian and ask her for a cup of tea. He found her sitting on her bed, playing the lute.

"In the outer court," she said, "they have been house warming and drinking wine. How is it that you have had nothing, but must come to me for tea?"

"To tell you the simple truth," Jingji said, "I was up before dawn and have been busy ever since. I never had a moment for food."

"Where is your father?" Jinlian said. Jingji told her that Ximen was resting in the inner court. "Well," she said, "since I see you have had nothing to eat, Chunmei must pick out some of my own pastries for you."

The young man sat on her bed, and a small table with four plates of light refreshments was brought in for him. As he began to eat them, he saw that Jinlian had been playing the lute, and asked her whether she would not sing for him. She laughed. "My dear good Brother," she said, "I don't belong to you. Why should I sing for you? When Father gets up, I shall tell him what you have asked."

Jingji smiled. He knelt before her and said, "Please, Mother, forgive your son. I will never offend again." Jinlian laughed at him.

Ever afterwards they were on terms of intimacy, taking tea and meals together almost every day. Jingji used to go to her room to joke with her, and they sat close together without the slightest scruple. All this time Yueniang treated the young man as though he had been her own son, never dreaming how utterly faithless he was.

CHAPTER 19
Ximen Qing's Vengeance

After many months of labor the work in Ximen Qing's garden was com-pleted. The place seemed quite new. So many people came to offer congratulations that the feasting lasted for several days. One day, about the beginning of the eighth month, Xia, the magistrate of the military court, celebrated his birthday in his new house. He engaged four singing girls, a band of musicians, and a troop of actors. Ximen Qing was invited, and set off early in the morning. At home Wu Yueniang prepared a feast for the ladies of the household, and they all went to the garden to admire its arrangement. There were flowers and trees, and buildings specially placed so that they afforded a beautiful view, and everything was delightful.

There was a gatehouse, fifteen feet high and broad around, with a belvedere in each of the four directions. There was an artificial mound and a lake beside it. Bamboos, with their light green foliage, stood out against the darker green of the pines. Summerhouses, high and flat-roofed, contrasted with buildings that, though imposing, were not so high. There was provision for each of the seasons. In the spring could be seen the swallows flitting through the halls, and peach blossoms striving to outdo the apricots in beauty. In summer, from the arbors, you could look down upon the running rivulets, and delight in the gay colors of the artemisia. In autumn, from the Hall of the Humming Bird, one might gaze upon masses of golden chrysanthemums. In winter there was the Tower of Hidden Spring, where the white plum blossom held out its dainty petals.

The narrow paths were carpeted with lovely flowers, and sweet-smelling trees drooped their branches over the carven doors. There were willow trees sporting in the wind, touching, as it were, their eyebrows; and cherries, like raindrops, peeping shyly out.

Before the hall, where the swallows played, the lantern flowers were breaking into blossom; behind the Tower of Hidden Spring white apricots were just coming out. The marigold was opening beside the mound, and the bamboo shoots were springing up beside the balustrade.

The purple swallows flew daintily between the hangings; the twittering orioles flashed amid the green shadows.

There were windows shaped like the moon, and caverns of snow; halls of the wind, and halls of the waters. There were arbors of white roses and ramblers intertwined, and the thousand-leaved peach stood face to face with the willow of the Three Springs. The pine trees formed a wall, and the bamboos a passage. There were winding streams and square ponds. Palms stood gloriously upon the steps, with sunflowers making the round after the sun. Fishes swimming among the reeds suddenly jumped, and the powdered butterflies danced in couples among the flowers.

The white peony blossomed like the face of Buddha, and lichee covered the branches like the head of the King of the Demons.

Yueniang led the others into the garden. They held each other's hands, walked on the beautiful paths, and sat on the soft fragrant moss. One leaned against an arbor and admired the view, then tossed a red cherry at the goldfish. Another rested on the balustrade and laughingly frightened the butterflies with her silken kerchief. Yueniang herself went to the highest point, called the Hall above the Clouds, and there played chess with Li Jiao'er and Meng Yulou. The others stood at the flower summerhouse and looked down upon the white roses, the peonies, the ramblers, and the other flowers. They looked at the bamboos that bore the cold like supermen, and the proud pine trees boldly contemptuous of the snow. Throughout the four seasons the flowers never faded, and at the eight festivals it always seemed like spring. There was too much to appreciate in a single visit: it needed to be enjoyed slowly.

Wine was brought. Yueniang took the place of honor, Li Jiao'er sat opposite and the other ladies on either side. "I forgot to invite our brother," Yueniang said, and sent Xiaoyu to the outer court to invite Chen Jingji to join them. He came, dressed in a light blue hat, a long purple gown, and black boots with white soles. When he had greeted them, he sat beside his wife. After the wine had been passed around, Yueniang again played chess with her stepdaughter and Li Jiao'er. Sun Xue'e and Meng Yulou went up to admire the view, and Pan Jinlian, alone with her white silk fan, played with the butterflies near the lake by the mound. Jingji crept up behind her quietly.

"Fifth Mother," he said suddenly, "you don't know how to catch butterflies. Let me catch one for you. They go up and down. They are not quite sure what they want, and wander this way and that."

Jinlian turned and looked at him. "You must wish to die before your time, you rogue," she said. "It is clear your life means nothing to you." Jingji laughed, went closer to her, then took her in his arms and kissed her. She pushed him away and the young man stumbled. At that moment, Yueniang saw them from the steps. "Fifth Sister," she called, "I have something to tell you. Come here!" Jinlian left Jingji and went up the steps.

When Jinlian had left him, Jingji went sadly to his own room, and wrote a poem to express his melancholy.

> I saw her with a flower in her hair
> With lips uncarmined though they seemed so red.
> Once before, I met her, then today again
> And thought she loved me, though I could not see the love.
> She may give herself to me, but it is not likely
> She may reject me, but I do not think she will.
> When can we meet? When is the time for meeting?
> I think of her although I cannot see her
> And when I've seen her, think of her again.

Ximen Qing, after Magistrate Xia's party, passed through South Lane. He went so often about the streets and lanes, that he knew all the ne'er-do-wells who haunted them. To two of them he often gave money—Lu Hua, otherwise known as Viper in the Grass, and Zhang Sheng, who was nicknamed Rat Scurry down the Street. They were both scoundrels who spent all their time in chicken stealing and mean thieveries of every kind. Today, they were gambling as Ximen Qing passed. Reining in his horse, he called to them. They ran to him at once, made a reverence, and asked where he had been.

"It is Magistrate Xia's birthday," Ximen said, "and he invited me to take wine with him. There is a little matter I should like you to attend to for me. Do you mind?"

"Your Lordship," they said, "you need not ask. We have received too many kindnesses at your hands. If there is anything we can do for you, even if it means going through fire and water, we will do it."

"Very well," Ximen said, "come and see me tomorrow and I will tell you what it is."

"Why wait till tomorrow?" they said; "please tell us now."

Ximen Qing lowered his voice and told them the story of Jiang Zhushan and Li Ping'er. "I want you to avenge my dishonor," he said, and pulling up his clothes, took about five taels of silver from his purse. "This will buy you some wine. If you do the business to my satisfaction, there shall be more for you."

Lu Hua would not take the money. "You have been so good to us," he said. "When you mentioned our doing something for you, I imagined you wished us to go to the Eastern Sea and take the horns from the Green Dragon, or to the Western Mountains, to draw the Magic Tiger's teeth— something really difficult. But there is nothing cannot accept your money for a job like this."

"If you will not take my money," Ximen said, "I sh it for me." He handed the money to Daian, and made i

Zhang Sheng stopped him. "Lu Hua," he said to his compa. don't understand his Lordship. If we refuse to take his money it will loo. as though we decline to do anything for him." They took the silver and made a profound reverence. "Your Lordship," they said, "wait for us. In less than a couple of days, we promise we'll bring a smile to your face." Zhang Sheng added that he hoped Ximen Qing would recommend them to Xia, and this he promised to do, a promise that he later redeemed.

When Ximen Qing reached home, the sun had set. Yueniang and the others went to the inner court, but Jinlian stayed in the summerhouse and watched the servants clear away the remains of the feast. Ximen went straight to the garden, and found her there.

"What have you been doing while I've been away?" he said.

Jinlian laughed. "The Great Lady brought us to see the garden," she said. "We did not expect you back so early."

Ximen Qing explained. "Xia was good enough to engage four singing girls, though there were only five guests. I remembered what a long way I had to come, and came back early."

Jinlian took his long gown. "If you have had no wine," she said, "I will order some for you." Ximen Qing told Chunmei to clear everything away, except some dessert, and a jar of grape wine.

He sat down on a chair, and gazed at Jinlian admiringly. She was wearing an incense-colored silken gown that opened down the middle, with varicolored ribbons at the sleeves. Below was a shimmering embroidered skirt, and beneath the skirt, red shoes with white high heels. On her head she wore a net of silvery silk, a gold inlaid comb, a plum-blossom pin, and many pretty ornaments. Her lips seemed redder, and her face whiter than ever before. Ximen was seized with sudden desire for her, took her hands, pulled her to him, and embraced her. When Chunmei brought the wine, they drank it together, and kissed more passionately still. Then Jinlian pulled up her skirts, and sat upon his knee. She passed wine from her own mouth to his, and picking a fresh lotus seed with her dainty fingers, offered it to him. But Ximen refused it; he said it was too bitter.

"My son," Jinlian said, laughing, "if you refuse anything your mother offers you, you are tempting the fates." But instead of the lotus seed, she gave him a walnut. Then Ximen wished to play with her bosom, and opening her silken gown, she uncovered her exquisite, flawless, fragrant breasts. He fondled them and kissed them, delighting in their firmness.

.ey sat together, and enjoyed each other's company. Ximen Qing was
y happy.

"I have something to tell you that will make you laugh," he said. "You
remember that Doctor Jiang set up a medicine shop. When I've done with
him, he'll be setting up a vegetable shop on his face." Jinlian asked him
what he meant, and he told her of the arrangement he had made with Lu
and Zhang.

"If you do that," said Jinlian, "you will arouse a good deal of ill feeling. Is it the Doctor Jiang who sometimes comes to see us when we are
ill? I have always thought him a most modest man. He always looks at the
ground when he examines us. You ought to sympathize with him, instead
of treating him like this."

"You don't understand his tricks," Ximen said. "You say he looks down,
but, don't you see, he looks down so that he can look at your feet?"

"What a nasty-minded fellow you are!" Jinlian said. "I don't believe he
ever thinks of women's feet. He is an educated man, and wouldn't dream
of such a thing."

"If you judge him by appearance, you make a mistake. He pretends to
be decorous, but he's a very dangerous fellow at heart."

They chattered and joked for a long time. Then the wine was finished,
and the table cleared, and they went to bed.

It was now two months since Li Ping'er had married the doctor. In the
early days of their marriage, he was very anxious to satisfy his wife. He
prepared love potions, bought some interesting pictures and other devices
for stimulating love, and did, in fact, everything he could to make the lady
happy. But Ximen Qing had been a more strenuous lover, and Jiang failed
to come up to her expectations. She came more and more to hate the sight
of him. She took the instruments of love and smashed them with a stone.
"There is no strength in your loins," she cried. "You are no better than an
eel. What is the use of buying things like these? You have deceived me. I
thought you a piece of good meat, but I find you are only good to look at,
not to eat. You are like a waxen spearhead, a dead turtle."

Several times she sent him away in the middle of the night, and he
had to go to the shop to sleep. She could only think of Ximen Qing, and
would not allow the doctor to enter her room. Every day she went most
carefully through his accounts.

It was on one such day as this, when Doctor Jiang had gone to sit
down in his shop, that two men appeared. They were both tipsy, swaying
from side to side, and their eyes stared wildly. They found chairs, and sat
down. "Have you any dog-yellow in your shop?" they said.

Zhushan laughed, and asked them not to make fun of him. "I have ox-yellow, but no dog-yellow," he said.

"Well, if you have no dog-yellow, show me some ice ashes."

"The drug shops," said the doctor, "sell ice pieces that come from Persia over the Northern Sea, but no ice ashes."

"Don't ask him for such things," the other man said. "The shop has only been open for a few days, how can you expect him to have such things? We have more important business to talk about."

"Brother Jiang," he continued, "do not pretend not to know what you're about. Three years ago, when your wife died, you borrowed thirty taels of silver from Brother Lu. That and the interest now make quite a lot of money. We have come to call for it. It might have seemed discourteous if we had asked you for it as soon as we came into the shop, and you might have thought we had no consideration for you, seeing that you have just married and opened this shop. So we had our little joke. We suppose you will admit your indebtedness. But if you don't, you will have to pay just the same."

The doctor was startled. "I've never borrowed any money from you," he said.

"If you had not, we shouldn't be asking you to pay. Don't forget the old saying: If there is no crack in the egg, the flies can't get in. It's no use saying that."

"But I do not even know your honorable names," the doctor said, "and I have certainly never had the honor of your acquaintance. Why do you ask me for this money?"

"Brother Jiang, you are taking up the wrong attitude. Remember the old saying that those in authority are never poor, and men who don't pay their debts are never rich. Just think how poor you used to be. You used to go around ringing a bell and selling your plasters, when, fortunately for you, you met brother Lu, and he befriended you. You would not be where you are today, if it had not been for him."

"I am Lu Hua," the other man said. "In such and such a year you borrowed thirty taels from me and spent the money on your wife's funeral. Now you owe me forty-eight taels, counting the interest, and I want the money."

"I never had the money," cried the doctor excitedly. "If you say I did, let me see the contract."

"I was the witness," Zhang Sheng said. He took a document from his sleeve and handed it to the doctor.

Zhushan's face became the color of wax. "You meat fit for the gallows! You low hounds!" he cried. "Whence have you sprung to cheat me?"

Lu Hua's fist flew over the counter into the doctor's face and the doctor's nose was twisted to one side. They pulled all the medicines from the shelves and threw them into the street.

"Robbers," Zhushan wailed, "how dare you steal my things?" He called his boy to help him, but Lu Hua cuffed the boy away, and he dared not come again.

Zhang Sheng pulled the doctor over the counter, and rescued him from Lu Hua. "Brother Lu," he said, "he has been very slow to repay this debt, but we might give him a few more days. What do you say, Brother Jiang?" he added, turning to the doctor.

"I never borrowed his money," Zhushan cried, "and if I did, why can't he talk about the matter quietly? Why does he behave like a savage?"

"Brother Jiang," Zhang Sheng said, "you talk as if you had been eating something bitter, and still had the taste in your mouth. If you had behaved reasonably, I would have asked Brother Lu to forgive you some of the interest, and you might have paid him in two or three installments. That would have been the proper method of procedure. Why did you refuse to admit the debt, and so rudely too? Did you really think that he would not ask for his money?"

"My temper got the better of me," Zhushan said. "I will go with him before the judge, and then we shall find out who had his money."

"Dear, dear!" said Zhang Sheng, "you must be drunk again."

Lu Hua suddenly let fly his fist; the doctor stretched his length on the ground and indeed nearly fell into the gutter. His hair was disarranged and his hat covered with dirt. "Oh, blue skies and glorious sun!" he cried. At that moment, the policeman arrived, and took them all into custody.

Li Ping'er, hearing the noise, went to the lattice and, peeping through, saw the policeman taking her husband away. This alarmed her, and she told old woman Feng to take down the shop signs. Meanwhile all the things in the street had been stolen. She hastily bolted the door and sat down in her own room.

Ximen Qing very soon learned what had happened. Early the next day he sent a man to the court with a message to his friend Xia, the magistrate. Xia took his place in the hall, and ordered the doctor and the accusers to be brought before him. After reading the accusation he questioned Zhushan. "You are Jiang," he said; "why did you not pay Lu Hua the money you owed, instead of striking him? A most improper proceeding!"

"I do not even know him," Zhushan said. "Certainly I never borrowed any money from him. I tried to explain, but he would not listen. He beat me and kicked me and stole my belongings."

The magistrate called Lu Hua. "What have you to say about it?" he asked.

"Indeed he did." Lu Hua said. "He spent this money on his wife's funeral. For three years he has kept putting me off. I heard he had married again and had a fine shop, so I went and asked for my money. He insulted me for all he was worth, and now he says I stole his things. Here is the contract, and Zhang Sheng is the witness. I beg your Worship to investigate the matter thoroughly." He brought out the document and handed it to the magistrate.

> "Jiang Wenhui, doctor of this town, writes this [it said]. His wife has died, and he has no money to pay for the funeral, therefore he engages, with Zhang Sheng as surety, to borrow thirty taels of pure silver from Lu Hua. The interest shall be three *fen* monthly. He will spend this money, and repay the thirty taels next year with the interest without any deduction. In witness whereof, this document is drawn up."

When the magistrate had read the paper, he banged his fist upon the table angrily. "Here," he cried, "are both the document and the surety. Do you think you can hoodwink me? I see you are a smooth-spoken rascal, but obviously you won't pay your debts." He told the attendants to pick out a strong bamboo and beat Jiang Zhushan with all their might. Three or four of them threw him to the ground and beat him severely thirty times, till his skin was torn and the blood flowed. Then the magistrate told two constables to take a white warrant board, and escort Zhushan to his house, there to collect the thirty taels for Lu Hua. If the money was not forthcoming, he was to be taken to prison.

The doctor, dragging his aching limbs, reached home, weeping. He begged Li Ping'er to give him the money for Lu Hua. She spat in his face and cursed him. "You shameless turtle," she cried, "have you ever given me any money that I should give some to you? I've known for a long time, you turtle, that you're nothing but a braggart and a sponger. Why, I must have been blind to marry a turtle like you, good to look at and useless for anything else."

The constables, who were standing outside, heard this squabbling and became more urgent. "If Jiang has no money," they said, "there is no use wasting time. We must get back to the court at once and let his Worship know." Zhushan went out to appease them and returned again to plead with Li Ping'er.

"Treat this matter in the spirit of charity," he begged, kneeling on the ground before her, "and let it be as an offering of thirty taels to the Holy Ones of the Four Mountains and the Five Shrines. If you will not, I must go back to the court, and how can I bear more punishment on my poor torn legs? It would mean my death."

Li Ping'er could hold out no longer, and gave him the thirty taels. He gave the money to Lu Hua in the presence of the constables. The contract was torn up and the matter ended.

After Lu Hua and Zhang Sheng had got the money they went straight to Ximen Qing. He offered them wine and food in the arbor, and they told him the whole story. He was delighted. "You have avenged me; that is all I want," he said, and when Lu Hua offered him the thirty taels, he refused them. "Keep the money to buy a jar of wine," he said, "and what I gave you too. One of these days I may want something more of you." They thanked him and went away to gamble.

After Jiang Zhushan had paid the money he returned, but Li Ping'er would have no more of him.

"I regard those thirty taels as money paid to rid me of a plague. Now you must go somewhere else, for if you stay here any longer, all I have in the house will not suffice to pay your debts."

The doctor wept bitterly. His legs pained him and he had nowhere to go, but he was obliged to find other quarters. Everything that Li Ping'er had given him he had to leave behind, and he hired a cart to take away his old medicine box and his mortar.

When he had gone, Li Ping'er told old woman Feng to throw a basin of water after him. "I am so glad that this plague is out of my sight," she said. She longed for Ximen Qing all the time, and when she heard that his difficulties were over, she was sorrier than ever. She languished so that she did not trouble about her tea or her food and left her eyebrows unpainted. She leaned upon the door and gazed till her eyes seemed to start out of her head, but nobody came.

One day Daian, riding past the house, saw that the gate was shut and the medicine shop closed. Everything seemed quiet. He went home and told Ximen Qing.

"I imagine," Ximen said, "that the little turtle has had such a good drubbing that he has to keep to his room. He won't be able to go out and attend to his business for a long time." He forgot all about the matter.

The fifteenth day of the eighth month was Yueniang's birthday, and many ladies came and were entertained in the great hall. Ximen Qing, who was still not on speaking terms with his wife, went to the house where Li Guijie lived, telling Daian to take back his horse and come again in the evening. He invited Ying Bojue and Xie Xida to play backgammon with him. Li Guiqing was there, and the two sisters together served the wine. After a while they all went to the courtyard to play Arrows through the Jar. In the afternoon Daian came back with Ximen Qing's horse, and found his master washing his hands in the back court. Ximen asked the lad what had happened at home during his absence. "Nothing particular," Daian said. "Most of the ladies have gone, and the Great Lady is in the inner court with Aunt Wu. Mistress Hua sent old woman Feng with a birthday present. There were four plates of fruits, two long-life noodles, a roll of silk, and a pair of shoes. Mother gave old woman Feng a *qian*. She said you were not at home, and did not send an invitation to Mistress Hua."

Ximen Qing saw that the boy's face was flushed. "Where have you been drinking?" he asked.

"Mistress Hua," said the boy, "told old woman Feng to ask me to go and see her. It was she who gave me the wine. I told her that I never drink, but she pressed me to drink a cup or two. That's what has made my face red. She is very sorry now for what has happened, and cried for a long time. I told you before, but you wouldn't believe me. After Doctor Jiang was at the court, the lady would have no more to do with him. She is very, very sorry and still wishes to marry you. She is much thinner than she was. She told me I must ask you to go and see her, and if you can, please tell me, because she is waiting to hear what you say."

"The rascally whore!" Ximen cried. "She has a man already. Why can't she leave me alone? If you are telling the truth, say I'm too busy to go. Say she need not send presents, just let her choose an auspicious day and I'll take the strumpet home."

Daian said that, as Li Ping'er was waiting for an answer, he would leave Ping'an and Huatong to go home with his master. "Go along, then," said Ximen, "it is all perfectly simple."

Daian went to the house in Lion Street, and told Li Ping'er what his master had said. She was delighted. "My good brother," she said, "I am grateful to you for what you have done for me." She went herself to the kitchen to cook something for the boy. "I have not enough boys here," she said, "and you must come one of these days to help me to get my things removed."

The next day she hired five or six porters to carry her belongings, and they were busy for four or five days. Ximen Qing said nothing to Yueniang, but simply gave orders that the things were to be put in the new house. On the twentieth day of the eighth month, he sent a large sedan chair for Li Ping'er, with a roll of silk, and four pairs of red lanterns. Daian, Ping'an, Huatong, and Laixing were sent to escort the sedan chair. It was afternoon when they arrived. Li Ping'er sent her two maids in charge of old woman Feng, and when the old woman returned, she got into the sedan chair, leaving her house in the care of the old woman and Tian Fu.

That day Ximen Qing stayed at home and sat in the new summer-house, wearing his everyday clothes and hat, waiting for Li Ping'er. The sedan chair reached the gate, but, for a long time, no one came out to receive it. Yulou went to Yueniang's room. "Sister," she said, "you are the mistress here. The woman has come, and, if you do not go out to welcome her, his Lordship will be angry. He is in the garden, and the sedan chair is at the gate. How can she come in if nobody goes out to receive her?"

Yueniang at last decided to go, fearing that if she did not, her husband would fly into a temper. So, after hesitating a while, she went to the gate to receive Li Ping'er. With a precious vase in her hands, the new wife went to the room which the maids had prepared for her, and there waited for Ximen Qing. He was still angry with her and would not go that night. The next day she was taken to Yueniang's room, and there was formally given her rank and place as the Sixth Lady in the household. For three days there were celebrations. Ximen Qing invited his relatives and friends, but still did not go to visit her. The first night he went to Jinlian's room.

"She is the last of us," Jinlian said, "and this is her first night. You should not let her room be empty."

"You don't realize that strumpet's eagerness," Ximen said. "I will leave her to herself for a day or two. Then I will go."

But even on the third day, when all the guests had left, instead of going to her, Ximen Qing went to Yulou's room.

Seeing that for three nights her husband kept away from her, Li Ping'er told her two maids to go to sleep, and, after sobbing for a long while, she stood upon her bed, and fastening her shoelaces to the beam, tried to hang herself.

The two maids woke. They saw that the lamp in their mistress's room was very low and got out of bed to turn it up. Then they saw the woman hanging there. They were frightened and ran at once to tell Chunmei. Jinlian got up and went to see Li Ping'er. She was hanging very stiff and straight above the bed, wearing a red dress. Jinlian and Chunmei quickly cut her down and laid her on the bed. After a while some saliva dribbled from her mouth and she began to come around.

Jinlian told Chunmei to go to the back court and ask Ximen Qing to come. He was drinking wine with Yulou and had not gone to bed. Yulou had been remonstrating with him. "You have married her," she said, "yet for three nights you do not go near her. She will be miserable and think that this is all our doing."

"You don't understand," Ximen said. "She is the sort of woman who, not content with the rice, must have the pan too. How do you expect me to be anything but annoyed? We were on the most intimate terms even before her husband's death, and I know all there is to know about her. Then she went and married that Doctor Jiang. Evidently I wasn't good enough for her. Now she wants me again."

"Oh, I understand how you feel," Yulou said, "but the other fellow deceived her."

While they were talking a knock came at the door. Yulou told her maid Lanxiang to see who was there. The maid came back and said that Chunmei had come to ask for her master because the Sixth Lady had hanged herself in her room.

"I told you so," Yulou said excitedly, urging Ximen Qing to go at once. "I told you to go to her, and you wouldn't listen to me. Now the trouble has begun." They took a lantern and went to the Sixth Lady's room.

Yueniang and Li Jiao'er also heard the news, and went to see the woman. When they arrived, Jinlian was holding her up. They asked whether she had been given any ginger broth. Jinlian told them that she had given her some as soon as she had been cut down. Li Ping'er made a gurgling noise and then began to show signs of coming around. Yueniang and the others were much relieved. They spoke consolingly to her and made her lie down. Then they went back to their own places.

The next day about noon Li Ping'er was persuaded to eat some gruel. "Don't give her a thought," Ximen Qing said to Li Jiao'er and the others. "She is playing this game in the hope of frightening me, but I will see she does not get away with it. Tonight I shall go to her room and see that she hangs herself again. If she refuses, she shall taste my whip. That's the only way to show her the kind of man I am."

When the ladies heard this, they were so afraid for Li Ping'er that the sweat rose upon their brows.

That night Ximen Qing took a whip and went to her room. Yulou and Jinlian told Chunmei to shut the door and allow no one to come in. They both stood outside and quietly listened to all that went on. Ximen went into the room where Li Ping'er was lying upon the bed, sobbing. She did not get up when he came in, and this annoyed him all the more. He ordered the two maids out of the room and sat down on a chair.

"Now, you strumpet," he shouted, pointing his finger at the woman, "you have already caused me trouble once. What do you mean by coming and hanging yourself in my house? You should have gone on living with your little turtle. Nobody asked you to come here. I have done you no harm. Why should you come here with your piddling tricks? Well, I've never yet seen a woman hang herself, and I'll begin by watching you." He threw a cord to her.

Li Ping'er remembered that Jiang Zhushan had told her of Ximen's prowess as a wife beater, and wondered what misdeed in a former existence had brought her to such a pass that day. She sobbed more loudly.

Ximen Qing, in a terrible rage, ordered her to get down from the bed, strip, and kneel before him. When she hesitated, he threw her to the ground and beat her several times. Then she took off her clothes and knelt down trembling. Ximen still sat still and related all her misdeeds. "I told you," he said, "that you must wait a while for me because I was busy. You paid no attention but married that fellow Jiang. If it had been anybody else, I would not have cared, but to marry a miserable creature like him . . . You took him to live in your own house and gave him money to set up a shop beneath my very eyes. I suppose you thought you would try to start a rival shop to mine."

"It is too late for me to be sorry now," the woman said. "But I did wait for you, and thought about you day and night till I became crazy. The garden of the noble family of Qiao is at the back of my house, and there were many foxes there, which came in the middle of the night in human form and sucked the marrow from my bones. When morning came, they disappeared. If you don't believe me, ask old woman Feng and my two maids. I nearly died, and they sent for Doctor Jiang to cure me. I was quite helpless and he deceived me. He told me you had gone to the Eastern Capital, and there was nothing for me to do but marry him. I didn't realize what a good-for-nothing braggart he was. Then someone came and set upon him at the door, there was trouble at the court, and it was all very troublesome for me. I lost my money and drove him away."

"You told him," Ximen said, "to accuse me of having detained your property. Why do you come back to me now?"

"Wherever did you hear that nonsense?" Li Ping'er cried. "I would have been torn in pieces first."

"It would not have mattered to me if you had," Ximen said. "You may have money enough to get a new husband when you want a change, but you shall not behave like that here. Let me tell you this. It was I who got the men to set upon Doctor Jiang. It was no trouble to me, but it was quite enough to set that fellow spinning round and round looking for a hole to crawl into. If I had taken the matter more seriously, you would have been taken to the court too, and made to give up everything you have."

"I knew it was your doing," Li Ping'er said, 'but forgive me, I beg you. If you treated me as you say, there would be nothing for me to do but die."

Ximen's ill temper was gradually dying away. "Tell me, you strumpet, which is the better man, Jiang or I?"

"How can he compare with you?" the woman said. "You are like the heavens, and he is nothing but a piece of clay. It was such a man as you who set the tiles upon the palace of the Jade Emperor in the thirty-third heaven, and he is fit only to dig coal for the King of Hell in the ninety-ninth abode beneath the earth. Don't mention yourself in the same breath with him. Why, such food as you have upon your table every day, he has never seen and never will see, though he live to be hundreds of years old. How can I compare him with you? Not only he, but Hua, my first husband too. Had he been the least like you, I should never have desired you. But you are just what I need. Ever since I came into your hands I have never ceased to think about you day and night."

With such words she made Ximen remember his old affection for her, and his heart was happy again. He threw the whip aside, lifted the woman up, made her put on her clothes again, and took her in his arms. "Daughter," he said, "you say but the truth. Indeed he has never seen a sky as large as a plate." He told Chunmei to set out a table and bring wine and food.

CHAPTER 20

The Reconciliation

They walk along the flowery glades
Where screening trees leave but a little space,
Hiding themselves from curious eyes
Always afraid lest others should see them.
The thorns upon the bushes cut and tear
They seek escape among the climbing roses.
They brush aside the rustling branches
Seeking to return again
And look for some forsaken corner.
The swallow, from his nest beneath the eaves,
Guides them to the silken curtains.

Li Ping'er, with her sweet ways and persuasive words, dispelled Ximen Qing's anger. He raised her up and made her dress again. They embraced and were perfectly happy. Ximen told Chunmei to set a table and go to the inner court for wine.

After Ximen Qing had gone in, Pan Jinlian and Meng Yulou stood outside the door to see what they could hear. As the other door was closed, there was no one but Chunmei about, and the two women peeped through the crack in the door. They could see the light but could not hear a word of what was said.

"Chunmei, the young rascal, is better off than we are," Jinlian said, "she can hear."

The maid stood outside the window for a while and then went over to them.

"What are they doing?" Jinlian whispered.

"Father made her take off her clothes and kneel down," Chunmei said. "At first she would not, and Father was angry and took the whip to her."

"Did she take her clothes off then?"

"Yes, when she saw that Father was really angry, she undressed and knelt down. Father asked her a lot of questions."

Yulou was afraid that Ximen would hear them, and, taking Jinlian by the hand, she drew her away to the other door.

It was about the twentieth day of the eighth month and the moon was late in rising. Jinlian and Yulou stood together in the dark, waiting for Chunmei.

"Sister," Jinlian said, "she thought she would get something good here. That's why she was so anxious to come. And now, at the very start, she has had a good thrashing. She seems to be one of those people who do not care for authority. If she does what she is told, all will be well, but if she behaves deceitfully, she will have to pay for it. Indeed, she will have to pay in any case. I remember how that young woman told stories to me and about me, and, although I was as careful as could be, I had to weep before him or I should not have been forgiven. You have been here for a long time. Do you understand him?"

The door opened. Chunmei came out and went to the back court. Jinlian, from the shadows, called to ask where she was going, but Chunmei only laughed and went on. Then Jinlian called her again, and this time she stayed. "She wept and told Father a long story," the maid said. "Now he is quite content. He has raised her up and made her put on her clothes again. He has told me to lay the table and bring them some wine."

"What a shameless creature!" Jinlian said to Yulou. "All that thunder, and so little rain to follow! It all ends in smoke. Nothing will come of it. She will just offer him wine. And you, you scamp," she said to Chunmei, "she has maids of her own, why should you fetch wine for her? When you get to the kitchen, that Xue'e woman will make a fuss, and I simply won't put up with it."

"I can't help it," Chunmei said, "I'm only doing what Father told me." She laughed and went away.

"The young rascal," Jinlian cried. "Ask her to do something that is her business and she is as lazy as a corpse. But when it's something she is not supposed to do, she rushes around and takes all the care in the world. That woman has two maids of her own. Why should Chunmei take this upon herself? She is a meddlesome young hussy."

"Oh, it is often so," Yulou said. "There is my maid Lanxiang. If I ask her to do anything for me, she takes no pains at all, but if *he* has any trick for her to play, she bustles about and doesn't mind what trouble she takes."

Yuxiao came to them. "Third Mother," she said to Yulou, "I have come to take you to your room."

"You frightened me, you little wretch," Yulou said. "Does your mistress know you're here?"

"I have just helped her to bed," the maid said, "and now I've come to see what is happening. I saw Chunmei going to the inner court. What is Father doing?"

Jinlian pointed to the door. "Go there," she said, "and you'll hear a strange story." Yuxiao wished to hear more, and Jinlian told her.

"Did Father really make her take off her clothes, and beat her?" the maid asked.

"He beat her," Yulou said, "because she would not take them off."

"Well," the maid said, laughing, "it is better to be beaten with them on than with them off. The bare skin is not too fond of punishment."

Chunmei brought the wine. Xiaoyu, with a square food box, came with her. They both went into the room.

"Look at those young rascals," Jinlian cried. "Why are they doing this? They are like rats flying in the skies. Take it in quickly," she said to Chunmei, "and let her own maids serve them. You must not occupy yourself there. I have something else for you to do."

Chunmei laughed and went in with Xiaoyu. After setting the things on the table they came out again, and her own maids served Li Ping'er and Ximen Qing. Yulou and Jinlian had many questions to ask Chunmei. Then Yuxiao said: "Third Mother, it is time for us to go," and they went away together. Jinlian told Chunmei to shut the door, and went to sleep by herself.

Ximen Qing and Li Ping'er drank together and talked till midnight, rejoicing in their love. Then they spread the coverlets and arranged the bed. In the bright candlelight they might have been the phoenix and his mate singing in harmony before a mirror. Fragrant incense was in the burner, and they were like a pair of butterflies dancing among the flowers. That night they took the silver lamp and gazed upon each other, fearful lest their coming together might be but fantasy.

Next day they slept till breakfast time. Then Li Ping'er got up and dressed her hair before the mirror. Yingchun brought in the breakfast. Li Ping'er rinsed her mouth and ate with Ximen, but very little. She told her maid to heat what remained of the wine, and drank it with her husband. After a little while she went on with her dressing. Then she opened her boxes and showed all her fine headdresses and clothes to Ximen Qing. There were a hundred pearls from the Western Ocean that had once belonged to Grand Secretary Liang, and a cap button of dark green that, she said, had been her father-in-law's. She weighed this and asked Ximen to take it to the silversmith's and have a pair of earrings made from it. Then she brought out a hairnet of gold thread that weighed about nine taels and asked him if the Great Lady or any of the others had a net like it. When she heard that they had silver nets but nothing to compare with hers, she said it would be unbecoming for her to wear it. "It will be better for you to take it to the silversmith's and get him to make a nine-phoenix pin, with pearls between the teeth. And with what is left he can make a comb like the Great Lady's, a Guanyin of gold and jade."

When Ximen Qing had taken the things and was about to go out, Li Ping'er said: "There is now nobody in my house. It would be well to send a man there to take care of it, and let Tian Fu come here to wait on me. Old woman Feng is too old to walk, and herself causes me more than a little anxiety."

Ximen Qing agreed and went out. On his way he came upon Jinlian, with her hair in disorder, standing by the gate.

"You are up very late, Brother," she called to him. "Where are you going?"

"I am going out on business," Ximen said.

"What is your hurry, you funny creature? Come here. I have something to say to you."

When Ximen saw that she was serious, he turned back and went with her into her room. She sat on a chair, and held his two hands.

"It is hard to find words bad enough for you," she said. "Are you afraid someone is going to put you in a pan and boil you, that you are in such a hurry to get away? Stay here. I want to tell you something."

"Oh, you little strumpet," Ximen said, "what is it you want? I have something to attend to, and you must wait till I come back."

He started out, but Jinlian caught him by the sleeve. It seemed very heavy. "What have you got there?" she asked. "Take it out and let me see."

"It is my purse," Ximen said.

Jinlian would not believe him. She put her hand into his sleeve and took out the golden hairnet. "This is her net," she said. "What are you going to do with it?"

"Well," Ximen said, "when I told her that none of you had one like it, she didn't care to wear it herself, and so she asked me to take it to the silversmith's and change it for something else."

Jinlian asked how much it weighed, and what Li Ping'er wished to have made instead of it. Ximen told her.

"For such a pin," Jinlian said, "three taels and five or six *qian* of gold will be quite enough. The Great Lady's comb has only one tael and six *qian* in it. You must have one made for me with what is to spare."

"But she wants a solid stem," Ximen said.

"Even if she does, it will only take three taels, and there will be enough left to make a pin for me."

"You little strumpet," Ximen said, laughing, "you are never satisfied unless you are getting something out of somebody. You're always on the make."

"My son," Jinlian said, "don't forget what your mother tells you. If I don't get my pin there will be trouble."

Ximen Qing put the net into his sleeve again and laughed. As he passed through the door, Jinlian called to him: "You have come out of this business rather easily. He asked her what she meant. "Well," she said, "yesterday there was a great deal of thunder but very little rain. You told her to hang herself, and here you are with her hairnet. She has twisted you around her little finger, and she isn't afraid of you in the least."

Ximen laughed. "You're talking nonsense," he said, and went out.

Yueniang, Yulou and Li Jiao'er were sitting together in Yueniang's room when there was some excitement among the boys. They were looking for Laiwang. Ping'an pushed aside the lattice and was going in. Yueniang said: "Why do you want him?" Ping'an told her that Ximen Qing wanted him at once. After some time Yueniang told the boy that she had sent Laiwang on an errand. She had told him to go with a present of oil and rice to the nuns.

"I will tell Father that you have sent Laiwang on some business," Ping'an said.

"Tell him what you like, you young scamp," Yueniang said. The boy went away.

"If I open my mouth," Yueniang said to Yulou and the others, "he says I take too much upon myself. If I do not, I feel I am not doing my duty. Now that woman has come here, of course her house ought to be sold. There is a tremendous fuss, ringing of bells and beating of drums, and somebody must be sent to take charge of the place. Old woman Feng is there, and an unmarried boy was chosen to keep her company. That was all that was necessary. The house won't run away. Now he must have Laiwang and his wife to go there. There is always something wrong with Laiwang's wife, and who's going to wait upon her if she has to stay in bed?"

"Lady," Yulou said, "it is not for me to say anything, but, after all, you are the mistress of this house and you ought not to refuse to speak to him. It has made us all very unhappy, and the boys don't know to whom they must go. He is all muddled these days, and you really must take our advice and speak to him again."

"Third Sister," Yueniang said, "you don't know what you're talking about. I did not begin this quarrel. He flew into a temper without any excuse at all. I am not afraid of him, and no matter what he does, I shall not look at him with a friendly eye. He has said insulting things about me behind my back and called me a whore. What right has he to say things like that? He has seven or eight women here and he says I am not a lady. But it has always been the same. Fall in with other people's wishes and they will say nice things about you: tell the truth and everybody will hate you.

I reproved him perfectly justly. I told him he had accepted things from her, bought her house, and that if he married her, all the gentlemen at the office would scorn him. Her mourning was not over, and I said it was not the right time to marry. I never dreamed that they were making plans the whole time. They used to meet regularly and I never knew a thing about it. It was like putting me inside a big jar. One day he would tell me he was at the bawdy house; the next night, he said, he was at another bawdy house. And all the time he was staying with her.

"Yes, he goes to the bawdy houses, where all the people are like beautiful foxes and behave like dragons and tigers. They swindle him and cheat him, and he thinks everything they do is perfect. I have done my duty by him and spoken to him fairly, and now he has not a word for me. But I want nothing from him. Let him give me three meals a day and I can do without a husband. Let him allow me to go my own way and he can go his."

Yulou and the others could think of no reply to make to this. After a while Li Ping'er came in, beautifully dressed. She wore a gown of red silk embroidered with gold and a skirt with an embroidered pattern of green leaves. Yingchun came with her, carrying a silver pot, and Xiuchun, with a box of tea leaves. They came to offer tea to Yueniang and the others. Yueniang told Xiaoyu to offer the Sixth Lady a chair. Then Sun Xue'e came and all the ladies had tea.

"Sister," Jinlian said to Li Ping'er, "you owe apologies to our Great Sister. Let me tell you that for a long time she and Father have not spoken to one another, and it is all on your account. We have done our best to smooth matters over. You must give a party and try to get the old couple to talk to one another again."

Li Ping'er agreed. She kowtowed four times before Yueniang. "Sister," Yueniang said, "she is teasing you. You must not urge me any more," she said to Jinlian. "I have taken an oath that I will not speak to him even if I live to be a hundred years old." There was nothing more to be said.

Jinlian took a brush and began to brush Li Ping'er's hair. She noticed that the new wife was wearing a set of golden hair ornaments with designs representing different insects, and a comb with an inlaid pattern showing the Three Friends of Winter, the bamboo, the plum and the pine.

"Sister," said Jinlian, "you should not wear these pins. They catch your hair. A golden Guanyin with a solid stem, such as the Great Lady wears, is much more suitable."

"I have thought of having one made like Great Sister's," Li Ping'er said.

Xiaoyu and Yuxiao, when they came in to wait upon the ladies, did not show due respect to Li Ping'er. Yuxiao said to her: "Sixth Mother, what office did your father-in-law hold at court?"

"He was in the Department of Forestry," said Li Ping'er.

"Ah," Yuxiao said, laughing, "so your acquaintance with the rod did not begin yesterday."

Then Xiaoyu began. "Last year," said she, "some old men, the elders of the village, were seeking you, to get you to go to the Eastern Capital."

Li Ping'er did not understand this remark. "Why were they seeking me?" she asked.

"Because you are so clever at dealing with floods," Xiaoyu said.

Then Yuxiao began again. "Where you come from, Mother, the ladies all worship the Thousand Buddhas. That, I suppose, is why you kowtowed so often yesterday."

And Xiaoyu said: "Yesterday, four officers were sent from the court to ask you to visit the Mongols in Tartary. Isn't that so?"

"I don't know what you mean," said Li Ping'er.

Xiaoyu laughed. "They said you knew how to speak the language."

Jinlian and Yulou were greatly amused at all this, but Yueniang upbraided her maids and told them to go and attend to their business. As for Li Ping'er, she flushed and paled in turns, and did not know whether she should stay or go away. After a little while she went back to her own room.

When Ximen Qing returned, he told her that he had given her ornaments to the silversmith. Then he said that on the twenty-fifth, he proposed to give a banquet and invite her late husband's eldest brother.

"There is no need to invite him again," Li Ping'er said, "I settled that with his wife, but, if you like to do so, by all means do.

"Old woman Feng can look after my house alone," she added; "all you need do is get someone to take turns with Tian Fu. There is no necessity to send Laiwang there. I hear his wife is not very strong and really not fit to go there."

"I did not know that," Ximen said. He called Ping'an and told him to go to the house on Lion Street every other day to relieve Tian Fu.

On the twenty-fifth Ximen Qing gave a banquet for all his relatives and friends. A band of players and four singing girls were engaged, Li Guijie, Wu Yin'er, Dong Yuxian and Han Jinchuan. They came about noon. The guests took tea under the awning, and, when they had all assembled, went to the great hall. The guests, who included the band of brothers as well as Ximen's relatives, sat at six tables. Ximen Qing himself sat in the host's place, with his son-in-law, Ben the Fourth, and Fu, the manager of his shop, at his table. The musicians played several melodies, and two youths, Li Ming and Wu Hui, sang a song. There was more music and then the four singing girls came to serve the wine.

"Today," said Ying Bojue, "is a very happy day in our brother's life. I say so with great diffidence, but I should very much like to pay my respects to our new sister-in-law and assure her of our affectionate regard. I do not wish to cause any inconvenience, but here are two venerable uncles, and I should like to know what they have come for if not to see her."

"My wife is not at all beautiful," Ximen said. "It will be better to dispense with this visit."

"Brother," Xie Xida said, "do not say that. We have told you what we wish. Why should we have come if we did not desire to see our sister-in-law? Then here is your honorable relative Hua the Elder. Once he was only a friend; now he is a relative. You cannot treat us as strangers. Please ask the lady to come and see us. There is nothing to be afraid of."

Ximen Qing laughed but did not move.

"Brother," Bojue said, "don't laugh. We have all brought our presents. We don't ask the lady to come out for nothing."

"Oh, you're talking nonsense," Ximen said. However, they pressed him again and again, and at last he told Daian to go to the inner court and ask Li Ping'er to come to them. There was a long delay. Then Daian came back and said that the Sixth Lady thought there was no need for such a ceremony.

"It is you, you little dog bone," Ying Bojue said. "You're playing tricks. You haven't been to the inner court at all. You have just come back and made up this story."

"I should not dare to do such a thing, Uncle," the boy said. "If you don't believe me, go yourself and ask her."

"You think I dare not go," Bojue said. "I know my way about your garden well enough. I will go and drag the lady out, whether you will or not."

"We have a strong dog and a fierce one," Daian said. "He will bite your legs."

Bojue left his seat and kicked Daian. "You young scamp," he said, laughing, "you have had your joke. Now be quick and ask the lady to come. If you don't succeed, I will give you twenty strokes with one of these palings."

The singing girls laughed. Daian went back a little way and looked to his master for instructions. Ximen Qing could not help himself. He told the boy to ask the Sixth Lady to dress and come to them. Daian went and after a while came back for Ximen Qing. All the menservants were dismissed and the second door was closed. Yulou and Jinlian urged Li Ping'er to go out, and arranged the flowers on her head. The servants spread beautiful rugs on the ground, and the four singing girls went to the inner court. They played their instruments and walked in front of Li Ping'er. The incense was delightfully fragrant and the music exquisite.

Li Ping'er wore a long gown of red silk embroidered in five colors. Her skirt was green and bore the design of the Hundred Flowers, with golden stems and leaves of many colors. She wore a girdle with a green jade clasp. On her wrists were golden bangles. There were pearls upon her breast and jade tinkled at the hem of her skirt. Pearls and flowers were piled high upon her hair, and two jewels were upon her brow. Pendants came down over her white cheeks. Tiny shoes, with embroidered love birds on them, peeped out from beneath her skirt. The four singing girls played their instruments about her. She looked like the stem of a blossom bending in the wind; her embroidered girdle flowed behind her. She greeted them all with a low reverence, and they quickly left their chairs to return her greeting.

Yulou, Jinlian and Li Jiao'er stood behind the screen with Yueniang to watch the proceedings. They heard the song of congratulation to one who has reached exalted rank, the song that declares that Heaven has joined these two together and compares them to the phoenix and his mate living together in wedded bliss for generation after generation.

"Sister," said Jinlian, "do you hear that? That is not a fitting song for this occasion, for if they are to live together for generation after generation, what about you?"

Yueniang, in spite of her equable temperament, could not help feeling annoyed. Ying Bojue, Xie Xida and the others paid compliments to Li Ping'er as though they hated themselves because they had only one mouth to sing her praises. "Is this Sister-in-law?" they said. "Why! in all the world, we have never seen anyone so beautiful. We need not speak of the sweetness of her nature and her virtue. And how exquisitely she carries herself. There is no other like her in all the world. Brother, we envy you. Now that we have seen this lady once, we shall be happy if we die tomorrow."

"Take the lady back to her room at once," they said to Daian. "We must not let her tire herself."

Yueniang heard this and cursed them for a pack of rogues.

Li Ping'er retired. The four singing girls, seeing that she was rich, flattered her in their turn, calling her Mother this and Mother that, arranging her ornaments and putting her clothes in order, leaving nothing undone.

Yueniang, feeling very unhappy, went to her own room. Daian and Ping'an brought to her presents, money, rolls of silk, dresses and boxes, but Yueniang would not look at them. All she said was: "You rascals! Why have you brought that stuff here? Take it to the outer court."

"Father told us to bring it here," Daian said.

Yueniang told Yuxiao to take the presents and put them on the bed. When Yueniang's brother, Wu the Elder, had had his second course, he went to pay a visit to his sister. She rose as soon as he came in and made a reverence to him. Then they sat down to talk.

"It was very kind of you to entertain my wife yesterday," said Wu the Elder, "and now my brother-in-law has done the same for me. My wife tells me that you have not been on speaking terms with your husband for some time, and I was thinking it would be my duty to remonstrate with you, when he happened to invite me here. Sister, if you persist in this course, you will lose all merit. There is an old saying that a man is a fool who fears his wife, but that a woman of gentle birth stands in awe of her husband. Obedience and virtue are the ordinary lot of woman. Whatever he does, you should not interfere. Take everything as a matter of course, and he will appreciate the good qualities that are in you."

"It is too late now to show him my good qualities," Yueniang said, "or I should not be treated with such contempt. Now, you see, he has a rich wife and I am treated as a maidservant, as if I didn't even exist. You need not worry. I shall put up with his treatment of me. He has changed his manner to me for some time now." She burst into tears.

"Sister," Uncle Wu said, "you are doing the wrong thing. You and I are not people of that sort. You must not behave like this. If you and your husband live together in harmony, it will redound to our credit."

He argued with Yueniang for a long time, and Xiaoyu brought him tea. When he had drunk it, a boy came from the hall to ask him to return to the party, so he took leave of his sister and went back. The feast continued until evening and then broke up. Li Ping'er gave each of the singing girls a handkerchief with a gold pattern, and five *qian*. They went away delighted.

Thereafter Ximen Qing spent every night with Li Ping'er. The others were quite happy about it except Jinlian, who secretly told stories to Yueniang about Li Ping'er, and to Li Ping'er about Yueniang, in the hope of stirring up trouble between them. Li Ping'er had no means of knowing the truth, so she fell into the trap, called Jinlian her sister, and became very intimate with her.

After his marriage with Li Ping'er, Ximen came into possession of more ill-gotten wealth, and was richer than ever. His house was refurnished, inside and out; rice and wheat were piled high in his barns; his mules and horses were in droves, and his maids and menservants would have made a small army.

Ximen Qing changed Tian Fu's name to Qintong. He bought two more boys, one called Qitong and the other Laian. He engaged Li Ming, Guijie's brother, to teach music to the maids. Chunmei was to learn the lute; Yuxiao, the cithern; Yingchun, the banjo; and Lanxiang, the four-stringed fiddle. Every day they dressed themselves beautifully and went to a room at the west side of the hall to study. Ximen gave Li Ming many meals and paid him five taels a month. He gave two thousand taels to Fu and Ben the Fourth, and instructed them to open a pawnshop. Chen Jingji, his son-in-law, kept all the keys and went out to collect the debts. Ben the Fourth kept the accounts and weighed the stock. Fu managed the medicine shop and the pawnshop, assayed the silver, and looked after the business generally. The medicine was stored in the loft above Jinlian's rooms. Shelves were made and put up in the loft over Li Ping'er's rooms, and on them were stored clothes, headdresses, curios, books and pictures from the pawnshop. Piles of silver came in every day.

Chen Jingji got up early every day and went to bed late. He was responsible for all the keys, and checked the accounts and the money. He was very clever at taking in and paying out, writing and making out accounts, and Ximen Qing was very pleased with him. One day when they were sitting together in the hall, Ximen said: "You have done very well since you have been here. If your father knew, he would be pleased. You know the saying that he who has a son must depend on that son, and he who has no son must depend on his son-in-law. If I have no child, this property will all come to you and your wife."

"Misfortune came upon me," Chen Jingji said, "and my family has had a very hard time. My father and my mother have both had to go far away, and I had to come to you. I have received the greatest kindness at your hands, and, whether I live or die, I can never hope to repay you. But I am young and inexperienced, and only ask that you will not be too severe with me. I dare not hope for anything beyond that."

Words of this kind were pleasing to Ximen Qing's ears, and he was more delighted than ever. Afterwards all the domestic affairs were entrusted to this young man. He dealt with the letters and present lists. Whenever Ximen's friends came to visit him, Jingji was invited to keep them company, and he was always about. Nobody could have suspected the treacherous villainy of this young man.

The time passed very quickly and it was soon the end of the eleventh month. Ximen Qing went to a party at Chang Zhijie's house. The party finished early, and, before it was time to light the lamps, he, with Ying Bojue, Xie Xida, and Zhu Shinian, got on their horses and started back. When they left the house, the snow clouds were very heavy.

"Brother," Ying Bojue said, "if we go home now there is nothing for us to do. It is a long time since we saw Guijie. It is going to snow. Let us go and see her, like Meng Hao-jan walking on the snow in search of Chunmei."

"It is a very good idea," Zhu Shinian said. "You give her twenty taels a month. If you never go there, she gets it all for nothing."

The three men badgered Ximen until he agreed to go to the house in East Street. It was dark when they got there. The maid was sweeping the floor in the hall. The old procuress and Guiqing came to greet them. They sat down.

"Guijie has enjoyed your hospitality," the old woman said, "and she thanks your Sixth Lady for the handkerchiefs and the flowers."

"I am sorry I treated her so shabbily," Ximen said, "but it was getting late, and, as soon as the guests left, I sent her home."

The old woman offered them tea and a maid set the table.

"Where is Guijie?" Ximen asked.

"She waited for you a long time," the old woman said, "but you did not come, and today, as it is her aunt's birthday, she has gone in a chair to wish her many happy returns."

As a matter of fact, Guijie had not gone to her aunt's. When she found that Ximen Qing did not come to see her for a long time, she welcomed the attentions of a gentleman called Ding Shuangqiao, the son of a silk merchant of Hangzhou. He had come with a thousand taels' worth of silk to sell, and was living at an inn. He defrauded his father and went to play in the bawdy house. He paid ten taels of silver and two dresses of heavy Hangzhou silk, and spent two nights with Guijie. He was, in fact, drinking in her room when Ximen suddenly arrived. The old woman sent them both to a secluded little room in the inner court to wait till he had gone.

Ximen Qing believed what the old woman told him. "If Guijie is not in," he said, "let us have some wine and we will wait for her." The old woman went to the kitchen and hastily got something ready. Guiqing played for them and sang a new song. They guessed fingers and drank.

Then something happened. Ximen Qing went to the back court to change his clothes and suddenly heard laughter coming from a room there. When he had done what he went to do, he crept to the window and peeped in. Guijie was drinking with a southerner who was wearing a square cap. Ximen could not contain himself. He went back again, threw over the wine table, and smashed all the plates and dishes to pieces. Then he called his four boys and told them to tear the curtains from the windows. His three friends tried to stop him, but Ximen was in a fury. He determined to tie the man and the girl together and throw them out of the door. Ding was not a very brave young man. When he heard the noise, he crawled under the bed and implored Guijie to save his life.

"Keep quiet," said Guijie, "Mother is here. It is quite a usual thing in our house. Let them make as much noise as they like, don't you stir."

The old woman saw Ximen devastating the place and still tried to lie and argue with him. He would not listen but urged his boys to break up the house. He would have struck the old woman, but fortunately for her his three friends prevented him. He made a great to-do, and swore that he would never enter the house again. Then he went home in the snow.

CHAPTER 21

Wu Yueniang Relents

The north wind pierces like an icy torrent
The powdered snow seems whiter
A steam of mist rises from the beasts
But it is warm within the silken curtains
Where dainty fingers tear apart fresh oranges
And pluck the lute strings.

Who goes to stand on guard?
A low voice asks.
The third night watch has sounded on the city wall.
It is better not to go. The horses slip upon the icy road
And there is no one now upon the way.

It was late when Ximen Qing set out for home. When he reached there, the boys opened the gate. He dismounted and, walking over the snow, found the door to the back court partly open. Everything seemed quiet and, thinking that this was strange, he stood there silently, hidden by the screen. As he waited, listening, Xiaoyu came from the room and set a table in the passage.

Since Wu Yueniang had ceased to speak to her husband, she had abstained from rich food three times a month, and, every day that had a seven in it, paid worship to her star and burned incense. This she did, imploring Heaven to change her husband's heart. Ximen Qing himself knew nothing of this. The maid set out the table, and, in a little while, Yueniang in her most beautiful dress came out and burned incense in the middle of the court. Then she bowed low towards the Heavens and prayed: "I am she who married Ximen Qing. My husband loves light women, and, though he is now of middle age, he has no son to carry on his name. He has six wives, but all are childless and there will be none to worship at our tomb. Day and night, my heart is heavy within me because I have no son to lean upon. Here then I swear: I will pray every night to the Three Great Lights of Heaven. I beseech you to save my husband. Make him amend his ways. Cause him to forsake things that are vain and turn with all his heart to the things of his own household. Let one of us six women, I care not which, soon bear a son that so our future may be secure. This is my only prayer."

> Secretly she went forth into the sweet night
> The courtyard was filled with fragrant mist
> And a strange light illumined the snow,
> There she prayed to Heaven,
> And paced in loneliness through the long night.

When he heard Yueniang's prayer, Ximen's heart was touched by shame. "Truly," he said to himself, "I have not appreciated her as I should. She loves me and is a true wife." He could hold back no longer. He came from behind the screen and took her in his arms.

Yueniang had not expected that he would come home while the snow was so heavy. She was startled and opened the door of her room, but her husband held her closely. "Sister," he said to her, "though I should die, I could never realize too well the goodness of your heart. You love me, and I have wronged you. I have made your heart cold. Now I am sorry."

"The snow is so thick it has made you mistake the door," Yueniang said. "This is not your room and I am not a respectable woman. What have you and I to do with one another? I have no wish to see you. Why should you come and bother me? Though I live for a thousand years I never wish to see your face again."

Ximen Qing carried her into her room. In the lamplight she looked even more beautiful. She was wearing a scarlet coat and a soft yellow skirt. There was a dainty ornament in her hair. He could not help loving her. "I have been a fool for a long time," he said. "I have not taken your good advice and I have misinterpreted your intentions. I have been like those who did not recognize the jade of the Jing Mountain and thought it but a piece of common stone. Now I know that you are indeed a lady. You must forgive me."

"I am not she whom your heart desires," Yueniang said. "I do not know what you are talking about. What good advice have I ever given you? If you insist on staying here, please do not speak to me. Indeed I find your presence most distasteful. Kindly remove yourself at once, or I shall be compelled to call the maid to drive you out."

"Today," Ximen said, "I have had my fill of anger. That is why I came home though the snow was so heavy. I should like to tell you what the trouble was about."

"Trouble or no trouble," Yueniang said, "I have no desire to hear you. I do not live for you. Pray go and tell the person who does."

Finding that Yueniang would not condescend even to look at him, Ximen Qing knelt down, like a little boy, crying, "Sister! Sister!" all the time.

Yueniang would have nothing to do with him. "You are an utterly shame-less fellow. I shall call the maid," she cried. But when Xiaoyu came in, Ximen Qing stood up and began to think of a plan for getting rid of her.

"It is snowing," he said. "Hadn't you better bring the table from the courtyard?"

"I have already done so," Xiaoyu told him.

Yueniang could not help laughing. "You worthless rascal," she said. "Now you're trying to play tricks with my maid." Xiaoyu disappeared and Ximen Qing again knelt down. "If it were not for common humanity," Yueniang said at last, "I would have nothing to do with you, not for a hundred years."

Ximen rose, found a seat for himself, and ordered Yuxiao to bring some tea. Then he told his wife what had happened that afternoon in the bawdy house. "I have taken an oath never to go there again," he said.

"I don't care whether you go or not," Yueniang retorted. "You have poured out gold and silver like water to get that girl, and the moment you stay away, she sets out to find another lover. And with women of that sort you can never be sure of their hearts, even if you can make sure of their bodies. You can't put a seal on her, and seal her up."

"You are quite right," Ximen said. He sent the maid away, and began to undress, imploring Yueniang to be gracious to him.

"Today," she said, "I have allowed you to sit on my bed. That is enough. I am surprised you dare ask for any more. I shall certainly never allow it."

"Look at this fellow," Ximen said, making his intentions still more obvious. "He's another who is angry and won't speak. He opens his eye, but not a word has he to say for himself."

"You dirty rascal!" Yueniang cried. "Do you think I would look at you, even with my eyes half shut?"

Ximen Qing was not in a mood to bandy words. He set her white legs over his shoulders, and had his way. Their delight in each other was like that of the butterfly, as it sips the nectar from the blossom. Beauty and love were theirs in the fullest measure. Fragrance as of orchid and musk seemed to pass from one to the other. Ximen Qing, in the seventh heaven of delight, murmured, "Darling," and Yueniang answered him in a soft low voice. Soon they were sleeping, their faces close pressed together.

The next morning, Meng Yulou went to see Pan Jinlian. Before she opened the door, she asked if the Fifth Lady was out of bed. Chunmei answered: "My mistress has just got up and is dressing her hair. Please come in." Yulou went in and found Jinlian at her toilet before the dressing table. "I have news for you," she said. "Have you heard anything?"

"How should I hear anything," Jinlian said, "living, as I do, tucked away in a corner? What is it?"

"Last night," Yulou said, "his Lordship came home about the second watch, went to the upper room and made his peace with the lady who lives there. He stayed all night."

"Oh!" Jinlian said, "when we proffered our humble advice, she swore that, though she lived a hundred years, nothing would induce her to speak to him. And now with no excuse at all and nobody to act as peacemaker, she goes and makes friends!"

"I heard all about it just now," Yulou said. "My maid Lanxiang happened to be in the kitchen and she heard the boys saying that our master and Ying Bojue went yesterday to drink at Guijie's place. He caught the wench about some dirty business and smashed up the house. Then he came back, though it was snowing hard. When he got to the door leading to the inner room, she who lives there was burning incense. I fancy he must have heard something she said. Anyhow, he went to her and, the maid tells me, they talked all night. He went down on his knees and she behaved most scandalously. It is all very well for her to go on in this way, but if anybody else behaved like that, she would have a great deal to say."

"There are a great many advantages in being the first wife," Jinlian said. "I wonder what gave her the idea of burning incense. If she really wished to pray she could have said her prayers in secret. There was no need for her to go singing them out so that her husband might hear her. Well, she has become reconciled to him on the sly, without any assistance from anybody. I thought she would hold out, but it was evidently all pretence."

"I don't think so," Yulou said. "She really wanted to make friends with him all the time, but, being the first wife, she didn't care to talk to us about it. She thought that if she allowed us to intervene, we should take liberties afterwards. She ought to have realized that what goes on between husband and wife concerns others besides themselves."

"We must not let this opportunity slip. Hurry up and finish your hair dressing. I will go and see the Sixth Lady. You and I will contribute five *qian*, but I shall ask Li Ping'er for a whole tael, because it is really all her fault. We will buy some wine and a few delicacies and then we'll go and offer wine to them and afterwards have a feast to enjoy the snow. We'll spend all day over it. What do you think?"

"A very good idea," Jinlian said. "But he may be busy today."

"How can he be busy on a day like this? When I came past their door, everything was quiet. Xiaoyu was taking them some water."

Jinlian hurriedly finished dressing her hair and went with Yulou to see Li Ping'er. She was still in bed, but her maid went in to say that they had come.

"What a lazy woman you are," they said as they went in. "There you are, lying in bed like a lazy dragon."

Jinlian put her hand under the bedclothes and discovered a ball of perfume that had been used to make the bed sweet. "Ah," she said, "you have been laying an egg, Sister." She pulled off the coverlets and looked down at the white body.

Li Ping'er hastily jumped out of bed and began to dress. Yulou scolded Jinlian. "Hurry up and dress," she said to Li Ping'er, "we have something to tell you. The master and mistress of this house made friends yesterday. We are going to give five *qian* each, but it will be more for you because you're really responsible for all the trouble. It is snowing hard. We are going to have a feast; invite the happy pair, and enjoy the beautiful snow at the same time. Doesn't that seem good to you?"

"Excellent," Li Ping'er said. "How much do you want from me?"

"A tael," Jinlian said. "Get it weighed out at once, because we must go and collect something from the others in the back court."

Li Ping'er quickly dressed. Then, calling her maid, she opened a chest and took out a piece of silver. Jinlian weighed it and found that it was rather more than a tael. Then Yulou asked Jinlian to help the Sixth Lady to dress her hair, and she herself went to the back court to try to get some money from Sun Xue'e and Li Jiao'er. Meanwhile Jinlian sat and watched Li Ping'er complete her toilet. After a very long time, Yulou came back.

"If I had known what would happen," she said, "I would never have started this business. It is a matter in which we are all equally concerned, yet anybody would have thought I was begging money for myself. The little whore said to me: 'I am a poor downtrodden creature. My husband never comes near me. Where do you think I'm going to find any money?' I talked to her for a long time but all I got out of her was this silver pin. Weigh it and see how much it's worth."

Jinlian took the scales and found it did not amount to four *qian*.

"What did you get from Li Jiao'er?" she asked.

"First she said she didn't have any money," Yulou told them. "'Though every day the money passes through my hands,' she said, 'it is all checked carefully, and I have to give back every bit left over. I have nothing at all of my own.' I told her that none of us had any money to spare. 'It's a matter that concerns us all,' I said, 'but if you don't wish to give anything, don't.' I lost my temper and went out. That frightened her and she sent a maid to bring me back. Then she gave me something, but it's all most annoying."

When Jinlian weighed the silver that Li Jiao'er had contributed, it turned out to be a little less than five *qian*.

"What a cunning wench she is," she cried. "Even if you did everything you could think of, she'd give you short measure. Now we haven't sufficient."

"Yes," Yulou said, "but when she is measuring other people's silver, she uses a measure large enough. Getting money out of her is like getting blood out of a stone. I wonder how many times she has been cursed for it."

Jinlian and Yulou put all the money together. It came to just over three taels. They sent a maid to fetch Daian.

"Yesterday," Jinlian said to him, "you went with your master to Li Guijie's house. What happened there to make him so angry?"

Daian told them the whole story. "Father got very angry," he said. "He told us to break all the windows, doors and partitions, and he would have tied the pair together if Uncle Ying hadn't stopped him. He was still furious when he got on his horse, and on the way home he swore he hadn't done with the whore yet."

"The rascally strumpet!" Jinlian cried. "I always thought she acted like a woman with a jar of honey and held on to it tightly, but this time she's let it drop. Did your master really say so?" she said to Daian. The boy assured her that he had told the truth. Then she began to scold him.

"You young scoundrel," she said; "no matter how wicked she may be, she is your master's girl and you have no right to call her names. I remember once when I asked you to do something for me, you said you were very busy and hadn't any time. But when your master handed you some silver and told you to take it to that girl, you called her Auntie Guijie, and were as sweet as you could be. Now she is out of favor and your master is angry with her, you call her a whore. One of these days I will tell him what you said."

"Oho!" Daian said, "so you, Fifth Mother, are beginning to take her part now. That is indeed like the sun rising in the west. If Father hadn't called her a whore I wouldn't have, either."

"Just because your master says things like that, you need not think you can do so," Jinlian said.

"If I had known you would take it this way, Lady, I would never have said a word."

"Be quiet, you young scamp," Yulou said. "Here are three taels and a *qian*. You and Laixing must go and make some purchases for us. We are giving a snow feast to your master and mistress. If you can keep your hands off the things you buy for us, I'll ask the Fifth Lady not to say anything to your master."

Daian swore that he would never dream of stealing anything, and, calling Laixing, went off with him to do the shopping.

As Ximen Qing was dressing in Yueniang's room, he saw Laixing going to the kitchen with chickens and ducks and Daian carrying a jar of Jinhua wine.

"What are those boys doing?" he asked the maid.

Yuxiao told him that the ladies were going to give a party to Yueniang and himself. Then he asked Daian where he had got the wine, and the boy told him that Yulou had given him money to buy it. "Dear, dear," Ximen said, "why go out to buy wine when there is so much in the house already? Take a key and go and get some jasmine wine from the front court. We will mix it with this."

Curtains and screens had been set out in the hall; the winter season awning, with its design of Chunmei, had been put in position, and the stove well supplied with charcoal. Food and wine were daintily arranged. The ladies came and invited Ximen Qing and Yueniang to join them. Li Jiao'er poured wine into the cups while Yulou held the wine jar. Jinlian served the dishes. Li Ping'er knelt down and offered a cup of wine to Ximen Qing. He took it and said, laughingly, "This is very kind of you, my child. You are indeed a dutiful daughter. But an ordinary reverence is enough."

"Who do you think is paying reverence to you, you overgrown boy?" Jinlian said. "Like the onion that grows by the south wall, the older you grow, the hotter you get. Why, if it were not for the Great Lady, we shouldn't be paying any reverence to you today." They offered Yueniang a cup of wine. She thanked them pleasantly and said she had never expected such kindness.

"It is nothing at all," Yulou said, smiling. "We thought we should like to offer this poor repast to your honorable selves this wintry weather. Please sit down, Sister, and accept our reverences." Yueniang did not wish to do this without making equal reverence in return. But Yulou said they would remain on their knees forever unless Yueniang sat down. At last, after much friendly argument, they were content with half the prescribed salutation.

"Sister," Jinlian said, "we ask you to forgive him for our sakes this once. If he is ever rude to you again we shall not bother about him any more." Then she turned to Ximen Qing. "Why do you sit there like a fool? Come down at once from that place of honor, offer a cup of wine to the Great Lady, and make your apologies."

Ximen Qing laughed. The wine was passed around and afterwards Yueniang, bidding Yuxiao take the jar, herself poured out the wine and offered it to the ladies in return. Xue'e knelt down to receive her cup, but the others took theirs without doing so. Then Ximen Qing and Yueniang sat down in the place of honor, and all the other ladies, with Ximen's daughter Ximen Dajie, sat on either side.

"Sixth Sister," Jinlian said to Li Ping'er, "you ought to offer a special cup of wine to the Great Lady."

Li Ping'e rose and was about to do as she was told, but Ximen Qing stopped her. "Don't pay any attention to that little strumpet. She is teasing you. You have already offered us wine once and there is no need to do so again." Li Ping'er sat down.

Chunmei, Yingchun, Yuxiao and Lanxiang then brought their instruments and sang the song of the Thousand Blossoms of the Pomegranate, which is all about a second honeymoon. Ximen Qing asked them who had suggested that song, and Yuxiao told him that Jinlian had done so. Ximen looked at Jinlian and told her he did not know what she was thinking about. Yueniang suddenly thought of Chen Jingji and sent a boy to fetch him. When he came, he made reverence to them all and sat beside his wife. Yueniang had wine and food set before him and soon the whole family was enjoying a very merry time. Through the window Ximen Qing looked out upon the snow. It was as white as cotton wool and the falling flakes seemed like the whirling petals of the pear blossom. It was a very beautiful sight.

> Snow like tender willow seeds
> Snow like down from a goose's back
> Falling softly with no more sound
> Than a crab that creeps over the sand.
> Piling up mountains of powdered jade
> And dressing wayfarers with glittering spangles
> Till they look like bees covered with pollen
> And the palaces are covered deep.
>
> The snowflakes whirl like a dragon of jade
> Tossing his scales high in the air
> The white powder scatters like the feathers
> That fall from a stork
> The lofty mansions are a mass of ice.
> So cold is it that the body tingles
> The earth shines like a silver ocean
> And the flame of the candle seems like a flower upon it.

Yueniang noticed that the snow lay deep upon the mound in the garden. She sent a maid for a teapot and herself put snow in it, and, from the snow, made boiling water with which she made most fragrant tea for all of them.

They were drinking this tea when Daian came and said that Li Ming had come and was awaiting instructions. Ximen gave orders that he should be brought in. He came, made reverence, and stood before them. "You have come at a good time," Ximen said. "Where have you been?"

"I have been at Master Liu's by the Wine and Vinegar Gate. I give lessons to his children and today I have been to see how they are getting on. I heard that your maids know several tunes but that their time is perhaps not quite perfect, so I thought I would come and see if I could help them at all."

Ximen Qing poured out for him a cup of tea, telling him to drink it and then come and sing a song. Li Ming took his cup of tea and retired to drink it. Then he came back, tuned his zither, cleared his throat, and stood before them, his feet close together. He sang to them of winter in the capital. When he had done, Ximen Qing made Xiaoyu pour wine into a silver peach-shaped cup, and Li Ming, upon his knees, drank it. Then Ximen took four dishes from the table, set them on a tray and gave them to Li Ming, who went outside to eat. A little later, having wiped his mouth on a napkin, he returned and stood by the screen. Ximen Qing told him of the trouble there had been with Li Guijie.

"Of that I know nothing," Li Ming said. "It is some time since I was at my sister's house. But I cannot believe it was Guijie's fault. It must have been the old woman. Please do not be angry with her. I will go and see her."

All day until the first night watch, they drank wine together and the ladies enjoyed themselves immensely. Then Chen Jingji and his wife went to the front court, and they drank no more. Ximen Qing gave Li Ming a final cup of wine and told him that, if he should go to Guijie's house, he must on no account say that Ximen Qing was at home. Li Ming promised, and Ximen sent a servant to take him to the gate. The ladies went to their apartments and Ximen Qing again went to Yueniang's room.

The next day it had ceased to snow. Guijie and her mother were still afraid that Ximen Qing would seek vengeance, so they sent a roast goose and a jar of wine to Ying Bojue and Xie Xida, begging them to go and see Ximen and ask him to pay them a visit that they might express their sorrow for what had happened. Yueniang had just finished dressing and was eating cake with her husband when Daian told them that the two friends had come. Ximen Qing put down his cake and was about to go to them, but Yueniang said: "I can't think what has brought those two villains here today. Finish your cake and let them wait. Why should you hurry? I can't imagine where they think they are going to take you on a snowy day like this." But Ximen told a boy to take food to the front court and said he would eat it there with Ying Bojue and Xie Xida. Then he got up to go. "Don't go out with them when you have finished your cake," Yueniang said. "Remember we are going to celebrate Yulou's birthday this evening." Ximen promised and went to greet his two friends.

"Brother," Ying Bojue said, "you were very angry yesterday. So were we, and we told them what we thought about them. We said you had spent a great deal of money in that house in times past and that, just because they had not seen you lately, there was no reason why they should start to sing another tune. Yet they took that Southerner in. Unfortunately for them, you caught them. We asked how they could expect that you would not be annoyed. And not only you, we said, but we were angry too. We gave them a good talking to, until they felt very much ashamed of themselves. This morning they sent for us, and both mother and daughter knelt before us and sobbed bitterly. They are very much afraid of what you will do, so they have prepared a simple little feast and have asked us to persuade you to go to see them. They are anxious to apologize."

"I have no intention of doing them any harm," Ximen Qing said, "but I shall never go to that house again."

"Brother," Ying Bojue said, "it is natural that you should be angry, but, as a matter of fact, it really was not Guijie's fault. That young man Ding had no intentions upon her. He is one of her sister's old lovers. But there was another young man on his father's boat, a young fellow called Chen, a son of Privy Counselor Chen, and Ding thought he would like to spend ten taels and give him a party at Guijie's. The very moment he came to give them the money you suddenly arrived. They lost their heads and hid the Southerner in the back room where you discovered him, but he never so much as laid a finger on Guijie. This morning both mother and daughter swore this to us. They prostrated themselves before us and begged us to persuade you to go and see them so that the whole unpleasant business may be cleared up and you will not be angry any more."

"I have taken an oath," Ximen Qing said. "I have promised my wife that I will not go there again. I am no longer angry. Please tell them so, and that they need not trouble themselves on my account. I am very busy and cannot go to see them."

Ying Bojue and Xie Xida became excited. They knelt down. "Brother," they said, "if you refuse to go just for a few moments it will look as if you pay no attention to us. Do please go." They worried him so much that he finally gave way and, when they had eaten their cakes, told Daian to bring his clothes.

Yueniang was sitting talking to Yulou. "Where is your master going?" she asked the boy. But he said he did not know and that he had only been told to bring the clothes.

"You are lying, you young rascal," Yueniang cried. "It is the Third Lady's birthday today, and, if your master comes home late, you shall be whipped."

"Why should I be whipped?" the boy said, "I can do nothing."

"When he heard his friends had come," Yueniang said, "he dashed out as though his life depended on it. He was just having lunch, but he left everything. Where they'll take him, I can't imagine, or when he'll come back." She went on with her preparations for the evening.

Ximen Qing and his two friends went to Guijie's house. A table with refreshments had already been set out in the hall and two other singing girls had been brought in. Guijie and her sister Guiqing, dressed in their best clothes, went out to welcome the visitors, and the old procuress knelt on the floor to show how sorry she was for what had happened.

"You owe me a good deal," Ying Bojue said to Guijie. 'I have hardly any mouth left, I have had to do so much talking to persuade your young man to come. Now you give him wine and leave me without. If I hadn't dug him out you would have cried yourself blind and had to go singing in the street. You'd better talk nicely to me."

"Oh, Ying, you beggar," Guijie said, "you're such a loathsome creature, I can't find words bad enough for you. Why should I go singing in the street, begging?"

"You little strumpet," Bojue said, "you'd say your prayers, then beat the priest, would you? There was nothing you wouldn't do for me until he came, but now your wings are dry, I don't count any more. Come here and give me a kiss to warm me a little." He caught her by the neck and kissed her. Guijie laughed. "Look what you're doing, you've spilt the wine all over his Lordship."

"Oh, you little wretch! You love him so much you're afraid a drop of wine might fall on him. All your nice words are for him—there are none for me. I might be the son of a concubine."

"Well, you may be my son," Guijie said.

"Come here and I'll tell you a story," Bojue said. "Once upon a time a crab and a frog swore they would be brothers. They decided that the one who could jump over a certain brook should be the elder brother. The frog tried several times and at last succeeded. Just as the crab was about to see what he could do, two girls came up to draw some water from the brook. They tied a string to the crab, but, when they had got the water they had come for, they forgot to take the crab with them. The frog came back to the water's edge. 'Why don't you jump?' he said. 'Of course I can jump it,' said the crab, 'but just for the moment, I can't. Those two little whores have tied me up.' "

Guijie and her sister went and slapped Ying Bojue. Ximen Qing laughed heartily.

In Ximen's house, Wu Yueniang prepared a feast in celebration of Meng Yulou's birthday. Aunt Wu and Aunt Yang were there, and two nuns, and they all sat together in the upper room. They waited for Ximen

Qing until sunset, but he did not come. Yueniang was much annoyed. Then Pan Jinlian took the hand of Li Ping'er and suggested that they should go to the gate and look out for him. Yueniang told them she wondered they had the patience to do so. Then Jinlian asked Yulou whether she would not go with them, but Yulou said she would wait until she had heard the nuns tell some stories. So Jinlian ceased to trouble them, though when they gathered around to hear the story, she asked the nuns not to waste any time. Nun Wang, who was sitting on the bed, told them one story, but when she had finished it, Jinlian said: "That's not much of a story, tell us another."

The nun told them another story. Then Jinlian, with Yulou and Li Ping'er, went to the gate to look for Ximen Qing.

"Where do you think he's gone today?" Yulou asked the others.

"I expect he's gone to that strumpet Guijie's house," Jinlian said.

"But he has sworn never to go there again," Yulou said. "I'm sure he hasn't gone there. What will you bet me?"

"Anything you like," Jinlian said. "Clasp hands on it. The Sixth Lady is the witness. I'm sure he has gone there today. The other day there was a row and that little scoundrel Li Ming came to see how the land lay. Those murderous ghosts Ying and Xie came here this morning and went off with him. They and that young strumpet have schemed to get him there so that they can apologize. Then he'll set the fire going in his old stove again. In my opinion, he'll stay there ever so long. Probably he won't come back at all today. It is silly of the Great Sister to wait for him."

"But if he doesn't come back," Yulou said, "he'll surely send a boy to tell us so."

While they were talking a seller of melon seeds came along, and they were buying some seeds from him when they suddenly caught sight of Ximen Qing, and all ran indoors. Ximen Qing was on horseback. He said to Daian: "Run and see who they are." Daian ran a little way, then came back and told Ximen that the three ladies were buying melon seeds. He got off his horse and went in by the second door. Yulou and Li Ping'er went to Yueniang's room and told her of Ximen's return, but Jinlian hid behind a screen, and, when Ximen Qing came up to it, jumped out and startled him.

"You frightened me, you little villain," Ximen cried. "What were you doing outside the gate?"

"Is that a question for *you* to ask?" Jinlian said. "You were late and we went to look for you."

Ximen went to join the ladies. Yueniang had everything ready and told Yuxiao to take the wine jar while she poured out wine for all of them.

Ximen Qing was the first and then the others in their due order. They took their places and Chunmei and Yingchun played and sang for them. After a little while the things were cleared away and the birthday wine for Yulou was brought in, with forty different dishes. It was excellent wine, and of a color as exquisite as that of the clouds at sunset. Aunt Wu sat in the place of honor and they drank until the first night watch. By this time Aunt Wu could drink no more and went to her own room, but the others stayed, dicing with Ximen Qing, guessing fingers, and making up charades.

Yueniang suggested that they should take the title of a song and the name of a domino and make them fit with a line of the "Story of the Western Pavilion." Whoever happened to hold the domino that was named must drink a cup of wine as a forfeit. She herself began. "The Sixth Lady is drunk. Yang Fei dropped her eight jewels, and her hair is caught by the roses."

No one held the "eight jewels," and Ximen Qing began: "The lovely maiden Yu watched the battle between Chu and Han. The chief marshal was wounded and the noise of gongs and drums seemed like the heavens quaking." The lady who held the "chief marshal" had to drink a cup of wine. They continued till the turn came around to Yulou.

"A beautiful woman leans upon the scarlet rail, holding her silken skirt. She prays that the winds of spring may bring the moon within her net of gauze." She herself had the "scarlet rail," and Yueniang told Xiaoyu to pour a cup of wine for her.

"Drink three great cups," she said. "Tonight your bridegroom will spend the night with you." She turned to Li Jiao'er and Jinlian, "When we have finished our wine, we will all escort them to their room."

"Your word is law, and must be obeyed," Jinlian said. Yulou was very shy.

Soon afterwards Yueniang and the others took Ximen Qing to the Third Lady's room. Yulou asked them to stay a while, but they would not, and Jinlian said jokingly: "Sleep well, my child. Tomorrow your mother will come and see you. Now don't be naughty." Then, to Yueniang, "My daughter is still very young. I hope you will excuse her for my sake."

"You bad girl," Yulou cried, "you're like old vinegar. Wait till tomorrow and see what I'll do to you."

"I'm only like a go-between on her way upstairs," Jinlian said, "on tenterhooks as you might say." Then they all ran away.

As they came to the entrance to the inner courtyard, Li Ping'er slipped and fell. "Sister," Jinlian cried, "you're as bad as a blind woman. Just one slip and down you fall. I'd come and help you, but I'm over my ankles in the snow, and my shoes are in such a mess!"

"It is all this show," Yueniang said. "I've told the boys about it twice, but the thievish little scamps haven't cleared it away. Now the Sixth Lady has fallen down. Get a lamp," she said to Xiaoyu, "and take the ladies to their rooms."

Ximen Qing overheard this. "Listen to that little strumpet," he said to Yulou. "She gets into the snow and pulls the others after her. Then she talks about people treading on her toes. I'm surprised the others don't tell her what they think about her. Yesterday she said she never told the maids to sing that song, but I know she did."

"What did she mean by it?" Yulou asked.

"Well, she was trying to make out that the Great Lady deliberately burned incense in such a way that I was sure to find her doing it."

"She knows the meaning of all the songs," Yulou said. "The rest of us don't."

"Ah," Ximen said, "you don't realize how eager that woman is to score over others." They went to bed together.

Xiaoyu got a lantern and took Jinlian and Li Ping'er over the snow to their rooms. Yueniang went to her own place. Jinlian, who was already half drunk, took her companion by the hand. "Sister," she said, "I am tipsy and you must come to my room with me." Li Ping'er told her she was not drunk, but went with her and sent Xiaoyu back. Jinlian gave the Sixth Lady tea.

"You remember," she said, "how once you found it hard to join us here. Now we walk upon the same path. I had much to put up with for your sake and everybody had something to say about me. Still, my heart is in the right place, and I wouldn't have it otherwise. Heaven, at least, knows the truth."

"I realize how kind you have been to me," Li Ping'er said, "I shall never dare forget it."

"I only want you to understand," Jinlian said.

Chunmei brought tea. When they had drunk it, Li Ping'er said good-bye and went to her own room. Jinlian got into bed alone.

CHAPTER 22
Song Huilian

The next day the birthday celebrations were continued. Aunt Wu, Aunt Yang and old woman Pan spent the day with the ladies of the household in the inner hall.

Some time before, Laiwang's wife had died of a wasting sickness and Yueniang had found a new wife for him. This was the daughter of Song Ren, a coffin seller of the town, and her name, like the Fifth Lady's, was Jinlian. Originally, Cai, the Junior Prefect, had bought her for a maid, but she misconducted herself, had to leave, and ultimately married Jiang Cong the cook. This Jiang Cong often worked for Ximen Qing, and so it came about that Laiwang was frequently at his house on some errand or other. On such occasions he would drink wine and chat with the cook's wife, and they got on very well together. One day when Jiang Cong had been drinking, there was a quarrel among the cooks about the sharing out of certain moneys, and he was killed. The other cooks escaped over the wall. His wife then went to Ximen Qing and asked him to communicate with the authorities. This he did; the cooks were arrested and sentenced to death. Laiwang told Wu Yueniang that the young widow was a good needlewoman, and she gave him five taels of silver, two dresses, four rolls of black and red cloth, and some headdresses, and told him to marry the woman. But she changed her name to Huilian, for, there being already one Jinlian in the household, it would have been confusing to have another.

Song Huilian was twenty-four years old, two years younger than Pan Jinlian. She had a clear white skin, and her body was admirably proportioned, not too tall and not too short, neither too plump nor too slender. Her feet were even tinier than those of Jinlian. She was intelligent and wide awake, and had excellent taste in self-adornment. But she was indeed a captain among those who dally with men and a leader of those who disturb the harmony of households.

When she first came to Ximen Qing's place, she worked with the other maids and serving women in the kitchen, as plainly dressed as the rest. But, after a while, she noticed Meng Yulou and Pan Jinlian and began to copy them, dressing her hair high upon her head, with a long ringlet on either side. And when she served the ladies with tea or water, Ximen Qing gazed at her and gazed again. One day he formed a plan. He decided to send Laiwang to Hangzhou with five hundred taels to buy some dragon robes of ceremony for the Imperial Tutor, and other clothes for the family, an errand that would occupy him for about six months. It was about the middle of the eleventh month when Laiwang at last set off, and thereafter Ximen Qing never ceased to think of the delights that awaited him in Huilian's arms.

This day, Yulou's birthday, Yueniang and the others were enjoying a feast in the inner hall. Ximen Qing did not appear and Yueniang told Yuxiao to prepare a meal for him in her room. Through the lattice he chanced to see Huilian. She was wearing a double coat of red silk and a purple skirt. "Is that Laiwang's new wife?" he asked Yuxiao. "Why does she wear a red coat with a purple skirt? It looks very odd. Tell your mistress she must give her a skirt of another color."

"Even that purple skirt she borrowed from me," Yuxiao said.

The birthday passed, and on one of the following days Yueniang went to visit a friend. That day Ximen Qing drank heavily and went home in the afternoon. As he reached the second door, Huilian came out and they bumped into each other. Ximen Qing threw his arm around her neck and kissed her. "My daughter," he murmured, "if you do what I wish, you shall have all the ornaments and clothes you can desire." The woman made no reply but pulled her hand away from Ximen Qing and ran off to the other courtyard. He went to his wife's room and told Yuxiao to bring him a roll of blue satin.

"Take this to Huilian," he said to the maid, "and tell her that the other day I saw her dressed very unbecomingly. She must make herself a new skirt of this silk."

Yuxiao took the roll and Huilian looked at it. It was of bright blue satin, with the flowers of the four seasons as a design.

"If I make a new skirt," she said, "how shall I explain matters to our mistress?"

"You need not worry about that," Yuxiao told her. "Father will make any explanation that is necessary. He says if you do what he tells you in this matter he will buy you anything you like. The Great Lady is not at home and he wishes to see you. What have you to say about it?"

Huilian smiled, but for a long time she did not answer. At last she said: "When is he coming? I must clean my room."

"He says he will not come here," Yuxiao said. "He is afraid one of the servants might see him He wants you to go to the grotto beneath the artificial mound. It is very quiet there and an excellent place for you to meet."

"But if the Fifth Lady and the Sixth Lady hear of this, they will be angry," Huilian said.

Yuxiao assured her, saying that Yulou and Jinlian were playing a game with Li Ping'er and that she need not fear she would be disturbed. So the matter was settled and Yuxiao went back to tell Ximen Qing. He and Huilian went to the grotto, and Yuxiao kept watch for them.

Jinlian and Yulou were playing with Li Ping'er when a maid came and told them that Ximen Qing had come home. They separated. Yulou went to the inner court. Jinlian first went to her room to powder her face, then she, too, went to the inner court. When she came to the second door, she found Xiaoyu standing outside Yueniang's rooms. She asked the maid if Ximen Qing was there, but Xiaoyu only waved her hand in the direction of the outer court. Jinlian understood and went to the little gate near the artificial mound. There Yuxiao stopped her. Jinlian suspected that Yuxiao herself was carrying on a secret intrigue with Ximen and prepared to force her way in.

"You mustn't go in," Yuxiao cried in great confusion, 'Father is very busy."

"What if he is?" Jinlian cried. "What do I care?"

She went in and tried to find him. When she came to the grotto, matters were reaching a climax, but Huilian, hearing someone about, hastily set her clothes in order and came out. She flushed when she saw the Fifth Lady.

"What are you doing here, you scoundrelly slut?" Jinlian said.

Huilian muttered something about looking for Huatong and ran away like a streak of smoke.

Jinlian went into the grotto and found Ximen Qing hastily adjusting his girdle.

"Oh, you shameless object," she said angrily, "is this the way you behave with your slaves? In the daytime too! I would have boxed her ears, but she ran away too quickly. So you're Huatong, are you? She's been looking for you. Now tell me the truth. How often has this happened before? You must tell me, or, when the Great Lady comes back, I'll tell her all about it. If I don't have that strumpet's face beaten till it's as plump as a pig's, I shall know what to think of myself. You wait till you think we are amusing ourselves and then you play your games here. But you can't escape your old mother's keen eyes.

Ximen Qing laughed. "Be quiet, you funny little rogue. Don't let the whole world hear about it. I give you my word this is the first time."

Jinlian declared she did not believe a word he said, and Ximen Qing went off, laughing. When she went to the inner court, she found all the maids talking. They said their master had come home and sent Yuxiao for a roll of satin, and they wondered whom it was for. Jinlian realized it must have been for Huilian, but she said nothing to Yulou.

From that day onwards Huilian prepared soup and food for Jinlian every day and sewed for her. When she went to play chess with Li Ping'er, the woman would help her with advice. And, whenever there was a suitable opportunity, Jinlian helped Ximen Qing in his amorous adventure, hoping thereby to make herself more secure in his favor.

Ximen kept his promise to Huilian. He bought her clothes, ornaments, and perfumed tea leaves, and gave her silver that she spent on artificial flowers and powder. So, in course of time, she adopted a style of dress quite unlike that to which her poverty had originally constrained her. Further, Ximen told Yueniang that Huilian could make excellent soup and suggested that, in future, she and Yuxiao should not be sent to the common kitchen with the rest but that they should attend to the provision of tea and water at the smaller fire, and generally confine themselves to attendance upon Yueniang.

It was the eighth day of the twelfth month, and Ximen Qing had made an appointment with Ying Bojue to attend the funeral of one of their notable fellow citizens. He told the boys to saddle two horses and waited for his friend. Bojue was late and, meanwhile, Li Ming arrived. Ximen sat by the side of the fire in the great hall and looked on while Li Ming gave a music lesson to Chunmei, Yuxiao, Yingchun and Lanxiang, who were all dressed for the occasion. His son-in-law, Chen Jingji, sat beside him and talked. After they had heard one tune, Bojue came in with his boy Ying Bao, carrying a rug. Chunmei and the other girls were about to retire, but Ximen Qing said: "This is only Uncle Ying. There's no need to run away from him. Come and greet him properly." Then Ximen and Ying Bojue exchanged greetings and sat down, and the four girls came and kowtowed. Bojue rose quickly to acknowledge their greeting.

"Brother," he said, "what a lucky man you are to have four young ladies so beautiful as these, each more beautiful than the other. What a pity it is I left my house in such a hurry that I forgot to bring any money with me. One of these days I will give you something to buy some powder and things with." Chunmei and the others withdrew. Then Chen Jingji greeted Bojue and sat down.

"What makes you so late?" Ximen said.

"My eldest daughter has been very ill," Bojue said, "but she is a little better now, so my wife has decided to bring her home for a change. This has made me rather busy. I had to get a chair and buy one or two things before I could come."

"Well," Ximen said, "I have waited a long time. We had better have some gruel." He gave orders that some should be brought.

Li Ming greeted Ying Bojue, who asked what he had been doing lately. They all chatted while the table was being set. Four bowls of gruel were brought, with ten plates of other refreshments. The bowls were made of silver, and the gruel was mixed with nuts of various kinds and fruits with white sugar on the top. Ying Bojue finished off the gruel and drank a small cup of wine. As half the wine still remained in the jar, Ximen told a boy to take it with the dishes that were left and give them to Li Ming in one of the side rooms. Then he dressed, and he and Ying Bojue mounted their horses and rode to the funeral.

For a while after Ximen had gone, Yuxiao and Lanxiang went on with their music, but soon they stopped and went to the room where Ximen's daughter Ximen Dajie lived. Chunmei was left alone with Li Ming who was teaching her to play the lute. Li Ming had had too much to drink and, when his hand became entangled in Chunmei's broad sleeve, he freed himself with undue clumsiness.

"How dare you touch my hand, you thievish turtle!" the girl cried. "You must be anxious to die. You seem to have very strange ideas about the kind of girl I am. Every day you have good wine and good food, but today you must have taken leave of your senses. Would you dare touch my hand! You put your shovel in the wrong place. Before you do a thing like that, you should ask leave. I will tell Father the very minute he comes home and he will send you packing. Do you think you're the only person who can teach us songs? We can find a teacher anywhere, and we don't need you, you ugly turtle."

She used the word *turtle* very freely, and Li Ming gathered up his things and escaped as quickly as he could.

Chunmei was very angry and, still cursing Li Ming, went to the inner court. Jinlian, Yulou, Li Ping'er and Huilian were playing chess in Jinlian's room when the girl came in.

"Whom are you cursing?" Jinlian said. "Who has annoyed you?"

"Who but that disgusting little turtle, Li Ming?" Chunmei said. "When Father went out, he had the kindness to leave food and wine and gruel for him. Yuxiao and the other girls behaved most unbecomingly. They might not have had any modesty at all. They played there for a while and then went off to our mistress's room. When that turtle saw there was nobody in the room, he touched my hand and laughed at me—he was quite drunk—but I cried and cursed him and he took his things and went. What a pity I didn't box his ears! The thievish turtle doesn't choose the right people to play his tricks with. I am not the kind of girl to stand that sort of thing. I'll beat his turtle's face till it is green."

"You silly girl," Jinlian said, "there is no reason why you should study music if you don't wish to. Why allow yourself to become so angry that your face goes yellow? We will tell Father. He will send the rascal about his business, and that will be the end of it. We are not having you taught music to make money, and I won't have a rapscallion like that behaving in such a way to one of my maids. I know the turtle. He's full to the very brim of vice."

"He is the brother of the Second Lady," Chunmei said, "but that doesn't trouble me. She can hardly have me beaten to avenge her brother."

"He is a music master, and gives lessons here," Huilian said. "He has no business to make free with any of the girls. No matter how little he may be paid, he should treat us with the same respect as his own father and mother. Besides, he is always having his meals here."

"Not only that," said Jinlian, "we pay him five taels of silver every month. He will come to a bad end if he goes on in this way. Is there one of our boys who would dare to show his teeth to his master? Is there one who would dare to joke with him? They know that if they did they would get a cursing if Father happened to be in a good temper, and a beating if he were in a bad one. This turtle is playing with fire, and Father will teach him how hot the fire is." She turned to Chunmei. "Why didn't you come here as soon as your master went out? Why did you stay and give that turtle a chance to play tricks?"

"It was all because of Yuxiao and the others," the maid said. "They stayed, and would not come."

"Where are they now?" Yulou asked. Chunmei told her that they had gone to Yueniang's room. Jinlian rose and went to see them. Li Ping'er also went away and sent to fetch Yingchun. In the evening when Ximen Qing returned, Jinlian told him what had happened. He sent for Laixing and gave instructions that Li Ming was not to be allowed to enter the house again.

CHAPTER 23
Ximen Qing's Dalliance
with Song Huilian

Winter at last gave place to spring. It was the beginning of a new year. Ximen Qing went to celebrate the festival with his friends, and Wu Yueniang paid a visit to her brother. In the afternoon Meng Yulou and Pan Jinlian played chess with Li Ping'er. When Yulou asked what should be the stakes, Jinlian said five *qian* of silver, three to be spent on wine, and the other two on a pig's head.

"We will ask Laiwang's wife to roast it for us," she said. "She can do it with a single faggot and make it very tender."

"But the Great Lady is not at home," Yulou said. "How can we do it in her absence?"

"We will save some for her," Jinlian said.

They began to play. They played three games and Li Ping'er lost. Jinlian told a maid to call Laixing, and gave him the money, telling him to buy wine, a pig's head, and four pig's trotters. When he had bought them, she said, he was to take them to Laiwang's wife, ask her to cook them and take them to the Third Lady's room. Yulou suggested another plan. "Sixth Sister," she said, "say that when she has cooked the head, she must put it in a container and bring it here. Li Jiao'er and Sun Xue'e will be there, and I am not sure we want them." Jinlian agreed.

After a while Laixing came back from his errand and took the pig's head to the kitchen. Song Huilian and Yuxiao were there, playing a game with melon seeds. "Sister Huilian," Laixing said, "the Fifth Lady and the Third Lady sent me to buy some delicacies. I have put them in the kitchen and the ladies wish you to cook them. When they are done, will you please take them to the Sixth Lady's room?"

"I am busy now," said Huilian, "I'm making a pair of shoes for my Lady. Ask somebody else to attend to it. Why come to me?"

"Well, please yourself," Laixing said, "here they are. I've got other things to see about." He went away.

"We had better stop this game," Yuxiao said, "and you go and cook the things. You know what a sharp tongue the Fifth Lady has. Don't set it wagging."

Huilian laughed. "I wonder how she knows that I can cook pig's head?" She went to the kitchen, filled a cauldron with water, cleaned the pig's head and the trotters, found a suitable faggot and put it underneath the oven. Then she filled a large bowl with salt, put spices into it and mixed the ingredients together. She put the pig's head into a container. In less than an hour it was so tender that the skin began to peel. With all the flavor of the spices it smelled exceedingly appetizing. She set the head on a large tray and put the tray, with saucers of ginger and onion, into a large square box. This she carried to the Sixth Lady's room. Then she warmed the wine and took that in. Yulou chose some of the tastiest part, put it on a dish, set aside a jar of wine, and told a maid to take it to Yueniang's room. Then they all sat down to enjoy their feast.

Huilian came in smiling. "How do you like my cooking, Ladies?" she asked.

"The Third Lady," Jinlian said, "was just saying how clever you are. It is as soft and tender as can be."

"Is it really true that you only use a single faggot?" Li Ping'er said.

"Hardly that," Huilian replied. "If I did, it would be overcooked."

Yulou told a maid to pour some wine for the woman, and Li Ping'er picked out some meat and invited her to try some of her own cooking.

"I knew," Huilian said, "that you did not like things too salty, but I did not make it quite tasty enough. However, next time, I shall know exactly what you like." She kowtowed three times and stood beside them.

They drank till evening when Yueniang returned. Then they went together to receive her. Xiaoyu showed her the delicacy that had been put aside for her. "We have been playing chess today," Yulou said, with a smile, "and this is what we won from the Sixth Lady. We saved some for you."

"It is hardly fair," Yueniang said, "that one should pay for what all enjoy. I'll tell you what. We will have a kind of festival, and each of us in turn shall give a party to the rest and we will have Miss Yu here to sing. That seems to me a better plan than gambling. What do you think?" They all agreed, and Yueniang continued: "Tomorrow is the fifth of the month, I will begin. Li Jiao'er can take the sixth, Yulou the seventh, and Jinlian the eighth."

"That will suit me very well," Jinlian said, "for it is my birthday and I shall kill two birds with one stone."

They approached Xue'e, but she did not welcome the suggestion. Yueniang said they would not ask her again and Li Ping'er should take her turn. Yulou said that the ninth would be Jinlian's birthday and perhaps her mother and Aunt Wu would come. It was decided that Li Ping'er should entertain them on the tenth.

On the following day Ximen Qing went to visit a friend and Yueniang gave her party. Miss Yu, the singer, sang and played for them. Then
came the turn of Li Jiao'er, Yulou, and Jinlian. On Jinlian's birthday old
woman Pan and Aunt Wu came to spend the day. Then it was the turn
of Li Ping'er. She sent Xiuchun twice to invite Sun Xue'e but, though she
promised to come, she did not.

"I told you she wouldn't come," Yulou said, "there is no use asking her.
She always tries to make out that we have all the money and she is as poor
as an unshod donkey. Since she chooses to take that attitude, we'd better
leave her alone."

"She is quite impossible," Yueniang said, "we won't bother about her
any more." They all went to visit Li Ping'er. Miss Yu went with them to
make music, and there were eight of them in all, including Ximen Dajie
and Aunt Wu. Ximen Qing himself was not at home and Yueniang told
Yuxiao that, if he should come in and ask for wine, she should see it was
given him.

It was afternoon when Ximen returned. When Yuxiao took his clothes,
he asked where Yueniang was, and she told him that all the ladies, with
their guests, were with Li Ping'er, taking wine.

"What kind of wine are they drinking?" Ximen asked. When he was
told, he called for a jar of Lily wine that Ying Bojue had brought, and told
Yuxiao to open it. He tasted a little and said: "This wine is just what ladies
like," and told the maids to take it to them. It happened that Huilian was
serving wine to the ladies, and when she saw Yuxiao bringing the new jar,
she very cunningly went to meet her. Yuxiao winked at her and pressed
her hand so that she understood that Ximen had returned. Yueniang asked
Yuxiao who had told her to bring the wine, and the girl told her. Then she
asked how long Ximen had been back. "If your master wants anything to
drink, set a table in my room. There is plenty to eat if he wants anything.
You can wait upon him." Yuxiao went away.

Huilian stayed a while and then said she was going to the kitchen to
make some tea. "There is some Liu'an tea in my room," Yueniang said,
"use that." Huilian went to the inner court. There, Yuxiao was standing
outside the door of the upper room, making a sign to her to go in. She
pushed aside the lattice and went in. Ximen Qing was drinking wine. She
went over to him and seated herself upon his knee, and they embraced
each other lovingly. She fondled him with her hand until it became evident he was greatly stirred, and, from her mouth, she passed wine to his.

"Father," she said, "I have used all the fragrant tea leaves you gave me
the other day; may I have some more? And have you any money? I owe
some to Xue."

"There are a few taels in my purse," Ximen said, "you may take them." Then he would have unloosed her girdle, but she restrained him, saying she was afraid someone might come.

"If you stay in tonight," Ximen said, "we can enjoy ourselves." Huilian shook her head. "There are so many difficulties in the inner court. We had better go again to the Fifth Lady's room."

While they were amusing themselves Yuxiao kept watch for them outside the door. Xue'e happened to come into the court and heard the sound of laughing and talking. At first she thought it was Yuxiao talking to Ximen Qing, but then she saw the maid standing by the door. She stopped, and Yuxiao began to fear that she would decide to go in. "The Sixth Lady has sent for you several times," she said. "Why won't you go?"

Xue'e laughed contemptuously. "I am one of those women who never have any luck," she said. "However speedy the horse I ride, I can never catch up with them. How can I play with them? They can have ten parties, while I haven't even the undergarments I need."

Ximen Qing coughed and Xue'e went back to her kitchen. Yuxiao pushed the lattice to one side, and Huilian seized the opportunity and slipped away.

She went to the kitchen to make some tea, and soon Xiaoyu came and said that Yueniang wanted to know why the tea was so long coming. "It is just ready," Huilian said, "I am only looking for some nuts." She found the nuts and, with Xiaoyu carrying the tray, took the tea to the ladies.

"Why has it taken you so long to make the tea?" Yueniang said.

"Father is drinking wine in your room," the woman said, "and I did not venture to go in. I had to wait for your maid to get the tea for me and then I had to go to the kitchen for the nuts."

The ladies drank the tea and began to play. Huilian leaned over the table and made comments on the game until Yulou grew angry. "Why must you put in your word when we are playing?" she said. "It is not your place to speak here." Huilian was abashed. She blushed and did not know what to do with herself. Finally she went away.

The ladies drank wine until nightfall. Then Ximen Qing came in. "You all look very jolly," he said, laughing. Aunt Wu stood up and offered her place to her brother-in-law. "The place for you to drink is in the inner court," Yueniang said. "Why do you, a man, come and join a party of ladies?"

"Very well! I will go,"Ximen said, and he went to Jinlian's room. She followed him. He was already half drunk.

"Little oily mouth," he said, taking her by the hands, "I want to ask you just one favor. I wished to enjoy Huilian in the inner court, but there was nowhere we could go. May we come here?"

"You are a dirty creature," Jinlian cried, "and I can't find words bad enough for you. I don't mind what you do with that woman elsewhere, but there is no place for you here. Besides, even if I were willing, that young scoundrel Chunmei would object. Ask her, if you don't believe me. If she doesn't mind, I will raise no difficulties."

"Very well," Ximen said, "you won't do what I wish. I shall have to spend the night in the grotto. Please ask the maids to take some bedclothes and light a fire for me there. It is rather chilly."

Jinlian laughed. "Really, I can't tell you what I think of you. That slave's wife might be your mother and you might be Wang Xiang, carrying out the duties of filial piety in winter. Only you'd rather lie on a warm bed than on ice."

"Don't tease me," Ximen Qing said, laughing, "but tell the maids to light a fire." Jinlian agreed, and when the ladies separated that night, she told Qiuju to take bedclothes and a stove to the grotto under the artificial mound. Huilian, after escorting Yueniang, Li Jiao'er and Yulou to their apartments, asked if there was anything more she could do for them, and was told to go to her bed in the front court. She stood there for a short time and then, seeing that no one was about, went swiftly to the artificial mound.

Huilian thought, when she went into the garden, that Ximen Qing had not come yet, so she did not close the gate, but when she reached the grotto she found he was already there. She went in. It was very cold and the ground was covered with dust. She took two sticks of incense from her sleeve, lighted them and set them in the ground, shivering although there was a stove. She first covered herself with the bedclothes and pulled a sable cloak over her, then Ximen shut the door of the grotto, got on to the bed, removed his long gown and unloosed the woman's girdle. She placed herself upon him with legs outstretched. Then they came together and enjoyed the work of love to the full.

Jinlian heard them go to the garden, took off her headdress, and going very softly, opened the garden gate and went to the mound. She did not trouble whether the moss made her feet cold, or whether the branches of the shrubs tore her skirt. She stood quietly outside the door and looked in. The light was burning brightly. She heard the woman say laughingly, "Showering ice upon an icy bed! You are in no better case than a beggar. You can find nowhere else to go, so you come to this icy hell. You are like a man who swallows a long string so that when he comes to die of starvation somebody will pull him out." Then she went on: "It is so cold! Let us go to sleep. You do nothing but look at my feet though you know them perfectly well already. I have no new shoes. Will you buy some tops for me, and let me show you what beautiful shoes I can make?"

"My child," Ximen said, "of course I will. You shall have all colors to-morrow. Your feet are smaller than the Fifth Lady's."

"There is no comparison between hers and mine," the woman said. "I tried on her shoes yesterday and found I could get into them with my own shoes on my feet. But, so long as the feet are straight, it doesn't matter much whether they are large or small."

Jinlian heard all this and was anxious to hear more.

"Was your Fifth Lady married before she came here?" she heard Huilian say.

"Yes," Ximen replied, "she is one of the changeable kind."

"But how charming she is," Huilian said, "I don't wonder that she and you are like dew and water together."

Jinlian listened and was almost paralyzed. "If I allow this strumpet to carry on like this," she said to herself, "she will be the end of me." She would have gone at once and taxed the couple with their misdeeds if she had not been afraid of Ximen's hasty temper. She knew that if she let the matter pass too long he would refuse to admit it, and decided to leave something behind to mark the fact that she had been there. The next day she would confront him with it. She went back to the garden gate, and, taking a silver pin from her hair, put it in the latch. Then she went to her own room, in a very evil humor.

The next morning Huilian got up and went out, her hair hastily arranged. When she came to the garden gate, she was startled. The gate had not been locked, yet though she pushed, she could not open it. She had to go back to Ximen Qing, who called to Chunmei on the other side of the wall to come and open the gate. Then he saw the pin and knew that it belonged to Jinlian. He realized that she knew everything that had happened the night before. As for Huilian, it was as though she carried a ghost child in her womb. In the outer court she met Ping'an coming from the rooms on the east side. He looked at her and smiled.

"Why are you laughing at me, you young rascal?" she cried.

"Sister," Ping'an said, "what is the matter with you? I was only smiling."

"Why should you smile without any reason, and before breakfast, too?"

"Well, Sister, I'm smiling because you look as if you had had nothing to eat for three days. There is a hungry look about your eyes. I hear you weren't in your room last night."

Huilian flushed, and cursed the boy. "You thievish, gawpy, ghost-catching young imp! What night was I not in my room?"

"Your door is locked this very moment," the boy said. "I've just seen it. How do you explain that?"

"I got up very early to go to the Fifth Lady's room and I haven't been able to get back before now. Where have you been?"

"I suppose," the boy said, "that the Fifth Lady sent for you to salt crabs because you are so clever at anything to do with legs. And she sent you to the gate to find a basket seller because you are so good at putting one and one together."

Huilian snatched up a door bar and chased Ping'an around the courtyard. "You young rascal," she cried, "I'll tell my husband about this and he will treat you as you deserve. You are mad."

"Don't be angry, Sister. By the way, whom did you say you'd tell?" This made her still more angry and she ran after him again.

Daian, who happened to come from the shop, took the bar from her and asked her why she wished to beat the boy.

"Ask the wicked little chatterbox himself," Huilian cried angrily. "I haven't a particle of strength left."

Meanwhile Ping'an took advantage of the opportunity, and made off.

"Don't be angry, Sister," Daian said. "Go to your room and dress your hair."

Huilian took some small change from her pocket. "Will you buy me a large bowl of soup?" she said.

"Certainly," the boy replied. He took the money, washed his face, and then went to buy the soup. When he brought it, Huilian gave half of it to him. She dressed her hair, then closed her door and went to the inner court to wait upon Yueniang.

Then she went to see Jinlian. The Fifth Lady was doing her hair, and Huilian served her most attentively, holding the mirror, carrying hot water and doing one thing and another. Jinlian never so much as glanced at her.

"May I put your sleeping shoes under the bedclothes?" Huilian said.

"Please yourself," Jinlian said. "If it is too much trouble, I'll tell my maid." Then she called to Qiuju: "Where are you, you thievish slave?"

"She is sweeping the floor," said Huilian, "and Sister Chunmei is dressing her hair."

"Please do not concern yourself about my maids, but go away," Jinlian said. "I will have my own maids to attend to me. Besides, my dirty place will soil your shoes. Hadn't you better go and wait upon his Lordship? He likes to have women of your sort about him. He and I are the dew-and-water kind of husband and wife, and I am a twice-married woman. You, Sister, are of a very different kind; you came in a sedan chair. You are the real wife."

When Huilian heard these bitter words, she knew that all the happenings of the night before were known to Jinlian. She threw herself upon her knees. "Mother," she cried, "you are my true mistress. Unless you raise your hand, there is no place for me to stand. Without your kind aid, I should never have been able to do what my master wished. The Great Lady is only a shadow, but you are my benefactress and I shall always be faithful to you. Mother, you may watch me as much as you like, and if ever you find me deceiving you, may I not die peacefully in my bed."

"I do not like to have dust thrown in my eyes," Jinlian said. "If my husband wants you I shall not interfere, but I will not have you playing tricks and putting me in an invidious position. You must think twice before you decide to come between us."

"Mother," Huilian said, "question me if you will. I shall not dare deceive you. Last night you did not really hear what was said."

"I don't believe you," Jinlian said. "Let me tell you this. One woman can never bind a man, and your master not only has several wives here, but a host of lady friends outside. But he always tells me what he does. There was a time when the Great Lady had some control over him, and in those days he used to tell her things, and did not tell me. You have not the authority of the Great Lady."

There was nothing Huilian could say. She stood there for a while, and then went away. As she came to the passage by the second door, she saw Ximen Qing.

"Oh, you good man," she said, "you have let other people know all that we did last night, and I have had to suffer in consequence. You should keep to yourself the things we say to one another, until you forget them. Why should you let everybody know? Your mouth runs over like a water trough, and I will never tell you anything again."

"What's that!" Ximen cried, "I don't know what you're talking about." Huilian scowled at him and went away.

She was very careful and cunning in her dealings with other people in the household. If she was buying anything at the gate she would call Fu "Master Fu" and Chen Jingji "Uncle." Ben the Fourth was always "Old Fourth." Now that she had had this affair with Ximen Qing, she was much less sedate in her manner, and was often at the gate joking with some man or other. She would go after Fu and say to him, "Master Fu, I wonder if you would mind buying some powder for me?" Fu was a simple-minded fellow and looked out for the powder seller for her, but he was not altogether comfortable about it at heart.

One day Daian said jokingly, "Sister, you should have been out with your scales earlier. The powder seller has gone."

"You rascal," Huilian said, "the Fifth Lady and the Sixth Lady have asked me to buy some powder for them. What do you mean by talking of two measures of rouge and three of powder? They powder their faces many times a day. I shall tell them what you say."

"Oh, Sister!" the boy said, "you always try to frighten me by talking about the Fifth Lady."

Once she said to Ben the Fourth: "Old Fourth, please keep a lookout for the flower seller, and buy me two branches of plum blossom and a couple of chrysanthemums." Ben the Fourth waited about for the flower seller, neglecting his own business. When the man came, he told her, and, standing by the second door, she picked out the flowers she liked best, and two purple and gold handkerchiefs. She spent seven *qian* and more. She took a piece of silver from her purse and asked Ben the Fourth to weigh it for her. He was busy upon his accounts, but left them, weighed the silver, and was about to cut off the amount she wanted. Then Daian came up.

"I will cut off the silver you want," he said. He took the piece, but instead of cutting it, looked at Huilian.

"Well," she said, "you thievish monkey! Why don't you cut it? Why stand there looking at me? Did you hear the dogs barking the night I stole the money?"

"I don't say you stole the silver," Daian said, "but somehow or other it seems familiar. It is just like some Father had in his purse. The other day, he had a piece cut into two at the lantern market. One piece he gave to the goldsmith and this is the other. I remember it perfectly."

"Don't you know that many things in this world look alike? What should I be doing with your master's silver?"

Daian laughed. "I know what that silver paid for," he said. Huilian slapped him. He cut the silver and gave the money to the flower seller, but made no offer to give Huilian the change.

"You rascal," she said, "you must be a brave man to dare to take my money."

"I am not robbing you," the boy said, "I am only going to buy some fruit."

"You thievish monkey," Huilian cried, "give it back to me, and I will give you something." When Daian handed back the silver, she gave him a small piece and put the rest back in her purse.

After that she often stood at the gate to buy artificial flowers and handkerchiefs, sometimes spending several taels. She would buy four or five measures of melon seeds and give them to the maids and serving women. For herself she bought a pearl headband and a pair of bright gold earrings. She wore red silk trousers and a broad-sleeved gown in which she kept fragrant tea leaves. She carried several perfume boxes. Every day she spent at least two or three *qian*, all of which came from Ximen Qing.

　　After Jinlian knew of her relations with Ximen, Huilian went to the Fifth Lady's room every day and waited on her with the utmost diligence. She served her with tea and water and sewed for her, doing many things that were quite unnecessary, and many things that she had no desire to do. She did not go to Yueniang even once a day, for all her time was spent with Jinlian, waiting upon her when she played chess or dominoes with Li Ping'er. Sometimes Ximen Qing would come in while they were playing, and then Jinlian would purposely ask Huilian to serve the wine. Sometimes they would sit and play together to please him.

CHAPTER 24

The Ladies Celebrate
the Feast of Lanterns

Candles blaze in silver sconces
Wine is heated in the jars
The guests are merry and their laughter never ceases.
Untrammeled hips sway as the willows of Zhang Tai
Unpainted lips sing as the spring in the imperial gardens
From the fragrance of their attire we know their will with us
Flowers fall from their hair and are gathered in silence.
If it were not for the delights of love
Would Han be sober after drinking?

The day came when the moon shines in the heavens and lanterns shine upon the earth. Ximen Qing had all his lanterns set out and a splendid feast prepared in the great hall. On the sixteenth day of the first month the whole household assembled, with Ximen Qing and Wu Yueniang in the place of honor, and the other ladies all beautifully dressed. The four maids who acted as the musicians of the family played and sang many songs about the lanterns. A small table was laid specially for Chen Jingji. The food was exquisite and the fruits appropriate to the season. Four maids served the wine, and Laiwang's wife Song Huilian sat on a chair outside the door, chewing melon seeds, waiting for the wine to be brought from the kitchen. It was her duty, when wine was wanted in the hall, to send Laian and Huatong to the kitchen to fetch it. She said: "The rascals have all run away; there is no one here." Then Ximen Qing saw Huatong bringing the wine, and asked him where he had been, saying he deserved a whipping. When the boy came out of the hall, he complained to Huilian.

"Sister," he said, "why did you tell Father stories about me? I haven't been away at all."

"I can't help that," Huilian said, "they called for wine and you were not there. If you are not to blame, who is?"

"Sister," said the boy, "it is very nice and tidy here, yet you are throwing down melon seeds. If Father sees it he will be angry again.

"Don't you bother about me, you young rascal," Huilian said. "If you won't sweep them away, I'll tell one of the other boys, and if Father sees them, I'll take all the responsibility."

"Oh, don't make a fuss about it," the boy said. "I'll sweep them away for you."

Ximen Qing saw that his son-in-law Chen Jingji had no wine and told Pan Jinlian to give him some. She stood up quickly, poured out a cup of wine and smilingly handed it to Jingji.

"Brother," she said, "Father says I must give you some wine. Now you must drink it."

Jingji took the cup and looked slyly at Jinlian. "Fifth Mother, please don't trouble. I will drink it."

Jinlian, with the light between Ximen Qing and herself, squeezed Jingji's hand as he took the cup from her. He pretended to be paying attention to the others, but touched her tiny feet.

"What shall we do if Father sees us?" Jinlian whispered with a smile. They made love in front of the others, without anyone knowing what they were about. But Huilian, who was standing outside the window, saw quite clearly everything that passed between them.

"This woman," she thought, "is always trying to get the better of me, and here she is, behaving like this with that young man. Next time she treats me badly, I shall know what to say."

They had been drinking for some time when a message came from Ying Bojue inviting Ximen Qing to go with him to see the lanterns. Ximen told Yueniang to enjoy herself with the others, and he, with Daian and Ping'an in attendance, went to join Bojue.

Yueniang and her companions went on with their feast till the stars grew dim and the full moon, rising in the east, made the courtyard bright as day. Then some of the women went to their rooms to change their dresses; others adorned themselves in the light of the moon, and others put flowers in their hair in the lantern light. Meng Yulou, Jinlian, Li Ping'er and Huilian stood in front of the great hall to watch Chen Jingji set off the fireworks.

Li Jiao'er, Sun Xue'e and Ximen Dajie went with Yueniang to the inner court.

"He is out," Jinlian said to the others. "Shall we ask the Great Lady to let us go to the street?"

"If you go," said Huilian, "please take me with you."

"If you wish to go, you must ask the Great Lady," Jinlian said. "If she and the Second Lady would like to go too, we will wait here for them."

Huilian was about to go to the inner court, but Yulou said: "She will do no good. I will go myself and ask them." Li Ping'er said: "I am going to my room to find a warmer cloak. It will be cold as the night gets older."

"Sister," Jinlian said: "if you have a cloak to spare, bring one for me. It will save my going back to my room." Li Ping'er promised, and went away.

Only Jinlian was left to watch Chen Jingji setting off the fireworks. She went over to him and pinched him slightly. "Brother," she said, laughing, "don't you feel cold with such thin clothes on?"

A boy called Little Iron Rod was jumping about begging Jingji to give him some fireworks. The young man thought that here was an opportunity. He gave the lad a few fireworks and told him to go and set them off outside the gate.

"So you think my clothes are too thin," he said to Jinlian. "Have you anything warmer for me?"

"You are determined to get something out of me," Jinlian said. "You touched my feet, and I did not complain. Now you have the audacity to ask me for clothes. I don't belong to you. Why should I give you clothes?"

"If you won't give me any, well and good," Jingji said, "but why try to frighten me?"

"Oh, you're like the birds that gather on the city walls, always afraid of something."

They were talking when Yulou and Huilian came back. "The Great Lady," Yulou said, "says she will not go out because she is not very well, but we may go if we promise to come back in good time. Li Jiao'er has a bad leg and she doesn't feel like walking."

"Well," Jinlian said, "if they won't go, we must go with the Sixth Lady; then, if he comes back, we shall be the only ones to blame. Do you think we should take Chunmei, Yuxiao, your maid Lanxiang, and the Sixth Lady's Yingchun?"

Xiaoyu came up and asked if she might go, and Yulou said she might if she obtained her mistress's permission. This she did, and came back to them, smiling.

Then the three ladies set off with their maids. The two boys Laian and Huatong escorted them with lanterns. Jingji set off several fireworks on the mounting stone.

"Uncle," Huilian cried, "wait a moment for me. I am just going to my room for a second."

"We are off now," Jingji said.

"If you don't wait for me, I will never love you again," Huilian cried. She ran to her room and changed into a dress of red silk with a white skirt, set a red and gold kerchief on her head, pins and flowers in her hair. Finally she put on a pair of gold lantern-shaped earrings. Then she joined the ladies in their walk "to gain immunity from the hundred sicknesses." The ladies all wore white silk gowns. They had masses of pearls and flowers on their heads. With their white faces and red lips they looked like angels in the moonlight.

Chen Jingji and Laixing walked beside them, setting off fireworks as they went along. There were lotuses that slowly threw forth fire, golden thread chrysanthemum, and orchids ten feet high. When they came to the street, there was a never-ending stream of incense, and the revelers were as plentiful as ants. Crackers exploded with a sound like thunder and the lanterns were bright with a thousand different hues. Flutes and drums sounded wildly. It was a splendid festival.

When the people in the street saw a procession advancing with lanterns of various colors, they imagined that it must have come from some noble household, and gave way immediately. "Uncle," Huilian said, "light a rocket for me." And a little later: "Uncle, set off a full moon for me." First, her ornaments fell off; then she lost a shoe, and had to wait while someone helped her on with it again. She jumped about and joked incessantly with Chen Jingji. Yulou did not approve of this behavior.

"Why do your shoes keep coming off?" she asked.

Yuxiao said, "She was afraid of soiling her own shoes, so she put a pair of the Fifth Lady's over them." Yulou demanded that she should come and show her feet.

"She asked me yesterday to give her a pair of my shoes," Jinlian said, "but I never dreamed the scamp would think of putting them on outside her own."

When Huilian pulled up her skirt, Yulou saw that she was indeed wearing two pairs of red shoes, bound to her ankles by green laces. She said no more.

After a while they crossed the street and went to the lantern fair. "Let us go first to the Sixth Lady's house in Lion Street," Jinlian said to Yulou. She ordered the boys to take them there. Old woman Feng had gone to bed and two girls who had been entrusted to her to sell were asleep with her, but when the boys knocked at the door, she got up hastily and opened it, and the ladies went in.

The old woman opened the stove to boil some water, then took a jar and was about to go out to buy some wine, but Yulou told her they did not wish for any wine, they had had so much at home before they came. "But we shall be glad to have some tea if you will give us some," she said.

"If you invite people to take wine with you, you must give them something to eat," Jinlian said.

"Yes," said Li Ping'er, "and if you think of giving us wine, we shall want a couple of large jars. No small ones for us!"

Yulou told the old woman that they were only teasing her. "Don't go," she said, "just make some tea for us." Then the old woman decided not to go.

"Why is it so long since you came to see me?" Li Ping'er asked old woman Feng. "What are you doing, these days?"

"You see these two girls," the old woman said. "Who is there to look after them if I go out?" Yulou asked who was selling them.

"One is a maid belonging to a neighbor," the old woman said. "She is thirteen years old, and they only want five taels of silver for her. The other is the wife of a servant in the Wang household. Her husband ran away, so they sent her to me. They ask ten taels for her."

"I know someone who wants a girl, so there is a chance for you," Yulou said.

"Who is that, Third Lady?" the old woman asked.

"The Second Lady has only one maid," Yulou said, "and that, of course, is not enough for her. She needs someone rather older, so you can sell the older of the two to her. How old is she?" The old woman said that she was seventeen. Tea was brought and she served it to the ladies.

Chunmei, Yuxiao and Ximen Dajie went upstairs to look out over the street. Then Chen Jingji warned the ladies that it was getting late, and almost time to return. Jinlian told him to mind his own business. However, she called down Chunmei and the others, and they left the house. As the old woman was seeing them to the door Li Ping'er asked where Ping'an was.

"I haven't seen him all day," the old woman said, "but then I often have to wait till midnight for him."

Laian told them that the boy had gone with his master to Ying's house.

"Lock your door, and go to bed," Li Ping'er said to the old woman, "he will not be back tonight. Come and see me tomorrow and bring the maid for the Second Lady. You know you are like the Abbot of the Stone Buddha Temple: you never do anything unless you are made." They waited till she had locked the gate, and then went home again.

When they reached their own gate, they found a woman called Han, the wife of a Mohammedan, making a terrible to-do. Her husband was away on duty with a Chamberlain of the Royal Stables, and she had been out on the walk to cure the hundred illnesses. She had come home drunk. Now she said that somebody had broken open her door, stolen her dog, and a lot of things were missing. She was sitting at the side of the road and cursing everybody. The ladies stopped and Jinlian told Laian to bring the woman over to them to tell them what was amiss. The woman came, made reverence and told her story. The ladies gave her some money and fruits, and Yulou told Laian to ask Jingji to take the woman home. Jingji made fun of the whole affair and wouldn't do anything for the woman, so Jinlian bade Laian take her home. "Come and see me tomorrow," she said. "You can do some washing for me, and I will tell my husband and see that you get your rights." At this the woman Han smiled, thanked them repeatedly, and went home.

The ladies went on. When they came to the gate, Ben the Fourth's wife was standing there. She smiled, made a reverence to them, and invited them to take tea with her. Yulou told her that they had been delayed by listening to Madam Han's story, and that it was too late for them to accept her invitation, though they thanked her very much. But Ben the Fourth's wife pressed them and at last they went in. In her room there was an image of the Buddha of the Eight Calamities, and another of the sage Guan. A snow-flower lantern hung by the door. When they had all sat down, she told her daughter, a girl of fourteen years called Changjie, to greet the ladies and hand around the tea. Yulou and Jinlian each gave the girl two flowers, and Li Ping'er gave her a handkerchief and a *qian* of silver, with which, she said, she might buy some melon seeds. Ben the Fourth's wife was delighted and thanked them repeatedly. After a while they left. Laixing met them at the gate, and, when they asked whether Ximen Qing had come home, told them he had not. They stood at the gate for a few moments while Chen Jingji set off two large chrysanthemum fireworks, a large orchid, and a golden goblet with a silver stem. Then they retired. It was the fourth night watch before Ximen Qing came back.

At the festival Chen Jingji and Jinlian had been laughing and chatting with Huilian, and he had already begun to feel some attraction for the woman. The next morning he dressed, and, before going to the shop, went to the inner court to pay his respects to Yueniang. When he came to her room, Li Jiao'er, Jinlian and Aunt Wu were there, about to have some tea. Yueniang herself had gone to burn incense at the shrine of Buddha. The young man greeted them politely.

"You're a nice man, Brother Chen," Jinlian said. "When I asked you to take home that Han woman last night, you wouldn't move an inch, and in the end I had to get one of the boys to do it. You could think of nothing but joking and chattering with Huilian. I wonder what the understanding is between you. Wait till the Great Lady comes back. You'll see whether I tell her or not."

"How can you say such a thing?" Jingji said. "After all that long walk my back was nearly broken. How many miles do you think it is from here to Lion Street? Yet in spite of my tiredness you asked me to take that woman home. It was only fair that one of the boys should do it. I had had hardly any sleep and it was already nearly daybreak."

They were still wrangling when Yueniang came back. Jingji made a reverence to her, and she asked him what had been the matter yesterday when Han's wife was drunk and cursing all the world. Jingji told her that the woman had been to a party, and, when she came back, discovered that someone had stolen her dog, so she sat on the pavement and cried and shouted and insulted everybody. "When her husband comes back today, I imagine he'll give her a drubbing. She hasn't got up yet."

"If we had not pressed her to go home," Jinlian said, "Father might have seen her, and then there would have been a fine to-do."

Yulou, Li Ping'er and Ximen Dajie came to tea with Yueniang. Jingji joined them and afterwards went with his wife to their own room.

"You rascal," his wife said, when they were alone, "what do you mean by fooling with Laiwang's wife? If my father hears about it, it will be all very well for that strumpet, but you won't know where to find a hole to die in."

A few days later, Ximen Qing had slept in the room of Li Ping'er, and was dressing, when a certain Captain Jing, who had recently been appointed to the district, came to call upon him. Ximen hastened to the hall to greet him, telling Ping'an to bring them tea. The boy went to the kitchen. Huilian, Yuxiao and Xiaoyu were playing in the courtyard. Xiaoyu was riding on Yuxiao's back laughing, and crying, "You bad girl, you've earned a beating. Why won't you let me beat you? Come here, Huilian, catch her by the leg and see what I do to her."

Ping'an intervened. "Sister Yuxiao," he said, "Captain Jing is in the hall, and Father has ordered me to take them some tea."

Yuxiao paid no attention, but went on playing with Xiaoyu.

"Captain Jing has been here a long time already," the boy said.

"Go to the kitchen for your tea," Huilian cried, "don't come and bother us. We only make tea for the ladies. We have nothing to do with the hall."

Ping'an went to the kitchen. Laibao's wife was on duty, but she told him she was busy cooking, and that he must go to the inner court.

"I have already asked them in the inner court," Ping'an said. "They say they have nothing to do with the hall. Huilian says it is your business to provide tea for that part of the house."

"Oh, that strumpet!" Laibao's wife cried. "She thinks she only has to say that she serves the Great Lady. I seem to be the only one in the kitchen. I am cooking for several people already, and I have plain food to get ready for Aunt Wu. How many hands do you think I have? If you want me to make tea, well and good, but why try to make out that I alone have to work in the kitchen? You have no right to treat me as if I were the scullery maid. You won't get any tea from me."

"Captain Jing has been here for hours, Sister," Ping'an said. "Please make the tea or Father will be dreadfully angry." The boy was pushed from

pillar to post. He had already wasted a long time. At last Yuxiao brought
what was needed, and Ping'an took it to the hall. Captain Jing was preparing to take his leave. Ximen Qing urged him to stay but the tea was cold.
Ximen scolded Ping'an and ordered him to change it, but, by the time the
fresh tea had been brought, Captain Jing had gone.

Ximen Qing went to the inner court to find out who was responsible,
and Ping'an told him that the scullery maid had made it. Then he went to
his own room and told Yueniang what had happened.

"Go to the kitchen," he said, "and find out who made the tea. When
you've done so, see that she has a beating."

Xiaoyu told her that it was the day for Laibao's wife to attend to the
cooking.

"Oh, the wretch," Yueniang cried, "she must be eager to die, making
tea like that."

She told Xiaoyu to fetch the woman. Laibao's wife came and knelt
before Yueniang in the courtyard.

"How many blows do you want?" Yueniang said. Laibao's wife said
the tea was cold because she had had to cook the dinner and also plain
food for Aunt Wu. Yueniang scolded her for a time and then forgave her.
Then she addressed all the maids and serving women. "Henceforth," she
said, "whenever visitors come to the hall, Yuxiao and Huilian must make
the tea, and those in the kitchen must see about the tea and food for our
own people."

Laibao's wife went back to the kitchen in a fury. As soon as Ximen
Qing had gone out, she went in a rage to the inner court. When she
found Huilian, she shook her finger at her. "You abandoned, scoundrelly
woman," she cried, "now you are satisfied. You have the luck. You do service for the mistress, and I am but the scullery maid. You told the boy to
come to me for tea, and it was you who told him to call me scullery maid.
Who are you to call me scullery maid? The cricket does not eat the flesh
of a spotted toad, for they are akin. You are not one of the master's ladies,
so why should you consider yourself superior to me? And if you were, I
shouldn't be afraid of you."

"You are talking nonsense," Huilian said. "You made the tea badly,
and Father didn't like it. What has that to do with me? Why vent your
spite on me?"

This made Laibao's wife more angry still. "You thievish whore," she
cried, "you wanted to get me a beating. You had a man on the sly when
you were with the Cai family, and your wickedness is past all bounds. Now
you come and play the same tricks here."

"Did you see me have a man on the sly?" Huilian said. "Well, dear Sister, you are yourself no virgin."

"No virgin?" Laibao's wife cried. "I'm better than you, anyway. You've had as many men as there are grains in a heap of corn. You can't set eyes upon a man without beginning your tricks. And you fancy nobody knows what you are up to. You have no respect for the ladies here, so why should you have any for us?"

"What are you talking about?" Huilian said. "In what way do I fail in respect to the ladies? Say all the nasty things you like. I don't care."

"No, you don't care," Laibao's wife shouted, "you don't care, because you have somebody behind you."

They went on quarreling until Xiaoyu asked Yueniang to intervene. "You rogues," Yueniang said, "instead of doing your work, you spend all your time squabbling. If your master hears of this, there will be more trouble. You have not been beaten yet, but you certainly will be. Do you wish to be beaten?"

"If I am beaten," Laibao's wife cried, "I will pull this woman's guts out. I will give my life to get even with her, and we will go together." She went back to the kitchen.

After this, Huilian was more arrogant than ever. Because of her relations with Ximen Qing, she thought the rest of the household unworthy of consideration. Every day she played with Yulou, Jinlian, Li Ping'er, Ximen Dajie and Chunmei.

A few days later old woman Feng brought the younger of her two maids, taking her first to Li Ping'er, and then to Li Jiao'er. Li Jiao'er paid five taels for the girl and kept her.

CHAPTER 25
Laiwang's Jealousy

The Feast of Lanterns was over and the Festival of Spring had come again. Ying Bojue came to ask Ximen Qing to go for a day in the country as the guest of Sun Guazui, and they went away together. Before the festival, Wu Yueniang had had a swing set up in the garden, and, while Ximen Qing was out, she took all the ladies to it that they might dispel that languor which the coming of spring seems to bring. The first to swing were Wu Yueniang herself and Meng Yulou, and, when they had done, she asked Li Jiao'er and Pan Jinlian to take their places. Li Jiao'er declined, saying she was not feeling well, so Yueniang asked Li Ping'er to be Jinlian's partner. Then Yulou cried, "Come here, Sister, and swing standing with me. But you mustn't laugh." They grasped the rope with their beautiful hands and stood on the board. Yueniang told Huilian and Chunmei to push the swing for them.

Jinlian laughed so much that Yueniang cried, "Don't laugh. It is dangerous. You will fall off." The words were hardly out of her mouth when Jinlian fell with a crash, for the board was slippery and she was wearing high-heeled shoes. But she caught the frame of the swing and saved herself from falling to the ground, though Yulou was nearly thrown off.

"Sister," Yueniang said, "I told you not to laugh. Now, you see, you've fallen." She turned to Li Jiao'er and the others.

"Never laugh when you're swinging," she said, "it makes the legs give way, and down you fall. I remember, when I was a girl, our neighbor Zhou had a swing in his garden. One spring holiday, his daughter and I and two or three other girls were swinging on it, and laughing just as the Fifth Lady was. Miss Zhou was thrown off. She fell across the board and broke her maidenhead. Later, when she married, people said she was not a pure girl, and she was divorced. Yes, it is a mistake to laugh, when one goes in for games of this sort."

"The Third Lady is no good," Jinlian cried, "I will swing standing with the Sixth Lady."

"Be careful, both of you," Yueniang said. She told Yuxiao and Chunmei to start them. Then Chen Jingji came.

"You are swinging, I see," he said.

"Yes," Yueniang said, "you have come at the right moment. You can push the swing for the ladies: the girls are not strong enough."

Jingji was as pleased as an old monk when the dinner bell goes. He gathered his clothes around him and hurried forward to offer his services. The first thing he did was to busy himself about Jinlian's skirt.

"Hold fast, Fifth Mother," he said, "I am going to push you." The swing flew up in the air so that the ladies looked like two winged angels. So high did it go that Li Ping'er was frightened.

"Brother," she cried, "I am falling, come and help me."

"Don't be alarmed, Lady, I will come in a moment," Jingji said. "If I am called first to one side and then to the other, I don't know where I am." He lifted Li Ping'er's skirts till her red trousers could be seen. Then he pushed the swing.

"Gently, Brother," Li Ping'er cried, "my legs are not very strong."

"Ah," said Jingji, "you shouldn't drink so much."

Then Jinlian complained that Li Ping'er was treading on her skirt, and they stopped swinging. Chunmei and Ximen Dajie took the places of the two ladies, and afterwards Yuxiao and Song Huilian swung standing. Huilian grasped the rope and, standing perfectly upright, danced upon the seat. She would have no one to push the swing for her, but herself drove it high into the air and down again. It was indeed a wonderful sight. Yueniang said to Yulou and Li Ping'er, "Just look at that woman. She certainly knows how to swing."

Laiwang had gone to Hangzhou to buy the clothes that were to be presented to the Imperial Tutor Cai. When they were ready, he had them packed in chests, and brought them back. As soon as he reached home they were unloaded, and he went to the inner court. Sun Xue'e was standing by the door of the hall. He made a reverence to her.

"Welcome home," she said, smiling graciously. "You must have had a very tiresome journey. It is only a short time since I saw you, but you have grown very stout."

"Where are my lord and my lady?" Laiwang asked.

"Your master has gone for a day in the country with Master Ying and the others," Xue'e said, "but your mistress and her daughter are swinging in the garden."

"Why do they play such games as that?" Laiwang said. Xue'e brought him a cup of tea and asked if he would like something to eat. "I will not have anything to eat," he said, "till I have seen the Great Lady, and I must go and wash first." Then he added: "I don't see my wife. Is she in the kitchen?"

Xue'e smiled sourly. "Your wife, indeed! Are you sure you still have a wife? She has become a great personage, and spends all her time playing chess and dominoes with the ladies. She doesn't condescend to come to the kitchen any more."

While they were talking Xiaoyu had gone to the garden to tell Yueniang that Laiwang had come. She came from the front court. Laiwang kowtowed and stood while she asked him about his journey. She gave him two jars of wine. Then Huilian came.

"You must be tired," Yueniang said. "Go to your room; wash and rest, and you can tell your master all about your business when he comes home."

Laiwang went to his room. Huilian gave him the key, and herself went to get him some water and unpack his luggage. "You black rogue," she said, "you have been away only a short time. What have you been eating to get as fat as this?" She helped him to change his clothes and prepared some food. When he had eaten something, he went to bed. The sun was setting when Ximen Qing came home. Laiwang got up and went to the front court to make his report.

"The birthday presents for the Imperial Tutor and the clothes for the members of his household are all in order," he said. "I had them packed, and brought them in four chests. They are at the customs office, and we must take porters to clear them."

Ximen Qing was pleased. Besides giving Laiwang money for the porters, and telling him to fetch the things next day, he gave him five taels of silver for himself and set him in charge of the buying department of the household. Laiwang had privately done a little business on his own account, and, secretly, he gave Xue'e two handkerchiefs, two pairs of silken trousers, four boxes of Hangzhou powder, and twenty cakes of rouge.

"Less than four months after you went away," Xue'e told him, "your wife began to carry on with his Lordship. Yuxiao was their go-between, and they made their nest in the Fifth Lady's room."

She told him how they had begun their naughty games in the grotto beneath the artificial mound, but had later made use of Jinlian's room, where they slept from morning till night and from night until morning.

"He has given her clothes," she said, "ornaments and artificial flowers, costing a lot of money, and she has been wearing them all the time. She is always giving the boys money and getting them to buy things for her, and she spends several *qian* of silver every day."

"No wonder her box is full of clothes and ornaments," Laiwang cried. "When I asked her where they came from, she said her mistress had given them to her."

"Mistress, indeed!" Xue'e said. "Master, more likely!"

Her words made a great impression on Laiwang. Wine helps a man to unburden his soul, and that night he drank deeply before he went to his room. He opened his wife's box, and found in it a roll of very handsome blue figured satin.

"Where did you get this satin?" he cried. "Who gave it you? Tell me the truth at once."

His wife did not know what was wrong, but she forced a smile and answered: "You funny old rascal. Why do you ask? It came from the inner court, and was given me to make a dress of. I haven't had time to make it up yet, so I put it in the chest. Where else do you think I could expect to get such a present?"

"You strumpet," Laiwang shouted, "don't try to keep up this pretense. Who gave it you, and where did you get these ornaments?"

"Pooh," said his wife, "you talk as if people had no relations of their own. Why, even if I had come out of a piece of stone, I should have come from somewhere. I borrowed these ornaments from one of my aunts. Where else do you think I got them?"

Laiwang struck her with his fist so that she all but fell. "Strumpet!" he cried, "you are trying to deceive me. I know for certain that you have been carrying on with that foul fellow. Yes, Yuxiao was the go-between. It was she who brought you this satin. You began in the garden, and afterwards amused yourselves all day long in the room of that whore Jinlian. Now, do you think you can deceive me any longer?"

"You wicked villain," Huilian cried, "you will come to a violent end, without a doubt. How dare you strike me? What have I done? You come and throw stones at me without the slightest cause. Explain yourself. Some backbiting sneak has been telling you a pack of lies about me, and you lay your hands on me. I assure you you shall not treat me as if I were dirt. If I am going to die, I will die clean. Ask anybody you like about the women of my family. If there is anything shady about me, my name is not Song. There is no reason at all for this fuss you are making. It's like a rainstorm without any wind. But there is something behind it, all the same. I suppose if it were suggested to you you would murder anybody?"

Laiwang did not know what to answer, and his wife went on: "I will tell you all there is to tell about this roll of blue satin. It was our mistress's birthday on the third day of the eleventh month, and she gave it me then because she saw me wearing a purple gown and skirt that I had borrowed from Yuxiao. She thought they did not suit me. I have been too busy ever since to make it up, and now I have put up with all this to-do. You have done me wrong. But I am not the sort to overlook a thing like this, and tomorrow you shall see. I'll let some of these people know what I think about them. My life is not worth living, and the sooner I find somebody to put an end to it, the better."

"If there is really nothing in it," Laiwang said, "there's no reason to make such a fuss. Get my bed ready."

"You scamp, you'll come to a bad end," Huilian said as she got the bed ready. "You go and drink a lot of wine and then come home and abuse your old woman instead of going quietly to bed." She hustled him off, and, in a very short time, he was snoring like thunder.

Unfaithful wives are always like this. However intelligent their husbands may be, with a few words their wives can twist things about in such a way that their husbands are completely hoodwinked. Such women are like the privy floor. They stink, but they hold their ground.

So Huilian made a fool of her husband and the night passed. Next day, she went to the inner court and asked Yuxiao who had been telling tales about her. As neither of them could fix upon the right person, she could only go about suspiciously, grumbling.

One day Yueniang wanted Xue'e and sent Xiaoyu to find her. Though the maid looked everywhere she failed to find her, until she went to the front court. There she saw Xue'e coming out of Laiwang's room. She supposed that the woman had been chatting with Laiwang's wife, but, when she reached the kitchen, Huilian was there, mincing meat. Meanwhile, in the front court, Ximen Qing had been talking to Master Qiao, who had come on behalf of a certain Wang Sifeng, a soda merchant of Yangzhou, who had been put in prison by the magistrate of that district. Qiao had brought two thousand taels of silver and wanted Ximen Qing to approach the Imperial Tutor, and secure the soda merchant's release. As soon as he had seen Master Qiao to the gate, Ximen called for Laiwang, who promptly came from his own room.

After this everybody knew that Xue'e and Laiwang were carrying on together.

One day when Laiwang had been drinking, he began to revile Ximen Qing before the servants in the front court. "When I was away," he said, "he got Yuxiao to take a roll of blue satin to my place and seduced my wife. At first, he had his way with her in the garden, but afterwards the Fifth Lady made a nest for them in her place. Let him look out for himself. If he falls into my hands, I will certainly kill him. My knife shall go in white, and it will be red when it comes out. Yes, and I'll kill that whore Pan as well, and get rid of the pair of them at the same time. You shall see whether I don't do as I say. I haven't forgotten how, when that whore Pan murdered her husband Wu Da, and her brother-in-law Wu Song brought an accusation against her, it was me they got to go to the Eastern Capital to get her off and have Wu Song banished. Now that she feels herself secure once more, she forgets all about the one who saved her life, and makes a whore of my wife. My hatred for her is as deep as the heavens. But there is a proverb which says that a man may as well be hung for a sheep as a lamb. I don't care whether I die or not, but I'll thrash his Majesty, even if I get chopped in ten thousand pieces."

Laiwang talked in this strain without realizing that anyone was eavesdropping, but Laixing overheard everything he said. Laixing was the servant to whom Ximen Qing had originally entrusted the business of buying and changing money for the household, but, after Ximen had fallen in love with Laiwang's wife, that business had been handed over to Laiwang. Since then Laiwang and Laixing had not been on the best of terms. So, when he had heard the kind of thing his rival was saying, Laixing slipped away to Jinlian's room. When he pulled up the lattice and came in, she was sitting with Yulou.

"What can I do for you?" she said. "Where is your master amusing himself today?"

"He has gone to a funeral with Uncle Ying," Laixing said. "Lady, I have something to tell you, but you must keep it to yourself, and not let anybody know I told you."

"If you have anything to say, let us hear it," Jinlian said.

"It is only this," Laixing said. "That rascal Laiwang got drunk somewhere yesterday, and made a fine hullabaloo, cursing everybody the whole day long. He wished to pick a quarrel with me but I came away and left him. In front of everybody he cursed Master, and you too, Fifth Mother."

"Why should the rogue curse me?" Jinlian said.

"I hardly like to tell you," Laixing said, "but since there is only the Third Lady here, and she is not a stranger, I will. He said Father had got him out of the way so as to be able to make love to his wife. He also said that you, Fifth Mother, had arranged everything for them, and allowed his wife to sleep with Father in your room from morning till night and from night till morning. He has got a knife to kill you both, and says it may be white when it goes in but it will be red when it comes out. He says you poisoned your first husband and sent him to the Eastern Capital to hush up the matter, and that though you owe your life to him, you only repay his kindness by injuries and help his wife to be unfaithful to him. I felt I ought to warn you. Fifth Mother, you must be continually on your guard against this fellow's plottings."

Yulou might have been plunged in a cold bath, she was so shocked when she heard this. Jinlian flushed beneath her powder and ground her silvery teeth. "The murderous villain," she cried, "I've never done him any harm in the past, and I'm not doing any now. If his master takes a fancy to his wife, what's that to do with me? That slave and I shall not both remain in Ximen's household. How dare he say I got him to save my life? You may go now," she said to Laixing, "and if your master asks you any questions when he comes back, be sure to tell him what you've told me."

"Fifth Mother," Laixing said, "I have only told the truth. I have repeated exactly what I heard. If Father questions me, I can only tell him what I have told you." He went to the front court.

"Is it true that there is anything between his master and that woman?" Yulou said.

"Did you ever know that unprincipled scamp to lose an opportunity of getting hold of a pretty woman?" Jinlian said. "Now he has given himself into that slave's hands. The strumpet was once a servant in Cai's house, and there she and her mistress played the whore together till they were found out and she was sent packing. Then she married Jiang Cong. Was one man enough for her? No, indeed, she must have lovers like grains of rice. She is up to every trick you could think of. That wretched husband of ours, who is cunning enough to deceive even the spirits—he could play tricks on a spook—told Yuxiao to take her a piece of satin to make a gown of. I meant to tell you this before. Don't you remember the day the Great Lady went to a party at Master Qiao's house? We were all playing chess in the front court when one of the maids came and said, 'Father has come back.' We stopped our game and I went to the inner court. Well, when I got to the gate, Xiaoyu was standing in the passage and, when I spoke to her, she didn't answer. She made some sort of a sign with her hand. I went on, and when I reached the garden, that little scamp Yuxiao was standing at the corner gate. She was keeping a lookout for them. Still I didn't realize what the game was and was going on, but Yuxiao got in my way and wouldn't let me go farther. 'Father is there,' she said. I cursed her, because I had an idea that she was up to some trick of her own, but when I did get in, there he was in the grotto with that woman. She blushed crimson when she saw me, and ran away. He didn't know what to say, and he had to listen to a few remarks from me, the shameless fellow."

"Afterwards the woman came to see me. She knelt down and begged me not to say anything to her mistress. Then, in the first month, he was going to bring the whore to spend the night with him in my room, but I and Chunmei told him plainly what we thought about him. We said, of course, we would not allow him to do anything of the sort. The wretch tried to get me mixed up in the business, but I was not going to have that pretty little whore carrying on with him in my place. Even if I had been willing, young Miss Chunmei would never have allowed it."

"No wonder the wicked little wretch never stands up when we come in," Yulou said. "I should never have dreamed of anything of the sort. It is most improper on his part to want her when he can get a woman anywhere. Look at the opportunity to talk scandal he gives the slaves!"

"Yes," Jinlian said, "but it is tit for tat. If he has fallen in love with the slave's wife, the slave has done as much for him. There's a nice little exchange going on. That little thief Xue'e has had plenty to say about us, but now even if I give her a smack on the face, she will have to keep her mouth shut."

"Shall we tell him or not?" Yulou said. "The Great Lady will not do anything about it, and if that fellow really has made up his mind, and we keep silence about it, Father will know nothing, and, some time or other, the slave will get him. I think you ought to mention it to him."

"If that slave were my father," Jinlian said, "I might possibly forgive him, but he isn't, and nothing will ever induce me to do so."

Late that evening Ximen Qing came home. He found Jinlian in her room, her cloudlike tresses in disorder, her fragrant cheeks heavy with slumber, and her eyes red like two peaches from weeping. When he asked what was amiss, she told him that Laiwang had got drunk and was going about saying he was going to kill his master. "Laixing heard this with his own ears," she said. "While you were stealing that slave's wife, he was doing as much for you. If the wretch only intended to murder you, I shouldn't worry so much, but he means to kill me too. If we don't do something about it at once, sooner or later we shall fall into his clutches. We have no eyes at the back of our heads."

"Who has been telling tales?" Ximen said.

"It's no use asking me," Jinlian said. "Ask Xiaoyu. The slave said several nasty things about me. For one thing he said I poisoned my husband and, after you married me, we sent him to find somebody to save my life. This is the sort of thing he has been saying all around the place. It is a good thing I have no children. That slave's scandal-mongering would not make good hearing for them. 'When your mother first came to this house,' he would say, 'she was in a very unpleasant predicament. She had to ask me to get her out of it. I saved her life.' And if he goes around talking in that strain, what about your good name? It won't be any too glorious. If you are devoid of decent feeling, I'm not, and if that is the sort of life I've got to live, well, I just won't live."

Ximen Qing listened. Then he went to the front court, called Laixing to a quiet spot, and asked him many questions about the matter. Laixing told him in detail everything that had happened. Ximen Qing went back to the inner court and questioned Xiaoyu. Her account of the matter agreed perfectly with that of Jinlian. She told him how she had seen Xue'e coming out of Laiwang's room one day when his wife was out. It was a fact, she said.

Ximen Qing flew into a rage. He gave Xue'e a drubbing till Yueniang made him desist. He took away her ornaments and fine dresses and made her work in the kitchen with the maid servants, and forbade her ever to come out. Later, in the inner court, he told Yuxiao to bring Huilian to him in secret, so that he could hear what she had to say.

"Oh dear! Oh dear!" she cried. "Father, you mustn't talk like that. I am ready to swear by all I love that he never said anything of the sort. He may have been drunk, but no matter what state he was in, he would never have forgotten himself so far as to curse you. Why, how could he accept favors from Zhou Wang and then turn around and accuse Zhou Wang of being a scoundrel? He is dependent upon you for his livelihood. Don't believe everything people say to you, Father. Who told you this story?"

Ximen Qing shut his mouth firmly. He would not answer until the woman pressed him. At last he said: "It was Laixing."

"Father," Huilian said, "you gave Laixing's job to us and he credits us with having got him out of it. He can't make so much money as he used to. So he hates us and spits out slanders against us with his bloody mouth. And you believe him! If my husband were really plotting a thing like that, I would never forgive him. Father, do what I tell you. Don't keep him here. Give him a few taels and send him away somewhere to act as your agent. When he has gone, you and I can talk together whenever we feel inclined, and it will be much pleasanter for both of us."

Ximen Qing thought this an excellent idea. "You are right, my child," he said, "I think I'll send him to the Capital to see the Imperial Tutor about this business of Wang Sifeng. He can take the birthday presents at the same time. But he has only just come back from Hangzhou and I didn't think it was fair to send him off again so soon. I made up my mind to send Laibao instead. But now you suggest it, I will send him to the Capital and, when he returns, he shall have a thousand taels of silver and I'll send him to Hangzhou with someone else to act as a manager, and set him up in the silk business there. Will that suit you?"

Huilian was delighted. "Nothing could be better," she cried. Ximen Qing saw that there was no one about. He took her in his arms and kissed her. She slipped her tongue into his mouth, and they exchanged a long passionate kiss. "You promised me a new hairnet," Huilian said. "Why haven't you got it for me? If you don't get it now, I never shall have one. I shall have to wear this old one every day."

"Don't be impatient," Ximen said, "tomorrow I will give the silver-smith eight taels of silver, and he shall make one for you. But your mistress will probably ask you where you got it. Then what will you say?"

"Don't worry," the woman said, "I shall find an answer. If anybody asks me, I shall say I borrowed it from my aunt. That will be all right." They talked a little longer and then parted.

Next day Ximen Qing took his seat in the hall and sent for Laiwang. "Get your clothes and luggage packed," he said. "Tomorrow is the twenty-eighth day of the third month, and you will start for the Capital to see the Imperial Tutor. When you come back, I am going to send you to do business at Hangzhou." Laiwang was very pleased. He bowed, and went back to his room to pack. Then he went out to buy a few things.

Laixing heard what was going on and went to tell Jinlian. She was told that Ximen Qing was in the bower in the garden and went there, but she could not find him. Chen Jingji was there, packing up the presents.

"Where is your father?" she said. "What is that you're packing up?"

"Father was here a moment ago," Jingji said. "He has gone to see the Great Lady and get the silver for that affair of Wang Sifeng. These are the presents for the Imperial Tutor."

"Who is going to take them?" Jinlian asked.

"I believe Father has told Laiwang to go," Jingji said.

As Jinlian was going down the steps towards the garden, she met Ximen Qing bringing the silver. She asked him to go to her room. "Whom are you sending to the Eastern Capital?" she said.

"Laiwang and Clerk Fu are going together," Ximen said. "You see, there are not only the presents, there's this silver to be spent for the soda merchant Wang Sifeng. Two will be safer than one."

"You always think you know best," Jinlian said. "Why don't you do what I tell you? You believe every word that strumpet tells you. There is not the slightest doubt she is thinking of her husband. Only a day or two ago that slave declared before all the servants in the house that you have taken his wife and he will have your money. If you lose your money, my good Brother, you will do so with your eyes open. You might as well make him a present of a thousand taels and have done with it. You want his wife. Very well. If you keep him here, it will be awkward, and, if you send him somewhere else, you won't be any better off. If you let him stay here, we shall never be safe against his evil designs, and if you send him away, he will run off with every penny of your money. So long as you are after his wife, he won't care a fig for anything you say. The best thing you can do is to get rid of him for good and all. You know the proverb: 'If you cut the grass, but do not pull up the roots, new shoots will spring up as before; but if you pull up the roots, there can be no new shoots to come up.' You would have no reason to be anxious, and you could do what you liked with the woman."

These words made Ximen Qing think.

CHAPTER 26
The Tragic End of Song Huilian

As Wu from Yue is parted, so I from my lord
Through the passing years the jade pillow marks our separation.
I climb the watchtower and look towards the north
I see but heavy mist and rain.
I turn again and cry to the moon hanging in the skies.

The night is dark and hides the spears beside the gate
I wander through the corridors and sleep alone.
I seek in vain for you in the inner chamber
My spirit goes to the waste lands and my soul to the waters.

After Pan Jinlian had talked to him, Ximen Qing changed his mind once more. The next day, though Laiwang, with his luggage all ready, waited for the order to start, noon passed, and still he received no word. At last Ximen Qing came and called Laiwang to him.

"During the night, I have been thinking the matter over," he said. "I remembered that you had only just come back from Hangzhou, and I decided that, instead of sending you to the Eastern Capital as I had intended, it would be too much for you, and I ought to send Laibao and give you a rest. Later on I will find something nearer home for you."

In matters of this sort, the master invariably has the last word. Laiwang could only acquiesce. Ximen gave the silver and the presents to Laibao and Clerk Fu, and, on the twenty-eighth day of the third month, they set out. Laiwang went back to his room in a temper, drank more than was good for him, and said all manner of foolish things, telling his wife he was going to kill Ximen Qing.

Huilian scolded him. "A dog that really means to bite never shows its teeth," she said. "You are talking nonsense. Remember the walls have ears. You are drunk again." She sent him to bed.

Next day, she went to Yuxiao's room in the inner court and asked her to go for Ximen Qing. They found a quiet place behind the kitchen wall where they could talk and Yuxiao kept watch for them by the door. Huilian was very angry.

"What a man you are!" she cried. "You promised me to let him go. Why have you changed your mind and sent somebody else instead? You have a mind just like a ball. It does nothing but bob up and down. You can't keep steady long enough to hold a candle. One of these days I shall build a temple in your honor and set up a banner pole, and bestow on you the title of Father of Lies. Never again will I believe a word you say. I did trust you, but evidently you don't care about me any more."

"Don't say that," Ximen Qing said, laughing, "it was not that I didn't want him to go, but I was afraid he didn't know his way about the Imperial Tutor's palace. That's the only reason I sent Laibao, and kept him at home. I'll see if I can't find some business for him here."

"What sort of business will you find for him?" Huilian cried. "Tell me."

"I will get a manager for him and set them up in a wineshop, not far away."

This delighted Huilian. She went back to her room and told Laiwang all about it. Then they waited for Ximen Qing's orders. One day Ximen called Laiwang to the front court. Lying on a table were six packets of silver. "My son," Ximen Qing said, "you must have had a very trying journey from Hangzhou. I did mean to send you to the Eastern Capital, but I thought perhaps you didn't know Cai's palace well enough, so I decided to send Laibao instead. Here are six packets of silver, three hundred taels altogether. Take them, find someone to act as your manager, and set up a wineshop somewhere not far away. You will bring the interest dutifully to me every month. That seems to me the best thing we can do for you."

Laiwang knelt down and kowtowed. He took the six packets of silver to his room. "He is using this business as a trap," he said to his wife. "He has given me these three hundred taels, and he says I am to find a manager and start a wineshop."

"You are a funny creature," his wife said. "It takes more than one shovel to dig a well; you must take your time. You have a business now and you will have to settle down, do your duty, and give up drinking so much wine. It's that which makes you talk so much nonsense."

"Well, I'm going to the street to find a partner," Laiwang said. He told his wife to put the silver in a chest. He went to the street but, though he looked about till late, he found nobody to suit him. Instead, he got very drunk and went home again. His wife sent him to bed, and, soon afterwards, Yuxiao called her away to the inner court.

Laiwang slept for a long time. It was the first night watch when he awoke. He was not yet sober and his head whirled. Suddenly he heard someone outside the window calling softly: "Brother Laiwang, why don't you get up and see what your wife is doing? That bad fellow has taken her to the garden again and, while you are asleep here, suspecting nothing, they are having a fine time." This made Laiwang wake up. He opened his eyes to see who was there. Huilian was not in the room. He decided that the voice must have been Xue'e's, and that she had come to tell him of something she had seen.

"You will be unfaithful before my very face, will you?" he cried, jumping out of bed in a fury. He opened the door and ran straight to the garden. He had just reached the garden gate when, suddenly, a stool was thrown out of the darkness and he was knocked down. At the same time a knife fell clattering on the ground. Servants came running from all directions, shouting: Thief! Thief!" and some of them pounced on him.

"It is only Laiwang," he cried. "I have come to look for my wife. Why are you seizing me?"

Nobody would listen to him, and he was dragged, struggling and fighting, to the great hall. There, among many brilliant lights, Ximen Qing sat, shouting, "Bring him in!"

"I woke up," Laiwang said, kneeling down, "and I couldn't see my wife anywhere, so I went to find her. What have I done to be seized and treated like a thief?"

Laixing produced the knife for his master to see. Ximen Qing cried angrily, "Animals one can deal with, but human beings are impossible. This fellow is a murderer. There was I, thinking he had just come back from Hangzhou, and giving him three hundred taels to set him up in business. Then, in the depth of night, he comes to murder me. If that was not what you were after," he said to Laiwang, "what were you doing with this knife?" He shouted to the attendants: "Take him to his room and bring me back my three hundred taels." The servants took Laiwang away.

Huilian was talking to Yuxiao in the inner court when she heard the news. She rushed at once to her room and, seeing what was happening, began to cry. "You went to bed drunk," she said. "What need was there for you to get up and start looking for me? Now you have fallen into a trap."

They opened the chest, took out the six packets of silver, and went back to the hall. Ximen Qing unwrapped the packets and examined the silver in the light of a lamp. Only one contained genuine silver, the others had nothing in them but tin.

"How dare you change my silver?" Ximen cried. "What have you done with my money? Tell me at once."

"Master," Laiwang sobbed, "you very kindly entrusted the silver to me so that I might set up in business. How could I think of cheating you and putting tin in its place?"

"You took a knife to murder me," Ximen cried. "Here it is. It is no use your trying to make excuses." He called forward Laixing, who knelt down and testified: "The other day, outside, didn't you say before a number of people that you were going to kill Master because he hadn't found anything for you to do?"

Laiwang gaped, his mouth wide open. "Now," Ximen Qing said, "the case is clear. The stolen property, the witness, the knife and the staves are all here. Chain him and put him into the gatehouse," he said to the servants. "Tomorrow I will write an accusation and send him before the magistrate."

At this moment, Huilian, her hair in disorder and her dress disarranged, ran into the hall and threw herself on her knees before Ximen Qing. "Father," she cried, "this is your doing. He was looking for me quite peacefully. Why should he be taken and treated as a thief? As for those six packets of silver, I was looking after them, and the original seal was never even broken. It cannot possibly have been changed. Though you may wish to get rid of the man, do not forget the justice of Heaven. What has he done? Why are you sending him to be beaten? Where are you going to send him now?"

Ximen Qing smiled sweetly upon her. "This has nothing to do with you, my good woman," he said. "Stand up. He has no regard for propriety, and he has been exceedingly impudent for some time. Now he has even attempted to murder me. But, of course, you know nothing about this. Be calm, you are not concerned in the matter at all." He said to Laian: "Take your sister very gently to her room, and see that she is not alarmed in any way."

Huilian, however, would not rise from her knees. "How stony-hearted you are, Father," she said. "If you will not listen to the priest's voice, at least hearken to the voice of Buddha. Won't you do this for me when I ask so earnestly? Though he did get drunk, he really would never have dreamed of doing a thing like this." Ximen Qing grew impatient and told Laian to pick her up and take her back to her room.

Next day Ximen wrote an accusation and told Laixing, as the witness, to take the papers and Laiwang to the court. "Upon a certain day," the accusation ran, "this man got drunk, and, in the middle of the night, made to kill his master with a knife. He is further charged with fraudulently changing money, etc." The party was about to set off for the court when Yueniang came into the hall. She pleaded earnestly with Ximen Qing. "If the slave has done wrong," she said, "we can deal with him here, and settle it ourselves without bothering the officers and disturbing the court."

"Woman," Ximen shouted, rolling his eyes, "you have no idea of what is fitting. This slave deliberately tried to kill me. Do you come here and ask me to forgive him?" He would not listen to her, and shouted to the servants: "Away with him to the court." Yueniang flushed and withdrew.

"What a cantankerous fellow the master of the house is," she said to Yulou and the others. "There is a nine-tailed fox at work somewhere. I wonder whose advice he is taking in this business. He is sending the slave away quite unjustifiably. It is all very well for him to say the slave is a thief, but he must prove it. Putting a man into a paper coffin like this is no way to behave. He is an unprincipled tyrant." Then Huilian came and knelt down, weeping.

"Stand up, my child," Yueniang said, "they can't execute your husband when they have examined him. That villain has been drinking something to make him crazy; he won't listen to a word I say. His wife, it would seem, is about of as much account as a private soldier in the army."

"Just now, your master is in a temper," Yulou said to the woman. "We can only win him over by degrees. Don't worry. Go to your room."

Laiwang was taken to the court. Ximen Qing had taken the precaution of sending Daian with a hundred measures of rice to Magistrate Xia and Captain He. They accepted the present. They took their places in the hall of audience and Laixing presented the accusation. The magistrates were told that Laiwang had been given a sum of money with which to establish a business, but that the sight of the silver had put the idea into his head of replacing it by tin. Then, it was said, he became afraid lest his master should find out, and, in the middle of the night, he took a knife and went creeping to the hall to murder his master. The two officers angrily summoned Laiwang before them. He knelt down and pleaded: "If you, heaven-born officers, will permit me to speak, I shall be able to explain everything; but if you will not, I dare not say a word."

"Now, fellow," Magistrate Xia said, "the stolen property and the evidence are both here. It is no use your attempting to clear yourself. All we want from you is the truth. Then, perhaps, we shall not be so hard on you."

Laiwang began to tell how Ximen Qing sent a piece of blue satin to his wife, Huilian, and had seduced her. "Now," he said, "he has accused me of this crime, so that he can get me out of the way and enjoy my wife as he pleases."

Magistrate Xia shouted at him and ordered the attendants to strike him on the mouth.

"You slave," he cried, "this is all part of your plot to murder your master. If it were not for him, you would not have a wife, and now he has given you a business as well. Yet instead of trying to repay his kindness, you get drunk, sneak into his bedroom in the middle of the night, with murder in your heart. Why, if all servants were like you, nobody would dare to keep one."

Laiwang went on saying that he was innocent, but the magistrate called upon Laixing to give his evidence, and, after that, there was nothing more he could say.

The magistrate ordered his attendants to pick out the cruelest thumbscrews they could find and apply them to Laiwang. Then he ordered twenty strokes of the weightiest bamboos. The poor man's skin was broken and his flesh torn. Blood poured from him. After this the jailers were told to put him into prison. Laian and Laixing went home and gave Ximen Qing a full account of the affair. Ximen was delighted. He gave orders that none of the servants should take bedclothes to Laiwang or even so much as a scrap of food. Moreover, they were not to tell Huilian that her husband had been beaten. All they were to say was that he would be out again in a few days.

After Laiwang's arrest, Huilian refused to dress her hair or wash her face. She would do nothing but shut herself in her room and cry, taking neither tea nor food. This alarmed Ximen Qing, and he sent Yuxiao and Ben the Fourth's wife several times to reason with her.

"Don't worry about your husband," they would say. "He got drunk and talked wildly, but our master has only sent him to prison to cool his heels for a few days. He will have him out again soon." Huilian did not believe them. She sent Laian to the prison with some food, and questioned him when he came back. He told her the same story. "My brother came before the magistrates, but they did not punish him. He says you must not worry about him; he will be out in two or three days."

After this, Huilian dried her tears, and every day painted her eyebrows carefully, powdered her face, and resumed her old lively ways.

One day, when Ximen Qing passed her door on his way home from somewhere, Huilian, who was standing under the eaves, called to him: "There is nobody in my room, Father. Won't you come in and sit down for a while?" Ximen went in and talked to her.

"My child," he said, still keeping up the pretense, "your mind ought to be quite at ease now. For your sake I have written to the court, and he has not received a single blow. He must stay in prison a day or two to teach him a lesson, and then he shall come out and I'll set him up in business."

Huilian threw her arms around his neck. "Dearest," she cried, "if you love me, let him come out soon. I don't care whether you set him up in business or not, but when he comes out, I will see he keeps away from drink, and he cannot object if you decide to send him away. If that is not good enough, find another wife for him and all will be well. I have not belonged to him for a long time."

"Very well, my precious one," Ximen said, "I am going to buy the house across the road that belongs to Master Qiao, and I will set aside three rooms for you there. When you are established there, we shall have greater freedom to enjoy ourselves."

"Do just what you like, darling," the woman cried. When they had said what they had to say, she closed the door. In the summer months, she wore nothing but an open skirt without trousers, so that, whenever she came together with Ximen Qing, he had only to pull aside the skirt and proceed. Then the girdle was unloosed and the jade treasure of Chen Fei disclosed: eyebrows with all the fragrance of Han Shu were brought near together. They were like a pair of love birds flying shoulder to shoulder, or the meeting of clouds and rain.

Huilian was wearing a perfume satchel of fine silk, embroidered in silver. There were fir and cypress leaves in it, and some fragrant herbs, and on it were embroidered the four words: "delicate," "fragrant," "beautiful" and "seductive." She gave it to Ximen Qing. He was so delighted that his one regret was that he could not there and then make oath that he would live and die together with her. He took a few taels of silver from his sleeve and gave them to her to buy delicacies, saying several times: "Don't worry any longer, or you will make yourself ill. I'll write to his Lordship Xia tomorrow, and have him set free." They talked for a while, and then Ximen Qing became alarmed lest anyone should come, and hurriedly went away. Now that she had extracted this promise from him, Huilian went once more to the inner court and made merry with the maids and serving women.

Yulou heard of this and went to tell Jinlian. "Sooner or later," she said, "Father will set the fellow free. He is going to buy Master Qiao's house opposite, and install the woman there. She is to have three rooms and a maid, silver headdresses and nets. She will be as good as we are. Did you ever hear of such a thing? And the Great Lady will do nothing to prevent it."

When Jinlian heard this, she flew into a fury. A dark flush deepened the redness of her cheeks. "Don't you imagine," she said, "that he will be able to do exactly what he likes! Here and now I tell you that if I let that thievish whore become Ximen Qing's seventh wife . . . my name is not Pan."

"Our husband is a bad lot," Yulou said, "and the Great Lady does nothing to keep him in order. As for us, we cannot fly, we can only walk. What can we do to stop him?"

"You haven't a good enough opinion of yourself," Jinlian said. "Why do you think we are alive? To live a hundred years so that others can make a meal of us? No, if he doesn't do what I tell him, I shall kill myself, and he will be responsible. I'm not far from it now."

Yulou laughed. "I'm afraid I'm not very brave. I haven't the courage to make him angry. I'll watch and see whether you're clever enough to deal with him."

That night Ximen Qing was sitting in his study in the Hall of the Kingfisher, about to send for his son-in-law to write a letter to Magistrate Xia. Jinlian suddenly appeared in front of him.

"What letter is this you are going to get Brother Chen to write?" she asked, leaning over the table.

Ximen Qing could not hide anything from her. "I have decided to let Laiwang come out of prison, when he has been beaten," he said. One of the boys was going to fetch Chen Jingji, but Jinlian stopped him.

"You flatter yourself," she said to Ximen, "that you are a very fine fellow, but, actually, you steer your course according to the wind and go wherever the current takes you. You will not do what I tell you, but you listen to everything that thievish strumpet says. What do you think you're doing? You may feed her on honey and sugar every day, but it will be her husband she really thinks about. Now listen to me. If you set that slave free you won't find it such an easy matter to enjoy his wife. There will be nothing to prevent his making a scandal. If you keep her here she will be neither one thing nor another. How do you propose to treat her? If you make her your concubine, he will be here: if she is to remain his wife, you have already made her so conceited that her airs and graces are unbearable to us all. As for the plan of keeping her for yourself and finding another wife for him, what is going to happen when you are sitting somewhere together and he comes in to serve you? Can he be anything but furious? And, when she sees him, is she to stand up or remain seated?"

"The whole thing is most improper, and, if it gets about, I hardly need say that all our friends and kinsmen will think very badly of you. Indeed, the whole household will look down upon you. If the master beam is not in position, the rafters cannot be expected to keep their place. If you are in earnest about the matter, you must not stick at a little harshness. Finish off the slave. Then you can embrace his wife with an easy mind."

Ximen Qing changed his mind again. The letter he sent to the magistrate asked him to reopen the case at the end of three months, and to put Laiwang to the torture. The unfortunate man was hardly treated as a human being. The two magistrates, the prosecutor, the police, and the jailers had all accepted presents from Ximen Qing, and were severe in consequence. But among them was a scrivener who came from Xiaoyi in Shanxi, Yin Zhi by name, a man both humane and incorruptible. He realized that Ximen had manufactured this trouble so that he could take possession of Laiwang's wife, and he declined to make out the papers that would have brought Laiwang before the magistrates. Indeed, he went so far as to tell them what he thought, so that they found it difficult to proceed as they had intended, and finally compromised by giving Laiwang forty strokes more and banishing him to Xuzhou. They accounted the alleged stolen property as seventeen taels of silver and five packets of tin and ordered Laixing to return it to his master. An official wrote the reply to the accusation, saying that Laiwang was being banished that day.

The two magistrates made out a warrant and sent two runners to bring out Laiwang. He was severely beaten and put into sealed fetters, and the men were ordered to start immediately for Xuzhou, and leave Laiwang in charge of the governor there. Laiwang had been so long in prison that he was in a wretched condition. His clothes were falling to pieces. There was no one to whom he could appeal for help.

"Brothers," he said to the two runners, "now that I have been through this trouble, I have not a penny in the world. I should like to get some traveling money for you. Will you have pity on me and take me to my master's house? My wife is there. She will give me clothes and things and I will sell them for journey money, and so make things more agreeable."

"You don't seem to realize," the runners told him, "that this is all your master's doing. He will give you neither your wife nor your boxes. Isn't there anyone else whom you can ask? We don't mind overlooking it for Master Yin's sake, and taking you there to get a little money and rice for the journey. Don't worry about traveling money for us."

"Brothers," Laiwang again said, "for pity's sake, take me to my master's door first. There are one or two neighbors whom I will ask to say a good word for me. Probably I won't get much, but I may get something."

The two runners agreed. Laiwang went to see Ying Bojue, but Bojue pretended not to be at home. Then he persuaded his two left-hand neighbors, Jia Renqing and Yi Mianzi, to go and plead with Ximen Qing that he might be allowed to have his wife and his possessions. Ximen would not even come out to see them and ordered his servants to drive them away from the door. Jia and Yi were so greatly abashed that they did not know what to do. Huilian, Laiwang's wife, was unaware of all this. She never heard a word of it, because Ximen had given orders that any servant who mentioned it to her should be given twenty strokes.

The two runners took Laiwang to the house of his father-in-law, the coffin merchant Song Ren. Laiwang wept as he told his father-in-law the story, and Song Ren gave a tael of silver to the runners and a peck of rice to his son-in-law for food upon the way. So, weeping and bewailing, Laiwang set out on the highway for Xuzhou, leaving Qinghe at the beginning of the fourth month.

Day after day Huilian expected her husband to come. She gave the boys food to take to him, but they ate it themselves as soon as they were outside the gate. They came back and said: "Brother enjoyed that food and all is well at the prison. He would have been out before this but the magistrates haven't been to the court for a few days. In any case, he will be home in a day or two."

Ximen Qing deceived her. "I have sent to the court," he told her, "and he will be out very soon now." Huilian believed them, but, one day, she heard a rumor that her husband had been taken out of prison and had been begging at the door for his clothes. No one knew where he had gone. She questioned the boys time after time, but none of them would speak. One day, however, she caught Daian as he was coming back from waiting upon his master, and said to him: "How is your brother getting on in prison, and when is he coming out?"

"Sister," Daian said, "I will tell you. By this time he has reached the River of Shifting Sand." Huilian pressed him, and at last Daian, with a great show of reluctance, told her how Laiwang had been beaten and banished to Xuzhou. "Don't get excited about it," the boy said, at the end, "and above all, don't let anybody know I told you."

It was more than Huilian could bear. She shut herself in her room and sobbed bitterly. "Oh, my man," she cried, "how could you fall into the trap and let yourself be treated so? All these years you have served him, and now you have not even a single suit of good clothes to cover you, and they have driven you far away. How bitter it is! Buried away as I am, I do not even know whether you are alive or dead." She sobbed a while. Then taking a long kerchief, she fastened it to the lintel of the door and hanged herself.

The Beanpole, Laizhao's wife, lived next door to Huilian. As she was coming from the inner court, she heard the woman weeping in her room. Then she noticed that the sound stopped and she could only hear a kind of gasping. She knocked at the door but there was no answer. She was frightened and made Ping'an, one of the boys, climb through the window and get into the room. Huilian, with all her clothes on, was hanging from the lintel. The boy cut her down at once and opened the door. They brought ginger broth and poured it down her throat, then sent word to the people in the inner court. Wu Yueniang, Li Jiao'er, Meng Yulou, Li Ping'er, Ximen Dajie, and the two maids, Yuxiao and Xiaoyu, all came to see, and Ben the Fourth's wife also came to look. The Beanpole was sitting on the floor supporting Huilian who was sobbing soundlessly. Yueniang spoke to her, but she only hung her head. A froth came from her mouth.

"What a foolish child you are," Yueniang said. "If there was anything wrong, you should have told me. What sense is there in behaving like this?"

She told Yuxiao to help support her, and said again: "Huilian, my child, if anything is troubling you, tell me what it is." But though she spoke several times, Huilian did not answer. After she had questioned her for a long time, the woman began to cry, making a great noise and beating her hands together. Yueniang told Yuxiao to help her to bed, but she would not go. Then Yueniang and the others spoke firmly to her, and went back to the inner court, leaving Yuxiao and Ben the Fourth's wife to look after the woman.

After a while Ximen Qing pulled up the lattice and came in. Huilian was still sitting on the cold floor, and he told Yuxiao to put her to bed.

"My mistress has told her to go to bed," Yuxiao said, "but she won't go."

"What an obstinate child you are," Ximen cried, "you'll get cold there on the ground. If you have anything to say to me, say it, and don't behave in this silly way."

Huilian shook her head. "Father," she said, "you are a fine fellow, and you have deceived me splendidly. Why do you call me your child? I am no child of yours. You are an executioner in disguise: to bury a man alive means nothing to you. And not only are you ready to put him to death, you must needs see his funeral also. Day after day, you lied to me. One day you said: 'He will be here tomorrow,' and the next day you said: 'He will be here tomorrow,' and I thought he really would come. Why have you sent him away and said nothing to me about it? You did it secretly, and had him sent far, far away, while I knew not a thing about it. To do a cruel thing like that you can have no conscience at all. Even after you had done your worst, you still kept the matter hidden from me. If you wished to get rid of us, why didn't you get rid of us both? Why keep me here?"

"My child," Ximen said, "I have no quarrel with you. That fellow was a scoundrel and I had to send him away. Settle down quietly. I will look after you." He said to Yuxiao: "You and Ben the Fourth's wife spend the night here and look after her. I will tell one of the boys to bring you some wine." He went out, and, after Ben the Fourth's wife had helped Huilian to bed, she and Yuxiao tried to console her.

Ximen Qing went to the shop and asked Fu for a thousand cash. With the money he bought a roast and had it put on a tray with a jar of wine, and told Laian to take the tray to the woman's room.

"Father told me to bring you this," the boy said. When Huilian saw the tray, she cursed him.

"You thievish young rascal. Take it away at once or I will throw it on the floor."

"Do keep it, Sister," Laian said, "I can't take it away again or Father will beat me."

He lay the tray on a table. Huilian jumped out of bed and took up the jar of wine. She was going to throw it on the floor but the Beanpole stopped her. Ben the Fourth's wife looked at the Beanpole and put her finger on her mouth. They were sitting together when Ben the Fourth's son came in and said to his mother: "Father has come home and wants his dinner." The two women went out. When they came to the Beanpole's door, Ximen's daughter Ximen Dajie was there gossiping with Laibao's wife. They asked Ben the Fourth's wife where she was going.

"My man has come home and wants his dinner," she said. "I am going to see what he wants and then I'm coming back again. I did not mean to stay, but his Lordship pressed me, otherwise I shouldn't have been there as long as this."

"What did Father say to her?" Laibao's wife said.

"I should never have thought Huilian was so peppery," Ben the Fourth's wife said. "She gave Father a piece of her mind and no mistake. There are very few serving women who would dare to say as much."

"She is not like other women," Laibao's wife said. "She has received his Lordship's special favors. You can't expect the rest of us to do what she can do." She went away. The Beanpole said to Ben the Fourth's wife: "Don't be long, Sister."

"You needn't trouble to say that," Ben the Fourth's wife said. "If I don't come back, Father will kill me."

Ximen Qing told Ben the Fourth's wife and the Beanpole to stay with Huilian, and late that night he sent Yuxiao to sleep there, hoping that the woman would gradually calm down.

"Sister," they said, "you are no fool. Why don't you take advantage of this opportunity while you have it? You are like a flower that has just blossomed. Our Master loves you and that is as Fate has decided. You cannot, of course, rank yourself among the ladies, but you are much better off than the rest of us. It will be far better for you to cast in your lot with Father than with a slave. Besides, he has already gone. You may feel a little sad—there's no harm in that—but if you keep on crying you will get in a bad way, and that will be just throwing your life away. There is an old saying: Strike the gong for a day, and be a priest for a day. After that, you need never bother yourself again about such things as virtue and chastity."

Huilian cried and sobbed. Days passed, and she still refused to take any food. Yuxiao told Ximen Qing and he sent Jinlian to talk to her. It was no use. Jinlian returned and said to him: "That whore can think of nothing but her husband. Everybody knows that after one night of marriage, the pleasure persists for a hundred nights; and lovers need walk but a hundred paces together for affection to remain with them forever. What hope do you think you have of capturing the heart of a woman as virtuous as this?"

Ximen Qing laughed. "Don't you believe it," he said. "If she is really so virtuous, why did she get rid of Jiang Cong the cook, and marry Lai-wang?"

He sat down in the hall and sent for all the boys. He determined to find out who had told Huilian of her husband's banishment. "If the culprit confesses," he said, "he shall not receive a single blow, but if he doesn't, and I find out who he is, there shall be thirty strokes for him and he shall be sent away from the house."

Shutong knelt down. "The other day," he said, "when Daian came back with you, I heard my sister asking him questions in the passage. It was he who let it out and told her."

"Go and find Daian," Ximen cried in a rage. But Daian had already heard what was going on and had run away to take refuge in Jinlian's room. She was washing her face when the boy came in.

"Mother, save me! Save me!" he cried, kneeling before her.

"What do you mean by coming and frightening me like this, you little rascal?" Jinlian said. "What have you been doing?"

"Father is going to thrash me because I told Huilian about Laiwang's being sent away. Mother, you must go and pacify him. If he sees me when he is in such a temper, he will certainly kill me."

"You funny little rascal," Jinlian said. "You're as scared as a ghost. I thought it must be something serious enough to shake heaven and earth, and it's only some trifling thing connected with that strumpet. Stay here."

Daian hid himself behind the door.

Ximen Qing created a terrible uproar in the front court when Daian was not to be found. He twice sent boys to Jinlian's room, but each time she drove them away with curses. Finally, with a horsewhip in his hand, he came along, like a whirlwind.

"Where is the slave?" he cried.

Jinlian did not pay the slightest attention to him. He went round and round, searching, and at last dragged Daian from behind the door. He was going to thrash the boy, but Jinlian snatched the whip from him and threw it on the top of the bed.

"You shameless creature," she said, "you are not fit to be a master. That whore spends her time thinking about her husband, and goes and hangs herself, and you try to vent your spite by ill-treating this boy. What harm has he done?"

Ximen Qing rolled his eyes about, but Jinlian said to the boy: "Get off to the front court, and go on with your work. Don't be afraid of him." Daian slipped away and went to the front court.

Jinlian could see that Ximen Qing still cared for Huilian, and decided upon a plot. She went to the inner court and told tales to Xue'e. "Laiwang's wife," she said, "is telling everybody that you were in love with her husband and created such a scandal that Father was angry and sent Laiwang away. You remember how he struck you and took away your ornaments and dresses. It was all her doing."

So Jinlian touched a very sore spot. She saw the effect she had produced and went off to Huilian with a different story.

"Xue'e," she said, "has been saying nasty things about you in the kitchen. She says you used to be a slave in the Cais' household and that you are an expert at stealing other people's husbands and carrying on with men. I heard her say: 'If she has not been playing tricks of that sort with our husband, why did he send Laiwang away? She had better save her tears to wash her feet.'"

In this way Jinlian stirred up hatred in their hearts. One day it became obvious that trouble was brewing.

It was the eighteenth day of the fourth month, and Li Jiao'er's birthday. The old procuress and her daughter Li Guijie came to congratulate their kinswoman. Yueniang asked them to stay and entertained them with the other ladies in the hall. Ximen Qing had gone to a banquet. Huilian had taken some food, and, that morning, spent a few moments in the inner court. Then she went back to her room and slept till the sun was low. The maids came several times to call her but she paid no attention and would not leave her room. At last Xue'e, who was only waiting for the opportunity, went to see her.

"You must be a person of most surpassing beauty, Sister," she said, "since you cannot be persuaded to accept our invitations." Huilian did not answer. She was lying on the bed with her face to the wall.

"Are you thinking of your husband, Laiwang?" Xue'e said. "It would have been better if you had thought of him before. If it hadn't been for you, this would never have happened and he would still be in Ximen's household."

Huilian remembered what Jinlian had told her. She jumped off the bed. "Why have you come here," she cried, "with your lewd tongue and your filthy temper? Even if I was the cause of his being sent away, it is not for you, of all people, to come and tell me so. You did not get off scot-free yourself. You ought to be very thankful that some people did not say all they knew. You are the last person to give yourself airs and talk about other people's misdeeds."

Xue'e lost her temper. "You thievish slave, you loose woman," she cried, "how dare you insult me?"

"I may be a slave and a loose woman," Huilian said, "but at least I am not a slave's mistress. I may have carried on with Master, but that is better than carrying on with a servant. You stole my husband and now you come here and make a song about it."

Xue'e was now almost beside herself. She dashed forward and struck Huilian in the face. The woman was taken by surprise and her cheeks flamed scarlet.

"Will you strike me?" she cried, and made for Xue'e with her head. They closed with one another and fought, till the Beanpole separated them. Then Yueniang came and upbraided them. "You ought to be ashamed of yourselves," she said. "You never stop to consider whether there are visitors here or not. Wait till your master comes home and you'll see whether I tell him or not."

Xue'e went to the inner court, and Yueniang, seeing how Huilian's hair was all in disorder, said, "Go and attend to your hair. Then come and join us."

Huilian did not reply. She took Yueniang politely to the door and went back into the room. She locked the door behind her and cried bitterly. It was now getting dark and the people in the inner court were busy with the evening meal. Huilian could bear no more. She took two long ribbons, like those used for binding the feet, tied them to the lintel of the door, and hanged herself. She was only twenty-five years old.

Later that evening as Yueniang was taking old woman Li and Guijie to the gate, she passed Huilian's door. It was shut and there was no sign of life. She wondered what had happened. When she had taken leave of her guests, she came back and knocked at the door. There was no reply. This frightened her and she told some of the boys to climb through the window. They cut the ribbons and took the woman down. For a long time they tried to bring her back to life, for they did not know how long she had been dead.

When Yueniang found that it was impossible to revive the woman, she was greatly upset, and told Laixing to take a horse at once and go for Ximen Qing. Xue'e, for her part, was very much afraid that, when he came, he would try to find out how this had happened. She paced up and down the hall and finally knelt down before Yueniang and begged her not to tell her husband of the quarrel. She was in such a state of terror that Yueniang began to feel sorry for her.

"You are afraid now," she said. "Why didn't you have a little less to say before?"

Then Ximen Qing came home. They told him that Huilian had been thinking about her husband and had cried the whole day. Then, at a time when everybody was busy, she had seized the opportunity and hanged herself. Nobody knew exactly when she did so.

"Oh, the silly woman!" Ximen cried, "the Fates have treated her hardly." He sent a servant to report the matter to Li, one of the local magistrates. "The family were entertaining visitors," he was told to say, "and this woman, who was responsible for the silver, lost a silver cup. She was afraid her master would punish her, and killed herself." At the same time he was to make the magistrate a present of thirty taels of silver. The magistrate acted as was expected of him and only sent one of his officers with a few coroner's men to view the corpse.

Ximen Qing bought a coffin and applied for a certificate. Then Ben the Fourth and Laixing took the body to the cemetery outside the city. They gave the firemen five *qian* of silver to burn the body. A heap of wood had already been piled around the coffin and they were just about to set fire to it, when Huilian's father, Song Ren the coffin dealer, suddenly came up and stopped them. There was something mysterious about his daughter's death, he said, and he accused Ximen Qing of abusing his authority and trying to seduce her. "My daughter," he said, "was an honest woman and repulsed him. She had met her death at his hands. I am going to take the matter to the Governor of the Province, so let no one presume to burn her body."

The firemen were afraid to complete their task and went away. Ben the Fourth and Laixing were obliged to leave the coffin in the temple. They went back to tell their master what had happened.

CHAPTER 27
The Garden of Delights

Laibao returned from the Eastern Capital and made his report to Ximen Qing. "When I reached the Capital," he said, "I went to see the Comptroller of the Household and gave him your letter. Then I was taken to the minister. When his Eminence had looked at the list of presents, he accepted them. Then I explained the case. His Eminence said: 'I will send at once to the Governor of Shandong and ask him to liberate the salt merchant Wang Sifeng of Yangzhou and the others.' Master Zhai sent his greetings to you. He says he would like to have a talk with you and that you ought to go to the Capital for his Eminence's birthday on the fifteenth day of the sixth month."

Ximen Qing was satisfied. He sent Laibao to tell Master Qiao. While he was speaking, Ben the Fourth and Laixing came in, but seeing their master occupied, they stood aside until Laibao had gone. Then Ximen Qing said to Ben the Fourth: "I suppose you have come back from the funeral?" Ben the Fourth hardly dared to speak, but Laixing came forward and whispered: "Song Ren came to the funeral pyre, and refused to allow the body to be burned. He said it was extremely irregular. He said other things that I should not like to repeat."

Ximen Qing was very angry. "What a detestable, hateful creature!" he cried. He sent a boy at once for Chen Jingji, told the young man to write a letter to Magistrate Li, and sent Laian with it to the Town Hall. The magistrate dispatched two runners who bound Song Ren and took him to the court. He was charged with blackmail and attempting to use the dead woman as a means of extorting money. He was brought in fetters to the Hall of Audience and there given twenty strokes so severe that the blood flowed down his legs in streams. The magistrate then bound him over never again to be a nuisance to Ximen Qing. At the same time he ordered police and firemen to go with Ximen's servants to the place of burning and burn the body. Song Ren, his legs all beaten and bleeding, crawled home. He was so exasperated that he took a fever and died, bitterly lamenting his fate.

Now that he had finally disposed of Huilian, Ximen Qing got ready gold and silver to the value of three hundred taels and sent for Silversmith

Gu and several others to make a set of silver figures for the birthday of the
Imperial Tutor. They worked beneath the awning at Ximen Qing's house.
Each of the figures was over a foot high. They also made a pair of golden
flagons with the character *Shou* engraved upon them. Ximen had bought
two pairs of peach-shaped cups of jade, two sets of crimson robes from
Hangzhou, and dragon cloaks embroidered in five colors. He still wanted
two rolls of a particular kind of black cloth and some crimson dragon silk,
but he could not find it at any price. Then Li Ping'er said to him, "I have
some sets of dragon robes that have never been made up. They are upstairs
in my place. Come and look at them."

Ximen Qing went with her and they picked out four sets, two of crimson silk and two of the special black cloth. They all were edged with gold
braid, and embroidered with five-colored dragons. They were certainly
much finer than anything they could have bought. Ximen Qing was delighted. He had them all packed up and Laibao and Clerk Fu left again for
the Eastern Capital on the twenty-eighth day of the fifth month.

Two days later it was the beginning of the sixth month. The weather
was very hot, and at noon the fiery sun was like a blazing umbrella in a
cloudless sky. Not a particle of cloud was to be seen and it seemed hot
enough to scorch the stones or to melt metal.

It was so hot that Ximen Qing did not go out. He stayed at home
with his hair undone and his clothes unbuttoned, trying to keep cool. He
sat in the bower by the Kingfisher Hall watching the boys watering the
flowers. In front of the Kingfisher Hall there was a bowl of sweet-smelling daphne. He told Laian to take a little watering can, and watched him
sprinkle the flowers.

Jinlian and Li Ping'er were both dressed in the lightest of silver silk,
with skirts of dark red and a fringe of gold thread. Li Ping'er was wearing
a short crimson cape and Jinlian had one of silver and red. Jinlian wore
nothing on her head but a blue Hangzhou headdress, through which four
braids of hair peeped out. On her brow were three flowers made of kingfisher feathers, which enhanced the beauty of her white face and glossy
hair, her red lips and pearly teeth. The two women came smiling, holding
each other's hands.

"You here, watering the flowers!" Jinlian cried, when she saw Ximen
Qing. "Why don't you go and dress your hair?"

"Tell one of the maids to bring me some water," Ximen said, "and I
will do my hair here."

"Put down your watering can," Jinlian said to Laian, "and send a maid
with some water and a comb. Be quick about it." Laian bowed and went
to do what he was told. Then Jinlian, seeing the sweet-smelling daphne,

was going to pick some to put in her hair, but Ximen Qing stopped her. "Don't touch them, little oily mouth. I will give one to each of you." He had already picked a few blossoms and put them into a crackleware vase.

"Ah, my son," Jinlian said, "so you've been plucking the flowers, have you? What do you mean by hiding them there instead of offering them to your mother?" She snatched one up and set it in her hair. Ximen Qing gave one to Li Ping'er. Then Chunmei came with a mirror and comb, and Qiuju brought water. Ximen gave three flowers to Chunmei, for Yueniang, Li Jiao'er and Yulou, and said: "Ask the Third Lady to come and play her zither for me."

"Chunmei can go to the Great Lady and Li Jiao'er, and if you want Yulou, I'll go and fetch her," Jinlian said. "When I come back, I shall expect another flower, and, if I bring someone to sing for you, still another one."

"Go first," Ximen said, "and we'll see about that when you come back."

"My son," Jinlian said, "wherever can you have been brought up? What a naughty boy to think of trying to cheat me like that! If I go and fetch Yulou, I shall never get one. No, let me have it first, and then I'll go."

"You wicked little rascal," Ximen Qing said, laughing, "even in trifles like this you will have your own way." He gave her the flower. Jinlian set it in her hair, and went towards the inner court, leaving Li Ping'er alone with Ximen Qing.

Through the light silk skirt, Ximen could see her crimson trousers; the sun's rays made them so transparent that he could clearly distinguish the cool flesh beneath them. The sight aroused his passion, and finding that they were alone, he stopped dressing his hair, and carried Li Ping'er to a long summer couch. He pulled aside her skirt, took down the crimson trousers, and played with her the game that is called Carrying Fire over the Mountains. They played for a long time without his bringing matters to a conclusion, and their pleasure was like that of a lovebird and his mate.

Jinlian did not go to the inner court. She went as far as the corner gate and then decided to give Yulou's flower to Chunmei. She went back on tiptoe to the Kingfisher Hall. There, she stood listening outside the window, and, for quite a long time, could hear the lovers amusing themselves.

"My darling," she heard Ximen Qing say to Li Ping'er, "above all else I love your little white bottom. I shall do my very utmost to give you pleasure today."

After a pause, she heard Li Ping'er say softly, "My dearest, you must be gentle with me, for I am really not too well. The other day you were rough with me, and my belly hurt so much that only during the last day or two has it begun to feel better."

"You are not well?" Ximen cried. "What do you mean?"

"I will not keep it from you any longer," Li Ping'er told him. "For a month now, I have been cherishing a little one within me. Please treat me with some indulgence."

Ximen Qing was delighted beyond all measure. "Why, my precious one," he said, "why didn't you tell me before? If that is how things are, I will bring this game to an end at once." His happiness reached its culmination and his joy was complete. He set both hands upon her legs, and the evidence of his delight was overwhelming. The woman beneath him raised herself to welcome it.

After a while, Jinlian could hear Ximen breathing heavily, and his lover's gentle voice, like an oriole's, answering him. No sound escaped her as she stood beneath the window. Yulou came up suddenly from behind. "What are you doing here?" she asked. Jinlian signed to her to be silent, and they both went into the summerhouse. Ximen Qing was a little taken aback and did not quite know what to do.

"What have you been doing all this long time I've been away?" Jinlian said. "How is it you haven't washed, or combed your hair?"

"I am waiting for a maid to bring me some jasmine soap," Ximen said.

"I have no patience with you," Jinlian cried. "Why must you have that particular kind of soap? Is that why your face is cleaner than some people's bottoms?"

Ximen Qing paid no attention to this remark, but, when he had finished dressing, sat down beside Yulou. "What have you been doing in the inner court?" he said. "Have you brought your zither?"

"I have been making a pearl flower for the Great Lady to wear at a party. Chunmei is bringing the zither."

Soon Chunmei came. She said she had given the flowers to the Great Lady and the Second Lady. Ximen told her to set out wine, and a bowl of ice with plums and melons in it was brought. In the cool summerhouse Ximen Qing enjoyed the society of his ladies.

"Why didn't you tell Chunmei to ask the Great Lady to come?" Yulou said. "She does not care for wine," Ximen Qing said, "I thought there was no purpose in troubling her."

Then Ximen took the seat of honor and the three women sat down facing him. The exquisite wine was poured out for them and many delicacies were placed before them. Jinlian would not sit on a chair but took a porcelain stool for herself.

"Come and sit on a chair," Yulou cried, "you will find that stool too cold."

"Don't worry," Jinlian said, "I am getting old. I've no reason to fear an internal chill or anything of that sort. Why should I?"

The wine was passed around three times and Ximen Qing told Chunmei to give Yulou her zither, and a lute to Jinlian. "Play the tune 'The God of Fire Rules the World and His Glory Fills the Void.'" Jinlian refused. "How well you must have been brought up," she cried, "to ask us to sing while you two sit there and enjoy yourselves. I will not play for you. Tell the Sixth Lady to play something."

"She doesn't know how to play," Ximen said.

"Well, even if she doesn't know how to play, she certainly knows how to count the beats," Jinlian said.

Ximen Qing laughed. "You little whore," he cried, "you always try to pick on something," but he told Chunmei to give Li Ping'er a pair of red ivory castanets. Then the two women began to play, spreading their exquisite fingers and slowly plucking the silken strings. They sang the song of "The Geese Flying Over the Sand," while Xiuchun stood at the side and fanned them. When the song was over, Ximen offered each of them a cup of wine. Jinlian went to the table, drank deeply of iced water, and ate some fruit.

"Why are you eating only cold things today?" Yulou said.

"Nothing of any particular interest is happening in my distinguished belly," Jinlian replied. "Why should I be afraid of cold things?"

Li Ping'er was so embarrassed that she became white and red in turns. Ximen Qing glanced sharply at Jinlian. "You little villain," he said, "you do nothing but talk nonsense."

"Brother," Jinlian said, "old women like me get nothing but dry meat to eat. We have to eat it sinew by sinew."

As they were drinking, the clouds began to gather. Far away the thunder rolled and suddenly a storm broke, drenching the flowers in front of the summerhouse.

In a few moments the rain stopped again. A rainbow appeared in the sky. The sun came out again, and in a twinkling the jasper steps glistened and a cool evening breeze freshened the courtyard. Xiaoyu came from the back court to call Yulou.

"The Great Lady wants me," Yulou said. "I have still some pearl flowers to finish. I must go now or she will be angry."

"I will go with you," Li Ping'er said. "I should like to see the flowers."

Ximen Qing said he would go with them too. He took the zither and asked Yulou to play. He beat time with his hands and they all sang together.

> It is evening.
> The storm has passed over the southern hall
> Red petals are floating on the surface of the pool.

Slowly the gentle thunder rolls away
The rain is over and the clouds disperse
The fragrance of water lilies comes to us over the distance.
The new moon is a crescent
Fresh from the perfumed bath, decked for the evening
Over the darkening courtyard it wanes
Yet will not go to rest.
In the shade of the willow the young cicada bursts into song
Fireflies hover over the ancestral halls.
Listen. Whence comes this song of Ling?
The painted boat is late returning
The jade cords sink lower and lower
The gentlefolk are silent.
A vision of delight.
Let us rise and take each other by the hand
And tire our hair.
The moon lights up the silken curtains.
But there are no sleepers there.
The brave mandarin duck tumbles the lotus leaves
On the gently rippling water
Sprinkling them with drops like pearls.
They give forth fragrance.
A perfumed breeze moves softly over the flower beds
Beside the summerhouse
How can our spirits fail to be refreshed?
Why crave for the islands of the blessed, the home of fairies?
Yet, when the west wind blows again, Autumn will come with it.
Though we perceive it not, the seasons change.

So singing, they reached the corner gate almost before they knew it. Yu-lou gave her zither to Chunmei and went to the inner court with Li Ping'er.

"Wait for me," Jinlian cried, "I am coming too," Ximen Qing caught her by the hand and pulled her back.

"So you would run away from me, little oily mouth," he cried. "I shall not let you go." He pulled so hard that she almost fell.

"You funny creature," Jinlian cried. "They are both going. Why won't you let me go?"

"We will drink a little wine together," Ximen said, "and play Flying Arrows Beneath the Tai Hu Rock."

"We can play quite well in the summerhouse," Jinlian said. "Why stay here? And it's no use asking this young scamp Chunmei to bring any wine. She won't do it."

Ximen Qing told Chunmei to go. She handed the zither to Jinlian and went off with her head in the air. Jinlian strummed the zither for a while. "I have learned a few bars from Yulou," she said. She saw how freshly the pomegranate flowers were blooming after the rain, and laughingly plucked one and set it in her hair. "I am an old lady, wearing on my brow a 'starving-for-three-days' flower."

Ximen Qing seized her tiny feet. "You little villain," he cried, "if I weren't afraid of somebody seeing us, I'd make you die of delight."

"Don't get so excited, you naughty fellow," Jinlian said. "Let me put down this zither." She laid the instrument beside a flower bed. "My son," she said, "you have only just finished amusing yourself with the Sixth Lady. Why should you come and plague me now?"

"You are still talking nonsense," Ximen said, "I never touched her."

"My boy," Jinlian said, "you may try as hard as you like, but you will never succeed in deceiving the God who watches over Hearth and Home. What is the use of trying to hoodwink an experienced old woman like me? When I went to the inner court to take that flower, the pair of you wasted no time."

"Oh, do not talk such rubbish," Ximen cried. He set her down among the flowers, and kissed her lips. She slipped her tongue into his mouth.

"Call me 'darling,' and I'll let you get up," he said. Jinlian could not help herself. She called him darling, but, she added, "It isn't me you really love, so why do you bother me?"

They amused themselves for a while, and then Jinlian suggested that they should go and play Flying Arrows in the Arbor of the Vines. She took the zither into her lap and played.

They walked side by side. Soon they had turned by the shaded pool and passed the Hall of the White Rose. Then they went in front of the Kingfisher Hall and came to the Arbor of the Vines. It was a very beautiful place.

They came to the arbor. There were four summer stools there, and near them a vase for the game of Flying Arrows. Jinlian set down the zither and played the arrow game with Ximen Qing. Then Chunmei came with wine, and Qiuju carrying a basket of delicacies, with a bowl of iced fruits.

"You went off in a huff, young woman," Jinlian said. "What has made you decide to bring the things?"

"We have looked everywhere for you," Chunmei said. "How were we to know that you'd take it into your head to come here?"

Qiuju set out the refreshments and Ximen Qing opened the basket. There were eight rows of exquisite fruits and sweetmeats in it, a little silver jar of grape wine, two small Jinlian cups and two pairs of chopsticks.

These they set upon a rustic table. Ximen and Jinlian sat down before it but went on with their game. They played Feathers through the Arch, The Geese Flying on their Backs, The Qiao Sisters Studying Their Books, and Yang Guifei Asleep in the Spring. Then they played The Dragon Entering His Cave and Pearls upon the Blind. Altogether, they had more than ten games. Then the wine went to Jinlian's head. The peaches began to bloom upon her cheeks, and her eyes lost their shyness. Ximen Qing thought he would like to drink the love potion known as the wine of the five fragrances, and told Chunmei to go and fetch it.

"Little oily mouth," Jinlian said, "you can do something for me too. In my room you will find a summer mat and a pillow. Bring them here. I feel very sleepy, and I think I shall lie down."

Chunmei professed to raise objections. "Oh dear," she said, "you give so many orders that nobody could possibly carry them all out."

"If you won't go," Ximen said, "send Qiuju. You bring the wine and we'll leave it at that." Chunmei went off, tossing her head. After a while Qiuju came back with the mat, the pillow and some coverlets. Jinlian ordered her to set them out. "Then fasten the garden gate and go to your room, and don't come back until I call you." Qiuju did as she was told, and went away.

Ximen Qing rose, and took off his jade-colored light gown. He hung it on the trellis, and went to wash his hands by the peony arbor. When he came back, Jinlian had already prepared the mat and its cushions inside the arbor of the vines, and had undressed till not a thread of silk remained upon her body. She lay flat on her back, a pair of crimson shoes still upon her feet, fanning herself with a white silk fan to gain some relief from the heat.

When Ximen Qing saw her, his wanton heart was quickly stirred, for the wine had not been without its effect upon him. He took off his clothes, and sat down on a stool, letting his toes play around the treasure of this beautiful flower.

Then proof of her pleasure oozed from her like the slime of a snail leaving its tortuous white trail. Ximen pulled off her decorated crimson shoes, loosened the ribbons that bound her feet and tied her ankles to the trellis, so that she looked like a golden dragon baring its claws. The gate of womanhood was open, its guardian was aroused, and a deep scarlet vale appeared.

Ximen Qing lay down and, taking his weapon in his hands, prepared to storm the breach, resting one hand upon the pillow, and proceeding to the attack as he had played Feathers through the Arch when at the Flying Arrow game. He strove with all his strength, till from the scene of combat a mist arose, spiraling, like an eel rising from the mud.

Jinlian beneath him never ceased to murmur, "Darling, my darling." Then, as he was just about to reap the fruits of victory, Chunmei came suddenly with the wine for which Ximen had asked. But when she saw them, she put down the jar of wine and fled to the top of the artificial mound, and there went into the arbor that was called the Land of Clouds. She rested her elbows on the chess table, and amused herself setting out the chessmen. Ximen Qing lifted his head and looked at her; then he beckoned her to come down, but she refused. "If you don't come down, I will make you," he cried. He left Jinlian and ran up the stone steps to the arbor. Chunmei fled down a tiny path to the right, through the grottos, till she reached a point halfway, where among the hanging foliage and flowers she tried to hide. Ximen Qing caught her there, and took her in his arms. "I've got you at last, little oily mouth," he cried. Then he carried her like a feather to the Arbor of the Vines.

"Have a cup of wine," he said, laughing, setting her on his knee, and they drank together mouth to mouth. Suddenly Chunmei saw that her mistress's feet were tied to the trellis.

"I don't know how you could do such a thing," she said. "It is the middle of the day, and if anybody should come in, what would they think of such goings on."

"Isn't the corner gate shut?" Ximen asked.

"Yes," Chunmei said, "I shut it when I came in."

"Now," Ximen said, "watch me. I'm going to play Flying Arrows with a living target. The game is called Striking the Silver Swan with a Golden Ball. Watch! If I hit the mark at the first shot, I shall treat myself to a cup of wine." He took a plum from the iced bowl, and cast it to the gate of womanhood. Three times he cast; three times he reached the inmost flower. One plum stuck there, but he neither removed it nor finished the work he had begun until the girl became faint and her distress from the effort was evident. Her starry eyes were half closed, and her body fell back limply upon the mat. "You are indeed a roguish enemy," she murmured. "You will be the death of me." Her voice trembled.

Ximen paid no attention to her, but told Chunmei to fan him, while he refreshed himself with wine. Then he lay down in an easy chair, and went to sleep. When Chunmei saw that he was asleep, she went softly over and touched him, then ran like a wisp of smoke to the Snow Grotto and so to the other side of the garden. There she heard someone knocking, opened the gate, and saw Li Ping'er.

Ximen Qing slept for an hour or so, and when he opened his eyes, Jinlian's white legs were still hanging from the trellis. Chunmei had gone. Again his passion was aroused.

"Now, you abandoned little creature," he cried, "I'll attend to you." He took out the plum, and gave it her to eat. Then, sitting on the pillow, he took from a pocket in his gown a case of love instruments. First he put on the clasp, and tied a sulfur ring about the root of evil. He refused to dismount her, but played so long about her entrance that she cried in fury. "My darling, my dearest, be a man quickly or I shall go mad. I see what it is. You are angry with me because of Li Ping'er. That is why you tease me like this. But now I have found how cunning you can be, I will never make you angry again."

"Ah," cried Ximen, laughing, "so you have learned your lesson. Well, speak nicely to me."

With one thrust he seemed to reach her inmost parts. Then he withdrew; searching in his pocket he found some of the powder that is called Delight of the Bedroom and Fragrance of the Penis, and applied it to the frog's mouth. He returned to the attack, and immediately a tall, proud warrior appeared, full of fire and fury; Ximen surveyed the struggle with admiration. She lay on the mat with half-closed eyes murmuring, "Oh my beloved darling! You don't know what you're putting into me. That thing has driven me to frenzy. Spare me, please." She spoke without shame, but Ximen instantly drove forward with full strength, his hands on the mat, tearing and digging, plunging into her depths a hundred times before withdrawing again. She wiped her wounds with a handkerchief, but in vain; the mat bore clear traces of battle, and the warrior, still erect and fierce, would not desist. "The time has come," cried Ximen, "the monk shall smite the timbrel." Suddenly he lunged, and reached the inmost citadel; for within the gate of womanhood there lies a citadel, like the heart of a flower, which, if touched by the conqueror, is infused with a wonderful pleasure. She felt pain and withdrew; but the sulfur ring broke inside her body with a crack.

She closed her eyes and her breath came faintly; only a faint murmur issued from her lips, the tip of her tongue became icy cold, and her body fell back apparently lifeless upon the mat.

Ximen Qing was alarmed. He hastily untied the ribbons, and removed the sulfur ring. It was broken into two pieces. Then he helped the woman to sit up, and at last her starry eyes began to gleam again, and she showed signs of life once more. In a caressing voice she said, "Darling, why did you treat me so cruelly today? You nearly killed me. You mustn't do this again. It is not simply fun. My head and eyes swim so that I hardly know where I am."

The sun was already setting. Ximen hastily helped her into her clothes, and then called Chunmei and Qiuju to come and take away the mat and the pillows. Then they supported her to her room. Chunmei came back to the garden to see that Qiuju removed all the empty cups. She was just shutting the garden gate, when suddenly Laizhao's little son Little Iron Rod jumped out of the summerhouse, and asked her to give him some fruits.

"What have you been doing, you young rascal?" Chunmei cried. She gave him a few peaches and plums. "Your father has been drinking," she told him, "and you had better run off, for he will certainly beat you if he sees you."

The little monkey took the fruit and disappeared. Chunmei fastened the garden gate, returned to her mistress and Ximen Qing, and helped them to retire.

CHAPTER 28
The Two Shoes

After Ximen Qing had taken Pan Jinlian to her room, he took off all his clothes. She wore only a piece of fine silk upon her breast. They sat down side by side and began to drink again. Ximen caressed her white throat with his hand, and they drank their wine, one from the other's mouth. They were profoundly happy in their love. Jinlian allowed her hair to fall about her; her delicate bosom was half disclosed, her eyes challenged him. She seemed like Yang Guifei inflamed by wine.

Her slender fingers played with the warrior between his thighs; it was exhausted after the battle. Still bound by the silver ring, it looked overworked but not quite spent. "Why don't you leave it in peace?" said Ximen. "It's your fault. You frightened it so much that it can hardly move."

"It can hardly move?" she replied. "What are you saying?"

"If it could move," said Ximen, "it would not be drooping like a fading flower, refusing to rise. Why don't you ask its pardon on bended knees?"

She looked at it and smiled. Then she squatted down, put her head on his thigh, undid his trousers and grasped the weary warrior. "You are he who raised his head so proudly, whose eye was so fierce that it terrified me. Now you pretend you are tired, and lie as if you were dead."

Meanwhile she played with it; she pressed it on her soft cheeks, caressed it with her hand, and then she brought it to her lips and kissed the frog's mouth. Immediately the warrior, boiling with passion, sprang up, its head was a talon, its eye was fire, its jaw bristled with hair, its body was stiff as iron.

Ximen Qing rested on a pillow and told Jinlian to go down on all fours, within the silken curtains, and put forth all her strength, the more to increase his pleasure. Immediately his passion blazed forth again, and again he engaged with the woman. "Darling," she pleaded with him, "you must spare me. Don't play with me again." That night their joy in each other was boundless.

The night passed. Next day Ximen Qing went out, and Jinlian got up about dinnertime. When she was ready to put on her shoes, she looked for the crimson pair she had been wearing the day before, but could not find them anywhere. She asked Chunmei where they were.

"When Father and I brought you back yesterday," Chunmei said, "Qiuju brought the coverlets and things."

Jinlian called Qiuju.

"I didn't notice you wearing any shoes when you came in," the maid said.

"Nonsense," Jinlian cried, "I didn't come in barefoot."

"Well, Lady, if you were wearing any shoes, they must be in your room."

"Don't be such a fool," Jinlian cried, "of course they must be here somewhere. Look for them."

Qiuju searched the different rooms, on the bed and under the bed, but could not find the odd shoe anywhere.

"There must have been a ghost in my room for my shoe to have vanished like this," Jinlian said. "Off my very feet too. What are you here for, you slave?"

"Probably you've forgotten, Mother, and left it somewhere in the garden," the maid suggested. "You weren't wearing it when you came in."

"You must be out of your senses," Jinlian cried. "Do you think I don't know whether I had my shoes on or not?" She turned to Chunmei: "Take the thievish slave with you and go and look in the garden. If you find it, well and good, but if it isn't found, she will have to kneel down in the courtyard with a piece of stone on her head."

Chunmei took Qiuju to the garden, but though they looked everywhere, and searched the Arbor of the Vines, they could not find the shoe.

After searching a long time they began to go back. On the way Chunmei scolded Qiuju. "You are like a go-between on the wrong track," she said. "What are you going to say now? You're as bad as old Goody Wang buying a mill. What's the good of it?"

"I'm sure I don't know who stole Mother's shoe," Qiuju said. "She wasn't wearing it when she came in. Perhaps you left the garden gate open and somebody got in and went off with it."

Chunmei spat in her face. "You slave," she cried, "you are frightened and you think you'll put the blame on me. Mother told me to open the door for her. What else could I do? Nobody could possibly have got in then. You brought the coverlets and you didn't take the trouble to look what you were doing. Now you make up a silly story like this."

She took Qiuju to her mistress and said that they had not been able to find the shoe. "Take her into the courtyard and make her kneel down," Jinlian cried.

The maid sobbed and cried. "Do let me go to the garden and look again," she begged. "Then, if I don't find it, punish me.

"Don't listen to her," Chunmei said, "she will never find it. We searched the garden so thoroughly that we could not have missed a needle."

"Why do you put in your spoke?" Qiuju cried. "If I don't find it, I'll ask Mother to beat me."

"Well," Jinlian said, "take her back once more, and let us see whether she finds it."

Chunmei took her to the garden. They looked beneath the artificial mound, around all the flowerbeds and under the evergreen hedges, but though they searched a long time, they found nothing. Qiuju began to get flustered. Chunmei boxed her ears twice, and began to drag her back to Jinlian.

"We haven't looked in the Snow Cave yet," Qiuju said.

"That is Father's summerhouse," Chunmei said. "Mother did not go there, and you will not find it there. You might just as well come with me and confess." But she went to the Snow Cave. Facing the door was a couch, and beside it a small table for incense. They looked around but saw nothing. Then they went to the bookshelves.

"Father's papers and visiting cards are on those shelves," Chunmei said. "It's no use looking there for Mother's shoe. You're just trying to put off the evil hour. If you upset those papers there will be more trouble, and you'll come to an evil end, for sure."

"Isn't this the shoe?" Qiuju cried. She pulled out a packet perfumed with incense and fragrant herbs, and gave it to Chunmei. "This must be it," she said, "and only a minute ago you were urging Mother to beat me."

Chunmei looked at it. There was no doubt about it, it was a crimson low-heeled shoe. "Yes," she said, "it is her shoe. How on earth did it get here? There's something very funny about this." They went back to Jinlian.

"Yes," she said, "this is my shoe, sure enough. Where did you find it?"

"We found it on the bookshelves in Father's summerhouse," Chunmei said. "It was among his visiting cards, wrapped up with sweet herbs and incense."

Jinlian took it in her hand and compared it with another of her shoes. They were both of crimson silk, embroidered with the flowers of the four seasons, the lower part white and also embroidered with flowers. The heels were green and the sides blue. The only difference between them was that the thread of the seam was green in one case and blue in the other, though, unless they were examined very carefully, it would have been impossible to tell them apart.

She tried on the shoe. It was a little tighter than her own. Then she realized that it must have belonged to Huilian. "This shoe belonged to Laiwang's wife," she said to herself. "I wonder when she gave it to that scoundrel. He did not dare bring it to any of the rooms, so he hid it. Now the slave has fished it out." She gazed at the shoe for a while. Then she said: "This is not my shoe. Go and kneel down at once, you slave." She told Chunmei to find a piece of stone and put it on the girl's head.

"But whose shoe is it, if it isn't yours?" Qiuju said. She wept. "I've found your shoe, yet you are going to beat me just the same. I wonder what you would do if I hadn't found it."

"Shut your mouth, you thievish slave," Jinlian shouted. Chunmei brought a large piece of stone and put it on the maid's head.

Jinlian found another pair of shoes and put them on. The room was oppressively hot, and she told Chunmei to take the dressing case to the summerhouse. She went there to dress her hair.

The same morning, Chen Jingji had to come from the shop to get some clothes. When he reached the corner gate that led into the garden, Little Iron Rod was playing there. The boy saw that he was carrying a pair of silver necklets.

"What is that you've got, Uncle?" he said. "Let me have it to play with."

"They are necklets somebody has pawned," Chen Jingji said, "and I'm taking them back."

"Give them to me, Uncle," the boy cried, "I will give you something nice instead."

"You silly boy," the man said, "they don't belong to me, but, if you like, I'll see if I can find another pair for you. What's this pretty thing you're going to give me?"

The little monkey took a crimson embroidered shoe from his girdle and showed it to Jingji. "Where did you find this?" Jingji said.

"I'll tell you, Uncle," the boy said, laughing. "I was playing in the garden yesterday, and I saw Father in the Arbor of the Vines with Fifth Mother. He had tied her feet and they were shaking and jumping about. Then Father went away, and I saw Auntie Chunmei and asked her for some fruit. I picked this up in the Arbor of the Vines."

Chen Jingji took it in his hand. It was curved like the crescent moon and as red as a fallen lotus blossom. As he held it on his palm, it seemed no more than three inches long. He knew it must belong to Jinlian.

"Give it to me," he said to the boy, "and tomorrow I'll find a splendid necklet for you to play with."

"Don't try to cheat me," the boy cried, "I shall ask you for it tomorrow."

"I won't cheat you," the man said, and the little monkey ran away to play.

Chen Jingji put the shoe in his sleeve. "I have had some fun with that woman more than once," he thought, "but I have never made quite sure of her. Each time when it has come to the point, she has managed to escape me. Now the Fates have been kind enough to put this shoe in my hands, and today, I'll go and try my luck with her in real earnest. This time, I imagine, I shall get her."

With the shoe in his sleeve, Chen Jingji went at once to Jinlian's room. As he passed the screen, he saw Qiuju kneeling in the courtyard. "Young Lady, what's the meaning of this?" he said, laughing. "Are you practicing weight-lifting because you've joined the army?"

Jinlian was upstairs. She heard this remark. "Who is that talking about practicing weight-lifting?" she said to Chunmei. "Surely the little wretch hasn't put it down?"

"No," Chunmei said, "the stone is still on her head. It is Master Chen."

"Come upstairs, Brother-in-law," Jinlian cried, "there is nobody here."

The young man gathered up his clothes and hastened upstairs. Jinlian was sitting near the open window with the blinds pulled down, dressing herself before a mirror. He came to her side, sat down on a stool, and watched her doing her coal-black hair, so long that it nearly touched the floor. She dressed it with red silk ribbons, setting on it a headdress of silver thread, and arranging the hair beneath, till it seemed like a sweet-scented cloud. In her hair she placed rose petals, and made four braids of it. She looked as beautiful as the living Guanyin. She finished her hair and put away the dressing case. Then she washed her hands, completed her dressing and told Chunmei to bring some tea for Chen Jingji. The young man smiled.

"Why are you laughing?" Jinlian cried.

"I'm laughing because I'm sure you have lost something."

"If I have lost something, you short-lived rascal," Jinlian said, "what business is it of yours? And, anyway, who told you about it?"

"Well," Jingji said, "if that's the way you look at it, treating my kind heart as if it were the entrails of a donkey, and talking in that nasty tone, I may as well be off."

He rose and started downstairs. Jinlian pulled him back again. "Don't make such a to-do," she said. "Now that Laiwang's wife is dead and you haven't anybody else to make love to, you condescend to call on your poor old mother. Well, you've guessed right this time. I have lost something."

Jingji took the shoe from his sleeve and dangled it in front of her. "Whose is this?" he said, laughing.

"Ah, you pretty rogue," Jinlian cried, "so it was you who stole my shoe, making me send my maids all over the place to look for it!"

"Why should I steal your shoe?" Jingji said.

"Well, you're the only person who ever comes to my room. It was you, you rat, who stole it."

"You ought to be ashamed of yourself," Jingji said. "I couldn't possibly have stolen it. I haven't been to your room for several days."

"You wait," Jinlian cried. "I'll tell your Father you stole my shoe, and we'll see if you say I ought to be ashamed of myself."

"You can't terrify me by using Father's name," Jingji said.

"Oh, aren't you brave? Though you knew quite well he was carrying on with Laiwang's wife, that didn't prevent you from finishing his work for him. After that, of course, you are not afraid of anybody. However, the proverb tells us that when a man sees his own belongings, he is entitled to take them back again. If you even suggest that you will not give it back, I will kill you."

"Lady," Jingji said, "you are so clever you might be a Mongol. There is nobody about, and we have an excellent opportunity to discuss the matter. If you want your shoe, what are you prepared to give me in exchange? If you don't give me something, not even lightning shall get it away from me."

"It's my shoe, you wretch," Jinlian cried, "and you must give it to me. What right have you to ask for anything in return?"

Jingji laughed. "Fifth Mother," he said, "I will have that handkerchief you have in your sleeve. If you give me that, I will let you have your shoe, like a good, dutiful son."

"But your Father knows this too well," Jinlian said. "I dare not give you this one. I'll find another one for you tomorrow."

"No," the young man said, "a hundred other handkerchiefs will not satisfy me. This is the one I want."

Jinlian laughed. "Oh, what a practiced villain you are. Well, I haven't the strength to quarrel with you." She took the handkerchief from her sleeve and gave it to him. It was of fine lace, with white silk needlework, and attached to it were three silver characters. She gave everything to him.

Jingji bowed low and took the handkerchief. Jinlian told him to take good care of it. "Don't let your wife see it," she said, "she has too sharp a tongue." Jingji promised and gave her the shoe. He told her that Little Iron Rod had picked it up in the garden and given it him in exchange for a necklet.

Jinlian flushed with anger. "The dirty little slave has made it quite black. I will tell his master to give him a thrashing."

"If you do," Jingji said, "it will be the end of me, for whether the boy gets beaten or not, I shall get the credit for the business, for it was I who told you. For goodness' sake, don't say anything about it."

"I will forgive a scorpion sooner than that little slave," Jinlian cried.

They were talking when Laian came to find Jingji. "Father is in the outer hall," he said, "and he is asking for Master Chen. He wants a present list written."

Jinlian hurried the young man away. She went downstairs and told Chunmei to fetch a rod so that she might beat Qiuju. Qiuju objected strongly. "I found your shoe, Mother," she cried. "Why should you still wish to beat me?"

Then Jinlian showed her the shoe she had just been given by Chen Jingji. "You thievish slave," she said, "if the other was my shoe, what is this?" The maid stared at it open-mouthed, and said: "It is very funny. Where has this third shoe come from?"

"You impudent hussy," Jinlian cried, "you tried to palm somebody else's shoe off on me. You might as well call me a three-legged fox." She would hear no more, but made Chunmei give the girl ten strokes.

Qiuju tried to protect her bottom, crying all the while to Chunmei: "It was you who left the gate open, and let somebody get in and steal the shoe. Now you tell Mother to beat me."

Chunmei cursed her: "No, it was you who brought in the coverlets. You lost the shoe, and you try to put the blame on me, when Mother gives you a few strokes. All this fuss about an old shoe. I suppose if Mother misses an earring or a ring some day, you'll still blame everybody but yourself. Mother is very kind to let you off so lightly. If I were she, I would send for one of the boys, and make him give you twenty or thirty stiff strokes, and then see how you'd like it." Qiuju swallowed down her anger and was silent.

Ximen Qing had sent for Jingji to pack up a roll of silk and other presents for Captain He, who had just been promoted to be magistrate at Huaian, with full rank. His kinsmen and friends were giving him a send-off at the Temple of Eternal Felicity.

When Ximen had sent Daian with the presents, he and Jingji dined together in the hall. Then he went to Jinlian's room. Jinlian, with much ado, told him how Little Iron Rod had picked up her shoe.

"It is all your fault, you good-for-nothing," she said, "that that little slave—he deserves to be cut into a thousand pieces— got my shoe. He has taken it outside and by this time everybody must have seen it. I found out about it and got it back. If you don't give him a taste of a thrashing, he will always be spoiled."

Ximen did not wait to ask how she came to hear about it, but went off in a temper to the front court. The little monkey suspected nothing and was playing on the stone steps. Ximen caught him by the plaits of his hair, struck him with his fist and kicked him till the boy squealed like a pig being killed. When he let him go, the little monkey lay fainting on the ground for some time. Laizhao and his wife came running along to rescue their child. After a while the boy came to himself, though his nose was still bleeding. His parents carried him to their room and asked him what it was all about, and so learned that he had picked up a shoe.

The Beanpole was furious. She went to the kitchen and made a tremendous fuss. She poured forth streams of curses.

"You thievish, death-dealing whore, you young turtle, what has my boy done that you should bear a grudge against him? He is only ten years old. What does he know about your cunt? You have kicked up all this fuss for nothing, and got him beaten till the blood is pouring from his nose. If he dies, you whorish turtle, I'll make you suffer. It shall be the worse for you."

When she had finished cursing in the kitchen, she went to the front court and continued there. If she had gone on for a couple of days she would not have exhausted herself.

Jinlian was drinking with Ximen Qing in her room, and heard nothing of all this. That night, as they were together on the bed, he noticed that she was wearing a pair of green silk bed shoes, with crimson tops. "Why do you wear shoes like that?" he cried. "I can't bear the sight of them."

"I only had one pair of red ones," Jinlian said, "and that little slave has ruined one of them. Where do you expect me to get another in place of it?"

"My child," Ximen said, "you must make another pair tomorrow and put them on at once. They make me feel so loving when I see you wearing them. You know your sweetheart can't bear to see shoes of any other color."

"What a funny slave you are," the woman said. "And that reminds me. There was something I meant to tell you, but I forgot all about it." She told Chunmei to bring the shoe and said to him: "Do you recognize this?"

"No," Ximen said, "I haven't a notion whose it is."

"Don't look at it as if it frightened you, then," Jinlian said. "You can't deceive me. That was a nice trick of yours! Huilian's stinking hoof, kept in your summerhouse, among your visiting cards, as if it were some precious jewel, wrapped up in paper and incense! Pray, what makes it so precious? When that thievish whore died, she went to the lowest depths of Hell." She pointed to Qiuju. "That slave thought it was mine and brought it to me, so I gave her a beating. Throw it away," she said to Chunmei.

Chunmei threw it on the floor and said to Qiuju: "I'll make you a present of it. You can wear it."

Qiuju picked it up. "Mother's shoe is so small, I couldn't even get one of my toes into it," she said.

"You slave," Jinlian cried, "how dare you call that vile creature 'Mother'? She must have been your master's mother in a former life, or he wouldn't be guarding her shoe as jealously as if it were a precious heirloom, the low fellow."

Qiuju took the shoe and was going out with it, but Jinlian called her back and told her to get a knife. "I'm going to cut that whore's shoe into little pieces and throw it in the privy. That will banish the thievish strumpet forever beyond the hills of Hades, so that never again can she come to life." She said to Ximen Qing: "If it distresses you so much to see me cut it, I will cut it all the more."

Ximen Qing laughed. "That's enough, you queer little slave," he said, "I don't feel in the least distressed."

"If you don't," Jinlian said, "take an oath on it. The whore is dead, and we don't know where she is. Why do you keep her shoe? Obviously because you like to look at it and remember her. I have spent many years with you but you don't really care for me. There is always another woman in your heart."

"You funny little strumpet," Ximen said, smiling. "Why do you say such things? She never did you any harm when she was alive."

He put his arm around her white neck and kissed her. Then the two once more did the work of clouds and rain.

CHAPTER 29
The Fortune-Teller

Next day Pan Jinlian rose early and set Ximen Qing upon his way. Then, taking her sewing basket, she went to the Kingfisher Hall, and, sitting down on the steps, began to design her shoes. She sent Chunmei to ask Li Ping'er to join her.

"What is that you're drawing?" Li Ping'er said.

"I am making a pair of crimson silk shoes with white flat soles, and on the toe I am going to embroider a cockatoo pecking at a peach."

"I have a piece of flowered crimson silk," Li Ping'er said. "I will copy your design, but I shall make my shoes with heels." She fetched her sewing basket and they sat down together. When Jinlian had drawn the pattern on one shoe, she asked Li Ping'er to draw the other. She said she was going to the inner court for Meng Yulou. "The other day," she said, "she told me she was going to make some shoes."

She went to the inner court and found Yulou in her room, bending over a table, putting the lining into a shoe.

"You are about early this morning," Yulou said.

"Yes," Jinlian said, "I was up early and saw Father off to Captain He's farewell party. Then I asked the Sixth Lady to come and work with me in the garden. It is cooler there. I have just finished drawing the pattern of one shoe and the Sixth Lady is doing the other for me. Now I've come for you. It will be jolly for us all to work together. What is that you're doing?"

"It is the mate to that black silk shoe I showed you yesterday," Yulou said.

"You do work hard," Jinlian said, "you have actually come to the lining already."

"I finished one yesterday and the other is half done," Yulou said.

Jinlian examined the shoe carefully. "What kind of a toe are you going to put on it?" she said.

"Oh, I am not like you two children," Yulou said. "You must have lots of flowers and pretty things. I am a staid old lady and shall simply have the toes of gilded sheep skin, bound around the edges with green thread. What would you suggest?"

"Oh, that will do well enough," Jinlian said, "but hurry up. Li Ping'er is waiting for us."

"Won't you sit down and drink a cup of tea first?"

"No," Jinlian said, "bring the tea with you, and drink it there."

Yulou told her maid to make some tea and bring it out to them. Holding hands, with the shoes in their sleeves, the two women went to the garden. As they passed Wu Yueniang, who was sitting under the eaves outside her own apartments, she asked where they were going. Jinlian told her that Li Ping'er had sent her for Yulou and that they were going to design some shoes. They went on to the garden. There they all sat down together, and looked at each other's work.

"Why do you always make crimson low-heeled shoes?" Yulou said to Jinlian. "They don't look nearly so pretty as the high-heeled ones. If you don't care for wooden soles, you can use felt, as I do."

"They are not walking-out shoes," Jinlian said, "they are for bedroom use. A little slave ruined my others, and Father told me to make some new ones."

"Speaking of shoes," Yulou said, "I hope the Sixth Lady will not think me a gossip, but yesterday you lost one of your shoes, and Father gave Little Iron Rod a beating. The boy fell down and lay in a faint for a long time. That upset Laizhao's wife, and she cursed like anything, up and down the back court. 'That whorish young turtle,' she cried, 'he has been telling tales about my boy and now the poor boy has had a thrashing. It's a good thing he didn't die, or that vile creature would have had to pay for it.' We couldn't make out whom she was cursing, but some time afterwards Little Iron Rod came along and the Great Lady asked him why Father had beaten him. 'I was playing in the garden,' he said, 'and I picked up a shoe. Uncle Chen came with a necklet and I asked him to give it to me for my shoe. I don't know who told Father and got me beaten.' Then he said he was looking for Uncle Chen so that he could get the necklet he had been promised, and ran off. You see the turtle in question is our brother-in-law. Fortunately, only Li Jiao'er was there, and not the Great Lady, or there would have been trouble."

"Why?" Jinlian said, "did the Great Lady have anything to say about it?"

"You may well ask that," Yulou said. "Indeed she had a good deal to say. She said: 'In this wretched household, there is now a nine-tailed fox who seems determined to rule the roost. I remember how comfortable everybody was when Laiwang came back from his journey to the south, until stories began to fly around. First that Laiwang's wife was flirting with his Lordship, then that he himself had got a knife and carried a club. All this ended in the poor man's being banished and his wife hanging herself. Now, all for the sake of a paltry shoe, she sets both heaven and earth in a turmoil. If she had been wearing the shoe in a proper and decent manner, it would not have been there for the boy to pick up. I suppose she was playing some dirty game in the garden with that man of hers, and drinking, and dropped her shoe. Now in order to keep the shameful business dark, she throws all the blame on the boy. After all, it is not a matter of any importance."

"She is talking out of her cunt," Jinlian cried. "What does she consider an important matter, I wonder. Surely murder is important enough, and the slave took a knife to murder his master." She turned to Yulou. "Sister, we have never had any secrets from one another. You remember how terrified we both were when Laixing came and told us, yet she, the first wife, talks in this strain. However, if it doesn't matter to her, it doesn't matter to me, and if the slaves like to kill their master, they may. That woman Huilian was one of her maids, but she never made the slightest attempt to control her, and the slave deceived her betters, and behaved badly to those beneath her. She flew into tempers first with one and then with another. Well, people must find somebody to let loose their hatred upon. If she is going to say nasty things about me, she will get as good as she gives. When that Huilian hanged herself, she didn't tell her husband the truth. She spent a lot of money hushing it up. If she hadn't done so, it would not have passed over so easily. She managed to scrape out of it, and now she puts on this high and mighty air. She accuses me of interfering with her husband. Well, if I don't make him kick out that slave and his wife, you can consider that I count for nothing. I don't intend to let myself be pushed down a well."

Yulou saw that Jinlian was growing purple with rage. "We are such firm friends, Sister," she said, "that I always tell you anything I hear, but when I do tell you things, you must keep them to yourself and not get so excited."

Jinlian did not take this advice. That night, when Ximen Qing came to her room, she told him the whole story. "Laizhao's wife," she said, "was screaming up and down the inner court that you had beaten her boy, and the first chance she got, you should pay for it."

Ximen Qing did not forget this. The next day he would have sent away Laizhao and his wife and child, but, fortunately, Yueniang persuaded him not to do so. Still, he would not keep Laizhao in the house, and sent him to take charge of the house in Lion Street in place of Ping'an whom he brought back and put in charge of the gate. Yueniang realized what had happened and was very angry with Jinlian.

One day Ximen was sitting in the front hall, when Ping'an came in and said: "Major Zhou has sent a fortune-telling gentleman, called Wu the Immortal. He is waiting at the gate to see you." Ximen gave orders that the man should be admitted, and, after looking at Major Zhou's card, he bade the fortune-teller welcome. Wu the Immortal was wearing a black Daoist hat, a long cloak, and straw sandals. He was girt by a girdle of yellow silk with two tassels, and carried a tortoiseshell fan. He stalked in with a majestic air. He seemed at least forty years of age. His spirit was as proud as the moon, and he was as venerable in appearance as the tall pines that grow upon the summit of Mount Hua.

There are always four marks by which an Immortal may be distinguished. His body is like the pine tree; his voice like a bell. When he is seated, he is like a bow, and when he walks, like the wind.

When Ximen Qing saw Wu the Immortal about to come in, he hurried down the steps to greet him and took him into the hall. The Immortal saluted Ximen with a religious reverence, and sat down. Tea was brought at once and Ximen said: "May I ask your Immortality's glorious and illustrious names? From what fairy country have you come, and how did you make the acquaintance of Major Zhou?"

The Immortal raised himself slightly. "I am called Wu," he said, "and my personal name is Shih. My name in religion is Shou Zhen. I was born in Xian Yu of Zhejiang, but while I was still a boy I went with my Master to the temple of the Purple Void on the Tiantai mountain. Afterwards, I wandered as a cloud over the earth, and have come at last to seek the Sacred Principle upon Taishan. On my way, I happened to pass through your esteemed city, and General Zhou was good enough to allow me to examine the eyes of his ladies. Then he bade me come to you to tell your fortune."

"Oh, Venerable Prince of the Immortals," Ximen Qing said, "to which school of magic do you belong, and what system of physiognomies do you follow?"

"I have a slight acquaintance with thirteen schools," the Immortal said, "and practice the method of Ma Yi. But I also understand the Liu Ren and the Magic Ke. I give my simples to cure people, but worldly wealth I never accept, knowing that I am upon this earth for but a short space."

Ximen Qing felt considerably more respect for his visitor. "You must indeed be a true Immortal," he said. He told his servants to prepare a table with monastic fare.

"But I have not yet performed my office," the Immortal said. "How can I eat your food?"

"Master," Ximen said, smiling, "you have come a long way, and I feel sure you have not yet breakfasted. There will be plenty of time afterwards for you to tell our fortunes." He sat down himself and shared the monastic fare with the Immortal. Then the table was cleared, and he called for writing materials.

"Sir," the Immortal said, "tell me first the eight words of moment in your honorable life, and I will relate the future for you." Ximen Qing told him the Eight Characters, saying that his animal was the Tiger, his age twenty-nine, and the hour of his birth noon on the twenty-eighth day of the seventh month. The Immortal silently made some calculations upon his fingers and said: "Sir, your horoscope would appear to show the year as *Wuyin,* the month as *Xinyu,* the day as *Renwu* and the hour as *Bingwu.* Now the twenty-third day of the seventh month is the Day of White Dew. We must therefore reckon your fate as from the eighth month. Taking the months in order, *Xinyu* is the controlling month, so obviously *Shangguan* is the controlling factor in your life. As Zi Ping says: wealth increases and riches multiply. You will obtain an official position. Then your luck will change again. Your fate depends upon *Shengong,* so your fortune starts from the seventh year *Xinyu.* Then at seventeen, it moves towards *Renxu,* at twenty-seven to *Guihai,* at thirty-seven to *Jiazi* and at forty-seven to *Yichou.* Your horoscope, Sir, as I see it, indicates that you will fill a position of authority and that you will be prosperous. Your Eight Characters are certainly clear and unusual. But though this is so, you are adversely affected by the Earth Element in *Wu,* seeing that you were born between the seventh and the eighth months, a fact that gives you too great physical vigor. Fortunately the day of your birth was *Renwu* and the Water Element of *Gui* comes between *Zi* and *Chou,* thus producing an equilibrium between water and fire, and putting beyond doubt the fact that you will profit by your abilities. The hour was *Bingwu,* and this fits in very well with *Xin,* so you may look forward to a career of great dignity: you will prosper, be happy, and at peace all your life. Your fortune will increase; you will obtain promotion, and you are destined to leave behind you an honorable descendant. Throughout your life you will be honest and fair dealing; when once you have made up your mind you will not change it. In joy you will be as agreeable as the breeze in spring, and in anger as terrible as the sudden thunder and the fierce lightning. You will enjoy many women, great wealth, and not a few of the insignia of office, and when at last you leave this world there will be two sons to speed you on your way. This year, *Ding* and *Ren* come together, and the fire of *Ding* will be in the ascendant. This means the coming of officials and ghosts, and certainly indicates your elevation to the clouds, or, otherwise, that you will receive an appointment and come into great wealth. Your fortune is now moving towards *Guihai,* so that the Earth of *Wu* moistened by the Water of *Gui,* and from the intermingling of water and earth, one naturally anticipates growth. I see the star of the Red Phoenix, and this is undoubtedly a sign of the coming of a son. Then, too, the controller of your life appears on horseback going towards *Shen,* so before the seventh month is out, these things will certainly come to pass."

"What about my life in the more distant future?" Ximen Qing said.

"Sir," the Immortal said, "I trust you will forgive me, but I am sorry to say that your Eight Characters do not go well with so much *Yin* water, and, when you reach the high tide of your fortune in the year *Jiazi,* the water will wash out the *Renwu* day, and the inconstant stars will then affect you. Before you reach your thirty-sixth year, you will suffer from sores, hemorrhage and wasting sickness."

"What then of the present?" Ximen said.

"This year you meet the five spirits of destruction. This means some slight trouble in your household. It will not be very serious, for the omens are favorable, and the trouble will pass away."

"Is there any great calamity in my life?" Ximen asked.

"Days lengthen into months, and months into years," the Immortal said, "it is hard indeed to prophesy."

Ximen Qing was satisfied. "Master," he said, "what do you read in my face?"

"Please turn your honorable countenance straight towards me," the Immortal said. Ximen Qing moved his chair slightly, and the Immortal said:

"What is this outward seeming? Without the mind it would be nothing, for outward seeming springeth from the heart. Whither the heart goeth, the appearance goeth also. I perceive that your Lordship's head is round, and your neck short. You are clearly a man favored by fortune. Your body is robust and your muscles strong, a sign that you are a man of heroic courage. Your brow is high and projecting, and all your life you will never lack raiment or wealth. Your chin is square and full, and in your old age you will fill an exalted office. Such are the good things I see. There are evil things also, but shall I venture to tell you these?"

"Pray tell me all, Immortal," Ximen said.

The Immortal asked Ximen Qing to take a few steps, and continued: "Your walk is like the shaking of the willow. It is a sign that you should outlive a wife, and if you do not do so, you will certainly suffer hurt. I trust you have already done so."

"I have," Ximen said.

The Immortal asked to see his hand, and Ximen Qing held it out. "Perfect wisdom," the Immortal said, "is always to be discerned by the skin and hair, and sorrow and happiness may be foretold by the hands and feet. Your hand is so fine and soft and firm, you are certainly destined by fortune for the enjoyment of wealth and happiness. Of your eyes, one is male and one female, a sign that you are wealthy and alert of mind. Each of your eyebrows has a fork, which shows that all through your life pleasure will mean much to you, but below them are three wrinkles, which mean that in middle age you will suffer a great loss. Your *Jianmen* is red; you will enjoy wealth and women all your life. Your brows are yellow, and in a few days you will receive an official appointment. There is red upon your *Sanyang,* and this very year a fine son will be born to you. One thing, which I hesitate to mention, is that your *Leitang* are thick and long, indicating a fondness for the flower maidens, but your nose, the star of wealth, would seem to promise a wealthy middle age. The *Zhengjiang* is hollowed, and from that we may foretell the fortunes and misfortunes of your next life."

The Immortal was silent. Ximen Qing asked if he would tell the fortunes of his ladies, and sent a servant to summon Wu Yueniang. She came with Li Jiao'er, Meng Yulou, Pan Jinlian, Li Ping'er, and Sun Xue'e, and they stood behind a curtain to listen. When the Immortal saw Yueniang, he quickly saluted her. He would not sit down in her presence, but stood to tell her fortune.

"Lady," he said, "your face is like the full moon, a sign that the household flourishes under your care. Your lips are like the red lotus, and so I know that you are prosperous and that you will have the dignity of motherhood. Your voice is sweet and fairy-like, and you will help your husband towards the attainment of happiness. Please show me your hands." Yueniang drew her delicate fingers from her sleeves. "Your hands," continued the Immortal, "are like dried ginger, a sign that you are well capable of controlling those under your charge. The hair upon your temples shines as does a mirror, which shows, according to the doctrine of Kun, that you are a very clever woman. These are the good points. There are others not so favorable, but these I hesitate to tell." Ximen Qing urged him to continue. "In your *Leitang* there is a mole, and if you were not so frequently ill, you would most certainly destroy your husband. There are wrinkles beneath your eyes, which show that your six relatives are as ice and as ashes."

> She stands erect, beautiful to see
> With footsteps slow and light, like a turtle coming from the water
> When she walks, the dust is not stirred. Her words are measured.
> The slender shoulders show that she must wed an honorable husband.

When Yueniang had withdrawn, Ximen Qing said: "There are still some ladies of lesser rank: will you see them?" Li Jiao'er came forward. The

Immortal looked at her for a long time, and said: "This lady's brows are very abrupt, and her nose is small. If she were not a concubine, she would certainly marry three husbands. She is plump and well favored, a sign that she will want for nothing. She enjoys comfort and is a peaceable person. Her shoulders are high and her voice is shrill, so, unless she is an orphan, she is a person of low degree. The bridge of her nose is rather low, and she will be poor, or die young." He asked her to walk a few steps, and said:

> The tapering brow, the sinuous back
> Show that in youth she trod the path of wind and dust.
> One of two things she must be, a girl from a house of evil fame
> Or a woman who stands behind the screen.

Li Jiao'er went back to her place, and Yueniang said to Yulou: "Now it is your turn."

"This lady," the Immortal said, "has forehead, nose and chin all well proportioned. She will have no anxiety about material things. The six natural treasures are full to overflowing and she will have fortune and honor in her old age. She will suffer little from sickness, for her mouth is favored by a bright and dazzling comet, and in truth her *Niangong* is smooth and beautiful. Kindly walk a step or two, Lady."

Then he said:

> Her mouth is like the character *Si*, her spirit pure and keen
> Her gentleness and charm are like a pearl resting on a palm
> Honor and dignity will be hers, wealth and prosperity.
> She will outlive two husbands.

When Yulou had retired, Jinlian was asked to take her place, but she laughed and refused. Yueniang pressed her, and finally she went out. The Immortal raised his head and gazed at her for a long time. Then he said slowly: "This lady's hair is thick and uncommonly heavy at the temples, and her glance is not direct. This is a sign of a very passionate nature. Her cheeks are full of charm, her eyebrows arched, and, even when she is standing still, her body quivers. The moles upon her face mean that she will be the end of her husbands, and her upper lip, which is short, indicates that her own life will not be long."

> Lightly and unrestrained she moves, craving the pleasures of love,
> Her eyes, sparkling like fragments of lacquer, show that she is the
>   cause of men's undoing
> Beneath the moon, before the stair, never can she be sated
> But, though she lives in a great mansion, her heart is not at rest.

Ximen Qing called for Li Ping'er, and asked the Immortal to predict her future. "Your complexion," the Immortal said, "is so sweet and fragrant that I know you for a maiden of high degree. Your bearing is modest, so that you may be told for a virtuous woman of high rank. Yet there is a sparkle in your eyes as though you had taken wine, and this suggests an engagement behind the mulberry tree. Your eyes are dark ringed, which shows that what happens to you each month gives trouble. Yet the sleeping silkworm is glossy and purple, and beyond a doubt you will bring forth a precious son. Your skin is white and your shoulders round, and your husband loves you dearly. You are often sick, for the roots are dark and deep, yet you constantly meet with omens of great joy, for the star of your fortune is bright and favorable. These are the points in your favor, but there are others not so favorable, and, Lady, you must be careful. The mountain root is black, and before your twenty-seventh year there are signs of tears, yet if you keep good counsel, you may survive the cock and dog years. Yet beware, beware!"

> Her countenance is like the flowers and the moon, yet she must
>   guard her plumage
> Close to her lover till life is done, like the phoenix and his mate.
> Trust in the wealth of the red doors
> And do not mix with humbler birds.

Li Ping'er withdrew, and Yueniang told Xue'e to take her place. The Immortal looked at her and said: "This lady's body is short and her voice shrill. Her brow is pointed and her nose small. Though she has come from the valley to the heights, her portion is of sneers and friendlessness. She manages her affairs well, and is not without guile, but she suffers from a fourfold "turn up," and it may be that disaster shall overtake her. The fourfold "turn up" is lips curling yet without an edge, ears curling yet without a curve, eyes turned up yet without a sparkle, nose turned up yet crooked."

> Her body is like a bird's, her waist like a wasp's. She is not of high
>   degree.
> Her eyes are like flowing waters; she is not chaste.
> She stands and leans upon the door
> If she does not become a maidservant, worse things will befall her.

Xue'e withdrew, and Yueniang told Ximen's daughter, Ximen Dajie, to come and let the Immortal see her.

"This lady's nose is low and flat," he said; "she will bring discredit upon her ancestors and ruin upon her household. Her voice is like a cracked gong, and all her family wealth will be dispersed. Her complexion is coarse; she will die young and in distress. She walks like the hopping of a sparrow, and though she lives in her own home, she is in need of food and clothing. Calamity will fall upon her before she is twenty-seven."

> Though she seems wise, she is not at peace with her husband
> Only the food and clothes her parents give keep warmth in her
> She is not handsome and honor will not visit her.
> Even if violent death should be spared her, there are hard times in store.

Then Chunmei came to be examined. The Immortal opened his eyes wide as he looked at her. She was about eighteen years old, he saw. A silver hairnet was on her head, a white gown with a peach-colored skirt, and a fine blue silk wrap. She made a reverence to him when she came forward. The Immortal gazed at her for a long time. At last he said:

"This young lady has the five sense organs well developed. She is exquisitely made. Her hair is fine, but her eyebrows are thick. This is a sign of hot temper. Her spirit is volatile and her eyes round. This denotes that she easily becomes excited. Her nose is straight: she will marry an officer of high rank and bear him a son. Her brows are prominent: this is a sign that she will wear a pearl headdress while she is still young. She walks like a flying angel; her voice is clear and her spirit pure. She will bring wealth to her husband, and by the age of twenty-seven will assuredly receive high honor. Unfortunately her left eye is rather large. This means that she lost her father in her childhood. And the right eye is small, which shows that her mother died when she was one year old. The mole beneath the left corner of her mouth is the sign of a quarrelsome disposition, but the mole on her right cheek indicates that she will be respected and loved by her husband as long as she lives."

> Her brow is high, the five sense organs as they should be
> Her lips are red as though with rouge; her steps are light.
> There will be wealth in plenty for her, and rich food
> And men of rank and dignity will love her all her days.

When the Immortal had said this, the women bit their nails and thought over his words. Ximen Qing put five taels of silver into a packet and offered it to the Immortal. He gave five *qian* to the Major's servant, with a visiting card to express his thanks. But the Immortal would not accept the silver. "I wander over the earth as a cloud," he said. "I take my meals, exposed to the winds, and my bed is in the dew. What use is money to me? I cannot take it."

Then Ximen gave him a roll of cloth with which to make himself a habit. This the Immortal accepted, and told his young disciple to take it. He made a reverence to Ximen Qing and thanked him. Ximen took him to the gate, and there the Immortal proudly took leave of him.

When Ximen Qing came back to the inner court, he asked Yueniang and the others what they thought of what the Immortal had said.

"He was clever enough," Yueniang said, "but I think he was mistaken about three people."

"Which three?" Ximen said.

"He said that the Sixth Lady was ill, but that she would bear a son. She is with child now, so that he may be partly right. Then he said that there are hard times in store for our daughter. I don't see how he can make that out. He told us that Chunmei would have a son. You have probably done your part, but I see no signs of her having a child. And certainly I don't believe what he said about her wearing a pearl headdress and being a lady. We have nobody in this household of official rank, so I don't know where the pearl headdress is coming from, and even if there were one, it would not be for her head."

Ximen Qing laughed. "He said that I should rise from the ground to the clouds, that position and wealth would come to me, but really, I don't see where they are coming from. It seems to me that when you and Chunmei were standing together he got mixed up because of your dresses. She was wearing a silver hairnet, and he thought she was our daughter. He thought she would probably marry into some family of position and so would come to wear a pearl headdress. People have always said that it is better for us when the fortune-tellers are wrong. If our minds and our appearance had any relation to one another our mind would be different every time the appearance changed. But since Major Zhou sent him here, we couldn't very well refuse to let him try his hand."

Yueniang had a meal served in the hall, and they all took part in it. Afterwards, Ximen Qing took a palm-leaf fan and strolled about the garden. When he came to the pavilion of the Glorious Landscape, near the great arbor, he pulled down the blinds and curtains. Outside, the flowering shrubs and trees cast a refreshing shade. In the depth of the foliage, a band of cicadas were singing, and from time to time the breeze wafted the fragrance of the flowers towards him.

Ximen Qing sat on a chair and fanned himself. Laian and Huatong came to the well to draw some water.

"Come here, one of you boys," Ximen said.

Laian came. "Go to the inner court," Ximen said to him, "and tell your sister Chunmei to bring me a pot of plum juice."

Some time afterwards, Chunmei, wearing her silver hairnet, came to him with a pot of plum juice. She was smiling. "Have you had anything to eat?" she said.

"Yes, I had something in the inner court."

Chunmei pretended to be annoyed. "You do not come to see us," she said, "you only send to us when you want plum juice. Wait till I make it cool enough."

Ximen Qing nodded. When the girl had made it ready, she came and rested on his chair. She took the palm-leaf fan from his hand and fanned him.

"What did the Great Lady say?" she asked.

"She talked about Wu the Immortal."

"Oh, that absurd monk said I should wear a pearl headdress, and the Great Lady said that even if there ever was one in this household, it wouldn't be for my head. But the proverb says we should never judge by appearances, and the water in the ocean cannot be measured with a pint pot. Even when you can't use a lathe, it is always possible to use a knife. It is a most uncertain business foretelling what is going to happen to people. Do you imagine I shall always be a slave in your household?"

"Little oily mouth," Ximen said to her, "if you give me a son, you shall wear a headdress, certainly." He took her in his arms and fondled her. "Where is your mistress?" he said, "I haven't seen her for some time."

"She told Qiuju to heat some water for a bath," Chunmei said, "but she got tired of waiting, and now she is asleep on the bed."

"When I have drunk this plum water, I'll go and play a trick on her," Ximen said.

Chunmei took the pot from the ice, and gave it to him. He drank a mouthful. It was so cold that he could feel it in his bones. It went through his body and made his teeth chatter. It seemed like gentle dew dropping upon his heart. After a while, he finished the plum water and, resting his hand on Chunmei's shoulder, went to Jinlian's room. She was asleep on the mother-of-pearl bed that he had recently bought for her. It was facing the door. Li Ping'er had a bed similar to this one and Jinlian had asked him to buy one for her. It cost something like sixty taels of silver. It was a four-poster and the panels all around it were made of mother-of-pearl cunningly designed to represent flowers, grasses and birds. The curtains were of purple silk, with silver hooks.

Jinlian was completely undressed, except for a light, scarlet vest. The bedclothes were of the finest silk and there was a Yin Yang pillow beneath her head. She lay upon the summer mattress, fast asleep. Seeing her, Ximen Qing's desire was stirred. He told Chunmei to close the door and go away, and quietly took off his own clothes. Then he took away the gossamer coverlet, got upon the bed, and admired the sight of his body beside that of his beloved. Then he played a trick on her. He parted her legs, gripped his penis and put it between them. She opened her eyes wide in astonishment, but Ximen had already moved in and out ten times.

"You strange rascal," Jinlian said, laughing, "when did you come in? I was asleep and didn't see you. Yes, sleeping so sweetly, yet you came and disturbed me."

"Since it is I, no harm is done," Ximen Qing said. "If it had been a stranger, you would pretend you didn't know the difference."

"What can I say to curse you?" Jinlian said. "Who do you think would be bold enough to come into my room? Only a rude man like you would do a thing of that sort."

After Jinlian had heard Ximen Qing, in the Kingfisher Hall, saying how white and beautiful Li Ping'er's body was, she had made a mixture of the hearts of jasmine flowers, cream and powder, and had rubbed it into her skin all over her body to make it smooth and white, so that she might be favored as Li Ping'er had been.

Her body now seemed as white as snow, with only a pair of scarlet sleeping shoes upon her feet. Ximen Qing squatted on the bed, and holding fast to her legs, plunged forward with all his might. He looked down so that he might enjoy the sight of what he was doing.

"Why are you looking at me, you funny creature?" Jinlian said. "My body is black, and cannot rival the Sixth Lady's white skin. I suppose that is why you are looking at it. Now that she is with child, you love and think only of her, and I am considered fit for nothing but the rubbish heap. You think you can treat me as you like."

"I am told you are waiting for a bath," Ximen Qing said. "Is that so?"

"Who told you?"

"Chunmei."

Then Jinlian asked if he would like to join her, and told the maid to bring the water. The bathtub was set down, the water poured in, and the two got down from the bed to bathe in the fragrant water. They played about as merrily as fishes. When they had spent some time washing themselves, Ximen Qing set Jinlian on the bathing board and, holding her feet in his two hands, mounted upon her and thrust forward. They jumped up and down, and shook about, two or three thousand times, making a noise like a crab crawling in the mud. Jinlian was afraid that her hair would be disarranged, so she put one hand on her head, and supported herself on the edge of the tub with the other. She made herself as charming as could be.

They played in the water for a long time. Then Ximen Qing yielded, and they stopped. They cleansed their bodies, and the bathtub was taken away. Ximen put on a short thin cotton coat and got on to the bed. A table was placed on it so that they might eat some fruit and drink wine. Jinlian bade Qiuju bring some white wine, and gave him some fruit pastries, because she thought he must be hungry. After a very long time, Qiuju brought a silver pot of wine. Jinlian poured out a cup. It was as cold as ice. She threw the wine in Qiuju's face, and it splashed all over her.

"You slave!" she cried, "you are not fit to live. What do you mean by bringing this cold wine for your father? I don't know what you're thinking about."

She told Chunmei to take the girl to the courtyard and make her kneel down there.

"I was only out of the room for a moment," Chunmei said to Qiuju, "getting some ribbons for mother's feet, and you go and upset the whole place like this."

"The other day," Qiuju said, pouting, "they wanted iced wine. How was I to know that they would want something different today?"

Jinlian heard this and cursed her. "What's that you say, you thievish slave? Come here!" She said to Chunmei, "Give her a good slapping, ten times on each side of her face."

"Oh, Mother," Chunmei said, "you can't even see the skin on her face, and it would make my hands dreadfully dirty. Won't you make her kneel down, and put a piece of stone on her head?"

Without more ado, Qiuju was dragged to the courtyard and made to kneel down with a piece of stone balanced on her head. Then Jinlian told Chunmei to warm the wine, and she drank a few cups with Ximen Qing. When they had had enough, the table was removed; they pulled down the curtains and told Chunmei to shut the door. Then they put their arms around each other's necks and entwined their legs. They were very tired and soon went to sleep.

CHAPTER 30
The Birth of Guan'ge

After their bath, Ximen Qing and Pan Jinlian went to sleep. Chunmei settled herself under the eaves outside their room and busied herself making shoes. After a while Qintong came to the door in the corner, looking about him as though he were in search of someone. "What do you want?" Chunmei said. The boy looked at Qiuju who was kneeling in the courtyard with a piece of stone balanced on her head, and, instead of answering, pointed to the maid. Chunmei scolded him.

"What do you want, you young rascal? Why do you wave your hands about like that?"

Qintong did not stop laughing for a long time, but at last he told her that Zhang An, the grave keeper, had called to see Ximen Qing.

"Oh," Chunmei said, "only Zhang An! And you make as much fuss as if it were a ghost. Don't make such a noise. They are both asleep, and, if you wake them up, there will be trouble. Tell Zhang An to wait."

The boy did as he was told, but, after waiting a long time, he came again to look in at the corner gate and asked Chunmei whether his master was not yet up.

"You little rogue," the maid cried, "you frightened me, rushing in suddenly like that. It's nothing but a trifle, yet you dash about like a homeless spirit."

"Zhang An wants to see Master, but he has to go to town too, and he's afraid he'll be too late."

"Well, they're both sound asleep, and I dare not wake them. Tell Zhang An to wait, and, if he is too late today, he must wait until tomorrow."

At that moment Ximen Qing woke up, and, hearing voices, called out to ask Chunmei who was there. The girl told him. "I will get up," Ximen said. "Let me have my clothes." When Chunmei had brought the clothes, Pan Jinlian asked what Zhang An had come about.

"The other day," Ximen said, "he came to tell me that the widow Zhao, who owns the property next to our family graves, is anxious to sell it. She asks three hundred taels and I am prepared to give two hundred and fifty, so I told Zhang An to go and talk the matter over with her. There is a spring on the land with four places where water can be drawn. If I buy the place, I shall join it up with our own and build a fair-sized arbor and a hall. I shall make an artificial mound, lay out gardens, put a cover over the well, and clear a space for practicing archery. I may make a ball ground where we can play when we feel like it. It will cost me quite a sum of money to do all I am thinking of doing."

"Buy it by all means," Jinlian said, "then we shall be able to have some fun when we go to visit our graves."

When Ximen Qing had gone to the outer court to see Zhang An, Jinlian got up, powdered her face and dressed her hair, and went to the courtyard to beat Qiuju. Chunmei went to bring Qintong with a rod.

"When I told you to bring your master some wine," Jinlian said to the maid, "why did you bring cold wine? One would think there was no discipline in the house at all. When I tell you to do anything, you stand there and argue, as brazen-faced as you can be.

"Give her twenty strokes," she cried to Qintong, "as hard as you can."

The boy had given the poor maid ten strokes when, fortunately, Li Ping'er came. With a smile, she bade him stop, and Qiuju was spared the ten remaining blows. Jinlian told her to kowtow to Li Ping'er, and then sent her to the kitchen.

"Old mother Pan," Li Ping'er said, "has come with a maid about fifteen years old, and our second sister has bought her for seven taels to wait upon her. She would like you to go and see her."

Together, they went off to the back court. Ximen Qing had given Li Jiao'er the money to buy a maid, who was given the name of Xiahua.

Laibao and Master Wu had set off upon their journey with the birthday presents. The weather was so hot that it was not an easy one. They ate when they were hungry, and when they were thirsty they drank, and so, after some days, came to the Eastern Capital. There they put up at an inn by the Gate of Ten Thousand Blessings. The next day they made ready their chests of presents and went straight to the Bridge of the Milky Way and the palace of the Imperial Tutor. Laibao, who had dressed himself in a suit of black clothes, asked Wu to look after the presents and went himself to the gate. He made a reverence to the gatekeeper who asked him whence he came.

"I am one of the household of Master Ximen who lives at Qinghe in Shandong. I have come with presents for the birthday of the venerable Imperial Tutor."

The gatekeeper upbraided him. "You scoundrelly rogue! What is Master Ximen to me, or Master Dongmen either? Let me tell you that my venerable lord has but one superior. All other men are far beneath him.

I don't care what a man's position is. He may be a duke or a prince, but when he comes here, he does not dare to flaunt himself as you have done. Stand back, fellow!"

Fortunately, among the officers who were standing by, there was one who knew Laibao, and he came up and smoothed the matter over.

"Don't let this disturb you," he said to Laibao. "This gentleman has only just come here and he does not know you. Wait a few moments and I will ask the Comptroller, Master Zhai, to come and see you."

Laibao took a tael of silver from his sleeve and gave it to the officer.

"Really, there is no need for this," the officer said, accepting it, "but if I may make a suggestion, you might offer something to these other two gentlemen, and so you will avoid any difficulty on their part."

Laibao brought out two more taels of silver and gave them to the officers. At this, the faces of the officers became more pleasant.

"So you have come from Qinghe," the gatekeeper said. "Wait a few moments and I will take you to see Master Zhai. His Eminence has just returned from the Temple of Ether, Glorious and Indefectible, where he has been offering incense. He is resting in his study."

Some time later Zhai came. He was wearing light shoes, white socks, and a devotional robe of black silk. Laibao knelt down before him. The Comptroller greeted him, and Laibao handed over the list of the presents he had brought, while servants came forward with two rolls of Nanjing silk and thirty taels of white gold.

"My master, Ximen Qing, offers this to you with his best respects. He knows that he has nothing in any way worthy to repay your kindness, but you may be willing to distribute these trifles among your servants. You had so much trouble over the affair of Wang the Fourth, the salt-merchant."

"I really cannot accept this present," the Comptroller said, and a little later, "Well, perhaps I must."

Laibao presented the list of gifts that his master had sent for the Imperial Tutor. When the Comptroller had examined it, he handed it back to Laibao and told him to have the presents carried to the inner courtyard and to wait there. To the west of the inner door was an antechamber where all who had business in that place were entertained. Here an attendant brought tea for Laibao and Wu. After a while Cai, the Imperial Tutor, came to the hall, and after the Comptroller had told him of their visit, Laibao and his companion were summoned. They knelt at the foot of the steps while the Comptroller gave the present list to the Imperial Tutor. Then the two men brought in the gifts, vases of shining yellow gold, cups of finest jade, figurines and the multicolored dragon robe of ceremony. There was silk from Nanjing glimmering with green and gold. This was not all. Provisions of meat and wine had been carefully preserved, and were piled high beside fresh and seasonable fruits. The Imperial Tutor could not fail to be pleased.

"I feel quite embarrassed by such splendid presents," he said. "You must really take them away."

Laibao and Wu kowtowed and said, "Our master, Ximen Qing, knows only too well that he has no adequate means of expressing his filial devotion to your Eminence. He sends these trifles in the hope that you may at least think them not unworthy to be distributed among your attendants."

"Then I will tell my servants to remove them," said the Imperial Tutor. A host of attendants carried the presents away. "A little while ago," he said, "there was a little business about some salt merchants at Zangzhou. I think I wrote to the Governor on your behalf. Was the result satisfactory?"

"Thanks to your Eminence's gracious intervention," Laibao said, "as soon as your dispatch arrived, the whole party was set at liberty."

"Your master has been at great trouble and expense on my account," the Imperial Tutor said, "and I have no means of expressing my kindly feeling towards him. Has he any official position?"

"What position should he hold?" Laibao said. "He is only a simple countryman."

"Since he has not," the Imperial Tutor said, "I shall see that he is given an appointment as a law officer in Shandong. He shall be made Deputy Captain in He Jin's place. Only yesterday his Majesty placed a few appointments at my disposal."

Laibao kowtowed and thanked the Imperial Tutor. "I am most grateful," he said, "for your Eminence's extreme magnanimity. If all the members of my master's household should throw ashes upon their heads and dust upon their bodies, they could never repay such kindness."

The Imperial Tutor called for writing materials and filled up a blank warrant of appointment. Then he said to Laibao: "You two have brought me these presents at great inconvenience to yourselves. Who is that kneeling behind you?"

Laibao was about to say that this was his partner when Wu himself came forward and said that he was related to Ximen Qing, and that his name was Wu Dian'en.

"So you are related to Ximen Qing?" said the Imperial Tutor. "Well, you look a very respectable person." He called for another blank warrant and told Wu that he was appointing him an officer of the Imperial Post for the district of Qinghe. This made Wu so excited that, in his thanks, he beat his head upon the ground as though he were pounding garlic in a mortar. Upon another blank the Imperial Tutor inscribed the name of

Laibao, appointing him tallyman at the palace of Duke Yun in Shandong. They both kowtowed and thanked his Eminence, and the documents were handed to them. They were told that the next day they must go to the Boards of War and Civil Service, that their papers might be duly registered and their credentials made out, after which they should assume their offices in due course. Finally the Imperial Tutor instructed his Comptroller to entertain the two men with food and drink, and gave each of them ten taels of silver for traveling money.

In such manner was the administration brought into disrepute during the reign of the Emperor Huizong. Faithless ministers held posts of most responsibility, and the court was besieged by sycophants and men of deceit. Worst of all were Gao, Yang, Zong and Cai. Abusing their position at Court they bartered offices and accepted bribes for setting prisoners at liberty. The bribery was utterly barefaced. Appointments were given to men by the scales, and the price demanded was according to the rank of the appointment. Pushful men and those skilled in intrigue took hold upon all the offices of greatest worth, while those who were competent, wise, capable, and honest might wait for years, and still receive nothing.

Thus social morals became corrupt. Rapacious officials and their foul underlings overran the empire. Pressgangs and forced labor weighed heavily on the people. Taxation increased, so that the people were impoverished, and bandits and thieves multiplied. The Empire was completely demoralized. So, because of these faithless ministers and men in office, the people of the Middle Kingdom were drenched with blood.

Zhai took Laibao and Wu to a room at the side of the courtyard, and there entertained them so liberally that they had as much as they could eat. He said to Laibao: "I should very much like to ask a favor of your master, but I don't know whether he would care to do it or not."

"Uncle Zhai," Laibao said, "how can you say such a thing? You have done so much with his Eminence on my master's behalf that I am sure he will be only too glad to do anything you like to ask."

"I am always ready to do anything I can for him," Zhai said. "Now, I have only one wife, and I am getting on in years. My wife is always ill and she has not borne a child. What I should like to ask is this: if your master knows of a pretty girl about fifteen or sixteen years old, perhaps he will be good enough to send her to me. I will gladly pay whatever expenses he may be put to."

He gave Laibao a letter and some presents for Ximen Qing, and offered the two men each five taels of silver as traveling money. Laibao steadily refused to accept it. "We have had a present from his Eminence," he said, "so, Uncle Zhai, pray do not press this upon us."

The Comptroller insisted. "That was his Eminence's own affair," he said, "this is mine. Let us not stand too much on ceremony."

By this time they had finished their meal and Zhai told them that he would send someone to their inn who would accompany them next day to the Boards of War and Civil Service so that they might set their papers in order, and be able to start straight away without having to return to the Imperial Tutor's palace.

"The Boards will be more expeditious," he said, "if I send an order with you." He called an officer called Li Zhongyu and said to him: "Go with these two gentlemen to their respective Boards to register their appointments and secure the necessary papers. Then report to me."

Laibao and Wu Dian'en took leave of the Comptroller and left the palace with the officer. They went to a wineshop in the street near the Bridge of the Heavenly River, and there Laibao offered entertainment to Li Zhongyu, and gave him three taels of silver. They arranged that, next morning very early, they would go first to the Board of Civil Service and then to the Board of War. So indeed they did, registered their names and secured their papers, for, when the officers of these Boards knew that they had come from the Imperial Tutor's palace, they did not dare delay, but quickly prepared the documents, which were as quickly sealed by the responsible officer and sent down to the other part of the office. In two days everything was settled. Then Laibao and Wu Dian'en hired animals and set off as fast as they could to Qinghe, traveling day and night in their anxiety to tell the happy news.

One very hot day in the hottest part of summer, Ximen Qing was at home admiring the lotus flowers and drinking cooling wine in the great arbor. Wu Yueniang sat with him in the place of honor and the other ladies, with Ximen Dajie, sat on either side. Chunmei, Yingchun, Yuxiao and Lanxiang were there to sing and play for them.

The ladies were drinking together when they suddenly missed Li Ping'er. Yueniang said to her maid: "Why has your mistress gone to her room?"

"She has a pain and has gone to lie down," the maid told her.

"Go quickly," Yueniang said, "and tell her not to lie down there but to come and enjoy the music with us."

Ximen Qing asked Yueniang what she was saying, and she told him.

"Our sister is about eight months gone with child," she said to Meng Yulou, "and I don't wish her to do anything that may harm it."

Jinlian cried: "Oh, Great Sister, it is far from eight months yet." And Ximen Qing said:

"If her time is still some way off, we must send and tell her to come and listen to the music."

Soon Li Ping'er came back again. "You must not catch a chill," Yue-niang said to her. "Drink a little warm wine and then you'll be all right."

Wine was poured for them all. Ximen Qing said to Chunmei: "Sing 'People All Dread the Summer Day' for me."

Chunmei and her companions had just touched the strings; they were opening their rosy lips and showing their white teeth, ready to begin: "All people . . . ," when Li Ping'er knitted her eyebrows in pain. She did not wait for the song to be finished, but went again to her room. Yueniang heard the song out, but she was uneasy about Li Ping'er and ordered Xiaoyu to go to her room. When the maid came back, she said that Li Ping'er was in severe pain and rolling about on the bed.

"I was sure her time had come," Yueniang said, excitedly, "and you said it was too soon. Send a boy to fetch the midwife."

Ximen Qing ordered Ping'an to run like the wind and fetch old woman Cai. They did not stay to finish their wine, but all went to the Sixth Lady's room.

"Sister," Yueniang said, "tell me how you feel."

"Great Sister, there is such a pain at the pit of my stomach and lower down that I feel as if all my insides were being dragged out of me."

"You had better get up," Yueniang urged. "Don't lie down any longer. It will not be good for the baby. I have sent for the midwife, and she will be here in a minute."

After a moment or two the pains grew worse and Yueniang asked anxiously: "Who has sent for the old woman? Why hasn't he come back?"

"Father told Laian to go," Daian said.

"You rascal," Yueniang cried. "Go and find him at once. What a silly thing to send a little slave on a business like this! Why, he doesn't know the difference between what is urgent and what is not."

"Get a mule quickly," Ximen Qing said to Daian, "and go yourself."

"Even when things are of the utmost urgency," Yueniang complained, "you go on in the same careless way."

Pan Jinlian was thoroughly annoyed when she realized that Li Ping'er was about to bear a child. She stayed in the room only a few minutes and then dragged Yulou out with her. They stood together beneath the eaves, where the breeze gave them a little coolness.

"How crowded it was in that room," Jinlian said, "it made the place so hot. Really, one would think they were watching an elephant laying galls, instead of an ordinary woman giving birth to an ordinary child."

At last Cai the midwife came. "Who is the mistress of the house?" she said.

"This is the Great Lady," Li Jiao'er said, indicating Yueniang.

The old woman knelt down and kowtowed, but Yueniang told her to waste no time on ceremony. "Why have you been so long?" she said. "Kindly come and examine your patient at once."

The midwife went to the bed and carefully examined Li Ping'er. Then she said: "The time has come. Great Lady, have you got ready the paper that will be needed when the child is born?"

"Yes," Yueniang said. She sent Xiaoyu to bring what was needed.

When the midwife came, Yulou said to Jinlian: "Here is the midwife. Let us go in." But Jinlian would not. "If you wish to see," she said, "go by yourself. I don't want to have anything to do with it. She is going to have a child and she is a favored person in consequence. I don't want to see her. I said that I did not think she had reached the time, and the Great Lady was furious with me. Whenever I think about it, it makes me wild."

"I said I thought it was the sixth month," Yulou said.

"Then you are a fool too," Jinlian said. "Let me see. It was the eighth month of last year when she first came here. She was not a virgin. She married after her husband's death and did not remain any too chaste. She may have been gotten with child two or three months before she came here. Yet they are all quite sure that this child belongs to the family. What I say is: if this really is an eighth-month baby, it may possibly bear some resemblance to our family. But if it is a sixth-month child, even if we get upon a bench to make a god, we still can't get near it by a head. But when a young animal once gets away from its native place, there's no tracing it."

As they were talking, Xiaoyu came bringing paper bandages and tiny bedclothes. "These are things the Great Lady prepared for her own use," Yulou said, "now she is giving them to the Sixth Lady."

"Oh," Jinlian said, "one is great and one is small. They seem to have a competition in this baby getting. Rather than produce nothing they would be satisfied with any bit of rubbish. I'm one of those hens that never lays an egg, yet does anybody dare to eat me? Look at them there, stretching and pulling, like a dog gnawing at a bladder. All this fuss and delight over nothing at all."

"What are you saying, Fifth Sister?" said Yulou. But Jinlian did not answer. She hung down her head and played with the ribbons on her skirt. Xue'e, who had heard that Li Ping'er was about to bear a child, came bustling over from the back court, hurrying so that she did not notice the step and nearly fell down.

"Look at that little toady," Jinlian said. "Why can't she walk decently instead of dashing along like that? She might be running for her life. If she falls down and knocks her teeth out, it will cost some money. Just because the Sixth Lady has a baby, one would imagine this wretched woman would get a ceremonial hat."

At last, the sound of a cry came to them from the room. The midwife said someone must tell the master to get ready a present for her, because the lady had borne a son. Then Yueniang took word to Ximen Qing, who quickly washed his hands and burned incense in a full burner before the shrine of Heaven and Earth and of his Ancestors, and vowed that he would offer a solemn thanksgiving of a hundred and twenty degrees, with prayers for the happiness and prosperity of mother and child, and that the birth might be without danger and accompanied by good fortune.

Now that Jinlian knew that the child was born and saw everyone in the household happily engaged about the mother and the child, she became angrier still, went to her own apartments, shut the door, threw herself upon the bed and began to sob. It was the twenty-third day of the sixth month, in the fourth year of the reign period Zhenghe.

Madam Cai washed the child, cut the navel string, disposed of the afterbirth, and then prepared soothing medicine for Li Ping'er. When all was done, Yueniang invited her to go to the inner court for refreshments. As she was about to go away, Ximen Qing gave her a piece of silver weighing five taels and promised that when she came again on the third day she should have a roll of silk. The old woman thanked him effusively and went away.

Ximen went to see the baby. It was very dainty and white, and he was delighted with his son. The whole household was elated. He spent that night in the apartments of Li Ping'er, and it seemed as though he could not take his eyes off his son. Before dawn he rose, had ten boxes made ready, and sent the boys to his neighbors and kinsmen with the noodles of good fortune.

As soon as Ying Bojue and Xie Xida received theirs and so learned that Ximen Qing had a son and heir, they set off, taking two steps in one, to offer their congratulations. Ximen entertained them in the arbor. When they had gone, he was about to send one of the boys to find a nurse, when old woman Xue came to introduce one. This was a woman of low degree, about thirty years old, who had lost her own child not a month before. Her husband was a poor soldier who was afraid that when he went to the wars there would be no one to look after his wife. He wanted no more than six taels of silver for her. Yueniang decided that the woman was clean and asked Ximen to pay the six taels and give her the charge of the newly born child. She was called Ruyi'er. Afterwards they sent for old woman Feng to work for Li Ping'er, promising her five *qian* of silver every month, besides her clothes.

They were all very busy when suddenly Ping'an came and told them that Laibao and Wu Dian'en had returned from the Eastern Capital. They were at the gate and had just dismounted. Soon they came in with the good news for Ximen Qing. When he questioned them, they told him all that had happened on their journey, and how the Imperial Tutor had given appointments not only to Ximen Qing but to themselves. Laibao produced the sealed documents that they had brought from the Boards of Civil Service and of War and laid them on the table.

Ximen Qing saw that there were many seals upon the papers, and it was clear that they had come from the court. He had been made a Deputy Captain. His brow lighted up and his face beamed. He took the document to show Yueniang and the others.

"The Imperial Tutor has been good enough to raise me to the position of a Deputy Captain, which is an appointment of the fifth grade," he said. "So now you are a real lady and must wear the ceremonial dress of your rank."

He told them also about the appointments that had been given to Laibao and Wu Dian'en. "Wu the Immortal," he said, "told us that I should be given a hat of ceremony and have the good fortune to rise from the ground to the clouds. Not more than half a month has gone by and two of his prophecies have come true already."

"The Sixth Lady has this boy," he said to Yueniang, "and he seems to be a good solid lad. After his washing on the third day, we will call him Guan'ge."

Laibao came in and kowtowed to Yueniang and the others. Ximen Qing told him to take the documents to Magistrate Xia the next day and told Wu to go to the town Hall. Then Laibao took leave of his master and went home.

The next day was the day for the solemn washing of the child. The neighbors and relatives all heard that Ximen Qing's wife had borne him a son and that he had been raised to official rank and they came, one and all, to offer their congratulations. All day long, people came and went without ceasing. As the proverb says: When fortune favors a man, so do other men; but when fortune departs, his friends depart too.

CHAPTER 31
Qintong Hides a Wine Pot

The next day Ximen Qing sent Laibao with the documents to the magistrate's court, and had a hat of ceremony made for himself. Then he sent for Zhao the tailor and gave him orders to make a colored cloak as quickly as possible. Several men were set to making girdles of office. That day Wu Dian'en went to call upon Ying Bojue and told him all about the appointment he had received. He begged Bojue to borrow some money for him from Ximen Qing so that he could expend whatever was necessary at his office. He promised to give Bojue ten taels for himself. So eager was he, that he knelt down before Bojue. Ying hastily raised him to his feet. "What could be more pleasant," he said, "than to do things for others? Thanks to Ximen's generosity, you have acquired this position, and this is no ordinary occasion. How much will you need?"

"I must own to you," Wu Dian'en said, "that, though my household manages to keep going, I have not a penny to spare. I shall have to give presents to my superiors in office and there must be a banquet. I shall need clothes and a horse. All this will cost seventy or eighty taels at least. I have made out a note, but without stating any definite amount. Do help me and I promise you shall be well repaid."

Ying Bojue looked at the note. "Brother Wu," he said, "I can't believe this is enough. You had better make it a hundred. I am sure that if I ask him, Master Ximen will not require interest from you, and you can pay him back in installments when you have taken up your duties. You will remember the proverb: Borrowed rice may be stored in the jar, but rice that has been begged will never find its way there."

Wu thanked his friend effusively and wrote a hundred taels upon the note of hand. They had tea and set off together to call upon Ximen Qing. Ping'an announced them, and as they went in they saw the tailors busy at their work. The Deputy Captain and his son-in-law were sitting under the eaves, watching a clerk writing visiting cards. The two visitors greeted them and then sat down to talk.

"Brother," Bojue said, "have you sent your papers to the office?"

"Yes," Ximen said, "I sent them to the courts this morning, and now I am arranging for Ben the Fourth to take my card to the Prefecture at

Dongping Fu and the District office here."

A boy brought tea. Bojue did not at once mention the business about which he had come, but went to watch the tailors at work upon the girdles. Ximen Qing saw him taking them in his hands and said with great pride: "What do you think of my new girdles?"

Bojue praised them: "Wherever did you get them, Brother? Each one seems to excel the other. Buckles as fine as these are not to be met with every day. And this rhinoceros horn; this button shaped like a stork's head! Why, you might take your money in your hand all around the Eastern Capital, and never be able to find anything like it. This is not flattery. Princes and nobles in the Capital have their girdles of jade and gold, but you would never find them with one of rhinoceros horn so good as this. And not the land rhinoceros ... this is the water kind, and ever so much more valuable. You know, the water rhinoceros they call *Tong Tian*. If you don't believe me, give me a cup of water. I will put the horn into it and you will see that it divides the water into two parts. It is indeed a priceless treasure. How much did you pay for it, Brother?"

Ximen Qing invited him to guess the price, but Bojue declared that such things had no definite price, and he could not possibly guess.

"I will tell you," Ximen Qing said. "It comes from the palace of the princely family Wang in the High Street. Yesterday someone heard that I was wanting a girdle and came to tell me about it. I sent Ben the Fourth, with seventy taels, to buy it, but they would not part with it for less than a hundred."

"Well," Ying Bojue said, "it would be a very difficult matter to find another so fine and beautiful. You will certainly look very grand when you go out in it, and your colleagues at the courts will fall in love with it." He went on in this strain for a long time and finally sat down.

"Have you taken your papers?" Ximen Qing said to Wu. Ying Bojue answered for him. "It was precisely because Brother Wu wishes to do so that he asked me to come here and trouble you. How extraordinarily kind to him you have been! You sent him to the Eastern Capital, and, though his appointment was actually given him by the Imperial Tutor, it really comes to him from you. It was a real piece of good luck. Whether he belongs to the first grade or the ninth, he is none the less an officer of the Court now. He has just told me that he wants to go to his office to make the acquaintance of his colleagues, but it will cost a lot of money to offer them a banquet and he doesn't know where to get it. One guest, Brother, does not inflict himself upon two hosts. For my sake, I want you to lend him a few taels so that he can enter upon his duties. Later, when he has taken up his appointment, there will be nothing too much for him to do for you. He has served your family long and well. Brother, you help many people in the Capital and elsewhere. If you will do nothing for him, it will be very awkward indeed for him."

He turned to Wu. "Brother Wu, bring out that charm of yours, and let his Lordship see it."

Wu Dian'en quickly drew out the paper and handed it to Ximen Qing. The sum of a hundred taels was mentioned, Ying Bojue's name appeared as witness, and interest was promised at the rate of five percent each month. Ximen took a pen and crossed out the part about the interest. "Since Brother Ying is the witness," he said, "I shall not ask you to do more than repay the hundred taels. I had thought you would need some money." He put the document in his sleeve.

As he was about to go to the inner court to get the money, there came an underling with a card from Magistrate Xia. He sent twelve soldiers to await Ximen's orders. The clerk asked when Ximen Qing proposed to enter upon his duties and what titles he would use. All the officials of the district were anxious to come and to congratulate him, and bring their present. Ximen sent for the Master of the Yin Yang, asked him to find a suitable date, and it was arranged that upon the morning of the second day of the seventh month he should take possession of his office. Ximen sent a card in return to the magistrate, gave five *qian* of silver to the underling, and sent him back again.

Chen Jingji brought a hundred taels and Ximen handed them to Wu Dian'en, saying: "Brother, take this and repay me." Wu Dian'en took the money and kowtowed. "I will not detain you," Ximen Qing said, "you have business of your own to attend to. But, Brother Ying, I have something to say to you."

Wu Dian'en went happily away with his money.

Ben the Fourth, who had been to the office at Dongping Fu, now came back and Ximen invited him to take a meal with them. Besides Ying Bojue, Xu the Master of the Yin Yang was there. While they were eating, Uncle Wu came to congratulate Ximen Qing. Then the Master of the Yin Yang took his leave, and, shortly afterwards, Ying Bojue also went away. He went straight to see Wu Dian'en, who had ten taels of silver ready waiting for him. He held it out with both hands. "If it had not been for the clever way you spoke for me," he said, "he might never have lent me this money." Then he set about making his robes of ceremony and selected a day on which to assume office.

Li, one of the magistrates of the district, now joined with his colleagues in sending a present of sheep, wine and other things to Ximen Qing. In addition, he sent with his card a youth about eighteen years of age. This was a native of Changshou in Xuzhou, and his name was Little Zhang Song. He had been one of the boys who waited upon the district officers. He was clear-skinned and good-looking. His face was white like powder, his teeth glistened, and his lips were red. He could read, write, and sing the songs of the south. He was wearing a gown of black silk with light shoes and white socks. Ximen Qing was very pleased to discover such an accomplished young man, and, sending a card of thanks to the magistrate, he at once took the boy into his service. He called him Shutong, and had new clothes, shoes, and a hat made for him. He decided that he would not have the young man to follow his horse like the other boys, but would use him rather as a secretary to take charge of his study, receive presents when they came, and take charge of the keys of the pavilions in the garden.

Zhu Shinian also recommended a boy to him. This one was only fourteen years old. Ximen Qing called him Qitong and appointed him to carry his visiting card case, and parcels, and to follow behind the horse with Qintong.

At last the day came when he was formally to take up his duties. A great banquet was given at the office and musicians were engaged from three of the bawdy houses. The party went on all day until sunset.

After this, Ximen Qing rode out every day upon a big white horse. He wore a black ceremonial hat and a robe of office with long-maned lions embroidered in five colors upon it. A girdle, four fingers broad, encircled his waist, and his feet were shod in white-soled boots. An escort of soldiers accompanied him and a large black fan was borne behind him. Men went before him, shouting to clear the way; others followed close upon his horse's heels. No less than ten were in attendance upon him. Up and down the streets he went.

As soon as he had left the office he went to see the Captain of the garrison and the various official personages of Qinghe. Then it was the turn of his kinsmen, friends and neighbors. It was a glorious occasion. Meanwhile, presents and visiting cards came to his house in shoals.

Now that he had definitely entered upon his duties, he went every day to the courts and took his seat in the great hall. There he examined official documents and attended to official business. The time passed very quickly.

Li Ping'er was now able to get up. Many ladies, both relatives and friends of the household, came with presents to celebrate the completion of the baby's first month of life. Li Guijie and Wu Yin'er, who had heard of Ximen's good fortune, made ready presents and came in their sedan chairs to congratulate him. Ximen Qing had a splendid feast prepared in the front hall for the ladies. Chunmei, Yingchun, Yuxiao and Lanxiang, all dressed in their most beautiful attire, served wine to the guests.

Every day as soon as Ximen Qing returned from the office, he took off his robes in the outer hall and Shutong took them, folded them, and put them away in the study. When he went to the inner court, he only kept on his hat. In the morning, he used to send a maid to the study to bring the clothes. A room at the side of the great hall had been specially arranged to serve him as a private room. There a bed, tables both large and small, chairs, screens, curtains, writing materials and books were set out, and, every night, Shutong slept at the foot of the bed. When Ximen slept in this room, he would send a maid in the morning to bring his clothes from the outer court. So, with all this sending backwards and forwards of clothes, Shutong, who was of very doubtful antecedents besides being taking in his ways and good looking, found plenty of opportunity to play tricks upon the maids from all the different rooms, and in particular, became a close friend of Yuxiao.

One day when this young man had just got up and was dressing his hair with red ribbon before a mirror on the windowsill, Yuxiao opened the door and came in. She saw that he was dressing his hair. "Ah, you young rascal," she said, "so you are still painting your eyebrows and your eyes. Father will be here as soon as he has finished breakfast."

Shutong paid no attention to her but went on dressing his hair.

"Where are Father's clothes?" she asked.

"By the side of the bed," the boy said.

"No, this is not the suit he wants today. He told me to ask you for the robe of black silk with the gold and embroidery down the front."

"They are in the cupboard," Shutong said, "I put them there only yesterday, and now he wants them again. Open the cupboard and get them yourself."

Yuxiao did not get the clothes. Instead she went over to the young man and watched him dressing his hair. "You funny thing," she said jokingly, "you are like a woman, putting red ribbons in your hair and making quite a headdress." She noticed that he was wearing a short coat of white material with two satchels for perfume, one of pink and one of green silk. "Give me the pink one," she said.

"You always want those things that people care most about," Shutong said.

"But you are a boy, and shouldn't wear such things," the maid said. "That pink one is much more suitable for me."

"That," Shutong cried, "is only a bag. What would you think if it were a husband?"

Yuxiao pinched him on the shoulder. "You young scamp," she said, "do not try to palm off your picture of the god of the door as if it were a genuine work of art." Without more ado, she broke the cord that held the two perfume bags and put them in her sleeve.

"Really," Shutong said, "your behavior is hardly becoming. You have broken my girdle."

Yuxiao slapped him playfully, but the young man was a little put out. "Sister," he said, "please do not play with me. I must finish doing my hair."

"Tell me," Yuxiao said, "have you heard where Father is going today?"

"Yes," the boy said, "he is going to say good-bye to Master Hua, the Deputy Assistant Magistrate for the district, for whom a farewell banquet is being given at Eunuch Xue's house. I expect he will be fairly late coming back as he is also going to Uncle Ying's to see about the payment for Master Qiao's house across the way. I should not be surprised if he drank wine there too."

"Well," Yuxiao said, "don't you go out. I may come and have a talk with you."

Yuxiao took the clothes, and went to the inner court.

Some time later Ximen Qing came. He told Shutong that he must not leave the house that day, and that he must write out twelve cards of invitation and put them in red envelopes. These invitations were all for gentlemen to come and celebrate Guan'ge's first month of life. Before he went out, Ximen Qing told Laixing to make all the necessary purchases, to engage extra cooks and, indeed, to do everything that was necessary. Daian and two soldiers were ordered to take out the invitations, and to engage singers. Qintong was to serve the guests with wine. After giving all these orders, Ximen Qing mounted his horse and set out.

Today was the ladies' party. Yueniang and her companions received their guests in the arbor. Tea was served there. The banquet was laid in the great hall, where gorgeous screens were set out, and cushions embroidered with lotus flowers. The four maids who were trained in music were told to be in attendance.

As soon as Ximen Qing returned in the afternoon, he had a box of wine and refreshments prepared, and asked Ying Bojue and Chen Jingji to go with him to Master Qiao's house, where he was to take seven hundred taels.

While the ladies were drinking, Yuxiao took a silver wine jar, a cup, and some pears, and went with them to the study. She expected to find Shutong. But when she opened the door, Shutong was not to be seen. She was afraid that someone might see her, so she quietly put down the things and slipped out again. Qintong, who was attending to the wine for the guests, saw her with his sharp eyes. He saw her go to the study and come back again. He thought that Shutong was there and ran to see him, but the young secretary, of course, was not there. Qintong spied a jar of warmed wine and some fruit at the foot of the bed. He hastily put the fruit into his sleeves, and, picking up the jar of wine, quietly made off with it to the Sixth Lady's room. The nurse Ruyi'er and Xiuchun were looking after the baby. Qintong asked where Yingchun was.

"She is serving wine in the hall," Xiuchun said. "What do you want with her?"

"I have something good here," Qintong said. "I want her to keep it for me."

"What is it?" Xiuchun said, but the boy would not show her.

At that moment, Yingchun came from the hall bringing a plate of hot goose and cakes made of rice flower and almonds for the nurse.

"What are you doing here, you young rascal?" she said. "You ought to be attending to your duties in the hall."

Qintong brought the wine jar from under his clothes. "Sister," he said, "please keep this for me."

"But this is the jar we use for heating wine in the hall," Yingchun said. "Why did you bring it here?"

"Sister," the boy said, "Yuxiao took it to the study for Shutong. She stole it and some pears and took them to him, but, when there was nobody about, I slipped in and took it. I want you to keep it for me, and if anybody comes looking for it, let them go away without it. It was a real piece of good luck for me." He showed the pears and oranges to Yingchun.

"Well," Yingchun said, "if anybody starts looking for this jar and there is trouble about it, it will be your lookout."

"I didn't steal it," Qintong said. "There's no reason why I should be worried. Let those who did steal it be alarmed. I am out of it. It won't be my legs that get the beating." He went away in a most cheerful frame of mind. Yingchun put the wine jar on a table.

In the evening when the guests had all gone, the silver was checked and one wine jar was missed. Yuxiao went to the study to look for it, but it was nowhere to be found. When she asked Shutong, he said he knew nothing about it and that he had not been there. Then the trouble began. Yuxiao accused Xiaoyu, and Xiaoyu cursed her. "You silly strumpet," she cried, "I was making tea all the time. You were serving wine. If the jar is lost, what has it to do with me?" They looked everywhere, but still it could not be found.

When Li Ping'er went to her room, Yingchun told her that Qintong had brought the jar there and asked her to keep it for him.

"The young rascal!" Li Ping'er cried. "Whatever made him bring it here? There is a terrible fuss in the inner court about it. Yuxiao says it is

Xiaoyu's fault, and Xiaoyu says it is Yuxiao's fault, and Yuxiao is taking all sorts of oaths and crying. You had better take it back at once or all the blame will be put on you."

While Yingchun was on her way to take the jar back to the inner court, Yuxiao and Xiaoyu had gone to see Yueniang, both talking away at one another as hard as they could.

"What," cried Yueniang, "are you still shouting? What were you doing to lose the jar?"

"I was serving wine in the hall," Yuxiao said, "and she was in charge of all the silver. Yet now the jar has been lost she says it is my fault."

"No," Xiaoyu said, "Aunt wanted tea, and I went to the inner court to take her some. You had the wine jar when it was lost. Your brains must have gone the way your dinner goes.

"There were no light-fingered people at today's party," Yueniang said. "Why should we lose a wine jar? We must wait till your master returns. When he hears what has been lost, certainly you will both get a beating."

In the middle of the squabble, Ximen Qing came in. He asked what the fuss was about, and Yueniang told him of the lost wine jar.

"You should keep calm," said Ximen. "What need is there for all this excitement?"

Jinlian interrupted. "If one jar is lost every time we have a party," she said, "you may be as rich as Wang the Millionaire, but you'll find that the early promise you seem to expect is not fulfilled."

In this way Jinlian was trying to be unpleasant. Li Ping'er had just borne a child and the losing of a wine jar at this particular time was of ill omen. Ximen Qing understood quite well what she meant, but he said nothing. Then Yingchun came in with the jar, and Yuxiao recognized it at once. When Yueniang asked where it had come from, Yingchun told them that Qintong had brought it to her mistress's room, but she did not know where he had found it. Yueniang asked where the boy was. Daian told her that it was his turn to go to the house in Lion Street, and he was there.

Jinlian sneered, and Ximen Qing asked what she was sneering about.

"Qintong," she said, "is one of her household, so it is natural that he should take the jar to her room. It must be plain to you what the jar was doing there. If I were you, I should send a boy to fetch that young slave, and beat him till the truth about the matter comes to light. If we blame these two maids, we shall be missing the mark completely."

This made Ximen Qing extremely angry. He glared at Jinlian. "I suppose you think the Sixth Lady coveted this jar for herself. Well, here it is. Let that be the end of the business. What need is there for you to try to make trouble?"

Jinlian flushed. "I didn't mean anything," she said. She went away in a very bad temper. When Chen Jingji came to discuss some business with Ximen Qing, she stood and talked bitterly with Meng Yulou.

"They will come to a bad end," she stormed. "The place is full of rogues and thieves. Why, she might have been going to die the other day. Now that she has this baby, she gives herself such airs one would think she had given birth to a prince. She looks like the goddess of Good Fortune whenever she meets us. She is too grand to condescend even to speak to us. And when she moves about, she opens her eyes as wide as two cunts and yells at everyone. We know she is rich. It seems to me she allows her boys and maids to carry on as they please, and if they rob all the rest of the household no one will hinder them."

Ximen Qing, who had finished talking to Jingji, went in the direction of the front court.

"You had better go," Yulou said. "He seems to be going to your room."

"Surely not," Jinlian said. "He finds it much pleasanter where the baby is. It is so cheerless where there is no baby."

At that moment, Chunmei came. "I told you he was going to your room," Yulou said, "and you wouldn't believe me. Now here is Chunmei come to fetch you!"

They called Chunmei and questioned her.

"I have come to ask Yuxiao for a handkerchief," she said.

"Where is your master?" Yulou said.

"He has gone to the Sixth Lady's room."

When Jinlian heard this, she became furiously angry. "The rogue," she cried. "May his legs be broken for a thousand years, and until the end of time he shall never cross my threshold again. May the rascal break the bones of his ankles."

"Why do you use these horrid words about him today?" Yulou said.

"You don't know that cheap bandit," Jinlian cried. "His mind is like a rat's belly, and his guts like a chicken's, not more than three inches long. We are all his wives. Why should he save all his favor for a woman who brings forth a seed wrapped in a bladder? Why should he raise one so high and kick the others into the mud?"

When Ximen Qing had gone to the front court, Eunuch Xue's servant came with a jar of rice wine, a sheep, two rolls of silk, a dish of lucky noodles and a dish of peaches. These were gifts to congratulate Ximen on the birth of his son, and his new appointment. Ximen gave a considerable present to the servant and dismissed him. Then he went to the inner court. Guijie and Wu Yin'er were about to go home. He asked them to stay.

"I have invited a number of gentlemen for the celebration," he said, "and there will be several performers of different kinds. I should like you two to serve the wine."

"If you wish us to stay," Guijie said, "I must arrange for someone to let my mother know so that she will not be anxious about us." Then she dismissed the two chair men.

The following day, the great hall was made ready for the feast. Silken screens were placed in position and embroidered cushions set around. Some time before, Ximen had made the acquaintance of Eunuch Liu, the controller of an Imperial brick manufactory. Both Liu and Xue had sent him presents, and Ximen, in return, had sent them cards of invitation. He had also asked Ying Bojue and Xie Xida to come and help him receive the guests. The two friends, dressed in suitable attire, came about dinnertime, and Ximen Qing asked them to sit down in the arbor and have tea.

"Whom have you invited today?" Ying Bojue said.

Ximen told them. "The two eunuchs Liu and Xue, Major Zhou, Jing Nanjiang, my colleagues, Magistrate Xia, Captain Zhang of the Militia and Captain Fan. My two brothers-in-law will be there too. Master Qiao has sent a man to say that he will not be able to come, so that, even including yourselves, there will be only a few guests."

The two Uncles Wu arrived. After greetings had been exchanged they all sat down. The servants set a table and served them with food.

When they had finished, Bojue said: "Has your young son been out yet, now that he is a month old?"

"Well," Ximen said, "the ladies were all anxious to see him. My wife thought we ought not to take him out lest he should catch cold, but the nurse said she did not think it would do him any harm, so he was wrapped up in a blanket and taken to my wife's room. This was just so that the day might be duly celebrated. He was taken back immediately."

"The other day," Bojue said, "you were good enough to send us an invitation, and my wife would have liked very much to come, but, unfortunately, she had a return of her old illness and could not get up. She was very upset about it, and before the guests arrive I take this opportunity of apologizing on her behalf. Won't you have your son brought here so that we may have a look at him?"

Ximen Qing sent word to the inner court that the baby was to be brought, but very carefully lest he should be frightened. "His two uncles are here," he said, "and also Brothers Ying and Xie, and they are anxious to see him."

Wu Yueniang bade the nurse Ruyi'er wrap the baby in a tiny shawl of fine red silk and take him to the corner door. There Daian received him and carried him to the arbor. They all looked at him. Guan'ge was dressed in a scarlet woolen vest. His skin was clear and his lips were red. He looked healthy. The guests paid him all sorts of compliments. The two Uncles Wu and Xie Xida each presented him with a stomach protector of figured satin with a small silver pendant attached. Ying Bojue had nothing better than a skein of five-colored threads and a few lucky coins. These things were all solemnly given to Daian for the child, and he was told to take Guan'ge back very carefully and be sure not to frighten him.

"The child looks very dignified and upstanding," said Ying Bojue. "He is obviously born to wear a hat of ceremony."

This pleased Ximen Qing immensely. He bowed in thanks to Ying Bojue.

Then news was brought that the two eunuchs had arrived. Ximen hastily put on his robes and went to the second door to welcome them. They were waiting, each in a sedan chair carried by four men. They were wearing robes with embroidered dragons, and were accompanied by a bodyguard with tasseled spears to clear the way. Ximen Qing asked them to go with him to the great hall. There he greeted them and offered tea. Then Major Zhou, Master Jing, Xia and the other military gentlemen arrived, all wearing their embroidered robes, with men attending them bearing staves and large fans, and runners shouting to clear the way. In a moment there was a crowd of attendants about the gate. Inside the courtyard there was a deafening sound of drums and instruments, and a never-ending succession of melodies and songs. Ximen Qing welcomed them in turn and introduced them to the two eunuchs Liu and Xue. At the upper end of the hall were twelve tables, and Ximen Qing, taking up a wine cup, prepared to put the guests in their proper places. The two eunuchs, Liu and Xue, repeatedly refused to take the places of honor. "Let others take them," they said. Major Zhou insisted that they should do so. "Most Worshipful Sirs," he said, "your age and dignity demand respect. As the proverb says: to be a Chamberlain at the Imperial Court for the space of three years confers more dignity than a barony. Obviously then, you must take the place of honor at once, and stand on ceremony no longer."

The two old gentlemen disputed for a long time over the first place. At last Xue said: "Brother Liu, since the other gentlemen will not take the upper seat, we must not be a nuisance to our host. Let us sit down."

They bowed politely to the guests. Liu took the left-hand place and Xue the right. Each placed a handkerchief on his knees and had a small boy to stand beside and fan him. When they had seated themselves, the others did so. Then the music blared in the courtyard, and food, exquisite and rare beyond description, was set before the guests. After the wine had gone around five times and three soup courses had been served, a troop of actors began their performance.

After the comedies, the two young singers, Li Ming and Wu Hui, came forward, one with a dulcimer, the other with a lute. Major Zhou raised his hand. "Most Worshipful Sirs," he said to the two eunuchs, "will you not tell these singers what songs they shall sing?"

"But only," Liu said, "when you have made your own choice."

"No," Major Zhou said, "it is right and fitting that you should give your orders first. Pray do not stand on ceremony."

"Well," Liu said, "I should like to hear 'Life Is Like a Dream.'"

Major Zhou demurred. "That is a song," he said, "for those who have withdrawn from the world and are weary of its enjoyments. This is a happy occasion for our excellent host Ximen. We are celebrating the birth of his son, and I really don't think it is suitable."

Liu tried again. "Can you sing," he asked the boys, "'Though He Is Not a Purple-girdled Minister of the First Eight Grades, He Governs the Young Ladies Who Wear Golden Pins in the Six Palaces'?"

Major Zhou objected again. "That alludes to Chen Lin and the dressing box, and is not suitable for an occasion like this."

"Send the two singers to me," Xue said, "and I will choose a song. Do you remember 'The World Is Full of Merriment, Yet Separation Is the Bitterest of All Life's Troubles'?"

Xia burst out laughing. "Most Worshipful Sir," he said, "that is worse still, for it speaks of separation."

"Well," Xue said, "we officials of the court are so wrapped up in our duties towards his Majesty that perhaps we don't know very much about songs and melodies. Let them sing what they like."

Xia, who was a magistrate and enjoyed such authority as a magistrate may claim, took advantage of his position and called for the thirty melodies. "Today," he said, "we are celebrating Master Ximen's appointment and at the same time the birth of his son. So let us have the song of the toy scepter."

"Why do you mention a 'toy scepter'?" Eunuch Xue said.

"Oh, Most Worshipful Sirs," Major Zhou said. "today our host's son is a month old. We have all been offering a little present in honor of the occasion."

"Is that so?" Xue said. "Brother Liu, we shall have to send a present tomorrow."

Ximen Qing thanked them. "This ignorant fellow has but a little dog. The occasion is not worthy of such honor, and I beg you not to trouble yourselves."

Daian was sent to the inner court to summon Wu Yin'er and Guijie to serve the wine. The two singing girls, as dainty as the flowers on the branches of a tree, kowtowed four times like a pair of candles. They took the wine jar and served wine to everyone and the two young musicians sang a new song. So delicate were their throats and so flexible, their voices echoed through the rafters.

That night with dancing and singing they enjoyed themselves immensely, and drank until the first watch of the night. Then Eunuch Xue stood up. "You have been exceedingly kind," he said, "and as this was a special occasion, we felt we ought to stay and enjoy ourselves, but now we must have outstayed our welcome and we will go."

"I have offered you the meanest of entertainments," Ximen said, "but you have condescended to visit me and my poor house has been illumined by your presence. I beg you, stay a little longer that my happiness may be complete." All the guests rose. "You have been extremely kind," they said, "but we really can drink no more wine." They bowed to Ximen Qing and thanked him. Ximen repeatedly urged them to stay, but in vain. So with his two brothers-in-law, he escorted them to the gate. The music rose to the skies, and outside the gateway on both sides, torches and lanterns blazed. The guests went away with men going before to guide them and men going behind to protect them. There was much shouting to clear the way.

CHAPTER 32
Li Guijie

After drinking their fill, the principal guests had gone away. Ximen Qing, however, pressed the two Uncles Wu, Ying Bojue and Xie Xida to remain. He told the musicians to go for their refreshment, bidding them come again next day. "I am entertaining the gentlemen from the District offices," he said, "and you must put on your best clothes. I will pay you for everything tomorrow."

The musicians answered: "Your servants will take the utmost care, and tomorrow we will dress ourselves in new clothes of the official type." They had food and wine, then kowtowed and went away. Soon afterwards, Li Guijie and Wu Yin'er came in side by side. They smiled and said: "Father, it is late and our sedan chairs have come for us. We must go."

"My children," Ying Bojue said, "your audacity surprises me. Here are two very worthy gentlemen, but instead of singing for them you just go off."

"Oh yes," said Guijie, "you would talk like that. We haven't been home for two days and mother will be wondering what has become of us."

"Why should she worry?" Bojue cried, "that yellow jade-colored old plum with a piece bitten out of her!"

"That is enough!" Ximen said, "let them go. They have had to work very hard these last few days. Li Ming and Wu Hui shall sing for us." He asked the two girls if they had had anything to eat. Guijie told him that Yueniang had given them refreshments. When they had kowtowed and were about to go away, Ximen Qing said: "I shall expect you the day after tomorrow. Bring another two girls with you. Han Jinchuan and Zheng Aixiang will do. I am inviting a few relatives and friends to dinner."

"You are lucky, you little strumpet," cried Ying Bojue, "you get away and do well out of it."

"I wonder what it is that makes you so clever," Guijie said. They laughed and went away.

"Whom are you going to invite, Brother?" Bojue said to Ximen Qing.

"Master Qiao, the two Uncles Wu, Brother Hua, Uncle Shen and the members of our brotherhood. We will spend the whole day enjoying ourselves."

"Though I realize that I am troubling you too greatly, "Bojue said, "I will come to assist you in receiving the guests."

Ximen Qing thanked him. Then Li Ming and Wu Hui came with their instruments and sang a few songs. Finally the men all went away.

The day when Ximen Qing had invited the officers from the District offices, Eunuch Xue was one of the first to arrive. Ximen offered him tea in the arbor. The eunuch asked whether his colleague Liu had sent a present. Then he asked to see the child that he might give him his blessing. Ximen Qing modestly deprecated such an honor, but at last told Daian to go to the inner court for the baby. The nurse brought the child to the corner gate where Daian received him and brought him to them. Xue looked at Guan'ge and praised him. "A very fine child!" he said. He called for his attendants. Two servants, dressed in black, brought a square gilt box, and from it took two packets of gifts. There was a length of royal silk, a roll of watered red silk, and four silver gilt coins, each with one of the lucky characters upon it: Good Fortune, Long Life, Health, and Peace. There was a small *Bo Lang* drum, painted in gold and various colors, and a set of amulets. "I am only a poor eunuch," he said, "and have nothing worth offering, but these trifles may serve to amuse your son."

Ximen Qing made a reverence to the eunuch and thanked him very heartily. When they had drunk tea, refreshments were served, but, before they had finished them, the expected guests were announced. Ximen Qing put straight his robes and went to the second door to welcome them. These were District Magistrate Li Datian, Assistant District Magistrate Qian Zheng, Chief Secretary Ren Tinggui, and Prison Governor Xia Tianji. They presented their cards and then went to the hall and greeted their host. Ximen asked Eunuch Xue to come and meet his guests, and the officers insisted that the old man should take the seat of honor. Among the guests was a graduate of the second degree named Shang.

When they had all taken their proper places, tea was served. After a while the sound of drums and music was heard in the courtyard. The actors came to offer wine to the chief guest and showed him their repertory. Eunuch Xue looked at it and bade them sing the song of Han Xiangzi attaining immortality. They danced to accompany this song. The performance was excellent. The eunuch was pleased and told his servant to give the musicians two strings of money. The party was very successful and did not break up until late.

Guijie went home. Now that Ximen Qing was an officer, she and her mother thought of a scheme for taking advantage of the situation. They bought four different kinds of presents and Guijie made a pair of shoes. The next day, she told her servant to put them in a box and, very early in the morning, got into a sedan chair and set off to ask Yueniang to accept her as a ward. She went in smiling, and kowtowed four times to Wu Yueniang, then to her and Ximen Qing together. Yueniang was greatly flattered.

"Only the other day," she said, "your mother sent me a valuable present and now you have gone to all this trouble to buy expensive gifts for me."

Guijie smiled. "Mother says that now his Lordship is an officer, of course he will not be able to come so often to see her. I have come to offer myself as his adopted daughter. Then there will be no difficulty about my coming here because we shall be relatives."

Yueniang told her to take off her long cloak and asked why Wu Yin'er and the others had not come with her.

"I spoke to Wu Yin'er about it yesterday," Guijie said. "I can't understand why she has not come. The other day, Father told me to bring Zheng Aixiang and Han Jinchuan. As I was coming along, I saw the chairs waiting outside their doors, so they are sure to be here before long."

Almost at that moment Wu Yin'er, Zheng Aixiang, and a young girl dressed in scarlet, came and kowtowed to Yueniang. They had brought their clothes in a bag. When Wu Yin'er saw Guijie sitting on the bed with her outdoor clothes already taken off, she said: "You are a fine friend, Sister Guijie. You would not wait, but came along without us."

"I was going to wait for you," Guijie said, "but when my mother saw the chair at the door she said: 'It looks to me as though your sister has already gone. You had better make haste.' I didn't realize you were not ready."

"She is not too late," Yueniang said, smiling. She asked the name of the newcomer. "She is Han Jinchuan's younger sister, Han Yuchuan," Wu Yin'er told her.

Yuxiao brought refreshments for the singing girls. Guijie, who was anxious to show that she was now the adopted daughter of Yueniang, sat on Yueniang's bed and helped Yuxiao to crack the nuts and put them into the fruit box. Wu Yin'er and the other girls sat together on a bench. Guijie lost no opportunity of making clear her new importance. "Sister Yuxiao," she would say, "would you mind giving me a cup of tea?" or "Sister Xiaoyu, may I have some water to rinse my hands?" Wu Yin'er and the others looked at her in astonishment, but Yueniang and Li Jiao'er were sitting opposite and they could say nothing.

"Sister Wu Yin'er," Guijie said, "you must get your instrument and sing a song for my mother. I have done my part already."

Again Wu Yin'er could not help herself. She picked up her instrument, and the four girls together sang the Eight Melodies of Ganzhou.

"What guests has Father invited today?" Wu Yin'er asked.

"They are all kinsmen and friends," Yueniang said.

"Are the two eunuchs coming?" Guijie said. Yueniang said no; that Xue had called the day before, but not Liu.

"His Lordship Liu is a fine man," Guijie said, "but Xue is always up to tricks. Sometimes he pinches me till I nearly faint."

"After all," Yueniang said, "he is a eunuch and there is something lacking about him. There is no harm in letting him have his little fun."

"You are right," Guijie said, "but sometimes I find him rather a nuisance."

Daian came for the box of fruits. When he saw the four girls sitting there, he said: "Half the guests are here already, and they are just about to take their places. Why do you not dress and go?"

Yueniang asked who had come, and Daian told her that Master Qiao, Uncle Hua, the two Uncles Wu and Uncle Xie were there. Guijie said: "What about Beggar Ying and Pockmarked Zhu? Have they come?"

"The ten gentlemen of the brotherhood are all here," Daian said. "Uncle Ying was here early and Father asked him to attend to a certain matter for him. He went away, but I think he will be back soon."

"Oh dear!" Guijie said, "every time I come into contact with those sharpers, I wonder how I shall be stung. I shall not go. I shall stay here and sing songs for Mother."

"You take too much upon yourself," Daian said. He took the fruit box and went back to the hall.

"Mother," Guijie said to Yueniang, "do you know that Pockmarked Zhu never allows his lips to stop moving when he is at a party? The others complain but he pays no attention. He and Greedy-Chops Sun have not an atom of shame about them."

"Yes," Zheng Aixiang said, "Pockmarked Zhu is always about with Ying. They came to our house the other day with Little Zhang the Second. Little Zhang had twenty taels and wanted my younger sister Zheng Aiyue. My mother told them that my sister had just been made a woman by a Southerner. It had only been a month before and the Southerner had not gone away yet, so we could do nothing for him. They would not listen to her, and my mother lost her temper, locked the door from the inside, and would have nothing to do with them. Young Master Zhang is very well off. He rides a great white horse and there are always four or five boys in attendance on him. Well, he simply sat down in our hall and refused to go away. Pockmarked Zhu knelt down in the courtyard and said: 'Old Lady, you must really come out and take this money. All we ask is to see Zheng Aiyue and have a cup of tea. Then we will go away.' This made us laugh like anything. He was like the man who comes to tell us about the floods.

He's an utterly shameless fellow."

"That young Zhang," Wu Yin'er said, "once had the *dong* cat."

"Yes," Zheng Aixiang said, "and set fire to the tiger's mouth, and then the turtle broke with her."

She turned to Guijie. "Yesterday I met Zhou Xiao outside our door and he told me to tell you that the other day he and Nie Yue went to call upon you, but you were not at home."

Guijie glanced sharply at her. "Why, of course," she said, "I was here that day. It was my sister Guiqing he went to see."

"If there is nothing between you," Aixiang said, "why are you always so friendly?"

"You are as fond of your joke as old Liu the Ninth. Do you think Zhou means anything to me? I should be ashamed to have anything to do with that fellow. There was a row, and he told everybody he was coming to see me. He was very much annoyed because I wouldn't let his mother say so. Of course, I can't help his coming to our house. But I should be a piece of stone, whatever he had to do with anyone else. If I were so foolish, it would be like looking towards the South and driving a nail into my bosom."

They all laughed. Yueniang, who had been sitting on the bed listening to them, said: "I have not understood a single word of what you have been saying all this time. I do not even know what language you are speaking."

The guests in the front court had now all arrived. Ximen Qing, dressed in his robes of ceremony, served them with wine. Master Qiao was asked to take the place of honor and he offered the first toast to Ximen Qing. The three singing girls came from the back court. They wore glittering pearl headdresses on their heads and their bodies were exquisitely perfumed with musk. Bojue, as soon as he saw them, said, jokingly: "Where have you three odd things come from? Stop. You may not come in. Why is Guijie not here?" Ximen Qing declared he did not know.

Zheng Aixiang took the zither, Wu Yin'er the lute, and Yuchuan the castanets. They opened their red lips, showed their pearly teeth, and sang.

Besides Master Qiao, who sat in the place of honor, all the members of the brotherhood were present, with Fu, the manager of the shop, and Ben the Fourth. There were fourteen guests, and eight tables. Ximen Qing sat in the host's seat. It was a very splendid feast. Charming voices, exquisite dancing, wine like rolling waves, and food piled up mountains high. When the wine had been passed several times and three songs had been sung, Ying Bojue said: "Host, do not allow them to sing any more. They sing the same tune over and over again like a dog scratching at the door. I have no patience for any more of it. Won't you ask one of the boys to bring three chairs, so that they can sit down and serve wine for us? That would be much better than this singing."

"Leave them alone, you dog," Ximen said. "Why should you upset the whole party?"

"Oh, Beggar Ying," Aixiang cried, "you're letting off fireworks from your behind. You can't wait till evening."

Bojue rose in his place. "You marvelous little strumpet," he cried, "evening or not evening, what has it to do with you, you mother's cunt? Come here, Daian. Bring the thumbscrews, and let them have a taste. Then they may serve the wine."

"Oh, you scamp," Aixiang cried, "you have lifted me right off the ground."

"Listen!" Ximen cried, "we have not all the time in the world. Serve us with wine at once. I will wait no longer."

Wu Yin'er poured wine for Master Qiao, Zheng Aixiang for the elder of the Wu brothers and Yuchuan for the younger, then they went to the others in turn. When Wu Yin'er gave wine to Ying Bojue, he asked her why Guijie had not come.

"The Great Lady has accepted her as a ward," Wu Yin'er said. "I will tell you about it, Uncle, but please keep it to yourself. She is up to some trick. The other day, when we left here, we went home together and it was arranged that we should all come together early today. This morning I dressed and waited for her. I never dreamed she would buy some presents and come here by herself. The result was that we were all late. We sent our maid to call for her, and she was told that Guijie had gone. My mother was very angry. I don't see why she should not have told us that she was going to be made a ward. We couldn't do anything about it. But she made a great secret of it and, when we were in the inner court, she sat on the Great Lady's bed and fussed about to show off her new dignity. She cracked the nuts, set the fruit boxes in order, did this, that, and the other thing and kept us at our distance. I really don't know exactly how it all came about, but the Sixth Lady told me that Guijie had made a pair of shoes for the Great Lady, bought a box of fruitcakes, two ducks, a pair of large hams and two bottles of wine, and brought them with her in a sedan chair very early this morning."

"So now she will not come," he said. "Well, I will see that the little strumpet does come. It looks to me as though she had arranged all this with her mother. She knows that Ximen has been given an appointment; she is anxious now that he has become powerful, and afraid he may not go to their house quite so often. So, to make sure that their relationship continues, she gets herself made his ward. Isn't that it? Now here is some advice for you. She has persuaded the Great Lady to accept her as a ward.

Tomorrow, get a few presents yourself and come here and ask the Sixth Lady to adopt you. You and she are connected through your relationship with your dead Uncle Hua, and it will be well for you to keep together. Don't let Guijie think you are annoyed."

"You are right," Wu Yin'er said. "I will tell my mother as soon as I get home."

She took the wine pot to the next guest. Yuchuan poured wine for Ying Bojue. "Sister," he said, "this is very kind of you. Pray do not make a reverence to me. What is your sister doing at home?"

"My sister has been at home for a long time," Yuchuan said. "She has not been out singing. Her time has been fully taken up."

"I remember," Bojue continued, "that I enjoyed your hospitality in the fifth month, but since then I have not seen her."

"The other day, Uncle, you came but you would not stay. You insisted on going away early."

"Well, as it happened," Ying Bojue said, "there was a little dispute that day, and I had some business with your uncle. Except for that I should certainly have stayed longer."

Yuchuan saw that Ying Bojue had finished his cup of wine and poured out another for him.

"It must be only a little," he said, "I dare not drink any more."

"Drink it slowly, Uncle," the girl said, "and when you have finished, I will sing you a song."

"Sister," Bojue said, "you seem to do just what I would have you do. I wonder how it is. You remember the proverb that says: We do not wish our children to make water of silver, or desire that their excrement should be of gold. All we ask is that they should be ready to act as the occasion demands. There can be no doubt that a girl like you need never be anxious about her livelihood. You are much more agreeable than that little strumpet Zheng Aixiang. That piece of mischief is simply trying to get out of singing."

"Beggar Ying, are you feeling ill?" Aixiang said. "How dare you insult me?"

"You dog," said Ximen Qing," you persuaded her to sing, and now you are teasing her,"

"Oh, that is all dead and done with," Bojue said. "She is serving the wine now. I was bound to ask her to sing. Now here I have three *qian* of silver. I will hire the little strumpet to turn the millstone like a ghost."

Yuchuan took up her lute and sang a short song. Then Bojue asked Ximen why he did not send for Guijie.

"She is not here today," Ximen said.

"But I have just been told that she is singing in the inner court. Why do you tell me such a lie?"

He told Daian to go to the inner court and fetch her. Daian made no move.

"Uncle Ying," he said, "you are mistaken. It was someone else who was singing for my mistress in the inner court."

"You rascally young oily mouth," Bojue cried, "so you too try to deceive me. Very well, I will go myself."

Zhu Shinian said to Ximen Qing: "Brother, please send for Guijie and ask her to serve wine to all of us. We will not ask her to sing, for I understand she has gone up in the world."

Ximen Qing was finally compelled to give way. He sent Daian to summon Guijie.

When the boy came to the inner court, Li Guijie was in Yueniang's room, playing the lute and singing for the ladies there. She asked Daian who had told him to come for her.

"Father said I was to ask you to come and serve one round of wine to his guests. Then you can come straight back."

"Mother," Guijie said to Yueniang, "you see Father is quite mad. I told him I would not go and yet he sends for me.

"The others urged him," Daian said. "They persuaded him to send me."

"You had better go, and serve them all with wine once, then come back," Yueniang said.

"If it is really Father who wants me," Guijie said, "I will go, but if it is that Beggar Ying, nothing he can do will ever persuade me, not if I live for a thousand years." She stood before Yueniang's mirror, repainted her face, and went to the hall.

The guests all gazed at her. Upon her head was a hairnet of silver thread; her pins and combs were gilt, and masses of pearls and emeralds were piled upon her hair. She wore a coat of "Lotus root" thread and a skirt of green satin. Her tiny feet were shod in scarlet shoes. She wore emerald pendants upon her cheeks. A strange fragrance came from her scented body.

Guijie kowtowed once towards the table, but it was carelessly done. She held a gilded fan before her face, assumed an air of modesty and dallied with her ornaments. Then she came and stood before Ximen Qing. He ordered Daian to place a chair with a cushion for her and asked her to pour a cup of wine for Master Qiao. But Qiao bowed hastily and said: "I must not trouble you, but will you not serve these other honorable gentlemen?"

"Of course she must begin with you," Ximen said.

Guijie lightly fluttered her silken sleeves and, taking a golden cup, raised it high in the air and handed it to Qiao.

"Most worthy Qiao," Bojue said, "pray be seated and let her stand beside you. These powdery-faced girls from the Li's house, it is their duty to serve wine. You must not indulge them."

"But, my dear Ying the Second," Qiao said, "this young lady is now the daughter of our honorable host. How can I trouble her? It would embarrass me."

"Do not worry yourself," Bojue said; "now that our honorable host has become an officer, she is not content to be a strumpet any longer; she must be his ward."

Guijie flushed. "Are you mad that you talk such nonsense?"

"But is this true?" Xie Xida cried. "I had heard nothing of it. Now all here, without exception, must all give five *fen* of silver to celebrate the occasion."

"It is a great thing to be an officer," Bojue interrupted. "Ever since the beginning of things people have never been afraid of officers in general, but only of those with whom they come into close contact. Now his Lordship has taken her as his ward, we shall have to sprinkle water on her body to wash the filth away."

"You talk the most arrant nonsense," Ximen Qing cried.

"Perhaps," Bojue returned, "but you can make an excellent knife out of barbarian iron."

Zheng Aixiang was pouring wine for Uncle Shen. "Beggar Ying," she said, "Sister Guijie is now his Lordship's ward. I advise you to become his adopted son, but, if you would rather, you can doubtless assume a more ambiguous relationship.

Bojue cursed her. "You little whore! Do you wish to die? Wait till I start on you, and then you'd better say your prayers."

"Curse him for me, Sister Aixiang," Guijie said.

"Don't worry about that looking-towards-Jiangnan tiger from the Ba Mountain, beshitten pants from the Eastern Hills."

"You little strumpet," cried Bojue. "Now you are even using the 'Confucius said' to curse me. I have said nothing. I am just a white ghost. I will tear the girdle that holds up your mother's trousers. Wait until tomorrow and see if I don't show you what I can do. Otherwise you will have no respect for me. You won't treat the general as a god."

"We had better not bother about him any more," Guijie said, "Little Brother's going to be angry."

Aixiang smiled. "Ah, dear Beggar Ying," she said, "you are like the devil in a cart with a lot of ugly-looking melons, so ugly that there are even none for you."

"You little crooked bone," Bojue said, "I can't deal with you all at once. I shall have to give way."

"You funny little pocketknife," Guijie said, "nice clean lips you've got. You have already broken everybody else's gums. Father, I'm surprised you don't beat him instead of sitting there, watching his naughty tricks."

Ximen Qing scolded him. "You dog, I asked her to come and pour wine, and you have no business to make game of her." He went over and slapped Ying Bojue.

"You thievish little strumpet. You simply depend upon your father's authority. Do you think I am afraid of you? Look at you, the heartfelt way you call him 'Father.'" Then he added: "Don't let her pass the wine. It is too good a job for her. Let us have the musical instruments and she shall sing a song for us. She has spent quite long enough in the inner court."

"Uncle," Yuchuan said, "you are like the soldier who came from Caozhou, managing everything the way you do."

So they drank wine and played and joked together.

After the birth of a son to Li Ping'er, Jinlian saw that Ximen Qing always slept in the Sixth Lady's apartments. She could not rid herself of her jealousy, and constantly thought of revenge. today she knew that Ximen Qing was entertaining guests in the front hall, and she stood before her toilet table painting her moth-like eyebrows carefully, dressing and redressing her hair, and putting a touch of color on her lips. Then she arranged her dress and went out from her room. As she passed Li Ping'er's room, she heard the baby crying. She went in and asked what was the matter with him.

"His mother has gone to the inner court," the nurse, Ruyi'er, said. "He wants her, and cries."

Jinlian smiled, went forward, and patted the baby.

"You are a real little man already," she said, "wanting your mother even at your age. Let us go to the inner court to find her."

"Fifth Mother," Ruyi'er said, "you had better not take him. He will make your clothes dirty."

Nonsense," Jinlian said, "I will put some more clothes on. It will be no trouble at all." She took the child to her breast, and went off with him to the inner court. When she reached the second door, she lifted him high in the air. Yueniang was sitting underneath the eaves, watching the maids and women cooking and changing the dishes. Jinlian looked at the baby, and smiled.

"Mother," she said, "what are you doing? The baby has come to look for his mother."

Yueniang looked at him. "Fifth Sister," she said, "what are you thinking about? His mother was not in her room, but you should not have brought him out. And why carry him up in the air like that? He will be frightened. His mother is inside, busy." She called to Li Ping'er and told her that her son had come to see her.

Li Ping'er hastily came out. When she saw Jinlian with the child, she said: "Oh, baby, you were quite happy with your nurse. Why should you want me? You will make your Fifth Mother's clothes dirty."

"He was crying," Jinlian said. "He wanted you, so I brought him along."

Li Ping'er opened her clothes and took the child. For a while, Yueniang played with him. Then she told his mother to take him to her own room, and be careful lest he should be frightened.

When Li Ping'er came to her own room, she said to Ruyi'er: "If the baby was crying, you should have done something to keep him quiet, and waited for me to come. Why did you get the Fifth Lady to bring him to the inner court?"

"I told her she should not do so," Ruyi'er said, "but she would not listen to me."

Li Ping'er watched the nurse feeding the child, and at last he went to sleep. Before he had been asleep very long, he woke from his dreams with a cry. In the middle of the night, he seemed first hot and then cold, and refused to take his nurse's milk. He would do nothing but cry, and Li Ping'er was alarmed about him.

When the party in the front court was over, Ximen Qing dismissed the four singers. Yueniang gave Guijie a dress of heavy silk and two taels of silver.

During the evening, Ximen Qing went to the rooms of Li Ping'er to see his son. The child was crying, but when he asked the reason, Li Ping'er did not tell him that Jinlian had taken him to the inner court.

"I don't know," she said, "what has made him cry and refuse to take his milk."

"Give him a few gentle pats," Ximen said. "That will make him sleep." Then he scolded the nurse. "You have not been careful enough of him. What have you been thinking about? You must have frightened him."

He went to the inner court to tell Yueniang. She, too, realized that the child had been frightened when Jinlian brought him to her room, yet she did not breathe a word of this to her husband. "I will send for old woman Liu tomorrow," she said, "she can look at him."

"You mustn't think of sending for that old rogue," Ximen said, "she will use the needle and the flame without hesitating. We must get the royal children's doctor to come and examine him."

Yueniang did not agree. "The child is only a month old," she said. "A doctor can't do him any good."

The next day, Ximen Qing went to his office and Yueniang told one of the boys to go for old woman Liu. The old woman said that the child had had a fright, and they gave her three *qian* of silver to make some soothing medicine for him. When he had taken the medicine, the boy slept quietly and kept down his milk. Li Ping'er smiled as though she felt like a stone that has come to rest at last upon the ground.

Chapter 33

Han Daoguo and His Wife

As soon as Ximen Qing reached home, he hurried to Wu Yueniang to ask if his little son was better. The doctor must be sent for at once, he said. But Yueniang told him that it was not necessary. She had sent for old woman Liu, and the baby, now that he had taken the medicine she had prepared, was sleeping peacefully and able to retain his food.

"I can't understand your faith in that old hag," Ximen cried. "She is far too ready with her lancings and cauteries. We ought to have the specialist who attends the children of the Royal House. If the child really is better, well and good, but if he is not, I'll have that old woman at the court and let her fingers feel the screws."

"How unreasonable you are with your scoldings and threats," Yueniang said. "I tell you the baby is much better now that he has taken her medicine. Why do you make all this fuss?"

A maid brought something to eat, and Ximen Qing was finishing it when Daian said that Ying Bojue had come. Ximen told one of the boys to take tea to the arbor and said he would join his friend there. He asked Yueniang to have the remaining dishes sent out to them. He sent for Chen Jingji to keep them company, saying that he himself would be there in a moment.

"Where did Ying the Second go for you yesterday, and what has brought him here again today?" Yueniang said.

Ximen told her. "Brother Ying knows a stranger from Huzhou called He who has five hundred taels' worth of raw silk and thread at an inn outside the city gate. He is in a hurry to go home and is prepared to sell his goods cheaply. I offered to pay four hundred and fifty taels and sent Laibao with Ying yesterday to let him see two bars of my silver as samples. The business was settled, and we are to pay for the goods today. The house in Lion Street is empty, and I propose to take two rooms on the street, set them in order, and open a shop there. Now that Laibao has got this appointment in Duke Yun's palace, I must look out for another manager, and arrange for him and one of the boys to keep the shop and look after the house at the same time."

Wu Yueniang agreed. Ximen said: "Brother Ying says he has a friend called Han who knows all there is to know about the thread business, but he has no money of his own and, for the moment, is out of work. Brother Ying says he is a capable business man, honest and straightforward; in fact, he recommends him very strongly. He is going to bring Han to see me, and we will fix up a contract."

He weighed the four hundred and fifty taels of silver and told Laibao to take them. Meanwhile Chen Jingji and Ying Bojue finished their meal in the arbor in a state of anxious impatience. They felt much happier when they saw the silver on the way. When Ximen Qing came, Bojue made a reverence to him and apologized for being late. He said that, after enjoying such hospitality the day before, he had found it hard to get up that morning.

"Well," Ximen said, "here are the four hundred and fifty taels. Laibao shall put them into a big sack. This is a day of happy omen, and I will hire a cart to bring back the goods, and put them away safely."

"You are very wise, Brother," Bojue said. "If we waste any time, I shouldn't be surprised to find that shifty fellow playing a trick on us. But if we get the stuff away, all will be well."

He and Laibao mounted their horses and went with the silver to the stranger's inn, and completed the transaction. As a matter of fact, Ying Bojue had made an arrangement of his own with He that the actual price should be four hundred and twenty taels, so that he got thirty taels for himself. He shared with Laibao the regular commission of five taels. They hired a cart and brought the merchandise to the city. They stored everything in the empty house in Lion Street, locked the door, and returned to give an account to Ximen Qing, who told Bojue to bring Han to see him on the next auspicious day.

Han was a short man, about thirty years of age, unguarded of speech and of a lively temperament. When Ximen Qing had made a contract with him, he and Laibao were given some money to engage workers to dye the thread. When everything was ready, the shop in Lion Street was opened, and there they dealt in threads of many colors, selling considerable quantities every day.

The time passed quickly. The sun and moon crossed and recrossed like the shuttles of a weaver. It was the fifteenth day of the eighth month, Wu Yueniang's birthday. A number of ladies had been invited, and Aunt Wu, Aunt Yang and old woman Pan were there. Two nuns were among the guests, and at night they used to recite the Buddhist scriptures for the edification of the others, continuing till the second or third night watch.

Ximen Qing, hearing that Aunt Wu was in Yueniang's room, did not go there, but to the apartments of Li Ping'er. She told him she was still anxious about the child, and suggested that he should go to Pan Jinlian instead. Ximen smiled, said he did not wish to be a nuisance, and did as he was told.

When Jinlian found her husband was coming, she was delighted. She might have discovered a hidden treasure. She hurriedly packed off her mother to sleep in one of the rooms belonging to Li Ping'er, lighted the silver lamp, delicately spread and smoothed the silken bedclothes, and perfumed her body daintily. She made the most intimate of preparations and awaited her master's pleasure.

That night they took their pleasure to the full. Jinlian was determined to gain possession of her husband's heart, so that he should go no more to the rooms of the others. He was like a wandering bee, stretching forth his proboscis among the tender petals that the winds of spring bestirred, or a flower-devouring butterfly, reveling by night within the deepest recesses of the blossoms.

When old woman Pan came, Li Ping'er asked her to come and sit on the bed, and told Yingchun to bring some refreshments. They talked till the night was late, and, the next morning, she gave the old lady a gown of white silk, two pieces of satin with which to make shoes, and a small sum of money. The old woman smiled and beamed delightedly. She took the things and showed them to her daughter. Jinlian said: "Mother, your eyes are too small and your skin too thin. How can you take gifts from her?"

"My good child," the old woman said, "other people are sorry for me and give me things. Why should you talk like this? What do you ever give me?"

"I have nothing to give you," Jinlian said. "You cannot compare me with the others. How can I possibly give you clothes when I have none to wear myself? But you go and accept favors from outsiders, and I shall have to get something ready—a few dishes and some wine, I suppose—and send them in return. If I don't, something will be said, and I can't have that."

She told Chunmei to prepare eight dishes, four boxes of fruits, and a jar of wine; then, seeing that Ximen Qing had gone, she ordered Qiuju to put them on a square tray and take them to Li Ping'er. "My mother and my grandmother," she was to say, "have nothing to do at the moment and would very much like to come and take wine with you."

Li Ping'er thanked her, and, in a few moments, Jinlian and old woman Pan came. When all three had taken their places, the wine was poured out and they talked together while Chunmei stood at hand to serve them.

Suddenly Qiuju came. "Brother-in-law is trying to find some clothes," she said to Chunmei. "He wants you to go and open the door of the room upstairs."

"When he has found the clothes," Jinlian said, "ask him to come here and take a cup of wine with us."

But when Chen Jingji had taken the clothes he wanted—they belonged to several different people—he hurried away, and Chunmei had to return to tell Jinlian that he would not come.

"He must come," the woman cried. She sent one of the maids for him. At last he did come and made a reverence to them.

Jinlian scolded him. "I was kind enough to send and invite you to take wine with us. Why wouldn't you come? Your luck will fail you." She told Chunmei to bring Jingji a large cup of wine. He put the clothes on the bed and sat down. Chunmei thought she would play a trick on him and brought a large bowl such as is used for tea and filled it to the brim with wine. Jingji was taken aback.

"Fifth Mother," he said, "if you insist upon my taking wine with you, I should much prefer a small cup. There are several people in the shop waiting for their clothes."

"Let them wait," Jinlian said. "I insist upon your drinking this large cup. A small cup will not do at all."

"Let our brother off with this one cup," old woman Pan said. "Perhaps his business is pressing."

"Don't believe a word he says," Jinlian cried. "What does he mean by being busy? He can drink good wine. If we gave him a pail of gold, he would drink it down to the second rib."

Jingji laughed and took the cup. Before he had drunk three mouthfuls, the old woman said to Chunmei: "Give your brother a pair of chopsticks. We can't have him drinking 'widow' wine."

Chunmei did not give him the chopsticks but, as a joke, took a couple of walnuts from the box and handed them to him.

"You think I can't crack them, do you?" he said, laughing, and putting them in his mouth, he broke them with one bite and ate them with his wine.

"You seem to have very good teeth still, young man," old woman Pan said, "I can't eat things that are at all hard, myself."

"There are only two things I can't eat," Jingji said: "stones like goose's eggs and ox horns."

Jinlian saw that he had finished his wine and told Chunmei to give him another cup. "The first cup was of my offering," said she. "You can't consider my mother and the Sixth Lady of less importance than myself. I don't wish to make you drink too much, so drink three cups and I will let you go."

"Really, Fifth Mother," Jingji said, "you must have mercy on me. I can't possibly drink any more. This cup I have already taken has made my face so red that I am afraid Father will be angry when he sees me."

"Are you afraid of your father?" Jinlian said. "I think not. By the way, where is he taking wine today?"

"He went to Master Wu's house this afternoon," Jingji said, "but now he is looking after the alterations that are being made in the house which used to belong to the Qiaos."

"They moved yesterday, didn't they?" Jinlian said. "Why haven't we sent them a present of tea?" Jingji told her that the tea had been sent that morning. Then Li Ping'er asked where they had gone. Jingji said that they had bought a very large house, as large in fact as Ximen's own, in the High Street. It had a frontage to the street of seven rooms and was five rooms deep. They went on talking and Jingji held his nose and swallowed another cup. Then, while Jinlian had her head turned away for a moment, he snatched the clothes from the bed and vanished like a cloud of smoke.

"Mother," Yingchun said, "he has gone off and forgotten to take the key." Jinlian took it and put it beneath her. "When he comes back to look for it," she said to Li Ping'er, "don't say a word. We will have some fun with him before I give it back."

"Don't tease him, Sister," old woman Pan said. "Give it to him."

Chen Jingji went back to the shop. He searched his sleeves and, of course, could not find the key. Finally he went back to Jinlian's room.

"Who's seen your old key?" she said. "What are you thinking about, putting it somewhere and then forgetting where you put it?"

"You must have left it in the room upstairs," Chunmei said.

"No," Jingji said, "I remember having it here."

"Ah, young man," Jinlian said, "the trouble with you is that a certain part of you is so large that you lose your brains when you really mean to get rid of something quite different. I wonder who it is, here or elsewhere, who makes you so absent-minded that your intelligence has got completely out of place."

"There are customers waiting for their clothes," Jingji said distractedly. "What shall I do? Father is not here, and I shall have to go and get a locksmith to force the door. Then we shall find out whether I left the key inside or not."

Li Ping'er could not help laughing. "Sixth Mother," Jingji cried, "you've picked it up. Do give it to me."

"I don't know what you're laughing about," Jinlian said. "You make it look as though we had his keys." Jingji became as excited as an ox prancing around a millstone. He looked at Jinlian and caught sight of the key string sticking out from beneath her.

"There's my key," he cried, but, before he could take it, she whipped it into her sleeve. She still refused to give it up.

"How can I possibly have your key?" she said. The young man was all of a flutter, like a chicken about to be killed stretching out its legs.

"They tell me," Jinlian said, "that you have a very sweet voice, and that you often sing for the boys in the shop. Why shouldn't you sing a song for me? Grandmother and the Sixth Lady are here, so you had better choose one of the latest and best. Then you shall have your key. If you will not sing, you may jump as far as the White Pagoda, but nothing shall induce me to give it to you."

So the young man was compelled to obey. "Very well," said he, "I do not propose to lose my life for it, so I will sing. As a matter of fact, I have such a stock of songs that I can sing you a hundred if you like."

"Boastful, short-lived rascal!" Jinlian said. She poured wine for all of them, saying to Jingji: "You had better take one more cup and then you will not be too shy to sing."

"No," Jingji said, "I'll finish the song first, and then I'll drink."

When he had done, he again asked Jinlian to give him the key. "Mother," he said, "give me the key now. I don't know what the clerks in the shop are doing, and Father may come at any moment."

"You think too much of yourself," Jinlian said, "and your tongue is too ready. If your father does come, and says anything to me about it, I shall tell him you got drunk, lost the key, and came here to look for it."

"Dear, dear!" cried Jingji "You might be an executioner, the way you play with your wretched victim." Then Li Ping'er and old woman Pan took pity on him and pleaded for him with Jinlian.

"If Grandmother and the Sixth Lady had not asked me," she said, "I would have made you sing till the sun went down. You have boasted that you know a hundred or two hundred songs, but so far you have only sung one. Yet you begin to spread your wings to take flight. I won't let you get the better of me."

Chen Jingji offered to sing another song. He had just finished it, and Jinlian was telling Chunmei to pour out another cup of wine for him, when Yueniang suddenly came from the inner court. Ruyi'er was sitting on the stone steps outside the door with Guan'ge in her arms. Yueniang scolded her.

"The baby is just getting a little better, and here you have him in a draft. Take him in at once."

Jinlian heard the voice and said: "Who is that?" One of the maids told her that Yueniang was coming. This put Jingji in a flurry. He hastily picked up the key and made for the door, but it was too late. The ladies were on their way to receive Yueniang.

"What are you doing here, Brother Chen?" she said.

Jinlian answered for him. "The Sixth Lady," she said, "was kind enough to entertain my mother, and brother-in-law came to look for some clothes. We asked him to take a cup of wine with us. Great Sister, will you not sit down too, and drink something? The wine is very mellow."

"I must not stay to drink," Yueniang said. "My sister-in-law and Aunt Yang are getting ready to go. I came to ask after the baby. I am anxious about him. Sister, why don't you take better care of him, instead of allowing the nurse to have him in a draft? The other day old woman Liu told us that he had a bad chill. You really must be more careful."

"I was taking a little wine with Grandmother," Li Ping'er said. "I never dreamed the rascally slave would take him out."

Yueniang stayed with them a few moments and then went again to the inner court. She sent Xiaoyu to ask the two ladies and old woman Pan to come. Jinlian and Li Ping'er powdered their faces and went with the old woman to the inner court. They drank wine with the two aunts until sunset. Then Yueniang and the others went with their guests to the gate and saw them off in their sedan chairs.

As they were standing at the gate, Meng Yulou said: "Great Sister, Father is not at home. He has gone to a banquet at Master Wu's. Why should we not go and have a look at Qiao's house on the other side of the road?" Yueniang asked the gatekeeper for the key and was told that Laixing was in the house watching the laborers at their work.

"Tell them to withdraw," Yueniang said. "We wish to see it."

"Oh, Mother," Ping'an said, "just go over. They are all busy sifting the sand in the fourth big room." Yueniang and the others were carried across in their chairs. They went in, and found themselves in a large hall. The house had two stories, and Yueniang decided to go upstairs. She had hardly gone halfway—the stairs were very steep—when she missed a step. She slipped and cried "Ah!" Then she gripped the banisters on either side. Yulou was startled and asked what was the matter, grasping one of Yueniang's arms to prevent her from falling. Yueniang was frightened. She would go no farther, and the others helped her down the stairs again. Her face was as pale as wax. Yulou said: "What made you slip, Great Sister? Have you hurt yourself?"

"No," Yueniang said, "I didn't fall, but I wrenched my waist. It gave me such a fright that my heart is in my mouth even yet. It is because the stairs are so steep. I was thinking of those in our own house, and I missed one. Luckily I was able to take hold of the railing, or I don't know what would have happened to me."

"We really ought not to have gone upstairs with you in your present condition," Li Jiao'er said. They took Yueniang home, but, when they were back, she cried that the pains in her belly were so severe she could not endure them. Ximen Qing had not yet returned, and they told a boy to run for old woman Liu.

"I am afraid you have hurt the baby," old woman Liu said. "Indeed, in my opinion the damage is fatal."

"I am more than five months on the way," Yueniang said, "and now I have slipped on the stairs and given myself a wrench."

The old woman suggested that, as it was too late to save the child, Yueniang should take some medicine and get rid of it. When Yueniang agreed, the old woman gave her two big black pills and told her to take them with a little herb wine. Just before midnight the medicine took effect and the child was delivered into one of the pails used for the horses. They took a light to look at it and found that it would have been a boy. Indeed, it was already a boy. Its shape was that of a perfect male child.

Fortunately, Ximen Qing had decided to spend the night with Yulou. The next morning, Yulou came to see Yueniang and asked how she felt. Yueniang told her the whole story.

"It is very sad," Yulou said. "Does Father know?"

"No," Yueniang said. "After the party he came to my room. He was going to take off his clothes, but I told him I did not feel very well and asked him to go somewhere else. Then he went to you. I said nothing to him about it. There is still a little pain."

"Perhaps you have not got rid of all the blood," Yulou said. "I think, if we had some wine heated and you take some medicine to warm you, you will soon be well again. But you must be careful for a few days, Sister, and keep to your room. You see, these miscarriages take longer to recover from than a regular birth. You must take particular care not to catch cold or you will be really ill."

"You are quite right," Yueniang said. "Don't mention the matter to anybody, for, if you do, the news will be spread abroad; people will talk of my 'nest being empty,' and everybody will have some comment to make." Nothing was said to Ximen Qing about the matter.

Clerk Han, whom Ximen Qing had recently engaged, was anything but a reliable character. He was the son of a needy fellow whom people nicknamed Han the Bald, and his personal name was Daoguo. He was a poor man, though there had been a time when he had served in Duke Yun's guard, a post that his grandfather had held before him. Now he was constrained to live in a mean alley off East Street. Though he was nothing but a man of straw, he had a good deal to say for himself, did not spare his words, and was careful to watch which way the wind blew. Trying to get money out of him was as futile as grasping at a shadow, or trying to lay hold of the wind, but, when he himself was getting money from anyone else, his hand burrowed far into the sack. Now that he had secured a post with Ximen Qing, he put on extra swagger. He had some clothes made, lifted his shoulders higher, and strolled jauntily through the streets. People changed his name to Show-off Han in consequence. His wife was a sister of Butcher Wang, the sixth in the family. She was tall, her face was dark and shaped like a melon seed; she was about twenty-eight years old. They had a little daughter. Han's younger brother, Han the Second, was known as Han the Trickster and belonged to one of the regular gambling sets. This young man had long made love to his brother's wife, and whenever Han Daoguo had gone to attend to the shop, he would come to the house and drink with his sister-in-law. He often stayed all night.

There were several high-spirited young fellows among the neighbors. They saw the woman painted and powdered, standing in her fine dresses at the door and ogling the passersby. Yet whenever they tried to make advances, they found her unkind and unresponsive. Indeed, she was so unsparing of her tongue that her young neighbors became irritated. In twos and threes they discussed the situation, and made up their minds to find out who was the favored suitor. It did not take them long to discover that it was her young brother-in-law.

Three rooms of the Hans' house looked upon the street; the rest of the house was bounded by the houses of the neighbors. At the back was a raised bank, and from this the young men watched, climbing upon the wall at night to look in. Sometimes, during the day, they would pretend to be catching butterflies on the bank, but actually they were trying to discover what was going on in the house. One day, Han the Second, knowing that his brother was out, bought some wine and took it to drink with his sister-in-law. They bolted the door and prepared to have a very merry time. But the young men were on the track, climbed over the wall, opened the back door, and all went in. When they burst open the door of the room, Han the Second tried to escape, but one of the young men knocked him down with a single blow. The woman was still upon the bed. She had no time to put on her clothes before one of the young ruffians was able to secure them. They bound the couple together with one cord. Before long the news spread all down the street and a crowd gathered before the door. While one asked what was amiss, another would go to have a look. In the crowd was an old man who, seeing the man and woman tied together, asked what was the matter. One of the more garrulous of the bystanders informed him.

"Venerable Sir," he said, "you may not know, but this is a case of un-lawful relationship between a man and his elder brother's wife."

"Dear, dear," the old man said, nodding his head, "a younger brother and his sister-in-law indeed. I fear they will have their necks stretched when the matter comes before the courts."

Unfortunately, the garrulous fellow knew all about the old man's rep-utation. He had three daughters-in-law, and his relations with all of them had been such that he had been given a rude nickname in consequence.

"Venerable Sir," the fellow said, "doubtless no one is better acquainted than yourself with the law on such matters. As you say, their necks will be stretched. But I wonder what is the punishment dealt out to a man who carries on with his sons' wives."

The old man decided that the conversation was taking an inconvenient turn. He bowed his head and went off without another word.

That day it was not Han Daoguo's turn to stay late at the shop, and he left for home early. It was about the middle of the eighth month and he was wearing a light silk gown and a new hat. Whisking his fan about and walking along the street with an air of consequence, he stopped now and again to exchange a few words with his friends, babbling away like a flowing brook. Then he chanced to meet two of his friends, one a certain Zhang the Second, who kept a paper shop, the other Bai the Fourth, a silversmith.

"Brother Han," Zhang said, "it is quite a while since I last met you. I hear you are now set up in a splendid establishment belonging to his Lord-ship Ximen Qing. It shows, I fear, a great lack of courtesy on my part that I have been so remiss in offering my hearty congratulations. Pray forgive me." He invited Han to take a seat.

Han Daoguo sat down on a bench, lifted up his head and fanned himself importantly. "Indeed," he said, "I recognize my own little worth. I place all my confidence in the generosity of others. That is how I have entered the service of my gracious master Ximen. We share the profits in the proportion of three to seven. His wealth is truly immense and he has numerous establishments of one sort and another. He thinks much of me and treats me on a different footing from others."

"I was given to understand," Bai the Fourth said, "that you were selling thread for him."

Han Daoguo smiled. "You don't understand, my dear brother. The thread business is only a sideline. As a matter of fact, I am in charge, and all the money that comes in and goes out passes through my hands. His Lordship always takes my advice and falls in with all my suggestions. Whatever the fates have in store, whether good fortune or ill, we meet it hand in hand. Why, he can't exist a single moment without me. Every day, when he comes back from his official duties, he sends and asks me to dine with him. Without my company he has not the heart to eat. We spend our time in his retiring room, eating and chatting at our ease, till the night is very late and he goes to the ladies' apartments. It was his lady's birthday the other day, and my wife went in a sedan chair to the party. Ximen's lady kept her so late that it was the second night watch before she returned.

"Ximen and I, in fact, are bosom friends, and there are no secrets between us. Perhaps I should not say so, but he even goes so far as to tell me all that happens on the most intimate occasions. Such things, indeed, form one of the most frequent subjects of conversation between us.

"I must say, of course, that I have always acted strictly as a man of honor, and have never been guilty of any kind of indiscretion. My sole desire has been to assist a man of high standing to acquire more wealth, with the object of succoring those in need and rescuing the drowning and the afflicted. In money matters, no matter what their nature, my hands are clean. Long ago I made up my mind that all my actions in such affairs should be strictly in accordance with the highest standards of probity. Even Fu cannot disregard my wishes. Please understand: I do not mean this as a boast; all I do is to carry out my master's wishes."

The conversation was proceeding pleasantly when a man rushed up in a great state of excitement. "What, Brother Han," he cried, "are you still gossiping here? I have been to the shop for you but missed you." He dragged Han Daoguo to a quiet corner and told him all that had been happening at home. "You will have to bestir yourself," he said, "and find somebody to get the matter settled. They are to come before the courts tomorrow morning."

Han Daoguo changed color. He sucked his tongue and stamped about, only wishing he could take wing and fly away. "Old Brother Han," cried Zhang, "why are you going? We haven't finished talking." Han raised his hands. "His Lordship is waiting for me. We have some important business to transact, and I am afraid I must leave you." He hurried away.

CHAPTER 34

Ximen Qing Administers Justice

Han Daoguo hastened to the Town Hall to see what he could find out. There he discovered that his wife and brother had both been thrown into prison.

He rushed back to the shop to ask Laibao's advice. "If I were you," Laibao said, "I should go and ask Uncle Ying to speak to our master about it. If he sends a card to the magistrate, I'm sure everything will be well, no matter how serious the case."

Han Daoguo went straight to Ying Bojue's house. He was told that Ying was out and nobody knew where he had gone. Perhaps he was at Ximen's house. Han said this was not so, and asked for Ying Bao. Ying Bao had gone with Bojue. This was very disturbing. Han decided to go and look for his man in the bawdy house. He the Second, the brother of He of Huzhou, had invited Ying Bojue to a party at a house in the Fourth Lane, and there Han Daoguo found him, well filled with wine, and red in the face. He took him aside and told him all his troubles.

"You are in a very serious position," Bojue said. "I can't do less than go with you." He said good-bye to He, and went with Han to his house, where he asked for all the details of the story.

"I very much fear," Han Daoguo said earnestly, "that the case will come up tomorrow. I can see only one means of escape, and that is if you will go to my master and ask him for a card to the magistrate. If all goes well, I will not forget you." He knelt down before Ying Bojue.

"My good lad," Bojue said, pulling him up, "of course I'll see what I can do for you. Write out a petition and don't say anything that isn't necessary. Say that you are often away from home, and, during your absence, a number of young scamps among your neighbors are always throwing bricks and tiles, and insulting your wife. This enraged your brother and he had a row with them, but, unfortunately, they seized him, kicked, pulled, and beat him, and finally tied him and your wife together. Then ask his Lordship to send a card to the magistrate to ask that your wife shall not be compelled to appear before the court. I am sure all will be well."

Han Daoguo took brush and ink, wrote quickly, and put the paper in his sleeve. Then Bojue went with him to call upon Ximen Qing. When they reached the house, they asked Ping'an, the doorkeeper, if his master was at home. "He is in his study in the garden," Ping'an said. "Please go straight in." Ying Bojue's visits to the house were so frequent that the dogs had ceased to bark at him. They went in by the second door, passed through the hall, and came to the Kingfisher Hall. Here Ximen Qing was wont to seek coolness in the hot summer days. There were blinds and curtains on both sides, flowers everywhere, and bamboo trees spread a pleasant cool shade. Huatong was sweeping the floor. When he saw the two men, he cried: "Uncle Ying and Uncle Han are here." They pulled up the blind and went in. Shutong asked them to be seated. "My father has just gone to the inner court," he said. Then he told Huatong to go and find Ximen Qing.

The boy went first to Jinlian's room and asked Chunmei if his master was there. Chunmei called him a thievish, deceitful little slave. "Father is in the Sixth Lady's room on the other side. You know that well enough. Why do you come here and ask?" The boy then went to the other side of the court. The maid Xiuchun was sitting on the steps. "Uncle Ying and Uncle Han are here," he said. "They are waiting for Father to come and talk to them."

"He is in the room," Xiuchun said, "watching my mistress make some clothes for the baby."

Ximen had taken two rolls of material, one of scarlet linen, and the other of light parrot-green silk, so that Li Ping'er might make some little shirts, a little gown, a vest and a hat for Guan'ge. They had laid a cover on the bed. The nurse was there with the baby, and Yingchun was ready with an iron. Xiuchun went in and quietly pulled the other maid's sleeve.

"Don't pull me," Yingchun said, "I shall drop the iron." Xiuchun told her that Huatong had come to say Master Ying wished to speak with his master.

"You naughty little slave," Li Ping'er said, "if Uncle Ying is here, why didn't you come and say so instead of pulling Yingchun by the sleeve?"

Ximen Qing told the boy to ask the two men to wait: he would join them in a few moments. He watched the women finish cutting out the clothes, and went to the study in his ordinary dress. When he had greeted Bojue, they sat down to take tea. Han Daoguo sat facing them. At last Ying Bojue said: "Brother Han, you have, I think, something to say. Pray tell his Lordship what it is."

Han Daoguo had just begun to say that certain wicked neighbors of his, whose names he didn't know . . . , when Bojue interrupted him. "My dear boy," he said, "you are going the wrong way about it. You shouldn't wrap up the bones of the affair, and simply show the flesh. Be perfectly frank. Brother Han has been spending most of his time at the shop. There was no one to look after his house except his wife and his little daughter. The neighbors are not by any means what they should be, and, when they saw that there was no man in the place, they began to throw bricks and tiles, and play tricks generally. His worthy younger brother, Han the Second, found this sort of behavior to be too much. He came to the house and told the rascals what he thought about them. Then they all set upon him, beat him nearly to death, and finally seized him and shut him up in jail. Now he has to appear before the magistrate in the morning. Brother Han came to me and wept and asked me to beg you to send a card to his Worship so that his reputation might in some degree be saved. If only his brother goes before the magistrate, it will not be so bad, but his wife should not be allowed to appear." He said to Han Daoguo: "Let your master see the paper you have written. Then he will send a man to get the matter arranged for you."

Han hastily took the paper from his sleeve, and knelt down before Ximen. "I have had the good fortune to be employed in this household," he said. "Will you not, for Master Ying's sake, deign to do something for me, and I and all my house will not forget your kindness so long as the teeth are in our mouths."

Ximen Qing pulled him up and read the paper. "The accused woman Wang," it said, "implored you of your goodness, to withdraw the prosecution." "That is not how you should write it," Ximen said. "Mention your brother only." He said to Ying Bojue: "I will certainly send a card to the court, but I think a much better plan would be to arrange for the charge to be altered so that the young man appears before me."

"Brother Han," Ying Bojue said, "your master's idea is excellent. You should make a reverence to him." Han Daoguo knelt down again and kowtowed.

Ximen ordered Daian to go at once for the officer of the police on duty, and, in a little while, a policeman in black clothes was ready in attendance. Ximen Qing called him forward. "Go to Han's house and find out to which quarter of the town it belongs. Then go to the officer of that quarter and tell him that it is my order that he shall release Mistress Han forthwith. Afterwards, take the names of the young men concerned, make the necessary alterations in the charge sheet, and see that all the rascals are brought to my court tomorrow for examination.

The officer went away. "Brother Han," Bojue said, "you had better go with him and see after things. I have something else to talk to his Lordship about."

Han Daoguo repeatedly thanked them both and went home with the policeman.

Ximen Qing and Bojue sat in the Kingfisher Hall, and Ximen told Daian to go to the Great Lady and ask for the wine that Eunuch Liu had sent. He was to ask for the mackerel too. Hearing the word "mackerel," Bojue lifted his hands.

"Oh dear," he said, "I haven't thanked you yet. Those two mackerel you sent me yesterday were excellent. I sent one of them to my brother, and told my wife to send a portion of the other to our dear daughter. The rest she minced, put in sweet oil and preserved in a porcelain jar, so that I may have some to eat whenever I feel like it, and if a friend should call, he too may have a little and participate in your generosity."

Ximen told him how the fish had been given him. "Liu Bohu," he said, "Eunuch Liu's brother, has done pretty well out of the Imperial osier beds. A short time ago he built a house at Wulitian. Unfortunately, he used the imperial timber to build his house, and Magistrate Xia, who, as you know, is a colleague of mine, got to know about it. Not only did he propose to fine Liu a hundred taels but also to send the papers to the Provincial Courts. This was very distressing to Eunuch Liu, and he came to see me about it. He brought a hundred taels with him and said there was nothing he desired more than to see the matter ended. Now I don't mind telling you, I don't do so badly out of my business, and the money he offered was nothing to me. Eunuch Liu is a friend of mine: we see a good deal of one another and he often gives me presents. When he asked me to help him, I could hardly turn a deaf ear. But I wouldn't touch a penny of his money. I told them to pull the house down as fast as they could. Liu the Third's servant was beaten forty stripes and that was the end of the matter. Eunuch Liu was very grateful. He killed a pig and sent it with a jar of lotus wine of his own brewing, two fish, about forty *jin* in weight, and two rolls of flowered silk, with gold embroidery. He came in person to thank me, and each of us appreciated the advantages of friendship a little better than we had done before."

"Brother," Ying Bojue said, "money means very little to you, but Xia has been a soldier. He has never had anything of his own, and now he must make what he can. Have you had much to do with him since you have held your present post?"

"We have tried a few cases together, some great, some small. On the whole he is fair enough, but he is too fond of taking little presents. To him, so long as he gets his fee, all cases are of the same complexion, and the parties are set free. It is quite contrary to justice, and I have protested several times. We are both, as I tell him, officials of no very high degree, yet we represent the law and we should maintain its dignity."

When wine and dishes had been set before them, Ximen poured the lotus wine into a golden cup. They drank together and chatted till after the first night watch.

Meanwhile the black-robed policeman did as he had been told. Han's wife was set free and allowed to go home. The officer in charge of the records was sent for; the young men's names were taken down and they were ordered to appear before the court the following morning. Then they began to look at one another. They knew that Han Daoguo was employed by Ximen Qing, and realized that he had secured Ximen's help. They saw that Han the Second alone was detained, and began to think that the matter would end badly for them.

The next day, Ximen Qing and Xia took their places in the great hall and the police brought in the culprits. Han the Second came first and knelt down before the dais. Xia read the charge.

"Ox Hide Alley, in the fourth quarter of the first ward. officer of the Records Xiu Zheng reports a breach of the peace by the following, Han the Second, Che Dan, Guan Shikuan, Yu Shou and Hao Xian."

He asked Han the Second how the trouble began.

"My brother is a tradesman," Han the Second said, "and he is seldom at home. Only a young girl and myself were there. There are a number of young ruffians living about there, and they used to gather around the door and sing lewd songs. At night they used to throw bricks at us and insult us in every conceivable way. One day when I was at my brother's house, I found these insults more than I could stand, and said a few words to that effect. The scoundrels would not listen to me. They threw me on the ground, kicked, and struck me. And now we are all before you. I pray, Sir, that you will establish the truth of the matter."

Xia asked the others what they had to say. "Your Worship," they cried, "do not believe these cunning stories. Han the Second is a gambler and a rogue. When his brother was out, he made love to his sister-in-law. As for her, she is always trying to show how clever she is and insulting her neighbors. Yesterday we caught them in the act, and her trousers are here for evidence."

At this, Xia asked the policeman why Mistress Han was not before the court. The policeman did not dare to say she had been released, so he said her feet were so small that she could only walk slowly and would come later. Han the Second looked at Ximen Qing. A few moments later, Ximen bowed to Xia. "Your Worship," he said, "it seems hardly necessary to bring the woman before us. I suppose she is a pretty woman, and these young rascals hoped to have some fun with her and were disappointed. They probably plotted this in revenge."

He called Che Dan forward and questioned him. "Where did you catch Han the Second?" he asked.

"We caught him in the woman's room," the man said. Then Ximen said to Han the Second: "What relation are you to this woman?" A police-man said that she was his sister-in-law. Then he asked the police: "How did these fellows get into her room?" The policeman told him that they had climbed over the wall.

Ximen put on an air of great indignation. "You scoundrels!" he cried, "since he is her brother-in-law, they are near relations. Why should he not go to see her? What is his business to you, you scamps? How dared you climb over the wall? The husband was out, and she had only a little daugh-ter in the house. It must have been one of two things. Either you intended to rob her, or you meant to rape her. Bring the rack," he shouted to the attendants, "rack each of them once, and give them twenty stripes with a heavy rod." Then they were all beaten and racked till their flesh was torn and the blood gushed forth. As none of them had been so punished from the day he left his mother's womb, they shrieked and yelled loudly enough to rend the skies and then lay groaning on the ground.

Ximen Qing did not give Xia an opportunity to speak, but ordered Han the Second to be taken away to await further examination. The other four were to be put in jail until they confessed. They bemoaned their fate, and their friends in the prison frightened them the more by saying that they would be banished and probably die in exile. This put them all in a terrible state, and, when their people sent food to them in prison, they se-cretly sent messages to their fathers or elder brothers to spend more money bribing the officials both high and low. Someone went and attempted to bribe Xia. "The woman's husband," said Xia, "is employed by his Lordship Ximen Qing. So long as he is concerned in the matter, I can do nothing. He is my colleague. You had better go and talk to him."

One of them thought of going to see Uncle Wu, but as for Ximen him-self, they knew that he was very rich, and dared not offer money to him. So the fathers and brothers of the poor young men were greatly put about and finally held a conference.

"It is no use going to Master Wu," one said, "he can do nothing for us. But they tell me that Ying, the silk merchant's brother, is on very friendly terms with Ximen. We had better get together as much silver as we can, and ask him to plead with Ximen for us. Then we may have some success."

Che, the wineshop keeper, Che Dan's father, acted as spokesman. The others contributed ten taels apiece, so that they had forty taels in all; then they went to Ying Bojue's house to implore him to intercede with Ximen. Bojue accepted the money and sent them away.

"You have already worked for Han against these people," his wife said. "How can you take their money now and act for them? Han will be very angry."

"Do you think I haven't foreseen that difficulty?" Ying Bojue said. "I know what to do." He weighed out fifteen taels of silver, wrapped them up, put them in his sleeve, and set off for Ximen Qing's house.

Ximen had not yet returned, and Ying went into the hall. Shutong was coming from the study in the west wing. The boy was wearing a tile-shaped hat, with a pin fashioned like a lotus. His gown was of Suzhou silk with a jade-colored jacket, summer shoes, and white socks.

"Pray sit down in the guest's place, Uncle Ying," he said. Then to Hua-tong: "Boy, go at once and bring some tea for Uncle Ying. If you stay there playing knucklebones, I shall tell Father the moment he comes in." Huatong went to get the tea.

"Is your Father not back yet from the courts?" Ying Bojue asked.

"A message has just come to say that, after leaving the office, he went with his Lordship Xia to make a call. Is there anything I can do for you, Uncle?"

"I want nothing," Ying Bojue said.

"Uncle," the boy said, "the other day you came here on Clerk Han's business. Yesterday my master had those fellows beaten and sent to prison. Tomorrow the papers will be made out and they will be sent for trial."

Ying Bojue took the boy aside. "I will tell you one thing," he said, "their people have heard that they are to be examined further, and they are very much alarmed. Last night they came to me, cried and knelt down before me, and begged me to speak to your master for them. I realized that as I had already taken a hand in the matter, I could do nothing for them without upsetting Han, so I suggested that they should give me fifteen taels of silver, thinking that I might come to you, and perhaps you might think fit to mention the matter to your father, and we shall see whether he takes pity on them or not."

He took the money from his sleeve and handed it to Shutong. The boy broke open the packet. The silver was in four large and four small pieces.

"Uncle Ying," he said, "I will, of course do anything you command, but I think I should have five taels more. Then I will mention the matter to Father, though, naturally, I can't say whether he will be willing to listen. Uncle Wu was here yesterday and Father refused him point-blank. My influence is no bigger than a sesame seed, so what can I do? Really, Uncle, I cannot expect to succeed without some help. I shall have to lay out the money on the Sixth Lady, who has just borne a son. We must get to work indirectly."

"Very well," Bojue said, "I will add a word too, but remember: they want their answer tonight."

"I don't know when Father will be back," Shutong said. "They may have to wait until tomorrow."

Bojue went away, and Shutong took the silver to the shop, keeping a tael and five *qian*. This he spent on a jar of wine, two roast ducks, and two chickens, two *qian* on fruit pastries and delicate pastry, and one on sweet rolls. He ordered these things to be sent to Laixing's room, and then went to ask Laixing's wife to set them out for him.

Jinlian was not at home that day. Early in the morning she had taken a sedan chair and gone outside the city to celebrate her mother's birthday. Shutong borrowed a square tray and sent Huatong with the delicacies to Li Ping'er. He himself took the jar of wine.

"Who has sent these things?" Li Ping'er said. Huatong told her they were a present from Shutong. "The young rascal!" Li Ping'er cried. "What does he mean by this?"

Then Shutong came in. Li Ping'er was sitting on a gilt bed, playing with the baby and a tortoiseshell cat.

"You young scamp," she said, "for whom have you brought all these things?"

Shutong laughed, but did not answer.

"Why don't you answer instead of standing there laughing?" Li Ping'er said.

"If it is not for you, for whom do you imagine I have brought them?"

"You rascal," Li Ping'er said, "I don't suppose you are doing this without a reason. If you don't explain yourself, I shall not accept them."

Shutong opened the wine jar, set down the dishes on a small table, and asked Yingchun to bring a silver wine pot. Then he poured out a cup of wine and offered it to Li Ping'er with both hands.

"When you have drunk this, I will tell you," he said, kneeling before her.

"Say what you have to say before I drink it," Li Ping'er said. "Otherwise, you may kneel there a hundred years, but I will have none of it. Stand up at once and tell me."

Shutong told her how Ying Bojue had spoken to him about the four prisoners. "He had already done something for Han, and he did not see how he could work for the other side too. He suggested that I should come to you. If Father questions you about it, don't say I told you, but tell him that Uncle Hua sent someone to see you about it. Meanwhile I will go to the study in the front court and write a petition, and show it to him. I will tell him that you gave it to me, and perhaps you will say anything else that seems necessary. After all, Father has already had the men punished, so if you persuade him to make an end of the matter and let them go, it will be a very gracious action."

"If that is all," Li Ping'er said, "there need be no difficulty. I will speak to your master as soon as he returns. There was no need for you to get all these things for me. You rogue, I suspect you've made something out of them."

"I will not deceive you, Lady," Shutong said. "They gave me five taels for myself."

"You are a clever young rascal, making money in this way." She would not drink a small cup, but made Yingchun bring a large one shaped like a flower. After drinking two cups herself she poured one out for Shutong.

"I dare not drink," the boy said. "It would make my face red, and I should not like my master to see me."

"What does it matter if I give it to you?" Li Ping'er said.

The boy kowtowed to her and drank the wine at a breath. Li Ping'er took some of each of the dishes and made the boy eat some. He drank two more cups of wine, then dared not drink any more, for fear his face should be red. Then he went to the shop where he had left half the cakes and dishes he had bought. He set them on the counter, bought another jar of wine, and invited Clerk Fu, Ben the Fourth, Chen Jingji, Laixing and Daian to have some. The dainties vanished like a whirlwind or like melting snow. He forgot to invite Ping'an, the gatekeeper, who sat outside the gate pulling a long face.

It was afternoon when Ximen Qing came back from visiting his friends. Ping'an saw him coming but gave no warning. Shutong heard the shouts of the attendants clearing the road for their master before he had time to put away the things. He had to rush out in a great hurry to take Ximen Qing's clothes.

When Ximen asked if anyone had called to see him, Shutong said: "No." Ximen Qing took off his hat and cloak and, after putting on a cap, went into his study and sat down. Shutong gave him a cup of tea. When he had drunk a mouthful, Ximen put it down. He noticed how red the boy's face was. "Where have you been drinking?" he said.

Shutong took a paper from beneath the ink slab on the table and gave it to his master. "The Sixth Lady gave me this," he said. "She told me Uncle Hua had sent it. It is about the four prisoners, and she asked me to take it and bring it before you. She gave a cup of wine, and that is why my face is red."

Ximen Qing looked at the paper. "The four accused implore your clemency," it said. When he had read it, he handed it back, and told Shutong to put it in the letter case and give it to the soldier-servant that he might be reminded about it next day. Shutong put the paper in the case, and came to stand beside his master.

After the wine he had drunk, the high color in his cheeks stood out in striking contrast to the fairness of his skin. Ximen could not resist the temptation. He drew the boy to his bosom, and kissed him passionately. Shutong had aromatic tea and some tablets of cinnamon in his mouth. His body was scented with a sweet fragrance. Ximen undid the boy's shirt, pulled down his multicolored trousers, and caressed him gently. "You must not drink so much wine," he said. "It will ruin your complexion."

"I will do your bidding in all things," the boy said.

Meanwhile, a horseman clothed in black rode up to the gate, dismounted, and bowed to Ping'an. "Is this the house of his Lordship Ximen Qing?" he said.

Ping'an was still sulking and pulling a long face, because Shutong had not invited him to the feast. He did not answer. The man waited a long time and finally said: "I have brought this letter from Major Zhou. Tomorrow there is to be a reception to General Xing Pingzhai at the Temple of Eternal Felicity. Three of the officers have given a tael of silver each towards the expenses, and I have come to see your master. Please be good enough to tell him. I will wait for his reply."

Ping'an took the paper and went in. Someone told him that Ximen was in the garden room, and he went into the garden past the pine tree grove. Huatong was sitting on the steps beside the window. He waved his hand and Ping'an suspected that something must be going on between his master and Shutong. He tiptoed to the window, peeped, and listened, and did not miss certain signs of agitation in the room. He heard Ximen Qing say: "Stand this way, my boy, and don't move." Then there was silence for a long time. At last Shutong came out to fetch water for Ximen Qing to wash his hands. When he saw Ping'an and Huatong standing at the window, he flushed, and hurried away to the inner court. Ping'an took in the subscription list and Ximen Qing set his signature to it.

"Go to the Second Lady for a tael of silver," he said. "Then get your brother-in-law to wrap it up and give it to the messenger." Ping'an went away.

When Shutong had brought the water, Ximen washed his hands and went to see Li Ping'er.

"If you would like something to drink, I will tell a maid to heat some wine," she said.

Ximen saw a jar of Jinhua wine underneath the table. "What is that?" he said.

Li Ping'er did not wish to tell him that Shutong had brought it. She said: "I thought I should like something to drink, so I sent a boy to the street to buy it. I opened it and drank a cup or two. Then I had had enough."

"We have plenty of wine in the outer court," Ximen said. "Why should you spend your money? I got forty jars of Heqing wine from Ding, the southerner, the other day. I haven't paid him for it yet, but the wine is all in the west wing. If you want any, you need only send a boy with a key to get some."

Plates of roast duck, chicken and fish were ready and Li Ping'er told Yingchun to prepare more. When the dishes were set on the table, she ate them with her husband. It did not occur to Ximen to ask where they had come from, for such things were plentiful in his house.

"Shutong has just given me a paper," he said as they were drinking. "He says you gave it him."

"Yes," said Li Ping'er, "Uncle Hua came and begged me to ask you to let those fellows go."

"Wu came yesterday about the same matter," Ximen said, "but I wouldn't promise him anything. I really intended to have the business still further examined but, since Hua has been here to ask, I will have them given another beating and set free."

"Why beat them again?" Li Ping'er said. "You have already punished them till they opened their mouths and showed all their teeth. Really, a most repulsive sight!"

"I don't care whether they show their teeth or not," Ximen said. "My office is not conducted on those lines, as other people, of greater dignity than they, have found before now."

"Brother," Li Ping'er said, "you are an officer of the law, I know, yet your office does not forbid you to show mercy. To be merciful is to be virtuous, and you must lay up a stock of virtue for our child's sake."

"What do you mean?" Ximen said.

"In the future, do not rack and beat the people as you have been doing, and, when you have a chance to be kind, take it. So, you will certainly lay up for yourself a treasure in heaven."

"If I do my duty, I must not be too lenient," Ximen said.

They were still drinking when Chunmei thrust aside the blind and came in. It seemed to her that Ximen and Li Ping'er were sitting in a very affectionate position. "Here you are enjoying your wine," she said. "You have forgotten all about sending a boy to meet my mistress. She has gone a long way outside the city, and only Laian is with her. She will be very late, I fear, but that doesn't seem to worry you."

Ximen saw that the girl's headdress was disarranged and her hair tumbling down. He laughed, and said: "You've been asleep, little oily mouth." Li Ping'er told her that the kerchief on her head needed to be set in order and added: "This is beautiful Jinhua wine. Won't you have a cup?"

"Drink a cup," Ximen Qing said, "and I will send some of the boys for your mistress."

Chunmei, with one hand on the table as she leaned over to pull up her shoes, declined. "I don't feel very well," she said, "and I have only just got up. I don't want anything to drink."

"It is very good wine, little oily mouth," Ximen said. Li Ping'er said: "Your mistress is not at home; why make all this fuss over a cup of wine?"

"Please drink the wine yourself, Sixth Lady. It makes no difference whether my mistress is at home or not. If she were at home and I were asked to drink when I did not feel well, I should refuse."

"If you will not have wine, have some tea," Ximen said. "I will tell Yingchun to send a boy for your mistress."

He passed his own cup to her. Chunmei took it reluctantly, drank a mouthful of tea, and set the cup down.

"You need not send Yingchun," she said, "I have brought Ping'an. He is bigger than the others."

Ximen called through the window and Ping'an answered. "If you go," Ximen said, "who will attend to the gate?"

"I have told Qitong to look after the gate," the boy replied.

"Very well," said Ximen, "take a lantern and go to meet your mistress."

When Ping'an had gone halfway, he met the sedan chair. He knew the two bearers. One was Zhang Chuan, the other Wei Cong.

"I have come to escort my mistress," he said, going forward and taking hold of the shafts.

"Who told you to come?" Pan Jinlian said. "Your father?"

"Not so much my father as my sister," the boy said.

"I suppose your father has not come back yet from the office," Jinlian said.

"Not come back, indeed!" the boy replied. "He came back very early and is now drinking good wine in the Sixth Lady's room. If Chunmei had not fetched me and insisted that I should be sent with a lantern to meet you, I shouldn't be here now. I knew you had nobody with you but Laian, that the road was bad and you ought to have somebody bigger, so I came."

"When you left the house, where was your master?"

"He was still in the Sixth Lady's room. He only sent me when Chunmei insisted."

Jinlian remained silent for a long time. Then she smiled, coldly. "The brigand seems to think I am a corpse already. He would spend every night in that strumpet's room if he could. She pins her faith to that water bladder of a baby, and I only hope she may not find out she has made a mistake. Zhang Chuan, you are one of the household and you have seen a good deal of the world. Why should they cut up a whole roll of silk to make clothes for that puling brat? Even Wang the millionaire wouldn't do a thing like that."

"Lady," Zhang Chuan said, "I should never have dared to mention the matter, if you had not done so, but you are certainly right. They should not. It is not the silk I am thinking about, but I am afraid they will spoil the baby. He has not gone through all his childish ailments yet, and he will not be reared without some trouble. I remember a sad case that happened last year. It was a very rich old gentleman who lived outside the Eastern gate, about sixty years old he was, living on a property that had belonged to his ancestors. He was as rich as rich could be, but he was childless. He kept his fast in the Eastern Temple and offered sacrifice in the Temple of the West. He made all manner of benefactions to religion, yet still no son was born to him. Then, suddenly, his third wife presented him with one and he was as delighted as our master has been. All day long, he would gaze upon that child and have him carried about in an embroidered silken cradle. He had three rooms for a nursery painted as white as driven snow. Three or four nurses were bought especially for the baby and, all day long, he was sheltered from the slightest breath of wind. Yet before he was three years old, he took the smallpox and died. I beg your pardon, but I can't help thinking it is better to bring up a baby a little more roughly."

"Roughly indeed!" Jinlian cried. "Their only trouble is that they can't keep him in a pile of gold."

"There is something else I have to tell you," Ping'an said. "If I do not, you will be angry with me when you hear about it. It is about that business of Clerk Han and the others. Father had the young men beaten and thrown into jail, and it was his intention to send the matter further. But this morning Uncle Ying came and had a talk with Shutong. I think he must have given Shutong a few taels, for he took quite a large packet of silver to the shop and had two or three taels cut off. He spent this on dainties that he got Laixing's wife to arrange, and took them, with a couple of jars of Jinhua wine, to the Sixth Lady's room. They drank some of the wine; then he went back to the shop and gave a party to his friends. When Father came back, the party broke up."

"Didn't he ask you to join the party?" Jinlian said.

"Ask me? Not he! He is the boldest of slaves and is not even afraid of you, so why should he bother about me? It is all Father's doing. I know that, for I caught the pair of them together in the study. He was once a servant at the officers' quarters, and you may be sure there is not much he does not know. If Father does not soon get rid of this slave, the whole household will suffer from his goings on."

"How long was he in the Sixth Lady's room, drinking?" Jinlian asked.

"A long time. When I saw him, he had evidently been drinking for a long time. His face was very red."

"Didn't your father speak to him about it?"

"My father's lips were sealed. How could he say anything?"

"Oh, the scoundrel! The shameless prince of all evil scoundrels!" Jinlian cried. "He must have a turn at everything. If ever you catch him and this slave playing their dirty games again, come and tell me at once."

Ping'an promised. "Please remember one thing," he said. "Don't let anyone know I told you." Then he went behind the sedan chair and they went on their way.

As soon as they reached home, Jinlian went to the inner court to pay her respects to the mistress of the house.

"What made you come back so soon?" Wu Yueniang said. "You might have spent another night."

"My mother asked me to stay," Jinlian said, "but one of my nieces was there, a girl about twelve years old, and I should have had to sleep in the same bed with her. Then, it seemed a very long way off, and I thought I had better come. My mother asked me to give you her compliments, and thank you for your kind presents."

She went in turn to the rooms of each of the other ladies, and finally to the front court. Ximen Qing was still talking to Li Ping'er.

When she came in, Li Ping'er quickly stood up and welcomed her with a smile. "Sister," she said, "you have come back very early. Won't you sit down and have a cup of wine?" She told Yingchun to give Jinlian a chair.

"I have had something to drink already," Jinlian said, "and, as for food, I've had enough for two. I won't sit down, thank you."

She turned and went out with her head in the air. Ximen Qing called her back. "What, you slave!" he cried. "Are you so bold that you decline to make your reverence to me when you return from your visits?"

"Make a reverence to you indeed!" said Jinlian. "If slaves are not bold, who should be?"

CHAPTER 35

The Favorite

Ximen Qing went early to his office. When they left the Great Hall, he spoke to his colleague Xia. "Che Dan and the others," he said, "have sent to me repeatedly to express their regret. I think we might be indulgent on this one occasion."

"I have had a number of visits too," said Xia, "but I hesitated to mention the matter to you. Since you have spoken of it, however, I suggest we have them before us, give them a beating, and let them go."

"An excellent idea, Sir," said Ximen.

They went back to the hall of audience and ordered the prisoners to be brought before them and made to kneel down. The unfortunate men were afraid of being punished again, and kowtowed. Ximen Qing did not give Xia time to speak, but said: "Why have you rogues sent so many people to us to plead on your behalf? I ought to send you for further trial, but this time I will forgive you. If ever you fall into my hands again, I shall send you to prison and there you shall die." He sent for Han the Second. The men, full of expressions of gratitude, ran off as though their lives depended on it. So this matter was happily settled.

Meanwhile Ying Bojue went to see Shutong and secretly gave him another five taels of silver. The boy put the silver into his sleeves, but Ping'an, who was watching from the gate, saw it. Shutong told Ying Bojue what he had done. Yesterday, he said, he had told his master about the whole affair, and the matter was to be settled that day.

"Their fathers and elder brothers told me," Ying Bojue said, "that they are very much afraid the rascals will have another beating."

"Do not worry," Shutong said. "I am prepared to promise that nothing more will happen to them."

Ying Bojue returned and told the good news to the young men's people. About midday, the four young men were all home again. They embraced their families and there was much weeping. They had lost more than a hundred taels of silver, and their legs were very sore. Never again did they give any trouble.

Before Ximen Qing came home, Shutong told Laian to sweep the study floor. From a box he took some delicacies that had been sent as a present and gave them to Laian. With a great show of secrecy and reluctance Laian said to Shutong: "Brother, there is one thing I wish to say to you. Yesterday, my brother, Ping'an, when he went to meet the Fifth Lady's chair, told her a long story of your misdeeds."

"What did he say?" Shutong asked.

"He said you took money from people and had the impertinence to buy presents of food that you gave to the Sixth Lady. When you were in her room, you drank for a long time and then went to the shop to eat, but didn't give him anything. He also said that you and Father had been playing tricks together in the study."

Shutong determined to remember this, but he said nothing. The next day Ximen Qing went early to a party that the officers had arranged at the Temple of Eternal Felicity to bid farewell to one of their number who was leaving for another post. He did not go to his office but returned early in the afternoon. When he dismounted, he said to Ping'an: "If anyone calls, tell him I am not at home." Then he went into the hall, and Shutong took his clothes. Ximen asked the boy whether there had been any visitors. "No," Shutong said, "but Mayor Xu has sent two baskets of crabs and some fresh fish. I gave his servant one of your cards. He gave me a *qian* of silver. And Uncle Wu has sent six invitations, one for each of the ladies, to a 'Third Day' party."[1]

Ximen Qing went to the inner court and Wu Yueniang showed him the cards of invitation.

"You must put on your best clothes and go," Ximen said. Then he went back to the study and sat down. Shutong made haste to burn incense in the burner and, with both hands, offered Ximen a cup of tea. When he had taken the tea, the boy gradually came closer and stood beside the table. After a while, Ximen pursed his lips. This was a sign to the boy to make fast the door. Then he drew the boy to his bosom and with one hand stroked his cheeks. He put his tongue into his mouth; the boy passed him a sweetmeat and stroked his erect penis.

"My son," Ximen said to him, "are you being well treated by the people here?"

The boy seized his opportunity. "There is one thing, but except to you, Father, I would not dare to mention it."

"Tell me," Ximen said. "Keep nothing back."

Then Shutong told him about Ping'an. "The other day, when you and I were here together, he and Huatong were secretly spying through

---

1. Uncle Wu's son, Wu Shunzhen, had married a young lady named Zheng, a niece of Master Qiao's wife. Ximen Qing had sent him some tea, and this was why invitations had been sent.

the window. When I went out to get water for you to wash your hands, I saw them. Besides that, he has treated me as a slave before outsiders, and bullied me in a hundred different ways."

Ximen Qing was very angry. "If I do not pull that slave's trousers down," he said, "I am not fit to be called a man."

Meanwhile Ping'an himself was not idle. He went quietly to Pan Jinlian and told her that his master and Shutong were again together. Jinlian ordered Chunmei to go at once to the front court and ask Ximen Qing to come and speak to her. As the maid passed the hedge, she saw Huatong making a pine tiger.

"What do you want, Sister?" he said. "Father is in the study."

Chunmei slapped his face. Ximen Qing, in the study, heard the rustling of skirts and knew that someone was coming. He hastily put Shutong aside, climbed upon his bed, and lay down. Shutong busied himself with the brushes and ink slabs on the table. Chunmei pushed open the door and went in.

"All very quiet," she said, "very quiet indeed! And the door shut too! Drawing the bonds of family closer, I suppose. My lady would like you to go and talk to her."

Ximen Qing did not move. "What does she want with me, little oily mouth?" he asked. "You go first and I will come in a moment. Let me have my rest."

Chunmei would have none of this. "If you will not come of your own free will, I shall have to drag you," she cried, and pulling and tugging, she forced Ximen Qing to go to Jinlian's room.

When they reached there, Jinlian said to her maid: "What was he doing in the front court?"

"He was with that boy in the study. They had the door shut, and everything was so quiet they might have been just on the point of catching a fly. I don't know what their little game was, but it looked to me as if there was something very close between them. When I went in, the boy was standing at the table pretending to write, and this one was lying on the bed. I had to drag him here, for he didn't want to come."

"Yes, he was afraid he would get into hot water if he did come," Jinlian said. "You shameless creature! Haven't you any self-respect left at all? In broad daylight, shutting yourself up in your study with that slave. What for? Just to make a beast of yourself with that mangy slave. And then, at night, you come to our place to sleep with us. A nice clean fellow!"

"You believe all that little oily-mouthed creature tells you," Ximen said. "I was simply lying on the bed and watching the boy write a visiting card."

"Why shut the door to write a visiting card?" Jinlian cried. "What secret, important words do you need for that? What three-legged Indra, or two-horned elephant, do you hide away in there that you are afraid someone may go in and see it? Tomorrow is Uncle Wu's birthday and we have all been invited to go there. Without making any bones about it, you can find something for me to offer when I go. If you will not, I will find some other husband who will. The Great Lady is going to give a dress and five *qian* of silver, and the others have flowers and ornaments to give. I am the only one who has nothing, and I had better stay at home."

"You may have a roll of fine red silk from the cupboard in the front court," Ximen Qing said.

"No," Jinlian cried, "I will not go at all if I have to take that red silk. Everyone will laugh at it."

"Be quiet and wait a minute," Ximen said. "I will go upstairs and get something for you. I am thinking about sending some presents to the Eastern Capital, some silk among them, and I will find something for you at the same time."

He went to the rooms of Li Ping'er, where he went upstairs and took two rolls of black silk woven with a gold thread, two of Nanjing colored silk, one of scarlet mixture, and one of kingfisher blue cloudy satin.

"I want to find a dress of taffeta for Jinlian to give as a present," he said to Li Ping'er. "If there isn't one, I must send a note to the silk shop and get one."

"There is no need to send to the silk shop," Li Ping'er said. "I have one, and a scarlet under-dress, and a blue skirt. There is no purpose in keeping one without the others, so she shall have them all." She took the clothes from a chest and herself carried them over to Jinlian.

"Sister," she said, "take either the under-dress or the skirt, whichever you like. We will wrap them up together and let the present be from both of us. That will save the trouble of going to the shop."

"But these are yours," Jinlian said, "1 cannot take them."

"Why say that?" Li Ping'er said. They argued pleasantly for some time, and at last Jinlian agreed. She asked Chen Jingji to write both their names on the card.

While this was happening, Bai Laiguang came to the gate.

"Is your master at home?" he said.

"No," said Ping'an, "he is not."

Bai Laiguang did not believe him and went into the house. There he found the window shut. "Well," he said, "it seems he really is not at home. Where has he gone?"

"He has gone outside the city to a farewell party," Ping'an said.

"Then he ought to be back soon," Bai Laiguang said.

"Uncle Bai," the boy said, "tell me what it is you wish to say, and I will give the message to my master when he comes back."

"Oh," Bai Laiguang said, "it is nothing very important, but I haven't seen him for a long time, so I thought I would call today. Since he is not here, I think I'll wait for him."

"I'm afraid he won't be back till very late," Ping'an said. "You will be tired of waiting."

Bai Laiguang paid no attention. He pushed open the door, went into the hall, and sat down on a chair. None of the boys did anything for him; they left him quite alone. But the Fates were kind to him. Ximen Qing and Yingchun, coming from the inner court with a roll of silk, passed the screen and came right upon him as he sat in the great hall. Yingchun put down the silk and hastily retired to the inner court.

"Isn't this my brother?" Bai Laiguang cried. "So you are at home after all."

There was no escape. Ximen Qing could only ask Bai Laiguang to be seated. Upon his head was a refurbished, remolded, ancient gauze hat, like those worn by the pilgrims to the summit of Taishan. He was wearing a white stuff gown that would hardly hold together and was fit only for the fire, the collar torn and the front all frayed. Upon his feet a pair of clapper-clopper black boots, out of shape and torn almost to shreds. And, inside the boots, socks like stirrups of yellow silk, which would not have imprisoned a fly.

They sat down, but Ximen Qing did not call for tea. Qintong was waiting beside him, and he ordered the boy to take the silk to the guestroom and ask Chen Jingji to wrap it up.

"I have not been to see you for a long time," Bai Laiguang said, waving his arms. "I am sorry."

"It is kind of you to remember me," Ximen Qing said. "Now that I have to go to the office every day, I have not much time to spend at home."

"What, Brother?" Bai Laiguang said. "Do you go to the office every day?"

"Yes," Ximen said, "I go twice every day and hear cases in the Hall. On the first and the fifteenth of every month I have to pay reverence to the tablets and to sign and stamp public documents and carry out public business, and attend to the police reports. Even when I get home, I have a great deal to do; I hardly have a moment's leisure. Today I have been outside the city with all the officers to say goodbye to Xu Nanxi, who has just been given a military appointment. The Governor of the Royal Estates, Eunuch Xue, has invited me to take wine with him tomorrow, but his place is so far away that I really shall not be able to get out there. The day after tomorrow I have to go and welcome the new provincial governor, and the same day the fourth son of the Imperial Tutor in the Eastern Capital is to marry a princess. Then Grand Marshal Tong's nephew, Tong Tianyin, has recently been promoted to be the controller of the Palace Guards. All this makes me very busy, what with presents and so on, and, the last few days, I have been tired to death."

They talked for a long time, and, at last, Laian brought some tea. Bai Laiguang had taken only one mouthful when Daian hurried into the room with a red card in his hand. "His Lordship Xia is here," he said. "He is dismounting outside the gate."

Ximen Qing hastily went to the inner court to put on his ceremonial clothes. Bai Laiguang retired to a room in the wing, and from there looked through the lattice. He saw Xia come into the great hall and Ximen Qing, dressed in his robes of ceremony, come to receive him. They greeted one another and sat down in the places of host and guest. Qitong brought cups of tea.

"Yesterday," Xia said, "we were talking about the reception of the new governor. Today I have learned that his name is Zeng, and that he graduated in the third degree in the year *Yiwei*. His warrant has already reached Dongchang, and all our colleagues are going out to welcome him. Though you and I are military officers, there are administrative duties attached to our appointments, and it is one of our duties to enforce the law, which makes us rather different from mere soldiers. I think, therefore, that we should go the day after tomorrow and find a place a little distance from the town, where we may offer the new governor a dinner of welcome."

"That is an excellent idea," Ximen Qing said, "but pray do not trouble yourself about the matter. I will find some temple or private estate, and send servants and cooks to make all the necessary preparations."

"It is extremely kind of you," Xia said.

They drank another cup of tea and the magistrate took his leave. Ximen went to the gate to see him off. Then he came in again and took off his robes. Bai Laiguang had not gone. He came back into the great hall, sat down, and said to Ximen:

"For the last month or two, Brother, you have not been to our meetings, and the brotherhood is practically at an end. Sun is certainly old, but he has no capacity for organization, and Brother Ying does not trouble. In the seventh month, we went to the Temple of the Jade Emperor to celebrate the *Zhongyuan*[2] and there were only three or four of us there including myself, and nobody with any money. All were empty-handed.

---

2. The fifteenth day of the seventh month.

We gave a great deal of trouble to Abbot Wu. He was very agreeable, and had engaged a storyteller specially for us, but he had to pay the man himself. The Abbot did not say anything, but we all felt most embarrassed. It was different when you were in charge. You always knew exactly what to do and how to do it. We hope it will not be long before you come and join us again."

"No, I think not," Ximen said, "the brotherhood had better be dissolved. I really have no time for things like that nowadays. If I can manage it, I will send a little offering to the Abbot as a thanks offering. But that must suffice. In the future you need not give me notice of any more of your meetings."

After this there was nothing for Bai Laiguang to say, yet he remained sitting there. Ximen Qing, seeing that he made no move, bade Qintong set a table in the side room. He had something to eat with Bai Laiguang, ordered wine to be warmed, and poured out several cups for him. At last, Bai Laiguang asked permission to leave. Ximen went with him only as far as the second door. "If you will excuse me," he said, "I will not go with you any farther. I have not my ceremonial hat and, in the circumstances, it would not be becoming that I should see you off." Then Bai Laiguang went away.

Ximen Qing returned to the great hall, pulled out a chair and sat on it. Then he shouted for Ping'an, over and over again. Ping'an came in and Ximen cursed him. "You thievish slave, how have you the audacity to stand there before me?" He called for his official attendants, and three or four men appeared immediately. Ping'an had no idea what was the matter, and was so terrified that his face became the color of wax. He knelt down.

"When I came home," Ximen Qing said, "I told you that if anyone called you were to say I was not at home. Why did you not obey me?"

"When Uncle Bai came," Ping'an said, "I told him you had gone outside the city to a farewell dinner, and had not yet returned. He would not believe me and forced his way in. Then I followed him and asked if he would leave a message with me. He said nothing, but opened the door of the hall, went in, and sat down. Just at that moment, unfortunately, you came and met him."

"Don't try and deceive me with a lot of words," Ximen cried. "You are a coward. Where were you gambling and drinking, that when somebody came you were not attending to your duties at the gate?" He ordered the men to go and smell Ping'an's breath. They did so, but said: "We cannot smell any wine."

"You two, who can use the rod, give this slave a fair and honest finger-squeezing."

Two of the soldiers seized Ping'an, and one put the thumbscrews on the lad's fingers. They turned the screw till he could bear the pain no longer and screamed: "Indeed, I told him you were out. He forced his way in."

The soldiers released the screws and knelt before Ximen. "It is done," they said.

"Give him fifty stripes," Ximen cried. The number was counted; they went to fifty and stopped.

"Give him twenty more," Ximen said. They did so. The boy's skin was torn; the flesh was bruised, and blood poured down his legs.

"Stop," Ximen cried.

The soldiers removed the thumbscrews and the boy screamed shrilly.

"You rascally slave," Ximen said, "you said you were at the gate. It is my belief that you are always trying to get money out of people, and so, spoiling my good name. Let me hear not so much as a whisper of anything of the sort. If I do, you shall lose your legs."

Ping'an kowtowed, rose, and, pulling up his trousers, made off as fast as he could.

Then Ximen Qing saw Huatong standing beside him.

"Down with him," he cried to the soldiers, "and put the thumbscrews on him." The boy began to howl like a pig being killed.

Pan Jinlian was coming from her room to the inner court and, as she passed the door that opened into the great hall, she saw Meng Yulou standing behind the screen listening with all her ears.

"What is going on?" Jinlian said.

"I am listening to Father. He is having Ping'an beaten, and setting the thumbscrews on Huatong. I don't know why."

Qitong passed by. Yulou stopped him and asked what the punishment was for.

"Father is angry because Ping'an let Bai Laiguang come in," the boy said.

"Oh, that is not the real reason," Jinlian said. "The boy must have ruined something very precious or he wouldn't be beaten like that. What a shameless fellow Father is. He pulls a long face to show that he is the master of the house, but he is utterly without shame."

"What do you mean by saying that the boy must have ruined something very precious?" Yulou said, when Qitong had gone.

"I was going to tell you," Jinlian said, "but so far I have not had a chance. The other day, I went to see my mother on her birthday. While I was away, that little slave Shutong accepted several taels of silver from somebody, and went and bought two boxes of food and a jar of Jinhua wine and took them to the Sixth Lady's room. She and the young rascal drank there for a long time. Then he went away. When our shameless husband came back, he had not a word to say, but he and the boy went off to the study in the garden, locked the door, and goodness only knows what they did there. Ping'an had to take him a visiting card, found the door shut, and was standing by the window when Shutong opened the door and saw him. I imagine the young rascal must have told that shameless fellow all about it and today he is having the boy punished in revenge. I am very much afraid that in the future that young man will make mischief for everybody in the household, and be getting everybody into trouble."

"That is a nice thing to say," Yulou said, laughing. "Of course, in a household like this, some of us are wise and some are foolish, but not all of us have evil minds."

"No, you are quite wrong," Jinlian said. "Let me tell you this. At the present time there are only two people he really and truly cares for. One is a member of the household, and the other is not. His mind dwells continually upon those two. When he sees them, he laughs, he talks. But the rest of us are out of luck. He treats us like black-eyed chickens. The robber! He will never come to a natural end. He is fickle because the foxes have got hold of him, and he has become just like themselves. Sister, mark my words. There is going to be serious trouble in this household. Today, I have had a bother with him over the present. As soon as he comes in, he goes to his study. Today, I sent Chunmei to ask him to come and see me. Would you believe it, even in broad daylight that little slave had fastened the door. Chunmei pushed it open, went in and gave him a shock. He opened his eyes very wide and didn't know what to do. When he came to me, I cursed him well, but he simply protested and excused himself as best he could. He offered me a piece of red silk, but I would not have it. Then he went to the Sixth Lady's room to find something for me. The brigand knew he was in the wrong, so he took a dress of material woven with gold thread from her chest, and she brought it to me herself. I refused to take it. 'Sister,' she said, 'why think twice about it? Take the gown or the skirt, whichever you like best, and when you have made your choice, we will go to Brother Chen and get him to write a card for us.' At last I gave way, and she persuaded me to take the gown."

"Well," Yulou said, "that seems fair enough. I think she treated you very well."

"You don't understand," Jinlian said. "We have to yield place to her. In these days, the whole world fears the wide-eyed *Jin Gang*, and nobody bothers about the Buddha whose eyes are closed. In these affairs between husband and wife, if one gives the other the least bit of rope, he becomes like General Wang's orderly and looks upon you as one not worth the trouble of even the crudest affection."

"Really," Yulou said, laughing, "you are as hot as pepper."

They both laughed. Then Xiaoyu came to invite them to go to Yueniang's room to eat crabs. She told them she was going to ask Li Ping'er
also. Hand in hand, they went to the inner court and found Wu Yueniang
and Li Jiao'er sitting beneath the eaves.

"What are you laughing about?" Yueniang asked.

"We are laughing at Father. He has been punishing Ping'an."

"No wonder I heard screams like those of a man running for his life,"
Yueniang said. "I didn't realize it was Ping'an being beaten. But why was
this?"

"Because he broke something precious," Jinlian said.

"What was this precious thing?" Yueniang asked, seriously, "and how
did he break it?"

Jinlian and Yulou broke into peals of laughter.

"I really don't understand why you find it so funny," Yueniang said, "or
why you don't tell me what the joke is."

"Great Sister," Yulou said, "you do not know, of course. Father was
beating the boy because he let Bai Laiguang come in."

"If that was all," Yueniang said, "well and good. But why did you talk
about his breaking something precious? Really, I never heard of such a
man. It would be far better if he sat on his behind in his own house instead of rushing into other people's houses when he has nothing to say
worth saying."

"He came to see Father," Laian said.

"Nobody had fallen out of bed," Yueniang said, "and nobody is going
to put up with behavior of that sort. It would be much nearer the mark to
say that he came to fill his belly."

After a while, Li Ping'er and Ximen Dajie came. They sat in a circle
and enjoyed the crabs. "There is some grape wine in my room," Yueniang
told Xiaoyu. "Get it and warm some for the ladies."

"Oh, but when we eat crabs," Jinlian said, "we ought to have Jinhua
wine." And, a little later: "It is a pity we have only this one course. How
much nicer it would be if we had roast duck with our wine."

"It is late now," Yueniang said, "how can we have roast duck?"

Li Ping'er flushed. The words were meant for her, and they showed
what was being thought of her. Yueniang was a simple-minded woman
and did not appreciate the meaning of what was said.

When Ping'an had been beaten, he went outside. Ben the Fourth,
Laixing, and the others hurried to discover why he had been punished.

"How should I know?" Ping'an said, weeping.

"I suppose Father was angry because you let Bai Laiguang come in,"
Laixing said.

"Well," Ping'an said, "I did all I could to stop him, but he insisted upon going in and then, unfortunately, Father came from the inner court and saw him. He had really nothing to talk about, but even after tea had been served he did not go away. Then his Lordship the Magistrate came and I was sure he would go, but he only retired to the wing room, and made no move to depart. Only when he had been given wine did he go. So I was punished like this. Father says I didn't stop him, but it was simply my bad luck that he would come in. Why should my poor legs be beaten for him? May heaven destroy this dog bone, may his sons become thieves and his daughters harlots! May the food he ate here break his backbone!"

"If his backbone breaks," Laixing said, "he will do well to dash in."

"May he choke and his gorge burst!" Ping'an cried. "Of all the shameless, faceless people in the world, there is none so shameless as this dog bone. He sneaks in so silently that the dog doesn't even bark: he shows his teeth and gobbles down our food. It was a beggar got him, and his rump will rot, the thievish turtle!"

"But if his rump does rot," Laixing said laughing, "none of us will ever know. He will tell us he is dribbling."

They all laughed.

"I suppose he has no rice to cook for his supper," Ping'an said. "How hungry his wife must be if he has nothing else to do but come to other people's houses to get food, and so save his own. This cannot go on. He had better let his wife keep another man on the quiet, and be himself a turtle. That would be more straightforward and he would not get himself cursed by the servants of other households."

Meanwhile Daian finished having his hair cut, paid the barber, and came away. To Ping'an he said: "I don't wish to say anything, but I can't help it. You are our master's servant. How is it you don't understand his temperament? You have no reason to complain. The proverb says: No one wants a boy to make water of gold and lay eggs of silver. What people do want is a boy who realizes what the situation is and acts accordingly. If Uncle Ying and Uncle Xie come, it is all right to let them come in whether Father is at home or not. They are good friends and have no secrets from one another, but as for the rest, if they come when our master has told you to say that he is not at home, why do you let them in? If he does not punish you, whom should he punish?"

Then Ben the Fourth made a joke. "Ping'an," he said, "you must learn how to be a little boy and play again. You see, he too knows how to play, and plays kickball all day."

They all laughed at this, and Ben the Fourth said: "You were punished for letting someone come in, but what had Huatong done? The fruit was not so tasty that you needed anyone else to help you enjoy it. When we have a banquet, we like to have others to keep us company, but I have never heard that the same thing is true when we are wearing thumbscrews."

Huatong rubbed his hands and cried. Daian said jokingly to him: "My son, stop crying. Your mother has brought you up too tenderly. Now somebody has given your fingers something to taste. Why don't you settle down to enjoy it?"

Ximen Qing watched Chen Jingji packing up the presents and the rolls of silk, and writing cards. The following day these gifts were to be sent to the Eastern Capital for their patrons there.

The next day, Ximen went to his office. Yueniang and the others, with pearls and jewels in their hair, and silk and embroidery upon their bodies, took sedan chairs to join the festivities at Aunt Wu's house. Laixing's wife, in a smaller chair, was in attendance upon them. Only Sun Xue'e and Ximen Dajie stayed at home to look after the house. In the morning, Han Daoguo sent a number of presents as a token of gratitude to Ximen. There was a jar of Jinhua wine, a teal, a pair of pig's trotters, four roast ducks, and four smoked fish. On the card that came with them was written: "The young student Han Daoguo kowtows and offers these." Because there was no one at home, Shutong did not accept them, and the boxes were set down. When Ximen Qing came back from the office, the boy showed them to him. Ximen bade Qintong go to the shop and bring Han Daoguo to him.

"What is this?" he said. "Why do you bring these presents? I cannot possibly accept them."

Han Daoguo made a reverence. "You have been extremely kind to me," he said. "You had compassion on me and avenged me. I and all my household are grateful to you. These trifles only express a tiny part of my gratitude. Take them, please, even if only as a joke."

"I cannot do so," Ximen Qing said. "You are associated with me in business, and that means that you are like one of my own household. Kindly send someone to take the things away."

Han Daoguo grew excited and insisted that Ximen Qing should accept them. After a long discussion, Ximen told one of the servants to take the ducks and the wine, but nothing more. The rest, he said, must all be taken back. Then he sent a boy with his card to invite Ying Bojue and Xie Xida. He said to Han Daoguo: "Tell Laibao to look after the shop this afternoon, and you come and join us."

"So besides not taking anything from me," Han Daoguo said, "you pile kindness after kindness upon me." He promised to come, and went away.

Ximen Qing bought many fresh fruits and dishes, and that afternoon, in the arbor by the Hall of the Kingfishers, they were all set out upon a square table. Ying Bojue and Xie Xida came early.

"Han has been at a great deal of trouble to buy presents for me," Ximen Qing said, "but I would not take them. He implored me to accept them, but I would only have the wine and ducks. I didn't wish to keep these all for myself, so I sent for you."

"He spoke about the matter to me," Ying Bojue said; "he said he was going to buy you some presents, but I told him you certainly would not accept them and that he should not take the trouble. Was I not right? I might have been in your very mind. You did refuse them."

They drank tea and played backgammon, and soon afterwards, Han Daoguo came. When they had greeted one another, he sat down. Ying Bojue and Xie Xida were in the places of honor, Ximen Qing in the host's seat, and Han Daoguo opposite. Four plates and four bowls were immediately brought in, with a host of dishes. Laian was told to open the jar of Jinhua wine, and heat it in a brass jar. Shutong was told to serve it.

"Go to the inner court," Ying Bojue said to Shutong, "and ask your mistress if she will not send some of her crabs for your Uncle Ying. Tell her I like them very much."

"You foolish dog," Ximen cried, "there are none left. Mayor Xu sent me a basket or two, but the ladies have eaten them all. We preserved the few that were left."

He told a boy to bring a few pickled crabs. "Today," he said, "the ladies have gone to a celebration at the Wus' house."

Before long, Huatong brought the pickled crabs. Ying Bojue and Xie Xida tried to see who could eat the faster, and ate them every one.

"Your Uncle Ying," Bojue said to Shutong, "never thinks of drinking wine without a song to it. You are always boasting of the way you can sing the songs of the South, but I have never heard you sing any. Let us have one today, and then I'll drink my wine."

Shutong began to beat time with his hands, and made ready to sing. Ying Bojue stopped him. "If that's the way you're going to sing, you may go on as long as you like, but I shan't pay any attention. When you play the part of a dragon, try to look like a dragon; and when you play the tiger, be a tiger. Off you go, get your face painted, and put on a girl's dress."

Shutong stood still, glancing at Ximen Qing to see what his master had to say to this. Ximen only laughed and cursed Ying Bojue, saying that he was just the kind of man who would seek to deprave a serving boy.

"Since he must have it so," he said to Shutong, "send Daian to the front court, and tell him to ask one of the maids for some clothes. Then go and paint your face."

Daian went first to Jinlian's rooms and asked Chunmei. She refused him. Then he went to Yueniang's apartments, and Yuxiao lent him four silver pins, a comb, a pendant, a pair of gilded imitation jade earrings, a scarlet double-fronted silk dress and a green skirt with purple trimmings. Then Shutong took powder and rouge to the study and dressed himself. So charmingly did he adorn himself that he looked exactly like a real girl. He went back to the table and offered a cup of wine to Ying Bojue with both hands. Then he cleared his throat and sang.

> Red withered leaves swirl down towards the water
> Though the plums are still young upon the branches.
> My brows lack color: who shall give it to them?
> Spring comes, and sorrow with it.
> Spring goes, but sorrow stays.
> Mountains and deep waters sunder us; we are together no more.
> I count the days until you come again
> And the tip of my brush is wounded by my grief.

Bojue applauded vigorously. "Anyone like you," he said to the boy, "need feel no shame when he eats his food. Your voice is as sweet as a flute, and the girls in the bawdy house simply cannot compare with you. Many, many times I have heard them sing, but there isn't one of them with a voice so sweet and rich as yours. Brother," he added, turning to Ximen Qing, "I don't wish to flatter you, but you really ought to be delighted to have such a boy in your household."

Ximen Qing smiled.

"Why do you smile?" Ying Bojue said. "I am perfectly serious. You must not undervalue this boy. You should regard him with unusual favor in all things. It was most fortunate that Li thought fit to send him to you. He did you a great favor."

"Yes, indeed," Ximen said. "Now, when I am out, this boy and my son-in-law are responsible for everything connected with the study. My son-in-law is mainly concerned with the shop."

Ying Bojue drank his wine and poured out two cups. "I shall be angry if you do not drink this," he said to Shutong. "Since I offer it to you, there is no reason why you should not."

Shutong looked at Ximen Qing.

"Since it is your uncle who offers it to you," Ximen said, "you had better drink it."

The boy knelt on one knee, gracefully bent his white neck, and sipped a mouthful, giving the rest of the wine back to Bojue. Then he turned to offer wine to Xie Xida, and sang another song.

"How old is this boy, Brother?" Bojue asked.

"Just sixteen," Ximen said.

Then Xie Xida asked the boy how many southern melodies he knew.

"Indeed, I know only a few," Shutong said. "I have sung for the amusement of Uncle Ying and yourself."

"You are certainly a clever boy," Xie Xida said, and he, in turn, offered Shutong some wine. Then the boy went to Han Daoguo, but Han Daoguo said: "How shall I take such a liberty in his Lordship's presence?"

"Today you are my guest," Ximen said.

"It is not to be thought of," Han Daoguo said, "your Lordship must drink first, and then perhaps I may make bold myself."

Shutong offered wine to his master, and again sang a song. When Ximen had drunk it, the boy went to Han Daoguo. Han stood up to take the wine. "Sit down," Bojue said. "The boy will sing for you." Han sat down, and Shutong sang again. Before the boy had finished his song, Han Daoguo had swallowed all his wine in one breath.

They were still drinking when Daian came and said: "Uncle Ben the Fourth is here, and would like to speak to you." Ximen gave orders that he was to be shown in. Ben the Fourth came in, made a reverence, and sat down. Daian brought chopsticks and a cup for him, and was told to go to the inner court for more dishes.

"How is the work getting on?" Ximen Qing asked Ben the Fourth.

"We are putting the tiles on the first story," Ben the Fourth said, "and yesterday we laid the foundations of the arbor. But we have not yet got the materials for the wings or for the back part of the living rooms. We are having to wait another five days for the flooring tiles: we cannot use any of the old ones. And we are still without some of the materials we need for the walls. We have earth enough to fill up the foundations and the artificial mound. Then we need a hundred cartloads of lime, and they will cost twenty taels of silver."

"Do not trouble about the lime," Ximen said. "When I go to the office tomorrow, I will order the lime burners to get it for you. Yesterday, Eunuch Liu of the brick kilns promised he would send me some. All you need to do is to tell him what you want and send a few taels, for this matter is as much one of friendship as of business. You will only need to buy the wood."

"Yesterday," Ben the Fourth said, "you told me to go outside the city to look at another place there. Early this morning Zhang An and I went. The place belongs to a noble family, but now the head of the family has died, and they are anxious to dispose of it. It is no use to us as it is, and I told them we should pull most of it down. They want five hundred taels for it but, in my opinion, if we decide to have it, we had better take some money with us and go to talk the matter over with them. We certainly ought to secure it for something like three hundred and fifty taels. Besides the wood, the tiles, bricks and mortar will amount to one or two hundred taels."

"Let me think whose house this is," Bojue said. "It must be Xiang the Fifth's. Xiang the Fifth was brought by somebody before the military court, and the case cost him a great deal of money. He used to keep Luo Cun there, and that is why he is so short of ready money. I'm sure he will be satisfied with three hundred taels. His hands are so cold that he will gladly welcome something to warm them."

"Tomorrow," Ximen said to Ben the Fourth, "you and Zhang An take two large bars of silver and go and talk to him. If he will accept three hundred taels, get on with the work."

After a while a bowl of soup and a plate of cakes were brought from the inner court. Ben the Fourth ate them, and then drank in company with the others. Shutong sang another song, and went away.

"It is very dull drinking wine like this," Ying Bojue said. "Won't you send for a dice box and let us have a game?"

Ximen Qing told Daian to go to the Sixth Lady's room and get a dice box. The boy brought it and set it down before Bojue. Then he went over and whispered to Ximen Qing: "Little Brother is crying, and Yingchun told me to ask you to send someone to fetch the Sixth Lady."

"Put down your wine jar," Ximen answered quickly, "and send a boy with a lantern at once. Where are the two boys?"

"Qintong and Qitong have already gone with lanterns to bring the ladies home," Daian said.

Ying Bojue noticed that there were six dice in the dice box. "I will cast a number," he said, "and I want the name of the tablet to agree with the number 1 throw. If there be anyone who cannot tell it, he must drink a cup of wine for forfeit, and the one next to him must sing a song. If he can't sing, he must tell a story instead."

"Ah, you funny dog," Ximen Qing cried, "you are too well versed in tricks."

"When the commander-in-chief lets forth a fart," Bojue said, "it must be obeyed as if it were the Emperor's command. It is no use your trying to keep me in order."

He said to Daian: "Pour a cup of wine as a punishment for your master, and then I will give my orders."

Ximen Qing laughed and drank the cup of wine.

"Listen, all of you," Bojue said, "I am going to give an order. If I make a mistake, I am ready to be punished for it. Here you are: 'Zhang Sheng got drunk and lay down in the Western Pavilion. How much did he drink? One large jar or two small ones?' Indeed it is a *yao* (one)."

Ximen Qing told Shutong to pour the wine, and Xie Xida had to sing.

Bojue drank the wine and passed the dice box to Xie Xida, that he might cast the dice. It was Ximen Qing's turn to sing. When he had thrown the dice, Xie Xida said: "Thanks be to Hong'er who helped me to bed. What time was it? The third night watch, and the fourth division thereof." Strangely enough, he really threw a four.

"Brother Xie," Bojue said, "that is four cups for you."

"Give me two," Xie Xida said, "I am no great drinker."

Shutong poured out two cups and Xie Xida drank one, then waited for Ximen Qing to sing. Meanwhile, he and Ying Bojue made short work of the nuts. Ximen Qing told them he could not sing, and would tell them a story, instead.

"There was once a man," he said, "who went to a fruit shop and asked the shopman if he had any olives. 'Yes,' said the shopman, and brought some out to show his customer. The man tasted a number of them. 'I am glad you like them,' said the shopman, 'but why don't you buy some, instead of popping them into your mouth like that?' 'I like them,' the customer said, 'because they are so soothing to the chest.' 'All you think about,' the shopman retorted, 'is soothing your chest. It never occurs to you that you are giving me a pain.' "

Everybody laughed. Ying Bojue said: "If you have a pain at the heart, order another two plates of nuts for us. I am like the old woman who went around picking up horses' droppings. The moister they are, the more drying they take."

Xie Xida drank the second cup, and it was Ximen Qing's turn to throw the dice. "I have left my gold pin and token behind. How much do they weigh? About fifty or sixty *qian*." He threw a five. Shutong poured out two half-cups of wine.

"Brother," Xie Xida said, "you are no poor drinker. If you drink only two cups it won't be fair, drink four. I offer them to you myself."

Then it was Han Daoguo's turn, but he asked Ben the Fourth to throw before him, for Ben the Fourth, he said, was older than he.

"I, too, cannot sing," Ben the Fourth said, "so I must tell a story." When Ximen Qing had drunk his two cups of wine, Ben the Fourth began. "Once upon a time a magistrate had to investigate a case of unlawful association. He asked the man how he set about the business. 'My head to the East,' said the man, 'and my feet to the East also.' 'Nonsense,' said the magistrate, 'whoever heard of going about sexual intercourse in that unsatisfactory way?' At that moment a man ran up and plumped himself on his knees before the magistrate and said: 'If you're in need of a clerk who knows how to be unsatisfactory, I'm the very man for you.'[3]

"Ah ha! Brother Pen," said Ying Bojue, "you don't intend to miss any chances! Your master is not an old man. You might be excused for anything else, but how can you think of getting a job like that which is evidently in your mind, in his household?"

Ben the Fourth was flustered. He blushed and said: "Uncle Ying, what do you mean? Such a thing never entered my head."

"What I said is like a scabbard made of sandalwood. The sword is gone and only the scabbard remains."

This made Ben the Fourth extremely uncomfortable, but he could not escape. He felt as though he were sitting on a cushion of needles. Ximen Qing finished his four cups of wine and it was Ben the Fourth's turn to throw the dice. Just as he was about to take them up, Laian came in and said that he was wanted by somebody from the tile works. Ben the Fourth was so anxious to get away that, as soon as he heard this, he ran off like a golden cicada breaking out of its chrysalis.

"Now that he has gone," Ximen Qing said, "it is your turn, Han." Han Daoguo took up the dice.

"I obey your orders," he said. "The old lady beat Hong Niang with a rod. How many blows did she administer? About forty or fifty."

"It is now my turn to sing," Bojue said, "but I shan't. I am going to tell a story." Then he said to Shutong: "Pour out wine for all of us, not excepting your master. Then listen to my story.

"Once a priest and his disciple went to a house to take some religious papers. When they came to their benefactor's door, they found that the pupil's girdle had become loose and the papers had fallen out. 'It looks as though you had no bottom,' the priest said to the young man. 'If I hadn't,' returned the pupil, 'you would not be able to exist for a single day.'"

"You dirty dog," Ximen cried, "but with a dog's mouth like yours, I suppose we must not expect elephant's teeth."

The party went on.

Daian went to the front court and called for Huatong. They set off with a lantern to Aunt Wu's house to find Li Ping'er. When they had told her that the baby was crying, she did not even wait to pay her respects to the young couple, but presented her gift and asked to be excused. The two Wu ladies would not let her go. "You must wait for the bride and bridegroom," they said.

---

3. Pun on the word *Xingfang*, which means "sexual intercourse" when expressed with one character, and a kind of clerk when another character is used.

Then Wu Yueniang intervened. "Please excuse her," she said, "there is no one at home, and the baby is crying for her. We will stay, for we have no such reason for anxiety." So the Wu ladies allowed Li Ping'er to go. Daian left Huatong, and he and Qintong accompanied the chair on its way home.

After the bridal pair had received them, Yueniang and the others set off in their four chairs, but they only had one lantern to guide them. It was the twenty-fourth day of the eighth month and extremely dark. Yueniang asked where the other lantern was. "Why have we only one?" she said.

"I brought two," Qitong said, "but Daian and Qintong took the other when they went back with the Sixth Lady."

Yueniang said no more, but Jinlian took up the matter. "How many did you bring from the house?" she asked the boy.

"Qintong and I brought two, then Daian and Huatong came and took one of them. Daian left Huatong behind, and went off with Qintong after the Sixth Lady's chair."

"Didn't Daian bring a lantern with him?" Jinlian said.

Then Huatong answered. "We did bring one."

"If he had one, why did he take another?"

"That is what I told him," said Qintong, "but he took it by force."

"You see how it is," Jinlian said to Yueniang. "That rascally Daian is trying to curry favor with her. When I get home, I shall have something to say about this."

"Oh," said Yueniang, "how easily you get excited. They are only boys, and their master sent for her. Why shouldn't they take the lanterns?"

"Really, Sister," Jinlian said, "that is no way to talk. The rest of us might put up with it, but you are the chief among us, and you ought to see that discipline is maintained in the family. If it were not dark, it would not matter, but it is dark, and here we are with four chairs and only one lantern. Really there is no excuse for it."

At length the chairs reached the door. Yueniang and Li Jiao'er went to their own rooms; Jinlian and Yulou got out together. As they went in, Jinlian asked where Daian was. Ping'an was telling her that the boy was serving in the back court when Daian came out. Jinlian cursed him roundly. "You flattering young ruffian. You keep your eyes open and think you'll wait on those who are in favor. But mind your step. You had one lantern. That was enough. The way you go on will not do at all. You took another lantern by brute force, and you changed the boys. So she got two lanterns for her one chair and we, with four chairs, had only one lantern. Do you consider we are not your master's ladies?"

"Mother," Daian said, "you have no reason to blame me. When Father heard the baby was crying, he told me to take a lantern and come at once to bring the Sixth Lady home. He was afraid the baby might make himself ill, crying. If Father hadn't told me to do so, I should never have dreamed of doing such a thing."

"Don't try to deceive me, you rascal," Jinlian cried. "He may have told you to bring her home, but he did not tell you to take all the lanterns. Little Brother, you are one of those birds that always fly to the places where things are going best. Don't make a mistake. You should put your hand to the cold stove as well as to the hot one. I suppose you think our luck is out."

"How can you say that?" Daian said. "If such a thing ever entered my mind, one day when I am riding my horse, may I fall off and break my ribs."

"You deceitful young scamp," Jinlian said, "don't try to go too fast. I shall keep my eye on you." She and Yulou went to the back.

"I always seem to get into scrapes of this kind," Daian said to the other servants. "Father told me to go and fetch the Sixth Lady, and now the Fifth Lady turns and scolds me."

At the second door, Yulou and Jinlian met Laian. They asked him where Ximen Qing was. The boy told them that he was with Ying Bojue, Xie Xida and Han Daoguo, drinking wine.

"Brother Shutong," he added, "has dressed up as a singing girl and is singing for them. Wouldn't you like to go and see?"

The two ladies went and peeped through the window. Ying Bojue, already drunk, sat in the upper seat. His hat was on one side and his head was bobbing about as though it were pulled by strings. Xie Xida could not keep his eyes open. Shutong was still dressed as a girl, serving wine and singing Southern melodies. Ximen Qing told Qintong to put some powder on Bojue's face. Afterwards, the boy made a circlet of grass and, stealing behind Bojue, put it on his head. Yulou and Jinlian, standing outside, could not help laughing. "The scoundrel!" they said. "Sin will be his companion as long as he lives. He behaves just about as badly as anybody could do."

Ximen Qing heard the laughter outside and sent a boy to see who was there, but the two women slipped away to the inner court.

It was the first night watch before the party broke up. Ximen Qing went to sleep in the Sixth Lady's room. When Jinlian went to her own apartment, she said to Chunmei: "What did the Sixth Lady say when she came home?"

"Nothing," Chunmei said.

Then Jinlian asked: "Did that shameless creature go to see her?"

"After the Sixth Lady came back," Chunmei said, "Father went twice to see her."

"Did the child really cry so much that he sent the boys to bring her home?"

"Yes," Chunmei said, "he screamed terribly this afternoon. Whether he was carried about or put in his cot, it made no difference. He cried, and no one could do anything for him. So somebody went and told Father, and he sent a boy to fetch her."

"In that case," Jinlian said, "all right. I suspected that that shameless creature had made up the whole thing so as to get her back. Whose clothes is Shutong wearing?"

"Daian came to me," Chunmei said, "but I soon packed him about his business. Finally, he got some from Yuxiao."

"If they ever come again," Jinlian said, "give nothing for that boy to wear." She realized that Ximen Qing was not coming to her that night, and she fastened her door and went angrily to bed.

To return to Ying Bojue. He had noticed that Ben the Fourth was in charge of all the work that was being done, and apparently making money thereby. Tomorrow he was going to take money to buy Xiang's house and would make at least several taels of silver out of that deal. So he was glad of the chance to score off Ben the Fourth, when he was so indiscreet as to tell that story, and to point out his little weaknesses. He had meant Ben the Fourth to know what he was doing. Ben the Fourth was greatly perturbed, and, the next day, he packed up three taels of silver and took them to Ying Bojue's house. Bojue pretended to be greatly surprised. "I have done nothing for you," he said, "why should you do this?"

"It is a long time since I made you any present," Ben the Fourth said, "and all I ask is that you will speak well of me to my master. If you will, I shall be eternally grateful to you."

Ying Bojue took the silver, offered a cup of tea to Ben the Fourth, and escorted him to the door. Then he took the silver to his room.

"If a husband does not make his power manifest," he told his wife, "the wife will never get a new dress. It was I who introduced that son of a dog Ben the Fourth to Ximen Qing, and now he has his finger in every pie. And everything that comes in, he puts into his own bowl, and never thinks any more about it. Ximen leaves all the work on the estate to him, and now he is going to buy Xiang the Fifth's place. He has done well for himself. But at the party yesterday, my chance came and I took it and showed him up. That frightened him and, as I expected, today he came and gave me three taels of silver. Now we can buy some cloth, and make clothes for the children through the winter."

CHAPTER 36
Ximen Qing Entertains the Laureate

My heart is oppressed when I think of the distance before me
My spirit shrinks with fear before the journey I must take.
How can I not dread the hardship of the way?
Yet always I think of my duty to my country.
Ji Bu never forgot his promise
Hou Ying was faithful to his word.
In human hearts devotion always conquers
And men give up the thought of gold.

The next morning, Ximen Qing went with his colleague Xia to welcome the new governor. He also went to see his new property and distributed gifts to all the workmen to show his appreciation of their labors. It was late when he reached home. As soon as he came to the gate, Ping'an told him that a messenger from Dongchangfu had brought a letter for him from Zhai, the Comptroller of the Imperial Tutor's household. "I took the letter to my mistress's room," he said. "Tomorrow about noon the messenger will call for your answer." Ximen Qing hastened to the upper room, opened the letter, and read it.

To be delivered at the mansion of the most worthy Ximen [it read]. For long I have been hearing of your fame and great renown, but it is long too since I beheld your glorious countenance. I have often benefited by your most gracious kindness, and it is almost impossible for me to express my sense of indebtedness.

Some time ago, you were good enough to convey to me your instructions, and I have engraved them upon my heart. In every possible manner, I have done my utmost to serve you with his Eminence. So now, if I may trouble you about a trifle, there is a matter that I have already mentioned to your worthy attendant, and, doubtless, you have done what I desired. I take this opportunity of sending you my humble card together with ten taels of gold. Now I await your convenience. Meanwhile, may I present my best respects and trust that your high-mightiness will condescend to reply. Your kindness shall be ever in my heart.

The new laureate, Cai Yiquan, is His Eminence's ward. He has just received the Imperial Command to return to his native place to visit his parents. He will pass by your honorable mansion and I trust you may find it possible to entertain him. He will be grateful for any kindness you may show him.

From my heart, the day after the Autumn Day, your servant Zhai Qian at the Capital.

When he had read this letter, Ximen Qing sighed. "Send a boy for a go-between at once," he cried. "However did I come to forget all about this matter?"

"What are you talking about?" Wu Yueniang said.

"Comptroller Zhai, of the Imperial Tutor's household," Ximen said, "wrote to me the other day. He said he had no son and asked me to find a young girl for him. He does not care whether she is rich or poor, and expense is no object with him. He simply wishes to find a good girl who will present him with a son and heir. He said if I told him what I spent on wedding presents he would repay me in full. And he said he would do all he could for me with the Imperial Tutor. But I have been so busy going to the office and attending to one matter and another, that I had forgotten all about it, and Laibao has not reminded me, since he is at the shop every day. Now Zhai has been put to the trouble of sending someone all this way with a letter, and he asks me what has been done in the matter, and sends a present of ten taels. Tomorrow the messenger is coming for an answer. What can I say to him? He will be very angry. Send at once for the go-between and tell her to find a girl without delay. She need not trouble about the girl's family. She must be a good girl and somewhere about sixteen or eighteen years old, that's all. Whatever it costs, I will pay. Wait! Why shouldn't we send him Xiuchun, the Sixth Lady's maid? She is a pretty girl."

"You lazybones!" Yueniang said, "what have you been thinking about? He asked you to get him a really fine girl, and you ought to have done so. But you yourself have not left Xiuchun alone; we can't send her. You must treat this business as one of real importance. Sometime in the future Zhai may be very useful to you. If you let your boat drift into the rapids, how can you use your oars? It isn't like buying ordinary merchandise, where you go to the market with your money and carry off what you like. When you are buying a girl, you must wait and give the go-between a chance, and see one after another. Some girls are good and some are bad. You don't seem to realize that it is not a simple matter."

"But he wants an answer tomorrow," Ximen Qing said. "What am I to say to him?"

"Have you been a magistrate all this time and can't manage a little affair like this? Tell the boy to be ready for the messenger when he comes; give him plenty of journey money and a letter saying that you have found the girl, but that her clothes and things are not ready yet, and you will send her as soon as they are. When the messenger has gone, you can get someone to find a girl for you. There will be plenty of time. That's the way out of your difficulty, and you will have done a good day's work."

Ximen Qing smiled. "You are right," he said. He sent for Chen Jingji to write the letter. Next day when the messenger came, Ximen Qing himself went to see him and questioned him. "When does the Laureate's boat arrive? I must get ready to welcome him."

"When I left the Capital," the man said, "he had just left the court. Master Zhai said he feared the Laureate might be short of money for his expenses, and perhaps you would lend him some. Then, perhaps, you will write to Master Zhai, and he will repay you."

"Tell Master Zhai," Ximen Qing said, "that no matter how much the Laureate needs, I will gladly lend it to him." He told Chen Jingji to take the messenger to an anteroom and entertain him. When he was ready to leave, Ximen gave him a letter and five taels of silver for journey money. The man made a reverence and set out well pleased upon his long journey.

It may be remembered that some time before, An Shen had passed the examination in the highest place, but that the censors had objected that he was the younger brother of An Zhun, who had been the first minister in the last reign. As a younger son of an evil party, they declared, he must not be placed at the head of all the scholars. Consequently, Huizong could not do otherwise than put Cai Yun in the position. Cai Yun then went to the palace of the Imperial Tutor to be his ward. Later, he was appointed head of the office of Secret Archives, and given leave to go and visit his parents.

Wu Yueniang sent a boy for the two old women Feng and Xue, and another marriage maker. She told them to make a thorough search for a good girl, and to bring her full particulars when they thought they had found one.

One day Ximen Qing instructed Laibao to go to the river to see what he could find out about Cai's boat. Cai was traveling on the same boat as An Zhun, who had been given the third degree at the same examination as himself. An was so poor that he had not remarried. He seemed to be unlucky in every way. He had left the Court to try to find a wife in his native place, and so the two scholars came to be traveling together on the same boat.

Laibao took Ximen Qing's card and went on board. He had a dinner sent from the shore.

Before the Laureate had left the Capital, Zhai had told him that at Qinghe he would meet a certain Captain Ximen, one of the Imperial Tutor's clients. "He is a rich man," Zhai had said, "and a very pleasant fellow. It was through his Eminence's influence that he came into his present position. I am sure that he will entertain you most hospitably if you should go there."

The Laureate had not forgotten this and he was delighted when he found that Ximen Qing's servant had come so far to meet him, bringing such a handsome present.

The next day, he and An came to call on Ximen Qing who had arranged a feast in their honor. Ximen had seen a number of actors and singers from Suzhou, and now he sent for four of them. Cai offered a present of a silk handkerchief, a number of books, and a pair of shoes. An brought a gift of books and a handkerchief, with four bags of young tea and four Hangzhou fans. Both the scholars wore robes of ceremony and black hats, and sent their cards before them. Ximen Qing, wearing his ceremonial hat, welcomed them and invited them to go to the great hall. There they made reverences to one another; the two young men offered their presents to Ximen Qing, and they all sat down in the proper order of guests and host.

"My friend Zhai at the Capital," the Laureate said to Ximen Qing, "has spoken very highly of you. He says your honorable family is the most important in Qinghe. Consequently, I have been longing to see you for some time, but this is the first opportunity I have had. Now that today I have been permitted to enter your hall, I feel that Heaven has indeed been gracious to me."

"You are unduly kind," Ximen said. "I had a letter from Master Zhai the other day telling me that your worthinesses were about to visit us on your emblossomed boat. I should have been there to welcome you, but, unfortunately, my official duties would not allow me. I must most humbly beg your pardon. May I be allowed the honor of knowing from what enchanted country and glorious family you worthy gentlemen come?"

"The humble student before you," Cai said, "is a native of Kuanglu in Chuzhou, and his poor name is Yiquan. I had the good fortune to take the first place in the examination and to receive an appointment as head of the Department of Secret Archives. At the moment, I am on leave, and on my way to visit my parents."

"The humble student before you," An said, in his turn, "is a native of Qiantang of Zhejiang, and his undistinguished name is Fengshan. I have just received the appointment of Inspector of the Board of Works. I, too, am on leave and am returning to marry in my native place. May we know your own honorable second name?"

"I am only a poor military officer of low rank," Ximen Qing said. "How should I dare to allow myself to be called by my second name?" When they pressed him, he said at last: "My poor name is Siquan. I have frequently been favored by the kindness of his Eminence through the good offices of Master Zhai, and, in that way, was granted my present appointment as Captain. I perform certain legal duties but am really quite unfitted for the post."

"Honored Sir," the Laureate said, "you are not a man of mean ambition, and your reputation for delicacy has long been known. Do not let us stand on ceremony with one another."

Ximen Qing invited them to take off their robes of ceremony in the pavilion in the garden. But the Laureate said: "I am anxious to get home and our boat is at the wharf. Really I ought to go now. Yet, since I have basked in the sunshine of your company, I feel I cannot leave you so soon. What shall I do? What shall I do?"

"If you two noble gentlemen," Ximen Qing said, "do not disdain this snail's abode, pray let the banner of literature rest here a while. Take a little food with me, and let a small repast of celery prove the earnest of my goodwill."

"Since we are offered such exalted hospitality," the Laureate said, "we humble students can do no less than obey your commands." They took off their ceremonial robes and sat down.

The servants brought more tea. Cai looked about him. The garden, the pool, the pavilions and the flowers stretched so far and were so luxuriant that he could not see everything at a single glance. "This is fairyland," he said delightedly. A table was set and they played chess.

After a while, Ximen said: "I have brought a few actors here today for your amusement."

"Where are they?" An said. "Why not send for them?"

In a moment the four actors appeared and kowtowed.

"Which of you take the part of the hero and heroine?" Cai said. "And what are your names?"

One replied: "I take the hero's part; my name is Gou Zixiao. This is the heroine and he is called Zhou Shun. This one takes the second part: he is called Yuan Dan, and the other, the young man, is Hu Zao."

An asked them where they came from. Gou Zixiao said they were from Suzhou. "Good!" said An. "Now go and dress and then play for us."

The four actors went away to dress. Ximen Qing told someone to find women's clothes and ornaments for them. He told Shutong to dress up too. So, three women and two men, they played from *The Incense Sachet*. At the upper end of the great hall two tables were set. The two scholars sat in the seats of honor, and Ximen Qing in the host's place. While they drank their wine the actors finished one act. An saw Shutong dressed as a girl and asked who he was.

"That is my boy Shutong," Ximen Qing told him. An called the boy to him and gave him some wine. "This boy excels all the boys I have ever seen," he said. Meanwhile Cai summoned the actors who had taken the parts of girls and gave wine to them. Then he called for the song of Chao Yuan. Gou Zixiao obeyed, and, clapping his hands, began.

> By the willows and the flowers
> The spider weaves a glistening web under the eaves.
> Beside the mountains and the waters
> The east wind is kind to the horse's back.
> But I must journey like a wandering spirit
> Dreaming about my home, whether I will or not.
> The geese are silent, and the fishes deep beneath the water
> And my heart is broken with the pain of separation
> The day is short. My mother, in the northern hall, wearies of her
>   dreams.
> When shall I come to the Ninth Palace of Gold?

Then An asked Shutong, if he knew the lines beginning: "The mercy of the gods is infinite" from *The Jade Bracelet*. "I do," Shutong said, and began.

> The mercy of the gods is infinite
> I met my father and my mother again
> It is a kindness man may seldom hope for.
> Fortune has given me a peaceful life, a worthy mate.
> I fly as the clouds fly in the wind
> My love to me is like a female phoenix to her mate.
> True it must be that not in this life marriages are made
> And, in my last life, I must have set the jade in Lantian.

An, who was from Hangzhou, was fond of boys. He was delighted with Shutong's singing, held his hand, and took wine from his mouth.

After a time they had all had wine enough, and Ximen Qing took his guests to look at the gardens. They played chess in the summerhouse. Ximen told the boys to bring two boxes filled with every kind of delicacy to eat with their wine.

"This is the first time we have met you," the Laureate said. "We must not place too great a strain upon your hospitality. It is late and we should go."

"Noble Cai," Ximen cried, "how can you think of going yet? Are you really thinking of going back to your boat?"

"I propose to spend the night in the Temple of Eternal Felicity, outside the walls," Cai said.

"It is too late for you to go outside the city now," Ximen Qing said. "Keep one or two of your attendants here and let the rest return tomorrow for you. Then we shall all be content."

"I greatly appreciate your kindness," Cai said, "but I hesitate to give you so much trouble." Nevertheless, he and his companion told their servants to go to the temple and spend the night there, and come again in the morning with their horses. They played two games of chess in the summerhouse, and the actors performed till it was late. Then Ximen paid and dismissed them. Shutong alone remained to serve wine and other things.

They drank till it was dark and the lamps were lighted. Then they went to change their clothes. The Laureate took Ximen Qing's hand and said to him:

"I am going home to see my parents, and I am a little short of money."

"Please do not let that trouble you," said Ximen, "I shall be only too glad to do what Master Zhai suggested."

He asked the scholars to go into the garden with him and led them around the white wall till they came to the Cave of Spring and into the Snow Cavern. There the lamps and candles were lighted. The place was comfortable and warm. A table was set with fruits and wine, and couches were arranged, with books and musical instruments. There they drank wine again and Shutong sang for them.

"Do you know the song about the Fairy Peaches touched with red?" the Laureate asked Shutong.

"Yes, I think I remember it," the boy answered, "it goes to the tune of the 'Moon in the Hall of Tapestries.'" He poured wine for them, then clapped his hands and began to sing.

An's feelings were indescribably moved. "The boy is perfectly adorable," he said to Ximen Qing. He emptied his cup.

Shutong was wearing a green gown with a red skirt, a golden ribbon at his waist. He raised the jade cup high in the air to offer wine to them, and then sang another song. They enjoyed themselves until far into the night. At last they were ready to go to bed. Ximen Qing had had silken coverlets prepared for them in the Cave of Spring and the Kingfisher Hall. He told Shutong and Daian to wait on them. Then he said good-night and went to the inner court.

The next morning the servants came for the two scholars, bringing horses and sedan chairs. Ximen Qing had food made ready in the great hall, and refreshments for all the attendants. Two boys brought in square boxes of presents. To the Laureate Cai he offered a roll of gold silk, and silk for making collars, perfume and a hundred taels of white gold. He gave to An a roll of colored satin, one piece of silk for collars, perfume, and thirty taels of white gold. The Laureate at first refused to accept it. "Ten taels will be quite sufficient for my needs," he said. "Why should you give me so much? You are too generous."

"Brother Cai," An said, "you accept, but I dare not."

Ximen Qing smiled. "These trifling things are nothing more than a token of my regard for you. You are going home and you are about to take a wife. I should like to help you to get a little tea."

The scholars rose and thanked him. "We shall never forget your kindness," they said. Then they bade their servants remove the presents. "We must go," Cai said to Ximen Qing, "and renounce the benefit of your instruction for a while. But before long we shall be returning to the Capital. Then, if a slight measure of advancement should come to us, we shall do something to return your kindness."

"I hope to behold the glory of your dignity again," An said.

"Indeed," Ximen said, "I only hope your honor has not been tarnished by this stay in my snail's nest. I beg your indulgence for all that has been done amiss. I would come to see you on your way, but, unfortunately, my duty calls me and I can only say good-bye."

He took them to the outer gate and watched them mount their horses.

CHAPTER 37

Wang Liu'er

Though she be dressed in rags, such is her charm
It makes its presence known.
The flashing eyes reveal the ardor of her love
And he who listens to the music of her soul
Must yield himself her prisoner forever.

They meet within the hall of flowers
The breeze is gentle and the moon is calm.
Softly they talk, and tenderly they smile,
Draw near the bed with phoenixes in flight
Embroidered on its curtains.
Then silently unloose the scented girdle.

After saying good-bye to his guests, Ximen Qing went out on horseback, wearing shades upon his eyes. Soldiers cleared the way for him. In the street he met old woman Feng and told one of the boys to stop her.

"What about this finding a girl for me?" he said. "How is it I have heard nothing from you before this?"

"During the last few days," the old woman said, "I have inspected several girls, but they all turned out to be the daughters either of butchers or of hawkers. Of course, they were out of the question. Then, fortunately, Heaven granted me a miracle, and I remembered a girl who lives quite close to me. She is a beauty of the very first order, and is but fifteen years old. Her animal is the Horse. If I had not happened to pass her door, and she had not invited me to call, I should not, even now, have thought of her. She has just reached the age for her hair to be dressed. She is as upright as the holder of a brush; her feet are tiny, and she knows how to paint her face most charmingly. Her little mouth is so dainty she might be an elf. Her mother says she was born on the fifth day of the fifth month. I think she is beautiful, and I'm sure you will fall in love with her yourself as soon as you set eyes on her."

"You crazy old woman," Ximen said, laughing, "I don't want to fall in love with her. I have plenty on my hands without her. As a matter of fact, Zhai, the comptroller of the Imperial Tutor's household in the Eastern

Capital, is anxious to ensure the continuance of his family, and he has asked me to find a girl for him. If you only find the right one, so much the better for you. Who is the girl? You must send me the necessary papers."

"She lives not a thousand miles away," the old woman said. "In fact, there is hardly a brick between us at this moment. She is the daughter of Han Daoguo who looks after your thread shop. If you wish, I will get her father to have the necessary papers made out, then we can fix a day and you can go to look her over."

"Very well," Ximen said, "go and see him, and if he has no objection, get him to give you the papers and bring them to my house."

Two days later Ximen was sitting in the great hall when old woman Feng came with the papers. In them the girl was described as "the maiden Han, fifteen years of age, whose birthday is the fifth day of the fifth month."

"I told her father what you said," the old woman began, "and he said that, thanks to your generosity, the girl has certainly a great future in store for her. But he is afraid that, being a poor man, he cannot provide what is necessary for the marriage."

"Go and tell him," Ximen said, "that I don't want a single thread from him. Everything she needs—clothes, ornaments, toilet boxes and every-thing else—shall be prepared here. Moreover, I will make him a present of twenty taels. If he provides her with shoes and socks, that will be all that is needed. As soon as everything is ready, we shall ask him to escort her to the Eastern Capital. You see, she is not going to be an ordinary concu-bine. The comptroller hopes that she will bear him a son and he will treat her as his wife. So long as she furnishes him with a boy or even a bit of a daughter, she will have nothing to worry about."

"When will you go and see her?" the old woman asked. "They would like to know so that they can make preparations."

"Since he has agreed, I may as well go tomorrow. Zhai is in a hurry for her. But tell Han not to make any preparations on my account. He need only offer me a cup of tea. Then I shall take my leave."

"Oh dear," the old woman cried, "it is not very often you condescend to go and see anyone. You may not want anything, but you must not rush away. He is one of your people; he can't allow you to go away with an empty stomach."

Ximen Qing explained that he was very busy, and the old woman went off to tell Wang Liu'er, Han Daoguo's wife, all that he had said.

"Don't tell stories," Wang Liu'er said.

"Indeed, he did say so," the old woman said. "Why should I deceive you? You know how busy he is, with people coming and going at his house all the time." Wang Liu'er gave the old lady some food and wine. Then she went away, promising to come the next morning to await the master.

That night, when Han Daoguo came home, his wife talked to him and they discussed the whole matter. In the morning he got up early, went to the High Well for some sweet water, and bought the finest nuts he could find. These he left at home, then went to the shop to attend to the business. His wife, alone in the house, dressed herself in her prettiest clothes, powdered her face, and made herself look very charming. She washed her hands, cleaned her fingernails, polished the teacups, cracked the nuts, and made some excellent tea. Then old woman Feng came and helped the woman to put everything in order.

Ximen Qing, when he came back from the office, put on plain clothes and set out on horseback. Daian and Qintong followed him. When they came to Han's house, he dismounted and went in. Old woman Feng received him and took him into the sitting room. He sat down. Soon Wang Liu'er and her daughter came to see him. Ximen Qing did not look at the girl; he could not take his eyes from the mother. She was wearing a coat of purple silk, a scarf of black and gold upon her shoulders, and a jade-colored skirt, beneath which Ximen could see two perfect little feet. She was tall, and her face, shaped like a melon seed, had a high color.

Ximen Qing was almost beside himself. He decided that, seeing what manner of woman Han Daoguo's wife was, it was not surprising that the young men who lived near her had been inclined to play tricks. The girl was very beautiful too, but this did not surprise him when he had seen the mother.

Wang Liu'er made a reverence to him and called her daughter forward. The girl kowtowed four times before Ximen, bowing as gracefully as a bunch of flowers before the wind. Then she rose and stood before him, and the old woman went to bring tea. Wang Liu'er rinsed the cup before she would allow the old woman to hand it to Ximen. Then Ximen looked the girl over from head to foot. The black hair was piled gracefully upon her head and her cheeks were delicately powdered. She seemed like a lonely flower, with a kind of quiet fascination. Her skin was like the purest jade, tender and fragrant.

Ximen told Daian to take from a box two silken handkerchiefs, four gold rings and twenty taels of white gold. He told the old woman to put them on a tray. From it Wang Liu'er took a ring that she set on her daughter's finger. The girl again made reverence to Ximen Qing, and withdrew.

"In a day or two," Ximen said, "I will ask you to bring your daughter to my house so that the necessary clothes may be prepared for her. Meanwhile, perhaps, you will be good enough to use this money to provide her with shoes and socks."

"All that we have upon our heads and all we wear upon our feet," Wang Liu'er said, kneeling down, "we owe to you. Now you have been kind enough to arrange this marriage for my daughter. Even if my husband and I laid down our lives, we could never sufficiently repay you for your kindness. Again I thank you for your precious gifts."

"Is your husband not at home?" Ximen said.

"No," the woman said, "this morning he told me what I must do in this matter, and then went to the shop. I will tell him to come and kowtow to you."

Ximen thought that the woman talked very charmingly. She called him Father in nearly every sentence. He was touched. "I must go now," he said, rising. "Please tell your husband what I have said."

Wang Liu'er pressed him to stay longer, but he would not. He went straight home to report the business to Wu Yueniang.

"Really," she said, "the marriage cord unites people, even when a thousand miles lies between them. Since you say this girl is very beautiful, we have not spent our labor in vain."

"As soon as possible," Ximen said, "we will bring her here so that her clothes may be made. I will take ten taels of silver at once and have them made into ornaments, rings, pins and other things."

"The sooner the better," Yueniang said, "then we will ask her father to go with her to the Eastern Capital. We need not send anyone else."

Ximen Qing thought it would be better to close the shop for a few days and let Laibao go too. He wished, he said, to make sure that a present he had recently sent had been safely delivered.

Two or three days later Ximen sent a boy to escort the girl. Her mother, Wang Liu'er, came with her, bringing a few small presents. When they came in, they kowtowed before Yueniang and the others.

"Father and Mother," Wang Liu'er said, "and you other ladies, I thank you for the kindness you have shown my daughter. My husband and I will be eternally grateful to you."

They took tea in Yueniang's room and then were entertained in the great hall. Li Jiao'er, Meng Yulou, Pan Jinlian and Li Ping'er joined them. Ximen Qing had provided rolls of red and green silk, material for undergarments, and Tailor Zhao had made two dresses of gold and silver-figured silk and a scarlet satin long gown. Wang Liu'er said a few words to reassure her daughter and went home.

Ximen bought for the girl a small suite of furniture, a gilded chest, a dressing mirror and a hand mirror, boxes, jars, and vessels of bronze and pewter, even a pail to serve a purpose we need not mention. In a few days, everything was ready; a letter was written to go with the party, and the tenth day of the ninth month appointed for the start.

Ximen borrowed four men and two non-commissioned officers from the local police office to act as escort. Han Daoguo and Laibao hired four horses, and, riding behind the wagons and the sedan chair, set off for the Eastern Capital.

Wang Liu'er was left alone. She felt very lonely as she went about her daily duties. For some days indeed, she wept nearly all the time.

One day, when Ximen Qing had nothing particular to do, he mounted his horse and rode down to Lion Street to see what was happening at the house there. Old woman Feng met him and brought him tea.

"I was very satisfied with the way you managed that little business the other day," he said. "Here is a tael of silver for you to buy some cloth." The old woman kowtowed and thanked him.

"Have you been to Han's house lately?" Ximen said.

"Oh yes," the old woman said, "I go every day to cheer up his wife. Now that her daughter has gone she is all by herself. She has never been separated from the girl before, and until the last day or two, she has been crying all the time. 'You have been to a good deal of trouble over my daughter's marriage,' she said to me. 'Has his Lordship given you your fee?' I told her you had been very busy, and I had thought it better not to trouble you. I said I knew it would be safe to wait, and, doubtless, when her husband returned, there would be something coming to me from that quarter."

"Of course that will be so," Ximen said. He looked cautiously around. Seeing there was no one about, he whispered: "When you have an opportunity, just let her know that I should very much like to call and see her. Tomorrow tell me what she says about it."

The old woman put her hand over her mouth and chuckled knowingly. "Now that your shovel has dug you up a golden baby, you want to dig again and find the mother. Well, this very evening, I'll see if I can do anything for you. I suppose you know who she is? She is a sister of Butcher Wang in the back street, the sixth of her family, and about twenty-nine years old. She dresses in smart clothes and may look rather forward, but, to the best of my knowledge, she is virtuous. If you like to come here tomorrow, I will see if I can't have some news for you." Ximen agreed, mounted his horse, and rode home.

When old woman Feng had dined, she locked up the house and set out to see the woman. Wang Liu'er opened the door and asked her to go in. "I cooked some noodles for you yesterday, and waited," she said, "but you never came."

"I meant to come," the old woman said, "but I was obliged to go and see someone else. What with one thing and another, I couldn't manage to get here."

"Well," Wang Liu'er said, "I have a rough meal ready. Will you have something?"

The old woman said she had just had dinner, and would have nothing but a cup of tea. Wang Liu'er made a cup of strong tea for her and ate her own dinner while the old woman sat and watched her.

"I feel very lonely," the woman said. "Always before, I have had my child to fall back upon. Now she has gone the place seems empty, and I have to do everything for myself. My face gets dirty, and everything is horrid. I'd rather die than live like this. She has gone so far away, and if I want to go and see her, I can't. How can I help being upset?" She began to cry.

"It has always been the same," old woman Feng said. "When there are boys in a family, it is always busy, but with girls, it is always lonely. For a girl, if she lives long enough, sooner or later will leave the home and go elsewhere. Things seem bad to you now, but you must remember that, when your daughter settles down in that palace and has borne a son or even a daughter, you and your husband will reap the benefit. When that time comes, you will have nothing to complain of."

"In families of rank," Wang Liu'er said, sadly, "there are always ups and downs. How can we ever say what will happen? Even if she prospers, how am I to know where my bones will be rotting, when that time comes?"

"Oh, don't talk like that," the old woman cried. "Your daughter is certainly not a bigger fool than anybody else. She is a clever needlewoman, and everybody has the fortune that is his due. There is nothing for you to worry about."

They chatted for a long time in this strain, and at last the old woman decided to broach more serious matters. "I hope you won't think I'm talking nonsense," she said, "but now that your husband is away, don't you feel lonely during the night?"

"Do you ask that?" Wang Liu'er cried. "Why, you're the very one who has made me so. Indeed, since you are responsible, I am expecting you to come and keep me company in the evenings."

"I'm afraid I can hardly do so," the old woman said, "but perhaps I know someone who can. You may not care about it, though."

"Whom do you mean?" Wang Liu'er said.

Old woman Feng put her hand before her mouth and laughed. "One host suffices for a single guest," she said. "I mean our master. Yesterday, he came to see me, and said you must be very lonely now that your daughter has gone away, and he would like to come and try to console you. What do you think? No one else is concerned in the matter, and if you are kind to him, you need never worry again about a livelihood. Indeed, if he comes often, he will probably buy you a house, and you will find it much more pleasant than living in a hole like this."

Wang Liu'er smiled. "He has already many ladies of his own, beautiful enough to be the wives of the gods. What can he want from an ugly thing like me?"

"You must not say that," the old woman said. "There is an old proverb that says: Beauty springeth from the lover's eyes. Fate has decided this for you. If he had not taken a fancy to you he would not have come to see me yesterday. He gave me a tael of silver, and said it was for arranging your daughter's marriage. Then, seeing there was no one to hear him, he spoke to me about yourself, and now he is only waiting for your answer. After all, it is like selling a field: a piece of business that depends solely on the will of the two parties concerned. It has nothing to do with me."

"Well," the woman said, "if he would really like to come, tell him I shall expect him tomorrow."

Old woman Feng, now that she had gained her point, stayed a little longer and then took her leave. The next day Ximen came again to see her and she told him the result of her visit. He was delighted and gave her another tael of silver to buy wine and food.

When Wang Liu'er knew that Ximen was coming, she swept out her room, burned fragrant incense, set clean hangings around the bed, and prepared some special tea. Old woman Feng came first, with a basket full of fresh vegetables and fruits. She went into the kitchen to prepare them. Wang Liu'er washed her hands, cleaned her nails and prepared some food. In the sitting room, she scrubbed and cleaned the tables and chairs till they shone.

It was afternoon when Ximen Qing came, dressed in his civilian clothes, and wearing shades upon his eyes. Daian and Qitong followed him. When Ximen had dismounted, he gave orders that the horses should be taken to the house in Lion Street and brought again that evening. He only kept Daian with him. Wang Liu'er, exquisitely dressed, came to the sitting room to welcome him.

"It was very kind of you to take so much trouble over my daughter's wedding," she said. "It is hard for me to find words to express my gratitude."

"Not at all," Ximen said politely, "I must ask you and your husband to pardon me for what I failed to do."

"What complaint could we possibly make," the woman said, "since everyone in our household is so much in your debt?" She kowtowed to him four times. Old woman Feng brought tea, and Wang Liu'er handed it to Ximen Qing. Meanwhile Daian saw the horses taken away, and bolted the gate.

Ximen Qing and the woman sat for a while, and at last she invited him to go and see her own room. The windows and doors were papered; there were a long bed and a few chests. On the wall were four pieces of tapestry that depicted Zhang Sheng meeting with Ying Ying, and bees and flowers. There were tables and tea tables, large mirrors and small, boxes and pewter, all set out in their proper places. A stick of incense was burning. In the place of honor was a chair, in which Ximen Qing sat down, while the woman again prepared some tea with walnuts and offered it to him, taking the cup when he had finished it.

Wang Liu'er sat down on the edge of the bed and chatted about matters of no particular importance. Ximen saw that she brought in all the trays herself.

"You ought to have someone to wait on you," he said.

"Ah," the woman said, "now my daughter has gone, things are certainly difficult. I have to do everything myself."

"You must not put yourself out," Ximen said. "I will arrange with old woman Feng to find a girl about thirteen or fourteen years old for you. She may be able to save you a little."

Wang Liu'er suggested that she must wait until her husband came back, but Ximen hastily assured her that not only would he make all the arrangements, but he would also pay the expenses.

"Have I not troubled you enough already?" the woman said.

Ximen Qing was delighted to discover how intelligent the woman seemed. When old woman Feng came in to set the table, he spoke to her about the girl.

"You must thank his Lordship," the old woman said. "Sister Jiao, down in the South of the city, has just the girl you need, thirteen years old, and she only asks four taels for her. In my opinion, that is the girl you should ask his Lordship to buy for you."

Wang Liu'er bowed to Ximen. Then the food was brought, and the wine heated. She poured out a full cup of wine and presented it to him with both hands. She was about to kneel before him, but he would not allow this.

"You have already made one reverence to me," he said; "there is no need for you to repeat it."

The woman smiled, and sat down upon a small bench. Old woman Feng brought the dishes from the kitchen, one by one, and finally a kind of savory paste. Wang Liu'er selected the tastiest morsels of meat, took some of the vegetables, rolled them up in the paste and handed the roll to Ximen on a small plate. They passed their wine cups to one another and drank together. Meanwhile old woman Feng offered Daian a chair in the kitchen, and saw that he was well fed.

When they had taken a few cups together, the woman moved her seat nearer to Ximen's, and they passed their wine from mouth to mouth. After making sure that there was no one about, Ximen threw his arms around her, kissed her and caressed her tongue with his own. She took the jade scepter into her hand. Their passions were stirred into flame. They drank no more, but saw to the fastenings upon the door. Then both took off their clothes, and the woman prepared the coverlets upon the bed. It was the hour before sunset. The wine had set Ximen Qing on fire. He took the silver clasp from its case, and put it in position, while the woman fondly touched him with her slender hands. She thought his weapon looked magnificent; the veins swelled with dark red blood, and the flesh was firm and powerful. She sat on his knees; they threw their arms around each other's necks, and kissed again. Then she raised one of her legs, and, with her hand, helped that sword to find its scabbard. For a while they jousted together. Ximen Qing allowed his hands to wander over the woman's body. It was very soft but firm. The hair was fine and delicate. Eventually he told her to lie on the bed; he pulled her legs around his body and threw himself fiercely into the struggle.

> The god of battle now holds sway over the green-clad bed.
> The coverlets, with silk-embroidered love birds, feel the press of strife.
> Heroes display their prowess on the coral pillows
> Striving for victory within the silken curtains.
> The hero dashes madly to the fray, plunges his spear with fury home.
> The heroine's heart beats wildly. She yawns and gapes and fain
> would all devour him.
> Then up he brings his pair of culverins, and lets them loose upon
> the enemy skulking in the trousers.
> The other raises her shield to meet the mad attack of the great
> general stationed beneath the navel.
> One plays the golden cockerel, standing on single leg, raising the
> other high, to show his mettle
> The other, like a stripped tree, with roots that spread in all directions, thrusts forth to meet the foe.
> When they have fought a while, the shining eyes are dimmed
> A single movement makes them squirm and quiver.
> Though their limbs tremble, they still fight on
> Clashing a hundred times, they cannot break away,
> Then, letting loose the dam, the captain of the scanty hair would
> drown his enemy in the flood.
> The general in black armor feigns to make a thrust, but turns aside
> and seeks to fly.

The warden of the navel is unhorsed, thrown down and ground to
    dust in but a moment.
Lord "warm and tight" now plays the fool, tumbling he falls to the
    far depths of the abyss.
The heavy mail is broken into pieces, like faded blossoms when
    the storm breaks on them
The silken cap gives way beneath the strain, like fallen leaves be-
    fore the raging winds
And Marshal "sulfurous," his crest awry, can find no place to flee.
Prince "Silver Armor" holds his ground, and swears he'll stand till
    death.
The skies are hidden by a sad dark cloud
The warriors roll stricken on the field.

Wang Liu'er liked one game more than any other. When she had
joined with him as lovers do, she wanted him to enjoy the flower in her
bottom while she played with the flower in her womb. Satisfied in this
way, she reached the blissful oblivion that is the aim of lovers. She used
to practice this game so often that in thirty days Han Daoguo would take
his pleasure at the front gate no more than three times. Apart from this,
she titillated his ivory scepter with her lips and fondled it all night with
never-failing desire; if its master flagged, her lips returned his strength.

Nothing could have given Ximen Qing greater pleasure. All that day
they played, till the watchman gave his first warning. Then he went home.

Before Ximen left her, Wang Liu'er asked him to come again the next
day, and to come early. She promised that if he did so, he should not go
away unsatisfied. Ximen could have asked for nothing better.

The next day he went to the thread shop in Lion Street, and took four
taels of silver. These he gave to old woman Feng, and told her to purchase
the maid. Two days later, Ximen, who could not forget the sweetness of
his last visit, went again to visit Wang Liu'er. Qitong and Daian went
with him. When they reached the house, he told Qitong to take his horse
to Lion Street. Old woman Feng came to attend to the wine and other
things, and set them out. By such small services as these, she hoped to
enrich her belly with oil and vegetables.

This time, Ximen Qing gave to Wang Liu'er a few taels of silver for
household expenses. It was day when he arrived, and night when he went
away. Not one word of the matter did he mention to any member of his
own household.

Old woman Feng went every day to work for Wang Liu'er, so she
seldom had time to go to Ximen Qing's house. Li Ping'er sent a boy two
or three times to summon her, but she was far too busy to come. Often,

indeed, she locked her door and stayed out all day. One day, Huatong ran across her in the street and made her go with him to Li Ping'er.

"Now, old woman," her mistress said, "for some days I have not seen even your shadow; what game is this you're playing? Every time I have sent after you, you have been out. It looks as if you didn't wish to come. Here I have been, as busy as could be, with a pile of clothes and the baby's bedclothes, all waiting for you to come and help the maids to wash them. And you never came."

"It is easy for you to talk, my lady," the old woman said, "but I have been like a scrivener running after a deserter. I am as busy as anybody can be. One day I seem to be a salt seller, and the next I have to turn myself into a carpenter. I don't have a moment."

"It is all very well," Li Ping'er said. "When I ask you to come, you say you are too busy, but I should like to know where you have been earning your daily bread these last few days."

"I am like a vase whose ears the wind has blown away; it can't get them back with its mouth.[1] I have not earned anything. You are angry with me, I see, but I simply have not had a chance to come and see you. I have been too busy to know where I am. The other day, the Great Lady gave me some money to buy her a cushion for her prayers, and I forgot all about it. When I did remember, yesterday, the rogue of a cushion seller had taken himself off, and I don't know what to say to her."

"Do you mean to say you have come without the cushion?" Li Ping'er said. "I should advise you to see if you can't find some monkey to run off with you. She gives you the money; you come empty-handed, and then pretend you don't know what you're about."

"I am going to give the Great Lady her money back," the old woman said. "Yesterday I went for a ride on a donkey and nearly fell off."

"If it happens again," said Li Ping'er, "you will certainly be killed."

Old woman Feng went to the inner court to see Wu Yueniang, but first she called at the kitchen. Yuxiao and Laixing's wife were sitting together. When they saw her, one of them said: "Why, here is old woman Feng! Well, honorable madam, and where have you been? The Sixth Lady is ready to eat you up."

The old woman greeted them. "I have just come from her," she said, "and a nice to-do she made."

"My mistress wants to know whether you have bought her cushion," Yuxiao said.

"Yesterday," the old woman said, "I took the money and went outside

---

1. i.e. I am not in a position to argue with you.

the city, but the cushion seller had sold his stock and gone home. He will not be here again before the third month next year. Here is the silver. Please take it, Sister."

"You marvelous old woman," Yuxiao said. "At the moment our master is weighing some silver. When he has gone, you had better see our mistress for yourself. Meanwhile, please sit down. By the way, it seems a long time since Han went off with that daughter of his. He ought to be back now, surely. When he does come, you will be in luck. He will certainly have to give you something."

"Something or nothing," the old woman said, "that is his concern. But he has only been gone about eight days. I don't see how he can be back before the end of the month."

Ximen Qing finished weighing the silver and gave it to Ben the Fourth to spend on the estate. Then he went out, and the old woman went to the upper room to see Wu Yueniang. She did not produce the money but said that the cushions which the merchant had were not good enough. The better ones were sold, and he had gone home to fetch some of an especially good quality. Yueniang was simple and unsuspecting. She said: "That is all right. Keep the money and bring me two cushions next year." She gave the old woman some cakes and old Feng then went back to see Li Ping'er.

"Did the Great Lady scold you?" Li Ping'er said.

"No," said the old woman. "I told her something that made her very happy and she gave me some tea and a few cakes."

"The cakes have come from the Qiao family," Li Ping'er said. "It was the day of the first full month for them yesterday. Well, old woman, your mouth has been stopped. You are like the mosquitoes that come in the fourth month, those that have such a deadly bite. Anyhow, now you are here, you must stay and wash some clothes for me."

"Put the things in soak," the old woman said, "and I will come early tomorrow. This afternoon, I have to go and do some business for a very special client of mine."

"Oh, you old rogue," Li Ping'er said, "you always find some excuse. If you do not turn up tomorrow, you shall see what happens."

The old woman laughed. She stayed a little longer talking with Li Ping'er, and then prepared to go. Her mistress asked her if she would have some food before she went, but she said she was not hungry, and would not stay. Really, she was wondering whether Ximen Qing might not be going to see Wang Liu'er, and she scuttled away as fast as her old legs would carry her.

CHAPTER 38

Pan Jinlian Is Melancholy

When old woman Feng came to the door beside the great hall, Daian was standing there with a tea tray in his hands, waiting. He looked at the old woman, made a face and said: "You go first. We shall start as soon as Father has finished talking to Uncle Ying. Qitong has already gone with the wine." The old woman quickened her pace and hurried away.

Ying Bojue had come to say that Li Zhi and Huang the Fourth, the contractors, had secured orders for the provision of thirty thousand lots of incense and wax for the annual contribution to the Emperor, in value about ten thousand taels. "Of course, there will be interest," he said, "and they are to be paid the money in Dongpingfu when the contract is completed. I have come to see what you think about it, and whether you would like to take a hand."

"Why should I?" Ximen said. "These contractors are all rogues. They will bribe the officials so as to get some advantage for themselves. Now that I am an official myself, I must not get mixed up in affairs of that sort."

"Brother," Ying Bojue said, "if you feel you cannot, I must ask somebody else. But I venture to ask you to lend two thousand taels, with interest at five per cent. to be paid monthly, and the capital to be repaid when they get their money. What do you say to that?"

"Since it is you who come to ask," Ximen said, "I think I might manage a thousand taels for them, but I am spending a great deal of money on my estate and have not much to spare."

Ying Bojue, seeing that his friend showed less disinclination in this matter, said: "If you can manage it, why not add five hundred more and make it fifteen hundred? They will not dare to be late with their payments."

"If they are late," Ximen said, "I shall know how to deal with them. Just one word, Brother Ying. If I let them have this money, I won't have them going here there and everywhere, using my name and doing dirty work under my banner. If I hear of anything of that sort, they will discover that the local jail is a most uncomfortable lodging."

"You should not say that, Brother," Ying Bojue said. "If they have responsibilities, they must carry them out. If they go about using your name, it will be all right for them, but if they do anything wrong, what shall I do? Please do not think any more about that, Brother. If there is anything wrong, I will answer for it. Now that you have made up your mind, I will bring them tomorrow to sign the document."

"Don't bring them tomorrow," Ximen Qing said, "I shall be busy. The day after will be more convenient."

Bojue went away, and Ximen Qing told Daian to saddle his horse. He put on his eyeshades and asked if Qitong had gone. "He came and took the net for the wine jar and went off with it," Daian said. He helped Ximen Qing on to his horse, and they set out for Ox-hide Alley.

One day Han the Second, Han Daoguo's younger brother, the ne'er-do-well, lost all his money gambling, drank till his eyes almost came out of his head, and then went to his brother's house to ask Wang Liu'er to give him some more wine. He took some little sausages from his sleeve and said: "Sister-in-law, my brother is away and I am going to drink a jar of wine with you."

The woman was afraid. She knew Ximen Qing was coming, and old woman Feng was in the kitchen. She would have nothing to do with him.

"I'm not going to drink," she said. "If you wish to, go and drink by yourself. I have no patience with you. Your brother is not at home. Why do you come here and bother me?"

Han the Second glared with his greedy eyes and refused to go away. Then, underneath the table, he saw a jar of wine, sealed and with a label of red paper. "Sister-in-law," he said, "where did you get that wine? Open it and have a pot warmed for me. You know how to enjoy yourself."

"You must not touch it," Wang Liu'er cried, "it came from the Master's. Your brother has not seen it yet, but when he comes back, you shall certainly have some of it."

"Why should I wait for my brother?" Han the Second cried. "I don't care if it belongs to the Emperor. I am going to have a cup."

He was going to remove the seal, but the woman snatched it out of his hand, and took it to her room. As she did so, she pushed Han the Second, and he fell to the ground, his face upturned to the skies. He had considerable difficulty in getting to his feet again, and his shame was turned to anger.

"You thievish whore!" he mumbled. "I am kind to you and bring you something to eat. I remember that you are lonely and come to have a drink with you. But instead of taking any interest in me, you knock me down. Let me tell you this. Don't you get on any high horse. I know you have a rich lover. That is why you won't have anything to do with me. You want to get me out of the way, so you insult me and push me about. You took very good care not to let me know. If you had done, you worthless wretch, you would have seen my knife go in white and come out red."

When Wang Liu'er heard him talking so unpleasantly, the color came into her cheeks and spread from her ears until her whole face was crimson. She took a dolly pin in her hand, beat him, and cursed him. "You starving thief! Where did you get drunk before coming here to spread your wild fire? I will never forgive you." Han the Second, mumbling and calling her evil names, finally went out, still cursing.

At that moment, Ximen Qing arrived. He saw what happened and asked who the man was. "Who is he, indeed?" Wang Liu'er cried. "Why, that Han the Second. He knew his brother was not at home, so when he had lost his money gambling, he got drunk and came here to knock me about. His brother often had to give him a thrashing when he was here."

When Han the Second saw Ximen Qing, he was off like a streak of smoke.

"The beggar!" Ximen Qing said, "tomorrow I will give him a little moral instruction at my office."

"I am sorry he made you angry," Wang Liu'er said.

"You don't know," Ximen said. "With fellows like that, one must not be too indulgent."

"You are right," the woman said, "it never pays to be generous with some people."

She asked Ximen Qing to go in and sit down. He told Qitong to take back his horse, and said to Daian: "You stand at the door, and, if you see even so much as that rascal's shadow, tie him up, and I'll have him before me at the office tomorrow."

"When he knows you are here," Daian said, "his spirit will not know where to hide itself."

Ximen Qing sat down, and Wang Liu'er made a reverence to him. Then she bade her young maid bring some tea with nuts for him. She told the girl to kowtow.

"She seems a good girl," Ximen said. "You must use her as you think fit." Then he added: "Old woman Feng is here. Why doesn't she bring the tea?"

"The old lady is in the kitchen," Wang Liu'er said. "She is doing some work I told her to do, and busy at the moment."

"That wine I told a boy to bring you," Ximen said, "was presented to me by a eunuch. It is 'Bamboo Leaves' wine, which has a good many drugs mixed with it and is very potent. The other day I found that the wine you have is not good enough for me, and so I sent this jar."

Wang Liu'er again made a reverence to him. "Thank you for the wine," she said. "We are unpretentious people, and live in this hole-and-corner street where there is no good wineshop at which I can get any of the best wine. If I want it, I have to go to the High Street to buy it."

"When your husband comes back," Ximen said, "I am going to arrange with him to buy a house in Lion Street, and then you can go to live there. It is near our own shop and in a good district for buying things."

"How kind of you, my lord, to think of me like that. I have been anxious for a long time to get away from this place. If we move, it will be easier for you to come and see me, and we shall escape people's chatter. Of course, my behavior is perfectly correct, and I don't care what they say. Father, do whatever seems good to you, whether my husband is at home or not."

They talked for a while, then Wang Liu'er set out a table in her own room, and invited Ximen to go in and take off his cloak. Wine and dishes were brought, and she poured wine for him and drank with him. She sat upon his knees, and so they drank. When they had had wine enough, they took off their clothes and went to the bed, where they played together merrily and without constraint. Wang Liu'er had placed soft bedclothes on her bed, and perfumed them with most powerful scent. Ximen Qing had discovered that she was well skilled in the arts of love, and was anxious to show her that he himself was no mean performer.

In his sleeve he had a silken kerchief. He opened it. Inside were a silver clasp, a lover's cap, a sulfur ring, a white silk ribbon with medicinal properties, and all manner of things for increasing passion. Wang Liu'er set her head upon the pillow.

She lifted her ivory-white legs to show her cock's tongue. Ximen asked whether he could put his medicine into it; he attached the silver clasp to the root of his penis, added the sulfur ring and smeared his belly with ointment from the navel downwards. She grasped his treasure and put it deep inside her, embracing him hard and long.

"Are your legs tired?" said Wang Liu'er. "Hold the bed; I'll move my body." And again, "I hope you're not in pain. Shouldn't I lift my legs higher?"

Ximen tied her leg to the bed and pressed down with his body. The juice of love flowed continually from her body like snail's slime. Something white came out too, and Ximen asked, "Why have you got so much of this?"

He was about to clean himself, but Wang Liu'er said, "Wait, I'll clean you in my own way," knelt down, and licked him clean with her sensuous tongue.

Then Ximen, again fired with desire, turned her over and started on the flower in her bottom. But the sulfur on his penis proved sticky, so progress was difficult and she grimaced with pain. He made little headway, and Wang Liu'er, feeling about with her hand, found that he had gone only halfway. She turned around and said, with a winning look, "Darling, please go in slowly. The root of your prick is bigger than I can take." Ximen lifted his legs so that he could see himself going in and out.

"Wang Liu'er, my daughter," he said, "there is nothing I enjoy more than this. It is well that I met you: you please me greatly. I will never leave you."

"Dearest," Wang Liu'er said, "my only fear is that you will tire of me and put me aside."

"If you had known me longer, you would know that I am not that kind of man."

They talked and sported together for a long time. "Unless you speak lovingly to me," Ximen said at last, "I will not yield to you." Then Wang Liu'er raised herself upon her hands to receive the stream of life. Ximen had such an orgasm that the liquid flowed like a torrent. He withdrew, still wearing the ring. Wang Liu'er washed him orally, and they lay down together.

Ximen Qing and Wang Liu'er embraced, and lay together till the second night watch. Then a boy came with a horse, and he went home.

The next day, when he reached his office, he sent two policemen to seize Han the Second. The young man was treated as a footpad, and, without any trial, the screws were put upon him and he was given twenty stripes. The blood ran down his legs. For a month he had to keep his bed. Indeed, he nearly died. This frightened him so much that he never again passed anywhere near the woman's door.

The days passed. Laibao, Han Daoguo and the others came back from the Eastern Capital and gave an account of their journey to Ximen Qing. "Comptroller Zhai," Han Daoguo said, "was very pleased with my daughter, and told us to thank you very much. We stayed a few days with him. Then he gave me a letter of thanks, and sent you a black horse as a present. Clerk Han got fifty taels of silver, and I got twenty as journey money."

"Money enough," said Ximen Qing. He read the letter of thanks. Ever afterwards, Zhai and Ximen Qing regarded one another as kinsmen and addressed each other as such.

Han Daoguo kowtowed to Ximen Qing and made ready to go. "Han," Ximen said, "the money is yours. A daughter like that is worth it."

Han Daoguo hesitated to take it. "Only the other day," he said, "you were good enough to lend me money. How can I take this now? I have already troubled you enough."

"If you do not take it, I shall be annoyed. Take it home with you, but do not spend it. I will tell you why later."

Han Daoguo expressed his gratitude and went away. His wife was very pleased to see him. She took his luggage, cleaned the dust from him, and asked him question after question about her daughter's affairs. Han Daoguo told her about the journey.

"It is an excellent household," he said. "When our daughter arrived, she was given three rooms for herself, and two maids to wait on her. As for clothes and jewels, they were too many for me to give you any idea of them. The day after her arrival she went to pay her respects to the Lady, and Comptroller Zhai was delighted with her. He asked us to stay a day or two, and entertained us so well that, even with the servants, there was too much for us. He gave me a present of fifty taels that I did not mean to keep, but our master would not have it, and told me to keep it."

He gave the money to his wife. She was as delighted as a piece of stone when at last it comes to rest upon the ground. "We must give a tael to old woman Feng," she said. "She has very kindly come here all the time you have been away. Our master has already given her one tael."

As they were talking, the little maid brought them tea. "Who is this?" Han Daoguo said.

"I have just bought her," his wife said, "and her name is Jin'er." Then she said to the girl: "Come here and kowtow to your father." The little girl did so and then retired to the kitchen.

Wang Liu'er told her husband all about her dealings with Ximen Qing. "Since you have been away," she said, "he has been here three or four times. He gave me four taels of silver to buy this little girl, and, every time he comes, he gives me a tael or two. That younger brother of ours, who does not know the difference between high and low, came piddling around. Master Ximen happened to see him, and he was haled to the office and well beaten there. Since then he has never dared to show his face again. Our master says this place is not very convenient, and he has promised to buy a house in the main street, and let us go there."

"I see now why he would not take the silver," Han Daoguo said, "but asked me to take it and not to spend it. Now I understand what he was thinking about."

"Well," Wang Liu'er said, "here are fifty taels. We will add a few more, and buy a really fine house. Then we shall have a comfortable life, good eating and fine clothes. It is obviously worth while my letting him have me."

"Tomorrow," Han Daoguo said, "if he should happen to come when I have gone to the shop, pretend that I know nothing about it, and don't treat him unkindly. Do everything he would have you do, for it is no easy matter making money nowadays, and I know no better way than this."

Wang Liu'er laughed. "You rascal. It is easy money for you, but you don't know the sufferings I have to endure." They both laughed heartily. She prepared supper, and they went to bed.

The next day Han went to Ximen's house to get the key, then opened the shop and gave old woman Feng a tael of silver for her pains.

⁂⁂⁂⁂⁂⁂

One day Magistrate Xia and Ximen Qing left the office together. Xia saw that his colleague was riding a big dappled black horse. "Why don't you ride your white horse now, but this black one? This is a fine horse, but I am not so sure about his mouth."

"I am letting my white horse have a few days' rest," Ximen said. "This one was sent to me by my kinsman Zhai at the Eastern Capital. He got it from General Liu of Xixia. It has good teeth, and is not too fast or too slow, but it has one slight defect; it won't let any other horse get near the manger. When I first had it, it lost its sleekness for a while, but it has been eating better these last few days."

"It seems to me to go very well," Magistrate Xia said, "but if I were you, I should keep it for riding about town and not take it too far. A horse like that would cost seventy or eighty taels to buy here. There has been something wrong with my horse, and before I could come to the office today, I had to borrow this one from a relative. It is a very poor beast."

"Don't let that upset you," Ximen Qing said. "I have another one at home, a chestnut. You shall have that."

Magistrate Xia bowed. "If you are really so kind, I must pay you, of course."

"Don't think of such a thing," Ximen said. "As soon as I get home, I will have it brought to you." They came to West Street and there separated.

When Ximen reached home, he told Daian to take the horse to his colleague Xia. The magistrate was very pleased and gave the boy a tael of silver. "Thank your master for me," he said, "and I will thank him myself when I see him at the office."

Two months went by. Magistrate Xia made some chrysanthemum wine, engaged two young actors, and invited Ximen Qing. Ximen dined at home, attended to some business, and then went to the party. Xia had prepared an excellent repast especially for Ximen Qing, and was very pleased when he arrived. He came down the steps to welcome his guests, and they greeted each other in the hall.

"Why have you been to so much trouble on my account?" Ximen said.

"I have simply made a little chrysanthemum wine," said Xia, "and thought I might perhaps invite you to my poor house for a talk. I have not invited anyone else." They took off their ceremonial clothes, and sat down in the places of guest and host. After tea, they played chess. Then they sat and drank wine while they talked. The young actors played and sang for them.

For a long time, Ximen Qing had not been to the apartments of Pan Jinlian. She felt the loneliness of her curtained bed, the coldness of its dainty coverlets. One day, she opened the corner gate and lighted the silver lamp in her room. She leaned upon the screen and played her lute. It was about midway between the second and the third night watches. Several times, she sent Chunmei to look for her husband, but Chunmei could never see him.

Through the long night she played her silver lute, but the room seemed so lonely that she could not bear to continue. Then she took the lute and laid it upon her knees. She played softly to herself and sang

> I rested sadly on the lattice
> Then sought my rest without undressing.

Suddenly, she thought she heard a sound on the gong outside and imagined it was Ximen's signal. Hastily, she bade Chunmei go out to see. "You were mistaken, Mother," Chunmei said when she returned, "it was only the wind. It is going to snow." Then Jinlian sang again.

> I hear the sound of the wind
> The snow is fluttering against my window
> And the ice flowers drifting one by one.

The lamp grew dim, and the incense burned out. She would have drawn the wick, but there was no sign of Ximen Qing. She could not summon energy enough to touch it. She sang again.

> I am too languid to trim the jeweled lamp
> I am too languid to light the incense
> I make shift to pass the night
> Dreading the morrow that must come.
> When I think of you, how shall my sadness end?
> When I think of you, my mind is consumed.
> You have despoiled my tender years, the flower of my youth
> You have deserted me.
> You have not fulfilled the promise you made in days gone by.

About the first night watch, Ximen Qing returned from Magistrate Xia's house. As he rode along, the sky was dark and lowering. The sleet covered his cloak and melted where it fell. He pressed his horse homeward. The boys carried lanterns for him. He did not go to the inner court but straight to the room of Li Ping'er. Li Ping'er welcomed him, brushed off the snow, and took his clothes. Dressed only in his silken gown, he sat on her bed and asked if the baby was asleep. "He has been playing for some time and now he has gone to sleep," Li Ping'er told him. Yingchun brought tea.

"Why have you come back from your party so early?" Li Ping'er said.

Ximen Qing said: "Some time ago, I gave Xia a horse, and today he gave a feast especially for me, and engaged two young actors. I saw that it was going to snow, so I came back in good time."

"Would you like to drink again?" Li Ping'er said. "I will tell the maid to heat some wine for you. You came back through the snow and you must not catch cold."

"We have some good grape wine," Ximen said. "Heat some of that for me. The wine I drank at Xia's place was homemade chrysanthemum wine, but I do not care much for its strong odor and I did not have enough to drink."

Yingchun set out a table with refreshments and fruits. Li Ping'er sat down on a little bench opposite Ximen. There was a small charcoal burner under the table. They sat together drinking. Meanwhile, Jinlian was cold and lonely in her room. She sat on the bed with her lute still upon her knees. The lamp had gone out, and the candles were dim. She would have gone to sleep, but she still hoped that Ximen might come. She was sleepy and cold. At last, she took off her headdress, tied her hair carelessly, pulled down the curtain, and sat on the bed with the bedclothes huddled over her.

> I cast myself upon the embroidered bed
> too sad to sleep.
> I draw the silken curtains.
> But there is only emptiness within them.
> Would that I had known his faithlessness before
> My trusting heart meets with an ill reward.

Again she sang:

> I hate him for his cruelty, so lightly he deserted me.
> In hours of idleness, our separation tortures me.

Once again, she bade Chunmei go outside to look for Ximen. "Go once more to see if Father is coming," she said. "Come back quickly and tell me."

The maid soon returned. "Mother," she said, "are you still thinking that Father is not back? He came back a long time ago and he is drinking in the Sixth Lady's room."

This was more than Jinlian could bear. It made her suffer as though her heart had been pierced by knives. Over and over again she cursed him for a fickle-hearted rogue. Tears rolled down her cheeks. She lifted her lute and sang.

> My heart aches. I cannot comfort it
> Sorrow and misery consume me utterly
> He casts aside the tender peach and seeks a bitter fruit.
> He, whom I made my guide, led me astray.
> When I think of you, my mind is consumed.
> You have despoiled my tender years, the flower of my youth
> You have deserted me.
> You have not fulfilled the promise you made in days gone by.

Ximen Qing suddenly heard the strains of the lute. "Who is playing the lute?" he asked.

"It is the Fifth Lady," Yingchun said.

"Hasn't the Fifth Lady gone to bed yet?" Li Ping'er said. "Go at once," she said to Xiuchun, "and ask her to come and take wine with us. Tell her I ask her to come."

Xiuchun went out, and Li Ping'er told Yingchun to place another seat for the Fifth Lady and to set out cup and chopsticks. When the maid came back, she said Jinlian would not come, she had gone to bed. "You go and ask her," Li Ping'er said to Yingchun. But Yingchun came back with the same story.

"The Fifth Lady has fastened the corner gate and blown out her lamp. She has gone to bed."

"Don't believe the little strumpet," Ximen Qing said. "Let us go and drag her out. We will make her come and then we will play chess with her."

He went with Li Ping'er to the corner gate. After they had knocked for a long time, Chunmei came and opened it. Ximen Qing took Li Ping'er by the hand, and they went together into Jinlian's room. She was sitting inside the bed curtains, with the lute beside her.

"You funny little strumpet," Ximen said, "why do we have to send for you three times, and still you won't come?"

Jinlian sat on the bed and did not make the slightest show of moving. She looked sulky. After a long wait, she said: "Unlucky people like me are only fit to be left in the cold. Let me live my own life. Don't trouble about me. Don't try to be kind to me. Save all your attentions for others."

"You marvelous little slave!" Ximen said, "you are like an eighty-year-old woman who has lost her teeth but can still make shift to chatter without them. Your Sixth Sister wants to play chess, and we have waited for you a long time."

"Yes, Sister," Li Ping'er said. "I have set out the chess, and we have nothing better to do. Let us play and win some wine to drink."

"Sister," Jinlian said, "please go away. I shall not come. You don't seem to realize that I am not very well. I need sleep. I have more to worry me than you have. These last few days I have had a wandering fit. Who but I would have to taste yellow soup and plain water? I have had to spend my days looking at my own face."

"There is nothing at all the matter with you," Ximen Qing said. "Why do you pretend to be ill? If you really are, tell me, and I will send for the doctor."

"You don't believe me, do you?" Jinlian said. "Chunmei, bring me my mirror and let me look at myself. I have been growing thinner and thinner day by day."

Chunmei brought her a mirror and she looked at her reflection in the lamplight. Ximen took the mirror from her and looked at himself in it. "I am not very thin," he said.

"You don't expect me to look like you, do you?" Jinlian said. "You drink wine day after day, and gobble down huge slices of meat. You have grown fat. Now you are making fun of me."

Ximen Qing said no more, but seated himself beside her on the bed. He put his arm around her neck and kissed her. He would have stretched out his hand to smooth her body, but she was still wearing her clothes. He put both hands around her waist. "My daughter," he said, "you really are thinner."

"How cold your hands are, you funny creature," Jinlian said. "You make me feel like ice. Did you think I was trying to deceive you? Nobody cares if I am sad, and my tears flow down to my own stomach."

She resisted for a little longer, but Ximen Qing dragged her bodily to the room of Li Ping'er. There they played chess and drank wine. When Jinlian had to go away, Li Ping'er noticed that her face was sour, and urged Ximen Qing to go with her.

CHAPTER 39
The Temple of the Jade Emperor

Ximen Qing stayed the night in Pan Jinlian's room. It seemed to her detestable that she could not unite herself even more completely with her lover. In a thousand delightful ways she made love to him: in ten thousand different manners she sported with him. Her tears fell softly on the silken coverlets, and her words were warm and gentle. She wished, more than all else, to win her husband utterly for herself.

She did not know, however, that Ximen was on such intimate terms with Wang Liu'er. He spent a hundred and twenty taels of silver on a house east of the stone bridge for Wang Liu'er to live in. Two rooms stood upon the street, and it was four rooms deep. There was a guest room, a shrine for the worship of Buddha and the ancestors, a bedroom, and a kitchen. When they removed there, the neighbors knew that Han Daoguo was Ximen Qing's clerk, and no one dared to behave other than kindly. Many sent boxes of tea and presents to celebrate the housewarming. They called Han Daoguo Brother Han or Son-in-law Han, and the young people addressed them as Uncle and Aunt.

Whenever Ximen Qing came to the house, Han Daoguo would sleep at the shop so as to allow complete freedom to his wife and her lover. Ximen came in the morning and went away in the evening and all the neighbors knew of it. Yet they were so in awe of his power and wealth that none of them dared to say a word. In less than a month, Ximen Qing visited the woman at least three or four times, and their passion for each other was as fiery as burning charcoal.

The end of the year was approaching, and Ximen was busy arranging to send presents to the Eastern Capital. He also prepared gifts for the civil officers of the district and those of his own department. About this time, Abbot Wu of the Temple of the Jade Emperor bade his novices take to Ximen Qing four boxes of gifts, "Heaven and Earth" pictures, charms for the coming spring, and prayers to the God of Fire. Ximen Qing was taking a meal in his wife's room when Daian brought a card upon which was written: "The unworthy priest, Wu Zongjia, offers these things with his most respectful compliments." Ximen Qing read it.

"This priest," he said, "has troubled himself on my account again."

He told Daian to ask Shutong to give a tael of silver with his card to the young novice.

"He is a priest," Wu Yueniang said, "and every new year and every festival you take presents from him. You would do well to make the sacrifice you promised when the Sixth Lady's baby was born."

"Thank you for reminding me," Ximen Qing said. "I did promise to make a first-class sacrifice, but I had forgotten all about it."

"You are a splendid example of gratitude," Yueniang said. "Whoever heard of anyone forgetting a promise of that kind? Your mouth makes promises readily, but your mind is elsewhere at the time. The gods do not forget. No wonder the baby is always cross. It must be because you have not kept your word."

"If you think that," Ximen said, "we will have the sacrifice at Abbot Wu's temple at the beginning of the new year."

"The Sixth Lady told me yesterday that the boy had not been very well," Yueniang said. "She was thinking about giving the boy a name."

"Well, we have the very place," Ximen Qing said. "We will enroll him at the Temple of the Jade Emperor." He said to Daian: "Who has come from the temple?"

"The novice Ying Chun," Daian told him.

Ximen Qing went out to see the young man. The novice kowtowed and said: "My master sends his compliments to you. He has nothing worthy to offer you, but ventures to send these trifles. They are for you to distribute among your servants."

Ximen Qing made a moderate reverence to Ying Chun, and asked him to thank the Abbot for his gifts. Then he invited the young novice to take a seat. Ying Chun bowed. "How dare I sit in your presence?" he said. But Ximen made him sit down, saying that he wished to talk to him. The novice was wearing a small hat and a long black gown. He was very modest in his bearing, and only after much hesitation was persuaded to take a chair and sit down. "What are your commands?" he asked. "In the first month of the new year," Ximen Qing said, "I wish to make a sacrifice, and would venture to ask your master to make the necessary arrangements. And I wish, too, to enroll my son's name in the register of your temple. But perhaps your master is too busy?"

The novice rose hastily. "Since such is your desire," he said, "even if we had other religious duties on that day, we should put them off."

"Then what about the ninth day?" Ximen Qing said. "Isn't that the birthday of the Gods?"

"Yes, that is the birthday of the Gods," the young priest said, "and it is written in the *Book of the Jade Casket* that upon that day we should pray the Gods to bless us, and the five blessings will descend together. It is an excellent day for fasting and worship. May I ask how many degrees of sacrifice you will require?"

"My son was born in the seventh month," Ximen Qing said. "At that time I vowed to make sacrifice of a hundred and twenty degrees."

"How many priests do you wish to take part in the sacrifice?"

"Let there be sixteen," Ximen Qing said.

A table was set, and the young priest was offered tea. Ximen gave him fifteen taels of silver for the expenses of the sacrifice, and one tael in return for the Abbot's gift. "There is no need for your master to prepare things," he said to the novice. "I myself will send paper offerings, incense and candles."

The young priest was so delighted that he completely forgot himself. He pissed himself and farted like thunder. He thanked Ximen Qing over and over again.

On the eighth day of the first month, Daian was sent to the temple with a measure of fine rice, a supply of paper money, and ten catties of official candles. He also took with him five catties of incense, and sixteen rolls of unbleached material for other things that were needed by the priests. In addition, Ximen Qing sent two rolls of brocade, two jars of Southern wine, four live geese, four live chickens, a set of pig's trotters, a leg of mutton and ten taels of silver. All this was for the enrollment of the baby's name.

Cards of invitation to the ceremony were sent to Uncle Wu, Uncle Hua, Ying Bojue and Xie Xida. Chen Jingji, on horseback, went to the temple to see that everything was in order.

The ninth day came. Ximen Qing did not go to his office, but rose very early, dressed, then mounted a great white horse and set off by the East Gate to the Temple of the Jade Emperor. Attendants marched before and behind him. Even from a far distance they could see the banners, decorations and arches that had been set up. Soon they reached the temple gate and Ximen dismounted.

Passing through the first gate, he came to another, the Gate of the Meteor, on either side of which were scarlet boards, seven feet long, with these words written upon them.

Then Ximen Qing came to the main sanctuary. There, written in twenty-four characters, they saw a sign:

> In gratitude to Heaven and Earth we offer our treasures.
> May our land be blessed and our benefactors rewarded.
> We take an ally to ourselves, and enroll his name.
> May all good fortune descend abundantly upon our altar.

On either side were scrolls, bearing the inscriptions:

> Established before the Heavens
> May we behold the majesty of DAO
> And manifest our singleness of heart

and

> Here is the honorable dwelling of the Most High,
> Here can we behold the glory of the Pure Cultivation,
> Here would we show our gratitude for every blessing.

Ximen Qing went up to the shrine. Before the table of incense stood a boy, with a ewer, in which Ximen Qing washed his hands. Then an acolyte knelt down and invited him to burn incense. Ximen Qing prostrated himself before the altar. Abbot Wu was wearing a hat of the Nine Yang Thunder, with rings of jade and a sky-blue vestment, broad-sleeved and embroidered with the crane and the twenty-eight stars. A silken girdle was about his waist. He came down from the lectern and made a priestly reverence to Ximen Qing.

"Unworthy priest that I am," he said, "your misdirected kindness has often made me its object, and I have frequently received precious gifts from you. Consequently I feel that if I refuse them, I shall not be truly sincere; and if I do accept them, I must be ashamed. It is my duty to pray that your son may have length of days. Why should you send me such valuable presents? I am truly embarrassed. Besides, your gifts for the purposes of the sacrifice have been far too generous."

"But it is I who feel grateful for the trouble you have taken," Ximen Qing said. "I have done nothing to repay you. These things are a very slight token of my appreciation, and nothing more."

After these polite exchanges, the priests who stood on either hand came to greet Ximen Qing, and he was invited to go to the Abbot's cell. This was a large hall, three rooms wide, called the Hall of Pine Trees and of Cranes. There tea was served.

Ximen Qing sat down and told Qitong to take a horse for Ying Bojue. "I don't think he can have a horse, so that is why he has not arrived yet."

"The donkey that Brother-in-law Chen rides, is here," Daian said.

"Very well," Ximen said, "let him take that." Qitong went away.

When the Abbot had finished his reading of the sacred books, he came to offer tea to Ximen and then sat down to talk. "Realizing the keenness of your desire to worship Heaven," he said, "I rose this morning at the fourth watch and read many sacred texts at the altar for you. Today is the third dawn and the ninth revolution, and I performed all the necessary exercises for the worship of the Jade Pivot. I also prepared a document with your son's birthday and his eight characters, and presented the name to the Three Most Mighty Ones. The name I chose for him was Wu Yingyuan, calling upon him every blessing, continual prosperity and strength of body. I made ready a sacrifice of twenty-four degrees to offer to Heaven and Earth, twelve more for the glory of the gods, and still another twenty-four for the dead. So we have a hundred and eighty degrees in all."

Ximen Qing thanked the Abbot. After a while the drum was heard, and he was asked to go to the altar to see the document of enrollment. He dressed himself in a scarlet robe of ceremony with a five-colored badge of rank. Then he fastened about himself the girdle with the buckle of gilded rhinoceros horn. When he came to the altar, a lector, robed in purple, began the reading of the sacred purpose.

> The devout Ximen Qing, dwelling in Xianpaifang of Qinghe in the Province of Shandong, venerating the sacred Principle, comes to implore a blessing, to offer sacrifice, and to pray for peace. He was born at the hour of midnight, on the twentieth day of the seventh month of the year *Bingyin*. His wife Wu was born at the hour of midnight, on the fifteenth day of the eighth month in the year *Wuzhen*.

There the lector stopped. "Have you," he said to Ximen Qing, "any other members of your household whom you would wish me to include?"

"Simply write this," Ximen said. "Li, born at the hour of dawn on the fifteenth day of the first month in the year *Xinwei,* and the boy Guan'ge, born at the hour of *Shen* on the twenty-third day of the seventh month in the year *Bingshen.*"

The lector repeated this after him and returned to his reading.

> This day, I, Ximen Qing, and all my household come to fulfill our humble duty and to do worship before the Mighty Creator. My life is but a particle of dust from the lowest order of the Three Forces. Yet when I go out and come in; when I rise from my bed or seek it, I am ever indebted to the protection of the Dragon Heaven. Seasons change from hot to cold, yet the mercy of the Almighty never faileth me.
>
> I have an appointment among the soldiery and a post in the Imperial Guard: I bask in the sunshine of the Emperor's favor; wealth and riches have come to me.
>
> Therefore, with humble devotion, I make this sacrifice towards the twenty-four regions in thankfulness for the great mercies bestowed on me by Heaven and Earth and to acclaim the benefits of the Kingly One. Twelve sacrifices I offer in honor of the True God whose birthday we celebrate this day.

May I be blessed by the Five Fortunes, may I prosper and the gifts of Heaven descend upon me.

On the twenty-third day of the seventh month last year, my second wife Li bore me a son, Guan'ge. At that time I prayed for her safe delivery and that good fortune might be with the child. This son, Guan'ge, I pray may be received into the religious life in the sanctuary of the Three Holy Ones, receiving the name Wu Yingyuan.

I vowed that I would make sacrifice of a hundred and twenty degrees that my seed may be continued after me and that this my son may enjoy length of days.

I desire to do worship to the spirits of three generations of the House of Ximen, to my grandfather Ximen Jingliang, to my grandmother Li, to my father Ximen Da and my mother Xia, to my late wife Chen, and all those who have died, one after the other. Whether they have ascended to Heaven I know not, or whether they have gone down to the place below. I offer twelve sacrifices that the omnipotent DAO may set them all upon the way of life. In all I offer a hundred and eighty degrees of sacrifice. Look graciously upon this petition and grant these blessings.

Upon this the ninth day of the first month in the third year of the reign Xuan He, the feast of the birthday of the Gods, in humble duty I come to the sanctuary of the Most Beneficent Jade Emperor, here, by the ministry of the priests, to give thanks to Heaven and Earth, and to pray that the Gods may bestow their blessing upon me and give me peace. Here I have enrolled the name of my son and recited the sacred scriptures that blessings may be multiplied. I have kept the great fast for a day and a night to invoke the glory of the Three Worlds and to welcome the Chariot of the God of Ten Thousand Heavens.

May He grant lasting peace to all my household and ensure that the Four Seasons shall be harmonious and fruitful.

For this I place my trust in the power of DAO and pray that manifold blessings may be bestowed.

This have I set down with faithful care.

When this had been read, the priests brought many talismans, petitions and papers and asked Ximen Qing to look at them one by one. There were between a hundred and eighty and a hundred and ninety of them, all well done and in excellent order. Then they showed him the talismans, petitions and papers for the enrollment of the child's name under the protection of the Three Holy Ones. The task was too great for Ximen Qing. He had observed the great care that the Abbot brought to his duties, so he contented himself with offering incense and signed the documents. He called for a roll of silk to be brought and given to Abbot Wu. The Abbot refused it for a long time, but finally bade a boy receive it.

Then a priest at the corner of the sanctuary beat the drum with a roaring like spring thunder and the others played their instruments. The Abbot vested himself in a scarlet robe with embroidery of the five colors, and red shoes. He took up an ivory scepter. Then he dispatched all the documents and went to the altar to await the coming of the Gods, and a bell was rung on either side. Ximen Qing was escorted to the altar, and there offered incense on both sides of the sanctuary of the Three Holy Ones. He opened his eyes wide and gazed at them. Ximen Qing went around the altar and offered incense. When he was done, the servers invited him to go to the Hall of the Pine Trees. In the innermost room, a fine carpet had been laid and animal charcoal was burning in the brazier. After a while Ying Bojue and Xie Xida arrived. They greeted Ximen Qing and each of them offered a star of silver as tea money. "We should have liked to send some tea," they said, "but it is a long way, and we offer this trifle instead."

Ximen Qing would have none of it. "Really," he said, "I have no patience with you. I invited you. Why should you do this? My relative Wu will bring something for tea, and that will be enough for all of us."

Ying Bojue hastily made reverence and said: "If you insist, we must take it back." Then he looked at Xie Xida. "It is your fault," he said, "I told you our brother would not accept it. Now, you see, he upbraids us."

Then Wu and Hua came, and each of them brought two boxes of fine cakes to have with tea. Ximen Qing asked Abbot Wu to accept them. After tea a vegetarian meal was prepared, and Ximen Qing and the others took part in it. The Abbot had engaged a storyteller, who told them all about Hong Men of the Han Dynasty.

When the Abbot had finished attending to the papers, he came in and sat down with them. He asked if Guan'ge himself was to be brought that day.

"No," Ximen Qing said, "he is very small, and my wife was afraid that the distance might be too much for him. But this afternoon his clothes are coming and we will offer them before the Three Holy Ones. I imagine that will have the same effect."

"I agree," Abbot Wu said, "it is the best thing you could do."

"In every other respect," Ximen Qing said, "the child is getting along very well, but he is much too easily alarmed. I have three or four maids and a nurse to look after him, but something is always disturbing him. We dare not let dogs or cats come anywhere near him."

"Rearing a child is no easy business," Uncle Wu said. Then Daian came and said that Li Guijie and Wu Yin'er had sent Li Ming and Wu Hui with tea. Ximen Qing ordered them to be brought in. The two boys came, carrying boxes, which they presented on their knees. When the boxes were opened, it was seen that they contained all kinds of delightful cakes, and tea with rose petals. Ximen Qing asked Abbot Wu to accept them.

"How did you come to know about this?" he asked Li Ming. "This morning," Li Ming said, "I met Uncle Chen riding along the street. He told me that you were performing your devotions here today, and I went home and told Guijie's mother. She told Wu Yin'er, and they asked us to come and bring you their best wishes. Really they would have come themselves, but it would have been hard for them to get here. These poor cakes are to be given to your servants."

Ximen Qing said that the two boys must have food, and the Abbot sent them to a room aside. Even the porters who had come with them were given a meal.

In the afternoon there were further devotions. The Abbot had prepared a large table of food, a jar of Jinhua wine, and, for the baby, a Daoist hat of black silk, with trimmings of gold, a black Daoist gown made of linen, and another of green cloudy silk. There were tiny black silk shoes and a yellow girdle, a yellow cord from the shrine of the Three Holy Ones, a purple cord from the Patroness of Children, and a silver necklet, on which was engraved: "Gold and jade fill the hall. Long Life, Honor and Riches be thine." There was a talisman of yellow silk with red characters to drive away devils. This bore the inscription: "God said the word" and "Long Life and Health." The parcels were tied with yellow string and set upon a square tray. Plates of fruit were on the table.

A boy was told to take from a bag copies upon red paper of all the texts they had been reciting, and the Abbot asked Ximen Qing to look at them. The papers were then put into boxes, and in all there were eight bundles to be sent to Ximen's house. Ximen was very pleased. He told Qitong to go at once and tell the people at home that the messenger must be given two handkerchiefs and a tael of silver.

This day was Pan Jinlian's birthday. Aunt Wu, old woman Pan, Aunt Yang and Miss Yu were sitting in Yueniang's room when the presents came from the temple. They set them on four tables, but even so there was not room for all. The ladies came to look at them.

"Come quickly, Sixth Sister," Jinlian said to Li Ping'er, "your baby's teacher has sent him some presents. Here is a little Daoist hat and robes. Oh, look! There are some little shoes too."

Yulou went forward and took the little shoes in her hands. "See how very careful those priests are," she said. "These little shoes with their white silk heels are done in *Daokou* work, and the laces in *Fangsheng*. The clouds are very well done. The priest who did this must have a wife. He could never do such good needlework himself."

"Nonsense," Wu Yueniang said, "if he is a monk, how can he have a wife? He must employ someone to do the work for him."

"If the Daoist monks have wives," Jinlian said, "Nun Wang here and the Abbess can make excellent girdles; must we assume that they have husbands?"

"Oh, the monks," Nun Wang said, "can go anywhere in those hats of theirs, but we of the Buddhist persuasion are recognized wherever we go."

"They tell me," Jinlian said, "that your convent, the Temple of Guanyin, is opposite the Daoist monastery. You remember the saying: ' When a house of nuns stands near a house of monks, something is bound to happen.' "

"The Fifth Lady loves to talk nonsense," Yueniang said.

"Ah," Jinlian said, "here is the purple cord talisman. With this the priest dedicates the child to Guanyin. And here is a silver necklet with a medal attached, and eight characters engraved upon it. How nice the baby will look when he puts it on. And on the back is the child's name—Wu—something —Yuan."

"That is the name the priest gave him," Qitong said. "Wu Yingyuan."

"Yes, the character is Ying," Jinlian said. "But the priest is certainly impertinent to change the baby's surname."

"That's what you think," Yueniang said. She asked Li Ping'er to bring Guan'ge, that they might see him dressed in his monastic habit. But Li Ping'er said: "He has just gone to sleep and I don't like to disturb him."

"It will do him no harm to wake him up," Jinlian said, and Li Ping'er then went to bring her son. Jinlian, who could read, took the parcels of red papers, pulled out the texts, and in one of the documents discovered that after Ximen Qing's name, only those of Wu Yueniang and Li Ping'er were mentioned. There were no others. This made her jealous.

"Look how that obstinate scoundrel arranges people in ranks and classes. Isn't it clear that he has his favorites. This paper mentions only one and the rest of us are left out. We don't count. We are pushed on one side."

"Is the Great Lady mentioned?" Meng Yulou asked. "Oh, it would be a joke if she were not there," Jinlian said.

"There is nothing the matter with it," Yueniang said. "If it mentions one of us, that is enough. Just because we have a regiment of women in the house, there is no reason why everybody's name should go down. The priests would laugh."

"We are no worse than anybody else," Jinlian said, "we all took the same length of time to come into the world."

Then Li Ping'er brought Guan'ge.

"Give me the clothes and I will dress him," Yulou said. Li Ping'er held the child while Yulou put on him the hat, the necklet and the two strings. The baby was frightened, closed his eyes, and, for a long time, held his breath. Yulou put on the little monastic dress.

"Take these papers and some paper money," Yueniang said, "and go to our domestic chapel and burn them there." Li Ping'er did so.

Yulou held the baby and played with him. "Now that you are wearing these clothes," she said to him, "you are a little priest."

"A little priest indeed!" Jinlian said, "rather the Great Omnipotent himself."

"Why do you say a thing like that?" Yueniang said seriously. "You must not talk in that way in the child's presence." Jinlian was abashed and said no more.

The wearing of these new clothes seemed to frighten the child and he began to cry. Li Ping'er came back, took him and undressed him. While she was doing so, he soiled her dress.

"Oh, you good little Wu Yingyuan," Yulou said, laughing, "if you're going to make messes, you must have something to sit on."

Yueniang bade Xiaoyu take paper, and put things to rights. Then the child lay on his mother's breast and went to sleep. Yueniang distributed all the cakes and invited Aunt Yang, Aunt Wu, and old woman Pan to come and eat the food that had been sent from the temple. It was growing dark.

The day before, Ximen Qing, in preparation for his sacrifice, had taken no meat or wine. Now, Jinlian, who had been unable to celebrate her birthday at the proper time, waited for him to come back from the temple that she might offer wine to him. She went and stood at the gate. About sunset, Daian and Chen Jingji came riding back. Jinlian asked Jingji if Ximen was returning.

"I don't think so," Jingji said. "When we left, the service was not over. They had only begun it, and I don't see how they can finish before the first night watch. Priests never let people go without a struggle. They want to thank the Gods and drink a cup of wine."

When Jinlian heard this, she said nothing but went to Yueniang's room in a bad temper. "I have just come from the gate," she said. "There I saw Brother-in-law Chen come back on horseback. He says that Father will not be here yet because the service is not finished. He himself came back before the others."

"That is all right," Yueniang said, "we shall be more at our ease. Tonight we will listen to these two nuns talking about religion and singing hymns."

Chen Jingji pulled the lattice aside and came in. He was a little tipsy.

"I have come," he said, "to pay my respects to Fifth Mother." He turned to his wife and asked her for a cup.

"Why should I get you a cup?" his wife said. "Kowtow to the Fifth Lady and I will offer the wine for you. Look at you! You are drunk! It is clear you found this sacrifice a splendid excuse for drinking. Coming back in a state like this!"

Yueniang asked him whether Ximen Qing was really not coming back, and whether Daian had returned.

"Father saw that the service would not be finished for some time," Jingji said, "and as he knew there was no man in the house, he told me to come back, and Daian to stay and wait upon him. The Abbot would not let me go. He pulled me and dragged me about, and gave me two or three great cups of wine. Then, at last, I got away."

Yueniang asked him how many people were at the temple. "Uncle Wu, and Uncle Hua, who lives outside the gates, Uncle Ying and Uncle Xie. The two young actors Li Ming and Wu Hui are there too. When the party will come to an end, I don't know. I only know that Uncle Wu was going home, and that Uncle Hua was not allowed to do so. In my opinion they will spend the night there."

Jinlian saw that Li Ping'er was not there.

"Why do you call him Uncle Hua?" she said to Chen Jingji. "What relation was he to the departed? You ought to know that he should be called Uncle Li."

"Fifth Mother," Jingji said, "you should take a lesson from the country girl who married Zheng En. Keep one eye open and the other shut."

"Kowtow and be off, you scamp," his wife said. "Don't come here with your scandalous talk."

Jingji asked Jinlian to take the proper position. He kowtowed four times, drunkenly, then went to the outer court.

After a while, candles and lamps were brought and the tables were set. They all ate noodles and wine, and then everything was cleared away. Yueniang told Xiaoyu to close the second door and put a small table on the bed. They all sat in a circle with the two nuns in the middle. They burned incense; then, with only two candles burning, listened to the two nuns telling religious stories. First the chief nun began. She told how the Thirty-second Sage came down from the Western Heaven to the Eastern World. Here he preached the teaching of the Buddha, the sacred doctrine of the Master, and the principle of retribution. She told the story of Master Zhang, a very wealthy man, giving one episode after another, very slowly. She spoke of the nobleman who was converted to the teaching of Buddha, left his house, his garden, and his belongings and went to lead a religious life in the Temple of the Yellow Plum.

When she had finished these stories, Nun Wang chanted a psalm. Then Yueniang said: "Teachers, you must be hungry, we had better have something to eat." She bade Xiaoyu bring four plates of vegetarian food and another four plates of buns and cakes, and asked Aunt Wu, Aunt Yang, and old woman Pan to join the two nuns.

"I have just had something to eat," Aunt Wu said. "Ask Aunt Yang. She has been fasting."

Yueniang put the cakes on small gilded plates and offered them first to Aunt Yang and then to the two nuns. "Take some more, old lady," she said to Aunt Yang, but the old lady protested that she had had enough.

"There are some bones on the plate," Aunt Yang said. "Please, Sister, take them away. I might put them in my mouth by mistake." This made everybody roar with laughter.

"Old Lady," Yueniang said, "this is vegetarian food made to look like meat. It has come from the temple, and there can't possibly be any harm in eating it."

"If it is really vegetarian," Aunt Yang said, "I will taste it. My eyes are so bad I thought it was meat."

As they were eating, Laixing's wife, Huixiu, came in.

"What do you want, you rogue?" said Yueniang. Huixiu said she had come to hear the nuns sing.

"How did you manage to get in, since the second door is closed?" Yueniang asked.

Yuxiao answered. "She was in the kitchen, putting out the fire."

"Then no wonder your nose and mouth are so black. You look like a spiritual drumstick. What use is there in your coming to listen to religious admonitions?"

The ladies and the maids still sat around the two nuns. When the cakes were done with, everything was cleared away; the lights were trimmed, and more incense burned. The two nuns beat small gongs and began their chanting again. They told how the nobleman Zhang, in the Temple of the Yellow Plum on the mountainside, spent all his days upon his knees listening to the sutras, and all his nights in meditation. They told how the Fourth Sage perceived that Zhang was no common man, so he took the nobleman among his disciples, gave him three precious favors and bade him go to the bank of the River of Foulness, there to find a womb wherein he might be born again. Then they told how the Virgin of a Thousand Pieces of Gold was washing clothes on the bank of the River of Foulness. She met a monk who begged for a place in which to live, and when she did not answer, the monk jumped into the river.

Jinlian was very sleepy, and her head kept nodding. After a while she went to her room to bed. Then Xiuchun came to tell Li Ping'er that Guan'ge had waked up, and she, too, went away. Only Li Jiao'er, Meng Yulou, Sun Xue'e, old woman Pan and the two aunts remained to listen to the end of the story.

They were told how, from the river, there came a big scaly fish, and the maiden ate it. Then she went home, and bore a child after ten months.

By this time Yueniang noticed that her stepdaughter had gone to bed, and Aunt Wu, who was lying on Yueniang's bed, was fast asleep. Aunt Yang was yawning and the candles had already been renewed twice. She asked Xiaoyu what time it was. "It is the fourth watch," Xiaoyu said, "and the cock has crowed."

Yueniang told the two nuns to take their books. Aunt Yang went to Yulou's room and Miss Yu to the inner court to sleep with Xue'e. The Abbess slept with Li Jiao'er, and Nun Wang remained with Yueniang. They waited for Xiaoyu to make them some tea and then went to bed. Aunt Wu slept in the inner room with Yuxiao.

"How did the Fifth Sage grow up?" Yueniang asked Nun Wang. "Did he become a true Immortal?"

Nun Wang told her how the maiden's parents drove her from their home, and how she went to Xianrenzhuang where the Fifth Sage was born. When he was six years old, he went to the River of Foulness, recovered his three precious gifts and returned again to the Temple of the Yellow Plum to listen to the teaching of the Fourth Sage. Afterwards he became an Immortal and took his mother with him to Paradise. Yueniang heard the whole story from beginning to end, and afterwards believed even more fervently in the teaching of Buddha.

CHAPTER 40
Wu Yueniang and the Nun

Nun Wang and Wu Yueniang lay together upon the same bed. "Lady," said the nun, "has any sign of good fortune yet been granted you?"

"Good fortune!" Yueniang said. "In the eighth month of last year we bought the house belonging to the Qiao family, on the other side of the street from here. I went to look at it, but I slipped on the stairs, and the child, which was about six or seven months on the way, came from me. Since then there has been no sign of another."

"If it was seven months on the way," the nun said, "it must have been well formed."

"It fell into the pail in the middle of the night," Yueniang said, "and when the maid brought the light near I saw it was a boy."

"What a sad affair," Nun Wang said. "But it seems to me not that you strained yourself, but that your womb is not so strong as it might be. It would be much better for you to have a child than any of the other ladies. The Sixth Lady has been here only a little while, and see how happy she is with her child."

"Heaven decides whether we shall bear children or not," Yueniang said.

"Never mind," the nun said, "I have a friend called Xue who makes excellent charms and medicine. Last year there was Secretary Chen's wife. She was well on in years and had never borne a son, though she had several miscarriages. After she had taken my friend Xue's charms, she had a very fine boy. Everybody was so pleased. But one of the ingredients is very difficult to get."

"What is that?" Yueniang asked.

"First we need the afterbirth of a boy. This must be washed in wine and burned to ashes. Then the ashes must be mingled with the charm and medicine, and, on the *Renzi* day, in absolute secrecy, so that no evil spirit may interfere, you must swallow them with a little yellow wine upon an empty stomach. After that, all you have to do is to make a note of the date, and you will find that in exactly one month you will conceive. It is always so."

"Is your friend a monk or a nun?" Yueniang said, "and where does he or she live?"

"She is a nun about seventy years old," Nun Wang replied, "and once she lived at the Dizang Temple. Now she has gone to be the Abbess of the Fahua Temple. She is wonderfully learned. She knows all the religious texts and stories and can preach upon the Diamond Sutra and the sacred doctrine of Cause and Effect. She can talk for a month without exhausting her stock of learning. She only visits families of distinction, and, sometimes when they get hold of her, they will not let her go for ten days or a fortnight.

"Will you go tomorrow and ask her to come here?" Yueniang said.

"I will," said the nun, "and, moreover, I will ask her for the charms and medicine you need. There is only the one thing that is difficult to get, and I don't know what we can do about that. I think we had better dig up the Sixth Lady's and use that."

"Why should I hurt others to benefit myself?" Yueniang said. "I will give you some money, and you must try to get another one for me somewhere."

"For things like that we must go to the midwives," the nun said. "I will get the medicine for you, and, if you take it, I give you my word that you will have a baby like a moon that not even ten bright stars can outshine."

"Don't mention the matter to anyone," Yueniang said.

"What are you thinking about, my good Lady?" the nun said. "I should never dream of mentioning it."

At last they went to sleep.

Next day, when Yueniang had just got up, Ximen Qing came back from the temple. Yueniang was dressing her hair. Yuxiao took his clothes and he sat down.

"Yesterday," Yueniang said, "the Fifth Lady wished to offer wine to you on her birthday. Why did you not come back?"

"The sacrifice was not over," Ximen Qing said, "and kinsman Wu had arranged to entertain us to dinner. We stayed all night drinking. Brother Hua, Ying Bojue and Xie Xida were there, and two young actors sang to us. This morning when I came back, Brother Ying and the others were still drinking there."

Yuxiao brought tea. That day Ximen did not go to the office. He went to his study, lay on the bed and slept. Pan Jinlian and Li Ping'er dressed their hair and went with the baby to Yueniang's room.

"His father has been back some time," Yueniang told them. "I asked him to have something to eat, but he would not. Now dinner is ready. Dress the baby in his Daoist robes; then take him to the front court and show him to his father."

"Let me put on the baby's clothes," Jinlian said. "I will go with you."

They dressed the child in his Daoist hat with its gold bands, the Daoist habit, with the necklet, the medals and the tiny shoes and socks. Jinlian wished to carry the baby, but Yueniang said: "Let his own mother carry him. Your yellow embroidered skirt might easily be soiled. If the baby wets it even a little, it will be ruined."

So Li Ping'er carried Guan'ge, and Jinlian went with them. When they came to the room in the wing, Shutong pulled aside the lattice and came out. Jinlian saw Ximen Qing asleep, his face turned to the wall.

"How soundly you sleep, you old beggar," she cried. "Here is a young priest come to pay you a call. Dinner is ready in the Great Lady's room, and he has come to ask you to go. Get up at once. Don't stay there sleeping."

Ximen Qing had been drinking all night, so that when his head touched the pillow he forgot how high the sky is and how thick the earth. He snored like thunder. Jinlian and Li Ping'er sat down on either side of the bed and put down Guan'ge before Ximen Qing's face. When he opened his eyes, there was Guan'ge dressed in his priestly robes. Ximen was so delighted that he opened his eyes wide and smiled. He took the child in his arms and kissed him.

"What a nice clean mouth to kiss the baby with!" Jinlian said. "Now little Master Priest, Wu Yingyuan, spit in his face and ask him over what field he has been toiling like an ox that he is so sleepy he would sleep all day. Yesterday poor Fifth Mother waited and waited for him. But he is so grand he would not come and kowtow to Fifth Mother."

"The service finished very late," Ximen said. "I had to thank all the gods, and we were drinking all through the night. My head is still heavy with wine and I should like to sleep a little longer because I have to go to a party at Master Shang's."

"You ought to have done with drinking for a while," Jinlian said.

"He sent me an invitation yesterday, and, if I do not go, he will be annoyed."

"Well, if you do go, you must come back at once. I shall expect you."

Li Ping'er said: "The Great Lady has had dinner prepared, and some bitter bamboo shoots specially for you. She wants you to go and have some."

"Really I don't feel like eating anything," Ximen Qing said, "but I will go and have some soup." He got up and went to the inner court.

When he had left, Jinlian sat on the bed and put her feet on the warmer below the floor. "This is indeed a warm bed," she said. Then she touched the mattress and cried: "The bed is quite hot." On a table was a small stove made of tiles, with a guard about it. She took it in her hands.

Then she said: "Sixth Sister, there is a box on that table with some fragrant tablets in it. Give it to me." She opened the box, took out a few tablets, and, wrapping them in her skirt, put them between her legs to perfume her body.

They sat there a long time till Li Ping'er said: "Let us go. He will be coming back in a moment."

"What if he does?" Jinlian said. "I don't care." But they took Guan'ge and went to the inner court.

When Ximen Qing had finished his dinner, he ordered a servant to get ready his horse. Then he went to Master Shang's house for the party. Old woman Pan left that afternoon. When Nun Wang was about to go, Yueniang told her she must not speak to the Reverend Mother about the arrangement between them. She gave the nun a tael of silver and asked her to remember the charms and the medicine. Nun Wang took the silver. "I cannot come before the sixteenth," she said, "but then I will bring what you wish for." Yueniang promised that she should have more silver, and the nuns went away.

My dear readers: monks, nuns and go-betweens should never be allowed to enter the palaces and dwellings of the gentry where there are ladies. They pretend to talk of religion and to tell edifying stories, but secretly they do all manner of mischief.

In the evening, Jinlian stood before her dressing table, dressed her hair in simple braids, powdered her face till it was as white as snow, and freshly painted her lips. She put on two earrings like tiny lanterns, set ornaments upon her cheeks, and bound her hair with a ribbon of purple and gold. Then she took a gown of scarlet woven with gold, and a skirt of blue satin. She dressed up like a maid, to make fun with Yueniang. She sent for Li Ping'er, who laughed until she shook.

"Sister," Li Ping'er said, "you look exactly like a maid. I have a red handkerchief in my room, and you shall have it to put over your head. Then I'll go to the back court and tell them that Father has bought a new maid. They will certainly be taken in."

Chunmei took a lantern and they went to the front court. When they came to the second door they met Chen Jingji. He laughed. "I should never have dreamed it was the Fifth Lady," he said.

"Come here, Brother-in-Law," Li Ping'er said, "I'll tell you what to do. You go in first and say so and so."

"Oh, I'll deceive them," Chen Jingji said.

He went before them to Yueniang's room. The people there were sitting on the bed drinking tea.

"Mother," said Jingji, "Father has gone and told old woman Xue to buy a maid for sixteen taels of silver. She is twenty-five years old and knows how to play and sing. She has just come in a sedan chair."

"Indeed?" Yueniang said. "Why didn't Xue come and tell me?"

"She was afraid you would scold her, so she only brought the sedan chair as far as the gate and then went away. The servants received the maid."

Aunt Wu was silent. Aunt Yang said: "He has so many wives already that I should have thought he had enough without buying another girl."

"My good Lady," Yueniang said, "you don't understand. If a man is rich, he may buy a hundred women and still not be satisfied. We are like a regiment of women soldiers."

"I will go and have a look at her," Yuxiao said. She went out, and saw Chunmei coming along in the moonlight, a lantern in her hand. Chunmei gave the lantern to Laian, and she and Li Ping'er assisted the new maid. The girl's head was covered with a red cloth, and she wore a scarlet gown. Yulou and Li Jiao'er were greatly excited. They came out to see. The maid came in. Yuxiao stood beside Yueniang.

"This is our mistress," she said to the maid. "Kowtow to her."

She took off the cloth that covered the new maid's head, and Jinlian gracefully kowtowed to Yueniang. But she could not help laughing.

"You maid," Meng Yulou said, "what do you mean by laughing instead of making your reverence?"

Yueniang laughed too. "Fifth Sister," she said, "you might have been a spirit, you deceived us all so well."

"She didn't deceive me," Yulou said.

"How could you tell?" said Aunt Yang.

"Because the Fifth Lady always kowtows in this way. She went backwards two steps and then bowed her body."

"You are quite right," Aunt Yang said, "but she certainly deceived me."

"She deceived me too," Li Jiao'er said. "I should never have recognized her with that cloth on her head, or until she laughed."

Qintong came with the wrapper and said his master had come.

"Hide yourself in the other room," Yulou said to Jinlian. "We will have some fun with him." Ximen Qing came in.

"Today," Yulou said to him, "Xue brought a maid in a sedan chair. She said you told her to buy her. You are not young, and the burden of the household is upon your shoulders. Why do you play games like this?"

"I never told her to buy a maid," Ximen said, laughing. "Do you believe everything that old rascal tells you?"

"Ask the Great Lady whether I am telling the truth or not," Yulou said. "The maid is here now. If you don't believe me, send for her." She said to

Yuxiao: "Go and bring the new maid to see your father."

Yuxiao laughed and put her hand before her mouth, but she did not go. She took a few steps forward, then came back again. "I don't think she will come," she said.

"You are a brave maid to disobey your master's orders," Yulou said. "I will go for her. If she will not do what she is told, she will be no use as a maid."

She went into the next room. Then they heard: "You wonderful creature. I won't go. And don't pull me about like that."

Then Yulou said: "You slave, where were you brought up? Wherever did you learn to be so stubborn as to refuse to do reverence to your master?" Jinlian was dragged out.

In the light of the lamp, Ximen saw that it was Jinlian dressed as a maid, her hair done as a servant's. He laughed till he could not open his eyes. Jinlian took a chair and sat down.

"You bold maid," Yulou said, "you have only just come to the house, and yet you take such liberties that you even dare to sit in your master's presence."

"This is your master," Yueniang said. "Kowtow to him."

Jinlian did not move. After a while, she went to Yueniang's room, took off her ornaments and redressed her hair. They all laughed.

"Today," Yueniang said to Ximen Qing, "the Qiaos have sent six cards of invitation asking us to go on the twelfth and see the lanterns. I think we ought to send them some presents first."

"Tell Laixing to buy some food and a jar of Jinhua wine. That will be enough. We will send invitations to Madam Qiao, Madam Zhou, Madam Jing, Madam Xia and Madam Zhang for the fourteenth. Aunt Wu will be able to stay until then. I will tell Ben the Fourth to get the firework makers to make some fireworks for us. We will engage the young actors from the household of the Wangs, and Li Guijie and Wu Yin'er can come. You can all stay at home, see the fireworks, and drink wine, and I, Brother Ying, and Brother Xie will go to a wineshop in Lion Street."

The tables were set and wine was brought. Jinlian served the wine and all the ladies drank her health. Ximen Qing thought how pretty she had looked in the lamplight, dressed as a maid, and his heart grew warm towards her. He looked meaningly at her. Jinlian realized what was in his mind and went to her own room. She dressed herself again, doing her hair after the manner of Hangzhou. She painted her lips and powdered her face. Then she prepared some especially dainty dishes, set out wine, and waited for her husband.

Before very long Ximen Qing came. He noticed that she had dressed her hair again, and was pleased. He sat down on a chair and took her upon his knee. They laughed and talked, and Chunmei brought in food and wine. Jinlian again offered wine to him.

"Little oily mouth," Ximen said, "you have offered me wine already in the outer court. Why do you take the trouble to do so again?"

Jinlian smiled. "That was nothing," she said. "There, you were drinking with the others. This is my special offering to you and to no one else. Year after year you have been good enough to spend your money on me, and I trust you have no reason to complain."

This speech delighted Ximen. He took the wine immediately and set the woman on his knees. Chunmei served the wine, and Qiuju served the dishes.

"The Qiaos have asked us all to go to their place on the twelfth," Jinlian said, "but I think only our Great Lady ought to go."

"Since you have all been invited," Ximen Qing said, "why shouldn't you all go? I will tell the nurse to take the baby, so that he will not cry for his mother."

"The Great Lady and the others all have dresses," Jinlian said. "I am like an old priest: I only have old ones. Not one of them is fit to be seen. Won't you give me some of the new clothes you have just had made in the South, or some material so that I can make a dress for myself? There is no sense in your hoarding it up. Surely you don't expect it to increase and multiply! When it is our turn to give a party, and all the honorable ladies come, I shall have to dress properly to receive them or they will laugh at me. I have spoken to you about it several times, but you never pay any attention."

Ximen Qing laughed. "I will send for the tailor tomorrow, and he shall make you some clothes."

"It will be too late tomorrow. There are only two days left."

"I will tell him to bring more tailors with him and make two or three dresses for you at once. The rest can be done more slowly."

"I have mentioned it before," Jinlian said. "This time I shall expect some first-class material. All the others have beautiful clothes, and I have none. You have never bothered about clothes for me."

Ximen Qing laughed. "Ah, little oily mouth," he said, "you always insist on having the best of everything."

They talked and drank till the first night watch. Then they went to bed, and were like the love bird and his mate beneath the bedclothes, or a couple of phoenixes behind the curtains. They sported wildly for half the night.

The next day, when Ximen Qing came back from the office, he opened his boxes and took out some rolls of southern silk, enough to make a long gown, a suit of figured satin, and another embroidered suit. For Yueniang he ordered two long-sleeved scarlet satin gowns and four embroidered dresses. Then, sitting under the arbor, he ordered Qintong to go for the tailor. The tailor came and kowtowed. He took his tape and scissors, covered the tables, and cut out the material. First he cut out the long-sleeved satin gown of five colors; then another with a stomacher embroidered with the head of a wild beast; a black cloak with the five colors and gold ribbons, with designs of gourds and flowers intertwined; a gown of scarlet satin woven with gold, and another stomacher with the head of a wild beast; and a skirt of light blue woven with gold. Then he prepared a gown with a stomacher of sandalwood color, with embroidered flowers, and a scarlet skirt to match, of the hundred flower design, and all the flowers had gold branches and green leaves. These were for Wu Yueniang. For Li Jiao'er, Meng Yulou, Pan Jinlian and Li Ping'er, a long-sleeved satin cloak of scarlet with the five colors, embroidered with flowers and birds, and two dresses of embroidered silk. There was no cloak for Sun Xue'e, and only one dress.

The tailor cut them out very quickly, though there were more than thirty pieces in all. Ximen Qing gave him five taels of silver, and then he brought another ten tailors to make up the clothes in his house.

CHAPTER 41

The Baby Guan'ge Is Betrothed

Ximen Qing watched the tailors as they hastily made up the dresses, and the work was finished in two days. On the twelfth, a messenger came from the Qiao household to renew the former invitation. That morning Ximen Qing had sent presents. Wu Yueniang, Aunt Wu, and the others set off together in six sedan chairs, leaving Sun Xue'e behind to look after the house. The nurse, Ruyi'er, took Guan'ge, and Laixing's wife, Huixiu, went with them to act as tiring maid. They too went in sedan chairs. At home Ximen Qing watched the firework makers making their fireworks, and superintended the hanging of the lanterns in the great hall. He sent a boy with his card to the house of the princely family of Wang to engage the actors.

In the afternoon he went to Pan Jinlian's room. Jinlian was not there, and Chunmei gave him something to eat.

"I have invited several ladies to come on the fourteenth," he told her. "You four girls must wear your best clothes when you wait upon them."

Chunmei leaned over the table. "You should say that to the other girls. There will be no dressing for me."

"Why?" said Ximen.

"The ladies will all be dressed in their new clothes," Chunmei said. "They will be very smart, and we shall look like burned paper. Everybody will laugh at us."

"But you all have dresses and ornaments, and pearls and flowers," Ximen Qing said.

"The ornaments are all right, but we have no clothes," Chunmei said. "I have only two old dresses and I am not fit to be seen."

"I see," Ximen said, laughing. "I have had clothes made for the ladies, and you are jealous, little oily mouth. Never mind. I am going to tell the tailor to make three dresses for my daughter, and you four girls shall each have a suit and a short dress of figured satin."

"Don't put me in the same class with the rest," Chunmei said. "I want a white silk coat and a scarlet-figured silk wrapper."

"If it were only for you," Ximen said, "it would be all right; but if you have one, my daughter will have to have one."

"Your daughter has one already," Chunmei said. "I have not. I don't see how she can object."

Ximen Qing took the keys and went upstairs. He chose enough material for five dresses and two figured satin wrappers, and took a roll of white silk for two double-breasted white cloaks. The wrappers for his daughter and Chunmei were scarlet; those for the other three maids were bluish green. There were scarlet satin short coats and light blue skirts for all of them, seventeen pieces of material in all. Ximen told the tailor to make the clothes, and gave him a roll of thin yellow silk for the tops of the skirts, and Hangzhou lining silk for the linings. Chunmei was satisfied. She laughed and talked all day with Ximen Qing and served him with wine when he wished for it.

Madam Qiao had invited several ladies to her party. There was the wife of Master Shang, Censor Song's wife, a young woman named Cui who was connected with the family, two nieces, Miss Duan and Wu Shunzhen's sister-in-law Zheng. She had engaged two singing girls to play for them. When Wu Yueniang, Aunt Wu, and the others arrived, Madam Qiao went to the second door to welcome them and took them to the great hall. There they exchanged greetings. She called Yueniang Aunt, and the others Second Aunt, and Third Aunt, and so on. Then she introduced the other ladies and took their places in due order. The maids brought tea, and Master Qiao came to greet the ladies. When they had greeted him, he told his wife to ask them to go to the inner room to take off their cloaks. A table was set, tea brought, and they all sat down to drink it. Ruyi'er and Huixiu looked after the baby and were entertained in another place.

After tea they came back to the great hall, where handsome screens were placed about and cushions embroidered with lotus flowers. Four tables were set and Yueniang was asked to take the place of honor. The eleven ladies all sat at one table, except for Miss Duan and Miss Zheng, who were at a table apart. The two singing girls sang for them. When soup and rice had been served, the cooks served up a crystal goose. Yueniang gave them two *qian* of silver. Then stewed trotters were served, and Yueniang gave the cooks another *qian*. Then came roast duck and again Yueniang gave the cooks a *qian*. After this course Madam Qiao rose and offered wine, first to Yueniang and then to Master Shang's wife. Yueniang left the table and went to the inner room to change her clothes and powder her face.

Yulou went to Madam Qiao's room, where Ruyi'er had the baby Guan'ge. He was in a small crib placed on the bed, and, lying beside him, was the little girl baby of the Qiaos. The two babies were playing together, putting out their hands to touch one another. This delighted Wu Yueniang and Meng Yulou. "These two babies," they said, "are like bride and bridegroom." Aunt Wu came in, and they said to her: "Come here, Aunt Wu, and look at this young couple."

"Yes," Aunt Wu said, smiling, "they are stretching out their hands and kicking their little heels, touching one another, just like a young husband and wife."

Madam Qiao and the other ladies heard what Aunt Wu said. "How might an inconsiderable family like mine," Madam Qiao said, "aspire so high as to ally itself with that of my aunts?"

"You are very kind," Yueniang said, "but indeed what manner of lady are you, and Miss Zheng too? I should very much like to enter into an alliance with this household, if only my son will not make your house ashamed. Do not say that."

Yulou pushed forward Li Ping'er. "Sister," she said, "what have you to say?" Li Ping'er smiled but said nothing.

"If Madam Qiao does not agree," Aunt Wu said, "I shall be very disappointed."

Master Shang's wife and the Censor's lady both said together: "For the sake of your kinswoman, Lady Wu, you must not stand too much on ceremony. Your Zhangjie was born in the eleventh month of last year."

"And our baby," Yueniang said, "was born on the twenty-third day of the sixth month. He is just five months older. Their ages could not be more suitable."

The others would allow no further parley. They urged Madam Qiao, Wu Yueniang and Li Ping'er to the great hall. There, pieces were cut from the bosoms of their dresses. The two singing girls sang for them and Master Qiao was told. He brought out fruits, three pieces of red cloth, and offered wine. Yueniang told Daian and Qintong to go home and refer the matter to their master. In a short time, two jars of wine, three rolls of silk, red and green thread, flowers of gold wire, and four large boxes of cakes and fruit were brought from Ximen's place, and the two households together hung up red charms and drank wine to celebrate their union.

Tall silver candlesticks blazed with light in the hall. Flower-shaped lamps burned brightly. Incense filled the air with delightful perfume. Smiling serenely, the two singing girls opened their ruby lips, showed their white teeth and gently plied their jade plectrums. They held their lutes in one hand and sang. The ladies put flowers and red talismans on the heads of Yueniang, Madam Qiao, and Li Ping'er. When wine had been served, the ladies made reverence to one another and began their banquet again. As the first course, the cook brought in a snowflake pie, filled with mincemeat. The word "Long Life" was fashioned upon it. There was lotus-seed soup, which looked as delightful as a pool, the seeds floating side by side upon its surface. Yueniang sat in the place of honor; she was very happy.

She told Daian to give the cook a roll of silk, and each of the singing girls a roll of silk also. They all kowtowed to thank her.

Madam Qiao would not allow the ladies to go. She took them to the inner court, where she had prepared all kinds of delightful refreshments for them. It was not until the first night watch that Yueniang was able to leave.

"My dear relative," she said to Madam Qiao, "you must come to our poor house tomorrow."

"You are very kind," Madam Qiao said. "My husband has spoken to me of your invitation, but I fear I am no fit person to come to your party just now. Perhaps you will allow me to come some other time."

"There will be no strangers present," Yueniang said. "Please do not stand on ceremony." Then she said to Aunt Wu: "There is no reason why you should leave when we do. You will be coming with Madam Qiao tomorrow."

"Madam Qiao," said Aunt Wu, "if you do not care to go tomorrow, any other day will serve as well, but the fifteenth is your new kinswoman's birthday, and that day you must not fail to go."

"Oh," Madam Qiao said, "if it is my relative's birthday, how should I dare not go?"

"If Madam Qiao does not come to see me, I shall blame you," Yueniang said to Aunt Wu. Then, leaving Aunt Wu behind, she said good-bye and got into her chair. Two soldiers carried a large red lantern before the sedan chair, and behind it were two boys with lanterns. Yueniang was at the head of the procession, then Li Jiao'er, Meng Yulou, Pan Jinlian and Li Ping'er each in her place. Then came the chairs with Ruyi'er and Huixiu. The nurse had Guan'ge closely wrapped in a red silk coverlet, and as still further protection against the cold, she had a brass warming pan in the chair. Two more boys followed her.

When they came to their gate and got out of their chairs, Ximen Qing was drinking in Yueniang's room. Yueniang and the others came in and made reverence to him. Then Yueniang sat down and all the maids came to kowtow to her. She told her husband about the betrothal. He asked what ladies had been present. She told him.

"This marriage," he said, "is all very well, but the families are not of equal rank."

"It was my sister-in-law's doing," Yueniang said. "She saw the Qiaos' baby lying on the same bed as Guan'ge, covered with the same bedclothes, so that the children looked like two young lovers, and she called to me to look at them. When we were having supper, we could not help talking about it, and it was arranged. I sent the boy to tell you and get you to send the boxes of fruits."

"Now that it has been settled," Ximen Qing said, "it doesn't matter, but there is a certain inequality of position. Qiao has some property, but he is only a private citizen, while I am an officer and have duties at the courts. If we have to ask him to a party here, he will wear an ordinary hat, and I don't see how I can invite him to sit with me. It will be most awkward. Only the other day Jing Nangang sent one of his people to try to arrange a marriage. His daughter was five months old, the same age as our own child, but I did not care much for the arrangement because the baby's mother is dead. Besides, she was not the daughter of the first wife. So I would make no promises. Now, without my knowing anything about it, you have gone and settled everything yourself."

"If you did not care for that child because she is a second wife's daughter, what are you going to do now?" Jinlian said. "The Qiao baby is a second wife's daughter too. It seems to me like Xian Daoshen and the God of Long Life, one complaining that the other is too tall, and the other objecting that the first is too short."

This made Ximen Qing very angry. "You strumpet," he shouted, "why don't you take yourself off? We are talking, but nobody asked you to put in your word."

Jinlian flushed and went out of the room. "Of course," she said, "I have no right to speak in this place, or in any other place, for that matter."

When, at the party, Jinlian saw the arrangements being made between Madam Qiao and Yueniang, and Li Ping'er wearing flowers and red charms upon her hair, it had made her very jealous. Now that Ximen Qing spoke angrily to her, she was still more upset and went to cry in Yueniang's inner room.

"Why has Aunt Wu not come back with you?" Ximen Qing asked Yueniang.

"Madam Qiao said she would not come tomorrow because we have ladies of rank coming, so I left Aunt Wu there, and they will come together."

"I told you there would be difficulties about precedence," Ximen said. "I don't know what you are going to do about it."

Some time later, Yulou went into the inner room and found Jinlian in tears. "Why are you so upset?" she said. "Let him say what he likes."

"You heard what I said to him," Jinlian cried. "It was nothing wrong. He said that child was not born in proper wedlock, and I said that neither was the Qiao baby. There is nothing there to complain about. But that bandit—he will come to a bad end—glared at me and swore without rhyme or reason. What does he mean by saying I had no right to speak? He has changed his tune completely. I'll see he gets paid back for it. There is that baby, a miserable, puny little thing that can do nothing but piddle, and they begin arranging a marriage for him. It is because they have so much money they don't know what to do with it. May he tear his coverlets and have nothing to cover him! May he be like a dog snapping at a bladder and get no joy out of it.

"Today the prospects of this marriage seem rosy. Let us hope they won't look different in time to come. They are behaving just like a man who puts out the light, blinks his eyes, and wonders what on earth is going to happen next. They think this is a good house to marry into; we shall see what they think in four or five years' time. This is the only child he has."

"In these days, people are always trying to be clever," Yulou said. "I don't care much for this sort of behavior, myself. It seems to me too early. The baby is so young. They might have dispensed with the cutting of the cloth. But perhaps they only want to be friendly and do this sort of thing for fun."

"If it is meant for fun, well and good," Jinlian said, "but why should that rascal curse me?"

"You shouldn't have said what you did say," Yulou said. "He couldn't help himself."

"I find it hard to say all I think about it," Jinlian said. "That woman is not a second wife any longer. She is the lady of the house. But even if Qiao's baby is the daughter of a second wife, there is no doubt she has old Qiao's blood in her veins. Whereas, in our household, people have not always gone straight, and who knows whose blood runs in our baby's veins?"

Yulou said nothing. They talked a while longer, then Jinlian went to her own room. Li Ping'er waited until Ximen Qing had gone away, then she kowtowed most gracefully to Yueniang.

"I am grateful to you," she said, "for all that you have done for my child today."

Yueniang smiled and returned her reverence. "It is you who are to be congratulated."

"You also, Sister," Li Ping'er said. She stood up while Yueniang and Li Jiao'er sat down to talk. Sun Xue'e and Ximen's daughter came in and kowtowed to Yueniang, making an equal reverence to Li Ping'er. Xiaoyu brought tea. While they were drinking it, Xiuchun came and said the baby needed his mother. Ximen Qing had told her to come.

"It was thoughtless of the nurse to take the child to my room," Li Ping'er said. "I ought to have gone with them, for I don't suppose there was a light."

"When they came home," Yueniang said, "I told Ruyi'er to take the child to your room. It was so late."

"I saw Ruyi'er with the baby," Xiaoyu said. "Laian was carrying a lantern for them."

"That is all right, then," Li Ping'er said, and went to join her baby. She found Ximen Qing in her room and the baby asleep at his nurse's breast.

"Why didn't you tell me you were going to bring the child here?" she said to the nurse.

Ruyi'er told her that Yueniang had seen Laian with a lantern and told her to bring the baby to his mother's room. "Young Master cried for a while," she said, "but I have got him to sleep now."

"Yes," Ximen Qing said, "the baby wanted you for a while, but he has gone to sleep now."

"He has been betrothed today," Li Ping'er said, "and I must kowtow to you." She knelt down. Ximen was very pleased with her and beamed with delight. He quickly raised her to her feet and sat beside her. They told Yingchun to set a table, and they drank together.

Jinlian went to her room in a most vicious temper. She knew that Ximen Qing was with Li Ping'er and, when Qiuju was a moment slow in opening the door for her, she boxed her ears and cursed her loudly.

"You thievish slave," she cried, "why did I have to knock so long before you opened the door? What are you here for? I shall not speak to you again." She went into her room and sat down. Chunmei came and gave her some tea.

"What was that thievish slave doing?" Jinlian said. "She was sitting in the courtyard," Chunmei said. "I told her to open the door for you, but she didn't pay any attention."

"Oh, I know," Jinlian cried; "just because he and I have had words, she is like Grand Marshal Dang eating a tablet. She thinks she will put on airs and annoy me."

Jinlian would have liked to give Qiuju a beating, but she was afraid Ximen Qing might hear. She said no more for the moment, but she was angry nonetheless. Then she undressed. Chunmei prepared her bed. She got into it and went to sleep.

Next day, when Ximen Qing had gone to his office, Jinlian made Qiuju balance a piece of stone on her head and kneel down in the courtyard. When she had finished dressing her hair, she told Chunmei to take down Qiuju's trousers and beat her with a thick stick.

"I shall soil my hands if I take down your trousers," Chunmei said to her fellow maid. She went to the front court and called for Huatong. The boy took down the girl's trousers while Jinlian stood by and cursed her.

"You thievish slave," she cried, "where did you learn to give yourself such airs? Others might forgive you, but I never will. Sister, you know I understand your little ways, and you would do well to restrain yourself. Who are you to put your face forward and show what a great person you are? Sister, don't count on getting help from any other quarter. I shall keep my eyes skinned and watch you." She struck and cursed her and cursed and struck her till Qiuju squealed like a pig being killed.

Meanwhile Li Ping'er had got up. The nurse was trying to rock the baby to sleep, but he kept on waking. She could hear Jinlian cursing Qiuju, and recognized all the references to herself in what was said. But she said nothing, and only covered Guan'ge's ears with her hand.

"Go and ask the Fifth Lady not to beat Qiuju," she said to Xiuchun. "Tell her the baby has just had his milk and is going to sleep."

Xiuchun gave the message, but Jinlian beat Qiuju more severely still. "You thievish slave," she cried, "you shout as loudly as though someone were sticking ten thousand knives into you. But I am a queer person; the louder you cry, the more I shall beat you. I did not expect outsiders to interfere because you were having a beating. Why do you come to have a look? My good sister, you ought to tell our husband to get rid of her."

Li Ping'er heard all this, and knew that the curses were aimed at her. She was so angry that her hands were as cold as ice, but she swallowed her anger and did not show any temper. That morning she had no tea. She carried Guan'ge in her arms and rocked him to sleep.

When Ximen Qing came back from his office, he went to see his son. The Sixth Lady's eyes were red with weeping, and she was lying on the bed.

"Why have you not dressed your hair?" he asked her. "The one in the upper room wishes to see you. And why are your eyes red?"

Instead of telling him about her trouble with Jinlian, Li Ping'er said she was not very well. Ximen told her that the Qiaos had sent some birthday presents for her, a roll of silk, two jars of southern wine, a plate of longevity peaches, another plate of noodles, and other dishes. "They have sent something for the baby too," he said, and told her all the different things that had come. "We have done nothing for them," he added, "and now they have sent all these things for your feast day. That is why the one in the upper room wishes to talk to you. They sent old woman Kong and Qiao Tong with the presents. Aunt Wu has come back. She says Madam Qiao cannot come until the day after tomorrow. She has a relative, Lady Qiao the Fifth, who is related in some way to the royal family. This Lady has heard about the betrothal and is very pleased. She is coming on the fifteenth too, so we must send a card to her."

Li Ping'er got up and slowly dressed her hair. Then she went to the inner court to see Aunt Wu and old woman Kong. They were having tea in Yueniang's room. The presents were set out there. She looked at them all. The cases were returned, and old woman Kong and Qiao Tong were each given two handkerchiefs and five *qian* of silver. When a card of thanks had been written out, they went away.

CHAPTER 42
Ximen Feasts in Lion Street

Stars and moon make glorious the sky
Ten thousand candles burn on earth.
Heavens and Earth make festival today.
Spring is the season of harmony.
Now people wear their finest clothes and even their horses are proud.
The days pass quickly: we must not spend them idly
White hair is a judge who spares no man.
Fools spend a thousand pieces of gold to buy a moment's happiness
And bid the watchman strike the night drum softly.

When the messengers from the Qiao family had been sent away, Ximen Qing went to the upper room to discuss matters with Wu Yueniang, Aunt Wu, and Li Ping'er.

"We must, of course, send them something in return for these presents," Yueniang said, "and something for the baby too, to show that we consider the betrothal definite. Besides, we do not wish to show ourselves behind them in courtesy."

"Yes," Aunt Wu said, "and we must send a marriage maker."

"They sent old woman Kong," Yueniang said. "Whom shall we send?"

"One guest never troubles more than one host," Ximen Qing said. "Old woman Feng is good enough for us." He had eight cards of invitation written; then he sent for old woman Feng, and told Daian to take the presents and the cards.

The invitations were for the fifteenth day. All the ladies who had been present at the Qiaos' party, and Lady Qiao the Fifth, were invited to celebrate the birthday of Li Ping'er and to enjoy the Feast of Lanterns. Ximen ordered Laixing to buy cakes and buns and fruits and food, two suits of silk clothes, a little scarlet cloak, a silk hat with golden ornaments, two lanterns made like sheep's horns, that came from Yunnan, a box of ribbons, a pair of tiny gold bracelets, and four gold and jade rings. These things were all packed up on the morning of the fourteenth, and Chen Jingji and Ben the Fourth were told to put on their black clothes and take them to the Qiaos.

Master Qiao received them well, and gave them presents of some value in return, particularly little things for the baby. While they were busying themselves with the presents, Ying Bojue came to talk to Ximen Qing about the money that had been lent to Huang the Fourth and Li Zhi. Seeing them so busy, he asked what it was all about. Ximen Qing told him about the betrothal.

"On the fifteenth," he said, "you must ask your Lady to come and spend an hour or two here."

"Your lady has only to give the command," Bojue said, "and my wife will come."

"A number of ladies are coming," Ximen said, "and I think we men had better go to Lion Street to see the lanterns." Ying Bojue agreed, and went away.

The same day Wu Yin'er brought four boxes of birthday presents to Li Ping'er and asked to be adopted as her ward. Li Ping'er accepted the presents and sent away the sedan chair. When, next day, Li Guijie came and found Wu Yin'er already there, she asked Wu Yueniang why she had come. Yueniang told her what had happened. Guijie made no comment but, all that day, she was sulky and would not speak to Wu Yin'er.

From the princely family of Wang there came a troop of twenty actors with two managers to direct the performance. They brought their chests of costumes. When they came and kowtowed to Ximen Qing, he told them to use the rooms in the west wing as their dressing rooms, and there they had their meals.

Major Zhou's wife, General Jing's mother and Captain Zhang's wife came. They all had soldiers to clear the way before their sedan chairs, and a number of attendants and serving women. Yueniang and the others, dressed in their long cloaks, came out to welcome their guests, and took them to the great hall where they exchanged greetings. Then they sat down and drank some tea, but not ceremonially, for they were waiting for the wife of Magistrate Xia. They waited a long time but she did not come. Two or three times they sent boys to see if she was coming. At last she came with soldiers to clear the way for her, and a number of attendants, with a woman to carry her dressing case. When she came into the great hall, she was received with music. There she greeted the other ladies, and they took their places according to their rank. They had tea under the awning and then went to the great hall, where Chunmei, Yuxiao, Yingchun, and Lanxiang, all exquisitely dressed, served them with tea and wine. The actors performed the *Story of the Western Pavilion*. It was a most brilliant scene.

Ximen Qing waited until the ladies had had tea, then mounted his horse, and went to the house in Lion Street. He had told Ying Bojue and

Xie Xida to meet him there. Some of his men had been told to take one of the four great fireworks to Lion Street and set up two for the entertainment of the ladies. The cooks were ordered to send two boxes of food and two jars of Jinhua wine. Two singing girls had been engaged, Dong Jiao'er and Han Yuchuan, and Daian had taken a sedan chair for Wang Liu'er.

"Aunt Han," Daian said when he met her, "Father has sent me to take you to see the fireworks this evening."

"But I don't know that I ought to go," Wang Liu'er said, smiling. "What do you think your Uncle Han will say about it?"

"Father has spoken to him already," Daian said. "He says you must dress and go. There are only to be two singing girls there, no one else."

Wang Liu'er did not move. Then Han Daoguo himself came in.

"Here is Uncle Han," Daian said. "Your wife will not believe what 1 say."

"Do you really wish me to go?" Wang Liu'er said to her husband.

"Well," he said, "his Lordship said that there is no one to look after the two singing girls. That's why he wants you. And you will see the fireworks this evening. Hurry up and dress. He told me to shut the shop and go there myself. We shall have a good time. Laibao has gone home already. It is his turn to watch the shop tonight."

"I don't know how long it will last," Wang Liu'er said. "We will go and stay a while and then come home. We can't leave the house without anyone to look after it and, besides, this is your day off and you must have some sleep."

She dressed and went with Daian to the house in Lion Street. Laizhao's wife, the Beanpole, was there. She had dusted the beds, changed the bedclothes and the curtains, burned incense to sweeten the rooms, hung up two lanterns, and put a brazier in the room. Wang Liu'er went in and sat down on the bed. The Beanpole made reverence to her and brought her tea.

When Ying Bojue and Ximen Qing had seen the lanterns, they came in and played backgammon in the upper room. Six windows were opened and the shades hung out before them. Below them they could see the lantern fair. It was a picture of gaiety and merriment. After playing a while, they had some food. Then they sat down to look at the lanterns through the blinds. While they were watching the crowd below, Ximen Qing suddenly saw Xie Xida, Zhu Shinian, and another man, who wore a scholar's hat, standing beneath the arch of lanterns. He pointed to them and said to Ying Bojue: "Do you know that fellow wearing a square hat?"

"He seems very familiar to me," Ying Bojue said, "but I don't know him."

Then Ximen Qing said to Daian: "Go down and ask your Uncle Xie to come, but don't let Pockmarked Zhu or the other man see you."

Daian crept downstairs like a young pickpocket and went out into the crowd. He waited till Pockmarked Zhu and the stranger were out of the way for a moment, then pulled Xie Xida by the sleeve. Xie Xida turned quickly and recognized Daian.

"Father and Uncle Ying would like to see you," the boy said.

"Very well, I understand," said Xie Xida. "Now slip away. I will go with these two as far as the place where the Plum Flowers are, and then I'll come to see your master."

Daian made off like a streak of smoke. Xie Xida, when he came to a more crowded place, turned aside and left Zhu Shinian and the other man looking for him. He went to the room where Ximen Qing and Ying Bojue were sitting, and made a reverence to them.

"I see you have come to look at the show, Brother," he said. "Why didn't you send me a message this morning?"

"There were a number of guests at my place all the morning," Ximen said, "and I couldn't find an opportunity to send you word. I did tell Brother Ying to invite you, but you were not at home. Did Pockmarked Zhu see you come here? Who is the man with the scholar's hat?"

"The man with the square hat," Xie Xida said, "is Wang the Third, of General Wang's family. He and Zhu came to see me because Wang is trying to borrow three hundred taels. He asked me, old Sun, and Pockmarked Zhu to be his guarantors. He is going to take a course of study at the military academy, and qualify for official rank. I was not interested in his business. I simply came with him to see the lanterns. When I heard you wished to see me, I went with them as far as the place where the Plum Flowers are and gave them the slip." He asked Bojue how long he had been there.

"Brother told me to come, to your house," Bojue said, "and I did so, but you were not at home. Then I came here. We have been playing backgammon."

"Have you had anything to eat?" Ximen Qing asked Xie Xida.

"When I left your place this morning," Xie Xida said, "I met those two, and I have had nothing to eat all day."

Ximen told Daian to go to the kitchen and ask for some food to be prepared. Before long it was brought. It was a very substantial meal, but Xie Xida soon disposed of it, cleaning up both inside and outside of all the dishes. The little soup that he had left, he put into his rice bowl, and so finished off everything. Daian cleared away, and Xie Xida went to stand beside his two friends. They were now playing backgammon again.

Meanwhile the two singing girls arrived, and the sedan chair men carried in their clothes. They came in smiling. Ying Bojue saw them through the window.

"What makes those little whores so late?" he said. Then to Daian: "Don't let them go to the inner court. Tell them to come up here and see me."

Xie Xida asked who they were. Daian told him, then ran downstairs and said to the singing girls: "Uncle Ying wants to see you." The two singing girls paid no attention, but went on to the inner court. They made a reverence the Beanpole, who took them to the inner room where Wang Liu'er was sitting, wearing a new-fashioned net upon her hair, a purple silk dress, a long black cloak, and a white ribboned skirt. Below the skirt her two tiny feet peeped out. Her hair came down rather low upon her cheeks, and her face was bright but not too highly painted. She looked like a person of the middle class. She was wearing two earrings, shaped like cloves.

They made the usual reverence to her and sat down on the bed. Little Iron Rod brought tea and Wang Liu'er drank it with them. The two girls looked at the woman from head to foot. After they had examined her well, they laughed. They had no idea who she was. Then Daian came and the girls secretly asked him. Daian did not know what story to tell. Finally he said: "The lady comes from my father's sister-in-law's. She has come to see the lanterns."

When the two girls heard this, they went back into the room.

"We did not realize you were our aunt," they said to Wang Liu'er, "and so we did not make the correct reverence to you. Please forgive us." Then they knelt down and kowtowed to her. Wang Liu'er hastily made a half reverence in return. Soup and dishes were brought and she ate with them. Afterwards they took their instruments and sang for her."

When Ying Bojue had finished his game of backgammon, he went downstairs to wash his hands. Hearing the sound of music coming from the inner court, he called Daian and said to him: "Tell me: to whom are those girls singing?" Daian laughed but did not answer for some time. At last he said: "You might be the Captain of Caozhou, the way you poke your nose into everything. Whether there is singing or not, it is no business of yours."

"You thievish young rascal," Ying Bojue said, "whether you tell me or not, you know I shall find out."

"Then why ask me?" Daian said, laughing.

Bojue went upstairs again. By this time, Ximen Qing and Xie Xida had played three games of backgammon. Then Li Ming and Wu Hui came in and kowtowed.

"Good!" said Ying Bojue, "you have come just in time. How did you know we were here?"

Li Ming, still upon his knees, said: "We went to his Lordship's house and there they told us that he was having a party here, so we came on to await his pleasure."

"Excellent!" Bojue said. "Stand up."

Then he said to Daian: "Go and ask your Uncle Han to come." Han Daoguo came, greeted them, and sat down.

The tables were laid; dishes appropriate to the season were brought in, and Qintong served wine. Ying Bojue and Xie Xida sat in the seats of honor—Ximen Qing in the host's place, and Han Daoguo opposite. When the wine had been heated, Daian was told to bid the singing girls come. The two girls, Dong Jiao'er and Han Yuchuan, came in, slowly and gracefully. They kowtowed, but not exactly in the direction of the two guests.

"I wondered who was here," Ying Bojue said. "Now I see it is only you two little whores. Why didn't you come when I sent for you? You are getting far too independent. If I don't take you in hand, you will become quite unbearable."

Dong Jiao'er laughed. "Brother," she said, "you are like a ghost playing his ghostly tricks on the other side of a wall. But you won't frighten me to death."

Han Yuchuan said: "You know, my dear slave, that you are like an animal's head picked up by the city wall, a fine specimen of an unwanted baby."

"Brother," Ying Bojue said to Ximen, "you have done more than you need today. Li Ming and Wu Hui are here, and that ought to be enough. What need have you of these two whores? Why not send them about their business at once? Tonight is the Feast of Lanterns, and they will have plenty of opportunity to go and beg elsewhere. But don't make them too late. Nobody will have them if they are too late."

"Brother," Yuchuan said, "how can you be so shameless? It wasn't you who sent for us, but Father. What business is it of yours?"

"Foolish little bone," Bojue said. "I happen to be here and you will have to wait on me whether you like it or not."

"You are like Tang, the fat man, who fell into a jar of vinegar and was sour all over," Yuchuan said.

"It is your heart that is sour, you thievish little strumpet," Bojue said. "But wait a while. I will show you something when you go home. I have two scores against you now, and you shall not escape me."

"What do you mean?" Dong Jiao'er said. "Tell me."

"I shall tell the policeman that you are breaking the law by night. He will arrest you and put the thumbscrews on you. And if that is not enough, I will spend a few coins on white wine and make your chair men drunk, and then you will wander all over the place, get home late, and have a beating waiting for you when you do get there."

"If we are late," Han Yuchuan said, "we shall not go. We shall stay here, or we shall ask Father to send us home and give mother a hundred cash. But it has nothing to do with you anyway. I like your impertinence!"

"Yes," Bojue said, "I suppose it is I who am the slave. Everything is topsy-turvy nowadays. I lose."

They laughed and talked. The two singing girls sang the songs of spring, and the men dined. Then Daian came and said: "Uncle Zhu is here." No one spoke. Zhu Shinian came upstairs and saw Ying Bojue and Xie Xida sitting in the places of honor.

"Ah!" said he, "a fine pair you are, stuffing yourselves with good food, but do you call yourselves men?" He turned to Xie Xida. "Brother, you are given an invitation and, without a word to us, you run away. We were looking for you everywhere, there by the Plum Flowers."

"It was quite by chance," Xie Xida said, "that I saw his Lordship and Brother Ying playing backgammon. I came up to greet them, and his Lordship made me stay."

Ximen Qing told Daian to bring a chair and invited Zhu Shinian to sit down. Cup and chopsticks were brought; Zhu sat down in the lower seat, and the cook brought something for him to eat. Ximen Qing had only one pie and a mouthful of soup. Li Ming was standing beside him, and he gave everything that was put before him to the young man to take away and eat. Ying Bojue, Xie Xida, Zhu Shinian and Han Daoguo each had a large bowl of soup, three large pastries, and four peach-blossom buns. They left one pie as ballast for the plate. Then all the food was cleared away and more wine was brought.

"Where did you leave him?" Xie Xida said to Zhu Shinian. "And how did you know I was here?"

"I searched everywhere for you," Zhu Shinian said, "and when I couldn't find you, I went to old Sun's place with Wang the Third. We met Master Xu Buyu. He borrowed the three hundred taels, but old Sun made a mistake in the contract."

"You must not put my name on it," Xie Xida said. "I will have nothing to do with it. You and old Sun are the guarantors and the commission will come to you. What mistake did you make?"

"I told him to write out the contract more or less indefinitely and make three conditions for repayment, but he didn't do so, and I made him write it out again."

"What were the three conditions?" Xie Xida said.

"First, when the wind blows away the stone roller and kills a single goose in the sky. Secondly, when a fish jumps from the bottom of the river to the bank; and thirdly, when the stones in the riverbed are so wa-ter-logged that they fall to pieces. When those three things happened, he was to pay his debt."

"Well," Xie Xida said, "if he wrote that, it was indefinite enough."

"It is not so indefinite as you think," Zhu Shinian said. "One day, if the weather is fine and the water low, and the authorities think fit to dig up the river, and the stones in the bed are broken by the workers with their tools, he will have to pay."

Everybody laughed. It was now growing dark and Ximen Qing told the boys to light the lanterns. They were sheep's horn lanterns, and very wonderfully made.

Yueniang sent Qitong and some soldiers with four boxes full of dainties. Ximen asked the boy if the ladies had finished their party, and who had told him to bring the things. "Great Mother told me to bring them for you to eat with your wine," Qitong said. "The ladies have not gone yet, and four acts of the play have been performed. My lady is entertaining her guests in the great hall. They are drinking there and watching the fireworks."

"Has anybody come to see the fireworks?" Ximen said.

"There is a crowd at the gate," the boy told him.

"I told four black-garbed soldiers to take their staves and keep order and not to allow the people to push one another about."

"Ping'an and the soldiers are keeping guard over the fireworks," Qitong said. "There is no disorder."

Ximen Qing gave orders that the table should be cleared and the boxes brought in. The cook brought some excellent fruit pasties. The two singing girls served wine. Ximen told Qitong to go home again. Then he and the others drank the warm wine, and enjoyed the delicacies Yueniang had sent. He told Li Ming and Wu Hui to sing the song of the lanterns. When the song was ended, they ate the pasties.

Han Daoguo was the first to go home. Ximen Qing told Laizhao to pull up the blinds downstairs and take out the fireworks. Ximen and his friends watched from the upper room, and sent word to Wang Liu'er, the singing girls, and the Beanpole to look on from below. Daian and Laizhao carried the firework to the middle of the street and there set light to it. People came crowding to see, shoulder to shoulder, for they were told that Ximen Qing was responsible for it.

Ying Bojue saw that Ximen Qing was a little tipsy. When the firework was burnt out, he went downstairs. Wang Liu'er was washing her hands. He dragged Xie Xida and Zhu Shinian away, without even waiting to say good-bye to his host.

"Where are you going, Uncles?" Daian said to him.

"Foolish boy," Ying Bojue whispered. "I have told you before. If I don't go, they will stay and stay, and it will be awkward. If your father asks for me, say we have all gone."

When the fireworks were done, Ximen Qing asked where Bojue was. "Uncle Ying and Uncle Xie have both gone," Daian said. "I tried to stop them, but they would not stay. They told me to thank you for them."

Ximen Qing said no more. He gave a great cup of wine to Li Ming and Wu Hui. "I am not giving you money today," he told them. "Come to me on the morning of the sixteenth. I am going to ask Uncle Ying and some of my friends that day."

"I must tell you, Father," Li Ming said, kneeling down, "that on the sixteenth, Wu Hui, Zuo Shun, Zheng Feng and I are all going to his Lordship Hu's place. Hu is the newly appointed governor of Dongpingfu. I am afraid we shall not be able to come until the evening."

"That is all right," Ximen said, "we are going to have our party in the evening, anyway. But you must not be too late."

The two boys promised. Then the two singing girls came to say good-bye. Ximen Qing said to them. "Tomorrow I am giving a party at my house to some ladies. Li Guijie and Wu Yin'er will be there, and I want you too." The two singing girls agreed, and went home.

Ximen Qing told Laizhao, Daian, and Qintong to clear everything away and blow out the lanterns and the lamps. Then he went to the back court. Little Iron Rod, who had been watching the fireworks, saw him come in. He ran upstairs, where his father was putting some food on a plate, with a jar of wine, and some pasties. These he took to another room. The boy asked his mother to give him some. But she boxed his ears twice and drove him out to play in the courtyard. He heard the sound of laughter coming from one of the rooms and thought it must be the singing girls. The door was shut, but he peeped through a crack. The room was brightly lighted by lamps and candles, and he could see Ximen Qing and Wang Liu'er busily engaged upon the bed.

Ximen leaned the woman over the edge of the bed, stripped off her underwear, put the clasp over his thing and began work on the flower in the back court. Back and forth, in and out—how could he stop after only a few hundred thrusts? The sounds of their banging away were clearly audible. From their rapid breathing and their behavior it looked as though they wished to break the bed in pieces.

The boy was looking on, when his mother caught him. She pulled him by the hair and dragged him to the front court. There she boxed his ears and cursed him. "You root of trouble, you little slave!" she cried. "Do you wish to die that you stand there and watch them?" She gave him some fruits and sweets and kept him carefully indoors. The boy was frightened, climbed into his bed, and went to sleep.

Ximen Qing and Wang Liu'er enjoyed themselves for a long time. Daian gave food and wine to the sedan chair men, and they took Wang Liu'er home. Then he and Qitong lighted their lanterns and went home with Ximen Qing.

CHAPTER 43

The Lost Bracelet

Sadness fills my heart
The love that came so lately soon has gone again
The past is past and nothing can bring it back.
Yellow chrysanthemums beside the fence
I know not whom your blossoms will delight
Wine for a time can banish sorrow
But sorrow returns before the wine is done.
I have waited long beside the balustrade.
The golden moonbeams slowly pass
And pure dew falls upon the dark green moss.

It was the third night watch when Ximen Qing returned. Wu Yueniang had not gone to bed. She was talking to Aunt Wu and the other ladies. Li Ping'er was there and offered wine to him. When Aunt Wu saw that Ximen had come, she went to her own room. Yueniang realized that Ximen was a little tipsy, but she took his cloak and told Li Ping'er to kowtow to him. Then they sat together for a while. He asked about the party, and Yuxiao brought tea. Then, seeing that Aunt Wu was staying in Yueniang's room, he went to sleep with Meng Yulou.

The next morning the cooks came early to prepare for the banquet. Ximen Qing went to his office to attend to the documents that needed to be dealt with. There Magistrate Xia thanked him. "My wife," he said, "enjoyed your very kind hospitality yesterday."

"I fear, the entertainment we could offer her was very poor," Ximen said, "I really should apologize." Then he went home.

Old woman Kong came before Lady Qiao the Fifth, and brought her presents. Ximen accepted them and gave a meal to all the servants. Old woman Kong went to rest in Yueniang's room. Then Miss Zheng came. She made a reverence to all the ladies and sat down to have tea.

Li Zhi and Huang the Fourth, having secured payment for their supplies of incense and wax, together with Ben the Fourth, brought the money from Dongpingfu. Ying Bojue was told of this and came with them to be present at the repayment of the debt. Ximen Qing told Chen Jingji to take a balance to the great hall and measure the silver. This was done and Ximen took the money. Huang the Fourth produced four gold bracelets weighing about thirty taels, and these were accepted as equal to a hundred and fifty taels of silver. They still owed Ximen about five hundred taels and asked to have their contract altered. "Come back after the festival," Ximen said to them, "and we will see about it. I am busy now." Li Zhi and Huang the Fourth addressed Ximen as "Old Father", thanked him very heartily, and went away.

Ying Bojue had not forgotten that the two men had promised him something for himself, and he thought this a very suitable opportunity to remind them of the fact. He was going out after them when Ximen Qing stopped him.

"Why did you three go away last night without saying a word to me?" he said.

"You were very hospitable yesterday," Bojue said. "I had a great deal to drink, and so had you. I knew you were going to have a party here today and that you would be wanted at home to make arrangements, so I thought we had better go. Today I suppose you have not been to your office; you must be very tired after your exertions."

"It was the third night watch when I returned," Ximen said, "but this morning I did go to the office to attend to some papers. I had a good deal of business there, and now I am hard at it getting ready for the banquet. I still have to go to the temple to offer the sacrifice appropriate to the festival and, after that, I have to go to Zhou Nanxuan's place for a party. I don't know how long it will take me."

"What powers of endurance you have," Ying Bojue said. "You really are a lucky fellow. I don't wish to flatter you, but I know no one else who could get through what you do."

They talked a while, then Ximen Qing invited Bojue to have a meal with him. Bojue excused himself.

"Why has your wife not come yet?" Ximen said.

"I ordered a sedan chair for her," Bojue said. "She must be on her way now." He made a reverence and went after Huang the Fourth and Li Zhi.

Ximen Qing examined the four golden bracelets and liked them very much. He thought of the luck that had lately come to him. Li Ping'er had borne him a son; he had been given an official appointment; he had betrothed his son to the baby Qiao, and now he had done an excellent piece of business. He put the gold bracelets in his sleeve and went to see Li Ping'er. As he passed Pan Jinlian's room, she came out.

"What have you there?" she called to him. "Come here and show me."

Ximen said he would be back in a moment and went on to see Li Ping'er.

Jinlian was disappointed when she found that he would not stop. "I wonder what treasure he has there to make him so excited," she said to herself. "Well, if you won't show me, all right. You little whippetysnip of a rogue, you'll break your leg if you don't look out. And if you go to her room, may you break both legs!"

When Ximen Qing came to her room, Li Ping'er had just finished dressing her hair and the nurse was playing with the baby. Ximen let the child play with the bracelets.

"Where did you get them?" the Sixth Lady said. "Take care the baby doesn't make his hands cold."

"I got them from Li Zhi and Huang the Fourth," Ximen said.

Li Ping'er was afraid they would make the baby's hands cold, so she took an embroidered handkerchief, wrapped them in it and then allowed him to play with them.

Daian came. "Yun has brought some horses for you to see," he said to his master.

"Where have they come from?" Ximen asked.

"He says his brother, Colonel Yun, has sent them."

Then Li Jiao'er, Meng Yulou, Aunt Wu and Miss Zheng came to see Guan'ge. Ximen Qing left the four bracelets and went to look at the horses. When all the ladies came in, Li Ping'er asked them to sit down and made a reverence to them, forgetting that the baby was still playing with the bracelets. After a while she discovered that one of them was missing. The nurse, Ruyi'er, said to her: "Have you one of those ornaments? I can only find three."

"No," Li Ping'er said, "I haven't one. I wrapped them all together in the handkerchief."

"Here is the handkerchief on the floor," Ruyi'er said, "but the other bracelet is not there."

There was immediately a terrible to-do. Ruyi'er questioned Yingchun, and Yingchun questioned old woman Feng.

"Ai ya, ai ya!" old woman Feng cried. "May I lose my sight if I have ever set eyes on them. All these years I've been coming here, I have never so much as touched a broken needle or a snapped thread. Your mother knows that I have never been greedy for gold. You are in charge of the baby. Why do you try to put the blame on me?"

Li Ping'er laughed. "Don't be so silly, old lady. But we have lost some gold ornaments." She turned to Yingchun. "Why are you making so much fuss about it, you rascal? We must wait until your master comes back. Probably he took it with him. But it is strange that he should only take one."

"What are you talking about?" Yulou asked.

"Our husband brought some gold ornaments here," Li Ping'er told her, "and he gave them to the baby to play with. That is all I know."

Ximen Qing went to the gate and looked at the horses. The servants were there, and he told the boys to put them through their paces.

"They may be Eastern horses," Ximen said, "but I don't think much of their condition. Besides, their action is anything but good. They can only walk. How much does your brother want for them?"

"Only seventy taels for the pair," Yun Lishou said.

"It is not a great amount," Ximen said, "but they can't trot. Take them back and wait till you get something with more style. Then let me know. It's not a question of price."

He went back to the house. A boy asked him to go and see Li Ping'er.

"Did you take away one of those gold ornaments?" she asked him. "There are only three here."

"I went to look at the horses," Ximen said, "I didn't take anything."

"Well, if you didn't, where has one of them gone? We have been looking for it everywhere."

"It was old woman Feng who took it," the nurse said. Old woman Feng began to cry and swore she had done nothing of the sort.

"Who did take it, then?" Ximen said. "Have another look for it."

"Aunt Wu and her sister-in-law came," the Lady of the Vass said, "and I asked them to sit down, forgetting all about the ornaments. I thought you must have taken it with you. So I never found out for a long time and, when I did, the ladies were upset and went away." She gave the other three bracelets to Ximen Qing.

Ben the Fourth came and gave a hundred taels to his master and Ximen went to the inner court to put the money away.

When she heard of the trouble in Li Ping'er's room, Jinlian, who could never leave ill alone, went to Yueniang and told her what she thought about it.

"Sister," she said, "see how that foolish thing behaves. No matter how rich he is, he should not give gold bracelets to the baby to play with."

"I have heard that a bracelet has been lost," Yueniang said, "but that's all. I have no idea what happened."

"Nor has anyone else," Jinlian said. "You didn't see him. I did. He came from the front court with those gold ornaments in his sleeve, looking like the eight barbarians on their way to pay tribute. I asked him what he had got there and would have looked at them, but he did not even turn his head. He dashed off to the Sixth Lady's room. Afterwards, I heard everybody talking about one of the things being lost. He had missed one and set them all looking for it. Even if he were as rich as Wang the Millionaire, he could not afford to throw gold away like this. Why, it must weigh ten taels and be worth at least fifty or sixty taels of silver. There will be a row about it yet. It is like a turtle escaping from a jar. The people in her room were all her own people, and she must take the responsibility for them."

As they were talking, Ximen Qing came in to give to Yueniang the hundred taels that Ben the Fourth had brought and the three remaining bracelets.

"I got these," he told his wife, "from Li Zhi and Huang the Fourth. There were four of them, but I gave them to the baby to play with and one is lost. I want you to send for all the maids in the house and question them. I am going to send a boy to the street for a piece of wolf's sinew. If the missing piece of gold is produced, well and good. Otherwise, I shall make good use of the wolf sinew."

"You ought never to have given the gold to the baby," his wife said. "It is cold and heavy, and it might have hurt the baby's hands or feet."

"No, you ought not to have given it to the child," Jinlian said, "but you could think of nothing but getting it to her room. I spoke to you and you wouldn't look at me. Just like a red-eyed soldier with some loot that he didn't wish anybody to see. Now that you have lost a piece of gold, you have the nerve to come here and tell the Great Lady about it. You ask her to examine all the maids. Well, if the maids don't laugh at you with their mouths, they will laugh at you with their cunts."

This made Ximen Qing angry. He took Jinlian by the hair and threw her on Yueniang's bed. He raised his hand threateningly and said: "I hate you. If it were not for what people would say, I would beat you to death, you bad little bone. You are always trying to show off your sharp tongue and interfering in matters that do not concern you."

Jinlian made a show of tears. "Because you are powerful and rich," she sobbed, "you have become cruel. You only think about being brutal to me. Your words are brave; you don't care whether you murder anybody or not. Go on, beat me, there is no one to hinder you. So long as I don't stop breathing, it will be all right, but if I do, my old mother will certainly come and ask you a few questions. No matter how rich and powerful you are, if my mother goes to the court and accuses you, you needn't think you will escape, just because you happen to be an officer. The post you hold is nothing very glorious and your ceremonial hat is a miserable thing. You can't stand a charge of murder against you. Even the Emperor has no right to murder his subjects."

Ximen Qing laughed. "Oh, how cleverly you talk, you bad little bone.
You say that my position is of no account, and that my ceremonial hat is
in rags. I will tell a maid to bring my hat, and then you'll see whether it
is in rags or not. Go and ask the people in Qinghe if I owe anybody any
money. You say I owe money."

"Why did you call me a bad little bone?" Jinlian lifted one of her feet.
"What is wrong with my feet? Why should you call me names like that?"

"You two are like a brass bowl and somebody banging it with an iron
broom handle," Yueniang said. "There is a proverb that says that the dev-
ilish man has a devil of his own, and, when he meets another devil, there is
nothing he can do. The stronger-mouthed always comes out on top. Sister,
your mouth is all you have to count on. If it were not quite so sharp, you
would be done."

Ximen Qing realized that there was nothing he could do, so he put on
his clothes and went out. On the way, Daian said to him: "A messenger has
come from Major Zhou asking you to go there after the sacrifice."

"Tell Jingji to take a horse and go to the sacrifice for me," Ximen said.
"I will go to Major Zhou's now."

The two stage managers and the actors from the princely family of
Wang came and kowtowed to Ximen Qing. He told Shutong to arrange
for them to have something to eat. "Amuse the ladies well," he said to
them, "and I will see that you are suitably rewarded. Do not open your
boxes in the upper room."

The two managers knelt down and said: "If we do not play our parts
well, we shall ask for no reward."

"This will make the second day they have played for us," Ximen said to
Shutong. "You may give them five taels of silver." He mounted his horse
and rode away.

Jinlian was sitting in Yueniang's room. "Why don't you go to your
room and powder your face?" Yueniang said to her. "Your eyes are all red,
and you will not be fit to see the guests when they come. Really, you ought
not to provoke him. I did the best I could for you. If I hadn't stopped him,
you would certainly have had a beating. There is always dog's hair on a
husband's face. He doesn't distinguish between the rights and the wrongs
of a case, but is always ready to trounce somebody. Why did you make
trouble with him just now? He lost his gold. Well, what if he did? It is no
business of yours whether he looked for it or not. It didn't happen in your
room, and there was no call for you to start arguing with him. You must
learn to keep your temper."

She calmed Jinlian, who went to her room to powder her face.

Shortly afterwards, Li Ping'er and Wu Yin'er, dressed for the party, came to Yueniang's room.

"How did the gold come to be lost?" the Great Lady said. "The Fifth Lady and he quarreled about it and nearly came to blows. I stopped them, and now he has gone out to a party somewhere. But he has sent a boy to buy a wolf's sinew and when he comes back tonight the maids will all be punished. What were the maids and serving women in your room about? They were supposed to be looking after the baby and they must have lost the gold. A piece of gold is not like a penny,"

"He gave the baby the four pieces of gold to play with," Li Ping'er said, "and I was busy entertaining Aunt Wu and Miss Zheng and the two other ladies. It was then one of the ornaments was lost. The maids say it was the nurse's fault, the nurse blames old woman Feng, and old woman Feng cries and says she is going to kill herself. It really is a most mysterious business, and I don't know whom to blame."

"I often play with the baby," Wu Yin'er said, "but thanks be to Heaven, I was dressing my hair in another room and kept out of it all. Otherwise, I should have been dragged into it and, even if you had said nothing, I should have felt very uncomfortable. People often lose money, but in such a household as yours it is most regrettable for such a thing to happen. If people outside hear about it, it will bring shame upon the household."

While they were talking, Han Yuchuan and Dong Jiao'er came, bringing their dresses with them. They kowtowed to Yueniang, Aunt Wu, and Li Ping'er and, rising, made a reverence to Wu Yin'er.

"You did not go home yesterday, Sister," they said to her.

"How did you know?" said Wu Yin'er.

"We went to the house in Lion Street," Dong Jiao'er said, "where the Feast of the Lanterns was held, and Father told us to come here today."

Yueniang asked them to sit down and Xiaoyu brought them tea. The two girls stood up to take the tea and made a reverence to Xiaoyu.

"At what time did you finish singing last night?" Wu Yin'er asked them.

"It was the second night watch when we reached home. We went with your younger brother, Wu Hui."

After they had talked for a short time, Yueniang said to Yuxiao: "See that they have their tea in good time." She was afraid it would be awkward if the guests arrived before they had had it. The table was set. There were two plates of spring dishes and four boxes of cakes. "Go to the Second Lady's room," Yueniang said to Xiaoyu, "and ask your sister Li Guijie to come and have tea."

Guijie and her aunt came in together. When they had made a reverence to everybody present, they sat down and had tea, and then the things were all cleared away. Yingchun, specially dressed for the occasion, came in carrying Guan'ge. The baby was wearing a silken cap of Good Fortune, with a gold brim, a long red gown, white silk socks and shoes. On his chest hung the cords and medals and on his wrists were little golden bangles.

"Well, my young lord," Li Ping'er said, "what have you come for? Nobody invited you." She took the child and set him on her knees. The baby saw that the room was full of people and looked at them one after another. Guijie, sitting on the bed, played with him. "Brother," she said, "you look at me so hard you must wish me to carry you." She held out her arms to him and the baby nestled to her breast.

"Ah," Aunt Wu said, laughing, "even a baby of his age seems to know the meaning of love."

"Think who is his father," Yueniang said. "When he grows up, he will assuredly be a very gay young man."

"If he is anything of the sort, I shall ask you to beat him," Yulou said.

"Baby," Li Ping'er said, "Sister is carrying you, and you must not soil her clothes. If you do, I shall beat you."

"I don't mind whether he does or not," Guijie said. "I love to have him in my arms and play with him."

Dong Jiao'er said: "We have been here a long time but we have not yet sung for the ladies." Han Yuchuan took her lute and Dong Jiao'er her zither: Wu Yin'er sang. She sang the song "Splendor of Riches Like the Moon at the Full. The Golden Chain Hangs on the Wu T'ung Tree." Her voice echoed through the rafters and stirred the dust there. It seemed powerful enough to pass through rocks and mount even to the skies.

Guan'ge was frightened. He lay still against Guijie's breast and dared not lift his head. Yueniang saw this. "Take the child," she said to Li Ping'er, "and let Yingchun take him to your room. What a delicate child he is. Look at his pale face." Li Ping'er took the baby. She bade Yingchun cover his ears with her hands and take him out.

The girls were still singing when Daian came in. "I have been to Mistress Qiao's," he said. "Mistress Chu and Master Shang's wife were ready; they were only waiting for Lady Qiao the Fifth. They will be here in a few moments. The musicians are ready both at the gate and in the hall. Ladies, you will do well to expect them at any moment."

Yueniang saw that many beautiful things were set about in the back hall, and the chairs put in their proper places. The lattices were suspended by golden chains and the air was sweetly perfumed. Chunmei, Yingchun, Yuxiao and Lanxiang were dressed in their new clothes. All the maids and serving women wore ornaments of gold and silver, and, in their dresses of green and gold, waited to do honor to the new relative of the household.

The first person to arrive was Ying Bojue's wife. Ying Bao was in attendance upon her. Yueniang welcomed her and took her to her room. Madam Ying made reverence after reverence to Yueniang. "We are always troubling you," she said, "troubling you beyond all reason."

"Not at all," Yueniang said, "it is we who are always troubling your worthy husband."

Soon they heard the shouts of men clearing the way; then the musicians in the outer hall began to play. Ping'an came and announced Lady Qiao's sedan chair. A host of people surrounded the five sedan chairs that had stopped outside the gate. The first was that of Lady Qiao the Fifth. It was covered with a canopy of sky-blue and had a double gold fringe around it. The men who cleared the way carried rattans. Behind the large chair were smaller ones for the maidservants. Then four soldiers with dressing cases and braziers. Then two black-robed attendants riding on ponies. After Lady Qiao the Fifth came Mistress Qiao, then Mistress Zhu, Master Shang's wife and Miss Duan, a sister-in-law of an officer named Cui.

Ximen Qing's six ladies, most exquisitely dressed and looking like jade carvings, came to the second door to welcome their guests and escorted Lady Qiao the Fifth to the hall. Lady Qiao was about seventy years old. She was not very tall. She wore a headdress of pearls with many precious stones and a scarlet gown embroidered in the palace fashion. Her hair was perfectly white and her eyebrows like two strips of snow. Her eyes were like autumn water, perhaps rather dark. Hair like a bundle of silk fell, not in too great abundance, over her temples. It was like the cloud resting on the Chu Mountain.

When they came to the hall, she made a reverence first to Aunt Wu, then to Wu Yueniang and the others. Yueniang asked Lady Qiao to accept a reverence from her, but the old lady refused. Even after much discussion, she would only accept a half reverence. Then Yueniang greeted Mistress Qiao in the manner appointed for relatives. After the greetings they thanked one another for the presents that had been exchanged. Then they took their seats. Lady Qiao the Fifth sat upon a chair with an embroidered cushion in front of the screen. Yueniang asked Mistress Qiao to sit next to her, but she said: "I must not sit next to the Fifth Lady, for I am her niece." Mistress Zhu and Master Shang's wife were invited to take the next places. They made a show of hesitation and the matter was settled after much discussion, with Lady Qiao the Fifth in the most honorable place and the others according to their rank.

In the midst of the hall was a great square stove with fire burning. It made the room as warm as though it were spring. Chunmei, Yuxiao, Yingchun and Lanxiang, dressed in their best clothes, served the wine.

"Will you not introduce me to your distinguished husband?" Lady
Qiao the Fifth said. "I should like to salute him in accordance with the
rites between relatives."

Yueniang told her that Ximen Qing had gone to his office and had
not yet returned.

"What office does he hold?" Lady Qiao asked.

"He was only a private citizen," Yueniang said, "but the Imperial Court
was gracious and made him Captain of a Thousand Families, and he has
duties at the law courts. I fear that this betrothal will lower the prestige
of your house."

"What is that you say?" Lady Qiao the Fifth said. "We are quite content to be allied to one of such high rank as your worthy husband. My
niece told me the other day about the matter and I was delighted. That is
why I have come to see you today, and I trust that in future we shall see
more of each other."

"My only fear," Yueniang said, "is that we shall damage your reputation."

"Do not say that," Lady Qiao replied, "even an Emperor sometimes
marries the daughter of a commoner. If you do not mind my telling you
rather a long story, I will explain to you that the present Empress of the
Eastern Palace is a niece of mine. Her parents died and I looked after her.
When my husband was alive, he succeeded to the post of High Commander. But he died, alas, when he was only fifty. I have no children and
have always lived with my nephews, of whom none is wealthy but this
one. Though he has no great position, he is able to live very comfortably,
and I don't think your family need be ashamed of him."

After they had talked for a while, Aunt Wu said to Yueniang: "Send
for the baby and let her Ladyship see him and give him her blessing." Li
Ping'er at once bade the nurse take the baby and kowtow to the old lady.
Lady Qiao the Fifth admired Guan'ge and said he was a very fine boy. She
told her servants to open her bag, and from it took a piece of yellow silk
shot with purple, such as is used at the Court, and a pair of golden armlets.
These she presented to the child. Yueniang thanked her. Then she asked
her to go to an inner room to change her clothes.

In the outer court four tables were laid and tea was waiting. Upon each
table there were forty dishes and every kind of delicacy imaginable. After
tea Yueniang took them to see the gardens.

By this time Chen Jingji had come back from the service at the temple,
and, when he had taken a religious meal, he, with Shutong and Daian,
arranged the tables in the outer hall. Then the ladies were invited to come
to dinner, and a very magnificent banquet they had.

Musicians and singers were posted near the tables. Wu Yueniang and Li Ping'er themselves served wine, while, outside the door, the musicians played. Then Mistress Qiao and the other ladies offered wine to Li Ping'er in celebration of her birthday and, afterwards, all took their places again. Guijie, Wu Yin'er, Han Yuchuan and Dong Jiao'er stood before them and sang the song "Long Mayest Thou Live Like the Southern Mountain." The actors brought the list of their plays, and Lady Qiao the Fifth asked them to play the drama "On the Night of the Feast of Lanterns, Wang Yueying Lost a Shoe." The cooks brought in small slices of roast goose, and were rewarded with five *qian* of silver. Five courses of meat were served and three of soup. The fourth act of the play was ended, and it began to grow dark. The candles in the hall and all kinds of lanterns were lighted. They looked like embroidered ribbons floating, like strings of color waving in the air. Then the full moon rose and the moonbeams mingled with the lights within the hall. The musicians took their instruments and played the melody of the lanterns.

When the music was done, Lady Qiao the Fifth and Mistress Qiao gave two taels of silver to the actors and two *qian* to each of the four singing girls. In the hall of the inner court, Yueniang had arranged for more tables to be prepared with fruits and other things. Now she asked the ladies to go there. The four tables were piled high; the singing girls sang, and the musicians played. They drank again.

Several times Lady Qiao said, "It is late, and I must go." At last Yueniang and the others were unable to dissuade her any longer, and they escorted her as far as the great gate. There they again offered her wine and stayed to see the fireworks. On both sides of the street, people were crowding, as close together as the scales on a fish, or as bees in a swarm. Ping'an and the soldiers kept the crowd back with their sticks, but still the people pushed forward. Then one of the fireworks was burnt out, and the people began gradually to drift away.

Lady Qiao and her companions said farewell to Yueniang, got into their chairs and departed. It was about the third night watch. Ying Bojue's wife went away too.

Yueniang and the others then went to the inner court and told Chen Jingji, Laixing, Shutong and Daian to see to the clearing away of everything and to give the actors and their two leaders refreshments, pay them five taels of silver for their performance, and dismiss them.

Yueniang said that some food and half a jar of wine that was left should be given to Clerk Fu, Ben the Fourth and Chen Jingji. "They have worked very hard," she said, "and it is only right that they should have a cup of wine." A table was set in the great hall. "I do not know when the master will return," Yueniang told them, "so do not put out the lanterns."

Clerk Fu, Ben the Fourth, Chen Jingji and Laibao sat in the upper seats, Laixing, Shutong, Daian and Ping'an in the lower. The wine was poured out.

"You had better put a man at the gate," Laibao said to Ping'an. "If our master comes home, there will be no one to receive him."

"It is all right," Ping'an said. "I have already posted Huatong there."

Then they amused themselves playing Guess Fingers and drinking wine.

"Don't let's guess fingers," Jingji said, "we must choose a quieter game. We shall be heard in the inner court if we make so much noise. Let each one recite a line of poetry. If he can do so, well and good, but if not, he must drink a large cup of wine. Now, Clerk Fu, you begin."

"At the Feast of Lanterns, I laughed at the streamers," Clerk Fu said. "Happiness in life is only for dreamers," added Ben the Fourth. "The moonlight and the lanterns are our joy today," said Jingji. "So we'll enjoy life as long as we may," said Laibao. "I invited my girl, why isn't she here?" said Laixing. "I, like the Great Lady, inspire with fear," Shutong continued. Then Daian said, "Though the wine has been left us, the lanterns are dim." "And the cup of enjoyment is full to the brim," Ping'an said.

They all laughed very merrily.

CHAPTER 44

The Thief Is Discovered

Chen Jingji and the others drank their wine in the outer court. Aunt Wu's sedan chair came for her. She got her things together and prepared to take her leave, but Wu Yueniang begged her not to go.

"Sister-in-law," she said, "please stay tonight. Go tomorrow instead."

"But I have stayed here and with the Qiaos for three or four days. There is no one at home, and your brother's business keeps him busy at the office. I hope you will all come to see me tomorrow, and in the evening we will walk off the hundred illnesses."

"We will gladly come," Yueniang said, "but it must be in the evening."

"No," Aunt Wu said, "come early in your sedan chairs, and you can return on foot in the evening."

Yueniang filled one box with the pasties that are made for the Feast of Lanterns and another with spiced cake, and ordered Laian to accompany Aunt Wu. Then Li Guijie and the other singing girls kowtowed to Yueniang and made ready to leave.

"Why are you in such a hurry?" Yueniang said. "You must wait for your father. He told me not to let you go before he came back. I fancy he has something to say to you, and I dare not let you go before he comes."

"But Father has gone to a party," Guijie said, "and there is no telling when he will return. I don't think we can wait for him. So please, Lady, let Wu Yin'er and me go. The others can stay. They only came today, but we have been here two days already, and I am sure my mother is anxious about me."

"I only want you to stay one night more," Yueniang said.

"Mother," Guijie said, "it is very kind of you, but there is no one at home. My sister is engaged elsewhere. I will sing a song for you, and then you will let me go, won't you?"

While they were talking, Chen Jingji came in to give an account of the money that he had spent on the servants. "I gave the sedan men one *qian* of silver apiece, so, in all, I paid out about ten packets, about three taels. Here are ten packets left." Yueniang took the silver.

"Uncle," Guijie said, "may I trouble you to go and see whether my sedan chair has come yet?"

"The chairs have come for the other girls," Jingji said, "but yours and Wu Yin'er's are not here. I don't know, but it is possible they may have been sent away again."

"Uncle," Guijie said, "either you have sent them away yourself, or you are deceiving us."

"If you don't believe me," Chen Jingji said, "go and see for yourself."

Then Qintong came with the wrapper and told them that Ximen Qing had returned. "It is a good thing you didn't go," Yueniang said. "There is your father."

Ximen Qing came in. He had drunk a great deal of wine. He sat on the upper side, and Han Yuchuan and Dong Jiao'er kowtowed to him.

"Have our guests gone?" Ximen asked his wife. "Why don't you make the girls sing?"

"They were just thinking of going home," Yueniang said.

"You and Wu Yin'er must not go away until the festival is over. The other two girls can go."

"There!" Yueniang said. "You wouldn't believe me. I might be always telling stories. You hear what he says." Guijie bent her head and said nothing.

Ximen Qing asked Daian if the sedan chairs had come for the girls. The boy told him that those for Dong Jiao'er and Yuchuan were waiting.

"I will not have any more wine," Ximen said, "but take your instruments and sing for me. Then two of you may go."

The four singers took their instruments and sang the twenty-eight verses from *Ten Bolts of Brocade*. The ladies sat and listened. Afterwards, Ximen Qing gave some silver to Yuchuan and Dong Jiao'er and let them go. The two other girls stayed.

Suddenly there was a great to-do in the outer court. Daian and Qintong, shouting, dragged in Xiahua, Li Jiao'er's maid.

"We had taken the two singing girls to the gate," they said, "and had our lanterns with us. When we passed the stable to give some hay to the horses, we found Xiahua there, hiding under the manger. We had no idea what she was doing there, and we were startled. We spoke to her, but she made no answer."

Ximen Qing went outside and sat down on a chair underneath the eaves. He summoned Qintong, and the boy brought out the girl. She knelt down.

"What were you doing in the outer court?" Ximen asked her. The maid was silent.

"I didn't send you to the stable," Li Jiao'er said. "Why did you go there?" The maid was frightened. Ximen Qing was determined to know what it was all about and told the boy to search her. Qintong pulled the girl down; there was a tinkle, and something fell to the ground. Daian picked it up. It was the gold bracelet. Ximen Qing looked at it in the light of the lantern and recognized it as the missing piece of gold.

"You slave!" he cried. "You stole it!"

"I picked it up," said the girl.

"Where did you pick it up?"

The girl made no reply. Ximen Qing was very angry. He sent Qintong for the thumbscrews. They were put on the girl's hands and turned till she screamed like a pig being killed. Again the screws were turned, and twenty times they ground her fingers. Yueniang did not dare to try to stop her husband, for she knew that he was drunk. When the girl could bear no more, she cried. "I picked it up in the Sixth Lady's room."

Ximen Qing had the thumbscrews removed, and told Li Jiao'er to take the girl away. "Tomorrow," he said, "I will send for the go-between and sell the slave. I won't have her here any more."

Li Jiao'er dared raise no objection. She said to the girl: "You thief! Who told you to go to the outer court? I know nothing of this. If you picked up the gold, why didn't you tell me at once?" Xiahua sobbed. "You may well cry," Li Jiao'er said. "You ought to be beaten to death."

"Stop!" Ximen Qing said. He gave the piece of gold to Yueniang and went to the apartments of Li Ping'er.

Yueniang told Xiaoyu to fasten the second door. "When did that maid go to the outer court?" she asked Yuxiao.

"When the Second Lady and the Third Lady went to the Sixth Lady's room," the maid answered, "Aunt Wu and our young lady went with them. That is when she went. Who would have dreamed of her stealing that piece of gold? She heard you say that Father had sent a boy to buy a piece of wolf sinew and she was frightened. In the kitchen she asked me what wolf sinew was. Everybody laughed, and we told her that wolf sinew was a part of the wolf's body. We said that when a person steals anything and won't give it up, a piece of wolf sinew is used to bind the thief's hands and feet. When she heard this, she must have become alarmed. So, when the two singers went away, she went out too. Seeing people at the gate, she must have hidden herself in the stable where the boys found her."

"It is very, very hard ever to know what people are really like," Yueniang said. "A young maid like that with such a thievish head and a rat's brain! It is disgraceful."

Li Jiao'er took Xiahua to her room. Guijie reproved her. "What a fool you must be," she said. "You are sixteen years old and you ought to know what you're about. How could you have been such an idiot? When you picked that thing up, you should have brought it here and given it to your mistress. Then, if it had been found out, she could have done something for you. Why didn't you tell her about it? Do you enjoy having thumbscrews put on you? You are an absolute fool. You know the proverb: 'A black-clothed man will stand beside a black pillar.' If it were not that you belong to these apartments, we shouldn't bother about you. But you do belong here, and now that you have been punished it brings shame upon us all."

Then she reproached her aunt. "You are no good either," she said. "If I'd been in your place, I shouldn't have allowed my maid to be punished. I should have dragged her to my room and punished her myself. Why are thumbscrews never put on other people's maids? Why is your maid picked out? You are too soft, and your nostrils have no breath in them. If they send your maid away, I suppose you will still say nothing. But if you won't say anything, I will. I am not going to have this girl turned out and everybody laughing at you. Meng Yulou and Pan Jinlian are like a couple of wolves. You can never hold your own against them."

She turned to the maid. "Do you wish to be sent away?" she said.

"No," said the maid.

"Well, in the future, you must consider nobody but your mistress. You must do everything she wants you to do. Then we will do our best for you."

"I will do everything you say," Xiahua said. When Ximen Qing came to Li Ping'er's room, he found her sitting on the bed with Wu Yin'er. He was going to take his clothes off and go to bed, but Li Ping'er said: "Wu Yin'er is here, and there is no room for you. Please go somewhere else."

"Why is there no room for me?" said Ximen. "One of you can sleep on one side, and one on the other, and I'll sleep in the middle. That will be all right."

Li Ping'er looked at him. "What bright ideas you do have," she said.

"Where shall I go, then?" said Ximen.

"Go and spend the night with the Fifth Lady," Li Ping'er said. Ximen Qing did not move for some time, then he said: "Very well, I don't want to trouble you. I'll go." He went to Pan Jinlian's room.

He might have been an angel from Heaven. Jinlian took his clothes and girdle. Then she arranged the bed and put silken bedclothes on it. She made tea and afterwards they went to bed.

When Ximen Qing had left, Li Ping'e and Wu Yin'er set out chessmen to play Elephant Chess. Li Ping'er told Yingchun to bring a box of fruits and heat a jar of Jinhua wine so that she might drink it with Wu Yin'er. "If you would like some food," she said to the girl, "I will have some prepared for you."

"I am not hungry, Mother," Wu Yin'er said. "Please don't trouble my sister."

"Your sister Wu Yin'er is not hungry," Li Ping'er said to Yingchun. "Bring her some fruit cakes on a tray." After a while the tray was brought and set beside them.

Li Ping'er and Wu Yin'er played one or two games. Then the wine was heated, and they drank together in silver cups.

"Give me my lute," Wu Yin'er said. "I will sing Mother a song."

"Perhaps you had better not sing," Li Ping'er said. "The baby is asleep and, besides, Father might hear and he won't like it. Let us play dice instead." She told Yingchun to bring the dice, and they threw the dice with wine for the wager. When they had played for some time, Wu Yin'er said to Yingchun: "Go to the other room and ask the nurse to come and have some wine with us."

But Yingchun said: "She is in bed with the baby. He has gone to sleep."

"Yes, she must look after the baby," said Li Ping'er. "Take a jar of wine to her. You don't realize how knowing the baby is. If he is left, he wakes up at once. One day, we three were asleep on the bed. His father moved slightly and the baby opened his eyes at once. He might have known. The nurse came and took him away, but he cried and would insist on having me to nurse him."

Wu Yin'er smiled. "Since you have had the baby, it must be awkward for you and Father. How often does he come to you?"

"He doesn't come very often," said Li Ping'er. "Sometimes several days pass and he only comes once or twice. But he often comes to see the baby. And sometimes my belly nearly bursts with anger, for now both he and the child get nothing but secret curses from some members of the household, not to speak of the curses I get. This has made me suffer a great deal, but I can't help it. I sometimes wish he didn't come at all, because, after he has spent the night here, the next day there is much raising of eyebrows and ugly looks, as much as to say that I monopolize him. That's why I urged him to go away just now.

"You don't know how it is, my dear. There are many people in this house and that means many tongues. Look at that business of the gold today. Someone who is jealous asked the Great Lady how it could be lost in my room. Luckily it turned out that Xiahua had taken it, so there was no mistaking green for red or black for white. Otherwise they would have said that one of my maids or my nurse or old woman Feng had taken it, as if they had caught a ghost. As it was, they made old woman Feng cry and talk about killing herself. She said she would not go away if the gold wasn't found. Now that it has been found, she has just taken a lantern and gone."

"Mother," said Wu Yin'er, "you must look well after the baby for Father's sake, and let people do what they like. The Great Lady never talks in this way. It is only the others who are jealous because you have a child. I only hope that Father will do what he thinks fit."

"If it hadn't been for your father and the Great Lady," Li Ping'er said, "the child would never have lived until today."

They talked and drank until the third night watch. Then they went to sleep.

CHAPTER 45

Beggar Ying and Wu Yin'er

The next day Ximen Qing did not go to his office. When he got up in the morning, he went to the front court and told Daian to take two presents of food to the Qiaos' house, one for Lady Qiao the Fifth and one for Mistress Qiao. Lady Qiao the Fifth gave the bearers two handkerchiefs and three *qian* of silver. Mistress Qiao gave them a roll of black cloth.

When Ying Bojue left Ximen, he hastened to Huang the Fourth's house. Huang had prepared and sealed ten taels of silver for him.

"His Lordship," he said, "told me to go and see him again after the festival. I think it will be all right about the five hundred tael contract, but what about the land tax?"

"How much will you need?" Bojue asked him.

"Brother Li," said Huang the Fourth, "does not understand. He talks about borrowing from some eunuch or other. But it seems to me that anywhere we shall have to pay five percent interest. We might as well do all our borrowing here and so save a good deal of commission. I want fifty silver ingots. In other words, I must borrow a thousand taels. I am prepared to pay interest monthly."

Ying Bojue nodded. "Don't worry," he said, "I will see about that. But there are six of you. How much do you propose to give me?"

"I will tell Brother Li that each of us must give you five taels."

"I think I can save that five taels for you by my cleverness," Bojue said. "One word from me will do all you require. My wife has gone to his Lordship's place today, so I shall not go now. But he has invited me to go tomorrow evening and see the lanterns with him. You two get up early, have some excellent dishes prepared and buy a jar of Jinhua wine. Don't engage any singing girls, because Li Guijie and Wu Yin'er will be there, but arrange for six musicians from the bawdy house. I will take everything for you. He is sure to invite you to his party. When we are all together, I shall only need to speak a sentence, or even half a sentence, and, I promise you, that will do the trick. You will get five hundred taels and make out your contract for a thousand. You pay thirty taels a month interest. It won't cost you any more than keeping a woman. The proverb says: Forgery is not one of the recognized fine arts, yet there is no genuine lacquer to be found anywhere. When you pay your tax, put plenty of wood in the incense and mix enough pine oil with the wax. Nobody is going to find out. We have no ambition to catch any fish; all we hope to do is to stir up the water a bit. A man who wants to borrow money has only to establish a reputation, and then everything is plain sailing."

They agreed upon this plan. The next day Li and Huang bought the presents and Ying Bojue got two boys to carry them to Ximen's house. When they arrived, Ximen was having the tables made ready in the outer court. Bojue made a reverence. "Yesterday," he said, "my wife must have greatly inconvenienced you. She came home quite late."

"I went to a party at Zhou Nanxuan's place," Ximen said. "It was the first night watch when I came back, so I didn't see any of my new relatives. They had left early. Today I am taking a holiday. That is why you don't find me at the office." They sat down. Bojue summoned the boys and told them to bring in the presents. The boxes were carried in and set down inside the second door.

"Brother Li and Brother Huang," said Bojue, "have repeatedly told me how grateful they are to you. They have nothing worthy to offer you, but they have bought these trifling things, and send them for you to dispose of among your servants." The two boys came forward and kowtowed.

"I have done nothing to deserve these gifts," said Ximen Qing, "and I can't possibly accept them. They must go back." "Brother," Bojue said, "if you will not accept the things, if you make the boys take them back again, my friends will die of shame. They were going to engage singing girls, but I told them not to. They have sent some musicians who are waiting outside for your orders at this moment."

"Well," said Ximen, "since they have sent the things, I can't very well send them back. I suppose we had better ask them to come and join us."

Ying Bojue immediately told Li's boy to go back to his master. "Tell him that his present has been accepted," Bojue said. "We are not sending anyone especially to invite him, but ask him and Uncle Huang to come here at once."

The boy brought in the presents. Ximen Qing told Daian to give him two *qian* of silver. Then he kowtowed and went upon his errand. The six musicians still waited for orders. Qitong brought tea, and Ximen and Ying Bojue drank it together. Then Ximen asked Bojue to go to the rooms in the eastern wing. "Have you seen Xie Xida today?" he asked.

"No," said Bojue, "I got up early this morning and went to Li's place to see about the presents, and I have been too busy to see him." Ximen Qing told Qitong to go at once and invite Xie Xida to join them.

Shutong set the table, and dinner was served. They ate it together, and afterwards everything was cleared away. They played double sixes for wine. Ying Bojue decided to speak before Xie Xida came. "How much can you give Li and Huang?" he said.

"I shall take back the old contract and give them another for five hundred taels."

"You can do that, of course," Ying Bojue said, "but it would be better to make the amount a thousand taels. It is easier to calculate the interest. Then, too, you have no use for that gold they brought you. Let them have it back, and count it as a hundred and fifty taels. If you do that, only a little more will be needed to make up the thousand."

"That is a good idea," Ximen said. "I will let them have another three hundred and fifty taels and make out the contract for a thousand. It is better than keeping gold where I have no use for it."

They were playing double sixes when Daian came in. He said: "Ben the Fourth is bringing a large marble screen with a shell base, two sets of bronze gongs, and some little bells. Their Highnesses, the Bai family, propose to pawn them with us for thirty taels, and Ben the Fourth wishes to know whether you are satisfied."

Ximen gave orders that the things should be brought in. Ben the Fourth and two other men carried them and set them down in the great hall. Ximen Qing and Ying Bojue stopped their game and went to see them. The screen was three feet wide and five feet high, made of a single piece of marble the size of a table. The frame had a pattern of conchs and was gilded, and the black and white markings in the marble were exquisitely delicate.

Bojue looked at it. After a while he said quietly to Ximen Qing: "Brother, if you look at it closely, you will see that the markings are exactly in the shape of a couching lion keeping guard over the house." They examined the bronze gongs and drums, decorated in gold and colors, and engraved with a cloud design. They were very handsome.

"I should have them if I were you, Brother," said Bojue. "You could not buy a screen like this for fifty taels, without taking the other things into account."

"But they may be redeemed," Ximen Qing said.

"Don't trouble about that," said Bojue. "It is like rattling down a steep hill in a carriage. If, after three years, they redeem them, the interest will amount to a tidy sum."

"Very well," Ximen said. "Tell Jingji to get the money ready for them."

Ximen Qing had the screen cleaned and put at the upper end of the great hall. He looked at it from all angles, and, indeed, the gold and green made a very harmonious and brilliant effect. He asked if the musicians had yet had their meal. One of the servants told him they were still eating. "When they are done, tell them to come and play for us," he said.

The big drum was taken out of the hall and a bronze gong and drums were set down under the eaves. When they were sounded, the noise went up to the skies, and the reverberations startled the birds of the air and the fishes under the water. Meanwhile, Xie Xida was announced. He came in and greeted his two friends.

"Come here, Brother Xie," Ximen Qing said, "and tell me how much you think this screen is worth." Xie Xida examined it carefully. He had nothing but good to say of it.

"Brother," he said, "you have a bargain here. It must be worth at least a hundred taels."

"Well, this," said Ying Bojue, "the two sets of drums and gongs and the bells have all been pawned together for thirty taels." Xie Xida clapped his hands.

"Buddha!" he cried. "What a bargain! Thirty taels! Why, it wouldn't buy the two sets of bronzes, not to mention the screen. Look at those two sets. How elaborately they are made. The red lacquer is all of the finest quality and there must be at least forty *jin* of musical bronze in them, and that is worth a lot of money. Really, everything comes in time to its proper owner. How lucky you are, Brother, to get these beautiful things so cheaply."

Ximen Qing asked them to go to the study. By this time Li and Huang had arrived. "Why did you trouble to give me those presents?" Ximen Qing said. "It really embarrassed me to accept them."

"We were ashamed to offer anything so trifling," said Li and Huang. "They were only intended for you to give your servants. We received your order to attend here and did not dare to disobey."

They sat down opposite. Huatong brought five cups of tea, and they drank together. Then Daian came and asked Ximen Qing where he wished to have the table placed. "Here," Ximen said. Daian and Qitong brought a square table and placed a small brazier beneath it. Ying Bojue and Xie Xida took the seats of honor. Ximen Qing took the host's seat, and Li and Huang sat opposite. There was an abundance of wine, and of food appropriate to the season, and every kind of delicacy. The musicians played outside the window. Ximen sent for Wu Yin'er to serve the wine.

Later that day there came a man from Li Guijie's house and the maid from Wu Yin'er's house, with sedan chairs to take the girls home. When Guijie heard that the man had come, she hurriedly went out and talked to him in a whisper for a long time. Then she went back to Wu Yueniang's room and said she must go home. Yueniang objected. "We are all going to Aunt Wu's house," she said, "and I want you to come with us. You will be too late to go home today. We shall come back without our chairs, for we are going to take the walk to banish the hundred illnesses."

"Mother," Guijie said, "let me explain. There really ought to be someone at our house. My sister is away. My fifth aunt has come, and there will be several other guests. They expect me. If they were not anxious to have me back, they would not have sent the man for me. If I were not engaged, I should be only too glad to stay for several days."

When Yueniang saw that Guijie was determined to go, she told Yuxiao to fill a box with the pasties specially made for the festival and another with sweet things. These were given to the man to carry. Then she gave Guijie a tael of silver and let her go.

Guijie said good-bye to Yueniang and the others, then went to see her aunt. Li Jiao'er went with her to the outer court and told Huatong to carry her things. When they came to the study door, the girl told Daian to ask Ximen Qing to come out. Daian slowly lifted the shutter and went in. "Guijie is going home and would like to speak to you," he said to Ximen.

"Guijie, you little whore!" Ying Bojue cried. "Are you still here?"

"She is just going," Ximen Qing said. Then he went out. Guijie kowtowed four times to him and thanked him for allowing her to come. "Can't you stay until tomorrow?" Ximen asked.

"My mother has sent a man with a sedan chair for me. She really needs me. But there is one thing I want to say to you before I go. It is about my aunt's maid. You really mustn't get rid of her. Last night my aunt gave her a very severe beating. She is so young, she really does not understand what she is doing. I gave her a good talking-to and told her she must change her ways, and she promised she would never do such a thing again. It will upset my aunt terribly if you send her away during this festival. She would have no maid, and, if the only poker you have is a wooden spoon, and a short one at that, it is still better than using the fingers. For my sake, Father, don't turn the girl away."

"If you wish it so much, I will allow her to stay," Ximen Qing said. He bade Daian tell Yueniang not to send for the go-between. Daian saw Huatong carrying Guijie's things.

"Give them to me," he said to the boy, "and you go to the inner court with the message." Huatong did as he was told. When Guijie had finished speaking to Ximen Qing, she went to the window.

"Beggar Ying," she called, "I have made no reverence to you, and now I, your mother, am going home."

"Drag the little creature back," cried Bojue. "Don't let her go until she has sung a song for me."

"You must wait," Guijie said. "When your mother has nothing to do, she will sing a song for you."

"What do you mean by going home in the middle of the day?" Ying Bojue said. "You must be expecting good fortune in the shape of a lover or two this evening."

"You dirty beggar," Guijie cried. She laughed and went away.

Daian went out with her and helped her into her sedan chair.

After Ximen Qing had spoken to Guijie, he went to the inner court to change his clothes. "That little whore Guijie is just like a thief who has escaped from jail," Ying Bojue said to Xie Xida. "She is more cunning than ever. On an occasion like this, you would expect her to stay, instead of which off she goes. I wonder who is waiting for her."

"I will tell you," Xie Xida said. He whispered something to Bojue.

"Don't speak too loud," said Bojue when he had heard a sentence or two. "Our brother knows nothing of this." They heard Ximen's footsteps and the conversation ended.

Ying Bojue embraced Wu Yin'er and drank wine with her mouth to mouth. "This is the daughter for me," he said. "Soft and gentle, a hundred times nicer than that little strumpet Guijie, whom even a dog will have nothing to do with."

Wu Yin'er laughed. "When it comes to bad language, Uncle," she said, "you are a master. When you say one you mean one, and when you say a hundred you mean a hundred. There are wise and foolish people everywhere, and we do well not to make comparisons. My sister Guijie has annoyed you."

"Don't talk to him, the dog," Ximen Qing said. "He is always grumbling about something."

"Don't pay any attention to him," Bojue said. "Don't you interfere with her. She is my little daughter. Come here, daughter, take your lute and sing me a song."

Wu Yin'er slowly stretched her jade fingers, gently touched the strings, and softly sang the song "The Willows Are Like Golden Tassels." She served wine to Ying Bojue, then to Xie Xida, and sang another song.

Meanwhile Huatong had gone to the inner court. All the ladies and the nuns were there, except Pan Jinlian. When the boy came, Yueniang was just about to tell old woman Feng to sell Xiahua. "Father bade me tell you not to send the girl away," Huatong said.

"But he told me to sell her," Yueniang said. "What has made him change his mind? Tell me. Who has been talking to him to make him change his mind like that?"

"I was helping Guijie to carry her things," the boy said. "It was she who told my father to keep the maid. Father told Daian to come and tell you, but instead of coming himself he made me come, and he went to the gate with her."

Yueniang was annoyed. "Daian is one of those slaves who try to be in with both sides," she said. "When I was angry and wouldn't send for the go-between, he told me his father insisted upon it. Now he is up to some trick or other. He has gone off with the girl. When he comes back, I will have a reckoning with him."

As she spoke, Wu Yin'er, who had finished singing, came in. "Your maid has come for you," Yueniang said to her. "Guijie has gone. Are you going too?"

"Mother," Wu Yin'er said, "I will stay if you like. Otherwise, you might think I did not appreciate the claims of courtesy." She asked her maid who had sent for her.

"Your mother sent me," the maid told her.

"Is there anything at home that calls for my presence?" said Wu Yin'er.

"No," replied the girl.

"Then, if not, why did you come for me? Go back. The lady here wishes me to stay. I am going to take the walk of the hundred illnesses with her and I will come home after that."

The maid was going away when Yueniang asked Wu Yin'er to call her back, that she might have something to eat. "The Great Lady is going to give you some food," Wu Yin'er said, "so wait. I want you to take my clothes with you. When you get home, tell my mother not to send a sedan chair for me. I shall come back on foot. Where is Wu Hui?"

"He has had some trouble with his eyes," the girl told her.

Yueniang told Yuxiao to take the girl to the back court. There they gave her two bowls of meat, a plate of bread and a jar of wine. Then they filled her boxes with pasties and tea cakes.

Wu Yin'er's clothes were in the rooms of Li Ping'er. Li Ping'er had taken a dress of fine silk woven with gold, two gold-fringed kerchiefs and a tael of silver, and these were all wrapped up together and given to Wu Yin'er. She was delighted. "Mother," she said, "don't give me these clothes." She smiled. "Really, I only want a white gown, so keep these silken dresses and give me an old white gown. I don't mind how old it is."

"My white gown is very big. It won't fit you," said Li Ping'er. She said to Yingchun: "Take the key, go to my large chest, and take from it a roll of white silk for your sister Wu Yin'er." To Wu Yin'er she said: "You must ask your mother to get the tailors to make two good gowns for you. Would you rather have figured or plain silk?"

"I should prefer plain, Mother," said Wu Yin'er. "Then it will match my wrapper." She smiled and said to Yingchun: "Sister, I have troubled you to go upstairs again for me. I have nothing with which to reward you, but I will sing you a song."

After a while Yingchun came down with a roll of plain white silk made on the broad looms of Songjiang. There was a label upon it that said: "Thirty-eight taels' weight." She gave it to Wu Yin'er, who kowtowed four times to Li Ping'er. Then she stood up again and made reverence several times to Yingchun.

"Wu Yin'er," said Li Ping'er, "take the other silken clothes too. Sooner or later you will need them when you are serving wine."

"You have already given me the white silk to make a dress. How can I accept these?" She again kowtowed to Li Ping'er.

After a while her servant had finished her meal, and Wu Yin'er gave her the clothes to carry home. "Why are you so pleased?" Yueniang asked her. "Don't imitate Guijie, who is full of self-conceit. Both yesterday and this morning, that girl has been like a raging tiger. She insisted on going home, and nothing we could do would stop her. She was so anxious to get away she didn't even sing properly, and, when her people came for her, she wouldn't wait to eat anything. Sister Wu Yin'er, you must not follow her example."

"Good Lady," Wu Yin'er said, "your palace is no ordinary house. We must remember the difference and, though we may give ourselves airs elsewhere, we should not do so here. Guijie is very young. She doesn't understand the ways of the world. Please, Lady, do not be angry with her."

While they were talking, a boy came with a message from Aunt Wu. "My mother hopes," he said, "that all you ladies, and Guijie and Wu Yin'er, will come early. She would like Lady Sun Xue'e to come too."

"Go home and tell your mistress," Yueniang said, "that we are now dressing. The Second Lady has a painful leg and she will not be able to come. My husband is entertaining some friends in the outer court today, so the Lady in charge of the kitchen will not be able to come either. Guijie has gone away, so, with my stepdaughter and Wu Yin'er, there will be six of us. Tell your mother she must not make any special preparations: we shall be quite content just to spend the evening with her." She asked the boy who was going to sing for them. The boy, Laiding, told them that it was Miss Yu. Then he went away.

Wu Yueniang, Meng Yulou, Pan Jinlian, Li Ping'er, her stepdaughter, and Wu Yin'er then set off. Before she went, she said to Ximen Qing: "I have told the nurse to look after the baby." They went to their sedan chairs, with the three boys, Daian, Qitong and Laian, and four soldiers. So they came to Aunt Wu's house.

CHAPTER 46

Daian in Trouble

Gongs and drums beat everywhere
In every house there is the sound of pipes and strings.
People go singing through the streets in bands
Young men and women play sweet melodies of the dance.
A mount of paper with gay colored streamers
Towers into the blue sky.
Incense from the royal palace rings its way heavenward over the
   assembled people
The precious moon sheds its soft brilliance within the courtyard
   and without.
Everywhere the scene is lovely.
This is the most glorious festival of the year
When we celebrate the first full moon.

Ximen Qing sent off Wu Yueniang and the others to the party at Aunt Wu's house. About sunset, Li Zhi and Huang the Fourth stood up to take their leave. Ying Bojue went out with them. "I have managed that business for you," he said, "and tomorrow you will get your five hundred taels." Li Zhi and Huang the Fourth bowed to him repeatedly and went away. Ying Bojue went back and drank wine with Xie Xida and Ximen Qing. Then Li Ming came in. "Here is young Li," Bojue said. Li Ming knelt down and kowtowed to them.

"Why has Wu Hui not come?" Ximen Qing asked him.

"He has not been able to go even to Dongpingfu," Li Ming said. "There is something wrong with his eyes. But I have brought Wang Zhu."

Wang Zhu was called in and, after he had kowtowed to Ximen and the others, he and Li Ming stood beside them.

"Your sister Li Guijie has just gone home," Ximen said to the boy. "Did you know?"

"I have only just returned from Dongpingfu," Li Ming said. "I came here as soon as I had washed my face, so I have heard nothing about her."

"I fear that these two boys have had nothing to eat," said Bojue. "Will you give orders for them to have some food?"

"Uncle," Shutong said, "a meal is being made ready for the musicians, and if these two wait a while they can eat with them."

Bojue told Shutong to bring a tray. He picked out some of the dishes and handed the food to Li Ming, telling him to take it away and eat it with his companion. Then he said to Shutong: "You foolish boy. People, like things, all belong to some definite class or other. You do not understand that, though they may come from the bawdy house, they are not on the same footing as the musicians. We cannot treat them in the same way, or it would look as though we were lacking in a sense of the fitness of things."

Ximen Qing tapped Bojue on the head. "You dog," he said, "you always look after actors because they belong to the same class as yourself and you know what they have to put up with."

"Stupid dog yourself!" Bojue said. "What do you know about it? Have you lived so long as a gay young man and still don't know the jingle: 'Be tender with the jade and loving to the flowers'? The more you love them, the more you get out of them, but treat them harshly and they wither away and die."

"Oh yes, my son," Ximen said, laughing, "no doubt you know all about that."

When Li Ming and Wang Zhu had finished their meal, Ying Bojue called them and asked them to sing a song he named to them. Wang Zhu took his lute and Li Ming his zither: they cleared their throats and sang. When they had finished, it was nearly evening.

Ximen Qing ordered the things to be cleared away and sent for Clerk Fu, Han Daoguo, Ben the Fourth and Chen Jingji. A great screen was set at the gate; two tables were placed there, and two sheep's horn lanterns hung. Food was piled abundantly upon the tables. Ximen Qing and Ying Bojue sat in the place of honor, and the clerks and managers on either side. On each side of the door hung twelve golden lotus lanterns. There was a small set piece of firework. This, Ximen said, was to be lighted when the ladies returned. The six musicians carried the bronze gongs and drums to the great gate. There they beat them for a short time, and then played their instruments. Delicate sweet strains came from them. Li Ming and Wang Zhu, the two young actors, played and sang the songs of the lanterns. And, of the people who passed along the street, none dared to raise his head to look. Ximen Qing was wearing a *zhongjing* hat, a velvet cloak and a white silk gown.

Daian and Ping'an set off the fireworks in turn, while two soldiers with rods kept back the crowd and would not allow them to push forward. In the cloudless sky the full moon appeared. There was great excitement in the street.

❀   ❀   ❀

The four maids, Chunmei, Yingchun, Yuxiao and Lanxiang, knowing that Yueniang was not at home and hearing the drums and music at the gate, and the fireworks, dressed themselves and looked out from behind the screen. Shutong and Huatong were heating wine at a brazier on the other side. Yuxiao and Shutong were old friends, and were always playing together. Now they had a struggle to see who could steal the other's melon seeds. Without caring what they were doing, they upset the wine jar on the fire. The fire sent forth a great flame, filling the whole place with smoke. Yuxiao laughed and Ximen Qing heard her. He told Daian to go and see who was laughing and what had caused the smoke.

Chunmei was wearing a new white cloak with a scarlet wrapper. When the wine jar was upset, she was sitting in a chair watching Yuxiao and Shutong playing together. Now she cursed her fellow maid. "Whenever you set eyes on a man, you lose your senses," she cried. "It was bad enough for you to upset the wine, without laughing. I don't know what there is to laugh about. You've put the fire out, and the ashes are coming down all over my head."

Yuxiao said nothing. She went to the back court. Shutong was rather anxious. He went to Ximen Qing and said: "I was warming the wine over the fire and the jar fell in." Ximen Qing asked no more questions, and that was the end of the matter.

Before the festival, Ben the Fourth's wife had learned that Yueniang would be away. She knew that the four maids, Chunmei, Yuxiao, Yingchun and Lanxiang, were all favorites of Ximen Qing, so she prepared some dainty dishes and told her daughter to go and ask the four maids to come and see her. The little girl was taken to Li Jiao'er. "I have no say in the matter," Li Jiao'er said. "I can do nothing; you must go and see what your master thinks about it." Then they went to Sun Xue'e, but she did not dare to take the responsibility. When the lanterns had been shown, Ben the Fourth's wife sent again to invite the four maids. Then Lanxiang urged Yuxiao, and Yuxiao urged Yingchun, and Yingchun urged Chunmei to go and plead with Li Jiao'er to ask Ximen Qing's permission. Chunmei refused to move. She was still angry with Yuxiao.

"You are like some poor beast who has never seen any food. You have never been to a feast and now you are anxious to have a sniff at one. It doesn't matter to me whether we go or not. I'm not going to ask anybody to help us. You are all fussing about like a lot of ghosts, and I'm sure I don't know what all the fuss is about. I have nothing but contempt for the lot of you."

Yingchun, Yuxiao and Lanxiang had all dressed in their best clothes, but they dared make no move. Chunmei sat still. Then Shutong came and said: "Ben the Fourth's wife has sent her little girl for you again. I don't mind if Father scolds me: I'll go and speak to him." He went to Ximen Qing and whispered, "Ben the Fourth's wife has sent an invitation to my four sisters, and they have sent me to ask if they may go."

"Tell them they may go," Ximen said. "But they must come back in good time, for there are not enough people to attend to the household."

Shutong hurried back. "I have managed that little business very well," he said. "One word from me, and you get permission. Father says you may dress up and go. But you must come back early."

Chunmei, at this, went slowly to her room to dress. Then, all together, the four girls came out. Shutong pulled the screen partly back for them so that they could pass. They came to Ben the Fourth's house and, to Mistress Ben, they might have been angels from Heaven. She took them to her room. Several snowball lanterns had been hung there and a table was spread with excellent food. Mistress Ben, when she spoke to them, addressed them as First Aunt, Second Aunt, and so on. They made reverences to one another. Han Huizi's wife had also been invited.

Chunmei and Yuxiao sat in the places of honor; Yingchun and Lanxiang sat opposite them. Mistress Ben and Mistress Han sat on either side. The little girl, Changjie, went backwards and forwards to heat the wine and serve the dishes.

Ximen Qing told the musicians to play the tune "The East Wind Is So Gentle That We Know Fair Weather Is Here."

Little cakes, made with roses, were brought and everybody ate some. They were sweet, fragrant and delicious, and melted as soon as they were put into the mouth.

Li Ming and Wu Hui took their instruments and sang the song. Their voices were melodious and their rhythm excellent.

Daian and Chen Jingji put some fireworks in their sleeves and called for two soldiers with lanterns to go with them to Aunt Wu's house. They were to escort Yueniang and the others on their way home. The ladies were drinking wine in the hall when Jingji arrived and, as the elder Wu was not at home, Jingji was invited to take wine with the younger brother. A table was set and the two men took cakes and wine together.

Daian went forward and said to Yueniang: "Father has sent me to escort you home. He wishes you to go home early. He thinks the streets will be crowded tonight."

Yueniang was still displeased with Daian, and would not speak to him. Aunt Wu told her servant Laiding to give the boy some food. "Wine, meat, soup and rice are all ready in the front court," Laiding said.

"Don't hurry," said Yueniang. "Why should you give him food as soon as he arrives? Let him wait in the front court until we are ready to go."

"Are you really so busy these days?" Aunt Wu said to Yueniang. "This is a great festival and it is well that we should sit together and enjoy ourselves. The Second Lady and the other lady are at home and there is nothing for you to be anxious about. Why should you think of going away so early? If we did not belong to the family, it would be another matter." Then she said to Miss Yu: "Sing a good song for the ladies." Yulou spoke. "The Sixth Lady is not at all pleased with her: she did not come to the birthday party." Miss Yu stood up and kowtowed four times to Li Ping'er.

"I have been ill," she said. "When this good lady invited me yesterday to come here, I was only just able to come. If I had not been ill I should certainly have come to kowtow to you."

"Miss Yu," Jinlian said, "since the Sixth Lady is displeased with you, you must sing a particularly good song. Then she may forgive you."

Li Ping'er laughed but said nothing. "Certainly," Miss Yu said. "Give me my lute and I will sing." Aunt Wu bade Miss Zheng pour out wine for the ladies. "They have had any for a long time," she said.

Miss Yu took her lute and sang "There Is a Storm upon the River." While she was singing, Yueniang said: "Why do I feel so cold now?"

"It is snowing," Laian said.

"Sister," Yulou said, "you should not be wearing such thin clothes. I have brought my heavy cloak."

"It is snowing," Yueniang said, "and we had better send the boys home for our fur coats."

Laian hurried out. He said to Daian: "The mistress says you are to go home and bring furs for the ladies."

Daian said to Qintong: "You go and get them. I'll stay here." Qintong did what he was told, without a word. After a while, Yueniang remembered that Jinlian did not possess a fur coat. She said to Laian: "Who has gone to get the coats?" Laian told her that Qintong had gone. "Why did he go without coming to me first?" Yueniang said.

Yulou said: "He has slipped off without a word. The Fifth Lady has no furs. We ought to have told the boy to bring the Great Lady's and not to bother about ours."

"Oh, we have a fur that someone has pawned," Yueniang said. "We will use that, and send for furs for everybody." Then she added: "Why did Daian send Qintong instead of going himself? Send him here."

When Daian came in, Yueniang scolded him severely. "You slave," she said, "what do you mean by ordering other people to do your work for you? You sent that slave away without asking my permission. You behave just like a cabinet minister. You are afraid you might disturb the set of your hat and so you tell someone else to go."

"You have no reason to be angry with me, Mother," Daian said. "If you had sent word for me to go, of course I should not have dared to disobey. Laian simply said that one of us must go."

"How brave Laian must have been to give you orders," said Yueniang. "Why, even I, who am the First Wife, do not venture to tell you to do anything. The truth is, we are too kind to you slaves, and you give yourselves airs in consequence. Your master has a picture of Buddha that was blackened by smoke and hung upon the wall. There are monks like that and there are benefactors like that. Your game is to curry favor with both sides at once, and you are so clever at it that your tongue might have been brought to a sharp point. You keep on the right side of those in the house and ally yourself with those without. You are idle, yet you must have your food. You are up to all kinds of dirty games on the sly, but don't think you deceive me. The other day, your master never told you to take Guijie home. What right had you to do so? One of the other boys was carrying her things and you snatched them out of his hands. It was none of your business whether we kept our maid or did not keep our maid. Why should you mix yourself up in that business? It was simply because someone suggested that you should. You thought you would get something out of it. You told someone else to come to me, because you thought that, if I had anything nasty to say, the one you sent would get it and not you. Now, can you say you don't play games like this?"

"That is Huatong's story," Daian said. "Father saw Huatong carrying her things, and he told me to see her home and Huatong to come back. You say, Mother, that whether you kept the maid or not was no business of mine. That is true. Why then should I bother about it?"

Yueniang was very angry and cursed him. "You thievish slave! Are you trying to argue with me? I have too much to do to say any more to you. You go too far. I tell you to do something: you don't do it; then you try to put me off with some cock-and-bull story. Wait! You shall see if I don't tell your father to treat you like a moldy sheep's head."

"Daian," Aunt Wu said, "go at once and bring your mother's fur cloak." Then she said to Yueniang: "Sister, tell him which one you wish him to bring for the Fifth Lady."

"Don't send him," Jinlian said. "I don't want any fur coat, and, if he does go home, let him bring my cloak. The fur coat is one that someone or other has pawned and I know nothing about it. If it is yellow dog's skin, people will laugh at me for wearing it. Besides, I can't keep it long; it will be redeemed."

"The fur coat I am thinking of is not one that has been pawned,"

Yueniang said. "It was brought in payment of debt by Li Zhi, who owed us sixteen taels of silver. It is the one Li Jiao'er wears that was pawned by General Wang's people." To Daian she said: "The fur coat is in the large chest. Ask Yuxiao to get it for you and bring my stepdaughter's coat too."

Daian went out with a very angry face. Chen Jingji asked him where he was going. "Such nasty temper!" said Daian. "Now all the work has to be done over again. Late though it is, I must run home." He went out. When he reached the house, Ximen Qing was still drinking at the gate. Fu and Yun had gone, but Ying Bojue, Xie Xida, Han Daoguo and Ben the Fourth were still there.

"Have the ladies come?" Ximen Qing asked.

"No," said Daian, "they have sent me for their fur coats." He went to the inner court.

Qintong arrived before Daian and went to the upper room for the furs. Xiaoyu was sitting sulkily upon the bed. "Those four strumpets," she told the boy, "have gone to Ben the Fourth's wife's to drink wine. I don't know where the fur coats are. You had better go there and ask them."

So Qintong went to Ben the Fourth's house. He did not knock at the door but stood quietly outside the window. Ben the Fourth's wife was saying: "My dear eldest aunt, and you, Second Aunt, is it because you despise the preparations I have made for you in this small mean hovel that you have had no wine for so long?"

"Fourth Sister," Chunmei said, "really we have had wine enough."

"Oh, how can you say that?" Mistress Ben said. "Why must you stand so much on ceremony here?" Then she said to Mistress Han: "You are my near neighbor and I look upon you as a second hostess. You must urge the Third and Fourth Aunts to drink. Don't sit there like a guest." She said to her little daughter: "Heat some wine and pour it out for your Third Aunt. But don't fill it quite full for your Fourth Aunt."

"I never drink wine," Lanxiang said.

"Ladies," said Mistress Ben, "you have gone hungry today because I have no good food to offer you. Please don't laugh at me on that account. I would have sent for some blind singers, but I was afraid the noise would disturb his Lordship. This is such a tiny place. Dear, dear! What a hard life poor people have!"

Qintong knocked at the door. The little girl went to see who was there. Qintong looked at her and smiled, but said nothing. "You funny creature," Yuxiao said, "what is it you want, standing there showing your teeth and grinning? Why don't you speak?"

"The ladies are drinking at Madam Wu's house," Qintong said. "When they saw it was snowing, they sent me for their furs. They all want them."

"They are in the gilded chest," Yuxiao said. "Ask Xiaoyu to give them to you."

"Xiaoyu told me to come here and ask you," Qintong said.

"Don't pay any attention to that little whore," said Yuxiao. "She knows well enough where they are."

"Your ladies have fur coats," Chunmei said, "and you must go and get them. My lady has none, so I can stay where I am."

"Go and ask Xiaoluan for the Third Lady's coat," Lanxiang said.

Yingchun gave Qintong a key. "Ask Xiuchun," she said, "to open the door of the inner room, and give you the Sixth Lady's fur coat."

Qintong went back to the inner court. Xiaoyu and Xiaoluan wrapped up the fur coats belonging to the Great Lady and Yulou and gave them to him. As he was coming away, he met Daian and asked what he had come for. "You may well ask," Daian said. "It was all your fault that I got a scolding from the Great Lady and was told to come and bring a coat for the Fifth Lady."

"I am going for the Sixth Lady's coat," Qintong said.

"Well," said Daian, "when you have got it, wait here for me and we will go together. If you go back before I do we shall have another taste of the Great Lady's temper." Daian went to the upper room. Xiaoyu was still sitting on the bed, warming her hands at the fire and biting melon seeds.

"Ah, Daian," she said, "so you have come too?"

"Yes," said the boy, "and I have a bellyful of anger. The Great Lady complains that I order other people about too much. She has sent me for the fur coat that Li Zhi brought in payment of a debt, because the Fifth Lady has none of her own. It is in the great chest."

"Yuxiao keeps the keys of the inner room," the girl said. "She and the others have gone to drink wine at Ben the Fourth's place. You will have to go to her."

"Qintong has gone to the Sixth Lady's room to get her furs," said Daian. "He will be back soon and he can go to Yuxiao. I am going to rest and get warm."

Xiaoyu invited Daian to sit on the bed. They sat close together and warmed their hands at the fire. "There is some wine in the jar," Xiaoyu said;."Would you like a drink?"

"You are very kind," said Daian. Xiaoyu got down from the bed, took the wine jar and set it on the fire. She opened the cupboard and took out a plate of preserved goose. There was nobody else about, and they kissed one another.

While Daian was drinking his wine, Qintong came back. Daian gave him a cup of wine and told him to go to Yuxiao to ask for a fur coat for the

Fifth Lady. Qintong left the other coats behind and went again to Ben the Fourth's place. Yuxiao cursed him. "You young jailbird!" she said. "What has brought you back here?" She refused to come with him, but gave him the keys. The boy returned and asked Xiaoyu to open the door. Xiaoyu did so and picked up the bundle of keys. For a long time she tried to open the chest, but without success. Again Qintong went to Ben the Fourth's place to Yuxiao. "These are not the keys," Yuxiao said. "The key of the chest is under the bed in the Great Lady's room."

When the boy returned this time, Xiaoyu began to curse. "The whore might be nailed there," she said. "Instead of coming herself, she lets me have all the trouble." She opened the chest, but the fur coat was not inside it. Qintong had to run backwards and forwards, and he too cursed. "If I am going to die," he said, "it will take me three days and three nights to do so. These young ladies are like the ghosts of some infectious disease. I'm almost exhausted." He said to Daian: "What a fine scolding we shall get from the Great Lady when we get back. She won't have a word to say against the maids. We shall have to take the blame for being late." He went back to Yuxiao. "There is no fur coat in the chest," he told her.

Yuxiao thought for a while. Then she laughed. "I forgot. It is in the chest in the other room."

Qintong went back again. "The whore is crazy," cried Xiaoyu. "Her naughty lover has been too much for her. First she tells us it is in one place and it is not. Then she tells us to look somewhere else." However, she found the coat and wrapped it up with Ximen Dajie's. She gave them both to Daian and Qintong, and the two boys took them to Aunt Wu's house.

Yueniang scolded them again. "You two thievish slaves have been putting your heads together. You didn't want to come."

Daian did not dare to say anything, but Qintong said: "We got all the other coats, but had to wait until the maid found this one." He produced it and Aunt Wu looked at it.

"This is a splendid coat," she said. "Why did you call it a yellow dog's skin, Fifth Sister? I should be very glad to have one like it."

"It is really new," Yueniang said. "A little worn, perhaps, at the front. We will replace that part by a golden stomacher and then it will be perfect."

Yulou said jokingly to Jinlian: "Come here, my child, and put this yellow dog's skin on you. Let mother see whether it suits you or not."

"I shall have to ask my husband for one," Jinlian said. "I don't care to wear other people's old clothes."

"You are too clever," Yulou said, laughing. "You ought to thank Buddha you have a coat like this." She put it on Jinlian. It was very large and cozy. Jinlian was somewhat appeased. Yueniang, Yulou and Li Ping'er put on their fur coats, all of which were made of sable. Then they said good-bye to the Wu ladies, and Yueniang gave Miss Yu two *qian* of silver.

Wu Yin'er said she too must say farewell. She knelt down and kow-towed to all the ladies. Aunt Wu gave her a set of silver flower ornaments; Yueniang and Li Ping'er each gave her a tael of silver. She again kowtowed and thanked them.

The two aunts and Miss Zheng would have taken the ladies to the gate, but Yueniang would not let them because it was snowing.

"A little while ago it was snowing very heavily," Qintong said. "Now it is more like rain. I am afraid the ladies' clothes will get wet, and I suggest borrowing umbrellas from our aunt." The younger uncle Wu quickly found some umbrellas and Qintong took them. Two soldiers with lanterns led the way. After passing through a few lanes, they came to the main street. Chen Jingji set off fireworks all along the road. He said to Wu Yin'er: "Sister Wu Yin'er, your home is not far away. Let us take you home."

"Where does she live?" said Yueniang.

"You go down this street," Jingji said, "and halfway down you come to a house with a high gateway. That is where she lives."

"I must say good-bye to you, ladies," Wu Yin'er said.

"Go straight home," Yueniang said. "Don't stop to make reverence to us. You have done so already, and the ground is wet. I will send a boy with you to see you to your door." She told Daian to go with the girl.

Then Jingji said: "Mother, I think I ought to go with Daian."

"Very well," said Yueniang, "you can both go with her." This was what Jingji was hoping for: he and Daian went off together.

Yueniang and the others went on their way. Jinlian said to Yueniang: "Mother, you talked about our taking her home. Why didn't we?" Yueniang laughed.

"What a child you are! I was only joking, and you took every word I said seriously. What kind of a place do you imagine this 'Home of Spring's Delights' to be? We could not possibly go there with her."

"But when men go to amuse themselves at such places," said Jinlian, "I have heard of their wives going after them and making a disturbance."

"Then, next time our lord goes there," Yueniang said, "you go and look for him. The chances are you will be driven out by another man who will take you for one of the ladies there."

They came to East Street. Outside the Qiaos' house, Madam Qiao herself and Miss Duan were standing. When they saw Yueniang and the others coming, they came forward and invited them to go in. Yueniang thanked them. "It is very kind of you," she said, "but it is late and we must not stay." Madam Qiao begged them not to stand on ceremony, and insisted that they should go in for a while. In her room, lanterns were hanging, and wine and fruit were set out upon the tables. Two singing girls were there to entertain the company.

At the gateway, Ximen Qing and his friends at last had wine enough. Ying Bojue and Xie Xida had been eating all day, and now the food had reached so high a point in their throats that they could not swallow another morsel. They saw that Ximen Qing was nodding in his chair and, not to miss a chance, they emptied the plates of fruit into their sleeves and went off with Han Daoguo. Only Ben the Fourth remained. He helped Ximen Qing to pay the musicians, told the boys to clear away, saw that the lanterns and candles were blown out and assisted Ximen Qing to the inner court.

Ping'an went to Ben the Fourth's place and said to the maids there: "Father has gone to the inner court. Why don't you come?"

When they heard this, Yuxiao, Yingchun and Lanxiang hurried away as fast as they could without even saying good-bye to Mistress Ben. They were off like a streak of smoke. Chunmei alone thanked Mistress Ben, and went back in a leisurely way. She overtook Lanxiang, who had been left behind because her shoe had come off. Chunmei scolded her. "You are like someone who steals a coffin for her own funeral," she said. "What kind of manners are these, letting your shoe fall off like that?"

When they came to the back court, they found that Ximen Qing had gone to Li Jiao'er's room, and all went in to kowtow to him. When the nun saw him come in, she left that room and went to Yueniang's room where she sat with Xiaoyu. When Yuxiao came in, she made a reverence to the nun.

"Sister," Xiaoyu said to her, "when Mother sent a boy for the ladies' furs, why didn't you come and look for them yourself instead of making me do so? I didn't know which was the key of the chest, and when I opened it, there was no coat inside. In the end, I found it in the great chest in the other room. You put the fur there, and you must have known where it was. You must have been off your head. You had food enough at Mistress Ben's, and now you are fatter than ever."

In truth, Yuxiao had had a good deal to eat, and her face was red. "You little whore," she cried, "what do you mean by behaving like a mad dog? If she didn't invite you, that's no reason why you should be angry with me. Do you think I wanted the whore to invite me?"

"Sisters," said the nun, "be calm, and do not let your master hear you. The ladies will be back in a moment and you had better have tea ready for them."

Then Qintong came with the wrappers. Yuxiao asked if the ladies had returned. The boy told her that Madam Qiao had kept them, and that they had gone in to take a cup of wine with her. They would probably be back soon, he said. The two maids stopped quarreling.

Before long, Yueniang returned from Madam Qiao's. When she reached the gate, Ben the Fourth's wife came out to welcome her. Then Chen Jingji and Ben the Fourth brought a small set of fireworks and set it off outside the gate. Afterwards, Yueniang went in, and Li Jiao'er and the nun came and made reverence to her. Xue'e kowtowed.

"Where is his Lordship?" Yueniang said to Li Jiao'er.

"He came to my room," Li Jiao'er said, "and I helped him to bed." Yueniang said no more.

Yingchun, Chunmei, Yuxiao and Lanxiang came to kowtow to their mistress.

"Madam Ben the Fourth sent these four maids an invitation," Li Jiao'er said. "They stayed a while and then came back."

For some time Yueniang did not speak. Then she said: "You wonderful little bitches. What do you mean by going? Who told you you might go?"

"They asked their master's permission before they went," Li Jiao'er said.

"Asked his permission!" said Yueniang. "What is the use of asking him? This house is like a temple where the doors are opened early on the first and fifteenth days of every month so that all the little ghosts can run away."

"Lady," the nun said, "these sisters are just like pictures; how can you speak of them as little ghosts?"

"They look like half-painted pictures to me," Yueniang said. "What right have they to go out for others to feast their eyes upon?"

Yulou saw that Yueniang was not in the best of tempers, and was the first to leave. Jinlian, Li Ping'er and Ximen Dajie went after her. Only the nun remained. She went to bed with Yueniang. The snow did not stop until the first night watch.

Next day, Ximen Qing went to his office. About midday, Yueniang, Yulou and Li Ping'er said good-bye to the nun. At the gate they saw an old country woman telling fortunes. She wore a pleated gown and a blue cloth skirt; there was a piece of black cloth over her head, and on her back she carried a bundle. She was walking along the street. Yueniang told a boy to go and bring her inside the second door to consult the divining diagram.

The old woman set out the spirit tortoise, and they asked her to tell their fortunes. She knelt down and kowtowed four times. "Lady, how old are you?" she asked Yueniang.

"Tell the fortune of a woman whose animal is the dragon," Yueniang said.

"If you speak of the great dragon," the old woman said, "the age is forty-two, but if it is the lesser dragon, it must be thirty."

"I am thirty," Yueniang said, "and I was born at midnight on the thirteenth day of the eighth month."

The old woman cast the spirit tortoise. It turned once, and she took up one of the divining cards. On it was a picture of a man and a woman in the place of the master, and a number of servants, some sitting, some standing. They were all watching gold and silver and treasure being put in safety.

"Lady," the old woman said, "you were born at the lucky hour of the *Wu* period. Now *Wu* and *Ji* together are like a great forest, and your being born in their conjunction means that you are a woman of benevolence and justice. You are generous and kind-hearted. You are charitable and devout and a supporter of the religious orders. You are, in fact, given to good works of every sort. All your life you have done your duties as a housewife; you are prepared to take the blame that others should have, and keep silence. Happiness and anger are both natural to you. But you do not manage your servants with great discretion. When you are pleased, you laugh long and heartily, and, when you are angry, you make a terrible to-do. In the early morning, when others are asleep, you burn fresh incense and wash the tripods. This while others sleep till the sun is long risen. Although by nature you are very quick, like wind and fire, yet you forget about a thing in a twinkling and you are ready to talk and laugh with anybody. There is a star of ill omen in the palace of diseases. You have to suffer from the babble of others. But you have a good heart, and so can overcome this, and you will live till you are seventy."

"Tell us whether this lady will have a son," Yulou said.

"I am sorry," said the old woman, "but there is something uncertain about the sign for children. I seem to see that she will have a son in a religious order to see her soul into the next world. But I doubt whether any other children she may have will live, no matter how many they may be."

"Your Wu Yingyuan is a priest already," Yulou said to Li Ping'er, smiling.

Yueniang said to Yulou: "Let her tell your fortune."

"Tell the fortune," said Yulou, "of a woman aged thirty-four, born at the hour of the tiger on the twenty-seventh day of the eleventh month."

The old woman again set the cards in order and cast the spirit tortoise. It stopped at the Star of Fate. She picked up a card on which was depicted a woman and three men. The first man was dressed as a traveling merchant, the second wore a red robe of ceremony, the third was a scholar. There was a room of gold and silver, and many servants stood on either hand.

"This lady was born in the year *Jiazi*," the old woman said, "and when *Jiazi* comes into conjunction with *Yichou*, it is like gold in the ocean. But there are three deaths and six injuries indicated by Fate. All will be well when you have been a widow."

"I have already been a widow once," Yulou said.

"You are gentle, kind and good-tempered," the old woman continued. "Nobody can tell whom you like and whom you dislike, because you never show it. You are respected by those below and loved by your husband, but, in spite of your kindness to others, you never win people's hearts. You must take the blame for what others do, and backbiters will make trouble for you. Though you suffer this, no one will admit that you are kind. But you are good-hearted, and though you will have to put up with trouble-makers, they will do you no real harm."

Yulou laughed. "Only a moment ago," she said, I asked for some money for the boys and there was trouble. I think that is what you must be thinking of when you talk about my being blamed for what others do."

"Can you tell us whether this lady will have a son?" Yueniang said.

"At the best, she will have a daughter," said the old woman. "Certainly not a son. But she will live long."

"Now tell this other lady's fortune," Yueniang said to the old woman. "Sixth Sister, tell her your eight words."

Li Ping'er laughed. "I am a sheep," she said.

"If you are a lamb," the old woman said, "you must be twenty-seven years old and you were born in the year *Xinwei*. What was the month?"

"Noon on the fifteenth day of the first month," Li Ping'er said.

The old woman spun the turtle. When it came to the Star of Fate, it stopped dead. She picked up a paper on which was a picture of one woman and three men. The first was wearing red, the second green and the third black. The woman was carrying a child. In a room filled with treasures of gold and silver there stood a demon with black face, long fangs, and red hair.

"This lady," the old woman said, "shows *Gengwu* in conjunction with *Xinwei*. It is as earth by the roadside. She is of high position and great wealth. She has food and clothing in plenty, and all her husbands are men of standing. There is virtue in her heart, and she does not care for money and treasure. Should she be robbed of them, she is happy nonetheless. Indeed, she will be angry if she is not. But she is plagued by people of little worth, and such people return her evil for good. Such evildoers disturb her peace, and begin their cunning tricks as soon as they have turned their eyes away from her. It is better to meet a tiger in a place where three roads meet, for then we can escape one way, than a man with a sword whose blade is double-edged.

"Lady, I hope you will forgive me. You are like a roll of fine red silk, yet one, alas, of no great length. You must exercise great self-control, and be on the lookout for danger to your child."

"My child has been enrolled at the Daoist Temple," Li Ping'er said.

"All to the good," the old woman said, "but I must warn you that this year you are under the spell of the *Jidu* star and there are signs of blood. You must be particularly careful in the seventh and eighth months. Then you must not see anything that might disturb you."

When the old woman had finished, Li Ping'er gave her five *fen*, and Yueniang and Yulou each gave her fifty coins. Then she was dismissed.

Jinlian and Ximen Dajie came. "No wonder I could not find you in the back court," Jinlian said, laughing. "You were all here."

"Yes," Yueniang said, "we came to say good-bye to the nun, and then we had our fortunes told. If you had been a little earlier, you too could have had your fortunes told."

"I don't want my fortune told," said Jinlian. "There is a proverb: 'Fortunes may be foretold, but not our conduct.' You remember how, some time ago, that priest said I had not long to live. It made me very depressed. But I don't care. If I die in the street, bury me there. If I die on the road, bury me there. If I fall into a ditch, the ditch will serve as a coffin."

She went with Yueniang to the inner court.

CHAPTER 47

The Villainy of Miao Qing

In the city of Guangling in Yangzhou in the province of Jiangnan, there lived a gentleman of standing in the official service whose name was Miao Tianxiu. He was extremely wealthy, a lover of poetry, and devoted to the Rites. He was now about forty years old, and his only child was a daughter, still unmarried. His wife suffered from a chronic wasting sickness, and the affairs of his household were entrusted to his favorite concubine, Diao the Seventh, who had originally been a woman of no great virtue. Master Miao had paid three hundred taels for her and was extremely fond of her.

One day, an old monk came to beg alms at the gate. He said that he came from the Temple of Thankfulness at the Eastern Capital. The monks there had determined to secure a golden Lohan, and he was traveling about begging for contributions.

Master Miao was no miser. He gave the monk fifty taels of silver.

"This is really more than I need," the old monk said. "Half of this amount will be sufficient for me."

But Miao said: "Don't say that, Master. If there is more money than you need for the image, let the rest be spent on sacrifices."

The monk made reverence to him and thanked him. As he was about to go away, he said, "Sir, beneath your left eye there is the sign of death. This presages great danger for you. You have been so generous to me that I can do no less than warn you. If you have business to do, on no account leave your native place. Be on your guard, be on your guard." He went away.

A few weeks later, Master Miao happened to go to his garden and there found his servant Miao Qing talking to his concubine Diao the Seventh beside a summerhouse. They had not expected that he would come upon them so suddenly, and so he caught them. Master Miao said nothing, but he gave his servant a tremendous thrashing and swore he would get rid of him. Miao Qing was greatly alarmed and went about asking his relatives and neighbors to intercede for him. In the end he was allowed to stay, but, ever afterwards, he hated his master.

Master Miao had a cousin named Huang Mei, a graduate from

Yangzhou. This man was a secretary at Kaifengfu, the Eastern Capital. He was a man of great learning and wide reading. One day he wrote to Master Miao suggesting that he should make a journey to the Capital, both for amusement and in the interests of his future career. Miao was delighted with the idea. He said to his wife and his concubine: "The Eastern Capital is the place for people of high standing, and there are hosts of interesting and beautiful things to see there. For a long time I have wanted to go there, but there was no particular reason why I should. Now my cousin sends me an invitation, and it is exactly what I should most enjoy."

"The other day," his wife said to him, "the monk told you that you were in grave danger and that you must not leave this place. It is a long way from here to the Capital, and there is plenty to busy you here at home. If you go away, you leave an invalid wife and a young daughter at home, and what we shall do if you go, I can't imagine. I think you ought to stay." But Master Miao did not agree. Indeed he almost lost his temper. "A man who lives in this world," he said, "should carry bow and arrows. It is a disgraceful thing if a man cannot wander over the world to see the glory of his native land. I have a heart in my bosom and something in my pocket, and I am sure to acquire both renown and a position. My cousin must have something good in store for me. Please say no more about it." He told Miao Qing to pack his clothes and get ready his baggage. So, with two chests of gold, silver, and other treasure, they had enough to load a boat. With a boy, Antong, and Miao Qing, he set off for the Eastern Capital. It was about the end of autumn and winter was near at hand, when he commended his household to the care of his wife and concubine, and chose a day to start upon his journey. Then he sailed from the wharf of Yangzhou. After a few days, they came to the lake of Xuzhou. The water was wild and the danger great.

When they had come to a place called Xiawan, Master Miao, seeing that it was late, ordered the boatman to lay up for the night. Now it was that his life was done, and the fate that he could not escape was upon him. The boatmen he had engaged, Chen the Third and Weng the Eighth, were both thieves. But, as the proverb says: 'The Devil cannot get into a house without someone to let him in.' Miao Qing had a burning hatred for his master and was waiting to get his revenge. He reflected that here was a chance for him. He might conspire with these two boatmen to push his master into the river, and so make an end of him, then he and the boatmen would share the plunder, and he would go home, murder his mistress, and enjoy his master's concubine and the property.

Miao Qing and the boatmen secretly made a plot. He said to them: "There are a thousand taels of silver in my master's chests. There is silk worth two thousand taels and many, many clothes. If you two will kill him, I am prepared to share with you."

The two men laughed. "We had that same idea before you spoke to us," they said.

That night it was very dark. Master Miao and the boy Antong were asleep in the cabin. Miao Qing was on watch. About the third night watch Miao Qing shouted: "Thief! Thief!" Master Miao woke from his dreams and pushed his head out of the cabin to look around. Chen stabbed him in the throat with a sharp knife. They threw him into the water. The boy Antong tried to escape, but Weng thrust at him with a stick, and he fell into the river.

Then the pair of ruffians went into the cabin, opened the chests and took out all that was valuable—gold and silver, silk and garments. These they counted and made ready to share. "If we keep these things," the two men said to Miao Qing, "we shall be identified. But you were his servant. You can take them and sell them in some market and nobody will suspect you." They shared the gold things among themselves and went home. Miao Qing boarded another boat and went to the wharf at Linqing. When the customs officers had examined him, he took all the things to an inn in the city of Qinghe. There he met some old merchants from Yangzhou. He told them that his master was coming later. Then he sold the property he had stolen.

The proverb says: Men think the world ought to be managed in such and such a way, but Providence thinks otherwise. Master Miao was a plain-living, good man, yet he was unexpectedly murdered by his own servant. Such a death was unnatural. He was to be blamed, because he did not take good advice when it was offered, but really there was no escape from the decision of Fate.

Antong was knocked senseless by the stick, but, though he fell into the water, he was not dead. He floated to a shallow place among the reeds. There came a fishing boat, and, in the boat, an old man. He wore on his head a round reed hat, and, on his body, a short coat of straw. When he heard a scream, he rowed his boat in the direction of the sound and found a boy of seventeen or eighteen years of age. He quickly pulled the boy out of the water and asked what had happened. The boy told him that he was the servant of Master Miao of Yangzhou, and that they had been robbed on the river. The old fisherman took the boy into his boat, gave him clothes and food and drink. Then he said: "Do you wish to go back or will you live here with me?"

Antong said: "My master has been murdered, and I can never see him again. What is the use of my going back? I will stay with you."

"Very well," said the fisherman. "Live with me, and we shall, in time, find out something about the robbers. Then we will make new arrangements."

Antong thanked the old man and went to live with him.

One day—it was the last day of the year—it was fated that something of importance should happen. The fisherman and Antong went down the river to sell fish. They came suddenly upon Chen the Third and Weng the Eighth drinking together on their boat. They were wearing the clothes of Antong's master. When they came on shore to buy fish, the boy recognized them. He secretly told the old man. "Now," he said, "my master's death shall be avenged."

"Write an accusation and bring them before the judge," the old man said.

Antong wrote down his charge and took the paper to the office of the Inspector of the River, Major Zhou. The Major saw that the boy brought no witness or evidence with him, so he would have nothing to do with the case, and the boy went to the magistrate's court. Magistrate Xia saw that the case was one of murder and robbery: he accepted the charge and, on the fourteenth day of the first month, sent the watch with Antong to arrest the murderers at Qinghe. When they were examined and saw Antong there, they did not wait to be tortured but told the truth at once. They said that Miao Qing had been concerned with them in the murder, that he had taken a share of the things and gone his own way. Magistrate Xia ordered them to be put back in prison and ordered Miao Qing's arrest. He decided to give sentence when Miao Qing had been brought before him.

It was about the time of the New Year Festival and all the officers were on holiday. For two days the public offices were closed. In the meantime somebody at the office told Miao Qing what had happened. Miao Qing was terrified. He locked up his room at the inn and hid himself in the house of a certain Yue the Third. This Yue the Third was a broker. He lived in Lion Street next door to Han Daoguo, and his wife was on very friendly terms with Wang Liu'er. She often visited Wang Liu'er, and Wang Liu'er, when she had nothing else to do, often visited her. They were on very close terms indeed.

Yue saw that Miao Qing seemed exceedingly distressed and asked him what the trouble was. Miao Qing told him. "Don't worry," Yue said. "My neighbor Han's wife is the mistress of Master Ximen, an officer of the court. Her husband is a servant of his, and both husband and wife are our very good friends. We agree with each other on all points. If I get you out of this trouble, how much are you prepared to offer? Tell me, and I will go and discuss the matter with him."

Miao Qing knelt down. "All I ask," he said, "is to be saved from this trouble. I will most surely give you a great reward and I shall never dare to forget your kindness."

They wrote out a supplication, parceled up fifty taels of silver, put them with two dresses of embroidered satin, and Yue told his wife to take them to Wang Liu'er. Wang Liu'er was delighted. She took the clothes, the silver and the paper, and waited for Ximen Qing to come.

For several days there was no sign of him but, on the evening of the seventeenth, Wang Liu'er saw Daian, with a wrapper, riding down the street. She went outside her door and called to him: "Where are you going?"

"I have been a long way with my master," the boy said. "We have just come back from Dongpingfu, where we took some presents."

"Has your father come back too?" Wang Liu'er asked.

"Father and Ben the Fourth have come back already," the boy said. Wang Liu'er took the boy into her house, told him all about the case and showed him the paper.

"Aunt Han," Daian said, "you may try to manage this affair, but you will not find it too easy. The two boatmen are already in prison and now this man is wanted. A few paltry taels are not enough for the servants. I want neither more nor less than twenty taels of silver, and then I will ask Father to come here and you can tell him all about it."

Wang Liu'er laughed. "You little oily mouth!" she said, "you may be hungry, but you must not be too greedy. If this case is settled, of course there will be something for you. Even if I get nothing myself, I will see that you get something."

"Aunt Han," said Daian, "don't misunderstand me. The proverb says: 'Honorable men are never ashamed to speak plainly.' The best thing we can do is to agree upon terms and then talk about the matter."

Wang Liu'er prepared some food and entertained Daian. "If I get a red face from drinking wine," the boy said, "my master will scold me."

"Don't trouble about that," Wang Liu'er said. "Tell him you have been here."

The boy drank one cup of wine and went away. As he went, the woman said to him: "Tell your father I am expecting him."

Daian went home, handed in the wrapper and waited for Ximen Qing to have his sleep out. When Ximen came to the room in the wing, the boy went to him quietly and said: "On my way home, Aunt Han stopped me and told me to ask you to go to see her. She has a very important matter to speak to you about."

"What is it?" Ximen said. "I will go."

Then District Examiner Liu came to borrow some silver. Ximen gave it to him and he went away. Ximen, wearing his eyeshades and a small hat, mounted his horse and went with Daian and Qintong to see Wang Liu'er. He went into the parlor and sat down, and Wang Liu'er came and made reverence to him. It was Han Daoguo's turn to sleep at the shop that night, so he did not return. Wang Liu'er had bought many things and had sent for old woman Feng to cook them. She hastened to bring tea for Ximen Qing. Ximen told Qintong to take his horse to the house opposite and to shut the gate.

At first the woman said nothing about the case. "You must be tired after so many parties during these last few days," she said. "I have heard about your young son's betrothal and must congratulate you."

"It was my relative Wu who suggested the marriage," Ximen said. "The Qiaos have only one daughter. It really is not the most suitable marriage, but I want to get the matter settled."

"It is not a bad marriage," Wang Liu'er said, "but you have a high position and it will be awkward, perhaps, when you meet them."

"That was what I thought," Ximen said.

They talked for a while and Wang Liu'er said, "It is rather cold here. Won't you come into the inner room?" They went into the inner room. There was a chair on either side and a brazier with burning coals. Hesitatingly, the woman showed him Miao Qing's paper. "This man, Miao Qing, asked Mistress Yue to come and see me about it," she said. "Miao Qing is staying with Yue. The two boatmen have accused him falsely. All he wants is to have his name kept out of this case. He sent me a little present and you must do something for him."

When he had read the paper, Ximen Qing said: "How much did he give you?" Wang Liu'er took the fifty taels from her box and showed them to him.

"If the case is settled, he promised to give me two dresses," she said.

Ximen Qing looked at the silver and laughed. "Why did you accept so small a sum?" he said. "You don't understand. This Miao Qing is the servant of Master Miao of Yangzhou. He and the two boatmen murdered their master and threw the body into the river. It is a case of murder and robbery. The corpse has not yet been found. The boy Antong was with them, and both the boy and the boatmen are anxious to get hold of Miao Qing. If he is arrested he will certainly get the punishment of the thousand slashes and the two boatmen will lose their heads. They say that Miao Qing has stuff worth two thousand taels. Why should he send you a paltry sum like this? Send it back to him at once."

Wang Liu'er went into the kitchen and told her maid to go for Mistress Yue. When Mistress Yue came, Wang Liu'er gave her the silver and told her what Ximen Qing had said. When the news was brought to Miao Qing, it was as though a pail of water had been poured over him from head to feet. He was absolutely terrified. He talked over the matter with Yue and said he would give up all he had if only he could save his life.

"Since Master Ximen says this," Yue said, "it is clear that a little more will be of no avail. It looks to me as though it will mean a thousand taels to the two officers, and another thousand taels for the underlings and the policemen."

"But I haven't sold all my things," Miao Qing said. "Where am I to find the ready money?" They told Mistress Yue to go back to Wang Liu'er and find out whether Ximen would accept the goods. "If so, Miao Qing will offer goods to the value of a thousand taels to him. If he will not have them, ask his Lordship to allow Miao Qing two or three days in which to sell them. Then he will go in person to his Lordship to offer the money."

Wang Liu'er took the list of the goods and showed it to Ximen. He looked at it. "In the circumstances," he said, "I will let him have a few days. Then he must bring the money to me himself."

Mistress Yue went back and told Miao Qing what had happened. He was greatly relieved.

Ximen Qing noticed that there was somebody in the next house, so he did not stay long. He drank a few cups of wine, then ordered his horse and went home.

The next day the office closed early, and he did not mention the matter at all. Miao Qing desperately urged Yue to sell the stolen property for him, and, in three days, everything was disposed of for seventeen hundred taels. He gave Wang Liu'er another fifty taels and four dresses of the finest material. On the nineteenth he put a thousand taels into four wine jars, bought a pig and, when it was dark, carried them to Ximen Qing. All the servants knew about the matter, so he gave Daian, Ping'an, Shutong and Qintong ten taels of silver apiece. Daian went to Wang Liu'er and got another ten taels from her.

Ximen Qing came out and sat under the awning. There was no light but the moon was just rising. The presents were brought to him and Miao Qing, dressed in black clothes, kowtowed. "I am so grateful for your generous kindness," he said, "that though my body were beaten to pieces, I could never repay you."

"Your case has not yet been investigated," Ximen said, "but the two boatmen still insist on the truth of what they have said. If you are arrested, you must inevitably be severely punished. But since you have come to me, I will see that your life is saved. You would not be satisfied if I did not take your present, but a half of it I must give to Magistrate Xia, my colleague.

You must stay here no longer, but get away as quickly as you can. Where do you live at Yangzhou?"

"I live within the city itself," Miao Qing said. He kowtowed again.

Ximen Qing called for some tea from the back court and Miao Qing drank it, standing beneath a pine tree. Then he kowtowed and prepared to take his leave. Ximen recalled him and said: "Have you attended to the officers of lower rank?" Miao Qing told him that he had. "Then you should go home at once," Ximen said.

Miao Qing gave fifty taels and the remainder of the silk to Yue and his wife. At the fifth night watch, they saddled a horse and he started for Yangzhou.

The next day Ximen Qing and Magistrate Xia left their office together. They were riding side by side. When they came to the middle of the High Street, Magistrate Xia was about to say good-bye to Ximen, but Ximen raised his whip and said: "Will you be kind enough to come to my house for a moment?" Xia went with him. They went into the hall and exchanged the appropriate greetings. Then Xia was asked to go to the arbor, and there he took off his long cloak. The servants brought tea and Daian and Shutong prepared a table.

"Really," Xia said, "I should not put you to all this trouble." Ximen Qing asked him not to say so. Two boys brought chicken, pigs' trotters, goose, duck, fish and other dishes on a large square tray. They ate some and everything was cleared away. Then they drank wine with dessert and fruits, using small golden cups and silver trays. Ximen pressed his colleague to drink more and more, and, while they were drinking, began to talk about the matter of Miao Qing.

"Yesterday," he said, "the fellow got some scholars to come here, and sent presents. I dared not make any decision myself, so I have asked you to come and talk about it." He showed Magistrate Xia the list of presents.

"I leave the decision to you," said Xia, when he had read the list.

"Well," Ximen said, "I suggest that, tomorrow, we send on those two robbers and leave Miao alone. We will ask someone to take Antong away. The matter can be settled when Master Miao's body is found. The present, of course, is yours."

"Not at all," Magistrate Xia said. "I agree with everything you say about the case, but why should you give me the present? You have done well. Certainly I shall not take it." They disputed politely for a long time, and at last Ximen said: "Perhaps we might share it." He put five hundred taels into a food box. Magistrate Xia stood up and made a reverence to him.

"You are very kind," he said, "and if I don't accept, you will take it unkindly. Thank you very much." He had some more wine and then went away.

Ximen Qing told Daian to take the food box to Magistrate Xia's as if he were taking wine. Xia himself came to receive it. He gave the boy a card in return and two taels of silver for himself. The four bearers each received four *qian* of silver. As the proverb says: Just as a pig's head will be cooked when the fire is hot enough, so a case will be settled when money enough is forthcoming.

So Ximen Qing and Xia arranged the matter. The next day they went to the office. The jailers, policemen, and attendants had all been bribed by Yue. In the hall of audience, the instruments of torture were all set out, and Chen and Weng, the two boatmen, were brought forward. When they were questioned, they still declared that they had murdered Master Miao at the instigation of Miao Qing. Ximen Qing professed to be very angry and ordered them to be beaten. "You two thieves have worked the river for years. You have pretended to carry travelers on your boat, but actually you have robbed and murdered. This boy says you killed Master Miao with a knife and threw his body into the water. You struck the boy himself with a stick. Here are the clothes of the boy's master for witness. Why do you still accuse somebody else?"

Then he called for Antong. "Who killed your master? Who pushed you into the water?"

"About the third night watch I heard Miao Qing shout. My master came out of the cabin, then Chen killed him and threw his body into the water. Weng struck me with a stick and I was thrown in too. He did not kill me. I do not know where Miao Qing is now."

"It is clear from what the boy says," Ximen Qing said, "that there is no way out for you." He had fetters put upon their legs and each of them was given thirty blows with a club. Their bones were broken and they screamed like pigs being killed.

The two robbers gave up half of the property they had stolen. They had already spent the rest. A document was written out to be sent with the men and the property to Dongpingfu. The magistrate at Dongpingfu, Hu Shiwen, was Ximen Qing's friend. He accepted the document without question. He sentenced Chen the Third and Weng the Eighth as thieves and murderers to have their heads cut off. Antong was allowed to go. Afterwards, the boy went to the Eastern Capital. There he accused Miao Qing of his master's murder, and of bribing the officers at Qinghe, and so escaping trial. A letter was written and joined to the lad's accusation; he was given money for his journey and sent to the supreme court of Shandong. Thus, more trouble was brewed for Miao Qing, and Ximen Qing was given considerable cause for anxiety in consequence of his action in the matter.

> Evil and good meet with their due reward
> Good Fortune and ill luck walk side by side
> But he who never walks in the wrong path
> Need have no fear when comes the summons in the night.

CHAPTER 48

The Censor's Accusation

Antong took the documents and the letter and set off for Shandong. He found that the Imperial Censor on circuit was at Dongchangfu. This was Ceng Xiaoxu, the son of the Censor, Ceng Bu. He had just taken a high place in the examination for the third literary degree, and was a very prudent and just official.

Antong thought that if he simply said he had come with a letter he would never be allowed to approach the Censor, and that it would be better for him to wait until the tablet was brought out. "Then," he said to himself, "I will kneel down, bring out my papers; the Censor will see them and justice will be done."

The boy put the accusation into his breast and took his stand outside the court. After a long time he heard the sound of the castanets announcing the opening of the court. The great gate was opened, Censor Ceng came to the great hall of audience, and a tablet was brought out upon which was written: "The cases of all princely families, princes and nobles." The second said: "The cases of civil and military officials," and the third: "Marriages, lands, and common cases." Then Antong followed the tablet and went in. He waited for all the cases to be decided, then knelt down in the hall before the dais. Attendants asked him what he wanted. He took the letter from his breast and held it up in both hands. The Censor said: "Bring me that letter." Then an officer quickly took the letter and set it down upon the table. The Censor opened it and read it. It said:

> Huang Duan, your humble fellow student of the arts, living at the Capital, with all due respect.
>
> To the exalted Censor Ceng. Greetings to your excellency from your younger brother. It is almost a year since your brightness illuminated me. Good friends seldom meet, and a joyful reunion is quickly ended. But the love of my heart is always with you. Last autumn your precious communication reached me. I opened it and read it, and my spirit seemed to wander till I spoke with you face to face. Some time ago you went to the South to see your honorable parents. Then I was told that you were on circuit in Shandong, and was pleased beyond all measure.

I congratulate you upon your magnificent loyalty and filial piety. Uprightness as keen as the wind and the frost keeps your mind forever glorious. Your worthy ambition is known and recognized at Court. Now you are going around the provinces and it is possible for you to discover the misdeeds of officials and correct evil customs that have become established. Since I love you, I feel that I must remind you. You are a man of great capacity and at the prime of life. Our Emperor has the wisdom of a Sage, and your father enjoys splendid health. You have a magnificent opportunity to display your learning to advantage and to establish the supremacy of law. You will not permit dishonorable officials to corrupt the administration of justice. You will not allow cunning and evil men to play their scurvy tricks. At this time, there is in Dongping a certain Miao Qing who has escaped the justice of the law. So wrong has been done to Miao Tianxiu, his master. It is beyond my understanding, how in an age of such splendor, these discreditable things can happen. You will, I am sure, go to that place and make examination into the matter, and so the wrongdoing will be set right. I have directed Antong to bring his accusation to you and beg you to examine it. This the sixteenth day of the second month.

When the Censor had finished reading the letter, he asked for the boy's accusation. The attendants came down and said to Antong: "His Excellency asks if you have brought an accusation." Antong took the paper from his breast and they handed it to the Censor.

When he had read it through, Ceng took a brush and wrote upon it: "The officers at Dongpingfu will examine this case justly. They will search for the corpse and examine it, sending their report to me in detail with all the documents." To the boy he said: "Go to Dongpingfu and wait there."

Antong kowtowed, then rose and went out by a side door. Censor Ceng put the papers together with his own notes into a folder, sealed it with his official seal, and gave it to one of his officers to take to Dongpingfu.

When Hu Shiwen, the magistrate of Dongpingfu, read the document that had come from his superior, he was so frightened that he did not know where to put his hands and feet. He sent at once for the Deputy of Yanggu, a certain Di Sibin. This man was a native of Wuyang in Henan, an honest-dealing official. He was not a lover of money, but somewhat hasty and stupid in his investigations of cases. Hence men called him Stupid Di.

Some time before this, Deputy Di had gone to Qinghe. When he was on the shore of the river west of the city, a whirlwind seemed to arise in front of his horse and, as he went along, the whirlwind went with him. "This is curious," Di said to himself, and, reining in his horse, he told one of his attendants to go after the wind to see where it went. The attendant followed the wind and, when it had nearly reached the wharf, it subsided. He came back and told Di what had happened. Di sent for some of the old men of the place and dug up the bank. They found a corpse with the mark of a knife clearly discernible in the throat. Di gave instructions to the coroner to hold an inquest upon it. "What is this place in front of us?" he asked the bystanders. They told him that it was a temple and not far distant. Di sent for the monks and questioned them. The monks told him that, in the tenth month of the previous winter, they had been setting lanterns on the water's edge when they saw a corpse floating down the river. It came to the shallows and the Abbot generously buried it. But of the cause of death they knew nothing.

"It is quite obvious," said Stupid Di, "that the monks themselves murdered the man and buried him there. He must have had money on him. But you will not tell the truth." Without listening to any of the monks' explanations, he had the screws put on the Abbot and gave him a hundred strokes of the rod. The other monks were each given twenty, and they were all thrown into prison. Then he reported the case to Censor Ceng.

The monks clamored for justice, and, when Ceng thought the case over, it occurred to him that, if they had really murdered the man, they would have thrown his body into the river and not buried it on the bank. Besides, it did not seem probable that so many people would conspire to murder one man.

The monks had now been in prison for almost two months. When Antong came, he was taken to identify the corpse. As soon as he saw it, he cried bitterly and said, "This is indeed my master. The thieves murdered him and the mark in his neck can still be seen." The body was carefully examined and a report sent to the Censor. The monks were set free.

Ceng read all the documents about the case. He examined Chen the Third and Weng the Eighth and they both said that the idea of murdering Master Miao had originated with Miao Qing.

The Censor was very angry. He sent a man with a warrant bidding him travel day and night and arrest Miao Qing at Yangzhou. And he wrote a report censuring all those who had accepted bribes and sold justice.

Wang Liu'er had received a hundred taels and four dresses from Miao Qing. She and her husband did not sleep all night. They talked about the ornaments, pins and rings she would have made; how they would send for the tailor to make some clothes; how she would have a new net for her hair, and spend sixteen taels on a new maid, Chunxiang, whom sooner or later she would give to Han Daoguo.

One day Ximen Qing came to see her, Wang Liu'er welcomed him and gave him tea. After a while he went to the inner court to wash his hands and saw a building being set up on the roof of a neighboring house. When he came back, he asked Wang Liu'er whose house it was. She told him it belonged to their neighbor, Yue. "Why should you allow them to interfere with your *fengshui?*" Ximen said. "Tell him to stop at once. If he refuses to pull it down, I will send the police to deal with him."

"We cannot talk to him like that," Wang Liu'er said afterwards to her husband. "He is our neighbor."

"The best thing we can do," Han Daoguo said, "is to get some wood, say nothing about it, and build another story ourselves. On the top of it we can dry our bean paste, and we can use the inside either as a stable or as a privy."

"That would be silly," Wang Liu'er said. "If we are going to build a roof, we might as well buy tiles and bricks and make two good rooms."

Han Daoguo agreed. They spent thirty taels, built their two rooms and put a flat roof over them. Ximen Qing told Daian to take wine, meat and cakes to give the workers as a reward. The matter was known to everyone who lived in the street.

Magistrate Xia, now that he had received several hundred taels, sent his son Xia Cheng'en to the military college. Every day the young man studied archery and horsemanship with his teachers and friends. Ximen Qing suggested to the two eunuchs, Liu and Xue, Major Zhou, General Jing and Captain Zhang, that they should send a present to Xia in congratulation. They gave him a large scroll.

At Ximen's burying place, he had recently built a mound, an arbor, and some rooms. He had not been to worship his ancestors since he had received his official appointment. Now he sent for Xu, the Master of the Yin Yang, to examine the site, built a gateway and made a path for the spirits. Around the gateway he planted peach trees, willows and pines. On either side he made a small embankment. At the Festival of the Dead he proposed to visit the grave and change the tablet. He prepared pigs and sheep and food.

The festival was on the sixth day of the third month. He sent out many invitations and arranged for a number of people to take the things out to the tomb—wine, rice, vegetables and so forth. He engaged musicians and actors, and arranged for several singing girls to be present. He invited a great number of guests, both men and women. Chunmei, Yingchun, Yuxiao and Lanxiang were to be there also. Twenty-four or more sedan chairs would be needed. But when there was question of the nurse's taking the baby Guan'ge, Wu Yueniang said to Ximen: "It will be better not to take the baby. He is not a year old yet, and old woman Liu tells me that the bones of his head have not yet grown together. He is very nervous, and, if we take him on such a long trip, I am afraid he will be frightened. We will leave him behind. The nurse and old woman Feng can stay at home and look after him so that his mother can go."

Ximen Qing would not agree. "Why are we going to the tombs of my ancestors at all?" he said. "I want both the baby and his mother to go and kowtow to my ancestors. You always believe everything that silly old woman tells you. If the baby's head is not strong enough, he must be wrapped up more carefully. He will be quite safe with his nurse in the sedan chair. There is nothing for you to worry about."

"Have it your own way," Yueniang said.

In the morning all the ladies came to Ximen Qing's house, and they started off together. They left the city by the southern gate, and, when they had gone about eight *li*, they could see the green pine trees that surrounded the tomb. There was the new gateway and the embankment on both sides. Stone walls encircled the tomb, and, in the middle, were the oratory and the way of the spirits. The perfume burners, candlesticks and utensils for the worship of the ancestral spirits were all of white alabaster. Over the gate was placed a new tablet that bore the inscription: "The Ancestral tombs of the valorous Commander Ximen." They went in and around beneath the interlaced branches of the trees. Ximen Qing, wearing his scarlet robes and girdle, set out the pigs, sheep, and food for the worship of his ancestors. First the gentlemen offered their worship, then the ladies. The musicians played. The baby was frightened and hid his face in his nurse's bosom. He whimpered, lying perfectly still.

"Sister," Yueniang whispered to Li Ping'er, "I should tell the nurse to take him away. Don't you see how terrified he is? I said we ought not to bring him, but his stupid father wouldn't listen to me. Now he is frightened into such a state."

Li Ping'er hurriedly told Daian to stop the beating of the drums and gongs. They covered the baby's ears and took him away.

After a time the service was ended. Master Xu read the oration and burned paper offerings. Then Ximen Qing invited the gentlemen to go to the front, and Yueniang invited the ladies to go to the back. They went through the gardens. There were pine trees and pine hedges, bamboos standing beside the paths, and many flowers and grasses.

Beneath the awning the actors played for the ladies, while four young actors entertained the gentlemen, playing instruments and singing in the great hall. Four singing girls served wine in turn for the gentlemen, and the four maids for the ladies. Then they stood at Ximen Dajie's table and had soup and cakes.

Pan Jinlian, Meng Yulou and Ximen Dajie went with Li Guijie and Wu Yin'er to the garden and played on the swings there. Behind the arbor, Ximen had arranged three rooms with furniture and beds, curtains, and things for the toilet. Here, the ladies might dress when they came to visit the tombs. The rooms were covered with paper so white that they seemed like caves of snow. Pictures and scrolls adorned the walls. To this place the nurse, Ruyi'er, brought the baby, and, on the gilded bed, the child lay upon a tiny blanket. Yingchun was there too, playing with the child. Jinlian, alone, came in from the garden, with peach flowers in her hand. When she saw Yingchun, she said: "So you are not attending to your duties in the hall."

"Chunmei, Lanxiang and Yuxiao are there," Yingchun said, "and my mistress told me to come here and look after the baby. I brought some cakes for the nurse."

The nurse welcomed Jinlian and stood up with the child. "Ah," Jinlian said, laughingly. "Ah, little oily mouth, the drums and the gongs frightened you. You're a brave young man, aren't you?" She opened her silken gown, took the child to her breast and kissed him.

Suddenly Chen Jingji pulled up the lattice and came in. When he saw Jinlian playing with the baby, he joined in the play too.

"Now, my young priest," Jinlian said, "let me see you kiss your brother-in-law."

Strangely enough, the child smiled at the young man. Jingji bent over and kissed him several times. Jinlian scolded him. Jingji smiled. "It is a good thing I didn't kiss the wrong person," he said.

Jinlian was afraid the nurse would hear him. She closed her fan and struck the young man. Jingji jumped like a fish. "I am not going to argue with you," Jinlian said.

"Very well," Jingji said, "but you ought to realize that I have feelings. I have only thin clothes on, and there was no need for you to hit me so hard."

"I have no intention of being kind to you," Jinlian said. "I shall hit you every time you offend me."

Ruyi'er saw them playing together and hastily took the child away from them. Jinlian and the young man laughed and joked together. She made the peach flowers into a garland and set it on his head without his noticing it. Jingji went out wearing it. Yulou, Ximen Dajie and Guijie met him. His wife looked at him. "Who did this?" she said. Jingji did not answer, but he took off the garland.

By this time four acts of the play had been performed, and it was beginning to grow dark. Ximen Qing told Ben the Fourth to give each of the chair men a cup of wine, four cakes, and a plate of cooked meat. When the chair men had eaten it, they took the ladies away. The servants followed on horseback. Laixing came with the cooks, bringing all the food boxes. Daian, Laian, Huatong and Qitong followed behind Yueniang's chair; Qintong, with four soldiers, followed behind Ximen Qing's horse. Ruyi'er had a small chair for herself and the baby, who was closely wrapped in bedclothes. Yueniang was still anxious about him and bade Huatong accompany the nurse's chair. She was afraid that they would find the streets very crowded when they came to the city.

When all the chairs had entered the city, those of the Qiao family went their own way. Yueniang reached home, but it was some time before Ximen Qing and Chen Jingji arrived.

When Ximen Qing dismounted, Ping'an said to him: "His Lordship Xia has been here and gone away. He sent messengers for you twice. I don't know what he wanted."

This made Ximen Qing thoughtful. He went to the great hall, where Shutong took his clothes. "What did his Lordship say when he was here?" Ximen asked the boy.

"He didn't say anything to me," Shutong said. "He only asked where you were. He suggested that I should go and ask you to come back because he had something very important to say to you. I told him that you had gone to the tombs to make offering to the dead and that you would be back this evening. He said he would come again. He has sent messengers twice, but I had to tell them you had not returned."

"What is this?" Ximen Qing said to himself.

He was thinking over the matter when Ping'an came and said Magistrate Xia had called once more. It was very dark. The magistrate was in plain clothes and had only two servants with him. When he entered the great hall, he greeted Ximen. "You have just returned from your glorious estate," he said. "Today I have been to worship at my ancestor's tombs," Ximen Qing said. "I ask your forgiveness for being absent when you called."

"I have come especially to bring you news," said Xia. "Shall we go into another room?"

Ximen Qing told Shutong to open the door, and they went in. He ordered all the servants to leave.

"This morning," Magistrate Xia said, "Li came to me and told me that the Censor has sent a report to the Eastern Capital accusing us both. I have had the document copied and here it is. Please read it."

Ximen Qing was alarmed. He paled. He took the paper to the lamp and read it. It said:

I, the Censor and Circuit Commissioner of Shandong, Ceng Xiaoxu, make accusation against certain rapacious and unworthy officials, and implore the Sacred Majesty to dismiss them that the dignity of the Law may be preserved.

I have been instructed that the duty of the Emperor is to go around the country and investigate the morals of the people. To check evil officials and enforce the law is the duty of the censors. In olden times it was written in the Book of Spring and Autumn that the Supreme Monarch went upon an inspection of the Empire and made the whole state subject to himself. So the morals of the people were improved and the exalted principle of the Ruler made manifest. The four peoples became obedient and all men recognized the rule of wisdom.

About a year ago the duty of going around all the districts of Shandong was entrusted to me. I have questioned the officials and found out the truth about the capacity of them all, whether military or civil. Now my tour of duty is almost at an end: I am continuing my investigations and would make report to Your Majesty. Especially would I, with Your Majesty's gracious permission, make the following accusations... .

Xia Yanling, captain of the Royal Guard and a principal magistrate in Shandong, is a man of no merit. He is rapacious and a man of evil conduct. People talk about his behavior and he is a disgrace to his position. Formerly, when he held office at the Capital, he committed many irregularities and was discovered by his subordinates. Now that he is employed in the courts of Shandong he is more rapacious than ever. He is always associating in evil with other officials. He has entered his son at the Military College by making false statements, and procured some other person to take the examination in his son's place, thus utterly demoralizing the students. He has allowed his servant Xia Shou to take bribes. The soldiers complain bitterly and his administration is extremely disorganized. When this Xia receives officers visiting his district, his face is as that of a slave and his knees as those of a maid. For this reason the people call him "Maid." When he investigates a case, his judgment is always uncertain, and his underlings call him "Wooden Image."

His Deputy, Captain Ximen Qing, was originally a street-corner lounger. He obtained his position by bribery and has thus improperly secured military rank. He cannot even distinguish between the flail and the corn. He cannot read a single character. He allows his wife and his concubines to play in the streets, and there have been scandals in his household. He drinks with singing girls in wineshops, and has disgraced the official class to which he belongs. Recently he has been associating with the wife of a certain Han Daoguo. He gives himself up completely to a dissolute life and cares nothing about his conduct. He took bribes from a certain Miao Qing and has irregularly allowed that fellow to escape the justice of the law. So Miao Qing's crime has never been punished.

These two rapacious and unworthy officers have long been the talk of the common people and they should be immediately dismissed from their posts. I pray Your Majesty to hear me, and instruct the Boards to examine these men closely. If it is found that what I have said is true, I pray Your Majesty to dismiss these two men. The morale of the service depends upon it. May the virtue of Your Majesty be glorious for ever and ever.

When he had finished reading this, Ximen Qing could only look at Magistrate Xia. He could find no words to say. "What shall we do?" said Xia.

"There is a proverb," Ximen Qing said, "that says: When soldiers come against us, we send out a general. When the flood comes, we build a dike. So, when in trouble, we must take steps to meet the situation. We must get ready presents and send them to the Imperial Tutor in the Eastern Capital."

Magistrate Xia hurried home and got ready two hundred taels of silver and two silver vases. Ximen prepared a chest full of gold, jade, and precious things, and three hundred taels of silver. Xia ordered his servant Shou, and Ximen his man Laibao, to take charge of these gifts. He had a letter written to the comptroller Zhai. The two men hired horses and went off, traveling as fast as they were able, to the Eastern Capital.

When the baby Guan'ge returned from the tomb, he cried all night and would not take his food. Everything he swallowed he disgorged again. Li Ping'er was alarmed. She came to Yueniang and told her.

"I said that a baby not a year old should not be taken outside the city," Yueniang said, "but the foolish man would not listen to me. He said the whole purpose of going to the tombs of his ancestors was that you and the child might offer worship there. He glared and shouted at me as if he were a savage. Now, what I anticipated has happened."

Li Ping'er did not know what to do.

Ximen Qing, after talking to Xia about the Censor's report, was getting the presents ready to send off. He felt very depressed about things in general. Now the baby was ill too.

Yueniang sent a boy for old woman Liu and also for a doctor who specialized in children's ailments. The gate was opened, and there was much shouting and running about all night. Old woman Liu said that the baby had been frightened and that he must have met the General of the Road. "It is of no great importance," she told them. " Burn a few paper offerings and we shall get rid of the devil, sure enough." She gave them two red pills, peppermint and lamp wick, and, when the baby had taken them, he quietened and went to sleep. He stopped crying and did not disgorge his milk any more. But the fever did not leave him. Li Ping'er gave old woman Liu a tael of silver for some papers. The old woman returned with her husband and another witch-woman. They burned the papers and danced the spirit dance in the arbor.

At the fifth night watch, Ximen Qing got up to see Laibao and Xia Shou away on their errand. Then he went to Magistrate Xia's, and together they went to Dongpingfu to Hu's place to hear what news there was of Miao Qing.

After Yueniang had been told that the baby had been frightened on the way home, she reproached Ruyi'er for not looking after the child properly. "He was frightened while he was in the sedan chair," she said. "If not, why should he not have got better?"

"I wrapped him up very carefully in the bedclothes," Ruyi'er said, "and he was not frightened. You sent Huatong to follow my chair, and he was all right then. It was only when we came into the city that he suddenly began to shiver. We were quite close to home. It was then he began to refuse his milk and to cry."

Laibao and Xia Shou made all the haste they could and reached the capital in six days. They went at once to the Imperial Tutor's palace, saw Comptroller Zhai, and handed over the presents to him. Zhai read Ximen Qing's letter. "The Censor's report has not yet reached the Capital," he said. "You had better stay here for a few days. The Imperial Tutor has recently sent a memorial to his Majesty that contains seven suggestions. This has not yet been returned. By the time it does return, perhaps the Censor's report will have arrived. I will warn his Eminence, and suggest that he should do no more than send the report to the Board of Military Affairs. Then I will send word to the Minister of War, Yu, and ask him to suppress it. Tell your master there is nothing to worry about. I can promise that nothing serious will come of the matter."

He entertained the two men. Then they went to their inn to rest and wait for further news.

One day, the Memorial of the Imperial Tutor Cai came back from the Court. Laibao asked one of the officers of the Imperial Tutor's household to copy it that he might take back a copy to Ximen Qing. Comptroller Zhai wrote a letter of thanks and gave Laibao five taels of silver. The two men went home again.

When they reached Qinghe, Ximen was living in a state of extreme anxiety. While they were away Magistrate Xia had been calling every day in the hope of hearing some news of their mission. The two men went at once to the inner court and Laibao gave Ximen an account of everything that had happened. "Master Zhai," he said, "read your letter, but he said there would be nothing very serious and certainly no need for you to be anxious. This Censor's tour of duty is nearly at an end and he will be succeeded by somebody else. His report has not yet reached the Capital, and, when it does, Master Zhai will speak to the Imperial Tutor and see that, however serious it may be, his Eminence sends it to the Board of Military Affairs. Zhai himself will go there and persuade the Minister to register it but not to let it go any further. So, no matter how serious the report may be, you will suffer no harm from it."

This was a great relief to Ximen Qing. He asked how it was that the Censor's report had not yet reached the Court. "When we went to the Capital," Laibao said, "we traveled posthaste and got there in five days. On our way back we met the couriers with the report. At least, we saw post-horses with bells and riders with yellow wrappers. The pennants bore pheasants' feathers."

"So long as the document reached the Capital after you did," Ximen said, "all will be well, but if you had been too late . . ."

"There is no need to worry," Laibao said. "I have other good news for you."

"What is that?" Ximen Qing asked.

"Recently, the Imperial Tutor sent a Memorial to the Emperor with seven suggestions that his Majesty will approve. The Imperial Tutor's relative Han, the Vice President of the Board of Domestic Affairs, proposes to open the salt monopoly in Shaanxi, and, in every district, to set up official granaries for the sale of rice. Wealthy people will pay their contribution of rice to these granaries and get their official receipt from them. The government will issue salt certificates. The old grain certificates will rate at seventy percent and the new ones at thirty. Some time ago, we and your relative Qiao put in to the excise office of Gao Yang thirty thousand grain certificates and thirty thousand salt certificates. The Board of Domestic Affairs has now appointed Cai, the President of the Academy, to be Salt Commissioner for the Two Huais. He is to leave the Capital shortly. He will certainly make an excellent inspector."

Ximen asked if this was true.

"If you do not believe me," Laibao said, "here is a copy of the document." He took a paper from a letter case and handed it to Ximen Qing. Ximen looked at it, and, as there were many unusual characters, sent for

Chen Jingji to read it for him. Jingji read half of it, and then stopped. So many of the characters were strange to him. Then Shutong was sent for, and he read it with perfect ease from start to finish, for he had come from a wealthy household and had been well taught. The paper said:

> The humble memorial of Cai Jing, Great Scholar of the Hall of Supreme Authority, Prime Minister, and Duke of Lu Guo.
>
> These foolish suggestions are put forward that he may expend his futile energies upon the securing of men of capacity; that an efficient administration may be secured; the financial state of the country strengthened, and the welfare of the people fostered.
>
> Thus may the glory of the Imperial Wisdom be made manifest:
>
> **First:** the public examinations should be abolished and men should be given appointments direct from the colleges.
>
> **Second:** the hitherto existing Board of Finance should be abolished.
>
> **Third:** the present trade in salt should be done away with.
>
> **Fourth:** the promulgation of a law upon coining.
>
> **Fifth:** the buying and selling of cereals should be placed upon a sound footing.

When Ximen Qing had heard this and had read Comptroller Zhai's letter again, he knew that his present had been safely delivered, and that President Cai had been appointed Salt Commissioner, and would pass through Qinghe on his way to assume office. He was delighted. He sent Xia Shou home to give the news to Magistrate Xia, and gave Laibao five taels of silver, two jars of wine and a piece of meat. Then Laibao went to his place to rest.

CHAPTER 49
The Monk from India

Xia Shou went home and told his master the news. Then Magistrate Xia came to Ximen Qing and thanked him. "You have saved my life," he said. "Without your influence and your authority, I should have been in a very grave position."

Ximen Qing laughed. "Do not mention it. We did nothing wrong and, though the Censor spoke harshly about us, the Imperial Tutor will arrange everything." He entertained his guest in the great hall. They laughed and talked, and it was evening before Xia went home. The next day they both went to their office and attended to their duties as before.

Censor Ceng saw that, though his report had reached the Court, nothing happened. He understood that bribery had been at work, and was very indignant. He knew, moreover, that the five suggestions of the Imperial Tutor would lead to serious trouble. They would work to the detriment of the common people and the advantage of the officials. So he went himself to the Capital to put his case before the Emperor, and presented a memorial suggesting that it was well for the country that money should circulate instead of being collected and hoarded in the Capital. The new method of dealing in foodstuffs he considered impracticable. The new coinage, in which each coin was worth ten pence, had many disadvantages, and free trade in salt ought not so frequently to be abolished. He pointed out that, when such raids are made upon the people's resources, the safety of the realm is endangered.

The Imperial Tutor was furious. He told the Emperor Huizong that the Censor was rebellious and undisciplined, that he was concerning himself unduly in matters of policy. He summoned Ceng to appear before the Board of Civil Service, which degraded him and made him Magistrate of Qingzhou in Shaanxi.

The Censor and Commissioner of Shaanxi, Song Pan, was the Imperial Tutor's brother-in-law. Cai Yu secretly ordered Song Pan to accuse Ceng. Ceng's servants were arrested and persuaded to bring false accusations against their master. His name was cut out of the roll and he was banished to the Salt Mountain. So did the Imperial Tutor get his revenge.

Ximen Qing told Han Daoguo and Cui Ben to go with Master Qiao's nephew and take the grain certificates to the officer of the Board of Domestic Affairs at Gaoyangguan and register them. Laibao stayed at home to attend to the preparations for a great banquet. He also went to find out whether there was any word of the arrival of the Salt Commissioner's boat.

One day Laibao heard that Cai and Song had started together from the Capital and had now reached Dongchangfu. He brought the news to Ximen Qing, and Ximen invited Magistrate Xia to accompany him. Laibao had already visited the Commissioner on his boat and presented some gifts. Ximen Qing and Xia journeyed for fifty *li* to receive the notables at the new wharf at Bojiacun. They went on board the boat and told Cai that they would like to invite his colleague Song. Cai agreed and said that it was their intention to visit the office of the prefecture together.

Hu, the magistrate of Dongpingfu, and all his officers, military and civil, from all the districts; the scholars, Buddhist and Daoist priests, and the Masters of the Yin Yang were present to welcome the notables. They sent in their cards. Major Zhou, General Jing, and Zhang, the Captain of Militia, with horses and men, attended in full state. People were sent in advance to spread the news, and even the chickens and ducks kept out of the way. There was music to welcome Song when he entered the prefectural office at Dongpingfu. The officers presented their credentials. Song spent the night resting and, the next day, the gatekeeper came to inform him that the Salt Commissioner had come to visit him.

Censor Song immediately came out to receive him. They greeted one another and took the places proper to host and guest.

"How long do you propose to stay here?" said Song.

"I shall probably stay a day or two," Cai said. "I have a friend at Qinghe, a certain Captain Ximen, a man of excellent character, wealthy but modest. He is under the protection of the Imperial Tutor, and that is how I know him. He was good enough to come a very long way to meet me and I am going to stay with him a while."

"What rank does this Ximen hold?" Song asked.

"He is a junior magistrate," Cai said. "One of those who came to pay their respects to you yesterday."

Song ordered a servant to bring him all the visiting cards. Among them he found the names of Ximen and Xia. "Is not this the man who is a friend of Zhai the Comptroller?" he said.

"Yes," Cai said. "As a matter of fact, he is outside now. He asked me to invite you to take dinner with him."

"As the Censor for this place," said Song, "I am afraid it would be hardly becoming for me to accept."

"Why should you be afraid?" said Cai. "Our friend Zhai would like it. What harm is there in it?"

They called for their sedan chairs and made ready to start together. As soon as their order for the sedan chairs came out, word was brought to Ximen Qing. He, Laibao and Ben the Fourth rode home in great haste to make everything ready for the banquet. Awnings had already been set up outside the gate, forming a gaily decorated reception room. Two bands of musicians had been engaged and actors and other performers were in attendance.

Censor Song did not bring all his attendants, only a few men with blue pennants to clear the way, and a few officers. He and Cai seated themselves in two large sedan chairs; attendants carrying huge umbrellas accompanied them, and so they came to Ximen Qing's house.

Everybody in Dongpingfu knew of this visit, and it was especially re- marked at Qinghe. Word went from mouth to mouth that the Censor was a friend of Ximen Qing and was coming to visit him at his house. The military officers, Zhou, Jing, and Zhang, were greatly excited, and sent soldiers, both horse and foot, to take post at each end of the street. Ximen Qing dressed in black robes, wearing his ceremonial girdle, went a considerable distance to meet his guests. Then the musicians began to play, the sedan chairs reached the gate. The two officers got down from their chairs. Both wore scarlet embroidered clothes, ceremonial hats and boots, and red girdles like a stork's beak. Attendants followed them, bear- ing two large fans.

The bamboo lattices were rolled high, and embroidered screens were placed in the great hall where the two guests were to be received. At the upper end two tables were set with delicacies and sweetmeats of the most delectable variety. The two officers bowed one to the other before they entered, and, when they went in, they made a reverence to Ximen Qing. Cai summoned his servant to offer the presents he had brought for Xi- men. There were two rolls of silk, a case of collected works of literature, four parcels of tender tea shoots, and an ink slab of Duanxi stone. Song presented a red visiting card on which was written: "The respectful com- pliments of Song Qiaonian."

"The Lanxiang of your name has long been known to me," Song said. "I have only just come to this place and I am ashamed to appear before you without some offering. My brother Cai urged me to come, however, and, but for him, I should not have had the pleasure of seeing your glori- ous countenance."

Ximen Qing fell upon his knees. "Your humble servant," he said, "is but a plain soldier, one subject to your commands. It is an honor to receive from you a visit which brings enlightenment to this poor hovel." He rose and bowed with the utmost politeness, and Censor Song returned his greeting.

Then Cai invited his companion to take the place of honor and took the seat beside him. Ximen respectfully seated himself with them. When they had drunk their tea, the musicians played and the drums were beaten. Ximen Qing offered his guests wine, and set places before the table. Servants carried in the food. The banquet surpassed all powers of description. Music, songs, dances and splendor seemed to be crowded within the confines of a tiny space, and there was a marvelous abundance of refreshment. To the servants of the two censors, Ximen gave fifty bottles of wine, five hundred cakes and a hundred measures of cooked meat, and these were taken away. The subordinate officers were entertained in other rooms. That day Ximen Qing expended a thousand taels of silver.

Censor Song was a native of Nanchang in Jiangxi, a volatile fellow. He did not stay long, and listened to but one act of the play. Then he stood up. Ximen Qing pressed him to stay, and Cai also tried to persuade him. "Brother," he said, "unless you have business to attend to, why not stay a little longer? Why go away so soon?"

"Brother," said Song, "you stay. I must go to my office and see about various matters."

Ximen Qing had bidden his servants pack two complete services of gold and silver in food boxes. There were twenty such boxes. For Song there was a whole set for the table, two jars of wine, two sheep, two pairs of golden flowers, two rolls of red silk, a set of gold dishes, two silver wine pots, ten silver wine cups, two small silver jars and a pair of ivory chopsticks. There was an exactly similar set for Cai. Ximen Qing presented his list of gifts.

"I dare not accept such a present," Song said. He looked at Cai.

"Brother," said Cai, "this is your sphere of jurisdiction, and it is right and proper that you should accept. But, for me, the case is different.'"

"They are but trifles," Ximen Qing said, "so that you may drink a cup of wine. Why treat the matter as one of ceremony?"

The two officers still hesitated, but the boxes were taken away and Song could only end by accepting them.

"I have never had the pleasure of meeting you before," he said, "yet you have entertained me nobly and given me this valuable present. I do not know how I can return such kindness, but I will endeavor to do so by degrees," He said to Cai: "Brother, I must go now, but do you stay here." Then he started. Ximen Qing would have taken him well on his way, but Song begged him not to do so, bowed, and got into his chair. Ximen Qing went back to Cai. They removed their robes of ceremony and went to sit under the arbor. The musicians were sent away and only the actors remained. Ximen called for food, and rare dishes and fruits were set before them. They settled down to enjoy their wine.

"Brother Song and I have visited you today," Cai said. "That was pleasure enough for us, but for all this excellent entertainment and the rest I don't know how to thank you."

Ximen Qing smiled. "I only fear that everything has been too poor for you. All I could do was but a slight indication of my feelings." Then he said: "What is his Lordship's honorable title?"

"His name is Songquan," Cai said. "He would not have come today, but I told him you were under the protection of the Prime Minister and he decided to come. He knows that you and Zhai are connected."

"My relative Zhai must have spoken to him," Ximen Qing said. "I must say his manner seems to me a little strange."

"He is from Jiangxi," Cai said, "but I don't think there is anything strange about him. Perhaps the first time he meets you he thinks he must stand on his dignity." He smiled.

"It is getting late," Ximen said, "and you cannot return to your boat tonight."

"The boat sails tomorrow morning," Cai said.

"Stay the night here," Ximen said, "and tomorrow I will take you to your boat."

"You are very kind indeed," Censor Cai said. He dismissed all his servants but two, bidding the others come for him the following morning.

When Ximen saw that they had gone, he whispered to Daian and told him to go to the bawdy house for Dong Jiao'er and Han Yuchuan. "Bring them in by the back door," he said, "and don't let anyone see you." The boy went away. Ximen returned to the table and drank wine with the Censor. The actors sang for them.

"How long did you stay at home?" Ximen asked, "and how is your lady mother?"

"My old mother is very well. I stayed about six months; then I went back to the Court. Unfortunately an accusation was brought against me by Cao He. I and thirteen others were brought before the Academy of History, and we were all reduced to provincial rank. That is how I came to be appointed Salt Commissioner. Song is a favorite of the Imperial Tutor."

"Where is venerable Master An now?" Ximen Qing said.

"An Fengshan has been appointed to the Board of Works," Cai said. "He has gone to Qingzhou as Superintendent of the Imperial Forests. That is quite a good post for him."

Ximen Qing called for the actors. When they had served wine, he asked them to sing "The Fisherman's Pride." While they were singing, Daian came and asked Ximen to go out and speak to him. "Dong Jiao'er and Han Yuchuan are here," he said. "They are in the Great Lady's room."

"Tell the sedan chair men to take the chairs away," said Ximen. Daian told him that he had already done this. Then Ximen went to his wife's room. The two singing girls kowtowed to him.

"Today," Ximen said to them, "I want you to wait upon his Excellency Cai. He is both Censor and Commissioner of Salt. If you are careful what you are about, he will certainly make you a handsome present."

Yuchuan laughed. "You need not be so explicit. We understand."

"He is a Southerner," Ximen Qing said, "and likes things done in the Southern style. You must not be too shy with your hands and feet."

"Mother," Dong Jiao'er said to Wu Yueniang, "do you hear that? Father is like one of those ram's-horn onions that is planted against a southern wall and grows hotter and hotter. We are to kowtow before a royal palace, but we mustn't drink the water in the well."

Ximen Qing laughed and went back to the outer court. When he came to the second door, he met Laibao and Chen Jingji with a visiting card. They gave the card to him and said: "Your relative, Master Qiao, says that if his Excellency the Censor is not engaged now will you please speak about this matter to him. He supposes that his Excellency will be going away tomorrow, and asked us to write this card." Ximen Qing told Laibao to go with him. The man waited outside the window of the arbor.

Ximen drank with Cai. After a while he said: "There is a little business I should like to mention, but I hesitate to trouble you."

"Tell me anything that is in your mind," said Cai. "Your commands shall be obeyed, whatever they may be."

"Last year," Ximen said, "one of my relatives paid the rice tribute and was given some salt certificates. He was appointed Collector at Yangzhou, within your jurisdiction. It would be very kind of you, when you take up your appointment, if you would let them have their salt a little earlier." He handed to Censor Cai the paper that Laibao had brought. It said: 'Laibao and Cui Ben are entitled to 30,000 *yin* of salt. May it be granted them as early as possible.' Censor Cai smiled.

"This is a trifle," he said, "I should like to see Laibao." Ximen Qing summoned Laibao to kowtow to the Censor. "When I get to Yangzhou," Cai said, "come to my office, and I will see that the matter is settled one month earlier for you than for anyone else."

"It is very kind of you," Ximen said, "but ten days would be quite sufficient."

Cai put the paper in his sleeve. Shutong served wine and the actors sang again. When the song was over, it was getting late. "I have burdened you for a whole day," Cai said, "and I must not drink any more." He stood up. The servants were about to light the lamps, but Ximen Qing stopped them.

"I am going to take his Excellency to the inner court to change his clothes," he said. He took Cai to the garden. They looked around it for a while, then Ximen took his guest to the Hall of the Kingfisher. The lattice was rolled down, candles were burning brightly, and wine and refreshments had been set out.

Ximen Qing dismissed the actors. Shutong saw that everything was cleared away in the arbor, and the corner gate was closed. The two singing girls, beautifully dressed, came to the steps and kowtowed four times to the Censor.

> Their faces so charming, their dresses gold embroidered
> They do not trouble the fragrant dust
> As they come down the stairs.
> With water splashes still wet upon their silken skirts
> As though they were just back from Wu Mountain
> Where they had brought the rain.

Cai seemed dumbfounded when he saw them. "You are too kind to me," he said. "This is indeed too much."

Ximen Qing smiled. "It is not very different," he said, "from that entertainment that once there was upon the Eastern Mountains."

"I fear I have not the learning of Wang Anshi," Cai said, "though you, Sir, have the elevated sensibilities of Wang Yuzhun." In the moonlight he took the hands of the two singing girls, feeling as excited as Liu Yuan at the Tiantai. They went into the Hall of the Kingfisher. Writing materials were lying there and, taking paper and brush, Cai prepared to write a poem to give to the girls. Ximen Qing told Shutong to take the ink slab, grind some thick ink, and arrange the flower-patterned paper. His Excellency was possessed of the accomplishments becoming his position. Taking the brush, he wrote without any hesitation, the characters springing like dragons beneath it. Under the lamplight he finished the poem without once stopping.

> Six months have passed since last I visited you
> But brush and paper wait for me in this room.
> The rain is over. Shutong is tending the sweet-smelling herbs
> The wind has changed. An angel walks among the flower beds.
> When I would drink my fill, the bells ring urgently
> When I have written my poem, the night watch will call me away

But when I go from you, I must expect new sorrow
I know not when I shall return.

When Cai had finished this poem, he bade Shutong put it on the wall
in memory of his visit. Then he asked the names of the two girls. One said:
"My name is Dong Jiao'er," and the other: "My name is Han Yuchuan."
Then Cai asked them by what familiar names they were called. "We are
but humble girls," Dong Jiao'er said, "it would not befit us to have familiar names." But the Censor pressed them, and at last Han Yuchuan said:
"Mine is Yuqing [Treasure of Jade]." Dong Jiao'er said: "Mine is Weixian
[Fairy of the Purple Flower]." The last one delighted Cai particularly, and
he did not forget it. He asked Shutong to bring the chess pieces and played
a game with Dong Jiao'er. Ximen Qing looked on while Yuchuan served
the wine and Shutong sang. The Censor won, and Dong Jiao'er had to
drink a cup of wine, but first she offered one to the victor. At the same
time Han Yuchuan offered a cup to Ximen Qing. They played a second
game. This time Dong Jiao'er won, and she quickly offered wine to the
Censor. Ximen drank again.

Then Cai said: "It is late and I can drink no more." They went out and
stood for a while amid the flowers. It was the middle of the fourth month,
and the moon had just risen.

"It is still early," Ximen Qing said, "and Han Yuchuan has not offered
wine to you yet."

"That is true," the Censor said. "Let her bring a cup here, and I will
drink it among the flowers."

Han Yuchuan brought a large gold cup shaped like a peach blossom
and offered it with her slender fingers. Dong Jiao'er stood beside her with
a dish of fruit. The Censor drank his wine and offered a cup to Dong Jiao'er. Then he said to Ximen Qing: "I have indeed taken too much wine.
Will you not ask your servants to clear away?" He took Ximen Qing's
hand. "You show me so much kindness," he said, "that my mind is confused. If you had not been by nature a scholar, you could not have been
so kind. I have not forgotten the loan you made me a few months ago. I
told the Comptroller all about it, and, if it should happen that promotion
comes to me, I shall never dare to forget your generosity."

"Please do not mention it," Ximen Qing said. "Think no more of it."

Han Yuchuan saw the Censor holding Dong Jiao'er 's hand. She knew
what this meant and went to the inner court. When she came to the Upper
Room, Yueniang said to her: "Why did you not stay?" Han Yuchuan smiled.

"He has Dong Jiao'er," she said. "I was not wanted any longer." A little
later, Ximen Qing said good night to the Salt Commissioner and came

in. He told Laixing to prepare food, wine, cakes and dishes, and, the next morning before dawn, to go with the cooks to the Temple of Eternal Felicity, where they would take leave of his Excellency. He must not forget the two young actors.

"But tomorrow is the Second Lady's birthday," Laixing said, "and there are not enough people to attend to things at home."

"Let Qitong buy the things," Ximen said. "The cooks must use the large oven."

Shutong and Daian cleared everything away and took a pot of excellent tea to Cai in the garden. In the Hall of the Kingfisher, the bed and furniture were arranged to perfection. Cai saw that Dong Jiao'er was carrying a speckled bamboo fan of gilded paper. On it was painted in black ink a picture of orchids growing beside a rivulet. She asked him to write a poem upon it for her. "I can't think what to write," he said. "I had better take your other name, Fairy of the Purple Flower." Taking up a brush, he wrote four columns upon the fan.

> All is still and silent in the courtyard
> The moonbeams cast their light upon the windows.
> They meet, so chance has ordered, and the night is early
> He of the purple shrub and the maid of purple blossom.

Dong Jiao'er made a reverence to the Censor and thanked him. They went to bed. Shutong, Daian and his Excellency's servants slept in a room near by.

The next morning the Censor gave Dong Jiao'er a tael of silver wrapped in red paper. She took it to the inner court and showed it to Ximen Qing. Ximen smiled. "He is a civil officer, and, of course, could not make you a very large present. This is as high a mark as you can expect." He told Yueniang to give each of the girls five *qian* of silver and let them out by the back way. Shutong brought water and aided his master to dress. Then Ximen Qing went to the great hall and ate rice gruel with Censor Cai.

Cai's servants came with horses and a sedan chair. He said good-bye to Ximen Qing and thanked him repeatedly.

"Please do not forget the matter of which I spoke to you yesterday," Ximen said. "I will write to you when you reach your post. And I am greatly obliged to you."

"There is no need to write," Cai said. "Send a servant with a blank sheet of paper and I will do anything you ask."

They mounted their horses and, followed by their attendants, went as far as the Temple of Eternal Felicity. There they lunched in the Abbot's parlor. Laixing and the cooks had made all kinds of preparations and the two young actors, Li Ming and Wu Hui, were waiting. They drank a few cups of wine together and Cai stood up. The horses and sedan chair were waiting outside the gate. Ximen Qing spoke to him about the Miao Qing affair. "Miao Qing," he said, "is a friend of mine who was falsely accused by the late censor. The papers for his arrest have been sent to Yangzhou. The case has already been settled here, so, if you should see his Excellency Song in Yangzhou, please speak in his favor. I shall be very grateful to you."

"Do not worry," Cai said. "When I see my brother Song, I will ask him to free Miao Qing if he should be arrested." Ximen Qing bowed and thanked him.

> Justice and friendship lie in opposing camps
> Friendship and justice cannot be reconciled.
> He who deals justly, loses all his friends
> He who to friendship yields, abandons justice.

(Some time later, when Censor Song was going to Jinan, he happened to be traveling on the same boat with Cai. The officers arrested Miao Qing, but Cai said to his friend: "This is an affair that goes back to Censor Ceng's administration. Why should you do anything about it?" So Miao Qing was set at liberty and orders were sent to Dongpingfu that the two boatmen were to be executed at once, and the boy Antong allowed to go.)

Ximen Qing would have gone all the way to the boat with Cai, but the Censor asked him not to do so. "Pray do not come any farther," he said. "We will part here."

"Take great care of yourself," Ximen Qing said. "I shall send my servant for news of you."

Cai got into his sedan chair and was carried away. Ximen Qing went back to the Abbot's rooms and the Abbot came to make reverence to him and offer tea. Ximen returned the greeting. He saw that the Abbot's eyebrows were white as snow. "Venerable Sir," he said, "how old are you?"

"The humble monk before you," replied the Abbot, "is seventy-four years of age."

"You seem very strong," Ximen said, and asked his name in religion.

"My name is Daojian," the Abbot said. Ximen asked how many novices the Abbot had.

"No more than two now," the Abbot said, "but there are more than thirty wandering priests in my temple."

"Your temple," Ximen Qing said, "is very large and spacious, but it seems to need repair."

"The truth is," the Abbot said, "that this temple was built by the venerable Zhou Xiu, but we have no fixed endowment, and it is almost utterly ruined now."

"So your temple belongs to Major Zhou? I remember now that his estate is quite close. You ought to ask him to open a subscription. I should be glad to help."

Daojian made a reverence and thanked him. Ximen Qing told Daian to give the Abbot a tael of silver. "I have given you much trouble today," he said. The Abbot apologized for the inadequacy of his preparations. Then Ximen told the priest that he would like to go to the inner court to change his clothes. Daojian told one of his novices to open the door. Behind the Abbot's quarters, Ximen found a large hall, as large as five rooms. A number of wandering monks were chanting from their sacred books and beating their wooden fish. Ximen looked around the hall. There was one monk of very curious appearance. His head was like a leopard's and his eyes were round. His color was that of purple liver, and upon his head he wore a cock's crest. His tattered robe was flesh-colored; his shaggy beard all matted together. By all seeming he might have been a veritable Arhat, a fiery-tempered dragon. He was lying upon the bench of contemplation, his head bowed and his shoulders hunched upon his chest. The stream of matter from his nostrils looked like chopsticks of jade.

Ximen Qing thought that this must certainly be a wonder-working monk, so unusual was his appearance. "I will arouse him," he said to himself, "and question him." Then, in a loud voice, he said to the holy man: "Where do you come from? Where is your monastery?" There was no answer. He repeated his questions, but still there was no reply. He asked a third time, and now the monk came down from the bench of contemplation, stretched himself, put forth a hand and straightened his body, and opened one eye. He made a slight inclination of the head to Ximen Qing and said in a hoarse voice:

"Why do you ask me these questions? I am only a poor monk. My name is everywhere the same. I come from a foreign land, from the deep pine forests of India, from the temple of the Frozen Mansions. I roam about the world, dispensing remedies to give ease to men. What would you say to me?"

"Since you have remedies to give ease to men," Ximen Qing said, "I should be glad to have something that would inspire me with new ardor. Have you any such medicine?"

"I have," the Indian Monk said.

"I should like to ask you to come to my house," Ximen Qing said. "Will you come?"

"I will come. I will come."

"If you are willing," Ximen Qing said, "let us start at once."

The Indian Monk rose, took his iron staff and a long leathern bag in which were two gourds of medicine, and they went out of the great hall. Ximen told Daian to bring two donkeys and bade him ride together with the monk.

"Not so," said the monk. "You go first on your horse. I need no animal on which to ride, but I shall be there before you."

"This must indeed be a wonder-working monk," Ximen said to himself, "or he would not make such rash promises." He was afraid the monk might go somewhere else, and told Daian to accompany him. He took leave of the Abbot and mounted his horse, and all his servants followed him. It was the seventeenth day of the fourth month, Wang Liu'er's birthday. It was also the birthday of Li Jiao'er, and a few ladies had come to congratulate her.

In the afternoon Wang Liu'er sent her brother Wang Jing to ask Ximen Qing to go and see her. She had no one else to send. "Go and look out for Daian," she told him, "and, if you do not see him, wait outside the gate."

Wang Jing waited at the gate. When he had waited two hours or so, Wu Yueniang and Li Jiao'er came out with old woman Li. Yueniang, seeing a small boy about fifteen years old, asked him what he wanted.

"I have come from the Han household to see my brother An," he said.

"Which brother An?" Yueniang asked.

Ping'an was standing near, and, fearing lest Yueniang should discover that the boy came from Wang Liu'er, he went forward and pushed him aside.

"He has come from Han Daoguo," he said. "He wants to see Daian to find out when Han is to come."

Yueniang was deceived. She said no more and went back into the house. Then Daian and the Indian Monk came to the gate. Daian's legs were very weary and his whole body was covered with sweat. He was in a very bad way, but the Indian Monk was perfectly comfortable and did not even puff. Ping'an told Daian about the visit from Wang Jing. "The Great Lady saw him, but, fortunately, I was here, and passed the matter over. Otherwise the cat would have been out of the bag. If Mother asks you any questions tell her the same story that I did."

Daian opened his eyes wide and fanned himself. "My luck is certainly out today," he said. "Father told me to bring this bald rascal home with me and we have walked all the way from the temple without stopping. I can hardly breathe. Father said we were to take two donkeys, but the monk would not hear of it. It is all very well for him to walk that long way, but my poor legs have certainly suffered. The soles are torn off my boots and my feet are torn too. What a dirty business!" "What does Father want with him?" Ping'an said.

"Who knows?" Daian said. "Perhaps he hopes to get some medicine out of him."

As they were talking, they heard the sound of the attendants clearing the way. Ximen Qing arrived. When he found the monk already there, he said: "Master, you are indeed a wonder worker to get here before I did." He asked the monk to go into the great hall. Ximen Qing gave his clothes to Shutong and changed his hat. He sat down with the monk, and they drank tea. The Indian Monk gazed around the great hall and saw how deep and spacious it was; how large and quiet the courtyard. Over the door hung a bamboo lattice made of shrimps' feelers with a tortoiseshell design. The floor was covered with rugs, with a pattern of lions rolling balls. In the middle of the hall was a table colored black, with dragonflies on the legs and the praying mantis upon the edges. There was a marble screen upon the table, with a fretted pattern and a base shaped like a mountain. Around it were several large cedar chairs, substantial and heavy, with eels' heads for decoration. The pictures on the walls were hung on purple rods bound with silk. The ends of the rolls were of cornelian.

When the Indian Monk had looked around him, Ximen Qing said to him: "Master, do you drink wine?"

"I drink wine and eat meat," the monk said.

Ximen sent a boy to the kitchen to tell them not to prepare vegetarian dishes but to bring wine and food. As it was Li Jiao'er's birthday, all kinds of food were already prepared. A table was set and the food brought. There were three or four plates of fruits, four smaller and four larger dishes to accompany the wine. There was one dish of fish head, one of preserved duck, one of chicken and one of sea perch. Then four dishes to be eaten with rice, one of little nuts of meat roasted with ram's-horn onions, one of little pasties of finely minced meat, shaped like a periwinkle, one of plump sausages, and one of bright and slippery eels. Then soup was brought. In the soup were two balls of meat and a garnished sausage between them. This soup was known as "The Dragon playing with two pearls." Then there was a great dish of stuffed buns with little openings at the top.

Ximen Qing asked the monk to eat, and bade Qintong bring a jar of wine with a round handle, a beak-shaped mouth and a neck like that of a chicken. The boy opened a large jar that had come from Yaozhou. From it he poured a tiny stream of wine as white as snow, extremely fortifying. He poured it into a high-stemmed cup shaped like a lotus upside down. He handed the cup to the Indian Monk, who took it and emptied it at one draft. More dishes were brought, one of sausages about an inch long, one of preserved goose neck. There were fruits for the monk to eat with his wine, grapes mottled as though they had the pox and red plums juicy at the center. Finally a great bowl of noodles and eels with vegetables.

The monk gobbled everything up till his eyes almost stood out of his head. Then he said: "I have had enough." Ximen Qing told a boy to clear away the table. Then he asked the monk to give him some medicines to enhance his skill in the arts of love.

"I have one medicine made by Laozi, to whom the Queen Mother of the West gave the secret. None are able to secure this medicine but those of whom I think well. You have been kind to me and I will give you a few pills." He took a gourd from his long bag and emptied about a hundred pills. "Take one on each occasion," he said, "but no more. Take it with a drop of spirits." He opened the other gourd and took from it some red powder about two *qian*'s weight. "Every time you use it," said the monk, "take two grains and no more. Should you feel a burning sensation, take your weapon in your hand and stroke your thighs a hundred times or so. Then all will be well. Be judicious in your use of these remedies and give none to anyone else."

Ximen Qing took the medicines in both hands. "Tell me," he said, "what is the merit of this medicine?"

> Shaped like an egg
> Yellow like a duck
> In three successive processes Laozi prepared it
> At the bidding of the Queen Mother.
> To him who glances at it heedlessly
> It seems like earth or dung
> But, when its merits are known, its worth is more than jewels.
> No gold will buy it
> And jade is valueless compared with it.
> Though you are girt with gold and robed in purple
> Though you are dressed in sable
> And ride upon the plumpest chargers,
> Though you uphold the pillars of the state
> Take but a speck of this, set it upon you, then
> Rush like a whirlwind to the bridal chamber
> There you will find spring always young
> All will be bright and gay.
> There will be no ruins on the jade mountain
> And the moonbeams will shine bright upon your window.
> The first engagement will leave you full of vigor
> The second, even stronger than before.

Though twelve exquisite beauties, all arrayed in scarlet, wait your
   onset,
You may enjoy each one, according to your fancy
And, all night through, erect your spear will stand.
Soon, new strength will be given to limbs and belly
It will refresh the testicles, invigorate the penis.
In a hundred days, hair and beard will be black once more
In a thousand days, your body will know its power.
Your teeth will be strong, your eyes more bright,
Your manhood stiffened. Then at the first planting
The seed will germinate.
I fear that this may seem beyond belief.
Pray try the medicine on the cat.
After three days he'll burn with fire
Four days will see him quite beyond control
And, if a white cat, he will soon be black
Then cease to piss and shit, and so will die.

Though in the summer you may sleep exposed
And in the winter plunge yourself in water
Yet, if you cannot keep your bowels free
Your hair you'll surely lose.

Each time, take but a grain or so.
Your weapon will be merciless.
Ten women in one night will be as one to you
You'll feel no slackening of vital power.
The old woman will knit her brows
The young one's strength will hardly stay the course.

When you are sated, and would give up the fight
Swallow a mouthful of cold water. Then withdraw your weapon
You will not be harmed.
In pleasure and enjoyment you will spend your nights
The joys of spring will fill the orchid chamber.
I make this gift only to those
Who worthily appreciate its qualities.
Take it, I pray, and may your manly vigor flourish evermore.

Ximen Qing listened. When the old monk had done, he asked for the
recipe. "When I send for a doctor," he said, "I insist upon having a good
one, and, when I have medicine, I like to know what it's made of. When I
have finished it, and can't get any more from you, it will be most awkward.
I don't mind how much you ask, you shall have it." He said to Daian: "Go

to the back and bring thirty taels of white gold." He offered the gold to the monk and again asked for the recipe. The monk laughed.

"I am a poor monk," he said, "and I roam all over the world. Gold is valueless to me. Keep your money." He rose and prepared to go away.

Ximen Qing saw that he would not get the recipe from the old man. He said: "If you will not take my gold, let me offer you a roll of cloth, fifteen feet long, to make a habit for yourself." He bade a servant bring a roll and presented it to the Indian Monk with both hands. The monk thanked him and made a reverence. Before he went away, he cautioned Ximen Qing, telling him not to take more than the proper dose. Then he picked up his long bag and his staff, went out of the door, and mysteriously disappeared.

CHAPTER 50
The Indian Monk's Medicine

Before she drew the perfumed curtains
And settled to the work of love,
Her brows were knit in sadness at the thought
The night would be so short.
She bade her lover hasten to the bed
And warm the silk-embroidered coverlets.
Then was their love as that of butterflies and bees.
They stripped themselves: their passion knew no bounds.
She left the lamp to burn beside the curtains
That he from time to time might gaze
Upon the beauty of her face.

It was the birthday of Li Jiao'er. Nun Wang came from the temple of Guanyin, bringing with her Nun Xue from the Temple of Lotus Blossoms. With them came two young novices, Miaofeng and Miaoqu. Wu Yueniang had been told that Xue was deeply versed in matters of religion and hastened to welcome her. The nun was wearing a religious hat, and a long robe the color of tea leaves. Her hair was tonsured. She was very stout and big. Her mouth was like that of a fish; her cheeks like those of a pig. When she came in, she made reverence to Yueniang and the others; and Yueniang and the others returned her greeting. The nun raised her eyebrows, closed her eyes, put on all sorts of airs, and spoke in an extremely affected voice. The ladies addressed her as "Noble Xue." She, in return, called Wu Yueniang Buddha of the Household or else My Lady. This made Yueniang think highly of her.

That day Aunt Wu and Aunt Yang had come to call and Yueniang entertained them so well that the tables overflowed. It was far beyond the ordinary range of entertainment.

The two novices, Miaofeng and Miaoqu, were no more than fourteen or fifteen years old, and they were very sedate. They were given something to eat and drink. Then everybody went to the upper room, and the ladies listened to a sermon from the nun.

Yueniang saw Shutong carrying things from the outer court and said to him: "Has that monk who eats meat and drinks wine gone yet?"

"Yes," Shutong said, "he has just gone. Father saw him to the door."

Aunt Wu asked: "Where did he meet that monk?"

"My husband went to see Censor Cai on his way," Yueniang said, "and he brought the monk back with him from the temple. He eats meat and drinks wine. My husband has been asking him for some medicine or other. The monk would take no money, and I have no idea how they got on with their business."

"The question of taking meat and wine is one of great delicacy," Nun Xue said. "Nuns generally observe the vow of abstinence, but monks do not seem to trouble much about it. As a matter of fact, the Scriptures say that, if we take but a mouthful of meat, we shall suffer for it in the next life."

"We eat meat every day," Aunt Wu said, "so we must be committing a great many sins."

"Oh, but it is different for you," the nun said. "You are able to enjoy meat as a reward for virtue in your last life. It is right and proper that you should enjoy both wealth and comfort. If plants are set in the ground in the spring, we may expect a harvest in the autumn."

Meanwhile, Ximen Qing had parted from the Indian monk and returned to his room. Daian whispered to him: "Aunt Han has sent her brother to ask you to go to her. It is her birthday today and she would very much like to see you."

Ximen Qing now had the medicine the monk had given him, and he desired nothing better than to try its effects. Wang Liu'er's invitation came at the right moment. He told Daian to prepare his horse and sent Qintong to the woman's house with a jar of wine. Then he went to Pan Jinlian's room for his case of instruments. Wearing plain clothes, with an ordinary hat and eyeshades, he rode to Wang Liu'er's house. When he got there, he told Qintong to stay and sent Daian back with the horse. "If anyone asks where I am," he told the boy, " say that I am going through the accounts at the house in Lion Street." Daian went back on his master's horse.

Wang Liu'er came out and kowtowed to Ximen Qing. Then she sat down beside him. "I only asked you to come that you might have some amusement," she said. "It was good of you to send the wine."

"I had forgotten that it is your birthday today," Ximen said. "I have been to say farewell to someone outside the city and have only this moment come back." He took a present from his sleeve and gave it to her. "I have brought you something," he said. The woman took the gift and examined it. It was a pair of gold pins with the lucky character *shou*.

"It is very pretty," Wang Liu'er said, and made a reverence to thank him. Ximen gave her five *qian* of silver and asked her to give a boy something and send him for a jar of Southern spirits. Wang Liu'er laughed. "Are you tired of ordinary wine," she said, "that you need Southern spirits?" But she hastened to give the boy five *fen* and sent him for the spirits. Then she took Ximen's cloak and asked him to go to the inner room. She made some excellent tea for him and set out a small table. They played dominoes for a while, then she warmed some wine.

Daian went home. He was very weary after walking so far with the monk. He went to sleep and slept till evening. Then he woke up, rubbed his eyes, and saw that it was late. He went to the inner court to get a lantern and make ready to go for Ximen Qing. But he stood there for a while without doing anything. Yueniang spoke to him. "Your father saw the monk to the door, but, instead of coming to change his clothes, he suddenly went out. Where did he go?"

"Father went to Lion Street to inspect the accounts," Daian said.

"He can't be inspecting accounts all day," said Yueniang.

"No," Daian said. "When he had finished the books, he had something to drink all by himself."

"All by himself, indeed!" Yueniang said. "You are lying. A boy came from Han Daoguo after him. What did he want?"

"The boy came to find out when Uncle Han would be here."

"You young rascal!" Yueniang said. "You are up to some trick or other."

Daian dared say no more. Yueniang told Xiaoyu to give him a lantern. "Tell your father," she said, "that the Second Lady is waiting for him to come and celebrate her birthday."

Daian went to the shop. Shutong and Clerk Fu were sitting behind the counter. On it were a bottle of wine, several dishes, and a plate of tripe. Ping'an came in bringing two jars of fish paste. "Excellent!" said Daian, putting down his lantern, "I have come just in time." Then he said jokingly to Shutong: "Ah, you naughty little strumpet. I have been looking everywhere for you, and you have been hiding here all this time, drinking."

"What did you want me for?" Shutong said. "Do you wish me to adopt you as my grandson for a while?"

"Little boy," Daian said, "would you bandy words with me ? I was looking for you because I want to do some business with your behind." He pushed him onto the couch and kissed him, but the boy freed himself.

"You queer creature," he said, "I find it hard to scold you as I should like. Now you've hurt my mouth and knocked my hat off."

Clerk Fu saw Shutong's hat on the ground. "Why, that's a new hat," he said, and told Ping'an to pick it up before somebody stepped on it.

Shutong picked up the hat and threw it on a couch. His face was very red.

"Well, you strumpet," Daian said, "I was only playing with you. Why do you get so angry?" He dragged Shutong to the bed and spat in his mouth. They overturned the wine, and it was spilled on the counter. Clerk Fu was afraid it would stain the account books. He hastily found a cloth and dried it up.

"Don't play the fool any more," he said, "or you will get angry with one another."

"I don't know where this strumpet can have been brought up," Daian said, "to make him as stubborn as this." Shutong's hair was in disorder.

"A game is a game," he said, "but this is not a game. You have filled my mouth with your filthy spittle."

"Ah, you slave," said Daian, "this is not the first time you have swallowed such a liquid. You are always doing it, and who can tell how often?"

Ping'an heated some wine and gave it to Daian. "Drink this and go for our master. You can settle with him when you come back."

"Yes," Daian said, "wait for me. When I come back, I will have a word with you. Unless I make you see spirits and ghosts, you will think I am not to be feared. I shall spit on you again. I am the son of no human parents, so I can do whatever I like." He drank his wine, summoned two small boys to accompany him with the lantern, and himself rode on horseback. When he came to Wang Liu'er's house, he knocked at the door and asked Qintong where their master was. "He is asleep," said Qintong. They shut the gate and went to the kitchen.

There, old woman Feng said to him: "Your Aunt Han waited a long time for you, but you did not come. Here is your supper." She took from a cupboard a plate of ass's flesh, a dish of cold roast chicken, two bowls of birthday noodles, and a pot of wine.

Daian drank some wine. Then he said to Qintong: "Come here. I can't drink all this wine. You must drink some for me."

"It is yours," said Qintong. "Drink it yourself." Daian said he had already had some wine. The two boys finished it off together.

Then Daian said to old woman Feng: "If you will excuse me, there is something I should like to tell you. You are really attached to the household of our Sixth Lady and are supposed to work only for her. But I am always finding you here working for Aunt Han. I am afraid I shall have to tell the Sixth Lady."

The old woman cut him short. "Oh, you funny young monkey," she said. "You keep quiet! If you say a word to her, she will never forgive me and I shall not be able to go and see her."

While Daian and old woman Feng were talking, Qintong slyly went to the window of the inner room, listened, and peeped in to see what was going on there.

Ximen Qing took a pill with the spirit, undressed himself and sat down on the side of the bed. Then he opened the case in which he kept his instruments. First he put the silver clasp on the root of his penis, and fixed a sulfur ring on top of it. Then he took a little of the red powder from a silver box, no more than the prescribed dose, and put it into the horse's eye. The medicine worked at once. The penis's erection was amazingly aggressive; its head swelled and the single eye opened wide; the lateral sinews stood out plainly; it was as dark as liver in color, seven inches long, and much thicker than usual. Ximen Qing was highly pleased: he decided that the medicine was a very fine thing. She sat naked on his knee, took his penis in her hands and said: "So this is why you wished to drink spirits. You wished to make him like this." She asked Ximen where he had obtained the medicine, and he told her about the Indian Monk.

She laid herself upon the bed, with two pillows under her. He wanted to put his penis to work, but its head was so swollen that it was a long time before he met with any success, and even then he made very little progress. Eventually the juices of love flowed from her and the path became gradually easier; the prick advanced, but its head was hardly covered. Then the wine that he had drunk came to the rescue; he withdrew a little, then plunged in deep and enjoyed untold rapture. She also had an exquisite orgasm; she lay on the bed as if unable to move, and said tearfully, "Dearest of men, your wonderful prick has killed me." Soon she whispered, "My darling, my dearest, would you like to enjoy the flower of my bottom?" He turned her onto her stomach and his penis returned to action, so violently that it made a loud noise. "Shove, darling, shove," cried Wang Liu'er, "don't be afraid. If you like, bring a candle, and the pleasure will be greater." The candle was moved nearer, and below him she opened her legs wide. Ximen withdrew and plunged in, while she moved her thighs to meet him and titillated the flower in her womb with her trembling hand.

"I am going to send your husband to Yangzhou," Ximen Qing said. "He shall go with Laibao and Cui Ben to get the salt. When that business is done, I will send him to Huzhou to buy some silk."

"Darling," said Wang Liu'er, "send him where you like. Why should you keep him here in idleness? But who will take charge of the shop?"

"I will put Ben the Fourth to look after the shop," Ximen said.

"Yes," said Wang Liu'er, "Ben the Fourth can look after it. That is a good idea."

So these two went about the business of love and Qintong watched them through the window. Daian came along from the kitchen and tapped

Qintong on the back. "You must not stand here," he said. "Come away before they get up." Qintong went with Daian, and Daian said to him: "In the lane behind here there is a bawdy house where there are two young girls who have but lately come. One day when I was riding that way, I happened to see them. It was at Long-legged Lu's place. One is called Jin'er and the other Sai'er. Neither of them is more than eighteen. We will make the other boys stay here, and we will go and have some fun with the girls."

They told the boys to watch the door, washed their hands, and said: "If we are wanted, come to the lane behind and call us." Then they went off to the lane. The moon was shining. The lane was known as Butterfly Alley. There were not more than ten houses in it and all were for the accommodation of the public.

Daian was a little drunk. He made a loud rat-tat at the door. Some time passed. The brothel keeper Wang Ba and the procuress Long-legged Lu had been weighing silver with a balance by the light of a candle when in rushed the two boys like a couple of demons. The light was blown out, but the brothel keeper recognized Daian as Ximen Qing's servant and asked them to take a seat.

"Call the two singing girls to sing us a song," said Daian.

"I am afraid you are too late, masters," Wang Ba the brothel keeper said. "They have both got visitors."

Daian wasted no words, but dashed into the inner room. There was no light but that of the moon, but he could see two men with white felt hats on the bed. One was actually lying on the bed and the other was taking off his boots. "Who is this?" one of them cried.

"My dagger to your mother's cunt," Daian said, and let fly his fist.

"Ai ya," cried the man. He ran away without troubling to put on his boots. The other got off the bed and ran away too. Daian demanded that the lamps be lit.

"The thieves, the rogues!" he cried. "How dare they ask who I am? I would have pulled out all their hair. It is lucky for them I let them get away. I ought to have sent them to the police court and let them taste the new thumbscrews there."

Long-legged Lu came and lighted the lamps. "Please do not be angry, young masters," she said. "They were strangers and did not know you. Don't treat it too seriously." She told the two girls to sing for the boys.

The two girls were wearing dresses of red and white, and their hair was done like a bundle of silk. "We did not expect you," they said. "It is late, and we have made no preparations." They brought four dishes of dried fruits, ducks' eggs, dried prawns and salt fish, besides pig's head and sausages. Daian looked closely at the girls. Sai'er had a tiny pink silk satchel for perfume, and he gave her his handkerchief in exchange for it. Then wine was brought. Sai'er took a cup and poured wine for Daian. Jin'er took up her lute, and, after offering wine to Qintong, sang this song:

> In the camp of the flowers of the mist
> Life is not easy.
> I may not choose to sit, or yet to stand
> All day I must be ready to welcome strangers.
> On me the fortune of this house depends
> When evening comes, the procuress
> Makes me give up my earnings.
> What does she care whether I live or die?
> I stand beside the gate till midnight
> When I come in, none asks if I am hungry.
> If I must live for but a few years more
> Among the flowers of the mist
> My life will be a living death.
> The tears drop from my cheeks like falling petals
> I cannot hold them back;
> Only when the iron tree comes into blossom,
> Will I ever get my reward.

Jin'er finished her song, and Sai'er gave Daian a cup of wine. Then she, in turn, took the lute and was about to sing when a boy suddenly came in. Daian rose and said to Sai'er: "I will come and see you another day." Then he went back to Wang Liu'er's house, where Ximen Qing had got up and was drinking with his lover.

The two boys went to the kitchen and asked old woman Feng if their master had called for them. "No," she said, "he asked if his horse had come, and I said it had. That was all."

The boys sat down and asked old woman Feng to give them some tea. While they were drinking it, Daian told the other boys to light the lantern and bring out the horse.

Ximen Qing got up to go. "The wine is good and hot," Wang Liu'er said to him. "Won't you drink another cup, or are you going to have more when you reach home?"

"No, I'm not going to drink any more at home," Ximen Qing said. He drank the cup she offered him.

"When will you come again?" the woman asked.

"I will come when I have sent your husband on this business." The maid brought a cup of tea so that Ximen Qing might rinse his mouth. Wang Liu'er took him to the door; he mounted his horse and rode home.

Pan Jinlian was listening with the others to Nun Xue and the two young novices singing their sacred songs when she suddenly remembered that Yueniang had scolded Daian and said she did not know what tricks he was playing. She went to her room and found that the love instruments had disappeared. She asked Chunmei about them. "Yes, Father came here," the maid said. "He looked in the drawers and in the bed, but I don't know where he found them."

"When did he come?" Jinlian asked.

"You were in the inner court with Nun Xue. I asked him what he was looking for, but he would not tell me."

"He has taken them to the bawdy house," Jinlian said. "I will find out when he comes back." She went back to the inner court.

It was very late when Ximen Qing returned. He did not go to the inner court. Qintong took a lantern to light him, and they went through the garden gate to the rooms of Li Ping'er. Qintong took his master's hat and clothes and gave them to Xiaoyu. When Yueniang saw the boy, she asked if his master had returned. "Yes," the boy said. "He has gone to the Sixth Lady's room."

"The fellow hasn't the slightest regard for decent behavior," Yueniang said. "Here we have all been waiting for him and he doesn't come."

Li Ping'er went quickly to her room and said to Ximen Qing: "The Second Lady is waiting to offer you wine on her birthday. Why have you come here?"

Ximen Qing laughed. "I have had too much wine already," he said. "I will see her tomorrow."

"Even so," said Li Ping'er, "you must come with me and take a cup of wine in the inner court. If you do not, you will offend the Second Lady." She compelled him to go. Li Jiao'er offered him wine.

"Have you been alone all this time?" Yueniang asked him.

"I have been drinking wine with Brother Ying," Ximen Qing told her.

"Of course!" Yueniang said. "I knew you couldn't be drinking by yourself." She said no more.

Ximen Qing did not stay very long. He staggered over to Li Ping'er's rooms. He had not fully eased himself when he was with Wang Liu'er, because of the Indian Monk's pill that he had taken. He had worked long and lustily, yet his weapon was harder than ever, as stiff as an iron rod. He went into the room, gave his clothes to Yingchun, and asked Li Ping'er to let him go to bed. She had not expected him and was already in bed with Guan'ge. Now she said to him: "Please go somewhere else. The baby has

just gone to sleep. Besides, I am not very well. Don't be silly. Go to somebody else." But Ximen embraced her and kissed her.

"I particularly want to stay here," he said. He showed her his weapon.
It gave her a start.

"However did you make it so big?" she said.

Ximen Qing laughed. He told her about the Indian Monk and said:
"If you won't let me sleep here, I shall die."

"But how can I?" Li Ping'er said. "I have been unwell for two days and
I am not better yet. When I am better, I will certainly sleep with you, but
please go to the Fifth Lady's room tonight. It is all the same to you."

"I don't know why," Ximen said, "but I feel I want you today. I am
afraid I must insist. Tell the maid to bring some water, wash yourself, and
we will sleep together."

"You make me laugh," Li Ping'er said. "You must be drunk or you
wouldn't behave so scandalously. Even if I do wash, it won't be very pleasant. If, at a time like this, my juices meet a man, bad luck follows. If this
means my death, I will certainly come and haunt you."

She could not get rid of him, and, at last, she told Yingchun to bring
some water, and washed herself. They got to bed together. Strangely
enough, the baby Guan'ge, who had gone to sleep, woke up the moment
she turned her head. This he did three times. Li Ping'er told Yingchun to
give him a comforter and take him to the nurse. Afterwards, they were able
to enjoy themselves more freely.

Ximen Qing sat down inside the net, and she got onto hands and
knees. He plunged in, admiring the ivory white of her legs in the candlelight. He maneuvered himself to enjoy the sight of the moving prick. He
reached halfway, but could go no further; she was afraid that blood would
flow, and tried to dry herself with a handkerchief. Ximen struggled for an
hour, and at last he held her legs apart and achieved so clear a passage that
they stroked each other with their pubic hair.

His orgasm was greater than imaginable, but she said, "Come carefully,
please, that hurts."

"Now you will have all of me", he replied. On the table there was a
cool potion; when he had drunk it the sperm flowed like water. His limbs
relaxed comfortably, and he felt as fresh as the spring. He was beginning
to appreciate the marvel of the Indian Monk's medicine. It was the third
night watch when he went to sleep.

When Jinlian knew that Ximen had gone to Li Ping'er, she was quite
sure that he had taken the instruments there. It never occurred to her that
he might have been elsewhere too. She bit her lips with her silvery teeth
and went to sleep.

That night Yueniang slept with the two nuns, Xue and Wang. Wang secretly gave her the afterbirth of a baby boy, which Nun Xue had made into a charm. Xue told Yueniang to pick out a *renzi* day, take the medicine with a little wine, and then sleep with her husband. "Do not let anyone know about this," she said, "and you will have a baby."

Yueniang took the medicine and thanked the two nuns. "I expected you in the first month," she said to Wang, "but you did not come."

"It is easy to promise," said Wang, "but not so easy to get such things as this. Fortunately Nun Xue was equal to the occasion. She gave an old woman three *qian* of silver and got this from a young lady who had just given birth to her first baby. We got alum water and cleaned it, and cooked it on two new tiles. Everything was done in proper form. We sifted it through a very fine sieve, mingled it with drugs and charms, and here it is."

Again Yueniang thanked them. Then she gave them two taels of silver and said: "If this is successful, Nun Xue shall have some yellow silk."

Nun Xue made a reverence to her. "Your Ladyship is very kind," she said. "Remember the proverb that says: 'Sometimes, though we try for ten days, it is impossible to sell a load of genuine stuff; yet in one day we can dispose of three loads that are not genuine.'

CHAPTER 51
Pan Jinlian Makes Mischief

Pan Jinlian was so angry when she thought that Ximen Qing had taken the love instruments to Li Ping'er that she tossed about the whole night through. She hated Li Ping'er. The next morning, when she knew that Ximen had gone to the office, she went to the inner court to see Wu Yueniang.

"The Sixth Lady," she said, "has been saying nasty things about you behind your back. She says you take undue advantage of your position and that you are overbearing. Last night, she says, our husband came in drunk and went to her room. She was in the inner court, and you shamed her before everybody there. She was angry, went to the other court and forced him to come to your room. He didn't wish to come, and went back again to her as soon as he could. They talked all night. He has given himself to her, heart, entrails and all."

This made Yueniang very angry. Aunt Wu and Meng Yulou were present, and she said to them: "You two were here yesterday. I said nothing that anyone could take exception to. When the boy brought the lantern, I asked him why his master had not come, and he said his master had gone to the Sixth Lady's room. Then I said: 'The Second Lady is expecting him and he ought to come.' There was nothing wrong about that. What does she mean by saying that I take undue advantage of my position? I used to think she was a good woman, but, evidently, I was judging by appearances, and did not realize what her mind was like. You never can tell. Now I see that she is like a needle hidden out of sight, a thorn in the flesh. How do I know what stories she may have been telling my husband? No wonder he was so anxious to go and see her yesterday. But never mind, my foolish lady. Even if he goes to you every day, it shall not worry me. You can have him, you people who cannot bear the strain of widowhood. Think of it! But when I first came here, and that rogue treated me without due respect, I managed to survive."

"Lady," Aunt Wu said, "say no more. There is the child, you know. Those in authority always have much to put up with. You are the mistress of the house, and the mistress is like a jar that has to hold all sorts of water. Both good and bad are your portion."

"One of these days," Yueniang said, "I will certainly ask her what she meant by saying I was overbearing."

This alarmed Jinlian. "Sister," she said, "you must forgive her. There is an old saying that tells us that the truly great do not concern themselves with the doings of those who are less worthy. And what person of that baser sort is without faults? We all suffer from the way she talks to our husband, especially I, who am her nearest neighbor. If I were as bad as she, there would be desperate trouble. And things are by no means better for us now that she has had this baby. She says more. She says that when her son grows up, there will be kindness for those who have been kind to her and revenge for those who have been unkind to her. We shall all die of starvation. But, of course, you knew nothing of this."

Aunt Wu said: "Lady, how can you say such things?" Yueniang said nothing.

When people get to discussing matters in this way, there are always some who speak for fire and some who speak for candles. Ximen's daughter, Ximen Dajie, was friendly with Li Ping'er, who had always given her needles, thread and cloth when she wanted them. She had given her fine silk and other things besides, and two or three excellent handkerchiefs. She never expected any return. So, when Ximen Dajie heard this conversation, she naturally went to tell Li Ping'er.

The Sixth Lady was sitting in her room making a charm for the baby to wear at the Dragon Boat Festival. She was also making different kinds of millet dumplings and delicacies to eat. When Ximen Dajie came in, she asked her to sit down, and told Yingchun to bring some tea.

"When we asked you to come and take tea with us, why didn't you come?" Ximen Dajie said.

"When your father went away, I began to make these things for the baby, now that it is cool."

"I want to tell you something," Ximen Dajie said. "Now, please realize, I don't wish to talk scandal, but have you done anything to displease the Fifth Lady? She has been telling the Great Lady that you said she was an interfering busybody. Mother is going to ask you what you meant by it. But when she asks you, don't tell her that I spoke to you about it, or she will be angry with me. You must think out your answer beforehand."

When Li Ping'er heard this, she could hardly hold her needle; she was so paralyzed by astonishment. For a long time she could not answer and tears rolled down her cheeks. "I never said a single word," she said at last. "Last night, I was in the inner court and the boy came to tell me that your father had gone to my room. I came and asked him to go to the inner court, and that was all. The Great Lady has been very kind to me. Do you think I don't know how to distinguish good from evil? How dare Jinlian say such things? I will have this out with her, face to face."

"She did seem to be disturbed when the Great Lady said she would talk to you about it," Ximen Dajie said. "If I were you, I should certainly challenge her."

"No," Li Ping'er said, "she is too clever for me. Her mouth is sharper than mine. Day and night she schemes to kill my child and me. I can only put my trust in Heaven. But one of these days she will be the end of me." She sobbed as she spoke.

Ximen Dajie stayed for a while to comfort her, then Xiaoyu came to ask them both to go to dinner. Li Ping'er put down her sewing and went with Ximen Dajie, but she could eat nothing and went back to her room to lie down.

When Ximen Qing came back from the office and found Li Ping'er lying on the bed, he asked Yingchun what was amiss. The maid told him that she had had nothing to eat. He became excited and asked: "Why couldn't you eat anything? Tell me. I see your eyes are very red. How are you feeling?"

Li Ping'er got up quickly, rubbed her eyes and said: "My eyes have been bothering me, but it is nothing very serious. I just wasn't hungry." She did not say a word about the trouble, but she could not get it out of her mind.

In the inner court, Ximen Dajie said to Yueniang: "I have been speaking to the Sixth Lady about the things the Fifth Lady says. She swears she never said anything, and cried bitterly. She says she could not possibly say anything of the sort after you have been so kind to her."

"I don't believe a word the Fifth Lady says," Aunt Wu said. "The Sixth Lady is much too good a woman to say things like that."

"I fancy there is some trouble between Li Ping'er and Jinlian," Yueniang said. "Perhaps Jinlian could not get her husband to go and visit her, and that is why she comes and tells me such tales. I am the one who has to suffer."

"You must be fair in your judgments, Lady," Aunt Wu said. "It would take a hundred like the Fifth Lady to make one like the Sixth. She has been here three years now, and never has she done anything she should not have done."

As they were talking, Qintong came in with a large parcel wrapped up in blue cloth. Yueniang asked him what was in it. "There are thirty thousand salt certificates here," the boy said. "Clerk Han and Cui Ben have been to have them registered at the Excise office. Father is giving them something to eat, and seeing about the money. The day after tomorrow is a lucky day, and they will start for Yangzhou."

"Master Ximen will be coming now," Aunt Wu said. "I had better go with the two holy teachers to the Second Lady's room." Before she finished speaking Ximen Qing appeared.

"What is that thievish, fat, bald-headed old whore Xue doing here?" he asked his wife.

"Why do you use such unbecoming language?" Yueniang said. "Since you do not offer them charity, there is no call for you to make such rude remarks. She has done you no harm. And how did you know her name?"

"Don't you know her history?" Ximen Qing said. "She got Counselor Chen's young daughter away to her temple where she carried on with some young fellow. For that she received three taels of silver. When the business came out, I had old Xue arrested. She was given twenty strokes and ordered to return to lay life and get married. I should like to know why she hasn't got married yet. Perhaps she would like me to put the thumbscrews on her."

"You must not speak evil of the servants of Buddha," Yueniang said. "She is religious and observes her vows. Why should she return to the secular life? You don't appreciate her holiness."

"Holiness!" said Ximen Qing. "Ask her how many men she welcomes in one night."

"Don't be so vulgar," Yueniang said, "or I shall tell you what I think of you." Then she said: "When are you going to send the men to Yangzhou?"

"I have sent Laibao to see our relative Qiao," Ximen said. "I want five hundred taels from him. I myself am contributing another five hundred taels: I shall send them off the day after tomorrow."

"Who is going to take charge of the shop?" Yueniang said.

Ximen told her that he had arranged for Ben the Fourth to do so. Then Yueniang opened a chest and took out the silver. It was weighed and wrapped up. Ximen gave each man five taels of silver as journey money.

Ying Bojue came while this was being done. "What are you doing, Brother?" he asked. Ximen Qing told him. "I congratulate you, Brother," Bojue said, bowing. "You will certainly do well out of the transaction."

Ximen Qing asked him to sit down and called for tea. Then he asked when Li and Huang were going to get their money. "Within a month, I expect," Ying Bojue said. "They told me yesterday that there is another contract going in Dongpingfu for twenty thousand lots of incense. They are very eager to get your backing to the extent of five hundred taels and, as soon as they get the money, they will bring it to you without even touching it."

"As you see," Ximen said, "I am sending people to Yangzhou and I have had to borrow five hundred taels from Qiao. How can I spare money for them?"

"Well," Ying Bojue said, "they said to me with much insistence that one guest does not trouble two hosts. If you do not do them this favor, they don't know where to get the money."

"Xu the Fourth, in East Street, outside the walls, owes me five hundred taels," Ximen Qing said. "They shall have that."

"Splendid," cried Ying Bojue.

At that moment Ping'an brought a visiting card and said that Xia Shou had come to invite Ximen Qing to go and visit Magistrate Xia next day. Ximen Qing looked at the card. "Good," he said.

"Brother," Ying Bojue said, "I have news for you. Have you heard about Li Guijie? Has she been here recently?"

"She has not been here since the end of the first month. I can't imagine what's been happening to her."

"General Wang's third son," Ying Bojue said, "is a nephew by marriage of Grand Marshal Huang of the Eastern Capital. In the first month, this young man went to the Capital to celebrate the New Year, and the old gentleman gave a thousand taels to the young couple as a New Year's gift. Oh, you have no idea of the beauty of Grand Marshal Huang's niece. No artist could paint more than a half of it. I have never seen so beautiful a woman. Since you have been staying at home with your own ladies, old Sun, Pockmarked Zhu, and Little Zhang have been spending all their time in the bawdy house with this young man. In Second Alley he has taken up with a girl called Qi Xiang'er, and sometimes he goes to Guijie's house. He stole his wife's ornaments and pawned them. This distressed his wife so much that she even tried to hang herself. The other day was the old gentleman's birthday. Wang's wife went to the Eastern Capital and told him all about it. The old gentleman was terribly annoyed. He had the names of all the naughty fellows set down and sent the paper to Marshal Zhu. Marshal Zhu has sent it here with orders to arrest the people named. So, yesterday, old Sun, Pockmarked Zhu and Little Zhang were arrested at Guijie's house. Guijie herself escaped to a neighbor's and spent the night there. They have asked me to come and beg you to help them."

"Only a month or two ago I said they were a pack of cadgers," Ximen Qing said. "Pockmarked Zhu even tried his tricks on me."

"I will be off," Ying Bojue said. "I expect Guijie will be coming to see you, and, whether you listen to her or not, she is sure to blame me for putting a finger in the pie."

"One moment," Ximen Qing said, "if you see Li, don't tell him I am going to let them have the money. Wait till I have got it from Xu, and then I'll talk to you again."

Bojue promised. As he went out of the gate, Guijie's sedan chair arrived. She was getting out of it, but Bojue went straight on.

Ximen Qing was telling Chen Jingji to go to Xu the Fourth's for the money when Qintong came and said: "The Great Lady would like to see you in the inner court. Guijie is here." Ximen went to the back court. Guijie was wearing a dun-colored dress. There was no powder on her face, and her head was hidden in a white kerchief. There were no ornaments in her hair and she seemed extremely miserable. She kowtowed to Ximen Qing.

"Whatever shall I do, Father?" she said, sobbing. "The fates have abandoned me. I was sitting quietly at home, when disaster seemed to drop suddenly from the skies. There is a certain young master Wang. He was a stranger to me, but, one day, old Sun and Pockmarked Zhu brought him to our house to see my sister. My sister was not at home, and I said to my mother: 'Don't let them in,' but, the older my mother grows, the bigger fool she becomes. It was the day of my aunt's birthday. I wanted to get into my sedan chair and come here, but Zhu went down on his knees and implored me not to come until I had at least given them a cup of tea. He made it impossible for me to get away. Suddenly, a number of policemen came to arrest them. Wang slipped away, and I managed to escape to a neighbor's house. When everything was quiet again, our servant came to take me home again. My mother was frightened out of her wits. She talked about killing herself.

"Today the runners came with a warrant from the office and spent the whole morning at our place questioning us. They mentioned my name and wanted to take me to the Eastern Capital. Father, you must take pity on me and save me. I don't know what to do. Mother, won't you say a word for me?"

Ximen Qing laughed. "Get up," he said. "What other names were there on the document?"

"Qi Xiang'er's name was there," Guijie said. "It was young Master Wang who made her a woman. But it was right for her name to be there, for she took his money. But if I ever took a penny from him, may my eyeballs fall out. And if I ever allowed him to set hands on me, may a beastly sore grow at every one of my pores."

"You really must do something for her," Yueniang said. "Don't make her take these terrible oaths."

"Has Qi Xiang'er been arrested?" Ximen Qing asked.

"Not yet," Guijie said. "She went to the Wangs' house."

"The best thing you can do," Ximen Qing said, "is to stay here for a few days, and I will see what I can do for you at the district office." He told Shutong to write a letter and go at once to the office to see Magistrate Li. He was to tell Li that Guijie was at Ximen Qing's house, and ask that she should not be arrested.

Shutong put on his black clothes and went on this errand. In a short time he was back again with a card from Li. "His Lordship told me," the boy said, "that he will gladly do anything else you wish, but he can't do this. In this case the document has come from the Eastern Capital. His Lordship must see that the people are arrested, and the best he can do for you is to allow her two days' grace. If you wish to do anything for her, you will have to send to the Capital."

When Ximen Qing heard this, he muttered a while. Then he said: "Laibao is about to go somewhere else, and I have no one to send to the Eastern Capital."

"Why not send the other two to Yangzhou, and keep Laibao?" Yueniang said, "Then he can go to the Eastern Capital for Guijie. There will still be the other two to go to Yangzhou. See how terrified the girl is."

Guijie kowtowed to Yueniang and Ximen Qing. Ximen sent for Laibao. "You will not go on the twentieth," he said. "I am going to send the others to Yangzhou, and you must set off tomorrow for the Eastern Capital to get this business of Guijie's settled. You will go and see Uncle Zhai and ask him to get the affair disposed of at the courts."

Guijie hastily made a reverence to Laibao. He made reverence in return and said: "I will start immediately."

Ximen Qing told Shutong to write a letter thanking Zhai for what he had done in the matter of Censor Ceng. He sealed up twenty taels of silver to go with the letter and gave it to Laibao. Guijie was greatly relieved. She offered five taels of silver to Laibao. "When you come back," she said, "my mother will reward you suitably." Ximen Qing took the five taels and returned them to the girl, telling Yueniang to give Laibao another five taels in place of them. "But this is quite wrong," Guijie said. "You are taking all this trouble on my account and I cannot allow you to spend your money as well."

"Do you think I don't have five taels," Ximen said, "so that I must ask you to pay him for me?"

Guijie put away her five taels and made reverence after reverence to Laibao. "Brother," she said, "please start early tomorrow. I am so afraid you may be too late."

"I will start at the fifth night watch, the break of dawn," Laibao said. He took the letter and went to Han Daoguo's house in Lion Street.

Wang Liu'er was making clothes in her room. She saw Laibao through the window and said to him: "What can we do for you? Please come in. My husband is not at home. He has gone to the tailor's for some clothes, but he will be back in a moment." She said to the maid: "Go to Xu's, the tailor's, and tell your father Uncle Bao is here."

"I have come to say that I am not going with him tomorrow. I have to go to the Eastern Capital instead. Guijie pleaded urgently with my master to do something for her, and I have been ordered to start tomorrow morning. Your husband and Cui will have to go by themselves and I shall join them later on. What are you making, Sister-in-law?"

"Underclothes for my husband," Wang Liu'er said.

"Tell him not to take much in the way of clothes," Laibao said. "The place to which we are going is the very home of silk, so why bother about clothes?"

As they were talking, Han Daoguo came in. The two men greeted one another, and Laibao told Han what he had told Wang Liu'er. "I will join you in Yangzhou," he said.

"Our master has given instructions that we are to stay at Wang Boru's inn," Han said. "Wang's father was a friend of his Lordship's father. He has a very large inn, and there are always many merchants there. Our money and our goods will be safe there. That is where you will find us."

"Sister-in-law," Laibao said to Wang Liu'er, "I am going to the Eastern Capital. Is there anything you would like me to take to your daughter?"

"Her father has had a pair of hairpins made, and I have made two pairs of shoes. Would you be so kind as to take them?" She wrapped them in a kerchief and gave them to Laibao. Then she told her maid to bring something to eat and to warm some wine. She laid down her sewing and set the table.

"Sister-in-law," Laibao said, "do not take any trouble on my account. I must not stay. I must go home and pack my luggage so as to be ready to start first thing in the morning."

Wang Liu'er smiled. "Why do you stand on ceremony with us? We are colleagues in business, and it is only right that we should entertain you and that you should drink a cup of wine with us." She said to Han Daoguo: "Now, old sobersides! Help me to get the table ready and ask Uncle Bao to sit down. Don't look as though you did not wish him to stay."

Dishes were brought, and they offered Laibao wine. Wang Liu'er sat with the two men. When Laibao had drunk a few cups, he said again that he must go. "It is late, and my house is shut up early." Han Daoguo asked what arrangements had been made about the horses, and Laibao told him that they were to be hired early the following morning. "If I were you," he said, "I should hand over the keys and the accounts to Ben the Fourth, and not go to the shop. Take a rest at home in preparation for your journey."

"I am going to give them to him tomorrow," Han Daoguo said.

Again Wang Liu'er urged Laibao to drink. "Just this one cup, Uncle," she said, "I will not ask you to drink any more."

"If I must drink," Laibao said, "may I have a cup of very hot wine?" Wang Liu'er poured the wine into the pot and told the little maid to heat it. Then she poured it out again and offered it with both hands to Laibao. "I am sorry that I have nothing better to offer you to eat," she said.

"I thank you, Sister-in-law," Laibao said. "We do not, of course, stand on ceremony since we are all members of one household." He took the wine and drank with Wang Liu'er. Then he got up. She gave him the shoes to take to her daughter.

"Go to the palace, Uncle," she said, "and see whether my daughter is well." Then she and her husband together took him to the gate. Laibao went home, packed his baggage, and, next day, set off for the Eastern Capital.

Uncle Wu came to talk to Ximen Qing. "A document," he said, "has come from the Capital to Dongpingfu appointing me Keeper of the Seals and Controller of the Granary in this city. I am to be on six months' probation and, if my work is well done, I am to be promoted; and, if not, reported by the Censor. Brother-in-law, if you can spare the money, I should be glad if you would lend me some. I will pay you back when I get paid myself."

"How much do you need?" Ximen Qing asked. "You shall have it."

"It is very kind of you, Brother-in-law. Perhaps twenty taels." They went together to Wu Yueniang's room. Yueniang took out twenty taels and gave them to her brother. Then they had tea, but, as there were lady guests, Uncle Wu could not stay in the inner court, and Yueniang asked her husband to entertain him in the great hall.

While they were drinking, Chen Jingji came in. He made a reverence to Uncle Wu, and said to Ximen Qing: "Xu asks to be allowed a few days in which to make his payment."

"Rubbish," Ximen said, "I need the money now. You will have to speak to him severely."

Uncle Wu asked Jingji to sit down and drink with them.

In the inner court, Aunt Wu and Aunt Yang, Ximen's ladies, and Guijie were drinking wine together. Miss Yu sang to them the first act in *The Western Wing* play cycle. When she had finished and laid down her lute, Meng Yulou gave her some wine. "What a terribly long ditty," she said, "I don't like you at all." Pan Jinlian, with a pair of large chopsticks, took a piece of meat and dangled it before Miss Yu's nose, to tease her.

"Sister," Guijie said to Yuxiao, "give me the lute, and I will sing a song for the ladies."

"But you are in trouble," Yueniang said. "You can't feel like singing."

"Now that you and Father have made things all right, I have nothing to worry about," Guijie said.

"Guijie," Yulou said, "I suppose you are able to change the parts you play so quickly because of where you come from. When you first came, your brows were knit and you would not even take a drop of tea. Now you laugh and talk readily enough."

Guijie stretched her delicate fingers, plucked the strings and sang to them. While she was singing, Qintong came with the things from the outer court. Yueniang asked if Uncle Wu had gone and was told that he had. "It must be time for my brother-in-law to come here," Aunt Wu said. "We had better go elsewhere." Qintong told them that Ximen Qing had gone to the Fifth Lady's room.

When she heard this, Jinlian was on tenterhooks. She lifted first one foot and then the other in her anxiety to get away, but she felt that it would not be polite to go. At last Yueniang said to her: "Get off to your room since he is there. Don't sit there looking like a guest who can get nothing to eat."

Jinlian tried to pretend to be in no great haste, but her feet carried her quickly away. When she came to her room, Ximen Qing had already taken some of the Indian Monk's medicine. Chunmei had taken his clothes and he was sitting on the bed.

"Ah, my son," Jinlian said, "you could not wait for your mother to come, but went to bed first. I have been drinking in the inner court. Guijie was singing there, and I have had several large cups of wine. I had to find my way here alone in the dark, one foot in the air and the other on the ground. Really, I don't know how I got here." She asked Chunmei for some tea. When the maid brought it, Jinlian drank it and made a sign to her. Chunmei understood and went to heat some water for her. The woman washed herself with sandalwood water and alum and took off her headdress so that her hair was held by a single golden pin. She stood before the mirror, reddened her lips and put some fragrant tea into her mouth. Then she came back and Chunmei brought her sleeping shoes. The maid went away and made fast the door behind her.

The woman took the lamp and set it beside the bed. Then she pulled down the curtains, took off her scarlet trousers, and stripped her jade body. Ximen Qing was sitting on the bed, the silver clasp in position upon a fierce-looking weapon. Jinlian was startled when she looked at it. It was too great for one hand to grasp, full-blooded and heavy. She stared at Ximen Qing and said: "I know what you've been doing. You've been taking some of that monk's medicine to make it like that. Then you think you'll come here to show what a mighty fellow you are. Fresh wine and fresh meat for others. I have to content myself with the defeated champion. I can serve the meanest of your purposes. Then you pretend to be fair to me. Why, the other day, when I was not in my room, you came and ran off with the instruments to the Sixth Lady's room and carried on your games there. And she pretends to be one of those pure, pious people. You wretched little creature, you can be twisted around anybody's finger. When I think about it, I swear I won't have anything to do with you for a hundred days."

Ximen Qing laughed. "Come here, you little strumpet," he said, "and see if your mouth can make this smaller; if you can, I'll give you a tael of silver."

"I'm ashamed of you, you rascal," she said. "How can it get smaller when you have drunk that potion?" But she lay on the bed and put his penis between her red lips. "It's so huge," she said, "that it hurts my mouth." Then she sucked and teased the prick's head with her tongue, licking the outer skin and rubbing it up and down with her lips. But, although she stroked the giant with her cheeks and played a thousand love games with it, it merely became longer and thicker. Ximen looked at her. Her beautiful body gleamed among the silk sheets. She took his hairy monster in her delicate fingers, put it between her lips, and took it all in her mouth; when she released it, it was limp.

Beside them lay a long-haired white cat. Watching the movement of this hairy thing, the cat crouched ready to spring. Ximen had a gold speckled fan in his hand and with it he teased the cat. Jinlian seized the fan and struck a hard blow at the cat. It ran quickly away. She looked up at Ximen Qing and said: "You terrible fellow. You are amusing yourself with me, and that isn't enough for you, you must play with the cat. Suppose it claws me. What then? Do you think I shall go on playing this game?"

"You funny little whore," Ximen said, "you would talk anybody to death."

"Why don't you ask Li Ping'er to play these games with you?" Jinlian went on. "You ask me every time you come here. What that medicine you have been taking may be I don't know; I could suck it all day without success."

Ximen took from his sleeve a little silver box and from it picked out with a toothpick some of the reddish ointment. He put it upon the horse's mouth. He lay down and made her ride on top of him. "Let me get into position first," she said. "If I do, perhaps you'll be able to penetrate me." But the head of his penis was so broad that they both struggled hard and long before even a little of it would go in. She rode on top of him, up and down, hither and thither, but could not conceal her pain. "Darling," she said, "that hurts me so much that I can't bear it any longer," and feeling around with her hand she found that less than half the penis was inside her. She collected some of her spittle and moistened the inside of her cunt with it to make the path easier. Then she moved up and down and gradually the penis went the whole way into her vagina.

"Darling," the woman said, "the medicine you always used to take gave me a tremendous feeling of burning inside, but this makes me feel a coldness that reaches even to my heart. My whole body seems numb. I shall certainly die at your hands today."

Ximen Qing laughed. "I will tell you a story," he said. "I heard it from Brother Ying. Once upon a time a man died and went down to the infernal regions. The King of Hades put an ass's skin upon his body and told him that in his next life he must be a donkey. But the record keeper looked in his books and found that the man still had thirty years to live. They sent him back to earth. His wife perceived that, except for his weapon, his body was as it had been before, but he had still the donkey's weapon. 'I will go back to Hell and change it,' he said to his wife. 'No, my dear,' said the wife. 'They might not let you come back again. I will put up with it somehow.' "

Jinlian struck him with the fan. "Beggar Ying's wife is able to put up with a donkey's weapon," she said. "That is obvious. You are a foul-mouthed thing, and I ought to hit you harder."

They went on with their work, but Ximen Qing did not give forth. He closed his eyes and made the woman move. She, wriggled and writhed with terrible moans. Then they changed places. He held her legs, and thrust in his penis with all his might. He worked hard in the face-down position, but he felt very little, and she did not become wet. They changed places again; she embraced his neck and hurled herself at him, put the tongue in the mouth, and pressed the whole penis inside herself. Then she whispered gently, "Darling, finish it off or I'll die." Soon she drooped; her tongue was as ice, and the juices of love flowed from her. Ximen felt that her cunt was warm, his passions were aroused, and he felt an enormous orgasm. Both their juices flowed like rivers. She mopped them up with a handkerchief. Then they embraced and kissed each other—but the penis was still erect. They slept for an hour; after that Jinlian, still unsated, climbed on top of him and played with him again. The juices again flowed, but at last began to exhaust themselves. Ximen Qing was undaunted. He could only marvel at the medicine that the Indian Monk had given him. Then they heard the cock crow. It was just before dawn.

"If it doesn't go down, come back to me tonight and my lips will make it do so."

"You can never do so," Ximen said, "there is only one thing that will."

Jinlian asked what that was, but he said: "This is not a thing to be told to other ears. Wait till tonight and I will tell you then."

In the morning he rose and Chunmei helped him to dress. Han Daoguo and Cui Ben were waiting. Ximen went out and gave them two letters, one to introduce them to Wang Boru, who kept the inn at Yangzhou, and the other to Miao Qing to ask if his affair had been settled satisfactorily. He told them that, if they needed more money, he would send it later by Laibao. "You said you were writing to Censor Cai," Cui Ben said, but Ximen said the letter had not been written and that he would send it by Laibao. Then the two men set out upon their journey.

Ximen Qing put on his hat and robe of ceremony and went to the office. He thanked Magistrate Xia for his invitation. "It will be a great honor if you visit me today," Xia said. "There will be no other guests." They attended to their business, then each went to his own home.

An official on horseback, carrying a parcel, with sweat rolling down his cheeks, came to the gate and asked Ping'an if Ximen Qing lived there. Ping'an asked his business. The man dismounted, bowed to Ping'an, and said: "I come from An, the Warden of the Royal Forests, with presents for your master. My master and Huang, the Controller of the Brick Fields, are now at Dongpingfu, at Master Hu's place, drinking wine. My master wishes to visit his Lordship, and I have come to see if he is at home." Ping'an asked for a card, and the man took one from the wrapper and gave it with the presents to the gatekeeper. The boy took them and showed them to Ximen Qing. On the list of presents he read: "Zhejiang silk, two rolls; four measures of Hu brocade; a scented girdle; and an ancient mirror." Ximen told him to give the messenger five *qian* of silver and a card in return, and to say that Ximen would be happy to receive his master. The man went away and Ximen hastily made the necessary preparations.

The two gentlemen arrived about noon. They came in sedan chairs with a fine array of umbrellas and men to clear the way for them. They sent in visiting cards with their names An Shen and Huang Baoguang. Both were dressed in ceremonial attire, with black hats and black boots. They got down from their sedan chairs and Ximen Qing went to the gate to meet them. They went into the hall and exchanged salutations. Then they sat down, Huang on the left and An on the right.

"Your fragrant renown has long been known to me," Huang said. "I am only sorry that my visit has been so long delayed."

"The kindness is on your side," Ximen said, "it was for me to come and see you first. May I ask your illustrious name?"

An answered for his colleague. "Brother Huang's name is Taiyu. It is expressive of the principle that earth is made peaceful by the glory that comes from Heaven."

"May I ask your name?" Huang said.

"My unworthy name," Ximen said, "is Siquan. I was so called because, on my poor estate, there is a well with four openings."

"The other day," An said, "I met Brother Cai. He told me how he and Song had inflicted themselves upon you."

"Yes," Ximen Qing said, "I had orders from my friend Zhai, and besides, his Excellency Song is my superior officer. It was only fitting that I should entertain them. When my servant was at the Capital, I heard of the exalted rank you had attained and I can only apologize for not having come in person to congratulate you. When did you set out?"

"Last year, after I left you, I went home to marry again. Then, in the first month of the new year I went to the Capital and was appointed to the Board of Works. Now I have been detailed to superintend the transport of the imperial timber from Jingzhou. I had to pass this way, and, of course, felt bound to come and pay my respects to you."

"I am grateful for your precious gifts," Ximen Qing said. He asked them to change their clothes, and summoned the servants to lay a table. But Huang rose, and An said: "Indeed, we have to go to drink wine with the prefect of Dongpingfu. We only called in passing, and we will trouble you some other day."

"It is a long way from here to Dongpingfu," Ximen Qing said, "and if you are not hungry yourselves, there are still your servants to consider. I shall not offer you anything very special, merely common, everyday food, and when your servants have been refreshed by a meal, you will travel more quickly." A table was set with food of all kinds, delicious dishes, soups, and pastries. Ximen took a small golden cup and offered three cups to each of them. The servants were entertained. Then the two officers stood up and An said:

"We are giving a little party tomorrow and should be very honored if you would come. The party will be at Chamberlain Liu's place. He is a friend of my brother Huang. Will you give us the pleasure of your company?"

"Since you are good enough to invite me," said Ximen, "I dare not refuse."

He escorted them to the gate. Just as they went away in their sedan chairs, a man came from Magistrate Xia to remind Ximen Qing. "I will come at once," he said. He ordered his horse to be brought, went to the inner court to change his clothes, then came out again and mounted. Qintong and Daian followed him, and soldiers went before him to clear the way. When he reached his colleague's house, he went to the hall. The two men saluted each other. Ximen said: "Their Lordships An and Huang have just been to see me. They stayed a long time or I should have been here earlier." Two tables were set in the hall. Ximen Qing sat on the left, and, next to him, the graduate Ni. They talked to one another and Ximen asked Ni his second name. "My name is Ni Peng, and my second name Shiyuan. I am also known as Guiyan. I am on the staff of the college of this prefecture, and at present am coaching his Lordship's son for his examination. I am ashamed to say I am too ignorant to have many friends." The two young actors came up and kowtowed.

When Jinlian had said good-bye to her husband, she went to bed again and did not get up before midday. Even then, she was too languid to dress her hair. She was afraid those in the inner court would remark it, so, when Yueniang sent for her to go to dinner, she would not go but said she was unwell. Not until afternoon did she go to the inner court.

Yueniang, taking advantage of Ximen Qing's absence, decided to hear Nun Xue expounding the teachings of Buddha and interpreting the *Diamond Sutra*. An altar was prepared and incense burned. The two nuns, Wang and Xue, sat down facing each other, and the two novices, Miaoqu and Miaofeng, stood beside them. The service began. All Ximen's ladies were present, with Aunt Wu and Aunt Yang. They gathered round and listened to Xue recite.

"It has been said," Xue began, "that lightning and brightness soon pass away but that stone and fire are everlasting. The withered blossom can never return to the tree on which it grew and flowing water can never go back to the spring from which it came. In painted halls and tapestried chambers, life is but emptiness. The noblest and the greatest die, and all is but a dream. Gold and jade are no more than fountains of trouble. Silken garments are wasted labor. Wives and children can never spend a hundred years together and, in the darkness beyond, a thousandfold sufferings await.

"When you have lain upon your dying bed and your spirit has gone to the realms below, only in history will your name be recorded. It will avail you nothing, and the yellow earth will cover your corrupting bones. Your fields and gardens, though they cover ten thousand acres, will be divided and cause strife among those who come after you. Your chests of silks and satins, though they are a thousand, will give you not a moment's pleasure. Before life is half done, white hairs assail us. When we have received the congratulations of one guest, he will be followed by another who comes to condole with our children. It is bitter, bitter, bitter. Our spirit is transformed into vapor and our body goes beneath the ground. On go the transmigrations, ceaselessly, and so our heads and countenances are ever changed.

"Hail to the limitless void of the Dharma Realm, to the Three Treasures of the Buddhas of Past and Future, the Dharma, and the Holy Orders.

"Oh, highest, deepest, most admirable Law! Through a hundred, a thousand, ten thousand ages, it is difficult of attainment. Let us now behold it, hearken to it, receive it, hold fast to it. Let us vow to grasp the Buddha's great Truth."

Then Nun Wang said: "Shakyamuni Buddha was the ancestor of all the Buddhas, the Founder of our religion. Do you know how he left his home? Hear me tell of it." Then Nun Xue sang:

> The Buddha Shakyamuni was a prince in India.
> He left his kingdom and went forth to the Himalayas
> Where he cut off his flesh to feed the eagles, magpies nested on his head.
> He cultivated his purity until the nine dragons spittle made him a body of gold,
> And became the Perfect One, the Buddha of the Great Vehicle.

Then Nun Wang said: "Now that you have heard of Shakyamuni, I will tell you how the Bodhisatva Guanyin strove after perfection, attained hundreds of manifestations, and attained the fullest power of the Path. Would you like to hear?"

Xue was about to sing again when Ping'an came rushing in and said: "His Excellency Song has sent two runners and a servant with a number of presents."

Yueniang was flurried. "Your father has gone to Magistrate Xia's," she said. "Who is there to accept the presents?"

Daian came in, put down his wrapper and said: "Don't worry, lady. I will take the card and go and tell my father. Meanwhile I will ask Master Chen to entertain the servants here." He took the card, mounted a horse, rode quickly to Xia's place and told his master. On the card was written: "A freshly slaughtered pig; two jars of Jinhua wine; four quires of writing paper and a miniature book." It was signed: "With the respects of the junior official Song Qiaonian." Ximen Qing told the boy to go home and ask Shutong to write a card with his full title, and give the servant three taels of silver and two handkerchiefs, and five *qian* to each of the runners.

Daian hurried home. He looked everywhere for Shutong but could not find him. This made him so excited that he ran around like an ox going around the grindstone. Nor could he find Chen Jingji. Clerk Fu had to come and entertain the men. Daian went to the inner court to get the silver and the handkerchiefs. There was nobody to wrap them up, and he had to go to the shop to have a parcel made of them. He asked Clerk Fu to write the necessary card. Then he asked Ping'an where Shutong was. "He was here when Master Chen was here," Ping'an said, "and when Master Chen went to get some money, he disappeared."

"I suppose the young rascal has gone off after some girl," Daian said.

At that moment, Chen Jingji and Shutong came riding along on the same mule. Daian scolded the boy and bade him quickly write the card. They dismissed the men who had brought the presents.

"You rascally young scamp," Daian said to Shutong. "You are too ready to roam about. When Father is not at home, you think you can go too. You have been after your girl, beyond a doubt. Father never told you to go out with Master Chen. Wait till he comes back and see what I tell him."

"Tell him what you like," Shutong said. "If you don't, I shall know you are afraid of me, and I shall consider you my boy."

"What, you dog!" Daian cried. "Do you dare me?" He went up to Shutong and kicked him. The pair rolled about on the ground struggling. Daian gained the upper hand and spat upon Shutong's face. "I am going for Father now," he said, "but when I come back I will settle my score with you."

In the inner court, Yueniang gave the two nuns some tea and refreshments, and they continued their hymns and their preachings. Jinlian grew impatient and tugged at Yulou, but Yulou would not move. Then she thought of suggesting to Li Ping'er that they might go, but she was afraid Yueniang would reprove her.

"Sixth Sister," Yueniang said, "she wants you to go with her. I think you had better go. She is so very impatient." Li Ping'er went out with Jinlian. Yueniang looked after them. "Now that the turnips are out of the way," she said, "we shall have more room. We don't want her here, jumping about like a rabbit. She is not the sort of woman to listen to religion."

Jinlian, holding Li Ping'er by the hand, came to the second door. "The Great Lady," she said, "is very fond of that sort of thing. But there isn't anybody dead in the household, and I don't see why we should have the nuns to read stuff of that sort. I have had enough of it; that's why I asked you to come out. Let us go and see what Ximen Dajie is doing." They passed through the great hall. There was a light in one of the side rooms. Ximen Dajie and Chen Jingji were quarreling over the disappearance of some money. Jinlian tapped at the window.

"So, instead of going to the inner court to hear the nuns, you are squabbling here."

Chen Jingji came out. "It is a lucky thing I didn't curse you. Fifth Mother and Sixth Mother, won't you come in?"

They found Ximen Dajie busy making shoes. "It is late and very hot," Jinlian said. "Why are you making shoes now?" She asked what they were quarreling about.

"Father told me to go outside the city walls to get some money," Chen Jingji said, "and my wife gave me three *qian* to buy her a handkerchief. Unfortunately, when I got there, I couldn't find the money. I couldn't buy it for her. When I got back, she said I had spent the money on some woman. She scolded me and made me take oath upon my body. When the maid was cleaning the floor, the money was found. She has taken it, yet still she tells me I must buy a handkerchief for her tomorrow. You two ladies can judge which of us is in the wrong."

"You thievish rascal," his wife said. "You say you don't keep a woman, but what were you doing out with Shutong? You must have heard Daian cursing him. I have no doubt that you and that boy went to some strumpet together. That's why you came back so late. Where is this money you were sent for?"

"Have you found the other money?" Jinlian asked.

"Yes, the maid picked it up when she was sweeping the floor. I have it now."

"Don't worry," Jinlian said to Jingji, "I will give you some money and you can buy two handkerchiefs for me." And Li Ping'er said:

"If there are handkerchiefs to be bought outside the city, please buy some for me."

"Outside the city," Jingji said, "there is a Kerchief Lane where some well-known merchants are having a special sale of kerchiefs of all sorts. Some are woven with gold; others have jade trimmings. They can supply as many as you like. Tell me what color you like and what kind of pattern you want and I will get them for you tomorrow."

"I will have an orange-colored one, with gold and green, and a phoenix among the flowers," Li Ping'er said.

"Mother," Jingji said, "orange and gold don't look at all well together."

"Mind your own business," said Li Ping'er. "I want another of pink wavy silk, with the design of Eight Precious Treasures, and still another of shimmering silk with gold and flowers."

"What design do you want, Fifth Mother?" Jingji asked Jinlian.

"I have only a little money, so two will be enough for me. One the color of jade, with edges of lace and gold."

"You are not an old woman," Jingji said. "What do you want with white?"

"Don't think you know better than I do," Jinlian said. "I shall use it when I have to wear mourning."

"Then you will need a colored one too."

"Yes, I want one of the most delicate purple grape shade, made of Si-chuan silk, gold and green, with a pattern of crossed squares, and in every square a pair of love symbols. On the lace I must have tassels and pearls and other bits of jewelry."

"Ai ya! Ai ya!" Chen Jingji cried. "You are like the melon-seed seller, who sneezed when he opened his box, and scattered the seeds all over the place."

"You horrid man," Jinlian said. "Since it is my money, I shall buy what I like. It is a question of taste and nothing to do with you."

Li Ping'er took a piece of silver from her purse and gave it to Jingji. "This will pay for the Fifth Lady's too," she said. Jinlian shook her head.

"No," she said, "I will pay for my own."

"We are asking Brother-in-law to buy them all at the same time. Why should you bother?"

"Even so," said Jingji, "it is more than enough." He took a balance and weighed the silver. It weighed a tael and nine *qian*.

"With the rest," Li Ping'er said, "buy two handkerchiefs for your wife."

Ximen Dajie stood up and made a reverence to Li Ping'er. "Now the Sixth Lady has paid for your handkerchiefs," Jinlian said to her, "you ought to hand over those three *qian* of silver. You and your husband can draw lots to decide which of you shall be our host. If it is not enough, we will ask the Sixth Lady for some more. Your father will be out tomorrow; we will buy roast duck and white wine and enjoy them together."

"Yes," said Jingji, "hand over that silver."

Ximen Dajie gave the silver to Jinlian, and Jinlian passed it to Li Ping'er for safe keeping. They found some cards, and Ximen Dajie and her husband played. Jinlian helped Ximen Dajie, and she won three games. Then they heard a knocking at the gate. Ximen Qing had returned. Jinlian and Li Ping'er went to their rooms and Jingji went to tell Ximen that Xu the Fourth would pay two hundred and fifty taels in a day or two, and the remainder the following month. Ximen Qing cursed, for he was drunk. He did not go to the inner court but straight to Jinlian's room.

CHAPTER 52

Ying Bojue Teases Li Guijie

That day, Ximen Qing had been entertained by Xia and presents had come to him from Censor Song. He was utterly delighted, and Xia was impressed. He shut the door and urged Ximen to drink more and more wine, refusing to let him go before midnight, the third night watch.

Pan Jinlian had taken off her headdress, prepared the bed and washed her cunt with perfumed water. She was waiting for Ximen Qing to come. When he came, he was drunk. She quickly undressed him; Chunmei brought him tea, and he went to bed. Jinlian, quite naked, sat on the side of the bed and bent over to tie the ribbons of her shoes to her white ankles. The shoes were low-heeled and scarlet. The sight aroused Ximen's passion, and his handle stood up sharply. He asked her for the love instruments, and she brought them out from beneath the bed and gave them to him. He put on two silver clasps, and then threw his arm around her. "Today," he said, "I want to play with the flower in the back court. Will you let me?"

"You shameless fellow," the woman said, "you have played that game often enough with Shutong. Why need you ask me? If that is what you want, go to the slave."

Ximen Qing laughed. "Little oily mouth," he said, "if you will let me do this, I shall want the boy no more. Don't you understand that I am particularly fond of this kind of play. I will only put it there for a little while."

Thus urged, the woman said: "I don't believe you can do it. Your thing is too big. But take the ring from its head and I will try."

Ximen Qing took off the sulfur ring and left only the clasps at the root. He told her to get onto the bed on hands and knees and raise her buttocks high. He rubbed his penis with spittle and moved in gradually. But its cruel, proud head refused to go farther than a little way. She grimaced and bit a handkerchief. "Darling," she said, "be careful not to go in too quickly; my bottom isn't like a door. I feel you inside me like a burning fire."

"Never mind," Ximen said, "tomorrow you shall have a dress of fine embroidery."

"I have clothes like that already," Jinlian said. "What I want is a dress like that of Li Guijie, a lined skirt of gold and silver with jade-colored ribbons and fur. It is very beautiful, and everybody but me has such a skirt. I don't know how much it will cost, but please buy me one."

"Don't worry," Ximen said, "I will buy one for you." He plunged violently forward.

The woman turned her head and looked at him. "Darling," she said, "it is painful enough. Why are you so violent? Won't you let yourself go now?"

But Ximen Qing would not. He held her legs while he looked at his penis going in and out, and cried, "Give me my way, you little strumpet, and call me 'darling.' Then you will have all of me."

The woman closed her eyes and said something like the whisper of a bird. She gently shook her willow-like waist and thrust her sweet body forward to meet his, her enticements and tender words beyond description. After a time, Ximen felt that the essence of his manhood was ready. He grasped her buttocks, then launched himself into her, with the sound of constant slapping against her buttocks. The woman under him could only mumble inarticulately. When the time came, he pulled her against himself and pushed it in to the root, into the final recess, enjoying exquisite pleasure. Contented, the semen flowed freely. The woman received it all, and they lay stuck together on the bed. After a long while he withdrew his penis, but it looked bloody, and liquid was oozing slowly from its mouth; she wiped it with a handkerchief, and they both slept.

The next day Ximen Qing went to his office. When he returned, invitations had come from the two dignitaries Huang and An, asking him to go early on the twenty-second to a party at Eunuch Liu's place. Ximen Qing dismissed the man who had brought the invitations, then went to the upper room and had some gruel. When he came to the great hall, he met Zhou the barber. Zhou knelt down and kowtowed. "You have come at the right moment," Ximen Qing said. "My hair needs attention."

They went to the Hall of the Kingfishers. Ximen sat down beneath an awning, took off his hat and hairnet and pulled down his hair. Barber Zhou took out his combs to dress it. He cleaned it and examined the color. When he knelt down to receive payment, he said: "There will be further promotion for you this year, my Lord, for your hair is in excellent condition." Ximen Qing was very pleased. When his hair had been combed, he told the barber to cleanse his ears and massage his body. The barber had his instruments with him and gave Ximen's body a thorough rolling. Then he exercised the muscles so that Ximen began to feel extremely fit everywhere. Ximen gave him five *qian* of silver and some food, and he was told to wait and shave the baby's head. Then Ximen Qing went to his study, lay down on a great marble bed, and fell asleep.

That day Aunt Yang went away and the two nuns Wang and Xue also made ready to go. Wu Yueniang packed their boxes with sweet things and cakes and gave each of them five *qian* of silver. To each of the novices she gave a small roll of cloth. As they were leaving, Xue told Yueniang not to fail to take the medicine on a *renzi* day and she would be sure to have a child.

"Lady Xue," Yueniang said, "my birthday comes in the eighth month. You must come to see me then. I want you especially." The nun made a reverence and promised to come. All the ladies went to see them off. Afterwards, Yueniang and Aunt Wu went back to the upper room, and the other ladies went to the garden with Guijie and the baby.

"Sister Guijie," Li Ping'er said, "won't you give me the baby?"

"No," said Guijie, "I love carrying him."

Yulou said: "Sister Guijie, you have not seen Father's new study yet."

Jinlian saw how beautifully the roses were blooming, and she plucked two of them for Guijie. They went along the pine-hedged walks till they came to the Hall of the Kingfishers. Beds, curtains, screens, tables, books, pictures, musical instruments and chess, were all tastefully set out. A silken net was held in position over the bed by two silver hooks, and the light summer pillows and mattress were spread upon it.

Ximen Qing was lying fast asleep. Beside him was a small gold incense burner in which some Dragon's Spittle incense was burning. The green windows were partly open, and light was reflected through them by the palm leaves outside. Jinlian took the incense box from the table and examined it. Li Ping'er and Meng Yulou sat down on chairs. Suddenly Ximen Qing turned over and saw the ladies. "What are you doing here?" he said.

"Sister Guijie wanted to see your study," Jinlian said. "So we brought her here." Then Ximen saw his son Guan'ge with them and played with him for a while.

Unexpectedly, Huatong came and said: "Uncle Ying is here." The ladies hurried away to the rooms of Li Ping'er. When Ying Bojue came to the pines, he saw Guijie with Guan'ge in her arms, and said to her maliciously:

"Ah, Guijie! So you are here! When did you come?"

Guijie did not stop. "Beggar Ying," she said, "pray don't meddle in my affairs."

"Your affairs or not, you little strumpet," Bojue said, "I am going to kiss you." He went up to her, but she pushed him away.

"You unpleasant fellow," she said, "if I were not afraid of frightening the baby, I would use my fan on you."

Then Ximen Qing came and said to Ying Bojue: "Don't frighten my son, you funny dog." He told Shutong to take the child to the Sixth Lady's room. The boy took him and carried him to his nurse, Ruyi'er, who was watching them from the corner. Ruyi'er took him away.

"What has happened about you?" Ying Bojue said to Guijie.

"Father was very kind. He has sent Brother Laibao to the Eastern Capital."

"That is good," Bojue said, "I suppose you are satisfied now."

Guijie would have gone to the inner court, but Bojue said: "Come here, you little strumpet, I want to talk to you."

"I shall be back before long," Guijie said. She went to visit Li Ping'er.

Ying Bojue made a reverence to Ximen Qing, and they sat down together. "Yesterday," Ximen said, "I went to Magistrate Xia's place. Censor Song sent me some presents. Among them was a pig. I didn't want to keep it too long so, this morning, I told the cook to cut it up and cook the head with peppers. Don't go away. I will send for Xie Xida and we will play backgammon." He said to Qintong: "Go and ask your Uncle Xie to come. Tell him Uncle Ying is here."

Bojue asked Ximen whether he had yet received Xu's money.

"The dog has only paid two hundred and fifty taels of what he owes me. You must tell your friends to wait a few days. I will get the rest for them somehow."

"That will be all right," Bojue said. "I should not be surprised if they brought you some present today."

"Don't let them spend their money on me," Ximen said. He asked if old Sun and Pockmarked Zhu had started or not.

"After they were arrested at Guijie's place, they spent a night in jail," Bojue said. "The next day they were taken to the Eastern Capital, three of them on one chain. It doesn't seem likely that any of them will come back as comfortable as he went. Trying to earn an honest living is not a simple matter in these days. What a hard time they will have. In this roasting weather, they have to bear that big iron chain, and they haven't a penny in their pockets. I can't think what will become of them."

"You funny dog," Ximen Qing said, laughing, "if they could not bear this punishment, why did they interfere with young Wang? They deserved all they get."

"You are right, Brother," Bojue said. "Flies can never make their way into an egg unless there is a crack in it. Why didn't Wang ask me and Xie Xida to go about with him? But the good go with the good, and the bad with the bad."

While they were talking, Xie Xida came. He sat down and fanned himself busily. "What has made you so hot?" Ximen Qing said to him.

"Ah, Brother, you don't know. Today, an unexpected trouble descended upon me. Early this morning, old woman Sun came to my house and said I had taken her husband away from her. That old whore! Her husband spent all his time at the bawdy house, ate and drank a tremendous lot, and spent all his money there. 'Have you come from Hell?' I said to her. 'Everybody knows you yourself have taken money from the people in the bawdy house.' I gave her a good talking-to and she went away. Then your boy came to invite me."

"I have just been saying to our brother," Bojue said, "that if we put newly vinted wine into two bottles, we shall see which is pure and which is not. Didn't I tell you that anybody who went about with young Wang would certainly get into trouble? Now it has happened, and they have nothing to complain about."

"I can't see how young Wang dared have anything to do with the girls," Ximen Qing said. "He is not properly grown up yet. Conduct like his would be shameful even in a corpse."

"The boy hasn't seen much of the world," Bojue said. "He is not like you. If I mentioned your name to him, he would be frightened to death."

The boys brought tea. Ximen Qing said: "You two play backgammon, and I will tell a boy to buy us some noodles." Qintong set the table, and Huatong brought four small dishes on a square tray, some garlic sauce, and a large bowl of stewed pork with a silver ladle in it. He set everything upon the table with three pairs of ivory chopsticks. The three men sat down and the boys brought three bowls of noodles. Each helped himself to the stew, the garlic sauce, and the vinegar. Ying Bojue and Xie Xida took up their chopsticks. In three helpings and two gulps each finished one bowl, and so on till they had had seven. They finished the seven before Ximen Qing had finished two.

"My sons," Ximen said, "how can you eat so much?"

"Brother," Ying Bojue said, "who has cooked these noodles? They are delicious."

"The stew is perfect," Xie Xida said. "It is most unfortunate that I have just had my dinner. I should have liked to eat another bowl."

The two friends felt hot and took off their coats. Qintong came to clear the table, and they asked him for water to rinse their mouths. "Cold tea will do," Xie Xida said, "but I won't have hot. It would make my breath smell of garlic." Huatong brought three cups of tea. Afterwards, they went to stroll among the flowers.

Huang the Fourth sent four boxes of presents to Ximen Qing, and Ping'an brought them in. There was a box of freshwater chestnuts, another box of a different kind of chestnut, four fine shad in ice, and a box of loquat fruits.

"What splendid delicacies!" Ying Bojue said. "I can't think how he managed to get them. Let me try one." He picked up several and handed two to Xie Xida. "There must be people who have never tasted such things in all their lives."

"You funny dog," Ximen Qing said. "I have not offered them to Buddha, yet you start tasting them."

"Why offer them to Buddha?" Bojue said. "They suit my palate admirably."

Ximen Qing told a boy to go to the inner court and get three *qian* of silver for the man who had brought the presents. "Who brought them?" Bojue said. "Was it Li Zhi or Huang Ning?"

"Huang Ning," said Ping'an.

"Lucky dog," Bojue said. "That's another three *qian* of silver for him." The two friends played backgammon, and Ximen Qing looked on.

After dinner, Yueniang and the others sat under the eaves. Little Zhou the barber peeped in from behind the screen. "Zhou," said Li Ping'er, "you have just come at the right moment. Come and shave my son's head. His hair is very long."

The barber came forward and kowtowed. "That is what Master said," he told them.

Yueniang said: "Sixth Sister, we must look at the calendar first and make sure that it is a lucky day."

Jinlian told Xiaoyu to fetch the calendar. When the maid brought it, Jinlian looked at it and said: "Today is the twenty-first day of the fourth month. It is a *gengxu* day, and under the influence of the Golden Dog. It is a good day for divine worship, for starting on a journey, making clothes, bathing, shaving and building. The afternoon is the most auspicious part of the day."

"In that case," Yueniang said, "the maid shall bring some hot water to wash the baby's head." She told the barber to amuse the baby while he was having his head shaved, and Xiaoyu to stand beside him with a kerchief to catch the hair. After a few strokes of the razor the child howled lustily. The barber was going on in spite of the crying, when, suddenly, the baby screamed and fell in a fit. No sound came from him and his face went purple. This frightened Li Ping'er. She cried: "Stop! Stop!" Zhou put his instruments together and went hastily away.

"The baby is not strong enough," Yueniang said. "We should have cut his hair ourselves instead of having him shaved. See what a state he's got into."

The baby gasped for a long time and at last began to howl again. Li Ping'er was greatly relieved. She began to play with him. "Did Little Zhou dare to come and shave my boy?" she said to him. "Did he shave half his head and treat him roughly? Let us bring him back and punish him." She took the child to Yueniang.

"You naughty little beggar," Yueniang said. "Crying like that when you are shaved. Now the part that has been left unshaven makes you look like a tonsured thief."

They played with him for a while, and Li Ping'er gave him to the nurse. "Don't give him any milk now," Yueniang said. "Let him sleep a while and then feed him." The nurse took him to the front court.

Laian came for the barber's instruments. "Zhou is so frightened that his face is as white as a sheet," he said. Yueniang asked whether the barber had been given anything to eat. "Yes," Laian said, "and my father has given him five *qian* of silver."

"Take him a pot of wine," said Yueniang. "We don't want to terrify him. He has a hard enough life." Xiaoyu heated some wine and gave it to Laian with a dish of preserved meat. The boy took it to the barber.

"Look at the calendar," Yueniang said to Jinlian," and tell me when the next *renzi* day is."

"It is the twenty-third," Jinlian said. "About the time of the day of Corn in the Ear. Why do you wish to know?"

"Oh, no particular reason," Yueniang said. "I was just wondering."

Guijie took the calendar and examined it. "The twenty-fourth is my mother's birthday. What a pity I won't be at home for it."

"The tenth of last month was your sister's birthday," Jinlian said. "Now it is your mother's. You people in the bawdy house suffer from two diseases on the same day and have three birthdays. In the daytime you have the money disease and at night the husband disease. In the morning, it is your mother's birthday; at noon, your sister's; and your own in the evening. It is very funny, all these birthdays coming in a lump. When your husband has any money, you had better make the best of the opportunity and celebrate all your birthdays together." Guijie laughed.

Ximen Qing sent Huatong to summon Guijie. She went to Yueniang's room to powder her face and then to the garden. Under the arbor a square table had been set, and on it were two large plates of roasted pork and many other dishes. The friends were eating, and Guijie served them with wine.

"Let me say this in your father's hearing," Ying Bojue said. "I am not talking for the sake of talking. I want to say that this business of yours is settled. Your father has done what was necessary at the district office, and you will not be arrested. But to whom do you owe this kindness? To me, who urged your father so strongly that he decided to intervene on your behalf. Now you must sing one of your favorite songs as a return to me, while I am drinking my wine."

Guijie laughed. "You ghostly beggar," she said. "You think too much of yourself. I don't believe Father pays the slightest attention to you."

"You little whore," Bojue said. "The sacred texts are not yet read, and already you would strike the priest. But don't go too far. Don't laugh at the priest because he hasn't got a mother-in-law. If I were a priest, I could deal with you myself, you young strumpet. And don't make fun of me. There are still some limbs that I can move."

Guijie struck him as hard as she could with the fan she held. Ximen Qing laughed. "You dog," he said, "your sons will be thieves and your daughters whores. And even that will not be as much as you deserve."

They all laughed. Guijie slowly took her lute and put it across her knees. She opened her scarlet lips and showed the whiteness of her teeth. Then she sang the song of the orioles.

> Who would have dreamed that this so fragrant body
> Could have been wasted and brought low by suffering?
> Her mirror is tarnished and she has no heart
> To polish it.
> She is too languid to adorn her face with powder,
> Too languid to set flowers in her hair.
> Her brows are knit in bitterness.

"You used to like him," Bojue said, "and you should be tender with him now. You ought not to treat him so unkindly."

"I don't know what you're talking about," Guijie said, and went on with her song.

> Most hard to bear is the sound of the horn
> Which the watchman blows on his Tower of vigil.
> It breaks her heart.

"Your heart is not broken yet," Bojue said, "but I warn you not to put too great a strain upon it. The string may break."

Guijie hit him hard. "You rascal," she scolded. "Are you quite mad today, that you fool with me like this?" She sang about the meeting of the virtuous guests.

> The windows are calm and silent
> The moon shines brightly.
> Alone, she leans upon the screen.
> She hears the sudden cry of a wild goose that has lost her mate,
> Calling outside the hall.
> It wakes her to the memory of ten thousand griefs.
> The night watch passes like an age
> The water clock moves slowly.
> She does not see the dimness of the lamps
> The burned-out ashes of the incense.
> She tries to sleep, but how can sleep
> Come peacefully to her?

"Oh, you foolish little whore," Bojue said, "why can't you sleep in peace? Nobody's arrested you yet. Why don't you sleep at home? You managed to escape into somebody's house, and still you are worried all day long. You won't be happy till the man comes back from the Eastern Capital."

This made Guijie angry. "Father," she said, "listen to Beggar Ying amusing himself at my expense. I don't know why he does it."

"Yes," Bojue said. "Now you realize that he is your father."

Guijie did not answer him. She took up her lute and went on with her song.

> When I think of him, when I think of him
> How can my heart not be troubled?
> When I am alone, when I am alone
> Tears fall from my cheeks like pearls.

"There was once a man," Bojue said, "who was always piddling. One day his mother died, and, in due observance of the rites, he slept before the coffin. He piddled again. Someone came and saw that the bedclothes were wet, and asked what had happened. The man didn't know what to say. 'Can't you see?' he said. 'It was the tears falling from my stomach.' It is just the same with your song. The girl could not think what to say, so she had to howl in secret."

"You shameless little boy," Guijie said. "Were you there to see? You're crazy." She continued her song.

> I hate him. I hate him.
> I can never tell the things he did.
> To this place I have fled, hating myself
> Because I dealt with him so faithfully.

"Oh, you foolish little whore," Bojue said. "In these days it is impossible to deceive even a three-year-old child. How could anyone expect you to be honest with the clients of your house of joy? Now I'll sing you one of the songs of the South."

> In these days we cannot say
> Who is straight and who is crooked.
> The world is full of cunning spooks
> And all pretend to love us dearly.
> They plot to bury us alive
>
> And put a jar upon our heads.
> The old whores think of nothing but cash
> And the poor little whores stretch out their necks
> To make the business flourish.
> Their bitterness is as great
> As that of drowning in the river.
> The grief we get of them
> Drives us to seek a well.
> When will their cup of bitterness be full?
> Far better would it be to live as horse or donkey.
> Than make a living by such dirty business.

Guijie began to cry. Ximen Qing slapped Ying Bojue and said, laughingly: "You will kill somebody with those silly jokes of yours." To Guijie he said: "Don't cry. Go on with your songs and don't mind him."

"Brother Ying," Xie Xida said, "why are you so rude to my daughter, treating her so unkindly? If you say another word, may you grow a big sore on your mouth."

After a while Guijie took up her lute again and sang:

> Men all say that he is noble and true . . .

Bojue began to say something, but Xie Xida clapped a hand to his mouth. He bade Guijie continue and pay no attention to Bojue.

> But the rogue is a deceiver.
> His eyes are open wide, but lips and heart
> Speak different stories.

Xie Xida took his hand away from Bojue's mouth. "If they did speak the same language, there would be no harm done," Bojue said. "But of course they never do. Why, the mouth might not agree even if your 'tiger's mouth' does—at least after two or three cones of moxa are burned there."

"Have you seen that done, you white-browed, red-eyed fellow?" said Guijie.

"Of course I've seen it. I saw it in the Hall of the Joy Star."

Ximen Qing and the others laughed. Guijie continued.

> He swore by mountain and by ocean.
> He lied as though he spoke the truth.
> Nearly did I suffer from love sickness for him,
> That deceiver.
> Now I know his deceit, but what can I do?

"What does life hold in store for you indeed?" Bojue said. "Why, he will certainly become a general one of these days."

Guijie sang again.

> Every day we are farther and farther apart.
> When shall we meet again?
> You have wronged me, who have waited for you
> With such longing and such patience.
> Even in my dreams I know
> The clouds and rain upon Wu Mountain
> Can never meet again.
> All my life long I must be
> The widowed phoenix, you my widower.

She brought the song to an end.

> Your love has waned, you leave me lonely.
> All that life meant is now but emptiness.

"Excellent! Excellent!" Xie Xida cried. "You take the lute," he said to Shutong," and I will offer her a cup of wine to put her in a better humor."

"Yes," said Bojue, "and I will offer her something to eat. I seem to be no use to anybody, so I'll make this offering as amends for my evil deeds."

"Go away, you beggar," Guijie said. "Who wants your attentions? First you strike a man with your fist and then pat him on the back."

Xie Xida offered Guijie three cups of wine one after the other. Then he said to Bojue: "We have still a couple of games to play." They began to play again. Ximen Qing made a sign to Guijie and went out.

"Brother," Bojue said, as Ximen was going, "if you are going to the inner court, bring me some fragrant tea leaves. The garlic I had is making my breath smell."

"Where am I to get any fragrant tea?" Ximen said.

"Now, Brother, don't try to hoodwink me. I happen to know that Liu, the educational officer at Hangzhou, sent you a lot. Surely you don't want to keep it all for yourself." Ximen Qing laughed and went away. Guijie went out too.

She plucked a few flowers and then disappeared. Bojue and Xie Xida played three games. Then, as Ximen Qing did not return, they said to Huatong: "What is your father doing in the inner court?"

"He will be back soon," the boy replied.

"Will he?" said Bojue. "There is something funny about this." He said to Xie Xida: "You wait here, and I'll go and look for him." Xie Xida and Huatong played chess together.

Ximen Qing had gone to Li Ping'er's room to get some of his medicine. Then he came to the Arbor of Wild Roses and there met Guijie. He took her to the Snow Cavern. He shut the door, sat down on a small bed, and took Guijie on his knee. He showed his weapon to her and she was startled by it. "How did you make it so huge?" she said. Ximen told her about the Indian Monk. Then he asked her to bend her white neck, open her red lips and toy with it for a while. He gently lifted her two tiny feet, raised her in his arms, set her upon a chair and got to work. Meanwhile, Ying Bojue was looking everywhere for him without success. At last, he went through a small grotto under the mound of greenery, and so came to the Arbor of Wild Roses. Then he passed the Arbor of Grapes and so came to the Snow Cavern. It was deeply hidden in the thicknesses of the bamboos and pine trees.

He could hear someone laughing softly, but could not make out where the sound was coming from. He went on tiptoe to the cavern and pulled up the lattice. But the door was fast. He could hear Guijie's trembling voice calling Ximen Qing her darling. "Oh, please be quick," he heard her say, "I am afraid of someone coming." Then Ying Bojue gave a shout and pushed open the door. Ximen Qing, with Guijie's legs around him, was doing splendid work.

"Quick," cried Bojue, "fetch some water. There is a fight going on here."

"You frightened me, you silly thing, rushing in like that," Guijie said.

"You said you wished to make an end quickly," said Bojue, "but it is not so easy as all that. Things have to reach a certain pitch first. You were afraid someone would come and catch you, and here I am. I shall have to come to an understanding with you."

"You funny dog," said Ximen, "be off at once. Don't play tricks and let all the servants know."

"You must talk to me nicely, you little whore," Bojue said, "or I shall shout at the top of my voice, and all the ladies will know. They have accepted you as a daughter, and have been good enough to let you stay here. Now, here you are stealing their man, and, if it comes out, I don't know what will happen to you."

"Go away, you beggar," Guijie said.

"I will go when you have given me a kiss," said Bojue. He kissed her and went out.

"Come back, you dog. Why don't you shut the door?"

Ying Bojue came back and shut the door. "Strike hard, my son," he said to Ximen Qing, "and if you demolish her bottom, it will not worry me."

He went as far as the pine trees and came back again. "Where are the fragrant tea leaves you promised me?"

"I will give them to you later," Ximen said. "Why do you need to come back again now?"

Bojue went off laughing. "Really," said Guijie, "the man does not know how to behave." For a full hour she sported with Ximen, and then they ate a red date that allowed them to reach a climax. They set their clothes in order and came out of the Cavern of Snow. Guijie took some fragrant tea leaves from his sleeve and put them in her own. Ximen Qing was bathed in sweat. He was puffing and blowing. He went to a blooming lantana and piddled. Guijie took a small mirror from her girdle, dressed her hair by the window and went to the inner court. Ximen Qing went to the rooms of Li Ping'er, washed his hands, and rejoined his friends. Ying Bojue again asked for the tea leaves.

"You beggar," Ximen Qing said, "you might be going to die if you didn't get it. What makes you such a nuisance?" He gave a pinch to each of them.

"Is this all?" Bojue said. "Well, never mind, I'll ask the little whore for some."

Li Ming came and kowtowed to them. "Where have you come from?" Bojue said, "and how is that business of yours going?"

"Thanks to Father's kindness," Li Ming said, "the officers have not interfered with us for the last day or two. We are waiting to hear from the Eastern Capital."

"Has that little wench Qi Xiang'er come out yet?" Bojue asked.

"No," said Li Ming, "she is still at Wang's place. Guijie is safe here. No one would dare to come to this house for her."

"It would have been very awkward," Bojue said, "but fortunately, I and Uncle Xie won over your father. We told him that if he did nothing to help your sister, no one would."

"Oh," Li Ming said, "without Father's help, it would have been hopeless. The old lady is not very bright, and, besides, what could she do?"

"If I am right, it is the old lady's birthday some time now," Bojue said. "I must persuade your father to go with me to congratulate her."

"Pray do not put yourself about," Li Ming said. "When this matter is settled, she and Guijie will invite you, of course."

"Then we will congratulate her afterwards," Bojue said. "Come and drink this cup of wine for me. I have been drinking all day and I can't drink any more." The boy took the silver cup and knelt down to drink it. Xie Xida told Qintong to give him another cup.

"I feel sure you have not had anything to eat," Bojue said to Li Ming. "Here is a plate of cakes." Xie Xida took two plates of roast pork and duck and handed them to Li Ming. With his chopsticks, Ying Bojue helped the boy to half a shad fish. "I can see you haven't tasted any of this fish this year," he said. "Here is something seasonable for you."

"You funny dog," Ximen Qing cried. "Why don't you give him all the fish and be done with it?"

"I will eat the rest myself when I feel hungry again, after I have had some more wine. Don't you realize that fish of this sort is only to be had once a year? Why! When you pick your teeth, it still tastes sweet. This is no ordinary fish. I very much doubt whether you could even find it at Court. Certainly I could not get any anywhere else but here."

Huatong brought more dishes, water chestnuts, lotus roots and Ioquat fruits. Before Ximen Qing had time to eat any of them, Ying Bojue had emptied the plate into his sleeve. "You must leave some for me," said Xie Xida, taking another dish and leaving only the loquats on the table. Ximen Qing took one and put it into his mouth, then gave the rest to Li Ming. He told Huatong to go to the kitchen and bring two Ioquat fruits for Li Ming, who, when he had eaten them, sang a song for which Ying Bojue specially asked. The three men drank until evening. Then rice gruel with dried peas was brought for them. When they had eaten it, Bojue and Xie Xida made ready to go.

"Brother," Bojue said, "I understand that you are taking wine with his Excellency An tomorrow. I will tell Li and Huang to come about their business the day after tomorrow." Ximen Qing nodded. They did not wait for him to take them to the door, but went away by themselves. Ximen Qing told Shutong to clear the table and went to Yulou's room.

The next morning he did not go to the office, but dressed immediately after breakfast and, with Shutong and Daian, rode to Eunuch Liu's place. It was distant from the city about forty *li*.

Jinlian took advantage of Ximen Qing's absence to ask Li Ping'er to spend the three *qian* of silver that Chen Jingji had lost, adding another seven *qian* to them. They asked Laixing to buy a roast duck, two chickens, a jar of Jinhua wine, a bottle of white wine, fruit pastries and other things, and arranged for his wife to prepare them. Then Jinlian said to Yueniang: "The other day, Ximen Dajie was playing cards with her husband, and won three *qian* of silver from him. The Sixth Lady has added some more to it, and we have arranged to have a little feast. We should be glad if you would come and enjoy it with us in the garden." So Wu Yueniang, Meng Yulou, Li Jiao'er, Sun Xue'e, Ximen Dajie and Li Guijie all went to the arbor and joined in the feast. They took some of the food to the artificial mound. There, some of them played chess and some played darts.

"Why has our host not come?" Yueniang said.

"Father sent him to Xu's for some money," Ximen Dajie said, "but I don't think he will be long."

Chen Jingji soon came. He made a reverence to the ladies and sat down beside his wife. He told Yueniang that he had brought two hundred and fifty taels from Xu and given them to Yuxiao. The wine was passed around, and they all enjoyed themselves immensely. Yueniang, Li Jiao'er, and Guijie played chess, Yulou and the others strolled about the garden admiring the flowers. Jinlian, alone, fanning herself with a white silk fan, went in search of coolness to the deepest part of the banana palm glade behind the artificial mound. She saw on the grass a wild purple flower that was very delightful and went to gather it. She did not imagine that when he saw her go, Chen Jingji would quietly follow her by impulse. Suddenly he spoke from behind her. "What are you looking for, my lady? The grass is slippery, and I shouldn't like you to fall. It would hurt me if you did."

Jinlian glanced at him over her shoulder. Half smiling, half reproving, she said: "Why should it hurt you if I fell, you young scamp? I don't need you to look after me. What are you doing here? Aren't you afraid somebody will see us? What about those handkerchiefs you were to buy for me?"

"Here are the handkerchiefs," Jingji said, smiling. He took them from his sleeve. "What will you give me for them?" He drew nearer, but she pushed him away. Just then, Li Ping'er with Guan'ge in her arms came through the pine alleys with the nurse. They could see the movement of the white fan in Jinlian's hand, but not that she was pushing Jingji aside with it. They thought she was catching butterflies.

"Fifth Mother," Li Ping'er said, "catch a butterfly for my baby."

Jingji hurriedly slipped behind the artificial mound. Jinlian wondered whether Li Ping'er had seen him. She said: "Has our brother given you any handkerchiefs?"

"No, no yet," Li Ping'er said.

"He has brought them," Jinlian said, "but he did not like to give them to us in front of his wife, so he gave them to me secretly." They sat down in the shade of the plantains, opened the packet, and divided them.

After a while Li Ping'er said to Ruyi'er: "It is very cool and pleasant here. Go and tell Yingchun to bring the baby's pillow and bed, and also a set of dominoes. I will have a game with the Fifth Lady. You stay in my room."

The nurse went away, and Yingchun came with the things. Li Ping'er spread out the bed and put the baby upon it. While the baby was playing, she had a game of dominoes with Jinlian. Then she told Yingchun to bring a pot of tea. Yulou, who was in the smaller arbor, caught sight of them. She beckoned to Li Ping'er. "Come here," she said, "I have something to tell you."

Li Ping'er left the baby in Jinlian's care and went to speak to Yulou. But Jinlian was thinking about Chen Jingji who was still hiding in the grotto, and she forgot about the baby. She hurried into the cave and said to Jingji: "There is nobody about now. Come out at once." Jingji asked her to go and look at a huge mushroom that he said was there. She went in. Then Jingji knelt down and begged Jinlian to grant him her favors. They kissed.

When Li Ping'er came to the arbor, Yueniang said to her: "Yulou has been playing darts with Guijie. She was beaten. We want you to play for her."

"But there is nobody to look after my baby," Li Ping'er said.

"Jinlian is there," Yulou said. "There is no reason why you should worry." Yueniang asked Yulou to go and look after the child.

"Bring him here," Li Ping'er said. She told Xiaoyu to bring the baby's bed. Yulou and the maid went to the grove of plantains. The baby was screaming upon his bed, and there was no sign of Jinlian. A big black cat stood beside the child. It ran away when they came near.

"Where is the Fifth Lady?" Yulou said. "She has left the baby here, and the cat has terrified him."

Jinlian hurried out of the grotto. "I have just been to wash my hands, that's all. Where is this cat that is supposed to have frightened the baby? What are you so excited about?"

Yulou did not look into the grotto. She picked up the baby and went back to the arbor, trying to pacify him. Xiaoyu brought the bed, and Jinlian, afraid that they would tell the true story, went with them.

"Why is the baby crying?" Yueniang said.

"When we got there," Yulou said, "there was a big black cat standing near his head."

"He must have been frightened," Yueniang said.

"But the Fifth Lady was looking after him," said Li Ping'er.

"She had gone into the grotto to wash her hands," Yulou said.

"How can you say such a thing!" Jinlian said. "And where is this cat of yours? The baby is hungry and wants some milk. That's all."

Yingchun brought tea, and Li Ping'er told the nurse to feed the child.

Chen Jingji, now that there was nobody about, came out of the grotto and slipped away between the pine hedges. Yueniang, seeing that the baby refused to feed and would do nothing but cry, told Li Ping'er to take him to her room and put him to sleep. The party broke up. Chen Jingji, who had been disappointed in his hopes of enjoying Jinlian, went sadly to his own room.

CHAPTER 53

Pan Jinlian Is Unfaithful

In the little courtyard the jade steps are deserted
At the corner of the wall a few orchids put forth new shoots.
Lilies and pomegranates blossom there
The flowers beloved by those who long for children.
Let not the wind and rain beat down those flowers
May Heaven foster them.
May they not turn into the cuckoo flowers
Whose colors quickly change
And whose fragrance fades away.

Ximen Qing went to take wine with the two dignitaries An and Huang. With the serving boys, he came to Eunuch Liu's place. The two gentlemen came out to welcome him. Eunuch Liu was acting as host, and he, too, came out to meet Ximen, taking him by the hand as soon as he dismounted. "We have been waiting for you for a long time," he said. "You are late."

"You are very kind," Ximen said, "but I had some trifling business to attend to at home and this caused me to keep you waiting. I am very, very sorry." They all bowed profoundly and went into the hall. Ximen Qing again made reverence to them. They asked him to take the seat of honor and Eunuch Liu to take the second place. Eunuch Liu declined.

"This is my house," he said, "and you are my guests."

An insisted: "It is your proper place," he said. Ximen Qing supported him.

"On the score of age alone," he said, "you should take it, most noble sir." Liu could protest no more.

"Then," he said, "I must be presumptuous enough to take the second place." Huang and An sat in the hosts' seats. Some young actors came and kowtowed. Tea was served and then wine.

When the tables had been laid, the young actors took their instruments, string and wind, tuned them and sang the song "In Springtime, the Gentle Rain Falls Softly." When the song was done, Liu raised his cup and asked the company to drink.

"What an exquisitely beautiful song that was. Quite incomparable!" An said. "It must have been written by a true scholar. And the singers' voices are so sweet. One can imagine them holding back the floating clouds. You will agree with me, I am sure, when I say that, in both respects, we have here an example of absolute beauty."

"With regard to that," Ximen Qing said, "I can express no opinion. But I certainly would call this a marvelous party, with you two gentlemen as hosts and noble Liu here as the master of the house."

"That is not quite a true statement of the case," Huang said. "This party is remarkable because of the presence at it of noble Liu, who has gone daily in and out of the purple forbidden city, and witnessed the appearance of the Dragon. Is he not an illustrious chamberlain? And here, too, is noble Ximen, whose gold is as a mountain and whose jade is beyond price. We may well compare him with Tao Zhu, a wealthy man indeed. We have here two men, one of unusually exalted rank, the other extremely rich. This is indeed cause for admiration."

They laughed heartily and drank together. One of the actors took a long flute and played a melodious tune. The others sang a new song, "Where the Peach Flowers and Willows Blossom beside the Stream." This song too, met with approval.

Chen Jingji was driven to desperation by the foiling of his desire to possess Pan Jinlian. Ximen Qing did not return, and Jingji went quietly backwards and forwards, continually peeping in at the inner court. Jinlian herself, after the advances the young man had made to her, was ill at ease. There was nobody about, and she pondered the matter, resting her cheeks upon her hands. Suddenly, in the darkness, Chen Jingji came in. It seemed as though he would have devoured her. Desperately, he came up behind her and took her in his arms. "Woman mine," he said, "it nearly killed me when Meng Yulou came and disturbed us."

Jinlian was startled, for she had not noticed his coming. When she turned her head and saw who it was, she was half frightened, half pleased. "You young thief," she said, "let me go. Someone will see us." But Jingji would not let her go. He fumbled at her trousers, trying to unloose them. Jinlian half yielded, half resisted, but he had already torn the ribbon that held them. She pretended to be alarmed. "You thief," she said. "Are you so ignorant of the laws of propriety that you dare thus to approach your mother?"

"Mother," Jingji said earnestly, "should you ask for my heart and liver that you might make them into soup, I would gladly cut them out of my body for you. You must be kind to me."

As he spoke, he brought forward that which was below his waist. It was firm, and he pushed it forward against the single garment Jinlian was wearing. The touch of it made her cheeks as rosy as the peach blossom. She still made a show of refusal, but, as he persisted in his entreaties, she could not keep her hand from touching him. Jingji pulled up her skirt and shoved with all his might. At the first thrust he gained access, for she had long been aroused and was already wet, so there was nothing in their way. They stood up against the railing and sported furiously. Jingji was not satisfied. "Lie on the ground," he said, "and I will give you all you want."

Jinlian feared that her hair would be disordered or that someone might come. "Not this time," she said. "Let us be content for now. We shall meet again." They called each other many tender names and played together for a long time. Then they heard voices on the other side of the wall and were compelled to separate. They were still unsatisfied. The noise they heard was that of Shutong and Daian coming in with Ximen's hat, girdle, and boxes. The two boys were tipsy and made a great deal of noise.

Yueniang heard them and thought that Ximen had come. She sent Xiaoyu to make sure. The boys told her he was on his way, that they had come before him. When Ximen came, he was drunk. He went to Yueniang's room and carried her to her bed. But it was the next day, which happened to be a *renzi* day, on which she wished him to come to her. So she said: "I am not very well. Go somewhere else tonight."

Ximen laughed. "Oh, I know," he said, "you don't want me because I am drunk. Very well. I won't upset you. I'll go away and come tomorrow."

Yueniang smiled. "Really I am not very well," she said. "It isn't that I do not want you. Do please come tomorrow."

Ximen Qing went to Jinlian. She was resting on the bed after her bout with Chen Jingji. She rose hastily and said: "I suppose you have just come back from the party?"

Ximen did not answer. He took her in his arms and kissed her. Then he touched her cunt. "You wicked little strumpet. Of whom have you been thinking that you are as wet as this?"

Jinlian said nothing. She pushed him aside and went to wash herself. The happiness they enjoyed that night is beyond description.

The next day was the twenty-third and a *renzi* day. Yueniang got up and dressed herself. She told Xiaoyu to set out a table, and on it she placed an incense burner and burned some precious incense. Then she placed on the table a volume of the Scripture of the White-robed Guanyin. Yueniang knelt towards the west, added more incense, and opened the book. She read it once and knelt down once, and so twenty-four times, reading and kneeling time and time again. She took the medicine from a small box, put it on the table and knelt down four times. Then she made this prayer: "The woman Wu prays to Heaven most high that, by the help of this medicine, prepared by the nuns Xue and Wang she may be blessed with a male child." She took the wine that Xiaoyu had warmed and knelt towards the west again. Then she swallowed the pills and the powders. When the medicine passed her throat, it tasted very fishy, and she had to gulp it down. She made reverence four times more, then went back to her own room and remained there.

The next day, when Ximen Qing had got up in Jinlian's room, he sent Shutong with a card to thank Huang and An for the banquet they had given him. Ying Bojue came. He made a reverence to Ximen and said: "Brother, what time was it when you came back from Liu's place yesterday?"

"They were very kind and pressed me to drink a great deal of wine," Ximen said. "I had a long way to come home, and it was after the first night watch when I got here. I was drunk. That is why I am so late getting up."

Daian brought breakfast, and the two friends ate it together. A servant came and announced their Excellencies An and Huang. Ximen Qing dressed, and told the servants to make haste and clear the table. Ying Bojue disappeared into another room. An and Huang got out of their chairs and greeted Ximen Qing. They came in, and the servants brought tea.

"We were lacking in politeness last night," the two gentlemen said.

"You were most kind," Ximen said, "and I was just thinking of coming to see you when you arrived."

"You cannot possibly have been satisfied with your entertainment or you would not have left so early," said An.

"I fear I was very drunk last night," Ximen said. "When it was time for me to leave, noble Liu gave me more than ten cups of grape wine. I was almost sick as I rode home, but I managed somehow to control myself. I have only just waked up and even now I am not quite sober."

They laughed, drank three cups of wine, then talked for a while and took their leave. Ying Bojue said he had business to attend to and went home.

Ximen Qing went to the inner court and had lunch. Afterwards, he got into a sedan chair and went to pay a return call upon An and Huang. He had two red present cards written and told Daian to buy two sets of presents. These he took with him.

That evening, when he came home, Yueniang had made every preparation for him. As soon as he arrived she told Xiaoyu to bring food and heat wine. Husband and wife sat together. "Last night," he said, "I was drunk and you wouldn't let me stay. You tried to pretend you were not well, but you were only fooling me."

"No," Yueniang said, "I really was not well. Why should husband and wife not be free and open with one another?"

Ximen Qing drank ten cups of wine, ate some fish and some duck, then would not eat any more. Yueniang told her maids to clear away. Xiaoyu perfumed the bedclothes. They bathed and went to bed. That night they enjoyed delight beyond all measure. Yueniang's monthly sickness was just over, and she had every reason to hope that the joy she sought would be granted her. She was as lively as a fish in the water. So a child was conceived.

The next day, when Ximen Qing got up, Yueniang prepared for him lamb, wine, eggs and kidneys, and he went to his office. When he returned, he went to Li Ping'er's room to see Guan'ge. He found her nursing the baby.

"Some time ago," she said to him, "I vowed to make a sacrifice, but I have not done so. These last few days, every time I go for a certain purpose, I lose a little blood. I ought to carry out my vow, but, so far, I have been too busy."

"If you like," Ximen Qing said, "I will send Daian for Nun Wang and you can talk to her about it." He gave the necessary instructions to Daian, and the boy went away at once.

Shutong came and said: "Uncle Ying and Uncle Chang are here." Ximen Qing went out to see them.

"The other day, when Xie Xida and I had wine with you," Bojue said, "I told you about that matter of Huang and Li, and you promised they should have the money."

"But where am I to find the money?" Ximen said.

"The other day you promised. Why have you changed your mind? Brother, don't try to pretend. You are such a rich man that it is no use your professing not to have any money. You must give them some."

Ximen Qing did not answer. He looked at Chang Zhijie.

"It is a long time since I last saw you," Chang Zhijie said. "How is your young son?"

"Thank you," Ximen said. "My wife has just been telling me that she is anxious to have a service for him. I have sent for a nun called Wang to see about it."

"When people have money," Ying Bojue said, "children make a great difference. When a child comes into the world, he needs the utmost care. It is like planting seeds. They must be watered when they are young if they are ever to come to anything. My little brother is more valuable than ten thousand pieces of gold. He is a pearl upon your palm. You can't help taking more care of him than common people do. There is always trouble with children in their second year, the sixth, and again in the ninth. There is always danger of smallpox and scarlet fever. Forgive my plain speaking, but I feel that you should indeed offer sacrifice for your child, and so secure the happiness that you have already. If my sister-in-law wishes it, it must be done. Then your troubles will end and the rearing of the baby will be a simple matter."

Daian came and said: "Nun Wang was not at the temple. She had gone to Wang's palace. I went there to look for her. After I had waited a long time, she came out and I gave her the message. She promised to come at once."

Ximen continued his conversation with Ying Bojue and Chang Zhijie. Shutong brought them tea.

"Brother," Ying Bojue said, "you have been very kind to me, but I have never ventured to ask you to come and see me, because my house is so unsuited for your entertainment. But if you are free tomorrow or the day after, I hope you and Brother Chang will come and spend a day with me in the country, and so give me an opportunity to show my friendship."

"I am sure you cannot fail to appreciate the motives of my friend Ying, and I hope you will accept his invitation," said Chang.

"I am not busy tomorrow," Ximen Qing said, "but I do not like to bother you."

"I cannot remember the number of times I have bothered you," Bojue said. "Besides, I am making no very great preparations. Just a poor cup of wine."

"I will keep tomorrow free for you," Ximen said.

"I have engaged the young actors," Bojue said, "but perhaps it would be more satisfactory to have two singing girls."

"Don't let that trouble you," Ximen said, "I will arrange for Wu Yin'er and Han Jinchuan to come." He told Qintong to go at once to the two singing girls and tell them that, the next day, they must go to the park outside the city.

Before long, Nun Wang came. She made a reverence to Ximen Qing. "You sent for me," she said. "May I hear your commands? I was at his Lordship Wang's place and could not get away before."

"This is the situation," Ximen Qing said. "When Guan'ge was born, we promised to have a service of thanksgiving, but we have been so busy that we omitted to do so. We wish to give thanks to Heaven for protecting him so far and letting him grow so big. In the first place, I wish to thank Buddha for his favor, and, secondly, to forestall any calamities and troubles that might be in store for him, and ensure his long life. So I sent for you."

"The young master's body is worth ten thousand pieces of gold," Nun Wang said, "and we must trust in Buddha's protection for him. Your Lordship may not know it, but in the Sacred Scriptures of Buddha it is written that in the world of men there prowl demons and devils whose business it is to inflict injuries upon people and destroy their children. When a child dies before its birth, or in its infancy, some demon is always responsible. The best thing we can do for your son will be to read the sacred texts and implore the assistance of Buddha. Anything else would be inappropriate."

"What is the most suitable form for our devotions to take?" Ximen Qing asked.

"First," Nun Wang said, "we will go through the scripture of the Master of Medicine. Then, I suggest that we prepare two Tuoluo charms. They cannot fail to be efficacious."

"And when will you begin reading the scriptures?"

"Tomorrow is an excellent day; I will have the service at my temple."

Ximen Qing agreed. Nun Wang went to the inner court to see Yueniang and the others. They were with Li Ping'er. She made a reverence to them all. Yueniang said: "We are anxious for you to do something for the baby. When will you do it?" Nun Wang said that she would begin at her temple the following day. Xiaoyu brought tea for her.

"Teacher," Li Ping'er said to her, "I have something to say to you." The nun begged her to speak. "Since I have had this baby," Li Ping'er said, "I have never been quite well. When you read the sacred scriptures, pray for me too. I will see that you are well paid for it."

"That will be no trouble," Nun Wang said. "When I write out the prayers, I will put down your name. That is all."

CHAPTER 54

Ying Bojue Gives a Party

Precious wine is worth a fortune
Let not the wine cups, then, stay idle in the hand
In the presence of the flowers.
Rise and dance and drink with the flowers.
The flowers are silent
They know men love them.

Let us not say farewell till we have drunk our fill.
Look at the flowers
Already one is faded.
Yet, though the flowers fade
Next year they will be as beautiful again.
So much cannot be said of these fair maidens.

It was arranged between Nun Wang, Li Ping'er and Wu Yueniang that the religious ceremony should be performed next day. Yueniang sent all the necessary things to the temple. She said to Chen Jingji: "Tomorrow the Sixth Lady is making intercession for a blessing on her child, and you must go to the service." But Jingji said:

"Father is going to the gardens outside the city, and I shall have to look after the shop. It would be better to ask someone else to go to the ceremony." As a matter of fact, Jingji, hearing that Ximen Qing was going to a party with Ying Bojue, thought it would be an excellent opportunity for him to amuse himself with Pan Jinlian. Yueniang believed that he really was going to look after the shop, so she did not press him any further. She told Shutong to go to the service.

While Ximen Qing, Ying Bojue and Chang Zhijie were still talking, Qintong came back. "I have been for the two singing girls," he said. "Wu Yin'er is not well. She will not be able to go tomorrow, and Han Jinchuan will take her place."

"You had better go and tell Dong Jiao'er," Ximen Qing said. Chang declared that as they were going outside the city they did not need a second girl. The two men went away.

The next day, Ximen Qing got up before dawn. Yueniang had arranged breakfast for him and, as soon as he had eaten it, he got into a sedan chair and went to the temple of Guanyin for the beginning of the service. Nun Wang came to the temple gate to meet him.

The nun read the prayers, and afterwards Ximen Qing went to change his clothes. Tea, cakes and fruits were brought for him, but he took only a mouthful of tea. Then he went back to his chair, bidding Shutong stay for the remainder of the service. When he reached home, the sun had only just risen, but Ying Bojue and Chang Zhijie had already arrived.

Ximen Qing laughed at them. "Who ever heard of invitations for breakfast?" he said. "It is true I am not busy today, but we can't go till afternoon."

"You don't understand, Brother," Ying Bojue said. "Twenty *li* outside the city there is a park belonging to a eunuch. It is beautiful and it is quiet. But it is so big that it would take two days at least to appreciate all its beauties. We must go early and spend all day there."

"Brother," Chang Zhijie said, "you have nothing particular to do today. That is why we came so early. Let us start at once."

"If you will have it so," said Ximen, "you go first and I will join you there."

The two men set out, but, sending the attendants in advance, they themselves went to the bawdy house and waited for Han Jinchuan to go with them. Ying Bojue had arranged for refreshments and engaged two actors.

Some time after Bojue had gone, Ximen Qing got into his sedan chair and went out of the city.

> A thousand trees cast a deep shadow
> And a brook meanders through them.
> White walls enclose the ever-blooming flowers
> And pleasant houses screen the quiet landscape.
> Peach flowers blossoming at Wuling
> Make the fisherman lose his way.
> Plum blossoms flowering on the Yu Mountains
> And the poets exchange verses in the sunshine.
> It is paradise on earth.

Ximen Qing could not help exclaiming at the beauty of the scenery. He got out of his sedan chair and went into the gardens. Ying Bojue and Chang Zhijie came to welcome him, and they went together to an arbor. Han Jinchuan and the actors kowtowed to him. Tea was served. Bojue would have had wine, but Ximen said: "There is no hurry. Let us take a stroll together." He took Han Jinchuan's hand and Ying Bojue led the way. They went to a verandah, then, following the vermilion railings, came to a place where there were many willow trees and an arbor of roses. They passed the Taihu stone and the Pavilion of the Pine Winds. So they came to the Pavilion of Unusual Characters. Behind this were about thirty plum trees, and among them a small high building called the Tower of the Plums. In this were many poems written by famous men. Ximen Qing studied them attentively. They went to the peony bed, where there were many different kinds of rare peonies. Then they turned to the north, and here was the bamboo grove with a small pavilion with the sign "Listen to the rustling of the bamboos," and a small arbor called the Coming of the Phœnix. The signs were all written by men of great renown for their skill with the brush. On the right was a goldfish pond and, on the bank, a small arbor with a sign: "Here you may enjoy the water." They leaned on the red railings for a while and watched the goldfish swimming about in the water. They made the pond seem like an embroidered coverlet. Ximen Qing was especially pleased with this. But Ying Bojue led him to another high building. This was the "Tower for Listening to the Moon." There were many poems by famous men here also, and panels of carved wood painted in characters of green. They went down from the building and turned towards the east. There they saw a great artificial mound with a cave in it called the Cave of the Eight Immortals. In the cave was a marble chess table. Iron flutes and brass long flutes hung upon the walls. It was a place where immortals might have dwelled. When they came out of it, they climbed the mound and from its summit could see the whole extent of the garden.

They had walked for some time, and Chang Zhijie said to Ximen Qing: "Brother, you must be tired. Let us rest in the arbor before we start out again."

"But we haven't been around one-tenth of the garden," Ximen Qing said. "How can we say that we are tired? Don't you know that sedan chair men walk a hundred *li* day?"

They laughed but went to the arbor. Ximen Qing took the place of honor with Chang Zhijie on one side of him and Ying Bojue on the other. Han Jinchuan sat beside Ximen "I must offer you my most sincere thanks for all your trouble," Ximen said to his hosts.

"Brother, it is not worth mentioning," said Bojue. "This is but a poor cup of wine that I am able to offer you."

They drank together, then the two actors came before them. They took their instruments and sang a new song: "Every Word Is Exquisite, Like a Pattern of Flowers." They sang very sweetly, and their voices lingered. Ximen Qing praised them. "It is a pity they are boys," Chang Zhijie said.

"If they were girls, no price would be too high for them."

"If they were girls," Ximen Qing said, "we should have asked them to sit down before this. We should not have allowed them to stand and sing."

"Brother," Bojue said, "you are an officer to the manner born, and what you say always bears the stamp of authority."

Everybody laughed. They drank their wine, and Bojue, taking a large cup, suggested that they should play the game of giving orders. Ximen was not anxious to begin, but Bojue pressed him, and at last he agreed. "I will take the words 'Wind,' 'Flower,' 'Snow' and 'Moon.' I will begin; Brother Chang shall be next; then our host, and, lastly, Han Jinchuan. Each must make a verse and bring into it one of my four words. When he begins, he must drink a cup; and, if he fails, he must drink a second cup and tell a story. If the story is a poor one, he must tell another. I will begin." He took his cup and drank it. "'The clouds are few, the wind gentle. It is nearly noon.' Now, Brother Chang, it is your turn."

Chang drank his cup and said: "Chasing the flowers and following the willows, I crossed the stream." Then it was the turn of the host. Ying Bojue drank his cup of wine, but he seemed dazed and could not get out a word.

"Brother Ying," Ximen Qing said, "you must pay your forfeit and drink another cup."

"Let me think a moment," Bojue said. He racked his brains, and Ximen asked him again. "Of the glory of Spring," he began, "a few degrees have been revealed."

Ximen Qing roared with laughter. "That doesn't include a single one of my words," he cried. "That verse won't do. You'll have to drink two cups."

They called for Bojue's story.

"Once there was a scholar on his way to the Capital," Bojue began. "His boat was anchored in the Yangzi. At nightfall he asked the boatman to go and anchor somewhere else, for, he said, 'There are bandits in this place.' 'Where?' said the boatman. 'Don't you see that inscription on the stone tablet there, "Bandits on the river"?' The boatman laughed and said: 'That isn't "bandits on the river." How could you make such a mistake? It is not "bandit" but "poem".' 'Well,' said the scholar, 'they both look alike to me.'"

"I don't believe any scholar would make such a mistake," Ximen Qing said, laughing.

"Brother Ying," said Chang Zhijie, "you must drink ten big cups."

"Why?" said Ying Bojue, astonished.

"Think for yourself," Chang Zhijie said.

Ximen Qing was reputed to be the wealthiest man in all Shandong, and, when Bojue had spoken in his story of the scholar's confusing the word "poem" for "bandit," he might have been taken to refer to Ximen Qing, for the word for a very wealthy man has the same sound.

Ximen Qing himself had not at once seen the point, but now he understood. Bojue realized that he had made a slip. He drank two cups of wine and asked to be forgiven.

"If you did not deserve to be punished, I would not punish you," Ximen Qing said, "but you do deserve it, and I cannot let you off."

Bojue felt uncomfortable, but he drank a few cups more. "You have too much to say," he said to Chang Zhijie.

"Now you must tell us another story," Ximen said. But Bojue was afraid to commit himself again. "Never mind," Ximen said, "it is only fun, come along." Bojue felt more at ease.

"When Confucius was traveling in the west," he began, "someone caught a unicorn. For some reason Confucius did not see it, and, day and night, he wept and cried bitterly in his house. His disciples were afraid that he would fall ill, so they got a bull, dressed it up in copper coins and tried to persuade him that this was the animal. But the moment Confucius set eyes on it, he saw through their trick. 'Obviously,' he said, 'this is a very wealthy bull, but why do you try to make out that it is a unicorn?'"

When he had finished his story, Bojue fell upon his knees before Ximen Qing. "I know I am not fit to live," he said, "but I really didn't mean any harm."

Ximen Qing laughed and told him to stand up. Han Jinchuan laughed too. "Beggar Ying," she said, "you are always trying to be smart at other people's expense. Now you've put your foot in it. Father, don't pay any heed to him."

Bojue was annoyed at this. He went to Han Jinchuan and struck her on the head. "That rascal Chang," he said, "is bad enough. There was no need for you, you little whore, to say anything more." He had hit her hard and hurt her. She dared not cry, but it was clear that she was very much put out.

"You dog," Ximen Qing said, laughing, "first you make rude jokes about me and then you begin hitting people. What punishment do you really want?"

Bojue laughed and put his arm around Han Jinchuan. "My daughter," he said, "where were you brought up with such tender care that you are ready to cry at a little tap like that? It surprises me that you are able to put up with things as big as a donkey's."

Han Jinchuan turned her head and looked scornfully at him. "Beggar," she said, "pray when were you there to see? You are talking nonsense. It is your wife who has to endure a thing as big as a donkey's."

"Why, of course I've seen," Bojue said, laughing. "The gentleman is famous for his beauty, his asininity, wealth, youth and idleness. He is just the sort of man you like. And that reminds me of another story. There was once a young lady whose thing was getting rather the worse for wear. Somebody told her that if she put a piece of alum into it, it would recover its former tightness. This the young lady did, but she found that it tightened her up so much that it hurt. This made her very sorrowful. She was standing outside her gate when a passerby said: 'That little whore is trying to look like Ba Wang.' The young lady heard him. 'What!' she said, 'Ba Wang indeed! Why, I can't even manage Fan Kuai!'"

They all laughed at this, even Han Jinchuan. Ying Bojue finished his wine and offered another cup to Ximen Qing, asking him to take the last turn in the game. "It is Han Jinchuan's turn," Ximen said. Jinchuan would not play, and Chang urged Ximen. Ximen drank a cup of wine and said: "Up the staircase of the clouds, let us go to the cavern of the immortals in the palace of the moon." So the game was finished.

Ximen Qing changed his clothes and went for a stroll. Bojue was still calling for more refreshment. Suddenly he noticed that Jinchuan had disappeared. He looked about and found that she had gone around the artificial mound and was relieving herself behind the arbor of roses. He picked a branch from a flowering shrub and quietly went over to her. Squatting down behind her, he touched the heart of her flower. Jinchuan was startled, jumped up before she had finished what she was about, and wet her drawers. At that moment Chang Zhijie crept up behind Bojue and pushed him so violently that he fell forward and caught all the piss in his face. He sprang to his feet, laughingly cursed Chang Zhijie, and ran after him to beat him. Ximen Qing stood beside a pine tree and roared with laughter. Even Han Jinchuan laughed and skipped with delight. "Beggar Ying," she said, "now you've got what you deserved." They went back to the table.

"Now, you dog," Ximen Qing said, "you have had your joke at our expense. What about telling us a story against yourself?"

"I don't mind in the least," Bojue said. "One day a rich man let out a fart. A man standing by, one who always lived by sponging on the rich man, said: 'I smell nothing.' This alarmed the rich man. 'That's bad,' he said. 'If there is no smell to my farts there must be something wrong with me. I must see a doctor.' 'Wait a moment,' said the sponger, 'I will make sure.' He put out his nose and pretended to sniff again. Then he smacked his lips. 'Ah,' said he, 'there is a splendid aftertaste. You have nothing to worry about.'"

They all laughed. Chang Zhijie said: "You have made rude remarks about our brother, but why should you draw a picture of me?" They all laughed again. Ying Bojue asked Chang Zhijie to guess fingers with Ximen Qing, and Han Jinchuan sang songs for them.

Chen Jingji, when he was sure that Ximen Qing had gone out, dressed himself and waited for an opportunity to approach Pan Jinlian. He dared not go to her openly, but went to the Snow Cavern hoping that she might be there. He waited for a long time but she did not come. At last he lost patience and went to her room. Fortunately, no one saw him. When he came to the door he could hear her singing in a low sweet voice: "Why did you love me and then forget me?" This seemed a proof that she really loved him. He rushed into the room and threw his arms about her. "How could I ever forget you?" he said. "Yesterday, my darling, the Great Lady told me to go to the temple of Guanyin, but I would not go. I was thinking of you all the time. Today, Father has gone to drink wine, and I went to the Snow Cavern to find you, but though I waited and watched until the eyes nearly came out of my head, your dainty shadow never appeared. Now I have thrown discretion to the winds and come to you here."

"Don't speak so loud," Jinlian said, "there will be trouble if you are heard."

Suddenly, through the window, she saw Xiaoyu coming with a roll of white silk. The girl turned and went away again. "That maid must have forgotten something," Jinlian said. "Did you see how she turned and went back?" She thought it probable that the girl would return. "You must go at once," she said. "We can do nothing now." Chen Jingji was made to vanish like a whiff of smoke. Jinlian was right. Yueniang had told Xiaoyu to take the silk to her so that she could draw the pattern of a skirt, but the girl had forgotten to bring the pattern and went back for it. Luckily, the maid did not catch Jinlian with Jingji. When she returned with the pattern, he had slipped away. But when Jinlian took the silk, her hands were trembling.

Ximen Qing and his friends were becoming tipsy, and he was anxious to go home. Bojue urged him to stay. He knelt down and said: "Brother, is it because you are angry with me on account of that joke I made about you that I can't persuade you to stay?"

Ximen laughed. "You dog," he said, "nobody bothers about what you say."

Bojue took a large cup and filled it for Ximen Qing. Chang Zhijie offered him some fruits. Ximen thanked his host and prepared to leave. He gave Han Jinchuan a tael of silver and told Daian to give the young actors three *qian* each. "I am drunk," he said as he got into his sedan chair. The two boys followed him. Bojue told the servants to clear away and dismissed the young actors. He rode back to the city beside Han Jinchuan's sedan chair.

When Ximen Qing reached home, the sun had set. He went to sleep with Li Ping'er. The next day she said to him: "Ever since the baby was born, there has been something wrong with me. When I look in the mirror, I see how pale my face is. I never want to eat or drink, and, when I try to walk, my legs seem to give way beneath me. If it is anything serious, what will become of my baby?"

Ximen saw that she was crying. "I will send for Doctor Ren," he said. "I am sure you will be all right when you have had some medicine." He told Shutong to write a letter and ask Dr. Ren to come. Shutong went on the errand, and Ximen Qing went to the hall. Ying Bojue came to thank him for coming to the party the day before, and Ximen, in return, thanked him. They sat and talked. Then Shutong came and said: "Doctor Ren is here." Ximen Qing at once went to receive him, introduced him to Ying Bojue, and the three men sat down together. Shutong brought tea.

"Kindly tell me who is ill," Dr. Ren said.

"My sixth wife is not feeling very well. I shall be grateful if you will make a careful examination."

"Is that the lady who had a baby?" Dr. Ren said.

"Yes," said Ximen, "but I don't know why she should not be well."

"Let me go and see her," the doctor said. Ximen Qing took him to Li Ping'er's room. The doctor sat by the bedside, and one of the maids opened the curtains very slightly. Li Ping'er put out her right hand and rested it upon a case of books wrapped in a handkerchief.

"First, I will try the pulse," Dr. Ren said. When he had found the place, he put three fingers on the pulse. He bent his head and examined it carefully for some time. Then he removed his hand, and Li Ping'er slowly withdrew hers. She stretched out her left hand, and laid it on the books. Dr. Ren examined it. Then he said to Ximen Qing: "I have now examined the lady's pulse and—I am very sorry— I must see her face."

"We are good friends," Ximen Qing said, "there need be no difficulty about that." He told the maids to pull the curtains aside. Dr. Ren looked at his patient. Her face was like a peach blossom, her eyebrows dark like willow leaves. He looked at her for a minute, then said to Ximen Qing: "I have seen your lady's face, but I have not come upon any sign of anything serious. I must have more details about her illness. We doctors have to find things out from our patients themselves."

Ximen Qing sent for Ruyi'er. She came in, dressed in her best clothes, made a reverence to the doctor and told him about her mistress's illness:

how her mouth was always parched, and how she suffered from sleeplessness. Dr. Ren stood up and bowed. He said to Ximen Qing: "I don't believe it is anything serious. In people of the common sort, their bodies are so tough that their blood can stand anything, and we can give them almost any kind of medicine. If we make a slight mistake, no great harm is done. But a lady like yours is more delicate. We must not allow the slightest possibility of error, for, if we give her anything that is not exactly what we should give, there may be serious danger. That is why I have to ask questions and find out what she has to say. It is essential. The other day, I went to see his Lordship Wang's wife. Her illness was very similar to your lady's. I asked a few questions, investigated the symptoms and examined her, and so got an excellent idea of the trouble. I went home, read some of the prescriptions of the ancients and compared them with my own ideas upon the subject. I gave her some medicine to get rid of her fever and something to strengthen her at the source of her weakness. The treatment was most effective. The lady took only three or four doses, and then she was completely recovered. His Lordship was most grateful. He sent me silks and money, and his lady sent me something too. He also sent me a special signboard and, when he gave it to me, the musicians played so loud that the sound reached the heavens. There was inscribed upon it: 'The Learned Doctor with Miraculous Powers.' A few days ago, a friend of mine came to see me, and he says the characters are done in the *Yan* style. Every character seems to stand out. When I was young, I did a great deal of reading. It was only because my family had come down in the world that I began to practice the art of medicine. I think I can prove that the title of learned doctor was not altogether undeserved."

"I feel more satisfied now that you tell me there is nothing serious," Ximen Qing said. "I may say, Doctor, that, though I have more than one wife, this is the only one for whom I really care. She has borne me a son and I look to her to rear him. We must not have any trouble. I have confidence in your remarkable skill. She shall be carefully looked after, and, when she gets well, you shall have a handsome fee. I am only a soldier and cannot attempt to rival his Lordship, but I know what is right and proper."

"Since you are so kind," Dr. Ren said, "I will not take any payment from you. Indeed I would rather that you should not even pay for the medicine."

Ximen Qing laughed heartily. "I am not the sort of man to take medicine for nothing," he said. "And that reminds me of a very interesting story. I once heard of a man who said that a cat with the mange can be cured by a certain black powder. Somebody asked him what would cure a mangy dog. 'Give it some white medicine,'[1] the other said. So, Doctor, you see white medicine is fit only for dogs."

Dr. Ren clapped his hands and laughed. "Then I don't know what you will do to me if my prescription happens to be for white medicine." They both laughed. "In that case, you will have to give me another sign instead of a fee," Dr. Ren said. They laughed again. The doctor got up and they came away.

---

1. This expression also means "medicine given gratis."

CHAPTER 55

The Imperial Tutor

When Dr. Ren had finished his examination of Li Ping'er, they went back again to the great hall and sat down. "I want you to tell me the truth," Ximen Qing said. "What do you think of the case?"

"The lady did not take sufficient care after the birth of her child," Dr. Ren said. "Now her blood is impoverished, and her face is pale. She has no appetite, and she does not care to move about. Her pulse beats strongly enough, but it is not steady. That is a symptom that her liver is inflamed and that her blood circulates irregularly. Without the most careful attention, I fear she will not get well."

"What medicine are you thinking of giving her?" Ximen Qing asked.

"The first thing to do is to break down the fever and stop the flow of blood. I shall use yellow cedar and *Jinmu* as the base and a few other things. I think she will be all right."

Ximen Qing told Shutong to seal a tael of silver and give it to the doctor for the medicine. The doctor left, and shortly afterwards the medicine arrived. It was made ready in the rooms of Li Ping'er. Ximen returned to Ying Bojue.

"Li and Huang came to me this morning," Bojue said. "They say they must have the money and asked me to plead with you to help them."

"I suppose I must do what you wish," Ximen said. "Tell them to come tomorrow." He went with Ying Bojue to another room and they had something to eat.

"Is Li Guijie still here?" Bojue asked. "It seems to me that the man who went to the Eastern Capital should be back by now."

"Yes," Ximen said, "I want him myself. I am anxious to send him to Yangzhou. I don't see how he can be much longer."

After the meal, Ying Bojue went away.

The next day when Ximen Qing returned from the office, Ying Bojue was already waiting for him with Li and Huang. When he came in, they rose. Ximen went to change his clothes. He asked Wu Yueniang for the two hundred and fifty taels that Xu had paid. He added another two hundred and fifty taels and told Chen Jingji to give the money to Li and Huang. "I am really very short of money," Ximen Qing told them, "and I am only giving you this because Brother Ying has pressed me to do so. I must have it back as soon as possible."

"You have been so kind to us," Li said, "that, of course, we shall not be slow to pay. As soon as we recover the money, we will bring it to you before we touch a penny ourselves." They checked the silver, thanked Ximen Qing repeatedly, and withdrew.

Ying Bojue was going too, but Ximen pressed him to stay. While they were talking, Ping'an came and said: "Laibao has come back from the Eastern Capital."

"There," Bojue said, "didn't I tell you yesterday that he was due back?"

Laibao came in and kowtowed to Ximen Qing. "Did you see Uncle Zhai? What happened about this business of Guijie's?" Ximen asked him.

"I saw Uncle Zhai himself," Laibao said. "As soon as he had read your letter, he sent a man to the Minister. I went with the man, and the Minister told me that he would have had all the prisoners released, seeing that we came from his Eminence's palace, but, unfortunately, the matter had been taken up by Grand Marshal Huang, and all he could do was to prevent any further pursuit of those who had escaped. He said he must keep in jail those who had already been taken. But eunuchs, he said, never carry things to a conclusion and, before long, the Grand Marshal will have forgotten all about the matter. Then it will be easy to settle the matter of the prisoners."

"In that case, Qi Xiang'er will not be arrested," Bojue said. "The little strumpet is in luck's way."

"Uncle Zhu and the others will probably receive some slight punishment," Laibao said, "but I don't think they will be sentenced." He took Zhai's letter from his pocket and gave it to his master.

"Old Sun and Pockmarked Zhu can never have dreamed that I would come to their rescue," Ximen Qing said.

"But you have such a kind heart, Brother," said Bojue.

"Uncle Zhai seemed very pleased to see me," Laibao continued. "He asked whether you were going to the Capital to congratulate the Imperial Tutor on his birthday. I did not dare to say you were not going, so I said very probably you were. Uncle Zhai said it would be very nice of you to go and see him."

"I never had any idea of going," Ximen Qing said, "but, after what you have said, I shall have to go." Then he said: "You must be tired. Go to the inner court for some refreshment and then rest. I shall want you to go to Yangzhou in a day or two."

Laibao went out. Ximen Qing went to tell Li Guijie. He said to Bojue: "You stay here. I shall be back in a moment." But Bojue was anxious to go after Li and Huang. He said: "I must go now, but I will come back." He went away.

When Ximen Qing came to Wu Yueniang's room, Guijie had already heard the news. She hastened to kowtow to Ximen Qing and Yueniang. "Father and Mother," she said, "it is only by your kindness that I have been rescued from desperate straits. I don't know what I can do for you in return."

"Since you came to us," Yueniang said, "we could do no less than get things put right for you. If we had not done our best, there would have been no point in your coming."

"Father and Mother," Guijie said, "you have saved my life, but that little whore Qi Xiang'er had no claim on you, and you have saved her too. She made a lot of money; she involved me in her own trouble, and we have treated her well. I can't help feeling she is in our debt."

"Yes, indeed," Ximen Qing said, laughing, "the little whore has come out of it very well."

They talked for a while, then Guijie prepared to go away. "My mother has not heard the news," she said. "I must go and tell her or she will go on worrying. I will come again with her to thank you."

"Very well," Ximen said. "I will not keep you. Go home and tell your mother."

"You must have something to eat before you go," Yueniang said. Guijie declined. Again she thanked Ximen Qing, Yueniang, and the others.

"You are safe now," Ximen Qing told her, "but see that in future you have nothing to do with that young man Wang."

"Father," Guijie said, "what are you talking about! How could I even let him touch me! Why! if I meet him in the street, I shall be done for. It was not I who asked him to come the other day."

"That is all right," Yueniang said. "Only don't see him any more. There is no need to be so positive about it." They sent for the sedan chair and saw the girl off.

Ximen Qing told Yueniang he was thinking of going to the Eastern Capital.

"If you make up your mind to go," said Yueniang, "we must begin to get things ready at once, or you will be rushed."

"I have already got ready the things for the Imperial Tutor's birthday, the dragon gong, the embroidered stuffs, and the golden flowers," Ximen said. "Only my personal baggage is not ready yet."

"Oh, your things will be no trouble," Yueniang told him. Ximen Qing went to see Li Ping'er.

The next day Ximen was sitting in the arbor. He told Chen Jingji to write a letter to Censor Cai. This was the letter for Laibao to take. He gave Laibao some money and told him to start for Yangzhou the following morning.

Several days passed. The Imperial Tutor's birthday was drawing near. Ximen Qing picked out an auspicious day and told Qintong, Daian, Shutong and Huatong that they were to accompany him. They were to get their things ready. Wu Yueniang, Meng Yulou, Pan Jinlian, and the others packed Ximen's clothes and the things he needed for the journey. With the presents there were more than twenty loads. On the eve of his departure, the ladies gave a feast in honor of their husband, and afterwards he went to Yueniang's room to sleep with her.

The next day he sent off in advance the loads and his baggage and procured a passport so that his things might be cleared through all the stages on the way. When he had attended to these details, he went to see Li Ping'er and his little son Guan'ge.

"Take care of yourself," he said to Li Ping'er. "Whenever you need any medicine, just send somebody to Doctor Ren. I shall be back before long."

Li Ping'er said good-bye to him with tears in her eyes. "Be careful on the way," she said to him. Then she went with him to the great hall where Yueniang, Yulou, Jinlian, and the others were waiting. All together they escorted him to the gate. Ximen got into a light sedan chair and, with the four boys on horseback, set out for the Eastern Capital. Every day they rose early to continue their journey, and every night they rested at an inn or post stage. The scenery was delightful. The travelers they met were mostly civil and military officers going with their presents to the Capital to congratulate the Imperial Tutor on his birthday.

In ten days they reached the Capital. They entered by the Gate of Ten Thousand Blessings, and, as it was late, they went straight to the Arch of Dragon Virtue to see Zhai.

When the Comptroller heard that Ximen Qing had come, he hurried out to welcome him. They greeted one another and tea was served. Ximen Qing told Daian to have the baggage brought in, but Zhai bade his own servants attend to it. A banquet was served in honor of Ximen's arrival. A table of carved horn was set and there were some very rare dishes. It would have been perfection if only there had been dragons' livers and phoenix marrow. Even the Imperial Tutor himself could not have done better. The servants brought wine. Zhai offered a cup to Heaven, then to Ximen Qing. Ximen offered a cup in return. Fruits and dishes followed one another like water flowing in a stream.

After drinking two cups of wine, Ximen Qing said: "I have come specially to celebrate his Eminence's birthday and have brought with me a few trifling gifts for him. But I am afraid he may refuse them, and, to be candid, I should like you to go to him and speak to him about me. Besides, I hope that his Eminence may take me under his guardianship. If he will do this, I shall be happy all the rest of my life. But it may be difficult to persuade him."

"There will be no difficulty," said Zhai. "Though his Eminence is the most powerful of his Majesty's subjects, he is somewhat susceptible to praise and flattery. Let him but see the value of the presents you have brought him, and not only will he accept you as his ward, he will see that you get promotion."

Ximen Qing was delighted to hear this. They went on drinking and, after some time, Ximen said he had drunk enough. Zhai pressed him to drink one more cup, but Ximen said he had serious business to attend to on the morrow and he dared not drink too much. But, being pressed, he did drink one cup more.

Zhai saw that the boys were served with refreshments and invited Ximen Qing to go and rest in a study in the inner court. A bed with silken curtains and bedclothes, exquisitely perfumed, had been made ready and there were many servants to wait upon him. Ximen Qing lay down alone upon the bed. This was something to which he was not accustomed, and he found it hard to pass the night. Before dawn he was anxious to get up, but all the doors were shut and he had to wait till sunrise. Then a man came with a key and opened the doors; boys came with water and towels, and Ximen Qing dressed. Zhai came in and sat with him. A servant brought a red box in which were thirty different kinds of delicacies and a silver wine pot. The wine was poured and they ate their breakfast.

"After breakfast," the Comptroller said, "I will go before you to the palace and speak to his Eminence about you. I will let you know when to send the presents."

Ximen thanked him. They took a few cups of wine with their breakfast and the table was cleared. "Sit here," Zhai said to Ximen Qing. "I must go, but I shall be back very soon." It was indeed only a short time before he was back again. "When I got to the palace," he said, "his Eminence was washing. There was a host of civil and military officers waiting to congratulate him on his birthday, but not one of them had seen him yet. I spoke of you to him, and you must go at once. There is a crowd at the palace. I will go first and you can join me there." He went away again.

Ximen Qing was delighted. He ordered his own servants and asked some of Zhai's servants to carry the presents to the palace. Dressed in ceremonial robes and hat, he got into his sedan chair. A host of officials, great and small, all come to congratulate the Prime Minister, were pressing shoulder to shoulder and back to back. In the distance Ximen Qing saw one officer, also sitting in a sedan chair, near the Arch of Dragon Virtue. When he looked more closely he recognized his old friend Miao of Yangzhou. At the same time Miao recognized him. They got down from their sedan chairs, bowed, and saluted one another. Miao was a rich man and now held a very comfortable position. He had attached himself to the Imperial Tutor's faction, and had come, like the rest, to congratulate his Eminence on his birthday. So they chanced to meet. They were both eager to get on to the palace and did little more than greet one another, exchange addresses, and then separate. Ximen Qing came to the palace, bowed, and entered through the Great Archway. There Zhai met him.

Ximen Qing noticed that the middle gate was shut and that the officers were all coming in by the gates at the side. He asked Zhai the meaning of this and was told that the Emperor had once passed through that door and, ever after, it must be closed to ordinary men. Ximen Qing followed the Comptroller through one door after another. Each was guarded by a military officer. There was excellent order everywhere. The military officers bowed to Zhai and asked who Ximen Qing was. Zhai told them that Ximen was his relative from Shandong, come to congratulate his Eminence. They went through more doors and down more passages. Everywhere were carven pillars and painted beams. Music could be heard faintly. It seemed to come from heaven. "The palace is far distant from any other place," Ximen said. "Where is the music coming from?"

"His Eminence," Zhai said, "has commanded the attendance of twenty-four girl dancers. They know all such dances as the Dance of the Evil One, the Rainbow Skirt Dance and the Dance of Guanyin. They play every day when my master breakfasts, dines, and sups. At present he is taking his breakfast."

Ximen Qing smelled some incense that he had never smelled before, and the music seemed nearer. "Step softly," said Zhai, "we are quite close to his Eminence's study."

They went through another passage and came to a great hall that seemed to Ximen Qing like the palace of the angels. Outside were storks and peacocks and many strange birds. There were the Hortensia flowers that confer Eternal Life, Flowers of the Sacred Cloud, and the *Fusang* Plant; flowers that never faded, blossoming so luxuriantly that the eye could scarce bear to dwell on them. Ximen Qing did not dare to press forward. He asked Zhai to go before him.

They went into the hall. In the midst of it stood a great throne with a tiger skin thrown over it, and, on the throne, sat a man robed in a gown with dragons embroidered upon it. This was his Eminence the Imperial

Tutor. Behind a screen were twenty or thirty exquisite maidens in a row, all dressed after the fashion of the court. Some held kerchiefs, and some held fans with which to refresh his Eminence. The Comptroller stood beside him, and Ximen Qing kowtowed four times. His Eminence rose and, standing upon a rug, returned the salutation. It was the first time they met.

The Comptroller approached the Imperial Tutor and whispered. Ximen Qing knew that he was being spoken about, and again kowtowed four times. Now the Imperial Tutor did not rise. It was a sign that he was prepared to accept Ximen as his ward. Then Ximen spoke and called him "Father."

"Your son," he said, "has nothing to offer. I have brought no more than a few trifles in honor of your most illustrious birthday. It is as though one brought a feather for ten thousand *li*. But may your Eminence live as long as the Mountains of the South!"

"You are very kind," the Imperial Tutor said. "Please sit down."

An attendant gave Ximen Qing a chair. He bowed twice and sat down. Tea was brought. Zhai went out and ordered the presents to be brought in. There were more than twenty loads. They were brought and laid before the steps. A small box was opened and the inventory taken from it. It said: One crimson dragon robe; one green dragon robe; twenty rolls of Han-figured satin; twenty rolls of Sichuan silk; twenty rolls of foreign cloth; other rolls, forty, both plain and figured; a girdle of a lion's head in jade; another girdle mounted in gold of tagaraka wood; of jade goblets and horn goblets, each ten pairs; four pairs of golden wine cups with flowers for decoration; ten fine pearls and two hundred taels of gold. These were the present.

The Imperial Tutor looked at the inventory and then at the twenty loads of offerings. He was pleased and thanked Ximen Qing. Then he told Zhai to have them sent to the treasury and called for wine to entertain Ximen Qing. But Ximen remarked that his Eminence was very busy. He rose and prepared to take his leave. "Very well," said the Imperial Tutor, "but come this afternoon." Ximen Qing bowed and went out, the Imperial Tutor taking a few steps with him. Zhai went farther, but he too was busy and had to return, and Ximen Qing went back alone to the house. There he took off his hat and girdle and had dinner. After dinner, he went to the study and slept for a while. Then a man came and asked him to go and see the Imperial Tutor. Ximen gave the man some gold and put on his robes. He told Daian to make up a number of parcels of silver and put them into a box. The four boys followed him as he made his way again in a sedan chair to the Imperial Tutor's palace.

His Eminence sent invitations to all who came to congratulate him upon his birthday, but these invitations were spread out over a period of three days. The first day was reserved for members of the Royal Household and the eunuchs, the second for ministers and officials of high rank, and the third for the commoner class of officers. But Ximen Qing was a stranger and had offered so magnificent a present that his Eminence was pleased with him and gave him a special invitation. He even came to receive his guest. Ximen very politely begged the Imperial Tutor to go before him. He bent his back and walked delicately.

"It has been very kind of you to come such a long way especially on my account, and to give me such a splendid present," his Eminence said. "I trust you will take a meal with me that I may at least show my inclination for you."

"My life in this world," Ximen said, "is entirely dependent upon your Eminence's kindness. The trifles I brought are not worth mentioning."

They chatted and joked together as though they really were father and son. The twenty-four beautiful maidens played for them, and attendants brought wine. His Eminence desired to offer Ximen a cup of wine. Ximen expressed his unworthiness, but, being pressed, rose and drank a single cup. They sat down. Then Ximen Qing bade Shutong bring a peach-shaped cup of gold. He filled it to the brim and, taking it, knelt down before his Eminence and said: "Live for a thousand years." The Imperial Tutor smiled.

"Stand up, my son," he said. He drank the wine.

Ximen Qing rose and took his place again. The food served was so rare and varied that it can hardly be described. Ximen Qing stayed until sunset. Then he distributed the packets of silver among the attendants and took his leave of the Imperial Tutor. "Father," he said, "you have much to do and I must not detain you. I shall not trouble you again." Then he left the palace and returned to Zhai's house.

The next day he decided to visit Master Miao and told Daian to find out where he was staying. Daian discovered that he was at a house outside the Imperial City belonging to a eunuch named Li. Ximen Qing went there with Daian. The boy presented Ximen's card and Master Miao came out. "I was hoping that some good friend would come and have a chat with me," he said. "You have come at the right moment." He insisted that Ximen should stay for dinner. There was a magnificent spread of food of every kind. Two very handsome singing boys came and sang several songs.

"These two foolish boys," Ximen Qing said, pointing to Daian and Qintong, "can only eat and drink. They cannot compare with your two boys."

Miao smiled. "I'm afraid they will not be of much use to you, but, if you really like them, I shall be only too glad to give them to you."

Ximen Qing said: " I dare not accept anything that you must appreciate so much yourself." They did not stop drinking till very late. Then Ximen said good-bye to Miao and returned to Zhai's house.

For eight or nine days, nearly all the important officials at the palace sent invitations to Ximen Qing. Then he felt anxious to get home and ordered Daian to pack up his baggage. The Comptroller pressed him to stay one day more. This he did. The two men drank together and treated one another as though they were blood relations. Then Ximen Qing set off on his way back to Shandong.

While Ximen Qing was away, Yueniang and the others stayed in their own rooms doing needlework, and none of them went out to play. So they waited for his return, all except Jinlian, who dressed herself exquisitely and mingled with the maids, sometimes playing at guessing fingers and sometimes at dominoes. She laughed and talked merrily, not caring what anybody thought about her. She was anxious to meet Chen Jingji, and every day went to the garden and many times to the cavern, hoping to find him there. Jingji was always thinking about her, and he went there frequently. Whenever they met they would play and kiss. But they were afraid of someone seeing them and dared not fully satisfy their longing for each other.

One day Yueniang, Yulou, and Li Ping'er were sitting together when, suddenly, Daian came in and kowtowed. "Father is nearly here," he told them.

"Where is he now?" Yueniang asked.

"I came first with the passports," Daian said. "He must still be twenty *li* away."

"Have you had anything to eat?" Yueniang asked.

"I have had breakfast but not lunch."

Yueniang ordered food to be prepared, then she, with the other ladies, went to the great hall to await her husband. They waited a long time.

At last Ximen Qing arrived. The ladies went out to welcome him. He made a reverence to Yueniang, then greeted all the others. Shutong, Qintong and Huatong kowtowed and went to the kitchen for something to eat. Ximen Qing told the ladies about the hardships of his journey, how he had stayed with Zhai, how the Imperial Tutor had invited him, and how he had gone to many parties with the eunuchs and other officials. Then he asked Li Ping'er about his baby. "And how do you feel," he said, "after taking Doctor Ren's medicine? Was it any good? Though my body went to the Eastern Capital, my heart was always here with you."

"The baby is well, and I am better than I was," Li Ping'er assured him.

Yueniang saw that all the luggage was brought in and the presents that

Ximen Qing had been given. She gave orders for a meal to be made ready for her husband.

That night the ladies gave a feast to celebrate his return. He went to Yueniang's room to sleep, and it seemed to them like a refreshing rain after a long period of drought, or the meeting of old friends in a strange land. They took extreme delight in one another.

The next day, Chen Jingji and his wife came to pay their respects to Ximen Qing and discussed business matters. Ying Bojue and Chang Zhijie heard that Ximen had returned, and they came to call. Ximen greeted them. "So long a journey must have been very trying," they said. Ximen told them about the beauty and greatness of the Eastern Capital and how the Imperial Tutor had accepted him as a ward. They congratulated him. Ximen asked them to stay and have some wine.

When Chang Zhijie was about to leave, he said to his host: "There is something I should like to ask you, but I don't know whether I should or not." He bent his head and seemed embarrassed.

"Please tell me what it is," Ximen said.

"Well," Chang Zhijie said, "my house is not so convenient as it might be. I should like to find another, but I have no money. Perhaps you will lend me some and let me pay you back with interest."

"Why talk about interest?" Ximen Qing said. "We are too good friends for that. But, at the moment, I simply haven't any ready money. You must wait till Han comes back, and I will certainly do what you wish." Ying Bojue and Chang Zhijie thanked him and went away.

Master Miao had promised to give two singing boys to Ximen Qing. But Ximen Qing had been so anxious to get home that he did not stay to say good-bye to Miao. Miao thought he was still at the Capital and sent his servants to Zhai's place to make inquiries. So he learned that Ximen Qing had gone. "A gentleman's word," he thought, "is like a whip on a mettle-some horse, I must do what I promised." He sent for the two singing boys and said to them: "I promised to give you to his Lordship Ximen Qing, and now I am going to send you to his place. You must pack your things."

The two boys knelt down. "We have been with you many years," they said. "You have done much for us and taught us to sing. Now you don't want us any longer: you are going to send us away." They wept.

Miao himself was not at all happy about it. "Don't think I wish to get rid of you," he said, "but a man must keep his word. We must observe the teaching of Confucius. He says: A man who does not keep his word is a man no longer. There is no help for it. We cannot disobey these precepts, and I must not take your point of view into account. I am going to write a letter and send you to him. I will ask him to treat you kindly."

The two boys could only submit. They stood up. Miao told his family tutor to write a letter for them to take to Ximen Qing. He also wrote a card to go with a present of silk, books and handkerchiefs. Then he ordered his servant Miao Shi to take the letter and the two boys to Ximen Qing. The boys said good-bye to their old master, shed many tears, then mounted their horses and set off for Shandong. When they reached Qing-he district, they dismounted and inquired where Ximen lived. Then they went to the house.

After Ximen's return from the Eastern Capital, he was very busy. Many people sent him presents and many sent him invitations. Every day three or four friends came to see him, and he could not even attend to his duties at the office. But this day things were easier and he had gone to the office. He went to the Great Hall and, with Magistrate Xia, examined some of the prisoners. After this, he got into his sedan chair and, with several policemen to clear his way, went home. When he reached home, Miao Shi and the two boys had been waiting for some time. They followed him into the hall. Miao Shi knelt down.

"I come from Master Miao of Yangzhou," he said. "This is his letter." He took out the letter and the list of presents.

"Please stand up," Ximen Qing said to him. He opened the letter and read it carefully, pleased that Master Miao had sent him the two boys. "It was quite by chance I met your master," he said. "We were very friendly and when we were drinking together he was good enough to promise me you two boys. Now he has sent you to me even all this long way. Your master is certainly a man whose words are worth a thousand gold pieces. It is most unusual."

The two boys came forward and kowtowed. "Our master bade us come and serve you," they said. "He asks that you will be kind to us."

Ximen Qing told them to rise. "I will see that you are given a worthy task," he said. He called for food and wine to be given them and Miao Shi, prepared some valuable presents for Master Miao, and had a letter written to accompany them. He told the two boys that they should serve him in his study.

❋   ❋   ❋

Han Daoguo's wife, Wang Liu'er, knew that Ximen was very busy and was anxious to find someone to take a message to him. Her young brother, Wang Jing, was a fine-looking lad about sixteen years old and, that same day, she decided to send him to Ximen Qing. Ximen accepted him and sent him to work in his study.

While Ximen Qing was making arrangements about these boys, Ying Bojue came to see him. Ximen told him how Master Miao had sent the two boys. He told Daian to bring refreshments and invite Bojue to dine. Then he asked the boys to sing some songs of the South. They came in and stood side by side with castanets in their hands. They sang "Last Night the Plums in the Garden Blossomed." Their voices were sweet, and the melody they sang was exquisite. Bojue was delighted. He jumped out of his chair. "Brother," he said, "what extraordinary luck to get two boys like this. It was indeed kind of Master Miao."

"I shall have to give him something in return," Ximen Qing said. He gave the two boys new names. One he called Chunhong and the other Chunyan. He told them to sing two or three short songs. The two men drank their wine after a while, and Ying Bojue went away.

CHAPTER 56
Chang Zhijie Buys a New House

Ximen Qing kept the two boys. He gave a letter of thanks to Miao Shi to take to his master with some presents, and some silver to Miao Shi himself. Then Miao Shi went home. Not long afterwards Chunyan died, and Chunhong was left alone.

Though Chang Zhijie had asked for Ximen Qing's help, the days passed and he was still without money. His landlord pressed him continually. Unfortunately for him, Ximen Qing, after coming back from the Eastern Capital, was kept busy going to one party after another. Chang Zhijie could not get hold of him. The proverb says: If friends meet, they cannot fail to help each other; but, when they do not meet, nothing is done. Chang Zhijie asked Ying Bojue to go to Ximen for him. Ximen was not at home. Chang Zhijie went mournfully home and his wife told him what she thought about him. "You call yourself a man," she said, "yet you can't get a house fit to live in, and here we are in utter misery. You have always bragged about your friendship with Master Ximen, but it doesn't look as though he would do much for you."

Chang Zhijie had a mouth but, after this, he dared not open it. He seemed dazed and did not utter a single word. The next day he got up very early in the morning and went to see Ying Bojue. He took him to a wine house and invited him to drink. "I do not wish to cause you any expense," Ying Bojue said, but Chang Zhijie pushed him into a chair. He ordered wine, a plate of smoked meat and another of fish. When they had drunk a few cups, Chang Zhijie said:

"I have bothered you several times to speak to his Lordship about my affairs, but, so far, we have not been able to see him and this business of my house is getting desperate. Last night my wife kept at me all night about it. I could not bear it. That is why I am up so early this morning. Now, Brother, won't you go to his Lordship again? I don't suppose he has gone out yet."

"Since you ask me," Bojue said, "I will certainly go, and I have no doubt we shall manage it today."

They drank more wine, then Ying Bojue said he must not drink too much so early in the day. Chang Zhijie pressed him to drink still one more cup, then he paid for the wine and they came out together and went to Ximen's house.

It was the beginning of autumn, and a pleasant wind was blowing from the west. Ximen Qing had been going to one party after another and was beginning to feel the strain. This day he had been invited by Eunuch Zhou, but he excused himself and did not go. Instead, he went to the garden with Wu Yueniang, Meng Yulou, Pan Jinlian, and Li Ping'er. They enjoyed the flowers and were all very happy together.

Chang Zhijie and Ying Bojue were delighted to find Ximen at home. They went to the hall and sat there for a long time, but there was no sign of Ximen Qing. Shutong and Huatong came in with a large chest filled with silken clothes. As they passed, they shouted: "We've been carrying these things half a day, and we're nowhere near finished yet." Bojue asked them where Ximen Qing was.

"He is amusing himself in the garden," Shutong said.

"Then may I trouble you to tell him we are here?"

The two boys went on with their chest. After a while Shutong came out again and said: "Father says, will you wait a moment and he will be with you." They waited and, at last, Ximen came to them. They bowed to him and sat down.

"Brother," Bojue said, "you have been drinking much wine these last few days, and you must be very busy. What are you doing at home today?"

"Since I saw you last," Ximen Qing said, "I have had invitations every day. I have been drinking too much, and I'm tired of it. Today I ought to have gone to another party, but I made some excuse for not going."

"I have just seen a chest full of clothes," Bojue said. "Where have they come from?"

"It is nearly autumn," Ximen Qing said, "and we must have autumn clothes, you know. Those you saw are my first wife's, but that was only half of them. We haven't finished them all yet."

Chang Zhijie put out his tongue. "With six wives you must have to have six chests. What a nuisance! We poor people find it bad enough even to get a roll of cloth. You must be a rich man, Brother." Ying Bojue and Ximen Qing laughed.

"How is it that the things from Yangzhou have not arrived yet?" Bojue said. "We know nothing of the way business has been going or whether Li and Huang have let you have their money yet."

"Perhaps the boat is delayed," Ximen said, "I have not heard a word, and I am rather worried. Li and Huang have told me that they will not get their money till next month."

Bojue drew nearer to Ximen Qing. "You may remember," he said, "that the other day Brother Chang asked your help. The last few days you have been very busy, and we have not had an opportunity of mentioning the matter to you. Brother Chang's landlord is being very harsh, his wife grumbles every day, and he is at his wits' end. The weather is getting colder and colder and his fur coat is still in the pawnshop. Brother, you must show your kindness to him. You can't have forgotten the proverb: If we would help a man, let it be when he most needs help. If you help him so that his wife ceases to nag at him and he can find a house to live in, all the more credit to you. Brother Chang has asked me to come and beg you to help him at once."

"I certainly did promise to help him," Ximen Qing said, "but I spent a great deal of money on my visit to the Eastern Capital and I shall have to wait until Han comes back. Why is Brother Chang in such a hurry?"

"It isn't Brother Chang: it's his wife. She is the one who grumbles. You must do something for him without delay."

Ximen Qing thought for a while. Then he said: "Well, perhaps I may just be able to manage it. How many rooms will they need?"

"They are only husband and wife," Bojue said. "They will need an outer room, a reception room, a bedroom and a kitchen. They can't do with less than four rooms. They must have three or four pieces of silver. Brother, do this for them. Help them to get a house at once."

"I can only let him have a few taels today," Ximen Qing said. "With them he can buy clothes and furniture. When he has got his house, he shall have some more."

Ying Bojue and Chang Zhijie stood up together and thanked him. Ximen Qing said to Shutong: "Go and ask the Great Lady to give you the silver that I have in a leather case." The boy went away and soon returned with the silver. "This is the money—about ten taels, I think— that I had at the Eastern Capital to give to the servants at his Eminence's Palace," Ximen Qing said. "Take it and buy a few things with it." He opened one of the packets and showed it to Chang Zhijie. "The silver is in packets of three or five *qian*," he said.

Chang Zhijie took them and put them in his pocket. He thanked Ximen Qing.

"Don't think I have deliberately kept you waiting," Ximen said. "But you hadn't fixed upon your house and I didn't have the money. When I do get some, you shall have more."

Chang Zhijie thanked him. They all sat down again.

"I have heard of men of past generations who were generous and open-handed," Bojue said. "The consequence was that their sons and grand-sons were an honor to their family, and improved and extended their patrimony. On the other hand, I have heard of others, mean men who hoarded away their gold and treasure, whose sons and grandsons were anything but desirable. Sometimes they failed to preserve even the tombs of their ancestors. The justice of Heaven is unfailing."

"Yes," Ximen Qing said, "money should be made to circulate. It ought not to be buried away in one place. It is given us to use. If one man keeps a huge store of it for himself, someone else must go short. It is a crime to hoard away money and treasure."

Shutong brought food for them and the three men ate it. Chang Zhijie stood up, the money in his pocket, and went away in great delight. When he got home, his wife came out shouting and scolding as usual. "Now you barren fig tree! you impecunious rascal!" she cried. "Would you go away and leave your wife to starve? You seem quite pleased with yourself, but you ought to be ashamed. Here we are with no house to live in and the landlord always badgering us. I suppose you think I like to hear the sort of thing he says."

Chang Zhijie did not open his mouth. He waited until his wife had finished, then quietly took the silver from his pocket and put it on the table. He opened the packet. "Hullo, my square-holed brother, my dear square-holed brother! How bright and good you look! You make my body tingle all over. What a pity I can't swallow you down with a drop of water. If only you'd come to me earlier, that whore would not have been so rude to me."

His wife saw him set down twelve or thirteen taels of silver. She dashed to the table and tried to grab them.

"Ah," said Chang, "you have been nagging at me all this time, yet, the moment you set eyes on the silver, you seem to have become quite friendly. Tomorrow I am going to buy some clothes and get a place to live by myself. I'm tired of putting up with your tricks."

Mistress Chang smiled sweetly at him. "Brother," she said, "where did you get this silver?"

But Chang had nothing to say to her.

"Are you angry with me, Brother? I only want us to get a home. Now the money is here we must talk the matter over. We will buy a house and settle down. Why are you so angry? I have been a good wife to you. If you are angry with me, you are unjust."

Chang did not speak.

The woman continued, but he paid not the slightest attention. She began to feel abashed and started to cry. Chang sighed.

"You woman," he said, "you do no work in the fields. You do not weave. All you do is nag at me."

Mistress Chang shed more tears. Then they both shut their mouths tight and sat there silently, for there was no one to make peace between them. But Chang began to reflect. "The woman," he said to himself, "is in a very difficult position. Perhaps I ought not to be angry with her even if she does grumble about everything. It seems hardly kind not to speak to her. If Ximen Qing got to know about it, he would undoubtedly say that I am to blame." He smiled and said to his wife: "I am joking with you. I am not angry really. But you so often talk to me in this horrible strain, and I have never complained. I have just gone out of your way. Now I'll tell you all about this money. This morning you were so cantankerous that I could stand it no longer. I went to Brother Ying, gave him a drink and then we went to see his Lordship. By a stroke of luck, his Lordship happened to be at home. He had not gone to a party. Brother Ying was most kind. He did his utmost with his Lordship, and I got this money. He has promised that, when we find a house, he will give me some more. These twelve taels are for expenses and buying the things we need immediately."

"Now that you have this money," his wife said, "we must take care not to waste it. First of all, we must buy some winter clothes so that we won't freeze."

"Yes," Chang Zhijie said, "I was just going to suggest that. Here are twelve taels. We can buy a few clothes and some furniture. When we get the new house and are ready to move in, we shall look more respectable. I don't know how to express my appreciation of his Lordship's kindness. We shall certainly have to send him an invitation when we get into our new house."

"We will see about that later," said his wife.

The woman asked him if he had had anything to eat. "Yes," Chang Zhijie said, "I had something with his Lordship. But, doubtless, you have not. I will take some money and go and buy you some rice."

"Be careful you don't lose it, and please come straight back."

Chang Zhijie took a basket and went down the street. He bought mutton at the butcher's and rice at the rice shop. He took them home. His wife came to the door to meet him.

"Why did you buy this piece of mutton?" she said.

"You said you had a hard life, and, really, I ought to have killed an ox or two for you. This is but a trifling piece of meat."

Mistress Chang shook her finger at him. "You hardhearted thief. You still hate me. But I don't believe there is anything you can do about it."

"Probably," said Chang, "I shan't forgive you though you call me Brother and Darling and ask for forgiveness a thousand times. I will show my authority."

The woman laughed and went to the well to draw some water. Then she cooked the food, set a piece of mutton on the table and asked him to have some. "I have just had something," he said. "Eat it all yourself." The woman ate the food alone. She cleared the table and told him to go and buy some clothes. Chang Zhijie took some silver and went down the street. He went to several shops before he found what he wanted. He bought a black silk gown for his wife, a green silk skirt, a blue jacket and a white silk skirt, five pieces in all. For himself he bought a goose-yellow coat and a clove-colored gown. All this, with a few other things, cost him five taels and six *qian*.

"The things are not a bargain, but they are worth the money," his wife said. She put the clothes into a chest and decided to go and buy furniture the next day. She was thoroughly delighted, and all her grumblings vanished in the Eastern Ocean.

When Chang Zhijie had gone, Ximen Qing and Ying Bojue still sat in the great hall. "Though I am only a military officer," Ximen said, "I have a fairly important position. I have made a number of friends in the Capital, and I am in close relation with the Imperial Tutor. Letters pour in upon me like a stream. I am too busy to attend to my own correspondence, and I must find a scholar who can save me the trouble. Unfortunately, I don't know any genuinely learned man. If you do, please say so."

"You have set me a very difficult problem," Bojue said. "We want a learned man, but he must be honest. He must be a man easy to get on with, yet one who does not talk too much. We must have someone who can keep his own counsel. And we don't want a man who is a profound scholar in deceit and cunning and a fool at everything else. I have a friend who is a graduate. He has, it is true, several times failed to pass the final examination, but he is a learned man and will stand comparison with Ban and Sima.[1] He is a follower of Confucius. He and I have been good friends for ages. So far as I remember, ten years ago he went in for the examination and the examiners spoke very highly of his work. Unfortunately, another man was slightly better than he was, and he failed. He has made several other attempts since then and he still reads though his hair is gray now. He owns about a hundred acres of land and three or four houses."

"If he is in comfortable circumstances, why should he take a job?" Ximen said.

"His land and his houses have been bought by wealthy families, and now his two hands are his only capital."

---

1. Ban Gu and Sima Qian.

"Why did you tell me he had land if he has sold it?"

"Well, if that doesn't appeal to you, perhaps this will. He has a pretty young wife about twenty years old, an excellent woman. She has two three-year-old babies."

"If he has a beautiful wife, he certainly won't come," Ximen Qing said.

"Fortunately, about a couple of years ago, his wife ran off to the Eastern Capital with another man. The two babies died of smallpox, so he is all alone in the world. I'm sure he will come."

"You are talking rubbish," Ximen said, laughing. "What is his name?"

"He is called Shui. His learning is incomparable. If you engage him, I guarantee your letters will be a source of pride to you. He is a very learned man indeed."

"I don't believe a word you say," Ximen said. "It is all a pack of lies. If you can remember anything he has written, tell me, and, if I think it is any good, I'll engage him and provide him with quarters. Since he is a single man, there will be no difficulty about that."

"I remember getting a letter from him asking me to help him to find a job," Bojue said. "I will tell you what I can remember of it."

> A letter this for Brother Ying.
> I think of you, but cannot find
> Words to express my feelings.
> All here are well.
> If you should hear of a job for a tutor
> Pray get it for me.
> I may flatter myself, but it seems to me
> My brush is as great as a beam.
> I do not write often, but when I do
> Look out for clouds and mist.

Ximen Qing roared with laughter. "If he wanted you to get him a job, why didn't he write a letter instead of sending you doggerel like that? Horrible doggerel too! I'm sure the fellow is both an ignoramus and a rogue."

"Oh, dear me, no," said Ying Bojue. "You must not judge him by that. He and I have been friends for three generations. We used to go to school together when we were boys. I remember our teacher saying that Ying and Shui were one as clever as the other. 'They will turn out well,' he used to say. We did our exercises and our compositions together and never felt the least bit jealous. You see, we are really good friends. We are never formal with one another. That's why he wrote me that little ditty. It's quite entertaining, isn't it?"

"Perhaps you can tell me what the fifth line means?" Ximen said.

"Ah, Brother," said Bojue, "don't you see? That is a very clever piece of character analysis. When you write *she* [residence] on the left-hand side and *guan* [official] on the right, and you have the other *guan* [a mansion]. He is saying to me, perfectly obviously: 'If you hear of a *guan*, a position, recommend me for it.' Not a single unnecessary word. How could he write more plainly what he wants to say?"

Ximen Qing could think of no further objection to make. He said to Ying Bojue: "What kind of man is he?"

"His behavior is even more admirable than his scholarship," Bojue said. "Two years ago he was tutor in the household of a certain Vice President Li. There were a host of beautiful maids there and several good-looking boys. Master Shui was there for four or five years and an impure thought about them never entered his head. In course of time the maids and boys were so impressed by his wisdom that they all deliberately set to work to seduce him. Master Shui is a soft-hearted man and he yielded. His employer drove him out and the neighbors said he was a scamp. As a matter of fact, even if a girl sits on his knee, he remains perfectly calm. If you engage him, let your maids and your boys go to him and you'll find out soon enough how he behaves."

Ximen Qing laughed. "You funny dog, you can never stop joking. The other day, my colleague Xia's tutor, Master Ni, told me of a friend of his called Wen. When he has been to see me, we will decide."

CHAPTER 57

Ximen Qing Becomes a Benefactor

The temple stands bare on the mountainside
There are shrines among the towering crags
But the Buddhas of days gone by can be discerned no more.
Their stone bodies are covered with moss
The ancient sanctuary stands alone
The image of the world-honored one is shrouded in dust,
As though he heard the mourning of the dragons and the ele-
    phants

And the hearts of the faithful are filled with sadness.
If a general goes to war in vain
Let him give freely the four gifts and tarry not.
I know that the fan palm tree
Still grows beside the lotus blossom tower.
Thus will he bring joy to the gods
And the demon host will bear no grudge against him.

In Dongpingfu of the province of Shandong there was a temple called
the Temple of Eternal Felicity. It was built in the second year of the
Putong reign of the Emperor Wu of the Liang dynasty. Its founder was a
certain patriarch named Wanhui [Returns-from-afar]. If you ask why the
patriarch was so called, I must tell you that, when he was about seven or
eight years old, his brother was sent to serve as a soldier in the marches. He
did not write to his family, and none knew whether he was alive or dead.
So his old mother was unhappy about him and often shed tears. One day
the younger boy said to his mother: "Mother, the world is at peace and
our life is comfortable. What makes you weep so much? Tell me and I will
share your grief."

"You are only a boy," his mother said, "and you do not know. When
your father died, your elder brother went to the marches. He was an officer in the army. For four or five years no word has come from him, and
I do not know whether he is alive or dead. How can I be happy?" She
cried again.

"If I had known this before, I would soon have put things right. Mother, tell me where my brother is, and I will go and find him and get a letter from him."

The old woman laughed before her tears had dried. "You foolish child!" she said, "if it were only a hundred *li* or so away, we could go. But he is in Manchuria and that is more than ten thousand *li* away. It would take a strong man five months to get there. You are only a boy, and you would never get there at all."

"If he is in Manchuria," said the boy, "Manchuria is not in the skies. I will go, and you shall have me back in no time." He fastened his shoes, straightened his coat, bowed to his mother, and went off like a streak of smoke. The old woman called him back but he did not answer, and when she ran after him she could not catch him. She was more melancholy than ever. Many of her neighbors came to console her. "The boy cannot possibly go very far," they said. "He is sure to come back." The old woman dried her eyes and sat down sadly.

The sun was sinking in the west when the old lady went out to see if she could see anything of him. In the distance was a faint shadow that might have been a boy. She besought Heaven and Earth and the Three Luminosities and said: "May my little son return as a reward for my fastings and my sacrifices." And indeed, her son suddenly stood before her.

"What, Mother," he said, "have you not gone to bed yet? Here I am, back from Manchuria, and here is the letter from my brother."

The old woman laughed. "You did right not to go, but don't tell me any more lies. You couldn't possibly go more than a thousand *li* in one day."

"So you don't believe me, Mother?" the boy said. He took a packet from his sleeve. In it was a letter. It had indeed been written by his brother. And he brought a shirt to be washed that was one the old woman remembered making. Everybody heard of this, and so the boy came to be called Wanhui. Afterwards, he became a monk and was known as Abbot Wanhui. He was a man of outstanding virtue and performed a number of striking miracles. Once he swallowed two pints of needles before the stone tiger of the Emperor Zhao, and once he brought three pagodas from his head before the heir apparent of the Emperor Wu of Liang. So the Temple of Eternal Felicity was built expressly for him and immense amounts of money were spent on its construction.

Years and months flew like a weaver's shuttles. The patriarch Wanhui went back to Paradise, and, one after the other, his pious monks passed away. There were left but a handful of idle scroungers who kept women, drank wine, and did everything that is unbecoming. It was not long before they reached such a pitch that they pawned their religious habits and sold their bells. The tiles and bricks of which the temple was built were sold for wine, and the rain and wind soon affected the sacred images. A place of veneration became the prey of mists and weeds. For forty years nobody troubled to rebuild it. Then there came a monk from India who was impressed with the greatness of China. He crossed the River of Shifting Sands and the Sea of the Zodiac, and, after traveling eight or nine years, came at last to China. Then he came to Shandong and so to the ruined temple. There, for nine years he stayed with his face to the wall and did not speak a single word.

One day, an idea suddenly came into his head and he said to himself: "This temple is utterly in ruins, and these hairless asses care only for eating and drinking. It has become a waste place. This is a sad business. If I do not make up my mind to do something about it, no one else will. I must go out. I hear that his Lordship Ximen, a military officer and a very rich man, one day when he was entertaining his Excellency Cai here, saw the ruin and spoke of restoring this temple. If I can only persuade him to take the initiative, everything will be plain sailing. I must go at once." He beat the gong, assembled all the monks in the Great Hall, and told them what his purpose was. He bade one of them bring him ink and a brush. Then he wrote an appeal for funds. This veritable Buddha of a monk then left his fellows, put on sandals and a straw hat, and went to see Ximen Qing.

Now to return to Ximen Qing. When Ying Bojue had left him, he went to Wu Yueniang's room and told his wife about Bojue's recommendation of Master Shui. Then he said: "When I came back from the Eastern Capital, my friends and relations all gave parties in my honor and we must do something in return. I am not particularly busy today and I think we might do it at once." He told Daian to see to the preparations, and sent the other boys around with invitations. Then he took Yueniang's hand and went to see Guan'ge in the rooms of Li Ping'er.

The Sixth Lady welcomed them smilingly, and told the nurse to bring out the baby. He had grown very handsome. The child smiled at them and went readily to Yueniang. She took him in her arms. "My son," she said, "you are a clever boy and you will do well. When you are grown up, you will be a good son to your mother."

"When he is grown up and gets a position, the robes of ceremony will be yours," Li Ping'er said.

"My son," Ximen Qing said, "don't follow in your father's footsteps. When you are a man, be a civil officer, not a military officer like me. Mine is a good post, but it has not the dignity of a civil officer's; and, though I am rich, I do not enjoy the respect that is paid to the others."

Pan Jinlian was standing outside and heard all this. She was very angry. "You shameless, boasting, dirty strumpet!" she muttered. "Do you think you are the only woman who can bear a child? He hasn't passed three yellow plum seasons or four summers yet. He isn't through smallpox, and his schooldays are not over. He lives still with the God of Hades. What right have you to talk about his getting a government appointment and your being honored as a lady? And that rascal has no shame. Why should the child get a civil position different from his own?"

While she was muttering angrily to herself, Daian came. "Fifth Mother," he said, "where is Father?"

"You little thief!" Jinlian cried, "how do I know where your father is? Do you expect to find him in my room? Why not with the honored lady to whom he pays so many delicate attentions? Why do you come and ask me?"

Daian saw that there was no purpose in his questioning her any further, and went to Li Ping'er's room. There he coughed warningly and said: "Uncle Ying is in the great hall."

"Why! He has only just gone," Ximen Qing said. "What has brought him back so soon?"

"He will tell you when he sees you," the boy said.

Ximen Qing left Yueniang and Li Ping'er and went to the outer court. He was just about to speak to Ying Bojue when the old monk arrived. Outside the gate, he called loudly upon Buddha and asked: "Is this the noble Ximen's house? Tell him, Master Comptroller, that I am here. Tell him that I will bless his son, send him prosperity and long life. I am a monk from the Eastern Capital come to ask for alms."

Ximen Qing was a man who never troubled about money. He was delighted to have a son and was only too glad to do anything he could for the child. The servants knew this well and they came and told him without hesitation. "Bring him in," Ximen said. The old monk came in and made reverence to Ximen Qing.

"I come from India," he said. "I was at the Eastern Capital for a while, but for nine years I have remained in solemn meditation at the Temple of Eternal Felicity. I have come to know the Sacred Principle. Now the temple is in ruins, and the rooms are falling down and it seemed right to me that, as a humble disciple of Buddha, I should do something for the temple. So I determined. The other day, you, my lord, took leave of some other noble gentlemen at the temple. You were sorry to find it in such disrepair, and it was your kind intention to assist us. At that moment the host of Buddhas were your witnesses. I remember that we read in the sacred scriptures: If the pious men and women of this generation spend their wealth for the glory of the image of Buddha, reward shall come to them; their sons and grandsons shall be fair and strong; they shall pass all their examinations and their wives shall be honored. I have come especially to you. Help me to accomplish this good deed, whether you give me five hundred or a thousand." He took out a silken cloth and, from it, the subscription list, and handed it with both hands to Ximen Qing.

Ximen was moved by the monk's words and gladly took the appeal. He told a boy to bring tea for the monk and meanwhile looked at what was written.

A humble supplication [he read]. When, after the White Horse had borne the Sacred Books here, the Religion of the Buddha was made known, the glorious doctrines that had come from India were established in their various schools. Then all the monks of this great country were converted to the teaching of the Buddha. The Three Thousand Worlds were beautified. Now we have seen that this temple is in ruins and no longer worthy of its great name.

If we do not give alms, how shall we pride ourselves that we are disciples of the Buddha and men of virtue? This Temple of Eternal Felicity is a religious foundation of great antiquity, a holy place of sacrifice. It was built in the days of the Emperor Wu of Liang, and its founder was the Great Teacher Wanhui. In those days it had splendid proportions and was modeled upon the garden of the Buddha himself. The floor was paved with gold and the adornments were of exquisite delicacy so that it resembled the monastery of Qi Yuan. The staircases were of white jade. Lofty towers soared to the heavens. So the religious atmosphere was made manifest in the skies. The foundations were solid and the main sanctuary could contain a thousand monks. The wings were magnificent with beautiful buildings. The cloisters were spotless and the whole building was like the dwelling of the Immortals.

In those days bells and drums announced the sacred principle of the Buddha and all men said: "Here is the abode of the Buddha in this world." The monks were learned, and it was a paradise upon earth. But now, many years have passed and things have altered. Evil monks gave way to drink and broke their vows; so fond of sleep were they and idle that they never swept their monastery. Gradually it declined; the number of the monks decreased. It became a desert place, and few came to worship there.

Snakes and rats made their holes in the walls; wind and rain wore them away. Pillars and walls, one after another, fell. The monks did nothing to repair them, and the place crumbled into ruin. Day succeeded day, year followed year, and none thought to restore the buildings. Instead, the painted balustrades and panels were burned by the monks themselves to heat wine and tea; great pillars and beams were taken to exchange for salt and rice. The weather tarnished the gold upon the Lohan's body; the rain streamed upon the Buddhas, and their bodies crumbled into dust. Alas, thus was so gorgeous and beautiful a place, a treasure-house of gold and color, transformed into a desert of weeds and brambles. Things prosper for a while and then decay, yet prosperity will return when ill fortune has done its worst.

This monk can no longer bear to see the ruin of the House of Buddha. He has sworn a great oath that he will go to all good people for their charity and stimulate their generous feelings. Whether they give a column, a beam, or simply wood; whatever it is, their names shall be remembered forever. Whether they contribute silver or cloth, whatever we receive, their names shall be entered upon the roll of benefactors.

Trusting in the might and the wisdom of the Buddha, we call down blessings upon all good people that they may prosper forever. We have confidence in the All-knowingness that father, son and grandson shall obtain high office and that their household shall be continued forever. They shall beget wise sons who shall bring repute upon their families; their gold shall be piled as high as mountains and, whatever they ask for, it shall be granted them.

You to whom this shall come, may the spirit of parsimony depart from you.

When Ximen Qing had finished reading, he laid the writing on the table very carefully.

"Though I cannot call myself a rich man," he said to the monk, "I have a few thousands. I am a military officer, and for long no son was born to me. Last year, my sixth wife bore a child and I was content. The other day I happened to come to your monastery to take leave of some friends, and I thought then of giving money for the restoration. It is good of you to come and see me. I shall not refuse."

He took a brush and wondered how much he should put down. Ying Bojue said: "Brother, since you seem so well disposed, why not pay the whole cost? I'm sure it would not be too much for you."

Ximen Qing laughed, the brush in his hand. "No," he said, "I cannot do that."

Bojue said: "Well, at least a thousand."

Again Ximen Qing laughed. "No, that's too much."

Then the monk spoke. "Noble sir," he said, "we monks of Buddha never press people to give. We take whatever they choose to give us. Write what you can afford. I only ask that you will commend the cause to your relatives and friends."

"You speak with wisdom, Master," Ximen said, "I will not give less than five hundred." This sum he wrote down. The monk thanked him. "All the eunuchs and officers of the prefecture and the district are friends of mine. Go and see them. I am sure they will put down three hundred, two hundred, one hundred, or at least fifty, and you will certainly be able to restore your monastery." He gave the monk some vegetarian food and saw him to the door.

When he returned to the hall, he said to Ying Bojue: "I was just wishing to see you when you came. When I came back from the Eastern Capital, my friends and relatives gave parties in my honor. Today I am making a return and I should like you to stay. The monk interrupted us."

"A good monk that," Bojue said. "Certainly a very holy man. I was quite touched while he was talking to you, and even I made my little contribution."

"What did you contribute?" Ximen Qing asked. "I didn't see you write it down."

Bojue laughed. "Ah, Brother," he said, "I fear that you do not understand. The Sacred Scriptures tell us that good will is the finest form of charity; then the teaching of religion; and, last of all, the giving of alms. Did I not urge you to give him money? That was charity of the first order."

Ximen Qing laughed. "You certainly did, but I don't believe there was any particular good will about it."

They both laughed. "I will stay until your guests come," Bojue said. "If you have anything to attend to, please don't mind me, but go and discuss it with your lady." Ximen left Bojue and went to the inner court. Jinlian was grumbling there, but he paid no attention. She yawned and went to her room to sleep.

Li Ping'er, Ruyi'er, and the maids were trying to amuse Guan'ge, who was crying. Yueniang and Sun Xue'e were superintending the cooks in the kitchen. Ximen Qing went to them and told them about the monk and the contribution he had made. He also told them the joke Ying Bojue had made. They laughed.

Yueniang was a good woman. She said something to Ximen Qing that touched him deeply.

"Brother," she said, "you have been blessed by Heaven. A son has been born to you. Now you have had this generous idea of giving your money and the whole household will be the better for it. But the more good ideas the better, while evil ideas should be uprooted utterly. Brother, in days past you have not been all that you ought to have been. You have gone after whores and behaved improperly. This must stop. Then you will grow in virtue, and it will be better for your son."

Ximen Qing laughed. "That's a nice way to talk. And you're quite wrong. The world is based upon the interaction of the male and female principles, and it is natural for men and women to be drawn together. Any irregular little affair that may happen in this present life was predetermined in a former one. It is all written down in the register of marriages. One cannot say that anything we do is out of depravity and evil passion. Besides, they tell me that gold is not despised, even in Paradise, and, in the ten regions of Hell, money is at a premium. So, if we are generous in almsgiving now, it won't do us any harm if we debauch the angels and run off with the daughters of the Mother of the Gods."

Yueniang laughed. "Dogs eat filth and think it's nice. They can't change their habits, because they are made that way."

They were still laughing when the two nuns, Wang and Xue, came in with a bowl. They greeted Yueniang and Ximen Qing. Yueniang asked them to sit down.

Nun Xue was not one who had been brought up in a convent from her youth. She had been a married woman, and her husband had sold buns outside a temple. But the business did not prosper, and she started a business of greater profit with the monks of the temple. Five or six of them enjoyed her favors. They used to send her bread and other things that the faithful had given them for sacrifice. They gave her money for ornaments and cloth that pious donors had presented to the temple, and she used the cloth to make shoes for her feet. All this was without her husband's knowledge. When he died, as she had developed a keen enthusiasm for monasticism, she became a nun. She sent about conducting services in pious households and assisting wicked women in their unlawful love affairs. Seeing that Ximen Qing was a wealthy man with several wives, she favored his household with very frequent visits, hoping always to get more money.

> The Buddhist nuns, of course, have not a hair
> Upon their heads.
> Night after night, they sport with the monks.
> Three bald heads
> The teacher and his two disciples.
> What are the little cymbals doing on the bed?

Nun Xue sat down and opened a small box. "We have really nothing to offer you," she said, "but I have brought a few fruits that have been offered to Buddha. They are perfectly fresh."

"It is good of you to come at all," Yueniang said. "There is no reason why you should trouble to bring presents."

Jinlian woke up and heard somebody talking. She thought it must be

Ximen Qing again with Li Ping'er, and she got up to peep at them. But Li Ping'er was playing with the baby. When she knew that the two nuns were there, she determined to ask their advice about the child and went to Yueniang's room. When she had come and greeted the nuns, Ximen told them about the monk who had come to ask for alms. Jinlian was annoyed and went off muttering to herself.

When Xue had listened to Ximen Qing, she rose and made a reverence to him. "With generosity such as yours," she said, "you must assuredly live a thousand years. You will have five sons and two daughters and they will live together with you. I have a suggestion to make. It will cost you very little, and it will make you even more prosperous. If you accept this suggestion, even old Gautama who lived an ascetic life upon the Mountains of Snow, or the great Kās´yapa who could sweep the ground with his beard, or the Second Great Teacher who cut himself to shreds to feed a tiger, or old Ji Gu who poured the yellow gold upon the ground, will not be able to rival you in merit."

Ximen Qing laughed. "Sit down, most worthy Sister," he said. "Tell me what I must do and I will do it."

"Our Lord Buddha," the nun began, "has given us the *Dharani Sutra* to teach men the way to Paradise. Because those who see with the eyes of the flesh do not truly see and cannot truly believe, the Lord Buddha gave this teaching urging men to serve him faithfully that so they may attain to Paradise and escape from the turning of the wheel. The Buddha said: He who reads this book or prints it for others to read shall receive blessings unbounded. And in that book are charms for the protection of children. If people would engender boys and girls, first they should secure this text and recite it. Then their children will be easy to rear. No calamities will fall on them and blessings will be showered upon them. I know that the type of this book still exists but no one has reprinted it. Now, my lord, if you will spend a little money and print a few thousand copies, they can be sewn and distributed and you will have done a truly meritorious work."

"I see no objection," Ximen said, "but first I must know how much the paper, the printing, and the binding will cost. Tell me that, and I will have the work done."

"My lord," Nun Xue said, "there is no need for you to be troubled with such details. Nine taels of silver will do to begin with. The printer can print a few thousand copies and, when the binding is finished, you can pay whatever else is needed."

Meanwhile Chen Jingji was looking for Ximen Qing. He came to the arbor, and there had the good fortune to find Jinlian. When she saw him, it was as though a cat suddenly espied a fish. Her melancholy disappeared at once, and the soft winds of Spring brought color to her face. They saw that no one was about, held each other's hands and kissed, but they feared lest Ximen Qing might suddenly appear and were like a couple of rats, glancing about on one side and another as though they watched for the cat. They realized that there was no possibility for them to go further. Chen Jingji ran away without telling Ximen Qing what he had come to say.

After hearing what Nun Xue had to say, Ximen was once more persuaded. He told Daian to take thirty taels of silver from a box and gave them to the nuns. "I will have five thousand copies printed," he said. "When the work is done, I will check the accounts."

Then Shutong came and said that all the guests had arrived. There were Uncle Wu, Uncle Hua, Xie Xida, Chang Zhijie and the others. Ximen hastily dressed and came out to see them. He ordered tables to be set and they took their places in due order. Then fish, meats and fruits were brought. Those who were present were all good friends, so formal politeness was dispensed with. They guessed fingers and played all sorts of games. Some of them sang songs. They all heartily enjoyed themselves.

CHAPTER 58

Zheng Aiyue

Ximen Qing drank wine with his friends and relatives and got very drunk. When the party was over, he went to Sun Xue'e's room. She was in the kitchen watching everything being cleared away, but, when she heard that Ximen had gone to her room, she hurried away. Miss Yu was in her room. Xue'e asked her to go to Wu Yueniang's room, where she could share a bed with Yuxiao and the other maid. There were only three rooms in Xue'e's apartment. One had a couch and another a *kang* or stove bed. It was more than a year since Ximen Qing had visited her. She quickly took his clothes and put them on a chair. Then she made the bed, washed herself with perfumed water, and went to make him some tea. When he had drunk it, they took off their clothes and went to bed.

The next day was the twenty-eighth, Ximen's birthday. When he had burned some paper offerings, a boy called Hu Xiu came with a message from Han Daoguo. The servants told Ximen Qing, and Ximen gave orders that he should be brought to the hall. He asked the boy where the boat was. Hu Xiu gave him a letter with some accounts. "Uncle Han has bought silk in Hangzhou worth ten thousand taels," he said. "He has brought it as far as Linqing and there he is waiting for money to pay the duty. Without it, he can't bring the goods to the city."

When Ximen Qing had read the letter and looked at the accounts, he was delighted. He ordered Qitong to give Hu Xiu something to eat and told the boy that, when he had done, he must go and take the news to Master Qiao. He himself went to see Yueniang. "Han," he said, "has arrived at Linqing and he has sent this boy Hu Xiu with the statements. We must get busy clearing the house opposite. We can store the goods there, and I must look about for a man to take charge of the shop."

"Yes," Yueniang said, "there is no time to lose. It is late enough already."

"I will talk to Brother Ying about it when he comes," Ximen said.

When Bojue came, Ximen took him to the hall and explained the situation.

"I came to congratulate you on your birthday," Bojue said. "But now that your goods have come, I have still further reason to congratulate you. Their arrival on such a day is a good omen. You say you need a man. I happen to have an old friend who is the very fellow for you. He knows the silk trade inside out, but he has had bad luck and is out of employment at the moment. He is about forty years old. He is a good judge of silver; he can write and keep accounts, and all things considered, he is an excellent business man. His name is Gan and his second name Chushen. He lives in a house of his own in Stone Bridge Alley."

"Splendid!" Ximen Qing said. "Tell him to come and see me tomorrow."

Li Ming, Wu Hui and Zheng Feng came and kowtowed. In a short time the other musicians followed them. They were entertained in one of the side rooms. Then one of the servants came and said he had been to summon the singing girls. "But I cannot get Zheng Aiyue to come," he said. "Her old woman says she was all dressed and ready to start, when somebody came from the princely family of Wang and took her away. So I only got Qi Xiang'er, Dong Jiao'er and Hong Si'er."

"What rubbish!" Ximen Qing declared. "Not come indeed! and why not?" He turned to Zheng Feng. "What does your sister mean by refusing to come? Is it true that anybody from Wang's place took her away?"

Zheng Feng knelt down. "I do not live at home," he said, "I know nothing about it."

"She thinks if she says she is going to sing at Wang's place, that will settle the matter and I shall not be able to touch her." Then he said to Daian: "Take my card and two soldiers and go to Wang's. Ask for the young lord Wang. Tell him that I am entertaining a few guests here today and that Zheng Aiyue promised to come. We should be very much obliged if he would see that she does come. If there is any demur, arrest the old woman and throw her into jail. Let her see how she likes that." He told Zheng Feng to go too. The boy dared not refuse, and went out with Daian.

"Brother," Zheng Feng said to Daian, "you go in, and I'll wait outside. I have no doubt that my lord Wang did send for her, but perhaps she has not gone yet. If she has not, tell her she really must come with us."

"If she has gone to Wang's place, I shall take my master's card there," Daian said, "but if she is still at home, you had better go and tell your mother to dress her quickly and we will all go back together. I will say what I can for you to Father, and it will be all right. You don't understand him. When he was at Master Xia's place, he arranged with her to come, and he is naturally annoyed when she does not turn up." Zheng Feng went home and Daian, with the two soldiers, followed him.

Meanwhile, Ximen Qing said to Ying Bojue: "The beastly little strumpet! She is ready enough to go and sing for others, but, when I tell her to come here, she won't come!"

"She is a little baggage," Bojue said. "But she is not very experienced, and does not realize what a great man you are.

"I met her at a party," Ximen said. "I thought she talked prettily so I told her to come and sing here, the young scamp."

"Brother," Bojue said, "the four wenches you have here today are as fine as any of their kind."

"But you haven't seen Zheng Aiyue, Uncle," Li Ming said.

"Oh, yes I have," Bojue said. "Your father and I went and drank wine at her place one day. She was very young then. But it is some years since I last saw her, and I don't know what she is like now."

"The girl is well made," Li Ming said, "but she puts on rather too much paint. She knows a few songs, but she is not half as good as Li Guijie. And what kind of a place does she imagine this house to be that she dares to refuse to come here? She ought to be grateful for the chance. She certainly does not know her luck."

While they were talking, Hu Xiu came back. "I have been to see Master Qiao," he said. "Now I await your orders."

Ximen Qing asked Chen Jingji to get fifty taels from Wu Yueniang and told Huatong to write a letter and seal it. Then he ordered a soldier to start early next morning and go with Hu Xiu to the customs office. "Go and see Master Qian," he said, "and ask him to be lenient when he looks over the goods."

Chen Jingji brought the money. It was handed to Hu Xiu, who took it with the letter and the papers connected with the payment of duty and arranged to leave the next morning.

Shortly after Hu Xiu's departure, they could hear the shouts of men clearing the way. Ping'an came and announced the two eunuchs, Liu and Xue. Ximen put on his robes and received the two eunuchs in the great hall. When they had exchanged greetings, he invited them to go to the arbor to take off their ceremonial robes. They sat down, the two eunuchs in two large chairs in the place of honor, Ying Bojue in a more lowly seat.

"Who is this gentleman?" said Xue.

"You met him last year," Ximen Qing said. "It is my old friend Ying the Second."

"Ah," said Xue, "the gentleman who made such excellent jokes!"

Bojue bowed. "Your Excellency has an excellent memory. It was I."

Tea was brought. Ping'an came and said: "Major Zhou has sent a man with a card to say that he is engaged elsewhere and will not be able to come early. He asks that you will please not wait for him."

Ximen Qing looked at the card. "Very good!" he said.

"Sir," Eunuch Xue said, "who is this who is coming late?"

"Zhou Nanxuan. He is engaged elsewhere and has sent a man to ask us not to wait for him."

"We will leave a place for him," said the eunuch.

Then Wang Jing brought two cards and said: "The two scholars have arrived." Ximen looked at the cards. On one was written Ni Peng, and, on the other, Wen Bigu. Wen was the man whom Master Ni wished to recommend to him. He hastened out to welcome them and found the two scholars in academic dress. He paid particular attention to Wen Bigu, who was a man of about forty years of age, of dignified and discreet appearance. There was hair upon his cheeks, and his manner was urbane and gentle.

> Though he possessed incomparable talents
> Often he went to the place where the Rites are despised.
> His name and his achievements held no glory
> And his ambition was, perforce, content with lowly things.
> His fortunes had declined, and with them self-respect.
> Philosophy and letters he left to Confucius.
> The career of a public officer,
> Or the desire to make a name for himself and his ancestors
> Such notions as these he cast into the East River.
> Now he foregathered with the scum of the earth
> Only money was his goal.
> Hail-fellow-well-met,
> Without a care for shame or prudence.
> He was tall of stature, and broad girdled
> He could see no one before him.
> He talked with an air and sang a pretty song
> But his brain was empty.
> Every three years, for the examination he would enter
> But even a low degree was too much for him.
> So now he has abandoned hope of climbing high
> And sits with others to drink a cup of wine
> To lessen melancholy,
> Like a retired minister
> Exiled to the mountains.

Ximen Qing took them to the hall and each of them offered him a book and a handkerchief as a birthday present. They sat down in the places appropriate to host and guests.

"I have often heard of your great learning," Ximen Qing said. "Will you tell me your honorable name?"

"My second name is Rixin," said Master Wen, "and Kuixuan is my honorific name."

"Master Kuixuan, in what department of learning do you excel?"

"I am only a mean scholar," Master Wen said, "so I have begun upon the Book of Changes. Your great renown has long been known to me, but I have never ventured to call upon you. Yesterday, my old school friend, Ni Guiyan, spoke to me of your extraordinary virtues, and I felt I must come and see you."

"It is very kind of you to pay me the first visit. I shall hope to return your call one of these days. I am a military officer and know little of literature, and I have no one able to attend properly to my correspondence. The other day when I was visiting my colleague Xia, I made the acquaintance of Master Ni, and he spoke most highly of your attainments. I intended to call upon you, but you have come to me first and been good enough to bring me these gifts. I don't know how to express my appreciation."

"You flatter me," said Wen. "I am really devoid of learning and virtue."

When they had drunk tea, Ximen asked them to go to the arbor where the two eunuchs were sitting. Xue suggested that they should take off their academic robes, and they took off their gowns and joined the party, only taking their seats after they had been pressed to do so for some time.

As they were chatting, Uncle Wu and Captain Fan arrived, and Daian and Zheng Feng came to say that the four singing girls were now all present. "Is it true," Ximen Qing asked, "that she had been sent for by the princely family of Wang?"

"Yes," Daian said, "but she had not started. I was about to arrest the old woman; that frightened them, and Zheng Aiyue decided to come with me."

Ximen Qing went out and stood on the steps to look at the four girls. They came forward together and kowtowed. Zheng Aiyue wore a long violet gown with a white-ribboned skirt beneath it. Her waist was like the willow, supple and full of the promise of delight. Her face was like a lotus blossom.

"Why did you not come when I sent for you?" Ximen Qing said to her. "Did you imagine you could escape me?"

Zheng Aiyue kowtowed without a word, then stood up and went smilingly to the inner court with the other girls. They kowtowed to Wu Yueniang and the others, and, finding Li Guijie and Wu Yin'er with the ladies, they greeted them too. "You came early," they said.

"We have been here two days," Guijie said. "What makes you so late?"

"It is all Zheng Aiyue's fault," said Dong Jiao'er. "We were ready, but she wouldn't come and we had to wait." Zheng Aiyue hid her face with her fan, laughed, but still said nothing.

"Who is this girl?" Yueniang said.

"Don't you know her, Mother?" said Dong Jiao'er. "She is Zheng Aix-iang's younger sister, and her name is Zheng Aiyue. It is only six months since she was made a woman."

"She has a very fine figure," Yueniang said.

Pan Jinlian pulled up Zheng Aiyue's skirt and looked at her tiny feet. "Your shoes are too pointed; they are not like ours," she said. "In ours the proportions are as they should be, but your heels are too large."

"How impertinent she is," Yueniang said to Aunt Wu. "Why should she interfere in matters that do not concern her?"

Jinlian took a gold pin shaped like a fish from Zheng Aiyue's head and said: "Where did you get this?"

"It was made by our own silversmith," Zheng Aiyue told her. Tea and cakes were brought, and Yueniang told Guijie and Wu Yin'er to join the others. The six singing girls sat down together.

After tea, Guijie and Wu Yin'er invited the other girls to go to the garden with them, but Dong Jiao'er said; "We must go to the outer court first." Li Guijie and Wu Yin'er went with Pan Jinlian and Meng Yulou. They kept away from the great arbor because there were many guests there, and, after looking at the flowers for a while, they went to Li Ping'er's room to see Guan'ge. The baby was ill again. He kept waking up out of a bad dream and he would not take his milk. Li Ping'er had to spend all her time in her own room looking after him. When they came, she asked them to sit down.

"Is the baby asleep?" Guijie said.

"He has been crying all day long, but he has gone to sleep now," Li Ping'er said.

"The Great Lady tells me she is going to send for old woman Liu," Yulou said. "Why don't you send a boy and ask her to come at once?"

"It is Father's birthday today," Li Ping'er said, I think I will wait until tomorrow."

Then the four singing girls came with Ximen Dajie and Xiaoyu. "So you are here," said Ximen Dajie. "We have been looking all around the garden for you."

"There were so many people about we did not stay long," Yulou said.

"What were you doing all that time in the inner court?" Guijie said to Hong Si'er.

"We were having tea in the Fourth Lady's room."

Pan Jinlian looked at Meng Yulou and Li Ping'er. Then she laughed. "Who told you she was the Fourth Lady?"

"She asked us to go and take tea in her room," Dong Jiao'er said, "and, since we had not been presented to her before, we asked her what was her position in the household and she said: 'I am the Fourth Lady.'"

"The hussy!" Jinlian cried. "It would have been more becoming if somebody else had said so for her. In this house she is of no account at all. Nobody calls her the Fourth Lady. But she has had her husband in her room for one night. Now she has managed to scrape a little color together and is all agog to start a dye works. If it hadn't been that Aunt Wu was in the Great Lady's room, Guijie in the Second Lady's room, Aunt Yang in the Third Lady's room, the Wu Yin'er in the Sixth Lady's room, and my mother in mine, he would never have dreamed of going to her."

"You ought to have seen her this morning," Yulou said. "When she had seen Father to her door, she flaunted herself about the courtyard, with a 'Here, Zhang!' and a 'Now, you Li!' making a tremendous fuss of herself."

"Well," Jinlian said, "the proverb says: Never indulge a slave, and never spoil a child." She said to Xiaoyu: "I hear your father told the Great Lady he was going to buy that woman a maid. Last night, when he was in her room, he found it a complete mess. He asked her, and the little strumpet seized the opportunity and told him she was so busy all day she had not time to clean her room. She said she only went there to sleep and that was all. So he said: 'Don't worry about that any more. I will ask the Great Lady to get you a maid.' Is this true?"

"I know nothing about it," Xiaoyu said. "Perhaps Yuxiao heard it."

"Your father would never have thought of going to her," Jinlian said to Guijie, "if all our rooms had not been occupied. I am not one to talk about people behind their backs, but she is a very undiscerning sort of woman. And she has a very nasty tongue. I never speak to her if I can avoid it."

Yingchun brought tea. While they were drinking it, sounds of music reached them from the outer court. The guests had all arrived and the banquet was ready. Daian came and called the four singing girls. Master Qiao did not come that day.

First there were some varied amusements, then music and songs and dances. After a few comic sketches, food was brought in. Cold appetizers were served, followed by a soup. Then Dr. Ren arrived, dressed in robes of ceremony. Ximen Qing took him to the great hall. Dr. Ren brought out a handkerchief with the symbol for longevity embroidered on it and offered it, with two pieces of white gold, to Ximen as a birthday present. "Yesterday," he said, "Han Mingchuan told me of your birthday. I am sorry I am so late."

"I am most grateful for your coming," Ximen Qing said. "With these delightful presents too. And I must congratulate you on the wonderful medicine you were good enough to send us."

Dr. Ren wished to offer a cup of wine to Ximen Qing as a mark of respect, but Ximen politely refused to allow it. Then Dr. Ren took off his ceremonial robes and they joined the others. He sat at the fourth seat on the left, next to Uncle Wu. When soup and rice had been served, Ximen Qing gave Dr. Ren's servant a box of food. Dr. Ren thanked him and told the servant to take it away.

Then the four singing girls sang a suite of birthday songs, accompanying themselves with stringed instruments. More food was brought and wine was passed around. The actors brought their repertory list and the eunuchs selected the play *Han Xiangzi Saves Chen Banjie*. When the first act was done, they heard the noise of men clearing the way. Ping'an came in to announce the arrival of Major Zhou. Ximen Qing hastened to welcome him and, without waiting for the usual greetings, asked him to take off his ceremonial clothes. "But let me first offer you a cup of wine," Major Zhou said.

"No," said Eunuch Xue, "do not offer him wine, noble Zhou. Greet each other with a simple reverence." This they did and Major Zhou bowed to the other guests. He sat down in the third place on the left. Food was brought for him, then soup, two types of snacks, two plates of meat, and two jars of wine. This was for Major Zhou's servants. Major Zhou thanked his host and bade his servant take the food away. They passed wine to each other. With singing, dancing and music, they had a very happy time.

They drank until sunset. Dr. Ren was the first to leave. Ximen Qing took him to the gate. "How is your lady?" the doctor said. "Is she better?"

"She was better immediately after she took your medicine," Ximen Qing said, "but for some reason or other she has been none too well these last few days. You must come and see her again." Dr. Ren mounted his horse and rode away.

The two scholars Ni and Wen rose. Ximen urged them to stay longer but they would not. Ximen went to see them off. "I will come and see you," he said to Wen. "I will have a study prepared for you to live in and you must bring your family. Every month I shall offer a small sum for your beans and water."

"You are most kind," said Master Wen.

Master Ni exclaimed: "A noble gentleman indeed, who recognizes literature so handsomely!"

When they had gone, Ximen Qing returned and drank with his guests. The party did not come to an end until the first night watch. The four singing girls went to Yueniang's room and sang a few songs for the ladies. In the front court, Ximen asked Ying Bojue and Uncle Wu to stay. He gave food to the actors and dismissed them. The servants cleared the tables and Ximen called for dessert. Then he bade Li Ming, Wu Hui and Zheng Feng come and sing, and gave them wine.

"Brother," Bojue said, "this has been a splendid entertainment and your guests have been well pleased."

Li Ming said that the two eunuchs, Liu and Xue, had been very generous in their presents and they had left a packet of silver for Guijie and Wu Yin'er. "His Excellency Xue is younger than the other," the boy said, "and that makes him more lively."

Huatong brought dessert. Bojue noticed some pastries among the different dishes. He picked out one and put it in his mouth. It melted away at once. It seemed like exquisite dew falling upon his heart. "This is excellent," he said.

"Oh, when it comes to eating, you know well enough how to pick out something good," Ximen said to him. "Your sixth mother made those."

Bojue laughed. "To show her daughterly devotion to me," he said. Then he said: "Uncle, won't you try one?" picked one out and put it into Uncle Wu's mouth. He gave one to Li Ming and Zheng Feng.

While they were drinking, Bojue said to Daian: "Go to the inner court and tell the four little strumpets to come here. I can do very well without them, but I want them to sing for your uncle. He cannot stay much longer and, after all, they have only sung one or two songs all day. It won't do to let them off too lightly."

Daian did not move. He said: "I did speak to them, but they are singing for the ladies now. Doubtless they will be here in a few moments."

"When did you speak to them, you young rascal?" Ying Bojue said. He told Wang Jing to go, but Wang Jing paid no attention. "You won't go, won't you?" said Bojue. "Then I will go myself." But, as he spoke, the scent of perfume came to them and they could hear laughing voices. The four singing girls came in, dabbing their faces with handkerchiefs.

"What!" cried Bojue, "are you going without singing for us? That's too much of a good thing! Your sedan chairs alone cost four *qian* of silver, and for that money we could buy quite a lot of rice, enough to keep your whole households for a month."

"Brother," Dong Jiao'er said, "if you think we can earn a living so easily as all that, why don't you come and join us?"

"It is very late," Hong Si'er said, "almost the second night watch. We really must go."

And Qi Xiang'er said: "We have to get up very early in the morning to go to a funeral."

"Whose funeral?" said Bojue.

"At a house where the doors open underneath the eaves," Qi Xiang'er replied.

"Doubtless young Master Wang's," said Bojue. "You got into trouble over that young man before, but luckily for you this gentleman sent to the Eastern Capital and had the matter hushed up for Li Guijie's sake. You were forgiven too. Now you put on the airs of a bird that has escaped from a cage."

Qi Xiang'er laughed. "Don't talk nonsense, old oily mouth!"

"Are you making fun of me because I am old?" Bojue said. "I fancy I still have some good points. Anyhow, I can manage you four little strumpets without any difficulty."

Qi Xiang'er laughed again. "Brother," she said, "I can't see you very well but it is obvious that you are boasting."

"When I spend my money," Bojue returned, "I insist upon having something worth paying for. You young strumpets of the Zheng family appear to have eaten something that makes you talk too much. You seem lost."

"After listening to you," said Dong Jiao'er, "she dare not open her mouth."

"I don't care whether she is afraid of me or not. Bring your instruments and each of you sing a song. Then I will let you go."

"Very well," Ximen Qing said, "two of you shall serve us with wine and the other two shall sing."

Then Qi Xiang'er said: "I and my sister will sing." Zheng Aiyue took her lute and Qi Xiang'er her zither. They sat down and sang very sweetly "Darkness Has Gone, the Dawn Is Here." Dong Jiao'er offered wine to Uncle Wu, and Hong Si'er to Ying Bojue.

After they had drunk several cups of wine and the girls had finished singing, Ximen Qing still pressed Uncle Wu to stay and sent for Chunhong to sing some songs of the South. Only then did he tell Qitong to saddle a horse and take a lantern to see Uncle Wu to his home. But Wu said: "Brother, don't order a horse for me. I will go with Brother Ying." Ximen bade Qitong accompany them with a lantern. He himself went as far as the gate with them. As they were standing at the gate, Ximen said to Ying Bojue:

"Don't forget about Gan. I am going to make a contract with him. Then I will join with my kinsman Qiao, and we will get the house ready for the storage of the goods."

"I will not forget," Bojue said. He went away with Uncle Wu. Qitong, carrying a lantern, went with them.

"My brother-in-law spoke about getting the house ready. What house does he mean?" Uncle Wu said.

"Han Daoguo has arrived with the goods he has bought," Ying Bojue said, "and his Lordship is going to start a silk shop in the house facing his own."

"When is he going to open it?" Uncle Wu said. "We are his kinsmen and friends, and we ought to do something to mark the occasion."

They left the main street and came to the lane in which Ying Bojue lived. Uncle Wu said to Qitong: "Take Uncle Ying to his door."

Bojue declined. "No," he said, "go with your uncle. I don't need a light. My house is close by." They separated and Qitong went with Uncle Wu.

Ximen Qing paid and dismissed Li Ming and the others and went to sleep in Yueniang's room.

The next day Ying Bojue brought Gan Chushen to see Ximen Qing. Gan was wearing black clothes. They discussed terms, then Ximen sent for Cui Ben and told him to go and see Master Qiao and find out what Qiao thought about the arrangement of the house, and when they should open their shop. "I will do everything your master wishes," Qiao said to Cui Ben. "He need not worry about me." So Ximen Qing made a contract with Gan, with Ying Bojue as the witness. It was decided that, out of the profits, three parts of every ten should be for Ximen Qing, three for Qiao, and the remaining four should be divided equally between Han Daoguo, Gan Chushen and Cui Ben. They set to work upon the warehouse, had signs painted, and only waited for the merchandise to come so that they might start business. At home, Ximen Qing cleared one of the courts for Master Wen to occupy as his secretary. He arranged to pay his new secretary three taels of silver as salary each month, and to make him appropriate gifts at the different seasons. Huatong was instructed to wait upon the scholar. When all these arrangements were completed, Ximen gave a series of parties.

After his birthday celebrations, he sent for Dr. Ren to see Li Ping'er. Then he went to the house opposite to see how the men were getting on with their work. Aunt Yang went home, but Guijie and Wu Yin'er still remained. Yueniang took three *qian* of silver and bought some crabs. She boiled them and, when dinnertime came, invited Aunt Wu, Guijie, Wu Yin'er and the ladies to come and enjoy them.

Yueniang had sent for old woman Liu to come and see Guan'ge. After taking tea, the old woman went with Li Ping'er to her apartments. The baby, she said, had been frightened and could not digest his food. She gave Li Ping'er some medicine for him. Yueniang gave her a small fee and dismissed her.

Meanwhile, Yulou, Jinlian, Guijie, Wu Yin'er and Ximen Dajie were in one of the flower arbors. They had a small table and played dominoes. Xue'e was there too. She lost her game and was made to drink seven or eight cups of wine. Then she went away and the others asked Li Ping'er to take her place. Jinlian asked Guijie and Wu Yin'er to sing for them. They made merry all day, and, at sunset, Yueniang had the food boxes of the two singing girls filled and sent them home.

Jinlian had had too much to drink. She saw her husband going again to Li Ping'er and remembered that, the same morning, he had sent for Dr. Ren to see her. She was consumed by jealousy but she dared not go to him because she knew the baby was not well. As she was going in the dark to her own room, she trod upon some filth. When she reached her room, she asked Chunmei for a light. Her scarlet silk shoes were ruined. Her eyebrows went up and her eyes opened wide. She told Chunmei to get a stick, take a lamp, close the corner door, and give the dog a beating. The dog set up a terrible howling. Li Ping'er sent Yingchun to say that the baby had just taken old woman Liu's medicine and gone to sleep. She asked that Jinlian would stop beating the dog. But Jinlian sat and made no answer. The dog beating continued. At last she allowed the dog to run away and began to grumble at Qiuju. The more she looked at her shoes, the more her anger increased. She called Qiuju and said: "It was your business to drive the dog out. What do you mean by letting him stay there? Is that dog your lover that you can't bear to part with him? My new shoes, that I've only worn for three or four days, are completely ruined. You know you ought to have had a light showing for me when I came in. Why did you pretend not to know I was coming?"

"Before you came," Chunmei said, "I told her to feed the dog and put him out. She wouldn't listen but looked at me like a fool."

"Oh, yes, the bold slave!" Jinlian cried. "I know you must be beaten before you will do anything. Come here and look at my shoes."

Qiuju went forward and stooped to look at them. Jinlian struck her in the face with one. The girl's face was cut: she drew back and tried to stop the blood with her hand.

"You slave! You slave! Would you try to escape me?" Jinlian cried. Then to Chunmei: "Pull her here: drag her here, and go get the whip. Take off her clothes and let me give her thirty stripes. If she tries to get away, I'll give her more."

Chunmei pulled off Qiuju's clothes. Jinlian bade her hold the girl's hands, and the blows fell upon her body like raindrops. Qiuju shrieked and cried like a pig being killed.

Guan'ge had only just closed his eyes, and now he was waked up by the noise. Once more Yingchun came to Jinlian. "Mother asks you please to forgive Qiuju. She is afraid the noise will frighten the baby."

Old woman Pan was lying on the bed in the inner room. When she heard the noise, she got up. She asked her daughter to stop, but Jinlian would not listen to her. When Li Ping'er sent her maid again, old woman Pan took the whip from her daughter's hands. "Daughter," she said, "don't beat the girl any more. Your sister is afraid that the noise will upset the baby. I don't mind your beating this donkey, but we must not harm the treasure of the household."

Jinlian was already wild enough, but when she heard her mother's words she was infuriated. Her mind was so enraged that her face became purple. She pushed her mother away and the old woman all but fell down. "You old fool," she screamed. "Keep yourself in your place and don't inter- fere with me. What treasure indeed? What donkey? You are in league with everybody else to injure me."

"Why! nothing of the sort," the old woman said. "I only come to get a little cold food. Why do you treat me so badly?"

"Take your old cunt off tomorrow," Jinlian said. "I can tell you that nobody is going to get the better of me in this place."

The old woman went to her room and wept. Jinlian went on beating Qiuju. She beat her twenty or thirty stripes with the whip, then gave her another ten with a cane. Qiuju's skin and flesh were torn before she let the girl go. Then she drove her nails into her cheeks and scratched her face all over.

Li Ping'er covered the baby's ears with her two hands. Tears coursed down her cheeks. She was furious, but she did not dare to say anything more.

That day Ximen Qing had been taking wine in the house opposite with Ying Bojue, Cui Ben and his new manager, Gan. Afterwards he went to sleep with Yulou.

The next day Major Zhou invited him to go to a birthday party and he went. Li Ping'er saw that her child was no better, although he had taken old woman Liu's medicine, and, as a result of the noise in the night, his eyes were upturned. The two nuns, Xue and Wang, came. Li Ping'er went to Yueniang's room and said: "Here are a pair of silver lions that I have taken from the baby's bed. I am going to give them to Sister Xue so as to have some Buddhist scriptures printed and given away in the temple on the fifteenth day of the eighth month."

Nun Xue took the silver lions and was going away with them when Yulou stopped her. "Wait a moment," she said. "Sister, you must get Ben the Fourth to weigh them. When we know the weight, Ben the Fourth can go with her and we shall know how much we shall have to pay for these copies of the scriptures. Ben the Fourth had better see to it, for our teacher, Xue, is not expert in such matters."

"You are right," Yueniang said. She sent Laian to fetch Ben the Fourth. When Ben the Fourth came, he made a reverence to the ladies and weighed the silver. It came to forty-one taels and five *qian*. Yueniang told him to go with Nun Xue to the printer to arrange for the printing of the texts.

Jinlian said to Yulou: "We will take the two teachers to the gate and then go to see Ximen Dajie. She is making shoes in her room." Holding each other's hands, they went to the outer court. Ben the Fourth and the two nuns went out, and Jinlian and Yulou went to the rooms at the side of the great hall. They found Ximen's daughter making shoes under the eaves. Jinlian picked up the shoes and looked at them. They were of green Nanjing silk.

"You shouldn't have made the designs in red," Yulou said. "Blue would have been better, for you will have to have red heels."

"I have a pair with red heels," Ximen Dajie said. "That is why I am making this pair in red with blue heels."

They sat down. Yulou asked if Chen Jingji was in. "He is asleep indoors," said Ximen Dajie. "He has been drinking somewhere, I don't know where."

"If I hadn't spoken as I did," Yulou said to Jinlian, "that foolish Sixth Sister of ours would have given all that silver to the nuns. If they had once gone off with it, we should never have seen them again. That is why I suggested sending Ben the Fourth with them. They could have taken refuge with some people of importance and we should never have been able to get them out again."

"The nuns would be fools if they didn't make money out of rich ladies," Jinlian said. "To get a sum like that from her is like pulling a hair out of a cow. She wishes to save the baby's life because she knows she will never get another if this one dies, even though she gives mountains and rivers for charity. This printing of a few texts is a trifle. In our house it seems that some people are allowed to set the house on fire, but we mayn't even light our lamps. You are no stranger and this is our sister, so there is no harm in my saying that that lady indulges herself too much. She sends for the doctor even in the early morning. Of course, it is no business of ours. What annoys me is the way she says in front of others: 'Your father comes to see the baby and wants to sleep with me, but I always send him to the other ladies.' I am good-natured enough in all conscience, yet she is always complaining about me. The Great Lady always seems to take her side. Yesterday, Father did not go to her room. What does she do but send a maid to the corner door to ask him to go and look at the baby. Then she took some medicine and told her husband to sleep with Wu Yin'er. You see how clever she is. He was delighted, of course, and the Great Lady didn't seem to mind. Yesterday, when I was going to my room, I got my shoes all dirty and told my maid to drive the dog out. That displeased her, and she sent Yingchun to say the noise was frightening the baby. That old fool of a mother of mine told me to stop and said she was afraid of frightening the precious treasure. I was angry. I said something nasty to my mother, and now she has gone off in a huff. The best thing she could do, perhaps. We can manage well enough without that poor old woman."

Yulou laughed. "How badly you have been brought up," she said. "You should not talk like that about your own mother."

"Well, she annoyed me. She always was deceitful and ready to take anybody's part but mine. Anyone who will give her half a bowl of rice can always count on her support. If anyone gives her a little something she likes, she will remember it with gratitude forever. As for the other, after that baby's birth she got our husband to stay there as if he had taken root. If he were to make her his first wife, she would throw us in the mud and trample on us. But Heaven has eyes, and that accounts for the baby's illness."

Then Ben the Fourth came back. He was on his way to Yueniang's room, but, seeing the three ladies, he stopped outside the second door and did not venture to go farther. Laian came and said: "Ladies, Ben the Fourth is here."

"Well, you rascal, let him come in," Jinlian said. "We saw him only a moment or two ago."

Laian told Ben the Fourth. He put something over his head and hurried through to the inner court to see Yueniang and Li Ping'er. He explained that the two nuns had given the printer forty-one taels and five *qian*. Five hundred copies were to be printed with silk covers, each of which would cost five *fen*, and a thousand copies in thinner silk that would cost three *fen* apiece. That would be fifty-five taels all together. We still have to pay the printer thirteen taels and five *qian*," he said. "He has promised to send all the copies here on the fourteenth."

Li Ping'er went to her room and brought a silver perfume box. She gave it to Ben the Fourth, who weighed it and found it to be fifteen taels. "Take it," Li Ping'er said, "pay the printer and keep the rest for your expenses when you go to the temple to give out the texts. It will save you the trouble of coming to ask me again." Ben the Fourth took the box. As he was going away, Li Ping'er said: "Fourth Brother, I thank you."

Ben the Fourth bowed. "You are very kind," he said. Then he went to the front court. There Jinlian and Yulou stopped him.

"Have you given the silver to the printer?" Yulou asked.

"Yes," he said. "I have arranged for the printing of fifteen hundred copies. I paid forty-one taels and five *qian,* and now the Sixth Lady has given me this silver box." Jinlian and Yulou looked at the box but said nothing. Ben the Fourth went out.

"Our Sixth Sister is wasting her money," Yulou said. "If the baby is destined to live, nothing can kill him. If he is destined to die, his life won't be saved by any distributing of texts. If she trusts the nuns, they will make a fool of her."

They got up. "Let us go and look out of the gate," Jinlian said. They asked Ximen Dajie to go with them but she declined. Pan Jinlian took Meng Yulou by the hand, and they went to the gate together. When they got there, she asked Ping'an if the house opposite had been made ready.

"Yesterday," Ping'an said, "Father made the workmen clear it out and fix up the rooms in the back court as a warehouse. The Master of the Yin Yang came and blessed the starting of operations. The ground floor is being divided into three rooms, and shelves are being set up for the silk. The rooms at the front are to be made into a shop, and the painters have been told to decorate them. Next month the shop will be opened."

Yulou asked if Master Wen's family had move in.

"Yes," Ping'an said, "they came yesterday. This morning Father gave instructions that they were to be supplied with a bed, two tables, and two chairs."

"Did you see his wife?" Jinlian said.

"She came in a sedan chair," Ping'an said, "and it was too dark for me to see her."

As they were talking, they heard 'Ting, Ting, Ting', and an old man came along shaking a brass rattle. "Here is the polisher of mirrors," Jinlian said to Ping'an. "My mirror needs polishing. It is very tarnished. I told you to look out for a polisher, and you forgot all about it. Now, the very minute we come here, one comes along."

Ping'an stopped the old man, who put down his things. "If you have any mirrors to clean," Jinlian said to Yulou, "tell the boys to bring them out." Then she said to Laian: "Go to my room and ask Chunmei for my mirrors, the large one and the two small ones and the square one I use for dressing. See that he gets a good polish on them."

Yulou said to him: "Go to my room and ask Lanxiang for my mirrors." Laian went and came back with mirrors large and small, eight altogether in his hands, and the square one pressed against his chest.

"You foolish boy," Jinlian said, "you can't carry all those mirrors. Why didn't you make two journeys? You will make dents in them, holding them all together like that."

"I have never seen that big mirror of yours," Yulou said to Jinlian. "Where did you get it?"

"It came from the pawnshop," Jinlian said. "I like its brightness. That's why I keep it in my room." She said to the boy: "Only three of those mirrors are mine."

Yulou said: "and only two are mine."

"Whose are the rest?" Jinlian said.

"The other two are Sister Chunmei's," the boy said. "She gave them to me so that they might be cleaned with yours."

"The cunning little wretch!" Jinlian said. "She never uses her own mirrors but always mine. That's why mine are so dull."

The boy gave the mirrors to the old man who sat down on a bench, brought out his quicksilver and, in a very short time, polished them all till they shone again. Jinlian took one up and looked at herself. The mirror was like pure clear water.

> The lotus and the water chestnut
> Cast their reflection on the water.
> The breeze brings ripples to the surface
> And the green shadows move darkly.
> In a pool of autumn waters the lotus appears
> Like Chang E in the moon.

She gave the mirrors to Laian to take back. Yulou told Ping'an to go to the shop and ask Fu for some coins for the old man. He took the money but did not move away. "Ask the old man why he doesn't go away," Yulou said to Ping'an. "Perhaps he thinks we have not paid him enough." The old man wept.

"My mistress wants to know why you are so distressed," Ping'an said to him.

"Brother," said the old man, "I am sixty-one years old, and I have a son who is twenty-one. He is unmarried but he will do nothing for a living. He gads about everywhere, and I have to come out to the street day after day to earn a little money to support him. He is such an undutiful son that he even takes my money and goes gambling with it. The other day he was mixed up in some trouble and they took him to the courts. There they dealt with him as a pickpocket and beat him twenty strokes. When he came home, he took his mother's clothes and pawned them all. That upset his mother so much she had to take to her bed and she has stayed there this last fortnight. I upbraided him and he went away. He did not come back and I have looked everywhere for him in vain. Sometimes I think I will not bother to look for him any more, but I am old and he is my only son. There is only he to take care of me in my old age. Yet when he is at home he makes me angry. Life isn't worth living. I suffer so much and have no place to complain. I would cry my heart out if I could."

"Go and ask him how old his wife is," Yulou said to Ping'an.

"She is fifty-five," the old man said. "She has no children of her own, and she has been ill ever since this trouble. She is getting better now, but I have nothing to give her to feed her. She keeps asking for dried meat. I have been begging everywhere these last few days, but nobody will give me any."

"Never mind," Yulou said, "I have some in my room." She told Laian to go and ask her maid for two pieces.

Jinlian said: "Would your wife like some millet gruel?"

"Would she not?" cried the old man. "Where is there any? If she could only have some, she would be delighted."

Jinlian told Laian to ask Chunmei for two measures of new millet from that which old woman Pan had brought her, and two dried melons. When he returned, he brought the preserved meat, two measures of millet and two pickled cucumbers. "Old man," he said, "you are in luck's way. If she doesn't feel well enough to eat this, she must be just getting over child-birth, and this millet will help settle her stomach."

The old man reached out both his hands and took what was brought for him. He put it with his tools, bowed to the ladies, slung everything over his shoulder and went off sounding his rattle.

"Mothers," said Ping'an, "you shouldn't have given him so much. He has defrauded you. His wife is a go-between. I saw her on the street only a day or two ago. She hasn't been at home at all."

"Why didn't you tell me so before, you rascal?" Jinlian said.

"I told him he was lucky to have met you two ladies," Ping'an said.

CHAPTER 59

The Death of Guan'ge

The maple leaves are turning red
The other leaves are already yellow.
Her hair is white as the morning frost
For he of whom she thinks
Is at the gate of the underworld
And she will see him no more.

Though she cries out her heart
There is none to carry her message to the other world.
It is far distant, and the way is covered
With the mist of sorrow.
The pearl is buried
And all earthly things are forgotten.
If her tears were drops of rain
They would fill the Eastern Ocean
With sorrow eternal.

The old mirror cleaner had just gone when suddenly a man came from the East galloping towards them on muleback. He was wearing eye-shades and a broad-brimmed hat. He pulled up at the gate and the two ladies hastily withdrew. When he took off the eyeshades, they knew it was Han Daoguo. Ping'an asked him if the merchandise had come.

"All the wagons are inside the city," Han said; "I want to know where we are to unload them."

"Our master is at Major Zhou's place," Ping'an said, "but he told me that everything has to be put into the house opposite. Please come in."

A moment later, Chen Jingji came to take Han Daoguo to see Wu Yue-niang. When he came out, he brushed the dust and dirt from his clothes and told Wang Jing to take his baggage home. Yueniang ordered a meal to be served for him. Soon all the wagons arrived. Chen Jingji took the key and unlocked the doors. The porters carried in box after box of merchandise, ten great wagonloads in all, and did not finish till evening. Cui Ben was there to help, and everybody took a hand in the work. The doors were locked again and sealed. Then the porters were paid and dismissed.

Daian went to Major Zhou's house to tell Ximen Qing that the goods had come, and Ximen, after drinking a few more cups of wine, came home. Han Daoguo was waiting for him in the great hall. They sat down and Han told his master the whole story from beginning to end.

"Did you give my letter to his Lordship Qian?" Ximen asked. "Did he make things easier?"

"Oh, yes!" Han Daoguo said. "Because of that letter, though we had ten wagonloads we paid very much less than the amount due. At the customs I reckoned two boxes as one, and we made out that only two-thirds of them contained silk and that the rest held only tea and incense. So, though we had ten big wagonloads we only paid thirty taels and five *qian* duty. His Lordship accepted my list without going through the boxes, and passed everything through."

Ximen Qing was delighted to hear this. "We must send his Lordship a handsome present," he said. He told Chen Jingji to entertain Han Daoguo and Cui Ben. Afterwards, Han Daoguo went home.

When Wang Liu'er heard that her husband had returned, she bade her maid prepare an especially good meal and waited until the evening. When he came in, he made a reverence before the domestic shrine, took off his clothes, washed, and they began to talk. Han Daoguo told his wife that his mission had been very successful. Wang Liu'er remarked that there seemed to be a good deal of money in his pockets. He told her he had bought two hundred taels' worth of goods on his own account, wine and rice and so forth. These he had left outside the city and, when he came to sell them, he would certainly do well out of them. Wang Liu'er was very pleased. "Wang Jing," she said, "tells me that there is now a new manager called Gan, and it has been arranged that we and Brother Cui are to share equally with him in the profits. This will be all to our advantage. The shop is to be opened next month."

"If there is someone here to look after the shop," Han Daoguo said, "we shall need a man to go to the South to make the necessary purchases. I suppose our master will send me."

"You silly fellow," Wang Liu'er said, "a man who is really capable always gets more work than other people. If our master trusts you, it is because you are such a clever businessman. The proverb says: No man can make money without working for it. If you are sent away for a year or two, I will speak to his Lordship and have you brought back; Gan or Laibao can be sent in your place. Then you will be able to work at home."

"Oh, I don't mind," Han Daoguo said. "After all, I have a good deal of experience in this outside trade."

"You must not let it upset you," his wife said. "You will have more to do than if you were at home."

Wine was brought. Husband and wife pledged each other. Then they went to bed and enjoyed a pleasant night.

The next day was the first of the eighth month. Ximen's merchandise had come and he was free. He decided to go and visit Zheng Aiyue. He quietly gave Daian three taels of silver and a light dress and told him to take them to the girl. When the old procuress heard that Ximen Qing was coming, she was delighted. He might have been a gift from Heaven. She took the presents and said to Daian: "Tell his Lordship that both my girls are waiting anxiously for him. He must come early." Daian returned and told Ximen Qing in his study.

That afternoon, Ximen told Daian to have his sedan chair brought around. He dressed in a large hat, a black summer gown, and a pair of black shoes with white soles. Before leaving he went to the house opposite and saw how the workers were getting on. Then he got into the chair and pulled down the bamboo blind. Qintong and Daian went with him. Wang Jing was left at home and Chunhong was sent in advance with Ximen Qing's things.

Zheng Aixiang, dressed in her best clothes, stood smiling at the door to receive Ximen Qing. She led him to the reception room and made reverence to him. Ximen told Qintong to take the chair home and return that evening with a horse. Only Daian and Chunhong remained.

The old procuress came to welcome Ximen. "My daughter troubled you the other day," she said, "and now you have been kind enough to visit us. But why did you send those presents? I must thank you very much indeed for the dress you sent my daughter."

"Why didn't she come when I sent for her?" Ximen said. "Why did you say she had to go to Wang's?"

"I haven't forgiven Dong Jiao'er and Li Guijie yet," the old woman said. "They never told us it was your birthday. So, that day, they both brought you presents and my poor girl had nothing to offer. Besides, if we had known, we should have got out of that engagement at Wang's place. You would certainly have had the first claim. Then you sent your servant for her. I got into a flurry, and, without letting Wang's people know anything about it, I sent her off to you by the back door."

"I spoke to her about it when I was taking wine with Magistrate Xia," Ximen said. "If it had not been for that, I should not have minded. What made me so angry was that she never sent me word, but simply stayed away. I want to know why that was."

"Since that little baggage has become a woman," the old woman said, "she has not been at all eager to go out to sing. She knew that there would be a number of guests at your house, and she was shy. She has been brought up very tenderly. She has only just got up now, as you see, and I had to urge her several times. I said to her: 'You must get up at once because his Lordship Ximen is coming,' but she has only just done so."

The maid brought tea, and Zheng Aixiang offered a cup to Ximen Qing. Then the old procuress invited him to go to the inner court. Zheng Aixiang took him to her sister's room. He saw a scroll hanging on the wall with the words "Aiyue Hall." He sat down; the lattice was raised, and Zheng Aiyue came in. She wore no net upon her hair. It was simply dressed in the fashion of Hangzhou. It shone with a glossy blackness, coil upon coil like a black mist. Her double-breasted gown was of white silk, and her skirt was purple with green embroidery. Beneath it he could see two small red shoes. When she moved, the tinkling of the pearls and jewels made her seem still more beautiful.

Zheng Aiyue came towards him and greeted him rather carelessly. Then she sat down, hiding her pale face behind a gilded fan. Ximen Qing looked at her and thought her more desirable than ever. His eyes sparkled, his mind was troubled, and he found it hard to contain himself. The maid brought tea. Zheng Aiyue drew her sleeve back a little and, with her dainty fingers, offered him a cup. She and her sister Zheng Aixiang each took a cup and drank together with Ximen Qing. Then the cups were removed. She asked him to take off his long gown and go to her room. Ximen summoned Daian to take his cloak and the boy put it over a chair.

In Zheng Aiyue's room the hangings, curtains and bedclothes were all of silk. It was a most attractive room and exquisitely perfumed. "Indeed," Ximen said, "this is a dwelling place for the Immortals to which no mortal man should come."

They talked and laughed together for a while. Then the maid came to set the table. The food was well chosen and well prepared. First, they offered him lotus-blossom cakes. Then Zheng Aiyue picked out a mincemeat roll and offered it to him on a golden plate. When the food was done with and everything cleared away, she laid a scarlet cloth on the table and brought out thirty-two ivory pieces and they played dominoes. After the game, wine was brought and many fine fruits. The wine was poured into a golden cup, and the two sisters offered it to him. Then they took their instruments, Zheng Aixiang a zither, and Zheng Aiyue a lute, and together sang the song "Love Is in Our Hearts." So from exquisite lips came exquisite melody. Their voices would have melted a piece of marble. When the song was over, they cast dice. Then Zheng Aixiang made a show of going to change her clothes and left Zheng Aiyue alone with Ximen Qing.

Ximen took from his sleeve a white silk kerchief in which was wrapped a tiny gold box. Zheng Aiyue thought there were fragrant tea leaves in it and was going to open it, but Ximen said: "That is not for tea leaves. It holds my medicine." He took a packet from his sleeve and unfolded it, taking from it a lozenge of fragrant tea that he handed to her. She wished for more and put her hand into his sleeve. She found a purple kerchief with a pair of gold toothpicks in it. She admired it exceedingly.

"Guijie and Wu Yin'er have kerchiefs like it," she said. "You must have given them to them."

"Yes," Ximen said, "they were brought from Yangzhou. I don't suppose there is anyone else who could have given them such kerchiefs. Have it if you like it. I will send one for your sister in the morning." He took the wine cup and drank wine with his medicine. He put his arms around Zheng Aiyue and they drank mouth to mouth. He stroked her breasts. They were small and very soft. He pulled aside her shift. Beneath it her skin was as clear as the whitest jade. His passion was aroused, and his penis rose in anticipation. He pulled down his trousers and asked her to stroke it, but it was so big that she was afraid. She put her arms around his neck and said, "My sweet, this is the first time we have met. Be merciful and give me only a half. If you put in all there is, you will kill me. You've made it that size with your medicine. Nothing else would make it so red, so hot, so fearful."

Ximen laughed and said, "Get down, girl, so that you can find out what it knows."

"Another time I will do that for you," Zheng Aiyue said, "for we shall meet as often as there are leaves upon the trees, but not today, the first time we have come together."

Ximen Qing was anxious to begin. Zheng Aiyue asked if he would not have more wine. "It is not wine I want," he said, "but to lie with you."

Zheng Aiyue summoned the maid to clear away the wine table and take off Ximen's boots. Meanwhile, she went to the inner court to take off her clothes and wash herself. When the maid had taken off his boots, Ximen gave her a piece of silver, then he got into bed and she lighted some incense. Zheng Aiyue came back and asked if he would like some tea. "It is not tea I want," he said. Then she fastened the door and pulled down the curtains, put the pillow on the bed and joined him there. They were like a pair of lovebirds or the phœnix and his mate.

Ximen Qing saw that the girl's skin was smooth and fine, and her cunt dainty and without a hair upon it. It was like a piece of pastry made of the finest flour, tender and delicate and perfectly adorable. He clasped her waist with both his arms. It was as soft as jade and fragrance issued from it. Not for a thousand gold pieces could such perfection have been bought. He wrapped her white legs around his body, put on the clasp, and surged to the inmost recess of her flower of pleasure. But his penis was so stiff that it could not enter. He struggled long, with little success. She grimaced, and, gripping the pillow, begged him to stop. This only made his movements fiercer.

They sported together until the third night watch. Then Ximen Qing went home.

The next day Wu Yueniang was sitting in her room with Meng Yulou, Pan Jinlian and Li Jiao'er. Daian came and asked for the silk that was to be sent as a present to Magistrate Xia upon his birthday.

"Yesterday your father called for his sedan chair," Yueniang said. "Where did he go? It was very late when he came back and I suspect he went to Han Daoguo's house. You young rascal, you are always trying to throw dust in my eyes when you go off with him on sly expeditions of that sort."

"No," Daian said, "it was not to Han Daoguo's house my father went, for Han has only just come home."

"Where did he go, then?"

Daian smiled. He made no answer and took away the silk.

"Great Sister," Jinlian said, "you will never get the truth out of that young scamp. But I believe the young Southerner went with him too. Send for the young Southerner. We may get the truth from him."

Chunhong was sent for, and Jinlian said to him: "Where did you go with your father yesterday? Tell us the truth or the Great Lady will have you beaten."

Chunhong knelt down. "Don't beat me, lady," he said, "I will tell you. Daian, Qintong and I went with Father through a great gateway. We went up several streets and down others, and at last we came to a house where the doors were partly open, protected by sharp-edged bars. Inside the door there stood a very beautiful young lady."

Jinlian laughed. "You rascal. Don't you know what a house like that is? Calling a singing girl a lady too!" Then she asked: "What did the girl look like? Have you ever seen her before?"

"I didn't recognize her," Chunhong said. "She wore a net upon her head just as you ladies do. When we went in, a white-haired old lady came and made reverence to Father. Then we went to the inner court. There was another young lady there, but she didn't wear a net. Her face was the shape of a melon seed and her lips were painted very red. She drank wine with Father."

"Where did you go then?" Jinlian asked.

"Daian, Qintong and I went to the old lady's room. She gave us wine and cakes."

This amused Yueniang and Yulou roared with laughter. They asked him if he knew the second of the two girls.

"She looked like one who was here the other day."

"Ha! Guijie!" Yulou said.

"So he went there, did he?" said Yueniang.

"But there is no half-finished gate at our house," Li Jiao'er said.

"Perhaps they have built one lately," Jinlian suggested.

When Ximen Qing returned, he went straight out again to congratulate Magistrate Xia upon his birthday.

Pan Jinlian had a long-haired white cat. It was white all over except for a black streak that went down from its head along its back. It was called Coal in the Snow and sometimes Snow Lion. It could pick up fans and handkerchiefs in its mouth. When Ximen Qing was away, Jinlian often took it to bed with her. It never made a mess of her clothes. When it was wanted, it would come at once, and when it was not wanted, it would go away at once. Sometimes the woman called it Snowy Bandit. It ate not ox liver or dried fish, but raw meat, and this made it fat and strong. So long was its hair that you could hide an egg in it. Jinlian was fond of this cat, and often used to wrap a piece of meat in a red handkerchief and made the cat pounce forward to snatch it.

Guan'ge had been ill, but, after taking old woman Liu's medicine, he improved considerably. Li Ping'er dressed him in a red silk shirt and put him on the bed to play. Yingchun and the nurse were there, and the nurse was having something to eat. Snow Lion was sitting on the bed. The baby was wearing a red shirt and moving about, and the cat imagined that the red shirt was the handkerchief in which Jinlian often wrapped up a piece of meat for him to play with. Suddenly, the cat pounced forward and scratched the child. The baby gave one shriek and began to choke. Then he had convulsions. The nurse was alarmed, put down the bowl she was holding, and took up the baby. She succeeded in stopping the convulsions, but the cat still came after the baby and tried to scratch him. Yingchun drove him away.

Ruyi'er thought that the baby would now be better, but he had one fit after another. She asked Yingchun to go at once to the inner court for Li Ping'er. When the maid told her mistress what had happened, Li Ping'er was terribly upset. Yueniang ran with her to her room. Guan'ge's eyes were turned so that the pupils could not be seen. There was foam on his lips and the only sound he made was like the chirping of a young chicken. His hands and feet were trembling.

Li Ping'er felt as if her heart had been cut by a knife. She rocked the child in her arms and kissed him. "Oh, my baby," she cried, "you were so well when I went to the inner court. What has made you have a fit like this?" Yingchun and Ruyi'er told her about the cat. Li Ping'er wept more bitterly than before. "Baby," she said, "nobody has loved you, and now you have fallen into this trap."

When Yueniang heard this, she said nothing, but sent for Jinlian and asked her whether it was her cat that had frightened the baby.

"Who said it was my cat?" Jinlian said.

Yueniang pointed to the nurse and Yingchun. "They said so," she said.

"Then they have too much to say," Jinlian cried. "My cat is asleep in my room. How can it have frightened the baby? What right have they to say such a thing? Just as, when they take a melon, they always pick out the soft spot, so, whenever anything goes wrong, the blame is put down to me."

"How did the cat get in here?" Yueniang said.

"It often comes," Yingchun told her.

"Then why hasn't it scratched the baby before?" Jinlian cried. "As for you, young woman, don't goggle at me like that. Don't raise your eyebrows and don't have so much to say. Oh, I never have any luck." She went angrily to her own room.

Jinlian had secretly trained her cat with intent to kill the baby. If the child died, she hoped to win back Ximen Qing. It was the same as the very old story in which Tu'an Gu trained a dog to kill Zhao Dun, the minister.

When Yueniang and the others saw the child in such a state, they poured ginger broth down his throat and sent Laian for old woman Liu. The old woman came and felt the baby's pulse. She tapped her foot upon the floor and said: "This is serious. I fear the child will die." She hastily made a decoction of peppermint and Jinlian, then she produced a ball of gold foil, pounded her decoction in a cup, and filled the gold foil with it. Yueniang took a golden pin to open the baby's mouth. It was tightly closed but they got the medicine down his throat. "If that cures him, well and good," said the old woman. "If it doesn't, I fear we shall have to burn moxa on him."

"We can't decide that," Yueniang said. "We shall have to wait until his father comes home or he will be angry."

"Mother," Li Ping'er cried, "we must save the child's life. If we wait, it may be too late. If Father scolds us, I will take all the blame."

"Well," Yueniang said, "it is your boy. I will leave it to you, for I dare not take the responsibility."

Old woman Liu burned moxa on the baby in five places, between his brows, on his neck, on both wrists and on his breast. Then he seemed to go to sleep. In the evening, when Ximen Qing arrived, he had not yet awakened. When the old woman knew that Ximen Qing had come, she took five *qian* of silver from Yueniang and slipped away by a back door. Ximen came to Yueniang's room and she told him all about the child. He hurried to Li Ping'er's room. Her eyes were very red. "What has made the boy ill?" Ximen asked her. She only wept and made no answer. Then he asked the maid and the nurse, but they dared not tell him. He noticed that the child's hands were scratched and that he was burned in several places. He rushed back to question Yueniang. She could keep silence no longer and told him about the cat. "Old woman Liu declared that the boy had been terrified," she said, "and that the only thing to do was to use the needle and burn moxa on him. She was afraid it would be too late if we waited for you. Since then the child has slept. He has not waked at all."

Ximen Qing flew into a furious rage. He dashed to Jinlian's room and, without a word, took the cat by the legs and dashed out its brains on the stone flags underneath the eaves. There was a crash. The cat's brain was scattered like ten thousand peach blossoms, and its teeth like broken jade.

When Jinlian saw her cat destroyed, she sat on her bed and did not move. "You thief," she muttered as Ximen Qing went away, "taking people's property and killing it. That's the sort of hero you are. All this fuss about a cat. Of course, the cat won't demand its life at your hands when it meets you in Hades! You treacherous villain! you changeable creature! You will come to a bad end."

Ximen Qing went back to the Sixth Lady's room. "You were looking after the baby," he said to Ruyi'er and Yingchun. "How did it happen that you allowed the cat to frighten and scratch him? Then you listened to old woman Liu and allowed her to burn the child. If he gets better, well and good. But if he doesn't, that old whore shall go to the courts and I'll have the screws on her."

"What would you have done," Li Ping'er said, "if you had thought the baby was at the point of death? Doctors only do the best they can to help people."

Li Ping'er had hoped that after the operation the child would be better, but the only result was to drive the trouble farther in. The convulsions developed into a slow fit. The child's water and motions issued freely and were strangely colored. His eyes opened and closed convulsively; he dozed, and took no food all day. In a terrible state of anxiety, Li Ping'er consulted fortune-tellers, but the omens were all unfavorable. Yueniang, without Ximen Qing's knowledge, again sent for old woman Liu to come and work a charm. Then they sent for a doctor who specialized in children's ailments. He proposed to blow some powder into the baby's nostrils. "If the child sneezes," he said, "well and good, but if he doesn't, I fear there is no hope." They blew the powder into the child's nostrils but nothing happened. Not once did he sneeze. Li Ping'er gazed and gazed at the child all day and all night. She never dried her tears and she never wished to eat or drink.

The fifteenth day of the eighth month was Yueniang's birthday, but she would not keep it. Her relatives sent presents but no invitations were sent to them. Only Aunt Wu, Aunt Yang and the two nuns came. The two nuns had not shared the money equally and they were not on the best of terms.

On the fourteenth, Ben the Fourth and Nun Xue went to the printer's and brought back with them fifteen hundred copies of the texts. Li Ping'er gave him a string of coppers to buy paper offerings, incense, and candles, and, on the fifteenth, he went with Chen Jingji to the temple, burned the paper offerings and the incense, and distributed the scriptures. Then he returned and told Li Ping'er what he had done. Every day the Qiao family sent old woman Kong to see Guan'ge. They recommended a certain Dr. Bao of the Imperial College of Medicine, who was a specialist in children's diseases. When he came, he called the illness by a long name and said that it was hopeless. They gave him five *qian* of silver and dismissed him. Then they tried to pour some medicine down the baby's throat, but he rejected it. He closed his eyes, clenched his teeth and made a gurgling noise. All night long Li Ping'er never took off her clothes. She carried the baby in her arms, crying all the time. Ximen Qing, except for his duty at the office, never went out, and, whenever he came back from the office, he went at once to see his son.

One night at the end of the eighth month Li Ping'er was lying on the bed with Guan'ge in her arms. A single lamp was burning on the table and the maids and the nurse were sound asleep. She looked at the window. The moonbeams shone through it and she could hear the mournful sound of the night watchman. To her sad heart it sounded like ten thousand knockings. Her grief was beyond expression.

> The Milky Way is still, is still.
> The stars are far, are far away.
> The gleaming moon casts her cool beams through the window
> And the cold night breeze drives through the door.
> On the watchtower the drum beats quickly
> One watch and then another.
> In someone's house, beating laundry,
> A thousand strokes, and then again a thousand strokes.
> The wind chimes ring under painted eaves:
> It breaks the grieving woman's heart.
> The lamp, burning on its silver stand,

Serves but to point out her unending sorrow.
One thought alone is in that heart
The longing for her child's recovery.

Li Ping'er lay on her bed half sleeping, half waking. She dreamed that her old husband Hua Zixu came to her door, wearing white, and looking as he had looked in life. "Strumpet," he said harshly, "what right had you to steal my wealth and give it to Ximen Qing? At this moment I go to accuse you." Li Ping'er seized him by the sleeve. "Good Brother," she pleaded, "be merciful." But Hua Zixu escaped from her. She woke to find her hand grasping Guan'ge's sleeve and knew it was a dream. "Strange! Strange!" she gasped. She heard the drum sounding the third night watch. Her hair was standing on end and her body was bathed in a cold sweat.

The next day when Ximen Qing came, she told him of her dream. "Where he is now we do not know," Ximen Qing said. "It was only your fancy. Try and be calm and do not worry so much. I will get Wu Yin'er to come and stay with you, and old woman Feng to come and wait on you." Daian was sent to bring Wu Yin'er.

That afternoon Guan'ge, lying upon his nurse's breast, seemed hardly able to breathe. Ruyi'er was frightened. She called Li Ping'er. "Mother," she cried, "look at the baby. His eyes are upturned and he seems able only to breathe out, not in." Li Ping'er took the child from her, weeping. She told the maid to go at once for Ximen Qing and tell him that the baby was dying.

Chang Zhijie was there, telling Ximen Qing how he had found a house with four rooms and needed thirty-five taels more. When Ximen heard how ill his son was, he said to Chang Zhijie: "You must go now. I cannot take you to the gate. I will send you the money and come to see you in your new house." He hurried to see Li Ping'er. Yueniang and the other ladies were already there, watching the child struggling in the last agony. Ximen Qing could not bear to look. He went into another room, sat down on a chair, and sighed deeply. Before he had time to drink half a cup of tea, Guan'ge died. It was around four in the afternoon of the twenty-third day of the eighth month. The boy had lived a mere fourteen months.

They all set up a great crying. Li Ping'er beat her ears, tore her cheeks, dashed her head upon the ground, and wept until she fell into a swoon. For a long time she stayed unconscious, then she came to herself and rocked the dead child in her arms, sobbing.

"Oh my poor unfortunate child," she cried, "my heart is broken. Why could I not die with you? I will not live long in this world. Why have you left me so cruelly?"

Ruyi'er and Yingchun cried bitterly. Ximen Qing told some of the boys to prepare a room at the side of the great hall, and was going to put the child upon his bed on two benches there, but Li Ping'er clung to him with both hands and would not let him go. "My unfortunate child, my precious baby," she cried, "you have taken my heart with you. Now all my labor is wasted. I can never see you more, my heart!"

Yueniang and the others cried with her and tried to console her. Ximen Qing, when he saw her torn face and her hair in disorder, said: "Do not take it so hard. He was not fated to be our child. We reared him for a spell but now his little life is done. Cry and be done with it. We cannot bring him back to life by weeping. Remember that you are dear to me. Now we must take him away and I must send for the Master of the Yin Yang." He asked what the time was and Yueniang told him.

"As I thought," Meng Yulou said, "he waited for this hour and then went. At this hour he was born and at this hour he has died. It was the twenty-third day too, only the month is different. He has lived one year and two months exactly."

When Li Ping'er saw the boys waiting to take the body of her child away, she began to cry again. "Oh, why must you be in such a hurry? Great Mother, put your hand upon him. He is still warm. Oh, my son! How can I give you up? You cannot leave me so cruelly." Again she threw herself upon the ground and sobbed bitterly.

The boys took Guan'ge and laid him in the room they had prepared. Yueniang said to Ximen Qing: "We must let our relatives the Qiaos know, and send for the priests."

"We will send for the priests tomorrow," Ximen said. He sent Daian to bear the news to Master Qiao. Xu, the Master of the Yin Yang, was summoned to write the certificate. Ben the Fourth was given ten taels of silver and told to buy a set of fir-wood boards and get the carpenters to make a little coffin for the child.

As soon as the Qiaos got the message, Mistress Qiao came. She cried. Yueniang and the others cried with her and told her all that had happened. Then Xu, the Master of the Yin Yang, came. "My young brother," he said, "departed this life exactly at the hour of the monkey." Yueniang told him to look at the black book. Master Xu took up his black book and read:

> The young master was born at the hour of the monkey on the twenty-third day of the sixth month of the *bingshen* year in the Zhenghe reign period, and died at the hour of the monkey on the twenty-third day of the eighth month of the *dingyu* year of the same reign. This combination of a *renzi* day and a *dingyu* month indicates that another

life and death are before him. We must have no mourners except the relatives, and, when he is put into the coffin, no one who was born under the sign of the Snake, the Dragon, the Rat or the Hare, must be present. It says in my black book that one who dies on a *renzi* day will go upwards to the Temple of the Precious Vase, or down to Qi (Shandong). In his previous existence he was a scion of the house of Cai in Yanzhou. He extorted money from people by violence and spent his substance in wild living. He paid no worship to Heaven and Earth and was lacking in due reverence for his kinsmen. He caught a chill, took to his bed, fouled his bedclothes, and died. He was born again, suffered from convulsions, and, ten days ago, some animal terrified him. On that day his evil star was in the ascendant; his spirit was taken from him. On that day, too, he was born again in a family named Wang. He will grow to be a military officer and live to be sixty-eight years old.

This was what Master Xu found in his book. He asked whether Ximen Qing intended to bury or burn the body the following day.

"I do not wish him to be taken from here tomorrow," Ximen Qing said. "I will have the appropriate ceremonies on the third day, and he shall be buried in my family sepulchre on the fifth day after his death."

"The twenty-seventh will be a *bingchen* day and not inauspicious so far as the members of your household are concerned," the Master of the Yin Yang said. "The burial should take place at noon." He wrote a certificate and the child was placed in the coffin. It was the third night watch. Li Ping'er went to her room and, weeping, gathered together some of the child's tiny religious garments and put them, with hat, shoes, and socks, into the coffin with him. It was nailed up. Everybody began to cry again. The Master of the Yin Yang went away.

The next day Ximen Qing was too busy to go to the office. Xia heard of his bereavement and came to offer his condolences. Ximen sent a man to give the news to Abbot Wu and ask him to send eight priests to sing a dirge on the third day after the decease. The Abbot and Master Qiao both offered the customary offering of three animals. The four uncles, Wu, Shen, Han, and Hua, did likewise and came to burn paper offerings. Ying Bojue, Xie Xida, Master Wen, Chang Zhijie, Han Daoguo, Gan, Ben the Fourth, Li and Huang, all made contributions and came in the evening to watch before the body with Ximen Qing. When the monks had performed their part and had gone away, the customary offerings were made before the baby's coffin. Ximen Qing had tables set in the great hall for the entertainment of those who had come to condole with him.

Li Guijie, Wu Yin'er, and Zheng Aiyue sent offerings.

Li Ping'er, thinking always of her child, was very sad. She would take

nothing to eat and cried so much that she lost her voice. Indeed Ximen
Qing was afraid she might try to kill herself, and told the nurse, the maids,
and Wu Yin'er to stay with her all day. He himself spent three nights with
her and did all he could to console her. Nun Xue read the *Lengyan Sutra* to
her and an exorcism for freeing the troubled spirit, and tried to persuade
her to stop crying. "This was not really your child," she said. "He was one
to whom you were beholden in a former existence. We read in the *Dharani Sutra* of a woman who bore three children, all of whom died before
they were two years old. She cried as she took the last dead baby to the
river's bank, and could not bear to cast it in. Then the Blessed One took
the form of a monk and said to her: 'You should not so bewail. This is not
your child, but one who was your enemy in your last life. Three times he
has come to you to try to bring about your death. If you do not believe
me, here is proof.' The Blessed One pointed at the baby and it appeared in
devil's form. Standing on the water, the devil cried to the woman: 'Because
you have read the *Dharani Sutra* with devotion, angels have watched over
you day and night and I have had no chance to kill you. Now the Blessed
One has changed my heart, and I will be your enemy no longer.' So saying,
he sank beneath the waters and disappeared. I assure you, this baby must
have been your enemy. He came to you to be an expense and a hurt to
your body. The other day you gave fifteen hundred copies of the *Dharani
Sutra* to be distributed, so establishing yourself in virtue, and, thereafter
he could no longer endure to be with you and so died. Now you will have
a child who will be your true child."

Li Ping'er listened but she did not forget Guan'ge. Whenever the baby's name was mentioned she wept.

Five days passed. On the morning of the twenty-seventh, eight small
boys wearing black gowns and white hats carried banners, white parasols,
white flowers and willows, and walked before the coffin of scarlet and
gold. A great red scroll was borne beneath a canopy and on it was inscribed: "The Coffin of a son of the house of Ximen." Abbot Wu had sent
twelve Daoist novices in black robes. They chanted exorcisms about the
coffin. Musicians played mournful tunes. Then came all the relatives and
Ximen Qing dressed in plain clothes. They went on foot to the end of the
street, near the city gate, and there got into carriages and mounted horses.

Ximen Qing feared that Li Ping'er would cry if she went to the grave
with them, so he would not let her go, but all the other ladies went in
sedan chairs. Sun Xue'e and Wu Yin'er stayed at home to keep company
with Li Ping'er. She, forbidden to go to the grave, went after the coffin
to the gate. There she cried: "Oh my baby, you have broken my heart,"
and fell swooning. As she fell, her head struck the gate; her cheeks were

bruised, and the golden pins fell out of her hair. Xue'e and Wu Yin'er went forward and lifted her up. They took her to her own room. There she saw the lonely bed with the little drum shaped like the God of Longevity lying upon it. This reminded her again of her lost child. She beat her hands upon the table and sobbed bitterly.

Wu Yin'er grasped her hands. "Mother," she said, "please don't cry any more. The baby has gone and cannot come back to you however much you cry. You must console yourself. Don't be so sad."

Xue'e said: "You are still young and you will certainly have another child. I must not say all I think, because, in this place, there are holes in the wall and eyes to look through them, but it was she who schemed for this and she will pay for it. It was she who killed the baby and the baby will demand his life from her. You and I have had much to suffer. She wants her husband all to herself and, whenever he goes to anyone else, she is very angry. You know that our husband has not been to me for a long time. Well, the other day he did come, and you saw what a fuss she made about it and what she said about me to his daughter. I say nothing, but I keep my eyes open and watch. We shall see to what sort of an end that strumpet comes."

"Yes," said Li Ping'er, "she has made me suffer. But I do not know when I shall die. It may be today or it may be tomorrow, and I cannot make trouble with her. I can only leave her to go her own way."

The nurse Ruyi'er came in. She knelt down and said: "There is something I must say to you. I have not dared to do so before. The baby is dead and that is bad luck for me. I am afraid his Lordship and the Great Lady will send me away. My husband is dead and I have nowhere to go."

Li Ping'er was distressed again. "The baby is dead," she said, "but I am still alive. And even if I should die tomorrow, you have served me well. I am sure they will not send you away. One of these day, the Great Lady may have a boy or a girl. They will let you be his nurse, and it will be all the same for you. There is no cause for you to worry."

This satisfied Ruyi'er.

Li Ping'er began to cry again. Wu Yin'er and Xue'e did their best to console her and tried to get her to eat something. They asked Yingchun to go to the inner court and bring some food. But when it was set upon the table Li Ping'er could not bring herself to eat any. She tried a few mouthfuls and then gave up the attempt.

When the funeral procession came to the grave, Ximen Qing asked Master Xu to determine the site. Guan'ge was buried beside the tomb of Ximen's first wife, the lady Chen.

Master Qiao and the other relatives made offerings at the tomb and

were entertained in the new arbor. When they returned, Li Ping'er came
to kowtow to Yueniang, Mistress Qiao and Uncle Wu. Again she wept.
"Lady," she said to Mistress Qiao, "who could have such evil fortune as
myself whose baby has died so young? Your daughter is widowed before
her marriage, and all that we have done for them is thrown away. I trust
you will not scorn me now."

"Lady," Mistress Qiao said, "you must not talk like that. We can never
be sure how long anyone will live. There is an old saying that those who
have arranged an alliance between their families can never cease to be
friends. You are not old. You will very likely bear another child. We must
be patient and not give way to melancholy." Mistress Qiao went home.

In the hall, Ximen Qing asked Xu, the Master of the Yin Yang, to purify the house. They hung yellow paper charms over all the doors to drive
away evil spirits. The charms said: 'The spirit of our departed one is thirty
feet high. It goes towards the northeast. If it meets the god of the day, it
will return and not go forth again. Or it will destroy it, and all will be well.
The relatives will have nothing: to fear.

Ximen Qing gave a roll of cloth and two taels of silver to Master Xu
and took him to the gate. That evening he went to Li Ping'er's room and
tried to comfort her. He was afraid she would be sad if she saw the baby's
toys, so he told Yingchun to put them all away.

CHAPTER 60

The Opening of the New Shop

After Guan'ge's death, Pan Jinlian was as pleased as could be. She would say, pretending to scold her maids: "Ha, you strumpet! You thought you were like the sun at its zenith, but now you are brought low. Now you are like a turtle dove brought down by the bow, stretching out its tongue in vain. You are like a chair without a back and nothing to lean upon. You are another old woman Wang, who sold her corn and can never have it again to grind, or an old procuress whose singing girls are dead who has no one else to depend upon. Yes, we are now on the same footing again."

Li Ping'er in her room could hear all this. She said nothing, but her tears flowed faster. With the anger in her heart and her great grief, her spirit drooped more and more and she had no peace even in her dreams. Her appetite decreased day by day. On the second day after Guan'ge's funeral, Wu Yin'er went away.

Old woman Feng brought a maid, thirteen years old, and sold her to Sun Xue'e for five taels of silver. She was given the name Cui'er.

Li Ping'er never ceased to think of her baby, and there was a furious hatred within her for Jinlian. So her old illness returned; she had a continual issue of blood. Ximen Qing sent for Dr. Ren, but his medicine did her no good. It was like watering a rock; the more medicine she took, the worse she became. In less than a fortnight, she grew very ill and thin. All her beauty and charm left her and she looked like a handful of bones. Her sorrow was too great for her to bear.

One day, at the beginning of the ninth month, it was cold and the west wind blew chill. She was in her room alone. The bed was cold: the lonely moon cast its beams upon the window. She was thinking of her baby and sighed deeply several times. Suddenly she seemed to hear someone tapping on the window. She called her maid, but the maids were sleeping soundly and there was no reply. She rose from her bed, put on her shoes and an embroidered gown, went to the door, opened it and looked out. Hua Zixu was there with Guan'ge in his arms. He told her that he had a new house and asked her to go with him. But she would not leave Ximen Qing. She refused him and tried to take the child from him. He pushed

her and made her fall upon the ground. Then she woke up and found it
was a dream. Her body was bathed in sweat and she sobbed till dawn.

About this time, the merchandise that Laibao had bought in Nanjing
arrived. Laibao sent Wang Xian before him to get the money to pay the
duty. Ximen Qing wrote a letter and sent it to Rong Hai with a hundred taels of silver. He sent presents of wine, silk, and other things to
the customs officer asking that, when the merchandise was checked, a
lenient reckoning might be made. The shop was ready, and it was arranged
that it should be opened on the fourth day of the ninth month. On that
day the merchandise was brought, twenty large loads of it. Kinsmen and
friends sent presents and scrolls to be hung up in the new shop, and there
were twenty guests or more. Magistrate Xia sent a man with gifts and red
favors; Master Qiao sent twelve musicians. Ximen Qing himself engaged
Li Ming, Wu Hui and Zheng Chun. The two clerks, Gan and Han, were
in the shop, one to check and test the silver, the other to determine the
price of the goods. Cui Ben received the goods and set them in their
proper place. Ximen Qing, in his ceremonial dress, burned paper offerings; then the relatives and friends offered the presents they had brought.
Fifteen tables were laid in the hall. There was an abundance of food and,
when all had taken their places, the musicians began to play. Everybody
seemed to be present and the seats were all occupied. The three singers
sang the song of the World's Beginning; the wine was passed around several times, and several courses of food were served. The musicians played
and those in the company urged each other to drink. Ying Bojue and Xie
Xida took the largest cups. They did not stop drinking till sunset. Then
the guests departed, but Ximen Qing urged Uncle Wu, Uncle Shen, Uncle
Han, Master Wen, Ying Bojue and Xie Xida to stay. The tables were relaid
and they sat down again. This was the first day the shop had been open,
and, when the clerks reckoned up, they found they had done business
to the value of more than five hundred taels of silver. Ximen Qing was
delighted. When the shop had been closed, he invited Gan, Han and Fu
with Cui Ben, Ben the Fourth and Chen Jingji to join their party. When
the musicians had finished playing, they were dismissed. Only the three
singers remained to sing for them.

   Ying Bojue was drunk. He went to the front to wash his hands. Then
he said to Li Ming: "Who is that good-looking young singer with his hair
in a knot?"

   "Uncle," Li Ming said, "don't you know him? That is Zheng Feng's
younger brother, Zheng Chun. A few days ago, his Lordship had a party
with Zheng Aiyue at Zheng's house."

"Ah," Bojue said, "now I understand why she was at the funeral the other day." He went back to join Ximen Qing and the others.

"I see I have to congratulate you on a new brother-in-law," he said to Ximen Qing.

Ximen Qing laughed. "Don't talk nonsense," he said. He told Wang Jing to give Bojue a large cup of wine.

"What do you think about it, venerable Uncle?" Bojue said to Uncle Wu. "Don't you think he is punishing me without due cause?"

"I am punishing you, you dog, because of the lies you tell," Ximen Qing said.

Ying Bojue bent his head, considered for a while and said: "Very well, I will drink it. I don't suppose it will kill me. But I never drink without music. Kindly tell Zheng Chun to sing me a song."

The three boys came in together. Bojue said to Li Ming: "You and Wu Hui can go away. I only want Zheng Chun. I want him to play the zither and sing a song for me."

Xie Xida said to Zheng Chun: "Come and sing for your Uncle Ying."

"Beggar Ying," said Ximen, "please understand that you will have to drink a cup of wine for every song he sings." He told Daian to set two great silver cups before Bojue. Zheng Chun took up his zither and sang.

> A girl of sixteen years or so
> Watching a pair of butterflies at play,
> On the white wall rested her dainty shoulders
> And dried her tears with tender fingers.
> To her slave she said
> Drive them away and make them play elsewhere.

When Zheng Chun had finished his song, he invited Ying Bojue to drink. Bojue did so. Daian quickly refilled his cup. Zheng Chun began again.

> He passed beyond the sculptured screen and came to her
> Leaning against the arbor of wild roses.
> Shyly she pretended to put straight her phœnix pins.
> She would not speak of what had passed the night before,
> But smiled and gathered flowers to cast at him.

Bojue drank another cup of wine. Then he turned to Xie Xida. "This is too much for me," he said. "Two great cups of wine are more than I can manage."

"What, you foolish beggar!" Xie Xida said. "When you can't drink, you would make me drink for you? I am not your slave."

"Foolish beggar yourself," Bojue said. "When one of these days I get an official position, you certainly will be my slave."

"Oh, you dog," Ximen Qing said, "the only appointment you'll ever get will be that of musician in a brothel."

"Well, my boy," Bojue said, "if I am you shall have the hall."

Ximen Qing laughed. He said to Daian: "Go and fetch the knuckle cracker and crack this rascally beggar's knuckles."

Xie Xida went quietly over and tapped Bojue on the head. "Beggar," he said, "Master Wen is here, yet you talk all this nonsense."

"Master Wen is a man of learning," Bojue said. "He won't mind our being frivolous."

"You two gentlemen are my patron's very good friends," Master Wen said. "It is right and fitting that you should behave like this when drinking wine. Otherwise, enjoyment never could reach the pitch we desire. Happiness is in our hearts but it demands expression, and, when it is expressed, it is natural that we should let go a little."

Uncle Shen said to Ximen Qing: "Now let us try something else. Allow us to have a game of some sort—dice, or guessing fingers, or dominoes, and then a poem or a song or a tongue twister. He who fails must drink. That is fair, and there will be no disputes."

"An excellent idea!" Ximen Qing said. He poured a cup of wine, set it before Uncle Wu and asked him to begin.

Uncle Wu took up the dice box and said: "Gentlemen, I will begin, and after me, everyone in turn. I must have the name of a flower to correspond to the markings of the dice. The first word of the second sentence must be the same as the last word of the first. It must be a quotation from a song or a poem. He who fails must drink a large cup of wine. Here goes: I cast the first and get one point red. The red plum blossoms stand beside the white plum blossoms."

Uncle Wu cast the dice and got a two. He drank a cup of wine and passed the box to Uncle Shen.

"For the second cast: upon one stem I see two lotus blossoms. 'The lotus blossoms are the delight of the gaily colored mandarin ducks.' "

He threw a two, drank two cups of wine and passed the dice to Uncle Han.

"For the third cast," said Uncle Han, "I have three spring plums. 'The plums fall, but I do not put straight my hat.' "

He cast the dice but did not say what turned up. Then he drank his wine and gave the box to Master Wen.

"The fourth cast makes the *Zhuang Yuan* red," said Master Wen. "'Red and purple are not the wear for common men.'"

Master Wen drank a cup of wine. It was Ying Bojue's turn. "I can't read a word," Bojue said. "You will get no quotation from me. I shall have to give you a tongue twister."

> Flip-flop, flip-flop, a fast-footed old fellow
> Bearing beans by the bushel in his right hand
> And a beggar's broad begging bag firm in his left
> Scuffled steadily straight to his front.
> A mangy mongrel, all yellow and white
> Bit the beggar's broad begging bag.
> Flip-flop, flip-flop, the fast-footed old fellow
> Dropped the basket with the bushel of beans
> Strove stoutly to stampede the mangy mongrel all yellow and white
> But who can say whether he beat the dog, or the dog beat him?

Ximen Qing laughed. "You boil-breaking, mad creature!" he said. "Have you ever seen a man drive off a dog with his fist?"

"Well, he shouldn't have gone out without a stick. Nowadays, all beggars take sticks with them. That's the only way they can deal with the dogs."

"Sir," said Xie Xida, "Beggar Ying is speaking for himself. He is the beggar here."

"We shall have to punish him," Ximen Qing said. "He hasn't played the game properly. Now, friend Xie, it is your turn."

"I will give you a better tongue twister than his," Xie Xida said.

> On the wall there is a bit of broken brick.
> Beside the wall there is a horse.
> If the bit of broken brick falls upon the horse,
> Will the bit of broken brick break the horse's back,
> Or will the horse break the bit of broken brick?

"You said mine was no good," Bojue said. "Do you flatter yourself that your 'bit of broken brick' was any better? If you ask me, your wife is that horse and I the bit of broken brick. I and your wife would make a fine pair. It would be a case of a skinny donkey going around a broken millstone."

"Your wife, the old whore," said Xie Xida, "has only black beans to feed the pigs with. If she offered them to a dog, the dog would refuse them."

They joked with one another and each filled up his own cup. It was Han Daoguo's turn. "Master, you are here," Han Daoguo said. "How dare I go before you?"

"Don't stand on ceremony," Ximen Qing told him. "We must follow the order of the game." Han Daoguo said:

"The fifth cast gives the winter plums. 'Among the plums, I meet an angel.'"

Then it was Ximen's turn. "I will throw a six," he said. "The sixth cast fills the sky with stars. 'The stars are cold: the dark green waters mirror them.'"

Ximen did throw a six. Ying Bojue said: "I am sure promotion will come to you this winter. Fortune will turn your way." He filled a cup for Ximen.

Li Ming and the other singers came and sang for them. The party did not break up until the night watch had sounded. Ximen Qing dismissed the boys, watched the servants clear everything away, and told the four clerks to take charge in turn and see carefully to the doors and windows. Then he went home.

The next day, Ying Bojue came with Li and Huang to make a settlement of their debt. They said to Ximen Qing: "So far we have only got back fourteen hundred and fifty taels. That is not enough to cover the expenses; we can only offer his Lordship three hundred and fifty. When we receive the next payment from the authorities, we will pay the remainder." Bojue spoke on their behalf, and Ximen Qing told Chen Jingji to weigh the money and accept it.

Huang and Li then went away, leaving the money on the table. Ximen Qing said to Ying Bojue: "Brother Chang told me that he had got a house. He wants thirty-five taels. He came the other day, but I could not attend to him because the baby was ill. I don't know whether he mentioned the matter to you or not."

"I told him he had no business to worry you when your little son was ill," Bojue said. "I said you couldn't be expected to discuss matters of that sort when you were so terribly anxious. 'Keep the landlord quiet,' I said to him, 'and I will see our brother and get it fixed up for you.'"

"We will have something to eat and then you can take him fifty taels," Ximen said. "This is an auspicious day and he can settle the matter now. Tell him to spend anything that is left over on setting up a small shop so that he can make a little money for himself. That ought to be enough for his wife and himself."

Bojue thanked him. Food was brought, and they ate it together. Afterwards, Ximen told Bojue that he would not detain him, and asked him to go and arrange about Chang's house.

"I should like one of your servants to go with me," Ying Bojue said.

"Nonsense," said Ximen Qing. "Put the money in your sleeve and take it to him. That's all that's necessary."

"I don't mean that," Bojue said, "but I have other matters to attend to. It is my cousin Du's birthday. I sent him a present this morning and he sent a boy to ask me to go and see him this afternoon. I shan't be able to come back and report to you. If you will let one of your boys come with me, he can come and tell you when we have arranged about the house."

"Wang Jing shall go with you," Ximen said.

Wang Jing went with Bojue to see Chang Zhijie. Chang was at home and invited Bojue to go in. Bojue showed him the money. "His Lordship," he said, "told me to come and arrange with you about the house. I am very busy and have to go and see my cousin Du. Let us get the matter settled quickly. Then I must go."

Chang Zhijie hastily told his wife to make some tea. "His Lordship is really very kind," he said. "I can't think of anyone else who would have done it." They drank their tea and went to New Market Street. There they signed the contract and paid the landlord. Bojue told Wang Jing to go home and report to his master; then he gave the remaining silver to Chang Zhijie and went to see his cousin. Ximen Qing looked at the contract and told Wang Jing to take it back to Chang Zhijie.

CHAPTER 61

Li Ping'er Falls Ill

The cricket chirps mournfully in the dew
It frightens her as she lies on the autumn pillow.
Her tears moisten the embroidered coverlets.
Lonely she lies, her exquisite limbs are cold.
The night seems as unending as her sorrow.
The rain pours down. The lamp is very dim.
She cannot sleep.
Now the crow cries and the golden pit is cold.

O ne night, when Han Daoguo was at home from the shop, his wife
Wang Liu'er said to him: "Through our master's kindness we have
made a good deal of money. I think we ought to prepare some sort of
a feast and invite him to come. Besides, he has just lost his son and we
should do something to console him. It need not be a very expensive
entertainment, but it should be well done. When the people at the shop
see it, they will realize that you are on very good terms with his Lordship.
Such friendships as that between our master and yourself are not by any
means usual. It will help when you go to the South."

"That is just what I have been thinking," Han Daoguo said. "Tomorrow is the fifth, but that is not a favorable day. Why don't we give our
party on the sixth? I will engage two singing girls and take my card around
myself and ask him to come. At night, I will go and sleep at the shop."

"Why should you engage singing girls?" Wang Liu'er said. "After dinner, he may wish to stay a while, and it will be awkward if there are singing
girls about. Our neighbor, Mistress Luo, knows a girl called Shen. She is
young and has an excellent voice. She has the advantage of being blind.
We might get her to come. We can send her away when we have done
with her."

Han Daoguo agreed. The night passed. The next day he went to the
shop and asked Master Wen to write an invitation card for him. Then he
went himself to Ximen Qing. "Tomorrow," he said, "I am arranging to
have a very small party, and I beg you to come." He handed his card to
Ximen Qing. Ximen looked at it.

"You should not take so much trouble," he said. "I shall be free tomorrow, and I will come as soon as I get back from the office." Han Daoguo went away. The next morning, he sent Hu Xiu to buy food and engaged a cook. He sent a sedan chair for Miss Shen. His wife and the maids prepared some excellent tea and waited for Ximen Qing.

In the afternoon, Qintong brought a jar of grape wine and, later, Ximen Qing came in a sedan chair, followed by Daian and Wang Jing. He was wearing a *zhongjing* hat, a black silk gown, and black shoes with white soles. Han Daoguo welcomed him and thanked him for the wine. Ximen sat down on a chair that was set by itself in the place of honor. Wang Liu'er, in a dainty dress, came and kowtowed four times to him. Then she went out to see about the tea. Wang Jing brought it, and Han Daoguo offered a cup to Ximen; then he sat down and took a cup himself. When they had drunk their tea, Wang Jing took the cups away.

"Both when I have been here and when I have been away," Han Daoguo said, "you have been very kind to me and my wife. I find it hard to express my gratitude. The other day, when your son died, I was not at home, and, unfortunately, my wife had a very bad cold and could not call to offer our sympathy. We have ventured to invite you today, partly in the hope of making you merry and partly as a sign of our sincere sympathy."

"You are both very kind," Ximen Qing said.

Wang Liu'er came and sat with them. "Have you told his Lordship?" she asked her husband.

"Not yet," he said.

"What is that?" Ximen Qing said.

"He was going to ask two singing girls to come, but I thought they might be in the way and I wouldn't let him send for them. We know a young lady who often visits my neighbor Luo, a certain Miss Shen. She knows all the latest songs. The other day, when I was at your house, I saw Miss Yu. She sings well, but not so well as Miss Shen. I have asked Miss Shen to come and sing for you. If you like her singing, you may think fit to get her to sing for your ladies."

Han Daoguo told Daian to take his master's cloak, and the table was laid. Hu Xiu brought in the food. Wang Liu'er opened the jar and heated the wine. She carried the pot and her husband offered a cup of wine to Ximen Qing. Then Miss Shen came. Her hair was dressed high upon her head, and the ornaments and flowers she wore were very simple. Her gown was green, her skirt red. Her feet were very small. Her cheeks were the color of peach flowers, and her eyebrows long. She kowtowed to Ximen Qing. He bade her rise and asked how old she was.

"I am twenty-one," she said.

"How many songs do you know?" Ximen asked.

"More than a hundred; some long, some short."

Ximen asked Han Daoguo to give her a seat, and, after making a reverence, she sat down. Then she took a zither and sang "The Arbor of Fragrance in Autumn." When they had finished their soup and other dishes had been brought, she sang "The Five Thousand Rebels." They drank again, and Ximen Qing asked her to put down the zither and sing a short song to the accompaniment of the lute. Miss Shen was anxious to display her skill. Gently waving her silken sleeves, she took up the lute delicately, tuned it softly, and sang. The song she sang was "Sheep upon the Mountains." Han Daoguo asked his wife to fill up a cup of wine and offer it to Ximen Qing.

Wang Liu'er said to Miss Shen: "You know another fine song. I should like you to sing it for his Lordship."

> At the first meeting with her lover
> No more than twice ten springs had welcomed her.
> Black is her hair like a black cloud
> Her cheeks as rosy as a peach blossom
> As tender as the soft shoots of the bamboo.
> If she had been born of a good family
> She would have been a great lady.
> Alas, she has thrown away her virtue in a house of ill fame.
> If she could give up that evil life and marry,
> It would be better than having always to dismiss one man
> To give welcome to another.

> At the first meeting with her lover
> She is as perfect as the moon, as graceful as a flower
> A jewel amid the dust and wind
> With a slim waist that a hand can encircle
> And a clever mind that needs no telling.
> He is full of regret that they did not meet before
> Now, as they lie on the bed drinking, they repine
> They pour their wine, sing softly to each other, and embrace.
> One looks long and is charmed
> The other gazes and is filled with delight.
> They know that their joy may last for but a moment
> And strive to throw foreboding to the winds.

The songs reminded Ximen Qing of his first meeting with Zheng Ai-yue. He was pleased. Wang Liu'er filled his cup again and said, smiling: "My Lord, do not hurry over your wine: Miss Shen has several songs to sing yet. She has only made a beginning. You may decide to send for her to sing for your ladies. In my opinion, she is certainly cleverer than Miss Yu."

"Miss Shen," Ximen Qing said, "if I send someone for you at the Double Ninth festival, will you come?"

"Whenever you think fit to command me, I will come," Miss Shen said.

Ximen Qing was pleased with the intelligent way she spoke. They drank again. Wang Liu'er thought that the girl's presence might prove hampering to her dealings with Ximen Qing, so, after a few more songs, she told her husband to send Daian with Miss Shen back to Mistress Luo's house. Ximen Qing gave her three *qian* of silver to buy strings for her instruments. When Miss Shen had thanked him, he told her that he would send someone for her on the eighth day. "My lord," Wang Liu'er said, "you need only tell Wang Jing. I will do the rest." Miss Shen went away. Han Daoguo went to the shop and left his wife alone with Ximen Qing. Wang Liu'er threw dice and drank with him. Their hearts began to grow warm. Ximen Qing pretended that he was going to change his clothes and went to her room. She followed him; they fastened the door and set to their pleasure. Wang Jing took a lamp and went to another room where he joined Daian and Qintong and drank wine with them.

The boy Hu Xiu stole a few cups of wine in the kitchen. Then he dismissed the cook and went to the room where Wang Liu'er had her domestic shrine. There he set down a mattress and went to sleep. But the room was next to Wang Liu'er's, and soon the boy woke up. He could hear sounds coming from the next room. Through a crack in the partition he could see a light. He thought that Ximen Qing had gone and that Han Daoguo was sleeping there. He took a pin and made a hole in the paper. Through the hole he peeped. The candles were shining brightly. He was surprised to see Ximen Qing sporting vigorously with his master's wife, whose legs were plainly to be seen over the frame of the bed. Ximen Qing was wearing a short silken vest and nothing at all upon the lower part of his body. At the edge of the bed, he was coming and going, plunging and prancing, making a considerable noise. The woman was saying all kinds of endearments to him. Hu Xiu heard: "My darling, if you would like to burn your naughty sweetheart, do so. Burn me whenever and wherever you like. I shall not forbid you. My body is all yours, and whatever you like to do with it, you may do."

"But your husband may not like it," Ximen Qing said.

"Even if that turtle had eight heads and eight galls, he would not dare not to like it; it is only by your bounty that he exists."

"If you will love me only," Ximen said, "I will send him and Laibao to stay in the South. I can keep them busy there buying merchandise for me."

"Then send him," the woman said. "Why should you keep him here? Send him away by all means, and when he comes back I will find another woman for him. I belong heart and soul to you, so I want him no longer. Do with me whatever you think fit, I shall be quite content. And if I lie to you, may this unworthy body rot utterly away."

"You need take no oaths," Ximen said.

Hu Xiu heard all that they said and saw all that they did.

Han Daoguo, before he left the house, had seen no sign of the boy and supposed that he had gone to the shop. But when he got to the shop and made inquiries of Wang Xian and Rong Hai, they told him that the boy was not there. Han Daoguo went home again and looked for Hu Xiu at the front and the back, but could see him nowhere. In the front court, Wang Jing, Daian and Qintong were drinking.

When Hu Xiu heard Han Daoguo coming, he hurriedly lay down again on his mattress and pretended to be asleep. His master came into the room with a light. There the boy was, snoring. Han Daoguo kicked him. "Get up at once, you rascal," he said. "I thought you were at the shop. You have no business here. You can find a place to sleep there. Get up and come with me." Hu Xiu got up, rubbed his eyes, and went to the shop with Han Daoguo.

Ximen Qing and Wang Liu'er enjoyed the pleasures of love for a long time. He burned the woman in three places, at the pit of the stomach, on the mount of Venus, and on the tail bone. Then she got up, dressed herself, and called her maid to bring water that she might wash her hands. Fresh wine was heated; food was brought, and they talked together. After drinking a few cups of wine, Ximen Qing mounted his horse and went away with the three boys, Daian, Wang Jing and Qintong. It was the second night watch when they reached home.

He went to see Li Ping'er. She was lying on her bed. She noticed that Ximen Qing had been drinking and asked where he had been.

"Han Daoguo invited me to go to his place. He wished to express his sympathy in the loss of our child. There was a young woman named Shen there. She sings very well, certainly more sweetly than Miss Yu, and I am going to send for her at the festival. She shall sing for you. I know how melancholy you have been, but now you must not think about the baby any longer."

He was going to tell Yingchun to take his clothes and make ready to go to bed with Li Ping'er. "No," she said, "I am still unwell, and the maid is making some medicine for me at this moment. Won't you go and sleep with someone else? You must have seen how ill I have been looking lately.

There is hardly any breath left in my body. You will take no more pleasure with me."

"My dearest one," Ximen said, "I love you too dearly ever to forsake you. I want to stay with you."

Li Ping'er looked at him and smiled. "Who can believe that deceitful tongue of yours?" she said. 'If I were to die tomorrow, would you not forget me? Wait till I am better and, if you still wish to sleep with me, you shall."

"Very well," Ximen said, "if you won't have me, I'll go to Pan Jinlian."

"Yes, do," Li Ping'er said. "That is exactly where you should go. She is waiting for you in a fever of anxiety. If you do not go, she will think I have prevented you.

"In that case, I will go now."

Li Ping'er smiled bitterly. "I was teasing you," she said. "But please go."

When he had gone, she got up and sat on the bed. Yingchun brought her medicine. She could not restrain her tears, and her fragrant cheeks were wet with them. She sighed as she took the medicine.

Jinlian had gone to bed when Ximen Qing came to her room. "You have gone to bed very early," he said.

"What kind of wind has blown you here?" she said. "Where have you been drinking today?"

"Han Daoguo asked me to go to his place," Ximen said. "He wished to distract me after my bereavement, and to make some return for the kindness I've shown him."

"Looking after his wife when he was away on business, I suppose!" Jinlian said.

"Oh, no," Ximen said, "between master and man, anything of that sort would be improper."

"Improper, do you say? Did you put a strap about your loins to make sure that you would not overstep the mark? It is no use trying to hood-wink me. I have known all about it for some time. On your birthday, that strumpet was here flaunting a pin with the character *shou* that you had secretly sneaked from Li Ping'er and given to her. The Great Lady and Meng Yulou both noticed it. I told her what I thought, and she flushed crimson. But I don't suppose she mentioned that to you. So that is where you have been today. Oh, you shameless fellow! A flat-footed, lanky, ugly-looking strumpet like that with the hair all over her forehead and lips as red as blood! What a woman! A great purple-faced wanton hussy. I can't imagine what you find in her. And you keep her brother here so that he can run messages between the pair of you."

Ximen Qing kept on denying. "You funny little slave," he said, laughing, "why do you talk such nonsense? There is nothing at all between us.

Besides, her husband was there today, and I did not even see her."

"You are lying again," Jinlian said. "Everybody knows her husband is a barefaced pander. He is the sort of man who guards his sheep and goes picking tinder at the same time. He lets you have his wife and takes your money. You silly fellow, you can only hear guns forty *li* away."

Ximen Qing undressed and sat down on the bed. Jinlian stretched out her arm and pulled down his trousers. She touched his staff. It was soft. The clasp was still about it.

"Oh, you dried duck, boiled in a cauldron!" she cried. "Your body may be exhausted, but your mouth is never so. Look at this gentleman! Not a word to say for himself! Now, you villain. How dare you play tricks with that strumpet all this time? See the state you've brought him to! And your mouth is as assured as ever. Will you take an oath? I will tell Chunmei to bring a cup of cold water. If you dare drink it, I will believe you. Salt is salt, and vinegar is vinegar all the world over. But I need not tell you that. You are like a bald-headed man putting on a wig. If I let you do as you would like to do, there won't be a woman in the world safe from you. You shameless scoundrel! It is a good thing you are a man. If you were a woman, you would be carrying on with every man in the street."

Ximen Qing laughed. He could not think of anything to say. He got ready for bed and told Chunmei to heat some wine. Then he took a pill from the little gold box, swallowed it and lay down on the bed.

"My dear," he said, "taste it. If you bring it to life again, good for you."

Jinlian swore she would do nothing of the sort. "You filthy creature! And it has just been busy in that dirty strumpet's mill. If I did a thing as foul as that, it would kill me.

"You funny little whore," Ximen said, "don't talk nonsense. I tell you I have had nothing to do with her."

"If you have not, why won't you take an oath?"

The argument continued for some time. Finally, she invited Ximen Qing to wash. He would not. She took a handkerchief from under the pillow and wiped his penis, then took it in her mouth so that it soon regained its fire. Ximen mounted her fiercely and began; pressing her legs with his arms, he moved his penis noisily. The candle gleamed; he rejoiced at the sight. She lay on the bed and moved up to meet him, arousing his passion still more. He put some of his red powder onto his prick, which he pushed in again. Gripping her legs, he thrust three hundred times. Jinlian's eyes closed and she began to tremble. "Darling," she whispered, "you must do no more. You should not have put the powder on him."

"Now, little strumpet," Ximen Qing cried, "are you afraid of me or not? Will you ever treat me disrespectfully again?"

"Darling, forgive me," Jinlian said. "I will never dare to talk like that again. Don't thrust so roughly, you will make my hair untidy."

They played happily far into the night, till at last they were tired and went to sleep.

On the day of the Double Ninth festival, the ninth day of the ninth month, Ximen Qing said to Wu Yueniang: "A day or two ago, when I was drinking wine with Han Daoguo, I saw a certain Miss Shen. She is good-looking and she sings well. I will send a boy for her and she shall stay a few days to sing for you." He told the cooks to prepare a feast, and tables were set in the garden in the Hall of the Lovely Prospect. There Ximen and his household kept the festival. Wang Jing brought Miss Shen. She kowtowed to all the ladies. Yueniang thought her very pretty and asked how many songs she knew. Miss Shen said she knew a great many. Yueniang offered her some refreshments and asked her to sing for a while in the inner court before she went to the garden.

Ximen Qing did not go to the office that day. He superintended the planting of the Qiujus and invited the ladies to go to the garden. Chunmei, Yuxiao, Yingchun and Lanxiang were there to serve the wine. Miss Shen sang, and accompanied herself on the lute.

Li Ping'er, who was still anything but well, did not come until she had been sent for several times. She was indeed not fit to come; her body was so weak that the wind might have blown her over. Everybody asked her to drink, but she could take only a little. Ximen Qing and Yueniang, seeing her so melancholy, did their best to encourage her. "Sister," they said, "you must cheer up. We have brought Miss Shen to sing for you."

"Tell her any song you like," Meng Yulou said. But Li Ping'er did not answer them.

While they were drinking, Wang Jing came and said that Ying Bojue and Chang Zhijie had come. "Tell them to wait for me in the small arbor," Ximen said, "I will be there in a minute."

"Uncle Chang has brought two boxes," Wang Jing said.

"He has brought me some presents because I have helped him to get a house," Ximen said to Yueniang.

"We must see about something for them to eat," Yueniang said. "We can't allow them to go away with empty stomachs. You go to them, and I will arrange for them to have some food."

Before Ximen left the ladies, he said to Miss Shen: "Sing the best of all your songs for the Sixth Lady." Then he went to see Bojue.

"Sister," Jinlian said to Li Ping'er, "tell Miss Shen what song you would like. Father sent for her specially on your account, and you must choose something."

Li Ping'er asked for the song "Red Dust in the Purple Street."

"Yes, I know it," Miss Shen said. She took up her lute and sang it with particular care. When the song was done, Yueniang said: "Sister, drink a cup of this wine. It is beautifully sweet." Li Ping'er could hardly refuse. She took a cup and drank a mouthful, no more. Soon she felt too ill to stay and went back to her room.

Ximen Qing went to the Hall of the Kingfisher. Ying Bojue and Chang Zhijie were standing beside a pine thicket admiring the chrysanthemums. Twenty pots of the most renowned blooms stood there, all more than seven feet high. Among them were such famous flowers as Scarlet Cloak, Doctor's Red, Purple Cloak, Golden Girdle, White *Fenshi* and Yellow *Fenshi,* and many others. Bojue and Chang Zhijie came forward and made a reverence to Ximen Qing, then Chang called the man who had come with him to bring the boxes.

"What is this?" Ximen Qing said.

Bojue answered. "Brother Chang," he said, "is eager to express his sense of your kindness in helping him to get a house. He had nothing to give you, but his wife has prepared this box of crabs and a couple of roast ducks and he asked me to come with him so that we can enjoy them together."

"Brother Chang," Ximen Qing said, "there was no need for you to trouble. Your wife is only just better. She should not have bothered to cook these things."

"I told him so," Ying Bojue said, "but he thought it would be better than anything else he could get."

Ximen Qing told a boy to open the box. There were forty large crabs, ready dressed with peppers, ginger, garlic and herbs, and prepared with oil, sauce and vinegar. They smelled very tasty and promised excellent eating. The two roast ducks were done in the most attractive style. Ximen Qing told Chunhong and Wang Jing to take them to the kitchen. He gave a small present to the porter and thanked Chang Zhijie. Qintong raised the lattice and they went into the Hall of the Kingfisher. Bojue could not find words to express his admiration of the chrysanthemums. He asked where they had come from. "Eunuch Liu, the warden of the brick kilns, sent me these twenty pots," Ximen told him. "Not only the plants but the pots as well."

"Indeed!" said Bojue. "They are the genuine official pottery too. The clay is of the highest quality: it is put through the finest of sieves and pressed by the workmen's feet. That is how such flower pots as these are made. They are made like Suzhou bricks, and they are by no means easy to get hold of these days."

Ximen Qing called for tea. "Brother Chang," he said, "when did you move into your new house?"

Bojue answered: "He moved in three days after the money was paid. Yesterday was a lucky day. He bought a number of things, and opened a small shop. Mistress Chang's younger brother keeps the books."

"We must buy presents and celebrate the occasion," Ximen said. "We don't want a crowd of people, Xie Xida perhaps, and you and I will arrange for food to be taken to Brother Chang's house, so that he may not be put to any expense. We will engage two singing girls and have a merry housewarming."

"I should have invited you myself," Chang said, "but I did not dare. The house is so small I thought you would not like it."

"Not at all!" Ximen said, "we don't wish you to spend your money. I will send word to Xie Xida myself." He said to Qintong: "Go and ask your Uncle Xie to come and see me."

"Which singing girls are you going to send for?" Ying Bojue asked.

Ximen Qing laughed. "Oh, Zheng Aiyue and Hong Si'er, I think."

"Brother," Bojue said, "you didn't wish to tell me which two girls you would have, but I guessed. Now what do you think of Zheng Aiyue? Is she more tasty than Li Guijie?"

"There is none better," Ximen said.

"Why wouldn't she talk to us on your birthday?" Bojue asked. "It seems to me she is a very cunning girl."

"Next time I go to see her," Ximen said, "I will take you with me. She and her sister play backgammon very well, and we will have a game with them."

"By all means," Bojue said. "I will certainly go and have a game with the young lady. I don't intend to let her off altogether."

"You naughty dog," said Ximen, "don't play your tricks on her."

Xie Xida came, made a reverence, and sat down. "Brother Chang has just bought a new house," Ximen said to him. "He has moved into it without a word to us. I suggest that we all contribute a small sum and I will have a feast prepared here and send it around to his house. We will engage two singing girls and have a gay time there. But he must not be put to any expense."

"Brother," Xie Xida said, "you have only to say the word and the money shall be sent to you at once. Will anyone else be at the party?"

"Nobody else," Ximen Qing said. "Each of us will give two pieces of silver."

"His place is not very big," Bojue said. "It will not hold many people."

Then Qintong came and said that Uncle Wu had come. Ximen told the boy to bring him in. Uncle Wu made reverence to the three guests, then to Ximen Qing, and sat down. A boy brought fresh tea, and they drank it together. Then Uncle Wu rose and said to Ximen Qing: "Brother, will you come with me to the inner court for a moment? I should like to speak to you." Ximen Qing got up, and they went to the inner court together. They went to Yueniang's room, but she was in the arbor with the other ladies drinking wine and listening to Miss Shen singing. When she was told that her brother had come, she went back to her room and told Xiaoyu to bring tea.

Uncle Wu took ten taels of silver from his sleeve and gave them to Yueniang. "I have only had three pieces of silver from the office," he said, "so I can only pay my brother these ten taels. I shall have to pay the remainder by degrees."

"There is no hurry about it, Brother-in-law," Ximen Qing said.

"I am afraid I am very late already," Uncle Wu said.

Ximen Qing asked him if the work upon the granary was finished. "There is still another month's work to be done," Uncle Wu told him.

"Well," said Ximen, "when it is complete, you will reap your reward."

"Brother-in-law," Uncle Wu said, "this year, I understand, a number of military officials are to be appointed. I hope you will do anything you can for me by way of recommendation."

"Certainly," Ximen Qing said, "anything I can do for you, I will."

"You will go to the outer court, Brother?" Yueniang said.

"Perhaps I had better not go," Uncle Wu said. "The other three gentlemen may have business to transact."

"No," Ximen said, "a short time ago, Brother Chang borrowed a few taels from me and took a new house. He has just moved into it, and today he brought me a present of food, and I asked them to stay and enjoy it. You will be very welcome." He took Uncle Wu to the outer court. Yueniang went and bade the cooks get food ready for them. Qintong and Wang Jing prepared the table. Ximen Qing gave orders that the cellar should be opened and a jar of chrysanthemum wine brought. It had been given to him by Magistrate Xia. The wine was brought and opened. It was pale green in color and very sweet. Before it was poured into the wine pot, a jar of cold water was mixed with it to make it milder. It had a very delicate flavor, finer than that of grape wine.

Ximen Qing told Wang Jing to give a small cup to Uncle Wu, then to Ying Bojue and the others. They sipped it and spoke of it appreciatively. Then food was brought, and after they had had some, the crabs and roast ducks were served. Ying Bojue urged Uncle Wu to eat freely. Xie Xida was astounded: he could not imagine how they could be made so tasty and tender.

"They are a present from Brother Chang," Ximen Qing said.

"I have lived to be fifty-two years old," Uncle Wu said, "and never in all my life have I known crabs cooked in this way to be so good."

"Brother," Ying Bojue said, "have you given the ladies a taste?"

"I have," said Ximen.

"Mistress Chang's cooking is really marvelous," said Bojue.

Chang Zhijie smiled. "Oh," said he, "my poor wife does not really cook very well. I brought these things thinking perhaps they might afford a little pleasure."

They enjoyed their crabs with the wine while, at Ximen Qing's bidding, Chunhong and Shutong sang Southern melodies. Bojue thought he heard music. "Is Li Guijie here?" he said. "Who else can be playing like that?"

"Listen again," Ximen Qing said.

"If it is not Guijie, it must be Wu Yin'er."

"You are guessing, Beggar Ying," Ximen said. "This girl is blind."

"It must be Miss Yu, then?" Bojue said.

"No, it is a Miss Shen. She is young and pretty and an excellent singer."

"Then why not tell her to sing a song for us?"

"I brought her here to sing for the ladies," Ximen said. "Your ears are very sharp if you can hear all this way off."

"Yes, my eyes are so clear that they can see a thousand *li* and my ears can hear a bee buzzing forty *li* away."

"Beggar," Xie Xida said, "you ears are as sharp as a rabbit's. Of course you can hear."

Then Bojue said: "Brother, you really must send for her. I should like to see her. Tell her to sing just one song for Uncle Wu. You can't refuse, for his sake."

At last, Ximen Qing told Wang Jing to go and ask Miss Shen to come and sing for Uncle Wu. She came, kowtowed, and sat down. Bojue asked her age and she told him she was twenty-one. Then he asked how many songs she knew and she said she knew a number for lute accompaniment, and more than a hundred short songs. "That is not bad," Bojue said.

"Miss Shen," Ximen Qing said, "we do not wish to put you to any trouble, but will you be good enough to take your lute and sing for us 'The Four Dreams and the Eight Spaces'?" He told Wang Jing to fill up his guests' glasses. Miss Shen played and sang sweetly.

When Li Ping'er reached her apartment, she went to wash her hands. Suddenly, the blood gushed from her, and her eyes were dazzled. She got up as quickly as she could, and pulled up her skirts, then fainted and struck the ground with her head. Yingchun was there and did what she could, but Li Ping'er hurt herself. Yingchun and Ruyi'er got her to bed. She lay there unconscious. Yingchun was frightened and told her fellow maid to go for Yueniang. All the ladies hurried to see what was amiss. Yingchun and the nurse were on the bed, holding up Li Ping'er.

"She was quite well a moment ago," Wu Yueniang said. "What has happened to make her like this?" Yingchun showed her the chamber pot. Yueniang was startled. "Perhaps," she said, "the blood has flowed more freely because of the wine she drank."

"But she only drank a little," Meng Yulou and Pan Jinlian said together. They made ginger broth and poured it down her throat, but it was a long time before she came around and was able to speak to them.

"Sister," Yueniang said, "what is the matter?"

"Nothing very much," Li Ping'er said. "I got up and pulled up my skirt. Then my eyes seemed to go black. Everything whirled round and round, and I couldn't keep myself from falling."

Yueniang was going to tell Daian to go for his master and also for Dr. Ren, but Li Ping'er said: "No, don't say anything about it. I should not like to disturb their party."

Yueniang told Yingchun to straighten the coverlets and help Li Ping'er to go to bed. She and the other ladies gave up their amusements and went to their own rooms.

Uncle Wu and the others stayed until the evening, then Ximen Qing went to Yueniang's room. She told him how Li Ping'er had fainted. Ximen went at once to see her. She was lying, pale as wax, upon the bed. She held him by the sleeve and cried. He asked her what the trouble was. "As soon as I came in," she said, "the blood poured from me like water. Then I fainted."

Ximen saw that her head was slightly bruised. "What were the maids doing to let you fall and hurt your face?" he said.

"It was a very good thing for me the maid and the nurse could come to my help," Li Ping'er said. "If they hadn't, I should have been very much worse hurt."

"I will send for Doctor Ren the first thing in the morning," Ximen said. He spent the night in her room, sleeping on another bed.

The following morning, after he had been to the office, Ximen sent Qintong for the doctor. It was a little after noon when Dr. Ren arrived. Ximen Qing received him in the great hall and they had tea. Then he sent a boy to tell the ladies. They had the room cleaned and incense burned, and Dr. Ren was asked to go and see Li Ping'er. When he had examined her, he came back to the great hall.

"The lady is much worse than she was before," he told Ximen Qing. "The trouble has gone to her liver and the lungs are much inflamed. The wood element gets stronger and stronger and the earth element weaker. Her blood is overheated and circulates too violently. It comes down like a mountain torrent and nothing can hold it back. If the blood that comes from her were dark in color, she might still be saved, but it seems lighter; it is, in fact, fresh blood. I will send her some medicine and, if it does her any good, there may be some hope. If it does not, I fear there is nothing I can do for her."

"Master," Ximen said, "I beg you to make some medicine for her with all the skill at your disposal. You shall be handsomely rewarded."

"Do not speak of reward," Dr. Ren said. "You and I are good friends. I will certainly do my best for her." They took more tea, and the doctor left. Ximen Qing told Qintong to take a roll of Hangzhou silk and two taels of white gold to the doctor and bring the medicine back with him. The medicine he brought was called a tonic for the spleen. Li Ping'er took it very hot, but the blood poured from her more than ever. Then Ximen Qing, very much distressed, sent for Dr. Hu, who lived in the same street. Dr. Hu said that anger had disorganized the pulse, and that the blood had become feverish. He too sent some medicine. Li Ping'er took it, but it was like a pebble thrown into the depths of the ocean.

Now that doctors were visiting the house all the time, Yueniang decided not to keep Miss Shen for more than one night. She gave her five *qian* of silver, some clothes and some ornaments. Miss Shen went away in a sedan chair, and a box of food was sent with her.

When Hua Ziyu was at the party given to celebrate the opening of the shop, he heard that Li Ping'er was ill. He told his wife, and his wife brought a box of presents and came to see the invalid. When she saw how thin and pale Li Ping'er had become, both women cried. Yueniang ordered tea and took Mistress Hua to the inner court.

Han Daoguo suggested to Ximen Qing that Dr. Zhao, a graduate of the Imperial College of Medicine and a specialist in the diseases of women, might be called in. "He is an expert on the pulse," he said. "My wife once had trouble of much the same sort and Doctor Zhao cured her. I commend him to you for your lady."

As soon as he heard this, Ximen Qing told Qintong and Wang Jing to go at once on horseback outside the Western Gate and ask Dr. Zhao to come. Then he sent for Ying Bojue and discussed the matter with him. "My sixth wife," he said, "is very ill. What can I do about it?"

"I heard she was better," Bojue said in surprise. "Is she worse again?"

"She has been very sad ever since the baby died," Ximen said, "and now her old trouble has returned. Yesterday, on the festival day, I got Miss Shen here especially for her. But she didn't take any interest. She went back to her own room and there fainted, fell on the floor, and bruised her face. I sent for Doctor Ren. He said she was worse than she had ever been. She took his medicine, but the blood only poured from her the more."

"I hear you sent for Doctor Hu, too," Bojue said. "What did he say?"

"He said that anger had disorganized her pulse. She took his medicine, but it did her no good. Today, my clerk Han recommended Doctor Zhao. His name is Chao Longgang and he is a specialist in women's diseases. I have sent two boys to fetch him. I am very very anxious about her. It is all on account of the baby. She thinks about him day and night. Women never know where to stop. I have tried to console her but she won't listen to me and I don't know what to do."

Ping'an came and announced Master Qiao. Ximen Qing took him to the hall and there they sat for a while with Ying Bojue.

"I hear that your Sixth Lady is not well," Master Qiao said. "I have come to inquire about her."

"It is the child's death," Ximen said. "It has made her so melancholy that an old trouble has returned. It was very kind of you to come."

"Have you sent for any particular doctor?" Master Qiao asked.

"First she took Doctor Ren's medicine," Ximen said. "Then, yesterday, I sent for Doctor Hu. There was no improvement, and now I have sent for Doctor Zhao."

Then Qiao said: "Near the office there lives an old gentleman named He who has a great knowledge of medicine. His son, He Qixuan, has become a very famous doctor. Why don't you ask him to come?"

"I will send for him when Doctor Zhao has gone."

"I would suggest having them together," Qiao said. "Then they can hold a consultation about the cause of the illness. They can prescribe afterwards, and their prescription ought to be effective."

"You are right," said Ximen. He told Daian to take his card and go with Qiao Tong to ask old master He to come. When Master He came, he bowed to Ximen Qing and Qiao, and they made him take the seat of honor. "It is several years since I last saw you," Ximen said politely, "and now your hair is quite white."

"How is your son doing?" Qiao asked the old man.

"He goes to the office every day," He said, "and that does not leave him much time for anything else. I myself have to go and see those patients who are not of official rank."

"You are very old," Ying Bojue said, "yet you seem very strong."

"Yes," said the old man, "I am eighty-one years old." They had tea and a boy was sent to give warning to the ladies. Then the old gentleman went to see Li Ping'er. He came back to the hall.

"I will tell you what is the matter with the lady," he said to Ximen Qing and Master Qiao. "The seed got into her blood. Then she had a fit of anger. This intermixture of anger and blood has caused the trouble. Whether I am correct or not, I do not know."

"Yes, you are right," Ximen Qing said, "but what I want to know is, can you cure her?"

Just then, Qintong and Wang Jing came back with Dr. Zhao. Old Master He asked who he was. "This is a doctor who was recommended to me by one of my clerks," Ximen Qing said. "Don't mention the fact that you have examined her. When he has seen her, you can consult with him."

Dr. Zhao came in and made a reverence to them all. The two old men, He and Qiao, sat in the places of honor, and made room on their left for Dr. Zhao. Ying Bojue sat on the right, and Ximen Qing in the host's place. Dr. Zhao asked the names.

"This is He, and I am Qiao," said Qiao.

"My name is Ying," said Ying Bojue. "I presume you are Doctor Zhao."

"I am," said Zhao, "and my second name is Longgang. My grandfather was an official in the Imperial College of Medicine; my father was a doctor of high standing, so that I have the experience of three generations behind me. Every day I work very hard upon the theories of Wang Shuhe, Dong Yuan, and Wu Tingzi. I read the poem upon the Nature of Medicine, the Su Wen of Huangdi, the Nan Jing, and, of living masters, the Secret Art of Dan Xi, the cure of heart troubles also by Dan Xi, Jie Gu's Secret of Pulse Examination, the Thirteen Prescriptions, and so forth. I have read nearly everything that is written about medicine, so that, when I have to prescribe, I have a very harmonious system at my disposal. My fingers are able to discern the most profound workings of the pulse. I can diagnose the conflict between Yin and Yang according to the seasons. I determine the sinking or the floating of the pulse according to internal and external relations. And, in cases of fever or chill, I leave no detail unconsidered. There is nothing about the pulse I do not know, but, really, I cannot attempt to explain how much I do know."

Old Master He listened attentively. "May I ask what is the first thing to be done in the consideration of a patient's case?" he said.

"According to the ancient masters," Dr. Zhao said, "when one deals with any patient, one should look at him, listen to him, question him, and examine him. Then a miraculous cure is certain. I always begin by asking my patient questions, then I feel his pulse and consider his general appearance. Unless we see a patient as Zi Ping, the reader of fortunes, sees him, it is impossible to be quite definite about the ailment."

"Please, doctor, come and see my wife," Ximen Qing said. He told Qintong to warn the ladies in the inner court, and took Dr. Zhao to see Li Ping'er. She had just gone to sleep and had to be waked up again. Then she sat up in bed propped up with pillows and bedclothes. Dr. Zhao examined first her left hand, then her right.

"Lady," he said, "please raise your head." Li Ping'er did what she was told. Then the doctor said to Ximen Qing: "Kindly ask the lady who I am."

"Who is this gentleman?" Ximen said to his wife.

Li Ping'er looked at Zhao. "A doctor, I suppose," she said.

"There!" said Dr. Zhao, "you have no need to worry, Sir. She can still distinguish between one person and another."

"Be very careful," Ximen said, "and your fee shall be correspondingly large."

Dr. Zhao studied Li Ping'er for a long time. "Judging by her general appearance and her pulse, I think she must be suffering from a fever or some wasting disease. She must have been ill either before she had a baby, or afterwards."

"You are quite wrong," Ximen Qing said. "Kindly examine her again."

Dr. Zhao gazed at Li Ping'er and murmured: "Why is her face so pale? Her stomach must be out of order— or is it her blood?"

"Let me tell you, Doctor," Ximen Qing said. "My wife suffers from an issue of blood. It is that which makes her so thin and weak. If you have any medicine that will do her any good, I will pay you well for it."

"I said it was the blood," Dr. Zhao said. "Have no fear. I have some excellent medicine."

Ximen Qing took him back to the hall. Old Master He and Master Qiao asked what the doctor thought.

"In my opinion she is discharging too much blood," Dr. Zhao said.

"And what medicine are you going to give her?" said the old gentleman.

"I have a perfectly wonderful medicine that will certainly cure the lady. It is made of these drugs—liquorice, spurge, *gangsha,* hellebore, croton, coriander flowers, a mixture of ginger juice with raw pinella, aconite and almond *tianma*. Make all these into a pill with honey and take it with spirit in the morning."

"But, it seems to me, those drugs are much too strong," the old gentleman said. "I can't believe that would do at all."

"Why not?" said Dr. Zhao. "Doctors have always agreed that strong medicine, bitter to the taste, is excellent for invalids."

Ximen Qing realized that the doctor was talking nothing but rubbish. He gave him two *qian* of silver and dismissed him. He did not go with him to the gate, but he made no complaint because Han Daoguo had recommended him.

"The man is a fool," he said to Master Qiao.

"I did not venture to say so before," old Doctor He said, "but the fellow is very well known outside the gate. People call him Zhao the Trickster. He is always defrauding people and strolling about the streets. What should he know of medicine? As for your lady's illness, I will make up some medicine for her when I get home. If, when she has taken it, the flow of blood stops and she feels more comfortable, I will continue the treatment, but, if this medicine does not help, there is nothing else I can do." Ximen Qing gave the old gentleman a tael of silver and he went away.

Daian was sent for the medicine. Li Ping'er took it that evening, but there was no improvement in her condition.

"Do not give her any more medicine," Yueniang said. "She has had nothing to eat or drink, and medicine on an empty stomach is useless. Don't you remember that Wu the Immortal said she would have a blood disorder when she was twenty-seven years old? She is twenty-seven now. You would do well to send for Wu again. He can tell us whether she will live or not. If some evil star is overshadowing her life, we will ask the Immortal to offer sacrifice for her."

Ximen Qing at once sent a boy with his card to make inquiry at Major Zhou's house. Major Zhou's people said that Wu was a man who never stayed long in the same place. "When he is here," they said, "he always lives at the Temple of the Guardian Spirits of the Soil, south of the city, but, in the fourth month of this year, he went to the Wudang Mountains. If it is a fortune you wish to have told, there is a certain Master Huang who lives at the Daoist temple. He is well skilled in the art. He will not accept more than three *qian* of silver, but he will not leave his temple."

This was reported to Ximen Qing. He immediately told Chen Jingji to take three *qian* of silver and go to the Daoist Temple to consult Master Huang.

Outside the temple hung a sign on which was written: "Here, by the divinely blessed method of the Book of Changes, the decrees of Fate are interpreted. The fee is three *qian*." Jingji went in and bowed to Master Huang. He gave him the three *qian*.

"The fortune I would ask you to tell," he said, "is that of a woman twenty-seven years old, born at noon on the fifteenth day of the first month."

Master Huang made a calculation upon the abacus and said: "In this fate we have the year *Xinwei*, the month *Gengyin*, the day *Xinmao*, and the hour *Jiawu.* The life would appear to be one in well-to-do circumstances. The fate seems to run in the years with a four. The fourth year is *Jiwei,* the fourteenth *Wuwu,* the twenty-fourth *Dingsi,* and the thirty-fourth *Bingchen.* This year is *Dingdu,* and the evil stars are all in the ascendant. The *Jidu* star commands her life, and the five evil spirits are always busy making trouble for her. The *Jidu* star is the star of darkness, its form is that of a bundle of tangled silk that has neither beginning nor end. There is a great deal of unhappiness and some illness. The first month, the second, third, seventh and ninth are all months in which illness appears. This year, too, is unpropitious as regards children. There are other sources of anxiety, quarrels, losses of property, and, because she is a woman, the situation is more disastrous."

Master Huang wrote down what he had said, and Chen Jingji went back with it. Ximen Qing was with Ying Bojue and Master Wen. When Jingji gave him the paper, he took it to the inner court and read it to Yue-niang. It was obvious that what destiny had in store for Li Ping'er was more to be feared than hoped for, and they were full of sorrow.

CHAPTER 62

The Death of the Sixth Lady

When Ximen Qing realized that no medicine seemed to cure Li Ping'er, and when all the fortune-tellers assured him that her case was hopeless, he did not know what to do. At first, Li Ping'er still tried to get up, dress, comb her hair, and leave her bed when she had to attend to the intimate details of her toilet, but, by degrees, she came to eat less and less and grew thinner and thinner. In a very short time, she who had been such a flower-like creature was faded and withered. She could no longer get out of bed. Papers were put on her mattress, and she told her maids to burn incense all the time so that there might not be an unpleasant odor. Ximen Qing saw that her arms were as thin as threads. He was nearly always in her room, weeping, and only went to his office every other day.

"Dear man," Li Ping'er said to him, "you must not neglect your duties. I am afraid you will get behind with your official business. Don't worry about me. I have this trouble, but if the blood will only stop, and I can manage to eat and drink a little, I shall be better. You are a man. It is not fitting that you should stay at home with me all the time."

"Sister," Ximen said, and he wept as he spoke, "how can I leave you when I see you like this?"

"Oh, you foolish man, if the Fates have decreed that I must die, who can prevent it? I only wish to say one thing to you. I don't know why, but, when I am alone, something terrible seems to overshadow me. Shadowy forms are always before my eyes and, at night, I am haunted by evil dreams. Men with swords and staves quarrel and struggle with me. They snatch my baby from my breast and make to throw me on the ground. Then my former husband comes and says that he has a new house and wants me to go with him. But I did not mean to tell you this."

"When a man dies," Ximen Qing said, "he is as a light blown out. No one can say whither he has gone. It is because you have been ill so long. You are weak. I don't believe any evil spirit really comes to trouble you. But I will get Abbot Wu to give me some charms and I will put them up at your door. Then we shall see if there are devils in this house."

He went to the outer court and told Daian to go to the Temple of the Jade King to get the charms.

On his way, Daian met Ying Bojue and Xie Xida. He hastily dismounted. "Where are you going?" Ying Bojue said to him. "Is your master at home?"

"Yes," said Daian, "and I am going to the Temple of the Jade King for some charms."

The two friends went on to see Ximen Qing.

"When Brother Xie heard how ill your lady is, he was terribly shocked," Bojue said. "We have come to ask how she is."

"These last few days," Ximen told them, "she has grown so thin that she looks like another woman. Really, I don't know what to do."

"Why did you send Daian to the temple?" Bojue said.

Ximen told them about the evil dreams Li Ping'er had. "I fear there may be devils about the house," he said, "so I have asked for some charms to drive them away."

"Oh," Xie Xida said, "I am sure it is only because she is so weak. There are no devils here."

Then Bojue said: "Brother, if you wish to get rid of devils, it is a very simple matter. Priest Pan, of the Temple of the Five Sacred Mountains outside the city gate, has power over the Five Thunders and he can exorcise devils of every sort. He is known as Pan the Expeller of Demons. With his charms and wonder-working philters he often gets people out of difficulties of this sort. Send for him, Brother, and then we shall know whether there are devils at work here or not. And indeed, if you ask him, he may be able to cure your lady."

"As soon as the boy comes back from Abbot Wu, I will send him with you to Pan," Ximen said.

"We won't wait for him," Bojue said. "I will go at once. I most sincerely hope that your lady may be cured, and, if there is anything I can do to help, I will do it, even if I have to go on my head instead of my feet." He went off with Xie Xida.

When Daian came back with the charms, they were put upon the door of Li Ping'er's rooms. But that night she was terrified once more. She said to Ximen Qing: "He has been with two other men to carry me off. They ran away as you came in."

"Don't believe it," Ximen Qing said. "Brother Ying says it is all due to your weakness. He tells me that he knows a priest called Pan who will give us some very efficacious charms and medicine, and who has the power to drive out devils. I have told Brother Ying to get him to come tomorrow morning, and I'm sure he will get rid of all the disturbing influences."

"Oh, Brother," said Li Ping'er, "send for him this very moment. The dead man has gone away in a fury, and I am afraid he will come back and take me with him. Send for him now."

"If you are afraid, I will send for Wu Yin'er to keep you company," Ximen said.

Li Ping'er shook her head. "I don't wish to trouble her," she said, "I shouldn't like her to lose business."

"What about old woman Feng, then?"

Li Ping'er nodded, and Ximen Qing sent Laian for the old woman. But the door was locked, and the old woman was not to be found. Laian told the Beanpole that, when she came back, she must be told to go at once to Ximen Qing's house because the Sixth Lady needed her. Ximen Qing told Daian that, early next morning, he must go with Ying Bojue to the Temple of the Five Sacred Mountains to bring the priest Pan.

The next day, Nun Wang came. She brought a box of specially treated rice, twenty large milk biscuits and a small box of preserved eggplants. When she arrived, Li Ping'er bade Yingchun help her to sit up in bed. Nun Wang made a reverence, and Li Ping'er asked her to sit down.

"Teacher," she said, "I have not seen you since you had those texts printed for me. Though I have been so very ill, you have never come to see me."

"I did not know about your illness, Lady," the nun said. "It was only yesterday that the Great Lady sent a servant to the convent and I heard for the first time that you were ill. And, speaking of the printing of those texts, you don't know what trouble I had with that wicked old nun Xue. You remember it was arranged that we should both make terms with the printer. I got nothing out of it, but she secretly persuaded the printer to give her five taels. She did not even let me see a penny. Lady, when that bad old woman dies, she will go to the very depths of Hell. She put me in such a state that I even forgot the Great Lady's birthday, and I did not come."

"Let her go her evil way," Li Ping'er said, "but do not quarrel with her."

"I had no intention of quarreling with her," the nun said.

"The Great Lady is annoyed with you," Li Ping'er said. "She says you have never read the scriptures for her."

"Oh, Buddha!" Nun Wang cried, "I don't profess to be a saint, but I should not dare to forget a thing like that. I have been reading them all the time. I only stopped yesterday when the month was up. I have just seen her and told her about my troubles. I told her that I had only just heard about your illness, and I have nothing to offer but this rice, the preserved fruits, and the biscuits you will perhaps make into sop. The Great Lady told Xiaoyu to bring me here to see you."

Xiaoyu opened the boxes. Li Ping'er looked at them and thanked the nun. Then the nun said: "Sister Yingchun, please go and warm two of these biscuits. I want to see your lady take something to eat."

Yingchun took away the things and Li Ping'er ordered tea to be brought for the nun.

"I have had tea in the Great Lady's room," the nun said. "I only want to see you eat some porridge."

Yingchun set the table and brought in four kinds of tea cakes for Nun Wang. For Li Ping'er she brought some porridge with a plate of preserved fruits and two steamed milk biscuits. There were two bowls of porridge and a pair of small ivory chopsticks. Yingchun and Ruyi'er held the bowls and assisted Li Ping'er. But she only took two or three mouthfuls of porridge and nibbled at the cakes. Then she shook her head and would eat no more. She told them to take the things away.

"We must eat and drink," Nun Wang said. "Do have a little more. This porridge is so good."

"I would if I could," Li Ping'er said.

Nun Wang helped to pull the bedclothes over her and, as she did so, noticed how wasted Li Ping'er had become. She was shocked. "Lady," she said, "you were fatter than this when I saw you last. What has made you so thin?"

"She was better for a while," Ruyi'er said. "Then something angered her, and her illness came back again. Father sent for the doctor and he gave her some medicine that made her very much better. But, in the eighth month, the baby took fright and was very ill. My lady watched him day and night and never slept at all. She hoped he would recover, but, alas, he died. Then she cried and sobbed all day. Then, too, she was made angry, and, all things considered, got into a state that no one could stand, even if she were strong as iron or stone. Anybody but my lady would have complained and so got rid of her trouble, but she never tells anybody, only reluctantly when she is made to do so."

"Who upset her?" the nun asked. "Your master loves her, and the Great Lady respects her. There are only the few other ladies, and I can't think any one of them would offend her."

"Ah, you don't know," Ruyi'er said. She told the younger maid to go and see if the door was fast and continued: "It was the Fifth Lady. It was her cat that scratched the baby and made him have a fit. Master came and asked my lady, but she would not tell him and, in the end, the Great Lady told him. He killed the cat. The Fifth Lady never relented. She went on making trouble with us. In the middle of the eighth month the baby died. The Fifth Lady was delighted and has insulted us every day since. We can hear clearly everything she says, and my lady cannot help being upset. She weeps nearly all the time. Anger and sorrow together have gradually brought her to this pass. Only Heaven knows what a good heart she has. She never shows an angry face to the other ladies. If she has nice clothes, she will not wear them unless the other ladies have dresses like them. There is not a single person in the house to whom my lady has not been kind at some time or another. The trouble is that, though they are ready enough to take things from her, they never have a kind word to say about her."

"What do you mean?" Nun Wang said.

"There is old lady Pan, the Fifth Lady's mother. Whenever Father stays the night in the Fifth Lady's room, the old lady comes and sleeps here. And when she goes away, my lady never lets her go without stuff for making clothes or shoes. She gives her money too. Yet the Fifth Lady never has a good word to say about it."

"Oh, woman!" cried Li Ping'er, "why do you have so much to say? Let them do what they like. Heaven is mighty, yet Heaven never boasts; and Earth is solid, yet Earth never speaks."

"Buddha!" said Nun Wang, "who would have known that you had such a sweet disposition? But Heaven has eyes. Heaven will see your good works and reward you."

"Teacher," Li Ping'er said, "what reward shall I receive? Not even my child is left to me. I suffer so much pain, and have an ailment so unpleasant that even as a spirit I shall be unclean. I am going to give you some money so that, when I am dead, you can employ a few nuns to read as many texts as you can find so that this nasty disease may not cling to me forever."

"You are looking too far ahead," Nun Wang said. "Your heart is so good that Heaven cannot fail to protect you."

While they were talking, Qintong came. "Father says this room must be cleaned," he told Yingchun. "Uncle Hua has come to see your lady. He is in the outer court now."

Nun Wang stood up. "I must go to the inner court," she said.

"Teacher," said Li Ping'er, "don't go away. I wish you to stay for a few days. There is something I should like to say to you." The nun promised to stay.

Ximen Qing brought in Uncle Hua. Li Ping'er lay still upon her bed and did not speak.

"I never knew you were ill until yesterday," Uncle Hua said. "I have come especially to see you."

"It is very good of you," Li Ping'er said. She turned her face to the wall.

Hua stayed a short time, then went back to the outer court with Ximen Qing. "Our late noble relative," he said to his host, "when he was Governor of Guangnan, had some *gynura* medicine. It is a certain cure for all those troubles from which women suffer. If she takes five *fen* of it, mixed with a little wine, it will stop that flow of blood. I know she has this medicine. Why has she not tried it?"

"She has tried it," Ximen Qing said. "Yesterday the Prefect Hu came to see me. I told him about her illness, and he, too, told me of some medicine. That was white cockscomb flowers. It is mixed with a little charcoal and taken with wine. She took it, and, for a day, the flow of blood ceased, but the next day it was worse than ever."

"It is a very difficult case," Hua Ziyu said. "I think, brother-in-law, that you would do well to look out for a coffin for her. I will send my wife to see her tomorrow." He went away.

While the nurse and Yingchun were changing the bed for Li Ping'er, old woman Feng came. She made a reverence, and Ruyi'er said to her: "You are a fine one, Mother Feng! You have never been near your mistress, and yesterday Master had to send for you. Laian said your door was locked. Where were you?"

"I can't tell you what a hard life I have," old woman Feng said. "Every day I go to the temple for my religious devotions. I set off in the morning and, for some reason or other, I never get back till night. When I get home, there is always some priest to come and see me. Father Zhang, or Father Li, or Father Wang."

"An old woman like you, and so many priests to visit you!" said Ruyi'er. "This is the first time we have heard of Father Wang."

Li Ping'er smiled. "The old woman always talks nonsense," she said.

Then Ruyi'er said: "Old woman, you refuse to come when you are sent for. For the last few days my lady has had nothing to eat, and she has been terribly depressed. You have only just come, yet you have made her laugh already. If you will only stay a few days, I'm sure she will soon be better."

"Yes," old woman Feng said, "I am a good doctor when it is a question of driving care away." She laughed. Then she looked at Li Ping'er. "Lady," she said, "I had hoped to find you better. Are you able to get out of bed when you wish to relieve nature?"

"If only she could, it would be splendid," Yingchun said. "Until a few days ago, she could just manage to get up, we helping her, of course, but lately she has not been able, and we have had to put papers in the bed."

As they were talking, Ximen Qing came in. "Old woman Feng," he said, "you ought to be here nearly all the time. Why have you been so long away?"

"My Lord," the old woman said, "you know this is the season for preserving vegetables. I have been preserving some, so that if anyone is brought to me, I shall be able to give her something to eat. I have no other way of buying them."

"Why didn't you tell me?" Ximen Qing said. "Yesterday I was having the vegetables on my farm dug up, and you might have had a bushel or two."

"I am greatly obliged to your Lordship," the old woman said. Then she went to another room. Ximen Qing sat down beside the bed and Yingchun burned incense.

"How do you feel today?" Ximen asked Li Ping'er. Then he said to Yingchun: "Has your mother had any gruel?" Yingchun told him that the nun had brought some milk biscuits but that her mistress had only tasted them and taken a tiny bit of porridge.

"Brother Ying and the boy went for Priest Pan," Ximen Qing said, "but he was not at his temple. Tomorrow I will send Laibao."

"Oh, do send for him at once," Li Ping'er said. "I see that dead man whenever I close my eyes."

"It is all because your mind is so enfeebled," Ximen said. "Try to pull yourself together and don't let such ideas get hold of you. When the priest comes he will exorcise any evil spirits there may be about. He will give you medicine too, and you will soon be well again."

"Brother," Li Ping'er said, "there is no hope for me. I had always hoped to live long years with you, and now I am dying when I am only twenty-seven. What an evil fate is mine that I must leave you! I shall go and never see you again until you come to the gate of the spirits." She held his hand in hers and cried, sobbing softly, for she was too weak to make a noise. Ximen cried with her.

"Sister," he said, "if there is anything that you would say to me, say it."

In the midst of their grief, Qintong came and said: "An officer has come from your court. He says that tomorrow is the fifteenth, and there is a great deal of important business to be done. They wish to know whether you will be there or not."

"I cannot go tomorrow," Ximen Qing said. "Give the man a card, and tell Magistrate Xia that he must do all that is necessary."

"Brother," said Li Ping'er, "you must go to your office and not neglect your duties. Though I am dying, I shall not be gone so soon."

"But I am going to stay and watch over you," Ximen said. "I want you to keep firm hold on yourself and not let your thoughts bother you so much. Uncle Hua told me that I should get the boards for your coffin and so keep the evil ones away. When I have done so, you will certainly begin to improve."

Li Ping'er nodded. "Very well," she said, "but don't let yourself be cheated. You must not spend more than ten taels on the wood. And, if you really look upon me as your wife, don't have my body burned, but lay me beside your dead wife. So, perhaps, I may benefit from some of the offerings made at her tomb. And do not spend too much money on those boards for my coffin. You have a great household, and you must think of the future."

These words pierced Ximen's heart as though they had been a sword. "Sister," he said, "why do you talk like this? Even if I were a poor man, I would not treat you so disgracefully."

Then Wu Yueniang came with a small box of apples. "My sister-in-law has sent these especially for you," she said to Li Ping'er. She told Yingchun to wash and peel them.

"It is very kind of Mistress Wu," Li Ping'er said. When Yingchun had peeled some of them, she cut them into slices, put them on a plate and tried to help Li Ping'er to eat one. But she could only suck it and spit it out. Yueniang was afraid they might be disturbing her, so she made her turn her face to the wall, and she and Ximen Qing went out to talk about her.

"I am afraid she is in a very bad way," Yueniang said. "You ought to go and buy some boards for her coffin before it is too late."

"So Brother Hua has just said, and I have spoken to her about it. She said I must not spend much money because I have so many people to provide for and I must think of the future. It went to my heart. But I think I will wait until Priest Pan has been, and then I'll see about the coffin."

"You don't realize the situation," Yueniang said. "Look how she has changed. She has lost appetite till she cannot even drink a drop of water. You still hope for her recovery. We must face the facts. If she does get better, we can give the coffin to somebody for charity. It will not cost us much."

"I will do what you say," Ximen Qing said. He went to the great hall and sent for Ben the Fourth. "You know who has good coffin boards for sale," he said. "Go with Chen Jingji, my son-in-law, and see if you can find a good set. Take the money with you."

"I believe that Captain Chen, in the Main Street, has some good boards," Ben the Fourth said.

Ximen Qing sent for Chen Jingji and said to him: "Go to the Great Lady and ask her for five pieces of silver. Then go to look at the boards with Ben the Fourth." Chen Jingji hurried away, got the money, and went out with Ben the Fourth. In the afternoon they came back.

"We went to Chen's place and looked at all the boards he has," Jingji said, "but we did not think them either particularly good or very cheap. On our way back we met Master Qiao. He told us that a scholar named Shang had a very fine set of boards. His father bought them at Chengdu in Sichuan, where he used to be a judge. He brought them for his own lady. There were two sets originally and they have used one. They are of the kind known as Peach Flower Cavern. The set is complete in five pieces—sides, cover, top and bottom. They are asking three hundred and seventy taels. We went with Master Qiao to see the set, and it certainly is a very fine one. Master Qiao bargained with Scholar Shang for a long time, and at last the scholar agreed to reduce his price by fifty taels. He would not have sold the boards at all, he said, if he had not wanted the money to pay for his expenses when he goes to the Capital next year to sit for the public examination."

"Take three hundred and twenty taels at once and secure the boards," Ximen Qing said. "There is no time to lose."

"He has taken two hundred and fifty taels as a deposit," Jingji said, "so that leaves us with seventy more to pay." They went again to the inner court and Yueniang gave them another seventy taels. Then they went to Master Shang's. That evening a number of porters brought the boards, carefully wrapped in red drugget. They set them down in the courtyard. Ximen Qing examined them and found them excellent. He sent for carpenters to saw them, and the wood gave out a delightful fragrance. The main piece was about five inches thick, two feet five inches broad and seven feet five inches long. Ximen Qing was quite satisfied. He sent for Ying Bojue to come and look at them and asked him if he had ever seen such a fine set of coffin boards in his life before. Bojue expressed his admiration.

"A perfect example of the fitness of things!" he exclaimed. "Everything in the world has its proper owner somewhere. You have bought these boards for my sister-in-law, and it is clear evidence that she did well when she married you."

Ximen said to the workmen: "Make these boards up carefully and you shall have five taels of silver." The workmen set to work with a will and soon had put the coffin together.

Ying Bojue said to Laibao: "Tomorrow morning go and see Priest Pan. If he will come, bring him with you. We must avoid all further delay." Then he stood with Ximen Qing and watched the carpenters working in the courtyard. It was the first night watch before he went away.

"Come early tomorrow," Ximen said to him. "The priest may be here early." Bojue promised and went away.

In the evening, old woman Feng and Nun Wang went to Li Ping'er's room. They had seen Ximen Qing in the front court. They proposed to stay the night with Li Ping'er, but she would not allow them. "This is a foul place," she said, "and it would be disagreeable for you. Go and sleep somewhere else." Ximen, seeing that the nun and the old woman were there, went to sleep with Pan Jinlian.

Li Ping'er told Yingchun to fasten the corner door and bolt it. Then she said: "Take a light and open my chest." Yingchun took out some dresses and ornaments. Li Ping'er asked the nun to go nearer and gave her five taels of silver and a roll of silk.

"When I am dead," she said, "read the texts for me, you and a few other nuns."

"Lady," Nun Wang said, "you are looking too far ahead. Heaven will take pity on you, and you will certainly get better."

"Keep the money," Li Ping'er said, "and say nothing about it to the Great Lady. Tell her I gave you the silk for the sacred offerings you made for me." Then she called old woman Feng. "Old Feng," she said, "you are my old nurse. You waited on me when I was a child. Now I am dying. I have nothing to give you but these old dresses and this pin. I give them to you as a keepsake. And here is some silver that you may buy yourself a coffin. You need have no anxiety. I will ask his Lordship to let you stay on in that house as caretaker. I'm sure he won't send you away."

Old woman Feng took the silver and the clothes and knelt down. Weeping, she said: "This is the end of me. As long as you have lived, I have always had someone to depend upon. If you die, I shan't know where to go."

Then Li Ping'er called the nurse and gave her a purple silk gown, a blue silk skirt, an old silk cloak, two gold-headed pins, and a silver ornament.

"You took care of my baby," she said, "and even when my baby died, I still hoped you might take care of another child of mine. I did not want you to leave me while I lived. But there is no hope for me now, and I am going to ask your master and mistress to keep you after my death, so that, if the Great Lady has a child, you may nurse it. I give you these clothes as a little token of remembrance. Do not think that I am mean."

Ruyi'er knelt down and kowtowed. She cried. "I hoped that I might serve you always," she said. "You have always been so kind to me. And it is really my fault that the little master died and you are so ill. Please speak to the Great Lady for me. My husband is dead, and, if I am sent away from here, there is nowhere for me to go." Then Ruyi'er took the clothes and the ornaments and stood, drying her tears.

Now Li Ping'er summoned Yingchun and Xiuchun. They came and knelt down beside the bed. "You two have served me since your childhood. You have served me well, but there is little I can do for you now. You have already clothes enough, and there is no need for me to give you more. Here, for each of you, are two pairs of gold pins and two gold flowers. As for you, Yingchun, your master has made a woman of you, so, of course, you will not leave here, and I will ask the Great Lady to look after you. And you, Xiuchun, I will ask the Great Lady to find a good home for you, for I would not have you stay on here to be ill used by anyone else. I don't wish my maids to suffer when I am gone, and I don't think you will find anyone else as indulgent as I have been."

Xiuchun knelt and cried. "Mother," she sobbed, "I would like to stay here forever."

"Oh, you silly maid! Whom will you serve when I have gone?"

"I will look after your tablet."

"My tablet will not be here for long. It will be burned and you will have to go away."

"Then I and Yingchun will both serve the Great Lady."

"That is one way," said Li Ping'er.

Xiuchun did not quite understand the situation. Yingchun took the ornaments and cried. She could not speak.

So Li Ping'er gave them all her last instructions. In the early morning, Ximen Qing came. She asked him about the coffin. "We bought the boards yesterday," he told her, "and the men are working on it now. Remember, it is to drive your illness away. When you get better, we shall give it away in charity."

"How much did it cost? I do not wish you to waste your money."

"Oh, not much," Ximen Qing said. "A hundred taels, or something like that."

"It is a great deal of money for so useless an end," Li Ping'er said. "Well, have it made up ready for my death."

Ximen Qing went out to see the carpenters at work. Yueniang and Li Jiao'er came to see her. It was clear that she was very ill indeed. "How do you feel today, Sister?" Yueniang asked.

Li Ping'er took her hand. "Mother," she said, "there is no hope for me."

The Great Lady wept. "Sister," she said, "is there anything you would like to say to me? Here is the Second Lady, too. Tell us both."

"I have nothing to say," Li Ping'er answered. "We have been sisters together for a few years and you have always been very kind to me. I had hoped we should grow old together, but the Fates were against me. My baby died, and now I am dying. When I am dead, my two maids will be left. The older of them has already been made a woman, and you will doubtless keep her in your apartments. As for the younger, keep her if you want her, but, otherwise, please find a young man for her and let her be free. I don't wish people to speak of her as a maid without a mistress. I say this because she has served me so long, and I shall be the easier after my death for telling you. Ruyi'er does not wish to leave, so, Mother, for the sake of the care she took of my baby and for my own sake, keep her to look after the child you will bear."

"Sister," said Yueniang, "think no more about any of these matters. I take them all upon myself. If you leave us, I will have Yingchun to live with me and Xiuchun shall wait upon the Second Lady. The maid the Second Lady has now is not as honest as she might be and she is lazy. One of these days I shall have to dismiss her. The nurse, Ruyi'er, as you have said, has nowhere else to go, and I will keep her whether I have a child or not. I will try and find a husband for her."

"Don't worry about any of these things," Li Jiao'er added. "The Great Lady and I will hold ourselves responsible. If Xiuchun comes to me, I will let her wait upon me, and treat her kindly."

Li Ping'er called the nurse and the two maids and bade them kowtow to the two ladies. Yueniang began to cry again.

Meng Yulou, Pan Jinlian, and Sun Xue'e then came to visit Li Ping'er and she said a few kind words to each of them. Then all but Yueniang went away. "Mother," Li Ping'er said to her softly, "if you bear a child, Mother, look carefully after him. Bring him up that he may continue the family after you. Do not be careless as I was, so that you suffer from the evil plottings of others."

"I understand, Sister," Yueniang said. These words made a great impression upon her, and, when Ximen Qing was dead, the remembrance of them was the reason why Jinlian was no longer allowed to live in the family.

While they were still talking, Qintong came and said they must burn incense. Priest Pan had come. Yueniang told the maids to clean the room, make tea, get pure water, and burn some precious incense. She and the other women went to the inner room to listen to what the priest should say. Ximen Qing brought him in.

The priest came in by the corner door, past the screen. Before he entered the room where Li Ping'er was, he went backward two steps before the stairs. Then he murmured something; the servants raised the lattice, and he went in. He sat down beside the sick woman's bed. It seemed as if all his strength was concentrated in his two eyes; it was a sign that he was summoning all the power of spiritual vision at his command. He held a sword in his hand, and his fingers were bent in a definite and peculiar position. He murmured again, and it seemed as though his eyes saw through everything. Then he went to the other room and set out the table for incense. Ximen Qing burned some incense and the priest set fire to a charm. Then he cried:

"Come quickly, all ye spirits that serve!"

He cast around him a mouthful of water. Immediately there seemed to be a whirlwind of furious intensity outside the room, and in the whirlwind some of the marshals of the host of angels.

"In this house of Ximen," said the priest, "a woman, Li, is ill. She has appealed to me. I bid you, bring the guardian of the soil and the six tutelaries of this household. Bring them that I may examine them and learn the reason for this illness. Go then, forthwith, and delay not."

The priest closed his eyes. His color changed, and he sat stiffly upright. He put his hands on the table and hammered with a piece of wood as a judge does when he tries a case. This he did for a long time. Then he came out. Ximen Qing invited him to go to the outer court and tell what he had seen in his vision.

"This woman," the priest said, "is suffering the punishment that has been due to her for several generations. She has been accused in Hades, and there is no devil's work here. I can do nothing."

"Master Priest," Ximen Qing said, "is there no sacrifice that you can offer?"

"Hatred and debt," said the priest, "always find their quarry. Even the officers of Hades themselves could do nothing." But when he saw how very much in earnest Ximen Qing was, he said: "How old is the lady?" Ximen told him she was twenty-seven. "Well," said the priest, "I will offer sacrifice to the star of her life, and we shall see the manner of its burning." Ximen Qing asked when he would do so and what he would need.

"Tonight, at the third night watch," the priest said. "I shall need some white powder to mark the boundary. I shall make an altar and cover it with yellow silk. Then I shall arrange the stars according to their order and make an offering of five kinds of grain and soup and dates. I shall need neither meat nor wine. I shall need a lamp to represent the light of her life, and twenty-seven lanterns. I shall require an umbrella to cover the lanterns. That is all. You must fast, put on black clothes and come here to make your obeisance. I will offer the sacrifice. See that dogs and chickens are kept away, for I do not wish to be disturbed."

Ximen went at once to get everything ready. He went to his study, bathed, and changed into clean clothes. He asked Ying Bojue to stay with him. They had a vegetarian meal with the priest and, about the third night watch, the altar and the lanterns were made ready. The priest took his seat upon a dais with the altar of the lanterns below him. They were set out according to the position of the stars. Over everything were three large umbrellas and, around the dais, the master stars, twelve in number. Below them were the lanterns representing the life of Li Ping'er. These were twenty-seven in number.

The priest recited a preamble. Then Ximen Qing, dressed in black clothes, came and knelt down. The servants all withdrew. None was allowed to remain. The lanterns were lighted. The priest sat on the seat, his head bent down, his sword in his hand. He murmured something,

then gazed at the sky and set his feet in a certain position. Three times he
burned incense that he might be granted knowledge of the three worlds.
And every command he gave sounded like thunder. It was a bright clear
night; the stars were shining in the heavens. Suddenly the whole world
darkened and a mighty hurricane blew.

> This is not the roaring of tigers
> Or the muttering of dragons
> But a wind that rushes through the doors
> And around the screens
> A wind that blasts the flowers, rips off the leaves
> And drives the clouds to leave the mountains
> And send rain to the ocean.
> The wild geese have lost their mates and cry bitterly
> The wild ducks and the herons are frightened
> And seek trees for refuge.
> The angel of the moon shuts her palace door in haste
> And the immortal Liezi cries for help
> Away in the sky.

Three times the wind blew. It was followed by an ice-cold blast that
put out all the twenty-seven lamps. The priest saw a man in white garments and two black-robed attendants with him. They came, bringing a
paper that they set down upon the table. The priest looked at it. It was
the final judgment of Hades. There were three seals upon the paper. He
came to Ximen Qing and said: "Your lady has sinned against Heaven. Our
prayers are useless. The light of her life has gone out. There is no hope, and
death is not far distant from her."

When he heard this, Ximen Qing bowed his head and was silent. He
wept. At last he said: "Teacher, you must help her."

"It is the will of Heaven," said the priest. "There is nothing I can do."
He asked to be allowed to go. Ximen Qing urged him to stay the night.
"Being a priest, to walk through the dew and pass the night upon the
mountains is nothing to me," the priest said. Ximen Qing could not persuade him to stay. He told his servants to give the priest a roll of cloth and
three taels of silver. "It is God's will that I should make use of the knowledge I possess," the priest said. "I have taken an oath that I will never take
anything from the world. I cannot accept your gift." But, being pressed, he
told a novice to accept the roll of cloth and make a gown for him. Before
he left he said to Ximen Qing: "Sir, you must not go to her room tonight.
If you go, you too will have trouble. Be cautious! Be cautious!" He went
out of the gate and walked swiftly away.

Ximen Qing went back to the courtyard. He saw that all the lanterns had been extinguished. This made him very sad, and he wept before Ying Bojue. "Brother, this is her destiny," Bojue said. "We cannot take her back against the will of Heaven. You must not be so sad. The fourth night watch has sounded." Then he said: "Brother, you are weary, go and rest. I will go away now and come again tomorrow morning."

"You must have a light," Ximen Qing said. He ordered Laian to take a lantern and light Ying Bojue home. Then he went back to his study. There he sat by himself with the light of a solitary candle. His heart was torn by distress, and he could only sigh. He thought how the priest had said to him that he must not go to his loved one's room. "But how can I desert her now?" he said to himself. "I will go and see her even if I die for it. She may wish to say something to me." So he went to the sickroom.

Li Ping'er was sleeping with her face to the wall, but she wakened when she heard Ximen Qing. She turned to him and said: "Brother, why have you come?" Then she asked him about the lanterns.

"Be easy in your mind," Ximen said. "There was nothing wrong with the lanterns."

"Brother," Li Ping'er said, "do not try to deceive me. I saw him who is dead come with two others and stir up trouble for me again. He told me that you had sent for a priest to get me back from death. But, he said, the accusation against me in Hades had been accepted and I could not escape him. He went off in a raging fury and said: 'Tomorrow I shall come and take you.'"

Ximen Qing sobbed aloud when he heard this. "Oh, Sister," he said, "do not worry about him. I had hoped that we should live long years together. I never thought you would go away and leave me. I would rather die myself. It would be better than this agony."

Li Ping'er put her hands upon Ximen's neck. "Brother," she said, "I had longed to live with you always, but now I am going away. Before I close my eyes I would say one thing to you. You have a great household, and you alone can control it. You must always be careful and not do things without thinking. And be kind to the Great Lady. I know that one day soon she will bear a child to you, and he will carry on your family after you are gone. You are an officer now, but you must not go drinking so much as you have been doing. You must come home early. Your household affairs are of more importance than feasting. If I could have lived, I would have given you counsel. When I am dead, I fear there will be none to advise you."

These words cut Ximen's heart like a sword. "Sister," he said, "I know it. But do not worry about me. Heaven has put an end to our happiness together. It will not permit us to be husband and wife any longer. This will kill me, even though it is the will of Heaven."

Li Ping'er spoke to him about Yingchun and Xiuchun. "I have spoken to the Great Lady," she said, "Yingchun is going to serve her, and Xiuchun the Second Lady. The Second Lady has promised me."

"Say no more of this, Sister," Ximen Qing said. "Nobody shall send your maids away when you are dead. I will not even allow the nurse to go. I mean them all to guard your tablet."

"What tablet?" said Li Ping'er. "There will be nothing but a wooden board, and it will be burned thirty-five days after my death."

"Oh, no!" Ximen said. "I shall keep it as long as I live and make offerings before it."

Then Li Ping'er said: "It is late now. Go and sleep."

"I don't wish to sleep," Ximen answered her. "I am going to stay and look after you."

"I am not likely to die yet," Li Ping'er said, "and there is such a nasty mess here, it will make you sick. Besides, you will be in the way when the maids have to attend to me."

So Ximen Qing told the maids to look well after their mistress and went to Yueniang's room. He told Yueniang about the sacrifice, and said: "I have been to her room. She is still able to speak quite well. Perhaps Heaven will, even yet, allow her to get better."

"Her eyes are sunken, her lips are parched, and her ears burn," Yueniang said. "I fear there is no hope. She has the kind of illness in which she is able to talk up to the last moment."

"She has been in this house only a few years," Ximen Qing said, "and she has never harmed anyone, whether of high or low degree. And so sweet is her nature that she has never spoken an unkind word about anyone. I cannot bear to lose her." He cried, and Yueniang cried with him.

✱ ✱ ✱

Li Ping'er asked Yingchun and the nurse to place her so that she faced the wall. Then she said: "What is the time?" The nurse told her:

"The cock has not yet crowed: it is the fourth night watch."

Yingchun put some new paper beneath her, and they helped her over till she faced the wall. Then they pulled the bedclothes over her. Everybody had been up all night. Old woman Feng and Nun Wang at last went to sleep. Yingchun and Xiuchun put something on the floor and slept there. In less than an hour, Yingchun dreamed that Li Ping'er got out of bed and touched her. "Look after my room," she said, "I am going now." Yingchun woke up with a start. The lamp was still burning on the table. She looked at the bed. Li Ping'er was there, facing the wall, but, when Yingchun put her hand over her mistress's mouth, she could feel no breath. She could not say when her lady had died.

So this beautiful and charming lady became a dream of the Spring.

Yingchun quickly woke the others. They saw that Li Ping'er was dead. She was lying in a pool of blood. They were greatly excited and ran to the inner court to tell Ximen Qing. He and Yueniang hurried to the room as fast as they could. They lifted the bedclothes. The Sixth Lady's face had not changed and there was still a little warmth in her body. There was a red stomacher about her. Ximen Qing did not trouble about the blood. He gathered her in his arms and kissed her.

"Oh, my ill-fated sister, my dear sweet sister! How could you leave me like this? I will die too. I know I have not long to live." He cried and threw himself into the air in his grief. Wu Yueniang cried; Li Jiao'er, Meng Yulou, Pan Jinlian, and Sun Xue'e, and the household, maids and nurse and all cried, so that the sound of their crying shook the earth.

"We did not know when she was going to die," Yueniang said, "so we never dressed her properly."

"Her body is warm," Yulou said, "I think she must have just gone. We must wait no longer but dress her now, while her body is limp."

Ximen Qing still held Li Ping'er in his arms. "Heaven wills my death," he was crying. "You have been in this house three years and not a single day's real pleasure have you had. It is all my fault."

This made Yueniang a little impatient with him. "Cry if you will, but put her down," she said. "You must not cry face to face with her like that. If the foul air from her mouth comes to you, it will make you ill. And what do you mean by saying that she never had a single happy day? If she did not, who did? We ourselves cannot decide how long we shall live. We shall all have to go the same way." She bade Yulou and Li Jiao'er take the key and get some clothes so that they might dress her. She told Jinlian to help dress her hair.

"Get the clothes she used to like best," Ximen Qing said.

Yueniang said to Li Jiao'er and Yulou: "Get that new scarlet silk gown, and the satin skirt of willow yellow, the clove-colored silk dress and the light blue skirt she used to wear when she used to visit Mistress Qiao, and the dresses that were made for her lately."

Yingchun took a light and Yulou the key, and they went to the room and opened a chest. After searching a long time, they found the three dresses, a purple silk vest, a white silk underskirt and a scarlet undergarment, with white silk socks and a pair of drawers. Li Jiao'er carried them to Yueniang who, with Jinlian, was dressing the dead woman's hair. They used four gold pins to keep in place a green kerchief.

"What kind of shoes must she have?" Li Jiao'er asked.

"She used to like that scarlet pair with high heels," Jinlian said. "She did not wear them more than twice. Let us have those."

"No," said Yueniang, "I will not have red shoes put on her. It would look as though we wished her to jump into the fire of Hell. Bring the violet shoes with high heels that she wore when she went to her sister-in-law's place." Li Jiao'er told Yingchun to bring those shoes. They all worked together dressing Li Ping'er.

Meanwhile, Ximen Qing sent the boys to the great hall. They took down the pictures and covered the screens. They got a large piece of board and carried it to the hall, then put a silken coverlet on the board and a paper cover over that. Then they prepared a table for incense and a lamp to be kept lighted continually. Ximen Qing appointed two boys to be with the body all the time, one to beat the gong, the other to keep paper offerings burning. Then he sent Daian for Xu, the Master of the Yin Yang.

Yueniang took all the clothes that were to go with the dead woman into the coffin, and locked up the rooms that had belonged to her. Only the bedroom was left unlocked. The maids and the nurse were placed in charge of it.

When old woman Feng saw that her mistress was dead, tears rolled down her nose like a river. Nun Wang muttered texts for the soul of Li Ping'er. There was the *Duoxinjing,* the *Yaoshijing,* the *Jieyuanjing,* the *Lengyanjing* and incantations to invoke the compassion of the Blessed One, that he might receive the dead lady's soul and set her on the right way in the realm of the dead.

In the great hall, Ximen Qing was beating his breast. He cried so much that he had no voice left, saying: "My kind, sweet sister!" It was nearly dawn.

Then the Master of the Yin Yang came. "I am sorry to hear of your lady's death," he said. "At what hour did she die?"

"We cannot say exactly," Ximen Qing told him. "I only know that she went to sleep about the beginning of the fourth night watch. Everybody was tired. There was no one awake when she died."

"It does not matter," the Master of the Yin Yang said. He asked a servant to give him a light. Then he lifted the paper coverlet. The fingers of Li Ping'er indicated the hour of the Ox.[1] "She died," he said, "two degrees after the fifth night watch. We may say that she died at the hour of the Ox." Ximen called for ink and brushes and asked Master Xu to write the

---

1. Between 1 and 3 a.m.

certificate. Xu asked for the dead lady's name and her eight characters. Then he wrote:

> The deceased lady Li, the wife of Ximen, was born at noon on the fif-teenth day of the first month in the year *Xinwei* of the reign *Yuanyu,* and died at midnight on the seventeenth day of the ninth month in the year *Dingyu* of the reign *Zhenghe*. This was a *Bingzi* day, and the order of the month *Wuzu,* Her spirit is ten feet high. It will be useless to wail for her until the mourning dress has been worn. And, when she is put into her coffin, none should be present whose animal is the Dragon, the Tiger, the Cock, or the Snake, unless he is a kinsman.

Yueniang told Daian to ask Master Xu to look into his black book and tell them the destiny of Li Ping'er. The Master of the Yin Yang opened his secret book and said: "This was the hour of the Ox on a *Bingzi* day. If the departed goes to Heaven, she will go to the Palace of the Precious Vase, but if to the world again, then to the land of Qi. In a former existence she was born as a man named Wang in Binzhou. As this man she killed a ewe with child, and, for that reason, her animal was the sheep. Though she married a rich man, she suffered much from illness and the backbitings of others. Her child lived for a very short time, and she has died from a combination of disease and anger. Nine days ago her soul went to a family named Yuan in Kaifengfu to be reborn as a girl. There she will suffer poverty, but, when she is twenty years old, she will marry a rich man, much older than herself. She will have an easy life and die when she is forty-two, again as the result of anger." He ended his reading of the black book. The ladies all sighed.

Yueniang inquired what would be a suitable day for the funeral. Xu asked how long they wished to keep the body at the house.

"I cannot let her go yet," Ximen Qing said, crying. "She must not be buried for thirty-five days, at least."

"If you keep her thirty-five days," Xu said, "there will be no day suit-able. But after twenty-eight days there is one. I suggest that you have her grave dug about noon on the eighth day of the tenth month and bury her on the twelfth, about the hour of two. Both those days are suitable from every point of view."

"Very well," Ximen said, "we will have the funeral on the twelfth day of the tenth month."

The Master of the Yin Yang wrote out his certificate and placed it on the dead woman's body. Then he said to Ximen Qing: "About the hour of the Dragon[2] on the nineteenth, we will put her in her coffin. Please have

---

2. 8 a.m.

everything ready." Then he went away. It was now broad daylight.

Ximen Qing told Qitong to get a horse and ride to tell Uncle Hua. Then he sent servants in all directions to give the news to his relatives, and a man to the office to ask for leave of absence. He sent Daian to Lion Street for twenty rolls of thin white cloth and thirty rolls of coarser material. He told Tailor Zhao to bring a number of assistant tailors and set to work in the rooms beside the hall to make hangings and curtains and tablecloths for the funeral, skirts and gowns for all the ladies, and a long gown of white cloth for every servant. He gave Ben the Fourth a hundred taels of silver and sent him to buy thirty rolls of linen and two hundred rolls of yellow funeral silk. He sent for the arbor builders to make a great arbor in the courtyard.

Ximen never ceased thinking of Li Ping'er, her appearance and her actions. Suddenly he thought of having a portrait of her painted. He summoned Laibao and said to him: "Where can we find a good artist to paint her portrait?"

Laibao said: "Once a man named Han painted some screens for us. He used to be employed in the Imperial Household. He was dismissed but he paints excellent portraits."

"If you know where he lives," Ximen said, "bring him here at once." Laibao went away.

Ximen Qing had not slept all night. What with his grief and what with the strain he had had, he became very irritable about the fifth night watch. He cursed the maids and kicked the boys. Still he remained in the great hall watching his wife's body. From time to time he sobbed aloud. Daian was there too, and he cried bitterly. Yueniang, Li Jiao'er, Yulou, and Jinlian busied themselves distributing mourning to the maids and serving women behind the curtain. They could hear Ximen Qing still crying though he had no voice left. They asked him if he would take some tea, but he would not answer.

"She is dead," Yueniang said to him, "and you will not bring her back to life by crying. You have not slept properly for several nights; you have not combed your hair or washed your face. This morning you have worked very hard and have had nothing at all to eat. It would be more than anybody could stand even if he were made of iron. Go and do your hair, and have something to eat. We will attend to things. You are not very strong, and if you have to take to your bed, I don't know what we shall do."

"He has not dressed his hair or washed his face," Yulou said.

"A moment ago," Yueniang told her, "I sent a boy to ask him to do so, but he kicked the boy out, and I dare not ask him again."

Then Jinlian spoke. "You may not know it, but a short time ago, I spoke to him quite kindly. I said, 'If you cry like this, you will lose your flesh and your bones too. You must eat something. You can see about things afterwards.' He opened his red eyes wide and called me a swine of a woman. I won't bother about him any more. The unreasonable fellow! There's nothing swinish about me. And he always talks about others upsetting him!"

"She died so suddenly that he is naturally rather upset," Yueniang said, "but he should keep the sorrow in his heart and not make such a fuss about it. You saw, dead though she was, he didn't care. He kissed her and cried so loud. Really, it is not good breeding. She had been here for three years, he said, and had never had a single day's happiness. I have no recollection of her ever having had to draw water or do any other hard work day by day."

"He loved her more than any of us," Yulou said, "but he was right. Such a woman as our Sixth Sister was!"

As they were talking, Chen Jingji came with nine rolls of white silk. "This silk," he said, "Father tells me, is for kerchiefs and skirts."

"Ask your father to come and have some food," Yueniang said to him as she took the silk. "He has had nothing to eat."

"I dare not," Jingji said. "When a boy went to ask him, he nearly killed him. I dare not go near him."

"If you won't go, I shall have to send somebody else."

After a while she called Daian and said to him: "Your father has not had anything to eat, and he has been crying so long. Take him some food. Master Wen is there now; try and get your father to have something to eat with him."

"We have been for Uncle Ying and Uncle Xie," the boy said. "As soon as they come, we will take some food in. They need only say a word or two, and I promise you, Father will eat something."

"You cunning young rogue," Yueniang said. "You are the worm in your father's stomach. It looks as though we poor old women are not as good as you are. How do you know he will eat when they come?"

"You don't realize, Mother, what good friends they are with Father. Whenever he gives a party, no matter who else is there, they are sure to be invited. If Father has three *qian* worth of food to eat, so have they; if he has only two *qian* worth, they have it just the same. However bad a temper he may be in, they have only to speak a few words, and he is laughing and smiling again."

Qitong brought Ying Bojue and Xie Xida. They went in, knelt down before the body, and wept for a long time. They bewailed their kind sister-in-law. Jinlian said: "The rascally oily-mouthed rogues! So we are not kind!" Then they stood up. Ximen Qing made a reverence to them and they cried again.

"How unhappy you must be, Brother," they said. They were asked to go to a room in the wing. There they greeted Master Wen and sat down.

"When did my sister-in-law die?" Bojue asked.

"It was sometime about the hour of the Ox," Ximen told them.

"It was after the fourth night watch when I got home," Bojue said. "My wife asked after her, and I said: 'By Heaven's will, the poor lady is at the point of death.' As soon as I went to sleep, I dreamed a dream. I dreamed you sent a boy to fetch me. He said you were giving a feast in your house to celebrate your promotion. I came at once. You were wearing scarlet robes. You took two jade pins from your sleeve and showed them to me. 'One is broken,' you said. I looked at them for a long time and then I said: 'It is a pity the broken one is made of jade, while the other is only crystal.' But you said: 'No, they are both made of jade.' I woke up feeling that the dream boded no good. My wife saw me sucking my lips and asked me whom I thought I was talking to. I said: 'You don't understand. Wait, and, when the dawn comes, I'll tell you.' Then the day broke, and I saw your boy coming dressed in white. It was a shock, but here you are wearing mourning dress."

"I too had a dream," Ximen Qing said, "it was rather like yours. I dreamed that my kinsman Zhai of the Eastern Capital sent me six pins. One of them was broken, and I said: 'What a pity!' Then I woke up. I was just telling my wife about the dream when she in the front court died. What an unkind Heaven to bring such a calamity upon me. I would rather have died myself. I only lost sight of her for a moment, and at that moment she died. Even in years to come, how shall I think of her without my heart breaking? I have never wronged anyone, why should Heaven snatch my loved ones from me? First my child is taken, now she lies here, dead. What have I to live for in this world? Even if my money reached to the North Star, what use is it to me?"

"Brother," Bojue said, "it is no use talking like this. You and she were such a perfect couple that, of course, you cannot help feeling miserable now that she has died so suddenly. But you have a fine home; you have an official appointment, and you have a houseful of people dependent upon you. If anything should happen to you, what would become of them? Remember the old saying: If one lives, three live; but if one dies, three die. Brother, you are an intelligent man and I do not need to tell you this. If you loved your wife dearly and you wish to do justice to that love, send for the Buddhist and the Daoist priests to read their dirges, and give her a splendid funeral. Then you will be easy in your mind because you will know that you have done well by my sister-in-law. I don't believe that there is anything else you can usefully do. You must see this, Brother."

Then Ximen Qing realized the situation and stopped crying. The servants brought tea and they drank it. Ximen told Daian to go to the inner court. "Bring some food," he said, "and I will eat it with your uncles and Master Wen."

"Haven't you had anything to eat yet?" Bojue asked.

"I have been busy all the time since you went away, and I haven't had a bite of anything."

"It was foolish of you," Bojue said. The proverb says: 'It is better to lose money than to be starved.' The dead are dead; the living must go on living. You must think of yourself."

CHAPTER 63

The Sixth Lady's Funeral

His loved one is gone
Darkly, darkly.
He thinks of her so far away
Bitterly, bitterly.
The realms of light and darkness are ten thousand miles apart
Each has its own sun, its own moon.

He seems to see her in the play
But the day is late.
So long have they been parted, he cannot tell
Whether his dream is true
When he dreams of her.

Ximen Qing dried his tears and sent a boy to the inner court to ask for food. The two brothers Wu came. They made obeisance before the body, then greeted Ximen Qing, and expressed their sympathy. Ximen took them to the room in the wing, and they sat down with the others.

Daian, when he came to the inner court, said to Wu Yueniang: "Mother, you ladies would not believe me. Now that Uncle Ying has come, a few words from him have made Father ask for something to eat."

"Oh, yes, you cunning little rogue," Pan Jinlian said, "you are always acting as a go-between for him, so of course you know him well."

"I have served my master ever since I was a child," Daian said. "I can't help knowing what is in his mind."

"Who is with him now?" Yueniang asked.

"The two uncles have just come," the boy said. "Master Wen is there, Uncle Ying, Uncle Xie, Clerk Han and brother-in-law. There are eight of them altogether."

"Ask your brother-in-law to come here to have something to eat," Yueniang said. "Why should he have to join that crowd?"

"He has already sat down," Daian said.

Yueniang told him to take some other boys and go to the kitchen for food. "Take some porridge for him," she said, "I don't suppose he had any rice this morning."

"But who is there to go with me?" Daian said. "I am the only one at home. Some of the boys have gone shopping, and others have gone with messages about our lady's death. Wang Jing has gone to Zhang's place to borrow a funeral gong."

"What about Shutong? Are you afraid of upsetting his dignity?"

"Shutong and Huatong are both in the death chamber. One is beating the gong, the other attending to the burning of incense and paper offerings. Father sent Chunhong with Ben the Fourth to change some silk. He didn't like the silk they brought. He is going to pay six *qian* a roll."

"I should have thought five *qian* a roll was quite enough," Yueniang said. "Why should he change it? Go and get Huatong and take the food to them at once. Don't waste time like this."

Daian and Huatong carried large plates and large bowls to the outer court and set them out on a square table. While the men were eating, Ping'an came with a large card. "His Lordship Xia has sent his secretary and a guard of honor to do your bidding," he said. Ximen Qing went to inspect them and gave orders that the man should be given three *qian* of silver and a card of thanks with the name in mourning. He asked the man to express his thanks to Xia.

They had finished their meal and everything was cleared away when the artist Han, whom Ximen Qing had sent for, came. Ximen greeted him and said: "May I trouble you to paint a portrait for me?" Han said he would do his best.

"You must not be too long setting to work," Uncle Wu said. "Her appearance may change."

"That does not matter in the least," Han said, "I can paint it without seeing her if necessary."

When they had finished their tea, Ping'an said that Uncle Hua had come. Ximen Qing and Hua Ziyu went together before the body and cried there. Then they greeted each other and sat down with the rest. Uncle Hua asked when Li Ping'er had died.

"It was about the hour of the Ox when she breathed her last," Ximen said. "She spoke quite sensibly up to the last. She went quietly to sleep, and when the maid got up to look at her, she was dead."

Uncle Hua saw the artist and a boy carrying a palette. He was taking brushes and colors from his sleeve. "I see you are having her portrait painted," Hua Ziyu said.

"I loved her so much that I must have one," Ximen Qing said. "It will remind me of her whenever I look at it."

He warned all the womenfolk to withdraw. Then the curtain was raised, and Ximen Qing took the artist, Uncle Hua and the others to the death chamber. The artist put aside the coverings and looked at Li Ping'er. A green handkerchief was bound about her head. Though she had been ill so long, her face still seemed as beautiful as when she was alive. Her pale yellow cheeks and her scarlet lips were as delightful as ever. Ximen Qing could not help weeping again. Laibao and Qintong stood beside the artist with his brushes and colors. Han looked once only, but that was enough for him. Those who were standing around asked him to begin his painting. "Sir," Ying Bojue said, "you will bear in mind that this is the face of an invalid. When she was in health, the lady's face was rounder. She was very beautiful."

"I need not trouble you for instructions," the artist said, "I think I know. May I ask if this is not the lady who went to the temple on the first day of the fifth month? I saw her then."

"Yes," Ximen said, "at that time she was still quite well. If you can remember her, paint two portraits, one full-length and one half-length. Then we can make our offerings before her picture. I will give you a roll of silk and ten taels of silver."

"I will do my best," the artist said. He sketched out a half-length figure, and it looked very handsome, the flesh like jade and almost fragrant. He showed them the sketch and they thought it very good indeed.

When Ximen Qing had examined it he told Daian to take it and show it to the ladies. "Let them see whether they think it good or not," he said. "If there is any little point they don't like about it, they have only to say so and it shall be put right."

Daian took the sketch to the inner court. "Father told me to bring this to you," he said. "He says if there is anything about it that seems to you not exactly like the Sixth Lady, you must say so, and he will get the artist to correct it."

"This seems to me very unnecessary," Yueniang said. "We do not know where the dead woman has gone. What need was there to have a portrait painted?"

"And where are the children to kowtow before it?" Jinlian said. "I suppose, when all six of us are dead, he will have six portraits made."

Meng Yulou and Li Jiao'er examined the picture. "Mother," they said, "it looks bright and lifelike, but the lips seem rather flat."

"Yes," said Yueniang, looking at it, "and the left side of her brow is not quite high enough. Her eyebrows were more curved. But how could the man draw such a picture when he had only glanced at her dead body?"

"He saw the Sixth Lady at the temple once and he has drawn her chiefly from memory," Daian told them.

Then Wang Jing came and asked the ladies if they had done with the portrait: his master wished to have it back. "Master Qiao has come," the boy said, "and he is anxious to see it."

Daian took the picture back to the outer court and told the artist that the ladies thought the lips too flat and the eyebrows not sufficiently arched. They thought, too, that the left side of the forehead was not high enough. Han said: "I can easily put that right." He took his brush and corrected the sketch. Then he showed it to Master Qiao.

"A fine portrait!" Qiao said. "It only lacks breath."

Ximen Qing was perfectly satisfied. He offered the artist three cups of wine, and entertained him. Then he gave him a roll of silk and ten taels of silver, telling him to finish the half-length portrait first, because he wished to put that up at once, and to complete the larger one in time for the funeral. Both were to be painted in green with ceremonial headdress and robes. They were to be on silk, and the rollers were to have ivory ends. The artist took the silver and told his boy to bring his things. Then he went away.

Master Qiao and the others went to look at the coffin. It was now finished. "I suppose that the informal ceremony of encoffining will take place today?" he said.

"Yes," said Ximen, "the undertakers are coming and we shall have the informal ceremony today. The formal ceremony will take place three days hence."

Qiao finished his tea and went away. Then the undertakers came. They rolled up the papers and set out the clothes. Ximen Qing himself performed the rite of "lighting the eyes" for Li Ping'er, and appointed Chen Jingji to take the part of her son and dry them for her. He took a bright pearl and put it into her mouth. So the informal ceremony was performed. The body was set up again, and the whole household bewailed the dead woman. Laixing had ordered various things to be made at the paper shop, four sets of gilt paper offerings, a washing basin, towels, combs, and figurines. These were set on either side of the body. Before it were incense burners, vases, candlesticks and incense boxes that the metal smiths had made. They were placed upon a table and looked very fine and bright. Ten taels of silver were given to the silversmith to make three sets of silver goblets.

Ximen Qing asked Ying Bojue to look after the account books and records for the funeral. He gave out five hundred taels of silver and a hundred strings of coppers. Clerk Gan was detailed to keep the accounts; Ben the Fourth and Laixing to buy what was necessary and keep in touch with the kitchen. Ying Bojue, Xie Xida, Master Wen and Clerk Gan were to act in turn as ushers. Cui Ben's duty was to attend to the accounts for the purchase of mourning. Laibao was to have charge of the temporary stores, Wang Jing to attend to the cellar, and Chunhong and Huatong were to be in attendance at the coffin. Ping'an and the soldiers of the guard were to sound the funeral gong, and bring incense and paper offerings for the guests who came. A writer and four soldiers were detailed to keep the visitors' book at the gateway, to see that the dates were correctly given when the religious ceremonies took place, and to hold the canopies and banners.

These orders were written on a sheet of paper and posted upon a screen, and all the different members of the household went about the duties that were appointed them.

Eunuch Xue sent men with sixty long poles, thirty bamboos, three hundred pieces of matting, and a hundred hempen ropes. Ximen Qing gave the man who brought them five *qian* of silver and a card of thanks for his master. He gave orders that a great shelter should be set up, which was to have a lofty center ridge and an entrance on either side. In the middle was to be a screen: in front of it a kitchen, and behind, a smaller shelter about the size of three rooms. Outside the great gateway was to be another temporary building, seven rooms wide.

Twelve priests from the Temple of Thanksgiving were summoned to sing the dirge. Two servants each day were to be employed doing nothing else but serve tea and water.

Uncle Hua and the younger Wu went away. Ximen Qing asked Master Wen to compose an obituary notice to be printed. Ximen Qing told him to write: "My humble wife has died." Master Wen wrote it without comment, then showed it to Ying Bojue.

"This will not do at all," Ying Bojue said. "It is contrary to polite usage. His wife is still alive and, if this is sent out in the way he wishes, people will talk. Uncle Wu, especially, will be offended. Don't do anything about it for the moment. I will speak to him later." They sat down again with Ximen Qing and, after a while, Ying Bojue went away.

That evening, Ximen Qing did not go to the inner court. He had a bed set up beside the body of Li Ping'er, put a screen around the bed, and so passed the night alone. The two boys Chunhong and Shutong attended him. The next morning he got up and went to Yueniang's room to wash. He dressed in a white hat and gown, with white shoes, white socks, and a white girdle.

Magistrate Xia came to offer his condolences. When Ximen Qing had greeted him, Master Wen came and they had tea together. When the magistrate went out and passed through the gate, he bade the writer do his work well and keep an eye on the soldiers of the guard. If any of them should absent himself, word must be brought him and he would have the man punished. When he had given these instructions, he mounted his horse and rode home.

Ximen Qing asked Master Wen to send out invitations for the funeral and sent servants around to ask the relatives to come on the third day after the death.

In the afternoon, the temple servants came and set out the place for the ceremony. They hung up pictures of Buddha and made other preparations.

When the news was brought to Wu Yin'er, she got into a sedan chair and came to bewail and burn paper offerings. She kowtowed to Yueniang and said, weeping: "How sorry I am that nobody told me sooner. I never knew my Sixth Mother was dead. It has upset me terribly."

"You were her ward," Yulou said, "and you ought to have come as soon as you knew that she was ill."

"Good Lady," Wu Yin'er said, "I swear I had no idea. If I had known, I should certainly have come."

"Well," said Yueniang, "whether you came or whether you did not, she did not forget you. She left a keepsake for you and I have put it aside." She told Xiaoyu to get the things that Li Ping'er had left for Wu Yin'er. Xiaoyu went to the inner room. When the parcel was opened, it was found to contain silken dresses, two gold pins, and a golden flower. Wu Yin'er looked at them and cried so bitterly that her tears fell like drops of rain.

"If I had only known that she was ill," she cried, "I would have come to wait on her." She thanked Yueniang. Yueniang gave her tea and asked her to stay until the third day after the death.

On the third day the priests beat their gongs and chanted a dirge. Paper money was hung up and everyone in the household put on mourning clothes. Chen Jingji, dressed in the deepest mourning, made obeisance before the pictures of Buddha. Neighbors, friends, kinsmen and the gentlemen from the office came to offer their sympathy and to make paper offerings. Not a few indeed made special offerings. Xu, the Master of the Yin Yang, was there early. When the great offering was over, the body was lifted into the coffin. Ximen Qing asked Yueniang for four more complete dresses to put into the coffin. In each corner of it was placed a piece of silver.

"Brother-in-law," Hua Ziyu said, "I should leave the silver out. Neither gold nor silver will stay there long."

But Ximen Qing would not listen. He insisted on placing the silver in the coffin. Then the board of the seven stars was placed in position and the lid of the coffin put in its place. The undertakers nailed it down with longevity nails on every side, and all the people cried aloud. Ximen Qing cried so much that he seemed demented. "Oh, my sweet sister," he sobbed repeatedly, "I shall never see you again." It was long before they finished their lamentations. They entertained Master Xu with vegetarian dishes, and he went away.

All the people belonging to the household and all who served in the shop wore mourning, and the incense wafted from the gate seemed like a white cloud. Master Wen acted as Master of the Ceremonies, and Du, a writer of the Great Secretariate, came to write the Sixth Lady's name upon the banner. Du's name was Zichun. In the reign of Zhenzong he had been an official at the Ninghe palace, but now he was living in retirement. Ximen Qing had sent a present of gold and silk and asked him to come. Special delicacies were prepared for his refreshment. When he arrived, Ximen offered him three cups of wine, and Ying Bojue and Master Wen sat down to keep him company. A piece of red silk was set before him, and upon this he was to write the obituary title for the dead lady.

Ximen Qing wished him to write: "The coffin of the Lady of Ximen, Captain of the Royal Guard."

"But we can't say that," Bojue objected. "The 'lady' is still alive."

"This lady bore a son," Master Du said. "It is perfectly in order. There can be no possible objection to the title."

They discussed the matter for some time and finally decided to write "wife" instead of "lady."

"'Lady' is the word used to designate one of official rank," Master Wen said, "and 'wife' one who lives in your apartments. Both are commonly used in a very wide sense."

Master Du wrote the inscription in white, except for the word "*Royal*," which he wrote in gold. Then the silken banner was hung before the coffin, and Du was asked to write the tablet. Afterwards, Ximen Qing thanked him very heartily, entertained him with food and wine, and he went away.

The same day, Master Qiao and the three uncles, Wu, Hua and Shen, came to make their offering of the three carcasses. Mistress Qiao, Aunt Hua, and the two ladies Wu came in sedan chairs to express their condolences. They wailed before the coffin, and Wu Yueniang and the others cried with them. Then they were asked to go to the inner court and there given tea and something to eat. They were all dressed in mourning, Uncle Hua and his wife in very deep mourning. Li Guijie had been sent word, and she came in a sedan chair to make paper offerings. When she found Wu Yin'er there, she said: "When did you come? Why didn't you tell me? You are a fine one, always looking out for yourself."

"I did not know my mother was dead," Wu Yin'er said. "If I had known, I should have been here before this." Yueniang took them to the inner court and entertained them there.

The seventh day came. Sixteen priests came from the Temple of Thanksgiving. Priest Lang was in charge of them and presided over the ceremony. They recited the Lotus Sutra and performed the ritual for the dead. The relatives, friends, and those who served in the shops attended again. Abbot Wu of the Temple of the Jade King came to make an offering, and also to secure an invitation for the second week's mind. Ximen Qing asked him to stay and gave him vegetarian food.

A boy came and said: "The artist has brought the portrait." Everybody examined it. The painting showed Li Ping'er in a golden ceremonial headdress, wearing pearl ornaments and a scarlet embroidered gown. Her face was as fair as though she lived. Ximen Qing was delighted. He set the picture up beside the coffin, and everybody said that the only thing it lacked was breath. Ximen entertained the artist and asked him to take even more pains with the large portrait.

"Be assured that I will take the utmost care over it," said the artist. Ximen gave him a handsome present, and he went away.

About noon, Master Qiao came to make his offering. He brought a pig, a sheep, and other things for sacrifice, gold and silver mountains, and paper offerings of all sorts, paper money and incense. There were fifty loads in all, and they created a great impression as they were brought with carriages and music. Ximen Qing and Chen Jingji, standing before the body, made reverence in return. Then Master Qiao invited Scholar Shang, President Zhu, Uncle Wu, Scholar Liu, Captain Hua, and his relative Duan, one after the other to offer incense. When the three offerings had been made, they all knelt down on the floor to hear the Master of the Yin Yang read the panegyric:

> On the twenty-second day of the ninth month of the seventh year of the reign Zhenghe, Qiao Hong and the other relatives, with all due reverence, offer the stiff-bristled and the soft-haired animals and other sacrifice of food before the coffin of the deceased lady, the wife of Ximen, and there bewail her loss.
>
> The deceased lady was generous and kind. She managed her household prudently. She governed those in subjection to her with sympathy and goodwill. She was, in truth, the very acme of perfection in womanhood and her good fame was on the lips of all who lived about her. Most glorious of women, most fragrant of blossoms!
>
> When she married, she lived in absolute harmony with her lord. To him she bore a son with the brightness of a river pearl. We trusted that they might live together in married blessedness until a ripe old age, but, suddenly, she fell ill and vanished like a dream.

How shall we restrain our grief when we realize the departure of a lady so estimable? My little daughter is still in her mother's arms, yet she is the bond between this departed lady and ourselves. It was the will of heaven that the marriage should never be consummated. We must live in different worlds, and we shall never meet again.

With this cup I would express all my love and sincerity. May she who is gone know this, come, and enjoy it!

After this offering, the gentlemen were taken to the temporary building and entertained. Then the ladies came. Mistress Qiao, Mistress Cui, President Zhu's wife, Scholar Shang's wife and Miss Duan came to make their offering to the dead. Drums and gongs were beaten, and a number of dancers dressed as spirits performed before the coffin. Yueniang accompanied the ladies and afterwards took them to the inner court and gave them tea. Then they were entertained.

While Ximen Qing was drinking with the others, he suddenly heard the funeral gong being sounded, and a servant hurried in to say that the prefect Hu had come and his sedan chair was waiting at the gate. Ximen Qing, wearing his mourning robes, went to the coffin to await his guest, and asked Master Wen to dress and go to receive the prefect. Servants came in with incense and paper offerings, and, behind them, the prefect in plain dress and gold-buckled girdle. A number of officials followed him, some to hold his robes, others to adjust his girdle, and so on. When the prefect came to the coffin, Chunhong knelt and offered him incense. The prefect took it and burned it before the body, twice making a reverence.

"I pray your Excellency to rise," Ximen Qing said. "I am very grateful to you." He made reverence in return.

"I only heard yesterday that your lady had died," the prefect said. "I am sorry I come so late."

"My wife's illness was incurable," Ximen said. "It is very good of you to come."

Master Wen was with them. They went to the hall and offered the prefect a cup of tea. Then he went away, Master Wen accompanying him to the gate.

That day the people who came to make offerings to the dead did not leave until the evening. The next day Zheng Aiyue came and burned paper offerings before the coffin. Yueniang saw that the girl made an offering of eight plates of cakes and three of other refreshments, and she called for a white silk skirt for the girl. Li Guijie and Wu Yin'er each made an offering of three *qian*. Yueniang told Ximen Qing, and he said: "Give each of them a silk skirt, no matter what they offer." Yueniang took them to the inner court, and there they had tea. In the evening, a number of friends and kinsmen came to spend the night. A troop of actors had been engaged and were waiting to perform their plays. Li Ming, Wu Hui, Zheng Feng and Zheng Chun were with them. Ximen Qing had fifteen tables arranged for his guests in the temporary building. Master Qiao was there, the two uncles Wu, Uncle Hua, Uncle Shen, Uncle Han, the two scholars Ni and Wen, Dr. Ren, Li and Huang, Ying Bojue, Xie Xida, Zhu Shinian, Sun Guozui, Bai Laiguang, Chang Zhijie, the clerks Fu, Han, and Gan, Ben the Fourth, the two nephews of Wu Shun, and six or seven others. The tables were all large, and more than ten great candles were lighted. The ladies were near the coffin, hidden from the view of the guests by screens and hangings, but so that they could watch the play.

All the guests made reverence to the dead, and Ximen Qing and Chen Jingji made reverence in return. Then everybody sat down and the actors and musicians began to play. The first play was the *Romance of Wei Gao and Yuxiao*, and their betrothal in two generations. First upon the stage came the hero Wei Gao and sang, then the heroine, Yuxiao, and she sang, too. The cooks brought soup and rice and meat and goose. Ying Bojue said to Ximen Qing: "I hear that the three young ladies from the bawdy-house are here. Why not ask them to come and offer a cup of wine to Master Qiao and the two Masters Wu? It is too great an indulgence to let them simply stay and listen to the play."

Ximen Qing would have told Daian to bring the girls, but Qiao said: "We can't do that. They have come to make offering to the dead, and we can't ask them to serve wine."

"Sir," Bojue said, "you are mistaken. Little whores of their sort must not be allowed to be idle." He turned to Daian. "Go at once and drag them out. Tell them: Uncle Ying says that, although you have come to pay your due respects to the Sixth Lady, you must come and do something for us as well."

Daian went, but he soon came back. "They say they will not come if Uncle Ying is here."

"In that case I must go myself," Bojue said. He stood up, walked two steps and sat down again.

Ximen Qing laughed. "Why have you come back?" he said.

"I had it in mind to go myself and fetch those little whores," Bojue said. "But wait till I think what I'm going to say, and then I'll go and let them have a piece of my mind." After a while, he told Daian to go again and ask them.

The three girls came slowly. They were all wearing white silk gowns and blue skirts. They greeted the company, then stood smiling.

"Since we are here, why didn't you come at once?" Bojue asked them. They did not answer. They served all the gentlemen with wine and then sat down together at one table. The music began again. Wei Gao and Bao Zhiben had come together to Yuxiao's house, and her mother had come out to welcome them.

Bao Zhiben said: "Go and fetch the girl out," and the old woman replied:

"Master Bao, you are lacking in courtesy. My daughter is not at every man's disposal. You should say, not: 'Fetch her out,' but, 'Please ask her if she will be so good as to come out.'"

This made Li Guijie laugh. "Master Bao," she said, "was like Beggar Ying. He did not know how to behave."

"You little whore," Bojue said, "if I don't know how to behave, why is your mother so much attached to me?"

"She is attached to you the other way around," said Guijie.

"Attend to the play," Ximen Qing said to them. "If you talk any more, you will have to be fined." Bojue kept silence.

The play went on. In the great hall, on one side of the large screen, sat the two aunts Wu, Aunt Yang, old woman Pan, another Aunt Wu, Aunt Meng, Miss Zheng and Miss Duan, with the ladies of Ximen's household. On the other side were Chunmei, Yuxiao, Lanxiang, Yingchun and Xiaoyu. They stood in a group and watched the play. A maid passed with a plate of fruits and a pot of tea. Chunmei stopped her and said: "For whom are you taking the tea?"

"The ladies on the other side want some," the maid replied.

Chunmei took a cup for herself. Xiaoyu had observed that the girl in the play was called Yuxiao. She took hold of her fellow maid and said to her: "You little whore! See, two men have come to visit you, and your wicked old woman wishes you to welcome them. Why don't you go?" She pushed Yuxiao, and she stumbled over Chunmei. Chunmei was holding the cup of tea in her hands and she spilled it over her clothes.

"What are you doing, spilling the tea all over me!" Chunmei cried. "It is only a matter of luck that you didn't make me break the teacup."

Ximen Qing heard the noise and sent Daian to see who was making it. The boy saw Chunmei sitting on a chair. "Go and tell our master," she said, "that that whore Yuxiao got quite out of control when she saw the man on the stage."

Ximen Qing heard what was said, but he was too much occupied to think about it. Yueniang came and scolded Yuxiao. "What have you been doing here all this time?" she said. "You ought to have gone to see who is in my room. Do you know who is there?"

"Yes," Yuxiao said, "your daughter has gone to the inner court, and the two nuns are in our room."

"There is always trouble if I let you stay and watch the plays," Yueniang said.

Then Chunmei, seeing Yueniang, rose and said: "Mother, you might think they were crazy. They seem to have forgotten both their senses and their manners. They laugh and talk and never trouble in the least whether the guests see them or not."

Yueniang scolded them again and went back to her place.

Master Qiao and Scholar Ni were the first to go away. Uncle Shen, Uncle Han and Dr. Ren were about to follow their example, but Ying Bojue stopped them. "Host," he said to Ximen Qing, "you must speak to them. I am only a friend, but I am not going yet. They are your relatives and they ought to stay. Uncle Shen lives within the walls. Even if Uncles Han and Hua and Doctor Ren live outside the city, it is so late now that they can't get out, so what's the use of their hurrying? Come back all of you and sit down. Besides, the play is not finished."

Ximen Qing told the boys to get four jars of Magu wine. When it was brought, he said: "We won't keep this any longer." He took a large cup, set it before Uncle Wu and said: "He who tries to break up this party shall be punished by Uncle Wu." So they all sat down again, and Ximen Qing bade Shutong tell the actors to perform the most lively part of their play. The music began, and one of the actors came to ask whether they should play the scene in which the portrait is painted. "I don't care what it is," Ximen Qing said, "but let it be something lively."

The girl, Yuxiao, again appeared upon the stage. While she was singing "Never more shall I see you in this world, so I make this portrait of you," Ximen suddenly thought of all the suffering through which Li Ping'er had gone, and he was moved to tears. He took a handkerchief from his sleeve and dried his eyes. Pan Jinlian saw him with her cold eyes. "Look at that rascal," she said to Yueniang, and pointed to him, "he even sheds tears when he hears something on the stage."

"In spite of all your cleverness," Meng Yulou said, "you don't appear to understand. Plays are intended to express sorrow, joy, separations and meetings. He saw something that touched his heart. He is not the first to weep when he sees a play. It is like thinking about a dead horse when we see a saddle."

"Oh, I don't believe a word of it," Jinlian said. "People who cry when they hear a tale or see a play are all pretending. If the actors can make people shed real tears, they must be very fine actors."

"Be quiet, ladies," Yueniang said. "Listen to the play."

"I can't think what makes this sister of ours so self-opinionated," Yulou said to Aunt Wu.

The play went on until the fifth night watch, and then the party began to break up. Ximen Qing took a large cup and, standing by the door, stopped his guests and pressed them to drink again. But, when he found he could keep them no longer, he allowed them to go. The servants cleared away, and Ximen told the actors to leave their boxes because he wished them to perform another day when the two eunuchs, Liu and Xue, were coming. The actors agreed, and, after being entertained with food and wine, went away. Li Ming and his three companions went home. It was nearly dawn and Ximen Qing went to the inner court to rest.

CHAPTER 64

Shutong Runs Away

The jade is perished and the pearls are lost
Sadly he thinks of it.
In public he sheds tears, and in secret mourns.
Often he painted butterflies playing on the wall
And remembered the joy of the love birds
In the green curtains.
Now, only in dreams may he enjoy her.
She may not hope to emulate Fei Yin
Red lips and pearly teeth have joined the yellow dust.
Mournfully he longs to meet her
In the world to come.

It was almost dawn when all the guests went home and Ximen Qing
went to rest. Daian took a large pot of wine and several dishes and went
to the shop to enjoy them with Clerk Fu and Chen Jingji. Clerk Fu was
getting old. He did not feel like sitting up any longer. He made his bed
and lay down, saying to Daian: "You and Ping'an had better have these
things. I don't believe Brother-in-law Chen is coming." Daian went to
fetch Ping'an. They encouraged one another to drink and finished everything off. Then they cleared away the dishes and plates, and Ping'an went
to his own place. Daian shut up the shop and went and lay on Clerk Fu's
bed, feet against feet.

"Well," Clerk Fu said, "the Sixth Lady is no more, but she has had a
good send-off. Her coffin and the funeral are as fine as anyone could desire."

"Yes," said Daian, "if she had lived longer, she might have been accounted a very fortunate woman. Father has been to all this expense, but,
after all, it was not his own money. She was very well off when she married him. I happen to be one of the few who know this. She had not only
money but gold, pearls, jade, embroideries and valuable ornaments of all
sorts. They were the attraction. It wasn't the lady, but her money that our
master wanted. But there wasn't a more agreeable lady in the whole household. She was unassuming and pleasant always. She had a smile and a kind
word for everybody she met, even the slaves. When she sent us out to buy
anything, she would pick up a piece of silver and hand it to us. And if we

said, as we sometimes did: 'Mother, won't you please weigh the silver?' she would smile and say: 'Take it away. Why should I weigh it? You wouldn't be working here if you didn't hope to make a little for yourselves now and again. So long as you bring me something good I won't worry.' Everybody in the place borrowed money from her, and nobody ever paid her back. She never troubled whether they did or not. The Great Lady and the Third Lady are generous too, but the Fifth Lady and the Second are as mean as mean can be. If it ever falls to them to run the household, we shall have a very bad time. The sort of thing they do is to give us short money when they send us out to buy things, nine *fen* or something like that when the thing they want costs a *qian*. I suppose we are expected to make up the difference ourselves."

"The Great Lady is not so bad as that," Clerk Fu said.

"She is not so bad as that, certainly," Daian said, "but she loses her temper very easily. When she is in a good mood, one can talk to her and find her very agreeable, but when she is displeased, she scolds everybody without exception. The dead lady was far better than she is, for she never did harm to anyone and often spoke kindly for us to our master. If we got into scrapes, no matter how awkward, we used to go to her, and she would speak to our master. He never refused anything she asked. But the Fifth Lady always has words upon her lips like 'Wait and see if I don't tell your father' or 'You shall have a beating.' Her maid Chunmei is another evil star. My word! They are a fine pair!"

"She has been here several years," Clerk Fu said.

"Yes, and you know what she was like when she came. She does not even treat her own mother decently. The poor old lady often goes away in tears. Now that the Sixth Lady is dead, I can see the Fifth Lady ruling the roost completely. Anyone who goes to clean up the garden will get a good cursing from her if he doesn't do it as she would have it."

Clerk Fu was soon fast asleep and snoring. Daian had had some wine. He, too, was not long before he closed his eyes and was dead to the world. The sun was high in the heavens before they woke.

Ximen Qing often slept beside the coffin. Every morning, Yuxiao came and took away the bedclothes, and Ximen Qing went to the inner court to dress. Then Shutong, his hair undressed, would come to play and joke with the maid, and Yuxiao would dally there a long time. But today, Ximen Qing did not sleep there but in Yueniang's room. Yuxiao got up before the others and slipped out quietly. She went with Shutong to the study in the garden and there they had a merry time together.

Pan Jinlian also got up early that day. She went to the hall and saw that the light before the coffin had gone out. The tables and chairs were in disorder. Nobody was to be seen but Huatong, who was busy sweeping.

"What are you doing here alone?" Jinlian said to him. "Where are the others?"

"They are not up yet," Huatong told her.

"Put down your broom," Jinlian said, "and go and ask Brother-in-law for a roll of white silk. I want it for my mother. I want a girdle for her too. She is probably going away today."

"I think Brother-in-law is still in bed, but I will go and see," Huatong said.

When he came back, he said: "Brother-in-law says it isn't his business. Shutong and Cui Ben are responsible for the mourning. You must ask Shutong."

"How do I know where he is?" Jinlian said. "Go and look for him."

Huatong looked into the room beside the hall and said: "He was in here a few moments ago. Perhaps he has gone to the garden to dress his hair."

"Go on with your work, and I'll go and look for him myself," Jinlian said. She went to the garden. When she came to the study, she heard the sound of somebody laughing. She pushed the door open, Shutong and Yuxiao were enjoying a full measure of delight.

"Ah, you slaves!" Jinlian said, "excellent work you're doing there!"

Shutong and Yuxiao were scared. They plumped down on their knees and begged to be forgiven.

"You slave," Jinlian said to Shutong, "go and get me a roll of white silk and another of cloth. I am going to give them to my mother when she goes away."

Shutong hastened to bring them for her, and she went to her own room. Yuxiao went with her, knelt down, and said: "Fifth Mother, please say nothing to my Father about this."

"Tell me," Jinlian said, "how often have you played this game with him? If you tell me the truth, I will say nothing."

Yuxiao told her the whole story.

"I will forgive you," Jinlian said, "on condition that you promise me three things."

"If you will only forgive me, I will do anything you wish," Yuxiao said.

"First, whatever happens in your mistress's room, whether important or unimportant, you must tell me all about it. If I hear it from anybody else, and you have not told me, I will never forgive you. Secondly, you must get anything I want. Thirdly, I wish to know how it is that your mistress, who was never with child before, is now going to have a baby."

"The truth is," Yuxiao told her, "that my mother took some medicine made out of an afterbirth that Nun Xue brought for her."

Jinlian did not forget this, but she did not say anything to Ximen Qing.

When Shutong saw that Jinlian took Yuxiao away with her, smiling in a manner that boded ill, he decided that the matter was going to have unpleasant consequences. He went to the study, opened the cabinet, and took a number of handkerchiefs, kerchiefs and pins, together with some of the presents that had come from relatives. He had about ten taels of silver of his own and he went to the shop and got another twenty by deceiving Clerk Fu, telling him that he had to buy some silk. He went outside the city, hired a mule for a long journey, and went to the river. There he took boat and went to Suzhou, his native place.

This day Li Guijie, Wu Yin'er, and Zheng Aiyue went away. The two eunuchs, Xue and Liu, sent food and paper offerings as offerings for the dead, and a tael of silver. They also sent two storytellers to discourse upon a religious theme, and announced that they would come in person to visit Ximen Qing. Ximen wished to send some silk to the eunuchs and looked about for Shutong who kept the keys. He could not find the boy. Clerk Fu told him: "This morning he asked me for twenty taels and said you had given him orders to buy some silk. He may have gone outside the city for it."

"I never gave him any such orders," Ximen Qing said. "How dared he ask you for the money?" He sent people to look for the boy in all the silk shops, but in vain.

"I always believed there was something crooked about that slave," Wu Yueniang said to Ximen. "He has got into a scrape of some sort, stolen the money and made off. Go and look around your study. Then we shall know if he has taken anything else."

Ximen Qing went to the study. The key was hanging on the wall. Handkerchiefs, presents, and pins had disappeared from the great cabinet. He was very angry and gave orders to the police to arrest the boy wherever they found him. But they never found him.

About noon, Eunuch Xue came in his sedan chair. Ximen Qing had invited Uncle Wu, Ying Bojue and Master Wen to meet him. The eunuch came to the coffin and made reverence. "I deeply sympathize with you," he said to Ximen Qing. "What was the cause of your lady's death?"

"She suffered, unfortunately, from an issue of blood," Ximen Qing said. "It is good of you to come."

"I had nothing worthy to offer," Xue said, "and such things as I have sent are merely to indicate something of what is in my mind." He looked at the portrait that hung before the coffin. "How beautiful she was. And how sad that, when she was still so young and seemed to have such a happy life before her, she should have died."

"Such are the changes and chances of life," said Master Wen, who was standing beside them. "Such is the inevitability of fate. Some are poor, others rich. Some live long; others only for a short while. Yet all are governed by their destiny. Even the sages must submit to fate."

Eunuch Xue turned and looked at the speaker. He noticed that Master Wen was wearing academic robes and said: "Brother, may I ask to which academy you belong?"

Master Wen bowed low. "I am a man of very small learning," he said, "and my name is inscribed only in the records of the academy of our prefecture."

Xue asked if he might look at the coffin. Ximen bade a servant draw back the curtains and the eunuch examined the coffin closely. "What a magnificent coffin!" he said. "How much did it cost?"

"I bought it from a relative," Ximen Qing said.

"Venerable Sir," Ying Bojue said, "guess how much it cost, and tell us where it came from and what the wood is called."

Xue again examined it very carefully. "I should say it came from Jianchang or, if not, from Zhenyuan," he said.

"If it had come from Zhenyuan," Bojue said, "it would not be so fine."

"I believe the best elm comes from Yangxuan," the eunuch said.

"The Yangxuan elm is short and thin. It is not to be compared with this. This is made of much finer wood called Peach Flower Cavern. The tree grows in Wuling in Huguang. Long, long ago an old fisherman came to that cavern and saw some maidens of the Qin dynasty who had gone there to escape the soldiery. It is a place to which travelers seldom go. The boards of which this coffin is made were seven feet long, four inches thick, and two feet five inches broad. His Lordship paid three hundred and seventy taels for them, although he is a kinsman of the owner. Ah, Venerable Sir, you should have seen it before it was made up. Such fragrance! Such exquisite markings on both sides of the wood!"

"Fate was generous in allowing this lady to enjoy so wonderful a coffin," the eunuch said. "We court chamberlains can hardly hope for such a funeral when our time comes."

"It is very kind of you to say so," Uncle Wu said, "but, Sir, you are in the closest relations with the Imperial Court, and we, who are merely officers of the external administration, can in no way approach you. You, Sir, were but lately basking in the favor of the Son of Heaven. To us, you represent His Majesty's precious words. His Excellency Tong has been given the title of Duke, and those who follow after him will wear ceremonial dress. There is, I am sure, a glorious future before you."

"May I ask your name?" the eunuch said, "you speak with great discretion."

"This is Wu, my wife's brother," Ximen said. "He is a captain in our district."

"Is he the dead lady's brother?" Xue asked.

Ximen Qing explained that Uncle Wu was his first wife's eldest brother.

"You must please excuse me, worthy Sir," Eunuch Xue said to Uncle Wu, bowing. Ximen Qing then took them all to the temporary hall. He offered a chair to the eunuch and the servants brought tea.

"I wonder why Liu has not come yet," Xue said. "I must send one of my servants for him." One of the eunuch's servants knelt down.

"I did go to bring His Worship," he said, "and his sedan chair was waiting for him. I am sure he will be here soon." Xue asked if the two storytellers had come. Ximen Qing told him that they had. They were summoned, and came to kowtow. Xue asked them if they had had anything to eat, and, when they told him that they had, bade them do what they had been sent to do with all due care, promising them a good reward.

"Venerable Sir," Ximen Qing said, "I have engaged some actors. Perhaps you would like to hear them."

"Where are they from?" the eunuch asked.

"They are a company from Haiyan," Ximen told him.

"These barbarous dialects sound so impossible," Xue said, "I can't understand a word they say. Poor devils of students, who put their noses to the grindstone for three years, and then wander all over the place for another nine, carrying a zither, a sword, and a box of books, then come to the capital for the examination, and, when they have got a job, have to leave their wife and children behind—they are the people to enjoy actors of this sort. I'm just a single old chamberlain. Why should I bother about them?"

Master Wen smiled. "Venerable Sir," he said, "I am afraid I cannot agree with you. When in Qi, do as the Qi people do. Even though you occupy such an exalted position, there is a possibility that these actors may amuse you."

Xue laughed and clapped his hands. "Ah," he said, "I had forgotten Master Wen. Of course he takes the part of the officers who serve away from the court."

"Scholars and officers stand or fall together," Master Wen said. "If you cut down a branch, you injure a hundred forests. When anything happens to the hare, the fox grieves. If you disapprove of one, you disapprove of all."

"Not at all," Xue said. "In the same place you find both fools and wise men."

At that moment a servant came and told them that Liu had come. Uncle Wu went out to welcome him. After making a reverence before the coffin, he greeted the others.

"What has made you so late?" Xue asked.

"Xu came to call on me. I could not get away without sitting down with him for a while."

They sat down, and the servants brought tea. Liu asked his attendants if the food to be offered to the dead was ready. The servant told him that everything was arranged. "Let us go and burn some paper offerings," Liu said.

"Venerable Sir," Ximen said, "do not disturb yourself to such an extent. You have already made reverence to her."

"I came for that purpose," Liu said. "I must offer something to her with my own hands."

A servant brought incense. The two eunuchs together offered it and three cups of wine to Li Ping'er. They made reverence again to the dead lady. Then Ximen prayed them to stand up. They made only two reverences, and Ximen Qing made reverence to them in return. Then they went back to the arbor. A table was set.

When the two eunuchs had taken their places, Master Wen, Uncle Wu and Ying Bojue sat down, Ximen Qing sat in the seat of the host. The music began and the actors brought out their list of plays. The two eunuchs went through the list and bade them play the *Story of the White Rabbit*. But before the play had proceeded very far, the two eunuchs were tired of it. They sent for the two storytellers, who played and told the story of how the snow stopped Han Wengong in Languan.

Eunuch Xue began to talk to his colleague. "Brother Liu," he said, "I don't suppose you have heard, but the other day, the tenth day of the eighth month, there was a terrible rainstorm, and the roof figures at the palace were struck by lightning. A number of people at the court died of fright. Even His Majesty was alarmed. He admonished all the officials to take the greatest care in the performance of their duties, ordered the *Lingshujing* to be read every day in Shangqing Palace, and forbade the killing of animals for sacrificial purposes for ten days. For the same space of time, the courts were not permitted to give sentence and no reports might be made to the Emperor.

"Then an ambassador came from the people of Jin and demanded the surrender of three of our towns. The old villain Cai Jing suggested that this should be agreed to. As for the troops that had been under Tong's command, the Censor Tan Ji, Huang An and others were to take them over. Tong was to withdraw from the three districts in question, but he refused to come back and the case has been referred to a council of ministers.

"The other day was the Winter Festival, and his Majesty went to the Temple of His Ancestors to offer sacrifice. There is a certain doctor in the Department of Imperial Ceremonies called Fang Zhen, and, in the morning, when he went to inspect the temple, he discovered blood issuing from the courses between the bricks. At the northeastern corner, the floor had given way. He told the Emperor about this, and one of the censors told His Majesty that this was a sign that Tong had assumed a power beyond his due, there being no justification for the appointment of a eunuch as a duke. After this, the Emperor at once sent an envoy with his Golden Decree summoning Tong to return."

"Well," Liu said, "you and I do our duty here. What happens at the Court is no concern of ours. Let us enjoy whatever the day brings forth. Even if the sky seems about to fall, still, as the proverb says, there are four giants to hold it up. It looks to me as if this Empire of Song would be ruined by busybody ministers. Let us drink."

He told the storytellers to sing the story of Li Bo and his fondness for wine. This they did. About sunset, the two eunuchs called for their sedan chairs. Ximen Qing could not persuade them to stay longer and went with them to the gate. When he returned, he gave orders for the candles to be lighted and sat down again with Uncle Wu, Ying Bojue and Master Wen. He sent boys to bring Clerk Fu, Clerk Gan, Han Daoguo, Ben the Fourth, Cui Ben and Chen Jingji. Then he bade the actors perform the play of the Jade Ring that they had played the day before.

"The eunuchs do not understand these Southern plays," he said to Ying Bojue. "If I had realized that, I would not have asked them to stay."

"Brother," Ying Bojue said, "they did not appreciate the compliment you were paying them. Eunuchs are very ignorant. They like such things as the story of Languan, simple tales, folk songs and all that sort of thing, but the higher forms of art, compositions of a really great order, are completely beyond them."

The music began, and the actors played that part of the Jade Ring that had not been finished the day before. Ximen Qing called for good wine to be brought.

Ying Bojue, sitting at Ximen's table, asked if the three singing girls were still there. "Why don't you send for them and make them serve the wine?" he said. But Ximen said: "You must be dreaming. They have been gone a long time."

"Then they only stayed a day or two," Bojue said.

"Wu Yin'er was here longest," Ximen Qing told him.

It was the third night watch before the party broke up. The play was finished. Ximen asked Uncle Wu to come early the following day to welcome the guests for him. Then he gave the actors four taels of silver and dismissed them.

The next day, Major Zhou, General Jing, Captain Zhang of the militia, and Magistrate Xia came with other officers to make their offering to the dead lady. They made a reverence before the coffin, and someone was appointed to read their panegyric. Ximen Qing offered them refreshment. Li Ming and the other three young actors were in attendance. It was about noon when the offerings were brought. Uncle Wu, Ying Bojue and Master Wen stood at the gate to welcome the officers. They came in and changed their clothes in the great hall. Then the offerings of food were set out, and they came together to make reverence before the coffin. Ximen Qing and Chen Jingji were there to return their salutation. The Master of Ceremonies conducted the appropriate ceremonies and, when the triple offering had been made, knelt down to read the panegyric. When it was done, Ximen Qing thanked his visitors, and the officers were taken to the temporary hall. They took off their robes and had tea. Tables were set, and they sat down to enjoy themselves. The young actors played and sang to them. About sunset they went away. Ximen Qing would have liked Uncle Wu and the others to stay, but Uncle Wu said: "It seems to me that we are all rather tired, especially you, and we must have a rest." He went away with the rest.

CHAPTER 65

The Burial of Li Ping'er

The twenty-eighth day of the tenth month was the fourteenth day after the death of Li Ping'er. This was the second week's mind, and Abbot Wu with sixteen monks from the Daoist Temple of the Jade King came to make sacrifice. They brought banners and set up an altar in the house. A letter came from Secretary An. Ximen Qing entertained the messenger and dismissed him.

Abbot Wu brought a table of food and a roll of silk as his personal offering. The monks sang dirges, and the abbot solemnly made reverence before the coffin. Ximen Qing and Chen Jingji returned the reverence.

"Teacher," Ximen said, "you should not have done so much. We really do not know how we can accept this offering."

"I am ashamed of my unworthiness to offer sacrifice for your lady," Abbot Wu said. "These little things are no more than a trifling indication of my regard for her." Ximen Qing accepted the offerings and the men who had brought the boxes were sent away. The monks busied themselves most diligently with their ceremonies. They sought the dead lady in the nine dungeons of Hell; they summoned her spirit; they prayed for her relief.

The next day, the first to arrive was Uncle Han, who lived outside the city gates. With him came Meng Yulou's brother, Meng Rui, who had returned from his business abroad. Hearing that there was a bereavement in Ximen Qing's household, he came with Uncle Han, brought an offering of his own, and asked to be permitted to wear mourning. After paying his respects to Ximen Qing, he went to see his sister. Later, Ximen Qing entertained him.

About noon, a number of civil officers came. There were Li Gongji, the District Magistrate; Qian Sicheng, the Assistant Magistrate; Ren Lianggui, the Deputy Assistant Magistrate; and the Jail Warden, Xia Gongji. The District Magistrate of Yanggu, Di Sixiu, came with them. The five gentlemen were all wearing mourning and brought with them presents and paper offerings. Ximen Qing, with Uncle Wu and Scholar Wen, entertained them, and three young actors sang for them.

While they were drinking, Ximen Qing was told that his Excellency, Huang, the Controller of the Brickfields, had come to offer his condolences. He hastily put on his mourning robes again and went to the coffin. Master Wen went out to the gate to welcome his Excellency. Servants came bringing incense, paper offerings, and silk, and they walked in procession to the coffin. Huang burned incense and made a reverence to the dead. Ximen Qing and Chen Jingji returned the reverence.

"I did not know that your lady was dead," Huang said, "or I should have been here sooner. I am sorry to be so late."

"It is a long time since I have been to see your Excellency," Ximen Qing said, "and now you come to me with such gifts. I don't know how to thank you." He took Huang to the hall. There Ximen Qing and Master Wen sat down with him, and the servants brought tea.

"Song Songyuan sends his love to you," Huang said. "He has heard of your lady's death and would have liked to come and see you, but he is very busy at the moment and has had to go to Jizhou. You may not have heard that His Majesty is going to set up an artificial mountain on the north of the imperial city. He has appointed Grand Marshal Zhu Mian to proceed south of the Yangzi River to collect the Taihu stones. The boats have been coming down one after another, and the first of them has now reached the Huai and will come down the river into Shandong. The stones are beautifully marked and in pieces about twenty feet long and several feet wide. Each piece is covered in yellow wrappings, and the boats, which are very many, all carry yellow flags. The river is shallow just now and people have been brought together from all around to tow the boats. It has been a most unpleasant time for officials and people alike, and the people, especially, are finding life very hard. Our friend Song has to see to everything himself and direct all the underlings in his district. There are so many orders and instructions that they would make a mountain. Song is busy all day and all night, and never has a moment to himself.

"Now, Grand Marshal Huang is coming from the Capital, and friend Song, with all his staff, is going to receive him. He has asked me to say that, as he has no other friend here to whom he is able to appeal, he hopes you will entertain the Grand Marshal."

He bade his servants summon the messengers whom Song had sent. Two officials in black robes came and knelt down. They brought presents of gold silk, incense, candles and paper. "These are the things Song has sent on his own account. The other parcels contain the presents from his staff. From the Provincial Treasurer and the Provincial Judge, twelve; and from the officers of the Prefecture, eight. In all there are twenty-two presents, a hundred and six taels."

He offered the gifts to Ximen Qing and again asked if he would entertain the Grand Marshal.

Ximen Qing hesitated. "I am in mourning, and I do not know what I ought to do. When is His Grace coming?"

"There is plenty of time," Huang said, "he won't be here for another six weeks. He has not left the Capital yet."

"My wife is to be buried on the twelfth day of the tenth month," Ximen Qing said. "Since you and his Lordship are good enough to give me such a proof of your confidence, I will do what you wish. But I cannot accept these presents. Say what you would have me do and I will make the necessary preparations."

"Nothing of the sort," Huang said. "Song asked me to approach you on the matter, and these presents have been sent by all the officers of the province. They are not from Song alone. You can't possibly refuse them. If you insist, I shall take them back and we will not ask you to do anything for us."

"In that case," Ximen Qing said, "I have no option in the matter." He told Daian and Wang Jing to remove the presents. Then he asked what preparations it would be necessary to make.

"For his Grace," said Huang, "a long state table. For Song, the Provincial Treasurer and the Provincial Judge, a table on the floor level, and, for the lower officers, tables of the common sort. We ourselves will provide for the servants and musicians. You need not trouble about them."

Tea was brought a second time and Huang stood up to take leave. Ximen Qing asked him to stay, but the Controller said: "I am on my way to see Shang Liutang. He used to hold the post I have now, and afterwards he was made a judge at Chengdu. His son, Liangquan, passed the examination when I did."

"I did not know you were a friend of Liangquan," Ximen Qing said. "He is a good friend of mine too."

Huang made ready to go. "Please give my respects to his Excellency Song," Ximen said, "and tell him I await his pleasure."

"When the time comes, he will send word," Huang said. "Do not be too extravagant in your preparations."

Ximen Qing escorted Huang to the gate. He mounted his horse and rode away.

When the magistrate and the officers heard that Huang had come with officials from the provincial government, they were tremendously alarmed, and ran away to hide in the small arbor near the artificial mound. They told their servants to take their horses and sedan chairs away. When Ximen Qing rejoined them, he told them that Song had asked him to entertain Grand Marshal Huang the following month. With one voice they made complaint: "Our district is poor enough already. If the Grand Marshal comes, we shall have to provide all kinds of things, banquets, materials and servants, and we shall have to extract the money from the people. What more dreadful calamity could have overtaken us? We only hope you will speak to his Excellency on our behalf, for we are all friends of yours." They went away.

The days passed until it was the twenty-first day after the death of Li Ping'er. The abbot Daojian of the Temple of Eternal Felicity outside the gates came with sixteen monks to perform the appropriate rites. They wore embroidered vestments and large hats, and, with their drums and great gongs, performed a very imposing ceremony.

On the twenty-eighth day the priests of Baoqing Temple came to sing the Buddhist liturgy for the dead. Ximen Qing was not at home. He had gone to the grave with Xu, the Master of the Yin Yang, to watch the pit being dug. He came back in the afternoon, and, in the evening, all the monks departed. The next day, he sent wine, food, and other things to the grave, and instructed his servants to put up a temporary building, the size of three rooms, near the site of the grave. The neighbors were entertained and, afterwards, everybody was given a present.

On the eleventh day, very early, a troop of singing boys came with their gongs and instruments to perform some farewell plays before the coffin. They played *The Five Demons Playing Pranks on Ban Guan*; *Zhang Tianshi Being Led Astray by Devils*; *Zhong Kui and the Little Ghosts*; *Laozi Passing over Han Guan*; *The Six Thieves Deceiving Amida*; *Plums in the Snow*; *Zhuangzi Dreaming of the Butterflies*; *The Heavenly Prince Sending Down Earth, Water, Fire, and Wind*; and many another. The ladies watched the plays from the other side of the screen. When they were over, all the relatives came and burned paper offerings before the coffin. They made loud lamentation.

The next day was the funeral. At a very early hour the obituary banner was brought out, together with a host of other banners and objects made of paper. Musicians and Buddhist and Daoist clergy came. Ximen Qing had arranged with Major Zhou for fifty soldiers, all fully equipped with arms and horses. Ten of them were on duty at the house; the other forty marched on either side of the coffin. Another twenty men from his own department marched in front and attended to the paper objects. Still another twenty had gone before to the funeral ground to guard the gate and receive the offerings that might be sent there.

Officers, scholars, relatives, friends and neighbors assembled for the funeral. There was a great din of horses and carriages arriving, and the street was full of people. Many more than a hundred sedan chairs brought ladies. Even the smaller sedan chairs of the singing girls might have been counted in scores.

Xu, the Master of the Yin Yang, selected the moment for the procession to start.

Ximen Qing gave directions for Sun Xue'e to stay at home with the two nuns.

Ping'an and two soldiers stood at the gate.

Chen Jingji, on his knees before the coffin, broke a cup into many pieces. Then sixty-four undertakers lifted the coffin upon their shoulders, their directors standing upon a raised platform and signaling instructions by striking a wooden gong. The priests of the Temple of Eternal Felicity chanted a dirge and the procession started down the main street and turned to the south. The masses of people on either side of the street seemed like a sea of men, a human mountain. The weather was fine, and it was a magnificently imposing funeral.

Banners bearing characters of gold; banners with characters of silver
Following close behind the coffin.
Parasols of white silk and parasols of green silk
Carried by those who walk before it.
Banners for worthiness fluttering in the breeze.
Cries and groans of lamentation all the way.
Soldiers marching to clear the road
Brandish staves of olive wood.
Acrobats coming to meet the god, trying to display their skill
Tumble and twist to left and right
With bodies lithe as falcons
Clambering like monkeys over their horses
Standing on their heads
Turning somersaults
Passing coins through their bellies
And standing on one leg like golden cockerels.
The people applaud
Each trying to praise more loudly than his neighbor.
Shoulder to shoulder and back to back
Wise and foolish undistinguishable
Nobles and commonalty, all are there to see.
Zhang the Fifth, the big blockhead
Puffing and blowing.
Li the Fourth, the dwarf
On his toes all the time.
White-haired old gentlemen

Propping their beards on their sticks.
Dark-haired beauties
With babes in their arms
All come to look at the funeral procession.

There were more than ten sedan chairs for Wu Yueniang, Li Jiao'er and the other ladies. They followed the coffin one behind the other. Ximen Qing, wearing a hempen hat and mourning dress, walked with the others immediately after it. Chen Jingji placed his hand upon the coffin, and so they came to the beginning of East Street. There Ximen Qing, in accordance with the Rites, called upon Abbot Wu of the Temple of the Jade King to set up the portrait. The Abbot wore a gown embroidered with a scarlet stork, a hat of the Nine Thunders, and a pair of orange-colored shoes. In his hand was an ivory tablet. He rode in a sedan chair carried by four men. He advanced towards the coffin, bearing the large portrait of Li Ping'er. Chen Jingji knelt down, and the procession halted. Then, while all listened attentively, the Abbot began to read.

"This is the dead lady of Ximen, officer of the Royal Guard. She was born at noon on the fifteenth day of the first month of the year *Xinwei,* and departed this life very early in the morning of the seventeenth day of the ninth month of the seventh year of the reign Zhenghe. She lived for twenty-seven years. The glorious dead was an excellent lady of high degree, most beautiful of wives. Nature endowed her with a loveliness like that of flowers and the moon. Her disposition was as fragrant as the orchid. In temper and behavior, she was gentle and sweet; in character, agreeable and harmonious. And as she was wise and gentle when in her own family, so, after her marriage, she lived most perfectly with her husband. A child she bore, like the jade of Lantian, but he drooped as the blossom of an orchid. We hoped that a hundred years of happy life might be before her, but, alas, she lived but twenty-seven. As the bright moon always fades, so the treasures of this world easily elude us. She, this excellent lady, died suddenly, for whether we die young or live to old age is for the Fates to decide.

"Now we bear her coffin through the streets, and mourning banners wave in the breeze. Her worthy husband laments before her bier, and her household, here in the street, are broken-hearted. So deep is their affection that they can never forget her. But lest, being dead, the remembrance of her appearance should be dimmed, we, who unworthily assume this hat and these ornaments of the Daoist faith, unworthily because we failed to restore her to health, can only, with all due reverence, follow the traditions of our ancestors and set forth her portrait for exhibition.

"We cannot bring back the butterfly of Zhuangzi's dream, but we hope that in Paradise she may partake of sweet dew and precious refreshment. When she comes face to face with the True God, she will be adorned with a hundred jewels and her pure spirit will not long remain in Hades. Then will her mind forget all things, for all things, in very truth, are but illusion.

"So, as her body is buried, may her spirit become a pure breeze. This true spirit will go away and return no more, and she will enter into eternal life. Hearken now, while we bid her a last farewell. We know not whither her spirit goeth, but her portrait will remain for people of future generations to gaze upon."

The sedan chair, with the Abbot sitting upright within it, slowly withdrew. The music played and there was a great lamentation. The funeral procession moved forward. When it came to the East Gate, the relatives and Ximen Qing mounted horses, but Chen Jingji continued on foot behind the coffin all the way to the grave. Captain Zhang and two hundred soldiers, and the two eunuchs, Liu and Xue, were at the burying place, stationed on the hillock. There they received the coffin with music. Paper offerings were burned, and the smoke reached the skies. When the body was brought to the hill, the undertakers set it down while Xu, the Master of the Yin Yang, went with them to examine the grave with a compass. When everything was ready, sacrifice was made to the god of the place; the coffin was lowered into the grave, and earth cast upon it.

Then Ximen Qing changed his clothes, and, taking two rolls of silk to Major Zhou, asked him to put the final dot upon the tablet. After this, the officials of Ximen's office, and his relatives and friends, offered wine to him. The music thundered and fireworks blazed everywhere. It was a magnificent scene.

After taking some refreshment, they prepared for the return journey. Yueniang sat in the Spirit's sedan chair, with the tablet and the banner. Chen Jingji went back with the Spirit's bed, the fourteen Daoist novices accompanying him, playing music all the way. Both uncles Wu, Master Qiao, uncles Hua, Shen and Meng, Ying Bojue and Xie Xida, Master Wen and the clerks, came back with Ximen Qing. The ladies' chairs followed. When they reached the gate, a fire was lighted. Then they went in, and set up the tablet in the room of Li Ping'er. Master Xu performed various ceremonies, purified the whole house, and set yellow charms upon all the doors to keep away evil spirits. He was given a roll of silk and five taels of silver, and went away. The other guests went too. Ximen Qing took twenty strings of small money, five for the policemen, five for the soldiers of his own department, and ten for those of Major Zhou. He sent a servant with his card to thank Major Zhou, Captain Zhang and Magistrate

Xia. He urged Master Qiao and the others to remain, but they declined and went away.

Laibao came. "The men who set up the temporary buildings await your orders," he said. "They propose to remove everything tomorrow."

"I do not wish them taken down yet," Ximen said. "Tell the men to come after I have entertained Censor Song."

In the inner court, Mistress Hua and Mistress Qiao waited to see the tablet set up, then they made a last lamentation and went away.

That evening, Ximen Qing, still thinking of Li Ping'er, went to her room. The tablet was placed in the position of honor, facing her portrait. The smaller portrait was next to the tablet. There was a small silver bed and silver coverlets in a shrine, complete in every way with ornaments, and, beneath it, a pair of tiny shoes. On a table were incense, flowers, candles, plates, bowls and all kinds of things offered to the dead. Ximen Qing cried again. He bade Yingchun make a bed for him opposite the tablet. In the middle of the night he watched the lonely lamp and the moon shining through the window. He tossed about on his bed and sighed. All the time, he thought of the beauty he had lost.

> Mournfully he sighed before her shuttered window
> Lonely and broken-hearted, like the phœnix
> That has lost his mate.
> The orchids are withered, and the rain of autumn falls
> The maple leaves drop into the river
> In the frosty night.
> Their longing to be together was in vain
> In this life he will never more behold her.
> If the dead know what passes in the world
> Then there must be two heartbroken lovers
> One still on earth, the other in the underworld.

When day came, Ximen Qing watched the maids offer food and tea to their dead mistress, and he took his own meals there. When he took up his chopsticks, he looked towards the tablet and invited his dead lady to eat with him. Seeing this, the maids and the nurse shed tears. When he was alone, Ruyi'er used to come and give him tea and things to eat. She would find means to touch him, and an excuse for saying something or other, and soon they were on very good terms with one another.

One day, Ximen Qing invited a number of ladies and gentlemen to a service at the grave, and, when he came back, he was drunk. Yingchun helped him to bed. In the middle of the night he wished for some tea, but Yingchun was not there and Ruyi'er brought it for him. She noticed that his bedclothes had almost fallen on the floor, so, when she had given him the teacup, she gathered them up for him. This touched him; he put his arms around her neck and kissed her. Then he slipped his tongue between her lips. She let it pass, but did not speak. Ximen told her to undress, and they got into bed together and played with great delight.

"Now my mistress is dead," Ruyi'er said, "I will stay here and serve you, if you love me."

"If you serve me well," said Ximen Qing, "you need not worry."

After this, the woman did all she could to give him satisfaction, and was ready to do everything he wished. This pleased him.

The next day she got up and brought his shoes and socks, made the bed, and would not allow Yingchun to do anything for him. Ximen took four pins that had belonged to Li Ping'er and gave them to her. She kowtowed and thanked him. Yingchun knew this and joined forces with her. Ruyi'er, realizing that her position was now secure, and that she no longer needed help from anyone else, became quite different in manner. Every day she dressed beautifully and mingled with the other maids. She talked and joked so much that Pan Jinlian remarked it.

One morning, Ximen Qing was sitting with Ying Bojue, when one of the servants told him that a man had come from Song the Censor. He had brought a set of gold and silver wine cups, a pair of gold wine pots, two pairs of gold goblets, ten pairs of small silver cups, two pairs of silver jars, four pairs of large silver cups, two rolls of scarlet silk, two rolls of gold silk, ten jars of wine, and two sheep. He said that the Grand Marshal's boat had now arrived at Dongchang, and brought a message asking Ximen Qing to prepare for his entertainment on the eighteenth. Ximen accepted all these things, and gave the man a tael of silver and his card. He ordered Ben the Fourth and Laixing to buy whatever might be necessary.

"Ever since my sixth wife's illness," Ximen said to Ying Bojue, "I have never had a moment to myself. Now the funeral is over, there comes this business, and I shall be more occupied than ever."

"You must not complain, Brother," Bojue said, "it is not of your seeking. They came to you. You will certainly have to spend a little money, but the presence of the high officers of the province will make your house glorious."

"That is not what is troubling me," Ximen said, "but I expected they would come sometime after the twentieth. If they come on the eighteenth, things will have to be done in a hurry. It will be the thirty-fifth day after her death, too. I have made arrangements for a service with Abbot Wu, and I cannot alter the date. Even if I could alter it, I couldn't manage with these two things coming on the same day."

"I don't see any difficulty about it," Bojue said. "My sister-in-law died on the seventeenth day of the ninth month, and the fifth week's mind will be on the twenty-first. You have this reception on the eighteenth and the service on the twentieth. That does not seem too late to me."

"Very well," Ximen said, "I will send a boy to explain matters to the Abbot."

"There is another matter," Bojue said. "His Holiness, Huang, who has been deputed by his Majesty to go to Taian to offer incense, and also to accomplish the solemn sacrifice to Heaven that lasts for seven days and seven nights, is staying at present at our temple here. Before he goes away, you might get Abbot Wu to invite His Holiness to come and hold a service here. We should be only too glad to have a cleric of such great renown."

"Yes," said Ximen, "everybody says that Huang is a real saint. I would ask him to come, but Abbot Wu, you know, sent me a number of presents the other day; he displayed the portrait of my dead wife, and his priests came to the funeral. There was nothing I could do in return for all these attentions except to ask him to come and perform the sacrifice. If I now invite Huang, I don't know how I can make things right with Wu."

"Ask Wu to arrange the whole affair," Ying Bojue said, "and suggest that he invites Huang for the final ceremony only. If you spend a few more taels, there need be no difficulty. And, after all, you are spending money for your wife and not for anybody else."

So Ximen Qing told Chen Jingji to write a letter to the Abbot, requesting him to invite Huang, and saying that the day for the service would be the twentieth. Twenty-four monks would be wanted and the service should last for a day and a night. Five taels more were sent with the letter, which Daian was ordered to deliver on horseback immediately. Ying Bojue went away and Ximen Qing joined Wu Yueniang in the inner court.

Yueniang told him that Ben the Fourth's wife had brought her daughter Changjie to present her on the occasion of her engagement. They had brought two boxes of presents with them. Ximen Qing asked to whom the girl was engaged.

Mistress Ben the Fourth and her daughter, who was wearing a red silken gown, a yellow skirt, and many ornaments upon her hair, came and kowtowed to Ximen Qing. Yueniang stood beside them. "I hear," she said, "that Magistrate Xia has made choice of this young lady. The arrangement was yesterday, and the wedding is to be upon the twenty-fourth. He gave only thirty taels of silver for her. She is good to look upon, and no one would think she was only fifteen. She seems more like sixteen or seventeen. She has grown so much in the short time since I saw her last."

"He told me the other day," Ximen Qing said, "that he was thinking of securing two young ladies and having them taught music, but I never thought of asking who they were."

Wu Yueniang entertained Mistress Ben the Fourth and her daughter, and Li Jiao'er, Meng Yulou, Pan Jinlian, Sun Xue'e and Ximen Dajie came and joined them. When Mistress Ben went away, Yueniang gave her a complete outfit of heavy silk and a tael of silver. Li Jiao'er and the other ladies all gave her something: flowers, ornaments, kerchiefs, powder, or something of the sort.

In the evening, Daian returned and said that Abbot Wu had accepted the silver. "His Holiness Huang," he said, "is still here and will remain until after the twentieth. They will come on the morning of the nineteenth and prepare the altar and the dais."

The next day, Ximen Qing gave instructions to the cooks, insisting that everything should be of the very best. At the great gate he set up a seven-storied pagoda, and, before the great hall, one of five stories.

On the seventeenth, there came two officers from Song to see what preparations had been made. At the upper part of the hall they saw a peacock screen. The floor was covered with colored rugs. The chair cushions and tablecloths were all embroidered. The food that had been prepared for the Grand Marshal was the finest imaginable and the delicacies were delightful to eat as well as to look at. Two smaller tables were set for the two provincial officers, and there were a few other tables for provincial officers of rank. Outside the hall, in the temporary building that had been put up, were a number of tables for five courses of food and five of dessert for the officials of the eight districts. When the officers had finished their inspection, Ximen Qing gave them tea, and they went back to report to their superiors.

The next day the provincial dignitaries came with a host of officers to await the arrival of the Grand Marshal's boat. They had with them a yellow banner with the words imperial commissioner, and before them was carried the imperial decree. The officers, guards and soldiers of every kind were in full dress, marching behind their banners. The procession stretched for miles.

Then came Grand Marshal Huang. He wore a robe with the scarlet dragon embroidered upon it and rode in a sedan chair carried by eight men. Another eight men marched beside it. This chair had a silver top and the canopy above it was tea-colored. A host of officers and attendants followed, all mounted upon splendid horses. The procession was as fine as a bouquet of ten thousand flowers. They marched along to the strains of martial music. The road was strewn with yellow sand. As the procession advanced, there was such a silence that even the dogs did not bark or the cocks crow. Not a soul dared step forward.

They passed through Dongpingfu and arrived at Qinghe. The officials of the district knelt on either side of the road, till the Grand Marshal's guard called out: "Stand up, stand up!" Messenger after messenger was dispatched to Ximen's house.

At last they arrived, and the noise of the music was great enough to reach the skies. Beside the gate, in double ranks on either side, stood officers robed in black. Ximen Qing himself, also in black robes and hat, bowed low to the dust. The soldiers marched past, and the Grand Marshal's chair appeared. The Grand Marshal came in, followed by a crowd of people of high and low degree. He entered the great hall and the music played again, stringed and wind instruments together.

First, the Governor of Shandong, Hou Meng, and the Censor, Song Qiaonian, came to greet the Grand Marshal, and he returned their salutations. Then the Provincial Treasurer of Shandong, Gong Qi; State Counselor He Qigao; Provincial Treasurer Chen Sizhen; State Counselor Li Kanting; Counselor Feng Tinggu; Counselor Wang Boyan and a number of other provincial officers came to salute his Excellency, and he received them with pleasant affability. They were followed by the Prefects of the eight Prefectures. These made reverence from the courtyard, and the Grand Marshal bowed low to them in return. The captains and military officers came then, but the Grand Marshal sat still and took no notice of them. All the officers went back to remain in waiting outside.

Ximen Qing and Xia came to offer tea to the Grand Marshal. The two officers of highest rank present, Hou and Song, themselves handed the cup to His Grace. The music played. Then they offered a golden flower, and wine in a goblet of jade. The Grand Marshal moved towards his table, and, when he had seated himself, the Governor, the Censor and the other officers sat down in due order. Ximen Qing sat down too. The manager of the company of actors brought his repertory and the dance began. Both dancing and music were extremely well performed. They played the first act of *Pei Jingong returns the Girdle*. When this was over, cooks brought meat, venison and pork, with all manner of sauces and dressings, soup, a hundred kinds of the richest and rarest of viands, with rice and *shaomai*. Then four actors, with zithers, flute, lute and cittern, sang songs unaccompanied by dancing. While two courses of soup were being served, the music played three times. Song appointed two officers to entertain the Grand Marshal's attendants in the temporary rooms, while Ximen Qing had arranged for the entertainment of the military officers in the outer court.

The Grand Marshal bade his attendant to distribute ten taels of silver among the servants. Then he called for his sedan chair and prepared to

leave. He could not be persuaded to remain longer, and the officers escorted him to the gate. Then the music played again; banners and insignia
were ranged in order on either side of the street. Officials went forward to
clear the way, and the soldiers set out with a fine martial step. A number of
officers prepared to mount their horses to accompany His Grace, but this
he would not allow. He stepped into his sedan chair and was carried away,
and all the soldiers were ordered to escort him to his boat. The two senior
officers, Hou and Song, had arranged for supplies of food, and these, with
their cards, they entrusted to Hu Shiwen, the Prefect of Dongpingfu, and
the Captain of the Bodyguard, Zhou Xiu, to take to the boat.

The Governor and the Censor returned to the hall and thanked Ximen
Qing. "This has really put you to grave inconvenience," they said, "and we
do not know how to thank you. You must tell us whether the money we
sent was adequate, so that we may make up any deficiency."

Ximen Qing bowed. "I am grateful to you," he said, "for entrusting to
me so pleasant a duty, and making so magnificent a present. I only fear
that, in my poor house, the entertainment has been unworthy of the occasion. Will you forgive me if there has been anything amiss?"

Song thanked him again, then called for his sedan chair and went away
with the Governor. All the other officers hastened after them. Ximen Qing
went back to the hall and gave food to the musicians and actors and they,
too, went away. Four young actors alone were bidden to stay. Then all that
belonged to the officers was taken away by their servants.

Seeing that it was still early, Ximen Qing had the tables cleared, and
the food collected upon four of them. Then he sent boys to invite Uncle
Wu, Ying Bojue, Xie Xida, Scholar Wen, the clerks, and his son-in-law,
Chen Jingji. Many of them had risen before dawn that day and had been
busy all the time, and he wished to offer them a feast in return. Before
long, they all arrived and sat down to drink.

"Brother," said Ying Bojue, "how long did the Grand Marshal stay?
Was he pleased with his entertainment?"

"I am sure His Grace must have been pleased when he saw such a
splendid feast," Han Daoguo said. "The Governor and the Censor were
perfectly satisfied. They thanked his Lordship repeatedly."

"I can think of no other house that could offer so magnificent a reception," Bojue said. "In the first place, no other house here is so spacious,
and, secondly, no other house could welcome so many official people. You
must have entertained at least a thousand today. Well, it may have been
rather expensive, but your fame will spread throughout the province."

"My old teacher Chen was here too," Scholar Wen said.

"Who was your teacher?" Ximen Qing asked him.

"Chen Zhenghui," Scholar Wen said. "He is the son of the censor, Chen Liaoweng, a native of Zhengcheng in Henan. When he was only eighteen years old, he passed the senior examination. Now he is President of the Board of Education and a very learned man."

"He is about twenty-four years old now," Ximen Qing said.

Food was brought in. While they were eating it, Ximen Qing sent for the four young actors and asked their names. They were Zhou Cai, Liang Duo, Ma Zhen and Han Bi. Ximen Qing said to the last of them: "Are you any relation of Han Jinchuan?"

Han Bi knelt down and said: "Han Jinchuan and Han Yuchuan are my younger sisters."

The mention of the girls' names reminded Ximen of Li Ping'er. It made him sad to think that on such a glorious occasion as this she was no longer with him. "Take your instruments," he said to the boys, and sing 'The Flowers of Luo-ang and the Moon of Liangyuan.'" Han Bi and Zhou Cai tuned their instruments and sang.

> Flowers of Luoyang
> Moon of Liangyuan.
> Perfect blossoms we may buy and keep a little while
> Bright moon, which, for a moment, we may borrow.
> The flowers on the trellis seem so beautiful
> We stretch out our wine cups to the full moon.
> The moon is full, and then it wanes
> The flowers blossom and then fade.
> Parting is the bitterest thing in life.
> The flowers fade, but Spring has still her beauty.
> The moon wanes slowly, but the Autumn Festival will come again.
> Only we mortals die and never return.

When the song was over, Bojue saw tears in Ximen Qing's eyes. "Brother," he said "you told them to sing that song. Are you still thinking about your dead lady?"

Ximen noticed the plates of dessert at the other side of the table. "Brother Ying," he said, "you think my mind is always upon her. Look at those dishes. When she was alive, she used to arrange them with her own hands. Now she is dead, the maids do it. You can see for yourself whether the dishes are properly set out or even fit to eat."

"Judging by this meal," Scholar Wen said, "I do not see that you have any reason to complain of your ladies."

"Brother," said Ying Bojue, "you cannot get over your grief at her loss, but to talk in this way is hardly fair to the other ladies."

As they talked and drank together, Pan Jinlian was listening to them behind a curtain, secretly. When she had heard what Ximen Qing said, she went straight to the inner court and told Wu Yueniang all about it.

"Let him say what he likes," said Yueniang, "it's no use your imagining you can do anything to stop him. While she was still living, she promised Xiuchun to the second lady. Now he says she has only been dead a little while and we must not give her maids to anybody yet. I said nothing, but you have seen for yourself what airs the nurse and those two maids have been giving themselves lately. If I begin to say a word to them, he says I am too rough with them."

"Ruyi'er has certainly been different the last few days," Jinlian said. "I am very much afraid she will turn out to be a troublesome baggage. He spends all his time with her. I hear, too, that he gave her two sets of pins and she put them in her hair so that everybody could see them."

"They are a rubbishy lot," Yueniang said, "and none of them seems to have any morals."

CHAPTER 66

The Solemn Sacrifice

His breast is filled with a thousand griefs.
The sun seems to hang over the treetops
Green leaves give shade and Spring has come
The grass grows thick and the oriole sings.
He cannot hear her dainty footsteps
The music of her voice comes to him only in dream
The mountain masses beyond the gate
Cannot bar the way to sorrow.

Ximen Qing was drinking wine with Uncle Wu, Ying Bojue and the others. He said to Han Daoguo: "When will the boats be ready to start? We must see about getting the goods packed up."

"Yesterday," Han Daoguo said, "I had word to say that the boats will sail on the twenty-fourth."

"After the twentieth we will have everything made ready," Ximen Qing said.

"Who is going this time?" Bojue asked.

"Three in all," Ximen told him. "I propose that Cui shall come back first next year with a cargo of merchandise from Hangzhou. Han Daoguo and Laibao are going on to Songjiang and elsewhere to buy cloth. We have silk enough already in store."

"Really, you are a wonderful manager," Bojue said. "The proverb says: A good businessman must think of everything."

It was now the first night watch. Uncle Wu rose. "Brother-in-law," he said, "you have been working very hard lately and we have all had quite enough to drink. I think we ought to leave you to rest."

Ximen Qing would not hear of their going. He ordered the young actors to pour out wine and sing more songs. But after three more cups of wine or so, they went away.

Ximen Qing offered six *qian* of silver to the four young actors, but they declined the money. "We came on the instructions of his Excellency," they said. "We have done no more than our duty. How can we accept a present from you?"

"It is true you have been on duty," Ximen said, "but I see no reason why you should not take the silver." The four actors took it, kowtowed and went away. Ximen Qing went to bed in the inner court.

The next day when he returned from the office, he found that Abbot Wu had sent one of his novices and two men to make preparations for the ceremony. Ximen Qing had monastic fare served to the novice, who afterwards went away. Ximen asked Scholar Wen to send invitations to kinsmen, friends and neighbors, both men and women. The cooks were instructed to make the necessary preparations and especially to prepare vegetarian food to be offered to the dead lady.

Before dawn next day the priests arrived. They went upon the dais, lighted candles and burned incense. Then they began to play their instruments and recite the appropriate prayers. Outside the gate hung a long banner with an inscription, and, on either side of the gateway, a scroll of yellow paper. Upon one was written: "By the gracious mercy of the Ruler of the East may the soul of this lady, in the light of dawn, ascend to the mansions of the blessed," and on the other: "By the efficacy of the *Nandan* may she be granted forgiveness of her offenses, that her spirit, strengthened and purified, may mount to the Heavens."

Over the dais on which the altar stood hung a scroll that announced that thirty-five texts, charms and spells were to be read to relieve from travail the soul of the dead lady, and that sacrifice would be made to bring her safely through the perils of Hades.

His Holiness Huang, wearing a scarlet robe with a gold girdle, and with many attendants following, arrived in a sedan chair shortly after sunrise. Abbot Wu and the other clergy went to receive him. They led him to the altar. Ximen Qing, in black robes, came to welcome him and offered him tea. The priests were given monastic fare beside the altar. The table on which the food was set was made of red lacquer and the table covers were all embroidered. Two boys waited beside the table. While the attendants were preparing the texts, Ximen Qing made his offering of a roll of gold silk.

Before he went up to the altar, his Holiness put on a Hat of the Nine Thunders and a scarlet vestment with golden clouds and the hundred cranes embroidered upon it. He recited the prologue; the priests washed their hands and offered incense. Then his Holiness incensed the altar. He burned spells to summon the angelic host, and with invocations and charms made announcement to the three Heavens and the ten Earths. They presented the three offerings. The music began, and incense was burned processionally. Ximen Qing and Chen Jingji both had censers, and soldiers marched before them. Before them and behind were borne four parasols of gold embroidery, and banners adorned with pearls. When the procession returned, they took their places, and the music struck up again. Then they went to the tablet of Li Ping'er and summoned her spirit to appear that they might assist her on her way to Paradise. A small table was set apart especially so that the dead lady's spirit might come there, listen to the reading of the scriptures, and hear the teaching of the true faith.

At noon, his Holiness, still wearing his hat and vestments, offered sacrifice to the stars and burned charms to dispatch angelic messengers to the underworld.

This holy man, Huang, was not more than thirty years old. His appearance was most remarkable. Vested in his robes and engaged in the execution of these ceremonies he looked almost divine.

After this, Abbot Wu read before the altar from the Heavenly Treasures from the Jade Book with the Tiger Seal. Then incense was burned again, and everyone went to the temporary hall for refreshment. The most imposing table was that of his Holiness; the Abbot's was slightly smaller. The others had ordinary tables. Ximen Qing offered his Holiness and the Abbot each a roll of satin, four pairs of flowers and four rolls of silk. The other priests each received a roll of cloth. Food for his Holiness and the Abbot was sent to the temple, and the priests bade their servers put their food into a large box. After the meal, they all went to take the air in the garden. The tables were cleared and fresh ones set for the entertainment of the kinsmen and friends who had come to the ceremony.

Meanwhile, a messenger arrived from the Eastern Capital with a letter from Zhai. Ximen Qing received him in the hall. He was an official of the Imperial Tutor's household, wearing a black gown, tight-fitting trousers, with a swastika hat and yellow boots. He was fully armed. He made a reverence to Ximen Qing, and Ximen returned his greeting. Then he produced a letter and ten taels of silver. Ximen Qing asked his name.

"My name is Wang Yu, and his Lordship Zhai has bidden me bring this letter to you. Until he heard the sad news of your lady's death from his Excellency An, he knew nothing about it."

"When did his Excellency's letter reach the Capital?" Ximen Qing asked.

"In the tenth month," the messenger said. "His Excellency completed his work as Warden of the Royal Forests within the year, and he has now been made Senior Secretary of the Board of Waterways. He will return to the Capital when he has finished his present work."

Ximen Qing told Laibao to entertain the messenger and said that he would give him a letter to take back the following day. The messenger asked where Han Daoguo lived, saying that he had a letter to deliver to him, and that he would like to see him at once because he had to return to the Capital with the least possible delay. Ximen sent for Han Daoguo and the two men had a meal together, after which the messenger went with Han Daoguo to his house.

Ximen was greatly pleased to receive this letter and showed it to Scholar Wen. "When you write the answer for me," he said, "the style must be as good as this. I am sending him ten kerchiefs, ten kerchiefs of silk, ten pairs of gold toothpicks and ten gold wine cups. The messenger will come tomorrow for my letter."

Scholar Wen read the letter:

> Zhai Qian, your kinsman in the Capital, presents his most humble salutations. At the onset of winter he sends this letter to his Lordship Ximen Siquan, officer of the Imperial Guard.
>
> Since we last parted at the Capital, there has been no opportunity for us to meet, and this is a matter of great regret to me. I have told my master how much I long to see you.
>
> The first sad news of your lady's death came to me from An Feng-shan. It distresses me beyond measure that I cannot come in person to offer my sympathy. It is most unfortunate, most unfortunate! I can only hope that you will not allow yourself to give way utterly to your grief. As a slight token of my feeling for you, I send a small present, which I trust you will accept.
>
> I am informed that your activities in the public service are so meritorious that the people of Qinghe cannot too loudly sing your praises. There can be no doubt that after the general inspection this year, you will receive promotion. The other day report was made of those officers whose work merited the highest approbation, and I asked my master to place your name in the list. When the work is completed, his Majesty will distribute awards and you will be given the post of Senior Magistrate. His Lordship Xia's period of office will shortly expire, and he will receive a higher appointment. I tell you this before the matter is made public.
>
> I trust this letter will give you pleasure, but pray keep its contents to yourself and do not say anything to his Lordship. Keep the matter a complete secret.
>
> The noble Yang died in prison on the twenty-ninth day of last month.

Scholar Wen finished reading this letter and was putting it into his sleeve when Ying Bojue took it from him and read it again. When he gave it back to the scholar, he said: "Sir, you must take great pains over the answer. There are many men of learning at the capital, and we mustn't have them laughing at us."

"I," said Scholar Wen, "am like a dog's tail. It can be used instead of ermine when there is no ermine to be had. There is little depth to my learning, and who am I to wield a battle ax among the military gentlemen? I can only do what my duty requires of me."

"Scholar Wen will do admirably anything he is asked to do," Ximen Qing said. "What do you understand about matters of this sort, you dog?"

When they had finished their meal, he told Laixing to give food to the kinsmen, friends and neighbors who had come. He bade Daian take return gifts to the singing girls who had sent presents. To each of them he gave a roll of cloth and a tael of silver. In the afternoon, he sent for Li Ming, Wu Hui and Zheng Feng.

The priests returned to the altar. They beat their drums, made obeisance to the gods, and chanted their texts. Then they set up lanterns, burned paper offerings, and so went on until it was dark. By the time they were done, it was already the first night watch. Uncle Hua decided to remain, Ximen Qing having detained him, but Master Qiao and Uncles Shen and Meng went away. The two uncles Wu, Ying Bojue, Xie Xida, Scholar Wen and Chang Zhijie stayed with the clerks to watch the ceremonies during the night.

In the great court, a high dais had been erected with a decorated arch. A tank of water and a pool of fire had been prepared with offerings of food for the spirits. The tablet of Li Ping'er was placed upon a table, and offerings of every sort were set out before it. Beside the tablet were three banners, one for her spirit, one red one, and one yellow one. There was an inscription that read: "Away, ye evil spirits! This is holy ground. The purification of the Southern Palace has here been made."

The priests played their instruments, sitting in two ranks. Beside them stood four young novices, one bearing a wand, another a basin, another a double-edged sword. His Holiness put on a golden miter for the banishment of demons, and an embroidered vestment. Then going up to the highest point, he chanted the following verses:

> May the mercy of the ineffable one descend
> And the gates to the passes of the underworld
> Shall open one by one.
> Novices, walking two by two, lead the way
> And the soul of the departed, purified and cleansed,
> Shall reach the abode of the blessed.

Then he burned incense again and sang: "The Mighty One hath revealed the way of truth and shown mercy to them that dwell in darkness. He hath said that all who mortify the flesh shall come to immortality. He bestoweth blessings upon the people, both of this world and of the world to come. His mercy is outpoured over all in danger, famine or distress. We burn incense, and implore the Most High, the Most Gracious, the Ineffable One, and all the Immortals in all the Worlds, to come to our aid this day. All we who live in this world of dust are fettered by the things of this world. Death is a mystery to us; we long for life. Few there are who plant good seed, and many are they who go on the wrong path. We are foolish and do not understand; we yield ourselves to greed and passion. We believe that we shall live forever and forget the death that cometh so easily. One day we die and all is over. Yet our sin remaineth, and we suffer punishment in Hell.

"Therefore, as Thou hast taught us, we make sacrifice for this dead woman. She departed and went to the world of darkness, and, if we offer not sacrifice for the remission of her sins, she must suffer the most dreadful torments. We implore Thee, O Most High, grant Thy mercy and save us who cry to Thee. Let Thy most gracious light shine upon us that we may be enlightened. Bid Thine angels be merciful unto us, and send forth Thy decree to the Powers of Hell that they cease their examination of her who is dead. Bid them open the prison gates and set the prisoner free. Pardon her sins and let hatred be stilled.

"Let all obey Thy commands and come forth from the gates of Hell.

"Let her pass over this fire that her weakness may become strength, and that she be not as a. faded flower.

"Grant unto her another life, and bring her safely to the shores of Truth.

"To this end we burn these sacred spells, beseeching Thee to hear our prayer."

The priests dipped the spirit's banner into the pool of water and burned charms. They took the red banner, put it into the pit of fire and burned charms again. Then they took the yellow banner. His Holiness said: "From Heaven cometh the water and from Earth the fire. From their meeting cometh life itself." So the ceremony came to an end. The tablet was carried over the decorated bridge to pay respect to the God and to take refuge with the Three Divinities of the Daoist Faith. Then five sets of offerings were made.

"Now," said his Holiness, "she has found the three refuges. We will pronounce the nine commandments." The nine commandments were read. The priests played their instruments and recited many charms. Then they implored a blessing upon the soul of the dead woman and all other souls.

His Holiness came down from the dais. The others, still playing their music, followed him and went out of the gate to burn paper money, treasure chests and other things. This was the end. The priests returned and took off their vestments. People from the temple rolled up the pictures.

In the great hall, Ximen Qing had ordered many tables to be prepared. The lights shone very brightly. The three young actors sang, and all the relatives and friends sat there. Ximen Qing offered his Holiness a cup of wine, with two rolls of silk and ten taels of silver. Upon his knees, he said: "Now that my dead wife has had the benefit of your blessing, she will be able to enter paradise. I am most grateful to you, and this offering is a token of my gratitude."

"I am ashamed," said his Holiness, "that my priest's robe should cover one so unworthy to profess Holy Religion. Not any virtue of mine but your own sincerity will send your wife to paradise. I feel that I ought not to accept your gift."

"It is but a trifle," Ximen Qing said, "and really utterly unworthy of you. I can only pray that you will smile and accept it."

His Holiness then bade his novices remove the gifts.

Ximen Qing offered a cup of wine to Abbot Wu, with a roll of silk and five taels of silver. Ten taels more were for the expenses of the ceremony.

"I will accept the fee and no more," said the Abbot. "You have always been extremely generous to me, and I could do no less than perform this ceremony for your lady. Indeed I ought not even to take the fee, so how dare I accept the rest?"

"Teacher," Ximen said, "though his Holiness performed the actual ceremony, you had all the trouble of the preparations. I must insist."

The Abbot was obliged to accept. He thanked Ximen Qing. Then Ximen offered wine to all the other priests, spreading the blessing, as it is said. Uncle Wu and Ying Bojue helped him, Uncle Wu passing the cups, and Bojue pouring out the wine. Xie Xida took around the food. They knelt down.

"Today," Bojue said, "we have done excellent work. We are delighted to have his Holiness with us, and we are greatly obliged to Abbot Wu for the trouble he has taken. I have no doubt that all that has been done will greatly benefit my dead sister-in-law. Though this is largely due to the supreme powers of his Holiness, yet, Brother, your earnest sincerity must have had its part." He offered a cup of wine to Ximen Qing.

"Gentlemen," Ximen said, "I have troubled you greatly these last few days and I do not know how to thank you." With these words he drained the cup.

Ying Bojue filled another cup. "Drink this, Brother, and make it a pair. I would not have you drink a single one." Xie Xida helped Ximen to some

food. In return, Ximen Qing offered wine to them, and they sat down.
The actors sang and the cooks brought more and more food. They guessed
fingers, played games and, with music and singing, drank until the second
night watch. Then Ximen Qing was drunk, and everybody went away. He
gave three *qian* of silver to the actors, and went to the inner court.

CHAPTER 67

Ximen Qing Dreams of Li Ping'er

The wind blows from the north
And the ground is covered with flakes of jade.
The white earth and the river are made one.
A cold mist rises above the waves: it is like a screen.
The mountains are covered with gray cloud
And the cloud links them with the water.
The withered grass seems to be dead.

His thoughts were far as the red cloud
The gentle spirit was sad, and the memory bitter
Night after night, only a kind dream
Could give him sleep.

Do not stand alone on the high building
When the moon is waning.
The wine descending to a sorrowing breast
Turns to tears of love.

Ximen Qing was very tired when he went to the inner court to sleep. He did not rise next day until the sun was high in the heavens. Laixing came and said to him: "The builders are here. They wish to know if they shall pull down the temporary buildings."

"Yes, tell them to demolish everything," Ximen answered angrily. "Why do you come and bother me?"

The builders unfastened the mats and ropes and took down the pine-wood posts. They carried them to the house on the other side of the road and there stored them.

Yuxiao came and said to Ximen: "The weather is very threatening." He told her to bring his clothes so that he might get up.

"You are very tired, and the weather looks bad," Wu Yueniang said. "Stay in bed. What is there for you to do if you get up so early? Don't go to the office today."

"I am not going to the office," Ximen said, "but Zhai's messenger is coming for my answer."

"Then you had better get up," Yueniang said, "and I will tell them to make some gruel for you."

Ximen Qing got up but did not wash. He put on a velvet gown and a felt hat and went to his study in the garden. Now that Shutong had gone, Ximen Qing had told Wang Jing to wait upon him in this study and Chunhong to look after the study in the outer court. In winter Ximen usually came to this garden study. There was a fire beneath the floor and a large bronze brazier. The winter blinds were drawn. In the middle room were some *jiazhi* peaches, chrysanthemums of many different kinds, a few slender bamboos of great delicacy, and orchids. Writing materials and vases with the plum-blossom pattern books, and musical instruments were set out with great care.

When Ximen Qing came in, Wang Jing hastened to burn incense in a small gold burner. Ximen bade him tell Laian to go for Ying Bojue. Then Ping'an came and told Wang Jing that Little Zhou, the barber, had come. Ximen Qing gave orders that he should be sent in. The barber came and kowtowed.

"You have come at the right moment," Ximen said to him. "Now comb my hair and massage my body." He asked the barber why it was so long since he had last been there.

"I heard that the Sixth Lady had died and that you were very busy."

Ximen Qing sat down on a comfortable chair, and Little Zhou dressed his hair. Laian came with Ying Bojue. Bojue was wearing a felt hat, a green velvet gown, and a pair of old black boots with palm-leaf galoshes over them. He made a reverence to Ximen Qing. Ximen, who was still having his hair dressed, told him not to stand on ceremony but to sit down. Ying Bojue pulled out a chair and sat down beside the brazier.

"Why are you dressed like this?" Ximen said.

"Don't you know?" said Bojue. "It is snowing and very cold. I did not get home before cockcrow, and this morning I did not feel at all anxious to get up. If you hadn't sent your boy, I should have been asleep still. You must be strong, or you wouldn't be able to get up so early. If I were in your place, I should never get up at all."

"No," said Ximen, "I don't suppose you would. You know all I have had to do of late. First the funeral, then Grand Marshal Huang to entertain, and now this last ceremony. I have had no rest at all. This morning, my wife said to me: 'You must be tired; stay in bed for a while,' but I remembered that Zhai's messenger was coming for an answer to the letter he brought, and I wanted to see the temporary buildings pulled down. On the twenty-fourth, Clerk Han and the others are to start for the South. Then, during the funeral ceremonies, my kinsmen and friends have been very kind. I ought to go and visit them but, in the circumstances, perhaps I may be excused. But at least I must go and see the officers of rank who came to the funeral."

"I am afraid you can't escape that," Bojue said, "but, as for the others, if I were you, I should get somebody to go and call on them on your behalf. You can thank them when you see them. They all know how busy you are, and they will understand."

As they were talking, Huatong brought two cups of milk with sugar and cream. Bojue took one. The milk was so white that it looked like goose fat with the cream floating on the top. "This is a great treat," he said. "Nice and hot too!" He drank the milk, and found it so sweet that he had no difficulty in finishing it. Little Zhou finished Ximen Qing's hair and began to clean his ears. Ximen set down his cup of milk.

"Drink your milk, Brother," Bojue said. "Don't let it get cold. A man like you ought to drink milk. It is so nourishing."

"I don't want it," Ximen Qing said. "You drink it. My gruel will be coming shortly."

Ying Bojue liked it very much. He picked up the cup and drank it straight off.

The barber finished cleaning Ximen's ears and took a roller to massage his body.

"Do you enjoy being rolled like this?" Bojue said.

"I have a good deal of pain in the back," Ximen said. "I need the massage."

"Well, you are very stout, and you have such rich food every day you must have a good deal of heat inside you."

"Doctor Ren has said to me more than once: 'Sir, though you seem so stout, you are really not very strong,' " Ximen Qing said. "He gave me a box of tonic, reinvigorating pills. He told me that these pills had originally been made for his Majesty by his Holiness Lin, and recommended me to take one every morning with human milk. But the last few days I have had so much to do I forgot all about the pills. You are always saying that I have too many ladies and that I see too much of them, but since the Sixth Lady died, I have had so much on my mind I have never thought about such things."

Then Han Daoguo came in. "I have just heard that our boat has been chartered," he said. "We shall be able to start on the twenty-fourth as we proposed."

Ximen Qing told Clerk Gan to go into the accounts, get the silver ready, and see that everything was packed up the following day. He said to Han Daoguo: "How much money have we made in our two shops?"

"About six thousand taels all together," Han Daoguo said.

Ximen told him to give two thousand taels to Cui Ben so that he could go and buy goods at Huzhou, and to take the remaining four thousand to buy cloth at Songjiang with Laibao. "You will come back by one of the first boats next year," he said. He told each of them to take five taels and go home to get ready.

"There is one matter I must mention," Han Daoguo said. "I am detailed to a tour of duty in Duke Yun's palace. They say I must go in person and will not accept substitute money. What shall I do?"

"You are in the same position as Laibao," Ximen said. "He gets out of it by simply paying three *qian* of silver every month."

"Brother Laibao was appointed by his Eminence the Imperial Tutor," Han Daoguo said. "The papers came, and the authorities at the palace dare not say a word. But I have to serve because my ancestors have always served. I can't do what he does."

"Go and write out a statement of your case and I will ask Doctor Ren to go to the palace and arrange matters with Master Wang. I am sure they will take your name off the register and allow you to give money in place of service. After that, you will only need to send a man there once a month."

Han Daoguo bowed and thanked him.

"Brother," Ying Bojue said, "if you can arrange this matter for him, he will be much easier in mind when he starts for the South."

By this time the massage was finished, and Ximen Qing went to the inner court to dress. He told a servant to give Little Zhou something to eat. Sometime later he returned, wearing a white velvet hat and a velvet cloak, and gave the barber three *qian* of silver. He told Wang Jing to go for Scholar Wen. The scholar came, wearing a tall hat and a broad girdle. They greeted one another, and a servant laid the table and brought in gruel. Ying Bojue and Scholar Wen sat in the places of honor, Ximen Qing in the host's seat, and Han Daoguo in the lower place. Ximen called for another bowl of gruel and a pair of chopsticks for Chen Jingji. Jingji, wearing a white hat and white gown, bowed to Bojue and the others and sat down beside Han Daoguo. They soon finished the gruel, and the things were cleared away. Han Daoguo left them.

Ximen Qing asked Scholar Wen whether he had written the letter. "I have a rough draft here," Scholar Wen said, "and when you have approved it, I will write it again." He took the draft from his sleeve and gave it to Ximen Qing. It read:

To the great and virtuous statesman, my worthy kinsman Yun Feng.

The time has flown since we parted at the Capital, and already half a year has passed. Sorrow has come upon me and I have lost my wife. You, from so great a distance, have been gracious enough to send an offering. And you have sent a letter that I value highly, an earnest of your kind feeling and generous actions. I am greatly indebted to you and shall never forget your kindness. My only fear is that my delinquencies in the office may bring disgrace upon you, since my position there is due to you. I trust that you will speak kindly for me to his Eminence. All that I have is of your giving.

I take this opportunity of asking after your well-being. I have thought of you continually.

With this letter I send ten silken Yangzhou handkerchiefs, ten of colored silk, twenty gold toothpicks and ten gold cups. These are but a slight token of my regard, and I trust you will accept them with indulgence.

Your kinsman Ximen Qing of Qinghe.

When Ximen Qing had read the letter, he told Jingji to pack up the presents. He asked Scholar Wen to copy the letter upon fine paper and seal it with his seal. Then he gave five taels of silver to the messenger Wang Yu.

The snow was heavier than before. Ximen invited Scholar Wen to stay with him in the study and admire the beauty of the landscape. The servants cleared the tables and brought wine. Then Ximen Qing saw someone peeping through the blind and asked who was there. Wang Jing told him it was Zheng Chun. Ximen called the boy in, and he came, carrying two boxes. He lifted them high before him, then knelt down before Ximen Qing. A small golden square box was opened and Ximen asked what was in it. "My sister Zheng Aiyue," said the boy, "knows how busy and tired you have been, and she sends you these two boxes of cakes." One of the two boxes contained pastries filled with fruits, and the other, pastries shaped like a spiral shell. "My sister prepared them with her own hands," Zheng Chun said. "She knows you like them and made them especially for you."

"It is only a day or two since you brought me some tea," Ximen said, "and now your sister has sent me these delightful pastries. I am very grateful to her."

"Splendid!" Ying Bojue said. "Hand them to me. I'll see what they're like. My daughter, who used to make these pastries so well, is dead, but now, I see, I have another daughter who knows how to make them." He picked up one and put it in his mouth. Then he took another and gave it to Scholar Wen, saying: "Here, old gentleman, try this. You will find it will make your teeth grow again and give new life to your flesh and bones. I give you my word: to have rare things like this is better than ten years added to one's life."

Scholar Wen put the pastry into his mouth. It seemed to melt at once. "Cakes like this," he said, "come from the West. They are not the kind of thing one sees every day. They ease the lungs and bring a feeling of genuine delight. A rarity indeed!"

"What is in the little box?" Ximen Qing asked Zheng Chun.

The boy knelt down again and handed the box to Ximen. "My sister has sent this for you alone," he said, softly.

Ximen Qing put the box on his knee, but, before he could open it, Ying Bojue snatched it away from him and opened it. There was a red silk handkerchief inside, embroidered with a pattern of entwined hearts, and in the handkerchief were melon seeds that Zheng Aiyue had cracked with her own teeth. Bojue tossed the handkerchief to Ximen Qing, grabbed two handfuls of melon seeds and crammed them into his mouth. Ximen Qing tried to stop him, but by this time there were only a few seeds left.

"You dog," cried Ximen, "are you starving? She sent them for me. Give them to me at once."

"It was my daughter who sent them," Bojue said, "so it is right and proper that I should have them. You, my son, have too many good things already."

"If Scholar Wen were not here," Ximen said, "I would tell you what I think about you. You dog, you really go beyond all bounds." He put the handkerchief in his sleeve and told Wang Jing to take the boxes to the inner court. Food and wine were brought. When they had drunk a cup of wine, Daian came and said that Li and Huang had come to pay their debt.

"How much have they brought?" Ximen Qing asked.

"They have brought a thousand taels," Daian said, "and they say they will pay more later."

"The ungodly scoundrels," Bojue cried, "they have deceived me. They never said a word to me about it. No wonder they did not put in an appearance during the ceremony. They must have been to Dongpingfu for the money. Take it, Brother, and have done with them. They have had credit enough. I shouldn't be surprised if, later, they weren't able to pay. I knew that Eunuch Xue was going to Dongpingfu to get some money for himself yesterday. I hoped that all the money would not go to that old ox, because I knew there wasn't any hope that you would get your money back if he got hold of it."

"I am not worrying about him," Ximen Qing said. "If they don't pay, I shall clap them into jail." He told Chen Jingji to get the scales and weigh the silver. "Then I will go and see them," he said.

Jingji came back. "I have weighed the silver," he said, "and there are exactly a thousand taels. I gave it to the Great Lady. Huang the Fourth says he would like to speak to you."

"Go and tell him I am entertaining some guests," Ximen Qing said. "He must come back after the twenty-fourth. I know he wants to get out of his contract."

"No," said Jingji. "He says it is another matter about which he would like to speak to you. It is a favor he wishes to ask."

"Then I will go and see him," Ximen said.

When he came to the hall, Huang the Fourth kowtowed and said: "I have now paid a thousand taels to your son-in-law, and I will pay shortly the remainder. There is another matter about which I should like to ask your help." He knelt down and burst into tears.

Ximen Qing raised him and asked what was the matter.

"My wife's father, Sun Qing, and his partner, Feng the Second, are in the cotton business at Dongchang. Feng the Second has a son, Feng Huai, a very unfilial fellow, who spends all his time at bawdy houses. One day he stole two bales of cotton. My father-in-law remonstrated with his partner, and Feng the Second gave his son a beating. Then the young man made trouble with my wife's brother, Sun Wen, and there was a fight. He knocked out one of my brother-in-law's teeth, but not before he had taken a hard knock on the head. Bystanders stopped the fight, and Feng's son went home, but something went wrong, and he died about a fortnight later. The dead young man's father-in-law is a notorious scamp of Hexi. His name is Bai the Fifth, but he is nicknamed Profiteer Bai and is a harborer of rogues and villains. He put up Feng the Second to bring an accusation, and Feng went to the court to accuse the Suns. The magistrate appointed Captain Li to investigate the case, but his Lordship was then awaiting the arrival of the Imperial barge and the matter was delegated to Tong, one of the magistrates of the Prefecture. Bai bribed the magistrate and persuaded some of the neighbors to give false evidence. They swore that, when the two young men were fighting, my father-in-law encouraged them. Tong has sent to arrest my father-in-law. I have come to you to beg you to have pity and write a letter to Captain Li on his behalf. What I suggest is that, when my father-in-law has been in prison for a few days, Captain Li should be approached again. In the first place, my father-in-law had nothing whatever to do with the fighting, and secondly, the young man died so long after the actual fight that it was beyond the recognized limit. Besides, his own father had punished him first, so that it cannot be definitely said that Sun Wen was the cause of his death."

Ximen Qing looked at the paper Huang the Fourth had brought. It said: 'Sun Qing and Sun Wen, now held in prison at Dongchang, implore your favor and your gracious help.'

"Captain Li was here only the other day," Ximen said. "It was the first time we had met, so we can hardly be called intimate friends. How can I approach him in this matter?"

Huang the Fourth knelt down again. He cried and said: "You must have compassion on them, or both father and son will perish. If Sun Wen cannot be saved, at least let us save my father-in-law. It will be a noble act on your part. My father-in-law is sixty years old. If he is kept in prison during the wintry weather, it will certainly kill him."

Ximen Qing thought for a long time. Then he said: "I will write to his Lordship Qian of the Customs. He will speak to Captain Li. They passed their examination in the same year."

Once more Huang the Fourth knelt down. He took from his sleeve a card that said: "A hundred sacks of finest rice." He handed this to Ximen Qing and then brought out two parcels of silver. Ximen said he wanted none of his money.

"If it is no use to you," Huang the Fourth said, "you might perhaps pass it on to his Lordship Qian."

"Don't trouble about that," Ximen said. "If the matter is settled, I will send him some presents."

Ying Bojue came through the corner door.

"Brother," he said, "do nothing for this fellow Huang the Fourth. He is the sort of man who never burns incense to Buddha yet comes to fall before the knees of Buddha when he is in difficulties. Remember that, when you had the service for your dead lady, he never even sent you tea. Nor did he come himself. Why should you trouble about him?"

Huang the Fourth bowed to Ying Bojue. "Good uncle!" he said, "this is a serious matter and you are sentencing men to death. For the last month this business has kept me on the run, and I couldn't find a moment to come here. Yesterday I went to the office for the money, and today I have come to pay my debt and to ask his Lordship's aid to save my father-in-law. His Lordship refuses to take my offering, and I fear he is not willing to help me."

Bojue saw a hundred taels of snow-white silver. "Brother," he said, "are you going to do anything for him?"

"I don't know Captain Li well enough," Ximen said, "but I will buy a present of some sort and ask Qian to do what he can. I don't think I can take this money from Huang the Fourth."

"Then you make a mistake," Bojue said. "He comes and asks you for help, and it is not right that you should be put to expense in the matter. If you refuse to accept it, it will look as though you thought the gift too small. Take my advice and accept the money. If you don't need it yourself, pass it on to his Lordship Qian. Now, in Brother Huang's presence, I say that the fate of his father- and brother-in-law is entirely a question of luck. There is no knowing whether, even if the letter is delivered, they will get off scot-free. His Lordship here is no money-grubber. I think you ought to offer us a feast at the bawdy house."

"Uncle," Huang the Fourth said, "if you do this for me, you may be sure I shall offer you wine. Indeed, I shall make my brother-in-law come and kowtow to you. I may tell you that I have busied myself day and night over this affair and, hitherto, I have failed to get anyone to help me. If you refuse, I shall not know where to turn."

"You silly thing!" Bojue said, "of course it is a serious matter for you. You sleep with his daughter."

"Yes, indeed," Huang the Fourth said, "and she cries all the time."

Ximen Qing yielded to Bojue's persuasion and took the card, but he still refused the silver. Huang the Fourth implored him to take it, and went out, leaving it behind. Ying Bojue called him back and asked when he wanted the letter.

"It is very urgent," Huang the Fourth said, "and I should like it at once. Tomorrow morning I will send my son with your servant to deliver it. I should like to speak to the servant you decide to send."

"I will write the letter now," Ximen said. He sent for Daian and said to him: "Tomorrow morning you will have to take a letter." Then Huang the Fourth spoke to the boy, and they went out. When he came to the gate, he asked Daian to get for him the purse in which he had brought the silver. The boy went to the inner court to ask Wu Yueniang for it. She was making clothes with her two maids. Daian waited, but Yueniang said to him:

"We are too busy. We can't give it you now. Tell him he shall have it tomorrow."

"But he wants it very urgently," Daian said. "He has to go to Dong-chang tomorrow, and he won't be able to come back. Please take the silver out of it and let me have the purse."

"Go and give him the thing and get rid of him," Yueniang said to Yuxiao.

Yuxiao went to the inner room and emptied the silver on to the bed. She brought the purse to Daian. "Take it away, you rascal," she said to him. "Nobody is going to eat it. What a nuisance you are!"

"If it hadn't been wanted, I shouldn't have troubled you," the boy said. He went out with the purse. When he reached the second door, a piece of silver, about three taels in weight, dropped out. One of the wrappers had been torn, and, when Yuxiao had emptied the silver in such a hurry, she did not notice that this piece had been left in the bottom of the bag. "What a stroke of luck," Daian said to himself. "Money for nothing!" He put it in his sleeve. He gave the purse to Huang the Fourth and promised to bring the letter the next morning.

Ximen Qing went back to the study and asked Scholar Wen to write the letter. Then he gave it to Daian.

They looked out over the snow. It seemed like willow fluff blowing in the wind, or withered pear blossoms dancing. Ximen Qing had a jar of doubly strong Magu wine opened, and told Chunhong to warm some. Meanwhile Zheng Chun played for them. Ximen Qing bade him play "The Wind Blows Softly through the Willows."

Qintong came and said that Han Daoguo had given him a paper to show his master. Ximen read it and said to the boy: "Take this to Doctor Ren's house and ask him to go to the palace and have Han's name taken off the list."

"It is too late now to go outside the city," Qintong said. "Shall I go to-morrow morning?"

Ximen Qing agreed. Then Laian brought a square box with several dishes and two large plates of pastries made of goose fat and rose flowers. Chen Jingji shared their meal. Ximen Qing told Wang Jing to give three dishes and some pastries to Zheng Chun and two large cups of wine. Zheng Chun knelt down and said: "I never drink wine."

"You foolish boy," Ying Bojue said, "it is very, very cold, and, besides, it is your father who offers it to you. You know your brother always has some."

"My brother may drink wine, but it is not for me," said the boy.

"Drink one cup," Bojue said, "and I will ask Wang Jing to drink the other for you."

But Wang Jing said he never touched wine.

"Foolish boy," Bojue said, "I am asking you to drink one for Zheng Chun. You ought to know by now that young people should not refuse anything their elders give them. You must drink it." He stood up. Wang Jing held his nose and swallowed the wine.

"Dog!" Ximen Qing said. "What right have you to force him to drink?"

The boy drank only half a cup. Ying Bojue told Chunhong to drink the rest and asked him to sing some Southern songs.

"Wait a moment," Ximen Qing said, "I am going to have a game with Scholar Wen, and he can sing while we drink. That will be fun." He told Wang Jing to get the dice box and asked Scholar Wen to throw the dice first.

"I dare not," said Wen. "I ought to ask Master Ying to begin. What is your honorable name, worthy Sir?"

"My poor name is Nanpo,"[1] Bojue said.

"I will explain it to you, Master," Ximen Qing said jokingly. "So many gentlemen come to his place that there is no chance for him to get at the thing he keeps under the bed. In the evening, when he can get at it, he dare not pour it out in the street for fear his neighbors will curse him, so he tells his maid to take it to the south and empty it against the granary wall. That's why his second name is Nanpo."

Scholar Wen laughed. "But that is a different *po*. The character for 'pouring' has the water radical on one side and the word *fa* on the other. This *po* has the earth radical and the word *pi*."

"*Pi* is the very word, Master," Ximen said. "There are always *pizi* (Southerners) with his wife."

"I did not mean that," Scholar Wen said, laughing.

"Master," Bojue said, "you don't know him. He is always making nasty jokes about people."

"A little joking serves to liven things up," the scholar said.

"Let us begin our game," Bojue said. "Don't bother about him. His mouth is always dribbling. Please begin. Don't stand on ceremony."

"When I throw the dice," Scholar Wen said, "we will have a quotation from some poem, or song, or some classical work, which must have the word 'snow' in it. If we can think of one, we drink a small cup; if not, a large one." He threw a one. "I know," he said, "it is long since snow fell on the wild bird's island." He passed the dice box to Ying Bojue, who threw a five.

Bojue thought for a long time but could not think what to say. "This is really terrible," he muttered. Finally he cried: 'I've got it! The plum flowers in the snow open their snow-white blossoms. What do you think of that?"

"That won't do," Scholar Wen said. "You said 'snow' twice."

"That's all right," Bojue said, "big snow and little snow!"

"What nonsense you always talk, you dog," Ximen said. He told Wang Jing to give Bojue a large cup of wine, and bade Chunhong sing a Southern song.

> The night was chill and the traveler hungry
> He went to the village to seek an inn.
> Snow hovers gently over the temples
> And drops thickly on the places for dancing.

---

1. This means, literally, "pouring at the south."

Now he must stay awhile.
On the bank of the river he goes cheerfully
To see the plum blossoms.
In the courtyard, people with silver candles
Go to appreciate the snow
White snow, falling endlessly
Dancing in the air like willow fluff.

Bojue was enjoying his wine when Laian brought fresh pastries and dessert. There were conch-shaped light pastries and things that looked like small black balls, wrapped in orange leaves. Bojue picked one up and put it to his nose. It smelled very sweet. He put it into his mouth. It tasted like honey, and he thought it most delicious. He could not imagine what it was. Ximen Qing told him to guess.

"Sugar-coated soap," Bojue said.

Ximen Qing laughed. "Sugar-coated soap would hardly be so pleasant," he said.

"I would say 'Plum pastry balls,' but there is a kernel."

"Come here, you dog, and I'll tell you," Ximen said, "for I don't suppose you will ever guess. They were brought for me from Hangzhou by one of my people, and are called coated plums. There are various kinds of medicine inside. The medicine is mixed with honey, and the plums are steeped in the mixture. Finally, they are covered with peppermint and orange leaves. That is why they taste so pleasant. Taken every morning, they are excellent for the chest. They get rid of foul breath, are useful against phlegm, tone down the effects of wine, and are splendid for the digestion. They are much better than plum pastry balls."

"How should I ever have thought of that if you hadn't told me?" Bojue said. "Master Wen, I think I'll have another." He said to Wang Jing: "Bring me some paper, I'm going to take a couple home to my wife." He picked up one of the shell-shaped pastries. "Is it true," he asked Zheng Chun, "that your sister made these herself?"

Zheng Chun knelt down and said: "Do you think I would lie to you? Zheng Aiyue spent hours over these few pastries."

"She did good work," Bojue said. "Look! They are marked exactly like real shells. The colors, red and white, stand out ever so clearly."

"My son," Ximen Qing said, "when you talk like this you make me think of her who is gone. She was the only one in my house who could make them, and, now she is no more, there is no one here to take her place."

"I told you sometime ago that that does not trouble me," Bojue said. "One of my daughters is dead, but there is still another to make such pastries for me. I must say you are a wonderful man to discover such wonderful people."

Ximen Qing laughed until his eyes were no more than a narrow slit. He slapped Ying Bojue and told him not to talk such nonsense. Scholar Wen said: "Gentlemen, no one can help seeing what good friends you are."

"Don't say that," Bojue said, "he is your nephew, you know."

"For twenty years, Master," Ximen Qing said, "I have been his step-father."

Seeing them making fun with one another, Chen Jingji stood up and went away. Scholar Wen put his hand before his mouth and laughed. Ying Bojue drank his wine. It was Ximen Qing's turn to throw the dice. He threw a seven. For a long time he racked his brains for a verse. Then he said: "I will give you a quotation from the 'Perfumed Girdle': 'The Lord of the East will go away, for the pear flowers look like snow.'"

"No," Ying Bojue said, "that won't do. The word 'snow' must be the ninth. You must drink a large cup." He filled a cup of wine to the brim, gave it to Ximen Qing, and told Chunhong to sing. "My child," he said to him, "if one may judge by the number of date stones in your belly, you must know more than a song or two." Chunhong sang another song.

It was getting dark and lights were brought. When Ximen Qing had finished his wine, Bojue said: "Your son-in-law has gone, so Scholar Wen will have to finish the game." Scholar Wen again threw a one. As he was thinking what to say, his eyes caught sight of a pair of scrolls hanging on the wall. On them was written, "The wind rustles the tender willows. It is night upon the bridge. The snowflakes gently touch the frozen plums. There is Spring in the tiny courtyard." He took the line beginning "Snow-flakes" for his quotation.

"We can't have that," Ying Bojue said. "That doesn't come from your memory. You must drink a large cup." Chunhong offered wine to Scholar Wen. He drank it, and it made him drowsy. He nodded his head. Then he got up and excused himself. Bojue would have kept him, but Ximen Qing said:

"No, a scholar is a man of education and cannot drink much wine." He told Huatong to take Master Wen home. This was what Scholar Wen desired. He got up and took leave of them.

Bojue said to Ximen Qing: "Scholar Wen is really a poor creature. He has had very little to drink, yet he is drunk already." He and Ximen Qing went on with their drinking.

At last Bojue himself stood up. "The ground is slippery, and I must go now," he said. "Don't forget, Brother, to see that Daian takes the letter tomorrow."

"Didn't you see me give it to him?" Ximen said. "He will go in the morning."

Ying Bojue pulled aside the lattice. The sky was full of clouds, and the ground was like ice. He asked for a lantern and for Zheng Chun to go with him. Ximen Qing gave the boy five *qian* of silver, and filled a jar with the coated plums and put them in a box for Zheng Aiyue. As they were going away, Ximen said to Bojue: "Be good with your younger brother."

"That is enough!" Bojue replied. "We are father and son and shall behave as such. But I may go and have a chat with that little whore Zheng Aiyue."

Qintong took them to the gate. Ximen Qing saw that the tables were cleared, then, supported by Laian, who carried a lantern, he went to the corner door. He passed by Jinlian's door, which was closed, and quietly went on to the rooms of Li Ping'er. He knocked gently and Yingchun opened the door. Laian went back. Ximen entered the room and looked at the portrait of his dead wife. He asked whether they had offered food before it. "We have just made an offering," Ruyi'er told him.

Ximen sat down on a chair and Yingchun brought him tea. He told her to help him undress. Ruyi'er, finding that he was going to spend the night, quickly made the bed and warmed it with a hot-water bottle. Then she helped him to bed, and Xiuchun went out to shut the corner door. The two maids went to sleep in the other room.

When he asked for more tea, the maids were too sleepy to wish to get it. They told Ruyi'er to hurry. She took off her clothes and got into bed with him. The wine he had drunk had aroused Ximen's passions. He took some of the secret medicine and put the clasp on his penis. She lay on her back, he parted her legs and pushed hard until her tongue froze and her cunt ran with abundant stream. She called him all the tender names she could think of. It was the middle of the night and so silent that the noise they made might have been heard far away. Ximen Qing found the woman's body as yielding as down. He put his arms around her and kissed her, then told her to squat upon the bed and suck. She did so, to his great satisfaction.

"My child," Ximen said to her, "your skin is as white as the Sixth Lady's was. Being with you is like being with her. Treat me well and faithfully, and I will be kind to you."

"You must not say that," Ruyi'er said. "Comparing me with her is like comparing Earth with Heaven. But my husband is dead, and, if you do not hate a creature so ugly as I am, look at me sometimes and I shall be more than content."

Ximen Qing asked how old she was.

"My animal is the Hare, and I am thirty-one."

"You are a year younger than I am," he said. He was delighted to find that not only did she talk sensibly, but she was no mean performer on the bed. Next morning she waited upon him hand and foot, put on his shoes and socks, and helped him to dress his hair. The two maids, Yingchun and Xiuchun, could not get near him. Ruyi'er asked him to give her some white silk to make a mourning gown for her dead mistress. Ximen Qing sent a boy to the shop to get three rolls of white silk so that both she and the maids might have white gowns. He gave them money and clothes and ornaments, and Wu Yueniang knew nothing about it.

But Pan Jinlian knew, and she went to see Yueniang. "You really must speak to him," she said. "The shameless fellow went and slept with that woman yesterday. The wretch might be starved. He is ready to carry on with anybody he can get. We can't let him go on like this. What shall we do if she has a baby? She would play the same game as Laiwang's wife did. We ought not to allow her such liberties."

"You always try to get me to do things of this sort," Yueniang said. "He is carrying on with this woman. You all want to keep in his good graces and let me bear the brunt. Why should I be such a fool? You tell me to talk to him about it. Well, I'm not going to do anything of the sort."

Jinlian went back to her room without another word.

The snow had stopped, and Ximen Qing told Daian to set out with the letter for Qian. When he returned from the office, Ping'an told him that Zhai's messenger had come for his answer. Ximen Qing gave it to him and asked why he had not come the day before. The messenger told him that he had been delayed because he had had to go to Governor Hou. He took Ximen's letter and went away.

When he had had his dinner, Ximen went to the shop and watched his men weighing out silver and packing up. On the twenty-fourth, they burned paper offerings and started for the South. Han Daoguo and Cui Ben took with them the two boys Rong Hai and Hu Xiu. Ximen gave them a letter and some presents for Miao Xiaohu.

By the twenty-sixth, Ximen had finished paying his visits of thanks to relatives and friends. One morning he was sitting in Yueniang's room, having his breakfast. His wife said to him: "The first day of next month is Zhangjie's birthday. We ought to send some sort of present to the Qiaos. The proverb says: 'Once a relative, always a relative,' and we ought not to cease these courtesies now that our baby is dead."

"I see no reason why we should," Ximen said. He told Laixing to buy enough presents to fill four boxes, silken clothes, two kerchiefs and a box of ornaments. Then he wrote a card and told Wang Jing to take the things to Master Qiao's house. After this he went to his study in the garden.

Daian came back. "His Lordship Qian," he said, "received your letter. He wrote a letter to Captain Li and gave it to the officer with whom Huang the Fourth's son-in-law went to Dongchangfu. Captain Li asked the magistrate Tong to send the prisoners and all the documents to him, so that he could go into the case himself. Old Sun was discharged and all that happened was that they had to give ten taels of silver to pay for the other man's funeral expenses. Sun Wen was sentenced for some trivial offense, given seventy stripes, and made to pay a small fine. The officer came back to tell his Lordship Qian, and now we have Captain Li's letter."

Ximen Qing was very pleased with Daian for handling the matter so adroitly. He opened the letter and read it. It was from Li to Qian and explained the situation.

> I have received your letter [it read] and the matter is now quite clear. Feng the Second beat his son and, when his son fought with Sun Wen, both parties received injuries. The man's death took place after the statutory limit. It would be unjust to condemn the other man to death, and I have adjudged that he shall pay Feng ten taels of silver towards the funeral expenses. So there is an end to the case.

The letter was signed Li Jiyuan.

Ximen Qing asked where Sun Wen was now.

"He went home as soon as he came out of prison," Daian said. "Tomorrow he is coming with Huang the Fourth to kowtow to you. Huang gave me a tael of silver."

Ximen Qing told the boy to spend the money on shoes and socks and anything else he needed; Daian made a reverence to his master and went away. Ximen Qing lay down on the bed and went to sleep. Wang Jing burned some incense in a small burner and went out quietly.

Suddenly, Ximen Qing heard someone pushing aside the lattice. Li Ping'er came in. She was wearing a violet coat and a white silk skirt. Her hair was disordered and her face very pale. She came forward and, standing beside the bed, said to him: Brother, you are sleeping here. I have come to see you. You know I was accused by that fellow, and I have been in prison. I still suffer from an issue of blood and I have suffered greatly, for I have been unable to escape from the unpleasantness. The other day you were kind enough to pray for mercy for me, and my sentence was reduced by three parts. Still that fellow insists that I must be punished severely. He demanded your arrest. I have come to warn you lest, sooner or later, you should fall into his hands. Now I am going to find a place for myself. Take care of yourself. Do not go to too many parties, and, when you go, come back early. Remember what I say." She threw her arms around him and sobbed.

"Sister," Ximen Qing cried, "tell me where you are going." But she pulled her hands away from him. He woke up and found it was a dream. And, when he woke, his eyes were filled with tears. From the shadow of the blind upon the floor, he knew that it was about noon. He was very sad.

> The snow has settled
> Its brightness shines upon the window.
> The fire is nearly out and the bed is cold.
> They meet again in a dream of love
> And the breeze sends the fragrance of plum blossom
> Through the curtains.

That morning they had sent presents to the Qiaos. Now Mistress Qiao sent Qiao Tong with an invitation to Yueniang and the other ladies. Yueniang was told that Ximen Qing was asleep in his study, so she did not wish to disturb him. She entertained Qiao Tong in the inner court. But Jinlian said: "Give me the card. I will go and see what he says." She came to the study and found Ximen lying on the bed. She sat down on the bed. "My son," she said, "you are talking to yourself. What is the matter with you? No wonder nobody ever sees you nowadays. You are too comfortable here."

As she talked, she looked more closely at him and saw that he had been crying. "What makes your eyes sore?" she said.

"Perhaps because I fell off the pillow," Ximen said.

"No, you have been crying."

"You silly slave," Ximen said. "Why should I cry?"

"You have been thinking of someone who is still dear to you."

"Don't talk nonsense about people dear to me or not dear to me," Ximen Qing said.

"You were thinking about Li Ping'er," Jinlian said. "And the nurse, Ruyi'er, is in your mind too. As for us, we find no place there. We don't count at all."

"Don't be so silly, you little strumpet," Ximen said. "I want to ask you something. That day when the Sixth Lady was put into her coffin, what clothes did you wear?"

"Why do you wish to know?"

"No particular reason," said Ximen, "I just wish to know."

"There must be some reason," Jinlian said. "Well, I wore silk, a white silk coat and a yellow silk skirt. And underneath, I wore a purple jacket, a white skirt and red vests." Ximen Qing nodded. "I have been an animal's doctor for twenty years," Jinlian continued, "but what is the matter with your donkey's stomach, I can't for the life of me make out. If you are not thinking about Li Ping'er, of whom are you thinking?"

"I have seen her in a dream," Ximen Qing said.

"Yes," Jinlian said, "that's just what you would do. When my nose tickles, it is a sign that I am going to sneeze. Now, even though she is dead, you still think of her warmly. It is a clear sign that you care nothing for the rest of us. When we die, nobody will bother about us."

Ximen Qing put his arms around her and kissed her. "Little oily mouth," he said, "you always think of something nasty to say."

"My son," Jinlian said, "I can see through you as clearly as I can see a cat with a black tail."

Their tongues met, and soon the sweetness softened their hearts. There was fragrance upon her lips, and the room in which they were was exquisitely perfumed. Ximen Qing was stirred. He kissed her. Then, lying on the bed, he displayed his penis and asked her to play with it. She bent her head and fondled it with her lips. She was wearing a gold tiger-headed pin. There were many pearls and plum flowers in her hair, and jewels and ornaments of all kinds on her head.

Suddenly, as they were sporting very pleasantly together, they heard Laian's voice saying that Ying Bojue had come. Ximen Qing told him to bring Bojue in, but Jinlian, greatly excited, cursed Laian. "Don't let him come until I am up," she cried.

"He is already in the courtyard," Laian said.

"Then tell him to keep out of the way."

Laian went to Ying Bojue. "Please wait outside a moment," he said. "There is someone in the study." Bojue went towards the pine hedges and looked at the bamboos, some of which were still covered with snow. Wang Jing pulled aside the lattice, and there was a rustle of skirts as Jinlian ran away like a wisp of mist.

Bojue came in and made a reverence to Ximen Qing. Then he sat down.

"It is several days since you were here," Ximen said. "Why is that?"

"Brother," Bojue said, "I am absolutely tired of life."

"Why?" Ximen asked.

"Lately," said Bojue, "I have been hard pressed for money, and, yesterday, without the slightest excuse, Chunhua went and had a baby. It would not have been so bad if it had been in the daytime, but it was in the middle of the night. She was in a bad way and I had to jump out of bed, get ready papers and bedclothes, and go out for the midwife. Ying Bao had gone with my brother to get some fodder, and there was I, as busy as could be, and not a soul to help me. I got a lantern and went down the street for old woman Feng. When she got there, the baby was born."

"A boy or a girl?" Ximen asked.

"A boy," Ying Bojue said.

"Well, you silly fellow, are you sorry to have a son? So that slave Chunhua has presented you with a son."

"*Aunt* Chun to you," said Bojue, laughing.

"Why did you marry her, you dog, if it is too much trouble for you to go for the midwife?"

"You don't seem to understand," Bojue said. "I am not like you, and, in this cold weather, I know it only too well. You are a rich man and a person of importance. When one of your ladies has a baby, it is as though fresh flowers were added to a piece of embroidered satin. Of course you are pleased. But poor people like us can't even bear the sight of our own shadows. What point is there in adding to our number? Each member of the household has to be fed and clothed. No! I feel as hard as hard can be. There's Ying Bao goes out to work every day. My brother never gives a thought to me. My eldest daughter has gone and got married, and now, Heaven be my witness! the second one is all ready to be. She will be thirteen years old at the end of this year. The other day some old woman came to ask about her. I said: 'There is no hurry. She is young enough yet. Don't worry me any more.' Then, if you please, this disgusting creature must choose to be born in the middle of the night. Heaven and earth seem dark to me. Where am I to turn for money? My wife saw me worrying, gave the old woman a silver pin, and sent her off. Tomorrow will be the baby's third day. A host of people know this and they are sure to come. And what about the ceremony when the child is a month old? When that day comes, the best thing I can do is to disappear and spend a few days at a temple."

Ximen Qing laughed. "If you do go," he said, "one of the priests will come and take your place in the bed. You seem to have some sense, you dog." He laughed again, but Bojue looked sulky and would not speak.

"Cheer up, my son," Ximen Qing said. "How much money do you need? You have only to say and you shall have it."

"Not very much," Bojue said.

"You must have enough to cover the expenses, or you will have to pawn your clothes again."

"Since you are so kind, Brother," Bojue said, "I think twenty taels will be sufficient. I did, in fact, write out a note, but I was ashamed to mention the matter, for I have troubled you so many times. I did not fill in the amount. Give me what you think fit, Brother."

"What are you talking about?" Ximen said. "We are friends, and I don't require any note from you."

As they were talking, Laian came in with tea. Ximen Qing told him to put down the cups and go for Wang Jing. When Wang Jing came, Ximen said to him: "Go to the inner court, and tell your mistress that, in the cabinet behind the bed, there are two packets of silver that came to me from his Excellency Song. Ask her to give you one of them."

The boy went away. He was soon back with the silver.

"Here are fifty taels," Ximen said, handing the packet to Ying Bojue. "Take them. I haven't opened the packet. You'd better open it yourself and see what is in it."

"But this is too much," Bojue said.

"You say your second daughter is growing up," said Ximen; "buy her some new clothes, and, later on, she will be glad of them."

"That is a good idea, Brother," Bojue said. He opened the packet. It was some of the silver that the officers had sent, divided into pieces of three taels each, of very fine quality. He was delighted and bowed to Ximen Qing. "Brother," he said, "how generous you are. No one else would help me as you do. But you will take this note, won't you?"

"You foolish lad," Ximen said, "why should I trouble about that? This is your parents' house or you would not come here to ask help so often. The baby does not belong only to you, he belongs to me too. It is my duty to help you rear him. When the ceremony of the first month is over, I will send for your wife. She will do for the interest on the money I have just given you."

"These last few days," Bojue said, "your aunt has been as thin as your mother."

They laughed and joked together. Then Bojue asked what had happened to Huang's relations.

"Qian wrote to Li," Ximen told him, "and Li sent for the accused and examined them himself. Both Sun Wen and his father were set free, with only ten taels to pay towards the funeral expenses."

"What luck for them!" Bojue exclaimed. "They would never find anybody else like you. No, not even if they took a lantern to look. And you wouldn't take anything from them, either dry or wet. But though you would not accept a present from them, you must take the money you had to spend on Qian. And don't forget to tell Huang he must give us a feast. If you won't tell him, I will. We have saved his brother-in-law's life, and that is no small matter."

Wu Yueniang was sitting in her room when Meng Yulou came. "My brother, Meng Rui, will soon be leaving for Sichuan and Guangtong," Yulou said. "He is going to buy stock. He has come to say good-bye and would like to see his Lordship. My brother is in my room. I don't know where his Lordship is. Will you send a boy for him?"

"He is with Ying the Second, in the garden," Yueniang said. "But, talking about asking him to come, Jinlian went to speak to him about the invitation Mistress Qiao sent us. Qiao Tong was here, waiting for the answer. I gave him tea, and we waited and waited, but she never came back. Qiao Tong lost patience and went off. A long time afterwards, I saw her and asked her if she had spoken to him about it. It was hard to get an answer out of her, but at last she said she had forgotten all about it. The card was still in her sleeve. She is like a donkey that has lost its tail. I don't know what she was doing with him, but she was there a very long time. She would tell me nothing, and I gave her a scolding. Then she went away."

After a while, Laian came in. Yueniang said to him: "Go and tell your father Uncle Meng is here."

When he heard this, Ximen Qing got up. He asked Bojue not to go away, saying he would be back in a moment. Then he went to the inner court. Yueniang told him about the invitation.

"Yes," Ximen Qing said, "but you must go alone. We are still in mourning, and it would not look well for a crowd to go."

Yueniang told him that Meng Rui was waiting to see him in Yulou's room. "He has come to say goodbye before he sets out to Sichuan and Guangtong," she said. She asked why he had sent for the silver.

"Last night Brother Ying's wife had a baby," Ximen said. "He needs some money. And he says that his second daughter is coming to a marriageable age. He is anxious about it."

"Brother Ying is getting on in years," Yueniang said. "Now that he has this child, his wife will be pleased. We must send her some rice to make gruel."

"Yes, indeed," Ximen said, "and we will ask Beggar Ying to send us an invitation to the ceremony of the first month. Then we shall see what Chunhua looks like."

"I don't suppose she's any different from any other woman," Yueniang said, laughing. "She has eyes and a nose, just like everybody else."

They sent Laian to ask Meng Rui to come. Meng Yulou came with her brother. When they had greeted one another and talked for a while, Ximen Qing took Uncle Meng to the study where Ying Bojue was. He told the boys to bring something to eat. The table was set and they sat down to drink. Ximen Qing told them to set an extra cover and sent Laian for Master Wen. But the boy came back and said the scholar had gone to call on Scholar Ni. Then Ximen said: "Go and fetch your brother-in-law." After a little while, Chen Jingji came. He greeted Meng Rui and sat down on the other side of the table.

"When are you starting?" Ximen Qing asked Meng Rui, "and how long do you expect to be away?"

"I am leaving on the second of next month," Meng Rui said, "but how long I shall be away I cannot tell. I am going to Jingzhou to buy paper, then to Sichuan and Guangtong for incense and wax. That will take me a year or two. When I have finished buying, I shall come back. I propose to go through Henan and Shaanxi by land but, when I come back, I shall come by water. That means taking the river to Jingzhou. I suppose, all together, it will be a journey of seven or eight thousand *li*."

Bojue asked how old he was. "I am twenty-six," the young man told him.

"You are a young man," Bojue said, "but you seem to know all there is to know about traveling and business. I myself have wasted my life at home."

More food was brought. Plates and dishes filled up the whole table. It was evening when Meng Rui went away. Ximen Qing took him to the gate and returned to Bojue. He happened to see two paper chests and told Jingji to fill them up. He asked Yueniang to get some of the clothes that had belonged to Li Ping'er and put them into the chests with some paper money. He said to Ying Bojue: "It is forty-two days now since she died. We haven't sent for any priests, but we are going to burn these chests."

"How quickly time passes," Bojue said. "It is more than a month since my sister-in-law died."

"Yes," Ximen Qing said, "the fifth of next month will be her last week's mind, and I must ask some priests to come and hold a service for her."

"This time, you ought to have the Buddhist priests," Bojue said.

"My wife tells me," Ximen said, "that when the sixth lady was alive, when her child was born and she suffered from continually flowing blood, she promised that our two nuns and some others should come and read prayers for her."

Bojue saw that it was getting late. "I must go," he said, "and you will have to be burning these papers for my sister-in-law." He bowed low and added: "Brother, you have been very kind to me and I will never forget it."

"Forget it or not," Ximen said, "don't try and make out that you are dreaming. When the time comes for the ceremony of the first month, all my ladies are going to take presents and congratulate you."

"There is no need for them to bring presents," Bojue said. "It will be good enough of them to come to my poor house."

"I tell you what," Ximen said; "you must dress up old Chunhua and fetch her along here for me to see."

"Your aunt tells me that, now she has a son, she won't require your services any more," Bojue said.

"Wait!" Ximen said. "I shall know how to deal with her when I see her."

Bojue laughed and went away. Ximen Qing told the boys to clear away. Then he went to the room of Li Ping'er. Chen Jingji and Laian had packed the paper chests. That day, offerings of paper things had been sent from all the neighboring temples. Ximen Qing watched Yingchun prepare the table and offer cakes, food, and soup to the dead lady. Incense was burned and candles lighted. Then he told Xiuchun to bid the ladies come and he, with them, burned paper offerings before the tablet. Chen Jingji took out the paper chests and burned them out of doors.

CHAPTER 68
The Party at Zheng Aiyue's House

So deep is her passion, even when she is old
She cannot restrain it.
The moon, the dew, the mist, the cloud,
In all of them is something to incite her love.
When a real man stands before her
How shall she control her yearning?

They whisper softly, one to the other,
Then love weaves its chains about them.
Even if their bowels were made of iron
They must melt.
It is time to say farewell
The water runs onward, but the flowers are faded.

When Ximen Qing had burned the paper offerings for Li Ping'er, he went to spend the night with Pan Jinlian. The next day, Ying Bojue sent him a present of lucky noodles. Then Huang the Fourth came with his brother-in-law, Sun Wenxiang. They kowtowed to Ximen Qing and offered a pig, a jar of wine, two roast geese, and two boxes of fruits. Ximen showed great reluctance to accept them, but Huang the Fourth fell on his knees and begged him to do so. "My Lord," he said, "you have saved our lives, and we and all our households feel that we must do something to show our gratitude. We can't think what to do. These are only trifles that you may care to give your servants." After much argument, Ximen Qing agreed to accept the pig and the wine, though only on the understanding that he would send them on to Qian.

"Well," Huang the Fourth said, "it would seem that since I cannot make you accept them, we shall have to take the rest away." Then he said: "When you are at liberty, we should very much like to give a little entertainment to Brother Ying and yourself."

"Oh, you mustn't pay attention to anything he suggests," Ximen Qing said. "He plays the fool too much. You have been good enough to offer me these presents, and there is no reason why you should go to all the trouble of entertaining me." Huang the Fourth and his brother-in-law thanked him repeatedly and went away.

On the first day of the eleventh month, when Ximen Qing had returned from the office, he set out again to take wine with Magistrate Li. Wu Yueniang, dressed in white, went alone to the Qiaos' to celebrate the birthday of Zhangjie. The same afternoon, Nun Xue came with two boxes of presents. She had heard that Yueniang wished to have a service on the fifth, and she slipped out quietly, without any of the other nuns knowing what she was about. As Yueniang was not at home, Li Jiao'er and Meng Yulou took tea with her. "The Great Lady," they said, "has gone to a birthday party at the Qiaos', but you must not go away, for she has something to say to you." The nun stayed.

Jinlian had not forgotten what Yuxiao had told her. She had said that Yueniang had conceived after taking some medicine the nuns had brought her. Ximen Qing had taken a fancy to the nurse, Ruyi'er, and Jinlian feared that the nurse might have a child, and win Ximen's favor for herself. So, secretly, she invited Nun Xue to go to her room, and gave her a tael of silver to get some medicine for her.

In the evening Yueniang returned and invited Xue to stay. The next day she asked Ximen Qing to give the nun five taels of silver. Xue, ignoring her sister in religion, Wang, arranged with eight other nuns to come to Ximen's house on the morning of the fifth. An altar was set up in the garden house. There they recited Dhāranīs from the Avatamsaka and Diamond Sutras and fulfilled the ceremonies of the Blood Vessel Sutra In the evening there was the ceremony of feeding the Hungry Ghosts. Aunt Wu, Aunt Hua, Uncle Wu, Ying Bojue and Scholar Wen were invited to eat monastic fare. The nuns chanted their liturgy, but used no musical instruments except the wooden fish and the sounding stone.

With Ying Bojue there came a servant from Huang the Fourth bringing a card of invitation. They were asked to go on the seventh to Zheng Aiyue's house. Ximen looked at the card and smiled. "I cannot go on the seventh," he said, "because I have an engagement at a birthday party on that day. But I shall be free tomorrow, if that will do. Will anybody else be there?"

"Only Li the Third and myself," Bojue said, "and four singing girls who will play selections from the *Story of the Western Pavilion*."

Ximen Qing gave orders that Huang the Fourth's messenger should be entertained, and then dismissed him. It was settled that the party should be held the following day.

"Huang the Fourth sent out some presents today, I believe," Bojue said.

"Yes," Ximen Qing said. "I didn't want to take anything, but he pressed me so hard that, in the end, I accepted a pig and some wine. I sent them with two rolls of white silk, two rolls of cloth made at the Eastern Capital, and fifty taels of silver to his Excellency Qian."

"Brother," Bojue said, "you wouldn't take their money in the first instance, and now you have given these four rolls of material to Qian. It will cost you at least thirty taels, all out of your own pocket. You treat them far too generously. Besides, you saved the lives of both father and son."

At sunset Ying Bojue went away. Ximen Qing asked him to come again the next day.

The nuns did not finish their service until the first night watch. Then they burned paper treasure chests and went away. Early next morning, Nun Wang, who had found out about the service that had been held the day before, came to complain. Xue, she said, had taken everything for herself, and she wanted her fee. Yueniang was surprised. "Why didn't you come yesterday?" she said. "I understood from Nun Xue that you had gone to a birthday party at Wang's place."

"That old whore Xue played a dirty trick on me," Nun Wang said. "She told me that the service was put off until today. Surely she hasn't taken all the money and not left me a penny?"

"I'm afraid you are too late," Yueniang said. "She had the money before the service, so that is all over and done with. But perhaps I can find a roll of cloth for you." She told Xiaoyu to give the nun a meal and to get the cloth for her.

Wang cursed and cursed. "The wicked old whore!" she cried. "She got the poor dead lady to have some scriptures printed and made a lot of money. She promised to share it with me, but every last bit of it went into her own pocket."

"That may be," said Yueniang, "but she told me that you had five taels for chanting texts to free the poor lady from her blood trouble. Why didn't you do it?"

"On the thirty-fifth day after the lady died," the nun said, "I and a number of other nuns kept chanting those texts for hour after hour in our temple."

"Why didn't you tell me so before?" Yueniang said. "I might have given you something for your pains."

Nun Wang said no more. She sat down, but could not keep still and, before very long, she went away to find Nun Xue and tell her exactly what she thought about her.

Ximen Qing came home from the office. He had hardly finished his meal when Ying Bojue arrived. Bojue was wearing a new silk hat, a gown the color of incense, and black boots with white soles. "It is past noon already," he said to Ximen Qing, "and time we were off. Huang has sent several times to summon us."

"We will take Master Wen with us," Ximen said. He told Wang Jing to go and summon the scholar, but, when the boy came back, he said Master Wen was not at home. He had gone to visit a friend.

"Don't let us wait for him," Bojue said. "These scholars are always running about visiting their friends. There is no telling when he will be back. We mustn't waste time."

Ximen Qing told Qintong to bring the yellow horse for Ying Bojue. "No," said Bojue. "None of your horses for me! When I go riding, I wobble about like the clapper of a bell. I'll go first, and you can come in a sedan chair at your leisure."

"Well, well," Ximen said, "do as you please."

Bojue went away and Ximen Qing called for his sedan chair. He ordered Qintong, Daian and four soldiers to attend him. Just as he was about to set out, Ping'an hurried in with a card. "The honorable gentleman from the Office of Works is on his way to see you," he said. "This is his card. His sedan chair will be here in a moment."

Ximen Qing ordered food to be prepared, and sent Laixing out to buy some special delicacies. An arrived, and Ximen Qing, wearing his ceremonial robes, went to meet him. An was wearing an embroidered ceremonial gown with a round collar, and a girdle with carved gold buckle. They sat down and the servants brought tea. The two men talked politely to one another.

"Sir," Ximen Qing said, "it was a great disappointment to me that I could not come in person to congratulate you upon your appointment. The other day you were good enough to write to me and send me presents on the occasion of my bereavement. I am very sorry indeed that I have not had any opportunity to show my appreciation of your kindness."

"I cannot say how much I regret that I could not come to the funeral," An said. "When I was at the Capital, I told the sad news to Zhai Yunfeng. Possibly he sent something to mark the occasion?"

"He did indeed," Ximen Qing said. "Even all that long way."

"I imagine that promotion is in store for you this year," An said.

"I am so unlettered and incompetent that I dare not hope for anything," Ximen said. "You, Sir, have been promoted, and at last you have an opportunity to display your talents. The splendid work you have done upon the river is well known."

"You flatter me," said An. "I am but a poor scholar, and, had it not been for his Eminence's kindness, I should never have been given that appointment. You can imagine what terribly hard work it has been in these days when people are so desperately poor. Then, a little while ago, his Majesty required marble. A great many of the bridges over the river had to be pulled down so that the boats could pass under them, and everywhere the Imperial vessels passed, officials and people had a very bad time. Again, the country is overrun by thieves and bandits, and things are at such a pass that even the most efficient administrator would find it impossible to do anything very much."

"Sir," said Ximen Qing, "a man of your undoubted gifts will certainly make short work of difficulties and obtain still further promotion. Does his Majesty's decree specify any particular time limit?"

"The work must be completed within three years," An said, "and the Emperor is going to appoint an envoy to make sacrifice to the God of the River."

While they were talking, Ximen Qing had ordered a table to be prepared, but An said: "It is very kind of you, but I am on my way to see Huang Taiyu."

Ximen Qing said: "You must stay long enough to take some light refreshment." A great number of delightful dainties were brought in, and wine was poured into golden cups. Meanwhile, An's attendants were entertained elsewhere. An drank three cups of wine and got up to go, promising to come again. Ximen Qing escorted him to the gate; he got into his sedan chair and was carried away.

Ximen Qing went back to the hall, took off his robes of ceremony, and put on a plain hat and a purple gown. He asked if Scholar Wen had returned. Daian said: "No, but Zheng Chun and Huang's boy, Laiding, have come for you. They have been waiting a long time." Ximen Qing went out, got into his sedan chair, and set off with his attendants for Zheng Aiyue's house.

When he arrived, the people of the house withdrew respectfully, one servant stood on either side of the door. Zheng Chun and Laiding went in to announce his coming. Ying Bojue was playing double-sixes with Li the Third, but, when they heard that Ximen Qing had come, they put aside their game. Zheng Aiyue and her sister Zheng Aixiang wore sealskin caps upon their hair, which was dressed in the style of Hangzhou. They looked as dainty as flowers. They both came out to welcome Ximen Qing and he got out of his sedan chair and went with them to the guest room. He had given orders that there should be no music upon his arrival, so the musicians did not play.

Li the Third and Huang the Fourth were the first to make reverence to him. Then came the old procuress, and lastly the two sisters. Two large chairs had been set in the place of honor and Ximen Qing and Ying Bojue sat down in them. Li, Huang, and the two girls sat opposite. When Daian asked if the sedan chair should be dismissed, Ximen said that the soldiers and the chair men might go away. He sent Qintong to see whether Master Wen had come home yet, saying that he was to be given the yellow horse to bring him more quickly.

Bojue asked what had kept Ximen so long. Ximen Qing told him about An's unexpected visit. Zheng Chun brought tea. Aixiang took a cup and offered it to Ying Bojue and Zheng Aiyue offered one to Ximen Qing. Bojue held out his hand for this one too. Then he said: "Oh, I beg your pardon. I thought it was meant for me."

"I would not pay you so much honor," said Aiyue.

"You never bother about anybody but this naughty husband of yours," Bojue said. "You ought to treat his friends as well as you treat him."

"I don't consider you are one of his friends," Aiyue said, laughing.

After tea, the four players kowtowed to Ximen Qing, and he asked their names. "When it is time for them to play," he said, "please tell them to use their drums only, no other instruments."

"Just as you wish," Huang the Fourth replied.

Thinking that Ximen might feel cold, the old procuress told Zheng Chun to pull down the blinds and put more coal upon the fire. Some of the band of ne'er-do-wells heard that Ximen Qing was at a party at Zheng Aiyue's house. They came to the door and poked their noses around the corner, but did not dare to go any farther. One of them, who knew Daian, asked the boy to speak to his master on their behalf. Daian went softly and told Ximen Qing, but the only response was a growl, and the men went off as fast as their legs would carry them.

Two tables were laid in the place of honor, one for Ximen Qing by himself, the other for Ying Bojue and Master Wen. The scholar had not yet come, but a place was left for him. Two other tables were set opposite, one for Li and Huang, the other for Zheng Aiyue and Aixiang. An excellent meal was served, and the tables were decorated with flowers in golden vases. Zheng Chun and Zheng Feng sang.

The party had just settled down when Scholar Wen arrived. He was wearing a tall hat, and a green gown. When he came in, he bowed to the company. "What makes you so late, Scholar?" Bojue said. "We have been waiting for you a long time."

"I am very sorry," Scholar Wen said, "I did not know you wanted me. I have been to see a poor old schoolfellow of mine. We talked about books and that made me late."

Huang the Fourth hastened to set a cup and chopsticks at Wen's place and the scholar sat down with Ying Bojue. Fresh dishes were brought for him. The two boys sang again. Afterwards the four singers began to play one of the acts of the *Story of the Western Pavilion*.

Then Daian came and said that Wu Yin'er had sent Wu Hui and another boy with some tea.

Zheng Aiyue's house and that of Wu Yin'er were in the same lane, only a short distance from one another. Wu Yin'er heard that Ximen Qing was taking wine at Zheng Aiyue's, and decided to send him some tea. Ximen called for the boys. They came and kowtowed. They told him their errand, then opened their tea baskets and each of them offered a cup of fragrant tea with melon seeds.

"What is Wu Yin'er doing today?" Ximen asked them.

"She is at home," the boy said.

Ximen Qing drank the tea and gave each of the boys three *qian* of silver. Then he told Daian and Wu Hui to go and fetch Wu Yin'er.

Zheng Aiyue was quick-witted enough to send Zheng Chun with them. "You go too," she told him, "and if she shows any signs of not wanting to come, tell her I won't love her any more."

"It makes me laugh," Ying Bojue said, "to think of you as partners in your particular trade."

"My good friend," Master Wen said, "you don't seem to understand. It is well known that people of the same profession and the same disposition are fondest of one another. He who finds he has more to hope from Heaven looks always Heavenward, and he whose help comes from the Earth, looks towards the Earth. It is perfectly natural that this young lady should invite another young lady to come and join her."

"Beggar Ying," said Zheng Aiyue, "you and Zheng Chun are just as much partners. You both are always to be found wherever there is anything to be had for the asking."

"My poor foolish child," Bojue said, "I was a rascal long before you were born. I was making love to your mother while you were still in her belly."

They laughed and joked till the players returned to play another act. Ximen Qing called the girl who played the part of Ying Ying and asked who she was. "Don't you recognize her, Father?" Aixiang said. "She is a niece of Han Jinchuan, and her name is Xiaochou. She is thirteen years old."

"She will turn out very well," Ximen said. "Even now, she has a most fascinating manner and she sings delightfully." He bade her serve wine to them. Huang the Fourth pressed everybody to eat and made himself most agreeable.

After a while, Wu Yin'er came. Upon her head was a white headdress with a band of pearls around it. She wore a white double-breasted silk coat with an embroidered hem. Beneath it, a light green silk skirt with a golden fringe. Her shoes were made of dark green silk. She smiled as she came and kowtowed to Ximen Qing. She made a reverence to the others. "You make me wild the very moment you come in," Ying Bojue said. "Am I the son of a concubine that you kowtow to his Lordship and only make a reverence to the rest of us? Really, you little strumpets give yourselves too many airs. If ever I am called upon to go to the court, I shan't forget this."

"Beggar Ying," Zheng Aiyue shouted at him, "you are nothing but an unmannerly scamp. In your slovenly rags, how can you expect to be taken for anyone of consequence?"

Once again the tables were set. Wu Yin'er sat down beside Ximen Qing. He noticed that she was wearing a white headdress and asked her for whom she was wearing mourning.

"Why, you must know," Wu Yin'er said, "it is for the Sixth Lady, of course."

This pleased Ximen Qing, and they talked together very fondly. Food was brought and Aiyue came to offer wine to Ximen. Wu Yin'er rose. "I must go and see my Aunt Zheng," she said. She went to the old procuress's room and made reverence to her. The old woman invited her to sit down and told a maid to bring a brazier, for she was afraid the girl might feel cold. After a while, Wu Yin'er went back to the others. Fresh courses were brought, but she took no more than a mouthful or two of soup and a piece of cake. Then she put down her chopsticks. "I understand you had a special service for my lady's last week's mind," she said to Ximen Qing.

"Yes," he said, "I must thank you for sending the tea."

"It was very poor tea I sent," Wu Yin'er said, "yet you thank me even for that. Rather should I thank you for the splendid presents you sent in return. They set my mother all in a flutter. I suggested to Zheng Aiyue and Li Guijie that they should send tea to you for my lady's last week's mind, but we did not know you were having any service."

"There were only a few nuns to chant a dirge," Ximen Qing said. "We did not invite any of our relatives and friends. I was overtired."

They drank their wine and talked. Wu Yin'er asked after Ximen's ladies. He told her they were all well.

"Father," Wu Yin'er said. "My lady died so suddenly, you must feel lonely when you go to her room. Do you still think about her?"

"Indeed I do," Ximen said. "The other day I was in my study, and, though it was broad daylight, I dreamed of her and found myself sobbing."

"I can quite understand," Wu Yin'er said. "You see, she died so suddenly."

"Now then!" Ying Bojue cried. "You two are talking about your loves while the rest of us are as dry as dry can be. If somebody doesn't come and offer me a cup of wine and sing a song, I shall go."

Li the Third and Huang the Fourth were greatly put out and hurriedly asked Aiyue and Aixiang to serve the wine. They sent for the musicians, and the two sisters, with Wu Yin'er, sat together near the fire and sang "Dallying with the Plum Blossoms." The sound of their voices was enough to break the rocks and make the clouds course more quickly. When they had finished their song, Ximen Qing said to Bojue: "You made them sing, now you must offer them wine."

"Oh, that's all right," Ying Bojue said. "They shall have all they want from me before they die. How would they like it? Shall I lie on my back with my limbs outstretched, or on my side, or shall I stand on one leg like a golden cockerel? I can do any of those things. Or perhaps they would like me to imitate a wild horse stampeding around the courtyard, a monkey offering nuts, a yellow dog piddling, or an angel pointing the way? Tell me, Brother, which way shall I deal with them?"

"I can't find words bad enough to curse you with, you dirty scoundrel!" Aixiang cried. "You are always talking nonsense."

Bojue put three cups on a plate. "Daughters," he said, "drink this from my hand. If you don't take it, I'll throw it all over you."

"I am not drinking any wine today," Aixiang said.

"Get down on your knees before my sister Aixiang and let me box your ears," Aiyue said. "Then I'll drink."

"And what do you say, Sister Wu Yin'er?" Bojue said.

"I am not very well today. I will only drink half a cup."

"If you don't go on your knees," Aiyue said, "you can implore me for a hundred days, but you won't get me to drink any."

"Uncle," Huang the Fourth said, "if you refuse to kneel down, it will show you don't know how to take a joke. Kneel down. I will ask them not to box your ears."

"I won't box his ears more than twice," Aiyue said, "that is, provided he kneels down."

"Master," Bojue said to Scholar Wen, "you see how these little strumpets carry things to extremes." There was no escape. He knelt down. Zheng Aiyue pulled up her sleeves and held out her slender hands.

"Now, you rascally beggar, will you ever be rude to me again? You must promise out loud, if you wish me to drink the wine." Bojue could not help himself. He promised that he would never be rude to her again. Zheng Aiyue slapped him twice, then drank the wine.

Bojue got up. "Well, most excellent little strumpet," he said, "are you going to drink all the wine and leave none for me?"

"Kneel down again," Aiyue said, "and I will give you another cup." She filled one and poured it down Bojue's mouth.

"Oh, you little whore," he cried, "you've spilled it all over my clothes. Let me tell you this is the very first time I've worn this suit. If you make a mess of it, I shall have to ask your sweetheart to buy me another one."

They laughed and went back to their places.

It was getting late, and lights were brought. Ximen Qing called for the dice box. He asked Scholar Wen to throw first, but Wen declined, saying it was not fitting that he should throw before his master. So Ximen Qing and Wu Yin'er played. They used twelve dice and played Catch the Red. Meanwhile, the four players sang and played. The wine was passed around again. Wu Yin'er went to Scholar Wen and played dice with him and Ying Bojue, while Aixiang went to Ximen Qing and guessed fingers with him. Then Aiyue went back to Ximen and played dice again. Wu Yin'er devoted herself to Li the Third and Huang the Fourth and offered wine to them.

Zheng Aiyue went to her room and dressed again. She put on a double-breasted coat of figured satin, a skirt of the color of the finest down, with blue spots and golden fringe. Her trousers were embroidered; her shoes scarlet, designed like a phoenix's bill. Upon her head she wore a small white sealskin cap. In the candlelight she looked more beautiful than ever. The sight of her aroused Ximen Qing's desire. He had drunk deeply, but he remembered what Li Ping'er had said to him in his dream: "When you are away from home, never drink too much." He got up and went to the inner court to wash his hands. The old procuress sent a maid with a lantern to light him, and Aiyue followed him. When he had done what he went to do, she held his hand, and they went together to her room. Moonlight was pouring through the windows, and the candles were burning brightly. The air was as warm as Spring, and sweetly perfumed. Ximen Qing took off his outer clothes and sat with her upon the bed, his legs intertwined with hers.

"Will you stay the night?" Aiyue asked.

"No, I must go home," Ximen said. "Wu Yin'er is here, and that makes me a little uncomfortable. Then I have to remember my official position. The Inspector is coming this year, and I must not run the risk of any scandal. I can only come to you in the daytime." He thanked her for the cakes she had sent. "But when I saw them," he said, "I could not help feeling sad. The Sixth Lady, when she was alive, was the only person who ever made them for me. Now she is dead, there is no one in my house who can do it."

"They are not hard to make, if you are careful about the right proportions," Aiyue said. "The melon seeds I sent you, I cracked with my own teeth. But I hear Beggar Ying ate them all."

"He did. The rascal took two handfuls and left me hardly any."

"Lucky for him," Aiyue said. "I might have sent them especially for him! Thank you very much for the coated plums. My mother took some and found them very good indeed. When she has a coughing fit, she coughs all through the night and upsets everybody in the house. But one of those coated plums in the mouth keeps her throat moist. My sister and I did not take many of them. We gave the jar to my mother because we thought it was good for her to take them morning and night."

"Tomorrow, I will send another jar for yourselves," Ximen promised.

"Have you been to see Li Guijie lately?" the girl asked.

"I have not seen her since the funeral."

"Did she send any tea for the fifth week's mind?"

"Yes, Li Ming brought it for her."

"I will tell you something," Aiyue said, "if you promise to keep it secret."

Ximen Qing asked what it was, but Aiyue thought for a while and then said she would not tell him. "If I do," she said, "it will look as though I talk about the other girls behind their backs."

Ximen put his arms around her. "Little oily mouth, tell me what you were going to say. I won't say a word to anybody."

They were talking when Ying Bojue burst into the room. "Ah, you good people! So you leave us behind and come here to talk secrets to one another?"

"Why do you always poke your nose into other people's business?" Aiyue said. "How dare you rush in here and frighten me like that?"

"You dog!" Ximen said. "Go back to the front court at once. What do you mean by leaving Master Wen and Wu Yin'er to come and see what we're about?"

Bojue sat down on the bed. "Let me kiss your arm," he said to Aiyue, "then I'll go away and leave you to amuse yourselves." He drew the girl's arm from her sleeve and praised it. "My child," he said, "one has only to see these hands of yours to realize that Heaven intended you for the life you lead."

"Oh, you rascal," Aiyue cried, "no words are bad enough for you."

Bojue took her hand and bit it. She cried out and cursed him. "Oh, vile Beggar Ying, you never stop playing these horrible tricks of yours." Then she said to Taohua, her maid: "Go after him and, when he is once outside the door, bolt it."

Then Aiyue told Ximen Qing all about Li Guijie and young master Wang. "Sun Guazui," she said, "Pockmarked Zhu, Little Zhang and some others went with young Master Wang to Guijie's place. He had given up Qi Xiang'er and taken on with Yuzhi, at the Qin's place. At both places, he has spent a great deal of money and, recently, he had to pawn his fur coat for thirty taels. He stole a pair of his mother's gold bracelets and gave them to Guijie for a month's enjoyment of her favors."

"The wicked little whore!" Ximen Qing said. "I told her to have nothing to do with that young scamp. She promised me faithfully she would give him up, and swore she would never see him again. She has deceived me."

"Father, don't be annoyed," Aiyue said. "I will tell you a way to get even with young master Wang. You will have no more reason to be angry."

Ximen Qing took her on his knees. "What is your idea?" he said. "Tell me."

"I will tell you if you promise not to say a word to anybody else, not even Beggar Ying. I don't want it to get about."

"I am not a fool," Ximen said. "Why should I mention it to anyone?"

"Master Wang's mother, Lady Lin, is not yet forty years old," Aiyue said. "She is a very fascinating woman. She pencils her eyebrows, paints her face, and gets herself up as cleverly as a fox. Her son spends all his time at the bawdy house and she receives gentlemen at home. She pretends to go to the nunnery, but, as a matter of fact, it is old woman Wen she really goes to see. That old woman arranges everything for her. I understand she is very expert in the arts of love. Now this is what I have to say. If you would like to make her acquaintance, it ought not to be very difficult. Then there is the young man's wife. She is about nineteen years old, and a niece of Grand Marshal Huang of the Eastern Capital. She is as pretty as a picture. She can play backgammon and chess, but she might as well be a widow, for her husband, young Wang, never spends any time with her. She is a very disappointed woman and more than twice has tried to hang herself. Somebody cut her down. If you can only get hold of the mother, you will not have much difficulty in making sure of the daughter."

Ximen Qing was delighted with the idea. He put his arms around Aiyue's neck. "How do you come to know all this, my child?" he said.

Aiyue often went to Wang's house herself, but she did not think fit to say so to Ximen Qing. "One of my friends told me," she said, "and once old woman Wen introduced me to her."

"Who was the man who visited her?" Ximen asked. "Was it Zhang the Second, the nephew of that wealthy Master Zhang of the High Street?"

"No," Aiyue said, "not that ugly fellow. His face is covered with pockmarks, and his eyes are all screwed up. He is not good-looking enough for an adventure of this sort. Nobody but the Jiang girls would take him on."

"Well, I can't guess who the man is," Ximen Qing said.

"I will tell you," Aiyue said. "He is a Southerner, the man who made a woman of me. He comes here on business twice a year, but he only stays here one or two nights. He is too fond of poaching."

Ximen was thrilled. "My child," he said, "you seem to be very fond of me, and I am going to give you thirty taels of silver every month. You can give the money to your mother and then it will not be necessary for you to have any other visitors. I will come and see you whenever I am free."

"Why so much as thirty or twenty taels, Father? A few taels for my mother will be enough. I shall be glad not to have to receive everybody who comes, and to belong to you alone."

"Most certainly I shall give you thirty taels," Ximen said. "Say no more about it."

They began to sport upon the bed. It was piled deep with coverlets. "Won't you take off your clothes, Father?" Aiyue asked.

"I am afraid I must keep my clothes on," Ximen Qing said. "They will be out of patience waiting for us." He pulled up the pillow for her. She took down her trousers and stretched herself upon her back. Ximen Qing lifted her dainty feet over his shoulders, then unloosed his blue silk trousers and put the clasp on his penis. The heart of the flower lay sweetly folded before him; the tender willow-like waist quivered.

> This is a flower so delicate
> It cannot endure violence.
> The wind of Spring blows over it unceasingly
> And when it reaches the flower's heart
> Still seems unsatisfied.
> There are no limits to their love.
> Softly she calls him her precious boy.
> There are no words can tell
> The happiness of this night of Spring.

For a long time their love followed its course to their great delight. Ximen Qing breathed heavily, and she made strange little noises without ceasing, her hair spread out over the pillow. "My love," she murmured, "do not be so furious." Then their satisfaction reached its height, and sperm flowed from him in a stream. The rain ceased, and the clouds dispersed. They rose, dressed themselves, and washed their hands. Then, hand in hand, they went back to the hall.

Wu Yin'er, Aixiang, Scholar Wen and Ying Bojue were throwing dice and guessing fingers, all the time encouraging one another to drink, and being very merry together. When Ximen Qing came in, they rose and begged him to sit down. "A nice thing!" Bojue said. "You leave us here all this time and then come to have some wine. To steady your head, I suppose."

"We have been talking," Ximen Qing said.

"Talking indeed!" Bojue said. "I know the sort of secrets you have to tell one another." He took a large cup of wine already warmed, and they invited Ximen to drink. The four players sang.

Then Daian came and said: "The sedan chair is here." Ximen Qing pursed his lips as a sign that he was ready and Daian went out to bid the soldiers light their lanterns. As Ximen had made clear his intention not to stay any longer, everyone stood up and drank with him. He ordered the four players to sing "When First We Met, Shyness Restrained Us." Then Xiaochou took her lute and sang.

When the song was done, Wu Yin'er offered Ximen Qing a cup of wine while Aixiang and Aiyue offered wine to Ying Bojue and Scholar Wen. Li and Huang drank too. The four players sang again. When the cup had been emptied, they urged each other to drink again and the wine passed around twice more. The singers sang two more songs, and the wine and the music were finished at the same time.

Then Ximen Qing made ready to go. He told Daian to give packets of silver, some large, some small, to all who had waited on him. There were three *qian* of silver for each of the four players, five for the cook, and three for Wu Hui, Zheng Chun, and Zheng Feng. There were two *qian* for all the other servants, except Zheng Aiyue's maid, Taohua, who was given three. They kowtowed to express their thanks. Huang the Fourth did not wish them to accept these presents yet. "Uncle Ying," he said to Bojue, "won't you say something to his Lordship? It is still early, and he must sit down, just to show that he enjoys our entertainment." He turned to Aiyue. "Sister, you must help me to persuade him to stay."

"I have tried already," Aiyue said, "but he will not."

"I shall be very busy tomorrow, and I must go," Ximen Qing said. He bowed to Huang the Fourth. "I have had a very pleasant time," he said.

"Indeed I fear you have been starved," Huang the Fourth said, "and that is why you won't stay. It seems obvious that we have entertained you very poorly."

The three girls kowtowed. "When you get home," they said, "please give our humble duty to the Great Lady and the others. When we are free, we will come to see them."

"Yes, do," Ximen said. "Come any time and spend the day."

Lanterns were brought, and Ximen Qing went down the steps. Old woman Zheng came to make a reverence to him. "My lord," she said, "why must you go in such a hurry? I fear our cooking cannot have pleased you. There is another course to come yet."

"I have had everything I wanted," Ximen said. "Unfortunately, I have to get up very early in the morning to go and attend to some important business at the office. Brother Ying has nothing to do: ask him to stay."

Ying Bojue was going away with Ximen Qing, but Huang the Fourth stopped him. "If you go too, Uncle," he said, "it will be the last straw."

"Don't keep me," Bojue said. "Try Scholar Wen. If you can persuade him to stay, I shall believe you are a hero."

Scholar Wen tried to slip away, but Huang the Fourth's boy and Laian caught him by the waist and held him. Ximen Qing reached the gate. He asked Qintong whether he had brought anything for Scholar Wen to ride. "There's a donkey here," Qintong said. "Huatong is in charge of it."

Ximen called out to Scholar Wen: "There is an animal here for you to ride. You and Brother Ying stay. I must go now." They all went with him to the gate. Zheng Aiyue was holding his hand. She gave it a squeeze. "Remember what I have told you," she said, "but keep it to yourself." She bade Zheng Chun go with Ximen to his house. Ximen got into his sedan chair and went away.

Outside the gate, Wu Yin'er said good-bye to everybody, and was going home with Wu Hui when Zheng Aiyue said: "If you see Guijie, don't say a word about this." Then they went back to their tables; the fire was replenished, and more wine poured out. With music, songs and wine, they passed the time very pleasantly, and the party did not break up until the third night watch. The entertainment cost Huang the Fourth about ten taels of silver.

Ximen Qing, with two soldiers carrying lanterns, reached home in his sedan chair, dismissed Zheng Chun, and went to bed.

The next day, Magistrate Xia sent a servant to ask Ximen Qing to go early to the office. There was a thief to be tried. He went, heard the case and did not return until midday. When he had finished dinner, Shen Ding came with a young man named Liu Bao, whom Uncle Shen introduced as a cook for the silk shop. Ximen Qing agreed to engage him and went to the study to get a return card to give to Shen Ding. There he found Daian and asked him what time Scholar Wen had come back the night before.

"I was in the shop," Daian said, "and had been in bed a long time before I heard Qintong knocking at the door of the house opposite. I think it must have been the third night watch. This morning, I asked him if he had been drunk. 'No,' he said, 'but Uncle Ying was, and he was sick all over the floor. Then Zheng Aiyue thought it was getting very late, and she sent Zheng Chun home with him.'" This made Ximen Qing laugh. He called the boy closer to him.

"You remember old woman Wen, who arranged my daughter's marriage. If you know where she lives, go and tell her I want her to come and see me at the house across the road."

"I don't know where she lives," Daian said, "but I will ask Brother-in-law."

"Yes, make sure, and then go right away," Ximen said.

Daian went to the shop and asked Chen Jingji where the old woman lived.

"What do you want with her?" Jingji said. "Go along East Street towards the south. Turn to the left when you have passed the bridge. You will find yourself on the Wangs' estate. In the middle of it is a guardhouse, and, close by, a small stone bridge. Cross the bridge and you will come to a lane that passes a nunnery. Go up there and the third house you come to will be a bean curd shop. A little farther along is a house with red doors. That is the place. Shout: 'Old Mother Wen,' and she will come out to you."

"It sounds like a witch directing a tinker," Daian said. "What a rigmarole! Tell me again. I shall never remember all that."

Jingji told him again.

"A fine walk!" Daian said. "I must have a horse." He went and got the big white horse, mounted it, whipped it up, and went off at a gallop. He followed all his instructions until he came to the guardhouse near the ruined stone bridge, and saw the red walls of the nunnery. He went up the lane until he reached a house with a sign to show that bean curd was sold there. Outside was an old woman drying horse dung.

"Does an old woman named Wen live about here?" Daian asked her.

"Yes," the old woman said. "The next house on the other side."

Daian went on and came to a house with red doors. He jumped down from his horse and knocked at the door with his whip. "Is Sister Wen at home?"

Wen Tang, the old woman's son, opened the door and asked Daian what he wanted.

"I have come from his Lordship Ximen to ask Madam Wen to go and see him at once," Daian said.

As soon as Wen Tang heard this, he asked Daian to go in. The boy tied up his horse and went into the house. Lucky papers were hanging up, and a number of people were engaged in reckoning up the amount of offerings. He waited some time, then a cup of tea was brought to him. "My mother is not at home," Wen Tang said, "but as soon as she comes back I will tell her, and she will come to see his Lordship tomorrow morning."

"If she is not at home," Daian said, "what is her donkey doing here?" He stood up and went to the inner court. Old Woman Wen was drinking tea with several other old women. She had no time to hide.

"Surely this is Sister Wen," Daian said. "Why was I told you were not at home?"

The old woman laughed and made a reverence. "Brother," she said, "would you mind going back and telling his Lordship that I have a party? I don't know what he wants, but I will come to see him tomorrow morning."

"I don't know what he wants you for," Daian said. "I only know he does want you. What an out-of-the-way hole of a place you live in. Getting here has made me quite exhausted."

"For the last few years," old woman Wen said, "when your master has bought any maids or arranged any marriages, he has always gone to Feng or Xue or Wang. He has ignored me completely. Why does he suddenly want me now? It is as though one saw beans burst before the pan is put on the fire. Perhaps, now that his Sixth Lady is dead, he wishes me to find him another lady to take her place?"

"I know nothing about that," Daian said. "You will find out when you see him."

"Well, Brother, sit down for a while and, when my guests go away, I'll go with you."

"My master wishes you to go at once," Daian said. "He told me so repeatedly. He is waiting to talk to you before he goes out."

"Stay until I've given you something to eat, then we'll start together."

"I don't want anything to eat."

Old woman Wen asked if Ximen's daughter had any children. Daian told her she had not. Then the old woman gave him some cakes and went to change her clothes. "You go first on your horse," she said, "and I'll follow on foot."

"Your donkey is here," Daian said. "Why don't you ride it?"

"My donkey?" said the old woman. "That donkey belongs to my neighbors of the bean curd shop. They leave it here to graze, and you think it is mine."

"But you used to have a donkey," the boy said.

"Yes, but sometime ago one of my young women hanged herself. I had to sell my old house to pay off her people, so you can hardly expect me to have kept the donkey."

"The house didn't matter very much," Daian said, "but I'm surprised you parted with the donkey. I should have thought you would have kept him with you day and night. If I'm not mistaken, that donkey was splendidly finished."

Old woman Wen laughed merrily. "Oh, you young monkey!" she cried, "I'm afraid you'll come to a bad end. I was taking you seriously. Well, it's some years since I saw you last and a fine clever-spoken lad you've become. You'll have to come to me when you think of finding a wife."

"My horse goes at a good pace, and you walk slowly. If you don't come soon, my master will be in a fine temper. Come on, up you get behind me."

"You young rascal," the old woman said, "I'm not your shadow. What do you think people in the street will say if they see me riding behind you?"

"Then hire this donkey. We will pay them when you get there."

"That sounds better," said the old woman. She told her son Wen Tang to saddle the donkey and put a pair of blinkers on him. Then she climbed on to his back and went with Daian to Ximen Qing.

CHAPTER 69
Lady Lin

When Daian and old woman Wen reached the house, Ping'an told them that Ximen Qing was at the shop across the road. Daian went to see him. He was in the study with Scholar Wen but, as soon as Daian came in, he went into another small room.

"Old woman Wen awaits your pleasure," Daian said to him. Ximen Qing bade the boy bring her in. The old woman raised the lattice quietly and came in. She kowtowed to him.

"Sister Wen," Ximen said, "it is a very long time since I saw you last."

"Yes," the old woman said. "I have been very busy."

"Where are you living now?" Ximen asked her.

"Unfortunately," the old woman said, "I had a lawsuit and was compelled to sell my old house. I am living now on the Wangs' estate, at the south end of the street."

"Stand up," Ximen said, "I have something to say to you." The old woman got up, and Ximen sent the boys out. Ping'an and Huatong went to the corner door, but Daian hid himself behind a curtain to listen.

"You frequently call to see ladies of quality," Ximen said. "Tell me, who are they?"

"The Princely family in the High Street, Major Zhou's, Master Qiao's, Master Chang's and Magistrate Xia's. I see them constantly."

"Do you happen to know the lady at General Wang's place?"

"She is one of my most regular patrons. The lady herself and her daughter-in-law are always buying flowers from me."

"If you know them well, I should like you to do something for me," Ximen said. He took up a piece of silver weighing five taels and gave it to her. "If you devise a scheme for getting the lady to your place, so that I can meet her only once, there will be more for you."

Old woman Wen laughed. "Who told you about her?" she said. "How did you come to hear of them?"

"There is a common saying," Ximen answered, "that as trees have their shadows, so people have their names. Why shouldn't I know of them?"

"The Lady is thirty-five years old," old woman Wen said, "and she is all you could desire. She is charming and intelligent, and she looks not a day over thirty. If she does carry on like this occasionally, she does so only in the strictest secrecy. Generally, when she goes out, she is accompanied by a train of servants. She goes wherever she has to go and comes straight back. Her son is now grown up, so, of course, she does not wish people to talk about her. Probably the stories you have heard are untrue. She has, indeed, a great big house and, when her son is not at home, it is possible a gentleman may sometimes come to visit her, but nobody ever hears about it. It would be quite impossible for her to come to my place. There are no conveniences there. Even if you offered me more money, I dare not take it. I would rather go and tell her what you have said to me."

"If you will not take my money, it means you will do nothing for me, and I shall be very much offended. Take it, and if this little business comes off, you shall have some silken clothes."

"You are so wealthy that that side of the affair does not trouble me," the old woman said. "I shall consider myself lucky if you so much as look my way." She knelt down and took the money. "I will go and speak to the lady. When I come back, I will tell you what she says."

"You must take every pains," Ximen said. "I shall expect you here. I won't send a boy for you."

"Very well," the old woman said. "Tomorrow perhaps, or maybe the day after. As soon as I am in a position to say anything, I will come and see you."

She went out. Daian came up and spoke to her. "Sister Wen," he said, "one tael is all I ask from you. It was I who told you to come, and you mustn't keep everything for yourself."

"You little monkey," old woman Wen said. "When we hear someone sifting grain on the other side of a wall, we have no means of telling whether the results are good or bad. It is just the same with this business." She went out, mounted the donkey, and her son led it away.

Ximen Qing and Scholar Wen chatted together for a while, then Magistrate Xia came. Ximen put on his hat and robes and went with Xia to see the Sub-Prefect Luo, whose name was Luo Wanxiang. It was late when he returned.

Old woman Wen was very pleased with the five taels she had received from Ximen Qing. In the afternoon when the tea party at her house was over, she went to call upon Lady Lin. She made a reverence to the lady, who asked why it was so long since she had called. Old woman Wen said she had been having a tea party and that she had been busy making preparations to go on a pilgrimage in the twelfth month.

"Why not send your son instead?" Lady Lin said.

"If I find I can't go, I shall have to send Wen Tang," the old woman said.

"When the time comes, I will give you some money for him."

The old woman thanked her. Lady Lin invited her to sit near the fire. The maid brought tea.

"Is the young master in?" old woman Wen asked, while she was drinking her tea.

"No," Lady Lin said, "he has not been home for two nights. He is always going with some villain or other to spend his nights in the haunts of vice. He seems to care nothing for his wife, who is an exquisite creature, and I don't know what can be done about it."

"Where is the young mistress?" the old woman said.

"She is in her room," Lady Lin said.

When the old woman was sure they were alone, she said: "I don't think you need worry any longer, Lady. I think I know a way to dispose of these bad companions, and get the young master back to his home, so that he never sets foot in a brothel again. But I dare not suggest it to you without your leave."

"I always listen to any suggestions you make," Lady Lin said. "If you have anything to say, speak out."

"His Lordship Ximen, who lives near the Town Hall," the old woman began, "is now an assistant magistrate and a military officer. He lends money to all the officials, and has four or five shops where he sells silks and medicines, cloth and thread. He has boats upon the river going up and down for his purchases. He buys salt from Yangzhou and incense and candles from Dongpingfu. Dozens of clerks are employed in his service. He is a ward of the Imperial Tutor Cai in the Eastern Capital, and a subordinate of Grand Marshal Zhu. He and Zhai, the Comptroller of the Imperial Tutor's household, are upon a footing of kinship. He is on friendly terms with the highest officers of the Province, not to mention their underlings. He has acre upon acre of property and so much rice that it rots in his barns. His wife, by his second marriage, is a daughter of Captain Wu. He has five or six ladies and scores of singing boys and dancing girls. There is continual feasting in his house. He is about thirty-one or thirty-two, in the very prime of life. He is tall and handsome, and he takes medicine to strengthen his weapon. In matters of love, none is more skilled than he. He plays backgammon and chess, and is an expert ballplayer. He is well up in the philosophers and every kind of amusement. He profits by everything he sees. Indeed, so clever a man can only be compared to a fine piece of jade or a lump of pure gold.

"Now, Lady, he has heard that your family has held high rank for generations, and he knows that the young master has been in the military academy. He would very much like to make your acquaintance. Of course, he cannot do that without a preliminary meeting. The other day he was given to understand that your birthday is not far distant. He would like to be allowed to come in a friendly way to celebrate the occasion. He spoke to me about the matter. I said to him: 'I can quite see that you don't feel you can call without an introduction of some sort. Let me go and speak to the lady and ask her leave.' Lady, I don't regard this simply as a question of becoming friendly with him. You will be able to ask him to help you to get rid of the young master's bad companions. I do not think a man of his sort will be in any way damaging to the good fame of your house."

Lady Lin was already persuaded, but she said to the old woman: "We have never met. How can we suddenly pick up an acquaintance?"

"That need not trouble you," the old woman said. "I will go to him and say that you would be glad of his help about an accusation you propose to send to the courts against these rascals, and that you would be very much obliged if he would come and talk the matter over with you."

Lady Lin was satisfied, and it was arranged that she should expect him two days later, in the evening.

At dinnertime next day, the old woman came to see Ximen Qing. He was in his study when Daian came to tell him that she had come. He went to the inner room and pulled down the lattice. The old woman came and kowtowed to him. Daian, who knew well enough what was afoot, went out. Old woman Wen told Ximen she had succeeded in persuading Lady Lin. She had spoken highly of him, she said, explained his position, praised his generosity and amiability, spoken of his gay and lively nature. "She believed what I told her," the old woman said, "and she is willing to meet you tomorrow night. Her son will not be at home. She will offer you a meal and make a show of discussing legal matters with you."

Ximen Qing was delighted. He told Daian to get two rolls of fine silk for the old woman.

"When you go tomorrow," the old woman said, "don't be too early. Go at night, when it is quiet in the streets, and enter the house by the back door. Close to the back door is a house belonging to a woman called Duan. I shall be waiting there for you. Knock at the door, and I will come out and take you to Lady Lin's house. We shall have to be careful that none of the neighbors see us."

"I understand," Ximen Qing said. "Go to Madam Duan's and wait there for me. Don't go away. I shall certainly not be late."

Old woman Wen went back to tell Lady Lin the result of her conversation with Ximen.

That night, Ximen Qing went to Li Jiao'er's room. He was impatient for the next day and was sparing in his attentions. When the day came, he

put on a white hat and went with Ying Bojue to Xie Xida's place to celebrate his birthday. Two singing girls were there. He drank only a few cups
of wine and, as soon as it was dark, escaped from the party and mounted
his horse. Daian and Qintong followed him. It was the nineteenth day
of the month, and the moon was full. He set eyeshades on his eyes and
turned into the road that led from the main street to Lady Lin's backdoor.
It was late, and the street was quiet. Before he came to the door, he pulled
up his horse and bade Daian knock at Madam Duan's door. This house
belonged to Lady Lin. Old woman Wen had introduced Madam Duan to
Lady Lin as a kind of guard for the back door and, whenever any business
of this sort was to be done, the back door was always the place chosen as
the rendezvous.

Old woman Wen heard the knocking and came to the door at once.
She waited until Ximen Qing had dismounted and taken off his eyeshades.
She told Qintong to wait with the horse beneath the eaves of a house close
by. Daian went to wait in Madam Duan's house. Then the old woman
took Ximen through the back door and fastened it securely behind them.
They went through a passage that led to a courtyard. On one side were
the five rooms that formed Lady Lin's apartments. The small door that
led to them was closed. Old women Wen knocked softly. The sound was
delightful to Ximen's ears. A maid came and opened the door. The old
woman took Ximen Qing to the hall. When the screen was pulled aside,
he saw that the place was brightly lit up by lamps and candles. In the place
of honor was a portrait of Wang Jingchong, Commander-in-Chief of Taiyuan, and Duke of Fenyang. He wore a red dragon embroidered gown,
with a jade girdle, and sat upon a great chair covered with a tiger skin,
reading a book upon the art of war. Had his beard been longer, he would
have looked like the God of War himself. Above the portrait was an inscription: "The Hall of Virtue and Righteousness." There were two scrolls
written in the Li style, of which one read: "The Tradition of Integrity in
this House stands ever firm as the pine tree and the bamboo." The other
bore the legend: "His services to his country were many as the stars and
glorious as the mountains."

Ximen Qing was looking at them when he heard a tinkling of the bells
upon the door. Old woman Wen brought him a cup of tea. "Please ask the
lady to come and see me," he said.

"Pray, Sir," the old woman said, "drink your tea. I have told her ladyship that you are here."

Lady Lin had hidden herself behind the door and was secretly taking
stock of him. She found him tall and good-looking. He was wearing a
white silk hat with sable ear covers, a purple woolen gown, and a pair of

black shoes with white soles. She liked the looks of him. She quietly summoned old woman Wen and asked for whom he was wearing the white hat.

"His Sixth Lady died in the ninth month," the old woman said, "but though she is no more, he has still as many ladies as there are fingers on his hand. He is like a quail just let out from his cage, smart at the attack."

Lady Lin was more pleased than ever. Old woman Wen urged her to come and see Ximen, but she said it would embarrass her and she would rather he came to her room. The old woman went back to Ximen Qing and said: "The Lady would like you to go to her." She pulled aside the screen and he went in.

There were red hangings about Lady Lin's room and the floor was covered with carpets and rugs. There was a delightful odor of orchids and perfume, and the atmosphere was as balmy as that of Spring. The bed had embroidered curtains. The screens shone like the moon. Lady Lin wore a headdress of gold thread and jade, a full gown of white silk, and a coat of figured satin, with a gold design upon an incense-colored background. Her skirt was of the scarlet satin worn by ladies of the court, and her white silk shoes were high heeled. She was, indeed, an exquisite woman of the embroidered chamber, a goddess who, as it were, made sacrifice of her body for the love of men.

Ximen Qing bowed. "Lady," he said, "will you not sit in the place that is your due, that I may make reverence to you?"

"My lord," she said, "I pray you, do not."

Ximen Qing kowtowed to her twice, and she returned his greeting. Then he sat down on a chair and she sat on the edge of a small couch shaped like a comb. She was on the other side from him, but not immediately facing him.

Old woman Wen saw that the door to the courtyard was safely fastened. The servants withdrew. The door that led to young master Wang's apartments was secured. A maid brought tea.

"The lady," old woman Wen said, "has heard of your name and your position as an officer of the law. She would be very glad to know if you are disposed to help her."

"Pray tell me what I can do," Ximen said.

Lady Lin spoke for herself. "In truth," she said, "though we have inherited a title, I have not been well off since my husband's death. My son was brought up without the discipline that would have been good for him, and even now he has not passed his examination. He has studied at the military academy, but I fear his education has been neglected. Then, too, he has fallen into the clutches of some very objectionable fellows. They have carried him off to places of ill-fame, and, over and over again, he has brought my family to the verge of ruin. There are times when I think of going to the courts to make accusation against him, but I feel I cannot bring shame upon my dead husband. I have asked you to come, and, since I am telling you the truth, it is the same as though I actually went to the court. I shall esteem it a great favor if you will rid my son of these evil companions and so enable him to make a fresh start. If he will only change his present mood and attend to his studies, he will become a worthy successor to a worthy family. If you can bring this about, I shall be eternally grateful and try to make you a suitable return."

"Most estimable lady," Ximen Qing said, "please do not speak of reward. For generations your family has been one of exalted rank. Your son is at the military academy now, and, of course, he ought to think of his future and the title that will come down to him. Unfortunately, he has got mixed up with a pack of rascals and is giving himself up to wine and undesirable young women. It is only because he is young. Now that you have issued your commands, I will go to the office and have the rascals punished. You shall have no further trouble."

Lady Lin stood up and made a reverence. "I hope to be allowed to make you a present," she said.

"Please don't mention it," Ximen said. "We are such good friends."

As they talked, they exchanged glances that were more than affectionate. Old woman Wen set the table and put wine upon it. Ximen Qing made a show of reluctance to accept such an honor. "This is my first visit," he said. "I have come empty-handed. How can I accept such kindness at your hands?"

"Indeed," Lady Lin said, "it is I who should apologize for being taken unawares and having nothing more than this poor wine to offer you. I can only hope that it will serve to keep out the cold."

The maid poured out the wine. Lady Lin rose to offer him a cup. He stood up too and said: "I should be the first to offer wine."

"Today, perhaps," old woman Wen said, "you may be dispensed from offering wine to her Ladyship. The fifteenth day of the eleventh month is her birthday and, I suppose, you will come to congratulate her."

"Why didn't you tell me so before?" Ximen said. "Why, this is the ninth. There are only six days left. Of course I shall come to pay my respects."

Lady Lin smiled. "You are too kind," she said.

Sixteen bowls of delightful food were brought. Candles in silver candlesticks burned brightly on the table; a golden brazier on the floor gave forth splendid heat. They offered wine to one another, played games, and guessed fingers. Their smiles and merriment were an omen of clouds and rain, and, as we know, wine never fails to arouse the passions. The water clock dripped and dripped; the moon cast its beams upon the window. Their minds were obsessed by the same idea. Old woman Wen had withdrawn, and, though they called her several times, she made no answer. Seeing that they were alone, Ximen Qing gradually moved his chair nearer and nearer to her; his words became more and more affectionate. He pressed her hands, touched her arm, drew closer. Then he put his arms about her neck. She smiled but did not repulse him. She opened her red lips and he slipped his tongue into her mouth. They kissed, and smiled still more lovingly.

Lady Lin got up and fastened the door. She took off her long gown and some of her ornaments. Gently, she pulled aside the bed curtains and spread the embroidered coverlets. The pillows were set at one end of the bed. There was a delightful odor of perfume. Their perfect bodies met in an embrace; he felt the sweetness of her breasts.

Ximen Qing had been warned of the woman's skill in matters of love, and had brought his instruments with him. With the secret drug to encourage him, his passion blazed like fire. Their outstretched limbs quivered with a madness like that of butterflies and bees.

Ximen spent himself to the utmost to satisfy the woman, and they went on till it was very late. Lady Lin's hair was disordered; her pins had fallen out of place. She seemed like a weary flower, a tired willow. They lay down quietly together.

When they were up again and had put on their clothes, Lady Lin snuffed the candles and unlocked the door. She dressed herself before a mirror and told a maid to bring water for them to wash their hands. Again they pressed each other to drink. Ximen Qing drank three cups and got up to leave. Lady Lin could not persuade him to stay. She asked him to visit her again. Ximen Qing bowed and promised to come. She went with him as far as the door into the courtyard. Old woman Wen opened the back door and told Daian and Qintong to bring their master's horse.

The watchman was already beating his rounds from street to street. It was very still and the sky was white with frost. Ximen Qing went home.

The next day, when he had gone through his ordinary business at the office, he summoned two police runners and ordered them to find out who had been going about with Wang the Third, and the places to which they resorted. "Report to me," he said, "when you have made inquiries." He explained this to his colleague Xia by saying that "Young Wang the Third appears to be neglecting his studies. Yesterday his mother sent a man to me to say that it is not really his fault, but that he has got into the clutches of a pack of rascals. Unless we make an example of them, I'm afraid they will be the ruin of this scion of a famous house."

"You are right. We will deal with them as they deserve," said Xia.

The runners, armed with Ximen Qing's order, went around to find out the names and, in the afternoon, they came to his house and made their report. Ximen Qing examined their list. Upon it were the names of Sun Guazui, Zhu Shinian, Little Zhang, Nie Yue, Xiang the Third, Yu Kuan and Mohammedan Bai. The girls were Li Guijie and Qin Yuzhi.

Ximen Qing took up a brush and crossed out the names of the two girls and of Sun Guazui and Zhu Shinian. Then he gave orders that all the others should be arrested and brought before him the following day.

In the evening, the runners discovered Wang the Third and the others drinking and playing ball at Li Guijie's house. They surrounded the house, and, in the middle of the night, raided it. They arrested Little Zhang, Nie Yue, Yu Kuan, Mohammedan Bai and Xiang the Third. Sun Guazui and Zhu Shinian crawled away to the back of the house, and Wang the Third crept beneath Guijie's bed. Guijie and the others were terrified and did not know what to do. They came out to ask what the raid meant, but Wang the Third, in his hiding place, dared not move an inch. The old procuress imagined that the runners must have come again at the orders of some authority in the Capital. Before dawn, she made Li Ming dress and take Wang the Third home.

The police took Little Zhang and the others and threw them into jail for the night. The next day, when Ximen Qing arrived at the office, he went with Magistrate Xia to the hall of audience. The underlings were all in attendance. The prisoners were dragged forward. Each of them was placed in the screws and then beaten twenty times. Their skin was torn, their flesh bruised, and blood streamed from them. There was such a sound of beating that it reached the skies, and the noise of their groanings shook the earth.

"You outrageous scoundrels!" Ximen Qing cried. "You are always leading astray young men of good family and taking them to the bawdy house. I ought to give you most severe punishment, but, for this once, I am being kind to you and letting you off with a few stripes. If ever you come into my hands again, I will have you put in the cangue and make a show of you outside the Town Hall." He bade the officials kick them out, and they ran for their lives.

Having settled this matter, Ximen Qing and Xia retired to a room to drink tea.

"Yesterday," Xia said, "I had a letter from my kinsman, Grand Secretary Cui, in which he says that a report upon our work has reached the capital, but, as yet, its consequences are unknown. I think we might send a man to Huaiqingfu to see whether any news is to be had from Lin

Cangfeng, our colleague there."

Ximen Qing agreed. They summoned a man and said to him: "Here are five *qian* of silver. Take them and go to Huaiqingfu and call upon Captain Lin. Take our cards and find out what you can about the report and when we are going to know what has happened in regard to it." The man took the silver and the cards, went to his room to get his things ready, called for a horse, and started on his journey. Ximen Qing and Magistrate Xia went home.

When Little Zhang and his friends escaped from the court, they could not imagine why they had, so unexpectedly, got into trouble. One blamed another, but they found it impossible to decide who had given them away.

"I think somebody in the Eastern Capital is responsible," Little Zhang said.

"No," said Mohammedan Bai, "if it had been that, we should not have got off so easily."

There is an old saying: Goldsmiths are the greatest thieves, and singing girls can never be outdone in cunning. So it was with these rascals. They were as artful as could be. Nie Yue hit upon the solution.

"I know what it is," he said. "Ximen Qing is anxious to put young Master Wang in his place. You see, he was playing with Ximen's own girl. When there is a fight between a dragon and a tiger, the little wolves come off badly."

"It sounds likely," Little Zhang said, "and we come off the worst. Sun Guazui and Zhu Shinian were there with us, but we were the only ones who got into trouble."

"Don't be silly!" Yu Kuan said, "you know they are friends of Ximen. If he had arrested them, they would have been on their knees and he would have been sitting there, and it would not have been very pleasant for him."

"Why weren't the girls taken?" Little Zhang said.

"He is very fond of both of them," Nie Yue said. "Guijie is his own girl, and he would never think of arresting her. It's no use complaining. Put the blame on our bad luck. It's that which has brought us to this pass. By the way, I noticed that Magistrate Xia never spoke a word. That is how I know this is one of Ximen's tricks, and his alone. Let us go to Guijie's house and see what Wang the Third has to say. We can't have our backs broken for nothing. If we don't get some money out of him, the girls will think we're fools."

They went to Guijie's house. The door was closed as though it were of iron. They knocked for a long time, and, at last, a maid came and asked who was there. She did not open the door.

"We have come to see Master Wang," Little Zhang said.

"He is not here," the maid said. "He went home last night. There is nobody here. I can't let you in."

They went to Wang's house and marched into the parlor. Wang the Third heard that they had come and hid himself in his own room, terrified. After a long delay, he sent a boy to say he was not at home.

"Ah," they cried in chorus, "if he is not at home, where is he? Send for him."

Yu Kuan said: "Look here! It's no use his pretending to be half asleep. We have been hauled before the courts, beaten and kicked. Now they want him there." He pulled up his gown and showed the boy his legs. "Go and tell your master that we have been beaten on his account," he roared.

One after the other, they lay down on the benches and groaned and yelled. Wang the Third was less inclined than ever to come out. He said to his mother: "Mother, you must save me."

"What can I do?" his mother said, "I am only a woman."

The men began to lose patience and demanded that Lady Lin should speak to them. She did not go to them, but spoke from behind a screen.

"Wait a while," she said. "Really, he is not at home. I know, for a fact, that he is at my estate outside the city. I will send for him."

"Do, Lady," Little Zhang said, "and please be quick about it. This business must be settled, and the only thing to do with a wart is to cut it. Your son is the cause of this trouble, and we have had to bear the brunt of it. We have been dismissed now, but the court has still to deal with him. Until he comes, there will be no end to the trouble."

Lady Lin bade her servants take them some tea. Wang the Third was as frightened as a ghost. He implored his mother to find someone to get him out of the difficulty. At last, Lady Lin said: "I believe old woman Wen knows his Lordship Ximen. Some years ago, she acted as intermediary in his daughter's marriage. She must know him well."

"If she does, send for her," Wang the Third said.

"But a few days ago," his mother said, "you insulted her and she has not been here since. You offended her. I don't see how I can ask her now, and I don't suppose she would come if I did."

"Good Mother," Wang the Third said, "this matter is extremely serious. Send for her, and I will beg her pardon."

Lady Lin sent Yong Ding, the boy, to fetch the old woman. Yong Ding went quietly out by the back gate and brought her.

"Old mother Wen," Wang the Third said, "you know his Lordship Ximen and you must save my life."

The old woman pretended she could do nothing. "I arranged his daughter's wedding some years ago, but I have hardly been to his house since. It is a very big establishment. I can hardly expect to go there very often."

Wang the Third knelt down. "Old mother Wen," he said, "if you will only help me, I will see you do not lose by it. I will remember your kindness as long as I live. These fellows are trying to get me to go to the court, and I don't want to go."

Old woman Wen looked at Lady Lin. "Yes," the young man's mother said, "help him if you can."

"I am not going alone," the old woman said. "Put on your hat and clothes, Sir. I will take you to see his Lordship, and you can settle the business for yourself. I will say what I can on your behalf and, doubtless, everything will soon be all right."

"These fellows are very anxious to find me," Wang the Third said. "I am afraid they will see us as we go out."

"Don't worry about that," old woman Wen said. "I will go and pacify them. I'll arrange for them to have something to eat and drink and, while they are eating, I'll get you out by the back door. They won't see us."

She went to the outer hall and made a reverence to Little Zhang and the others. "I have come on behalf of her Ladyship," she said to them, "to assure you that the young gentleman is not at home. She has sent for him, and he will be here shortly. Sit down a while. We know you have suffered, but, when the young master comes back, he will certainly make it up to you. We don't blame you for coming since you have been mixed up in this affair. Besides, you came by order of the court and not of your own accord. I'm sure that, when the young master comes back, it will all end happily."

When they heard this, they cried, with one accord: "Old woman, you are talking sense. If you had come before and spoken to us in this strain, we should not have been so impatient and ill-mannered. But, you see, we could get nothing out of them but: 'He is not at home.' Nothing else. And it looked as if we were held responsible for all the trouble. He was the cause of our being beaten, and now the police are after him. What's the use his trying to get out of it with a 'not at home'? Does he get someone else to take his place when he is eating meat or drinking wine? Old woman, you seem to see things in the proper light. Here is a hint for you. If he likes to spend a little money and get the matter settled, well and good. It might even be managed without his seeing us, if he doesn't wish to do so. This is a military court, and things are more easily settled in it."

"Brothers," the old woman said, "there is much wisdom in what you say. I will ask the lady to have food and wine served for your entertainment. You must be hungry."

"Old mother," they said, "you seem to be sympathetic. To tell the truth, not a drop of water has passed our lips since we left the court."

Old woman Wen went back to the inner court, and foraged about till she got two *qian* worth of wine, one *qian* worth of cakes, and several large plates of pork, mutton, and beef. These were taken to the men, and she encouraged them to set to. Meanwhile, Wang the Third dressed himself in academic robes and wrote a petition. Old woman Wen smuggled him through the inner court. He put on a pair of eyeshades and they walked to Ximen's house.

When they reached the gateway, Ping'an, who knew old woman Wen, said: "My master is in the great hall. What do you want with him?"

The old woman handed him a visiting card and said: "Brother, kindly take this to your master." She asked Wang the Third to give two *qian* of silver to the boy. Ping'an took the card to Ximen Qing. Ximen looked at it. It bore the inscription: 'The young student, Wang Cai.'

He sent for old woman Wen, and she told him what had happened. He went into the hall and sent the boy to ask Wang the Third to go in. He did not change his clothes before going to receive the visitor. When he saw Wang the Third dressed in full ceremonial attire, he said to the old woman: "Sister Wen, why didn't you tell me? I am not suitably dressed." He said to the servants: "Bring my clothes at once." Wang the Third hastily stopped them.

"Uncle," he said, "pray don't trouble. I have come to see you, but I beg you not to put yourself to any inconvenience."

When they were in the great hall, Wang the Third insisted upon making a most profound reverence to Ximen Qing. Ximen smiled. "This is my house," he said, "I can't possibly allow it." He made the first reverence himself.

"How sorry I am that I have never called on you before," Wang the Third began.

"I hardly feel that we are strangers," Ximen said.

Again, Wang the Third pressed Ximen Qing to accept the honor. "I am your nephew," he said, "and you must accept it. It will show that you forgive me for having troubled you."

They compromised. Ximen Qing asked the young man to sit down. Wang the Third sat politely upon the edge of his chair. Tea was brought.

"I am very anxious for your assistance," Wang the Third said, taking a paper from his sleeve. He handed it to Ximen Qing and knelt down.

Ximen pulled him up again. "Tell me what I can do for you," he said.

"I am utterly ashamed of myself," Wang the Third said. "Only for the sake of my ancestors and their good fame do I venture to ask your forgiveness. Save me from the courts, and I will remember your kindness forever. I am afraid, afraid."

Ximen Qing unrolled the paper and looked at it. The five names were written on it.

"What?" he said. "These rogues again? I have given them one beating today. Why have they come to you?"

"They said that, when you had done with them, you ordered them to come for me. They are at my house now, roaring and shrieking insults. They demand money. There was nothing I could do but come and implore your help." He brought out a list of presents and gave it to Ximen Qing.

"Why do you offer me this?" Ximen said. "When I threw out those rogues, I had no idea they would come and make trouble with you." He returned the list of presents to the young man. "Go home," he said, "I will send and have the scoundrels arrested at once. I hope I may see you again soon."

"Since you have been so kind," the young man said, "I will certainly come to offer my thanks." He went out uttering innumerable protestations of gratitude.

Ximen Qing went with him as far as the second door. "I will not go farther with you," he said, "since I am not wearing my ceremonial dress." Wang the Third put on his eyeshades and went away with a boy. Old woman Wen waited to see Ximen Qing. "Not a word to those fellows," he said to her, "I am sending men to arrest them at once." Old woman Wen rejoined Wang the Third.

Ximen Qing sent four soldiers and a sergeant to the young man's house. The rascals were drinking and making a terrible din. The soldiers went in and arrested them. So frightened were they when the chains were put on them that they became as pale as death.

"Wang the Third has deceived us finely," they said. "He got us to stay here and then played this trick upon us."

"No nonsense now!" said the soldiers, "you had better beg for mercy from his Lordship Ximen."

"You are right," Little Zhang said.

They came to Ximen's house. The soldiers and Ping'an held out their hands for money, saying if they did not get it, they would not take them in. The men could not help themselves. Some took off their cloaks, others gave their pins, and, at last, word was taken to Ximen Qing. There was a long delay, then Ximen Qing came to the hall and they were taken in. They fell upon their knees.

"Now, you rogues," Ximen said, "I sent you about your business, and you went and pretended you had come from me, in an attempt to get money from these people. How much did you get? If you don't tell me, it will mean the screws again."

At this, the soldiers got busy with the thumbscrews, new and strong ones. Little Zhang and his companions kowtowed and begged for mercy. "We didn't get a penny," they said. "It is true we told them the court had ordered us to go there, but they only gave us something to eat. We never asked for anything else."

"You had no business there at all," Ximen Qing said. "You scoundrelly fellows are always leading honest young men astray. I loathe the very sight of you. If you do not confess, you shall be thrown into jail and, tomorrow, I will try you and have cangues put about your necks."

They all cried: "Heaven have mercy on us! Be merciful, and we will never go and cause them trouble again. Even if we don't get the cangue, to have to go to jail at a cold season like this will certainly be the death of us."

"Once again I forgive you," Ximen Qing said, "but you must repent and give up your evil ways. Henceforth, devote yourselves to steady honest work and don't go leading young men into evil courses. If you come before me again, I will have you beaten to death." He told the soldiers to kick them out. They ran for their lives. Ximen Qing went to the inner court.

"Who was your young visitor?" Wu Yueniang asked him.

"It was Wang the Third, the heir to General Wang. You remember the trouble there was sometime ago at Li Guijie's house? It was the same young man. He has been keeping that little strumpet and giving her thirty taels a month. No wonder she has been behaving so strangely. She had this young fellow completely at her feet. I found out about it and sent to arrest the rogues and have them brought before me. I had them beaten. Then they went to the Wangs' place and created a disturbance in the hope of getting money out of the young man. They told him I wanted him. He has never been before the court, and he was frightened and came with old woman Wen to ask me to help him. He brought fifty taels. I had the fellows re-arrested and put a stop to their games. They will make no more trouble. But what an unfortunate thing for that family to have such a bad young man. His grandfather was a man of great eminence, a general, in fact. This young man is at the military academy, but he never gives a thought to his career, neglects his flower-like young wife, and goes with these rascals to the bawdy house every night. All these bad habits before he is twenty."

"You seem to me like a young blackbird making disparaging remarks about a black pig," Yueniang said. "You only see things from your own point of view. You fancy yourself an angel, but, to me, you and he appear to have drunk from the same well. Are you a better man than he is that you should find fault with his goings on?"

Ximen Qing made no reply to this. Food was brought. Then Laian came and said Ying Bojue had come. "Take him to the study. I will be there in a few minutes," Ximen said to the boy. Wang Jing opened the study and showed in Bojue. Sometime later, Ximen Qing joined him. The two men sat down to talk.

"Why did you leave Brother Xie's place so early the other day?" Bojue asked.

"I have been very busy, and it is almost time for the inspection. I have sent people to the Capital to see what they can find out. You mustn't compare me with yourself, you, who never have anything to do."

"Has there been anything of interest at the office lately?" Ying Bojue said.

"There is always something," Ximen Qing said.

"I hear you had Little Zhang and some others arrested at Guijie's place the other evening. Old Sun and Zhu escaped, but the others got a beating at the office. When they had left there, they went and made trouble at Wang's place. Why wouldn't you tell me?"

"You dog!" Ximen said, "where did you hear all this? You have got hold of the wrong story, It was not my court, but Major Zhou's."

"Nothing of the sort," Bojue said, "Major Zhou had nothing to do with it."

"Perhaps somebody came from the Eastern Capital."

"Li Ming told me all about it this morning," Bojue said. "He said his people were in a terrible state, and Guijie, who was almost frightened to death, is still in bed. They thought the runners had come from the Eastern Capital but, this morning, they found it was your office."

"I haven't been to the office for several days," Ximen Qing said. "I know nothing about it. As for Guijie, she swore an oath that she would never have anything more to do with Wang the Third. I don't believe she is so frightened that she is still in bed."

Ying Bojue caught the flicker of a smile about Ximen's lips. "Brother," he said, "you almost took me in. Do tell me. How did old Sun and Zhu manage to escape? I can't believe the runners are so careless when they arrest people. You had a finger in the pie somewhere. You evidently determined to punish the sheep so as to teach the young horses a lesson. I suppose you meant to frighten Guijie, and let her realize what a powerful man you are. You wouldn't go so far as to arrest her—that would have been too hard, so you treat one set of people in one way and another set in another way. If old Sun and Zhu meet you, they wont know what to say for themselves. It was a very clever move on your part, making a show of repairing the bridge in one place and secretly posting your soldiers in another. Without flattering you, Brother, I must say it was a very clever scheme. A brilliant man never gives himself away. If you had done this openly, there would be nothing very remarkable about it. How deep you are, and how you understand human nature!"

Ximen Qing laughed softly. "There is nothing in that," he said.

"Surely someone gave you a hint?" Bojue said. "You would never have known so much about it otherwise. Why, neither ghosts nor gods could ever have found it out."

"You dog," Ximen said, "if people don't wish things of this sort to come out, they had better refrain from doing them."

"Aren't you going to have Wang the Third before the court?"

"Why should I?" Ximen said. "When the case was first brought to my notice, I crossed out the names of Wang the Third, Zhu, old Sun, Li Gui-jie and Qin Yuzhi. I only had those few scamps arrested."

"Why did they make trouble with Wang the Third?"

"They hoped to get money out of him. But Wang the Third came to see me. He kowtowed and begged my pardon, so I had the rogues arrested once more and told them I would have cangues put about their necks. They begged for mercy and swore they would never go near him again. As for Wang the Third, he addressed me as 'Uncle' before he said a word. He brought me a present list representing about fifty taels, but I told him to take it away. He has promised to ask me to go to his place so that he may thank me."

Bojue was surprised. "Did he really and truly apologize to you?" he said.

"Do you think I'm lying to you?" Ximen Qing said. He told Wang Jing to go and get Wang the Third's card. Wang Jing came back with the card. Bojue examined it. "The young student, Wang Cai," it said.

"Really, it was a brilliant scheme," he said.

"If you see any of them," Ximen Qing said, "don't tell them I know all that is to be known."

"I understand," Bojue said. "You don't wish them to realize it was all your idea. Of course, I won't say a word."

They had tea. Then Bojue said: "I must go. Old Sun and Zhu might come to see you. If they do, don't tell them I have been here."

"I shall not see them, if they do come," Ximen said. He sent a boy to tell the doorkeeper that, if the two men came, they were to be told he was not at home.

After this, Ximen Qing did not go near Li Guijie. When he had a party at his house, he did not engage Li Ming. Relations between them were completely broken off.

CHAPTER 70
Ximen Qing Visits the Capital

The Emperor said
That he would choose strong men and scholars,
That the wise should be as his arms and legs.
Now the art of letters is purified,
Rites and Music have regained their influence.
Men of nobility go to the palace
And the gate of guests is entered by men of worth.
The royal bounty is bestowed upon the people
Beyond all expectation.
The benevolence of the Ruler is above all things.

Ximen Qing had sent a man to Huaiqing to get news from Captain Lin. The captain gave him a copy of the Imperial Gazette and five *qian* of silver, and the man traveled back post-haste to Qinghe. Xia and Ximen Qing were waiting for him at the office. They opened the envelope. First they read the document that dealt with the inspection of the officials in their district. It related his Majesty's approval of the project to investigate the conduct of the officers, and spoke of Xia and Ximen Qing in these terms:

Xia Yanling, Captain and Magistrate in the Province of Shandong. An officer of excellent reputation and considerable experience. In a former appointment he kept his district in admirable order, and, in the position he now holds, has done even better. He deserves promotion as a thoroughly capable official and one worthy of high rank in the service.

Ximen Qing, Vice Captain and Deputy Magistrate, is also an efficient officer. He is renowned for the subtlety of his judgments, and, being a wealthy man, he does not accept bribes. He is attentive to his duties and carries them out satisfactorily. He has never received a penny that is not justly his due. He maintains the dignity of the law and the people respect him. His promotion to the full rank of Captain is suggested, and he should be confirmed in his appointment as Magistrate.

Ximen Qing was delighted with his promotion. But Magistrate Xia, when he learned that he had been appointed to the Imperial Escort, changed color and could not speak for several minutes.

The other document was from the Office of Works. It related his Majesty's satisfaction with the work that had been done in the transport of materials for the North Mount, ordered that half the taxes should be remitted in districts that had suffered from the work of transport, and that the dikes and weirs that had been destroyed should be replaced by officers of the Office of Works and the Provincial Authorities. Among the rewards granted in this document was a step in rank to Ximen Qing.

When Xia and Ximen had finished reading it, they went home. That afternoon, Wang the Third sent old woman Wen and a boy to invite Ximen Qing to go and see him on the eleventh of the month. He wished, he said, to express his gratitude for the favor Ximen Qing had done him. Ximen accepted the invitation with considerable pleasure, thinking that, in good time, Wang the Third's wife would fall into his hands.

On the evening of the tenth, orders came from Headquarters in the Eastern Capital summoning all the military officers of the Province to the Capital. They were to arrive before the day of the Winter Festival, and to attend at Court to express their gratitude to the Emperor. The order declared that anyone who arrived late would be punished.

The next day Ximen Qing went to discuss the matter with Magistrate Xia, then both men went home and set about the preparation of their luggage. They made ready presents and prepared to start in good time.

Ximen Qing sent Daian for old woman Wen and asked her to tell Wang the Third that he would be unable to keep his engagement because he had to go to the Eastern Capital to see the Emperor. The old woman hurried to Wang the Third and told him. Wang the Third said he would renew his invitation when Ximen came back.

Ximen Qing summoned Ben the Fourth and told him he was going to take him to the Eastern Capital. He gave him five taels of silver for household expenses. Daian and Wang Jing were also detailed to go, but Chunhong was left behind. Ximen asked Major Zhou for an escort of four horse soldiers. Sedan chairs and horses were made ready.

Magistrate Xia took with him only Xia Shou, but, in all, there were more than twenty attendants.

They started from Qinghe on the twelfth. It was winter and the days were short, but they traveled night and day. At Huaiqing they hoped to join Captain Lin, but he had started before them. They went on. When it was particularly cold, they stayed in their sedan chairs, but, on the warmer days, they rode on horseback.

At last they reached the Eastern Capital and entered the city by the gate of Ten Thousand Blessings. Ximen Qing proposed to stay at a temple, but Xia insisted that they should go together to his kinsman, Secretary Cui. Ximen, who did not know Cui, sent his card before him. When they reached the house, the Secretary was at home. He came out to welcome them and led them to the hall. They exchanged greetings. Cui said how delighted he was to see Magistrate Xia; they sat down, and tea was brought.

"May I know your honorable name?" Cui said, bowing to Ximen Qing.

"My humble name is Siquan," Ximen said. He asked Cui's name.

"I am a very insignificant fellow," Cui said, "and I am living in retirement. My humble name is Shouyu, and I am also called Xunzhai. My kinsman, Xia, has often told me of your preeminent virtue. I trust your favor may always uphold and support him."

"He has taught me all I know," Ximen Qing said. "Now that he has been promoted, I shall be dependent upon him in many ways. I owe him much."

"Why do you flatter me?" Xia said. "It would seem as though we were strangers."

"Siquan is right," Cui said, "you are his senior in rank."

They laughed. Their luggage was carried into the house. It was growing late. Secretary Cui ordered a meal to be prepared for them and they spent the night in his house.

The next morning they set off very early with their presents and visiting cards to the palace of the Imperial Tutor. His Eminence was still at the Court, but officers and people flocked like bees outside his palace. Xia and Ximen Qing had great difficulty in forcing their way through the crowd. They made a present to the gatekeeper, and their cards were taken in.

Zhai came out to greet them and took them to his own house. Magistrate Xia saluted him and Ximen Qing greeted him. They sat down. Xia presented his list of gifts. He offered two rolls of golden satin, two rolls of figured satin to the Imperial Tutor and ten taels of silver to Zhai. Ximen Qing had brought a roll of scarlet silk with embroidered dragons, a roll of black silk, also embroidered, and two rolls of official silk for the Imperial Tutor. To Zhai he offered a roll of dark green velvet and thirty taels of silver.

Zhai told the servants to take the presents for the Imperial Tutor to his palace, and to inscribe their names in the visitors' book. He accepted the velvet that Ximen Qing had brought for him, but would not take the silver from either of them.

"It would not be right," he said. "If I took money from you, it would look as though we were not good friends."

He told a servant to prepare a meal for them. "Today," he said, "his Majesty has set the finishing touch to the building he began at the behest of Heaven, and the title is being set up. His Eminence is presiding over the sacrifice. He will not be able to get away before the afternoon. When he comes back, he is going with Li Bangyan to a party at the palace of the Zhengs, who are connected with the Imperial Household. I doubt whether you will care to wait so long, and your other business may be delayed. Do not wait. When his Eminence is at liberty, I will speak to him for you. That will be just as good as if you saw him yourselves."

"It is extremely kind of you, kinsman," Ximen Qing said.

Zhai asked Ximen where he was staying. Ximen told him he was with Xia at Secretary Cui's house.

The meal was now ready. There were a great many dishes, prepared in the manner of the court and served in huge plates and dishes. The food was delicious. When Ximen and his colleague had drunk three cups of wine, they rose and prepared to leave, but Zhai begged them to stay and pressed them to drink again.

"Kinsman," Ximen Qing said, "when shall I be able to see his Majesty?"

"You will not be so fortunate as his Lordship Xia," the Comptroller said. "He is now one of the officers of the Capital. You and the newly appointed Vice Captain, He Yongshou, Chamberlain He's nephew, who are law officers—he is to be your assistant—will have to wait until his Lordship Xia has seen his Majesty. He will wait for you and, after your audience, you will get your commissions together. Whatever you wish to do after that, you will have to consult his Lordship."

Xia listened but said nothing.

"Kinsman," Ximen Qing said, "will it be possible for me to see his Majesty when he has returned from the worship of Heaven on the day of the Winter Festival?"

"Can you wait all that time?" Zhai said. "When he comes back, all the officials of the Empire will offer their congratulations and there will probably be a royal banquet. I don't see how you can wait till then. You had better go to the Registry today, and tomorrow go to Court and see his Majesty. Then you will be able to go home as soon as you have secured your papers."

"Thank you," Ximen said, "I will do as you command. I don't know how I can ever repay your kindness."

As they were going away, the Comptroller took Ximen Qing aside. "When I sent you that letter," he said reproachfully, "didn't I tell you to be most careful and not let your colleague know what should have been a secret between ourselves? What made you tell Xia? He wrote to his Holiness Lin, and Lin persuaded Marshal Zhu to come to his Eminence and say that Xia did not wish to come to the Capital to take a post in the Imperial Escort. He wished to remain another three years at Qinghe. Chamberlain He brought the matter before his Majesty's favorite concubine, and she herself approached both Marshal Zhu and his Eminence and urged the appointment of He Yongshou as the deputy. This produced a most awkward situation. His Eminence was placed in a very difficult position. If I had not spoken to his Eminence on your behalf, and persuaded him to refuse Lin's petition, you would have found yourself without any appointment at all, my dear kinsman."

Ximen Qing was greatly disturbed. "I am most grateful to you," he said, "but, really, I never mentioned the matter to anyone. I can't imagine how it came out."

"If a man doesn't keep things like that secret, so much the worse for him," Zhai said. "You must be more careful in the future."

Ximen Qing thanked him again and went away with Xia. They returned to Cui's house. Ximen sent Ben the Fourth to the Registry to put down their names, and the next day, he and Xia, dressed in black robes and hats of ceremony, went to the Imperial Palace to express their gratitude for his Majesty's favor.

As they were coming out by the West Gate, a man in plain clothes came up and said: "Which of you gentlemen is Master Ximen, the law officer from Shandong?"

Ben the Fourth asked the man who he was.

"I am from Chamberlain He, the Bailiff of the Imperial Palace. He would like to speak to Master Ximen."

The words were hardly out of his mouth before a eunuch, wearing a scarlet robe embroidered with dragons, a ceremonial hat, and black boots, came out upon the Imperial roadway and said: "Greetings, my lord Ximen."

Ximen Qing left Magistrate Xia. The eunuch took him by the hand and led him to a place apart. The eunuch bowed and Ximen knelt down to make a reverence in return.

"You do not know me, my Lord," the eunuch said, "I am He, the Bailiff of the Imperial Palace, and the Chamberlain of his Majesty's fourth lady. Recently, when I had completed my service, his Majesty was graciously pleased to appoint my nephew, He Yongshou, Vice Captain and Deputy Magistrate in your district of Qinghe. He will be your colleague."

"I must apologize for not recognizing your Excellency," Ximen Qing said. He bowed again. "This is a prohibited place and I cannot salute you here in a manner befitting your dignity. I trust you will allow me to visit you in your own palace."

They sat down and a servant brought tea. A food box was opened and many delicacies were set upon a table. Cups and chopsticks were brought.

"We will not use the small cups," the eunuch said, "I know you have just come from the Court, and you must be feeling cold. Besides, I have made such meager preparation for you, that it would not be right. Such food as this will only give you an appetite."

"I must not put you to any trouble," Ximen said.

Eunuch He filled a large cup and offered it to Ximen Qing.

"Since you are so gracious," Ximen said, "I must accept it, but I have to call upon a number of other officers, and I fear my face will be unbecomingly red."

"Oh, a cup or two to keep out the cold will not do you any harm. My nephew is very young," the eunuch continued, "He knows nothing of the law. I shall consider it a favor to myself if you will teach him whatever is necessary for him to know."

"Your Excellency," Ximen said, "pray do not be formal with me. Your nephew may be young, but I have no doubt that, having been brought up in so exalted a household, he is extremely intelligent."

"That is very kind of you. But the proverb says: Though we keep learning to the end of our days, we still know very little. The things one should know are as many as the hairs on an ox. Even Confucius was only able to acquire a legful. I am afraid he is sure to make mistakes, and I hope you will correct him."

"At your Excellency's service," Ximen Qing said. "Will you be good enough to tell me where your palace is situated, that I may come and call upon you?"

"My humble dwelling is in the Wenhuafang, east of the Bridge of the Heavenly River. There are two lions outside the door. We use them as mounting blocks. Tell me where you are staying, and I will send someone to call on you."

"Secretary Cui has been good enough to give me a room," Ximen Qing told him.

He drank a large cup of wine and rose. Eunuch He took him to the gate. "Do not forget what I have said," the eunuch said. "Perhaps you will wait for my nephew and get your commissions together."

"Certainly," Ximen said.

He left the palace and went to the Ministry of War, where he found Xia. They went together to pay their respects to the officials of the Ministry. When they came to the office of their own regiment, they went to call upon Grand Marshal Zhu. They handed in their records of service and then visited the Military Secretary and other officials.

It was now late in the afternoon. Xia changed his clothes, put on the robes of his new office, and sent in his card to the Grand Marshal. Zhu would not allow him to kowtow. Xia reported the date upon which he would enter upon his duties and came away. Ximen Qing was waiting for him. Ximen hesitated to ride side by side with Xia any longer. He asked him to mount his horse first, but Xia insisted that they should go together as before. Ximen kept addressing him as 'Sir' and 'My Lord' till Xia said: "Siquan, you and I have always been colleagues. Why do you speak to me in this formal way?"

"You are of higher rank now, and it is right that I should. Now that your Lordship has attained this high position, you will not be returning to Shandong, I suppose. When will you bring your family here?"

"I would have brought them with me, but there is nobody to look after my house," Xia said. "I think I shall stay with relatives here and send for my family next year. Perhaps you will be good enough to keep an eye on them. If you can find anyone who will buy my house, I hope you will sell it for me. I shall be glad to make it worth your while."

"How much is your house worth?" Ximen asked.

"I paid one thousand three hundred taels for it," Xia said. "Then I built another wing, and that cost me two hundred taels more. I am prepared to sell it for what it cost."

They went back to Secretary Cui's house. Wang Jing reported that Master He had been to call upon Ximen. "I told him," the boy said, "that you were not yet back from the Ministry. He asked me to present his compliments to his Lordship Xia, and left two cards. A man came and brought two rolls of silk from him."

Ximen Qing told Wang Jing to get two rolls of Nanjing five-colored silk, and wrote a card to go with them. He had something to eat as quickly as possible and hastened to the eunuch's house. When he entered the great hall, Captain He came out to greet him. The young man was dressed in black ceremonial hat and boots. He seemed not more than twenty years old and looked so handsome that one might have thought his face was powdered and his lips rouged. He saluted Ximen Qing modestly yet with the utmost grace.

Ximen told Daian to bring in the presents. "I hear that you have been good enough to call upon me and to bring me most precious gifts," he said. "I am sorry I was not there to receive you. This morning, his Excellency your uncle was kind enough to entertain me at the palace. I am grateful to him."

Captain He made a reverence. "I have been made an officer of the lowest grade," he said, "and count myself supremely fortunate to have been appointed to your office. I hope to benefit by your instruction."

They continued to exchange compliments.

"My lord," Captain He said, "have you called upon the Grand Marshal?"

"Yes," Ximen Qing said. "I went to the Ministry immediately after leaving his Excellency, your uncle. I went to our headquarters, handed in my record of service and called on the officers there. When I came away, it was my intention to call upon you. I never dreamed you would call on me first."

"Did you go to the Palace with his Lordship Xia?"

"Yes," Ximen Qing said. "We went together to the court, but as he has been appointed to the Imperial Escort, when we called at the Ministry, we handed in our papers and sent in our cards separately."

"Do we send presents to the Minister, or wait till we receive our commissions?" Captain He said.

"My kinsman tells me," Ximen Qing said, "that we should send our presents first. Then the Marshal will present us at court, and afterwards we shall get out commissions."

"In that case," He said, "we had better send our presents tomorrow morning."

They discussed the question of a suitable present. Captain He decided to offer two rolls of silk and a jade buckle. Ximen Qing would offer a roll of scarlet satin, a roll of black silk and a gold ring inlaid with jade. Each would offer four jars of Jinhua wine in addition. They arranged to meet outside the Marshal's house. They had tea, and Ximen Qing took leave of his new colleague and went home. He said nothing to Xia of the arrangements he had made.

The next morning, Ximen Qing went to Captain He's place. He had prepared an excellent meal, and Ximen Qing and his servants were admirably provided for. Ben the Fourth and He's servants were given charge of the presents, and Ximen Qing and He Yongshou went together to the Marshal's house.

Marshal Zhu was not at home. Officials of every grade were waiting with their presents in a crowd outside the gate. Captain He and Ximen Qing dismounted and went into a nearby house, whose master they knew. They sent a man to watch for the Minister's return. They waited until the afternoon. Then the man came running to say that the Marshal was coming back from the sacrifice by the South Gate. Already, he said, orders were being given to clear the way for him.

Soon afterwards, the man came again. "The Marshal has reached the Bridge of the Heavenly River," he said. There came an escort of officials and soldiers, with banners and weapons. They marched in pairs, shouting. Then, still a long way off, Ximen and his companion could see Marshal Zhu. He was sitting in a sedan chair carried by eight footmen; another eight footmen followed. He was wearing a ceremonial hat and a scarlet gown; a piece of white jade formed the clasp of his girdle. He wore a golden fish, the insignia of his office, and looked extremely dignified.

The escort reached the gate and halted. Then they turned inwards to form a guard. There was perfect silence among the onlookers. No one dared even to cough. The officers came forward to greet the Grand Marshal and knelt on the ground before him. As the sedan chair approached, the command was given to stand up, and the officers immediately obeyed. The sound of their acclamations reached the skies.

Suddenly there came from the east the strains of music. The principal officers in the Minister's department had arranged for this in honor of the exalted rank that had been conferred upon him by the Emperor's recent decree, and also to celebrate his son's entry into official life.

When the Minister got down from his sedan chair, the music stopped. The officers were preparing to present themselves to him when, suddenly, a messenger in black clothes, carrying two red cards, rushed forward and handed the cards to another official. "Their Excellencies, Chang of the Board of Rites and Vice Chancellor Cai, are here." The man went into the house to give warning to his master. Then, in two sedan chairs, came Zhang Bangchang and Cai Yu. They were both wearing scarlet ceremonial robes with peacocks embroidered upon them. One had a buckle of rhinoceros horn upon his girdle, the other, one of gold.

Following them came Wang Zudao, President of the Board of Civil Service, with Han Lü the Minister of the Left, and Yin Jing, the Minister of the Right. Marshal Zhu offered them tea, and they came away at once.

Then came the Duke of Xiguo, a kinsman of the Imperial House, the President of the Privy Council, Zheng Juzhong, and the Master of the Household, the Imperial Son-in-law, Wang Jinqing. They all wore girdles with jade buckles. Zheng rode in a sedan chair, but the others were on horseback.

When they had gone, the six officers of the Marshal's own department paid their respects to him. First came the Commander-in-chief of the troops at the Capital, Sun Rong; then, in order, Liang Yinglong, Commissioner of Police; and the others, all wearing red cloaks and fur hats. Sun Rong had a jade buckle to his girdle by virtue of his rank, but the rest wore gold buckles. They all brought presents.

There was music within the palace as the generals, wearing golden flowers, offered wine to the Grand Marshal. There was music in the courtyard while the banquet proceeded within. When they had offered wine, the generals sat down. Five singers came in, and to the accompaniment of lute and zither, sang a song in celebration of the occasion, beating time with ivory castanets.

When the wine had been passed three times, the song ended. The six generals rose and the Grand Marshal went with them as far as the gate. Then he returned to the hall, and the music died away. A servant told him that many officers wished to see him. He ordered a great table to be brought and set in the middle of the hall.

"Let the noblemen of the Court and those of high family be first admitted," he commanded.

They came in, and retired again immediately. Then all the officers of his own department were introduced. They came with their cards, and these were handed to him. Then came the law officers of the thirteen provinces in relays. Ximen Qing and Captain He were in the fifth party. Their presents were brought in, and an attendant took the list and placed it on the table. They came in and stood at the foot of the steps waiting for their names to be announced. While they waited, Ximen looked up and admired the magnificent proportions of the great hall and the great red sign with four characters upon it that had been written by the Emperor's own hand. Their names were called and the two men went forward, bowed, knelt down and waited.

"Why have you two gentlemen troubled the venerable chamberlain to send me a present?" the Grand Marshal said. He told his servants to take their gifts. "Do your duty, and I will treat you justly," he told them. "Stay until you have been to the Court and, afterwards, come to my Ministry for your papers."

The two men acknowledged the command the Marshal gave them. Then the attendants warned them to withdraw, and they went out by a door on the left. As they passed through the gateway, Ben the Fourth and the other servants were carrying out the empty boxes. They were about to go away, when a man, carrying a red card, galloped towards them. "Their Excellencies Wang and Gao are coming," he cried as he passed.

Ximen Qing and Captain He went into a house to watch the two noblemen pass. Soldiers cleared the way. Then came Wang Hua, Duke of Longxi, Commander of the Royal Guard, and Marshal Gao Qiu. They rode in sedan chairs, and wore red jade buckles on their girdles. The officers rushed out of the palace in a crowd, and Ximen Qing and Captain He lost sight of the two dignitaries. They went to a quiet place, took their horses from the servants, and rode home.

CHAPTER 71
The Son of Heaven

The flowers droop and the sweet grass is faded
He is a stranger in a strange place.
In the little courtyard
He thinks of her whom he has lost.
It is evening, and his tears
Drop red as blood.
Mountain and river are parted
His eyes are dim, his spirit ill at ease.
It seems that her sweet spirit has vanished utterly.

When, at the fifth night watch, he woke from his dream
His heart was broken.
The wind brought the sound of horns
And swept away the moon and the plum blossom.

Ximen Qing and Captain He came to the principal street. He asked Ximen to take wine with him at his house, but Ximen Qing very politely declined. Then He bade his servant take Ximen's bridle. "You must come," he said, "I am anxious to talk to you." So they went to He's place, and Ben the Fourth took the empty present boxes back to Secretary Cui's house.

Captain He had made special preparations for his guest. In the great hall, animal charcoal was burning in the braziers, and the smoke of incense went curling upwards from golden burners. There was a table in the middle of the hall, and beside it two other tables, one nearer the door and the other at one side. Bowls piled with rare fruits stood on the tables and flowers in golden vases.

"Are you entertaining any other guests?" Ximen Qing asked Captain He.

"No," He said. "My old uncle will dine with us when he comes back."

"Since we are to be colleagues," Ximen Qing said, "you should not have gone to all this trouble on my account."

"I beg your pardon," He said, "but, as a matter of fact, my venerable uncle has done this."

When they had drunk tea, Ximen asked if he might pay his respects to the eunuch. He said he would not be long and, in a short time, Eunuch He came from the back of the house. He was wearing a green dragon gown, ceremonial hat and boots, and a jewel at his girdle. Ximen Qing bowed to him and asked leave to kowtow, but the eunuch would not allow him to do so.

"Your Excellency is distinguished both by age and virtue," Ximen Qing said. "You are a nobleman of the Court and, as your nephew and I are colleagues, you must permit me to do so."

They wrangled for some time, and, at last, the old eunuch accepted a compromise. He asked Ximen Qing to take the place of honor, seated himself in the host's chair, and put his nephew on one side. Ximen Qing protested. "We are fellow officers," he said. "I cannot allow him to take a lower position than myself. It would be seemly so far as your Excellency and he are concerned, for you are uncle and nephew, but it is not right for me."

The eunuch smiled. "Sir," he said, "you seem to understand the Rites very well. I am an old fellow. I will take the lower place and let the officer take mine."

"That would be even more insupportable," Ximen said. They finally sat down as they had before.

"It is cold," the eunuch said to the servants, "put more coal on the fire."

The servants brought fine water-polished charcoal and put it in the brazier. They pulled down the oiled-paper blind outside the hall. It was so arranged that, when the sun shone, it shone through the paper and gave light to the hall.

"Sir," the eunuch said, "will you take off your ceremonial clothes?"

"I have nothing underneath," Ximen said, "I must send my servant for something."

"Don't trouble to do that," the eunuch said. He bade one of his servants bring his green gown.

Ximen Qing smiled. "How dare I put on the robes of your Excellency's rank?"

"Don't let that worry you," the eunuch said. "Put it on by all means. His Majesty gave me this new robe yesterday. I shall have no further use for the old one, and I should be glad if you would accept it and use it as a cloak."

When the servant brought it, Ximen Qing took off his ceremonial clothes and gave them to Daian. He put on the green robe, bowed to express his thanks to the eunuch and asked him, in turn, to take off his robes of ceremony. Tea was brought again.

"Let the boys come in," the eunuch commanded.

He had twelve boys being trained as singers. They were brought in by their instructors. They kowtowed. The eunuch bade them begin, and they went to their places. The eunuch himself prepared to offer wine to Ximen Qing, but Ximen hastily begged him not to do so.

"Your Excellency, pray do not offer me wine yourself," he said. "The Captain will do it for you. I shall be more than happy if you set the cup on the table before me."

"I must do so," the eunuch said. "My nephew has now secured his first appointment. He is quite ignorant. I am placing my confidence in your kind assistance. With it, I am sure, all will be well."

"Your Excellency," Ximen said, "the old proverb says: When men become fellow officers, there will be friendship between them and their descendants for three generations. I am in your hands. How can I fail to do my utmost for your nephew?"

"You are both in the service of his Majesty," the eunuch said. "For that reason, you must help one another."

Ximen Qing did not wait for the eunuch to pour the wine for him. He took the cup from his hands and set it down on the table. In his turn, he offered a cup to the eunuch and to Captain He. They bowed to each other and sat down.

After a prelude, three boys and their instructors played the banjo and the lute and sang the songs "Visiting Zhao Pu" and "The Silken Hangings in the Palace of Crystal." When they had finished their songs they withdrew.

The wine was passed several times and the second course brought. It was growing dark, and the lamps were lighted. Ximen Qing told Daian to give some money to the cooks and the musicians. He rose and said: "I have troubled you sufficiently. I must go now."

The old eunuch would not hear of this. "I happen to be free today," he said, "and I wish you to stay. I have not made any special preparations for you. This is very ordinary food, and I fear you must be starved."

"Starved!" Ximen cried, "starved, with all this delightful food. I only wish to go back and rest because, tomorrow morning, I have to go with your nephew to pay a round of visits, have our names registered, and get the necessary documents."

"If you are going to be occupied with my nephew," the eunuch said, "why not send for your luggage and spend a few days here? There is a small apartment in my garden that you would find very quiet. You could discuss everything you have to discuss with my nephew, and you would find it most convenient."

"I should very much like to come," Ximen Qing said, "but I must not offend his Lordship Xia. If I come here, he may regard it as a sign that I am no longer anxious to be on good terms with him."

"Oh, you mustn't bother about that," the eunuch said. "Men who have been together in the same office are separated one morning, and, the same evening, do not even bow to one another. Officers come and go. You have served with him; he is now promoted and you succeed him. That's all there is to it. If he thinks otherwise, he is not a reasonable man. No, we must have the pleasure of your company for the night. I shall not allow you to go."

He said to his attendants: "Give something to eat to his Lordship's servants, and send somebody for his luggage. Get the apartment ready in the courtyard of the western garden, make up beds there, and get a fire going."

One word from his Excellency was sufficient. A hundred eyes were on the watch. Servants hurried to do his bidding.

"Your Excellency," Ximen Qing said, "this is very kind of you, but I am sure Xia will be displeased."

"He has nothing more to do with your office," the eunuch said. "It doesn't matter what he thinks. He is now officer of the Imperial Escort, and has no more to do with affairs of the law. I don't believe he will mind in the least."

The eunuch said no more, but sent Daian and the other servant to have their evening meal. A number of other servants took poles and ropes and went to Cui's place for Ximen Qing's things.

"There is one point I wish especially to mention to you," the eunuch said. "When my nephew assumes office, he will need a house. I hope you will help him to find one. I am anxious that his family should join him at Qinghe as soon as possible. I think he had better go with you, and I will arrange for his family to follow when you have secured a house for them. It is not a very large household, only about thirty people, including all the servants."

"How much is your Excellency prepared to spend?" Ximen said.

"I suppose something more than a thousand."

"Now that Xia is going to remain in the Capital," Ximen said, "he will be getting rid of his house. You might buy that. It would be to the advantage of both parties. It is a good-sized house, seven rooms wide and five deep. When you go in by the second door, there is a large hall with side rooms. The living rooms branch out in different directions behind that, and there are quite a number of other rooms. The house is in a good broad street. It ought to suit Captain He very well."

"How much does Xia want for it?" the eunuch said.

"He told me he paid thirteen hundred for it," Ximen said, "and later, he built an extra wing and made a garden. If your Excellency cares for the idea, I should offer any sum you consider suitable."

"I will leave the matter to you," the eunuch said. "You shall arrange it for me. I am at home now, so why not send someone to tell Xia we think of buying his house and ask him for the title deeds? We shall be lucky if we get it. My nephew will have somewhere to live as soon as he gets to Qinghe."

Daian and a host of servants came with Ximen's luggage. Ximen Qing asked him if Ben the Fourth and Wang Jing had come.

"Wang Jing is here," Daian said, "but Ben the Fourth is still at Secretary Cui's house, making arrangements about the sedan chair."

Ximen Qing said softly to Daian: "Go and see his Lordship Xia, and ask him for the title deeds of his house. His Excellency here would like to see them. Bring Ben the Fourth back with you."

Daian went. Ben the Fourth, wearing black clothes and a small hat, soon came back with him. He brought the document.

"His Lordship Xia," Ben the Fourth said, "told us to say that, since his Excellency would like to have the house, there will be no difficulty about the price. Here are the title deeds. He says that, though he built the wings and spent a great deal of money on the place, he will leave the price to you."

Ximen Qing handed the papers to the eunuch. The sum mentioned was twelve hundred taels.

"Xia has lived in the house a good many years," the eunuch said, "and I expect it needs doing up. But since you, Sir, are seeing the business through for me, I will give him the price he paid for it."

Ben the Fourth knelt down. "Your Excellency does well," he said. "The proverb says: The establishment of an estate is an expensive business, and though in a thousand years, a house may change hands a hundred times, each new master will have it redone his own way from top to bottom."

"Who are you?" said the eunuch. "You talk like a man of sense. You are right when you say that a man who is setting up an establishment mustn't mind how much he spends. What is your name?"

"He is called Ben the Fourth," Ximen Qing said.

"Well, I don't see that we need look any further," the eunuch said. "You shall act as our representative, and get the thing fixed up for us. This is an auspicious day, and I will pay Xia his money."

"It is late now," Ximen said, "why not pay him tomorrow?"

"No," the eunuch said, "I have to be at the Palace before dawn tomorrow. It is the day when all the officers come to pay their duty to his

Majesty. We will settle with him today."

"At what time will the Emperor come out tomorrow?" Ximen Qing asked.

"His Majesty will go to make sacrifice about midnight," the eunuch said. "An hour or two before dawn he will return and breakfast at the Palace. Then he will hold his court. All the officers of the Empire come at the Winter Festival to offer their congratulations. All the Ministers and some of the higher officials will remain for a banquet. You gentlemen simply attend the court."

The eunuch told Captain He to put twenty-four large bars of silver into a box, and ordered two servants to go with Ben the Fourth and Daian and take the money to Xia at Secretary Cui's house.

Xia was pleased. He signed the document and gave it to Ben the Fourth to take back to the eunuch. The eunuch, too, was satisfied. He gave ten taels of silver to Ben the Fourth and three taels each to Daian and Wang Jing.

"They are only boys," Ximen Qing said, "your Excellency should not have troubled to give them anything."

"It is only something to buy food with," the eunuch said.

The three kowtowed and thanked him.

Then the eunuch bowed to Ximen Qing. "I am placing all my confidence in your kindness," he said.

"I am entirely at your Excellency's service," Ximen Qing said.

"Now, Sir," the eunuch said, "please ask Xia to have his place made free as soon as possible so that I can make arrangements for my nephew's family to take possession."

"I will certainly tell him," Ximen Qing said. "Perhaps, when Captain He arrives at Qinghe, he will stay a few days at the office while Xia's family make their preparations to leave for the Capital. Then we will have the place put in order, and you will send your nephew's family."

"No," the eunuch said, "I think we will leave the question of repairs until next year. I will send his family before then. He will not be comfortable if he has to live so long alone at the office."

It was now the first night watch. Ximen Qing said: "Will not your Excellency retire and take some rest? I have had wine enough."

The eunuch went to bed, but Captain He bade the musicians play, and went on drinking with Ximen Qing. When it was time to go to bed, Ximen Qing went to the garden. There was a small three-roomed apartment used as a study. The garden was very delightful with its buildings, arbors, lake, hillocks, flowers, and woods. Candles burned brightly in the study, and fragrant incense burned. It was quiet and delightful. Captain

He chatted for a while with Ximen Qing, and they took tea together. Then he said good night and went to his own rooms to sleep.

Ximen Qing took off his hat, girdle and clothes and went to bed. Wang Jing and Daian waited on him, then went to their own place.

Ximen Qing, lying on the bed, watched the moonbeams playing on the windows. He tossed about but could not sleep. He heard the drip, drip, drip of the water clock. He saw the tall shadows of the plants upon the casement. The cold wind rattled the windowpanes. He had now been away from home for some time and was thinking of calling Wang Jing to sleep with him. Suddenly, he heard a woman speaking very softly outside the window. He wrapped his cloak around him, put on his slippers, and quietly opened the door. He looked out. Li Ping'er stood there, her hair like mist. She was dressed in simple, beautiful clothes, and a white coat covered her snow-white body. She wore soft slippers, yellow in color, upon her dainty feet. She stood there in the moonlight.

Ximen Qing went forward, took her into the study and kissed her. "My darling!" he cried, "what has brought you here?"

"I have sought you," she said, "because I wanted to tell you that I have a new home now. I was anxious to let you know, because, sooner or later, I must go to it."

"Where is this house?" Ximen asked her.

"Not far from here. It is in the middle of the Zaofu Lane, east of the main street."

Ximen Qing put his arms about her, and they went to bed that they might enjoy each other the more fully. When they had taken their pleasure, she made her clothes tidy and dressed her hair, but she was loath to go away.

"Brother," she said to Ximen Qing, "don't forget what I said to you. Do not drink wine late at night. Go home early. That fellow is only waiting his chance to destroy you. Remember."

Holding each other by the hand, they went to the main street. The moon shone so brightly that it might have been day. They came to a lane leading eastwards from the street. In the middle of it was a house with white double doors. Li Ping'er pointed to it. "That is the house," she said. She loosed her hand from his, and ran in. Ximen dashed forward to stop her.

Then he awoke. It was a dream. The moon was still shining upon the window; the flowers cast a deeper shadow than before. He passed his hand over the bedclothes. There was a pool upon them that seemed to show that all had not been in his imagination. He could still smell the delicate scent of her body upon the bed, and the lips which she had kissed were still sweet. He was very sad, but restrained his sobs.

There was no sleep for Ximen Qing. He longed for the day to break. At last, when dawn was near, he began to doze.

The next morning, Captain He sent his own servants to help Ximen to dress, and himself came early to call upon him. They drank tea and breakfasted together.

"Why does his Excellency not come?" Ximen asked.

"He went to the court before it was light," Captain He said.

They were served with gruel; then with buns stuffed with forcemeat, and soup of chickens' brains. They called for their horses, put on their ceremonial dress and went to the Ministry with their servants following. When they came out, Captain He went home, but Ximen went to the Xiang Guo Temple to visit the Abbot, Zhi Yun. The Abbot entertained him with monastic fare, but Ximen Qing would only eat one cake and gave the rest to his servants. Then he went away, passing through the main street on his way to Secretary Cui's house to see Xia. They went through the Zaofu Lane. Halfway down it, he saw a house with white double doors exactly like the one he had seen in his dream. An old woman was selling bean curd nearby, and Ximen told Daian to ask her who lived in that house. "It is General Yuan's house," the old woman said.

Ximen Qing sighed with curiosity and amazement. He came to Secretary Cui's house. Xia was setting out to pay a call. He immediately ordered his servant to take the horses away, and took Ximen Qing to the great hall. Ximen told Daian to bring the presents that he wished to offer to Xia upon his appointment. There was one roll of black silk and another of figured silk.

"I have not congratulated you," Xia said to him, "yet you do so much for me. Yesterday you took a great deal of trouble over my house."

"Chamberlain He asked me about a house," Ximen said, "and I told him about yours. He asked for the title deeds, and agreed to the price without the slightest ado. That is just like a eunuch. They think they can build a bridge in a couple of seconds. But, after all, it was to your advantage."

They laughed. "I have not yet called on Captain He," Xia said. "Is he going back with you?"

"Yes," Ximen said. "And his family will follow later. His Excellency told me to ask you to be so good as to vacate the place as soon as you can so that he can send the Captain's family. Until you have done so he will have to stay at the office."

"That will not be very long," Xia said. "I am looking for a house here and, as soon as I find one, I will send for my family. I don't see why the house should not be ready for him next month."

Ximen Qing rose. He left a card for Cui. Xia took him to the gate and waited till he had mounted his horse. Ximen Qing went back to Captain He's house. He was waiting to entertain him. Ximen told him that Xia had promised that his house should be free the following month. The Captain was delighted. "It is all due to your good offices," he said.

After dinner, while they were playing chess in the great hall, a servant came and said that a number of presents had come from the Imperial Tutor's comptroller Zhai. They had been taken to Cui's house, and the Secretary had sent them on. Ximen Qing looked at the list. A roll of gold silk, a roll of patterned hempen material, a pig, a sheep, a jar of palace wine, and two boxes of cakes. All these were set down upon the card, and at the end of the list was written: "Your kinsman Zhai Qian makes most humble salutation."

"Your master has troubled himself once again on my account," Ximen Qing said to the servants who brought the things. He accepted the gifts, wrote a return card, and gave two taels to the servant and five *qian* to each of the porters. To the servant he said: "You will understand that, as I am a stranger here and not versed in the usual customs, I am ashamed to offer such a reward." The man kowtowed and accepted the money.

Wang Jing, who was standing beside his master, whispered: "I was told to go to the palace to see Han Aijie. I have brought something for her."

"What have you brought?" Ximen asked him.

"Two pairs of home-made shoes," Wang Jing said.

"That is not enough," Ximen said. He told Daian to look in his chest and take out two jars of rose-flower biscuits. He gave them to Wang Jing, with a card of thanks for the presents, and the boy put on black robes and went to the Imperial Tutor's palace with the servant.

Ximen wrote a card and sent it, with the sheep and a jar of wine, to Secretary Cui. He told a servant to offer the pig, a jar of wine, and the boxes of cakes to the eunuch. "We are such good friends," Captain He said to him, "that really there is no need for you to do anything of the sort."

Wang Jing came to the palace, and was received by Han Aijie in the great hall. She was dressed so exquisitely that she looked like a tree of jade, not at all like the girl who had lived with her mother at Qinghe. She had grown taller. She asked the boy many questions about her family, and gave him some food. She thought Wang Jing's clothes were very thin. She brought a blue silk gown, lined with fur, and gave it to him with five taels of silver. When the boy got back, he showed the cloak to Ximen Qing.

Captain He and Ximen were playing chess, when, suddenly, there was shouting outside. The doorkeeper came in and said: "His Lordship Xia has come to call." He handed one card to Ximen Qing and another to Captain

He. They hurried to the great hall to meet Xia. He thanked him for the expedition with which he had settled the question of the house. Xia presented gifts to each of them, and they thanked him cordially. Then he gave ten taels of silver to Ben the Fourth, Daian, and Wang Jing. They had tea, and Xia asked if he might see the old eunuch, but He said:

"His Excellency is at the Palace now." Then Xia presented a red card.

"Please give my humble respects to his Excellency," he said. "I am sorry I am too late to see him." He took leave of them.

Captain He immediately sent him a present in return. It was getting late. Captain He entertained Ximen Qing in one of the small rooms in the garden. During the meal, the boys sang for them, and it was the second night watch before they went to bed.

Ximen Qing had not forgotten what had happened the night before. He told Wang Jing to bring his bedclothes to the study and sleep there. In the middle of the night the boy went to him. They kissed each other and he found the boy's lips very fragrant.

The next morning, Ximen was up before dawn and joined Captain He. They went together to the Palace to wait for the opening of the East Gate. After a while the gates of the Throne Hall were swung open, and they heard the sound of gongs and cymbals. Then the Gate of Heaven was opened, and they caught a glimpse of the most glorious and august diadem. The Son of Heaven was returning from the altar of the south, and all his officers, civil and military, waited to receive him. Gongs were beaten and bells rung, as the Emperor came back to his palace to receive the homage of his officers. Clouds of incense streamed towards the skies. The great ceremonial fans waved to and fro.

His Majesty ascended the throne, and the cracking of whips gave the signal for silence. The officers, holding their tablets of office before their breasts, made five salutations and kowtowed three times before the throne, doing homage to the Sacred Majesty.

Then, from the palace, came an officer and spoke the words of the Emperor that all might hear them.

"We have reigned for twenty years," he said, "and at last We have completed the building of the *Genjue*. Heaven has been Our helper. Now as We enter upon another new year, We pray that the good fortune Heaven has bestowed Upon Us, may be shared by you."

There came out from among a group of high officials, one whose ceremonial boots trod proudly, whose sleeves waved in the breeze. This was Cai Jing, the Chancellor, Minister of the Left, President of the Board of Civil Service, Imperial Tutor and Duke of Lu. Carrying his ivory tablet low before him, he knelt down upon the golden steps.

"May Your Majesty live forever! In awe and humility, we kowtow before the Son of Heaven. As Your Majesty has said, you have governed this Empire for twenty years. During those years the Empire has enjoyed peace and prosperity, and the harvests have been plentiful. Heaven has observed Your Majesty's conduct, appreciated Your Majesty's labors, and given many signs of favor. There has been no war or disturbance upon the frontier, and people from all lands have come to pay tribute before Your Heavenly Throne. Your Majesty's palace is as a mountain of silver towering in the sky, and Your Majesty's capital of jade is unique in all the world.

"The Most Precious and Sacred Will is expressed in Your Majesty's exalted palace; purple candles have been burned in the palace of Heaven. How fortunate are we, that we should live in a world so blessed.

"The relations between Your Majesty and the people are perfect. We pray that You may be spared to live as the mountains, that the light of the sun and the moon may always shine upon us. Your Majesty's graciousness is beyond our power to express: we can only enjoy the blessings that come to us through it. We offer Your Majesty our most humble congratulations and praise."

There was a long delay. Then the Emperor's word was announced to them again.

"You, Our worthy officers, have offered Us your praises. Once again, We appreciate your loyalty and fidelity. We are content. It is Our purpose upon the first day of the New Year to change the title of Our reign to the first year of Chonghe. This We shall duly make known to Heaven. There shall be a general amnesty throughout the Empire, and reward for all those who serve Us."

After listening to this, the Chancellor withdrew.

"It is his Majesty's command," the herald said, "that if anyone has any business to bring forward, he shall do so now. Otherwise his Majesty will retire."

A man stepped out of the crowd, wearing a scarlet gown, with a jade clasp to his girdle, and a golden fish as his badge of office. He lowered his ivory tablet and bowed towards the Emperor, then knelt upon the golden steps.

"Zhu Mian, Grand Marshal, Commander-in-Chief of the Royal Guard, presents twenty-six magistrates to Your Majesty. Inspection has been made of their work, and the question of their promotion or dismissal determined. They have come to the Capital to obtain their new commissions, and since I dare not myself make the decision, I bring them before Your Majesty and await Your Majesty's command.

The twenty-six magistrates knelt down behind the Grand Marshal.

After a while, the Imperial Decree issued. "Let them be given their commissions in accordance with precedent."

Marshal Zhu retired.

The Emperor waved his arms, and the officers withdrew. His Majesty went into the palace.

The officers poured out of the two gates, headed by twelve elephants that marched unattended. The grooms and servants of the Ministers hurried to the service of their masters. There was a crowd of carriages outside the palace gates, and the shouting of the people made a noise like a storm at sea, while the neighing of their horses seemed like an earthquake. The magistrates came out and mounted their horses, and all rode together to their headquarters to wait for orders. A messenger came out to them. "The Grand Marshal," he told them, "will not be here. He is going to celebrate the Winter Festival at the Imperial Tutor's palace." The magistrates dispersed.

Ximen Qing returned to Captain He's place and spent another day there. The next day, they went together to their headquarters and secured their documents. Ximen went to say good-bye to Zhai, then went back to pack up his luggage, so that he would be ready to return to Qinghe with Captain He.

That evening, the old eunuch entertained them to dinner. He bade his nephew consult Ximen Qing in all things, and not make any decisions for himself.

On the twentieth day of the eleventh month, they set out for Qinghe, with more than twenty servants following them. They traveled upon the high road to Shandong. It was the season of greatest cold and every drop of water was frozen. They saw nothing but barren hills and deserted paths. Upon the withered trees only the blackbirds sat in the feeble sunshine. Snow and frozen clouds hung above the river. Over one hill they went, and found another one before them. They passed one village, and came to another. When they had crossed the Yellow River and had come to a town on the other side, they were suddenly overtaken by a violent windstorm.

> Not this the roaring of the tiger
> Or the muttering of the dragon.
> The cold air stung their faces; the sharp wind
> Pierced their very hearts.
> There was at first no sign of its coming
> But soon the mist and cloud were swept away.
> It rocked the trees and made mad the sea
> It hustled the pebbles and urged the stones

And the skies were dark.
The high trees moaned without ceasing
And the lonely goose lay broken in the ditch.
The sand drove across the ground
The dust screened the sky.
The small stones were flung about as in a whirlwind
And the dust was as the dust set up
By millions of soldiers on the march.
This tempest was so violent
It smashed the trees on the frontier of hell
And carried away the dust from the palace
Of the god of the underworld.
Chang E, the angel of the moon,
Shut the doors of her palace in haste.
Liezi, walking in the skies,
Called out for help.
The Jade Monarch could hardly stay
On the summit of the Koulkun Mountains.
Heaven and Earth alike
Were in a mad confusion.

Ximen Qing and Captain He were in sedan chairs, wrapped in rugs and blankets. The wind was so fearful that they could not advance even a single step. It was late, and they feared that highwaymen might come out from the woods and attack them. Ximen Qing sent some of his men forward to try to find a shelter for the night, saying that they would go on again when the wind abated. It was some time before a place was found. Then they discovered an old monastery with a few bare willow trees outside it. The walls were half in ruins.

The walls and the memorials were covered with rank grass
The corridors and the ancient sanctuaries were on the point of
   falling.
The monks at midnight had no light.
When the moon had set, it made the heart grieve
To see the monks at meditation.

The two officers hastened there. It was called the Temple of the Yellow Dragon. There were only a few monks, engaged in meditation without fire and without light. The rooms were nearly all in ruins, and many of them were patched with boards.

The abbot came to welcome them and made a fire to make them some tea. Hay was brought for their horses. When the tea was ready, Ximen

Qing took from his bag preserved chicken, meat, cakes and fruit, and Captain He and he made their supper on this food, together with some porridge that the abbot prepared for them. They stayed the night in this place.

The next day, the wind had stopped and the skies were clear. They gave the monks a tael of silver, and set out again.

CHAPTER 72

Pan Jinlian Quarrels with Ruyi'er

They flourish their arms and shrug their shoulders
Sometimes warm and sometimes cold.
Even a eunuch may raise a family
And a stone virgin bring forth a child.
Loss of power is the one thing to escape.
To some, their own children are not so much to be loved
As other people's children.
Father and Mother are not of great account
At any moment their own children
May pass them by.

While Ximen Qing was away, Wu Yueniang was a little anxious. There were so many ladies in the household, and she was afraid there might be trouble. She exhorted them all to keep the peace, and made sure that the main gate was closed and the back door locked, every night. The ladies stayed at home, doing needlework. Whenever Chen Jingji had to go to the inner court for clothes or anything, Yueniang took care that either Chunhong or Laian went with him. She was particularly careful about the closing of doors and windows and made quite sure that everything was safe.

Pan Jinlian could see nothing of Jingji.

One day, the nurse, Ruyi'er, gave her an opportunity to make trouble. Yueniang took some of Ximen Qing's clothes, shirts, and underclothes to Ruyi'er, and told her and Madam Han to wash and iron them. Chunmei was washing at the same time, and she sent Qiuju to borrow the dolly pin. Ruyi'er and Yingchun were using it, and they would not give it up. "You borrowed it only the other day," Ruyi'er said, "and here you are, after it again. We have all these shirts and clothes of our master's to do while Madam Han is here."

Qiuju, in a very ill humor, went back and said to Chunmei: "You are always sending me there to borrow things, and now they won't lend me the dolly pin. Yingchun was willing enough. It was Ruyi'er who wouldn't do it."

"What's that?" Chunmei cried. "Why shouldn't we borrow a lamp in the daytime? She won't lend us a dolly pin, won't she? Here I am with Mother's foot binders to wash. What am I going to beat them with? Go to the inner court and borrow one from somebody else."

Jinlian was washing her feet in her room. She overheard this. She hated Ruyi'er and was glad of the opportunity to make trouble. "How dare that strumpet refuse to lend us the dolly pin?" she cried. "Go yourself. And, if she makes any bones about it, curse her well. That ought to settle her."

Chunmei dashed away like a whirlwind. "Who is the stranger in this house?" she said, "are you or are we? You refuse to lend me this dolly pin. That means, I suppose, that there is a new mistress here now."

"If I hadn't been using it," Ruyi'er said, "I shouldn't have kept it."

She got angry in her turn. "The Great Lady," she said, "thought that, with Sister Han here, it was a splendid opportunity to get these shirts and trousers washed. I told Qiuju she could have the dolly pin as soon as I had finished with it. Then she went and told you I wouldn't lend it to her. It was a lie. Yingchun heard what I said."

Jinlian came along. "Now, woman," she said, "don't try any tricks on me. Since your mistress died, you have been taking her place in this apartment. You are washing his Lordship's clothes. I suppose you are trying to make out that, if you didn't, nobody else would. We might all be dead, and you the only one to attend to his clothes. I know. You think you will be able to score over the rest of us. But you needn't think you're going to frighten me by games of this sort."

"Fifth Lady," Ruyi'er said, "it is really nothing of the sort. If the Great Lady had not given me orders, you don't think I should have taken it upon myself?"

"You wicked bone," Jinlian cried, "you have far too much to say. I ask you: who was it served his Lordship with tea in the middle of the night? Who made his bed for him? Who asked him for a new dress? You think I don't know the games you play with him on the sly. But I do know, and I'm not afraid to say so."

"My mistress died, even though she had borne a son," Ruyi'er said. "What chance have I against you?"

This made Jinlian wild. Her face, which was already red, became redder. She ran forward, caught Ruyi'er by the hair, and thumped her in the belly. Fortunately, Madam Han was there to separate them. Jinlian went on cursing. "You shameless strumpet! You husband-stealer! We have been neglected long enough, and now you try to get our husband away from us. What are you doing here at all? Even if you are Laiwang's wife come to life again, I'm not afraid of you."

Ruyi'er cried. She put her hair straight. "I have not been long in this household," she said. "I don't know anything about Laiwang's wife. I only know I came here as a nurse."

"If you are a nurse, you should behave as a nurse," Jinlian said. "Why do you set the whole place on its head like a disturbing spirit? I know what I'm about, and I'll see you don't get away with it."

Meng Yulou came from the inner court. "Sister," she said, "I asked you to play chess with me. Why didn't you come? What is the matter?" She pulled Jinlian away to her own room.

When they had sat down, she asked Jinlian what was wrong. The woman was now calmer. Chunmei brought them tea.

"See!" Jinlian said. "That strumpet has made my hands quite cold. I can't lift my cup. I was in my room, making a pattern for my shoes, when your maid came for me. I told her I was going to lie down and rest a while before I came. I lay on the bed, but did not go to sleep. Chunmei was washing my skirt, and I told her she might as well wash my foot binders too. A few moments later, I heard a great to-do, and found that Qiuju had gone to borrow a dolly pin, and the woman wouldn't lend it to her. She said we had had it the other day, and she wasn't going to lend it to us again because she was washing his Lordship's clothes. That annoyed me, and I told Chunmei to go and curse her. You see, she has been misbehaving herself for some time, and I was determined to teach her a lesson. What sort of a woman does she think she is? His Lordship never married her. She is worse than Laiwang's wife, and I wasn't going to forgive her. She wouldn't give way, and I gave her a real good cursing. If Madam Han hadn't been there to stop me, I would have pulled the strumpet's guts out. The Great Lady is very much to blame. You remember how she spoiled Laiwang's wife by being too indulgent. When I had a row with her, all the blame fell upon me. The Great Lady even went so far as to say I was responsible for Laiwang being kicked out. Now she is dealing with this woman as she dealt with Laiwang's wife. If the woman is a nurse, let her mind her own business. We are not going to let her carry on before our very eyes. We are not going to have dust thrown in our eyes. The shameless hussy! Her mistress is dead, but she still stays on in that apartment. Every time he comes home, he goes and bows to the portrait and mumbles something or other. Nobody knows what he says. During the night he asks for tea and this strumpet ups and gets it for him. Then she pulls the bedclothes over him, and they start their tricks. It is the maids' business to serve tea. Why should she take it upon herself? Why did she ask him for a new dress? The shameless fellow went to the shop immediately and got a roll of silk for her. You remember the last week's mind for Li Ping'er. He went there to burn some paper things for her. The maid and this strumpet were lying on the same bed, playing knuckle-bones. Did he say a word to stop them? Not he! He said: 'You can have the food and wine that have been offered to the dead lady.' That's how he treats them. One day I overheard the strumpet saying: 'I wonder what is keeping his Lordship so long. We must be ready for him.' I went in, and she was alarmed and didn't say any more. What a woman! The rascally strumpet! But he is so anxious for fresh meat he will take anything that comes along. He never troubles whether it is good or bad. The lustful fellow! The strumpet says her husband is dead; but who was that fellow with a baby in his arms looking around the gate the other day? She is deceiving us. She is like Li Ping'er come to life again, quite a changed woman. And the Great Lady spends all her time in her own room and acts as though she were deaf and dumb. Whenever we go and say anything to her, she says: 'You are mistaken.'"

Yulou could not help laughing. "How do you manage to get all this information?" she said.

"It's common gossip," Jinlian said. "Everybody knows it. If you bury a body in the snow, it always turns up again when the snow melts."

"She said her husband was dead," Yulou said. "Who is this husband, then?"

"The clouds never disperse unless there is wind," Jinlian said, "and business is never done without telling a lot of lies. She would never have got the job if she hadn't deceived us. You remember what she looked like when she first came. Half starved, yellow-faced, as thin as a lath, and her limbs shaking. Now she has enjoyed good food for a couple of years, she starts stealing our husband. If we don't put a stop to it, she will have a baby one of these days, and, if that happens, where shall we be? And whose baby would it be?"

"There is something in what you say," Yulou said, laughing. They stayed talking for a while and then went to the inner court to play chess.

One afternoon, Ximen Qing reached Qinghe. He told Ben the Fourth and Wang Jing to take the luggage home, and went with Captain He to the office. He helped to make the necessary arrangements there, then mounted his horse and rode home.

Wu Yueniang received him in the hall and gave him water to wash his face. He ordered a maid to set up a table in the courtyard that he might offer incense to Heaven and Earth in thanksgiving for his safe return. Yueniang asked him why he did this.

"Oh, it was terrible," Ximen Qing said, "I very nearly lost my life. On the twenty-third, when we had crossed the Yellow River and come to the place called the Town of the Eight Corners, there was a frightful storm. Dust and sand filled our eyes and we could make no progress at all. It was late and for a hundred miles we had not seen a soul. We were alarmed because we had so much luggage and we were afraid highwaymen might suddenly attack us. Then we came to an old monastery. The monks were so poor that they were going without light. The only thing they could give us was porridge. We spent the night there and started off again the next morning. The wind had stopped. It was a much worse journey than the last one. The last was during the hot season, but it was more agreeable than this, because, not only was the weather terribly cold this time, but we always felt so insecure. It was a good thing for us we were on the plain when the storm arose. If it had come on while we were crossing the Yellow River, I don't know what might have happened. I vowed to offer a pig and a sheep to Heaven and Earth on the first day of the twelfth month."

"Why did you go to the office before you came home?" Yueniang asked.

"Magistrate Xia has been promoted to be an officer of the Imperial Escort," Ximen said. "That is an appointment in the Capital and he is not coming back here. The new captain is He Yingshou, a nephew of Eunuch He. He is a boy of about twenty. He is quite ignorant and the old eunuch begged me to look after him. I couldn't leave him to find his own way to the office. He knows nothing about the place. He has bought Xia's house for twelve hundred taels. I arranged it all for him. He is going to send for his family as soon as Xia's people have left.

"I can't imagine who told Xia about these promotions. He sent a large sum of money to his Holiness Lin, and his Holiness told Marshal Zhu that he would like to retain his present position for another three years instead of going to the Capital. The Marshal spoke to his Eminence about the matter and it made matters most awkward. If it hadn't been for our kinsman Zhai speaking on my behalf, I might have lost my position. Our kinsman was very much annoyed. He said I had been very careless. I can't think who told Magistrate Xia."

"If you will forgive my saying so," his wife said, "you are indeed careless. Whenever you hear anything, you tell it first to one person and then to another. You like to show people how rich and powerful you are. You carelessly let things slip, and those who hear do not lose the opportunity. Then there is trouble. People worm secrets out of you and go off and use the information to their own advantage. You never hear about it till they have done all they wish to do."

"When I left Magistrate Xia," Ximen said, "he begged me repeatedly to do anything I could for his family. We must send them a present and call."

"It will be Mistress Xia's birthday on the second of next month,"

Yueniang said. "We will go then. As for you, you must be careful. Remember the saying: Never let people know more than a quarter of what you know yourself. Even your own wife may take advantage of you, not to mention other people."

As they were talking, Daian came and said: "Ben the Fourth would like to know if you are going to his Lordship Xia's place."

"Tell him to go when he has had something to eat," Ximen said.

Li Jiao'er, Meng Yulou, Pan Jinlian and Ximen Dajie came to welcome him home. They sat down together and talked.

Ximen Qing remembered that the last time he had returned from the Eastern Capital, Li Ping'er was still alive. He went to her room, bowed before her tablet and wept. Ruyi'er, Yingchun, and Xiuchun came to kowtow to him. Then Yueniang sent Xiaoyu to ask him to go to dinner in the inner court. He gave orders that those who had accompanied him on his journey should be given five taels of silver.

He sent a card to Major Zhou, and told Laixing to get half a pig, half a sheep, forty measures of fine flour, a sack of white rice, a jar of wine, two hams, two geese, ten chickens, and take them, with a supply of condiments, to Captain He. He also sent a cook.

He was in the hall when Qintong came and said that Scholar Wen and Ying Bojue had come to see him. Ximen Qing ordered the boy to bring them in. They bowed several times and said: "What a rough journey you must have had." Ximen thanked them for looking after his house in his absence.

"This morning, when I awoke," Bojue said, "I heard the crying of the magpies on the roof, and my wife said to me: 'I expect that means his Lordship Ximen is back. Why don't you go and see?' I said: 'Brother started on the twelfth and he hasn't been away a fortnight yet. How can he be back already?' 'Well,' my wife said, 'whether he is back or not, you must go.' She told me to dress and come, and here you are. I congratulate you."

He saw the wine and rice and other things collected outside the hall. "To whom are you sending these things?" he said.

"I came back with Captain He, the new magistrate," Ximen said. "His family has not come yet and he is staying at the office for the time being. I am sending him some provisions. I have invited him to dinner tomorrow, and I am going to ask you and Uncle Wu to come too."

"I must remind you," Bojue said, "that Uncle Wu and you are officers. Master Wen wears a scholar's hat. I am only a private person, and it seems hardly fitting that I should join you. I don't know what he may think. He may laugh at me."

"If that's all that is worrying you," Ximen said, laughing, "I will lend you my silk hat, and, when Captain He asks who you are, I'll tell him you're my eldest son. Will that suit you?"

They laughed. "I am serious," Bojue said. "My size in hats is eight and three-tenths. Yours won't fit me."

"I take a hat eight and three-tenths too," Scholar Wen said. "Perhaps you would like my scholar's hat!"

"No," Ximen Qing said. "Don't let him have it. When he goes to pawn himself, he might wear it."

"Well said, Sir," Scholar Wen said, "the joke is on both of us."

Tea was brought. "I suppose his Lordship Xia will stay at the Capital," Scholar Wen said, "or is he coming back

"He is now an officer of the Imperial Escort," Ximen said. "He wears embroidered robes and carries a wand. It is an exalted position and he will not come back."

He looked at the card that was to go with the provisions for Captain He, and bade Daian take them. Then he went with Ying Bojue and Scholar Wen to the side room and sat down on the stove bed. He sent Qintong to tell Wu Hui, Zheng Chun, Zheng Feng and Zuo Shun that they would be wanted the following day. The table was set and they began to drink. Ximen told a servant to get another pair of chopsticks and invite his son-in-law.

Chen Jingji came and sat down with them. They sat near the fire and, while the wine went around, Ximen Qing told them of the dangers he had passed through.

"Brother," Bojue said, "you have a heart stout enough to carry you through a hundred dangers. Even if there had been ruffians about, they could not have harmed you."

"'If a good man were to govern the country for a hundred years,'" Scholar Wen said, "'he would be able to make evil men into peaceful citizens, and could do away with the punishment of death.'[1] You are doing the Emperor's service, and Heaven will not let you come to harm."

Ximen Qing asked how things had been in the household.

"There was nothing of any consequence," Jingji said. "His Excellency An of the Office of Works sent twice to ask if you had returned. Only yesterday a man came from him, and I told him you were not back."

Then Ping'an came and said that the junior officers and their men were outside. Ximen Qing went to the hall and gave orders that the two officers should be admitted. They came and knelt down. "When will you assume your office?" they asked, "and what money will you require?"

---

1. A quotation from the *Analects of Confucius*, Book XIII, Chap. 11.

"Let everything be as before," Ximen told them.

"Last year, you were alone," they said, "but now you are promoted to a higher office, and Captain He comes to the office also. It is not the same. There are two officers instead of one."

"Take ten taels more, then," Ximen Qing said.

As the two men were going away, Ximen stopped them. "You had better ask Captain He when he wishes to assume office."

"Captain He says on the twenty-sixth," they said.

"Very well. See that everything is ready on that day." When the two junior officers had gone, Master Qiao came. Ximen Qing asked him to stay, but he went away as soon as he had taken tea. Ximen Qing went back to Ying Bojue and Scholar Wen, and they drank together until evening. That night, Ximen slept with Yueniang

Old woman Wen heard that Ximen had returned. She told Wang the Third, and he sent a card of invitation to Ximen Qing. In return, Ximen sent Daian with a pair of pig's trotters, two live fish, two roast ducks and a jar of wine as a belated birthday present to Lady Lin. Lady Lin gave Daian three *qian* of silver.

The next day Ximen Qing entertained Captain He to dinner. It was laid in the great hall. Very careful preparations had been made. Uncle Wu, Ying Bojue, and Scholar Wen came early and took tea with Ximen Qing. He sent a man to remind Captain He. Then the singing boys came and kowtowed to Ximen.

"Why haven't you engaged Li Ming today?" Bojue asked.

"If he doesn't come of his own accord, I shall not send for him," Ximen said.

Ping'an brought a card and announced Major Zhou. Uncle Wu, Scholar Wen, and Ying Bojue withdrew to a side room while Ximen Qing put on his ceremonial clothes and went to receive Major Zhou in the great hall. The Major congratulated Ximen on his promotion, and Ximen thanked him for the men who had acted as his escort on the journey to the Capital. They sat down and Zhou asked what he had seen at the Capital and in the Court. When Ximen had told him, he said: "I suppose Xia will be taking his family to the Capital?"

"Yes," Ximen said, "but not before next month. For the time being, Captain He is living at the office, but he has bought Xia's house. I made the arrangement myself."

"Excellent!" Major Zhou said. Seeing the tables all set out, he asked what guests Ximen was expecting.

"It is only a very plain meal in honor of Captain He," Ximen said. "It is the least I can do seeing that we are both in the same office."

When Major Zhou had drunk his tea, he stood up. "One of these days," he said, "I shall bring the officers of my command to offer you two gentlemen our congratulations."

"You are too kind," Ximen said. Thank you for troubling to come and see me."

They bowed to each other. Major Zhou went away and Ximen Qing rejoined his three friends.

It was late in the afternoon when Captain He came. Ximen Qing introduced Uncle Wu and the others and they exchanged greetings. After tea, they took off their ceremonial clothes. Captain He soon realized that Ximen Qing was a very rich man, so splendid was the repast served to him. There were four singing boys playing different instruments. They drank together till the first night watch, then Captain He went back to the office. Uncle Wu, Ying Bojue, and Scholar Wen went away at the same time. Ximen Qing dismissed the singing boys, told the servants to clear everything away, and went to Pan Jinlian's room.

Jinlian had taken particular pains to make herself look pretty and she had washed her body with perfumed water. She was expecting him and, when he came, she smiled sweetly. She took his clothes and told Chunmei to make tea. They went to bed, and, under the coverlets, embraced and pressed their tender bodies closely together. She used every one of her hundred charms to give him pleasure. They enjoyed each other for a while, then Ximen Qing found that he could not sleep. He told her how he had longed for her while he had been away. Then, as he was still unsatisfied, he asked her to play the flute for him. She was ready to do anything he asked, so that she might the more firmly establish her hold over him. They had been separated for a long time. She had been starved for love so long that passion set her afire. She would have made herself a part of him. She grasped his penis and wanted to suck it almost all night. He wished to make water, but she would not let him go. "Darling," she said, "never mind how much there is; my mouth can take it all. It is chilly tonight and you might take cold if you got out of bed. It would be more trouble."

Ximen Qing was delighted. "Dearest," he said, "I don't believe anyone else would love me as you do." He made water into her mouth and she drank it gradually. "Do you like it?' said Ximen.

"It is a little bitter," she replied. "Give me some fragrant tea leaves to take the taste away."

"The tea leaves are in my white silk coat," Ximen said. "Get them for yourself." Jinlian pulled the coat to her, took the tea leaves, and put them into her mouth.

Readers, concubines are always ready to lead their husbands on and to bewitch them. To this end, they will go to any length of shamelessness and endure any shameful thing. Such practices would be abhorrent to a real wife who had married her husband in the proper way.

Ximen Qing and Jinlian enjoyed ecstasies of pleasure that night.

The next day, Ximen Qing went to the office with Captain He. It was their first appearance in their new posts. There was a banquet, and musicians played for them. In the afternoon Ximen went home and the soldiers of his office sent a present of food. Wang the Third sent a man to ask him to dinner. Ximen was about to leave for Wang's house, when a servant came and announced the arrival of An, of the Office of Works. Ximen Qing hurriedly put on his robes and went to welcome him.

An, who now held the rank of a Vice President, wore a girdle with a golden clasp, and a silver pheasant as the badge of his office. He was followed by a host of officers. They entered the hall, smiling, and congratulating one another.

"I have asked several times when you were expected to return," An said, when they had sat down, "but I was told you were not yet back."

"I could not leave the Capital until I had been presented at Court," Ximen said.

"I wanted to ask a favor of you," An said. "Cai Xiaotang, his Eminence's ninth son, is governor of Jiujiang. He is on his way to the Capital and I have had a letter from him to say he will be here very shortly. Song Songquan, Qian Yunye, Huang Taiyu and I would like to entertain him. But, for that, we should need your house, and I don't know whether you would be willing to lend it to us or not."

"Certainly you may have it," Ximen said. "When is he coming?"

"On the twenty-seventh," An said. "I will send the necessary money tomorrow. It is extremely kind of you."

They drank tea, and Vice President An went away.

Ximen Qing went to Lady Lin's house and sent in his card. Wang the Third came out to receive him and took him to the great hall. Above the place of honor hung a golden scroll with the words: "The Hall of Loyalty Continuing." There were other scrolls on either side. One said, "The Wind and Frost wear down the mighty Trees," and the other, "Mountains and Rivers, Girdles and Whetstones are always new."

Wang the Third made a reverence to Ximen Qing and asked him to take the place of honor. Tea was brought, and he himself handed it. After tea they talked for a while until dinner was served. Two boys sang to them.

"Will you not ask her Ladyship to come?" Ximen Qing said.

Wang the Third sent a servant to invite his mother to join them.

Very soon the servant returned. "Her Ladyship asks that you will go to the inner court to see her," he said.

Wang the Third asked Ximen Qing to go, and Ximen asked Wang the Third to lead the way. So they went to the hall.

Lady Lin was wearing pearls and ornaments on her head, a scarlet, straight-sleeved gown, and a girdle decorated with gold and green jade. She wore a silken skirt embroidered with the design of the hundred flowers. Her face was powdered till it was as white as silver. Ximen Qing prepared to make a reverence to her and asked her to take the place of honor. "You are my guest," she said. "The place of honor is due to you." Finally, they made equal reverences, and sat down.

"My young son," Lady Lin said, "is very inexperienced. He was unfortunate enough to incur your displeasure, but you were generous and punished the fellows who led him astray. I don't know how to thank you. I have prepared this very simple entertainment for you, but I feel that really I should kowtow. Why have you sent me presents? I shall feel embarrassed if I accept them, and lacking in courtesy if I decline them."

"I had to go to the Eastern Capital on duty," Ximen Qing said, "I could not come to congratulate you on your birthday. These trifling presents you speak of are really intended for your servants."

Old woman Wen was standing beside Lady Lin. Ximen said to her: "Madam Wen, please give me a cup that I may offer her Ladyship some wine." He called Daian, who brought a dress of very fashionable style, embroidered with gold. This was put on a tray, and offered to Lady Lin. The dress was so bright that it was dazzling to the eyes. Lady Lin was delighted. Old woman Wen brought gold and silver cups. Wang the Third was going to send for the boys to sing, but Lady Lin said it would be better if they played outside. When Ximen had offered wine to her, she offered it to him in return. Then Wang the Third offered wine to him. Ximen would have made a reverence to the young man in return, but Lady Lin said:

"My lord, you must stand and allow him to pay you the respect that is your due."

"I dare not," Ximen Qing said, "the Rites do not allow it."

"My lord," Lady Lin said, "surely you are wrong. Your rank is now such that you might be his father. My son, in his earlier youth, was very poorly educated. He never associated with gentlemen. If you are well disposed to him, you may, perhaps, be willing to teach him something of the ways of the world. I would even venture to suggest that you might take him under your guardianship and treat him as your son. If he gets into trouble, correct him. I will not stand in your way."

"Lady," Ximen Qing said, "you speak wisely, but your son is really both intelligent and amiable. He is still young and only on the threshold of life. As he acquires more experience, he will amend his ways. You must not worry about him."

Ximen Qing was persuaded to take the place of honor. Wang the Third offered him three cups of wine and made reverence to him four times. Then Ximen Qing made a reverence to Lady Lin, and she, smilingly, returned it. After this, whenever Wang the Third was in the presence of Ximen Qing, he called him Father.

After this simple ceremony, Lady Lin bade her son take Ximen Qing to the outer court to take off his ceremonial clothes. Daian brought a hat and he changed. The two men sat down, and the singing boys played and sang for them. When the cooks brought in food, Daian gave them a small present of money. When five courses had been served, and the singers had sung two songs, lights were brought. Ximen Qing stood up to take leave, but Wang the Third begged him not to go so pressingly that he remained. The young man took him to a small courtyard attached to the study. There were only three rooms, but there were delightful flowers and trees about, and the furniture was very handsome. A golden sign bore the words: "San-quan's Ship of Poesy." There were five old pictures on the walls.

Ximen Qing asked who Sanquan was. Wang the Third was reluctant to tell him, but at last he said: "It is your son's name." Ximen Qing said nothing.

Tall jars were brought. They played darts and drank, and the singing boys sang for them again. Lady Lin, in the inner court, looked after the cooks and servants, sending them with dishes and fruits.

It was the second night watch before Ximen Qing went away. He was almost tipsy. He distributed money to the cooks and singers, and went home.

When he reached home, he went at once to Jinlian's room. She had not gone to bed, but had taken off her headdress and painted her face very delicately. She had made tea and burned incense in a golden burner. Now she was waiting for him, and when he came, she was delighted. She took his clothes and told Chunmei to make him a special cup of Sparrow-Tongue Tea. Chunmei helped him to take off his clothes and girdle. He went to bed. Jinlian took off her ornaments, put on a pair of bed shoes, and went to bed too. They lay down together and entwined their legs. Ximen Qing made a pillow of one arm and pressed her close to him with the other. Her body seemed to him as smooth as a piece of soft jade. His breast touched hers; their cheeks were close together. They kissed; their hearts seemed to melt away within them, and they were thrilled to the very center of their beings.

"My child," Ximen said, "did you ever think of me when I was away?"

"I never forgot you for a single second. The nights seemed so long. When I lay down, I could not sleep. I heated my bed and made it as warm as I could, but I still felt cold, so cold, indeed, that I could not stretch my legs out. I had to suffer and keep them drawn up. I kept thinking you would come, but you never came. Oh, many tears fell upon this pillow. Then dear little Chunmei saw how melancholy I was and sighing, and she cheered me as best she could. She used to play chess with me in the evenings. We stayed up till the first night watch, then went to bed and slept together. That was how I felt, Brother. I wonder how it was with you.

"Little oily mouth," Ximen said, "I have several wives, but, as everyone knows, I love you best."

"No, you are deceiving me," Jinlian said. "You are like a boy who takes rice from the bowl but keeps his eyes on the jar all the time. You think I don't know it. Do you remember how you and Laiwang's wife were as close together as honey and oil mingled? You never thought about me then. Li Ping'er had a baby, and you treated me like a black-eyed hen. Now they are gone, and I am still strong and well. You are like a willow catkin blown about by the wind. You have been secretly carrying on with Ruyi'er. You don't seem to care what sort of creature she is. After all, she is only a nurse, and, besides, she has a husband. If you take her on, one of these days her husband will bring all his sheep outside your door. You are an officer now. What are you going to do when the scandalmongers begin to talk about it? When you were away, that woman quarreled with me, screamed at me, and wouldn't give way an inch. That was when I sent Chunmei to borrow a dolly pin from her."

"Dear, dear!" Ximen Qing said. "It doesn't matter who she is, she must not forget that she is a servant here. I am surprised she had the audacity to quarrel with you. If you raise your hand, it should be a sign to her to pass, and if you lower it, she should know that she is barred from going any farther."

"Oh, you can always talk!" Jinlian said. "Now that Li Ping'er is dead, Ruyi'er has taken her mistress's place. I suppose you said to her: 'Serve me well, and you shall have everything that belonged to your mistress.' Did you say that?"

"Don't be so silly. I said nothing of the sort. If you will forgive her, I will make her come and kowtow to you tomorrow."

"I don't want her apologies. I forbid you to go to her."

"When I go there to sleep," Ximen Qing said, "I have no other purpose than to remember your dead sister. I go to look at her tablet, and I have nothing whatever to do with the woman."

"You are such a liar, I don't believe you," Jinlian said. "It is more than a hundred days since Li Ping'er died. Why should you go to gaze upon her tablet? You don't go to watch before the tablet, you go to make the place like a miller's grinding place. Before midnight we hear the sound of the bell and, after midnight, the sound of the winnowing."

Ximen Qing pulled her to him and kissed her. "You funny little strumpet," he said "where did you get such sharp ears?"

He told her to turn over, and inserted his penis from behind. He held her legs and moved in and out noisily. "Do you fear me or not?" he cried. "Will you try to control my actions any more?"

"If I didn't," Jinlian said, "you would fly off in the air. I know you can't give the woman up, but, if you wish to have her, you must ask my permission, and, if she asks you for anything, you must tell me before you give it to her. I won't have you giving her things without my knowledge. If you do, and I find out, you shall see whether I make trouble or not. I and that strumpet will die together. It is the story of Li Ping'er over again. You could think of no one but her, and I was as little to you as the lowest of your women. You rotten peach! You are like bean sprouts that haven't been tied with proper string. But your old mother is too clever for you."

Ximen Qing laughed. It was the third night watch before they were content to put their arms around one another and go to sleep. They slept till nearly dawn.

Before it was light, Jinlian, still hungry for more, fondled his weapon with her slender fingers till it was ready once more for action.

"Darling," she said, "I want to lie on you." She climbed on to him, and played the game of making a candle upside down. She put her arms around his neck and wriggled about. She asked him to grip her firmly by the waist. Then she lifted herself up and dropped herself again; soon his penis entered her up to its very root, and the only part that stayed outside was that bound by the clasp.

"Darling," she said, "I will make a red silk belt for you, and you can keep in it the medicine the monk gave you. And I will make two supports that you can tie at the root of it and fasten around your waist. When they are tightly tied, it will be soft and go in all the way. Don't you think that better than this clasp, which is so hard and such a nuisance?"

"Yes, my child, make it by all means. The medicine is in my little box. Put it in for yourself."

"Come back tonight," Jinlian said, "and we will see what it is like."

Daian came with a card and asked Chunmei if his master was out of bed. "His Excellency An," he said, "has sent money, two jars of wine, and four pots of flowers."

"Father is not up yet," Chunmei told him. "Ask the man to wait."

"He has a long way to go," Daian said. "He is on his way to the new wharf."

Ximen Qing overheard this. He asked what was the matter, and the card was brought to him. Upon it was written: 'I send you eight taels for the refreshment of Xiaotang. The food for the others may be what is customary. I trust you will instruct your servants to make careful preparations, and thank you for your kindness. I send you also four pots with seasonable flowers in the hope that you will like them. The two jars of wine may, perhaps, serve for the entertainment of the guests. Please accept them indulgently.

Ximen Qing got up. He did not dress his hair but, putting on a felt hat and a gown, went to the hall. He sent for his Excellency's messenger. The man presented the silver and the pots of flowers. One contained red plum, another white plum, the third jasmine and the fourth, magnolia. And there were two jars of Southern wine. Ximen was very pleased. He gave the man a card in return and five *qian* of silver for himself.

"When will the gentlemen arrive?" he asked. "Will it be necessary to engage actors?"

"Their Excellencies will be early," the man said. "They would like to have the Haiyan company." He went away.

Ximen Qing told the servants to take the flowers to his study and sent Daian to engage the actors. As it was Meng Yulou's birthday, he arranged for them to come in the evening also. Laian was sent to buy provisions.

We now return to Ying Bojue. On the twenty-eighth day of the month, his baby would be one month old, and there was to be a celebration. He took five cards and sent Ying Bao with a box to the house opposite Ximen Qing's. He was going to ask Scholar Wen to write invitations to Ximen's five ladies.

He had left his own house and turned into the street when he heard a voice behind him calling: "Uncle! Uncle!" It was Li Ming. Bojue stopped, and Li Ming asked where he was going.

"I am going to see Scholar Wen on business," Bojue said.

"I was just coming to see you," Li Ming said. "There is something I want to tell you."

Ying Bojue saw a porter carrying a box behind Li Ming, and he took Li Ming to his house. The boy kowtowed to him and presented the box. There were two roast ducks and two bottles of spirits in it.

"I have nothing but these trifles to offer you," Li Ming said, "but I should like to ask your help." He knelt down and could not be persuaded to rise. Bojue finally pulled him up.

"You silly boy. If you have anything to say, say it. There was no need for you to bring these presents."

"I have served his Lordship Ximen ever since I was a little boy," Li Ming said. "Now he is giving his patronage to others and leaving me out in the cold. I have nothing to do with Li Guijie's affairs. We are not in the same boat. His Lordship is angry with her, and he seems to be angry with me too. I have had no opportunity to explain matters. So I have come to you. I beg you to go and speak for me. Tell him that I had nothing to do with Guijie's naughty behavior. Since I have incurred his displeasure, all the boys in my business make fun of me."

"You haven't been to his place for a long time," Bojue said.

"No," the boy said.

"That explains why, the other day, when Captain He was at his place, I only saw Wu Hui, Zheng Chun, Zheng Feng and Zuo Shun. You were not there, and I asked why. His Lordship told me that you never came near the place and he wasn't going to send for you. Now, you silly boy, pull yourself together and don't be such a blockhead."

"When he didn't send for me," Li Ming said, "I felt too shy to go of my own accord. The other four were there two or three days ago and, today, I find Laian is engaging two of them for the Third Lady's birthday. There is a party tomorrow, and the four boys will be there again without me. I am very miserable about it. Uncle, I want you to explain matters for me. I will come and kowtow to you again."

"I spend all my time helping others," Bojue said, "and I will do the best I can for you. I have done many, many things for people, and this trifling business of yours is nothing at all. Take these presents away. I know how you get your money, and I won't take them. Come with me, and let me make everything all right."

"I will not go unless you accept my present," Li Ming said. "You do not need the things, of course, but I am anxious to show my humble respect for you."

He implored Ying Bojue to take them, and, at last, Bojue did so. He gave thirty coppers to the porter who had carried the box. Then they set out together. They went first to the house opposite Ximen Qing's. They went into the courtyard. Bojue knocked at the door and asked if Scholar Wen was at home. The scholar was in the study, writing a card. "Please come in," he cried. Huatong opened the door, and Bojue went into the study. Scholar Wen greeted him. They sat down, and the scholar said: "You are early today. What have you been doing?"

"I have come to ask you to write a few invitations with your masterly brush. It will be the end of my little son's first month of life on the twenty-eighth, and I am inviting his Lordship's ladies."

"Give me the cards," Scholar Wen said, "I will write them for you with pleasure."

Bojue told Ying Bao to take out the cards and give them to Scholar Wen. The scholar took them to the inner room and had written two when Qitong came hurrying in and said: "Master, please write another two cards for my lady. She wishes to invite Mistress Qiao and Mistress Wu. Did you give Qintong the cards for Mistress Han and Mistress Meng?"

"Yes," Scholar Wen said, "they were sent off sometime ago."

"Master," Qitong said, "when you have finished those two cards, please write another four. They are for Mistress Huang the Fourth, Mistress Fu, Mistress Han, and Mistress Gan. Laian will come for them."

Qitong went away and Laian came for the four cards. Bojue said to him: "Is your master at home or at the office?"

"He has not been to the office today," Laian said. "He is in the hall receiving presents."

"It was very late when his Lordship came back from Wang's place last night," Scholar Wen said.

"Which Wang's?" Bojue asked.

"The general's," Scholar Wen told him.

This was the first Ying Bojue had heard of this business.

When Scholar Wen had finished the cards for Laian, he began again on those for Ying Bojue. When they were done, Bojue went across the road to Ximen's house with Li Ming.

Ximen Qing's hair was still undressed. He was in the hall, accepting presents and sending cards in return. Tables were being set out for the reception. He asked Bojue to sit down. Bojue thanked him for the gifts he had sent some days before and asked why the tables were being arranged. Ximen told him that his Excellency An was making use of the house for a reception to the Imperial Tutor's son.

"Are you having actors or singing boys?" Bojue asked.

"We are having the Haiyan company of actors," Ximen Qing said, "but I have engaged four singing boys as well."

"Who are they, Brother?" Bojue asked.

"Wu Hui, Zheng Feng, Zheng Chun and Zuo Shun," Ximen said.

"Why not Li Ming?"

"He has climbed too high to care about my patronage any more," Ximen said.

"Why should you say that, Brother?" Bojue said. "He can hardly come if you don't send for him. I didn't know you were angry with him. And the business for which you are angry with him is really not his concern at all.

He can't help what happens at the bawdy house. We must not be unfair to him. This morning he called at my house and said, with tears in his eyes, that, apart from the relations that have existed between you and his sister, he has served you himself for several years. Now, he says, you send for the others and will have nothing to do with him. He swore on his oath that he had nothing to do with that business at the house. If you are angry with him, it will be very awkward indeed for him. He is only a boy. He can't earn a great amount of money and, if you stop sending for him, his position will be impossible."

"Li Ming, come here!" he called. "Tell your father all about it. Why are you hiding there? Come here, I tell you. Even an ugly bride must meet her father-in-law sometime."

Li Ming was standing outside the hall. He bowed and then stood upright, like the image of a little devil. He had been listening to what they were saying and, when Bojue called him, he came in quickly and knelt down. He kowtowed repeatedly.

"Father," he said, "you must think about this again. If I had anything to do with that business, may my bones be broken to pieces by horses or carts, and may I die at the hand of the executioner. Your kindness to me in the past has always been so splendid. My people and I can never repay you. If you are angry with me, the others in my profession will laugh at me and look down on me. I can never find another master like you."

He cried aloud, knelt on the floor, and would not get up.

"We must settle this," Bojue said. "A gentleman never holds a lesser man's faults against him. Besides, it wasn't his fault and, even if it had been, you would have to forgive him now that he comes to apologize." He said to Li Ming: "I am wearing black clothes so I have to stand near a black pillar. Now you have spoken to your father, I am sure he won't be angry with you any more. But, in future, you must take care."

"Yes, Uncle," Li Ming said, "I will amend my ways."

"Since your uncle asks me to forgive you, I will do so," Ximen said slowly. "Stand up."

"Kowtow," Bojue said.

Li Ming kowtowed and rose to his feet.

Ying Bojue asked Ying Bao for the cards of invitation and gave them to Ximen Qing. "It will be my baby's month-day on the twenty-eighth," he said. "I am inviting my sisters-in-law to my humble dwelling."

Ximen Qing looked at the cards, and told Laian to take them with the box to Wu Yueniang. "I don't think they will be able to come that day," he said. "Tomorrow is the Third Lady's birthday, and there is this reception as well. On the twenty-eighth, my wife is going to call on Mistress Xia. I don't see how she can manage to come to your place."

"Brother," Bojue said, "would you seek my death? If my sister-in-law won't go, whom else can I count upon? Since the fruits are in the garden, I will go myself and ask them."

But Laian came in with the box empty. "The Great Lady says I am to tell Uncle Ying she accepts his kind invitation."

Bojue gave the empty box to Ying Bao. "Brother," he said, laughing, "you are always making game of me. If my sister-in-law had really refused to come, I would have bashed my head against the wall, and she would have been compelled to give way."

"Stay till I have done my hair," Ximen Qing said to Bojue, "and we will have something to eat." He went to the inner court.

"Now what?" Bojue said to Li Ming. "If it hadn't been for me, he would not have forgiven you. Don't mind what he says. Wealthy people are always bad-tempered, but you mustn't forget the proverb: An angry fist will never smite a smiling face. In these days, people like to be flattered. Even if you have money and set yourself up in business, you have always to be agreeable to your customers. If you pull a long face, nobody will bother about you. What you have to do is to fit yourself to circumstances and make yourself as adaptable as running water. Then you will make money. If you always try to ride the high horse, others will get good food but you will starve. You have served his Lordship for a long time, but you don't understand him yet. Tell Li Guijie to come tomorrow. If she is hot upon your heels, she will kill two birds with one stone. It is the Third Lady's birthday. She can come to congratulate her and apologize to him at the same time. Then everything will be well."

"Uncle," Li Ming said, "you are right. I will go home at once and tell my aunt."

Laian came in to set the table. "Uncle Ying," he said, "if you will wait a few moments, Father will be here."

Soon Ximen came in, properly dressed. They sat down.

"I haven't seen old Sun and Pockmarked Zhu for a long time," Ximen said.

"I told them to come," Bojue said, "but they declared you were offended with them. I told them that, thanks to your generosity, when the mosquitoes and grasshoppers were brought before the court, they were allowed to escape. They swore to me they would never have anything to do with young master Wang again. I hear you were at Wang's place yesterday. I hadn't known of it before."

"Yes," Ximen said. "There was a little party, and I was invited. I was asked if I would take the young man under my protection and treat him as a son. I didn't get back until the second night watch. Why shouldn't they go there any more? They can go if they like. It won't worry me. Why should I bother about the young man? I'm not really his father."

"If you mean what you say, Brother," Bojue said, "I am sure they will come to apologize and explain the whole business."

"There is nothing for them to apologize about," Ximen said. "Tell them to come, that's all."

Daian brought the food. There were all sorts of delicious things. Ximen Qing had porridge, and Bojue, rice.

"Why haven't the two singing boys come yet?" Ximen asked.

"They are here," Laian said.

"Go and have something to eat with them," Ximen said to Li Ming. One was Han Zuo, the other Shao Qian. They came and kowtowed before Ximen Qing, then went to have their dinner. Before long, Ying Bojue stood up. "I must be going now," he said, "I expect my people are waiting anxiously for me. In humble families like ours, it is very hard to get anything done. We have to buy everything. Buy, buy, buy from the bottom of the cooking stove to the sitting-room door."

"Go and do what you have to do," Ximen said, "and come back this evening to kowtow to the Third Lady and show what a good son you are."

"I will certainly come," Bojue said, "and my wife will send some presents." He went away.

CHAPTER 73
Qiuju in Trouble

I was called a great lover
I remembered my love.
He who called me a great lover and accepted my love
That man despised me.
Because I am a great lover
My love grows ever deeper and stronger
If I die of love I shall not complain
My love shall be ever steadfast.

When Ying Bojue had gone, Ximen Qing went to the Cave of Spring to watch the masons putting in a warm bed. It was heated by a furnace outside the wall, so that the flowers should not be spoiled by the smoke.

Ping'an brought him a card and told him that Major Zhou had sent a present. There was a box with five separate contributions from Major Zhou himself, General Jing, Captain Zhang, and the two eunuchs, Liu and Xue. Each of them sent five *xing* and two handkerchiefs. Ximen told a servant to accept the things, and gave a card to the man who had brought them.

Aunt Yang, Aunt Wu and old woman Pan came early. Nun Xue, Nun Wang, the two novices, Miao Qu and Miao Feng, and Miss Yu came with gifts for Meng Yulou. Wu Yueniang gave them tea in her own room. The ladies were all there to welcome the guests, but after tea they went to their own rooms.

Pan Jinlian was eager to make the red silk belt she had promised Ximen Qing. She went to her room and brought out her sewing box. From it she took a piece of red sarcenet. Then, from a porcelain box, she took some of the aphrodisiac drug and sewed it, with fine delicate stitches, into the material. Everything was now ready for the work of darkness. Suddenly, Nun Xue came to the door. She had brought Jinlian the potion she was to take to make her conceive. They sat down to talk. Nun Xue saw that nobody was about.

"Wait until a *Renzi* day," she whispered. "Then take it before you have anything to eat. That night, sleep with your husband and you will conceive without fail. The Great Lady has a big belly. It was I who gave her the medicine. And I will tell you something else. Make yourself a little bag, and I will give you a spell written in red ink to put in it. Carry it on your body, and you will bear a son. You have my word for that. It has never been known to fail."

Jinlian was delighted. She put the medicine and the charm into a box. Then she consulted a calendar. The next *Renzi* day was the twenty-ninth. She gave the nun three *qian* of silver. "This is very little," she said. "It will buy you some vegetarian food. But when I have a baby, I will give you some silk to make clothes with."

"Don't trouble about that," the nun said, "I am not so greedy as Nun Wang. You remember when I held that service for the dead lady. She said I had done her out of it, and quarreled with me. Now, she never meets me without saying something horrid. But she can go to Hell. I am not going to argue with her. My only aim in life is to do all the good I can and save people from misfortune."

"Do the best you can," Jinlian said. "We can't expect everybody to be as kind as we are. Don't mention this business to her."

"Oh, I shall say nothing about it," Xue said. "It shall be a secret between ourselves. Last year, when I did this for the Great Lady, Wang said I had been too well paid, and nagged at me until I gave her half of what I got. A fine god-fearing creature she is! She never fasts, and she is far too fond of money. She takes alms from everybody and never does anything in return. When she dies and is born again, she will be something worse than a horned animal. I'm sure of it."

Jinlian told Chunmei to give the nun some tea. When she had drunk it, she went to Li Ping'er's room to pay her respects to the tablet. Then she went back to the inner court.

In the afternoon, Yueniang had tables laid in her room and invited all the ladies and the nuns. She also had a table set in the middle room and a fire lit, so that they could drink wine there in honor of Yulou's birthday.

The wine was poured into jade cups. Yulou, herself like a jade statue, raised a cup aloft. She offered it to Ximen Qing. Then she made a reverence to each of the other ladies in turn. Jingji and his wife were there. They greeted her. They all sat down, and special birthday dishes were brought in. While they were drinking, Laian came in with a box and said Ying Bao had brought presents. Ximen Qing asked Yueniang to accept them. He told Laian to get an invitation card written for Mistress Ying, and to invite Ying Bojue and Uncle Wu to come also.

"I know Mistress Ying will not come," he said, "so we had better ask Uncle Ying. We will send presents in return another day." Laian gave Ying

Bao a card, and the boy went home.

Ximen Qing remembered Yulou's last birthday, when Li Ping'er was still alive. Now, all the other ladies were there, but she was gone. The thought grieved him and he shed tears.

Li Ming and the other two boys came in. "Can you sing the song of the lovebirds?" Yueniang asked them. Han Zuo said he knew it, took up his instrument and was going to sing, but Ximen Qing stopped him.

"No," he said. "Sing 'I Remember the Flute Playing.'" The boys changed the tune and sang: "I remember the flute playing. Where is that exquisite creature now?" They went on till they came to the line: "For me she took off her silken skirt. There was blood on the red azalea flower."

Jinlian knew that Ximen Qing was thinking about Li Ping'er. and when this line was sung she deliberately teased him.

"My son," she said, "you are like Zhu Bajie sitting in a butcher's shop without a fire. No one could look as sour as you do. She wasn't a virgin: she was a married woman. Why do you think of the blood on the red azalea in connection with her? That is going too far. You are a shameless piece of goods."

"Listen to the song, you slave. I wasn't thinking anything of the sort."

The two boys sang: "The lovesick maiden in the palace made up her mind to run away. But how shall I do so? I must gather the flowers upon the walls."

Ximen Qing listened with bowed head. When the song was over, Jinlian was so jealous she could not leave him alone. They began to bicker. Yueniang would not have this. "Sister," she said, "be silent. What are you squabbling about? Aunt Yang and my sister-in-law are in the other room with nobody to keep them company. Perhaps two of you will go and join them. I will come myself in a few moments."

Jinlian and Li Jiao'er went to the inner room.

Laian came back. "I took the card to Mistress Ying," he said. "Uncle Ying and Uncle Wu are coming."

"Go and fetch Master Wen," Ximen Qing said to him. He said to Yueniang: "Tell the cooks to bring food to the outer court. I will take my friends there."

Then, with Li Ming, he went to the room in the eastern wing. Bojue was waiting for him. Ximen thanked him for his presents and told him he must let Mistress Ying come the following day.

"I'm afraid she won't be able to come," Bojue said. "There is nobody she can leave behind to look after the house."

Master Wen came in. Bojue bowed to him and said: "I am afraid I was a great trouble to you this morning."

"Not at all," Master Wen said. "It was a pleasure."

Uncle Wu came and sat down. Qintong brought lights, and they all sat around the fire. Laian brought wine and cups and set them on the table.

Ying Bojue noticed that Ximen Qing was wearing a dark green silken gown with a dragon in five colors embroidered upon it, over his white jacket. The dragon's claws were outstretched, and it showed its teeth. The head and horns were noble and impressive. The whiskers were bristling and the hair stood on end. The gold and green seemed alive and the dragon was coiled around Ximen Qing's body. Bojue was almost startled. "Where did you get that gown?" he said.

Ximen Qing stood up. "Look at it," he said. "Can you guess where it came from?"

"I have no idea," Bojue said.

"Eunuch He of the Eastern Capital gave it to me," Ximen said. "I was drinking with him one very cold day, and he gave it to me then. It is, as you see, a flying dragon. The Emperor had given him another, and he had no further use for this. But it was a great honor to me."

"It must be worth some money," Bojue said. "Brother, it is a good omen. One of these days, you will become governor of a province and wear a dragon robe and a jade girdle. You will go a long way yet."

Qintong warmed wine and set the cups before them. Li Ming sang.

"I must go and offer a cup of wine to your Third Lady," Ying Bojue said. "Then I'll come back and join you."

"My son," Ximen said to him, "if you have such a sense of filial devotion, go, and don't talk so much about it."

"I wouldn't mind going and kowtowing to her," Bojue said, "if the others wouldn't be jealous. But, as a matter of fact, it wouldn't do for me to kowtow to her, because I am the one in authority here. You must go and do it for me."

Ximen Qing tapped him on the head. "You dog," he said, "what do you care about authority?"

"I care a great deal," Bojue said. "Haven't you just hit me on the head?"

They laughed and joked together. Qintong brought them some birthday noodles. Ximen Qing pressed them to set to, and went to eat his own with the ladies in the inner court. Li Ming had something to eat too, then came back to sing for them again. Ying Bojue asked Uncle Wu to tell him what to sing.

"I will be kind to him," Uncle Wu said. "He may sing anything he knows."

"Uncle Wu is very fond of 'The Earthen Jar,'" Ximen Qing said. He told Qintong to fill up the cups. Li Ming tuned his instrument and sang:

"She looked out over the countryside, and spoke no word. All day she stood there, and her lovely face grew sad." Then Li Ming withdrew.

Laian came and said: "In the kitchen they want to know how many cooks you will need tomorrow."

"Six cooks and two scullions," Ximen said. "We must have five especially good courses."

Laian went away.

"Who will be your guests tomorrow?" Uncle Wu said.

Ximen Qing told him that Vice President An had invited the Imperial Tutor's ninth son.

"I am glad his Excellency will be taking wine here," Uncle Wu said.

"Why?"

"Because of that old business of the granary," Wu said. "My work is controlled by his Excellency's department. I should be glad if you would ask him to look indulgently on me, and tell him that I hope he will speak well of my work when the inspection is over. I shall be very much obliged to you."

"Let me have your record of service," Ximen Qing said. "I will speak to him for you."

Uncle Wu rose and bowed to Ximen.

"You ought to be satisfied," Bojue said to him. "His Lordship wouldn't do it for anybody but you. But, after all, if he doesn't look after your interests, whom will he bother about? A little effort on his part and, I'm sure, everything will turn out well."

They went on drinking until the second night watch. When Li Ming was about to go away, Ximen told him to come the following day. Li Ming went out. The boys cleared everything away. When the ladies in Yueniang's room heard that the guests in the outer court had gone, they went to their own apartments.

Pan Jinlian expected Ximen Qing to go to her room and hurried there but, as she reached the second door, she saw Ximen Qing going towards Wu Yueniang's room. She hid herself behind the shadow wall and watched him pass. Then she went quietly after him. Yuxiao was standing at the door.

"Why haven't you gone to your room, Fifth Mother?" she said. "Where is Grandmother?"

"Oh, that old thing has a pain," Jinlian said, "she has gone to bed."

She heard Yueniang say: "What made you send for those two new boys? They are no use at all. They sing the same old tune over and over again."

"When you told them to sing 'The Lotus Pool,' they were not so bad," Meng Yulou said. What are the little turtles called? They did nothing but play about all the time they were here."

"One is Han Zuo, and the other Shao Qian," Ximen Qing said.

"They might call themselves by any name," Yueniang said. "We know nothing whatever about them."

Jinlian tiptoed into the room, and stood behind the bed. Suddenly she said: "Sister, you told them to sing a song. He stopped them and told them to sing 'I Remember the Flute Playing.' That confused the little turtles. They didn't know whom to obey."

Yulou turned around quickly. "Where have you come from?" she said. "You gave me a fright, speaking suddenly like that. You might have been a ghost. How long have you been there?"

"The Fifth Lady has been standing behind you a long time," Xiaoyu said.

Jinlian nodded her head. "My son," she said, "don't think yourself so clever. You always flatter yourself that nobody sees through your little tricks. What right had you to compare her to a virgin in the palace? She and I were both in the same boat; we had both been married before. How could she take off her skirt for you, so that you saw the blood upon the red azalea? I should like to know how you would prove that. I can put up with a good deal, but this is too much. You told your friends that, since she died, you have never been able to enjoy your favorite dishes. Now that Butcher Wang is dead, you have to eat your pork with the hair on. Have you had nothing but dung to eat? You regard us as beneath contempt. We don't mind that. But the Great Lady manages the household for you, and you pay no heed to her. She who is dead is the only one worth thinking about. Why didn't you save her when she was dying? How did you live before you met her? Now everything is wrong. Whenever her name is mentioned, you are upset. But you have taken someone to fill her place and, what's more, you seem very glad of the chance. It looks as though the only water fit to be drunk in this house comes from her room."

"Sister," Yueniang said, "the good are short-lived; the wicked live a thousand years. If you have not a lathe to turn a ball, you must shape it with a chisel. Since we are dull and don't suit him, he must do as he pleases."

"I don't want to be nasty," Jinlian said, "but the things he says are so hurtful. I can't let them go by."

"When did I say anything of the sort, you little strumpet?" Ximen Qing said, laughing.

"The day you entertained his Grace Huang," Jinlian answered, "you were talking to Ying the Second and Scholar Wen. If she were here, you wouldn't care if the rest of us died tomorrow. You had better marry somebody to take her place, you rascally scamp."

Ximen Qing jumped up and kicked her. She ran away as quickly as she could. Ximen followed her, but when he reached the door she had disappeared. Chunmei was there. He put his hand on the maid's shoulder and went back to the inner court.

Yueniang saw that he was drunk and was anxious to get rid of him because she wished to listen to the nuns. She told Xiaoyu to take a light and take him away. Jinlian and Yuxiao were standing in a dark passage, and Ximen Qing passed them without seeing them.

"Father seems to be going to your room," Yuxiao said.

"Yes, he is drunk. He can go to bed. I am in no hurry."

"Mother, wait here a moment for me," Yuxiao said, "I am going to get some fruit for you to give the old lady." She brought the fruit. Jinlian put it in her sleeve, and went to her room. On the way, she met Xiaoyu, coming back.

"Father is looking for you," the maid said.

Jinlian came to her door but did not go in. She peeped through the window. Ximen Qing was on the bed amusing himself with Chunmei. She did not wish to disturb them, so she went around to the other room and gave the fruit to Qiuju. She asked whether old woman Pan was in bed, and the maid told her she had been asleep for a long time. Jinlian bade her put the fruit away and went back to the inner court. The ladies were all assembled, Nun Xue was sitting on the bed, and incense was burning on a small table. They were listening with great attention to the nun's words.

Jinlian came in suddenly, smiling. "You have had trouble already," Yueniang said to her. "He has gone to your room. Why have you come back here instead of seeing that he gets to sleep? I am very much afraid he will beat you."

"Do you think he'd dare?" Jinlian said, smiling.

"You talked to him too roughly," Yueniang said. "He was drunk and, if he had got into a rage, he would certainly have beaten you. We were all very anxious. You really are naughty."

"I am not afraid of him, even when he is in a temper," Jinlian said. "And what a performance! You told the boys to sing one song. He stopped them and told them to sing another to suit himself. It is the Third Lady's birthday and not the time for songs of that sort. The dead are dead. He is always trying to show how much he thought about her, and I don't like it."

"What is the matter, ladies?" Aunt Wu said. "I don't understand. His Lordship came in and suddenly went out again."

"Sister," Yueniang said, "you don't understand. He remembered that, on the Third Lady's last birthday, Li Ping'er was still alive. He cried because she was not here today. He told the boys to sing 'I Remember the Flute Playing.' The Fifth Lady didn't like it and began an argument with him. He flew into a temper and kicked her. Then she ran away."

"Lady," Aunt Yang said, "you should let your husband do what he pleases. What is the use of arguing with him? I can understand how sad he must have felt at the Sixth Lady's death, after you had all been so long together."

"We should never have thought of complaining about the song," Yulou said, "but Jinlian knows all the allusions. She realized that, when he picked out that particular one, he wished to praise her who is dead, and even went so far as to compare her with an historical personage. The song describes their loves, and tells how they lived for one another. It was too much for the Fifth Lady, and she quarreled with him. That caused all the trouble."

"How clever you are, Sister," Aunt Yang said to Jinlian.

"There are no songs she doesn't know," Yueniang said. "Give her the first line and she can always tell you the last. Whenever my husband calls for a song, there is always trouble. She knows what is in his mind. She often makes him angry."

"Of all my children," Yulou said, jokingly, "this is the only one who has any brains."

"I make trouble for everybody," Jinlian said, laughing, "and now you laugh at me."

"Sister," Aunt Yang said, "you must let your husband have his own way. The proverb says: One night of married bliss, and love stays for a hundred nights. Even if husband and wife live together only a short time, they must love one another. When the Sixth Lady died so suddenly, it must have seemed to him as though he had lost one of his fingers. It is only natural that he should grieve when he thinks about her."

"Let him think about her, by all means," Jinlian said, "but with moderation. We are all his ladies. He ought not to exalt one and treat the rest of us like dirt. He was angry because we didn't wear mourning for her long enough. We did so for fifty days. Why shouldn't that have been enough?"

"You must not be too hard on him," Aunt Yang said.

"How quickly time flies," Aunt Wu said. "It must be nearly a hundred days since she died."

"When is the hundredth day?" Aunt Yang said.

"The twenty-sixth day of the twelfth month," Yueniang said.

"We ought to have a service for her," Nun Wang said.

"We can't have a service every time," Yueniang said. "Perhaps we will have one on New Year's Day."

Xiaoyu brought tea and gave each of them a cup. When they had drunk it, Yueniang washed her hands and burned incense. Nun Xue preached to them again. After some opening verses, she told them how the holy man, Wu Jie, broke his vows and fell in love with Hong Lian, and how, in a later life, he became Dong Po. She went on for a long time.

Lanxiang brought two boxes of vegetarian food and cakes. She took the incense burner from the table and put down the food and a pot of tea. The nuns had this, then the maid brought food and a jar of wine for the other ladies as they sat around the fire.

Yueniang cast dice with her sister-in-law, and Jinlian guessed fingers with Li Jiao'er. Yuxiao stood behind Jinlian's chair to serve the wine and, at the same time, suggested how she should play. Li Jiao'er was beaten.

"I will guess fingers with her now," Yulou said. "She seems to win all the time. But I won't have her putting her fingers in her sleeves, or Yuxiao standing behind her, either."

Jinlian was beaten and was made to drink several cups of wine. She went to her room. She had to knock at the corner gate for a long time before Qiuju, rubbing her eyes, came to open it.

"You have been to bed, you slave," Jinlian said.

"No," said Qiuju.

"You are lying, you have only just this moment got up. What an idle good-for-nothing you are! You didn't even come to meet me. Has your father gone to bed?"

"He has been in bed a long time," Qiuju said.

Jinlian went to the inner room, pulled up her skirts, and warmed herself at the fire. Then she demanded tea. Qiuju hastily poured out a cup for her.

"Your hands are dirty, and I don't want stewed tea. Go and tell Chunmei to get the small kettle and boil some fresh water. Put some more tea leaves in the pot and make it strong."

"Chunmei has gone to bed. Shall I wake her?"

"No, don't disturb her. Let her sleep."

Qiuju went in. Chunmei was sleeping at Ximen Qing's feet. Qiuju woke her up. "Mother has come," she said. "She wants some tea. Get up at once."

Chunmei spat at her and cursed her.

"You slave! What do you mean by coming here and startling me like that? 'Mother has come,' indeed! Well, what about it?"

She got up, however, and slowly dressed herself. Then she went to Jinlian and stood, rubbing her eyes. Jinlian scolded Qiuju.

"You saw she was asleep, you slave. Why did you wake her?" Then she said to Chunmei: "The kerchief on your head is rumpled. Pull it down a little. And what have you done with the other earring?"

Chunmei looked at herself and saw that one of her earrings had gone. She took a light and went into the other room to look for it. After searching a long time, she found it on the footstool.

"Where did you find it?" Jinlian asked.

"It was Qiuju's fault," Chunmei said. "She woke me up suddenly and my earring caught in the curtain hook. I found it on the footstool."

"I told her not to wake you," Jinlian said, "but she didn't pay any attention."

"She said you wanted some tea."

"I wouldn't let her make it. She has such dirty hands."

Chunmei filled the small kettle and put it on the fire. She put coal on the brazier, and the water was soon boiling. She washed a cup, made some very strong tea, and gave it to her mistress.

"Has your father been in bed long?" Jinlian asked.

"Yes, I helped him to bed a long time ago. He asked where you were, and I told you you were still in the inner court."

Jinlian drank her tea. "Yuxiao gave me some fruits and things for my mother. I gave them to this slave. Did she hand them over to you?"

"No, I haven't seen them. I have no idea what she's done with them."

"Where are the fruits?" Jinlian said to Qiuju.

"I put them in the cabinet," the maid said. She went and brought them. Jinlian counted them and found that an orange was missing. She asked what had become of it.

"I took them and put them in the cabinet just as you gave them to me," Qiuju said. "Surely you don't think I was so near starvation I had to go and eat it."

"You thief!" Jinlian cried. "You are far too cheeky. If you haven't stolen it, where is it? When I gave them to you, I counted them. Why is there one short? Did you think I brought them for you?"

She turned to Chunmei. "Give her ten slaps on each side of her face."

"I should soil my hands if I touched those dirty cheeks," Chunmei said.

"Send her to me, then," Jinlian said.

Chunmei pushed the girl to her mistress and Jinlian pinched her cheeks.

"Did you eat that orange, you thief? Tell me the truth, and I will let you off. Otherwise, I will get the whip and beat you without mercy. Don't think I'm drunk. You deliberately stole that orange, and now you are trying to deceive me."

"Am I drunk?" she asked Chunmei.

"Certainly not," Chunmei said. "You are perfectly sober. It might be well to look in her sleeves. We might find some orange peel there."

Jinlian took Qiuju's sleeves and began to feel in them. Qiuju, in a great flurry, struggled to prevent her. Chunmei caught her hand. They found some orange peel.

Jinlian pinched the girl's face as hard as she could, and boxed her ears. "You thievish slave!" she cried. "You are as ignorant as can be, yet you are cunning enough when it comes to cheating and stealing. I catch you red-handed, and you still try to make excuses. I am going to have my tea, so I shall not punish you now. I'll deal with you tomorrow."

"Mother," Chunmei said, "don't let her escape you. The best thing we can do is to take off all her clothes and get one of the men to give her a good thrashing. If we do that, she may learn to have some respect for us. If we use a stick as though we were prodding a monkey, she won't take it seriously."

Qiuju's face was swollen. She went to the kitchen, sulking. Jinlian divided an orange into two parts and gave one to Chunmei. She gave her half the apples and pomegranates, saying: "These are for you. My mother can have the rest." Chunmei put them into her sleeve without looking at them, as though they were of no consequence at all. Jinlian was going to give her some of the other things, but Chunmei asked her not to.

"I don't care much for sweet things," she said. "Please give them to Grandmother."

Then Jinlian went to the chamber and made water. She asked Chunmei to get a tub of water so that she could wash. Then she asked what the time was.

"I have been asleep some time," the maid said, "it must be about the third night watch."

Jinlian took down her hair, and went to the inner room. The lamp was nearly out. She pulled up the wick. Then she went to the bed. Ximen Qing was snoring. She undressed and lay down beside him. After a while, she began to toy with his weapon. But Ximen had been playing with Chunmei; she could not excite it, for it was too soft. She was fiery with wine, and squatting on her heels on the bed she put the prick in her mouth. She titillated the hole, moved the head backwards and forwards, and sucked it inside and outside without ceasing. Ximen Qing woke up.

"Now, you funny little strumpet, where have you been all this time?"

"We were drinking in the inner court," Jinlian said. "The Third Lady gave us a feast and Miss Yu sang. We guessed fingers, threw dice, and played for a long time. I beat Li Jiao'er, but Yulou beat me. I had to drink a few cups of wine. Lucky for you that you got away and came here to sleep in peace, but don't think I will let you escape."

"Have you made the belt of ribbon?" Ximen said.

"Yes, it is here." She took it from underneath the bedclothes, showed it to him, then tied it about his prick and around his waist. She tied it very tightly.

"Have you taken anything?" she asked him.

He told her that he had, and she continued her attentions until the sinews of the prick stiffened and it surged erect, a fingerbreadth longer than usual. She lay on his body, but the penis was so big that she had to stretch her cunt with both hands before it would fit. But when it entered she embraced his neck and asked him to hold her around the waist; and gradually the prick, pressing on one side, pressed from the other, buried itself completely. "Darling," she said, "put a silk cloak below yourself." Ximen folded a red gown twice and put it beneath his thighs. She started again, and absorbed the whole prick. "Delight of my heart," she said, "feel. It's gone right in. It has filled me completely. Are you satisfied?"

Ximen felt with his hand and found that the penis had entered so far that nothing, not even a hair's breadth, remained outside. Only the testicles were left, and he was suffused with deepest pleasure.

"I'm cold," she said. "Let us move the candle. It was nicer in summer." And again, "Don't you think this ribbon is better than the clasp? It doesn't hurt me, and makes your prick longer. If you don't believe me, put your hand on my belly. I can feel it touching my bowels. Embrace me and let me sleep on top of you."

"Sleep, girl," said Ximen. "I'll hold you."

She put her tongue in his mouth, closed her eyes, put her arms around him, and slept. But soon desire woke her. She pressed his shoulders, sat up, and bounced up and down so fast that his penis went right in and out. "I am dying, my dearest," she cried. Man and woman enjoyed three hundred thrusts, and Ximen was the first to withdraw from the struggle. "Embrace me," she said, and gave him a breast to suck. Then she relaxed, and the juices of love flowed from her. A stag seemed to leap within her. Her arms and legs were limp; her hair covered her body. The penis, although it had withdrawn, was still erect, and she wiped it with a handkerchief. "What shall we do, darling?" she said. "It is not enough for you even yet."

"Let us go to sleep now," Ximen said. "We will settle that question afterwards."

"I feel as though I were paralyzed," Jinlian said.

So the mystery of clouds and rain was performed once more. They lay down to sleep and did not wake again till dawn.

CHAPTER 74

Li Guijie Is Forgiven

Wealth and dignity are as the dew of morning
Friends and companions as the gathering of sand.
It is better to sit before a bamboo window
And meditate upon some sacred book.

Contemplation benefits the soul as truly
As any listening to sermons.
When the soul is purified, you may make a cup of tea.
The crowing of the cock is all you fear
For in the morning the entanglement of earthly things
Is as a bundle of hemp.

At dawn, Pan Jinlian and Ximen Qing awoke. Jinlian saw that his weapon was still upright like a ramrod. "Darling," she said, "you must forgive me, but I can stand no more. I shall suck your prick."

"Suck it," said Ximen. "If you can soften it, all will be well." She squatted on her buttocks, put her hand between his legs, and took his prick in her mouth. She played with it for a whole hour, but it did not flag. Ximen held her white neck and dragged his prick this way and that inside her mouth with all his might. Soon her lips were wet with white spittle, and the prick was as red as they.

"Ying the Second has invited us to go and see his wife," Jinlian said. "Are we going?"

"Why not?" Ximen Qing said.

"I have a favor to ask of you," Jinlian said. "I wonder whether you will grant it me."

"What is it, you little strumpet?"

"Will you give me the Sixth Lady's fur coat? If we go, they will all be wearing fur coats, and I have none."

"We have the coat that General Wang's people pawned. Won't that do?"

"I don't want that. Li Jiao'er can have it. Let Sun Xue'e have the one Li Jiao'er had and give me the one that belonged to the Sixth Lady. I will make a pair of scarlet sleeves, with golden storks to go with it, and wear a white silk skirt. If you give it to me, it will be a proof that it has been worthwhile being your wife all this long time."

"You little strumpet, you never lose a chance of doing well for yourself. That fur coat is worth at least sixty taels of silver. If you put it on, will you look well in it?"

"You rascal," Jinlian said, "you would give things to any other woman. I am your wife and, if I wear it, so much the more credit to you. If you talk like this, I shall be angry with you."

"One moment you ask for something, and the next you are riding the high horse."

"I am not a maid. There is no reason why you shouldn't do something when I ask you."

She softened the penis with her cheeks and put it in her mouth. She teased the hole and titillated the sensitive spot with her tongue. She held it firmly between her lips and moved it gently. Ximen was delighted; his pleasure mounted, and he prepared to give way.

"Hold tight and let the sperm come out," he cried, and at once the sperm flowed into her mouth. After a while she swallowed it.

It was the day of the reception. Ximen Qing dressed and went out. Jinlian stayed in bed.

"Bring me the coat now," she said. "If you put it off, you will be too busy."

Ximen went to the room of Li Ping'er. The nurse and the maids were up, making tea to set before their mistress's tablet. Ruyi'er was dressed and her face and eyebrows painted. She smiled and offered him a cup of tea, and talked to him as he drank it. Ximen Qing told Yingchun to get the key. Ruyi'er asked him why he wanted it.

"I am going to give the Fifth Lady the fur coat," he said.

"The sable coat?" Ruyi'er asked.

"Yes," Ximen Qing said, "I am giving it her because she wants it."

Yingchun went to do his bidding. He took Ruyi'er on his knee and touched her breast. "My child," he said, "though you have had a baby, your breasts are still small." They kissed each other.

"I have noticed that you often go to her and seldom to the other ladies," Ruyi'er said. "She would be very pleasant if she were not so suspicious and touchy. The other day, when you were away, she quarreled with me about the dolly pin. Fortunately, Sister Han and the Third Lady were there to separate us. I did not mention the matter to you when you came back. I can't imagine who told her that you care for me, or when she found out. Has she spoken to you about it?"

"Yes, she has," Ximen Qing said. "I think the best thing you can do is to go to her and say you're sorry. She can never resist flattery, and she is very easily pleased. Her mouth may be sharp, but her heart is in the right place."

"That is so," Ruyi'er said. "We had that quarrel, but the next day, when you came home, she was quite pleasant. She said you were very fond of her, but that the other ladies were not able to rival me. I was to tell her everything, she said, and she would be my friend."

"In that case, there is nothing to bother about," Ximen Qing said. "I will come to you tonight."

"Are you sure?" Ruyi'er said. "Don't tease me."

"Why should I tease you?" Ximen said.

Yingchun brought the key. Ximen Qing told her to open the cabinet door and take out the fur coat. The maid shook it, then wrapped it up again.

"I badly need a good skirt and coat," Ruyi'er said softly. "Will you get one for me while there is a chance? And I should like a short coat, if there is one, belonging to my mistress."

Ximen Qing brought out a light blue silk coat, a yellow skirt of soft silk, a pair of embroidered drawers and some blue trousers. He gave them to Ruyi'er. She kowtowed and thanked him. He locked up the cabinet.

Ruyi'er took the fur coat to Jinlian. She was getting up, dressing her feet as she sat on the bed. When Chunmei told her Ruyi'er had come with a fur coat, she understood. Ruyi'er went in.

"Did your father send you?" Jinlian said.

"Yes, he told me to bring you this fur coat."

"Did he give you anything?"

"He gave me a dress for the new year, and told me to come and kowtow to you."

"There is no need for that," Jinlian said. "Your master has taken a fancy to you. Well, there is an old saying that, though there are many boats on the river, they do not block it; and though there are many carriages upon a road, there is still room for traffic. If it amuses you to go in for this kind of thing, do so, but you must do nothing that will injure me. I shall not bother about you any more, and I shall do nothing to interfere with you."

"My mistress is dead," Ruyi'er said, "and though the Great Lady still keeps me here, you are the one on whom I really depend. If you help me, I shall never dare to be ungracious in return. Falling leaves always come back to the root again."

"Perhaps you had better tell the Great Lady about the clothes he gave you," Jinlian said.

"I asked her to give me some clothes, and she said Father would give me some when he was free."

"That is all right, then," Jinlian said. Ruyi'er went back to her room. Ximen Qing had gone to the great hall.

"When you went for the key," Ruyi'er said to Yingchun, "did the Great Lady say anything?"

"She asked what he wanted it for. I didn't tell her about the coat. I said I didn't know. She said no more."

Ximen Qing, in the great hall, watched the preparations for the banquet. The actors of the Haiyan company, Zhang Mei, Zhou Shun, Gou Zixiao, came with their properties, and Li Ming and the other boys also came and kowtowed to Ximen Qing. He ordered food to be given to all of them, then told Li Ming and three others to perform in the outer hall, and Zuo Shun to entertain the ladies at the back.

Han Daoguo's wife, Wang Liu'er, could not come that day. She bought two boxes of presents and sent Miss Shen, in a sedan chair, with her boy Jin Cai, to congratulate Meng Yulou on her birthday. Wang Jing took them in and dismissed the chair men. Aunt Han and Aunt Meng came, then Mistress Fu, Mistress Gan, Cui Ben's wife, Miss Duan, and Mistress Ben the Fourth.

Ximen Qing, who was in the great hall, saw Daian taking in a short lady who wore a silver-gray coat and a red skirt. Her face was not powdered and her eyes were very narrow. She looked rather like Zheng Aixiang. As she was in the passage, Ximen Qing asked who the lady was. Daian told him it was Ben the Fourth's wife. Ximen said no more. They went on to the inner court to see Wu Yueniang, in whose room all the ladies were having tea. Ximen Qing himself came for porridge. He gave Yueniang the key.

"Why did you wish to open the cabinet?" his wife asked.

"Pan Jinlian told me she was going to Brother Ying's place. She wanted the Sixth Lady's fur coat."

Yueniang looked at him sharply. "You don't keep your word," she said. "When she died, you were very angry if anyone suggested getting rid of her maids, but now it seems all right for you to give her clothes away. Why doesn't the Fifth Lady wear her own fur coat? It is a good thing the owner of the coat is dead. If she were alive, I don't know what Jinlian would do."

Ximen Qing could not think of any answer to make to this.

Then a servant came to say that Liu, the Provincial Director of Studies, had come to pay back some money, and Ximen went to the great hall to receive him. Daian brought a card and said that people had come from General Wang's place with presents. Ximen asked what the presents were. The boy said: a roll of silk, a jar of wine, and food. Ximen told Wang Jing to give the messenger a card in return and five *qian* of silver for himself.

Then Li Guijie came, with the house porter, bringing four boxes of presents. Daian took the wrapper. "Please step into the passage, Aunt Guijie," he said hastily. "There is a gentleman in the hall." Guijie went into the passage and Daian carried the boxes to Yueniang's room.

"Has your father seen them?" Yueniang asked.

"No," Daian said, "he has a gentleman with him."

Yueniang told him to put the boxes in an adjoining room.

When his visitor had gone, Ximen Qing came to have something to eat.

"Guijie has come and brought some presents," Yueniang told him.

"This is the first I have heard of it," Ximen Qing said.

Yueniang told Xiaoyu to open the boxes. There were buns with mincemeat, a special birthday gift; crystallized roses; two roast ducks, and a pair of pig's trotters. Guijie came in from the other room, pearls and jewels all over her head. She was wearing a scarlet double-breasted coat and a blue silk skirt. She kowtowed four times to Ximen Qing.

"That will do," Ximen said. "Why did you go to all this expense?"

"Guijie has just told me she is afraid you are still angry with her," Yueniang said. "It was really not her fault at all, but her mother's. Guijie had a headache and, that day, Wang the Third and his friends were on their way to Sesame's place, and called in to have some tea as they were passing. Then the trouble began, but she never saw him."

"She didn't see him this time, and she didn't see him that time!" Ximen Qing said. "I don't know how she has the face to say so. I'm not interested any more. In a place like yours, everything is all right so long as the money comes in. I'm not angry with you in the least."

Guijie knelt on the ground and refused to get up. "Father," she said, "you are right. But may I rot to pieces if I ever let that fellow touch me! May every pore of my skin come out in boils! It is all that old whore's doing. She has no sense at all. She would let anybody in, no matter whether he is handsome or hideous. That is what has made you so angry."

"Now she is here," Yueniang said, "let us consider the matter ended. Don't be angry with her any more."

"Stand up, and I'll forgive you," Ximen Qing said.

But Guijie, with her most winning manner, said: "You must smile at me, Father. Then I'll get up. If you won't, I shall stay here for a year."

Jinlian joined them.

"Guijie," she said, "stand up. If you kneel there, and use pretty words to him, he will make all the more fuss. Now you are kneeling before him, but, I tell you, in future when he comes to you, make him kneel down before you and keep him there."

Ximen Qing and Yueniang laughed. Guijie rose to her feet.

Daian came. He was greatly excited. "Their Excellencies have arrived," he said. Ximen Qing put on his robes and went to meet them.

"From today," Guijie said to Yueniang, "I will give up my father if I may be your daughter."

"I don't believe in your oaths," Yueniang said. "You forget them as soon as you have taken them. He went to see you twice, and you were not there."

"Heavens!" Guijie cried, "when did he come to my place and find me not there? If he did, may I die this very moment. Somebody has been telling lies. He must have gone to some other place. I know he went to Zheng Aiyue's house and played with the girls there. They are jealous, Probably they are responsible for the whole affair. I don't see how Father could be angry with me otherwise."

"Why don't you girls attend to your business, instead of talking scandal about one another?" Jinlian said.

"Mother, you don't know. There is always jealousy among people of our profession. Each one is anxious to get the better of the others. Whenever one seems to be securing a little favor, the others conspire to cast her down."

Yueniang gave her tea.

Ximen Qing took Censor Song and Vice President An to the great hall. After the usual greetings, each of them presented him with a roll of silk and a case of books. They saw that the tables were very well set out, and thanked him repeatedly. Then they sat down to tea.

"I have still another favor to ask you," Song said. "Hou Shiquan has just been appointed Master of the Court of Sacrificial Worship. I and those under me would like to entertain him, if possible, here at your house, on the thirtieth. He is to leave for the Eastern Capital on the second of next month. Will you do this for us?"

"Your Excellency has only to command, and I obey," Ximen Qing said.

"The money is here," Song said. He summoned an attendant, who brought twelve taels of silver, which the officers had contributed. "We should like one large table and six small tables. Perhaps a few actors."

Ximen Qing promised to make the necessary arrangements. He took his guests to the arbor. Before long, Assistant Secretary Qian arrived. The three gentlemen played chess together.

Song was impressed by the magnificence and convenience of Ximen Qing's house. The books, pictures and furniture were all the best of their kind. In front of the screen stood a gilded tripod with the figures of the Eight Immortals. It was of very fine workmanship and several feet high.

Incense was burning in it, and the smoke came out through the mouths of deer and storks. He went and examined it more closely.

"This tripod is beautifully made," he said to Ximen Qing. He turned to the others. "I wrote some time ago to Brother Liu to ask him to get me a pair of tripods like this. I am going to present them to Cai, but they haven't come yet. Siquan, where did you get yours?"

"It came from a man in Huai," Ximen Qing said.

They went on with their game. Ximen Qing ordered some dainty cakes and other refreshments to be brought, and bade the actors sing songs of the South.

"Our guest has not come yet," Song said. "It won't look right if we meet him with red faces."

"I don't believe a cup will do us any harm," An said. "It is terribly cold."

Song was about to send someone to hasten his guest, but one of his attendants said: "We have been already. Their Excellencies are playing chess, but they will be here soon." An told the actors to sing the Spring Song. Before it was over, Cai and Huang were announced. Song ordered everything to be cleared away. They put their robes straight and went out to welcome their guest.

Cai was wearing a plain gown and a gold-buckled girdle. He presented a card to Ximen Qing. An said: "This is his Lordship Ximen. He holds the office of Captain and is one of his Eminence's wards." Cai bowed to Ximen.

"I have long wished to meet you," he said.

Ximen Qing replied: "I shall do myself the honor of paying you a visit." After these greetings, they took off their ceremonial clothes, tea was brought, and they sat down to talk. Sometime afterwards, the tables were laid, and Cai took the place of honor. Cooks brought soup and cutlets and rice. The actors came with their list of plays, and Cai bade them play the story of the two faithful lovers. They played two acts, and the wine went around several times. Then the singers came and sang "With a Whip of Jade and a Prancing Steed, He Leaves the Imperial City." Cai laughed.

"Songyuan," he said, "this promises well for you. The black horse is a censor's horse, and the third noble seems like Liu of the long beard."

An said: "But we can't say that this is the day on which the Magistrate of Jiangzhou made his black gown wet with tears."

Everybody laughed. Ximen Qing told Chunhong to sing "We Have Made Report to the Golden Gate of Peace upon the Frontier."

Song was delighted. He said to Ximen Qing: "What a charming boy!"

"Ximen said: "He is one of my household, and comes from Yangzhou." Song took the boy's hand, and asked him to pour wine for him. Then he gave him three *qian* of silver, and the boy kowtowed to thank him.

The sun was going down. Cai saw that it was getting late, and told his servant to bring his clothes. He made ready to go. The others tried to persuade him to stay, but in vain. They went with him to the gate. Two officials were bidden to take presents to the wharf. As Song was going, he said to Ximen Qing: "I will not thank you today, since I am putting you to still further trouble." Then they all went away.

Ximen Qing went back and dismissed the actors. "I shall want you again the day after tomorrow," he said to them. "Be sure to bring some especially good singers. His Excellency is going to invite Governor Hou."

He called for wine and sent Daian for Scholar Wen. He sent Laian for Ying Bojue. The two men came almost at the same moment, made a reverence to their host, and sat down. The three boys sang and wine was served.

"The ladies are all coming to see you tomorrow," Ximen Qing said to Ying Bojue. "Have you engaged any singers or entertainers for them?"

"That's a nice thing to ask!" Bojue said. "How can you expect me to do all that, when I'm so poor? I've engaged a couple of singers, and I hope my sisters-in-law will come early."

In the inner court, the two Mistresses Meng were the first to go away. Aunt Yang was about to follow them, but Wu Yueniang asked her to stay longer. "Nun Xue has sent her novices to fetch the sacred texts," she said, "and you might as well stay and hear them read this evening."

"I should very much like to stay," Aunt Yang said, "but I have been asked to go to my nephew's betrothal party tomorrow. I cannot very well fail to go."

When she had gone, the ladies drank together. When the lamps were brought, the wives of the three clerks went away. Miss Duan stayed, and old woman Pan went to Jinlian's room. Aunt Wu, L Guijie, Miss Shen, Miss Yu, the nuns, Meng Yulou, Li Jiao'er, and Pan Jinlian, were left in Wu Yueniang's room.

When the boys began to bring in the things, they knew that the party in the outer court had broken up. Jinlian hurriedly went out and stood silently at the corner door. Ximen Qing, supported by Laian with a lantern, came rolling by. He had meant to go and see Ruyi'er, but, seeing Jinlian, he took her hand and went to her room. Laian went on to Yueniang's room to give her the cups and chopsticks.

Yueniang thought Ximen Qing was coming to her room, and she had sent Miss Shen, Miss Yu, and Guijie to stay with Li Jiao'er. "Is your father coming?" she said to Laian.

"He has gone to the Fifth Lady's room," Laian told her. Yueniang was annoyed.

"The fellow doesn't know what he's doing," she said to Yulou. "I was sure he would come here and go with you. I can't imagine why he has gone to her again. But, now I come to think of it, she has been looking lovesick these last few days. She doesn't seem able to leave him for a moment."

"Oh, never mind, Sister," Yulou said, "if we talk like this, it will look as though we wished to beat her at her own game. Didn't you notice how the nun poked fun at us, saying that, no matter where he went, he could not go beyond these six rooms? Let him do what he likes. We cannot control him."

"They must have arranged it beforehand," Yueniang said. "When she heard that the party in the outer court was over, she dashed out as though her life depended on it." She said to Xiaoyu: "There is no one in the kitchen. Shut the second door and tell the nuns to come. We will listen to their preaching." She asked Li Jiao'er, Miss Shen, Miss Duan, and Miss Yu to come back again.

"I have sent one of the young nuns to fetch the *True History of the Lady Huang*," she said. "Unfortunately, Aunt Yang has left us."

She told Yuxiao to make some good tea.

"You and I will take our turn with the tea," Yulou said to Li Jiao'er. "We must not trouble the Great Lady all the time." So they gave orders for tea. The table was set. The three nuns came and sat on the bed with their legs crossed, and the other ladies sat down and disposed themselves to listen. Yueniang washed her hands and burned incense. Then Nun Xue opened the text of the *True Story of the Lady Huang* and read:

We know that the Law never perisheth. It proceedeth into the void. The DAO is without life, and, when it giveth life, it advantageth us in no way. From the Holy Body are manifested the Eight Incarnations, and from the Eight Incarnations is manifested the Holy Body. Such is the brightness of the Lamp of Wisdom that it openeth a window to the world: so clear is the Mirror of Buddha that it shineth to the bottom of the dark way.

A hundred years is as the twinkling of an eye.

The four bodies of illusion are but shadows.

Yet, every day, people busy themselves in the dust; they make haste all day to compass their own ends. They know not what they do.

Only Nature is glorious and perfect.

As for them, they pursue the six roots of vanity and concupiscence. Though their achievements and their renown are known to all the world, yet they are but a dream. Though their dignity and their wealth make men amazed, they cannot escape a sudden end. As wind and fire they die away, and there is no exception either for old or young. The water wears away many a mountain.

After this, the nun read some short homilies and sang hymns. Then she began to tell the story of the Lady Huang, whence she sprang, how she read the sacred books and gave alms. How she died and was born again as a man, and how five men and women went up to Heaven at the same moment. She did not end her story before the second night watch.

Li Jiao'er's maid brought tea for the ladies, and Yulou's maid brought fruit and food, a large jar of wine, and a big pot of tea. Yueniang told Yuxiao to give the nuns cakes and dainties to eat with the tea.

"Now that the teachers have done," Guijie said, "it is my turn to offer you a song."

"You are very kind," Yueniang said.

"I will sing first," Miss Yu said.

"Very well," said Yueniang.

Then Miss Shen said: "When she has finished, I will sing."

Guijie would not have this. "What song would you like, Mother?" she asked. Yueniang asked her to sing "The Stillness of the Late Night Watch." Guijie offered wine to all the ladies, then took her lute and sang to them. When she had finished, Miss Yu was about to take the lute, but Miss Shen took it from her.

"I will sing 'The Hanging of the Portraits in the Twelfth Month.' She began: "The fifteenth day of the first month is the merry Feast of Lanterns. We take handfuls of incense and do homage to Heaven and Earth."

Aunt Wu was sleepy. Before Miss Shen had finished, she drank her tea and went to Yueniang's bedroom to sleep. Afterwards, Guijie went to sleep with Li Jiao'er, Miss Duan with Yulou. The nuns went to Xue'e and Miss Yu and Miss Shen to Yuxiao. Yueniang herself slept with her sister-in-law.

There is an ancient tradition that when a woman is with child she should never sit down on one side, or lie on one side. She should never listen to exciting music or look upon any immodest color. She should occupy all her time with poetry and books, with gold and jade. If she does this, she will give birth to a boy or a girl who will be intelligent and good. This we call the education of the child in the womb. Now that Yueniang was with child, she should not have allowed the nuns to tell these stories of life, death and reincarnation. In consequence of this, one of the Holy Ones came to her and, afterwards, her son mysteriously disappeared, so that the family of Ximen came to an end. It was very sad.

CHAPTER 75

Pan Jinlian Quarrels
with Wu Yueniang

Butterflies hover in couples among the flowers beside the stream
South of the hills and west of the river.
The wind and the moon are distraught with love.
In the ancient palace
The beautiful woman is filled with discontent
Clouds and rain are in wild confusion.
She opens her fragrant mouth, and the words flow from her lips
She presses her delicate cheeks in wild abandon.
Say not that the life of love is without substance
When one oriole has finished its song,
Another takes up the melody.

Pan Jinlian met Ximen at the corner door and went with him to her room. He sat down on the bed. "Why don't you undress?" she said to him.

He smiled and kissed her. "I came to tell you I am going somewhere else tonight. Please give me my love instruments."

"You rascal," Jinlian said, "do you think you can get around me with soft words like these? If I had not been standing at the door, you would have been with her already. You would never have come near me. I know. This morning you arranged everything with that evil slut. That was why she brought me the fur coat and kowtowed to me. What do you take me for? You won't get over me in that sort of way. When Li Ping'er was alive, I counted for nothing. But that bird is no longer in the nest. I'm not going to make the same mistake a second time."

"Rubbish!" Ximen Qing said, laughing. "If she hadn't come and kowtowed to you, you would have had just as much to say."

Jinlian was silent for a long time. "I will let you go, but you shall not have the instruments," she said at last. "You want to use them for your dirty work with that bad bone. When you come back to me, they will be filthy."

"But I am so accustomed to them I don't know what to do without them."

He badgered her for a long time, and she gave him the silver clasp. "Take it, if you must have it," she said. Ximen Qing put it into his sleeve and went out staggering.

Jinlian called him back. "Tell me. Are you going to spend all night with her? If you do, you'll have all the maids laughing at you. You'd better stay a little while and then send her packing."

"I shall not stay very long," Ximen Qing said. He went out again.

Again Jinlian called him back. "Come here," she said, "I am talking to you. Why are you in such a hurry?"

"What do you want now?" Ximen Qing said.

"I am allowing you to go and sleep with her, but I forbid you to talk a lot of nonsense. If you do, she will give herself airs in front of me again. If I find out you have done anything of the sort, I will bite off your weapon the next time you come to me."

"Oh, you funny little whore," Ximen Qing said, "you talk enough to kill anybody." He went out.

"Let him go," Chunmei said. "Why do you try to keep him in order? You know the old saying: if a mother-in-law has too much to say, the daughter-in-law will become deaf. If you go on like that, people will only hate you more. Let us have a game of chess."

She told Qiuju to shut the corner door. Then they sat at the table and played chess.

Ximen Qing went to Li Ping'er's room and pulled aside the shutter. Ruyi'er, Yingchun, and Xiuchun were having supper on the bed. When Ximen came in, they all got up.

"Don't mind me," Ximen Qing said. He went to the inner room and sat down in a chair before the tablet of his dead wife. After a while, Ruyi'er came out to him.

"It is cold here, Father," she said, smiling, "come into the other room."

Ximen Qing put his arms around her and kissed her. They went into the other room together. Tea was boiling on the fire and Yingchun offered him some. Ruyi'er stood before the bed, near the fire.

"You have had no wine," she said. "We have had a pot of Jinhua wine and some food for my dead lady and we kept some for you."

"You take the food and give me some of the fruit," Ximen Qing said. "I don't want any Jinhua wine." Then he said to Xiuchun: "Take a lantern and go to my study. There is a jar of grape wine there. Ask Wang Jing for it and warm some for me."

Yingchun set the table. "Sister," Ruyi'er said to her, "open the boxes and let me find something for Father to eat with his wine." She picked out some special dainties and fruits and put them on the table. Then

Xiuchun came with the wine, opened the jar and warmed some. Ruyi'er poured out a cup and offered it to Ximen Qing. He tasted it and found it very good. Ruyi'er stood beside the table to wait on him. She gave him some chestnuts.

Yingchun knew why he had come and went to spend the night with Xiuchun. When she had gone away and there was no one else in the room, he made the woman sit on his knee and they drank wine from mouth to mouth. He unfastened her dress and uncovered her tender white bosom. He touched her nipples. "My child," he said, "I know nothing so sweet as your lovely white skin. It is as beautiful as your lady's, and when I hold you in my arms I feel as if I held her."

Ruyi'er smiled. "No, Father, hers was whiter than mine. The Fifth Lady is beautiful, but her skin is not so pure. It is not so white as the Third Lady's. But the Third Lady, unfortunately, has a few pock marks on her face. Sun Xue'e is white and pretty." Then she said: "Yingchun is going to give me one of her ornaments. I wish you would give me the golden tiger that belonged to my dead lady. It is something to be worn in the new year, and I would like her to have it."

"If you have nothing to wear, I will give the silversmith some gold and get him to make something for you. The Great Lady has all your lady's ornaments. I can hardly ask her for them."

"I should like a gold tiger," Ruyi'er said. She stood up and kowtowed to him.

When they had been drinking for some time, she said: "Father, will you ask my sisters to come and have some wine with us? They will be unhappy if you don't."

Ximen Qing called Yingchun, but there was no answer. Ruyi'er went to the kitchen and told the two girls that their master wanted them. Yingchun came. Ximen Qing asked Ruyi'er to give her some wine and a plate of food. Yingchun took them, standing. "Please make Xiuchun come," Ruyi'er said, "I should like to offer her something." The maid went away but returned and said Xiuchun would not come. Then she took her bedclothes and went to the kitchen to sleep with Xiuchun.

Ximen Qing drank more wine. Then Ruyi'er cleared everything away and gave him some tea. She found fresh silken bedclothes, and an embroidered pillow. She warmed them and asked him whether he would rather sleep on the large bed or the small one. "I prefer the small one," he said. Ruyi'er put the bedclothes on the small bed and helped him to undress. She went to the other room to wash, came back, and fastened the door. When she had put the lamp beside the bed, she undressed and got into bed with him.

The woman touched the warrior. The clasp was already in position. It was very hard and frisky and she felt pleased and terrified at the same time. They kissed each other and set to. Ximen, seeing her lying on the bed without any clothes on, was afraid she might catch cold. He picked up her vest and covered her breast with it. Then he took her by the legs and thrust forward violently. Ruyi'er gasped for breath and her face became very red.

"Mother gave me that vest," she said.

"My dear," said Ximen, "never mind about that. Tomorrow, I will give you half a roll of red silk to make underwear, and you shall wear that when you wait on me."

"Thank you," Ruyi'er said.

"I have forgotten how old you are," Ximen Qing said. "What is your surname, and your place in the family? I only remember that your husband's name was Xiong."

"Yes," Ruyi'er said, "his name was Xiong Wang'er. My own name is Zhang, and I am the fourth child. I am thirty-two years old."

"A year older than I am," he said.

They went on with their lovemaking, and he called her Zhang the Fourth. "My daughter," he said, "serve me well, and, when the Great Lady's baby is born, you shall have charge of it. And, if you yourself bear a son to me, I will make you one of my ladies and you shall take the dead lady's place."

"My husband is dead, and I have no relatives of my own," Ruyi'er said. "I have no other wish than to serve you, and I never want to leave you. If you take pity on me, I shall always be grateful."

Ximen Qing was very pleased with the way she spoke. He grasped her white legs firmly and plunged forward violently again. She murmured softly and her starry eyes grew dim. Soon he asked her to lie down with legs spread-eagled like a mare's, and, covered with a red blanket, he rode her. He thrust with his prick, pressing on as he fondled her white buttocks in the candlelight. "Call me your darling without stopping," he said. "Let me bury myself in you." She rose to receive him, and called him her darling in a trembling voice. They played for a whole hour before Ximen wished to yield. At last he withdrew his prick, and she wiped it with a handkerchief. They slept in each other's arms. Before dawn she woke up excited and put his prick in her mouth. "Your Fifth Mother," said Ximen, "sucks all night. She does not let me get up if I want to piss because she is afraid that I'll catch cold, and she drinks my water."

"What does that matter?" she cried. "I'm also thirsty"; and Ximen made water in her mouth. They made love in every possible way.

The next day, she rose first, opened the door and lit a fire. Then she helped Ximen Qing to dress. He went to the front court and told Daian to send Ben the Fourth with two soldiers to take the golden tripod with his card to Censor Song's place. "When they have delivered it," he said, "they must wait for a return card." He told Chen Jingji to pack up a roll of gold silk and a roll of colored satin. He bade Qintong get a horse ready and take them to his Excellency Cai. Then he took breakfast in Yueniang's room.

"I don't see how we can all go to see Mistress Ying," Yueniang said, "Somebody must stay at home to keep Aunt Wu company."

"But I have got five presents ready," Ximen Qing said. "Of course, you must all go. My daughter is here. She can stay with Aunt Wu. I have promised Brother Ying." Yueniang said no more.

Guijie came and kowtowed to them. "I am going home today, Mother," she said.

"There is no hurry," Yueniang said. "Stay another day."

"My mother is not well," Guijie said, "and there is no one to look after her. I will come and see you again in the fifth month."

She kowtowed to Ximen Qing. Yueniang gave her some cakes and a tael of silver. When she had had some tea, she went away.

Ximen Qing had put on his ceremonial clothes and was on his way to the outer court when Ping'an came and said that General Jing had come. Ximen Qing went to greet him, and they made reverences to one another in the great hall.

"I haven't been to see you, and I have not yet congratulated you upon your promotion," General Jing said.

"And I have not called to thank you for sending me such a splendid present," Ximen Qing replied.

When they had exchanged greetings and taken tea, General Jing said: "I see your horse is waiting for you. Where are you going?"

"Yesterday," Ximen said, "Censor Song and their Excellencies An, Qian, and Huang, used my house for a reception to Cai the new Governor. Cai is the Imperial Tutor's ninth son. He gave me a card, and I am going to call upon him. I must go now because he may be leaving at any moment."

"I have come to ask a favor of you," General Jing said. "You know that Song's term of office will expire early in the new year. I expect there will be an inspection of all the officers, and I have come to you in the hope that you will mention my name to him. I discovered that he was here yesterday, and that is why I have called. If any promotion comes to me, I shall owe it to you."

"We are good friends," Ximen Qing said, "I shall be glad to do anything I can. Give me your record of service. He will be coming here for another party the day after tomorrow and I will speak to him then."

Jing rose and bowed. "I am very much obliged to you. Here is my record of service." He took it from an attendant and handed it to Ximen Qing. It said:

> Jing Zhong, Garrison Commander of Qinghe, and officer in command of troops in various districts of Shandong. Thirty-two years of age. Born at Tanzhou. In consequence of the exploits of his ancestors, he was given the rank of captain. He passed through the military academy and has been promoted by degrees to his present post in command of troops in Jizhou, etc.

When Ximen Qing had read this, Jing brought out a list of presents and asked him to accept them. Ximen saw: "Two hundred measures of fine rice."

"What is this?" he said, "I cannot possibly accept it. If I did, there would be no point whatever in our friendship."

"Siquan," Jing said, "if you do not want it, you can give it to his Excellency. You must not refuse. If you do, I will never trouble you again."

After much demur, Ximen accepted. "When I have spoken to him, I will let you know," he said.

They drank tea again, and Jing went away. Ximen Qing mounted his horse and, with Qintong in attendance, went to see Governor Cai.

When Ximen had gone, Yuxiao, who had helped him to dress, went to see Jinlian.

"Mother," she said, "why didn't you stay longer in the inner court last night? Mother said several nasty things about you. She said that, as soon as you heard Father coming from the other court, you dashed after him. She said you got hold of him so tightly that you wouldn't let him go, even to the Third Lady, whose birthday it was. And the Third Lady said she wasn't going to enter into a competition with you; he might go to any room he liked."

"What can I do to clear myself?" Jinlian said. "They are not blind. Why couldn't they see that he never came here at all?"

"He comes to you so often," Yuxiao said. "And now the Sixth Lady is dead, they don't see where else he can go."

"Chickens cannot piddle, but they have to get rid of their water somehow," Jinlian said. "One woman has died, but there is another to take her place."

"Mother was angry with you because you asked for the fur coat without speaking to her about it first. She scolded Father when he gave back the key. She said it was lucky for you the Sixth Lady was dead or you wouldn't have had a chance to get the things. If she had been alive, you would only have been able to look at them."

"How absurd!" Jinlian said. "He is at liberty to do what he thinks fit. She is not my mother-in-law. It is not for her to control me. So she said I wouldn't let him go, did she? Well, I didn't put a cord about him. What nonsense!"

"I have come to tell you this so that you will know how matters stand. You mustn't mention it to anybody else. Guijie has gone, and the Great Lady is getting ready to go out. You will have to get ready too."

Yuxiao went away again. Jinlian decked herself with flowers and ornaments and powdered her face before the mirror. She told Chunmei to go and ask Yulou what color she was going to wear.

"Since we are still in mourning, Father wishes us all to wear plain clothes," Yulou said.

The ladies decided to wear white hairnets with pearl bandeaux, and plain-colored clothes. Yueniang alone wore a white headdress with a gold top, an embroidered coat, and a green skirt. One large sedan chair and four small ones were waiting for them. They took leave of Aunt Wu, the nuns, and old woman Pan, and set out to Ying Bojue's house to celebrate his baby's first month.

Ruyi'er and Yingchun had the food that Ximen Qing had left and a jar of Jinhua wine. They set out these things, took another pot of grape wine from the jar, and, at midday, invited old woman Pan, Chunmei, and Miss Yu to come and enjoy them. Miss Yu played and sang for them.

"I understand that Miss Shen sings that song about hanging up the portraits very well," Chunmei said, as they were enjoying their meal. "Why shouldn't we send for her and get her to sing to us?"

Yingchun was going to send Xiuchun but, at that moment, Chunhong came in to warm his hands at the fire.

"Now, you thievish little Southerner," Chunmei said to him, "didn't you go with the ladies?"

"No," Chunhong said, "Father told Wang Jing to go and said I was to stay here."

"You must be frozen, you little Southerner, or you wouldn't have come to warm your hands." She asked Yingchun to give him some wine. "When he has had it," she said, "we will get him to go for Miss Shen, and she shall come to sing for Grandmother."

When Chunhong had drunk his wine, he went to the inner court. Miss Shen was drinking tea with Aunt Wu, Ximen Dajie, Yuxiao, and the nuns.

"Sister Shen," Chunhong said, "my aunt wants you to go and sing for her."

"Your aunt is here," Miss Shen said. "What are you talking about?"

"I mean Aunt Chunmei," the boy said.

"Why does she want me?" Miss Shen said. "Miss Yu is there."

"Go, Miss Shen," Aunt Wu said, "and come back to us later." But Miss Shen would not go.

Chunhong went back and told Chunmei that he could not persuade her to come.

"Tell her I want her. Then she will come," Chunmei said.

"I did tell her, but she wouldn't pay any attention. When I said my aunt wanted her, she cried: 'What aunt are you talking about?' I said: 'Aunt Chunmei.' Then she said: 'Why should I bother about her? Miss Yu is there, and that's enough. Who is she to have the audacity to send for me? I am busy. I'm singing for Aunt Wu.' Aunt Wu told her to come, but she wouldn't."

Chunmei flew into a temper. Her ears grew red, and her face became purple. Nobody could stop her. She rushed to Yueniang's room, shook her finger at Miss Shen, and upbraided her.

"How dare you say to the boy: 'What aunt are you talking about?' and: 'How has she the audacity to send for me?' Who are you? Are you a general's wife that I have no right to send for you? You are just a thievish strumpet who runs around from one family to another. Before you have been here any time at all, you begin trying to give yourself airs. What songs do you think you know? You know about a couple of lines, one here and one there. The sort of stuff you sing is the veriest doggerel, never written down on paper. You know a few heathenish songs and a few crazy tunes, and you make all this fuss. I have heard some of the finest singers there are. You simply don't count. That whore, Wang Liu'er, may think a lot about you, but, I assure you, I don't. I don't care how much you try to follow in her footsteps, I'm not afraid of you. Get out of here at once."

Aunt Wu checked her. "You must not be so uncivil," she said.

Miss Shen, surprised at being scolded in this way, could only blink. She was angry but she dared not speak. At last she said: "Sister seems to be very annoyed, but I didn't say anything wrong to the boy. Why does she come and insult me like this? If this is no place for me, there are plenty of other places I can go to."

This made Chunmei more angry still. "You wandering vagabond of a strumpet! If you are such a high-principled woman, why do you go begging clothes and food outside your own family? Get out of here and never come back again."

"I don't depend upon this place for my living," Miss Shen said.

"If you did, I should tell the boys to pull your hair out."

"You maid," Aunt Wu said, "what makes you so uncivil today? Go to the other court."

Chunmei did not move. Miss Shen cried and got down from the bed. She said good-bye to Aunt Wu, packed her clothes, and went away without waiting for a sedan chair. Aunt Wu told Ping'an to send Huatong with her to Han Daoguo's house.

Chunmei, still fuming, went back to the outer court. Aunt Wu looked at Ximen Dajie and Yuxiao. "Chunmei must have been drinking," she said. "She would not have been so unmannerly if she hadn't. It made me very uncomfortable. She ought to have let Miss Shen go in her own good time. Why should she tell her to get out at once? She wouldn't even let a boy take her away. It is too bad."

"I imagine they have been drinking," Yuxiao said.

When Chunmei got back to her party, she said: "I wish I had boxed her ears. Then she would have known what sort of woman I am. I wasn't going to let her get away with behavior like that."

"You must remember that, when you cut one branch of a tree, you hurt the other branches," Yingchun said. "Don't forget Miss Yu is here."

"Miss Yu is a very different sort," Chunmei said. "She has been coming here for years and everybody likes her. She never refuses to sing if she is asked. She is not in the least like that strumpet. What songs does she know? Always the same few lines from the same few ditties, extremely vulgar, and not at all the sort of thing to be Song in a decent house like this. I don't want to hear her sing. I believe she is trying to put herself in Miss Yu's place."

"That is true enough," Miss Yu said. "Last night, when the Great Lady asked me to sing, she took the lute away from me. But don't be angry with her. She has no idea how she ought to behave here, and she doesn't know the respect that is due to you."

"That's what I told her," Chunmei said. "I said: 'Go and tell Han Daoguo's wife. I don't care.'"

"Sister," old woman Pan said, "why let yourself be so upset?"

"Let me give you a cup of wine to make you calmer," said Ruyi'er.

"This daughter of mine always flies into a temper when she is provoked," Yingchun said. "Now, Miss Yu, pick out one of your best songs and sing it for her."

Miss Yu took up her lute. "I will sing 'Ying Ying Made Trouble in the Bedchamber' for Grandmother and Sister Chunmei."

"Sing it well and you shall have some wine," Ruyi'er told her.

Yingchun took a cup of wine and said to Chunmei: "Now, Sister, no more tempers. Drink this cup of wine from your mother's hand."

This made Chunmei laugh. "You little strumpet!" she said, "how dare you call yourself my mother? Miss Yu, don't sing that song. Sing 'The River Is in Flood, and the Water Has Reached My Door.'"

Miss Yu took her lute and sang the first line: 'The flowers are dainty and the moon delightful.' They enjoyed their wine.

When Ximen Qing returned from the wharf where he had visited Cai, Ping'an said: "A messenger has been from Captain He to ask you to go early to the office tomorrow. Some robbers have been arrested, and they are to be tried. Prefect Hu has sent a hundred copies of the new calendar; and General Jing, a pig, a jar of wine, and four packets of silver. I gave them to brother-in-law, and he took them to the inner court. We did not send a card in return because the servant said he would call again this evening. I gave a return card and a *qian* of silver to his Lordship Hu's servant. Your kinsman, Master Qiao, has sent a card asking you to take wine with him tomorrow."

Then Daian came, bringing a return card from Song. "I took the things to his office," the boy said. "His Excellency said he would settle up with you tomorrow, and he gave me and the men five *qian* of silver and a hundred copies of the new calendar."

Ximen Qing went into the great hall. Chunhong hurried to warn Chunmei and the others.

"Are you still drinking?" he said. "Father has come back."

"What if he has, you little Southerner?" Chunmei said. "He won't interfere with us. The ladies are not at home, and he won't come here."

They went on drinking and joking, and nobody left the party. Ximen Qing went to Yueniang's room. Aunt Wu and the nuns went to the adjoining room. Yuxiao took his clothes and got something ready for him to eat.

Ximen Qing summoned Laixing and said to him: "You must see about preparing another feast. On the thirtieth, Censor Song is going to have a party here, and, on the first, the two eunuchs, Liu and Xue, Major Zhou and the others, are coming."

When Laixing had gone, Yuxiao asked Ximen what kind of wine he would like.

"Open the jar that General Jing has just sent," he told her. "I would like to taste it and see if it is any good."

Then Laian came and said he was going to take a man to meet Yueniang and the other ladies. Yuxiao asked him to unseal the jar. Then she poured out some wine and handed it to her master. It was a beautiful shade of green, and rather pungent. Ximen Qing asked for more. Food was brought, and he had his meal. Laian took some soldiers with lanterns to escort the ladies home.

They came in, wearing their fur coats. Sun Xue'e was the only one to kowtow to Ximen and Wu Yueniang. Then she went to the other room to see Aunt Wu and the nuns. Yueniang sat down and said: "Mistress Ying seemed very glad to see us. Her neighbor, Madam Ma, and Brother Ying's sister-in-law, Miss Du, and several other ladies were there, perhaps ten in all. There were two singing girls. The baby is big and chubby, but Chunhua seems thinner and darker than she used to be. Her long face is not very beautiful. It looks just like a donkey's. She is not at all well, and the household is in a mess, for there are not enough people to look after it. When we came away, Brother Ying kowtowed and thanked us most effusively. He asked us to thank you for the presents you had sent."

"Did Chunhua dress and come out to see you?" Ximen Qing asked.

"Of course, she did. She has eyes and a nose like everybody else. She is not a spirit. Why shouldn't she come out to see us?"

"Oh, the poor maid!" Ximen said. "If I put a few black beans on her, I'm sure some pig would run off with her."

"You shouldn't talk like that," Yueniang said. "You always try to make it appear that nobody is worth looking at except your own wives."

Wang Jing, who was standing beside them, said: "When Uncle Ying saw the ladies coming, he didn't come out to welcome them. He ran to a little room and peeped through the window. I caught him there, and I said: 'Old gentleman, you are lacking in propriety. 'What are you looking for?' He kicked me out."

"The rascal!" Ximen Qing said, laughing. "When he comes tomorrow, I will cover his face with dust."

"Yes," Wang Jing said, and laughed too.

Yueniang shouted at him. "Don't tell such lies, you young rascal. He didn't look at us at all. You are telling stories. We never saw him all day long, except when we were leaving and he came to kowtow to us."

Wang Jing went away. Yueniang got up and went to see her sister-in-law and the nuns in the next room. Ximen Dajie, Yuxiao, and the maids and serving women came to kowtow to her.

"Where is Miss Shen?" Yueniang said.

Nobody answered. At last Yuxiao said: "Miss Shen has gone."

"Why didn't she wait for me?" Yueniang asked.

Aunt Wu saw that the business could not be kept hidden. She told Yueniang of the quarrel between Chunmei and Miss Shen. Yueniang was angry. "If she didn't wish to sing, why should she?" she said. "The maid has no business to be so conceited and undisciplined as to curse her. The master of this house does not behave properly himself, and the maids do what they like. The whole household is topsy-turvy." She turned to Jinlian: "You ought to keep her in order instead of letting her behave so outrageously."

"I have never seen such a blind mule as Miss Shen," Jinlian said, laughing. "If the wind didn't blow, the trees wouldn't shake. She goes from one person's door to another, and singing is her business. When she is asked to sing, she should do so with a good grace. If she made a fuss and gave herself airs, Chunmei was right to tell her what she thought about her."

"All very well," Yueniang said, "but if she goes on like this, people, whether good or bad, simply won't stand it. They'll go away. You will do nothing to keep her in order."

"I don't see why I should punish my maid because she put this blind strumpet in her place."

Yueniang grew angry. Her face flushed.

"Very well, spoil your maid, and she will drive all our relatives and neighbors away."

She went to Ximen Qing, and he asked her what was the matter.

"I expect you know," Yueniang said. "You have such polite young ladies for your maids. Now, one of them has been cursing Miss Shen and making her go away."

"But why wouldn't she sing for her?" Ximen said, smiling. "Don't worry. Tomorrow, I'll send her two taels of silver, and that will put matters right."

"Miss Shen's box is still here. She didn't take it away," Yueniang said. She saw that Ximen Qing was laughing. "There you are, laughing, instead of sending for the maid and giving her a scolding. I don't see anything to laugh at."

Li Jiao'er and Yulou were there but, seeing how angry Yueniang was, they went to their own rooms. Ximen Qing went on drinking wine. Yueniang went to the inner room to take off her ornaments and ceremonial dress.

"Where have those four packets of silver on the chest come from?" she said to Yuxiao.

Ximen Qing answered her. "General Jing sent them. He wants me to speak to Song for him."

"Brother-in-law brought them. I forgot to tell you," Yuxiao said.

"Silver belonging to other people should always be put in the chest at once," Yueniang said.

Yuxiao put it in the chest.

Jinlian was still sitting there, waiting for Ximen Qing to go to the outer court. It was a *Renzi* day. She was going to take the medicine Nun Xue had given her and hoped that, after she had slept with him, she would conceive.

Ximen Qing showed no sign of moving. At last, she pulled aside the lattice. "If you are not coming, I shall go," she said. "I haven't patience to wait any longer."

"You go first," Ximen Qing said. "I will come when I've finished my wine."

Jinlian went away. Then Yueniang said: "I don't wish you to go to her. I have something to say to you. The pair of you wear the same pair of trousers, and you are making my life unbearable. She even has the audacity to come to my room and call you away. The shameless hussy! She might be your only wife and the rest of us nobodies. You are a foolish scamp. No wonder people talk about you behind your back. We are all your wives and you ought to treat us decently. You needn't make everybody aware of the fact that she has got you body and soul. Since you came back from the Eastern Capital, you haven't spent a single night in the inner court. Naturally people are annoyed. You should put fire into the cold stove before you begin on the hot one. You have no right to allow one woman to monopolize you. So far as I am concerned, it doesn't matter. I don't care for games of this sort, but the others will not stand it. They don't say anything, but they think a great deal. Yulou didn't eat a thing all the time we were at Brother Ying's place. She has probably caught a chill on the stomach. Mistress Ying gave her two cups of wine, but she couldn't keep it down. Will you go and see her?"

"Is that true?" Ximen Qing said. "Have these things taken away. I won't drink any more." He went at once to Yulou's room. She was undressed and lying on the bed, sick. She was retching painfully. "My child, how do you feel?" Ximen said. "I will send for a doctor for you." Yulou was vomiting. She did not answer. He helped her to lie down, but she pressed her hands to her breast.

"My dear, how are you? Tell me."

"I have a good deal of pain. Why do you ask? Go and attend to your own affairs."

"I didn't know," Ximen said. "The Great Lady has only just told me."

"Of course you didn't know," Yulou said. "I am not your wife. You only love the one who has established herself in your heart."

Ximen Qing took her in his arms and kissed her. "Don't tease me," he said. "Lanxiang, make some strong tea for your mother at once."

"I have some already made," Lanxiang said. She brought a cup. Ximen took it and held it to Yulou's lips.

"Give it to me," she said, "I will drink it by myself. Don't try to be pleasant. Go and sell your hot buns where they are wanted. I am not jealous. The sun must have risen in the west today, since you come to see me. I can't imagine why the Great Lady said anything to you about it."

"You don't understand," Ximen Qing said. "The last few days, I have really been too busy to come."

"Yes," Yulou said, "you have too much to think about; you can't think about anyone but your sweetheart. We are stale. We're only fit to be thrown into the dustbin. Perhaps in ten years' time you will remember us."

Ximen Qing still went on kissing her. "Go away," she said, "I can't bear the smell of the wine you've been drinking. I have had nothing to eat all day and I haven't strength enough to play with you."

"If you have had nothing to eat, let me tell the maid to bring something. I haven't had my supper yet. I will have it with you."

"No," Yulou said. "I feel too ill. If you want anything to eat, go and have it elsewhere."

"If you won't eat," Ximen said, "neither will I. Let us go to bed. Tomorrow I will send for Doctor Ren."

"Doctor Ren or Doctor Li, it's all the same to me. I shall send for old woman Liu. She'll give me medicine that will cure me."

"Lie down," Ximen said, "and let me stroke your stomach. That will make you better. You know I am an expert at massage." Then he suddenly remembered. "The other day," he said, "Liu, the Director of Studies, gave me ten cow-bezoar pills from Guangdong. If you take one with some wine, you will be all right in no time." He said to Lanxiang: "Go to the Great Lady and ask her for the medicine in the porcelain jar. And bring some wine with you."

"I'm sure you will be well as soon as you have taken it," he said to Yulou.

"I can't think of anything horrid enough to say to you," Yulou said. "What do you know about medicine? And, if you want wine, there is some here."

Lanxiang came back with two pills. Ximen Qing made her heat the wine. He took off the outer wax. There was a golden pill inside it. He gave it to Yulou.

"Now heat another cup of wine for me," he said to Lanxiang. "I am going to take some medicine myself."

Yulou looked at him. "You dirty creature! If you are going to take medicine, go somewhere else to do it. What do you think you're going to do here? You've decided I'm not going to die just yet, so you think you'll begin your tricks. In spite of all the pain I've had, you are ready to begin. No, I'll have none of it."

Ximen Qing laughed. "Very well, my dear. I won't take any medicine. We'll go to bed."

When she had taken the pill, they went to bed. Ximen Qing fondled her soft breasts. With one hand he pressed her sweet nipples, and, with the other, drew her white neck closer.

"How do you feel now that you've taken the pill?" he said.

"Not so bad as I did, but still bad enough."

"Don't worry," Ximen said, "you'll soon be better. Today, while you were out, I gave Laixing fifty taels of silver. We are going to give a banquet for Song the day after tomorrow. On the first of next month we must burn paper offerings, and, on the third, we must devote a couple of days to entertaining people. We can't accept presents and give nothing in return."

"What do I care whether you have people coming or not?" Yulou said. "On the twentieth, I am going to get the boys to settle up the accounts, and I shall give up this housekeeping business. You will probably hand it over to Jinlian. It is time she did some work. Only yesterday she was saying there was nothing very hard about it, and there is no reason why I should always be bothered with it."

"You shouldn't pay any attention to that little whore," Ximen said. "She is always bragging, but, if she is given anything of importance to do, she can't do it. If you really mean to hand it over to her, wait until these parties are over."

"Oh, you are very clever, Brother," Yulou said. "You pretend you don't love her more than the rest of us, but now you are giving yourself away. You say I am to hand the accounts over to her when the parties are over. Why should I have all the hard work? In the morning, when I am dressing my hair, the boys come in and out, measuring silver and getting change. It takes my breath away and uses me up. And nobody even says: 'Well done!'"

"My child," Ximen said, "don't you know the saying: 'When anyone has managed the house for three years, even the dog hates him'?"

He slowly lifted up one of her legs and put it over his arm. He embraced her, still holding it. He saw that she was wearing a pair of red silk slippers. "My child," he said, "what could be more delightful to me than this white leg? If I had all the women in the world to choose from, I could never find one so tender and so lovable as you."

"Oh, chatterbox!" Yulou said. "Do you imagine anybody believes that wooly mouth of yours? Other women have legs just as white. You really mean that my skin is rough, and you are calling black white."

"My dear, if I am lying to you, may I die this minute!"

"Don't take any oaths," Yulou said.

Ximen Qing put on the clasp and slipped his staff into her.

"I know the fellow you are," Yulou cried. "You always come to this." Then she saw the clasp. "When did you put that thing on? Take it off at once." But Ximen ignored her words, grasped her legs, and strove with all his might. Soon her juices of love flowed with a sound like that of a dog eating a fowl. She wiped her cunt with a handkerchief. She trembled and could not speak.

"Don't go any further, darling," she said. "My back has recently been hurting and some white fluid has been escaping."

"We will get some medicine from Doctor Ren tomorrow. That will cure it."

Yueniang was talking to Aunt Wu and the nuns. By degrees they came to the subject of Chunmei and Miss Shen, and the whole story came out.

"Chunmei was really very rude," Aunt Wu said. "She insulted Miss Shen in words that cut like knives. I was obliged to interfere. It was not surprising that Miss Shen was angry. I would never have believed that Chunmei could curse people like that. I'm sure she must have been drinking."

"Yes," Xiaoyu said, "she and four others were drinking."

"It is all that unreasonable fellow's fault," Yueniang said. "He has encouraged her to give herself such airs. She doesn't care who it is. She won't suffer anybody to speak to her. I shouldn't be surprised if, in the future, all sorts of people don't get driven away, and nobody will have anything to do with us. Miss Shen is a girl who goes from one house to another. It won't be very pleasant for us if this story gets about. People will say Ximen Qing's wife must be a dreadful creature. In this household, it is impossible to say who is master and who the slave. People will not say she is an undutiful slave, but that we are a bad bunch. And what will that mean?"

"Never mind," Aunt Wu said, "since your husband says nothing about it, why should we bother?"

The ladies went to their own rooms to sleep.

When Jinlian realized that Yueniang had prevented Ximen Qing from going to her, so that she missed the *Renzi* day, she was very angry. Very early the next morning, she told Laian to fetch a sedan chair for old woman Pan.

When Yueniang got up, the nuns were ready to go away. She gave each of them some cakes and five *qian* of silver, and promised that Nun Xue should hold a service in her own temple in the first month. She gave her another tael of silver to buy incense, candles and paper things, and said she would send oil, wheat flour, rice, and vegetarian food as an offering.

The nuns had tea with Aunt Wu in the upper room, and Yueniang sent for Li Jiao'er, Yulou, and Ximen's daughter, Ximen Dajie.

"How do you feel after taking the pill?" she asked Yulou. "Is your stomach still painful?"

"I brought up a little water this morning," Yulou said, "but I feel better now."

Yueniang told Yuxiao to go for Jinlian and old woman Pan. Yuxiao said: "Xiaoyu is seeing about the buns. I will go myself." She went to Jinlian's room.

"Where is Grandmother?" she said. "They want you to go and have tea with them."

"I sent her away this morning," Jinlian said.

"Why did you send her away without telling anybody?" Yuxiao said.

"Why should she stay any longer? She seems to have made herself a nuisance."

"But I have a piece of dried meat and four preserved melons for her. I never dreamed she would go. You keep them for her." The maid gave the food to Jinlian, who put it in a drawer.

"Last night, when you had gone away," Yuxiao said, "the Great Lady told Father you were the one who governed this household, and that you and he wore the same pair of trousers. She said you were a shameless thing, monopolizing him as you did, so that he was afraid to go to the inner court. She persuaded him to go and sleep in the Third Lady's room. Then she told Aunt Wu and the nuns that you spoiled Chunmei so much that she even dared to insult Miss Shen. Father is going to send a tael of silver to Miss Shen to make things all right."

Yuxiao went back to Yueniang and said that the Fifth Lady was coming, but that her mother had gone home.

Yueniang looked at Aunt Wu. "You see! I said something to her yesterday, and now she flies into a temper and sends her mother away without a word to me. She must be up to something, but what form the storm will take I can't think."

Yueniang did not know it, but Jinlian was already in the room on the other side of the lattice. She came in suddenly.

"Great Sister," she said, "I have sent my mother home. Did you say that I monopolize our husband? I wish to know."

"Yes, I did say so," Yueniang said. "What about it? Ever since he came back from the Eastern Capital, he has spent all his time in your room. He never comes near the inner court. Do you flatter yourself that you are his only wife, and the rest of us nothing? Whether the others realize what you are about, I don't know, but I do. A few days ago, when Guijie went away, my sister-in-law asked me why she was in such a hurry and why our husband was angry with her. I told her I didn't know. You pushed yourself forward and said you were the only one who knew all about it. Of course you know. You never lose hold of him for a moment."

"If he didn't wish to come to my room," Jinlian said, "do you imagine I should keep him there with a pig's-hair cord? Do you suggest that I am a whore?"

"Aren't you?" Yueniang said. "Yesterday, when he was here, you pulled the lattice aside and dashed in to take him away. What do you mean by it? Our husband is a man. He does a man's work. What crime has he committed that you should tie him with a cord of pig's hair? You foolish creature! I said nothing about it until you made me do so. On the sly, you asked him for a fur coat. You didn't say a word to me about it, even when you put it on. If everybody behaved like that, my function here might as well be to look after the ducks. It is time you realized that, even in a poor house, there must be someone in authority. You allowed your maid to sleep with him. It was like cat and rat sleeping together. You indulge her in every possible way, and now she has the audacity to insult people. Yet you still stick up for her and won't be contradicted."

"What about my maid?" Jinlian cried. "You think she is bad, and you would like to get rid of me. As for that fur coat, I did ask him for it, but it wasn't only to get that for me that he opened the door. He got clothes for other people too. Why don't you mention that fact? I spoil my maid. I am a whore. And I make my husband happy. Why don't you say that woman is a whore too?"

Yueniang became more and more angry. Her cheeks became crimson. "No," she said, "not you, but I am the whore! But when I married him, I was a virgin, not a married woman who got him into her clutches. I am no whorish husband-stealer. It is clear enough which of us is a whore and which is virtuous."

"Sister, don't lose control of yourself," Aunt Wu said.

But Yueniang went on. "You have killed one husband already, and now you are trying to kill another."

"Mother," Yulou said, "why are you so angry today, beating us all with the same stick? You, Fifth Lady, must give way to the Great Lady. You must not quarrel with her."

"The proverb says: When there is fighting, no hand is gentle: when there is quarreling, no words are soft," Aunt Wu said. "When you quarrel like this, it makes your relatives ashamed. If you won't pay any attention to me, I shall take it that you are angry with me and call for my sedan chair and go home."

Li Jiao'er hastily begged her not to do so.

Jinlian sat down on the floor and rolled about. She banged her face on the ground and knocked the hairnet from her head. She cried aloud.

"Let me die!" she shouted. "Why should I go on living a miserable life like this? You were married in due and proper manner: I only followed him to the house. Very well! There need be no more difficulty, I will ask him to set me free. I will go, but I fear that, if you imagine you will capture a husband thereby, you are mistaken."

"Now, you disturber of the peace," Yueniang said, "before one can get a word out, you pour forth a stream of words. You roll about on the floor. You put all the blame on us. Will you ask my husband to divorce me? Don't think anybody is afraid of you, even if you are so clever."

"No, indeed!" Jinlian cried, "you are the only good and virtuous woman here. Who would dare to quarrel with you?"

"Am I not good and virtuous? Do you suggest that I have had a lover in this house?" Yueniang was growing still more angry.

"If you haven't, has anybody else? Let me see you point to any lover I have had."

When the quarrel had reached this pitch, Yulou went forward and tried to pull Jinlian away. "Don't behave like this," she said. "These holy nuns will be ashamed of you. Stand up, and I will go with you to your room."

Jinlian would not get up. Yulou and Yuxiao pulled her up. They took her to her own room.

"Sister," Aunt Wu said to Yueniang, "you ought not to get into a state like this when you are in such delicate health. There is really nothing very much the matter. When you sisters are happy, I am content; but, if you spend all the time quarreling and will not listen to what I say, I shall not be able to come any more."

The nuns gave their novices something to eat. Then they took their boxes and came to say good-bye to Yueniang. "Teachers," Yueniang said, "you must not scorn me."

"There is some smoke to every fire," Nun Xue said. "A tiny flame in our mind can give rise to much smoke. My advice is: give way to each other. As Buddha says: Our minds should be as calm as a ship at anchor. We must cleanse our hearts and make them pure. If we leave the lock open and loose the chain, ten thousand diamond clubs can not control us. The first step towards Buddhahood is self-control. Thank you for all your kindness to us. We hope you will be very well."

They made reverence to Yueniang, and she returned it. "I feel that, this time, I have entertained you very poorly," she said, "but I will send you something later." She asked Li Jiao'er and Ximen Dajie to see the nuns to the gate. "Mind the dog," she said.

When the nuns had gone, she sat down again with Aunt Wu. "This business has made my arms numb and my fingers as cold as ice," she said. "I only had a mouthful of tea this morning, and there is nothing but that in my stomach."

"Over and over again, I have advised you not to quarrel," Aunt Wu said. "You never listen to me. Now you are getting near your time. Why do you make this trouble?"

"You saw the whole affair," Yueniang said. "Am I the one who causes the trouble? You might as well talk about a thief arresting a policeman. I can give way to everybody but nobody will give way to me. There is only one husband here, and she wants him all for herself. She schemes and plots with that maid of hers. They do things that no other person would ever dream of doing. Though they are women, they have no idea of decency. She never looks at herself, but opens her mouth and pours forth insults. When Li Ping'er was alive, she was constantly having rows with her. She was always coming and telling me one thing and another that Li Ping'er had done wrong. She is the kind of woman who is always causing trouble. She has an animal's heart and a human face. She never admits saying anything. She takes such dreadful oaths they would frighten anybody. But I will keep my eyes open and watch her. I will see what sort of an end she comes to. When we had tea, I sent for her mother. How could I have dreamed she would send her away? She was all ready to make trouble with me. She sneaked up here determined to do so. Well! I am not afraid of her. Let her tell my husband, and he can divorce me."

"We were all in the room," Yuxiao said. "I was standing near the fire, but I did not hear the Fifth Lady come in. I never heard a sound."

"She walks like a spirit," Xue'e said. "She always wears felt shoes, so she doesn't make any sound. Don't you remember the trouble she used to make for me when she first came here? She said all sorts of things about me behind my back, and my husband beat me twice in consequence. At that time, Sister, you said it was my fault."

"She is accustomed to burying people alive," Yueniang said. "Today she thought she would try her hand on me. You saw her beating her head on the ground and rolling about. When he comes back and finds out about it, I shall come off worst."

"You mustn't say that, Mother," Li Jiao'er said, "the world cannot be turned upside down."

"You don't know," Yueniang said. "She is one of those nine-tailed foxes. Better people than I have died at her hands. How shall I escape? What flesh and bones have I that they can withstand her? You have been here several years, and you came from the bawdy house, but you are worth a dozen of her. See how desperate she was yesterday. She dashed into my room and called him. She said: 'I'm not going to wait for you if you don't come.' It looked as though he belonged to her, and she had the right to have him. I shouldn't care if he hadn't gone to her room every night since he came back from the Eastern Capital. Even when it was somebody's birthday, she wouldn't let him go. She wants all ten fingers to put into her own mouth."

"Why do you worry about it so much?" Aunt Wu said. "You are nearly always ill. Let him do what he likes. If you are trying to fight other people's battles, you will be the one to suffer."

Yuxiao brought some food, but Yueniang would not touch it. "My head aches, and my heart feels very queer," she said. She told Yuxiao to put a pillow on the bed so that she might lie down, and asked Li Jiao'er to keep Aunt Wu company. Miss Yu was going, so Yueniang gave orders that a box of cakes and five *qian* of silver should be given to her. Then the girl went away.

It was about noon when Ximen Qing came home after trying the case at his office. General Jing's man came to ask for his return card. Ximen Qing said to him: "Thank your master for these valuable presents, but they are really too much. I should like you to take them back now, and I will accept them when I have been able to do what he wishes."

"My master gave me no orders," the man said, "and I dare not take them back. It will be just as well if they are kept here."

"In that case," Ximen Qing said, "thank your master for me. Here is a card to take back to him." He gave the man a tael of silver.

Then he went to Yueniang's room. She was lying on the bed. He spoke to her several times, but she would not answer. He asked the maids what was wrong, but none dared to tell him. Then he went to Jinlian's room. She, too, was lying on the bed, and her hair was in disorder. He asked her what the trouble was, and again he got no answer. Then he went to pack up some silver, and, when General Jing's man had gone, he went to Yulou's room. Yulou knew that the secret could not be kept so she told him about the quarrel between Yueniang and Jinlian.

In a great state of excitement, Ximen Qing went to Yueniang's room again. He held her up in his arms. "Why did you have this quarrel?" he said. "You know you are not in a fit state of health. Why do you take that little strumpet seriously? Why did you have a row with her?"

"I did not quarrel with her," Yueniang said. "It was she who started the trouble, I didn't go to her: she came to me. If you wish to prove it, ask the others. This morning, out of kindness, I got tea ready and asked her mother to come and join us, but, in a temper, she had sent her mother away. Then she came herself, tossing her head and shouting. She rolled about on the floor and beat her head on the ground. She got her hairnet in a mess. It was a marvel she didn't strike me, and, if it hadn't been for the others keeping us apart, we might have rolled about together. She is so used to bullying people that she thinks she can bully me. She said several times that you married her irregularly and that she would ask you to divorce her and she would go away. For one word I said, she said ten. Her mouth was like the Huai River in flood. How could a weak person like me withstand her? She knows how to put the blame on others. She made me so angry I didn't know where I was. As for this baby, he will never be born, not even if he is a prince. She made me so ill my belly feels ready to burst, and my guts hurt as though they were dropping out of me. My head aches and my arms are numb. I have just come back from the closet, but the child didn't come away. It would have been better if it had come, then I shouldn't have been troubled any longer with it. Tonight I will get a cord and hang myself. Then you will be free to go to her. If I don't hang myself, I shall surely be murdered as Li Ping'er was. I know you will think things very unfortunate if you can't get rid of more than one wife in three years."

Ximen Qing was terribly excited. He put his arms around Yueniang. "Good Sister," he said, "don't worry about that little whore. She doesn't know the difference between high and low, what is sweet and what is sour. Don't be angry. You are worth more to me than all the others put together. I will go and beat her."

"Dare you?" Yueniang said. "She will tie you with a pig's-hair cord."

"Let her say so to me," Ximen said. "If I get angry with her, I will kick her till she doesn't know where she is. How do you feel now? Have you had anything to eat?"

"I haven't tasted a thing," Yueniang said. "This morning, I got the tea ready and waited for her mother. Then she came and screamed at me. Now I feel very ill. My belly hurts and my head aches. My arms are all numb. If you don't believe me, come here and feel my hands. They are still cold."

Ximen Qing stamped his feet on the ground. "What shall I do?" he cried. "I know. I'll send the boys for Doctor Ren."

"What is the use of sending for Doctor Ren? He can do nothing. If it is to live, it will live, and, if not, it will die. If it dies, so much the better for everybody. A wife is like the paint on the walls. When it is faded, another coat is put on. If I die, you will make her your first wife. She is clever enough to manage this household."

"I'm surprised you have patience even to quarrel with her," Ximen Qing said. "You ought to treat her as dung and leave her alone. If we don't send for Doctor Ren, the anger will get into your system and we shan't be able to get it out again. Then it will be too late to do anything."

"Send for old woman Liu, and I will take her medicine," Yueniang said. "I will ask her to use a needle on my head and get rid of the headache."

"That's absurd," Ximen Qing said. "What does that old whore know about women's ailments? I shall send a boy with a horse for Doctor Ren at once."

"You can do so if you like, but I won't see him."

Ximen Qing paid no attention. He went to the outer court and said to Qintong: "Get a horse at once and go for Doctor Ren. Be quick. Bring him back with you." Qintong got a horse and was away like a cloud of smoke. Ximen Qing went back to Yueniang's room and told the maids to make some gruel. But when the gruel was brought, Yueniang would not eat it.

Qintong came back and said Doctor Ren was at the palace and his people said he would come the next morning.

Yueniang saw that messengers had come several times from Master Qiao to invite Ximen Qing. "The doctor will be here tomorrow," she said. "You had better go or our kinsman Qiao will be angry."

"If I go, who will see to you?"

Yueniang laughed. "You silly fellow," she said. "None of this. Off you go. There is nothing seriously wrong with me. Leave me alone. Perhaps I shall feel better. If I do, I'll get up and have something to eat with my sister-in-law. Don't be so excited."

Ximen Qing said to Yuxiao: "Go for Aunt Wu at once, and ask her to stay with your mother. Where is Miss Yu? Tell her to come and sing for your mother."

"Miss Yu has been gone a long time," Yuxiao said.

"Who told her to go?" Ximen said, "I wanted her here for another two days." He kicked Yuxiao.

"She saw this was no place to be at, so she went away," Yueniang said. "Yuxiao is not to blame."

"You wouldn't kick the one who insulted Miss Shen," Yuxiao murmured.

Ximen Qing pretended not to hear this. He dressed and went to Master Qiao's house. Before the first night watch, he returned and went to Yueniang's room. Yueniang was sitting with Aunt Wu, Yulou and Li Jiao'er. Aunt Wu hurriedly went away as soon as he came in.

"How do you feel now?" Ximen Qing said.

"I have had two mouthfuls of gruel with my sister-in-law," Yueniang said, "and my stomach feels rather easier. But I still have the headache and backache."

"That is all right," Ximen said, "Doctor Ren will be here tomorrow and he will give you some medicine to expel the anger and strengthen your womb. You will soon be well again."

"I told you I didn't want the doctor, but you would send for him. This is nothing serious, and I don't want any man to come and fiddle with me. You will see whether I am able to go out or not tomorrow. What did kinsman Qiao want with you?"

"Oh, it was only an entertainment to celebrate my coming back from the Eastern Capital. He was very kind, and had made a lot of preparations. There were two singing girls, and his Honor Zhu was there. But I was so anxious about you, I couldn't eat a thing. I had a few cups of wine and came back as soon as I could."

"You smooth-tongued rascal," Yueniang said. "These flowery phrases and flattering expressions are too much for me. What is making you so extraordinarily pleasant? Even if I were one of Buddha's incarnations, you would give me no place in your heart. If I died, you wouldn't think me worth a jar of earthenware. What did Qiao say to you?"

"He is thinking of applying for honorary rank, and he has prepared thirty taels of silver. He wants me to speak to Prefect Hu about it. I told him there would be no trouble about that because, yesterday, Hu sent me a hundred copies of the new calendar, and I hadn't sent him anything in return yet. When I did, I said, I would send a card and ask him for a nomination. Qiao wouldn't agree. He said he must offer his thirty taels. If I help him, he said, it would be very much to his advantage."

"Did you take his money?" Yueniang said. "You ought to do something for him if he asks you."

"He is going to send the money tomorrow. He was going to send presents too, but I stopped him. I think if I send Hu a pig and a jar of wine, that ought to be enough."

That night, Ximen Qing stayed with Yueniang.

The next day was Censor Song's party. Tables were arranged in the great hall, and everything was made ready. Thirty musicians from the Prefecture came early in the morning, with four conductors and four soldiers. Shortly afterwards, Dr. Ren came on horseback. Ximen Qing took him to the hall, and they greeted one another.

"Your servant called for me yesterday," Dr. Ren said, "but I was on duty. When I came home last night, I found your card, and I have come this morning without waiting for my carriage. May I ask who is ill?"

"My first wife has suddenly become disturbed in health, and I should be glad if you would examine her," Ximen said.

They drank tea. Then Dr. Ren said: "Yesterday, Mingchuan told me you had been promoted. I must congratulate you now and send my presents later."

"It is really not an occasion for celebration," Ximen said, "I am so ill-fitted for the office I hold."

He said to Qintong: "Go to the inner court and tell the Great Lady that Doctor Ren has come. Ask them to get the room ready." Qintong went. Aunt Wu, Li Jiao'er and Meng Yulou were with Wu Yueniang. He gave them Ximen's message. Yueniang did not move.

"I told him not to send for the doctor," she said. "I don't want any man here, staring at me and putting his fingers on my hand. I want some medicine from old woman Liu, nothing more. Why should he make a fuss like this to satisfy that man's curiosity?"

"But he is here now, Mother," Yulou said, "we can't tell him to go away without your seeing him."

Aunt Wu also insisted. "He is a physician to the royal family," she said. "You must let him feel your pulse. We don't know what is wrong, or where the trouble lies. This is the only way we can find out. It will be good for you to take his medicine and put your blood and air in order. You mustn't let the thing go too far. Old woman Liu knows nothing about medicine."

Yueniang went to dress her hair and put on her headdress. Yuxiao held the mirror for her, and Yulou climbed on the bed and brushed her back hair. Li Jiao'er arranged her ornaments, and Xue'e put her clothes straight. In a very short time she looked like a carving in jade.

CHAPTER 76

Master Wen Falls into Disgrace

The golden cups are always in their hands
They pledge each other without ceasing.
No thought of earthly things disturbs their quiet hearts.
Year after year, men are the same
In every place, the same flowers bloom.
Let us sing and recite poems
To increase the joy that comes from this inspired wine
And when we have drunk our fill,
Call for the flute and strings.
When we are in our cups, things are today
As they were yesterday.
Only the scholar Wen is here no more.

When Ximen Qing found that Wu Yueniang was not yet ready, he came himself to hurry her. When she was dressed, he asked Dr. Ren to come. Yueniang came from her bedroom and made a reverence towards the visitor. Dr. Ren turned and bowed. Yueniang sat down on a chair facing the doctor, and Qintong put an embroidered cushion on the table. She held out her arm, and Dr. Ren felt her pulse. After this, she made a reverence and went back to her room. One of the boys brought the doctor tea.

"Your lady," said Dr. Ren, "appears to be suffering from disorder both of air and blood. Her pulse is feeble and sluggish. As regards the air, it is partly because she is with child, but also because she has not been taking sufficient nourishment. Then, too, she has been angry and so stirred up the fire in her liver. This makes her head and eyes ache. She takes things too seriously, and the result of this is a certain melancholy in the abdominal region. The blood and air in her body are not evenly matched."

Yueniang sent Qintong to tell the doctor that her head ached, her arms were numb, and her belly very painful. She had backache and no appetite.

"This is evident," the doctor said. "I have already said as much."

"As you say, she is with child," Ximen Qing said. "Indeed, she is near her time. She has had occasion to be angry, and her anger has been unable to find a satisfactory outlet. She feels depressed in consequence. I hope, Doctor, you will give her the best medicine you can think of. I shall be more than grateful."

"I will do what I can," the doctor said. "I will send her something to make her stomach easier, to set the air in the right channels and, generally, to strengthen her internally. But when the lady has taken the medicine, she must avoid all further occasion of anger, and she must be careful what she eats."

"You will remember the baby, Doctor?" Ximen said.

"My medicine will nourish and soothe it."

"My third wife, too, has pains in the stomach," Ximen Qing said. "If you have anything likely to do her good, will you be so kind as to prescribe for her?"

"Certainly. I will send her some pills," Dr.. Ren said.

He went to the outer court. On the way, he saw the company of musicians and asked Ximen Qing whom he was entertaining.

"His Excellency Song and his officers are entertaining Governor Hou here today," Ximen told him.

The doctor was astonished. His respect for Ximen Qing increased accordingly. Indeed, when he was taken to the gate, he bowed so often that he paid twice the usual degree of honor to his patron.

Ximen Qing went back, packed up a tael of silver and two handkerchiefs, and told Qintong to take them on horseback to the doctor's house and bring back the medicine.

Li Jiao'er, Meng Yulou and the other ladies were busy in Yueniang's room, getting the fruit ready and cleaning the silver.

"You didn't want to come out to see the doctor," Yulou said to Yueniang, "but, you see, he knew exactly what was wrong the moment he looked at you."

"I am not a good respectable wife," Yueniang said, "and, if I am going to die, why don't you let me die in peace? That woman said I was not her mother-in-law. The only difference between us, I suppose, is that I am eight months older than she is. If she hadn't made sure of our husband, do you think she would have dared to shout and rave at me as she did? If you hadn't taken her away, I should not have escaped in ten years. If I am to die, let me die. As the proverb says: when one cock dies, there is always another to take his place, and the new cock's crowing is sweeter than the last. When I am dead and she has taken my place, all will be peace and quietness. When the turnips are pulled up, there will be more room in the field."

"Oh, Great Sister, you mustn't talk like that," Yulou said. "I will answer for her. I admit she often behaves badly, and she is always trying to score over people, but she isn't so bad as she sounds. You mustn't fall out with her completely."

"Isn't she as clever as you are? I tell you she is cunning personified. If she were not, she wouldn't always be sneaking up to listen to other people's conversation. And why should she say such horrid things?"

"Mother, you are the mistress here. You are the source from which we draw our water, and you must not be ungenerous. A gentleman can afford to be indulgent to ten commoner folk. If you raise your hand, she may pass, but if you are as obstinate as she is, she can never get by."

"No, our husband is behind her," Yueniang said, "I, the first wife, must stand aside."

"That is not true," Yulou persisted. "Now that you are not very well, he does not even venture to go near her."

"Why?" Yueniang said. "She talked about binding him with a pig's-hair cord. He is a wild horse. When he loves a woman he must have her, and no power on earth can stop him. If we try to do anything about it, we are called whores for our pains."

"Mother," Yulou said, "you have got this off your chest, and now the anger must be out of your system. I will go and fetch her. She shall kow-tow and say she's sorry. Aunt Wu is here, and I want you both to smile at each other in her presence. If you refuse to make up this quarrel, you will put our husband in a very awkward position. He won't know what to do. When he wants to go to her, he will be afraid of your displeasure, and, if he doesn't go, she won't have anything to do with him. Here we are, all busy getting things ready for the party, and she is in her room, doing nothing. We can't have her staying there any longer. Am I not right, Aunt Wu?"

"Sister," Aunt Wu said to Yueniang, "the Third Lady is right. It isn't simply a misunderstanding between you two ladies. It puts your husband in a hole, and makes it very embarrassing for him whichever of you he goes to see."

Yueniang did not speak until Yulou was on the point of going for Pan Jinlian. Then she said: "Don't go. It is of no consequence whether she comes or not."

"She will not dare refuse to come," Yulou said. "If she does, I'll drag her here with a pig's-hair cord."

She went straight to Jinlian's room. Jinlian had not dressed her hair. There was no powder on her face, and she was sitting on the bed, alone.

"Fifth Sister," Yulou said, "why are you making such a fool of yourself? Get your hair done. There is to be a party in the outer court, and we are all very busy, yet you stay here, nursing your temper, instead of coming to help us. I have spoken to the Great Lady, and now you must come with me and see her. Keep your temper and try to look pleasant. Don't forget: Pleasant words and pretty phrases make the coldest day warm; but unkind hurtful words make it cold even in the sixth month. You have quarreled, but if you insist on being obstinate, where is it all going to end? People enjoy flattery, just as Buddha enjoys incense. Come and say you're sorry, and let us have an end to the business. It will be very awkward for our husband if you don't. He will not come to see you if he is afraid she will be angry."

"I can't make any show against her," Jinlian said. "She says she is the only duly married wife here. You and I are dewdrops. We are nobodies, not worthy to lick her boots."

"I told her she was killing several birds with one stone," Yulou said. "His Lordship is my second husband, I admit, but it wasn't I who made the advances. When we were married, I had a proper witness and a go-between. I did not come into the family by the back door. But don't cut off one branch and damage the whole tree. The Great Lady is angry with you, but some of us are not. And don't carry things to extremes. We have to keep our eyes open and see what we're about. We must make sure of our ground. It was a mistake to quarrel before the nuns and Miss Yu. Each of us has his reputation to think about, as every tree has its own bark. The Great Lady is not very well, and, if you don't go and see her, I can't tell what the consequences may be. We have to be together, like the lips on one's mouth. Dress your hair. We will go and see her."

Jinlian sat and thought for a long time. Then she swallowed her anger, went to her dressing table to brush her hair, and put on her net. She dressed and went to the upper room with Yulou. The Third Lady pulled aside the lattice.

"I have brought her," she said. "She did not dare refuse to come. Come, my child, and kowtow to your mother." Then she said to Yueniang: "My daughter is young. She hardly knows the difference between right and wrong. Otherwise she would not have offended you. Won't you forgive her this time? If she is ever rude to you again, you may punish her as much as you please. I will not raise a finger to stop you."

Jinlian kowtowed four times to Yueniang. Then she jumped up and slapped Yulou. "You little strumpet!" she cried, "do you think I would have you for a mother?"

The ladies laughed. Even Yueniang could not help smiling.

"You slave!" Yulou said, "your mistress gives you back her favor, then you jump up and beat your mother."

"It is splendid to see you sisters all merry together," Aunt Wu said. "The Great Lady sometimes says more than she means, but you must make allowances for her, and give way a little. Then everything will be well. The proverb says: The peony is beautiful, but it must have leaves for its beauty to appear."

"If she had not said anything, I should not have quarreled with her," Yueniang said.

"Mother," Jinlian said, "you are the Heaven and I the Earth. Forgive me. I am just a stupid creature."

Yulou patted her on the back. "Now you speak like my daughter. But we have no time to talk. We have been working a long time, and it is your turn to help us."

Jinlian climbed on to the bed beside Yulou and helped her to arrange the fruit in the boxes.

When Qintong came back with the medicine, Ximen looked at the note that came with it, and told the boy to take it to Yueniang.

"So there is some for you, too?" Yueniang said to Yulou.

"Yes," Yulou said, "I have my old trouble again, and I asked Father to get me some pills from Doctor Ren.

"It is because you didn't eat anything the other day," Yueniang said. "You must have caught a chill."

Song was the first to arrive. Ximen Qing took him to the arbor, and they sat down.

"Thank you for sending the tripod," Song said, "I must pay you for it."

"How can I accept money for it?" Ximen said. "I was afraid you would refuse it, even as a gift."

"You are really too kind," Song said. He bowed and thanked Ximen Qing.

When they had had tea, they talked about the official affairs of the district and the condition of the people. Song asked about the local dignitaries. "Prefect Hu is very well liked," Ximen Qing said, "and District Magistrate Li is most conscientious in his work. I have not had much to do with the others."

"You know Major Zhou," Censor Song said. "What do you think of him?"

"He is an experienced soldier," Ximen Qing said, "but I should hardly say that he is so efficient as Jing of Jizhou. Jing passed the military examination when he was still quite young, and he is as capable as he is brave. Perhaps your Excellency will keep an eye on him."

"Are you speaking of Jing Zhong? Do you know him?"

"He is a friend of mine," Ximen said. "Yesterday he brought a card and asked me to speak to your Excellency on his behalf."

"I have heard that he is a good officer," the Censor said. "Is there anyone else?"

"There is my wife's brother, Wu Kai. He is a Captain here and in charge of the alterations to the granary. He is due for promotion, and, if your Excellency helps him, I shall be involved in his honor."

"As he is your kinsman," Song said, "I will not only recommend him for promotion, but see that he gets an appointment worth having."

Ximen Qing bowed and thanked him. He gave the Censor the two men's records of service. Song handed them to one of his officers and said they were to be brought before him when he prepared his report. Ximen Qing quietly told a servant to give that officer three taels of silver.

Then they heard music, and a servant came to tell them that the Provincial Officers had arrived. Ximen Qing went to receive them while Song went to the garden gate to look on. When the officers had exchanged greetings, they looked around the great hall. There was a large table in the middle magnificently set out, and a smaller table only a little less splendid. They were very pleased. They thanked Ximen Qing and said that they must send him more money.

"We certainly have not sent him sufficient for all this," Censor Song said, "but, for my sake, Siquan, do not ask them for any more."

"I should not dream of accepting any more," Ximen Qing said.

They sat down in places according to their rank and tea was brought. A man was sent to invite Governor Hou. After some delay the messenger came riding on horseback and told them that the Governor was on his way. The musicians played together and all the officers went out to the gate to wait for him. Censor Song stood alone at the second door.

Cavalry with blue pennons trotted by. Then Governor Hou came wearing a scarlet robe with a peacock embroidered upon it, sable ear covers, and a girdle with a buckle of pure gold. He was in a sedan chair borne by four men. When he had got down from his carriage, the officers escorted him to the great hall. Censor Song was wearing a scarlet robe embroidered with gold clouds. The buckle on his girdle was of rhinoceros horn. Each invited the other to precede him, and at last they entered the hall together. When the two high officers had greeted one another, the others came to make their reverences. Ximen Qing was the last. The Governor remembered him from the day of the reception to Huang, and he told one of his officers to give Ximen a card, on which was written: "Your friend, Hou Meng." Ximen took the card with both hands and gave it to a servant.

They all took off their ceremonial robes, and the Governor sat down in the place of honor. The other officers ranged themselves on either hand. Censor Song took the place of the host. After tea had been served the musicians played and Song offered his guest wine, flowers and silk. He ordered food to be sent to the Governor's office. Then the banquet was served. The dishes were all garnished with flowers.

The dancers performed exceedingly well. Then the Haiyan actors came and kowtowed and presented their list. The Governor told them to play *The Duke of Jin Returned the Girdle*. The banquet proceeded. When two acts had been performed, Governor Hou ordered five taels of silver to be distributed among the cooks, waiters, musicians, and servants. Then he put on his ceremonial robes again and took leave of the company. All the officers went with him to the gate. When he had gone, Song and the rest thanked Ximen Qing again and went away.

Ximen Qing returned to the great hall and dismissed the musicians. It was still early and he said: "Don't take any of the things away." He sent boys for Uncle Wu, Ying Bojue, Fu, Gan, Ben the Fourth, and his son-in-law, Chen Jingji. He told the actors to have something to eat, and bade them, when his guests arrived, play *Han Xizai Entertained Scholar Tao by Night*. Then he sent for Chunmei to decorate the hall, that he might enjoy the beauty of the flowers while he was drinking.

The three clerks came first, then Scholar Wen, the two Wu brothers, and Ying Bojue made a reverence to Ximen and said: "I am sorry I was only able to offer your ladies such poor entertainment the other day. Thank you for the splendid presents you sent."

Ximen Qing laughed. "You dog!" he said. "What did you mean by peeping at my ladies through the window?"

"You don't believe that!" Bojue said. "I know who told you." He pointed to Wang Jing. "It was that dog. You wait and, one of these days, I'll bite you."

They sat down and had tea. Uncle Wu wished to go and see his sister in the inner court, and Ximen Qing took him there. On the way he told him what he had said to Censor Song. "His Excellency took your record of service," he said, "and I gave three taels of silver to the officer in whose charge he left it. He has your papers and Jing's. The Censor promised that there shall be something for you when he sends his report."

Uncle Wu was delighted. He bowed to Ximen and said: "This is very kind of you."

"I only had to say: 'This is my wife's brother,' and he said at once: 'Since he is a kinsman of yours, I must certainly do something for him.'"

They came to the upper room, and Wu Yueniang made a reverence to her brother.

"It is time you went home," Uncle Wu said to his wife. "There is nobody to see after the house, and you have been here too long already."

"She won't let me go away," Aunt Wu said. "She says I must stay until the third."

"Then you must be sure to come home on the fourth," Uncle Wu said.

He went back to the outer court and drank with the others. The actors played and then performed as Ximen had told them. When the excitement of the play was at its height, Daian came in. "Qiao Tong has come from Master Qiao and would like to speak to you," he said. Ximen Qing left his friends and went to see the boy.

"My father says he did not give you the money yesterday," Qiao Tong said, "so he has sent me with it now. There are thirty taels here and five more for the less important officers."

"I am going to see Prefect Hu about it tomorrow morning," Ximen said. "I think he will do what we wish, and there will be no need to give any money to anyone else. Take these five taels back." He told Daian to give food and wine to Qiao Tong.

Two acts of the play had now been performed, and it was about the first night watch. The guests took their leave, and Ximen Qing ordered everything to be cleared away. Then he went to Yueniang. She was sitting with her sister-in-law, but Aunt Wu withdrew at once.

"I have managed that business of your brother's with Censor Song," Ximen said to his wife. "His Excellency said that not only would he see that he got promotion, but that he would appoint him to some post worth having. So now he is sure of a military appointment. I have told your brother about it, and he is delighted."

"But he has no money," Yueniang said. "Where is he going to find two or three hundred taels?"

"There is no need for him to spend any money," Ximen Qing said. "I told the Censor that he was your brother, and his Excellency promised me that he would attend to the matter himself."

"Do what you think best," Yueniang said, "it is not my business."

"Yuxiao," Ximen said, "get that medicine ready for your mother. I want to see her take it."

"Go away and don't make a fuss," Yueniang said, "I will take the medicine when I go to bed."

Ximen Qing was on the point of going when Yueniang called him back.

"Where are you going?" she said. "If you are going to her, you had better think twice about it. She has just apologized to me, and if you go to her, it will look as if you go to make things right with her."

"I am not going to her," Ximen said.

"Where are you going, then?" Yueniang said. "I don't want you to go to that woman Ruyi'er either. Yesterday, in my sister-in-law's presence, the Fifth Lady said some very horrid things to me. She said I allowed Ruyi'er to take liberties, to please you."

"Surely you don't take seriously the things that little strumpet says?"

"Do what I tell you," Yueniang said. "I won't have you going to the front court, and I don't want you here. You must spend the night with Li Jiao'er. You may do what you like after that." Ximen was obliged to go and sleep with Li Jiao'er.

The next day was the eleventh of the twelfth month. Ximen Qing went early to the office and, with Captain He, busied himself with official papers. He was there all morning. When he came back, he got ready the presents, a pig, wine, and thirty taels of silver, and told Daian to take them to Hu, the Prefect of Dongpingfu. Hu accepted the presents and immediately sent the necessary papers.

Meanwhile, Ximen Qing sent for Xu, the Master of the Yin Yang, and set out pigs, lamb, wine and fruits in the great hall, and burned paper offerings as a sacrifice. When the ceremony was over, Xu went away.

The document that Daian brought back with him bore several seals. It referred to Qiao Hong as an officer in the District administration. Ximen told Daian to take two boxes of the food that had been offered at the sacrifice, to Qiao and to ask him to come and see the document. He also told a servant to take a box of food to Uncle Wu, Scholar Wen, Ying Bojue, Xie Xida, and the clerks. Then he sent invitation cards to Major Zhou, General Jing, Captain Zhang, Eunuchs Liu and Xue, Captain He and Captain Fan, Uncle Wu, Kinsman Qiao, and Wang the Third asking them to a celebration on the third of the month. He engaged musicians and four singers.

This day, Meng Yulou gave up the housekeeping accounts. She handed them over to Ximen Qing and told him to give them to Pan Jinlian. Then she went to see Wu Yueniang.

"Do you feel better, Mother, now you have taken the medicine?" she said.

"Yes," Yueniang said, "people say that women always get better when they have a man doctor to attend them, and it seems to be true. I am certainly better. My headache has gone, and my stomach feels much easier."

"Ah!" Yulou said, "it looks to me as if all you wanted was a man to hold your hand."

Even Aunt Wu laughed at this.

Then Ximen Qing came with the accounts. "You must attend to the matter yourself," Yueniang told him. "I don't know whose turn it is, and I can't imagine whom to give the accounts to. Nobody wants to be bothered with them."

Ximen took thirty taels of silver and thirty strings of coppers and gave them to Jinlian.

When Qiao came, Ximen took him to the great hall and showed him the document that Prefect Hu had sent. It said: "Honorary Lieutenant Qiao Hong has made a contribution of thirty measures of fine rice to the quartermaster's department, in accordance with regulations." Qiao was very pleased and bowed his thanks to Ximen Qing. He told Qiao Tong to take the paper home with the greatest care. "Now I can wear ceremonial dress," he said to Ximen, "and, when you have a party here, I shall be able to come."

"You must come early on the third," Ximen said to him.

When they had had tea, Ximen Qing told Qintong to set a table in the side room. "Kinsman," he said to Qiao, "let us go to the west room. It is warmer there." They went together to the study.

Then Ying Bojue came with a few presents. "The brothers have sent them," he said. Ximen looked at them. Abbot Wu's name was the first on the list: then came Ying Bojue, Xie Xida, Zhu Shinian, Sun Guazui, Chang Zhijie, Bai Laiguang, Li the Third, Huang the Fourth and Du the Third.

"I still have some more people to invite," Ximen said. "There are the younger Uncle Wu, Uncle Shen, Doctor Ren, Hua, Scholar Wen and the three clerks, more than twenty altogether. I must ask them all on the fourth." He gave the presents to a servant and told Qintong to go to Uncle Wu and tell him that Master Qiao was there. Then he asked if Scholar Wen was at home.

"No," Laian said, "he has gone out to see a friend.

After a while, Uncle Wu arrived and, with Chen Jingji they sat down to drink. While they were drinking, Ximen said to Uncle Wu: "We have to congratulate Kinsman Qiao here. He has got his papers today. We must buy some presents and give a party for him."

"It is a very insignificant matter," Qiao said. "You must not trouble to do anything of the sort."

Then a man came from the Town Hall with two hundred and fifty copies of the new calendar. Ximen gave the man a return card and sent him away.

"We haven't seen the new calendar yet," Ying Bojue said.

Ximen gave fifty copies to Uncle Wu, Qiao, and Ying Bojue. Bojue noticed that the new year was described as the first year of the reign of Chonghe, and that it would have an intercalary month.

They went on playing games, guessing fingers, and drinking until it was late. Qiao went away first, but Uncle Wu and Ying Bojue did not go until the first night watch. Ximen Qing told a servant to get a horse ready early the next morning and ask Captain He to come that they might go together to take leave of Governor Hou. Then he told Laian and Chunhong that they must accompany Yueniang when she went to Mistress Xia. Four soldiers were to go with them.

He went to Jinlian's room. She had taken off her headdress; her hair was disarranged; there was no powder on her face, and she was lying, with all her clothes on, on the bed. There was no light in the room and everything was very still. Ximen called Chunmei, but there was no answer. Then he saw Jinlian on the bed and spoke to her. There was no answer. He sat down on the bed.

"Little oily mouth, why are you treating me like this? Why don't you answer me?"

He lifted her in his arms and asked what was the matter. Jinlian turned her face away. Fragrant tears rolled down her cheeks, one after another. If Ximen Qing had been made of iron or stone, he would have melted. He put his arms around her neck.

"Funny little oily mouth. Why did you quarrel with her?"

For a long time, Jinlian did not answer. Then she said: "Who says I quarreled with her? It was she who began by finding fault with me, insulting me before a host of people. She said I was one of the husband-hunting devils, and that was how I got you. She said she was a real wife, properly married to you. Who told you to come here again? Go to her. If you go to her, perhaps I shall not be accused of monopolizing you. She said you always came to me. You know quite well you haven't been near the place these last few nights. And she tells lies. She said I asked you for the fur coat and never said anything to her about it. I am not her slave. Why should I go and kowtow to her and ask her to give me a fur coat? Chunmei scolded that scamp of a blind woman, and she said I didn't train her properly. She talked a lot of nonsense. If you were a real man, you would settle this sort of thing with your fist, and there wouldn't be all these rows and troubles. I suppose we must keep ourselves in our proper places. The proverb says: Things that are bought cheap are sold cheap; and things that are easily come by are easily forgotten. I came here as a second wife and now I am not to be allowed to breathe. Yesterday, she flew into a temper. Who was in her room all the time? Who sent for Doctor Ren? Who offered to do everything she wanted? Poor me! I was left in this miserable hole and nobody cared what happened to me. Oh, I know you! Then people come and ask me to go and apologize to her!"

Tears rolled down her flower-like face. She lay on Ximen Qing's breast and sobbed. She wiped her nose and dried her tears continually. Ximen kept his arms about her and comforted her.

"It is all right, my child," he said, "I have been very busy. You must forgive one another. I'm not going to say who is to blame. I was coming to see you yesterday but she said I was coming to apologize to you and would not let me come. So I went to Li Jiao'er, but all the time I was there, I was thinking of you."

"I know you now," the woman said. "You pretend to love me but, really, you love her. She is going to have a baby, and I am only a straw and cannot compare with her in any sort of way."

Ximen Qing hugged her. "Don't talk such nonsense, little oily mouth," he said.

Qiuju brought tea. "Ha!" said Ximen "here's a nice clean little slave! Who told her to bring the tea? Where is Chunmei?"

"You do well to ask for Chunmei?" Jinlian said "I shouldn't be surprised if she were dying by now. She has had nothing to eat for three or four days. She is in bed in the other room. She only wants to die. She thinks that's the best thing she can do now that your first wife has insulted her before everybody. She has done nothing but cry ever since."

"Is that true?" Ximen Qing said.

"Go and see for yourself."

Ximen got up and went to the other room. Chunmei was lying on the bed, her face unpowdered and her hair falling down.

"Get up, little oily mouth," he said. He called her by name, but she did not answer and pretended to be asleep. He tried to lift her in his arms but she struggled and stiffened herself till her back was like the backbone of a carp. She nearly knocked Ximen Qing onto the floor. Fortunately, he had firm hold of her and the bed prevented him from falling.

"Let me go," Chunmei cried. "Why do you come here to see a slave? You will soil your hands."

"Because the Great Lady scolded you a little," Ximen Qing said, "that's no reason why you should be so angry and refuse to eat anything."

"It doesn't matter to you whether I eat or not, Chunmei said. "I am a slave, and if I die, I die. But slave though I may be, I have done nothing wrong. Why should I be insulted because I told that blind vagabond what I thought about her? And the Great Lady found fault with my mother too, and said that she didn't keep me in order. Is it right that I should be punished because I cursed that blind scamp? Wait and see whether I don't point my finger at Han Daoguo's wife and insult her, when she comes here. She is responsible for all this trouble. It was she who introduced that blind creature."

"Yes, she introduced Miss Shen, it is true," Ximen said, "but there was no harm in that. How was she going to know that you would quarrel?"

"I should not have insulted her if she had been reasonable," Chunmei said, "but she was so obstinate."

"Well," Ximen said, "now that I'm here, won't you give me a cup of tea? I can't drink the tea Qiuju brought. Her hands are too dirty."

"You will have to drink it. When the butcher is dead, you must eat your pork with the bristles on it. I can't get up. How can I make tea for you?"

"Who told you to stop eating?" Ximen Qing said. "Come into the other room and let us eat and drink. Qiuju shall go for dishes and wine and cakes and fruit and soup."

He did not wait for further argument but took Chunmei's hand and went with her to Jinlian. He told Qiuju to take a box and go to the kitchen. When she came back, he bade Chunmei put slices of chicken with meat and fish, together with pickled bamboo shoots and radishes, and make a large bowl of soup. The dishes were set on the table with rice and warm buns.

Ximen Qing sat down beside Jinlian, and Chunmei sat facing them. They encouraged one another to drink and did not make an end for a long time. Then they went to bed.

Ximen rose early next morning. Captain He came in good time, and, after drinking a cup of wine, they set out beyond the walls to pay their respects to Governor Hou. Yueniang sent presents to Mistress Xia, then dressed and went in a large sedan chair to see her. Laian and Chunhong went with her, and four soldiers cleared the way. Daian and Wang Jing were left at home. About midday, old woman Wang, the tea seller, came with He the Ninth, and asked if Ximen Qing was at home.

"What wind has blown you here?" Daian said to them. "We don't see you very often."

"Old He wishes to see your master about a matter concerning his younger brother," old woman Wang said. "We should not have come otherwise."

"His Lordship has gone to say good-bye to Governor Hou," Daian said, "and the Great Lady has gone out too. But wait a moment, and I will tell the Fifth Lady."

When he came back, he said: "The Fifth Lady would like to see you."

"I will go and see her," old woman Wang said, "but you must take me in. I am afraid of the dogs."

Daian took the old woman to the garden, pulled aside the lattice and showed her into Jinlian's room. Jinlian was wearing a fur cap and silken clothes and looked very pretty. She was sitting on the bed with her feet on a footstool. Old woman Wang knelt down before her. Jinlian returned her greeting, and old woman Wang sat down beside her on the bed.

"It is a very long time since I saw you last," Jinlian said.

"I have wished to see you for a long time," the old woman said, "but I didn't venture to come. Have you any children?"

"I wish I had," Jinlian said, "but I have only had two miscarriages. Is your son married?"

"No," the old woman said, "I have not arranged a marriage for him yet. He has just come back from Huai. He made some money, and now he has bought a donkey and started a flour mill. I understand his Lordship is not at home."

"No, he has had to go outside the city today. The Great Lady is out, too. What did you want with him?"

"He the Ninth asked me to come and see his Lordship," old woman Wang said. "His brother, He the Tenth, has got mixed up in a case of theft. He has been taken to the courts and charged with being a receiver of stolen property. But he had nothing whatever to do with the matter, and we have come to ask his Lordship to get him off. He must not believe what the thieves say. When He the Tenth gets out of prison, he will come, with presents, to kowtow to his Lordship. Here is the paper."

Jinlian looked at it. "Give it to me," she said, "I will give it to my husband, with my own hands."

"He the Ninth is waiting outside," old woman Wang said. "I will tell him to come again tomorrow."

Qiuju brought the old woman a cup of tea. "Are you happy here, lady?" old woman Wang said. "Happy!" Jinlian said. "If there were not so many squabbles, I should be happy enough. But I have trouble of some sort every day."

"You have only to open your mouth when the food is brought to you, and to dip your hand when water is poured out for you. You have ornaments of gold and silver, and maids to wait upon you. What possible trouble can you have?"

"The proverb says, that where there is more than one wife, the first wife is the only one who counts for anything. The others do not matter. When you have more than one spoon in a bowl, they are bound to clash. What can one expect but difficulties of one sort or another?"

"My good Lady," old woman Wang said, "you are cleverer than anyone I know. Your husband is prosperous, and you must have a splendid life. Well, I will tell He the Ninth to come again tomorrow." She got up to go away.

"Don't be in such a hurry," Jinlian said. "Stay a while."

"I mustn't keep old He waiting too long," the old woman said, "I will come and see you some other day."

She went out. When she came to the gate, she spoke to Daian. The boy promised to speak to his master as soon as he came in. "Brother An," old He said, "I will come back tomorrow morning." Then he went off with old woman Wang.

In the evening, Ximen Qing returned. He went to Jinlian's room, and she gave him the paper. He handed it to a servant and said that it was to be given to him next day at the office.

When he had told Chen Jingji to send out the invitations, he gave Qintong a tael of silver and a box of cakes to take to Han Daoguo's house for Miss Shen. He was careful not to let Chunmei know what he was doing.

Wang Liu'er smiled and accepted the things. "Miss Shen will not be angry any more now," she said. "Tell your father and mother she is sorry if she annoyed Chunmei."

When Yueniang came back, she greeted Aunt Wu and the other ladies. Then Ximen Qing came and she made a reverence to him.

"Mistress Xia was very cordial indeed," she said. "There were a number of neighbors and relatives there, all ladies. Magistrate Xia has written to them and enclosed a letter for you that they are going to send tomorrow. They propose to start for the capital on the sixth or seventh of this month. Mistress Xia is very anxious that Ben the Fourth should go to the Capital with them. She will send him back immediately. By the way, Ben the Fourth's daughter is quite grown up now. I didn't know her. I thought she looked at me peculiarly when she gave me tea. Mistress Xia calls her Happy Cloud. She bade her kowtow to me, and the girl set down her tray and kowtowed four times. I gave her two gold flowers. Mistress Xia was pleased that I treated her maid so kindly. She is very fond of the girl and has regarded her rather as a daughter than as a maid."

"She is a lucky girl to have found such a comfortable place," Ximen Qing said. "In some places, she would have been more likely to be scolded."

Yueniang looked at him. "You mean I scold that beloved maid of yours, I suppose?"

Ximen Qing laughed. "If she takes Ben the Fourth, who is going to look after the shop?"

"Oh, close it for a few days," Yueniang said.

"No, I won't close it. This is the New Year season and there is a good deal of trade about. But we'll talk about that tomorrow."

Yueniang went to change her dress and then sat down with Aunt Wu. Her maids and women came to kowtow to her. That night, Ximen Qing slept with Sun Xue'e.

The next morning he went to the office. He the Ninth came again to the house and gave Daian a tael of silver. "I told my master about the matter," Daian said, "and I think there is no doubt your brother will be set free. You had better go to the office and see." He the Ninth went away at once.

When Ximen Qing reached his office, he had the thieves brought before him, put their legs in the press, and ordered each of them to be given twenty severe blows. He let He the Tenth go free and put a monk of the Temple of the Mighty Blossom in his place, on the score that the thieves had passed a night in that temple. It was as though Master Zhang drank the wine and Master Li got tipsy, and like people complaining of the willow, when the branches fall from the mulberry tree.

That day, when Ximen Qing was home again, he sent for the four singing girls, Wu Yin'er, Zheng Aiyue, Hong Si'er and Qi Xiang'er. They came about midday, and went at once to kowtow to Yueniang and Aunt Wu. Yueniang gave them tea, and they played and sang for the ladies. Then Ximen Qing came, and the four girls put down their instruments and kowtowed to him.

"You are late today," Yueniang said.

"Yes, I had several cases to deal with. There was the one old woman Wang came about yesterday. I let He the Ninth's brother go, though the thieves insisted that what they had said was true. Anyhow, I put them on the rack and ordered them twenty blows. I put a monk in He the Tenth's place, and, tomorrow, I shall send the documents in the case to Dongpingfu. Then there was another bad case, one of a woman carrying on with her daughter's husband. The man is only just over twenty and his name is Zong Deyuan. He was living with his wife's people. The mother died, and the father married again, a woman called Zhou. A year after this marriage, the father died too. Zhou was young and could not control herself and she began to carry on with the young man. They punished one of their maids, and the maid told everybody what was going on. The neighbors accused them and, today, I have extracted a confession from them and sent them to Dongpingfu. It is a very near relationship, and I'm afraid they will both be hanged."

"In my opinion," Jinlian said, "the maid who spread the scandal ought to be beaten to death. It was her duty as a maid to be loyal to her employers. Instead, her chattering will have caused the death of two human beings."

"I don't agree," Yueniang said, "the lower classes will never respect their betters when these do not behave properly. If a bitch will not have it, the dog cannot get his way. It was the woman's fault. If she had behaved with decorum, no one would have dared approach her."

"You are right, Mother," one of the singing girls said, smiling. "Even we singing girls do not receive our patrons' friends. And, in the family, one should be still more careful."

Ximen Qing had something to eat. Then music was heard in the front court. General Jing had arrived. Ximen hastily dressed and went out to welcome him. When they had drunk their tea, he said to Jing: "Censor Song accepted your record of service and promised to do what we asked. You will undoubtedly be promoted very soon."

"I am very grateful to you," Jing said. "I shall never forget how kind you have been in this matter."

"I mentioned Zhou to his Excellency," Ximen said. "It may be that something will come to him too."

The two eunuchs, Liu and Xue, came then. As they were escorted to the great hall, the musicians played. They both wore dark dragon gowns and gemmed girdles. When they had taken their places, Major Zhou arrived. They chatted together. "Yesterday," Jing said to Major Zhou, "Si-quan was good enough to speak highly of you to Censor Song, who had a party here. Now Song will certainly remember you, and you cannot fail to receive promotion."

Major Zhou bowed and thanked Ximen Qing. Then Captain Zhang, Captain He, Captain Fan, Wang the Third, Uncle Wu and Kinsman Qiao came, one after the other. Qiao was wearing ceremonial dress, and four servants attended him. When he had greeted the others, he made a special reverence to Ximen Qing. People asked what appointment he held, and Ximen said: "My kinsman has just had honorary rank conferred upon him."

"Since he is your kinsman, we must congratulate him," Major Zhou said.

"I appreciate your kindness immensely," Qiao said, "but please do not trouble."

They all sat down according to their rank. After they had taken tea, wine was brought. The host offered it to his guests, and they all sat down again. Wang the Third refused to sit with them.

"You must sit down," Ximen said to him. "This is not a formal party and I wish you to help me to entertain my guests."

Then Wang the Third was compelled to sit down with them. When the soup course was finished, the musicians played different tunes and the four singing girls sang for them. Eunuch Liu, who sat in the place of honor, distributed money to the musicians and singers. It was a merry party and the guests did not leave until the first night watch. Then Ximen

Qing paid the musicians and dismissed them, and the four singing girls went and played for a while to entertain the ladies. Yueniang asked Wu Yin'er to stay but let the others go. On their way, they went to the hall to say good-bye to Ximen Qing.

"I want you to come again tomorrow," Ximen said to Zheng Aiyue. "Bring Li Guijie with you."

"I know why you didn't send for Guijie today," the girl said. "It was because Wang the Third was here. It is rather late in the day for you to be taking precautions. What guests are you expecting tomorrow?"

"Nobody but relatives and friends," Ximen Qing said.

"I suppose Beggar Ying will be here," Zheng Aiyue said. "I won't come if that hateful fellow is here."

"No, he won't be here tomorrow."

"If I thought he was going to be here, I wouldn't come," Zheng Aiyue said. She kowtowed to Ximen and went away. He ordered the things to be cleared away, then went to Li Ping'er's room and slept with Ruyi'er.

The next day he went early to the office and sent the prisoners to Dongpingfu. Then he went home to the party. All the guests arrived. There were twelve tables. Three singing girls came, Li Guijie, Wu Yin'er, and Zheng Aiyue, and three boys, Li Ming, Wu Hui, and Zheng Feng.

While they were drinking, Ping'an came and said: "Uncle Yun has come to see you. He has inherited a title and has brought presents with him."

Ximen Qing told the boy to bring him in.

Yun Lishou was wearing a black silk ceremonial gown and a girdle with a gold buckle. Servants with presents followed him, and he handed the list to Ximen Qing. Upon it was written: 'Yun Lishou, who has recently inherited the rank of officer of the royal guard and subprefect of Qinghe in Shandong, presents his humble compliments and offers ten sable skins, a sea fish, a parcel of dried shrimps, four preserved geese, ten preserved ducks, and two blinds of oiled paper.'

Ximen Qing told his servants to take the gifts and thanked Yun Lishou.

"I only came back yesterday," Yun said, "and I have come at once to see you." He made a reverence to Ximen Qing. Then he said: "You have been very kind to me, and these things are intended as a slight token of my gratitude." He greeted the others.

Now that Yun Lishou had succeeded to a title, Ximen Qing treated him with more respect. He asked him to sit at the same table with the younger Uncle Wu. A cup and chopsticks were at once brought in for him, and Ximen Qing ordered food to be given to his servants. Then Ximen asked how he had come into the title.

"I am indebted to the kindness of his Excellency Yu of the Ministry of

War," Yun Lishou said. "My elder brother, who was in his department, died, and his Excellency appointed me to carry on the ancestral title and take up his appointment. Now I am in the office of the writer to the signet."

Ximen Qing was pleased. "I congratulate you," he said, "and I must give a special party in your honor."

All the guests invited him to drink with them and the singers were bidden to offer him wine. Before long, Yun Lishou was tipsy. Ying Bojue might have been on the end of a string. He stood up and sat down again and joked and swore at the singing girls all the time. It was a very merry party; they all drank a great deal of wine, and nobody went away before the second night watch. Ximen Qing sent away the three singers and went to sleep in Yueniang's room.

The next day he was up late. He had his breakfast and was going to call on Yun Lishou when Daian came and told him that Ben the Fourth wished to speak to him. Ximen knew that he wished to speak about acting as an escort to Mistress Xia. He went to the great hall. Ben the Fourth gave Xia's letter to Ximen Qing. "His Lordship would like me to escort his family to the Eastern Capital, if you have no objection," he said.

Ximen Qing read the letter. It thanked him for looking after Xia's family and asked that Ben the Fourth might be allowed to take them to the Capital.

"Since he asks for you, I suppose you must go," Ximen Qing said. "When do they propose to start?"

"They sent for me this morning," Ben the Fourth said, "and told me they proposed to leave on the sixth. I hope to get back in about a fortnight." He gave the keys of the shop to Ximen Qing.

"Very well," Ximen said, "I will ask the younger Uncle Wu to look after the shop."

Ben the Fourth went home to see about his luggage, and Ximen Qing, in his ceremonial robes, went to call on Yun Lishou.

That day, Aunt Wu was going home, and a sedan chair came to fetch her. Yueniang filled two boxes with delicacies, and went with her sister-in-law to the gate. Huatong was standing there, sobbing bitterly. Ping'an was pulling him and shaking him, but the boy only cried the louder. When Aunt Wu had gone, Yueniang came back and said to Ping'an: "What is the matter? Why are you pulling him about like that? You have made him cry."

"Scholar Wen wants him, and he won't go," Ping'an said. "He stays here and answers me back all the time."

"Leave him alone," Yueniang said to Ping'an. She turned to the boy and asked him: "Why do you stand here crying? If Master Wen sends for you, you must go."

"It is not your business," Huatong cried to Ping'an, "and I won't go. Why do you keep bullying me?"

"Why won't you go?" Yueniang said.

The boy would not answer.

Then Jinlian came along. "You sly young rascal!" she said. "Why don't you answer the Great Lady?"

Ping'an boxed his ears, and the boy cried louder than ever.

"Don't hit him," Yueniang said, "let him explain himself quietly. Tell me, why won't you go?"

Then Daian came back with Ximen's horse.

"Is your father back?" Yueniang asked him.

"No," Daian said, "he is taking wine with Uncle Yun. I have brought back his ceremonial clothes and am going to take him his soft hat."

Then he saw the boy crying. "Hullo, my boy," he said, "what are you crying for? Is something hurting you?"

"Master Wen has called for him and he won't go," Ping'an said. "He stays there and is rude to me."

"Brother," Daian said, "when Master Wen sends for you, you must be on your guard. Scholar Wen is renowned for his fondness for hole-and-corner work. He can't live without it. But you have put up with it before, why can't you do so today?"

"You rascal!" Yueniang said to Daian. "What do you mean?"

"Ask him, Mother," Daian said.

Jinlian, who was one of those people who always want to know everything, drew the boy aside and said to him: "Boy, tell me the truth. What does he want you for? If you won't tell me, I shall ask the Great Lady to have you beaten."

"He keeps on coming up to me," said the boy, "and wants me to submit to him. He shoves his penis up my ass so roughly that today it's swollen and hurts. When I ask him to take it out, he refuses and presses it up and down."

"You thievish slave," Yueniang said, when she heard this. "Get away from me. I'm surprised at you, Sister, wanting to know things like that. I am ashamed of you. I was so ignorant I didn't realize what you were talking about and listened to every word you said. A splendid fellow that Scholar Wen must be. We let him have this boy, and this is the sort of thing he does."

"Oh, Mother," Jinlian said, "they all go in for this sort of thing. Even the beggars in their hovels."

"But this Southerner is a married man," Yulou said. "Why should he do it?"

"He has been here a long time, but we have never seen his wife," Jinlian said.

"No, ladies," Ping'an said, "and you are not likely to see her. He locks the door every time he goes out. I have only seen her once. She was going in a sedan chair to see her mother. She came back before the evening. She never goes out, but I have sometimes seen her in the evening emptying the chamber pots outside the door."

"She can't be a very respectable woman," Jinlian said, 'if she would marry a man like that. Why, she can never see the light of day. Her room must be as bad as a prison.'

The ladies went back to the inner court.

It was sunset when Ximen Qing came back.

"Have you been all this time at Yun's place?" Yueniang asked him.

"Yes," Ximen said. "He opened a jar of wine and insisted on my having something to eat. Now that Jing has been promoted, Yun will have charge of the seals. I and Qiao will get some presents ready and I will arrange for the officers to present him with a congratulatory scroll. I must ask Wen Guixuan to write it."

"Wen Guixuan or Wu Guixuan," Yueniang said. "The fellow is an atrocious scoundrel. If people get to hear of his goings on, we shall all be disgraced."

"What are you talking about?" Ximen Qing said, alarmed.

"Don't ask me. Ask the boy."

"What boy?" Ximen said.

Jinlian explained. "What boy!" she said. "Why! Huatong, of course. When we took Aunt Wu to the gate, we found him there, crying, and he told us what that Southerner had done to him."

Ximen Qing found it hard to believe. "Let us have the boy here," he said, "and I'll talk to him." He sent Daian for Huatong and threatened to put on the thumbscrews.

"What have you been doing with that man?" he said. "Tell me the truth."

"He gave me wine to drink and then misused me," Huatong said. "Today, he tried to do it again, but I got away and would not go back. He told Ping'an to make me go back, and Ping'an hit me. The ladies saw him. And he kept on asking me things about your ladies, but I wouldn't tell him. Yesterday, when you had a party, he told me to steal some of the silver for him. A short time ago, he went to see Scholar Ni and showed him your letters, and Scholar Ni told Magistrate Xia what was in them."

Ah!" Ximen Qing said. "It is easy enough to paint the tiger's skin, but who can paint the bones inside that skin? We may know people's faces but never their minds. I treated him as a man. How could I tell that he was a dog in human form? I won't have him here a moment longer."

"Get up!" he shouted to Huatong. "And never go near him again."

The boy kowtowed and went out.

"No wonder, the other day, when Kinsman Zhai scolded me for not being discreet, I couldn't imagine who had given away my secrets," Ximen said to Yueniang. "It was this dog bone. Why should I keep him here?"

"What is the use of asking me that?" Yueniang said. "You have no son for him to teach; why should you keep that fellow here to write your present lists for you? He lives at your expense and plays dirty tricks of this sort."

"Say no more about it," Ximen said. "Tomorrow he shall go."

He sent for Ping'an. "Go and tell Scholar Wen," he said, "that I need his house as a storehouse and he must go elsewhere. If he comes to see me, tell him I am out."

Ximen Qing told his wife that Ben the Fourth had called to see him and said that he was going to the Capital with the Xia family on the sixth. "I think I will ask your younger brother to look after the shop," he said. "What do you think?"

"I shall not express any opinion," Yueniang said. "If you want him, send for him. He is my brother, and somebody is sure to say I favor him."

Ximen Qing told Qitong to go and ask Uncle Wu the Second to come and see him. When the young man came, Ximen went with him to the great hall and took wine with him. Then he gave him the keys and asked him to go to the shop in Lion Street next morning.

Scholar Wen was very much upset, especially when he found that Huatong did not go near him. Then the next day, Ping'an came and said: "His Lordship says he is going to use this house as a storehouse, and I am to tell you to find somewhere else to live."

The scholar was greatly disturbed and changed color. He realized that Huatong must be the cause. He put on his scholar's gown and hat and went to see Ximen Qing.

"My master is at the office," Qintong told him.

When Ximen Qing came back from the office, Scholar Wen again dressed up and went across, with a long letter. He gave the letter to Qintong, but Qintong would not take it. "My master has just come back from the office," he said. "He is very tired and I dare not disturb him."

Scholar Wen understood what this meant. He went to Scholar Ni to ask his advice, and then went back to the house he had lived in before.

CHAPTER 77

Ximen Qing Visits Zheng Aiyue in the Snow

At the end of the year
The plums and the snow match themselves in beauty.
Under the moon they are white with the same whiteness.
When the wind blows, the tender petals half emerge
They have not the wildness of the willow catkins.

The shadow of a pair of sparrows
Seems like a snow-white parrot.
The snowflakes in the moonbeams
Glitter like a mass of crystal.
Above the flowers they know how to find sweetness
Like a pair of mandarin ducks.

Scholar Wen was not permitted to see Ximen Qing, so, greatly ashamed, he had to go back to live in his old house. Ximen turned the rooms he had left into additional reception rooms for his own use.

One day, Scholar Shang came to see him. He was going to the Eastern Capital to enter for an examination, and he wanted Ximen to lend him a leather trunk and a warm cloak. Ximen asked him to sit down, and they had tea.

"I am anxious to have two appropriate compositions written to congratulate my kinsman Qiao and my friend Yun Lishou," Ximen said. "Qiao has recently been granted honorary rank, and Yun has come into the family title. Perhaps one of your friends would not mind doing this for me. I should be glad to make it worth his while."

Shang smiled. "You need not speak of reward," he said. "My schoolfellow, Nie Lianghu, who is a graduate of the military academy and tutor to my son, is very learned. I will speak to him about it, and all you need do is to send the materials to him."

Ximen Qing thanked him and he went away. Then Ximen sent Qintong with the scrolls, enclosing two handkerchiefs and five *qian* of silver, and, at the same time, sent the leather trunk and the coat to Scholar Shang. Two days later the scrolls were returned. Ximen Qing hung them on the wall and was very well satisfied with the composition and the writing of the golden characters.

Ying Bojue came to see him. "When are we going to have the feast in congratulation of Master Qiao and Brother Yun?" he said. "Are the scrolls ready? Why haven't I seen Scholar Wen lately?"

"Don't mention Scholar Wen to me," Ximen said. "He is a dirty dog." He told Bojue the whole story.

"Brother," Bojue said, "I told you the fellow could not be trusted. He is very sly. It is a good thing you have such sharp eyes, or he would certainly have ruined your boys. But who will write the scrolls for you?"

"Scholar Shang was here yesterday," Ximen told him. "He told me his friend Nie Lianghu was very well educated, and I asked him to write the scrolls. He has now finished them. Come and have a look." He took Bojue to the hall. Bojue thought they were admirable.

"Everything seems to be ready," he said. "Don't wait too long before you send them. We must let our friends have plenty of time to make preparations."

"Tomorrow is a good day," Ximen said. "I will send them then."

As they were talking, a servant came in to say that Xia's son had called to say good-bye. "He said," the man told them, "that they proposed to leave for the Capital on the sixth. I told him you were not at home, and he said, would you be good enough to ask Captain He to send someone to take charge of the house."

Ximen Qing looked at the card and said: "Now I must get ready two sets of presents, one for Xia and one for Shang." He told Qintong to go out and buy them and to tell Chen Jingji to send them with his compliments. Then he went to the study to have something to eat with Ying Bojue.

Ping'an came hurrying in with three cards. "Counselor Wang, General Li and Vice president An have come to see you," he said. Ximen Qing looked at the cards. They bore the names of Wang Boyan, Li Qiyuan, and An Shen. He hastily put on his ceremonial dress.

"Brother," Bojue said. "You seem to be very busy. I had better go."

"I will see you tomorrow," Ximen said, and went to receive his three visitors. He took them to the great hall. There they thanked Ximen Qing for the trouble he had taken, drank tea, and sat down to talk.

"Li, Wang, and I have come to trouble you again," An said. "Magistrate Zhao has been appointed to the Lord Chamberlain's office, and we should like to use your house for a reception. We have invited him on the ninth. Five tables will be needed and we will provide the actors. Will you be so kind as to allow us to do this?"

"The house shall be put in order for you, and I await your instructions," Ximen said.

An told his attendants to present three taels of silver, and Ximen Qing accepted them. Then the three officers went away. When they came to the gate, Li said to Ximen Qing: "The other day I had a letter from Qian Longye. He told me that a certain Sun Wenxiang was one of your underlings. I set him free. Did he tell you?"

"Yes, indeed," Ximen Qing said. "And I am very much obliged to you. One of these days I will come especially to thank you."

"You must not trouble," Li said, "we are very good friends." They got into their sedan chairs and were carried away.

Pan Jinlian had now taken charge of the housekeeping accounts. She began by buying a new pair of scales. Every day, when the boys brought vegetables, or things for the house, she insisted on having them shown to her, and would not hand over the money until she was satisfied. She did not count the money herself but made Chunmei do so. The maid measured the silver. Curses rained upon the boys' heads, and she was always saying she would tell Ximen Qing to beat them. The boys grumbled a great deal. "It was very much better in the Third Lady's time," they said.

The next day, when Ximen Qing had finished his work at the office, he said to Captain He: "Xia's family are now ready to start, and you should send somebody to take over their house."

"I have already sent one of my servants," Captain He said. "They sent word to me yesterday."

"Shall we go and look at it?" Ximen Qing said.

They left the office together and went on horseback to Xia's house. It was empty except for a few servants, and Ximen Qing showed Captain He how it was arranged. They went to the garden. It seemed very bare.

"When you move in," Ximen Qing said, "you will have to plant some flowers and trees here, and make a place where you can really enjoy yourself. These arbors need to be repaired."

"Yes," He said, "I shall set to work as soon as the Spring comes. I shall build a pavilion in the hope that you will often come and spend your leisure with me."

When they had finished their inspection of the house, He bade his servants clean the place and keep all the doors and windows shut. He made up his mind to write to his uncle and ask him to send his family before the New Year. He himself proposed to take up his quarters there the next day. The two officers took leave of one another. Ximen Qing went home and Captain He went back to the office.

When Ximen reached home, He the Ninth had come to thank him with a roll of silk, four dishes of food and a jar of wine. Eunuch Liu's servant had brought a box of candles, twenty tablecloths, eighty packets of official incense, a box of precious incense, a jar of homemade wine, and a pig. When Ximen Qing came in, Eunuch Liu's servant kowtowed and said: "My master presents his compliments and sends these trifles for you to give to your servants."

"The other day," Ximen said, "I allowed your master to leave my table hungry, yet still he sends me these delightful presents."

He told his servants to take the things and asked Liu's man to wait a moment. Huatong brought the man a cup of tea and Ximen Qing gave him a return card and five *qian* of silver. Then he ordered He the Ninth to be shown in. When old He came, Ximen took his hand and went with him to the hall. Old He knelt down. "Your Lordship," he said, "has shown the generosity of Heaven in saving my younger brother's life. I shall never forget your kindness."

He begged Ximen Qing to allow him to express his gratitude in the humblest manner, but Ximen would not have this and dragged He the Ninth to his feet. "Old Ninth," he said, "we are very good friends, and you must not think of it. Please sit down."

"I am so contemptible a creature," He the Ninth said. "How shall I sit in your presence?"

He remained on his feet, so Ximen Qing remained standing also and drank a cup of tea with him. "Why did you bring me these presents?" he said. "I will not take them. If anyone interferes with you in any way, let me know, and I will see that you are protected. And, if you have any business at the Town Hall, send me word, and I will write to Li on your behalf."

"It is very kind of you," He the Ninth said, "but I am an old man now and I have handed over my office to my son He Qin."

"That was wise," Ximen Qing said, "you did well to retire. Since you will not take all the presents away, I will accept the jar of wine, but you must take away the rest. I won't detain you any longer."

He the Ninth thanked him repeatedly and went away. Ximen Qing sat in the great hall watching his servants packing up presents, fruit boxes, flowers, sheep, wine, scrolls, and money. He told Daian to take one set to Qiao's place, and sent Wang Jing with the other to Yun Lishou. Daian returned with five *qian* of silver that Qiao had given him, and then Wang Jing came. Yun Lishou had given him tea, a roll of black cloth, and a pair of shoes. He brought a return card. "Master Yun," he said, "sends his love. He is going to send you an invitation later."

Ximen Qing was pleased. He went to the inner court for dinner.

"Ben the Fourth has gone," he said to Yueniang, "and Uncle Wu the Second is at the shop. I have nothing else to do today, so I will go and see him."

"Very well," Yueniang said, "tell him that, if he wants anything to eat or drink, he need only tell one of the boys to ask me for it."

Ximen Qing called for his horse, put on a felt hat, sable ear covers, a dark gown, and black boots with white soles, and went to Lion Street. Qintong and Daian followed him.

Uncle Wu and Laizhao were there. A sign was hanging outside the shop, and people came to buy silk, thread, and cotton wool. Trade was so flourishing that there were almost too many people to be served.

Ximen Qing dismounted, watched the people for a while, then went and sat down at the back of the shop. Uncle Wu the Second came to him. "We are doing twenty to thirty taels' worth of business a day," he said.

"I hope you are taking the greatest pains over Uncle Wu's food," Ximen Qing said to Laizhao's wife.

It was very cloudy, bitterly cold, and almost snowing. Ximen Qing decided to go and see Zheng Aiyue. "Go back and get my fur rug," he said to Qintong, "and ask the Great Lady to give you something for Uncle Wu to eat." Qintong went home. He was soon back with the fur rug, and a box of food and wine for Uncle Wu. Ximen Qing drank a few cups with his brother-in-law. "I suppose you will spend the night here," he said. "See that you enjoy yourself. I must be off now." He put on his eyeshades, mounted his horse, and, still followed by Daian and Qintong, went to Zheng Aiyue's house. When he came to East Street, it was already snowing.

> Far and wide the bitter frost
> Encompasses the earth.
> The snow falls exquisitely
> A flake and then another flake
> Like the willow catkin and the cotton fluff
> Each flake as big as a pussy willow.
> The bamboos, the trees, the cottages
> Slowly succumb beneath the weight of snow.
> The rich say it will drive away calamity
> And grumble that there is no more of it
> Sit by their stoves with choice charcoal to warm them
> Wearing coats of sable and embroidered mantles
> Twirling a sprig of plum blossom
> Between their fingers
> And singing of good omen of prosperity
> Heedless of the poor.
> And poets lie at ease
> And make a lot of verses.

The snow seemed like a mass of tiny fragments of jade. Ximen Qing walked over it and went into Zheng Aiyue's house. As soon as he had dismounted, a maid had rushed in and told her mistress that he was there. The old procuress came out to welcome him and took him to the hall. There she greeted him and thanked him for the presents he had sent and for his kindness to Zheng Aiyue. "Your Great Lady and the Third Lady gave her flowers," she said.

Ximen Qing answered politely and sat down. He told Daian to take the horse to the inner court.

"Please come to the upper room," the old woman said. "Zheng Aiyue has just got up. She is dressing her hair. We expected you yesterday, and she waited for you all day. Today she did not feel very well, so she did not get up till late."

Ximen Qing went in. The windows were partly open, and all the blinds were drawn. There was a bronze brazier on the floor with charcoal burning in it. He took the place of honor. Zheng Aixiang came in and offered him some tea. Then Zheng Aiyue, very daintily dressed, with plumflower ornaments, gold pins, and a sealskin cap. Her hair seemed like the mist; her form as though it were carved from a block of jade. She smiled and made a reverence to Ximen Qing.

"Father," she said, "I was late the other day. Your party went on so long and, when I went to the ladies' court, the Great Lady kept me and insisted that I should have something to eat. I did not get home until the third night watch."

"Little oily mouth," Ximen said, "you and Li Guijie boxed Beggar Ying's ears very soundly."

"Yes," Zheng Aiyue said. "He is always saying such nasty things. Pockmarked Zhu was drunk too. He said he was going to see us safely home. I told him we had people with lanterns to take us home, and we didn't need him."

"Yesterday, I heard he had gone with Wang the Third to the house in the main street to see one of the girls," Ximen said.

"He only stayed one night and then he was done with her. Now he has taken up with Sesame."

They talked for a while, then Zheng Aiyue said: "Father, you must be cold here. Come into the inner room."

Ximen Qing went in. He took off his fur coat and sat down beside the fire with Zheng Aiyue. The air was deliciously scented. After a while, a maid brought food, and the two sisters and Ximen Qing ate it together. Zheng Aiyue offered him another half-bowlful, but he told her that he had had some cakes before he came out. "I meant to come and see you before," he said, "but the weather was so bad."

"You never sent me word, Father," Aiyue said, "and I waited for you all day. Today, when I didn't expect you, you came."

"Two friends came to see me yesterday, and I couldn't get away."

"I am going to ask a favor of you," Aiyue said. "Will you give me a sable fur? I want one to wear about my neck."

"That is easily done," Ximen said. "My friend Yun, who has just come back from the north, brought me some excellent specimens the other day. The ladies want some and, when they make up their own, I will ask them to make one for you."

"You don't say you will give me one," Aixiang said, "but I suppose you only think about Aiyue."

"You shall each have one," Ximen said.

The two girls stood up and made reverence to him.

"Don't tell Guijie or Wu Yin'er," Ximen said to them.

"The other day, when Guijie saw that Wu Yin'er was staying at your house," Aiyue said, "she asked me how long I thought she would stay. I told her. I told her, too, that when you invited Major Zhou, we four singing girls were there, but you didn't send for her because Wang the Third was there. Yesterday, when there were only relatives and friends, you did send for her. She didn't know what to say."

"You said exactly the right thing," Ximen Qing said. "I gave up sending for her brother Li Ming, but he persuaded Uncle Ying to come and speak for him. Then, on my third lady's birthday, Guijie herself came with presents and begged to be forgiven. The ladies pleaded for her. I didn't say anything but I deliberately asked Wu Yin'er to stay, just to show Guijie what I thought about things."

"I forgot the Third Lady's birthday," Zheng Aiyue said, "I didn't send her anything."

"Tomorrow my friend Yun will be giving a party," Ximen said. "Perhaps you and Wu Yin'er will come and sing for us."

"I shall be there," Aiyue said.

She got thirty-two ivory tablets and played with Ximen Qing. Aixiang sat with them and joined in the game. Wine was brought and the two girls offered it to him. Then they tuned their lutes and sang. When the song was done, they brought the dice box and threw dice with him. They drank together and grew more and more gay. Suddenly, Ximen Qing saw a picture of the Moon Maiden over the bed and, underneath it, a poem.

Here is a beauty, fair beyond all others
The gentle breeze blows aside her crimson skirt.

It is the third month of Spring and the flowers bloom
In the golden valley.
The moon shines and the shadows of the flowers move
The night is at its best.
The essences of jade and snow are combined in her
Her learning and her beauty surpass those of Wen Jun.
Love in youth should be kept as a precious thing
And the lover should not wander with the white cloud.

Beneath the poem was written: "Sanquan, after drinking, wrote these words."

"I suppose Sanquan is Wang the Third," Ximen Qing said.

"Yes, but he wrote this a long time ago," Zheng Aiyue said, hastily. "He calls himself Xiaoxuan now. He has explained to everybody that your honorific name is Siquan and he has given up his old name to save you annoyance." She took a brush and crossed out the word "San."

Ximen Qing was pleased. "I didn't know he had changed his name," he said.

"I shouldn't have known if somebody or other hadn't told me," Zheng Aiyue said. "I understand his father's name was Yixuan, and that is why he calls himself Xiaoxuan."

By this time Aixiang had left them and Aiyue was alone with Ximen Qing. They sat side-by-side, drinking and throwing dice.

"Lady Lin is very fond of lovemaking," Ximen said. "The other day, I went and took wine with Wang the Third, and she invited me to go to the inner court to see her. She asked me to take the young man under my protection, and made him do reverence to me as to a father. She said I was to give him instruction and advice."

Zheng Aiyue clapped her hands in delight. "You have me to thank for that," she said, smiling. "One of these days you will have his wife."

"Yes, but I must burn a stick of incense to her first," Ximen said. "When the New Year comes, I am going to invite her to my house to see the lanterns and to drink wine with my ladies. Then we shall see what happens."

"Father," Aiyue said, "you have no idea how beautiful that young lady is. She is more exquisite and dainty than any figures painted on a lantern. She is only nineteen, yet she has to live like a widow. Wang the Third never spends a night at home. If you devote a little time and attention to her, she will certainly be yours."

They drew closer and closer together. A maid brought fruit. Aiyue offered some to him. She passed honey lozenges from her own tongue to his. She unloosed his trousers with delicate fingers, took out his penis, and stroked it gently until it stood erect, proud and purple. He asked her to suck it; she bent her head, opened her red lips and took in half the penis, which moved this way and that with a pleasant sound. Before long, Ximen's passion was fully roused and he was ready for more serious things. Aiyue went to the back, and Ximen Qing also went out to change his clothes. It was snowing harder than ever.

When they were both back, Aiyue helped him to undress and he got into bed. Aiyue, when she had washed her cunt, closed the door and got into bed too.

It was the first night watch before they had done. Then they got up and put on their clothes, and Aiyue dressed her hair again. The maid came in and gave them something to eat. Ximen Qing drank some wine and asked Daian if umbrellas and lanterns were there. Daian told him that Qintong had just brought them. The old procuress and Zheng Aiyue went with Ximen to the gate and watched him mount his horse.

"Father," Aiyue said, "whenever you want me, let me know in good time."

Ximen Qing promised, then, holding an umbrella over his head, rode away over the snow. When he got home, he told Yueniang he had been drinking with Wu the Second.

The next day was the eighth. Ximen was told that Captain He had transferred his things to Xia's house, and sent him some presents. Then Ying Bojue came. It was very cold, and Ximen asked him to come to the study and sit by the fire. He told the boys to bring breakfast.

"I have sent all the things to my kinsman Qiao and Brother Yun," he said. "I gave them two *qian* of silver as a contribution from you, so you need not trouble to send them anything. Now you have only to wait until they send you an invitation."

Bojue thanked him. "What did his Excellency An want with you yesterday?" he said. "And who were the other visitors?"

"The others were General Li and Counselor Wang. They are both Zhejiiang men. They want me to give a party for a certain magistrate Zhao who has been appointed to the Lord Chamberlain's office. He was a prefect in their native place. I could not very well refuse them. They gave me three taels of silver towards the expenses."

"Civil officers are always stingy," Bojue said. "Their three taels will go no way at all. You will have to spend your own money."

"This Li," Ximen Qing said, "is the man who tried Sun Wenxiang, Huang the Fourth's brother-in-law. He reminded me that he had set the young man free."

"I see," Bojue said. "So naturally, he is careful not to forget it. You will have to give them the party if only for that reason." Then he said to Ying Bao: "Show the man in."

"Who is this?" Ximen asked.

"A young man," Bojue said. "He comes of a very decent family. His parents are dead, and he has been with the princely family of Wang since he was a child. He is married. He could not get on with the others and now he is out of work and finds it hard to get a job. He is a friend of Ying Bao, and asked Ying Bao to find him one. This morning Ying Bao asked me to recommend him to you, but I told him I didn't know whether you were in need of anybody."

"What is his name?" he said to Ying Bao. "Bring him in."

"His name is Laiyu," Ying Bao said.

Laiyu knelt down outside the lattice and kowtowed to Ximen Qing.

"He is a strong lad," Bojue said. "He looks as if he could carry a heavy load. How old are you?"

"I am twenty," Laiyu said.

"Have you any children?" Bojue asked him.

"No, I have only my wife."

"His wife is nineteen," Ying Bao said, "she is a good cook and she sews well."

Ximen Qing was impressed by Laiyu's appearance; he liked the way the young man bowed and stood upright again. He seemed an honest fellow.

"Since Uncle Ying has brought you to me, I will engage you," he said. "Mind that you serve me faithfully. Choose an auspicious day, then have the hiring contract made out and come with your wife."

Laiyu kowtowed. Ximen Qing sent him with Qintong to the inner court to kowtow to Wu Yueniang and the others. Yueniang gave him the apartment that Laiwang had had. Ying Bojue went away, and Laiyu and Ying Bao got the hiring contract written and gave it to Ximen Qing. Ximen called the young man Laijue.

We have now to speak of Mistress Ben the Fourth. After her young daughter had taken service with the Xia family, she had to depend upon Ping'an, Laian, or Huatong to run errands for her. Indeed, at one time or another, nearly all Ximen Qing's boys might have been found drinking wine in her place. She was a good-natured woman and used to cook food for them and give them tea or water whenever they asked for it. When Ben the Fourth came back from the shop, he often saw the boys about but did not give the matter a moment's thought. Now he was away, they all came to see what they could do for her. Daian and Ping'an, especially, were frequently about the place.

On the ninth, there was the reception that An, Li and Wang had asked Ximen Qing to give for Magistrate Zhao. Laijue and his wife came early in the morning. The wife went to the inner court to kowtow to Yueniang and the other ladies. She was wearing a purple coat, a black cape, and a green skirt. She was short and her face was shaped like a melon seed. She was carefully powdered, and her feet were very small. Yueniang inquired whether she could sew and asked a number of questions about housework. Her answers were perfectly satisfactory. Yueniang gave her the name Hui-yuan and bade her take her turn in the kitchen every third day.

About this time, Aunt Yang died. Antong brought them the news. Ximen Qing sent an offering of food and five taels of silver, and Wu Yue-niang, Li Jiao'er, Meng Yulou, and Pan Jinlian went to the funeral. Qin-tong, Qitong, Laijue and Laian went with them.

Ximen Qing, in the silk shop, watched the tailors making fur necklets for Yueniang. The first one they made he gave to Daian and told him to take it, with ten taels of silver, as a New Year gift to Zheng Aiyue. The people at the bawdy house made much of Daian and gave him five *qian* of silver. When he came back, he said to Ximen Qing: "Sister Zheng Aiyue is very grateful to you. She told me to say she was sorry she had entertained you so poorly the other day. She gave me three *qian* of silver."

"Keep it," Ximen Qing said. "By the way, now that Ben the Fourth is not at home, what are you doing at his house all the time?"

"When Mistress Ben's daughter went away," Daian said, "there was no one she could ask to do anything for her. So we are always ready to run an errand when it is necessary."

"That is right," Ximen said. "You must do all you can to help her now she has nobody else to do things for her."

He whispered to the boy: "Go and talk to her and say I should like to go and see her. See how she takes it. If she is well disposed, ask her to give you a handkerchief for me."

Daian went to see Mistress Ben the Fourth, and Ximen Qing went home.

Wang Jing had brought from the silversmith's a golden tiger and four pairs of pins with gold heads and silver stems. He gave them to Ximen Qing. Ximen put two pairs of pins away in his study and went with the others to Li Ping'er's room. He gave the tiger and one pair of pins to Ruyi'er and the other pair of pins to Yingchun. They kowtowed and thanked him. Ximen asked Yingchun to give him something to eat and afterwards went to the study and sat down. Daian came in quietly, but he said nothing, because Wang Jing was there. Ximen Qing told Wang Jing to go to the inner court for some tea.

"I told her what you said," Daian said. "She smiled. She said she would expect you this evening and gave me this handkerchief."

He handed to Ximen Qing a red embroidered silk handkerchief, wrapped in red paper. Ximen Qing put it to his nose and found it fragrant. He was delighted and put it into his sleeve. Wang Jing brought tea, and he drank it. Then he went back to the shop to watch the tailors at work.

He was told that Uncle Hua had come to see him, and gave orders that he should be brought in. They went into a small room and Huatong brought them tea.

"I have heard of a merchant with five hundred sacks of Wuxi rice," Hua Ziyu said. "Now that the river is frozen, he is anxious to sell it as soon as he can and get home again. I thought you might like to buy it, since it is so cheap."

"I don't need any rice now," Ximen said. "When the river is frozen, nobody buys rice. The price will go down again as soon as the ice melts. And, besides, I have no spare cash at the moment."

He told Daian to set a table and go for some food, and sent Huatong for Ying Bojue. When Ying Bojue came, the three men sat around the fire drinking. Ximen Qing called for some wheaten cakes. After a while, a novice from Abbot Wu's temple, Yingchun, came with presents and charms for the New Year. Ximen Qing asked him to sit down with them and have some wine. Then he asked him to arrange for a memorial service on the hundredth day after Li Ping'er's death, and gave him the necessary money.

At sunset, Hua Ziyu and Yingchun went away. Clerk Gan shut up the shop and joined Ximen and Bojue. They threw dice and guessed fingers. Lights were brought. Then Laian came and said that Yueniang and the other ladies had come back.

"Where have they been?" Ying Bojue asked.

"Aunt Yang is dead," Ximen said. "This is her third day. I sent an offering of food and money, and the ladies have been to offer their sympathy."

"How old was she?" Bojue asked.

"Seventy-five or seventy-six," Ximen said. "She had no children of her own and lived with her nephew. I gave her a coffin. I had it made for her several years ago."

"For an old lady to have a coffin is like having treasure in a chest," Bojue said. "It was very kind of you."

They drank more wine, and at last Ying Bojue and Clerk Gan went away. When Ximen himself left the shop, he told Wang Xian to be very careful about the fire and the candles. Wang Xian bolted the door after him.

Ximen Qing could see nobody about, and he went hurriedly to Ben the Fourth's place. The woman was standing at the door when she heard the door of the shop close and saw Ximen Qing coming out of the dark. She hastily opened her door and Ximen went quickly in. She shut the door again and said: "Please come in."

A door led to an inner room in which were a small bed and a bright fire. There was a lamp on the table. Mistress Ben was wearing a golden band about her hair, a purple silk coat, and a jade-colored skirt. She made reverence to Ximen Qing and offered him a cup of tea. "I hope my neighbor, Mistress Han, will not know anything about this," she said.

"You need not be afraid," Ximen Qing said. "It was quite dark when I came across. Nobody could have seen me." He kissed her and embraced her. Then he pulled aside the coverlet, laid her on the bed, twined her legs around his shoulders and went to work; for the clasp was already on. It was not long before the juices of love flowed from her so freely that they wet his trousers. Ximen extracted his penis and took some powder from his box; putting it in the usual place he returned to the attack. The powder held the fluid back, so things went more easily. She held his penis in her cunt and whispered words of endearment. Ximen, excited by the wine he had drunk, held her legs and pushed forward vigorously. He thrust with all his might almost three hundred times, until her disheveled hair covered his shoulders and her tongue was too cold to speak. Ximen was hardly breathing, but suddenly the sperm flowed forth and gave him an exquisite orgasm. After a long pause, he took out his penis and the juices of love flowed, but she wiped them away with her handkerchief. They both dressed, and she dried her face with balsam.

Ximen Qing gave her a few taels of silver and two pairs of gold-headed pins, and told her to buy flowers and ornaments for the New Year. She thanked him and quietly let him out. Daian was waiting for him in the shop. As soon as the boy heard Ben the Fourth's door open, he opened the gate and let Ximen Qing in. Ximen was sure that nobody had seen him, and afterwards went several times to see Mistress Ben and sported with her more than once. But, as the proverb says: If you would have no one discover your secret, never do anything that you do not wish to have known. Mistress Han found out what was going on, and she told Pan Jinlian. Jinlian did not say a word to Ximen Qing.

On the fifteenth, Qiao sent an invitation to Ximen, and he went with Ying Bojue and Uncle Wu. It was a large party and there were many people drinking and listening to the plays. The guests did not leave until the second night watch. The next day Qiao sent each of them a present of food.

At the beginning of this month, Cui Ben, who had bought silk and other merchandise to the value of two thousand taels of silver, loaded them upon a boat and started back. When the boat reached Linqing, he left the boy Rong Hai in charge of the merchandise, hired a horse, and came to ask for money to pay the duty. When he came to the gate, Qintong cried:

"What, are you back, Brother Cui? Come in. I will go and tell the master. He is in the shop."

But when Qintong came to the shop, Ximen Qing was not there. He asked Ping'an, and Ping'an said his master had gone to the inner court. Then Qintong went to Yueniang, but she said: "Your Father went out this morning and has not come back yet." The boy went to all the rooms, the garden, and the studies, but he could not find Ximen Qing. He went back to the gate.

"I'll be killed if I can tell you where he is," he said. "I can't find him anywhere. How he has managed to vanish in broad daylight is more than I can understand. And here is Brother Cui waiting for him."

Daian knew where his master was, but he said nothing.

Then Ximen appeared suddenly, and the boys were astonished. He had been amusing himself with Mistress Ben the Fourth. Ping'an made a face at Qintong. He and the other boys were worried for Qintong's sake. If Cui Ben, they thought, had gone away, there would be punishment in store for Qintong. Fortunately, Cui Ben had not gone away. He kowtowed to Ximen Qing and handed him the accounts.

"The boats are at the wharf," he said, "and I need money to pay both freight and duty. We set off together on the first day of the month and separated at Yangzhou. The others went on to Hangzhou. I stayed a couple of days at Miao Qing's. He has spent ten taels of silver on a Yangzhou girl for you. She is sixteen years old, the daughter of a captain there, and her name is Chuyun. I can't tell you how beautiful she is. I can only say that her face is like a flower, her skin like jade, her eyes like stars, her eyebrows like the new moon, her waist like the willow, and her feet hardly three inches long. She is so beautiful that the fish when they see her sink to the depths of the river, and geese fall stricken to the ground. She is pretty enough to make the moon retire in shame and the flowers hang their heads. She knows three thousand short songs and eight hundred long ones. At the moment she is at Miao Qing's house, and he is getting ready ornaments and clothes to send with her. He is going to send her with Laibao in the spring, in the hope that she will amuse you when you feel the need of amusement."

Ximen Qing was delighted. "You should have brought her with you," he said, "and there was no need for him to bother to buy clothes and ornaments for her. Do you think I couldn't provide her with things of that sort, myself?"

Ximen Qing loathed himself because he had no wings to fly to Yangzhou, to bring back the girl and amuse himself with her.

He gave Cui Ben something to eat and five taels of silver to pay the duty and freight. He also gave him a letter to the officer at the wharf, asking him to be lenient. Cui Ben took it to Assistant Secretary Qian.

Ping'an noticed that Ximen Qing did not call for Qintong. "My boy," he said, "I could never have believed you'd be so lucky. His Lordship must be in a good temper today or you would have been tied up and beaten."

Qintong laughed. "You know his Lordship too well," he said.

It was the twentieth of the month when the merchandise arrived. It was stored in the house in Lion Street. Ximen Qing was busy preparing presents for the New Year, when a man came from General Jing. He was anxious to know whether the Imperial Rescript had come in response to the report that Censor Song had made. "My master says, perhaps you will send someone to the provincial office to find out." Ximen Qing sent a man with five *qian* of silver to the provincial office, and he found that the Imperial Rescript had arrived the day before. He made a copy and brought it back. It was a very long document, and, in the course of it, reference was made to Major Zhou, General Jing and Uncle Wu. They were all spoken of in terms of high praise and recommended for promotion.

Ximen Qing read the document with great satisfaction. He went to the inner court and said to Wu Yueniang: "Censor Song's recommendations have come. He has suggested your brother for promotion, and that he be given charge of the commissariat in this district. Zhou and Jing are commended too, and they will both be promoted. I am going to send a boy for your brother so that I can tell him."

"Yes, do," Yueniang said, "I will get the maids to prepare wine and food for you. But, if he takes up this new office, won't he need money?"

"Don't worry about that," Ximen said, "I will lend him anything he needs."

After a while, Uncle Wu came, and Ximen Qing showed him the Imperial Rescript. Uncle Wu thanked Ximen and Wu Yueniang. "I shall never be able to forget your kindness," he told them both.

"If there is anything you need, let me know," Ximen Qing said.

Uncle Wu thanked him again. They sat down with Yueniang in her room and had a meal there. Ximen asked Chen Jingji to make a copy of the document for Uncle Wu, and then sent it to Major Zhou and General Jing.

CHAPTER 78
Pan Jinlian and Her Mother

Uncle Wu went away in the evening. The next day, Jing came to thank Ximen Qing. "I read the Imperial Rescript yesterday," he said, "and was greatly pleased. It is all due to your kindness, and I can never forget the fact." He drank some tea and rose. "When is Master Yun going to invite us to take wine with him?" he asked.

"It is so close to the New Year that we are all busy," Ximen Qing said. "He will probably put it off until afterwards." Jing went away.

Ximen Qing killed a pig and sent it with two jars of wine, a roll of red silk, a roll of black silk, and a hundred fruit pastries to Censor Song. Chunhong took them with Ximen's card to the Censor's office. The officers took the boy in, and Song saw him in the hall at the back. While he was writing a note in return, he gave the boy some tea and three *qian* of silver. Then Chunhong came back and gave Ximen Qing the card. It said:

> To the most exalted and noble Ximen. Twice already I have enjoyed your magnificent hospitality, and I do not know how to thank you. Now, you send me presents that I feel I have no right to accept. You may, perhaps, have learned that I have recommended your kinsman and Jing. I am anxious to see you that we may talk about the matter. With most cordial thanks I now send back to you your servant. Your friend, Song Qiaonian.

The Censor sent a man with a hundred copies of the new calendar, forty thousand sheets of paper, and a pig.

One day a document arrived, confirming Uncle Wu in his new appointment. Ximen Qing went to call upon him, taking thirty taels of silver and four rolls of silk. On the twenty-fourth, Ximen Qing set seals upon his office and prepared a feast for his kinsmen and friends. When Uncle Wu returned from assuming office, Ximen invited him, and there was another celebration.

Now Captain He's family arrived. Ximen Qing sent tea to them in Wu Yueniang's name. On the twenty-sixth, Abbot Wu and twelve priests came to read the office for the hundredth day after the death of Li Ping'er. A host of relatives and friends came that day to offer tea to Ximen Qing.

They, in turn, were asked to eat vegetarian food, and all went away the same evening. On the twenty-seventh, Ximen sent presents to his relatives and friends. He sent half a pig, half a sheep, a jar of wine, a sack of rice and a tael of silver to Ying Bojue, Xie Xida, Chang Zhijie, Clerk Fu, Clerk Gan, Han Daoguo, Ben the Fourth and Cui Ben. To Li Guijie, Wu Yin'er, and Zheng Aiyue, he sent a dress and three taels of silver each.

Yueniang wished Nun Xue to hold a service in her temple and sent Laian to her with oil, rice, flour and money.

The end of the year was drawing near. The moon lit up the plum blossom by the windows, and the wind howled through the snow-covered eaves. There was the noise of fireworks everywhere, and every household set up charms and spells for the Spring.

Ximen Qing burned paper offerings and went to Li Ping'er's room to make an offering to his dead wife. Then he assembled the whole household in the inner hall. The servants, boys, maids, and serving women came to kowtow to Ximen Qing and Wu Yueniang. Then husband and wife distributed kerchiefs, handkerchiefs, and money to all their household.

The next day was the first of the first month of the first year of the reign period Chonghe. Ximen Qing rose very early, dressed himself in his robes, and made sacrifice to Heaven and Earth. After breakfast, he got on his horse and went to the Censor's office to wish Song a happy New Year. The ladies rose early too. They dressed up and put on flowers and ornaments. They wore silken skirts and embroidered gowns, and looked very beautiful and charming. They came to kowtow to Yueniang.

Ping'an and one of the men from the office were at the gate to receive the New Year cards and write the names of the callers in a book. They were also ready to receive the officers and others who came to congratulate Ximen Qing at the New Year.

Daian and Wang Jing, wearing new clothes, new hats, and new boots, were outside the gate, playing shuttlecock, lighting bonfires, and chewing melon seeds. The clerks came and everybody connected with the houses. They were received by Chen Jingji.

About noon Ximen Qing returned from his calls upon the Censor and other officers. As soon as he had dismounted, Wang the Third came to offer his good wishes. Ximen Qing took him to the great hall, and there the young man kowtowed to him. Then Wang the Third asked to be allowed to see Yueniang, and Ximen took him to the inner court. When they returned to the hall, Ximen gave him wine.

They had drunk only one cup when Captain He was announced. Ximen Qing told Chen Jingji to entertain Wang the Third, while he himself went to receive Captain He. Wang the Third went away when he had drunk a little more wine. Then Jing and Yun and Qiao came, one after the other. Ximen Qing was kept busy entertaining them until evening, and, by that time, he was almost tipsy. He spent the night with Yueniang.

The next day, he went out again making New Year calls and did not return until late. When he reached home, Uncle Han, Ying Bojue, Xie Xida, Chang Zhijie, and Hua Ziyu were there, and Jingji was talking to them. When Ximen came in, they greeted one another, and wine was brought. Uncle Han and Hua Ziyu lived outside the city gates and they left early. But Ying Bojue, Xie Xida, and Chang Zhijie lingered. Uncle Wu the Second came. He went to the inner court to greet his sister, then joined the others. After a while he went away.

By the time Ximen Qing took Bojue and the others to the gate, he was drunk. Daian was there, and Ximen squeezed his hand. The boy knew what this meant and said: "There is nobody there."

Ximen went at once to Mistress Ben the Fourth. She was waiting for him. Neither of them wasted any words: they undressed and set to work immediately. She was full of lust; she spread-eagled her thighs, opened her cunt with both hands, and let him reach her inmost recesses. Warm liquid oozed from her and wet the sheet. He put some powder on the head of his penis, gripped her body with both arms, and thrust so hard that the whole penis went in; not a hair's breadth stayed outside. The woman opened her eyes wide and called him Darling. Ximen asked her what her maiden name had been. "My mothers name was Ye," she said, "I was fifth child."

After that, Ximen Qing kept murmuring: "Ye the Fifth, Ye the Fifth."

Once, this woman had been a nurse. She had misbehaved with Ben the Fourth; then they had run away, and he had taken her to live with him as his wife. She was now thirty-two years old, and very well skilled in the arts of love. She called Ximen Qing by the sweetest names. He was delighted and yielded. He took his penis out of his trousers and was about to wipe it clean, but she interrupted him and said, "Don't wipe it; I'll suck it for you." Ximen wished for nothing more, so she bent down, took the penis with both hands and sucked it until it was quite clean. Then he pulled up his trousers.

"Why has my husband not come back yet?" Mistress Ben said.

"I expected him before this," Ximen said. "Possibly his Lordship Xia has kept him."

He gave her two or three taels of silver. "I should have liked to give you some clothes," he said, "but Ben the Fourth might find out, so I am giving you this money to buy some for yourself."

She opened the door for him and he went away. Daian was waiting in the shop and took his master into the house.

If the upper beams lean to one side, the lower ones also will give way. Mistress Ben the Fourth had misconducted herself with Daian even before she had dealings with Ximen Qing. Now, as soon as Daian had taken his master into the house, seeing that Clerk Fu was not in the shop, he took two jars of wine and went with Ping'an to see her. They drank until the second night watch. Ping'an went to the shop to sleep and Daian stayed with the woman.

"I have allowed your master to come to me," she said to him, "but I am very much afraid my neighbor, Mistress Han, will tell the ladies. Then they will treat me as they treat Clerk Han's wife, and I shall never be able to hold up my head again."

"The only two who count are the Great Lady and the Fifth Lady," Daian said. "There is nothing wrong with the Great Lady, but the Fifth is very sly. This is what I should do. Now that it is the New Year, buy something for the Great Lady. She is very fond of fruit pastries. Spend a *qian* or so on them and some fine melon seeds and take them to her. On the ninth, it will be the Fifth Lady's birthday. Take her some little presents and I will give her a box of melon seeds for you. That will stop their mouths."

The woman approved this plan, and the next day, when Ximen Qing was out, Daian took the boxes to Yueniang. When she asked where they came from, he told her Mistress Ben the Fourth had sent them.

"Why should she spend her money buying things for me?" Yueniang said, "especially when her husband is not at home." She accepted the presents and gave Daian two boxes of fruit and other things to take back, telling him to thank Mistress Ben the Fourth.

When Ximen Qing returned from his round of visits, Abbot Wu called to wish him the compliments of the season. They took wine in the hall and Abbot Wu went away. Ximen Qing told Daian to take a horse and go to see old woman Wen. "Tell her I want to go and see Lady Lin," he said. "What shall I do about it?"

"You need not bother, Father," the boy said, "I met old woman Wen riding past here on a donkey. She told me that Wang the Third is setting off tomorrow for the Eastern Capital to pay a visit to Marshal Huang, Lady Lin would like you to go and see her on the sixth. Old woman Wen will be there herself."

"Is this true?" Ximen Qing said.

"Should I dare to lie to you?" Daian replied.

Ximen Qing went to the inner court, but he had hardly reached his wife's room before Daian came to tell him that Uncle Wu had come. Wu was dressed in ceremonial robes, wearing a girdle with a gold buckle. He made reverence to Ximen Qing and said: "It is entirely due to your kindness that I find myself in this position today. Thank you for the presents you sent me. I am sorry I was not at home yesterday when you called. Today, I have come especially to pay my respects. Forgive me for being late." He knelt down and kowtowed.

Ximen Qing knelt down too. "Uncle," he said, "you have my heartiest congratulations. You must not worry about the question of money."

Wu Yueniang kowtowed to her brother. Uncle Wu hastily made a half-return to her, and asked her not to pay him the full honor. "That is quite enough for me," he said. "Your brother and sister-in-law are always coming here and troubling you. Now I am old, I depend upon your generosity."

Yueniang said: "Brother, I only trust you will forgive me when I fail to do things to your liking."

"Sister," Uncle Wu said, "you must not talk like that. Have we not troubled you enough already?"

"It is rather late, Uncle," Ximen Qing said. "You can't go anywhere else now. Take off your ceremonial clothes and come and sit down for a while."

They did not know that Meng Yulou and Pan Jinlian were there. When these two ladies found that Uncle Wu was going into the inner room, they came out hastily, kowtowed to Uncle Wu, and went away.

Ximen Qing and Uncle Wu went in and sat by the fire. The table was set, and the two maids, Yuxiao and Xiaoyu, came and kowtowed to Uncle Wu. Yueniang offered her brother a small gold cup of wine. Ximen Qing took the host's place, and Uncle Wu invited his sister to sit down. Yueniang asked to be excused for a moment and went into the other room for some fruit.

"Everything seems to be going well," Ximen Qing said to his brother-in-law as they drank their wine.

"It is all due to you," Uncle Wu said. "I have been to headquarters and I find that things are practically settled at the Capital. I haven't yet been to my own office of the commissariat. Tomorrow is an auspicious day, and I propose to break the seals and then go home to prepare some boxes and send them to the granary. Then I will see all the keepers of the granary and give them their orders. Ding, who used to be in charge, was reported upon adversely by Governor Hou and dismissed. I have taken his place. I have to go through all the books and give instructions to the keepers. I am making a thorough clearance of old records and reports so as to be ready for the new harvest when autumn comes.

"How many acres have you under your control?" Ximen Qing asked.

"The system of local supplies for the troops to avoid the trouble and expense of transport was established in the most remote times," Uncle

Wu said. "Originally, contributions of grain were only made in autumn. Wang Anshi, when he was Minister, introduced the early grain system, which calculated for another contribution in the summer. In Jizhou, not counting barren land and marshes, we have twenty-seven thousand acres, and each acre must make a contribution of one tael and eight *qian*, so all together we have more than five hundred taels. At the end of the year we send the contribution to Dongpingfu. There, arrangements are made for buying grain and hay for the horses."

"Is there anything left over?" Ximen asked.

"There are some people not on the register," Uncle Wu said, "and people in general are very sly. If you treat them firmly and insist upon good measure, there is likely to be trouble."

"But I suppose there will be something to make it worth your while."

"To tell you the truth," Uncle Wu said, "if things are properly managed, I think I ought to make more than a hundred taels every year, besides chickens, pigs, geese and wine. Those things are presents, of course, and do not count. But I shall have to rely upon your assistance.

"I shall be very glad to do anything I can, if you can only make something out of it," Ximen said.

They drank until lights were brought, and then Uncle Wu went away. Ximen Qing went to Jinlian.

The next day he went to the office, removed the seals, and set to work again upon official business. An invitation came from Yun Lishou asking him to take wine with the other officers on the fifth. Captain He's wife invited Yueniang and the other ladies to visit her on the sixth.

Ximen Qing went with Ying Bojue and Uncle Wu to take wine with Yun Lishou. Yun had borrowed a house and engaged musicians to entertain his guests. The party did not break up until late. All the time, Ximen Qing was longing for the morrow.

The next day, Yueniang went to see Captain He's wife. Ximen Qing, dressed in his finest clothes, mounted a horse, put on his eyeshades, and went to Lady Lin's house. Daian and Qintong attended him. Wang the Third was not at home. Ximen sent in his card. Old woman Wen took it to Lady Lin. He was asked to go in, and taken through the great hall to the inner court, and into a room the floor of which was covered by rugs. The hangings and curtains were red. Lady Lin was wearing a scarlet straight-sleeved gown and her hair was piled up with pearls and ornaments. They greeted one another, then sat down and drank tea. The boys took the horse to the stable. After tea, Lady Lin begged Ximen to take off his ceremonial clothes and go to her room.

"My son," she said, "has gone to the Eastern Capital to wish his father-in-law the compliments of the season. He will be back after the festival."

Ximen Qing called Daian to take his long cloak. Beneath it he was wearing a white silk coat and a sky-blue gown embroidered with flying fish. It was very handsome.

The table was set and maids brought wine and dishes. Lady Lin offered him wine with her delicate hands; passionate glances flashed from her eyes. They guessed fingers, threw dice, and talked sweetly to one another. Spring was in the air. Then they began to glance sideways at one another and their heads whirled.

It was almost sunset. Silver candlesticks were brought. Daian and Qintong were being looked after by old woman Wen. Wang the Third's wife was in another apartment. She was served by her own maids and women and did not come to them. Lady Lin closed the door. After that, no servant would dare to come in. Then, stirred by the wine, they went to the inner room, pulled aside the embroidered curtains, and shut the windows. They turned up the lamps and closed the doors. Ximen Qing took off his clothes and got on to the bed; Lady Lin washed herself carefully, and then joined him. Ximen had come for this purpose; he had brought his instruments with him. He had taken some of his secret medicine, and the silver clasp was ready for action. He pulled up her legs and put his strong prick before her cunt, then reared up and thrust it in noisily. The woman called him her darling without ceasing.

Ximen burned grains of incense on her belly and by the hole of her cunt. He told her he was going to give a party and that he would like to invite her son's wife and herself to come and see the lanterns. The woman was so enraptured that she promised they would both go. Ximen Qing got up, drank with her until the second night watch, then mounted his horse and rode home. He went out by the back way.

When he got home, Ping'an said: "Eunuch Xue has sent a card to ask you to go to his country place to enjoy the signs of the approach of Spring. And Uncle Yun has sent five cards of invitation asking the ladies to a party."

Ximen went to Yueniang's room. Yulou and Jinlian were there. Yueniang had returned from Captain He's place and was talking to them. When Ximen came in, she rose and made a reverence to him.

"Where have you been all this time?" she said.

Ximen could think of no better excuse than that he had been drinking at Ying Bojue's house.

Yueniang told him about the party at Captain He's. "Mistress He," she said, "is very young. I don't believe she is more than eighteen. She is as beautiful and charming as a painted figure. She is well up in affairs of the day as well as those of the past. She was so sweet and pleasant to me she might have known me for a long time. It is two years since she married Captain He. She has four maids, two nurses, and two serving women."

"She is a niece of Eunuch Lan," Ximen Qing said. "When she married He, the eunuch gave her a very considerable dowry."

"Tomorrow," Yueniang said, "your friend Yun's wife has asked us to go and see her. There are five cards. Shall we go?"

"Yes, indeed," Ximen said. "All of you, if you are invited."

"I think Sun Xue'e ought to stay at home," Yueniang said. "It is the New Year, and, if anybody should call, there would be no one here."

"Very well. Xue'e shall stay at home and the rest of you can go. Eunuch Xue has asked me to go and see him, but I don't feel much like going. I don't know whether it is the Spring air or not, but the last few days I have had a good deal of pain in my legs and loins."

"There may be something wrong with your lungs," Yueniang said. "Don't waste any time but get Doctor Ren to give you some medicine."

"Oh, I don't think it is anything serious. If I leave it alone, it will get better of itself. If it doesn't, I will ask him for something later on. I think we might give a party for the Feast of Lanterns and invite some ladies, Mistress Ho, Mistress Zhou, Mistress Jing, Mistress Zhang, Mistress Yun, Lady Lin, Aunt Wu and Mistress Cui. What about the twelfth or the thirteenth? We can make a show of lanterns and have some of the actors from the royal household. Last year, we had a few large set pieces, and Ben the Fourth looked after them. This year he is at the Eastern Capital, and we shall have to find someone else."

"Since Ben the Fourth is not here, why not ask his wife?" Jinlian said. "She would do as well."

Ximen Qing looked at her. "You little strumpet!" he said. "You can't speak three sentences without making yourself objectionable."

Yueniang did not seem to be very interested, and the matter dropped.

"We have never seen Wang the Third's mother," Yueniang said. "What is the idea of asking her? I don't suppose she will come."

"Since Wang the Third is now my ward, we may as well send her an invitation," Ximen Qing said. "Whether she comes or not is her affair."

"I don't think I shall go to Yun's place tomorrow," Yueniang said. "I am getting near my time. If I get into a crowd, people may talk."

"You need not worry," Yulou said. "You are not very big. The baby is not due this month, and it is the New Year. Why not be merry and go?"

Ximen Qing drank a cup of tea and went to sleep with Xue'e. When Jinlian saw this, she went away with Ximen Dajie. Ximen asked Xue'e to pinch and rub his body for a long time.

The next day Ying Bojue came. "Mistress Yun," he said, "has sent a card to my wife to ask her to go and help her entertain your ladies. But my wife has only a few old dresses, and this is not a very suitable time to wear them. People would laugh at her. I have come to see if you would mind lending her some of your ladies' clothes and a few ornaments and things. Then she can wear them."

Ximen Qing said to Wang Jing: "Go and ask the Great Lady."

"Ying Bao is here with a box," Bojue said. "Take it, Brother, and bring something back in it."

Wang Jing took the box and went to the inner court. After a while he returned and handed the box to Ying Bao. "There are some silken clothes and a set of ornaments inside," he said. Ying Bao took them away and Bojue sat down to have tea with Ximen Qing.

"Eunuch Xue has asked me to go to his place outside the city to enjoy the coming of Spring," Ximen Qing said, "but I have too much to do. My kinsman, Wu, has invited me to go and take part in a service at his place on the ninth, but I can't go to that either. I must send my son-in-law instead. I don't know whether I have been drinking too much, but my back aches very badly and I feel too lazy to move."

"You have been drinking too much, Brother," Bojue said. "You must drink less."

"It is the New Year and I can't help myself," Ximen said. "Wherever I go, drink is pressed upon me."

Then Daian came in with a box. "Captain He," he said, "has sent you an invitation to a party on the ninth."

"There you are!" Ximen said. "Another invitation. And I can't refuse."

He opened the case. There were three cards inside it. One, a large red one, said: "To his Lordship, my colleague Siquan"; another: "To his Worship, Wu"; and the third, "To my good friend, the worthy Ying." They all ended with the words "your friend He Yingshou kowtows."

Daian said: "The messenger said he did not know the other addresses, so he brought all the cards here. He said he would be much obliged if we would forward them."

"What shall I do?" Ying Bojue said. "I have never sent the Captain any present. How can I accept his invitation?"

"I will give you something for Ying Bao to take to him. That will be all right."

Ximen told Wang Jing to wrap up two *qian* of silver and a handkerchief, and to write Bojue's name on a card. "Perhaps you will take this card with you. I will not send it," he said to Ying Bojue. He told Daian to take the other card to Uncle Wu. Wang Jing gave the packet to Ying Bojue.

Bojue bowed to Ximen Qing and thanked him. Then he went away.

"I will come early, and we will start together," he said as he was leaving.

In the afternoon Yueniang and the others dressed and set out. They had one large sedan chair and three small ones. They took Laijue's wife to act as their maid, and she, too, had a small sedan chair. Four soldiers went before them to clear the way, and Qintong, Chunhong, Qitong, and Laian followed them. So they came to Yun Lishou's house.

When they had gone, Ximen Qing said to Ping'an, the gatekeeper: "No matter who comes to see me, you must say that I am not at home. Just accept any cards that may be brought."

Ping'an had had such instructions before, and he had learned his lesson. He did not dare to leave the gate. He sat down and, whenever a visitor came, said his master was not at home.

Ximen Qing's legs were still painful. He remembered that he had some long-lasting medicine that a doctor had once given him, to be taken with the milk of a woman. He went to Li Ping'er's room and asked Ruyi'er to give him some of hers. Ruyi'er was dressed in her holiday clothes. She at once gave him some milk and gave him what he needed for the medicine. Ximen sat by the fire and told Yingchun to bring him something to eat. Yingchun did so, then went to play chess with Chunmei. She knew that Ruyi'er would give him any water or tea he might want. When the maid had gone, Ximen lay down on the bed, pulled down his trousers, took out his prick, and asked her to take it in her mouth while he took some wine in his. "Suck it for me thoroughly," he said, "and I'll give you a decorated cloak to wear on holiday." "Certainly," she replied. "I want to suck it again and again." "My child," Ximen Qing said, "I should like to burn some incense on your body."

"Do what you like," the woman said.

Ximen Qing made fast the door, then took off his cloak and trousers. She lay on the bed, and Ximen took from his pocket three grains of incense, soaked in wine, which were left over from the time when he had his pleasure with Mistress Lin. He took off her clothes and put one grain of incense on her bosom, another on her belly, and the third in her cunt; then he burned them all. He put his prick in her cunt, bent down to look, and thrust vigorously; then he took a mirror to see better, and it was not long before the incense had burned down to her skin; she grimaced and ground her teeth in pain, and at last she said in a trembling voice, "Stop, I can't stand it any longer."

"Zhang the Fourth, you strumpet, whose woman are you?" Ximen Qing cried.

"I am yours."

"Say that you once belonged to Xiong Wang, but now you belong to me."

"This strumpet once was Xiong Wang's wife, but now she belongs to this darling."

"Do I know how to deal with a woman?"

"Yes, my darling, you know well how to treat a woman's cunt."

So they talked, in a manner we cannot describe. His penis was so long and thick that it filled her whole cunt. He traveled up and down, making the heart of her flower now red as a parrot's tongue, now black as a bat's wing. It was a delightful and wonderful sight. He held her legs; bodies squeezed together, and his prick went in right to its root. Her eyes opened wide, and love juices flowed from her. Ximen reached his orgasm, and his sperm flowed like a river.

After he had burned her in this way, he opened the cabinet and gave her a silk embroidered cape.

In the evening, Yueniang and the others came back. "Mistress Yun is going to have a baby," Yueniang told her husband. "Today, when we offered wine to one another, we agreed that, when the babies arrive, if one is a boy and the other a girl, we will arrange a marriage between them. If they are both boys, they shall go to the same school, and if girls, they shall be like sisters, do their needlework, and play together. Mistress Ying was our witness."

Ximen Qing smiled.

The next day was the day before Jinlian's birthday. Ximen Qing went to the office in the morning and told the boys to get out and clean all the lanterns and put them up. He told Laixing to buy fruits and to arrange with the singing boys to come in the evening.

Early that morning, Jinlian got up and dressed, putting on flowers and powdering her face till it was very white. Her lips were red; the sleeves of her coat green. She came to the great hall to watch Daian and Qintong putting up the lanterns. She smiled and said: "I see you are getting ready for the Feast of Lanterns."

"Yes," Qintong said, "today is the eve of your birthday, and Father said we were to get out the lanterns and have them up ready for your party tomorrow. This evening I am coming to kowtow to you. I'm sure you will have something for me."

"If it is a beating you want, yes, indeed; but if money, it is no use coming to me," Jinlian said.

"Mother," Qintong said, "you never speak without using the word 'beating.' We are your children and you ought to be kind to us instead of talking to us about beatings."

"Shut your mouth and get on with your lanterns," Jinlian said. "And don't set about your work in that offhand way. The lanterns will not stay up. The other day, when Cui Ben came and you said: 'How can the master have vanished in broad daylight?' you very nearly got a thrashing. If you don't put up these lanterns properly, you won't escape a thrashing this time."

"Mother," Qintong said, "you always use ill-omened words. My life is precarious enough as it is, and your words make it seem still less secure."

"You have a wonderful way of finding out things, Mother," Daian said. "How did you come to hear that?"

"Outside the palace there is a pine tree, and inside it, a great bell," Jinlian said. "The pine tree's shadow is easy to recognize, and the sound of the bell, easy to hear. So it is with things in this house. Yesterday, your master said to the Great Lady: 'Last year, Ben the Fourth was here to see about the big fireworks. Now he is away and there is nobody to see to them.' I said: 'Even if Ben the Fourth is not at home, his wife will do as well. Why don't you send for her?'"

"What are you suggesting now, Mother?" Daian said. "You surely can't think of such a thing. Ben the Fourth is one of our clerks."

"What am I suggesting now, indeed?" Jinlian said. "It is true, isn't it? A lovely state of affairs! He goes beyond all limits."

"Mother," Qintong said, "don't believe everything you hear. We must not let this reach Ben the Fourth's ears."

"That silly turtle!" Jinlian said. "What's the harm if that fellow does get to know? I say he is a turtle, and everybody knows that that is exactly what he is. He doesn't worry when he goes to the Eastern Capital. He knows that, when he leaves his wife behind, her cunt will not be unemployed. Don't argue with me, you scamp. You all help your father in these games. And when you arrange things of this sort for him, you get your own fingers in the pie. Isn't that so? You say I know too much. It is perfectly clear why that woman sent presents to the Great Lady the other day. I understand she is sending me some melon seeds to keep my mouth shut. She is very clever at these underhand games, but my first guess is that Daian devised the whole scheme."

"You must be fair, Mother," Daian said. "Why should I do anything of the sort? I have never been to her place unless there was something important to be done. Don't believe everything Mohammedan Han's wife tells you. She and Mistress Ben the Fourth have had quarrels over their children. As the proverb says: It is easy for people to pick a quarrel, but hard to keep on good terms. If the roof falls, it does not necessarily follow that somebody must be hurt; but an evil tongue, incessantly wagging, will be the death of anyone in time. In cases like this, if you believe a thing, it is true; if you do not believe it, it is false. Mistress Ben the Fourth is a very pleasant woman. She has been here some time and she is always kind. We all go to her for tea and things, and I can't believe we all have improper dealings with her. She hasn't a house big enough to hold us all."

"Oh, I know the bleary-eyed strumpet," Jinlian said. "She is no bigger than half a brick, but she blinks her watery eyes and seems to make people do what she wishes. She and that hashed-up, melon-faced Han Daoguo's wife! I know their tricks. I keep my eyes open. How can I fail to see?"

At that moment, Xiaoyu came up and said: "The Great Lady is asking for you. Grandmother Pan has come, and she wants to pay the sedan chair men."

"I have been standing here all this time," Jinlian said. "How was it I didn't see her?"

"She went in by the passage," Qintong said. "She needs six *fen* of silver for the sedan chair."

"Where does she expect me to get the money?" Jinlian cried. "Why doesn't she bring her own money when she goes out to visit people?"

She went to the inner court to see her mother, but she would not give her any money.

"Give the old lady a *qian* of silver and put it down in the accounts," Yueniang said.

"No, I'm not going to upset our husband," Jinlian said. "He knows exactly how much money he gives me. He gave it to me to buy things with, not to pay for sedan chairs."

They all sat down and looked at one another. The sedan chair men kept pressing for their money. They wanted to go away. At last, Yulou could bear it no longer. She took a *qian* of silver from her sleeve and dismissed the men.

After a while, the two aunts Wu and the nun came. Yueniang gave them tea. Old woman Pan went to her daughter's room. Jinlian upbraided her harshly.

"Who told you to come, if you haven't money enough to pay for your chair? You come here, and people laugh at you. You have no shame at all."

"Daughter," old woman Pan said, "you never give me any money. Where am I to get it? Indeed, I found it very hard even to get presents to bring with me."

"It's no use looking to me for money," Jinlian said. "Money doesn't come my way. There are seven holes here and eight eyes trying to find them. In the future, come when you know you have money to pay for your chair and, if you haven't any, stay away. I'm sure nobody in this house is dying to see you, so you needn't make an exhibition of yourself. Though the god of war may have sold bean curd, it was the man himself who counted, not the stuff he sold. I can't put up with the insulting things people say. There was trouble the other day, after you had gone away. Did you know that? I am like the droppings that fall from a donkey. They look very fine and large, but there's nothing inside."

The old woman began to cry. "Mother," Chunmei said to Jinlian, "what is the matter with you today? Why are you scolding Grandmother so?" She did her best to console the old lady, took her to the inner room, and made her sit down on the bed. Then she gave her a cup of tea. The old woman was so upset that she went to sleep and did not wake up till she was called to dinner. Then she went to the inner court.

When Ximen Qing came back from the office, he had his meal in Yueniang's room. Daian brought him a card and said that Jing had called to see him. Upon the card was written: "The recently promoted Commander of the troops in the southeast and Superintendent of Communications, Jing Zhong, presents his humble respects." Ximen hastily put on his ceremonial clothes and went to welcome him. Jing was wearing a scarlet gown, with a unicorn embroidered upon it, and a girdle with a gold buckle. He was accompanied by a host of officials and soldiers. They greeted each other in the hall, then sat down, and tea was brought.

"The documents reached me the day before yesterday," Jing said. "I have not yet been to my new office, but I felt I must come especially to thank you."

"I must congratulate you, General," Ximen said. "It is only right and fitting that a man so capable as yourself should be appointed to a more responsible post. Your appointment sheds glory even upon myself. I must give a party in your honor."

He asked Jing to take off his ceremonial clothes and stay to dinner. At the same time he ordered a servant to set the table. Jing would not stay. "I came to thank you," he said, "before I went to anyone else, but I have a great deal to attend to. I will come and see you another day." He prepared to say good-bye, but Ximen Qing would not have it. He told a servant to take his guest's ceremonial robes and set the table at once. Charcoal was put into the brazier; the blinds were drawn. Jade-like wine was poured from a golden jar and food brought in a precious dish.

The wine had just been served when the two boys, Zheng Chun and Wang Xiang, came in and kowtowed. "What makes you so late?" Ximen Qing asked Zheng Chun. "And who is this other boy?"

"He is Wang Xiang, a brother of Wang Gui," Zheng Chun said.

Ximen told them to bring their instruments and sing, and the two boys sang the song "This Delightful Weather." Servants brought two trays of food and two jars of wine for the people who had come with General Jing.

"This is really too much," Jing said. "I have troubled you enough. Why should you give food to all my people?" He ordered them to come and kowtow to Ximen Qing.

"Tomorrow or the day after," Ximen said, "my wife is going to invite your lady to come and enjoy the Feast of Lanterns. I hope you will persuade her to come. There will be your lady, Mistress Zhang, Captain He's wife, and the two ladies of my kinsman Wu, nobody else."

"If any invitation comes from your lady, my humble wife will be sure to come," Jing said.

"Why has Zhou not been given an appointment yet?" Ximen Qing asked.

"I am told he is to receive an appointment in the Capital in three months' time," Jing said.

"I am glad to hear it," Ximen said.

Jing stood up and said good-bye. Ximen Qing took him to the gate. Then, with the soldiers clearing the way for him, he went away.

That evening, they kept the eve of Jinlian's birthday. The two boys sang in the inner court. When the wine had been passed around, Ximen Qing went to her room. Aunt Wu, old woman Pan, Ximen Dajie, Miss Yu, and the two nuns stayed in Yueniang's room while Jinlian went to her own to drink with Ximen Qing. She offered him wine and kowtowed to him. After a while old woman Pan came, and Jinlian sent her to sleep in the Sixth Lady's room, so that she herself could drink and sport with Ximen.

The old woman went to the Sixth Lady's room, and Ruyi'er and Yingchun helped her to get into the warm bed. But, before she did so, she looked at Li Ping'er's tablet in the outer room with many offerings set out before it. The portrait was hanging there. The old woman made a reverence to it. "Sister," she said, "you are safe in paradise now." Then she came and sat on the bed and said to Ruyi'er and Yingchun: "Your mistress is a happy woman. She is dead, but her husband has many prayers said for her and makes offerings to show he still remembers her."

"The other day we observed my mistress's hundredth day," Ruyi'er said. "Why didn't you come? Aunt Hua and Aunt Wu were here; there were twelve priests to read the prayers. They played instruments and waved banners about. It was really a splendid ceremony, and didn't come to an end before the evening."

"It was the New Year season," old woman Pan said. "I couldn't leave the boy at home alone. That is why I didn't come. But where is Aunt Yang today?"

"Didn't you hear that Aunt Yang had died?" Ruyi'er said. "On my mistress's hundredth day she didn't come, and, only a few days ago, all our ladies went to her funeral."

"What a sad thing!" old woman Pan said. "I believe she was even older than I am. I never knew she was dead. No wonder I missed her today."

"Grandmother," Ruyi'er said, "we have some sweet wine. Would you like some?" Then she said to Yingchun: "Sister, will you put a small table on the bed and warm some sweet wine for Grandmother?"

The wine was brought, and, while she was drinking it, the old woman said: "Your mistress was a very good woman. She was kind and sweet. When I came here, she never treated me as a stranger. She used to give me hot tea and hot water, and she would be angry if I wouldn't take them. And at night she would stay awake and talk to me. When I was going away she always gave me something. Why, Sisters, even this gown I am wearing now, she gave me. My own daughter never gives me so much as the half of a broken needle. That is the truth. If I were starving, she wouldn't give me a penny. She would see my eyes drop out on the ground first. When your lady was alive, my daughter used to scold me for a miser and say I was always trying to get things out of her. I know she has a lot of money, but, in spite of it, she would not give me even the few *fen* I needed to pay for my sedan chair. She bit her lips and said she had no money. In the end, the lady in the east room gave me a *qian* and paid off the chair men.

"When I went to her room, she gave me a fine dressing down. She said I was to come if I had money and to stay away if I hadn't. Let me tell you this: when I go away this time, I shall never come back. I won't come here to be insulted. I give her up entirely. There are many cruel people in the world but none so cruel as she is. Sisters, I tell you: if I die tomorrow, I don't know what the end of her will be. She will never take advice from anybody. You know, her father died when she was seven years old, and, from that day to this, I've never thought about anybody but her. When she was young, I taught her needlework and sent her to school. I dressed her carefully and took care that her hands and feet were well kept. She has been clever enough to rise to the position she holds now, and see how she treats her poor mother. Her eyes are never kind when they look on me."

"Did your daughter go to school?" Ruyi'er said. "Now I understand why she is able to read all the characters."

"Yes, she went to school when she was seven years old, and she spent three years there. She learned composition and how to read poems and songs and literature of all sorts."

As they were talking, there came a knock at the door. "Who is there?" Ruyi'er said. "Go and see, Xiuchun."

Xiuchun went to the door. When she came back, she said: "Sister

Chunmei is here." Ruyi'er squeezed the old woman's hand.

"Don't say anything," she whispered. "Chunmei is here."

"She and my daughter walk with the same leg," the old woman said.

When Chunmei came in, she found them drinking wine with the old woman. "I have come to see how Grandmother is," she said. Ruyi'er asked her to sit down. Chunmei arranged her skirt and sat down on the bed, with an air of great self-importance.

Yingchun sat next to Chunmei, Ruyi'er on the left-hand side, and the old woman in the middle.

"Have your father and mother gone to bed?" the old woman said.

"Yes," Chunmei said, "I waited on them till they were in bed and then I came to see you. I have got some dishes and a cup of wine ready for you." She said to Xiuchun: "The dishes are all ready. Go and ask Qiuju for them." Xiuchun went out. She soon returned carrying a jar of wine. Qiuju brought a food box.

"Go back now," Chunmei said to Qiuju, "and, if they want me, come and tell me."

Qiuju went back. The dishes were put on the table. Xiuchun went to fasten the door, then came and joined them. When the wine was heated, Chunmei offered a cup to old woman Pan, then to Ruyi'er, Yingchun, and Xiuchun. She picked out all the tasty bits from the dishes and offered them to the old woman and the others. "Grandmother, do have some," she said. "I assure you it has been prepared especially for you."

"Sister," the old woman said, "your mistress never bothers about what I eat, but you take pity on a poor old widow. I foresee that you will make progress day by day. My daughter has not a human heart. I have always been miserable on her account. Whenever I offer her advice, she storms at me. Sister, you know I came today to see her, not to cadge a few bits of cold food. And you see how she has treated me."

"Grandmother," Chunmei said, "you don't understand. You only see one side: the other is hidden from you. My mistress is one of those people who are never satisfied so long as they are in a subordinate position. Compared with the Great Lady, who has money in plenty, she is in a most unfortunate position. My mistress is really poor, though you think she has a good deal and will not give you any. I know her better than anyone else does. My father leaves a great deal of money in her hands, but she will not touch a penny of it for her own purposes. If she wishes to buy flowers and things of that sort, she asks him straight out, instead of using his money and saying nothing about it. She will not allow the servants any handle against her. Grandmother, if you are angry with her, you are unjust. I am not standing up for her. I only want you to realize what the position is."

"Perhaps the old lady did not quite understand her daughter," Ruyi'er said. "After all, you are mother and daughter. If she had money, she would surely give it to you before anybody else. When you, old lady, come to your end, the Fifth Lady will have no one of her own to come and see her. She will be like the rest of us who have lost our mothers."

"I am old," the old woman said, "and I don't know whether I shall die today or tomorrow. I am not angry with her."

Chunmei saw that the old woman was becoming maudlin after her few cups of wine. She said to Yingchun: "Get the dice box and let us throw dice." They got a box with forty dice. Chunmei played with Ruyi'er, then with Yingchun. They drank great cups of wine, and, before long, their peach-flower cheeks were flushed. They finished the jar. Yingchun brought half a jar of Magu wine, and they finished that too. By the second night watch, old woman Pan could not stay awake any longer. Her body swayed backwards and forwards; her head began to nod. The party broke up.

When Chunmei went home, she opened the corner door and went through the courtyard. Qiuju was in the middle room, standing on a small bench and peeping through the partition. She was spying on the pair in the other room, and was very interested in the remarks they made to one another and the different sounds she heard. Just when she was most delighted, Chunmei came up and slapped her face. "You young rascal!" she said. "What do you mean by listening there?"

Qiuju was taken by surprise. She stared at Chunmei and said: "I was dozing. I wasn't listening at all. Why do you come and hit me?"

Jinlian overheard this. She called out to Chunmei: "Who is talking there?"

"I have told Qiuju to shut the door, but she won't move," Chunmei said.

Qiuju glared and went to shut the door. Chunmei took off the ornaments in her hair and went to bed.

The next day was Jinlian's birthday. Mistress Fu, Mistress Gan, Ben the Fourth's wife, Cui Ben's wife, Miss Duan, Miss Zheng, and the younger Wu's wife, came to congratulate her. Ximen Qing, with Uncle Wu and Ying Bojue, dressed in their best clothes, went on horseback to Captain He's place. There were a great many guests, and four singing girls were there to entertain them. Major Zhou was present. In the evening, when the party broke up, Ximen Qing came back and spent the night with Ruyi'er.

On the tenth he sent out cards to invite the ladies.

"Why should we not invite Aunt Meng?" Yueniang said, "and my sister-in-law too? They will be very upset if they find we've left them out."

"You are quite right," Ximen said. He asked Jingji to write two more invitations and Qintong took them.

Jinlian overheard this and was annoyed. She went to her own room and urged old woman Pan to go away at once. As the old woman was leaving, Yueniang said to her: "Grandmother, why are you going away in such a hurry? You must stay another day at least."

"Great Sister," Jinlian said, "It is the New Year, and there is nobody to look after her boy. Please don't keep her."

Yueniang gave the old woman two boxes of cakes and a *qian* of silver for her sedan chair, and took her to the gate.

When the old woman had gone away, Jinlian said to Li Jiao'er: "The Great Lady is inviting her rich relations for the Feast of Lanterns, and my old mother would be out of place. I couldn't let her stay. When the guests come, I can't say she is a guest too, because her clothes make it quite obvious that she isn't. And I can't tell them she is one of the women from the kitchen, because she isn't that. It puts me in a very awkward position."

Ximen Qing told Daian to take two cards to Wang the Third's place, one for Lady Lin and one for the younger lady, whose family name was Huang. He also told Daian to go to the bawdy house to tell Li Guijie, Wu Yin'er, Zheng Aiyue, and another girl to come, as well as the three boys, Li Ming, Wu Hui and Zheng Chun.

That day, Ben the Fourth came back from the Eastern Capital. In his best clothes, he came to kowtow to Ximen Qing and gave him a letter from Xia.

"What has kept you so long at the Capital?" Ximen asked him.

"I caught a very bad cold," Ben the Fourth said, "and I wasn't well enough to leave before the second of this month. His Lordship Xia sends you his best wishes and thanks you for looking after his house."

Ximen Qing gave Ben the Fourth the keys of the thread shop again, but he set apart another room so that Uncle Wu the Second could sell silk there. He was going to let Uncle Wu the Second do business with Laibao when Laibao came back with merchandise from the South. He asked Ben the Fourth to get the firework makers to put up two set pieces ready for the party on the twelfth.

Then Ying Bojue came with Li the Third, who thanked Ximen Qing for all he had done for him in the past. They sat down and had tea. Ying Bojue began: "Brother Li knows of a piece of business, and he is anxious to find out if you would be interested in it."

"What is the business?" Ximen Qing said.

"A document has come from the Eastern Capital," Li the Third said "requiring the Thirteen Provinces each to send to the capital historic works of art to the value of tens of thousands of taels. Our Prefecture of Dong-pingfu is to provide twenty thousand taels' worth. The order is still in the governor's hands and has not been sent down to the lower authorities. Zhang the Second, in the High Street, proposes to expend a hundred taels in getting the contract. There is about ten thousand taels profit to be made. I thought I would come with Uncle Ying to let you know about this so that, if you feel inclined, we can go into the business with Zhang the Second. It would mean five thousand taels from each of you. Brother Ying, Huang the Fourth, and I myself, would be your associates, and Zhang the Second would have two men in with him. We should share the profits in the proportion of two and eight. What do you think about it?"

"What kind of works of art do they want?" Ximen Qing said.

"Perhaps your Lordship has not heard," Li the Third said. "The work on North Mount has just been finished at the Imperial City, and its name has been changed to the 'Mountain of Long Life.' A number of buildings are to be constructed there, the Palace of the Pure and Precious Secret, the Hall of the Immortals, and the Sanctuary of the Jade Spirit. There is also to be a dressing chamber for the Lady An. All these buildings are to be adorned with rare beasts and birds, Zhou bronzes, and Shang tripods, Han seals, and Qin incense burners, stone drums of the Xuanwang period, bronzes and copper of the successive dynasties—antiquities, in fact, of every sort. It is a very great undertaking, and his Majesty is going to spend a great deal of money."

"I think it would be better if I managed the whole business myself," Ximen said. "I might as well provide the ten or twenty thousand taels and go in for the thing with my own people."

"It certainly would be better," Li the Third said. "We need say nothing about it, and Brother Ying, Brother Huang and I will give you our assistance. Then there will be no outsiders."

"Will you bring in one of your own people?" Bojue asked.

"When we have made all the arrangements, we will have Ben the Fourth to help us," Ximen said. He asked where the orders were.

"They are still at the Censor's office," Li the Third said. "They have not been sent on yet."

"That doesn't matter," Ximen said. "I will write to Song and send him some presents. That will be all right."

"But you must act at once," Li the Third said. "As the proverb says: Soldiers must always be on the alert, and he who cooks his rice first will be the first to eat. If we don't look out, somebody may get the job before us."

Ximen Qing laughed. "Don't worry about that," he said. "Even if the orders had been sent to the office of the Prefecture, Song would recall them for me. Besides, Hu, the Prefect, is a friend of mine."

He asked Li the Third and Ying Bojue to stay for a meal, and it was settled that Ximen Qing should send his letter the following day.

"I must tell you one thing," Li the Third said, "His Excellency is not at his office now. The day before yesterday, he set out for an inspection at Yanzhou."

"You shall go yourself with one of my boys tomorrow," Ximen said.

"Very well," Li the Third said, "I expect we shall manage it in five or six days. Whom will you send with me? Give him the letter and let him come and spend the night at my house so that we can start early in the morning."

"The only one of my servants whom his Excellency knows is Chunhong, and he likes him. I will send him and Laijue with you."

Ximen summoned the two boys and told them that they were to go on a journey with Li the Third and that they must spend the night at his house.

"You do well," Bojue said. "We must waste no time, for, in matters like this, the man with the fastest legs has the advantage."

When they had had something to eat, Ying Bojue and Li the Third went away. Ximen Qing told his son-in-law to write the letter, then measured about ten taels of gold leaf and gave it with the letter to Chunhong and Laijue.

"See that you go quickly and warily," he said to them, "and come back as soon as you have got the document. If it has been sent to the Prefecture before you get there, ask his Excellency to give you a letter to the Prefect, instructing him to let us have it."

"I understand," Laijue said, "I have been to Yanzhou before, on an errand for Counselor Xu."

They went to Li the Third's house and, the next day, hired horses and set out.

On the twelfth, Ximen Qing gave a party and did not go to the office. He invited Uncle Wu, Ying Bojue, Xie Xida, and Chang Zhijie to come in the evening. Early in the morning, the musicians of the princely household of Wang came and, when the ladies arrived, they sounded the bronze drums and gongs in their honor. A servant came from Major Zhou to say that Mistress Zhou had trouble with her eyes and would not be able to come. But Mistress Jing, Mistress Zhang, Mistress Yun, Mistress Qiao, Mistress Cui and Aunts Wu and Meng came early. Captain He's wife, Lady Lin, and Wang the Third's wife did not arrive so early, so Ximen Qing sent soldiers several times to urge them to come, and dispatched old woman Wen to Lady Lin.

About noon, Lady Lin came in a large sedan chair, with a smaller chair following. After he had greeted her, Ximen Qing asked why her daughter-in-law had not come.

"My son is not at home and she is obliged to stay there," Lady Lin said.

Sometime afterwards, Captain He's wife came. She was in a sedan chair carried by four men. Behind her came a smaller one with a serving woman. A number of soldiers followed with her dressing case, and servants walked beside the chair. The chair was brought to the second door; the lady got out, and the musicians played. Wu Yueniang and the others went to the second door to welcome her. Ximen Qing stood quietly in one of the side rooms, and looked at the young lady through the blind. She was not more than twenty years old, tall and slender, and she looked as pretty as a jade carving. There were masses of pearls and ornaments on her hair. She wore a red gown with long sleeves embroidered in five colors. Her girdle was set with gold and jade, and below it was a blue skirt. As she moved, the tinkle of jade could be heard, and she brought with her the fragrance of orchid and musk.

> Gracious and charming
> Dainty and alert
> Of manner fascinating
> And of figure perfect
> With eyebrows long and delicate, arching on the temples
> Eyes, like a phoenix's, delicately sloping.
> Her voice was as sweet
> As that of an oriole flying in the sunshine.
> Her tender waist like the willow
> Playing in the wind.
> From the host of the most elegant she came
> Without a trace of arrogance or common breeding
> As though one bred in a thicket of pearls.
> Her dress was chaste and dignified.
> She was like a cherry tree in full bloom
> Of whom no one knows how many flowers
> Blossom in one night.
> Like a willow slow in budding
> So that no one can tell how far advanced
> Is Spring.
> Her lotus feet moved lightly
> Gaily as the fairies.
> With skirt raised just a little
> Like the "Water-Moon" Guanyin.
> A flower among flowers
> But what the flowers do not know, she knows.
> A precious jade among jades
> But with a fragrance that no jade possesses.

Ximen Qing was entranced. Although he had not touched her, his heart was hers. Yueniang and the others took her to the inner hall and there they greeted one another. Then Ximen Qing was sent for. He hastily put straight his hat and clothes and rushed in. To him the young lady seemed like a tree of jade come to this world from paradise, an angel from the Wu Mountain. He bowed very low. His heart was beating fast and his eyes were dazzled. It was all he could do to control himself. When he had greeted her, he withdrew.

Yueniang entertained her guests in the arbor. They had tea. Then the musicians played and the guests took their places in the great hall. Lady Lin sat in the place of honor. The actors played two acts of *Little T'ien Hsiang Worshipping the Stars at Midnight*. Then the four singing girls came to sing the song of the lanterns.

Meanwhile, Ximen Qing and his friends were drinking wine elsewhere, and the three boys, Li Ming, Wu Hui, and Zheng Chun, sang for them. But, all the time, Ximen Qing was peeping through the window into the great hall.

Readers, the moon cannot always be at the full, and the most glorious clouds are soon dispersed. Happiness reaches its height, but sorrow follows after. So, too, when ill fortune reaches its climax, consolation is at hand. This is the will of Heaven. Ximen Qing thought of nothing but of gaining renown and increasing his riches: he spent himself in luxurious living and the pursuit of women, and never checked himself. He did not realize that Heaven abhors extremes. But the officers of Hell were coming to summon him. His days were nearly done.

That evening, the lanterns were lighted and the boys sang. Even before the first night watch, Ximen Qing was snoring as he sat with the others. Bojue, trying to rouse him, asked him to play games and guess fingers.

"What makes you so sleepy, Brother?" he said. "Are you not happy today?"

"I did not sleep very well last night," Ximen said. "Today, I don't seem to have any energy."

The four singing girls came to them. Bojue bade two of them sing and the other two serve the wine. They were drinking happily when Daian came and said: "Lady Lin and Mistress He are going." Ximen Qing hastily left the table and stood in the shadow beside the second door to watch them go. Yueniang and the others came with them and, when they reached the courtyard, they waited for a while to look at the fireworks. Mistress He had changed her clothes. She was wearing a scarlet cloak with sables. Lady Lin wore a white silk coat with sable cape, gold pins, and jade ornaments. Servants, with lanterns, took the ladies to their chairs.

Ximen Qing looked at them with starving eyes; his mouth watered so that he could hardly swallow. But they were beyond his reach. At that moment—it might have happened in a fairy tale—Laijue's wife, seeing that the ladies had gone, came from the inner court. So she met Ximen Qing and could not get away. She was a pretty young woman and Ximen had long desired to possess her. She was not so sprightly as Laiwang's wife had been, but she was not far behind her. Ximen was stirred by the wine he had drunk. He took the woman in his arms, carried her into her room, and kissed her.

This woman had once been a maid in a princely household, but she had carried on with her master and had been sent away through the jealousy of the other servants. Today the same fate overtook her, and she had to yield. She slipped her tongue into his mouth. They both undressed. Ximen put her on the edge of the bed and raised her legs. Then he took his pleasure of her.

CHAPTER 79

The End of Ximen Qing

Men born in the south and the north
Travel different roads.
There is no certainty in the life of man
Creation disposes of us as it chooses
Lifts us up and sets us down,
Makes us lie outstretched or stand upright.
It is the same wherever we go.

We sigh in vain, thinking of what is past,
For fame and wealth and dignity
Are not things to be sought.
Whatever the course of our life may be, whether misery or joy
We must follow it.

Whether we live in splendid palaces
Or ride on steeds caparisoned with gold
Or inhabit humble dwellings
Or live in small thatched cottages
All will still shed tears.

When Ximen Qing had finished with the woman, he went back to drink with Uncle Wu and the others. The ladies stayed for a while, ate some dumplings in celebration of the Lunar Festival, and then went away. Chen Jingji saw that the actors were given a meal, and dismissed them with two taels of silver. The four singing girls and the three men stayed on, singing and serving wine for the men.

"Tomorrow is Brother Hua's birthday," Bojue said to Ximen Qing. "Have you sent him a present?"

"Yes, I sent him something this morning."

"Uncle Hua has sent you a card of invitation," Daian said.

"Are you going, Brother?" Bojue said. "If so, I will come for you and we will go together."

"I can't tell you now," Ximen said. "I advise you to go alone."

After a while the four singing girls went to the inner court, leaving only the three boys to entertain the men. Ximen Qing was very sleepy and nodded all the time.

"Brother-in-law," Uncle Wu said, "you are tired. We had better go."

Ximen Qing would not let them go before the second night watch. Then he sent away the singing girls and gave the boys two large cups of wine each and six *qian* of silver. As they were going away, he said to Li Ming: "I shall want you here on the fifteenth. I am going to invite their Lordships Zhou, Jing, He, and some others on that day. Don't forget. And I want you to engage four singing girls for me."

Li Ming knelt down and asked whom he would like to have. "There is that girl from the Fans' house," Ximen said, "and Qin Yuzhi, and, at Captain He's the other day, I saw a girl called Feng Jinbao. Then there is Lü Sai'er. They will do."

When Li Ming had gone, Ximen Qing went to Wu Yueniang's room.

"Lady Lin and Mistress Jing seemed to enjoy themselves," Yueniang said to him. "They did not go until very late, and Mistress Jing thanked me repeatedly. She said you had been extraordinarily helpful to her husband, and they would never forget your kindness. General Jing is going next month to the Huai country to see about the transport of the grain. Mistress He drank plenty of wine. She seems to have taken a fancy to the Fifth Lady. I took her to the garden and showed her the artificial mound. She gave some very generous gifts to the servants."

Ximen Qing spent the night with Yueniang. During the night she dreamed, and when daybreak came, she told her dream to her husband. "It may have been because Lady Lin was wearing a red cloak," she said, "but I dreamed that Li Ping'er took a red cloak from her box and dressed me in it. Pan Jinlian snatched it away from me and put it on herself. That made me angry, and I said to her: 'You have her fur coat already. Why should you want this too?' Then Jinlian grew angry and tore the cloak. I began to shout. Then I woke and found it was a dream."

"Don't let the dream worry you," Ximen said. "I will give you a coat. When people dream about a thing, it is always because they would like to possess it."

He got up, but his head was heavy, and he did not feel like going to the office. When he had dressed, he went to the study and sat down. Yuxiao brought him some of Ruyi'er's milk in a little jar, and Ximen took it with his medicine. Then he lay on the bed, and Wang Jing softly tapped his master's legs. When Yuxiao came, the boy withdrew. Ximen Qing gave her a pair of gold pins and four silver rings, and asked her to take them to Laijue's wife. Yuxiao realized that he was again repeating the experience he had had with Laiwang's wife. When she came back, she said: "She has accepted your gifts and is coming to kowtow to you." Then she took the empty jar and went away.

Yueniang had ordered Xiaoyu to cook some gruel for Ximen Qing, but he would not come and take it. Wang Jing had brought a packet from his sister, Wang Liu'er, and told his master she was anxious to see him. Ximen Qing opened the packet. In it was a tress of glossy dark hair, tied with five-colored silk, with a lovers' knot of silken ribbon. There was also an embroidered purple bag with two openings, filled with melon seeds. Ximen Qing examined everything very carefully. He was pleased. He put the bag on the shelf and the hair in his sleeve.

Suddenly Yueniang came into the room. Ximen was still lying on the bed, with Wang Jing working on his legs. "Why don't you come to breakfast instead of staying here?" she said. "What is it that makes you so languid?"

"I don't know. But I feel wretched and my legs hurt."

"Perhaps it is the weather," Yueniang said. "But now you are taking the medicine, you will soon be well again." She took him to her room and they had breakfast there.

"It is the New Year," Yueniang said, "and you ought to be merry. Why don't you go and see Uncle Hua? It is his birthday today. Or send for Brother Ying to come and have a chat."

"Ying is not at home today," Ximen said. "He has gone to Hua's place. Make something for me to eat, and I will go to the shop and see Uncle Wu the Second."

"Very well," Yueniang said, "order your horse. I will tell the maids to prepare something."

Ximen Qing told Daian to saddle his horse, then he dressed and went to Lion Street. The Feast of Lanterns was in full swing, and the street was very busy. The sound of horses and carriages was like thunder, and the lanterns were as beautiful as embroidered silk. People swarmed like ants.

Ximen looked at the lanterns, then went to the shop. Uncle Wu and Ben the Fourth were doing a very brisk trade. Laizhao's wife made a fire in the parlor and brought tea. After a while, Yueniang sent Qintong and Laian with two boxes of food. There was some Southern bean wine in the shop, and they opened a jar of this and went upstairs. Ximen Qing drank with Uncle Wu and Ben the Fourth and looked out at the lanterns. People were pressing up and down the street below.

Ximen Qing sent Wang Jing with a message to Wang Liu'er. When she heard, he was coming she hastily made preparations. Ximen told Laizhao to let Uncle Wu and Ben the Fourth have the rest of the food, and bade Qintong take a jar of wine to Han Daoguo's house. Then he mounted his horse and rode there. Wang Liu'er, all dressed up, welcomed him and kowtowed four times.

"Thank you for your presents," Ximen Qing said. "But why haven't you been to my house? I have twice sent you an invitation."

"Though I didn't go, no one came to urge me," Wang Liu'er said. "And I have not been very well these last few days. I have no appetite and I don't feel able to do anything that requires the slightest exertion."

"You must be thinking of your husband," Ximen said.

"Thinking of my husband!" Wang Liu'er cried. "It is because you have not been to see me. I thought I must have done something to annoy you. You have been treating me like the ring on a hairnet, which is always put out of sight. But perhaps you have another woman now."

Ximen Qing laughed. "Another woman?" he said. "No, all through this festival there have been so many parties that I have been too busy to come."

"You had a number of ladies yesterday, I hear," the woman said.

"Yes, my wife has been visiting them, and we had to do something in return."

"How many ladies were there?"

Ximen told her about the party.

"So, when you have a party for the Feast of Lanterns, you invite everybody of any importance, but you don't ask me."

"Oh, you mustn't let that upset you," Ximen said. "There will be another party on the sixteenth, and the wives of those who work with me will all be invited. I shall not allow you to refuse."

"If your lady sends me a card, how dare I refuse?" Wang Liu'er said. "By the way, the other day, one of your maids insulted Miss Shen, and she complained to me most bitterly about it. As a matter of fact, she did not wish to go that day, and I persuaded her. After the trouble she came here and cried till I didn't know what to do. Then you were kind enough to send a box and a tael of silver, and that put matters right. Your maid seems to have been in a very bad temper. She ought to know that, before she beats a dog, it is well to look and see what the master thinks about the matter."

"That little oily mouth has a very sharp tongue," Ximen Qing said. "She even treats me like that sometimes. But Miss Shen herself was in the wrong. She was asked to sing and she should have sung. When she refused, of course people got angry. She said a few things to the maid, too."

"She told me she never opened her mouth," Wang Liu'er said. "She said the maid came and insulted her and shook her fist at her. When she came here, tears were rolling down her cheeks and she never stopped blowing her nose. I kept her here for the night and then took her home."

The maid brought tea and old woman Feng came and kowtowed to Ximen Qing. He gave her a piece of silver worth about three or four *qian*. "You have not been to my place since your mistress died," he said.

"Where should I go now that she is dead?" the old woman said. "But I often come here to talk to this lady."

They took Ximen Qing into the inner room and asked whether he had had anything to eat.

"I had some gruel this morning," he said, "and, just before I came here, I had some cakes with Uncle Wu the Second. I am not particularly hungry."

Still, the table was set. The woman asked Wang Jing to open the jar of bean wine, and heated some. They sat down to drink.

"Did you get the things I sent you?" Wang Liu'er said. "I cut off a lock of my own hair and arranged it with my own hands. I thought you would like it."

"It was very kind of you," Ximen said.

When they had drunk wine enough, and there was nobody in the room, Ximen Qing took the ribbon from his sleeve, put it around his penis and tied it around his waist. Then he drank some medicine mixed with wine. Wang Liu'er stroked the prick, which quickly became proud and erect. The veins stood out; it looked like a piece of purple liver. The silk ribbon had far more effect than the clasp. Ximen Qing lifted her onto his lap and pressed his prick into her cunt. They drank wine, each from the other's mouth, and their tongues played together.

In the evening, old woman Feng made some dumplings with pork and radishes for them. Wang Liu'er ate some with him and, when the maid had cleared away, they went to the bed. They pulled aside the silken curtains and took off their clothes. The woman knew that Ximen Qing liked to do things in the light, and she set the lamp on a small table near the bed. Then she made fast the door and went to wash her cunt. When she came back, she took off her trousers and went to bed. They lay down together and put their arms around one another. Ximen Qing was still thinking of Captain He's wife and his passion blazed like fire. His penis was very hard. He told her to get onto hands and knees like a horse, and he plunged to the flower in her bottom. He did this six hundred times, while her behind showed its noisy approbation. She felt down her body, played with the flower in her belly, and called him endearing names unceasingly.

Still Ximen was not content. He sat up, put on a white short coat and set a pillow beneath him. Then he bade the woman turn over and tied her feet with two ribbons to the bedposts. He began by playing the game of the golden dragon stretching its claws, and thrust this way and that, sometimes plunging deep, sometimes just a little way. He was afraid she might catch cold and wrapped a red silk coat about her body. He brought the light nearer and bent his head to watch the movements. Whenever he took out his penis, he put it in again right up to the hilt; he did this six hundred times. The woman, her voice trembling, called him every endearing word she could think of. Soon he withdrew completely and put some of the red powder on the tip of his penis; when it was set in motion again it so stimulated her cunt that she could hardly bear it. She climbed on top of him and begged him to go in deeper; but he deliberately played about the opening, touching the treasure inside only lightly and refusing to go in further. Love juices flowed from her like slime from a snail. In the candlelight Ximen beheld her white legs raised about his body on either side. He saw them quivering in response to his movements, which became still more violent.

"Do you love me, you strumpet?" he asked her.

"I have been thinking about you all the time," she said. "I can only hope that you will be like the pine tree and the cypress, evergreen. Do not weary of me and give me up. If you should do that, it would kill me. I dare not tell this to anyone else, and nobody knows it. And I shall not tell that turtle of mine. He is away and he has money. He has other women and need not bother about me."

"My child," Ximen said, "if you will give yourself entirely to me, I will find another wife for him when he comes back and then you can belong to me always."

"Darling," Wang Liu'er said, "do get him another wife. Whether you take me into your household or leave me outside does not matter. Do as you please. I give my worthless body to you utterly and entirely and I will do anything you wish."

"I know you," Ximen Qing said.

They went on for a very long time. Then Ximen unloosed the ribbons that tied her feet, and they went to sleep together. About the third night watch he got up, put on his clothes, and washed his hands. Wang Liu'er opened the door and bade the maid bring them wine and food. They drank again. After more than ten cups of wine, Ximen began to feel tipsy and asked for tea to rinse his mouth. He took a paper from his sleeve and gave it to Wang Liu'er. "Take this to clerk Gan, and ask him for a dress," he said. "You can choose your own pattern and design." She thanked him, and he went away. Wang Jing carried a lantern and Daian and Qintong led his horse, one on either side.

It was the third night watch. Dark clouds covered the sky, and the light of the moon could hardly pierce them. The street was deserted; only the barking of dogs could be heard in the distance. Ximen Qing went westwards. Suddenly, as he came near the stone bridge, a whirlwind swept before his horse. It was like a dark form advancing from the bridge to attack him. His horse was startled and reared. Ximen shuddered. He whipped his horse. It shook its mane. Daian and Qintong clung to the bridle with all their strength, but they could not hold it, and the horse galloped wildly till it came to Ximen's gateway. Then it stopped. Wang Jing, with the lantern, was left far behind. When Ximen Qing dismounted, his legs were almost useless, and servants came out to help him in. He went to Pan Jinlian's room.

Jinlian had come back from the inner court, but she had not gone to bed. She was lying upon her bed, dressed, waiting for Ximen Qing. When he came, she got up at once. She took his clothes and saw that he was drunk, but she asked no questions. Ximen put his hands on her shoulders and drew her towards him.

"You little strumpet!" he murmured, "your darling is drunk. Get the bed ready: I want to go to sleep."

She helped him to bed, and, as soon as he was on it, he began to snore like thunder. She could do nothing to wake him, so she took off her clothes and went to bed too. She played delicately with his weapon, but it was as limp as cotton wool and had not the slightest spirit. She tossed about on the bed, consumed with passionate desire, almost beside herself. She pressed his prick, rubbed it up and down, bent her head to suck it; it was in vain. This made her wild beyond description. She shook him for a long time and at last he awoke. She asked him where his medicine was. Ximen, still very drunk, cursed her.

"You little strumpet!" he cried, "what do you want that for? You would like me to play with you, I suppose, but today your darling is far too tired for anything of that sort. The medicine is in the little gold box in my sleeve. Give it to me. You will be in luck if you make my prick stand up."

Jinlian looked for the little gold box and, when she found it, opened it. There were only three or four pills left. She took a wine pot and poured out two cups of wine. She took one pill herself, leaving three. Then she made the terrible mistake of giving him all three. She was afraid anything less would have no effect. Ximen shut his eyes and swallowed them. Before he could have drunk a cup of tea, the medicine began to take effect. Jinlian tied the silken ribbon for him and his staff stood up. He was still asleep. She mounted upon his body, put some powder on the top of his penis, and put that in her cunt; immediately it penetrated right to the heart of her. Her body seemed to melt away with delight. Then, with her two hands grasping his legs, she moved up and down about two hundred times. First it was difficult, because she was dry, but soon the juices of love flowed and moistened her cunt. Ximen Qing let her do everything she wished, but he himself was perfectly inert. She could bear it no longer. She put her tongue into his mouth. She held his neck and shook it. She writhed on his penis, which was entirely inside her cunt; only the two testicles remained outside. She caressed it with her hand, and it looked remarkably fine. The juices flowed; in no time she had used up five handkerchiefs. Still Ximen persevered, although the head of his prick was swollen and hotter than burning coal. The ribbon felt so tight that he asked her to remove it, but the penis stayed erect, and he asked her to suck it. She bent down and, taking it in her lips, sucked it and moved up and down. Suddenly the white sperm squirted out like living silver; she took it in her mouth and could not swallow it fast enough. At first it was sperm, and then it became an unceasing flow of blood. Ximen Qing had fainted and his limbs were stiff outstretched.

Jinlian was frightened. She hastily gave him some red dates. Blood followed sperm, cold air followed blood. Jinlian was terrified. She threw her arms around him and cried: "Darling, how do you feel?"

It was some time before Ximen came to himself. He said: "My head and eyes spin. I wonder what is the matter."

"What makes you yield so much today?" Jinlian said. "You must have taken too much medicine."

Readers, there is a limit to our energy, but none to our desires. A man who sets no bounds to his passion cannot live more than a short time. Ximen had given himself to the enjoyment of women, and he did not realize that he was like a lantern whose oil is exhausted and whose light is failing. Now his seed was used up, there was nothing in store for him but death. As we said at the beginning of this book:

> Beautiful is this maiden; her tender form gives promise of sweet
>   womanhood,
> But a two-edged sword lurks between her thighs, whereby destruc-
>   tion comes to foolish men.
> No head falls to that sword: its work is done in secret,
> Yet it drains the very marrow from men's bones.

The next morning, when Ximen Qing got up and went to dress, he suddenly felt dizzy and almost fell forward. Fortunately, Chunmei caught him and he did not actually fall. He sat down on a chair, and it was some time before he recovered. Jinlian was again frightened.

"You must be hungry," she said. "Stay here, and tell me what you would like to eat. I will not let you go until you have had something."

She told Qiuju to go to the kitchen for gruel.

"I want some gruel," Qiuju said to Sun Xue'e. "Father fainted and now he has asked for gruel."

Wu Yueniang heard this and came at once to ask Qiuju what was the matter. The maid told her how Ximen had nearly fallen when he was doing his hair. Yueniang was greatly upset. She urged Xue'e to hurry with the gruel and went at once to see her husband in Jinlian's room. He was still sitting on the chair.

"What is the matter?" Yueniang said.

"I don't know," Ximen said, "but my head feels very bad."

"It was fortunate Chunmei and I were there to catch him, or he would have hurt himself badly," Jinlian said. "He is so heavy."

"Perhaps his head is dizzy from drinking too much wine last night," Yueniang said.

"Yes," Jinlian said. "Where did you go drinking yesterday, that you came in so late?"

"He had something to eat in the shop with my brother," Yueniang said.

Chunmei brought the gruel. She gave some to Ximen Qing, but he ate only half a bowl and then set it aside.

"How does your head feel?" Yueniang asked him.

"It is not so bad now," he said, "but I don't seem to have any strength or energy at all."

"Don't go to the office today," Yueniang said.

"No, I won't. I'll go to the outer court and get Jingji to write some invitations. I am going to ask Zhou and Jing and Captain He to come on the fifteenth."

"You haven't had your medicine," Yueniang said. "Get some milk. You must take that. I think you must have been overdoing things the last few days."

She told Chunmei to get some milk from Ruyi'er, and the maid brought it in a bowl. Ximen took it with his medicine and went to the outer court. Chunmei helped him. When they came to the corner gate that led to the garden, his eyes clouded over; his body seemed to collapse, and he could not hold himself up. Chunmei took him back again.

"Listen to me," Yueniang said. "You must have a rest. We will postpone these invitations. There is no real need to write them now. Do absolutely nothing, and don't go out. And tell me anything you would like to eat. I'll make it for you."

"I don't want anything," Ximen said.

Yueniang went to the inner court and questioned Jinlian. She asked whether Ximen Qing had been drunk when he came in the previous night, whether he had had any more to drink, and if he had busied himself with her.

Jinlian was so full of denials that she hated herself because she had only one mouth to express them.

"Oh, no, Sister," she said. "He came back so late and he was so drunk that he never thought of such a thing. He asked me for more wine, but I gave him tea instead. I told him there was no wine and he must go to sleep. I have had nothing to do with him since you spoke to me the other day. I don't like to say anything, but I fancy he had been somewhere before he came home. But I'm not at all sure. I can only tell you that I had nothing to do with him in that way."

Wu Yueniang and Meng Yulou sent for Daian and Qintong and questioned them closely.

"Where did your father go drinking yesterday?" the Great Lady asked. "Tell me the truth. If you don't, and anything happens, I shall hold you two responsible."

Daian refused to say anything except that his master had gone to Lion Street and had taken wine there with Uncle Wu the Second and Ben the Fourth. Yueniang sent for her brother. "Do you know," she asked him, "if your brother-in-law went anywhere else after he took wine with you?"

"He stayed only a short time with us," Uncle Wu said. "Then he went away again."

This made Yueniang very angry. As soon as her brother had gone, she sent for the two boys again. She scolded them severely and threatened them with a beating. This frightened them, and they confessed that Ximen had been to see Han Daoguo's wife. Jinlian was waiting for this.

"Now, Sister," she said, "you see you have been blaming me, and I am innocent. The one who is really guilty is laughing at us. Just as every tree has its own bark, so each one of us has his own face to consider. How can you think that I exist only for things of that sort? You might perhaps ask these two slaves where our husband was the other day when you went to see Mistress He. It was very late when he came back and I don't believe he had been paying New Year calls."

Before Qintong had time to speak, Daian told them how his master had been carrying on with Lady Lin.

"No wonder he was so anxious we should send her an invitation," Yueniang said. "I said to him: 'We have never met her, and she certainly won't come.' Of course, we never dreamed of what was going on. No wonder that, in spite of her age, she paints her eyebrows and powders her face till it looks like the plaster on the wall. The old strumpet!"

"I have never heard of anybody like her," Yulou said, "and with a grown-up son too! It would be better for her to marry again than to carry on in this shameless way."

"The old whore doesn't know what shame is," Jinlian said.

"I didn't think she would come," Yueniang said, "yet she had the audacity to do so."

"Sister," Jinlian said, "now you see who is black and who is white. You scolded me when it was Han Daoguo's wife who was really to blame. It looks as though, in this household, almost everybody has a lover in secret. They are turtles openly and even send their young turtles here so that those young turtles can help them in their evil games."

"It is not for you to call Wang the Third's mother a whore," Yueniang said. "She told me that, when you were young, you were a maid at her place."

Jinlian's face became scarlet. "The old whore is mad," she said. "When was I ever at her place? My aunt was a neighbor of hers, and when I used to go and stay with my aunt, I occasionally went to the Lin woman's garden to play with other little girls. I come from her place, do I? Why, I know nothing whatever about her. She is just a blind old strumpet."

"You have too much to say," Yueniang said. "I only told you what she said, and there is no need for you to make such a fuss about it."

Jinlian was silent.

Yueniang told Xue'e to make some meat-stuffed dumplings for Ximen Qing. As she passed the second door, she saw Ping'an going to the garden. She stopped him and asked what he was about.

"Li Ming has engaged four singing girls for the party on the fifteenth and has come to know if everything is all right," Ping'an told her. "I told him the invitations had not been sent out yet, but he wouldn't be satisfied with that and asked me to go and see Father."

"Party?" Yueniang said. "What party, you rascal? What are you going to ask? Go and tell that young turtle to be off about his business? What is all the excitement about?"

Ping'an ran away in bewilderment.

Yueniang went back to Jinlian's room. She told Ximen Qing that Li Ming had come to inquire about the singing girls. "I told him we shouldn't need any as the party had been postponed," she said.

Ximen Qing nodded. He expected to be better in a day or two, but when one day had passed his warrior swelled up and there were red scrofulous spots on it. The testicles were swollen too, and as bright-colored as a tomato. When he pissed, it hurt like the cutting of a knife, and this pain he felt every time. The soldiers came to take him to the office, and were grieved to hear of his illness.

"You must do what I tell you," Yueniang said to him. "Send a card to Captain He and tell him that you must rest at home until you are stronger. And we must send at once for Doctor Ren, and get him to give you some medicine. This is serious, and we must not put off any longer. You can't go on in this state. You haven't had a proper meal for two or three days. Besides, you really are very much swollen."

But Ximen would not send for the doctor. He said: "Oh, it is nothing very serious. I shall be better in a few days and ready to go out."

He sent a card to the office excusing himself. He was very irritable and impatient at being in bed.

Ying Bojue heard he was not well and came to see him. Ximen asked him to come in. Bojue bowed and said: "I didn't know you were not well. So that is why you didn't go to Uncle Hua's place the other day."

"I should certainly have gone if I had been well," Ximen Qing said. "I don't know why, but I have not had energy enough even to move."

"What is the trouble, Brother?" Bojue asked him.

"Nothing very particular?" Ximen said. "My head feels heavy; my limbs seem to give way under me, and I can't seem to walk."

"Your face is flushed," Bojue said, "and judging by that, I think you must have some fever. Have you sent for a doctor?"

"No," Ximen said, "my wife talked about sending for Doctor Ren, but I told her not to bother because it wasn't serious enough."

"You are wrong, Brother," Bojue said. "You must send for him at once and let him have a look at you and give you some medicine to get rid of this fever. It is Spring now and a dangerous season for the lungs. I met Li Ming yesterday. He told me he had been bidden to engage some singing girls for a party you were giving today, but that you were not well and the party had been put off. That gave me quite a shock, and I came to see you at once."

"I haven't been to the office," Ximen said. "I sent a card of excuse."

"You certainly must not go out," Bojue said. "You need a rest."

After drinking tea, Bojue said he must go and that he would come again. "Li Guijie and Wu Yin'er will come and see you, I'm sure," he said. Ximen Qing asked him to stay and have something to eat, but he said he would rather not, and went away.

Then Ximen told Qintong to go for Dr. Ren. The doctor came and felt his pulse. "The fever is mounting," the doctor said, "and there is exhaustion of the fluid in your testicles. It is clearly a case of sexual exhaustion. I will give you something to supply the missing element."

He went away. Ximen Qing sent him five *qian* of silver, and a boy brought back the medicine. After taking it his head felt better, but his body was so weak that he could not get up. His prick swelled more and more and it was increasingly difficult for him to make water.

In the afternoon Li Guijie and Wu Yin'er came with presents. When they had kowtowed to Ximen Qing, they asked how he was.

"It is very good of you, Sisters, to come and see me, but why did you bother to buy presents?" he said. "For some reason I seem to have a little fever."

"Perhaps you have been drinking too much wine during the New Year celebrations," Guijie said. "You will be all right if you don't drink any more for a few days."

They went to the Sixth Lady's room. There they found Yueniang and the others, and were asked to go and take tea in the inner court. Afterwards they went back to Ximen Qing.

Then Ying Bojue, Xie Xida, and Chang Zhijie came. Ximen Qing told Yuxiao to prop him up in bed and asked the three men to stay for wine.

"Brother," Xie Xida said, "have you had any rice gruel?"

Yuxiao turned her head away and did not answer. Ximen Qing said: "No, I have not had any. I couldn't eat it."

"Well, send for some," Xie Xida said. "We will have some with you."

After a while, the rice gruel was brought. Ximen ate half a bowl and set it down again.

Guijie and Wu Yin'er had gone to join Yueniang in the Sixth Lady's room. Bojue asked where they were. Ximen Qing told him.

"Go and tell them to come and sing a song for your father," Bojue said to Laian.

But Yueniang would not let the girls go. She thought that Ximen Qing was in no condition to listen to songs, and told Laian to say to Ying Bojue that the girls were having something to eat with her.

When the three friends had drunk some wine, one of them said: "Brother, you will be tired if we keep you sitting up. We will go now and you must lie down for a while." Ximen thanked them for coming, and they went away.

When Ying Bojue came to the door of the smaller courtyard, he called Daian and said to him: "I don't like the look of your father's face at all. Go and tell the Great Lady she ought to send for a doctor at once. Hu, in the High Street, is very good in fever cases. I suggest you send for him, but you mustn't waste any time."

Daian went at once and told his mistress. She went to Ximen Qing. "Brother Ying says that Doctor Hu is very good in fever cases," she said to him. "Why shouldn't we send for him?"

"Why should we?" Ximen Qing replied. "He didn't do Li Ping'er the slightest good."

"Medicine will only cure cases that can be cured," Yueniang said, "and Buddha saves only those who merit salvation. You do not think he is any good, but, if he cures you, that is all we care about."

"Very well, send for him," Ximen Qing said.

In a short time, Qitong brought the doctor. Uncle Wu was there, and he was present while the doctor examined Ximen's pulse.

"The poison is concentrated in the lower parts," Dr. Hu said to Uncle Wu and Chen Jingji. "Something must be done at once, or he will begin to make blood all the time instead of water. This has been caused by his indulging in sexual intercourse without first making water."

They gave him five *qian* of silver for medicine and made Ximen Qing take it. But it was like throwing a piece of stone into the sea. He could not make water at all. Yueniang was very much alarmed. She sent away the two singing girls and sent a messenger for He Qixuan, the son of old He. He told them that there was an accumulation of poison in the male organ and that the bladder was very much inflamed. The fever was driving the poison downwards. Ximen's veins, the doctor said, were filled with poisonous matter, and his heart and kidneys were completely out of harmony.

They gave the doctor five *qian* of silver. Ximen drank the prescribed medicine, but the penis stayed erect, as if made of imperishable iron. Throughout the night, in her ignorance of the harm she was doing, she played with him, mounted his body, and put his candle into herself. He fainted several times.

The next day, Captain He came to see him. When a boy came in to announce him, Yueniang said: "Captain He has come to see you. This is not a fit place to receive anybody. Shall I take you to the inner court?"

Ximen Qing nodded. Yueniang put some clothes on him and she and Pan Jinlian helped him to go to the upper room. There they made a bed, cleaned out the place, and burned incense. Chen Jingji took in Captain He.

"Sir," the Captain said, "I will not exchange formal greetings with you today. How do you feel?"

"My head is better," Ximen said, "but I have still a great deal of pain down below."

"It looks like a case of poisoned urine," Captain He said. "Now it so happens that, yesterday, a friend of mine called to see me on his way to Dongchangfu to visit his people. He comes from Fenzhou in Shaanxi and his name is Liu Juzhai. He is very well versed in troubles of this kind. May I send him to see you?"

"It is very good of you," Ximen Qing said. "I will send someone to ask him to come."

Captain He drank his tea. "Sir," he said, "you must take great care of yourself. Don't bother about things at the office. I can manage quite well."

Ximen Qing raised his hand. "You are very kind," he said.

When Captain He had gone, Ximen told Daian to take a card and go with one of Ho's servants for Liu Juzhai. Liu felt his pulse, put some medicine upon the affected part, and gave him a dose of something to be taken with water. Ximen Qing gave him a roll of Hangzhou silk and a tael of silver. He took the first dose, but there was no improvement.

That day, Zheng Aiyue brought him a pair of young pigeons and a box of fruit pastries. She came in a sedan chair. When she had kowtowed to him, she said: "I did not know you were ill. That excellent pair, Li Guijie and Wu Yin'er, came before me, yet they never said a word to me about it. That is why I did not come before."

"Why have you troubled to bring these things for me?" Ximen said.

"They are not intended as proper presents," Zheng Aiyue said, smiling. "They are only something for you to taste."

"We are very anxious for him to take something, but he doesn't seem able to do so," Yueniang said. "This morning he has only had a mouthful of rice gruel. The doctor has just gone."

"Mother, will you ask one of your maids to cook these young pigeons? They are very tender, and perhaps he will try one of them with his gruel. You must eat something," she said to Ximen Qing. "You are a big man, like a mountain of gold, and you have a whole household dependent on you."

"He has no appetite," Yueniang said.

"Father," Zheng Aiyue said, "listen to me. You must eat something even if you don't feel like it. We are human beings. We have no roots such as plants have, and we must eat and drink to live. If you don't eat anything, you will waste away."

Before long, one of the young pigeons was cooked. Xiaoyu brought it with the rice gruel and some preserved fruits. Zheng Aiyue jumped on to the bed and sat down on her heels before Ximen Qing. She took the bowl in her hand and tried to make him eat. He did his best, but could only swallow a few spoonfuls of gruel and a little pigeon. Then he shook his head and would try no more.

"You need two things to make you better," Zheng Aiyue said, "medicine and food. I am glad to see you take even a little."

"He would not have eaten anything at all if you had not come," Yuxiao said.

Zheng Aiyue had some tea, then Yueniang entertained her and sent her away with five *qian* of silver. Before she left, the girl went and kowtowed to Ximen Qing. "Be patient," she said, "I will come again soon."

That evening, Ximen Qing took a second dose of Dr.. Liu's medicine. But his body began to ache all over and he groaned the whole night through. In the fifth night watch, his testicles swelled up and burst and blood poured upon the bedclothes. Sores came out on the end of his penis, and a yellow liquid came from them. The whole household rushed in a turmoil to his bedside. They realized that the medicine had done him no good and sent for old woman Liu to light a spirit lamp that they might know whether he would live or die. Then they sent a boy to Major Zhou's house to find out where the Immortal Wu was. They remembered how he had told them long ago that Ximen Qing would suffer as he was doing, and now his prophecy was fulfilled. Ben the Fourth told them that there was no need to send the boy to Major Zhou's place. The holy man was staying at the temple of the local god outside the walls. "He is spending his time there," Ben the Fourth said, "telling fortunes, curing the sick, and practicing divination. He never cares what people pay him, but goes wherever he is wanted."

Yueniang sent Qintong to ask him to come.

When the Immortal came, he looked at Ximen Qing and found him entirely changed. His face was worn and thin, and his spirits low. He was lying on the bed with a kerchief tied about his head. The Immortal felt his pulse.

"Sir," he said, "you are ill because you have taken too much wine and had too much to do with women. Now your vital fluid is exhausted and a furious fever has taken hold upon the instrument of your passion. I fear I can do nothing for you. Your case is hopeless."

"If you can give him no medicine to make him well," Yueniang said, "perhaps you will tell us what the Fates say of him."

The Immortal made calculations upon his fingers and reckoned Ximen's eight characters. "His animal is the Tiger," he said, "he was born on the *renwu* day of the *wushen* month, of the *bingyin* year, and at the *bingchen* hour. The present year is *wuxu*, and he is thirty-three years old. But for calculating his fate we must take the year as *guihai*, and this is unfavorable, viewed in regard to the position of fire and earth. In this year, the *wu* earth is in conflict with the *ren* water. And this month happens to be *wuyin*, so that there are three *wus*, all against him. He cannot withstand them."

> Now he comes into conflict with the star of evil omen
> His body is light and yet heavy. He is in desperate straits.
> Beware the day and the hour of the planet Jupiter
> For then the gods will knit their brows.

"Since the Fates are of such evil omen, is there nothing you can do for him?" Yueniang asked.

"The White Tiger is standing before him at this moment, and the Angel of Death is presiding over his destiny. Heaven itself can do nothing now, and even the Year Star Jupiter could not avert calamity. It is the will of Heaven, and neither god nor spirit can alter it."

Yueniang gave the Immortal a roll of cloth, and he went away. She sought diviners and soothsayers, but everywhere she was told that the omens were against her husband's life. That night, she burned incense in the courtyard and took an oath before Heaven. "If my husband recovers," she swore, "I will go every year for three years to the peak in Tai'an District to offer incense and a robe to the Goddess there." And Yulou took an oath to offer sacrifice to the stars every seventh day. Only Jinlian and Li Jiao'er did not take any oaths.

At one time, when Ximen was in a half-fainting state, he thought he saw Hua Zixu and Wu Da standing before him, come to demand payment of the debt he owed them. He would not speak of this but asked that he should not be left alone.

Once, when Yueniang was out of the room, he took Jinlian's hand, and cried. "My love," he said, "when I am dead, you sisters must keep my tablet and stay together."

Jinlian was very sorrowful. "I am afraid I shall not be wanted here any longer," she said.

"When the Great Lady comes, I will speak to her," Ximen said.

When Yueniang came back, she found them both with eyes red with crying. "Tell me what you want," she said. "We have been together as husband and wife so long now."

Ximen sobbed quietly. "I know I am going to die," he said, "and I want to say this. When your baby is born, I should like you all to stay here and bring him up together. You must not let the household go to pieces so that the neighbors come to look down upon it." He pointed to Jinlian. "Forgive her for all the things she has done wrong."

Yueniang could restrain herself no longer. Tears rolled down her cheeks like pearls. She sobbed aloud. Ximen asked her to summon Chen Jingji. When the young man came, Ximen said: "My son, if I had a son of my own, I could count on him. But, as yet, I have no son, and I must put all my trust in you. I look upon you as my own son and, if anything should happen to me, it will be for you to bury me. Afterwards, stay here and help your mother and keep up the good renown of this house. The silk shop is worth fifty thousand taels, but part of that belongs to our kinsman Qiao. Tell Fu to dispose of as much stock as is necessary, pay off our kinsman, then close the shop. The thread shop of which Ben the Fourth is in charge is worth six thousand five hundred taels, and the silk shop that Uncle Wu the Second looks after, five thousand taels. Both those shops should be closed as soon as the stuff can be sold. If Li the Third gets the contract we have spoken about, it will be better not to go further in the matter. Ask Uncle Ying to get somebody else to take it up. Li the Third and Huang the Fourth still owe me five hundred taels with interest amounting to another hundred and fifty. Ask them for payment. You and Clerk Fu can look after the household and the two shops that are here. The pawnshop is worth about twenty thousand taels and the medicine shop five thousand. Clerk Han and Laibao are still in Songjiang. When the river is free from ice, fetch them home again. They have about four thousand taels' worth of merchandise. Sell it and give the money to your mother. Liu, the Director of Studies, owes me three hundred taels. Hua owes me fifty. Xu the Fourth, outside the city, owes me, including interest due, about three hundred and forty. We have all the necessary documents, and you can ask them for payment at once. It will be best to sell the two houses, the one in Lion Street and the one opposite, because they will be too much for your mother to control."

Then he began to cry. Jingji promised to do all that Ximen had said. Clerk Fu, Clerk Gan, Uncle Wu the Second, Ben the Fourth and Cui Ben came to see him. He gave each of them his instructions, and each one in turn told him not to be alarmed because he was not really very ill. A great many people came to visit him and, when they saw how ill he was, went away sighing.

Yueniang still hoped that Ximen might get better, but Heaven had destined him for no more than thirty-three years of life. In the fifth night watch on the twenty-first day of the first month, the fever consumed him. He panted like an ox and so continued for a long time. He lingered on until mid morning, and then, alas and alack, his breathing ceased and he passed away.

Ximen Qing died before a coffin had been made ready for him. Yueniang hurriedly sent for Wu the Second and Ben the Fourth, opened a chest, and took out four bars of silver. These she gave to the two men and told them to buy a set of coffin boards. They had hardly left her when she felt a severe pain in her belly. She hurried to her room, lay down on the bed, and lost consciousness. Yulou, Jinlian and Xue'e were in the other room, dressing Ximen Qing in his robes. When Xiaoyu told them that the Great Lady was lying on the bed, Yulou and Li Jiao'er hurriedly went to her. They saw her with her hand pressed to her stomach, and knew that her time had come. Yulou left Li Jiao'er to look after Yueniang while she went to send a boy for old woman Cai. Li Jiao'er sent Yuxiao for Ruyi'er and, when Yulou returned, she had disappeared.

Yueniang was unconscious; the chest was lying open, and there was nobody about. Li Jiao'er took five bars of silver and went off with them to her own room. She came back with some paper.

"I could not find any paper here, so I went to my own room to get some," she said to Yulou.

Yulou suspected nothing. She looked after Yueniang and made everything ready. Yueniang's pains increased and the baby was born almost as soon as old woman Cai came.

Ximen Qing was laid out, stiff and cold, in the other room, and the whole household began to bemoan him.

Old woman Cai attended to the baby, cut the navel string, and they made a soothing drink for Yueniang and helped her to bed. Yueniang gave the old woman three taels of silver, but this did not satisfy her.

"When the other lady had a baby, you gave me more than this," she said. "I want now what I had then. Besides, this is your own baby."

"Things are different now," Yueniang said. "My husband is dead. Take this, and, when you come on the third day, I will give you another tael, no more."

"I would rather have a dress," the old woman said. She thanked the ladies and went away.

When Yueniang was a little better, she noticed that the chest was open. She scolded Yuxiao. "You should not have left the chest open with so many people about when I was unconscious. Hadn't you sense enough to lock it up?"

"I was sure you had locked it," Yuxiao said, "and I didn't give it a thought." She took the key and locked it.

When Yulou saw that Yueniang was in a suspicious mood, she did not stay very long. She said to Jinlian: "You see the sort of woman the Great Lady is. The moment her husband is dead, she begins to suspect people." She had no idea that Li Jiao'er had stolen five bars of silver.

Uncle Wu the Second and Ben the Fourth went to see Shang and bought from him a set of coffin boards. They engaged carpenters to make them up, and the boys carried Ximen Qing to the great hall. Then they sent for Xu, the Master of the Yin Yang, to write his certificate. Uncle Wu came too, and he, his brother, and the clerks were all very busy in the outer hall. They took down the lanterns, rolled up the pictures, placed a sheet of paper over Ximen's body, and set lamps and incense on a table before it. Laian was left to strike the bell.

The Master of the Yin Yang looked at Ximen's hands and declared that he had died exactly at the hour of the Dragon, and that no harm would come to anyone in the household. After consulting Yueniang, he decided that Ximen should be put in his coffin on the third day. The grave was to be dug on the sixteenth of the second month, and the funeral held on the thirtieth. There would thus be more than four complete weeks between Ximen's death and his burial.

When Xu had gone away, they began to send out the sad news to all their friends and acquaintances. They sent the seal of his office to Captain He. Everyone in the household dressed in mourning, and a temporary building was set up.

On the third day Buddhist monks came to hold the first service and to burn paper money. Chen Jingji was dressed as Ximen's son, and stood before the body to receive those who came. Yueniang was not able to appear but was in a small room near by. Li Jiao'er and Yulou entertained the ladies. Jinlian, who was now in charge of the household funds, took in all the offerings that people sent. Xue'e stayed in the kitchen and superintended the preparation of tea and food for the visitors. Clerk Fu and Uncle Wu the Second kept the accounts. Ben the Fourth saw that mourning was distributed to the proper people. Laixing was responsible for the supply of provisions. Uncle Wu and Clerk Gan entertained the men who came.

When old woman Cai came to wash the baby, Yueniang gave her a silken dress and dismissed her. She called the baby Xiaoge.[1] The neighbors sent noodles as a token of congratulation. The news that Ximen Qing's first wife had borne a child immediately after his death had quickly spread. People said it was a very strange thing that a child should be born almost at the very moment of his father's death.

When Ying Bojue heard of Ximen's death, he came to bemoan his friend. The two uncles Wu were watching an artist paint a portrait of Ximen Qing.

"What a sad business!" Bojue said to them. "Even in my dreams I cannot bring myself to believe that our brother has gone." He asked to be allowed to pay his respects to Yueniang.

"My sister cannot appear," Uncle Wu said. "She gave birth to a son the very day of her husband's death."

This was a surprise to Bojue. "Really?" he said. "That means that our brother has an heir to all his property."

Chen Jingji, in the deepest mourning, came and kowtowed to Ying Bojue.

"You have all my sympathy," Bojue said to him. "Your father is dead and your ladies are like stagnant water. You must be very careful. Do not do things as you yourself think they ought to be done. Consult your two

---

1. Filial Devotion

uncles here. If you will forgive me for saying so, you are still very young and have hardly sufficient experience in business and affairs."

"No, Brother," Uncle Wu said, "I have too much other business to attend to. His mother is here."

"The Great Lady is here, it is true," Bojue said, "but she cannot attend to affairs outside the house. You will have to do what you can for her and you will remember the maxim that the uncle on the mother's side must always take a great part in the control of the family. You are not a stranger: you are the child's own uncle and the most important person in the household. Nobody here stands higher than you do." He asked when the funeral was to be.

"The grave will be dug on the sixteenth and the funeral will be on the thirtieth," he was told.

When the Master of the Yin Yang came again, Ximen Qing was put into his coffin and it was nailed up with longevity nails. The coffin was set in position, with a tablet bearing the words "General Ximen."

Captain He came and made reverence to the body. Uncle Wu and Ying Bojue gave him tea. Captain He asked about the funeral and gave orders that the soldiers who had been on duty at Ximen's house should remain there. Nobody was to go away before the day of the funeral. He appointed two sergeants to command the soldiers and declared that he would punish anyone who should dare to misbehave.

"If there is anyone who owes money, let me know," he said to Uncle Wu. "I will see what I can do to secure payment."

He went back to the office and sent a report of Ximen's death to the Eastern Capital.

When Laijue, Chunhong and Li the Third came to Yanzhou, they gave their letter and the present to the Censor. Song read it. It was a request that Ximen Qing might have the commission for the purchase of antiquities. "It is too late," he said to himself, "I have already given instructions about the matter to the Prefect." Then he saw that there were ten taels of gold leaf, and decided that it would be a pity to refuse. He told Chunhong, Laijue and Li the Third to wait and sent one of his officers in all haste to bring back the document from Dongpingfu. When it arrived, he gave it with a letter to Chunhong, together with a tael of silver for traveling money. The journey between the two places took about ten days, and when they reached Qinghe again they learned that Ximen Qing was dead. He had been dead three days, and, at that moment, service was being held for him.

Li the Third had an idea. He said to Laijue and Chunhong: "Let us keep this document and say his Excellency would not let us have it. Then we can take it to Chang. If you two don't care to come with me, I will give each of you ten taels and you can go home and keep your mouths shut."

Laijue did not object, but Chunhong would have nothing to do with the scheme. He would not promise anything.

When they came to the gate, paper money was hanging up and the monks were busy at their prayers. There were many people present. Li the Third went home, but Laijue and Chunhong came in and kowtowed to Uncle Wu and Chen Jingji. They were asked about the document and where Li the Third was, and, before Laijue could say anything, Chunhong handed the letter and the document to Uncle Wu. He told him that Li the Third had offered him ten taels to keep the letter and go to Chang's place with him. "I told him I would not do anything so shameful," the boy said, "and came straight to you.

Uncle Wu went to the inner court. "This young lad is really extraordinarily honest," he said to Yueniang, "but what a dirty trick of that wicked fellow Li the Third, as soon as he heard of your husband's death!"

He went to Ying Bojue. "We have a note," he said, "showing that Li the Third and Huang the Fourth still owe us six hundred and fifty taels. As Captain He has advised, we will send the note to his office and ask him to make them pay. He will certainly not refuse, seeing that he was the dead man's colleague."

"Li the Third certainly ought not to have done such a thing, but do not make too much of it, Uncle," Bojue said. "I will go and speak to him about it."

He went to Li the Third's house, and they sent for Huang the Fourth. "You should not have offered the boys money," Bojue said. "That gave them a hold over you. Now you are like the man who was too slow to catch the fox and only came in for the smell. They are talking about going to the courts, and you know how those officials look after one another. These were in the same office, and you would have no chance at all. Listen to me. Send twenty taels quietly to Uncle Wu. Consider it as money you might have had to spend at Yanzhou. I understand that Ximen's people are not going on with the business, and all we have to do is to get the document and go and see Chang. You must scrape together two hundred taels and take some food to offer to the dead. Give them the two hundred taels and ask them to make a new arrangement with regard to the rest, telling them that you will pay the balance by degrees as your business progresses. That seems to me to be the best thing you can do and you will save your face at the same time."

"You are right, Brother," Huang the Fourth said. "Brother Li, you were in too much of a hurry."

That evening, Huang the Fourth and Ying Bojue went to see Uncle Wu, taking with them twenty taels of silver. They told him they wanted the document and asked his help. Uncle Wu knew that Yueniang did not propose to go any further in the matter, and, when he saw the silver before him, he promised to help them, and accepted it. Next day, Li the Third and Huang the Fourth came to Ximen's house with two hundred taels of silver and an offering of food. Uncle Wu told Yueniang. The old contract was torn up and a new one made in which it was stated that they owed four hundred taels, which they were to pay in installments. Yueniang forgave them the remaining fifty. The document was given to Ying Bojue and he went with Li the Third and Huang the Fourth to make a bargain with Chang.

CHAPTER 80

Li Jiao'er Goes Back to the Bawdy House

Like a woman in wine she swayed
And thought of the joys of past days.
The memory of them was beyond endurance.
There was silence in the high buildings
The Spring rain was falling.
At midnight, through the distant window, a dim light flickered.
She leaned against the pillar, and the breeze blew softly
She wandered through the passages, and her thoughts were troubled.
Through the window she could hear the sound of the snuffers,
But, when she beat upon the railing, no answer came.

On the seventh day after Ximen Qing's death, sixteen Buddhist monks came to hold a service. Ying Bojue brought together Xie Xida, Hua Tzū-yu, Zhu Shinian, Sun Tianhua, Chang Zhijie, and Bai Laiguang, and they all sat down. Bojue said to them: "His Lordship is dead, and this is his first week's mind. We were his friends. He gave us food, money, things for our use, and now and again he lent us money. Now he is dead, and it is impossible for us to ignore the fact. If we throw a little dust, it will get into people's eyes. If we do nothing, he will certainly want to know why, when we come to meet him before the face of the god of Hell. I suggest that we all contribute one *qian* of silver. There are seven of us and that will make seven *qian*. With that, we can buy presents and a scroll and get Master Shui to write something appropriate upon it. Then we will go and make our offering to the dead and, in return, we shall get a mourning handkerchief that will cost them at least seven *fen*. What do you think?"

"It is an excellent idea, Brother," they all agreed. They gave their money to Ying Bojue to buy the things that had been agreed upon and left it to him to make the necessary arrangements. Shui was quite well aware that Ying Bojue had been one of Ximen's companions in evil doing, and the panegyric he composed was full of satire. In due course Bojue and the rest brought their presents and set them out before the body. Chen Jingji, in mourning robes, received them. Bojue, as the leader, was the first to offer incense, and the others followed him. As none of them knew how to read, they had no idea what the panegyric said. So, when they made the offering of wine, they produced it and handed it over to someone else to read.

In the first year of the reign of Chonghe [it said], being the year *Wuxu,* in the second month, *Wuzi,* and the third day, *Gengyin,* we, Ying Bojue, Xie Xida, Hua Ziyu, Zhu Shinian, Sun Tianhua, Chang Zhijie, and Bai Laiguang reverently lay our offering of wine and food before the coffin of his Lordship Ximen, officer of the Royal Guard, and say:

He who is dead was a man of unimpeachable honor all his days. He never sacrificed the weak, nor did he surrender to the strong. He was a man of firmness and determination. He gave water to those who thirsted and distributed the essence of his glorious being to those in need of it. His chests and boxes were mighty: his appearance was elevated and proud. Whenever he came upon pleasant things, he rose to meet them; and when he came upon things that were dark, he withdrew. He lived in the company of silken trousers, and stored his wealth in the treasury of the loins. He had eight horns and needed not to scratch or dig; and when he came upon a flea or a louse, the itching was more than he could stand.

Now we humble fellows received many kindnesses at his hands. We were forever going with him to the chamber under the loins; we slept with him among the willows, and joyed with him among the flowers. We hoped that he might long lift his crest and fight valiantly. How could we foretell that he would suffer from this fatal sickness? Now his limbs are outstretched and he is gone; we are left behind trembling like doves upon our feet. We have no place to go; the camp of mist and flowers seems remote from us. No longer can we draw near to the red walls of the bawdy house. No longer can we go to battle with the tender jade. We cannot go hand in hand to warm and fragrant places. For him our heads are bent and our limbs weakened; he has made us lonely beyond all power to tell.

Now we have come to offer wine as milk and food. His spirit knows what we do, so we invite it to come here and partake of these our offerings.

After this, Chen Jingji came and made a reverence to express his thanks. Then he took them to the temporary building and entertained them to a substantial meal.

This day, the old procuress Li heard of Ximen's death and sent Li Guijie and Li Guiqing with offerings to lay before his body. Wu Yueniang could not come out, and they were entertained by Li Jiao'er and Meng Yulou.

"Mother says," the two girls told Li Jiao'er, "that now his Lordship is dead there is no sense in your staying here any longer. You are one of us. The proverb says: However large the arbor, no party can last forever. Mother says: Give your things to Li Ming and don't be silly about it. Yang-zhou is a pleasant place, but one can't live there forever. Sooner or later, you will have to leave here." Li Jiao'er considered the matter.

The same day, Han Daoguo's wife, Wang Liu'er, came to burn some paper offerings for Ximen Qing. She was dressed in mourning. She set the things upon the table and stood waiting for a long time, but nobody came to greet her. The fact was that Wang Jing had already been dismissed, and the boys were all unwilling to tell their mistress that Wang Liu'er had come. Only Laian did not know this, and he went to Yueniang's room and said: "Aunt Han has come to burn paper offerings for my father. She has been standing there a long time, and Uncle Wu said I was to come and tell you."

Yueniang was still very angry with Wang Liu'er. She said to the boy: "Go away, slave! What do you mean by talking to me about Aunt Cunt or Aunt Devil? She is a husband-stealing whore, one of those creatures who bring families to destruction. She separates father from son, husband from wife, and then has the audacity to come here and offer her cuntish paper offerings!"

Laian did not know what to do. He went back to Uncle Wu, who asked him if he had spoken to the ladies. Laian made a face, and waited for a moment before he replied. Then he said: "All I got from the Great Lady was curses." Then Uncle Wu himself went to see his sister.

"What is this?" he said. "You ought not to use such language. It has always been conceded that though a man may himself be bad, the ceremonies he performs are none the worse for that. This woman's husband has a lot of your money and, if you behave like this to her, your good name will suffer. You must not do it. If you don't feel like going out to her yourself, tell the Second Lady or the Third to entertain her. Why make such a fuss about it? It may make people think very badly of you."

Wu Yueniang said nothing, but sometime later Meng Yulou went out to receive Wang Liu'er. They sat down and drank tea, but Wang Liu'er realized what was intended, and went away as soon as she could.

Guijie, Guiqing, and Wu Yin'er were in the upper room while Yue-niang was calling Han Daoguo's wife every possible kind of whore, and they thought it likely that her remarks might be intended to apply to them also. Before sunset the two sisters prepared to go home, but Yueniang said: "There will be many people here tonight. Stay and watch the puppet plays and go home tomorrow."

Guijie and Wu Yin'er decided to stay, but Guiqing went home. In the evening, when the monks had done, more than twenty of Ximen's relatives and friends assembled. The puppet players came, and, while the party was proceeding in the temporary building, they played *How a Dog Was Killed to Teach a Lesson to the Husband*. The ladies sat in the hall in which the coffin lay. The lattice was drawn across, and their tables were placed near the screen.

Li Ming and Wu Hui were there, and did not go away that night. The guests, when they arrived, first made an offering to the dead. Then they sat around the tables, and candles were brought. It was the third night watch before the play was finished.

After Ximen Qing's death, Chen Jingji joked and trifled with Pan Jinlian every day. Sometimes, even before the coffin, they exchanged meaningful glances. Sometimes they made merry behind the screen. Now, when the guests were going away, and the ladies withdrawing to the inner court, Jinlian came close to Jingji and pinched him. "My son," she said, "tonight your mother will give you what you want. Your wife is here, so you must come to my place."

Jingji was delighted. He went to open the gate, and Jinlian ran through the darkness to her room. They did not utter a word, but undressed and lay down on the bed. Jingji did everything to her perfect satisfaction.

> For two years they had known each other
> And now today they come together
> And their eager love is satisfied at last.
> She gently moves her slender hips
> He hastens to extend the precious scepter.
> Then, ears pressed close to listen, they speak their love
> Pledging their troth eternally upon the pillow.
> She lets the butterfly possess her
> Most exquisitely giving proof of her delight.
> The rain is furious, the clouds submissive.
> She plays a thousand, nay ten thousand, loving tricks.
> "Darling," he whispers once and once again,
> "My own heart," she answers, with a warm embrace.
> The willow now puts forth new foliage
> And the blossom retains its brilliant redness.

When they had done, Jinlian was afraid someone might come, and hurried again to the inner court. Next morning, the young man came very early to her room. She was still in bed and he peeped through the window. The red bedclothes covered her like a crimson cloud, and her cheeks were like jade.

"Oh, what a splendid housekeeper you are," he cried. "Not out of bed yet! And today our kinsman Qiao is coming to make his reverence to the dead, and the Great Lady says we are to get rid of the food that Li the Third and Huang the Fourth offered yesterday. Get up and let me have the key."

Jinlian told Chunmei to go and open the door upstairs; she put her lips to the window and the young man kissed her.

> They hate to hear the cuckoo through the lattice of pearl
> For their hearts are sewn together as by a needle
> And their love bound as things are bound by glue.
> He looks upon her smiling face
> Its dimples rival the dainty eyebrows.
> How delicate those tender fingers.
> The ornaments of jade release their hold
> And the dark hair falls tumbling.
> The languid air gives place to passion
> And the paleness changes to a rosy flush.
> He touches her sweet lips
> And the fragrance of them stays upon his own.
> Even the memory of that touch
> Brings sweetness to his mouth.

Chunmei opened the door and Jingji went to the outer court to watch the table being properly cleared. Then the food came from Qiao. Both Qiao himself and his wife offered it to the dead man. The two uncles Wu and Clerk Gan took the guests to the temporary building and there entertained them. Li Ming and Wu Hui played and sang.

This day, Zheng Aiyue came to make her offering. Yueniang asked Yulou to give the girl a mourning dress. Then she went to join the ladies. When she saw Guijie and Wu Yin'er already there, she said: "Why didn't you tell me? If I had known, I should have been here before. A nice pair you are, not to say a word to me about it!"

When she found that Yueniang had a baby, she said: "Now, mother, you have both joy and pain together. It is indeed sad that my father should die so young, but at least you now have a son to support you, and you need not worry any more."

Yueniang gave the girls mourning, and kept them until the evening.

The next day was the third of the second month, the second week's mind for Ximen Qing. Sixteen monks came from the Temple of the Jade King. Captain He invited the two eunuchs, Liu and Xue, Major Zhou, General Jing, Captain Zhang, Yun Lishou, and other military officers, to go with him and offer food and a panegyric to their dead colleague. There was nobody to stop them and, dressed up like a lot of monkeys, they burned incense and kowtowed. Chen Jingji made a reverence to them in return. They were entertained and then went away.

Yueniang knew only too well that, of all the people who knew Ximen Qing, officers, friends, and servants alike, there were very few who were not seeking their own ends. She could trust none of them. But she believed Shutong to be honest and reliable, and appointed him to attend upon Li Jiao'er, giving him the keys of the Sixth Lady's rooms.

> The water flows peacefully below the Xiang Wang Tai.
> From the same love there spring two kinds of sadness.
> The moon knows not the changes of mortal life
> And in the depth of night
> Still casts her beams upon the whitewashed walls.

Li Ming pretended to be helping Ximen's people, but secretly told Li Jiao'er to give him the things she was going to take away with her. He stayed for two or three days and did not go home. Yueniang knew nothing of this. The others were unwilling to mention the matter to her, for Li Jiao'er had not been guiltless in her dealings with the younger of Yueniang's brothers.

The ninth day of the month was the third week's mind, and again there was a religious service. There was none for the fourth week. On the sixteenth, Chen Jingji went to attend the digging of the grave. On the thirtieth, Ximen Qing was buried. There were many paper offerings, and a good number of people attended, but it was not such a magnificent occasion as when Li Ping'er was taken out to be buried. The Abbot of the Temple of Eternal Felicity officiated. He sat in a sedan chair and recited the scriptures in a loud voice. Then Chen Jingji broke a paper bowl and the coffin was taken out. The members of the household set up a wailing, and Yueniang, in her sedan chair, followed close behind the coffin. Then came the chairs of the other ladies. The body was taken straight outside the city and buried. Chen Jingji offered a roll of silk to Yun Lishou and asked him to complete the tablet. Xu, the Master of the Yin Yang, directed the funeral. It was sad to see how few people made offerings at the graveside. Uncle Wu, Qiao, Captain He, Uncle Shen and Uncle Han were the only ones to do so, except for Ximen's clerks. Abbot Wu left twelve young monks to perform the ceremony of the return; the tablet was set up in the upper room, and Master Xu purified the house. Then the relatives and friends went away.

Every day Yueniang and the others, dressed in their mourning, made offerings before the tablet. After the first visit to the grave, the soldiers went back to the office. For the fifth week's mind, Yueniang sent for the nuns Xue and Wang, and the Abbess and twelve nuns came to speed Ximen Qing on his way to paradise.

While the funeral party was being held, Guiqing and Guijie secretly said to Li Jiao'er: "Mother says you have nothing much of great value, and there is no reason why you should remain any longer in Ximen's house. Think what it means. You have no child, and there is no sense in staying on as a widow. Mother thinks the easiest plan is to start a quarrel and just break with them. Yesterday, Ying Bojue came and said that Zhang who lives in the High Street was minded to spend five hundred taels on getting you for his second wife. He will give you control of his household. Mother thinks you would do well there. There is no point in staying at Ximen's house all your life. We who come from the bawdy house have always to work on the principle. Welcome the new and give up the old. We must make up to those who are rich and powerful: we can't afford to waste our time."

After Ximen Qing's fifth week's mind, Li Jiao'er remembered this. She did not bother about the household but let things go as they would.

"The other day," Pan Jinlian said to Sun Xue'e, "I saw Li Jiao'er talking to Uncle Wu the Second in the small room at our family grave."

Chunmei saw her handing Li Ming a parcel behind the screen in the great hall. He tucked it away underneath his clothes and went off with it.

Yueniang was told of these things. She scolded Uncle Wu the Second, and would not let him have any more to do with the shop. She told Ping'an that Li Ming was not to be allowed to enter the house again. Li Jiao'er was first ashamed and then angry. She had been waiting for an opportunity to make trouble, and now she had it.

One day, when Yueniang was having tea with Aunt Wu, she asked Yulou to join them, but did not ask Li Jiao'er. This made the woman very angry. She shouted at Yueniang and thumped the table upon which Ximen's tablet rested. At the third night watch, she said she was going to hang herself. Her maid went to tell Yueniang, who was very much upset. She consulted her brother, and they sent for old woman Li and told her to take Li Jiao'er away. The old woman feared that Yueniang would not allow her to take her clothes and ornaments.

"My girl has been here and suffered from ill usage and backbiting, and you are not going to get rid of her so easily. She must have some money to wash away her shame."

Uncle Wu, in view of his official standing, would not say anything either way, and, after much haggling, Yueniang let Li Jiao'er go with clothes, ornaments, boxes, bed, and furniture. She would not let the two maids go, though Li Jiao'er tried to insist.

"No," she said, "certainly not. If you do take them, I shall bring an accusation against you for procuring young maids to be whores."

This frightened the old procuress. She said no more, but smiled and thanked Yueniang. Li Jiao'er got into a sedan chair and was carried to her old home.

Readers, singing girls make their living by selling their charms. With them it is purely a business. In the morning, they receive Chang the dissolute, and in the evening Li the ne'er-do-well. At the front door they welcome the father, and by the back door they let in the son. They forget their old clients and love the new. It is their nature to keep their eyes open when there is any money about. Even if a man loves them with his whole heart and does everything in his power to make them true, their hearts can never be secured. They steal the very food from a man's mouth, and as soon as he is dead, they quarrel and go away, back to their old business.

> I laugh at the flowers of the mist
> Which no one can keep for long.
> Every night they find a new bridegroom.
> Their jade-like arms are the pillow for a thousand men
> Their ruby lips are enjoyed by ten thousand guests.
> Their seductions are many
> And their hearts are false.
> You may devise a host of schemes to hold them
> But you can never keep them
> From longing for their old haunts.

When Li Jiao'er had gone, Yueniang sobbed aloud and the other ladies tried to console her. "Sister," Jinlian said, "don't let it upset you so much. The proverb says that when a man marries a whore, it is like trying to keep a seagull away from the water. When it cannot get to the water, it still thinks about the eastern ocean. All this was his fault."

While they were busied over this, Ping'an came and announced that his Excellency Cai, the Salt Commissioner, had come. "He is in the great hall," the boy said. "I told him that master had died. He asked when, and I said on the twenty-first day of the first month, and that we were now in the fifth week after his death. He asked me if the tablet had been set up, and I told him it was in the inner court. He wishes to pay reverence to it."

"Go and tell your brother-in-law to see him," Yueniang said.

Jingji put on mourning clothes and went to receive Cai. After a while, the inner court was made ready and Cai was invited to go there. He kowtowed before the tablet. Yueniang in return made reverence to him. He did not speak to her, except to invite her to retire. Then he said to Jingji: "Your father was very kind to me, and today, on my way to the Eastern Capital, I stayed especially to thank him. I never dreamed that I should find him dead. What was the cause of his death?"

"Inflammation of the lungs," Jingji told him.

"How very sad!" said Commissioner Cai.

He called his servants, and they brought him two rolls of Hangzhou silk, a pair of woolen socks, four fish, and four jars of preserved food. "These trifles," he said, "I offer to him who is dead." Then he gave Jingji fifty taels of silver. "Your father," he said, "was good enough to lend me this, and now that I have been paid myself, I return the money to set the seal upon our friendship." He asked Ping'an to take the money.

"Your Excellency is over-conscientious," Jingji said.

Yueniang told him to take Cai to the outer court, but the Commissioner said that he could not stay and would only drink a cup of tea. The servant brought the tea, and Cai went away.

Yueniang was half pleased, half sad when she received these fifty taels of silver. She reflected that if Ximen Qing had been alive he would never have allowed such a nobleman to go away without staying for something to eat. He would have remained, she thought, and enjoyed the pleasures of the table for many an hour. Now, he had stood up and gone. Though she still was rich, there was no man to entertain such guests.

When Ying Bojue heard that Li Jiao'er had gone back to the bawdy house, he went to tell Zhang the Second. Zhang took five taels of silver and went to spend the night with her. He was one year younger than Ximen Qing. His animal was the Hare, and he was thirty-two. Li Jiao'er was thirty-four, but the old procuress told him she was twenty-eight and warned Ying Bojue not to let him know the truth. So Zhang the Second paid three hundred taels and took Li Jiao'er for his second wife.

Zhu Shinian and Sun Guazui took Wang the Third to Li Guijie's house, and he attached himself to her again.

Then Ying Bojue, Li the Third, and Huang the Fourth borrowed five thousand taels from Eunuch Xu, and another five thousand from Zhang the Second, and began the business of purchasing antiquities for the authorities. Every day they went riding about on magnificent horses and calling at one bawdy house after another.

Zhang the Second, now that Ximen Qing was dead, spent five thousand taels in bribing Zheng, one of the royal family in the Eastern Capital, so as to secure the appointment that Ximen Qing had held. He did much work upon his garden and rebuilt his house, and Bojue was there nearly every day. Bojue told him everything he knew about Ximen's household.

"His Fifth Lady," he said, "is as beautiful as a painting. She knows poems, songs, literature, philosophy, games, backgammon and chess. She can write very beautifully and play the lute exquisitely. She is not more than thirty years old and much more charming than any singing girl."

Zhang the Second was greatly impressed and wondered what he could do to get her for himself.

"Is that the woman who was once the wife of Wu Da the cake seller?" he asked.

"Yes," Bojue said. "She has been in Ximen's household for five or six years. I don't know whether she would be inclined to consider another marriage."

"Please find out for me," Zhang the Second said. "If she has any such idea, let me know at once, and I will marry her."

"I have a man still in that household," Ying Bojue said. "His name is Laijue. I will tell him. And if he can do anything in the matter, I will certainly let you know. It would be much better for you to marry her than some singing girl. When Ximen Qing married her, he had considerable trouble, but things are never the same twice, and what will happen on this occasion, I cannot say. But anyone who gets hold of a beauty like this will be a lucky fellow. You are a man of position, and you certainly ought to have someone like her to enhance its splendor. Otherwise, all your wealth is wasted. I will tell Laijue to find out what he can for us. If there is the slightest whisper of the word marriage, I will see what my sweet words and honeyed phrases can do to inflame that amorous heart. It may cost you a few hundred taels, but it will be worth it."

Readers, all those who live upon others are men who seek for power and money. In their time, Ximen Qing and Ying Bojue had been like blood brothers. They might have been glued together, so close was their affection. Day after day, Bojue took his meals with Ximen, and was given clothes. Now, when his friend had only just died, almost before his body was cold, Bojue was planning to bring disgrace upon him. With friends, it is only too possible to know the face and to know nothing about the heart, just as an artist may paint the outside of a tiger, but must leave the bones unseen.

CHAPTER 81
Han Daoguo Defrauds Wu Yueniang

Han Daoguo and Laibao had taken four thousand taels of Ximen Qing's money and gone south of the river to buy goods. When they came to Yangzhou, they went at once to see Miao Qing, proposing to stay with him. Miao Qing remembered how Ximen had saved his life, and treated the two men with very great kindness. He bought a girl called Chuyun and took her to his house, intending to make a present of her to Ximen Qing in return for the favors he had received from him.

Han Daoguo and Laibao neglected their business and amused themselves with the young ladies of the town. But when winter came, they grew homesick and got busy buying silk and cloth, which they brought back to Miao Qing's place, proposing to start home again when they had bought enough.

Han Daoguo grew very attached to a girl called Wang Yuzhi, who lived at an old established bawdy house of Yangzhou, and Laibao to Xiaohong, the younger sister of a girl called Lin Caihong. One day, they asked Miao Qing and a salt merchant named Wang Haifeng, to go for a day's amusement on the Baoying lake. When they came back, they went to the bawdy house. It happened to be the birthday of Wang Yuzhi's mother, and Han Daoguo decided to invite a number of other men and have a party to celebrate the occasion. So he sent his boy Hu Xiu to ask two merchants, Wang Dongqiao and Qian Qingchuan, but before the boy himself came back, the two merchants arrived with Wang Haifeng. It was nearly sunset when the boy came.

"What has made you so late?" Han Daoguo, who had had a good deal of wine, said to him. "Where have you been drinking? I can smell the wine in your breath. My guests have been here some time already: they came long before you showed any signs of turning up. I will deal with you tomorrow."

Hu Xiu looked at Han Daoguo out of the corners of his eyes and went out. "It's all very well for you to scold me," he muttered, "when your own wife is in bed with another man. Here you are enjoying yourself, while in your house at home, your master is enjoying your wife. He only sent you here because he wanted her. You are happy here and you never think of the burden she has to bear."

The old procuress heard this and dragged the boy to the courtyard. "Master Hu," she said, "you are drunk. Go and sleep." But Hu Xiu shouted and struggled and would not go. Han Daoguo, who was entertaining his friends, heard the noise, and it made him very angry. He came out and kicked the boy.

"You slave," he cried, "I can hire anybody to take your place for five *fen* of silver a day. I don't need to keep you. Get out of here!"

Hu Xiu would not go. "You would dare to send me away, would you?" he shouted. "Have you found anything wrong in the way I've handled the money? Here you are, spending money on women, and you dare to drive me away. You will see whether I tell our master or not."

Laibao came out and took Han Daoguo away. Then he came back and said to Hu Xiu: "You rascal, this is just drunken brawling."

"Uncle," said Hu Xiu, "don't you meddle in this. I am not drunk, but I'll show him what I think of him."

Laibao hustled him into the house and made him lie down and go to sleep. Han Daoguo was very anxious that his friends should not lose their respect for him. He and Laibao entertained them; the three singing girls sang and danced for them, and they played all kinds of games. At the third night watch, the party broke up.

The next day, Han Daoguo would have punished Hu Xiu, but the boy swore he did not remember a word of what he had said, and Miao Qing intervened on his behalf. In due course, they finished their purchases. The goods were packed up and loaded upon the boat. But Chuyun, whom Miao Qing had bought to present to Ximen Qing, suddenly fell ill and could not go with them. "When she is better," Miao Qing said, "I will send her to your master."

He wrote a letter and prepared some presents, then saw the two men and Hu Xiu start back to Qinghe. The three singing girls also went to see them off.

It was the tenth day of the first month when they left Yangzhou. One day, they came to Linjiang lock. Han Daoguo was standing in the bows of the boat, when he saw his neighbor Yan the Fourth on a boat coming towards them. This Yan was coming to meet some official, and when he saw Han Daoguo, he bowed and shouted: "Han, your master died in the first month." The two boats passed so quickly that there was no chance for any further conversation. Han did not say a word to Laibao.

This was a very dry year in Henan and Shandong. There were no crops on the land; the cotton was a failure, and the fields were bare. The price of material went up and every roll of cloth fetched three-tenths more than its regular price. Merchants took their money with them and set out to buy goods even many miles away.

"We have four thousand taels' worth of goods," Han Daoguo said to Laibao. "Here we can get three-tenths more than the regular price and I think we should do well to sell half of what we have. We shall have less duty to pay and I don't believe we are at all likely to do any better at home. It would be a pity to let this opportunity slip."

"You are quite right," Laibao said, "but our master may be annoyed when we get home."

"If he is," Han Daoguo said, "I will take the blame."

Laibao said no more, and they sold a thousand taels' worth of cloth in that place.

"You and Hu Xiu stay here until the duty is paid," Han Daoguo said then, "and I will take the boy Wang Han, together with the thousand taels we have just got, overland to our master."

"When you get there," Laibao said, "ask him for a letter to Officer Qian so that we have not to pay so much duty and can get our boats through before the others."

Han Daoguo promised, and he and the boy packed some of their things, loaded them upon a mule, and started overland for Qinghe. At last, they reached the southern gate of the city about sunset and met Ximen's grave keeper, Zhang An, pushing a wheelbarrow in which were rice, wine, and boxes of food. He was taking them outside the city.

"What! Are you back, Uncle Han?" the grave keeper cried, when he saw Han Daoguo.

Han noted that the man was wearing mourning and asked the reason.

"Our master is dead," Zhang An said, "and tomorrow, the ninth day of the third month, will be his last week's mind. The Great Lady has sent me with these things to the grave because they are coming tomorrow to burn paper offerings for him."

"What a terrible business! What a terrible business!" Han Daoguo said.

He found, as he went home down the street, that everybody was talking about Ximen Qing's death. When he came to the crossroads, he thought for a while. "If I go to Ximen's place," he said to himself, "he is dead. Besides, it is very late and I had better go home and see what my wife has to say. It won't be too late if I go to my master's place tomorrow." So he and Wang Han drove the mules to Lion Street to his own house. When they reached there, they dismounted, knocked until the door was opened, then dismissed the porters, and Wang Han carried in the luggage. Han's wife welcomed him. He made reverence to the family god, then Wang Liu'er helped him to take off his outer clothes, and the maid brought tea. He told his wife all about his journey.

"I met Brother Yan and Zhang An," he said, "and so learned of our master's death. What did he die of? He was quite well when I went away."

"Heaven sends unexpected weather," Wang Liu'er said, "and human beings have many changes of fortune. Nobody dare prophesy about his own end."

Han Daoguo opened his luggage and brought out clothes and silk. He took out the thousand taels, one packet after another, and put them on the bed. His wife opened them and saw the shining silver.

"What is this?" she said.

"As soon as I heard of our master's death, I sold part of the merchandise for a thousand taels," Han Daoguo told her. He put down another hundred taels of his own.

"When I was away," he continued, "did he come to see how you were getting on?"

"Everything was all right so long as he was alive," the woman said. "Do you intend to give them all that silver?"

"I was going to see what you thought about it. I think if I gave them half, that would be quite enough."

"You silly fellow," Wang Liu'er said, "don't be such a fool. The master is dead now and we have really no more obligation to them. If you give them half, you may get into trouble because they may want to know where the rest is. Let us make up our minds, take the thousand taels, hire a mule or two, and go to the Eastern Capital. We will go to our daughter's place, and I don't imagine our own kinsfolk will turn us away."

"But we can't dispose of this house in such a short time," Han Daoguo said.

"What's to prevent us sending for your brother, you silly fellow?" Wang Liu'er said. "We can leave a few taels with him and he can look after the house. That's quite simple. If anybody from Ximen's family makes inquiries, they can be told we have gone to the Eastern Capital because our daughter was anxious to see us. We have no cause to be afraid."

"But I owe a great deal to my master's kindness," Han Daoguo said. "I don't like the idea of turning around on him and acting so deceitfully."

"If you are going to think about principles, you will starve," Wang Liu'er said. "He amused himself with your wife, and now you take his money. So you are quits. The other day, I bought presents and paper offerings and went to offer my sympathy. That whore, his first wife, kept me waiting for hours and insulted me most disagreeably. I did not know what to do with myself. At last, the Third Lady came out and sat down with me, but I came home as soon as I could. If that counts for anything, you certainly ought to take this money."

Han Daoguo said no more. They made their decision that very night. Before it was light, they sent for Han the Second, gave him twenty taels of silver to carry on with, and gave the house into his charge. Han the Second was quite agreeable. He told them to go their way and he would see after everything. So Han Daoguo and his wife, with the boy Wang Han and the two maids, set off for the Eastern Capital. They hired two large carts to carry their trunks and boxes, and left the city at daybreak.

That day, Wu Yueniang with her little son, Meng Yulou, Pan Jinlian, Ximen Dajie, and Ruyi'er, went with Chen Jingji to burn paper offerings at Ximen Qing's grave. While they were there, Zhang An told Yueniang that he had met Han Daoguo the night before.

"If he is back," Yueniang said, "why hasn't he been to see me? Perhaps he will come during the day."

She burned the paper offerings but did not stay very long at the grave. When she got home, she told Chen Jingji to go and see Han Daoguo and find out where the boats were. Jingji went and knocked at the door, but for a long time no one answered. At last Han the Second opened the door.

"My brother and his wife," he said, "have gone to the Eastern Capital to see their daughter. I know nothing at all about the boats."

Jingji went back and told Yueniang. She was greatly worried and told Chen Jingji to take a horse and go to the river to find out whether the boats had arrived. As soon as he came to the wharf, Jingji found Laibao and the boat there.

"Brother Han has already taken a thousand taels to you," Laibao said.

"We haven't seen anything of him," Jingji said. "Zhang An, the grave keeper, saw him and, when we went to the grave, we heard he had come back. The Great Lady sent me to his house, but they had taken all their belongings and gone to the Eastern Capital with the silver. Father is dead, and this is his last week's mind. The Great Lady was worried and sent me to see if the boats had arrived."

Laibao said nothing. He thought: "The fellow deceived me. Now I see why he suggested selling a thousand taels' worth of goods. He made up his mind that very moment. Really, even though men meet face to face, their minds might be a thousand miles apart."

So Laibao heard of his master's death. He decided to take Chen Jingji to the wine house and the bawdy house. Secretly, he removed eight hundred taels' worth of merchandise, sealed it up, and stored it at an inn. Then they went to the customs office, paid the duty, and their boat was allowed to proceed. They loaded their merchandise upon carts and so brought it to the city. The stuff was stored in one of the rooms in the eastern wing of Ximen's house.

After Ximen's death, the shop in Lion Street had been closed. Clerk Gan and Cui Ben got rid of all the goods in the other silk shop, paid over the money fairly, then gave up their jobs and went home. The house was sold. The medicine shop was still kept open, and Chen Jingji and Clerk Fu looked after it.

Laibao's wife had a son called Sengbao, now five years old. Han Daoguo's wife had a niece who was four years old. Their parents had arranged that these two children should some day marry. Yueniang did not know this.

When Laibao handed over the merchandise, he put all the blame on Han Daoguo. "He sold two thousand taels' worth of goods," he told Yueniang. She repeatedly urged him to go to the Eastern Capital to get the money out of Han Daoguo.

"It is better for me to keep away," Laibao said. "Their kinsman is a member of the Imperial Tutor's household, and nobody dare touch them. If I were to go, it would look as though I wished to make trouble. We have every reason to be satisfied that they don't come to us for something, and we must not stir up trouble."

"But it was my husband who arranged this marriage for Zhai," Yueniang said. "Surely he would remember that."

"Han's daughter is a favorite there," Laibao said, "and she would certainly take her parents' side. She will do nothing to help us. The best thing you can do is to keep quiet about the matter. Regard it as a dead loss, and say no more about it."

Yueniang could not think of anything else to say, so she said no more. She told him to try to find some customers to buy the merchandise he had brought. A number of people came, and Yueniang told Chen Jingji to deal with them. There was a long discussion, and in the end, they all said they did not want the stuff and took their money away.

"Your son-in-law is not sufficiently experienced," Laibao said to Yueniang. "I have been doing this sort of thing for years, and I know all there is to know about it. In business, the principle is: sell first and be sorry later. Don't let us be sorry first, and sell afterwards. The stuff is here, and if we can do even moderately well out of it, we ought to be content. If the price is set too high, so that customers won't make a deal, that is not good business. You must forgive me, but you are young and don't understand business. Don't think for a moment that I am ready to yield the advantage to others. I'm not; I simply want to sell the stuff and get it out of the way."

After this, Chen Jingji did no more in the matter. Laibao did not wait for Yueniang's instructions, but took over the abacus and brought the customers back again. They measured out two thousand taels, Jingji counted it, it was given to Yueniang, and they went off with the goods.

Yueniang offered Laibao twenty-three taels, but he put on an air of great dignity and refused to take it. "No, Lady," he said, "my master is dead, and your property is like stagnant water. Don't give me the money. You need it; I do not."

One evening, Laibao came in, very drunk. He went to Yueniang's room and put his hand on the bed. "Lady," he said, "you are very young. Your husband is dead, and you have only the baby. Don't you ever feel lonely?" Yueniang did not answer.

A letter came from Zhai at the Eastern Capital. It said that he had heard of Ximen Qing's death, and that Han Daoguo had told him there were still some very beautiful girls in the household. He would like to know the price put upon them, said that he would pay it, and asked for the girls to be sent to the Eastern Capital to amuse the old lady. Yueniang did not know what to do. She sent for Laibao. This time the man did not even address her as Lady. "Woman," he said, "if you do not send the girls, there will be serious trouble. It is all the fault of the dead old man. He was always trying to show off. Whenever he invited anyone here, he always had his own musicians. Everybody knew it. Now Han's daughter is at the palace; it is quite natural that she should tell the old lady. Now, perhaps, you realize the truth of what I was saying the other day. Here they are coming to ask us for something. If you don't do what he says, he will get someone from the local office to come and demand the girls. Then it will be too late, even if you give them up. I don't suggest you should send them all; a couple will probably satisfy him."

Yueniang wondered. She could not well spare Lanxiang, who was the Third Lady's maid, or Chunmei, who waited on the Fifth Lady. She wanted Xiuchun to look after the baby. She asked her own maid, Yuxiao, and Yingchun if they would go, and they both agreed. Then Yueniang told Laibao to hire suitable conveyances and take the two girls to the Eastern Capital. This he did and, on the way, enjoyed them both.

They reached the Capital, and Laibao went to see Han Daoguo and his wife. They talked over what had happened.

"If you hadn't prevented them," Han Daoguo said, "something disagreeable might have happened. Of course, I'm not in the least afraid of them."

Zhai was delighted with the two girls, both of whom were very beautiful. One could play the zither and the other the banjo. Neither was more than eighteen years old. He took them to the palace to wait upon the old lady, and she gave two bars of silver for them. Laibao took the silver home, but he only gave one of the bars to Yueniang. He tried to frighten her by saying: "If I hadn't gone, you would never have had this silver. The Hans are very rich and comfortable there. They have a house all to themselves and a host of maids and servants to wait on them. Master Zhai calls them Father and Mother. Their daughter goes to the palace to see the old lady every day. They are on such good terms that she is always going about with the old lady. When she asks for one thing, they give her ten. She chooses the kinds of food she likes best and clothes in the latest style. She has learned how to write and do sums. When luck is on one's side, cleverness always follows. She is tall and very pretty. When I saw her the other day, she was just as beautiful to look at as a tree of jade, and so charming and pleasant. She called me Uncle Bao. Those two girls of ours will have to ask her for their needles and thread."

Yueniang thanked him and gave him food and wine. When he refused to take her money, she gave him a roll of silk for his wife to make into clothes.

One day, Laibao and Liu Cang, his wife's brother, went to the river and brought away all the merchandise that had been left at the inn, and sold it for eight hundred taels of silver. Then he secretly bought a house, opened a store near Liu Cang's house, and gave parties to his friends every day. His wife used to tell Yueniang that she was going to see her mother, but really she went to the new house. There, she changed her ornaments, dressed up in pearls and gold and silver, and went to see Wang Liu'er's mother. This old lady was known as Old Sow Wang. They discussed the marriage between the young children. Whenever she went there, she went in a sedan chair and, when she came back, she dressed again in her ordinary clothes and returned to Ximen's house. Yueniang knew nothing of all this.

Laibao himself was always getting drunk and, on several occasions, came to Yueniang's room and made improper overtures to her. If Yueniang had not been a virtuous woman, she would have been caught by his bait and would assuredly have been seduced.

Then some of the other women told Wu Yueniang how Laibao's wife had arranged this marriage for her child, and how she was going about in gold and silver, showing every sign of great wealth. Pan Jinlian also told her several times, but she would not believe a word of it. Laibao's wife heard of this, and made a terrible to-do in the kitchen, abusing high and low alike.

Laibao himself began to swagger. He went about bragging. "You people are all very well at talking in bed, but that's about all you can do. I went on the water and come back with the cash. If it hadn't been for me, Clerk Han would have walked off with all of it. His mouth was as wide open as a pair of the largest pincers. He would have gone off with all of it to the Eastern Capital, and it would have been just as if the whole lot had fallen into the water without so much as a splash. Yet nobody has a kind word for me. You talk about my getting money by robbing my master, and things of that sort. The one who cuts off the leg doesn't know, and the one whose leg is cut off doesn't know either. The proverb says: Don't believe scandalmongers or you will lose your calabash. Don't believe lies, or you will lose your net. Some backbiting women have been saying that we have suddenly got very rich and been fixing up a marriage. Why, she goes and borrows, as any poor priest might do, clothes and ornaments from her sister. People talk about our using our master's money because they want to get us kicked out. But don't worry. If we do leave here, Heaven will give no grass to the waterfowl. I shall wash my eyes and keep an eye on those strumpets who are shut up here."

Yueniang came to hear of this kind of talk and was anxious to find out what it meant. Laibao's wife quarreled with everybody and talked about killing herself. And the man treated her without any respect when he found her by herself. Yueniang was very angry, but she did not know what to do. Finally, she decided to send Laibao and his wife away. Then the man openly carried on business with his brother-in-law, and they did a roaring trade during the shortage of cloth.

CHAPTER 82
Pan Jinlian Makes Love
with Chen Jingji

Now that Pan Jinlian had tasted the joys of love with Chen Jingji, never a day passed that did not witness some new proof of the passion that united them. Sometimes they would stand, close pressed together, and gaze into each other's laughing eyes; sometimes they sat, and so made love, giving each other gentle slaps and pinchings, with occasional ticklings, feeling themselves free of all restraint. If others were present and they could not speak the words they longed to speak, they would write short notes of love, and drop them on the floor, each picking up the other's. One day—it was about the fourth month—Jinlian took a silk handkerchief, and in it wrapped a powder satchel, in which she had placed a lock of hair and some fragrant pine leaves. She intended to give this to Jingji with her own hands, but, finding he was not in his room, she threw it through the window. When the young man returned, it lay there in its paper wrappings, and, when he opened it, he found the satchel and the handkerchief. There was a short poem with the gifts.

> This kerchief of silver silk and this perfume satchel
> Are for you.
> The lock of hair is a memory of our first mating.
> The pine leaves mark my trust
> That you will remember forever.
> I write my love with my tears.
> In the deep night I am alone with my shadow.
> Do not let the night pass in vain,
> But come quickly to the arbor of roses.

To the young man this seemed a clear sign that she wished him to go to the arbor. He took a piece of fancy paper and wrote a poem in reply. Then he went to the garden but found that Wu Yueniang was paying a visit to his loved one. At first, indeed, he did not know this, and when he reached the garden gate called: "Darling, are you there?" Fortunately, only Jinlian heard him and, hurriedly lifting the lattice, she came out and made a warning sign to him with her hands.

"Oh, it is you!" she said. "I suppose you are looking for your wife. She was here a moment ago, but now she has gone to the garden to pick some flowers." The young man silently handed his poem to her, and she put it in her sleeve.

"What did he want?" Yueniang said. Jinlian said he was looking for his wife, and that she had told him he would find her in the garden. So Yueniang was deceived. Soon she went away, and Jinlian took from her sleeve the packet Chen Jingji had given her. It was a golden fan, with green rushes beside a flowing stream painted upon it. Accompanying it was a poem.

> On this white silk are painted dark bamboos
> And green rushes that seem to be alive
> With gold and silver to enhance their brightness.
> Will you not use this, darling, when the day is hot
> Not to bring cooling breezes, but to give you shade?
> When people throng around you, put it in your sleeve
> Let it refresh you when you are alone.
> I could not bear to think
> That vulgar hands might snatch it from your own.

When she had read this poem, Jinlian plied her maids, Chunmei and Qiuju, with wine, and when it grew late, sent them to another room to sleep. Then alone, she opened wide the green windows and lighted long tapering candles. She made ready the bed and perfumed it, then bathed and went out to stand beside the flower pleasance to await a fitting moment.

That night, Ximen's daughter had gone to Yueniang's room to hear the exhortations of Sister Wang, the nun. Only the maid, Yuanxiao, was left with Chen Jingji. He gave her a kerchief and said: "You stay where you are, I am going to play chess with the Fifth Lady. If your mistress should return, come and tell me at once." Then he went to the garden. The flowers in the moonlight cast their shadows, some long, some short. He found his way to the Rose Arbor but, long before he reached it, could see Jinlian, uncovered, standing there, her glorious tresses waving in the gentle breeze. He approached quietly, then suddenly dashed forward and took her in his arms. Jinlian was taken by surprise.

"Oh," she cried, "you young villain, what do you mean by rushing out and frightening me like that? It is a good thing it is I, with whom you know you can do what you like, but would you have dared to do it with anybody else?"

Jingji had taken more wine than usual that evening. "I don't think it would have mattered very much if it had been somebody else," he laughed.

Then, hand in hand, they walked towards her room. It was brightly lighted by the candles on the table, and refreshments lay ready before them. They made fast the corner gate; then sat side by side and began to drink.

"Where is your wife?" Jinlian said.

"She has gone to hear the reading of the sacred texts," Jingji answered. "I told Yuanxiao that she must come and warn me at once if it became necessary. She thinks I have come to play chess with you."

They drank wine together in great content, for, as the proverb says: If the drinking of tea leads to frivolity, wine opens wide the floodgates of passion. As the olive-colored wine coursed through their veins, the ruddy hue of the peach flower mounted to their cheeks. One would seek a kiss; the other would not seem too shy. At last they snuffed out the candles and went to bed.

> When he came in,
> He took me in his arms and carried me
> And set me down upon his knee.
> I spread the silken coverlets, and that gay lover
> Well proved his valiance in the bed.
> He lifted up my feet, yes, lifted up my feet,
> Disordering my hair and putting out of place
> The knot that bound it.

Their passage at arms over, Yuanxiao came and knocked at the door, telling them that Jingji's wife had returned. He dressed hastily and went away.

> The bees that buzz so wildly and the merry butterflies
> We often see
> But, sometimes, they are hidden from our eyes
> When they plunge deep within the pear blossom.

The three rooms on the upper floor of Jinlian's apartments were arranged, with the middle one as the place for family worship, and the others as storerooms for drugs and incense.

One day the Fates decided that something should happen. Jinlian and Chen Jingji were so much in love with one another that nothing could keep them long apart. Every day they met at her place. One morning Jinlian dressed and went upstairs to offer incense before the image of Guanyin. At the same time, Chen Jingji came to take some of the stores. So they met. There was nobody in sight, so Jinlian decided that she had burned incense enough. Instead, she threw her arms around her lover and kissed him, calling him her precious sweetheart, while he called her his own true darling. After a while they said to one another: "There seems to be no one here," took off their clothes, and found a convenient bench. Then they began a merry game. Over his shoulders two small feet were raised and all was going well. But were it not for the unexpected, there would never be any story to tell. Just at the moment when their happiness seemed about to reach its height, Chunmei came with a box to get some tea. The couple were disturbed, but it was too late for them to do anything. Chunmei discreetly but hastily withdrew. Jingji put on his clothes again, and Jinlian did likewise. It was she who took the situation in hand.

"Chunmei, my dear girl," she called, "come here a moment. I have something to say to you."

Chunmei came back. "My dear good sister," Jinlian said, "this gentleman, as you know, is not a stranger. I must tell you the plain truth. We are lovers, and we cannot do without each other. You must keep this to yourself and not breathe a word to a soul."

"Mother," Chunmei said, "why need you say that? I have served you all these years. Do you think I do not know you well enough? Of course, I shall tell no one."

"If you really mean to keep our secret," Jinlian said, "you must prove it to me. Here is the man, lie with him and I will believe you."

Chunmei flushed till her face was now pale, now red, but she could not refuse. Indeed she made the necessary preparations herself, lay down on the bench and yielded before the young man's impetuosity. So that day, Chen Jingji came into full possession of two priceless pearls. What could he do but thread them?

Afterwards, they went their ways. In the days that followed, the two women often brought the young man there, but they hid the matter from the maid Qiuju.

On the first day of the sixth month, old woman Pan died, and the news was brought to Ximen's household. Wu Yueniang prepared the prescribed offerings for the dead and told Pan Jinlian to take a sedan chair and attend the funeral outside the city. Two days later she came back and went to Yueniang's room, and talked there for a long time. Then she left Yueniang, but when she had passed through the great hall, she felt sorely pressed by Nature, pulled up her skirts and gave herself relief beside the wall. After Ximen Qing's death, few people came to see them, and the gate of honor and the doors that led to the great hall were kept shut. Chen Jingji lived in the rooms in the Eastern wing. He had just got up when suddenly he heard the sound of rushing water. Putting his head quietly out of the window, he saw that Jinlian was responsible for it. "What is this wild beast I see?" he laughed. "Mind you pull your skirts high enough.

They might get wet." Jinlian hastily arranged her clothes and went over to the window.

"What!" she cried. "You still here! You are just getting up, I suppose. A nice life you lead. Is your wife about?"

"Yes," Jingji said. "It was very late when we came back from the Great Lady's rooms last night. I had to go too, for the Great Lady asked me to go and hear the *Hong Luo* Sutra read by the nuns. I stayed so long, I was ready to drop, and this morning I did not feel like getting up."

"What a liar you are, you rogue," Jinlian said. "I was not at home yesterday, but I swear you never went to hear any sutras read. The maids tell me you went to dine with Meng Yulou."

"Nothing of the sort," the young man retorted. "My wife will tell you that I went to see the Lady of the House. I never went near the Third Lady's room."

As he talked, he climbed onto the bed. His weapon was at the ready, and he thrust it through the window.

"Oh, you, who will meet an early end," Jinlian cried, "what do you mean by bringing out that old fellow. You gave me quite a fright. Take it back at once, or I will put a needle through it and hurt you."

Jingji laughed. "You don't seem very fond of him today, but you must be generous and treat him kindly."

"Jailbird!" Jinlian cried. She took a small brass mirror from her sleeve, and set it on the windowsill, pretending to powder her face, but in reality doing something quite different. The young man found her attentions most pleasurable, and they were feeling very pleased with one another when they heard footsteps. Jinlian hurriedly took up her mirror and the young man withdrew. It was Laian.

"Fu would like you to take a meal with him," the boy said.

"I am dressing my hair now," Jingji said." Tell him not to wait. I will be with him in a moment." The boy went away and Jinlian cautiously returned. "Tonight," she said, "don't go out. I want you, and will send Chunmei to give you warning. There is something I wish to say to you." Jingji promised to come and, when he had finished combing his hair, went off to attend to some business at the shop. Jinlian went to her own room.

That night was very dark, and the weather very sultry. Jinlian told Chunmei to heat some water for a bath, and dressed her nails. Then she had a light mattress set upon her bed, drove off the mosquitoes, and pulled down the net. She placed some incense in the small burner.

"Mother," Chunmei said, "do you know that this is the first day of the hottest season of the year? Would you like some 'Touch-me-not' to stain your fingers? If you would, I'll get some for you."

"Where?" Jinlian said.

"There is some in the great courtyard. I will get it for you at once."

"Tell Qiuju to get the pestle and mortar ready to pound some garlic," Jinlian said, adding softly: "Go to the East wing and tell your brother to come. I have something to say to him." Chunmei went out to do her bidding and, while she was away, the woman bathed her fragrant body. At last the maid returned with the flowers and told Qiuju what to do with them. Jinlian gave Chunmei a few cups of wine and told her to sleep that night in the kitchen. Then, by the light of the candles, she stained her delicate fingers, while the maid, at her direction, took a bench into the courtyard, with a mattress and some pillows. It was now the first night watch, and everything was silent as the stars moved slowly across the heavens. On either side of the Milky Way the stars of the Heavenly Lovers took up their station. The fragrance of flowers came over the wall, and a little band of glowworms gave their dainty light. Jinlian threw herself upon the mattress, fanned herself and waited. The maid closed the corner gate, but did not bolt it.

> Beneath the moon she stood and waited.
> The wind came and opened the gate
> And, on the walls, the shadows of the flowers moved.
> She thought her precious lover was come.

Chen Jingji had told her he would give warning of his coming by shaking the branches of a flowering shrub. So, when at last Jinlian saw them move, she knew he was there. She coughed gently, and the young man came in and sat beside her. She asked whom he had left at home. "My wife is not there," Jingji said, "but I told Yuanxiao that if anything should happen she must come and tell me at once." He asked if Qiuju had gone to bed, and the woman told him she was already fast asleep. They kissed each other and, there in the courtyard, enjoyed the pleasures of love without so much as a single garment to hinder them.

> Their two hearts beat as one
> They pressed together fragrant shoulders
> And touched each other's cheeks.
> He grasped that perfumed breast, smooth as the softest down,
> And found it perfect.
> He raised those tiny feet, took off the embroidered shoes,
> And jade met jade as precious as itself.
> Each burning tongue sought sweetness from its mate.
> Then like mad phoenixes they took their fill of love
> And, when the storm was past,

She whispered to her lover, bidding him
To come again and not delay.

When they were done, Jinlian brought five taels of silver in small pieces and gave them to Chen Jingji.

"My mother has just died," she said. "My husband, when he was alive, provided a coffin for her. She was placed in it the third day after her death and, by our mistress's orders, I was present. I have only returned today. Tomorrow she is to be buried, but the Great Lady says that as we are still in mourning for your father, she cannot let me go. So here are five taels. I want you to go and see about things tomorrow. Pay the undertakers with this money and see the matter through. If you go, I shall be as satisfied as if I went myself."

"It will be no trouble," Jingji said, taking the money. "I will go early and, when all is over, I will come and tell you about it." Then it suddenly occurred to him that his wife might be returning, so he went away.

The next day, it was still morning when he came back. Indeed so early was it that Jinlian had not finished dressing. The young man gave her two branches of jasmine that he had plucked at the temple. "Did you actually see the coffin put in the earth?"

"That is what I went for," Jingji returned. "If I hadn't seen the old lady buried, should I have dared to come and tell you so? I did not spend all the money. There is still about a tael left, and I gave it to your sister. She told me to thank you."

Jinlian, now that her mother was buried, shed a few tears. Then she told Chunmei to put the flowers into a vase and bring the young man some tea. Jingji took some refreshment and then went away.

From that day, the pair seemed more closely drawn together than ever. One day—it was in the seventh month—Jinlian sent the young man a message asking him on no account to fail to visit her that evening. He promised, but unfortunately Cui Ben and a few other friends carried him off for a day in the country and, when he came back, he was so drunk that he could only throw himself on the bed and fall into a sound sleep. When night fell, Jinlian came to see where he was and found him lying on the bed in such a drunken sleep she could not waken him. By chance she thought to see what might be in his sleeve and there discovered a pin with a gold head shaped like a lotus. On it was engraved this legend:

Horses with golden bridles neigh on the tender grass.
The season of apricot blossom brings great joy
To those who live in towers of jade.

She took the pin to the light and examined it. It belonged to Yu-lou. "Where has he got this?" she wondered. There must, she decided, be something between them or it could not have found its way into Jingji's hands. "No wonder that he has seemed somewhat lacking in manly vigor lately," she said to herself. "I must leave a few words behind me to show I have been here. I think I'll write a line or two on the wall and, next time I see him, I'll drag the truth out of him." Then with a brush she wrote:

> I came alone to visit you, and found you sleeping,
> Came like an angel from the skies.
> It was in vain. You are like Xiang Wang
> There is no spirit to you.
> Day and night I offer you my love
> And you reject it.

She went back to her room. Not long afterwards Jingji woke up, considerably more sober. He lighted a candle, suddenly remembering his tryst with Jinlian. Then he saw the poem written on the wall, the ink still wet, and knew she had been there. The young man felt extremely annoyed with himself. "It is about the first night watch," he said, remembering that his wife and the maid were still with Yueniang. "If I go, I shall find the corner gate closed." He went to the garden and shook the flowering shrub, but there was no response. Taking a large stone to step on, he climbed over the white wall. Jinlian, finding him drunk, had been very disappointed. She had gone back sadly and thrown herself on the bed fully dressed.

Jingji climbed over the wall. Nobody was to be seen in the courtyard: the two maids had gone to bed. He walked on tiptoe and found that the door had not been bolted, so he pushed it open and, by the moonlight that streamed upon the bed, saw Jinlian lying there. "Darling," he cried several times, but there was no reply. "Don't be angry with me," the young man went on. "Cui Ben asked me to go and practice archery outside the city, and I had too much to drink. I am very sorry I didn't come when I should have, and as for your visiting my room, I never knew it." There was still no answer. The young man was greatly upset. He knelt on the floor and kept repeating the same words over and over again.

"You deceitful scamp," Jinlian cried at last, slapping him in the face with the back of her hand, "be quiet. I don't want the maids to hear all about it. There is someone else now, and you care for me no longer. Where have you been today?"

"Really," Jingji assured her, "Cui Ben did take me outside the city. They gave me a lot of wine, and I got drunk and went to sleep. I beg your pardon for not coming. As soon as I saw the poem on the wall, I knew you were annoyed."

"Oh, you deceitful rascal!" Jinlian cried. "Be quiet and don't argue. Slippery as you are, you shan't escape me this time. If, as you say, you were drinking with those fellows and nowhere else, where did you get the pin in your sleeve?"

"I picked it up in the garden two or three days ago."

"In the garden, did you? Well, go to the garden and pick up another one like it and bring it to me. Then I may believe you. This belongs to Yulou, the little strumpet. It's hers beyond a doubt. Why, her name is on it, so what is the use of trying to deceive me? Of course, you and she are carrying on together. Once before I had to speak to you about her, and you swore you had never touched her. But, if that is so, how does this pin come into your possession? I suppose you've told her everything about me. That's why she was laughing at me the other day. Henceforth, my dear Sir, you are you and I am I. Kindly relieve me of your presence."

Jingji swore by all the gods and began to cry. "If I, Chen Jingji, have had the least little thing to do with her, may I die before my thirtieth year; may I have boils the size of bowls; when I want soup, may it turn to water, and when I want water, may there be no water." Still Jinlian refused to believe him.

"You deceitful rubbish," she scolded. "Oaths like that are the kind people take when they want to get rid of the toothache. I wonder you're not ashamed to say such things."

They went on squabbling till it was very late. The young man undressed and lay down beside her, but she turned away and would not answer him, though he kept repeating Lady this and Lady that. Indeed, she slapped his face. After that he did not dare to speak or even to move. When daybreak came, he feared the maids might be getting up, so he climbed over the wall and went back to his own place.

CHAPTER 83
Qiuju Spies on Pan Jinlian

Such love as this the world has seldom known
Alas, when things we treasure seem to be in our hands
We lose them.
Tears flow and the west wind carries them away
Like raindrops falling on Yangtai.

The moon has its mountains, its fullness, its waning
Mankind has happiness, sorrow, and parting.
When they whisper to each other before the fire
The gods know.
Do not say, then, this is the best time of all.

When, at dawn, Pan Jinlian saw Chen Jingji climb over the wall and go away, her heart relented. It was the fifteenth day of the seventh month, the Festival of All Souls, and Wu Yueniang went in her sedan chair to the temple where Nun Xue lived, to burn some paper treasure chests for Ximen Qing. Jinlian and the others went to the outer gate to see Yueniang start, but when Meng Yulou, Sun Xue'e, and Ximen Dajie came back, Pan Jinlian waited. At the second door, she met Chen Jingji. He had been to the apartments that once belonged to Li Ping'er to get some clothes that were needed in the pawnshop.

"Yesterday I said a few words to you," she said, "and you flew into a rage, and dashed away ever so early. Does that mean you have finished with me?"

"Dear Lady," Jingji said, "how can you say such things? Last night, I never had a wink of sleep. You were so cruel that I nearly died. Look at the marks of your slaps on my face still."

"Scamp," Jinlian said, "if it is true that there is nothing between you, what gave you such a hangdog expression, and why did you run away?"

"The sun was rising," Jingji said, "and if I had not gone then, somebody might have seen me. I assure you, I have never even touched her."

"Then come and see me this evening, and you shall give an account of yourself again."

"You plagued me so much all night," Jingji said, "I never closed my eyes. Now, I shall have to try to get a little sleep in broad daylight."

"Come and see me again," Jinlian said, "and we will clear up this business."

She went to her room, and Jingji took the clothes to the pawnshop. He was busy for a long time, but at last was able to return to his own room. There he threw himself on the bed and went to sleep. It was almost sunset when he woke up. He was anxious to go to Jinlian when, suddenly, dark clouds gathered in the sky and it began to rain.

Jingji looked at the pouring rain. "Oh, what vile weather!" he said to himself. "She was all ready and waiting for me to go and explain things, and now it is raining. What wretched luck I have." He waited and waited, but the rain did not stop. At the first night watch, it was still coming down in torrents, and water was streaming from the roof. At last he could wait no longer. He took a red rug and wrapped it around himself. By this time Yueniang had come home and Jingji's wife and maid were both with her in the inner court. He locked the door, and went to the garden by the gate in the western corner. Still the drenching rain poured down. He pushed open the gate leading to Jinlian's rooms. She knew that he would come, and had told Chunmei to give Qiuju plenty of wine and send her to bed. None of the doors was locked, and Jingji was able to walk straight in.

The windows were partly open and candles were burning brightly. Fruits and refreshments were set out on a table, and golden cups for the wine. Jinlian and Jingji sat down side by side.

"Tell me," she said to him, "if you have had nothing to do with Yulou, how do you come to have her pin?"

"I picked it up by the white rose arbor in the garden. I swear it. May I die this very moment if I lie to you."

"If that is true," Jinlian said, "keep the thing. I don't want it. But remember this: whatever happens, you must not lose the little perfume satchel I gave you to keep your pins in. If anything happens to that, you will know what to expect."

They drank together and played chess. Before the first night watch was over they went to bed and there sported very merrily, spending half the night in transports of delight. In days gone by, Jinlian, by constant diligent practice, had acquired a most marvelous skill in all the arts of love, and this night it was made manifest to her young lover.

Qiuju woke. She could hear a man's voice in the other room, but could not quite sure whose it was. Before dawn, she got up to make water, and heard the door of her mistress's room being softly opened. The rain had not stopped, but there was a glimmer of moonlight, and through the window she caught a glimpse of a figure wrapped in a red rug. It seemed very like Chen Jingji.

"So it is he who comes night after night to sleep with my lady," she said to herself. "She is always boasting about her virtue, yet here she is carrying on with her son-in-law."

The next morning she went to the kitchen and told her story to Xiaoyu. Xiaoyu was very friendly with Chunmei, and repeated the story to her. "Qiuju," she said, "says that your lady is carrying on with young master Chen. He spent last night with her and did not go away till this morning. You know his wife and her maid were not in their rooms last night."

Chunmei went back and told Jinlian what she had heard. "Mother," she said, "you will have to beat that slave. She can't be allowed to spread this tale all around the place. It might be disastrous for you."

Jinlian, furiously angry, summoned Qiuju. The girl knelt down. "I told you to go and make some gruel," the woman said, "and you have broken the pot. What is the matter with you? Is the hole in your bottom so large that all your brains have fallen out? I fancy your hide is beginning to tickle because it hasn't had a good drubbing for so long." She found a rod and with it gave Qiuju thirty hard blows. The maid squealed like a pig being killed, and her body was bruised.

"Mother," Chunmei said, "if you don't beat her harder than this, it will only allay that tickling. Why not take her clothes off and get one of the boys to give her twenty or thirty strokes with a good thick stick? Then she will begin to know what's what. If you give her gentle taps like this, you'll never make the water muddy. This is nothing more than play. Bold as she is, she seems to have no fear of you." Then she turned to Qiuju. "You are a slave," she said to Qiuju, "and you ought to know that you should never talk to outsiders about anything that happens in your own house. Why, if all maids were like you, people might as well keep a whistle."

"I never said anything," Qiuju cried.

"Still obstinate!" Jinlian said, "you master-murdering slave! Let's have no more from you."

Qiuju went to the kitchen.

One day, about the time of the Autumn Festival, Jinlian secretly arranged with Jingji to come and drink wine with her and enjoy the moonlight. They played Turtle Chess with Chunmei. It was very late when they went to bed, and they did not get up until it was time for morning tea. This was only asking for trouble. Again Qiuju discovered them, and she went at once to Yueniang's room to tell her. But Yueniang was dressing her hair and Xiaoyu was standing at the door. Qiuju took Xiaoyu aside and said: "Brother-in-law has spent the night with my lady again, and they have not got up even yet. It is just as I told you the other day, yet I was beaten for my pains. Today I can prove what I say. This is no lie. I want the Great Lady to go and see for herself."

"Oh, you goggle-eyed slave!" Xiaoyu cried. "Here you are again with scandalous tales about your mistress. The Great Lady is doing her hair. Get off with you."

"What is she talking about?" Yueniang asked.

Xiaoyu was obliged to make some answer, so she said: "The Fifth Lady sent Qiuju to ask you to go and see her." Yueniang finished dressing and then hurried to the outer court to see what Jinlian wanted. Chunmei fortunately happened to see her coming. She rushed in and told Jinlian. The woman was still in bed with Jingji, and they were greatly alarmed when they heard that Yueniang was on her way. Jingji, rolled himself up in the coverlets and hid himself completely, and Jinlian made Chunmei set a table on the bed. She herself pretended to be making a pearl ornament.

Yueniang came in and sat down. "You are very late this morning," she said. "I wondered what you were doing. I see you are making an ornament." She took the work in her hands and examined it. "It is really very well made," she said. "There is the sesame flower in the middle, borders of squares on either side and, all around, bees resting on chrysanthemum flowers, and hearts interlaced. It is very pretty indeed. You must make one for me."

When Jinlian realized that Yueniang was speaking pleasantly, her heart began to beat more quietly. She told Chunmei to bring some tea. Yueniang drank it and shortly afterwards went away. "Sister," she said as she was going, "when you have dressed your hair, come and see me." Jinlian promised, and as soon as Yueniang had gone, she made Jingji get up and slip away. Both she and Chunmei had had such a terrible fright that they were bathed in sweat.

"The Great Lady has never been to see me before unless she had something definite to say. I wonder what made her come so early today."

"That slave has been at her tricks again," Chunmei said.

Before long, Xiaoyu came and told them what had happened. "Qiuju came," she said, "and talked about brother-in-law being here all day and all night. I scolded her for saying such things, but she still went on. Then the Great Lady asked what it was all about, and the only thing I could say was that you had sent to ask her to come and see you. Lady, you must be on your guard against such backbitings. And you must watch that slave."

Though Yueniang did not believe Qiuju, she was not quite easy in her mind because she realized that Jinlian was a young woman and easily carried away. Her husband was dead. If anything of the sort should happen, she was afraid the story would get out and there would be a scandal. Besides, she thought about Ximen Dajie. She would not allow her to go far away, and she gave the young couple the room that Li Jiao'er once had, so that henceforth they should live in the inner part of the house. Only when Clerk Fu went home did she allow Jingji to sleep at the shop. When the young man had to come for clothes or medicines or anything, Daian always came with him. The windows and doors were all securely fastened, and the maids and serving women were not permitted to go out without very good cause. The household, in fact, was governed much more strictly, and this made it practically impossible for Jinlian and Jingji to indulge their very warm affection for each other. They found, as we so often find, that the joys of this life seldom attain their fullest realization, and that fine weather never lasts very long.

For a month after Qiuju had told of the secret attachment between Jinlian and Chen Jingji, they never had an opportunity of meeting. At last Jinlian could bear the separation no longer. She was lonely behind her embroidered curtains and desolate in her painted chamber. She was afflicted by lovesickness, and became too languid to powder her face. She ate less food and drank less tea than was her custom. She grew thinner and thinner, and the girdle around her waist grew looser and looser. So languid was she that she would lie down on her bed and stay there for hours at a time.

"Mother," Chunmei said, "nothing can be done by worrying. The Great Lady has sent for the two nuns and I hear that tonight they are to stay and read the scriptures. This means that the door to the inner court will be closed early. I will pretend to go to the stable to get some straw to fill a mattress, but really I will go to the shop and ask young master Chen to come and see you. What do you think?"

"Good sister," Jinlian said, "do, for pity's sake, tell him to come. I will never forget how well and kindly you have served me."

"There is no need to say that, Mother," Chunmei said. "You and I are really but one. Father is dead, and whether you go up or down in the world, I shall always be ready to go with you and to stay wherever you may stay."

"If you feel like that, what more could I desire?" Jinlian said.

That evening, she went to Yueniang's room, but soon she excused herself, saying that she did not feel very well and went to her own place. She was like a cicada escaping from its chrysalis. Yueniang closed the door of the inner court very early and dismissed the maids and serving women.

Then she settled down to listen to the nuns.

"Good sister," Jinlian said to Chunmei, "go at once and bring him to me."

"First I must give Qiuju some wine and get her comfortably out of the way. Then I will go." She heated two large cups of wine, gave them to Qiuju, and hustled her into the kitchen. Then she took a basket and went to the outer court. She filled the basket with straw and went stealthily to the pawnshop. She knocked softly at the door. Clerk Fu was not there and Jingji was alone. He had just gone to bed when he heard the knock. He recognized Chunmei's voice and, when he opened the door, found that it was indeed she.

"Come in," he said, smiling, "there is no one here but myself."

Chunmei went in. She asked where the boys were.

"Daian and Ping'an are both at the medicine shop," Jingji told her, "and I am left here to bear my loneliness as best I can."

"My mistress sends her love to you," Chunmei said, "and says what a fine person you must be to let all these days pass without coming near her. She says she supposes that, now you have Yulou, you don't care about her any more."

"Oh, what a thing to say!" Jingji said. "Ever since that last time I have been afraid, and the Great Lady keeps the doors and windows so tightly shut that I dare not move."

"For some days," Chunmei said, "my mistress has been miserable. She is restless all the time and never eats a thing. And when she has anything to do, she doesn't seem to know how to set about it. Today the Great Lady is busy listening to the nuns, but my mistress has gone back to her room and wants to see you there. She has sent me especially to ask you to go to her."

"I am grateful for her love," Jingji said. "You go first and I will follow in a few moments."

He opened the cabinet and took out a white silk kerchief and a pair of silver toothpicks. He gave these to Chunmei and embraced her. Then he lifted her on to the bed and kissed her. They were very well pleased with one another.

When they had amused themselves for a while, Chunmei went back with the straw. "Brother-in-law," she said to Jinlian, "was delighted to see me. He says he will come, and gave me this kerchief and these toothpicks."

"Keep a good lookout," Jinlian said. "He may come any moment."

It was the twelfth day of the ninth month, and the moon was very bright. Jingji went first to the medicine shop and ordered Ping'an to take his place at the pawnshop. He told the boy that the Great Lady had sent for him to listen to the exhortations of the two nuns. Then he went to

Jinlian. He knew that the main garden gate would be shut, so he went in by the other and, when he came to Jinlian's apartments, shook the hibiscus tree as a signal. Chunmei came out to welcome him and took him into the room. Jinlian was standing at the door. "Oh, villain," she said to him with a smile, "how kind you are to stay away from me for so long."

"I wished to come ever so much," Jingji said, "but I was afraid I should get you into trouble." They held each other's hands and went into the room together. Chunmei closed the door in the corner and set food and wine on the table. Jinlian and Jingji sat down side by side and Chunmei opposite. They poured the wine and passed the cups to one another. When they had had wine enough, a sidelong look came into the woman's eyes and her cloudlike hair seemed to lose its tidiness. She brought out the love instruments that had once belonged to Ximen Qing. The Case for Mutual Enjoyment was there, the Trembling Voice and Lovely Eyes, the silver clasp and the Bell of Excitement. In the candlelight, Jinlian stripped herself of all her clothes and lay naked upon a "drunken old gentleman's chair." Jingji, too, took off his clothes. They found a set of twenty-four pictures representing the pleasures of love, and endeavored to reproduce in real life the joys depicted in the paintings.

"Go behind him and push," Jinlian said to Chunmei. "I'm afraid he must be exhausted."

Chunmei, indeed, gave the young man a push forward. So the warrior stood inside her cunt; he plunged up and down, and gave both of them a most delightful orgasm.

Qiuju, who was in the kitchen at the back, suddenly wished to make water and got up, but she found the door closed on the outer side, and could not open it at first. Finally, she put her hand around and succeeded in working back the bolt. It was quite light in the courtyard, and she went across on tiptoe to the other room. Peeping through the window, she could see candles shining brightly and three people in the room, all merrily drunk, and not a stitch of clothing on them. They seemed to be enjoying themselves immensely. Jinlian and Chen Jingji were plunging and rearing, and Chunmei, behind the young man, was rendering every assistance in her power, and in this way the three worked together.

"These are the people who make themselves out to be so good, while I am beaten," Qiuju said to herself. "But this time I have caught them in the act and tomorrow morning I will go and tell the Great Lady. She won't say I'm lying now."

She watched them until she was quite satisfied, and then went back to the kitchen and to bed.

The three others went merrily on until the third night watch. In the morning, Chunmei was the first to get out of bed. When she came to the kitchen, she found the door open. She questioned Qiuju, and the girl said: "Oh, yes! I had to get up in the night, and I pushed it open and went into the yard."

"You slave!" Chunmei said, "couldn't you see the chamber pot in the room here?"

"I didn't know it was there," Qiuju declared, and they squabbled for a long time. Jingji went away.

Then Jinlian asked Chunmei what all the noise was about, and Chunmei told her how Qiuju had opened the door. Jinlian was greatly annoyed and determined to beat the girl again, but Qiuju went to the inner court and told the whole story to Yueniang.

"You slave who would be the death of your mistress," Yueniang said. "Only the other day you came to me with a long cock-and-bull story. You said your mistress was carrying on with my son-in-law, and that he was with her all night and all day. So I went there: your mistress was in bed busy making an ornament, and my son-in-law was nowhere to be seen. When he did appear, he came from another part of the house altogether. You deceitful slave! My son-in-law is not a sugar figure that can be hidden away anywhere. Are you trying to throw dust in my eyes? If people knew the truth of this, they would know that you are a traitor to your mistress. But if they did not know, they would say: 'When Ximen Qing was alive, he had dealings with many women. And now, though he has been dead only a short time, his own wives are behaving in a most disorderly fashion.' They would even cast doubts upon my own child."

She was going to punish Qiuju, but the girl ran away in alarm and never dared to go to the Great Lady again. When Jinlian heard that Yueniang had refused to believe what Qiuju told her, she was even bolder than before. But Jingji's wife heard whispers, and asked her husband questions.

"Surely, you don't believe that story!" he said. "Why, I spent the whole time at the shop. How could I go to the garden? Besides, you know the garden door has been shut all the time."

"I won't argue with you," his wife said. "If I hear anything more and find that the Great Lady will not believe you, you can keep away from me."

"If I have done anything wrong," Jingji said, "sooner or later it will come out. You ought to refuse to listen to such scandal. You know the Great Lady doesn't believe it."

"I only hope you are telling the truth," his wife said.

CHAPTER 84
Wu Yueniang's Pilgrimage

One day, Wu Yueniang sent for Uncle Wu and told him she wished to go and offer incense at the temple at Taianzhou. When Ximen Qing was desperately ill, she had promised to make sacrifice there.

"If you go, I must go with you," Uncle Wu said. They got ready offerings, incense, candles, and paper things, and decided that Daian and Laian should go with them. They hired three horses, and a sedan chair for Yueniang. Before they left, Yueniang told Meng Yulou, Pan Jinlian, and Sun Xue'e to look well after the house, and Ruyi'er and the maids to take care of Xiaoge. They were to fasten the doors early and not to leave the house.

"You must stay at home," she said to Chen Jingji, "and keep the gate with Clerk Fu. I shall make my offerings on the morning of the fifteenth, which means that I shall be back here at the end of the month."

On the eve of her departure, she took leave of Ximen Qing's tablet, and drank wine with the ladies. She gave all the keys to Xiaoyu. They started before dawn and, leaving the city, set out on the high road. It was the end of autumn: the days were short and the weather cold. Though they only halted once during the day, they could not cover more than sixty or seventy *li,* and, when the sun set, they went to an inn or the house of some villager to spend the night and started again early the next day. It was almost wintry weather, and the wild geese seemed chill and full of sadness. The leaves had withered on the trees; the countryside was bare and melancholy, and there was a great air of mourning everywhere.

After some days, they reached Taianzhou. From there they could see Taishan, the most renowned of all the mountains in the world. It stood deep-rooted in the earth, and its summit pierced the heart of the sky. It is between the states of Qi and Lu, and the very air about it is holy. Uncle Wu saw that it was late, and they went to an inn. The next day they rose very early and went up the mountain to the Daiyo Temple built upon the mountainside. Dynasty after dynasty had venerated this temple, and generation after generation had worshipped there.

Uncle Wu took Yueniang there. She offered incense before the principal shrine and visited all the sacred images. A priest read her declaration. She burned paper money in all the chapels and partook of monastic food.

Then she went with Uncle Wu to climb to the highest peak of the mountain. They went up the forty-nine winding paths, clinging to the ivy and scrambling past the vines, and at last caught sight of the Palace of Niangniang far above them in the sky. They had still forty or fifty *li* to go. Wind and cloud, thunder and rain, were all beneath them now. It had been the hour of the Dragon[1] when they left the Daiyo Temple. It was the hour of the Monkey[2] when they came to the Golden Palace of Niangniang. There was a red sign over the entrance with these words emblazoned in gold upon it: "The Palace of Radiant Sunset." They went inside and gazed upon the figure of Niangniang.

Wu Yueniang made obeisance. A Daoist priest came and stood beside her. He was a short man, about forty years of age, with three wisps of beard. His eyes were very light and his teeth white. He wore a hat with a pin, and a purple gown. His shoes were embroidered in a cloud design. He read Yueniang's declaration; then they burned incense in a golden burner, and gold and silver papers, and a boy was told to take away the offering.

This priest was really a very bad man. He was the principal disciple of the Abbot of the Daiyo Temple, and his name was Shi Bocai. He was immoderately fond of women and money, and a fellow completely absorbed in the affairs of this world and the pursuit of power. In this district there was an outrageous scoundrel called Yin Tianxi, a brother-in-law of Gao Lien, the local magistrate. This scoundrel was the leader of a band of villains who haunted the neighborhood of the two temples, armed with bows and arrows, and accompanied by hawks and dogs. They preyed especially on women pilgrims, and nobody had the courage to complain about them. The priest, Shi Bocai, allowed them to use his place for their evil purposes. He devised all manner of schemes for getting women to his rooms, and then handed them over to the scoundrel Yin to do what he liked with. He saw that Yueniang was beautiful and that she was in mourning. She must be, he decided, a lady of good family and wealthy. She had only a white-haired old gentleman and two boys to protect her. So he went up, made a reverence to her, thanked her for her offering, and asked her to take tea in his room.

Uncle Wu thanked him. "It is very kind of you," he said, "but we must go down at once."

"There is still plenty of time," the priest said, and took them to his apartments.

The room he led them into was very white and clean. In the place of honor was a couch with embroidery of sesame flowers upon it, and yellow

1. 5–7 a.m.
2. 3–5 p.m.

hangings. Over a small table was a picture of Dongbin playing with white peony flowers. On either side was a scroll. One bore the words: "The Pure Wind made his sleeves dance like storks," and the other "In the Moonlight, he discussed the Holy Scriptures." The priest asked their names.

"My name is Wu," Uncle Wu said, "and this is my sister who has come to make sacrifice for her late husband. But we must not impose upon your kindness."

"Since you are so closely related," the priest said, "perhaps you would not mind both taking the place of honor." He himself sat down in the host's place and told one of the novices to bring tea. There were two novices, one called Guo Shouqing and the other Guo Shouli. They were about sixteen years old and very handsome. They wore black silk hats and long gowns, light shoes, and white socks, and used a great deal of perfume. They served the visitors who came to the temple with tea, water, and wine, and the guests who stayed the night there were accustomed to employ them for the basest uses. These two boys closed the door and brought in a number of delightful vegetarian dishes. They offered Uncle Wu and Yueniang excellent tea made of spring water. When the tea had been cleared away, they at once brought wine and a host of dishes, chicken, goose, duck, and fish. They poured the golden wine into amber cups.

When the wine appeared, Yueniang decided that it was time to go. She called Daian, and upon a red lacquer tray the boy offered the priest a roll of cloth and two taels of silver. Uncle Wu begged him to accept them. "Do not trouble to offer us wine and food," he said. "It is late and we must go back."

The priest thanked them. "Only by the grace of Niangniang," he said, "am I in charge of this temple. I live upon the charity of others and, if I may not spend what comes to me upon entertainment, upon what shall I spend it? I have offered you the very simplest of fare, yet you give me valuable presents. I really don't know whether I can accept them or not."

When they urged him to do so, he told the boys to take the presents. "But you must sit down," he said, "and have some wine, so that I may show how kindly I feel towards you."

Uncle Wu could not refuse, and they sat down again. Hot dishes were brought. The priest said to the boys: "This wine is not good enough. Go and open that jar of lotus wine that his Lordship Xu sent me, and offer some to this gentleman."

The boys brought another jar and warmed some of the wine. The priest filled a cup and offered it with both hands to Yueniang. She was unwilling to take it, and Uncle Wu explained that she never drank wine.

"Lady," the priest said, "after so trying a journey you must take some."

He then offered half a cup and Yueniang took it. He filled another and offered it to Uncle Wu, saying: "My lord, try this wine and tell me what you think of it."

Uncle Wu tasted it. It was very sweet and well bodied. "It is excellent," he said.

"It was given to me by Xu, the Prefect of Qingzhou," the priest said. "His lady, and his son and daughter, come to offer sacrifice here every year, and he is one of my most intimate friends. His daughter's baby has been placed under the protection of Niangniang. They regard me as a hardworking, plain fellow, but they appreciate my sincerity and love and respect me. You see the government has cut down the revenue of these two temples by half, but, fortunately, this excellent prefect wrote and arranged that the whole of it should be left to us. So we have money enough to burn incense to Niangniang, and what is left we spend upon the entertainment of pilgrims."

While they were talking, the two boys and the porters were entertained elsewhere. There was as much as they could eat. Uncle Wu drank a few cups of wine and then again prepared to take his leave. It was getting late.

"The sun has gone down," the priest said. "It is too late for you to go down the mountain now. Will you not spend the night here and start to-morrow morning? That will be much pleasanter for you."

"I have left some luggage at the inn," Uncle Wu said, "and I am rather anxious about it."

The priest smiled. "Don't worry about that," he said. "I give you my word that it will be perfectly safe. When the people in the villages know you are at my place, they will be afraid of me. I could very quickly get hold of anybody who might steal your property and bring them before the local courts."

Uncle Wu said no more. The priest offered him another large cup of wine, but, realizing that it was very potent, he excused himself, saying he was tipsy enough already and that he must go and change his clothes. He went to the back part of the building and looked around. Yueniang was very tired. She went to lie down on the couch and the priest closed the door and went away.

Suddenly Yueniang heard a noise. It was a man creeping through a little door behind the bed. His face was red and bearded. He was about thirty years old, and wore a black hat and a purple gown. He took Yueniang in his two hands.

"I am Yin Tianxi, at your service," he said, "the brother-in-law of Magistrate Gao. I heard that you were a lady of good birth and very beautiful, and I was anxious to make your acquaintance. Now I have seen you, I realize my good fortune. If you are kind to me, I shall never forget it."

He pressed her down on the couch and would have forced her. Yueniang was frightened and cried aloud. "In this world of peace and brightness, would you dare to assault a woman of good birth?" she cried. She tried to escape, but the man prevented her. He knelt down.

"Lady," he said, "do not make such a noise. Take pity on me, and listen to my urging."

Yueniang only cried the louder: "Help! Help!" Laian and Daian recognized their mistress's voice and dashed to the back to call Uncle Wu. "Uncle," they cried, "come at once. Our lady is fighting with someone in the priest's room."

Uncle Wu hurried as fast as he could. He pushed the door but could not open it. He could hear Yueniang crying: "Why are you trying to keep me here?"

"Sister, don't be afraid," Uncle Wu shouted. "I am here." He picked up a piece of rock and forced open the door. When Yin Tianxi saw that someone was coming, he released Yueniang and slipped quickly away through the back. There were many ways of escape. Uncle Wu came in. "Sister," he cried, "has he done you any harm?"

"No," Yueniang said, "but he has got away."

Then Uncle Wu tried to find the priest, but the priest eluded him and sent his young novices to face the trouble. Uncle Wu was terribly angry. He bade Laian and Daian break all the windows and doors in the temple, and then took Yueniang away. She got into her sedan chair and they went down the mountain as fast as they could. It was about sunset when they left the temple and midnight when they came to their inn. Uncle Wu told the people of the inn what had happened. They were greatly disturbed. "You should not have challenged that evil star, Yin," they said. "He is the magistrate's brother-in-law, and everybody knows his goings-on. When you have gone, we shall suffer. He will not let you go for nothing."

Uncle Wu paid the reckoning and gave the innkeeper an extra tael. Then all the luggage was packed up; Yueniang got into her sedan chair, and they set off posthaste.

Yin Tianxi was angry. He gathered twenty or thirty of his men, all armed with swords and clubs, and they raced down the mountainside. Meanwhile, Uncle Wu and his people went straight on. About the fourth night watch, they came to a clearing and saw, afar off, a light shining through the forest. They went towards the light and came to a cave in which an old monk was reading the sacred scriptures by candlelight.

"Venerable Teacher," they said to him, "we have been to offer sacrifice at the temple, and now evil men are pursuing us. We have lost our way in the darkness. Will you tell us where we are, and how we can get from here to Qinghe?"

"You are on the eastern spur of Taishan," the old monk told them. "This cave is known as the Xuejian Cave, and I am called the Holy Man of Xuejian, though my real name is Pujing. I have been here for thirty years, mortifying the flesh. It is good fortune that has brought you to me. Do not go farther. There are many wild beasts on these mountain slopes, and it will be better for you to start tomorrow. The high road to Qinghe is not far from here."

"But I am afraid those evil men may find us," Uncle Wu said.

The old man looked about him. "Do not let that trouble you," he said. "The scoundrels have gone home already." He asked Yueniang's name.

"She is my sister," Uncle Wu said, "the widow of Ximen Qing. She came to offer sacrifice for her husband. Venerable Teacher, you have saved our lives, and we can never cease to be grateful to you."

They spent the night in the cave. Before dawn, Yueniang offered the old monk a roll of cloth. He would not accept it.

"I want one of your sons to be my disciple," he said.

"My sister has only one child," Uncle Wu said, "and she hopes to bring him up to continue the family. If she had another son, she would certainly give him to you."

"My baby is still very young," Yueniang said. "He is not a year old yet. He cannot come to you."

"I don't want him now," the old monk said, "I only ask for your promise that I shall have him in fifteen years' time."

Yueniang decided that she would settle that when the fifteen years were over. She made an indefinite kind of promise. Then they said good-bye to the old monk and set out along the high road to Qinghe.

CHAPTER 85
Chunmei Is Dismissed

The wheel of passion turns and never stops
And those who watch are oft bewildered.
The fortune of a man is subject to many vicissitudes
And when it is all but attained
It comes to naught.
Man finds it hard to hold his head aloft
While strangers look on coldly
And there is none to sympathize.

All through the day
Her brows were knit in sorrow.
She leaned on all the railings
Knowing not what to do.
She can only hope that the moon still shines
Over the five lakes
She must have patience, the time will come
When she will realize the debt of love.

Pan Jinlian and Chen Jingji followed one another about like a cock and a hen. One day, Jinlian felt a sudden pain and realized that her belly was growing bigger. She felt languid and tired and disinclined to eat anything. She sent for Chen Jingji.

"These last few days," she said, "I have been hardly able to keep my eyes open. My belly is getting big, and I can feel something moving inside it. I have no appetite and my body feels very heavy. When your father was alive, I got some medicine from Nun Xue to make me have a child, and nothing happened. Now he is dead, and I have been carrying on with you only a short time, yet I am with child. It was the third month, I think, when I was last unwell, and that would make the child about six months on the way. Now I, who have always laughed at other people, look like being laughed at myself. Pull yourself together. The Great Lady has not come back yet. Go and get some medicine to get rid of it. If I have the child, it will be the end of me, and I shall never be able to lift my head and look people in the face again."

"We have all sorts of medicines in the shop," Jingji said, "but I don't know which is the right one. And I haven't any sort of prescription for that purpose. Doctor Hu, in the High Street, is a specialist in women's troubles. I will go to him and ask him for something to put you right. He knows us quite well."

"Well, be quick about it, Brother," Jinlian said. "You must do something to save my life."

Jingji took three *qian* of silver and went at once to see Dr. Hu. The doctor was at home. He knew that Chen Jingji was Ximen Qing's son-in-law and took the young man in.

"It is a long time since I last saw you," he said. "What can I do for you?"

"I have come to trouble you for an abortive," Jingji said. "Here is the money. Thank you very much."

"The people of this world," Dr. Hu said, "regard the saving of life as a very noble thing. Everybody comes to ask for medicine to help them to get babies. Why do you come and ask for the very opposite? I have none."

Jingji gave the doctor another two *qian*. "Don't let us talk about nobility," he said. "If I am asking for it, it is because I want it. A young woman I know would find it very awkward if she should have a baby, and she wishes to make sure that she does not."

"I will give you some of the medicine that people call 'Clear all out,'" Dr. Hu said, taking the money. "Let her take it and, in the time it would take her to walk five *li*, the child will come away."

He gave Jingji two doses. The young man said goodbye and hurried back to give the medicine to Jinlian. In the evening she took it with some hot water. Immediately she began to feel pain. She lay down on the bed, and Chunmei pressed her belly. In a very short time, she called for the pail, and the child came away. She told Qiuju that she had been unwell and bade her throw everything into the privy. The next day, when the privy cleaners came, they found a white, well-nourished infant. As the proverb says: Good news is never heard outside the door, but bad news travels a thousand miles. In a very few days, nearly everyone in the household knew that Jinlian had been carrying on with Chen Jingji and had had a baby.

When Wu Yueniang came back, it was the tenth month and she had been absent for a fortnight. She was welcomed as though she had fallen from the skies. She made obeisance to the gods and burned incense, then went to visit Ximen Qing's tablet. Afterwards, she told Meng Yulou and the others of her adventures at the temple. She sobbed as she did so. Then the people of the house came to see her, and Ruyi'er brought Xiaoge. Mother and child came together again.

When she had burned some paper offerings, she gave her brother food and wine and he went home. In the evening, the ladies entertained Yueniang. She was weary after her long journey and the fright she had had, and for two or three days was not at all well. Qiuju, who had heard about the relations between her mistress and Chen Jingji, was very anxious to tell Yueniang all about them. She came to Yueniang's door, but Xiaoyu spat in her face and boxed her ears.

"Get off at once, you scandalmongering slave!" she cried. "My mistress is not well after her long journey, and she is still in bed. If you make her angry, it will be the worse for you."

Qiuju swallowed her anger and went away.

One day, Chen Jingji came for some clothes, and Jinlian and he again amused themselves upstairs. While they were enjoying themselves to the utmost, Qiuju again went to the inner court, and asked Yueniang to come and see for herself.

"Lady," she said, "I have warned you several times, but you would not listen. When you were away, they used to sleep together from morning till night and from night till morning. She even got in the family way. She and Chunmei have both been at the same tricks. Now they are upstairs doing wicked things together. If you do not believe me, come and see for yourself."

Yueniang hurried to the outer court. The couple upstairs were busily engaged, but Chunmei happened to see Yueniang coming and rushed upstairs to warn them. They were greatly alarmed and could think of no place in which to hide. Jingji could only pick up some clothes and run downstairs.

"My son," Yueniang said, "what are you doing here? You seem to have a very poor memory."

"Someone is waiting in the shop and there was no one else to come and get the clothes," Jingji said.

"Didn't I give definite orders always to send a boy for the clothes?" Yueniang said. "What right have you in the room of this woman who has lost her husband? You are utterly shameless."

Chen Jingji ran away as fast as his legs would carry him, and Jinlian stayed upstairs, not daring to come down. At last, however, she did come down, and Yueniang scolded her severely.

"Sister," she said, "you must give up this shameless way of behaving. You and I are widows, and things are very different now from when our husband was alive. Even vases and jars have ears. Why do you associate with this young man? The servants are all saying the most terrible things about you. The proverb says that a man without character is like iron without any strength, and that a woman without character is as soft as honey. When we behave with proper decorum, people will do what they are told without our having to go to extremes, but, if we do not so behave, they will not obey, however severe our orders. If you were straightforward and conducted yourself decently, nobody would dare to say a word about you. I have been told this several times before, but I would never believe it. Now I have seen with my own eyes, and there is no choice left to me. Make up your mind that you will so live as to maintain our dead husband's good name. Take my own case. If I had been a wicked woman, I should never have come back here when that bad man assaulted me."

Jinlian flushed and paled in turns. She was full of denials. "I was burning incense upstairs when he came for some clothes, and I had no conversation at all with him."

There was a good deal of argument, and then Yueniang went away.

In the evening, when Ximen Dajie and Jingji were in their own apartment together, Ximen Dajie said to him: "You villain! Will you still dare to say that I have no proofs? Will you argue with me now? What were you doing upstairs with her today? I can't find words bad enough for you. The best thing would be to put you and her together in a big jar. And that whore, who has stolen my husband, swaggers about in my presence! She is like a tile out of the privy, hard and stinking. She always thinks she is better than anybody else. Do you think you will continue to have your meals here with me?"

"You whore!" Jingji said, in a fury, "isn't my money kept here? I'm not begging for food in this place." He went away in a very bad temper.

After that time, he always stayed at the shop and never came to get anything. Daian and Ping'an were sent to bring anything that was needed. Even the midday meal was served at the shop. Clerk Fu used to take some money and go to the street for noodles, then take them back with him. It was one of those cases where, as when there is a fight between a dragon and a tiger, the little wolf suffers. All the doors and windows were kept shut, even before the sun went down. And so the lovemaking between Chen Jingji and Jinlian was interrupted again.

There was a house belonging to Chen Jingji, which was lived in by his mother's brother. This was a man named Chang, who had no work to do and spent all his time at home. To him Jingji went night and morning for his meals. Wu Yueniang asked no questions. Pan Jinlian and the young man were separated for about a month. She was desperately lonely. Each day seemed like a whole season, and each night was like half a summer. She could not bear the loneliness, and passion raged within her. There was no way she could see him. She could not send out a message, and he could not come near her.

One day, the young man saw old woman Xue going past the door and it occurred to him that she might be able to take a letter to tell Jinlian how much he loved her and how greatly he was distressed by their separation. As soon as he had an opportunity, he pretended to be going out to collect some money, but actually he took a donkey and went to see the old woman. When he came to her door, he tied up the donkey and asked if the old woman was at home. Her son, Xue Ji, and his wife were sitting on the bed nursing their baby. There were two girls in the room, waiting to be sold. When the young woman heard somebody asking for old woman Xue, she went out to see who it was.

"I should like to know if Madam Xue is at home," Jingji said.

The young woman asked him to go in. "Mother has gone to change some ornaments and to collect some money," she said. "If there is anything we can do for you, I will send for her." She made tea for Chen Jingji.

After a while, old woman Xue came back. She made a reverence to Jingji and said: "What wind has blown you here?" She bade her daughter-in-law make him a cup of tea, but the young woman told her she had already done so.

"I would not trouble you," Jingji said, "except on a matter of some importance. You know I have been on very close terms with the Fifth Lady for a long time. Now Qiuju has been blabbing, and we cannot get a chance to meet. The Great Lady and my wife, too, are treating me very badly. I can't live without that woman, yet we have been parted all this time and have no way even of sending a message one to the other. I have thought of sending a letter, but there is no one I can trust it with. So I have come to you. I am sure you can help me."

He took a tael of silver from his sleeve. "This," he said, "may serve to buy you a cup of tea."

The old woman laughed and clapped her hands. "I never heard of such a thing," she said, "a son-in-law carrying on with his mother. Tell me, however did you manage to get her?"

"Sister Xue," Jingji said, "this is not a joke. Here is my letter. You must take it to her for me."

The old woman took the note. "I have not been to see the Great Lady since she returned. I will go to pay her my respects."

"When shall I expect the answer?" Jingji said.

"I will come to your shop and tell you there," the old woman said.

Jingji mounted his donkey and went back to the shop. The next day, old woman Xue took her box and went to Ximen's house. First she went to see Yueniang, then Yulou, and finally Jinlian.

Jinlian was eating some rice gruel and talking to Chunmei, who was trying to make her more cheerful. "Mother," she said, "don't let yourself be so upset. Right or wrong, let people talk if they feel like it. After Father died, the Great Lady had a baby. Did anybody suggest there was anything wrong about that? She cannot control the things we do in secret. Cheer up. If the skies fall, there is always one who upholds them to put them back again. So long as we're alive let us be as merry as we can."

She heated some wine and gave a cup to her mistress. "Drink this," she said, "and drown your sorrow."

Then she looked out into the courtyard. Two small dogs were there, seemingly glued together.

"There!" she said, "even animals must have their enjoyment. Why not we human beings?"

Then old woman Xue came. She made a reverence to Jinlian and again to Chunmei. "I see you are having some fun," she said. Then she saw the two dogs.

"A good omen for this house," she said. "When one sees a thing like that, one ceases to feel lonely."

"You have not been here for a long time," Jinlian said. "What has brought you today?" She asked old woman Xue to sit down.

"I don't know what I have been doing all the time," old woman Xue said, "but I am never idle. I wasn't able to come and see your Great Lady when she came back from her pilgrimage. I have just come from her, and she was quite annoyed with me. The Third Lady was there too. She bought a pair of ornaments and some ribbon from me. She is a good lady, that. She just handed me eight *qian* of silver. But the lady Sun Xue'e, who bought two pairs of flowers in the eighth month and still owes me two *qian* for them, doesn't want to pay me. So mean she is! But why were you not in the inner court?"

"I have not been very well lately," Jinlian said. "I didn't feel like leaving my room."

Chunmei heated a cup of wine and gave it to the old woman. Old Xue made a reverence and thanked her. "Ought I to take it, when I have only just come in?" she said.

"It will bring you a good baby," Jinlian said.

"No more babies for me," old woman Xue said, "but my daughter-in-law had one a little while ago. He is two months old. I expect you have been very lonely since your husband's death, Lady?"

"Naturally," Jinlian said. "We have to suffer now in all kinds of ways. There are too many talkers in this household. The Great Lady herself, since her child has been born, has been quite a different woman. We are not so friendly as we used to be. As I told you, I have not been well lately, but we had a quarrel and that is one reason why I have not been near her."

"It was all Qiuju's fault," Chunmei said. "When the Great Lady was away, that slave told a pack of lies about my mistress, and even dragged me into it. It is most provoking."

"She is your maid," old woman Xue said. "How dare she say things about her mistress? One who wears a black gown should stand by a black pillar. She ought not to do things like that."

"Go and have a look," Jinlian said to Chunmei. "She may be listening to us again."

"No," Chunmei said, "she is in the kitchen, picking rice. She is like a torn sack or a leaking manger, going about and telling everybody our business."

"Since there is nobody here, I have something to tell you," the old woman said. "Yesterday, Master Chen came to my house. He told me your maid Qiuju had got you into this pickle. He said that the Great Lady had scolded him, and that she kept the doors and windows tightly closed. He said he was no longer allowed to come here for clothes and medicine, and that his wife had gone to live in a room in the east wing. Nobody sends him anything to eat, and he has to go to his Uncle Zhang's for his meals. It is not right that the Great Lady should not trust her own son-in-law but put all her confidence in the boys. He told me it was ever so long since he had seen you, and that he is dying to do so. He sends this letter and his love. Don't worry, he says. Now that the master is dead, you would perhaps be wise to come out into the open. There is nothing to fear. Sometimes, we are afraid of the incense making too much smoke, but now there is no reason why it should not."

She took Jingji's letter from her sleeve and gave it to Jinlian. It was in the form of a poem written to the meter of "The Embroidered Scarlet Shoe."

> The fires of hell consume me
> The waters beneath the dark blue bridge are almost to my neck.
> What we have to do, let us do quickly
> For scandal spreads over the districts of the south
> And there is no avoiding it.
> Let us then complete the work of joy
> For if we do it not, it is as though we did.

When Jinlian read this, she put it into her sleeve.

"He would like you to give him some token, or write a few words to him," the old woman said. "Otherwise, he will not believe that I have given you the message."

Jinlian told Chunmei to drink with old woman Xue and herself went to the inner room. She came back with a white silk handkerchief and a gold ring. On the handkerchief, she wrote a poem to express her love. When she had finished, she wrapped the handkerchief and the ring up together and gave them to the old woman.

"Give him my love," she said, "and bid him be patient. Tell him if he keeps going to his uncle's for his meals, his uncle may get tired of him and say: 'You are doing your father-in-law's business, why do you come here to eat?' It looks as though our people have not food enough to feed themselves. So tell him not to go to his uncle, but to take some money from the shop and spend it on food and cakes and things to eat with Clerk Fu. And tell him to come to the house as usual. If he does not come, it will look as though he were afraid of somebody here."

The old woman promised to tell him all these things. Then Jinlian gave her five *qian* of silver, and she went to the shop to make her report to Chen Jingji.

They found a quiet place, and old woman Xue gave him the things that Jinlian had sent. "The Fifth Lady says you must be patient," she told him. "Don't allow yourself to be drawn into a quarrel. Come to the house as usual and don't go to your uncle's for your meals. It may displease him."

She showed him the five *qian* of silver Jinlian had given her. "You see there are no secrets between us," she said. "I am sure things will go well with you, and I tell you about this money because, if she told you about it herself sometime, it would look bad for me."

"I am very grateful to you, old lady," Jingji said, and bowed low to old woman Xue.

She had hardly taken two steps away from him when she came back. "I nearly forgot one very important thing," she said. "When I came away, the Great Lady sent Xiuchun after me. She told me to sell Chunmei. She said that the maid, as well as the mistress, had been carrying on with you."

"Take her to your house," Jingji said, "and I will come and see her there."

The old woman went home.

That evening, when the moon was shining, old woman Xue came to take Chunmei away. First she went to Yueniang's room.

"We paid sixteen taels of silver for her," Yueniang said, "and I will take sixteen taels now."

Then she said to Xiaoyu: "Go and tell Chunmei. She is to go without her clothes."

Old woman Xue went to Jinlian and broke the news to her. "The Great Lady," she said, "has told me to take Chunmei away because she helped you to receive your lover secretly. She is only asking the price for which she bought her."

Jinlian opened her eyes very wide, but she could not speak. Then she began to cry. "Oh, Sister Xue," she said, "you see the kind of treatment we receive now that my husband is dead. It is only a few months since he died, yet now they mean to rob me of my maid. How utterly heartless the Great Lady is. She thinks that, now she has a child of her own, she can drag us all through the mud. But Li Ping'er's child died when it was only eighteen months old. Children have been known to die of smallpox, and we never know what Heaven may have in store for us. She will do well not to raise her hopes too high."

"I suppose his Lordship, when he was alive, took his pleasure with Sister Chunmei," the old woman said.

"'Took his pleasure' indeed!" Jinlian cried. "He treated her like part of himself. She had only to say one word and he believed ten. When she asked for one thing, he gave her a dozen. Even his wives were less considered than she was. If she suggested that he should give one of the boys ten strokes of the rod, he would not dare to *give* them five."

"The Great Lady is in the wrong, then," old woman Xue said. "You say his Lordship had taken his pleasure of her, yet the Great Lady is sending her away without boxes and without any clothes. She is to go just as she came. The neighbors will think that very strange, I'm sure."

"Did she tell you Chunmei was not to be allowed to take away her clothes?" Jinlian cried.

"Yes, that was her order. Xiaoyu is coming to see about it."

Chunmei heard the whole of this conversation, but she did not shed a single tear. When she saw how her mistress was crying, she said: "Mother, why do you cry? You must not worry about me when I have gone away. It would make you ill and, if you are ill, there will be no one to look after you. Let me go. I don't want any clothes. A good man will not eat food that other people throw to him, and a good girl does not wear her wedding dress."

Then Xiaoyu came. "Mother," she said, "surely you are not going to pay any attention to what the Great Lady says now. She is obstinate at the moment. Sister Chunmei has served you well. Take some of the best clothes, and let Madam Xue take them away for Chunmei as a parting gift from you. She is going away now, and there is no reason why we should say anything to the Great Lady about it."

"You are very kind," Jinlian said.

"Lady," Xiaoyu said, "we never know what is coming to us. We are like frogs and crickets living here. A fox is sorrowful when it sees a dead rabbit;

creatures are always sympathetic with their own kind."

They filled Chunmei's box with the things like kerchiefs and ornaments that had belonged to her. Jinlian gave her two of her own best dresses and some socks, making a large parcel of them. She gave her pins and rings and earrings. Xiaoyu took two pins from her hair and gave them to the girl. The pearls and headdresses and embroidered clothes she took back to Yueniang.

Chunmei said good-bye to Jinlian. Xiaoyu cried. When they were on their way to the gate, Jinlian wanted her to go and say good-bye to Yueniang and the others, but Xiaoyu advised them not to do so. Chunmei walked proudly behind old woman Xue and never turned her head. Jinlian and Xiaoyu went with her to the gate. Then Xiaoyu went back to Yueniang. "She has gone now," she said, "and she has left all her clothes behind." Jinlian returned to her room. She had been accustomed to talking to Chunmei, and now Chunmei was taken away from her. She was very lonely and cried bitterly.

CHAPTER 86

Pan Jinlian Leaves the House of Ximen

Chen Jingji, one morning after breakfast, pretended that he had money to collect, took a horse, and went to old woman Xue's house. The old woman was at home and asked him to come in. Jingji tethered his horse outside and went in. After he had taken tea, the old woman said: "What can I do for you, Brother-in-law?"

"I was out collecting some money," Jingji said, "and thought I would call to see you. I hear the maid came to you yesterday. Is she still here?"

"Yes, I have not found a master for her yet."

"I should like to see her. May I have a word with her?"

The old woman pretended to hesitate. "Good Brother-in-law," she said, "the Great Lady gave me very strict instructions. She said that this maid was being sent away because she and you had been misbehaving yourselves. I wasn't to let you see her. So go away, please. She might be sending some of her boys here. If they came and saw you, there would be trouble for me when they went back and told the Great Lady. I should never be able to go there again."

The young man smiled and took a tael of silver from his sleeve. "Buy yourself a cup of tea with this," he said, "I will give you more, later."

Then the old woman agreed. "I am not in any need of money at the moment," she said. "Perhaps you will keep it for me and give it me some other time. But one thing I do want. At the end of last year, I pawned two pairs of embroidered pillow ends at your pawnshop. That is about twelve months ago and, including the interest, I should probably have to pay eight *qian* of silver. Will you get them for me?"

"You shall have them tomorrow," Jingji said.

The old woman asked him to go to the inner room, and there he found Chunmei. She told her daughter-in-law to cook something for them, and went off herself to buy cakes, wine, and meat for Chen Jingji and Chunmei.

"Brother," Chunmei said, when she saw Jingji, "a fine fellow you are! Nobody but a murderer would have brought my mistress and me to such a pass that we can neither rise nor fall. Now the secret is out, and you see how people hate us."

"Sister, you have finished with that household now, and I don't see why I should bother about it any more. In this world, we have to go our own ways. See that Madam Xue finds a good home for you. When the fruit of the fields has been dug up and taken away, it can never return whence it came. That is how it is with me. I shall go to the Eastern Capital to see what my father has to say. Then I shall come back and divorce my wife, and claim the boxes and things that those people have of mine."

Old woman Xue soon came back with the refreshments. A table was set and the pair sat down and drank together. Old woman Xue joined them, and they chatted together.

"The Great Lady is very unfeeling," the old woman said. "To a beautiful girl like you, she might at least have given ornaments and clothes. It will be very awkward when you have to go to a new master's house. And she asked the same money for you as she paid. It is like pouring clean water from one cup to another. Some is bound to be spilled on the way. Yes, indeed, she is very, very mean. When you came away with me, Xiaoyu asked your mistress to give you two dresses. Without them, you wouldn't have had a rag to put on when you go to your new home."

When they had had wine enough, old woman Xue told her daughter-in-law to take the baby away, and left them alone to amuse themselves.

She was afraid that Yueniang might send someone to see what was happening, so she would not let Jingji stay very long. He mounted his horse and went home. In a day or two he gave Chunmei two kerchiefs and two pairs of drawers, and got the pillow ends for old woman Xue. He gave the old woman some money to buy wine for him to drink with Chunmei. Unfortunately, Yueniang sent Laian to the house to find out why the old woman had not found a master for Chunmei. Laian saw Jingji's horse outside, and went back at once and told his mistress.

Yueniang was very angry, and sent one boy after another to fetch the old woman. When she came, Yueniang scolded her severely.

"You have the maid, yet you keep putting off finding a master for her. You think you'll make a little extra money for yourself by keeping her to carry on with some young rascal. If you can't attend to this business, let me have the maid back again and I'll give the job to old woman Feng. You'll never be allowed near the place again."

Then old woman Xue plied her go-between's mouth. "Heaven! Heaven!" she cried. "Your ladyship really must not blame me. Do you think I would chase the god of wealth away with a stick? You were kind enough to give me this job, and I should never have the boldness not to get on with it. Yesterday, I took the maid to several places, but I didn't succeed in selling her. You ask sixteen taels for her, but I haven't got money enough to pay for her before I sell her."

"The boys tell me," Yueniang said, "that young Chen has been hanging about your place drinking with the maid."

"Ai ya!" the old woman cried. "What a lie! He certainly called to see me because he had to bring me two pillow ends that I left at your pawnshop twelve months ago. Since he had done me that favor, I asked him to have a cup of tea, but he would not and rode away on his horse at once. He did not drink wine at my place. What stories your boys have been telling you!"

Yueniang did not say anything for a long time. At last she said slowly: "I should not be surprised if that young man's passion put wrong ideas into his head."

"I am not a three-year-old child," old woman Xue said, "and it was easy to see what the position was. You gave me your orders, and I had to carry them out. He didn't stay a single minute at my house, just handed me the pillow ends, and went away without even a cup of tea. He hadn't time to see the maid. Really, Lady, you must make sure of the facts before you blame me. Now, his Lordship Zhou wants a girl to ensure the continuance of his family, but he does not want to pay more than twelve taels. I might get thirteen taels out of him. His Lordship has been here to parties and seen her. He liked her appearance: she is beautiful and can sing sweetly, or he would not have offered so much. You must remember that she is not a virgin, and we can hardly expect so high a price from anybody else."

Yueniang agreed to accept this sum and, the next day, old woman Xue took Chunmei to Major Zhou's house. The girl was beautifully painted and wore a headdress of pearls and ornaments. She was dressed in a red silk coat and blue silk skirt. Her shoes were small and pointed. Major Zhou thought her more beautiful than ever. He gave the old woman a piece of silver worth about fifty taels.

Old woman Xue took the silver back to her own place, cut off a piece amounting to thirteen taels, and gave it to Yueniang. She brought another tael with her, and told Yueniang that Major Zhou had given it to her as a reward for her services. She asked Yueniang for something more, and was given five *qian* of silver. So, all together, she made thirty-seven taels and five *qian* from this deal. Such is the way of go-betweens, nine out of ten of whom make their living in this way.

Chunmei was lost to Chen Jingji, and Jinlian was out of his reach. Yueniang was very careful about doors and windows. Every evening she took a lantern, went around the whole house, and made sure that all the doors were bolted before she went to bed. Jingji was powerless, and it made him very impatient. He quarreled with his wife.

"Strumpet!" he shouted. "Let me tell you straight out that I am the son-in-law in this family. I'm not a beggar. I'm sick of the place, and your people are keeping all my chests full of gold and silver. You are my wife, but do you take my part? No, you talk about my begging my food here. Do I ever eat a thing without rendering service in return?"

His wife cried.

It was the twenty-seventh day of the eleventh month, Meng Yulou's birthday. She got ready some dishes and wine and, out of the kindness of her heart, told Chunhong to take it to the shop for Clerk Fu and Chen Jingji. Yueniang tried to stop her. "That young man is a scoundrel," she said. "Don't have any dealings with him. If you would like to send something to Clerk Fu, well and good, but don't give that young man anything."

Yulou did not pay any heed. She told Chunhong to take the things to them. The boy put down the food on the counter of the shop. When Jingji had finished the jar of wine, he was still not satisfied and told the boy to go back and ask for more.

"I have had enough," Clerk Fu said. "I don't think we need ask for any more."

But Jingji insisted, and Laian was sent to ask for more wine. Sometime later he came back. "There is no more wine in the inner court," he told them. Jingji was already half tipsy. He again told the boy to go and fetch more wine, but the boy did not move. Then Jingji took some of his own money and bought wine. As he drank it, he cursed Laian.

"You wait, you thievish slave! Your mistress treats me badly, and you, you slave, think you can look down on me too. You won't go and do what I ask you. You know I am the son-in-law in this family. I am tired of eating and drinking in this haphazard way. You know how they treated me when my father-in-law was alive. Now he is dead, they sing a very different tune. Nobody bothers about me any more, and all they want is to get rid of me. My mother-in-law believes every little story the slaves carry to her. She entrusts her business to slaves and has no confidence in me. Let her do as she likes: I have patience enough to endure this injustice."

Clerk Fu tried to cheer the young man. "You mustn't talk like that," he said. "If they don't respect you, whom do they respect? I am sure they must be busy now. It is not that they don't want to give you the wine. Your scolding the boy doesn't matter, but the walls have ears. If anybody hears you, they will say: 'That young man is drunk again.'"

"Old friend," Jingji said, "you don't understand. I may have wine in my belly but I know what I'm talking about. My mother-in-law listens to every bit of tittle-tattle, and believes that everything about me is bad. She thinks that it is I who have made a fool of other people and not others who have made a fool of me. But if I amuse myself with every woman in that household, and she brings a case against me in the courts, it is no more than a case of carrying on with one's late father-in-law's women, and that is only a matter of imprudence. First, I shall divorce her daughter. Then I shall go to the courts myself, or else to the Eastern Capital, and I shall accuse her of detaining many chests full of gold and silver that ought either to belong to me or be given to the authorities, since they came from Yang Jian. If I do that, her house will be confiscated, and all the women will be sold. I am not hoping to catch any fish: all I wish is to stir up the mud. If she had any sense, she would treat me as her son-in-law as she used to do, then everything would be all right."

Clerk Fu did not care for the tone the young man was taking. "Brother-in-law," he said, "you are certainly drunk, and you are talking without thinking."

Chen Jingji opened his eyes wide and glared at Clerk Fu. "You thievish old dog!" he said haughtily. "Do you suggest that I am drunk, and don't know what I'm talking about? Well, it is not any wine of yours I'm drinking. Even if I am a scoundrel, I am still the honorable son-in-law of this household and you are a paid hireling. Will you dare to treat me badly too? You old dog! Wait! During the last few years, you have made money enough out of my father-in-law, and you have eaten his food. Now you have evil ideas in your head and you think, if you get rid of me as soon as you can, you will be able to make yourself the only man who can transact business here. If I send an accusation to the courts, you may be sure your name will be on it."

Clerk Fu was not a very brave man and, seeing that things did not seem to be taking a good turn, he put on his clothes and went home as fast as he could. The boy cleared the things away and took them to the inner court. Jingji lay down on the bed and went to sleep.

The next day, very early, Clerk Fu went to Yueniang and told her what had happened. There were tears in his eyes when he suggested that he should go away, give up the business, and hand over the accounts to her.

"Go on as usual," Yueniang said to him gently. "Treat that rogue as though he were some stinking offal, and don't pay the slightest attention to him. He came here because he was in trouble with the authorities, and only intended to spend a short time here. I should like to know where are all these treasures he spoke to you about. All I know of are my daughter's furniture and a few trunks. I remember how his father got away. We were terrified lest somebody should find out and spread the news about him. We were worried day and night. When he came here, he was only sixteen or seventeen years old and like a hunted animal. He has lived on my husband's kindness ever since, and everything he knows about business he has learned here. Now that his wings have grown, he means to repay our kindness by hatred, and to pay no account to all the things we have done for him. What a young man! He seems to have no conscience and to disregard the principle of Heaven utterly. I am watching, and I shall see whether Heaven prospers him or not. My friend, go on as you always have done, and pay no heed to him. The time will come when that young man will feel ashamed of himself."

One day, something seemed destined to happen. There were a number of people in the pawnshop redeeming their things. Ruyi'er came with a pot of tea for Clerk Fu, carrying the baby Xiaoge in her arms. The baby howled, and she put the pot down on the table.

"Baby," Chen Jingji said, "don't cry." Then he turned to the people who were there and said, with a half-serious air: "Doesn't it seem clear that he is my own child? When I tell him to stop crying, he stops."

Nobody made any answer.

"Brother-in-law," Ruyi'er said, "I suppose you think that is a clever thing to say. You don't know your place. I shall tell my mistress about this."

Jingji went over and kicked her twice. He laughed and said: "You thievish creature! So I had no right to talk in that way, hadn't I? Well, now I am kicking your backside so as to make a sound that people should listen to."

The nurse picked up the baby and went to the inner court and told Yueniang all about it. She cried. "That is how he talked about the baby before all those people," she said.

Yueniang was dressing her hair before a mirror. When she heard this, she could not speak. Suddenly she fell forward on the floor in a faint. Xiaoyu was greatly alarmed. She called for nearly everybody in the house, and they picked up Yueniang and put her on the bed. Sun Xue'e jumped on the bed and lifted her up and down. After a while they were able to pour some ginger water down her throat. At last Yueniang came around, but her breath came with difficulty. She sobbed, but could not cry out. Ruyi'er repeated Jingji's remarks to Yulou and Xue'e. "I reproved him," she said, "and he came and kicked me. I nearly fainted on the spot."

When the others had gone away, Xue'e stayed to look after Yueniang. "Lady, it is no use being angry with him," she said. "It would be most serious if you fell ill of anger. That fellow is annoyed because you sold Chunmei and because he cannot get here to see that strumpet Jinlian. That is why he says things of this sort. Now let us make an end of this business once and for all. Your stepdaughter is married to him. We have to regard her as a piece of land that has been sold, and we cannot help her very much. As the proverb says: when once the frog gets into the water, it must take the consequences. But why should we keep that young man here any longer? Send for him. Let us give him a sound drubbing and drive him away. Then send for old woman Wang to take that strumpet away and sell her to anybody who will buy her. When we have got rid of these evil elements, we may have peace. I see no reason why we should deliberately keep them there. If we do, we may all suffer in the future."

"You are right," Yueniang said.

They decided upon a plan. The next day, Yueniang gave her maids and women clubs, seven or eight of them altogether, and hid them about the place. Then she sent Laian to summon Chen Jingji. The second door was closed when the young man went in.

"Kneel down," Yueniang said.

The young man refused, and turned his head impudently away, without speaking.

"You know what you have done?" Yueniang said.

Jingji paid no heed.

Yueniang was furious. With Xue'e, Laixing's wife, Laizhao's wife, Xiaoyu, Xiuchun and some others, she caught hold of him and threw him to the ground. Clubs, long and short, descended furiously upon him. Ximen Dajie went away and never spoke a word to save her husband.

In desperation, the young man pulled down his trousers and displayed his manhood. This startled the women; they all threw down their clubs and ran in every direction. Yueniang was annoyed, but she could not help being amused. She called him a turtle with nothing to boast of, but Jingji was pleased with himself. "If I had not thought of that," he said to himself, "I should never have got away alive." He got up and ran away, holding his trousers up with one hand. Yueniang told some of the boys to go after him and see that he cleared his accounts and handed them over to Clerk Fu.

It was now clear to Chen Jingji that he could stay there no longer. He packed his clothes and his belongings and, without saying good-bye to anyone, left Ximen Qing's house in a very bad temper. He went to stay at his Uncle Zhang's.

When Jinlian heard this, she was more melancholy and depressed than ever. Yueniang did what Xue'e had suggested, and sent Daian for old woman Wang.

The old woman had given up her tea business since she had come into some money. Her son, Wang Chao, who had been to the Huai country with some merchants, had come back with a hundred taels that he had stolen. Old woman Wang bought two donkeys, millstones and sieves, and had set herself up as a miller. When she heard that Ximen's people wished to see her, she hurriedly dressed and went with Daian.

"Brother," she said, as they went along, "it can't be very long since I saw you last, but I see, from your hair, that you have now reached man's estate. Are you married yet?"

"No," Daian said.

"Why have they sent for me?" the old woman said. "Your father is dead. Is the Fifth Lady going to have a baby and wants me to be the midwife?"

"The Fifth Lady is not going to have a son," Daian said. "She has had rather too much of a son-in-law. The Great Lady is going to ask you to take her away."

"Heavens!" old woman Wang cried. "I was sure she would not be able to hold herself in check after your master died. Dogs can never get out of their habit of sniffing about the filth. So she has been misbehaving herself. I know the young man. What is his name?"

"Chen Jingji," Daian said.

"Oh yes, now I remember. Last year I went to see your master with old He the Ninth. Your master was not at home, and that strumpet took me to her room. She didn't give me a thing, not even a needle. All she gave me was a cup of tea. I came away. I thought she was settled there for a thousand years, and now she is to be sent away. Oh, what a splendid whore! It was I who arranged her marriage, and really she ought not to have treated me like that, even if I had been somebody else."

"She and the young man made such a scandal they nearly killed the Great Lady," Daian said. "Now he has been kicked out, and my mistress wants you to take this one away."

"When she came, she came in a sedan chair," the old woman said, "and she will have to leave in one. And she will have some things to take. I suppose they will give her some boxes?"

"Of course," Daian said, "but the Great Lady will tell you all about that."

So they came to the house. The old woman went to see Yueniang, made a reverence, and sat down. The maid brought tea.

"Old woman Wang," Yueniang said, "I should not have asked you to come except for a matter of some importance." She told her all about the business of Jinlian. "When she came here," she said, "you brought her. I didn't wish to bring anyone else into the matter, so I sent for you to take her away. I don't care whether she marries again or not, I only wish to see the last of her. My husband is dead, and I can't control so many people. I don't care how much my husband spent on her, but I think he must have spent enough to make a woman of silver. I leave the matter entirely in your hands. Give me whatever you get for her and I will spend the money on services for my dead husband. So perhaps some good will come of it."

"I see, Lady," the old woman said, "it isn't that you want the money. You are just anxious to get rid of the cause of so much trouble. I understand, and I will do what you desire. This is a good day, and I may as well take her with me now. But when she came, she had some property of her own and she came in a sedan chair. She must have a chair now."

"She may have her boxes, but she will get no sedan chair from me," Yueniang said.

"You say this because you are angry," old woman Wang said, "but you must let her have a chair, or, when the neighbors see it, they will laugh at you."

Yueniang said nothing. After a while she sent Xiuchun to fetch Jinlian.

When the woman saw old woman Wang there, she was excited. She made a reverence to Yueniang and sat down.

"Lady," old woman Wang said, "you must get your things together. The Great Lady has told me to take you away with me."

"My husband died only a short time ago," Jinlian said, "and I have done nothing wrong. Why should I be driven away like this without the slightest cause?"

"There is no use pretending you do not know what it is for," the old woman said. "When a snake goes through a hole in the wall, it knows what it's about. You know what you have done."

"Don't talk such nonsense," Jinlian said. "It is no use your using high-flown language with me. You are the very one who is always helping people to do things they should not."

There has never been a time when a feast did not come to an end. The beams that stand out are those that decay first. Trees cast their shadow, and each one of us has his own reputation to save. Flies cannot get into an egg if there is no crack in it.

Jinlian saw that things were in a bad way for her. She realized that now she must leave this house. "If you must beat a man," she said, "do not strike him on the face; and if you quarrel with anyone, do not talk about his faults. You have the upper hand now, but do not abuse your power. I have been here many years. Why should you drive me away without mercy, because you listen to the tittle-tattle of slaves and serving women? I will go. It is all the same to me. I warn you, though, that you and others will have to stay here to the ends of your lives. See that you don't bring scandal upon yourselves."

Yueniang went to her room. She got out two boxes, a small table, four dresses, a few ornaments, earrings and pins and a set of bedclothes. She filled up the boxes with shoes and socks. She told Qiuju to come to her, and Jinlian's room was locked up.

Jinlian dressed and said good-bye to Yueniang. Then she went to Ximen Qing's tablet and sobbed. Afterwards, she went to see Yulou. They had been sisters for a long time, and now, when they had to part, they both shed tears. Without saying anything to Yueniang, Yulou gave her a pair of gold pins, a light blue silk dress, and a red skirt.

"Sister," she said, "we shall have few chances to see each other in the future. Look for a good home and go forward. The proverb says: every banquet must come to an end, and now we must say good-bye. When you find a home, ask someone to let me know. When I go out, I may be able to come and see you. We love one another as sisters."

They left one another in tears. Xiaoyu went with Jinlian to the gate and quietly gave her two gold hairpins. "Sister," Jinlian said to her, "you are very kind." Old woman Wang had already found somebody to carry the things. Only Yulou and Xiaoyu saw Jinlian get into her sedan chair.

When the woman came to old woman Wang's house, she was taken to the inner room and they slept together during the night.

Wang Chao was now grown up and his hair was dressed as a man's. But he was not yet married, and slept in the other room. The day after her arrival, Jinlian dressed very daintily and stood looking out from behind the lattice. She had nothing to do and spent her time painting her eyebrows or playing the lute. When old woman Wang was not at home, she would play chess or dominoes with Wang Chao. The old woman busied herself feeding the donkeys and sifting the flour and did not pay much attention. So, in a few days, Jinlian was engaged in a love affair with Wang Chao. At night, when old woman Wang was asleep, Jinlian would pretend to get out of bed to make water, but really she went to the other room and sported with Wang Chao. Once the bed made such a noise that old woman Wang woke up.

"What is that noise?" she cried.

"The cat is catching a rat underneath the cabinet," Wang Chao answered.

Old woman Wang, half asleep, murmured: "Ever since I have had that wheat flour there, I have been worried about it. I can't even sleep at nights now."

After a while, the noise began once more, and the old woman again called out to know what was the matter.

"The cat has caught the rat and taken it under the bed."

The old woman listened attentively, and indeed the sound was like that of a cat worrying a rat. She said no more. Jinlian finished what she had begun, crept quietly into bed and went to sleep.

The rat is small
But bolder than it looks,
Hungry and eager, ready for any prank.
When anyone appears,
It beats retreat and hides.
Its scufflings in the depth of night
Disturb good honest slumberers.
Oblivious of the rules of good behavior
It loves to find a hole in which to hide
And always takes the most delight
In stolen sweets.

When Chen Jingji heard that Jinlian had left Ximen's household and was now at old woman Wang's, he took two strings of coppers and went to call there. Old woman Wang was at the door sweeping up the donkey's droppings. Jingji bowed low.

"Brother, what can I do for you?" the old woman said.

"I should like a word with you," Jingji said.

The old woman took him into the house.

"I understand," Jingji said, "that the Fifth Lady of his late Lordship Ximen is here, looking for a husband. Is that so?"

"What is your relationship to her?" the old woman asked.

"I am her younger brother," Jingji said, smiling.

The old woman looked at him from head to foot. "I never knew she had a brother," she said. "Don't try to hoodwink me. Are you not Ximen's son-in-law? Your name is Chen, and you have come here to get her for yourself. You can't deceive me like that."

Jingji, still smiling, brought out the two strings of coppers and held them out to the old woman. "This may serve to buy you some tea," he said. "I only wish to see her for a moment. Later on, I will reward you more suitably."

When the old woman saw the money, she protested more strongly. "Don't talk about rewards to me," she said. "The Great Lady told me that nobody must be allowed to see her. If you really wish to speak to her, give me five taels of silver, and if you wish to speak to her a second time, that will be another five taels. If you wish to marry her, it will cost you a hundred taels with ten for myself. I shall not do this business for nothing. These two strings of coppers won't even make a splash if you throw them into the water."

Jingji saw that the old woman had a good deal to say, and that she would not accept what he had brought. He took from his hair a pair of silver pins with gold heads, worth five *qian*. He knelt down.

"Old Mother Wang," he said, "take this. I will give you another tael another day. Just let me see her for a moment. There is something I must say to her."

The old woman took the pins and the money. "Go in," she said. "Speak to her and then come out again. I can't have you sitting there making faces at her. And I must have the other money tomorrow." She pulled aside the lattice and allowed Jingji to go in.

Jinlian was sitting on the bed. "You splendid fellow!" she said to Chen Jingji, "you have brought me to such a pass that, if I go forward, there is no village ahead of me, and, if I go back, no inn where I can rest. I don't know what to do, and everybody has heard this scandal about us. You never came to see me. I am a poor, helpless woman with nowhere to go. Whose fault is it?" She clung to Jingji and sobbed. This annoyed old woman Wang very much. She was afraid someone might hear.

"Sister," Jingji said, "I have sacrificed my skin and flesh and suffered from anger and shame on your account. I would have come to see you if I could. Yesterday, I went to old woman Xue's place, and they told me that Chunmei had been sold to some military gentleman. It was there I heard that you had left Ximen's house and were staying here to find a husband. I came at once to see you. I want to discuss matters with you. We love one another and we cannot bear to be parted. Now, I propose to divorce Ximen's daughter, and then I shall go to them for the money and things they have of mine. If they refuse, I will go to the Eastern Capital and accuse them before the courts. If that business is ever taken to law, they will be done for, even if they give up the stuff. When I get the money, I will marry you. I see no reason why we should not be happy together for ever and ever."

"Old woman Wang wants a hundred taels," Jinlian said. "Have you got so much?"

"Why does she ask so much?" Jingji said.

"Your mother-in-law told me," the old woman said, "that when Master Ximen got this woman, he spent more money than would have built a woman of silver. She insists upon a hundred taels and not a penny less."

"Old Mother," Jingji said, "I am crazy about this lady. We cannot live without one another. I see we are at your mercy. I will give you half the money, fifty or sixty taels. Then I will go to my uncle and arrange to have a small house and marry the lady. It is a beautiful idea, and you must soften your heart a little."

"Fifty or sixty taels, did you say?" the old woman cried. "Even if you offered eighty, you would not get her. Yesterday, a silk merchant from Huzhou, a man called He, offered seventy for her. Then Zhang the Second of the High Street, who is an officer, sent two of his men and offered eighty. They brought the money with them, but I would not take it and they had to go away. You are only a boy. You don't know what you're talking about. You come here and think you'll make a fool of me. You know I am not likely to be hard."

She set out for the street. "Whenever did anybody hear of a son-in-law wanting his mother-in-law?" she said loudly. "He thinks he'll come farting here, does he?"

Jingji was alarmed and dragged the old woman back. He knelt down before her. "Old Mother," he said, "don't say another word. You shall have your hundred taels. You know my father is at the Eastern Capital. I will go to him tomorrow and get the money."

"You must be quick or you'll be too late," Jinlian said. "Someone else will get me, and I can never belong to you."

"I will get a horse and start at once," Jingji promised. "I shall be back in less than a fortnight."

"Let me tell you this," old woman Wang said. "If you are the first to cook the rice, you will be the first to eat it. Remember, that doesn't include the ten taels for myself."

"Do not mention it again," Jingji said. "If you will only help me, I shall never forget your kindness."

Jingji went away. He went home, packed his luggage, and the next day hired a horse and set off for the Eastern Capital to get the money.

CHAPTER 87
Wu Song Avenges His Brother

My home is far away. In this harassed world
We are dispersed, some to the east some to the west.
They who still live seek to have news of one another
But the dead are become dust,
And the poor are ruined.

At last the hero returns
He has walked for long.
The road was deserted and at sunset
The air was full of sadness.
Foxes he met, both large and small, which glared at him,
Their hair on end.
But a good sword have I, and I can deal with them.

Chen Jingji took a horse and set out with one of his uncle's servants. The day after Wu Yueniang had sent Pan Jinlian away, she sent Chunhong for old woman Xue. She had decided to sell Qiuju. When Chunhong came to the High Street, he met Ying Bojue. The man stopped him and asked him where he was going.

"The Great Lady has told me to go for old woman Xue," the boy said.

"Why?" Bojue asked.

"She is going to sell the Fifth Lady's maid Qiuju."

"Why did they send the Fifth Lady away?" Bojue said.

"She and my brother-in-law carried on together secretly, but the Great Lady found out about it," Chunhong said. "First, she dealt with Chunmei. Then, she gave the young man a beating and drove him away. And finally, she got rid of the Fifth Lady."

Ying Bojue nodded his head. "So there was something between the Fifth Lady and Master Chen," he said. "Really, there is no telling what people will do." Then he said to Chunhong: "My boy, now that your master is dead, why do you stay there? You will never do any good. I know you would prefer to be in the South. Why don't you go to your native place and get a job there?"

"You are right," Chunhong said. "Now that my master is dead, the Great Lady is very severe with us. Nearly all the businesses have been closed down, and several houses have been sold. Qintong and Huatong have gone, and, indeed, they don't need so many people about the place. I should have liked to go to the South, but I couldn't think of anyone who would take me there. And I don't know the people here very well, which makes it difficult for me to get a job in these parts."

"You silly boy!" Bojue said. "One who does not keep his eyes open will always be in difficulties. If you go to the South, you will have to cross ten thousand rivers and climb a thousand mountains. Why go there? You can sing, and there will be no difficulty in finding another master for you. I can tell you of one, straight off. There is his Lordship Zhang the Second of the High Street. He is very rich and now holds the office your master used to hold. Your Second Lady married him as his second wife. Let me introduce you to him. When he finds that you can sing the Southern tunes, I guarantee that he will take you on at once, and keep you as one of his most favored boys. He is very different from your old master, good-tempered and young. He is very generous and agreeable. You will certainly be in luck's way if you get him for a master."

Chunhong knelt down and kowtowed to Ying Bojue. "Uncle," he said, "I shall count upon your help. If I find a place with Master Zhang, I will buy you a present."

Bojue pulled the boy up. "Stand up, you silly boy," he said. "I am only too glad to be able to help people. I don't want any presents from you, for I know you haven't any money."

"If I go away, I expect the Great Lady will find out a number of things I have done wrong," the boy said.

"Don't worry about that," Bojue said. "I will go and see Master Zhang, and get a tael of silver and a card from him. If he sends them to your mistress, she will not dare to take any money. She will give you up for nothing."

The boy went on to old woman Xue's house. The old woman went to see Yueniang and took Qiuju away. She sold the girl for five taels of silver and paid the money to Yueniang.

Then Ying Bojue took Chunhong to Zhang the Second's house. When Zhang the Second found that the boy was intelligent and could sing the songs of the South, he told him to stay. He sent a tael and a card to Ximen's place and asked for the boy's luggage.

Yueniang was entertaining Yun Lishou's wife. Yun Lishou was now an assistant magistrate at Qinghe. After Ximen's death, knowing that Yueniang was a very rich widow, he struck up a friendship with her. That was why his wife had come to see Yueniang that day with eight presents. She wished to arrange a marriage between Yueniang's son and her own child who was two months old. They settled the matter as they were drinking together, and Mistress Yun gave Yueniang two gold rings as an engagement token.

Daian brought in Zhang the Second's card and the tael of silver. "Chunhong has gone to Zhang's place, and they have come to ask for his clothes."

Yueniang knew that Zhang the Second was now an officer, and she did not dare refuse to give up the boy. She would not take the money, and gave the boy's things to the messenger.

Sometime before all this, Ying Bojue had told Zhang the Second about Jinlian. "She is very beautiful," he said. "She plays the lute excellently, and she knows all about such things as poetry and games, and she can write. She is quite young and she won't like being a widow. Now I hear she has come out, after a quarrel with Ximen's first wife. She is at old woman Wang's place now."

One after another, Zhang the Second sent men to old woman Wang with money in their hands, but old woman Wang told them that Mistress Ximen would not take less than a hundred taels. They came again and offered eighty taels. Still old woman Wang would not agree. Then Chunhong came to Zhang's house and told his new master that Jinlian had been sent away because she had been carrying on an intrigue with her son-in-law. Zhang the Second gave up the idea of marrying Jinlian.

"I have a fifteen-year-old son," he said to Ying Bojue. "He is at school now. I couldn't do with a woman like that in the house."

Then Li Jiao'er told him that Jinlian had poisoned her first husband before she went to Ximen Qing, that she had misconducted herself with the boys, and murdered another lady and her child. Zhang the Second was even more determined not to marry Jinlian.

Major Zhou was delighted with Chunmei. He found her pretty, intelligent, and attractive. He gave her three rooms and a young maid, and stayed with her for three whole days. He had two dresses made for her. When old woman Xue went to see him, he gave her five *qian* of silver. He bought a maid for Chunmei and established her as his third wife. His first wife was blind. She ate vegetarian food, devoted herself to religion, and did not concern herself with household affairs at all. Chunmei lived in the western wing and Major Zhou, who was very fond of her, gave her all the keys.

One day, old woman Xue came and told Chunmei that Jinlian had left Ximen's house and was at old woman Wang's place. That night, Chunmei wept and said to Major Zhou: "My old mistress and I were together all those years and she never spoke a harsh word to me. I might have been her daughter. I believed that she and I would never see one another again, but now she too has left Ximen's house. If you marry her, we can live together most happily. She is very beautiful. She knows all about poetry and music, and she is clever and charming in every way. Her animal is the Dragon, so she is now thirty-two years old. If she comes, I will gladly take rank below her."

Major Zhou was impressed. He sent his servants, Zhang Sheng and Li An, with two handkerchiefs and two *qian* of silver, to old woman Wang's house to see Jinlian. They told him that she really was extraordinarily beautiful. The old woman still demanded a hundred taels, and Zhang Sheng and Li An discussed the matter with her for a long time. They offered eighty taels, but old woman Wang would not accept it. She declared that Mistress Ximen insisted upon a hundred taels. "You will have to pay the hundred," she said, "but you need not bother about my fee. Heaven will not allow me to go unrewarded for my pains."

Zhang Sheng and Li An took back the money to the Major, and he decided to let the matter rest for a day or two. But Chunmei cried every evening. "You must give a few more taels," she said. "If she comes here to live with me, I shall die happy."

So this time the Major sent his bailiff, Zhou Zhong, with Zhang Sheng and Li An. They offered the old woman ninety taels. This made her still more grasping.

"If ninety taels would have done, I could have sold her long ago," she said. "His Lordship Chang would have paid that."

This made Zhou Zhong angry. He told Li An to wrap up the money again. "Do you think that I, a three-legged frog, am not able to find a two-legged woman?" he said. "You old whore! You don't seem to realize whom you are dealing with. Would you talk about Zhang the Second to me? Do you imagine that my master cannot do what he likes with you? It is simply because his new wife has asked him to do this. He doesn't want the woman so much as all that."

"We have been here several times," Li An said, "and that seems to have made you get rather above yourself, you old whore."

He took Zhou Zhong's hand. "Come, let us go and tell our master," he said. "Let him get this old whore to his office and give her a beating."

But the old woman was still thinking of what Chen Jingji had promised and, in spite of all their abuse, she would not budge. The men went back to Major Zhou. "We offered her ninety taels," they said, "but she would not agree."

"Take a hundred taels and a sedan chair tomorrow," Major Zhou said, "and bring the woman here."

"Master," Zhou Chung said, "if you give her a hundred taels, she will certainly demand another five for herself. Leave her alone for a few days and we shall see if she is still so stupid. If she is, have her brought to your office and try the effect of the thumbscrews. Then she will be afraid of you."

> We know not what life has in store for us
> No one can tell what brings good fortune
> And what brings evil.
> But at last comes the reward alike of good and evil
> Sometimes at once and sometimes long delayed.

We have now to speak again of Wu Song. When he reached Mengzhou, the place to which he had been banished, he was fortunate enough to come under the charge of Shi En, the son of the Chief Jailer. On a certain occasion this Shi En and a man called Jiang Menshen had trouble at a drinking house. Shi En was hurt, but Wu Song came to his aid and Jiang Menshen was beaten. Later, Jiang's sister became a concubine of General Zhang, and, when Wu Song was working for the general, he was accused of stealing and sentenced to serve as a soldier. On his way into this further banishment, Wu Song killed two officials at Feiyunpu. Then he went back and killed all General Zhang's and Jiang Menshen's people, and afterwards took refuge at Shi En's house. Shi En gave him a letter and a leather trunk containing a hundred taels of silver and told him to go to Anping fortress, and see the officer in command there, a certain Liu Gao. On his way, he heard that the Emperor's successor had been proclaimed at the Imperial Palace, and that the Emperor, besides making sacrifice to Heaven, had declared a general amnesty. So Wu Song came home.

When he came to Qinghe, he gave the officers his papers and was reinstated in his old position at the Town Hall. He went to see his neighbor Yao, who had been looking after Ying'er. The girl was now about nineteen years old. Wu Song took her and settled down. He heard that Ximen Qing was dead and that Jinlian was no longer living in that household, but had gone to old woman Wang's house, and was trying to find a new husband. Then Wu Song determined upon revenge.

He put on a hat, and dressed himself well, and went to see what he could see at old woman Wang's house. Jinlian was standing behind the lattice and, when she saw Wu Song, went at once to the inner room. Wu Song pulled aside the lattice and said: "Is old woman Wang at home?"

The old woman was busy preparing dinner. "Who is there?" she said. But, as soon as she had spoken, she recognized Wu Song and made a reverence to him. Wu Song bowed low in return.

"Brother Wu, when did you get back?" the old woman said. "I am delighted to see you."

"My offense has been pardoned," Wu Song said, "so I was able to come home again. I got here yesterday. Thank you for having looked after my brother's house. I will reward you later."

The old woman smiled. "Brother," she said, "you are even better look-ing than you used to be. There is hair on your lip; you have become quite stout, and you have acquired most elegant manners." She took him into the house and offered him tea.

"There is something I want to talk to you about," Wu Song said.

"What is it?"

"I hear that Ximen Qing is dead and that my sister-in-law is back with you again. Will you let her know that I should like to marry her? Ying'er is grown up now and needs somebody to look after her and find her a husband. So we shall avoid people's rude remarks."

At first, old woman Wang decided she would not tell Wu Song the true story. "She is here," she said, "but I am not at all sure that she feels inclined to marry again." But when she found that Wu Song was ready enough to pay, she said: "I will broach the matter to her gradually."

On the other side of the lattice, Jinlian heard all that was said. She heard Wu Song say that he wanted to marry her in order to have someone to lock after Ying'er. She noticed that, after these years of absence, Wu Song seemed a more powerful man than ever. He spoke very agreeably. He seems to have given up his old ideas, she thought, and now is ready for marriage. So she did not wait for old woman Wang to call her, but came out of her own accord. She made a reverence to Wu Song.

"Am I right, Uncle, in understanding that you wish to take me to look after Ying'er and see about her marriage?"

"You must know," old woman Wang interrupted, "that Mistress Ximen wants a hundred taels."

"That seems a great deal," Wu Song suggested.

"Ximen spent so much money on her that he could have made a woman of silver with it," old woman Wang said.

"Well, we won't haggle," Wu Song said. "I want my sister-in-law, and I don't mind spending the money. And you shall have five taels for yourself."

This made the old woman so pleased that she farted and piddled with delight. "Brother Wu," she said, "I know no other man who has such in-telligence as yours. You are a man, and you have been abroad a few years and seen the world."

Jinlian went to the inner room, made some strong tea, and offered it to Wu Song with both hands.

"Ximen's people are anxious to have the matter settled as soon as possible," the old woman said, "and there are four or five people falling over themselves to marry her. I refused them all because they would not pay the price. If you want her, you must let me have your money at once. As you know, the first man to cook the rice is the first to eat it. Heaven brings you together, so don't let anybody else do you out of such a good match."

"Yes," Jinlian said, "if you want me, you must not waste any time."

"I will bring the money tomorrow and take you away tomorrow night," Wu Song said.

Old woman Wang could not believe Wu Song had so much money. The next day he opened the leather trunk and took out the hundred taels that Shi En had given him. He added to it another five taels of his own and went to see old woman Wang. He asked for scales to measure the silver. When the old woman saw the table piled up with white silver, she said to herself: "That Chen Jingji promised me a hundred taels. But he has had to go to the Eastern Capital for it, and there is no telling when he will be back. Why should I not take the chance while I have it?" When the five taels for herself was produced, she accepted it and thanked Wu Song most profusely.

"Brother Wu," she said, "you know how to deal with me."

"Mother," Wu Song said, "take the money. I will take my sister-in-law today."

"Don't be in too much of a hurry, Brother," the old woman said. "You are like a man who lets off fireworks in some dark corner because he hasn't patience enough to wait for the evening. You must wait until I have paid the money to Ximen's people. Then you may take her. And what a fine bridegroom you are, with that smart hat!"

Wu Song grew impatient. Jinlian joked with him. When he had gone away, the old woman thought: "Mistress Ximen said I was to get rid of this woman and never said a word about the price. Now is my chance. I will give her twenty taels and keep the rest for myself."

She took twenty taels to Yueniang, who asked the name of the purchaser.

"Lady," old woman Wang said, "the hares scamper about over the hills but in the end they go back to their own holes. She is going back to the old food she used to eat: she is going to marry her husband's brother."

When Wu Yueniang heard this, she was sorry. She knew that when an enemy meets an enemy, they look closely one at the other. Afterwards, she said to Meng Yulou: "Jinlian will die at this man's hands. He is a man ready to kill for no reason whatever, and he will not spare her."

Old woman Wang went home and told her son Wang Chao to take Jinlian's belongings to Wu Song. The bridegroom had prepared a feast for them. In the evening, the old woman took Jinlian to him. She was no longer in mourning. She wore a new headdress, red clothes, and there was a veil on her head. When they came into the middle room, the candles were burning brightly.

Then they saw Wu Da's tablet on the table. This made them wonder. They felt as though someone were pulling out their hair and sticking knives into their flesh. When they had gone to the inner room, Wu Song told Ying'er to fasten all the doors.

"I must be going now," the old woman said. "There is nobody to look after my house."

"Stay and have something to drink, old Mother," Wu Song said. He told Ying'er to set the dishes on the table and heat some wine. Yet, when the wine was brought, he did not ask them to drink, but poured himself cup after cup and drank them all down.

"I have had quite enough to eat, Brother Wu," the old woman said, "I must go now and leave you two to enjoy yourselves."

"Old woman," Wu Song said, "don't be a fool. I, Wu the Second, have something to say to you." With a crash Wu Song drew out a knife, two feet long, with a very sharp blade. Grasping the knife in one hand, he seized the old woman with the other. His eyes were wide open and his hair stood on end.

"Old woman," he said, "you need not be surprised. Just as a debt finds out those who owe it, so hatred never fails to meet its object. Don't pretend to be a fool. It was your hand that ended my brother's life."

"Brother Wu," the old woman said, "it is getting late, and you are drunk. You shouldn't play with knives. It isn't funny."

"Be silent, old woman," Wu Song said. "I, Wu the Second, am not afraid of death. I will deal with that creature first, and with you, you old sow, later. Move a single inch, and you shall feel my knife."

Then he turned to Jinlian. "Listen, you whore," he said. "How did you murder my brother? Tell me the truth and I will forgive you."

"Uncle, don't be silly," Jinlian said. "How can you fry beans in a cold pan? Your brother died from heart trouble. I had nothing to do with it."

Almost before the words were out of her mouth, there was a crash. Wu Song banged the knife upon the table, seized the woman by her hair with his left hand, and grasped her breasts with his right. Then he kicked over the table. Dishes and cups crashed to the ground. Jinlian was not very strong. He lifted her like a feather from the other side of the table. Then he dragged her to the middle room, before the table on which Wu Da's tablet stood. Old woman Wang saw that he was in a mad rage and would have run away, but the door had been locked and Wu Song, striding after her, caught her. He threw her to the floor and, with his girdle, tied her up till she looked like a monkey offering a fruit. She could not get away.

"Oh, Sir," she cried, "don't be angry with me. This lady is responsible for the murder. It was all her doing. My hands are clean."

"You old bitch," Wu Song cried. "I know everything, and it is no use your lying to me. It was you who told Ximen Qing to have me banished. But I am here, and where is Ximen Qing?"

"I will kill you first," he said to Jinlian, "and then this old bitch."

He picked up the knife and brandished it twice before her face.

"Uncle, forgive me, and let me get up," she cried. "I promise I will tell you."

Wu Song picked her up. He stripped her of her clothes and made her kneel down before the tablet.

"Speak quickly, whore!" he shouted at her.

Now her spirit had left her. She told Wu Song everything; how, when she had been pulling up the lattice, the pole had struck Ximen Qing, how she had made clothes, and how the intrigue between them had begun. Then she said how Ximen Qing had kicked Wu Da in the chest, and old woman Wang had shown her how to poison him. Then, how they had burned his body, and Ximen Qing had married her. Meanwhile old woman Wang was sobbing. "Oh, you fool," she cried, "you have told him the truth. What can I do now?"

Wu Song, before the tablet, grasped the woman by the hair. With his other hand, he sprinkled wine upon the ground and set fire to some paper money.

"Brother," he said, "your spirit cannot be far away. This day Wu Song avenges you."

When Jinlian heard this, she was desperate and began to shriek. Wu Song took a handful of dust from the incense burner and threw it into her mouth so that she could not make any more noise. He tugged at her hair and threw her down upon the ground again. As she struggled with him, her hair was disordered and the pins and earrings fell out. Wu Song thought it possible that she might try to run away, and kicked her in the ribs. Then he stamped upon her arms with both his feet.

"You whore," he cried, "you make yourself out to be a very clever woman. I would like to know what sort of heart you have, and I will see."

He tore her arms apart, and thrust the knife deep into her soft white bosom. One slash, and there was a bleeding hole in her breast. Blood gushed forth. Now the woman's starry eyes were almost closed and her feet seemed to tremble. Wu Song took the knife in his teeth, tore open her breast with both hands, and dragged the heart and entrails from her body. The blood streamed from them as he set them on the table before the tablet. Then, with a single stroke, he cut off her head. The blood flowed over the floor.

Ying'er looked in, terrified, and covered her face with her hands.

A violent man, this Wu Song. And how sad, the case of this woman who, when the breath was still in her body, could use it in a thousand ways. Now she was powerless. She was only thirty-two years old. When his hand fell, her young life ended. The knife struck, and she was no more. Her spirit fled to the palace of the King of Hell, and her spirit vanished to the city of the dead. It was like the breaking of the golden branches of the willow by the snow in springtime, or the jade-like blossom rent and torn by the wild wind as the year goes out. We know not where her loveliness vanished that night, or where her sweet spirit went.

When Wu Song killed Jinlian, old woman Wang shouted, "Murder." Then he went to her, and struck off her head. He dragged away the body, then thrust his knife through the woman's heart, and pinned it to the eaves at the back of the house. It was the first night watch. He took Ying'er into the other room. "I am frightened, Uncle," she said. "My child," Wu Song said, "I can do nothing for you."

Then he jumped over the wall and went into old woman Wang's house. He wished to kill Wang Chao. But it seemed that Wang Chao's end was not to be yet. When he heard his mother's shrieks, he knew that Wu Song was killing her. He came to the front door but would not open it. He knocked at the back, but there was no answer. Then he rushed to the street to find a policeman. Meanwhile, the neighbors on either side knew that Wu Song was killing somebody, but none of them dared to interfere.

When Wu Song reached old woman Wang's room, he found a light burning, but there was nobody there. He opened her chest, took out the clothes and strewed them on the floor. Then he found the silver, about eighty-five taels, for the old woman had only given Yueniang twenty. But he took ornaments, pins and earrings. Then, taking his knife, he jumped over the wall at the back. About the fifth night watch, he left the city, and went to Shizipo, where Zhang Qing and his wife lived. Then he became a monk. Afterwards, he went to Liangshan and joined the bandits.

CHAPTER 88

Chunmei Mourns for Pan Jinlian

For a moment he beheld her in a dream
But, when he woke, he knew that there was no one.
He turned and tossed and could not sleep
Then threw his clothes about him and paced the floor.

The morning breeze is sharp
The moonbeams dim.
He lies alone, wakeful, till morning breaks
But she of whom he dreamed
Does not return.

When Wang Chao and the police came to Wu Song's place, the doors were still fastened. In old woman Wang's house, money and things were missing and clothes were strewn over the floor. They realized that Wu Song had murdered the woman and gone off with the money. They forced the door and found the two bodies on the floor, covered with blood. The entrails of Pan Jinlian were pinned to the eaves at the back of the house, and Ying'er was still shut up in the room. She could only cry when they questioned her. The next morning they brought the matter before the notice of the magistrate and produced such evidence as they could get.

This magistrate had been recently appointed, and his name was Li Changqi. He was a native of Zaoqiang in the prefecture of Chending. When he heard of the murder, he sent his runners to summon the neighbors and the members of both families. So Wang Chao and Ying'er came before the magistrate. The house and the bodies were examined. The magistrate declared that Wu Song, when drunk, had killed the women Pan and Wang. He ordered the bodies to be buried temporarily, and issued a warrant for Wu Song's arrest, offering a reward of fifty taels of silver for his apprehension.

Zhang Sheng and Li An took a hundred taels with them and went to old woman Wang's house again. But when they got there, they found that the two women had been killed and that the local officials were examining the bodies and taking steps to arrest the murderer. They went back and told their master. When Chunmei heard the news, she wept for three days and would neither eat nor drink. Major Zhou was much disturbed and sent for all kinds of different entertainers to amuse her, but they could not assuage her grief. Every day she sent Zhang Sheng and Li An to see if Wu Song had been arrested.

Meanwhile, Chen Jingji had gone to the Eastern Capital to get some money so that he could marry Jinlian. On the way, he met Chen Ding, a servant of his family, who was coming to tell him that his father was very ill and that his mother wanted him to take up the responsibilities of the household. Then Jingji traveled with even more haste than before. At last he came to the Eastern Capital and hurried to the house of his uncle, Zhang Shilian. But his uncle was dead, and his aunt told him that his father had died three days before. They were all wearing mourning clothes.

Jingji made a reverence before his father's tablet, and kowtowed to his mother and his aunt. His mother realized that he was now a grown man, cried with him, and talked about the matters that needed to be decided. "I am happy and sad at the same time," she said. When Jingji asked her what she meant, she said she was happy because the announcement of the Emperor's successor meant a general amnesty for all prisoners, and sad because of the death of Jingji's father and uncle. "Your aunt is now a widow," she said, "and we shall not be able to stay here any longer. You must take your father's body and bury it at our old home."

If I take the coffin and all the other things, Jingji thought, it will mean a long and slow journey, and I shall be too late to marry. I had better take the chests and valuables and go and marry Jinlian at once. Then I can come back for the coffin, and I shall not be too late.

When he had thought the matter over, he said to his mother: "The country is overridden by bandits and thieves and it is not at all safe to travel. If I take both the coffin and the boxes at the same time, they are likely to attract attention, and what can I do if anything happens? I suggest we do things more gradually. To begin with, I will get two carts and take all these trunks and things and go and see about a house for you. Then I will come back and take you, Chen Ding, and the coffin, at the beginning of next year. When we are settled, we will put the coffin into a monastery and offer sacrifice, then build a tomb and bury it."

His mother, being a woman, was deceived by these smooth-sounding words. She let him take everything away, two cartloads in all. They put banners on the carts to make it seem as though they were pilgrims and, on the first day of the twelfth month, Chen Jingji left the Capital.

When he reached Qinghe, he went to tell his Uncle Zhang that his father was dead, and that his mother and his father's body were coming shortly. "I have brought these things," he said, "so as to make everything ready for my mother."

"In that case," his uncle said, "I must go back to my own house." He bade his servants make preparations at once for the removal.

When his uncle had gone, Jingji was delighted. "Now I have got rid of that old fellow," he said to himself, "I can marry Jinlian straightaway and have a good time. My father is dead and my mother treats me with every indulgence. I will begin by divorcing my wife, and then send an accusation against my mother-in-law. She has no hold on me now since my family is no longer under the ban."

People decide upon courses of action like this, but Heaven often thinks otherwise. Jingji took a hundred taels for old woman Wang, and went to Amethyst Street. But when he got there, there were two rough graves outside the door, each with a spear and a large lantern upon it. On the door itself was pasted a notice that said: "Murder! The murderer Wu Song has killed Pan and Wang. Anyone who arrests him, or gives notice of his whereabouts, will receive a reward of fifty taels of silver."

Jingji looked at the notice. He was as if rooted to the ground. Two men came out of a tent.

"Who are you?" they cried. "Why are you looking at the notice? We haven't arrested anybody yet. Who are you?" They looked as though they would lay hands on Jingji. He ran away. When he came to a wine house, not far from the stone bridge, he saw a man dressed in black coming towards him.

"What are you doing here, Brother?" the man said. "You seem very brave."

Jingji saw that it was a great friend of his, a man called Yang the Second, who was nicknamed Iron Claw. They greeted one another, and Yang the Second asked Jingji where he had been. Jingji told him that he had been to the Eastern Capital, and that his father had died. Then he said: "This woman who has been killed was my father-in-law's wife. This is the first I have heard of it. I have only just read the notice."

"It was her brother, Wu Song, who came back from banishment and murdered her," Yang the Second said. "I don't know why he did it. He even killed old woman Wang. I know Wu Song had a niece, for she has been living with my uncle, Yao the Second, for the last three or four years. Wu Song ran away as soon as he had murdered the two women, and my aunt got the girl away from the authorities and found a husband for her. The two bodies, as you see, are still here. The police will have a very difficult task looking out for Wu Song all the time, and I doubt whether he will ever be caught."

Yang the Second asked Jingji to go and drink with him in the wine house. Now that the young man knew his lover was dead, he was very much upset and could not drink much. He drank three cups or so and then left Yang the Second and went home. That evening he bought some paper money. Then he went to the stone bridge not far from old woman Wang's door. "Sister Pan," he said, "your young brother, Chen Jingji, comes to offer you this paper money. It was because my coming back was so delayed that you met your death. Now you are dead, you will become a goddess. Use your spiritual power to help those who seek to arrest Wu Song. When he is found, I will go to the place of execution to see him cut to pieces. Only then shall I be satisfied."

He sobbed and set fire to the paper money. Then he went home, shut the gate, and went to his own room. He went to sleep. Jinlian appeared to him, wearing a simple dress, and covered with blood. She said to him, with tears: "Brother, I died such a bitter death. I longed to live with you, but, alas, before you came back, that fellow Wu Song murdered me. The underworld will not take me in, so all day I must wander about, and all night I seek for shelter everywhere and try to beg a little water to drink. I thank you for burning paper money for me. My murderer has not been found, and still my body lies in the street. If you think of our past love, buy a coffin and bury me properly, that I may not lie there exposed any longer."

"Sister," Jingji said, "you know that I would gladly bury you, but I am afraid of my mother-in-law, that cruel, heartless woman. If she hears of it, she will seek to do me some evil, and this would be an opportunity. Sister, go to Major Zhou's place. See Chunmei and ask her to have your body buried."

"I have been there," Jinlian cried, "and I could not get in. The god of the gate stopped me. But I will go again."

Jingji still cried and tried to hold her hand and talk to her, but the smell of the blood on her body came to him, and she escaped from him. He woke up and found it was a dream. The night watchman's drum was sounding the third night watch.

"How strange!" he said to himself. "Did I not see my sister? Did she not tell me all about this tragedy and ask me to bury her? But I do not know when Wu Song will be arrested. It is a sad business."

Search was kept up for Wu Song, but two months passed and there was no sign of him. At last there came news that he had gone to Liangshan and joined the bandits, and the policemen told the magistrate. Then the magistrate gave orders that the bodies might now be taken away and buried by their families. Wang Chao took away his mother's body, but there was no one to bury Jinlian.

Chunmei had been sending Zhang Sheng and Li An nearly every day to the Town Hall for news. Each time they could only report that the murderer had not been caught and that the bodies were still there. The police were keeping watch over them and nobody dared move them. At the beginning of the first month, Chunmei had a dream. Pan Jinlian came to her, covered with blood and her hair in disorder. "Sister," the woman said, "I had such a sad death. It was hard for me to come and see you because the god of the gate would not let me in. Now my enemy, Wu Song, has escaped. My body still lies in the street, blown by the wind and drenched by the rain. Dogs and fowls come and stand over me. I have no near relations, and there is no one to take me away. If you still remember the friendship there used to be between us, buy a coffin and bury me somewhere. Then, in Hades, I can close my eyes and mouth in peace." As she said this, she cried bitterly.

Chunmei wished to take her hand and ask her many things, but Jinlian slipped away from her. She woke up and knew it was a dream. She was still crying.

She did not know what the dream meant until the next day. Then she said to Zhang Sheng and Li An: "Go and see whether the bodies of those two women are still there."

When they came back, the men told her: "The murderer has escaped and the two bodies could not lie there forever with the police keeping watch over them, so the magistrate has ordered the relatives to take them away. The old woman's son has taken away his mother's body, but the other woman is still there."

"Now," Chunmei said, "I am going to ask you two to do something for me. If you do it, I will see you are well paid for it."

The two men knelt down. "Lady," they said, "you need not talk of payment. If you will speak kindly of us to our master, we shall be grateful and, if you tell us to go through fire or water, we are ready to do it."

Chunmei went into her room and got ten taels of silver and two rolls of cloth.

"The dead woman was really my sister," she said to them. "She married Ximen Qing and, after his death, left his household. Then she was murdered. Don't say anything to your master, but go and buy a coffin with this money, put her body into it, and take her outside the city. Find a suitable place and bury her there. I will pay you well."

"We will go and do so at once," the men said.

"I am afraid the magistrate will not let us take the body away," Li An said. "We ought to have a card from our master to give him."

"Oh, we will tell him that the dead woman is our lady's sister," Zhang Sheng said. "I don't believe the magistrate will make any objection. We shan't need a card."

They took the money and went to the Town Hall.

"It is my belief that the dead woman must have been a friend of the master's young lady," Zhang Sheng said to Li An. "They probably lived together. That is why she is so concerned about this dead woman. Perhaps you remember that when the woman was killed, our lady cried for three or four days and wouldn't eat anything. The master sent for all sorts of people to come and amuse her, but they couldn't do anything. Now there is nobody to bury the woman and she wants to do it. If we manage this business, she will certainly say a kind word for us to our master. It is a stroke of luck for us, because he never refuses her anything. He considers her more than the other ladies."

They came to the Town Hall and sent in their petition. "The dead woman's sister is the Major's wife," they said. "It is by her orders that we have come to ask for leave to remove the body."

They paid six taels for a coffin. Then they dug up the body, put the woman's entrails back into it, and sewed up the gash with thread. Finally they wrapped her in a shroud and put her into the coffin.

"Our best plan," Zhang Sheng said, "will be to bury her at the Temple of Eternal Felicity, where our master worships. There is room there."

They hired two men to carry the coffin to the temple and said to the Abbot that they would like to bury the body there, since it was that of their young mistress's sister. The Abbot pointed out a place behind the temple, near a poplar tree, and there they buried her. Then they went back and told Chunmei all they had done. "We bought a coffin and buried her," they said, "and we have still four taels left."

"It is very kind of you," Chunmei said. "Will you take the four taels and give two to the Abbot and ask him to read a dirge to help her on her way to paradise?" She gave the two men each a tael and a present of food besides.

The two men knelt down. "We have done nothing," they said, "and we dare not take these gifts. We only ask that you should speak well of us to our master."

"I shall be angry if you do not," Chunmei said.

So the two men kowtowed and took the money. Then they went to drink, and said how kind their mistress was. The next day, Zhang Sheng took the silver and asked the Abbot to hold a service for the dead woman. Chunmei gave them five *qian* of silver to get paper money to burn for her.

❊   ❊   ❊

Chen Ding reached Qinghe about this time. He brought with him Chen Jingji's family and his father's coffin. He set down the coffin at this same

Temple of Eternal Felicity where, after a funeral service had been held, they proposed to bury it. When Jingji heard of their arrival, he brought in the luggage and kowtowed to his mother.

"Why did you not come to meet me?" she asked.

"I haven't been well, and there is no one to look after the house," he said.

"Where is your uncle?"

"When he found you were coming, he went back to his old house."

"You should not have allowed him to do so," Mistress Chen said. "He might just as well have stayed."

Then Zhang came to see his sister; they embraced each other and wept. Then they sat down together to talk.

The next day, Jingji's mother told him to take five taels of silver and some paper money and give them to the Abbot to hold a service for his father. Jingji set out on horseback. On the way, he met two of his friends, Lu and Yang. He dismounted, and greeted them. They asked him where he was going.

"My father's body is at the temple outside the city," Jingji told them. "Tomorrow will be the twentieth, and my father's last week's mind, so my mother has asked me to take some money to the Abbot for the ceremony."

"We are very sorry," the two men said. "We had no idea your father's coffin had arrived. When will the funeral be?"

"Not for a few days yet," Jingji said. "We shall not bury him until after this ceremony."

The two men bowed to him and were going on, but he called them back. "Yang," he said, "do you know who has taken away the body of that woman Pan?"

"About a fortnight ago," Yang said, "when it was clear that the police would not be able to lay hands on Wu Song, I told the magistrate, and the magistrate told the relatives they might remove the bodies. Old woman Wang's body was taken by her son, but the other remained for several days. Then somebody from Major Zhou's place brought a coffin and buried it at the Temple of Eternal Felicity outside the city."

Then Jingji guessed that Chunmei had taken it. "Are there many Temples of Eternal Felicity outside the city?" he asked.

"There is only one," Yang told him, "the one where Major Zhou worships. How many would you like?"

Jingji was delighted. It seemed to him that it was by a special dispensation of providence that Jinlian should be buried there. They went their ways. Jingji mounted his horse and rode on to the temple. Before he mentioned the service for his father, he said to the Abbot: "I hear that Major

Zhou's people have buried a woman here recently. Can you tell me where the grave is?"

"Behind the temple, under the poplar tree," the Abbot told him. "The dead woman was the young lady's sister."

Jingji did not go to his father's coffin, but took the paper money and other offerings to Jinlian's grave. There he burned the paper money for her. "Sister," he cried, "this is your young brother, Chen Jingji, come to make an offering to you. Find a pleasant place in which to live, and spend the money when you are in need of it."

Then he went to the place where his father's coffin rested and burned paper money there. He gave the money to the monks and said: "May we have eight monks on the twentieth, to perform the service for the last week's mind?" The Abbot took the money and went to see about preparing the necessary things. Jingji went home and told his mother.

On the twentieth day, they all went to the temple for the service. When it was over, they selected a day of good omen and buried the dead gentleman in his ancestral tomb. After this they went home and mother and son settled down in their house.

At the beginning of the second month it was very warm. Wu Yueniang, Meng Yulou, Sun Xue'e, and Ximen Dajie, with Xiaoyu, went and stood at the gate to look down the street. Everything seemed lively and busy. They suddenly caught sight of a crowd of people following a monk. He was very fat and tall; there were three bronze figures on his head, and lamps all over his body. His robes were apricot colored and had broad sleeves. His feet were bare, and his ankles splashed with mud.

> He sits and gives himself to meditation
> Expounds the sacred scriptures, preaches the gospel.
> Broad shoulders, sunken eyes
> Themselves exemplify the manner of the Buddha.
> He begs his food and preaches
> According to the rule of his religion.
> By day he goes with staff and tinkling bell
> At night brings out the spear and club.
> Outside the door he beats his bald head to the ground
> On the street he strikes his lips.
> Reality is emptiness
> And emptiness reality.
> Who shall say what happens to this earthly life?
> Some go, some come
> Some come, some go.

> But who has found a welcome
> In the paradise of the west?

When he saw Yueniang and the other women standing at the gate, he came over to them and saluted them.

"Most charitable ladies," he said. "I see that you belong to an exalted family. This is a most opportune meeting. I have come from Mount Wu begging for alms, because I seek to build a temple for the ten Lords of Virtue and the Three Precious Ones. I rely entirely upon the charitable, who cultivate the field of generosity and give me alms. So this admirable work will be brought to a happy end, and a reward in the next life assured. I am but a wandering monk."

Yueniang told Xiaoyu to go and get a hat, a pair of shoes, a string of coppers, and a measure of white rice. She was always inclined to be generous to monks, and this one attracted her. She kept a store of hats and shoes especially for them. When Xiaoyu brought the things, Yueniang said: "Ask his Reverence to come and take them."

"You, monk, who will become a donkey in your next life," Xiaoyu said in her sweetest voice, "come here. My lady offers you these things. Why don't you kowtow to her?"

Yueniang scolded her. "You little scamp," she said. "He is a monk, a disciple of Buddha. You mustn't talk to him like that. It is his duty to ask for alms. You little strumpet, you will certainly be punished sooner or later."

Xiaoyu laughed. "That thievish monk!" she said. "What does he mean by letting his eyes roam over my body from head to feet?"

The monk accepted the gifts in both hands, made a reverence, and thanked them.

"Shaven rogue!" Xiaoyu said to him. "Where are your manners? There are several ladies here, as you see. Why do you content yourself with bowing twice to us, and why don't you make a reverence to me?"

"Do be quiet, you little rascal," Yueniang said. "He is a son of Buddha, and you have no right to expect a reverence from him."

"Lady," Xiaoyu said, "if he is a son of Buddha, who are Buddha's daughters?"

"The nuns are Buddha's daughters," Yueniang said.

"Oh, now I understand," Xiaoyu said. "Nun Xue and Nun Wang and the Abbess are all Buddha's daughters, are they? Well, I wonder who are Buddha's sons-in-law?"

Yueniang could not help laughing. "You little strumpet!" she said, "It is only lately you have learned to talk such nonsense. You are always being rude nowadays."

"You mustn't scold me only, Lady," Xiaoyu said. "That monk, with his thievish eyes, is looking at me all the time."

"If he looks at you," Yulou said, "I suppose it is because he wishes to make you give up the things of this world."

"Then I will go with him," Xiaoyu said.

They all laughed, but Yueniang said. "You are a little strumpet. You are always insulting monks and saying wicked things about Buddha."

The monk took the things and went away haughtily, the three images on his head. "Lady," Xiaoyu said, "that thievish monk had another look at me before he went away. Really, you shouldn't scold me."

As they were standing there, old woman Xue came to them, carrying her box of artificial flowers. She made a reverence to them.

"What have you been doing?" Yueniang asked. "It is a long time since I even saw your shadow."

"I hardly know myself what I have been doing," the old woman said. "A few days ago, his Lordship Zhang the Second, the new magistrate, was arranging a marriage with the Xu family. Xu's niece is going to marry Zhang's son. Old woman Wen arranged that. Yesterday was the third day and they had a splendid banquet. The young lady at the Major's place sent for me, but I was too busy to go."

"Where are you going now?" Yueniang said.

"I have come especially to see you," old woman Xue said. "There is something I want to talk to you about."

"Come in, then," Yueniang said, and took the old woman to her room. When she had had tea, the old woman said: "Lady, there is something you don't know. Last year, your kinsman Chen, at the Eastern Capital, died. His wife sent for your son-in-law to bring his father's body and the whole household here. They reached here in the first month, held a service, and buried the old gentleman. I thought that, if you had known, you would certainly have gone to burn some paper offerings for the old gentleman."

"But I would never have known, if you hadn't come to tell me," Yueniang said. "How was I to hear of it? I heard that Pan Jinlian had been killed by her first husband's brother, and that she and old woman Wang had been buried, but I have heard nothing of what happened since."

"If the Fifth Lady had not misbehaved herself and had stayed here, it would have been much better for her," the old woman said. "But she forgot her womanly virtue and behaved so badly that you had to send her away. If she had still been living with you, her brother-in-law would not have had a chance to kill her. Indeed, debts always demand that they who owe shall pay, and hatred never fails to find its victim. But Chunmei did not forget how she had loved that lady in the past. She bought a coffin and buried Jinlian, or the body would be lying there still. Wu Song has not been caught, and there was nobody else to care about her."

"Chunmei has only been at Major Zhou's house a short time," Xue'e said. "How comes she to be in such a position that she can afford to buy a coffin and bury the woman? Didn't the Major have anything to say in the matter? How does he treat her?"

"Ah! You can't imagine how fond he is of her," the old woman said. "He spends every night with her and obeys her slightest wish. As soon as she went there and he found how beautiful she was, he gave her three rooms and a maid. He spent three nights with her and had all the clothes she needed for a year made for her. On the third day he gave a feast and presented me with a tael of silver and a roll of silk. His first wife is now about fifty. She is blind, eats vegetarian food, and does not take any part in the management of the house. His second wife, Sun, has a little daughter and spends all her time looking after the child. Chunmei has all the keys. The Major does everything she suggests, and she never has any difficulty in getting money out of him."

Yueniang and Xue'e said nothing. When the old woman was preparing to go away, Yueniang said: "Come again tomorrow. I will get a food offering ready, a roll of silk, and some paper money, and you must go with my daughter to offer them to her dead father-in-law."

"Won't you go yourself, Lady?" the old woman said.

"Tell them I am not very well," Yueniang said. "I will go and see them another day."

"Then tell your daughter to have everything ready. I will be here about dinnertime."

"Where are you going now?" Yueniang asked. "Must you always be going to the Major's place?"

"If I don't go, they will be angry with me. They have sent for me several times."

"Why do they send for you?" Yueniang said.

"Lady, Chunmei is now four or five months gone with child and the Major is delighted. I shall certainly get a present when I get there."

The old woman went off with her box. "What a liar that old strumpet is!" Xue'e said. "Chunmei has only been there a short time. How can she be so far gone with child? The Captain has more than one wife already. Is it likely that he devotes himself entirely to her?"

"He has a first wife, and another lady who has a little girl "Yueniang said.

"These go-betweens," Xue'e said, "always talk about water a foot deep having waves ten feet high."

CHAPTER 89
Wu Yueniang Meets Chunmei Again

A beautiful woman's lot is grievous.
Alas, that one so exquisite
Should turn to a handful of yellow dust.
Is it that Heaven pays no heed,
That good and evil are but matters of chance?
It granted her beauty and intelligence
Then let her go as though she had been nothing.
It seems unjust.
And when we ask the Heavens why it happens,
No answer is vouchsafed us.

It is sad.
The beauty of the earth combined with Heaven's fragrance
Passes like the seasons.
They are many who lie buried.
May we not ask where there is gaiety?
Yet there are palaces where people dance and sing,
Where people walk in springtime on the purple path,
And, in the evening, sit beside green-painted windows,
Graceful and exquisite.
Surely the life of man seems purposeless,
Now as in the days long past.

Wu Yueniang prepared the food offering and paper things, and Ximen Dajie, in mourning dress, went in a sedan chair to her husband's house, with old woman Xue in attendance. When they came to the house, Chen Jingji was standing outside the door. He asked the old woman where the things had come from. She made a reverence.

"Your mother-in-law has sent them as an offering to your late father," she said, "and your wife has come too."

"Curses on my mother-in-law!" Jingji cried. "She is half a month too late. It is as if she set up the god of the door on the sixteenth day of the first month. My father has been buried a long time, and she comes now with her tribute of respect."

"Good Brother-in-law, as your wife's mother says, now she is a widow she is like a crab without legs. She knew nothing about your father's coffin coming, and you must forgive her if she is late."

As they were talking, Ximen Dajie's sedan chair came up.

"Who is this?" Jingji said.

"Whom do you expect? Your mother-in-law is not well and she has sent your wife to come and burn paper offerings for your father."

"Take the whore away," Jingji said scornfully. "Better people than she have died by thousands. What have I to do with her?"

"You should not talk like that. When a woman marries a man, she does so to live with him."

"I don't want anything to do with the whore. Be off at once."

The chair men were standing by, and Chen Jingji went up and kicked them. "Take her away," he cried, "or I will break your beggarly legs and pull that whore's hair out.

The sedan-chair men could only take the chair away. By the time old woman Xue was able to speak to Jingji's mother, it had been gone for some time. The old woman could do nothing, so she gave the things to Mistress Chen and came back to tell Yueniang what had happened.

Yueniang was so angry that she nearly fainted. "The rogue is utterly unprincipled!" she cried. "He came here to escape the law, and his father-in-law kept him all those years. This is how he repays us. What a pity that my dead husband kept such a rascal in the place and so gave us all this trouble today. It puts me in the position of a rotten rat, and he dares to insult me."

"Daughter," she said to Ximen Dajie, "you saw with your own eyes that neither my husband nor I ever treated him badly. So long as you live, you belong to the Chen family, and, when you die, you will be a Chen ghost. I can't keep you here. Go to him tomorrow. Don't be afraid. I don't think he will be quite so desperate as to push you into a well. He dare not kill you, because, fortunately, law still has some force in this world."

The next day Yueniang told Daian to go with her daughter. The young woman went in a sedan chair. When they came to the house, Jingji was out. He had gone to his father's grave to put earth on the mound. His mother was a lady of breeding and received her daughter-in-law.

"Go home and tell your mistress that I am very much obliged to her," she said to Daian. "Ask her not to be angry with the young man. He had taken too much to drink yesterday and that is why he behaved so strangely. I will bring him around by degrees." She gave Daian something to eat and dismissed him.

In the evening Chen Jingji came back. The moment he saw his wife he began to kick her and curse.

"You whore!" he cried, "why have you come back? You told me I begged my food from your family. The real truth is that your people have stolen a lot of my property, and that is how they got their wealth. If your people won't keep a son-in-law for nothing, why should I keep you now, you whore? Better people than you have died by thousands, yes, and by tens of thousands."

Then his wife cursed him in return. "You shameless rascal, you unprincipled scamp!" she cried. "Just because that strumpet was murdered, why do you vent your spite on me?"

Jingji pulled her hair and struck her violently with his fist. His mother came and tried to separate them, but he pushed her away and threw her on the floor. The old lady cried. "You rascal! Are your eyes so red that you do not even know your own mother?"

That same night Ximen Dajie was sent back again. Her husband said to her: "If you don't make them give me back my things, I will kill you." This frightened her so much that she stayed at home and never again tried to go and see her husband.

At the Festival of Pure Brightness in the third month, Yueniang prepared incense, candles, paper money, and other things and went outside the city to offer them at her dead husband's grave. She left Sun Xue'e, Ximen Dajie, and one or two maids to look after the house. She, with Meng Yulou, Xiaoyu, and the nurse Ruyi'er carrying the baby, went to the grave in sedan chairs. She asked Uncle Wu and Aunt Wu to go and join them there.

When they came outside the city, everything looked beautiful. The willows were green and the flowers fresh. Hosts of people were celebrating the coming of Spring, for there is no season more delightful. Then the sun is beautiful and the wind gentle, as the eyes of the willow open and the hearts of the flowers are unfolded. The very earth seems perfumed. A myriad flowers seem to compete with each other for the prize of beauty; the herbs put forth new shoots. They are the message of Spring. The light is soft and bright; the scenery warm and perfectly harmonious. The little peach flowers have painted their faces a deep red; the young willows bend their slender waists, tender and narrow as the palace gates. Orioles sing a hundred melodies, and wake people from their midday dreams. Purple swallows sing, and the melancholy of early spring is banished. The sun makes the days longer and warmer, and little yellow ducks splash in the pools. Through the green duckweed they dash. Beyond the river on some estate, we know not whose, the swing hangs high among the mist of green willows.

It is the festival of Spring
And mist is everywhere.
Outside the town the gentle breeze blows away the paper money
And hangs it in the trees.
People laugh and sing on the tender grass.
It is the season of apricot blossom
When the rain comes suddenly
And suddenly is gone again.
The gentle oriole chatters in the cherry trees,
Under the willows, guests who have drunk their fill
Sleep on the riverbank.
Charming women are busy to the strains of music
They bring a rope and make it fast, Swing to and fro
Like a flight of angels.

Yueniang and the others came to Wuliyuan, where the grave was. Daian took the food boxes to the kitchen; they made a fire and the cooks prepared the dishes. Meanwhile, Yueniang, Yulou, Xiaoyu, and Ruyi'er with the baby, went to the hall. There they had tea and waited for Aunt Wu. Daian set out the offerings before Ximen Qing's grave, and still they waited for Aunt Wu. She was delayed because she had not been able to get a sedan chair, and it was almost noon before she came along with Uncle Wu, both on donkeyback.

"I don't know how you manage to ride a donkey," Yueniang said to her.

Aunt Wu drank some tea, then she changed her clothes and they all went together to make their offering. Yueniang took five sticks of incense, kept one for herself, and gave the others, one to Yulou, one to Ruyi'er for the baby, and one each to her brother and his wife. She first put incense in the burner and bowed before the grave. "Brother," she said, "when you were alive, you were a man; now you are a spirit. Today is the Festival of Spring. Your dutiful wife Wu, sister Meng, and your son Xiaoge, who is now a year old, have come to your grave to burn paper money for you. Protect your son's life, that he may live long and come to do worship at your grave. Brother, you and I were once husband and wife. I treasure in my memory the remembrance of your features and your way of speaking, and I am sad."

She covered her face and sobbed. Then Yulou came forward, offered incense, made a reverence and cried with Yueniang. The nurse, Ruyi'er, with the baby in her arms, knelt down. Uncle Wu and Aunt Wu also offered incense and made reverence. Then they went to the arbor and there had food and wine. Yueniang asked Uncle Wu and Aunt Wu to take the places of honor. She and Yulou sat opposite, Xiaoyu and Ruyi'er and Aunt Wu's old maid sat at the side.

That day, Major Zhou also went to visit his ancestral tombs. Before the festival, Chunmei slept with him. She pretended to have a dream and cried during the night. Zhou asked her what was the matter.

"I had a dream," Chunmei said, "and in my dream, my mother came to me. She cried and said to me that she had brought me up, yet I was not going to burn paper offerings for her at the Festival of Spring. Then I cried and awoke."

"If she brought you up, you must do your duty as a daughter. But where is she buried?"

"At the Temple of Eternal Felicity outside the Southern Gate."

"Then you must not trouble any more," Major Zhou said. "That temple is my own place of worship. Tomorrow, I shall be going there to visit our family tombs and I will tell a servant to take something to the place where your mother is buried."

The next day, the Major told his servants to take food, wine, and fruit and go to his ancestral tombs outside the city. At the grave he had a large house with halls, rooms and a garden, a place for worship, and shrines. His two wives and Chunmei went with him each in a sedan chair carried by four men. Soldiers marched before them.

Yueniang drank wine with Uncle Wu and Aunt Wu. She was afraid it was getting late, and told Daian and Laian to clear everything away. They went to the village of Apricot Blossom. There was a hill near the village and a wineshop at the foot of the hill. Many people were strolling about, and she told the servants to take their food there. Aunt Wu had no sedan chair, so they all walked and the sedan chairs followed empty behind them. Uncle Wu came last, leading the two donkeys. They walked over the green grass for about three *li*, then came to the Peach Flower inn, and, when they had gone five *li*, saw the village of Apricot Blossom. The red and green dresses of the people seemed like masses of flowers and willows. They had all come to visit their graves. In the distance they could see a temple beneath the shade of a locust tree. It was a building of more than usual magnificence.

Yueniang asked what this building was called.

"It is the place where Major Zhou worships," Uncle Wu said, "and it is called the Temple of Eternal Felicity. Don't you remember how, when my brother-in-law was alive, he gave a great deal of money to repair the building? That is why it looks so new and beautiful."

"Let us go and have a look at it," Yueniang said.

Some of the novices saw them coming and went to tell the Abbot. When he saw a number of people coming, he came out to receive them.

He made a reverence to Uncle Wu and then to Yueniang, and told one of the young monks to unlock all the shrines that they might see the different images of Buddha. When they had had tea, all the doors were opened. Yueniang and the others looked everywhere. Then they went back to the Abbot's apartments, and he offered them tea.

"May I ask your name in religion?" Uncle Wu said.

"My name is Daojian," the Abbot said, "and this monastery is the place of worship of his most generous lordship Major Zhou. Under my instruction are more than a hundred monks, and, at the back, is a place for the wandering monks who come here to meditate. They make intercession for the charitable." He asked them if they would not take something to eat.

"We must not put you to inconvenience," Yueniang said. She took five *qian* of silver and asked Uncle Wu to give them to the Abbot. "It is only a trifle to pay for incense to burn before the Buddhas," she said.

The Abbot made a reverence. "I have really nothing to offer you," he said, "but I should be glad if you would take a cup of tea. Thank you for this gift."

Novices set the table and brought vegetarian food and cakes. The Abbot sat down with them and took up his chopsticks to encourage them to eat something.

Suddenly two men in black clothes burst into the room and shouted in a voice like thunder. "Teacher, why don't you come out to welcome the young lady?"

The Abbot put on his robes and hat, told the young monks to clear everything away, and asked the ladies to go into a small room.

"I must go and see the young lady," he said. "When she has finished her worship, I will come back to you."

Uncle Wu suggested that they should leave, but the Abbot would not hear of it.

The monks, ringing bells and beating drums, went to the main gate to receive the visitor. A host of men in black clothes followed a large sedan chair, coming from the east like a flying cloud. The chair men's clothes were wet with sweat.

The Abbot bowed. "I did not know you were coming, Lady," he said. "I beg your pardon for not being ready to welcome you."

"Teacher," Chunmei said, who was sitting in the sedan chair, "I am sorry to put you to so much trouble."

The servants took the offerings and went to the back of the temple where Pan Jinlian was buried. They set out paper money and other offerings before the grave. Chunmei did not go into the temple but straight around to the back. There she left the sedan chair. The servants stood ready to do anything she might wish and, slowly and gracefully, she walked between them to the grave. There she offered incense and made reverence four times.

"Mother," she said, "I have come to offer paper money for you. I trust that you may rest in paradise and make use of this money when you are in need. If I had only known you would be killed, I would have made a plan to bring you to me. It is my fault that I was too late. Now I repent, but it is still too late."

She told the servants to burn the paper money, and sobbed loudly.

Yueniang, in the temple, only knew that some young lady had come and that the Abbot had gone to meet her. When he did not come back, she asked the young monk what was happening.

"A little while ago," the young monk said, "the young lady buried one of her sisters. It is the Festival of Spring today, and she has come to burn paper offerings."

"I should not be surprised if this were Chunmei," Yulou said.

"But she has no sister buried here," Yueniang said. "What is the young lady's name?" she asked the young monk.

"Her name is Pang," the young monk said. "A few days ago she gave the Abbot five taels of silver to hold a service for her sister."

"I remember our husband telling me that Chunmei's family name was Pang," Yulou said. "It must be she."

As they were talking, the Abbot returned and told the young monk to prepare tea. A sedan chair was brought to the second door and Yueniang and Yulou looked through the lattice to see what manner of young lady this might be. They recognized Chunmei. She was taller than before. Her face was like the full moon and she looked as exquisite as a figure of jade. Her head was covered with pearls and ornaments, and phoenix pins were thrust obliquely through her hair. She wore a crimson embroidered coat and a blue skirt with trimmings of gold, and little ornaments that tinkled as she walked. She was very different from the Chunmei they had known.

The Abbot set a large chair in the place of honor and asked Chunmei to sit down in it. The young monk made a reverence to her and brought tea. The Abbot offered it with his own hands. "Really," he said, "I did not expect you today. You must forgive me for not coming to meet you."

"I feel that I have been a great trouble to you," Chunmei said. "The other day I asked you to hold a service for me."

"That was nothing," the Abbot said. "I should have done it out of gratitude for the kindness you have shown. We had eight monks, and in the evening, when the ceremony was over, I burned paper offerings. Then I sent your servant away and bade him tell you all about it."

Chunmei drank tea, and the young monk took away the teacup. But the Abbot sat with her and talked, and Yueniang and the others could not come away. Yueniang was afraid because it was getting very late, and she bade the young monk go and tell the Abbot she would like to say good-bye to him. The Abbot would not hear of it.

"May I mention something to you?" he said to Chunmei.

"Say anything you like, Teacher," Chunmei said.

"There are a few ladies here who came to see the place. We did not know you were coming. Now they wish to go away."

"Teacher," Chunmei said, "why do you not ask them to come and see me?"

The Abbot went and told Yueniang what Chunmei had said, but Yueniang did not wish to go. "It is late and we must go home," she said. "We have not time to come and see her."

The Abbot was very much embarrassed. He felt that he had accepted Yueniang's money and had entertained her very inadequately. He implored them to go and see Chunmei. Then they could refuse no longer. Yueniang, Yulou, and Aunt Wu came out.

"Mothers and Aunt!" Chunmei cried. She made Aunt Wu take the place of honor, then, like a branch of blossoms, swaying in the wind, knelt down and kowtowed. Aunt Wu hastily greeted her in return.

"Sister," she said, "things are very different now. I dare now allow you to make such reverence to me."

"Good Aunt," Chunmei said, "you must not say that. I am not that sort of woman. I know the correct behavior of an inferior to a superior."

When she had kowtowed to Aunt Wu, she turned to Yueniang and Yulou. They wished to salute her, but she would have none of it. She kowtowed to them four times. They helped her to her feet.

"I did not know you were here," Chunmei said. "If I had known, I would have asked you to come before."

"Sister," Yueniang said, "since you left us, I have not been able to come and call on you. I am sorry."

"Lady," Chunmei said, "who am I that you should call on me? Why should you be sorry?"

Then she saw Ruyi'er with the baby Xiaoge. "The young master is quite big now," she said.

"Come here and make a reverence to your sister," Yueniang said to Xiaoyu. Then Xiaoyu and Ruyi'er, both smiling, came and made a reverence to Chunmei and she returned their greeting.

"Sister," Yueniang said, "you should accept their reverence."

Then Chunmei took a silver pin with a gold head from her hair and put it in Xiaoge's cap.

"You must thank your sister," Yueniang said. "Why don't you say something to your sister?"

Then, indeed, the baby did babble something. Yueniang was very pleased.

"Sister," Yulou said, "if you had not come here today, we might never have met."

"I came because my mother is buried behind this monastery," Chunmei said. "I lived with her for several years and she had no relatives of her own. The least I could do was to come and burn some papers for her."

"Now I remember," Yueniang said. "Some years ago your mother died, and you told us you did not know where she was buried."

"You don't understand, Sister," Yulou said. "She means our sister Pan. It is due to her kindness that Jinlian is buried here."

Yueniang said no more.

"Would anyone else have been as kind as you, Sister?" Aunt Wu said. "You did not forget one who had been your friend, and you gave her burial. And at this festival you have come to burn paper offerings for her."

"Lady," Chunmei said, "you know how well she treated me when she was alive. It was such a tragic end. Her body was lying there exposed. I could do no less for her than bury her."

The Abbot told the young monks to set the table again. They brought in two large tables with all kinds of vegetarian dishes and cakes. The tea was made with golden tea leaves as tiny as sparrows' tongues, and the purest of water. They enjoyed their food and, when they had finished, the things were taken away. Uncle Wu was entertained elsewhere by some of the monks.

Yulou rose and said she would like to see the grave of Jinlian. She wished to burn paper offerings too, for they had been as sisters. But seeing that Yueniang did not intend to go, Yulou took five fens of silver from her sleeve and asked one of the young monks to buy some paper money.

"Don't trouble to buy any, Lady," the Abbot said. "I have plenty. Take what you wish."

Then Yulou gave the money to the young monk and asked him to lead the way to the grave under the poplar tree. There she found a mound of yellow earth about three feet high and a few grasses growing on it. She offered incense and burned some paper money. Then she made a reverence, and said: "Sister, I did not know that you were buried here. By chance I came to this monastery, and now I offer you this paper money. May it be of use to you." She sobbed loudly.

When Ruyi'er saw that Yulou had gone to the back, she decided to go too. Yueniang, who was talking to Chunmei, said to the nurse: "Don't take the baby, you may frighten him."

"Don't be alarmed, Lady," Ruyi'er said. "I will see he comes to no harm."

Then she went to the grave, where Yulou was burning paper offerings and weeping as she did so.

The ladies changed their clothes and powdered their faces. Chunmei ordered one of her servants to bring a food box, and all kinds of dainties were set out on the table before them. Wine was heated. The cups were of silver; the chopsticks of ivory. She asked Aunt Wu, Yueniang, and Yulou to take the places of honor, and she took the hostess's seat. Ruyi'er and Xiaoyu sat at the side. Uncle Wu had wine in another room.

While they were drinking, two servants came in and knelt down. "Our master would like you to come and see some performers," they said. "The other ladies are there already, and he asks you to come at once."

Chunmei showed no sign of hurry. "Very well," she said, "you may go back to him."

The two men did not dare to go away, and waited outside the door. Aunt Wu and Yueniang rose. "Sister," they said, "we have troubled you long enough. It is late, and you have other matters to attend to. We must go."

Chunmei would not listen, and still told her servants to fill the cups with wine. "Ladies," she said, "it was not easy for us to meet, but now that we have chanced to come upon each other, I trust we may keep on good terms. I have no relatives of my own, and perhaps you will allow me to come and see you on your birthdays."

"Sister," Yueniang said, "it is extremely kind of you to suggest it, but I dare not put you to so much inconvenience. Will you not allow me to come to you first?"

Yueniang drank another cup of wine and then said she could drink no more. "Aunt Wu has no sedan chair," she said. "It will be very awkward if we are late."

"If she has no chair, I shall be glad to let her have one of my ponies," Chunmei said.

Aunt Wu thanked her and declined. They stood up again and made ready to go. Chunmei sent for the Abbot and gave him a roll of cloth and five *qian* of silver. He thanked her and went with all the ladies as far as the main gateway. There Yueniang said good-bye to Chunmei. The girl watched Yueniang and the others get into their sedan chairs, and then got into her own. The two parties went in different directions. Chunmei with her servants went to Xinzhuang.

CHAPTER 90
Sun Xue'e's Elopement

The dodder clings to the raspberry bush
Its tendrils are not very long.
To lose one's virtue at a rake's hands
Is worse than to be thrown out in the street.

In the night he is kind to me
But the mattress of my bed is not warm enough.
He comes in the evening and goes in the morning
Is this not too hasty of him?
I am going to my end
And the old pain stabs my heart.

Uncle Wu took Wu Yueniang and the others along the bank shaded by many great trees. Daian had already prepared for them at a small hill not far from the wineshop in the village of Apricot Blossom, where everything was busy and lively. He had been waiting for them a long time. Then the sedan chairs arrived with Yueniang and the other ladies, and the donkeys with Uncle Wu and Aunt Wu. He asked Yueniang why they were so late, and she told him of the meeting with Chunmei at the Temple of Eternal Felicity. Wine was served and they all sat down in the open air.

While they were drinking, they could watch the carriages with gaily decorated wheels, and people coming and going. From the hillock on which they were, the people in the street seemed like a sea or a mountain of human beings. Some were standing in a ring watching performing horses. Among them was the son of the magistrate, a young man called Li Gongbi. He was about thirty years old, and a student at the Imperial Academy of Learning. But he was a gay and dissolute young fellow, who cared more about hawks and dogs and horses than for the study of poetry and literature. He was always to be seen about the streets, and people called him Li the Wastrel. Today he was wearing a light silk gown, a palm hat with a gold button, and yellow boots. He was with a man named He Buwei, and they had with them a party of twenty or thirty lusty fellows with crossbows, blowpipes, balls, and quarterstaffs watching Li Gui putting the horses through their paces. Then they performed all sorts of tricks, fighting with spears and staves. The men and women standing by laughed and cheered.

This Li Gui was nicknamed the Demon of Shandong. He wore a hat with a swastika badge, a purple shirt, and an embroidered waistcoat, and was riding a silver-maned horse. He carried a shining spear with a red handle, and behind him were several streamers flying in the wind. He was displaying his skill for the benefit of the people in the street.

The young man Li was looking at this show when suddenly he raised his head and saw the ladies on the hill. One was rather taller than the others, and he could not take his eyes from her. He did not speak, but wondered to what family she belonged and whether she was married. Then he whispered to Little Zhang, one of the men with him: "Go and see who those three people in white are, standing on the hill. When you have made sure, come back and tell me."

Little Zhang hurried away. When he came back, he said: "They are members of Ximen Qing's family. The old man is Wu, the short woman is Yueniang, the first wife, and the tall one with pockmarks on her face, the third wife, Yulou. Of course, they are widows now."

Li felt particularly attracted to Yulou. He gave some money to Little Zhang.

When Yueniang and Uncle Wu had watched the show for some time, they told Daian to pack up the things, and the ladies went to their sedan chairs. Then they went home, as sunset was drawing near.

Sun Xue'e and Ximen Dajie had been left at home. They had nothing special to do, and about midday went to the gate and stood there. As Fate would have it, a mirror man came along. In those days, the people who sold powder, flowers and ornaments, and those who polished mirrors, all had a sign to show who they were.

"My mirror is very tarnished," Ximen Dajie said, and told Ping'an to fetch the man to polish it. He laid down his pack. "I am not a mirror polisher," he said, "I sell gold and silver ornaments and artificial flowers." He stood and looked hard at Xue'e.

"If you are not a mirror polisher," she said, "be off with you. What do you mean by staring at me like that?"

"Lady," the man said, "don't you remember me?"

"Your face seems familiar, but I can't quite remember you," Ximen Dajie said.

"I am Laiwang, who used to serve his Lordship," the man said.

"You have been away so many years you have grown fat," Xue'e said.

"When I left here, I went to my native place Xuzhou. But I could not get work there and took service with a nobleman who had an appointment at the Eastern Capital. I went there with him. On the way his father died and he had to go back again. Then I went to a silversmith and learned this trade. Business is very slack and my master told me to try and sell these things in the streets. I have seen you several times but felt shy about making myself known. If you had not stopped me today, I should not have dared to come to you."

"Now I know you," Xue'e said, "but I should not have known you if you had not told me. Why shouldn't you come? You are an old member of this household. What have you got there? Bring them in and let us see."

Laiwang took his boxes into the courtyard, opened them and, putting the gold and silver ornaments on a tray, showed them to the ladies. They were excellently made. When Ximen Dajie and Xue'e had looked at them, they said: "If you have any artificial flowers, we should like to see them too." Laiwang opened another box. He had all kinds of flowers, some to wear on the forehead, some large enough to make a complete headdress, others in the form of different insects. Ximen Dajie picked out two pairs of flowers for her hair, and Xue'e a pair of jade phoenixes and a pair of gold fish. Ximen Dajie paid for what she took, but Xue'e asked Laiwang to come another day for his money, one tael and two *qian*.

"The Great Lady and the others have gone to your master's grave to burn paper money," she told him.

"I heard last year that my master was dead," Laiwang said. "I suppose the Great Lady's baby is quite big now."

"He is eighteen months old, and the whole household treats him as though he were a pearl or some other jewel. The future of this house rests wholly upon him."

While they were talking, Laizhao's wife brought a cup of tea for Laiwang. He took the tea and made a reverence. Laizhao came out to talk to him. "Come tomorrow and see the Great Lady," he said. Then Laiwang picked up his boxes and went away.

In the evening Yueniang came back. Xue'e and Ximen Dajie and the maids kowtowed to her. Daian could not keep up with the men carrying the boxes, so he hired a donkey. When he reached home, the porters were dismissed.

"Today at the temple," Yueniang told her daughter and Xue'e, "we met Chunmei. Jinlian is buried at the back, and we never knew. Chunmei went to burn some paper money for her and we met her quite by accident. We were very friendly. The Abbot offered us vegetarian food, then Chunmei called for her servants, and they must have set out thirty or forty dishes. We could not drink all the wine she offered us. She looked at the baby and gave him some pins. She was most agreeable. And what a number of servants she had! She was in a large sedan chair with ever so many attendants following it. She is taller and stouter than she used to be, and her face seems whiter and fuller."

"She had not forgotten us," Aunt Wu said. "I remember when she was here, she was much more efficient and a much better talker than any of the other maids. She spoke so gently and quietly. Even then I knew she was a capable girl. Now she has been lucky her intelligence is more evident than ever."

"Sister," Yulou said, "she told me that she has not been unwell for six months. Her fortune is made. I understand she expects to have a baby in the eighth or the ninth month. The Major is delighted. So what old woman Xue said happens to be true."

"Today, while you were out," Xue'e said, "Ximen Dajie and I were standing at the gate and saw Laiwang. He is a silversmith now, and was selling gold and silver ornaments and flowers in the street. At first, I didn't recognize him. I bought a few things. He asked after you and I told him you had gone to the grave."

"Why didn't you ask him to wait for me?" Yueniang said.

"I told him to come again tomorrow." While they were talking, Ruyi'er came to them. "The baby has been asleep ever since we came in," she said, "and I can't get him to wake. His breath seems cold, but his body is as hot as fire."

Yueniang was frightened. She went to the bed and picked up the child. She kissed him and could feel a cold sweat on his body, though he seemed feverish.

"You wicked woman!" she said irritably to Ruyi'er. "He must have got cold in the chair."

"He could not," Ruyi'er said. "I had him well wrapped up in the bed-clothes."

"Well, perhaps when you took him to the grave he got a fright. I told you not to take him, but instead of listening to me you rushed off like a mad woman."

"Xiaoyu knows I had only had him there for a minute or two. How could he be frightened?"

"Don't argue," Yueniang cried. "Whether you had him there a short time or not, he is frightened now."

She called for Laian and sent him for old woman Liu. When the old woman came, she felt the baby's pulse and examined his body. "He has caught a chill," she said, "and would seem to have met an evil spirit." She gave them two red pills and asked them to give them to the child with ginger water. The nurse was told to put the baby to bed. During the night he began to sweat and his body became cooler. They gave the old woman some tea and three *qian* of silver and asked her to come the next day. The whole household was in a state of excitement. Some got up and some lay down, and they were running about half the night.

Next day, Laiwang came to the gate with his wares. Yesterday," he said to Laizhao, "Lady Xue'e bought something from me and told me to call today for the money. And I should like to see the Great Lady."

"Come another day," Laizhao said, "the young master is not well. They had to send for old woman Liu last night, and they were worried and busy all night. He is better today, but I don't think they will feel like seeing you."

As they were talking, Yueniang, Yulou and Xue'e came along with old woman Liu. Laiwang knelt down and kowtowed to Yueniang and Yulou.

"I haven't seen you for a long time," Yueniang said. "Why haven't you been to call on me?"

Laiwang told Yueniang of his adventures. "I felt shy about coming," he said.

"You are an old servant of ours," Yueniang said, "and your master is dead now. Your trouble was really due to that wicked woman Pan, who would carry fire to one place and water to another. Your good wife hanged herself and you were banished. But Heaven could not allow such a creature to live, and now she is dead too."

"I need not say anything, Mother," Laiwang said. "You understand so well."

When they had talked for a while, Yueniang asked what he had to sell. He showed her and she picked out ornaments to the value of three taels and two *qian* and paid him for them. Then she asked him to go to the second door, and told Xiaoyu to give him a pot of wine and some cakes. Xue'e went to the kitchen and herself gave him a large bowl of meat. When he had had a good meal, he kowtowed and prepared to go away. Yueniang and Yulou went to the inner court, but Xue'e stayed and talked to him.

"Come here as often as you like," she said to him. "There is nothing to fear. I will send you a message by Laizhao's wife. Tomorrow evening I will wait for you in the little room by the wall not far from this door." They exchanged glances, and Laiwang knew what the woman meant. He asked if the second door would be closed in the evening.

"Come to Laizhao's room," Xue'e said, "and, in the evening, take a ladder and climb over the wall. I will help you down on this side. I shall have something to tell you when we meet."

Laiwang was delighted. He said good-bye to Xue'e and took away his boxes.

The next day he did not bother to do any business. He came to Ximen's house and, when Laizhao came out, he bowed to him.

"I haven't seen you for a long time, Brother Laiwang," Laizhao said.

Laiwang smiled. "I would not have come except to ask Lady Xue'e for some money."

Laiwang took the man to his own rooms.

"Where is my sister-in-law?" Laiwang said.

"My wife is always in the kitchen during the day," Laizhao told him.

Laiwang gave him a tael of silver. "This is to buy a pot of wine for your wife and yourself."

"But a pot of wine doesn't cost so much as that," Laizhao said. He called his son, Little Iron Rod. The boy was now fifteen years old. He took a pot and went out to buy some wine. Then he went to the kitchen to see his mother.

Laizhao's wife came out with some hot rice and a large bowl of stew with two other dishes. "Oh, I see you are here, Brother Wang," she said.

Laizhao showed his wife the silver and said: "Our brother has given us this to buy some wine."

"I don't think we ought to take it," she said, smiling. "We have done nothing for you." She put a small table on the bed and asked Laiwang to sit down. Then she set out food and wine. Laiwang filled a cup and offered it to Laizhao, then he filled another and offered it to the woman.

"It is a very long time since we were last together," he said politely. "I fear this poor cup of wine is all I can offer you."

"I am not the sort of person who cares too much for wine and meat," Laizhao's wife said. "You are a friend, and you must tell me the truth. Yesterday, the lady told me that she and you still love one another. She has trusted my husband and myself to help you. There had better not be any pretence between us. As the proverb says: If a man wishes to find the track down the mountainside, he must ask a practiced guide. If you two meet here and you get anything out of it, don't keep everything for yourself, but let us have at least a taste of the gravy. We have to be responsible for you."

Laiwang knelt down. "Brother and Sister," he said, "if you help me, I will never forget." Then they had their meal. Laizhao's wife went to the inner court again and talked to Xue'e. Then she returned and told Laiwang to come to her rooms that evening. When the second door was closed and the people in the inner court had gone to bed, he would be able to get over the wall and join his beloved.

Laiwang went away. That night, he came again to Laizhao's rooms and bought wine for him and his wife. They drank until it was late, without anybody knowing that he was there. Then the gate was closed, the second door fastened, and everybody went to bed.

Xue'e and Laiwang had arranged a signal. When he heard a cough on the other side of the wall, he climbed up a ladder and got over the white wall in the dark. Xue'e had a bench waiting for him on the other side. They went to a small harness room near by. There they embraced and began to make love more earnestly. Neither had a mate, and their passion was ready to burst into flame. Laiwang's spear was hard and strong. They sported for a long time; then the moment of greatest happiness came to him, and he yielded to her.

Xue'e gave him some gold and silver ornaments, a few taels of silver, and two suits of clothes. "Come again tomorrow night," she said to him, "and I will have something more valuable for you. Take it and find a place for us to live. I know that this family can hardly prosper now. I will leave it, and we will get a house and marry. You are a silversmith and we shall not have to worry about a living."

"I have an aunt outside the East Gate," Laiwang said. "She is a famous midwife. Her place is out of the way, and I suggest that we go there. We will stay there a while until we know whether there is going to be trouble and, if not, I will take you to my native place. There I will buy a few acres of land, and we will work on that."

He climbed over the wall again and went back to Laizhao. There he stayed till dawn and slipped away as soon as the gate was opened.

The next evening he came again. He went as before to Laizhao's rooms, then over the wall, and they made merry again. So they went on for a long time. They stole a number of valuable things, gold, silver and clothes, and Laizhao and his wife had their share.

One day Yueniang was very depressed because the baby was ill again. She went to bed very early. Ximen Dajie's maid had been given to Xue'e, and Li Jiao'er's maid had been given to Ximen Dajie because Chen Jingji had wanted her. Today, Xue'e sent her maid to bed. She took a number of earrings, pins and ornaments and put them into a box. Then she covered her head with a kerchief. She had arranged with Laiwang that they should meet in Laizhao's place and run away.

"That is all very well," Laizhao said. "You can get away easily enough, but I am in charge of the gate, and how can I let you escape like a pair of wild ducks? The Great Lady is sure to find out, and what am I to say to her when she asks me about it? You had better get over the roof. Smash a few tiles, and then there will be something to show the way you went."

"That is a good idea, Brother," Laiwang said.

Xue'e gave Laizhao and his wife a silver cup, gold earrings, a black silk coat, and a yellow silk skirt. They waited until the fifth night watch, when it was very dark, and then climbed over to Laizhao's place. Laizhao heated two big cups of wine and gave one to each of them. "Drink this," he said. "It will strengthen you for what you are going to do."

At the fifth night watch, each of them took some incense, then they got a ladder and climbed out on to the roof. Step by step they climbed up, breaking a few tiles as they went. When they came to the other side, there seemed to be nobody about, no watchman in the street. Laiwang got down first, then helped Xue'e, who climbed down with her feet on his shoulders. When they came to the street a watchman stopped them and asked where they were going. Xue'e was alarmed, but Laiwang was cool enough. He held out the incense he had brought and said: "We are husband and wife going to offer incense at the temple outside the city. That is why we are up so early."

"What have you in those parcels? "the watchman asked them.

"Incense and paper money," Laiwang said.

"If you are husband and wife and are going to the temple, it is a good work and you may go," the watchman said.

At that, Laiwang took Xue'e's hand and they hurried off as fast as they could go. By the time they came to the city gate, it had just been opened. They went out, turned up one street and down another, and so came to the place where Laiwang's aunt lived. It was a very lonely place: there were only a few ramshackle houses. They came at last to the house of Midwife Qu. The door was shut, but they knocked and, after a while, the old woman, who had just got up, came and opened the door. There stood Laiwang with a woman.

Laiwang's real name was Zheng Wang. "This is my wife, whom I have lately married," he said. "Can you let us have a room? We should like to stay here for a few days while we look for a house."

He gave the old woman three taels of silver for expenses. When she saw the money, old woman Qu could not refuse to let them stay. But, one night, her son, Qu Dang, who had seen that Laiwang seemed to have a great deal of gold and silver, forced the door, stole the valuables, and went gambling. He was arrested and brought before the magistrate. The magistrate, Li, realized that the things must have been stolen and ordered runners to go with Qu Dang to the old woman's house. They arrested Laiwang and Xue'e. The woman was so frightened that her face became the color of wax. She put on plain clothes, covered her face with a veil, took off her rings, and gave them to the runners. Then they were taken before the magistrate, and people came to hear of the matter. Some recognized them and said: "Surely that is one of Ximen Qing's women. She has been carrying on with one of the servants, the fellow Laiwang, now called Zheng Wang. They stole some things and ran away. Then Qu Dang stole the stuff from them again and now they have to go before the magistrate."

One man told ten, and ten told a hundred, and so the news spread like wildfire.

When Xue'e had run away, her maid discovered that the most valuable ornaments had been taken away and that clothes were strewn about the floor. She went to tell Yueniang.

"You slept with her," Yueniang said, in astonishment: "how was it you didn't notice when she went away?"

"She said she wished to be alone," the maid said. "She went out quietly and then came back. I had no idea what she was doing."

Yueniang sent for Laizhao. "You are in charge of the gate," she said to him. "Why didn't you know that somebody was running away?"

"I have locked up the gate every night," Laizhao said. "She must have flown."

Then they discovered that some of the tiles were broken on the roof, and realized that Xue'e had escaped that way. They did not wish to send anybody to find out where she had gone, and made no fuss about the matter.

In his court, the magistrate tried the case. First, he had Qu Dang beaten, and that young man gave up four gold ornaments, three of silver, a pair of gold rings, a silver cup, five taels of silver, two suits of clothes, a handkerchief, and a box. From Laiwang the magistrate took thirty taels of silver, a pair of gold pins, a gold figurine, and four rings. From Xue'e, he took a gold ornament, a pair of silver bracelets, five pairs of gold buttons, four pairs of silver pins, and some silver. From old woman Qu, he took three taels of silver. His verdict was that Laiwang had stolen these things and abducted a woman, and Qu Dang had stolen the stuff from him. The two men were sentenced to imprisonment for five years and the property confiscated. Xue'e and old woman Qu were beaten and the old woman confessed. The magistrate sent to Ximen's house to ask them to take Xue'e away.

Yueniang sent for Uncle Wu and discussed the situation with him. They decided that, since everybody had heard about the matter, they would not take Xue'e back. She had disgraced the family and done injury to the reputation of her dead husband. So they gave something to the runners and asked them to get the magistrate to hand Xue'e over to the official go-between to sell.

Chunmei heard that Xue'e had been carried off by Laiwang and all that had happened afterwards. She made up her mind to buy the woman and set her to work in her kitchen. Thus she would have her revenge.

"This woman is a very good cook," she said to her husband. "She is clever at getting tea and meals ready, and I think we might buy her."

Major Zhou sent Zhang Sheng and Li An to the magistrate with a card. When Li learned who it was who wished to buy the woman, he asked for only eight taels of silver. The men paid the money and took Xue'e to Zhou's house. First they presented her to the first and second ladies, then they took her to Chunmei.

Chunmei was in her room, getting up from a gilded bed with silken curtains. The maids took in Xue'e. She recognized Chunmei, bowed her head, and kowtowed four times. Chunmei opened her eyes wide. Then she sent for the chief of the serving women. "Pull down this strumpet's hair," she cried, "and take off those clothes. Then let her serve in the kitchen, keeping up the fire, and cooking."

Xue'e could only swallow her resentment. It has always been possible for one who begins by sweeping up the rice to become the governor of a granary. Xue'e realized her position. How she was standing beneath low eaves and must perforce bow her head. She took off her headdress and changed her clothes, and went to the kitchen sadly and bitterly.

CHAPTER 91
Meng Yulou Marries Again

One day, Chen Jingji heard of this business of Sun Xue'e from old woman Xue. He sent the old woman with a message to Wu Yueniang. "Your son-in-law says he does not mean to have anything more to do with your daughter. He is going to the Provincial Governor to say that, when your husband was alive, he had a number of chests of gold and silver left with him by old master Chen."

This was one more worry for Yueniang. Xue'e had run away with Lai-wang; the boy Laian had run away; Laixing's wife had died and the funeral was only just over. When she heard the message old woman Xue had brought, she was alarmed, sent at once for a sedan chair, and told Ximen Dajie to go to Chen's house. Daian and other servants carried all the things belonging to her to Chen Jingji.

"These things were her dowry," Jingji said. "The things I am asking for are those I gave into their keeping."

"Your mother-in-law told me," old woman Xue said, "that in her husband's time these were the only things they had. She has never seen anything else."

Then Jingji claimed his wife's maid. Old woman Xue and Daian went back to Yueniang and told her. She refused to give up the girl. "She was Li Jiao'er's maid," she said, "and now she is looking after my baby. If he must have somebody, he may have Zhongqiu. She has been my daughter's maid."

Jingji refused to have Zhongqiu, and old woman Xue was kept going backwards and forwards between the two houses. At last Jingji's mother said to Daian: "Brother, go and tell your mistress that she has several maids. Why does she insist on keeping that particular one to look after her baby? And I don't see why she should keep Zhongqiu either, since Zhongqiu was my daughter-in-law's maid and was made a woman by my son."

Daian went and told Yueniang. Then she gave way and sent Yuanxiao. Jingji was very pleased with himself. "It is settled on my own terms after all," he said.

❀　　　❀　　　❀

We now return to Magistrate Li's son. He had seen Wu Yueniang and Meng Yulou outside the city at the Festival of Spring. They were both beautiful and dressed alike, and he knew that they had been Ximen Qing's wives. He liked Yulou because she was tall. Her face was like a melon seed and she seemed charming and gay.

This young man's wife had died sometime before, and he had been looking about for a wife but could find no one who pleased him sufficiently. He was greatly taken with Yulou but did not know how to approach her. Besides, he did not know whether she wished to remarry.

Then he heard that Xue'e had been brought before his father's court. She was one of Ximen's wives also. He succeeded in persuading his father to return all the stolen property to Ximen's people. But Yueniang was afraid to have anything to do with the courts and would not send a man to claim the things. The young man was disappointed. The stolen goods were confiscated and Xue'e was sold. Then he talked over the situation with one of the officers called Yu.

"Why don't you send old Tao, the go-between, to Ximen's house to arrange the matter?" Yu said. "Tell the old woman that, if she brings the matter off, she shall have five taels of silver and be freed from her official work."

The young man spoke to old woman Tao, and the old woman was so delighted that she ran to Ximen's house as if she had had wings. Laizhao was at the door. The old woman made a reverence to him. "May I know if this is Ximen's house?" she said.

"Who are you?" Laizhao said. "What do you want? My master is dead."

"Will you kindly go and tell the lady that I am Tao, the official go-between. My young master tells me that one of the ladies is thinking of remarrying, and I have come to see about it."

"Old woman," Laizhao shouted, "you seem to have lost your manners. My master has been dead more than a year now. There are two ladies here, and neither of them wishes to remarry. You know the proverb: Howling wind and driving rain do not beat upon a widow's door. You are trifling and talking nonsense about marriage. Be off with you, and quickly. If the ladies hear of this, you may get a beating."

The old woman smiled. "The governor may be wrong," she said, "and his deputy too, but the messenger is always right. I should not have come if my young master had not sent me. Whether they wish to marry or not, kindly go and tell them. Then I will go back and let my young master know what they say."

"To do something for others is sometimes advantageous to oneself," Laizhao said. "Wait here, and I will go and tell them. One of the ladies has a baby. The other has not. I have no notion which it is you want."

"My young master told me that he saw her in the country at the Spring Festival. She has a few marks on her face."

Laizhao went and told Yueniang that the official go-between wished to see her. Yueniang was startled. "Nothing that is said here ever goes beyond these walls," she said. "What do they know of us?"

"The woman says they saw a lady with a few marks on her face, at the Festival of Spring."

"That is Sister Meng," Yueniang said. "I shall never remarry."

She went to Yulou. "Sister," she said, "I have something to tell you. A go-between has come, and she says Magistrate Li's son saw you at the Festival of Spring. She says you would like to remarry. Is that true?"

Now, as chance would have it, Yulou had noticed the young man that day and thought how gay and handsome he seemed. He was about the same age as herself, a good horseman, and skilled with the bow. When they looked at each other, they seemed to establish an understanding. But she had not known whether he was married or not. She had said to herself: "My husband is dead, and I have no child of my own. The Great Lady has a son, but, when he grows up, he will do his duty by his own mother and I shall be like a fallen tree that gives no shade, or as if I drew water in a bamboo basket. Since Yueniang has had this child, she does not behave to me as she used to do. It will be well for me to take a step forward and make sure of a home in which to spend my old age. Why should I be so foolish as to stay here? There is nothing here for me, and I am wasting my time."

She was thinking exactly this when Yueniang came and spoke to her. The man whom Yueniang mentioned was the very young man she had seen at the Festival of Spring. She was pleased but also a little ashamed. She said to Yueniang: "Don't believe a word of it. I have never even thought of remarrying." But she blushed.

"It is a matter entirely for you to decide," Yueniang said. "I have no authority over you." She told Laizhao to bring the go-between to the inner court.

Old woman Tao made a reverence to Yueniang and sat down. A maid brought tea, and Yueniang said: "What can I do for you?"

"I should not come to such a magnificent palace as this unless I had something of great importance to say," the old woman said. "I was ordered to come by his Lordship. It is said that there is a lady here who would like to marry again."

"It is possible that the lady may care to remarry," said Yueniang, "but she has never spoken of the matter to anyone. How did your young master come to know of it?"

"He only told me that he saw a lady at the festival. She was tall and had a face shaped like a melon seed, with a few white marks upon it. I think this must be the lady."

Then Yueniang understood that it must be Yulou. She took the woman to Yulou's room. There they sat down and, after a while, Yulou came out to them beautifully dressed. The old woman made a reverence to her.

"This is the lady," she said. "She is unusually beautiful and well worthy to be my young master's first wife."

Yulou smiled. "Don't be silly," she said. "Tell me how old the gentleman is. Has he been married before? Has he any women in his household? What is his name and what his position? Don't waste time. Tell me the truth."

"Heaven!" the old woman cried. "I am the official go-between. I'm not like the rest of them. I never tell lies. I say what I know and nothing else. The magistrate is over fifty, and this is his only son. The young gentleman's animal is the Horse, and he is now thirty-one. He was born at the hour of the Dragon on the twenty-third day of the first month. He is a student at the Imperial Academy of Learning and will shortly take his degree. He has a bellyful of literature, and is very skilled at archery and horseman-ship. There is nothing about philosophy he doesn't know. His wife died two years ago, and now he has only a young girl to look after him. She is quite a common sort of girl, and he wants a wife to manage things. He has sent me here especially to ask you to marry him. If you are willing, my master says you shall be excused from paying taxes on your land, houses and property, and if anyone harms you in any way, you have only to point to him and he will be arrested and punished at once."

"Has the young gentleman any children?" Yulou asked. "And what is his native place? I ask this because when their term of office here expires, they will probably go away, and I do not wish to go very far. All my peo-ple live here."

"He has no children," old woman Tao said, "and his home is in the Zaoqiang district of Zhengdingfu. It is about six or seven hundred *li* on the other side of the river. They own miles and miles of land, have herds of mules and horses, and a host of people. The Imperial sign stands over all the arches. It is a splendid and glorious place. If you become his first wife, and he gets an official appointment, you will wear ceremonial dress and drive a carriage like a lady. Is that not good enough for you?"

Yulou made up her mind. She told Lanxiang to bring the old woman tea and cakes. "I must apologize for asking so many questions," she said, "but really go-betweens are such clever liars, and I did not wish to be deceived."

"Lady," the old woman said, "you should look carefully. Then you would see that the pure are pure and the foul, foul. Only too often the bad ones bring disrepute upon the good ones. I never lie, I have always set out to be an honest go-between. If you have made up your mind, please write a note and I will give it to the young master."

Yulou found a piece of scarlet silk and told Daian to take it to the shop and get Clerk Fu to write her eight characters upon it.

"When you came here," Yueniang said, "old woman Xue acted as your go-between. We will send for her, and then she and Madam Tao together can take your eight characters. That will look more dignified."

After a while, old woman Xue came. She made a reverence to old woman Tao. As they belonged to the same profession, it was arranged that they should take the note to the Town Hall together.

On the way, old woman Tao said to her companion: "Did you arrange this lady's marriage on the previous occasion?"

"I did," old woman Xue said.

"What family did she come from? Was she a virgin?"

"She is a Yang," old woman Xue said.

Then old woman Tao noticed that the characters on the silk showed that Yulou was born at the hour of the Rat on the twenty-seventh day of the eleventh month, so she was now thirty-seven years old.

"I am afraid my master will think she is rather old," she said. "He is only thirty-one, and she is six years older. Had we not better go to a for-tune-teller and find out whether the parties are suited to one another? If the dates don't work out, we will make her a little younger. I shan't con-sider that anything wrong."

The two women went on, but they did not meet any fortune-tellers in the street. But from a distance they saw a black tent to the south of the road. Outside it were two signs. They bore the inscriptions: "I foretell good and evil fortune as Zi Ping. With an iron pen, I determine whether honor or ill-fame will come. To all who come to have their fortunes told, I tell the truth without fear and without favor." In the tent there was a table, and beside it sat a man who could write and tell fortunes. They went to him and he asked them to sit down.

"We have come to ask about the destiny of a woman," old woman Xue said, taking from her sleeve three *fen* of silver. "This is only a trifle, but please take it. I have very little money with me."

The man asked the eight characters. Tao gave him the card, on which the eight characters were written.

"I see this is a marriage," the man said. Then he began to calculate on his fingers and set out the counters on the abacus. "The woman is now thirty-seven years old," he said. "She was born at the hour of the Rat, on the twenty-seventh day of the eleventh month. The month is *Jiazi*, the day *Xinmao* and the hour *Gengzi*. She is an honorable woman. Working backwards, as one does with the life of a woman, we find that she is now at the period *Bingshen*. *Bing* comes in conjunction with *Xin,* which shows that she is destined to enjoy power and dignity and to be a lady. She has several husband stars, yet her influence is always happy for her husbands and they will love her. In these two years there seems to be an adverse influence. Has anything happened?"

"Two husbands have died already," old woman Xue said.

"That is good," the man said.

"Will she bear a child?" old woman Xue asked.

"Not yet. She will not have a child until she is forty-one. Then she will have a son who will comfort her declining days. Her fate seems to be excellent. She will be very rich and of high rank." He took a brush and wrote four lines.

> Her charm is worthy to be compared with the beauty of the plum.
> Three times the red silk is taken away, and twice she paints her
>   brows.
> We shall see the day when the horse's head is raised in victory
> Then she will cast aside the covering of *Yin* and be free.

"Master," old woman Xue said, "what do you mean by those two last lines? We don't understand. Would you mind explaining?"

"I spoke of the 'horse's head' because the lady is going to marry a man whose animal is the Horse. Afterwards, she will live a life of ease. By 'the covering of Yin' I make reference to the man whose animal was the Tiger. That man is dead, and though he loved her, she was only a concubine in his household. From now onward, she will have a happy life. She will live to be sixty-eight and her son will close her eyes. Husband and wife will live together till they die."

"The man she is going to marry has indeed the horse for his animal," the old women cried, "but we are afraid he will think her too old. Can you make her a few years younger?"

"I will make her thirty-four," the man said.

"If you do that, will that fit in with the Horse?" old woman Xue said.

"Yes," the man said, "the *Ding* fire meets the *Geng* gold. From the gold melted in the fire, a precious jewel is made. It will be all right." He put down Yulou's age as thirty-four. The two old women went on to the Town Hall. There they were taken to the young man. He asked who old woman Xue was.

"She is the go-between of the other party," old woman Tao said. She told the young man the result of her visit. "The lady is very beautiful," she said, "but she is slightly older than you. I did not venture to settle the matter without your consent. Here is the card."

Li looked at it. "Born at the hour of the Rat, the twenty-seventh day
of the eleventh month, thirty-four years of age," it said.

"That is all right," the young man said. "She is only two or three years
older than I am."

"Yes, my lord," old woman Xue said hastily, "and doubtless you remember the proverb: When the wife is two years older than her husband,
his wealth will be increased, and if she is three years older, she will be like a
mountain of gold. The lady is very beautiful and has a perfect disposition.
I need hardly say that she knows how to read and can manage a household
very economically."

"You need say no more," the young man said. "I have seen her myself.
We must select a day of good omen for the betrothal."

"When shall we come to receive your orders?" the old women said.

"We will not waste any time. Come two days from now."

He gave each of them a tael of silver for her pains, and they went off
in high spirits.

Li was very pleased that his marriage was now so far advanced. He consulted with He Buwei and then told his father. Then he sent for the Master
of the Yin Yang, who selected the eighth day of the fourth month for the
betrothal and the fifteenth for the wedding. He made a handsome present
to He Buwei and Little Zhang to buy tea and wine and other things. The
two go-betweens went to Ximen's place and told Yueniang and Yulou the
days that had been selected. On the eighth day of the fourth month, sixteen dishes of fruits and cakes, a gold headdress, a set of gold ornaments,
a cornelian girdle, a set of little bells, gold bracelets and silver pins, two
scarlet ceremonial cloaks, four embroidered dresses, thirty taels of silver,
rolls of silk and cotton, were made into twenty separate parcels. He Buwei
and the two women took them all to Ximen's house.

On the fifteenth, a number of servants from the Town Hall came to
take Meng Yulou's things away. Yueniang made them take everything that
had belonged to Yulou. Ximen Qing had given his daughter one of the lacquer beds, and now Yueniang gave Yulou the bed decorated with mother
of pearl that had been in Jinlian's room. Yulou wished to take Lanxiang
with her and leave the younger of her maids to Yueniang. But Yueniang
would not agree.

"No," she said, "I will not take your maid. I have Zhongqiu and Xiuchun and the nurse to look after the baby, and they are all I need."

Then Yulou sent all her things away, leaving two little silver pots as
playthings for the baby. That evening there came for her a sedan chair
carried by four men, with eight men from the Town Hall, and four pairs

of red lanterns to attend her. Yulou put on her golden headdress, ornaments, and pearls. Then she dressed in a straight-sleeved scarlet gown. First she went to say farewell to Ximen Qing's tablet; then she kowtowed to Yueniang.

"Sister Meng," Yueniang said, "you are cruel. You are leaving me here alone, and I have no friend left." They held each other's hands and cried.

All the household went with her to the gate, and there an old woman put a veil of red silk on her head and gave her a golden vase to carry. As Yueniang was a widow, she did not go out, but asked Aunt Meng to take Yulou to her new husband.

"That is Master Ximen's third lady," the people in the street said to one another. "Now she is marrying the magistrate's son. This is the wedding day." Some said it was good, and some that it was bad. Those who considered it good said: "Ximen Qing was a very pleasant fellow. He is dead now, and his first wife lives on at his home as his widow. She could not possibly manage the household if it remained so big, so she lets the ladies go their own way, and all is as it should be."

Those who considered it bad said: "Now, even Ximen Qing's wives are remarrying. He was a most unprincipled fellow. He lived for money and to seduce other people's wives and daughters, and, now he is dead, his wives remarry and take his property with them. Some have married; some have run away; some have carried on intrigues with impossible people; some have even descended to theft. They are like the feathers of a chicken, all scattered to the winds. As the proverb says: we may have to wait thirty years for our reward, but, in this case, we see the reward today."

Aunt Meng came with the sedan chair to the Town Hall. The beds and furniture were all in their proper places. She was asked to take wine and then went home. Li gave the two old women Xue and Tao each five taels and a roll of silk, and they went home too. The young couple became husband and wife that same night and enjoyed each other as fishes enjoy water. Next day, Yueniang sent tea and food to Yulou, since Aunt Yang, who would have done it, was now dead. The three Aunt Mengs also sent tea. Then they received an invitation from the Town Hall asking them to go on the third day of the wedding. There was a very grand dinner; musicians and singing girls were present to perform plays and music. Yueniang dressed in pearls and put on a scarlet cloak, an embroidered skirt, and a girdle with a gold buckle, and went in a large sedan chair to the Town Hall. The ladies were entertained in the great hall and the magistrate's wife was there to receive them.

When Yueniang got home after this very lively feast, she went to the inner court. It was so quiet that not a sound could be heard. She remembered how busy all the ladies had been in Ximen Qing's lifetime, and how, when she had come back from a party, they had all come to welcome her home. Indeed, one long bench had not been enough for the ladies to sit on. Now they were all gone. She went to Ximen Qing's tablet and sobbed.

Young Master Li and Yulou, both very lively by nature, were delighted with each other. They were so much attracted one to the other that they found it hard to separate even for a moment. The young man looked closely at Yulou and, the more he looked at her, the more he loved her. And her two maids were very pretty too. Lanxiang was now eighteen. He was so delighted he did not know what to do with himself.

The young man's first wife, when she died, left an old maid called Yuzan. She was now about thirty years old. She painted her face till she looked like a demon. She used to dress her hair in a number of knots, then, around it, she put a handkerchief, and tied it with a gold ribbon as if it had been a hairnet. She wore the strangest green and red clothes and shoes like boats, with four eyes. Each of them was at least one foot two inches long. When she was in the presence of anyone, she shivered and shook, talked in a quavering voice, and behaved in the queerest manner. Before the young master had married again, it was she who served him every day with food and tea. She was very industrious, and smiled and talked even when she did not mean to. When Yulou came, and her young master attached himself so firmly to her, it was a very great trouble to Yuzan. She was furious.

One day, when the young man was reading in his study, she went to the kitchen and made a special cup of tea. She put the teacup on a tray and took it to the study. She put on a smiling face, pulled aside the lattice, and went to offer the tea. But the young man, after reading a while, had gone to sleep on the table.

"Master," she said, "nobody cares for you as I do. I have made you such a nice cup of tea. Your newly married wife is still comfortably asleep in bed. Why don't you order her maids to make some tea for you?"

The young man was half asleep and did not answer. "You old beggar," she said, "you have been so busy all night that you are tired out now. That's why you go to sleep in the daytime. Wake up and have this cup of tea."

Then the young man woke up and saw the maid.

"Put down that tea and go away, you dirty slave," he said.

Yuzan flushed, put down the tea, and went out in a bad temper. "You don't appreciate my kindness," she said. "I had the best of intentions when I made you this tea, and yet you shout at me. I may be ugly, but as the proverb says: an ugly person is a jewel in the household, but the beauty is a source of trouble. I may be ugly, but you used to like me well enough."

The young man kicked her. Yuzan pulled a face long enough to reach the ceiling. She never painted her face again, nor did she make any more tea. When she saw Yulou, she never addressed her as "Lady," but just said "You" and "I." She used to seat herself on Yulou's bed. Yulou said nothing.

Then she said, one day, to her mistress's two maids: "Don't call me Sister, call me Aunt. I am only slightly inferior to your mother and you must call me Aunt when your father is away. You must do what I tell you and work hard. If you don't obey me, you shall have a taste of my shovel."

She tried very hard to make up to the young man but he would have nothing to do with her. Then she was annoyed and would not get out of bed until noon. She refused to cook and would not scrub the floors.

"Don't bother about her," Yulou said to her maids. "Go yourselves to the kitchen and do the cooking and take the food to your master."

Yuzan was terribly jealous. She used to go to the kitchen, break the plates, and curse and beat the maids. "You thievish little whores!" she cried, "you must know that I was here before any of you. Your mother was not here before I was. Now you get hold of everything and don't exert yourselves in the least. The First Lady never used to call me Yuzan, but although you have been here only a few days, you have the audacity to call me by my name. I am not your servant. Before you came, I used to sleep with the young master. We slept together every night and did not get up till breakfasttime. We were like sugar and honey together, and I managed everything. Now you have come and smashed the honey jar and broken the relations between us. I am driven to a cold room where I have to put benches together to make a bed. I never enjoy my master's weapon any more. Indeed, I've forgotten what it is like. There is no place where I can say what I think. When she was in Ximen's family she was only the third lady, and I know she was called Yulou. I know it. And now that she comes here, she ought to control herself a little instead of boasting and ordering people about."

Yulou heard all this. It made her angry but she would not speak to her husband about it. One day, when it was very hot, the young man ordered them to heat some water and bring the bathtub so that he could take a bath with Yulou.

"Tell Lanxiang to go and do it," Yulou said. "Don't ask your own maid."

"No," the young man said, "it is her business to do it. I can't have her going on like this."

When Yuzan heard her master asking for water so that he could have a bath with his wife, she was very annoyed. She brought the tub and plumped it on the floor. Then she heated a great cauldron of water.

"I have never seen such a strumpet," she grumbled. "Always trying to harm me in some cunning way. What a strumpet she must be, washing herself nearly every day. Look at me! I slept with my master for months and months and never used a drop of water. But I didn't offend the eyes of Buddha. This whore has been trying to quarrel with me for a long time." She cursed all the way from the kitchen to the bedroom. Yulou heard her and said nothing, but the young man heard her too, and he was very angry. Though he had no clothes on, he picked up a stick and went out. Yulou tried to stop him.

"Don't be angry with her," she said. "It will be more trouble than it is worth if you go out now, when you are so hot, and catch a chill."

But the young man found it too much. "No," he said, "the ill-mannered slave!" He went out and seized her by the hair. Then he threw her to the ground, and blows fell from his stick like raindrops. Yulou tried to get him to stop, but she did not succeed until the maid had received thirty blows.

Then the maid knelt down before him. "Don't beat me any more, Master," she said. "I know you don't want me any more, and I will go away."

This made the young man angrier than ever and he struck her again.

"Since she is ready to go away," Yulou said, "don't beat her. And don't let yourself get into such a state."

The young man sent for old woman Tao to take the maid away. She was sold for eight taels of silver, and old Tao gave the money to the young man.

CHAPTER 92
Meng Yulou Outwits Chen Jingji

The savage tiger trusts to its own strength
But often is taken unawares.
It growls like thunder then, but that is all,
For the chains are set upon its legs.
When we see the tiger sleeping,
Its eyes have not the fierceness that we know.
The life of man is in worse case
Should evil men then not take heed?

Ximen Dajie came to Chen Jingji with all her belongings, but they were continually quarreling. He had asked his mother to give him some money to set him up in business. His Uncle Zhang borrowed fifty taels of silver from Mistress Chen and asked Jingji to find some work for him. One day, Jingji got drunk and quarreled with his uncle. This upset the uncle very much. He went elsewhere to borrow money and repaid the fifty taels he had had from his sister. This so distressed Mistress Chen that she fell ill. She had to go to bed; the doctors were sent for, and she took their medicine. Her son worried her so much about money that she gave him two hundred taels and Chen Ding was bidden to start a cloth shop at the front of the house. Jingji invited Lu the Third and Yang, and other foxy and doggish friends, to come to the shop, play the lute, gamble, and dice. This happened every day and, as they drank until midnight, the money was soon gone. Chen Ding told his mistress what was happening, and she placed her confidence in him. But Jingji accused Chen Ding and his wife of making money for themselves out of the dyeing of the cloth, and dismissed them. Then he asked Yang the Elder, whose name was Yang Guanyan, to be his manager.

This man's nickname was Iron Fingernails. He was a thorough-paced rascal, a magnificent liar, and skilled in the art of making something out of nothing. When he promised anything to anyone, they had as much chance of getting it as of catching a shadow, but when he made up his mind to get money out of anybody, it seemed as easy as if he took it from a sack.

Chen Jingji got another three hundred taels from his mother, so now his business had cost five hundred taels. First he had to go to buy cloth at Linqing. Yang went home, packed his baggage, then went back to Jingji and they started together for Linqing to buy what they needed. It was a place of considerable importance and a center of trade. People came to it from all sides. There were thirty-two flower and willow streets and seventy-two halls of music. Jingji was still young and only too glad to go with Yang to places of this sort instead of occupying himself with the purchases he had to make.

One day they went to a house where they saw a girl called Feng Jinbao. She was attractive and beautiful, and perfect from every point of view. They asked how old she was.

"She is my own daughter," the old procuress told them, "and my only source of livelihood. She is just sixteen years old."

Jingji was entranced. He gave the old woman five taels of silver and spent several nights with Feng Jinbao. When Yang saw how absorbed in the girl the young man was, so that he could not be persuaded to leave her, he suggested that Jingji should marry the girl and take her home with him. The old procuress demanded a hundred and twenty taels, but, after some discussion, she came down to a hundred. Jingji paid the money and took away the girl. She sat in a sedan chair; Yang and Jingji rode on horseback with the cloth they had bought. They cracked their whips, set their horses at the gallop, and were very pleased with themselves.

When they got home, Mistress Chen was so much upset to find that they had only bought a small supply of merchandise and that her son had married a singing girl that she died. Jingji bought a coffin, put his mother in it, called in some monks to hold a service and buried her in about a week's time. Her brother Zhang remembered how kind she had been to him and made no trouble with Jingji.

As soon as the young man came back from the grave, he set up his mother's tablet in the upper room and gave the other two rooms to Feng Jinbao, leaving only a little room for his wife. Then he bought a maid called Chongxi for Feng Jinbao. Yang looked after the shop and Jingji stayed at home and enjoyed the finest of food and drink. He spent every night with the singing girl and paid not the slightest attention to his wife.

One day he heard that Meng Yulou had married the magistrate's son and taken with her a considerable amount of property. Then the magistrate's term of office expired, and he was made Sub-Prefect at Yanzhou. He went to take up this new appointment. This reminded Jingji that he had once picked up one of Yulou's pins in the garden. He decided that he would take this pin with him to Yanzhou, and, with that as his evidence, claim that Yulou had had an intrigue with him and had given him the pin. He would say that everything she had brought with her from Ximen's household really belonged to Yang Jian and should have been confiscated. The magistrate Li, he thought, was only a civil officer and not one of very high rank, and a few sharp words would induce him to order his son to give up Yulou. "Then," the young man said to himself, "I will bring her back with me and, with Feng Jinbao, I shall have two women for my enjoyment." Unfortunately for him, the matter did not turn out as pleasantly as he expected.

He opened his mother's chests and took a thousand taels of silver. He gave a hundred to Feng Jinbao and re-engaged Chen Ding to look after the shop. Then he and Yang, with his servant Chen An, took the remaining nine hundred taels and set off for Huzhou at the time of the Autumn Festival. There they bought silk of various kinds enough to load half a boat. Then they came to the wharf of Qingjiang. They moored their boat and went to an inn kept by a man called Chen the Second. They ordered chickens to be killed and called for wine, and Jingji and Yang the Elder drank together.

While they were drinking, Jingji said to his friend: "You stay here a few days and keep an eye on the boat, and Chen An and I will go to visit my sister who is married to a nobleman at Yanzhou. We shall be back in three or four days."

"Yes, Brother, go by all means," Yang said. "I will wait for you and, when you come back, we will start for home."

So Jingji took his money and some presents and set out for Yanzhou. When he came to the city, he lodged at a temple. He heard that the new Sub-Prefect Li had entered upon his office a month before, but that his family had only arrived three days ago. Jingji wasted no time. He bought some food, put it with two rolls of silk and two jars of wine, and gave them to Chen An to carry. Then he dressed in his best clothes, and so, looking very handsome, came to the Prefecture. There he bowed to the gatekeeper.

"Excuse me," he said, "but I am a relative of your master's daughter-in-law."

The gatekeeper went at once to tell his master. The young man was in his study, reading. When he was told that his wife's brother had come, he ordered the servants to take the presents, and told the gatekeeper to introduce the visitor. He put on his ceremonial dress.

Jingji was taken to the hall, and there he and Master Li made reverence to one another.

"When I married," Master Li said, "I was not aware that my wife had a brother."

"I was away then," Jingji said, "buying goods in Sichuan and

Guangdong. I was away about a year and did not know that my sister had married. I am sorry. But now I have brought a few trifles and have come in the hope of seeing my sister."

"I am only sorry I did not know you before," Master Li said.

When they had had tea, the young man ordered a servant to take the presents and the card to Yulou. She was in her room when the message came.

"It must be my brother, Meng Rui, who has come all this way to see me," she said. She looked at the card, and it bore Meng Rui's name. She gave instructions that the visitor should be taken in, told Lanxiang to see that the great hall was tidy, and, when she had dressed, went to see her brother. Through the lattice, she saw her husband with a young man. It was not her brother but Chen Jingji.

"What can this young man be doing here?" she said to herself. "I must go and see. Even if we are not relatives, we belong to the same part of the world, and whether the water tastes sweet or not, it is the water of my native place. Though he is not my brother, he is my son-in-law."

She went in and greeted Chen Jingji.

"Sister," he said, "I did not know that you were married and living here."

The words were hardly out of his mouth when a servant came and told Li that another guest had arrived. He asked his wife to entertain her brother and went to receive the other visitor.

"What wind blows you here?" Yulou said.

When they had exchanged greetings, Yulou asked him to sit down, and told Lanxiang to bring some tea. They talked about the affairs of the family. Yulou inquired after Ximen Dajie, and Jingji told her how his wife and all her belongings had been sent to him. Yulou told him that she had met Chunmei at the Temple of Eternal Felicity at the Festival of Spring, and that she had burned paper offerings there for Pan Jinlian.

"I often used to tell the Great Lady that she should love you as well as her daughter-in-law," she said. "After all, you are her son-in-law and not a stranger. But she would believe the gossip that came to her ears, and that is how you came to be sent away. I never heard anything about your property."

"It is true that I did have dealings with Jinlian," Jingji said. "The Great Lady believed what the slaves said and drove me away. Then Wu Song killed Jinlian. If she had still been in that house, Wu Song, however bold a man he may be, would never have dared to go and kill her. That is a fact I shall never forget. Now Jinlian is dead and in Hades, and she will never forgive."

"Well, it is all over and done with now," Yulou said; "as the proverb says: hatred should be forgotten and not made more intense."

The maids brought food and wine and set it on the table. Yulou poured out a cup of wine and offered it to Jingji with both hands. "Brother-in-law," she said, "you have come a long way and spent much money on me. Please accept this poor cup of wine." Jingji bowed to her and took it. Then he poured out a cup for her. He noticed that she always addressed him as Brother-in-law. "Why doesn't the strumpet take the hint?" he said to himself. "Now let us see what happens."

The wine was passed three times, and they had reached the fifth course. They seemed to be getting on very well. Jingji's face was flushed with wine and, as the proverb says: wine makes desire as deep as the sea and stirs up lust as high as the heavens. There was nobody about, and he began to make evil suggestions.

"I have thought of you," he said, "as a thirsty man thinks of water, as a man seeks refreshment from the blazing heat. You remember how, when my father-in-law was alive, we used to sit close together playing chess. We never thought we should have to separate, and that you would be in the east and I in the west."

"No, Brother-in-law," Yulou said, "but don't forget the difference between right and wrong."

Jingji smiled, took some fragrant tea from his sleeve and gave it to Yulou. "Sister," he said, "if you will have pity on me, take this tea." He knelt down before her.

Yulou flushed, and threw the tea on the floor. "Evidently, you have no idea how to behave in a proper manner," she said. "I was good enough to offer you wine, and now you think you can behave as you like with me." She got up from the table and prepared to go to her room.

When Jingji found that she would not do what he wished, he picked up the tea. "I came here to see you," he said, "but how you have changed. I suppose now you have married the son of a Sub-Prefect I'm not good enough for you any more. When you were the third lady in Ximen Qing's household, things were very different, weren't they?"

He took the silver pin from his sleeve and held it out. "Whose is this pin?" he cried. "If you never had anything to do with me, what am I doing with it? Your name is on it. You and that woman plotted together to share between you all the precious things I left there. They belonged to Yang Jian, and the authorities should have had them. Now you have brought them to this new husband of yours, but wait and see whether I don't bring you to the place where you belong."

Yulou heard this. She knew that the pin was really hers. It was a pin with a gold head shaped like a lotus. She remembered losing it in the garden, but had no idea how Jingji had got hold of it. She was afraid the servants might hear of it, so she smiled at him. She even went over to him and took his hand.

"Good Brother-in-law," she said, "why did you take me seriously? I was joking."

She looked around, saw that there was nobody about, and said quietly: "If you care for me, I care for you too." No more was said. They put their arms about one another and kissed. Jingji put out his tongue like a snake's and made her take it into her mouth.

"You must call me your dearest husband, or I will not believe you," he said.

"Hush!" Yulou said. "Somebody will hear us."

"On a boat in the river I have some goods that I have bought," Jingji said. "We will go to it together. This evening, you can disguise yourself as a servant and come with me. I don't see why we should not. He is only a civil official and will not make any trouble. He won't dare to come and arrest us."

"Very well," Yulou said. "I agree. Come for me this evening and wait at the back of the house. First of all, I will throw a parcel of valuables over the wall. Then I will dress as a servant and come to you by the door and we will go to your boat."

Readers, when a beautiful woman takes an idea firmly into her head, even if the walls are ten thousand feet high, she cannot be prevented from carrying it out. But if she rejects it, you may be sitting in the same room with her, yet it will be as though a thousand mountains kept you apart.

If Yulou had married a fool, a man who was not so attractive as Chen Jingji, Jingji would certainly have succeeded in seducing her, but she had married young Li, who not only had a future in store for him, but was a brisk and lively fellow. She loved him and was quite content with her marriage. There was no reason why she should yield to Jingji. The unfortunate young man told her all his plans, but she deceived him.

When Jingji had drunk more wine, he went away. Young Master Li took him to the gate, and he went away with Chen An.

"Where is your brother staying?" Master Li asked his wife. "I must call on him tomorrow and take some sort of a present."

"He is not my brother at all," Yulou said. "He is Ximen Qing's son-in-law, and he came here because he wanted me to run away with him. I told him I would wait for him this evening at the back of the house. I mean to cheat him so that he is arrested as a thief and got rid of finally."

"Really, the fellow goes beyond all bounds," Master Li said. "But without my going to see him, he will come of his own accord and meet his death at my hands." He went out and told a trusted servant.

Jingji suspected nothing. At the third night watch, he came to the back of the house with Chen An. He coughed and Yulou answered. Then, over the wall, some silver was lowered at the end of a rope. It was about two hundred taels and had been taken from the official treasury. Jingji had hardly told Chen An to take it, when the watchman's alarm sounded, and four or five tall fellows came running out, crying: "Thief! Thief!" They seized Jingji and Chen An. The matter was reported to the Sub-Prefect, and he gave orders that the men should be thrown into jail and brought up for examination the next day.

The Prefect of Yanzou was called Xu Feng. He came from Lintao in Shaanxi. He had taken his examination in *Gengxu*, and was a very just and honorable man. He came to the hall of justice, and all the officers attended him. Sub-Prefect Li came and signed his name in the register. Then an official came and told Xu about the case, and Jingji was brought in.

"Last night," the official said, "about the third night watch, these two men, whose names we now know to be Chen Jingji and Chen An, broke open the treasury door and stole about two hundred taels of silver that are the proceeds of other cases. Then they jumped over the wall, but were caught and arrested."

The Prefect ordered his men to bring forward the thieves, and Chen Jingji and Chen An were hustled towards him. They knelt down. The Prefect saw that Jingji was only a young man and very good-looking. "Young fellow," he said, "where do you come from? What do you mean by coming to a government building to steal money belonging to the treasury? Have you anything to say?"

Jingji kowtowed again and again and protested he was innocent.

"How can you be innocent?" the Prefect said. "You stole the money, didn't you?"

Then the Sub-Prefect, who was sitting beside Xu, bowed and said: "My lord, ask him no more. The silver was found upon him. Why do you hesitate to punish him?"

The Prefect ordered Jingji to be given twenty strokes.

"Men are hard creatures," the Sub-Prefect said. "They never confess without a good beating. This young man, you see, is no exception to the rule."

The attendants threw Jingji to the ground and beat him with a thick cane. He yelled and shrieked. "I never realized what that strumpet Meng was up to," he cried. "It is she who has done this. Oh dear! Oh dear!"

Now Xu was a man who had taken a degree and, when he heard this, he thought there must be something underneath. When the young man had had ten strokes, he gave orders that he should be taken back to prison and brought up again the next day.

"That, I suggest, is the wrong course," the Sub-Prefect said. "The proverb tells us that men's hearts are as hard as iron, but the law is heavy as a mountain. If you give him one night, he will take back his confession in the morning."

"I know what I am doing," the Prefect said, and again told the jailers to put Jingji into prison. He was somewhat suspicious as to what was behind this case, and sent a man he trusted to the prison to ask Jingji what it was all about. The man disguised himself as one of the prisoners and spent the night with Chen Jingji.

"Brother," he said, "you are a young man and you do not look like a thief. I believe you are innocent."

"It is a long story," Jingji said. "I am the son-in-law of Ximen Qing of Qinghe. The woman Meng, who married Sub-Prefect Li's son, was one of my father-in-law's wives. Once she had a love affair with me, and now she has brought ten chests of gold and silver and precious things to Li's son. Those things once belonged to Yang Chien, and he left them in my father-in-law's care. I came here to ask for them, but they laid this trap for me and I fell into it. They arrested me as a thief and made me confess. Oh dear! Oh dear! Now I can see the blue sky and the sun no more."

The Prefect's servant went back and told all this to his master.

"When he mentioned the woman Meng, I wondered what there was at the back of it," the Prefect said.

The next day, he came again to the hall, and Chen Jingji and Chen An were brought before him. The Prefect extracted the real truth from the young man and set him free. The Sub-Prefect, who did not know what had happened, said: "My lord, he stole the money. Why do you let him go?"

The Prefect rebuked his assistant before all the other officers. "I am the Prefect here," he said, "and I serve his Majesty faithfully. It is not my business to take up your private quarrels, and to brand this innocent young man as a thief. Your son married a woman named Meng, one of Ximen Qing's concubines, and she brought with her many things that ought to have been handed over to the government. This young man is Ximen Qing's son-in-law, and he came to claim them. You have no right whatever to make him out a thief and try to have him punished as such. I am not here to do your dirty work. You are an officer and you have children, and you are trying to forward your children's interests. If this is the way you do it, it is an offense against justice."

The Sub-Prefect was ashamed. He flushed and bowed his head. It was a great blow to his pride, and he dared not say a word. Chen Jingji and Chen An went away.

When the Prefect had retired, Li went home in a furious temper. "This is the son you have reared for me," he cried to his wife. "He has caused the Prefect to insult me in the presence of all the officers. It nearly killed me."

His wife was upset and asked what was the matter.

The Sub-Prefect sent for his son and told the servants to bring him a thick rod. "Now!" he cried. "That thief you said you caught is Ximen Qing's son-in-law. That woman of yours brought many things away from Ximen's house and the young man said in the court that they had belonged to the criminal Yang Chien. He came here to demand them. You told me that he stole silver from the treasury and got me to treat him as a thief. I knew nothing at all of the truth, and the result is that I have been disgraced by the Prefect before all the officers of the court. That is what my son does for me, and I have only been in this post a few months. What use is such a son to me?"

He ordered his servants to beat the young man, and the blows rained down upon him. His flesh and skin were torn and the blood gushed out. The old lady could not bear the sight, and sobbed and tried to make her husband stop. Yulou stood, weeping, at the corner door.

When the young man had been given thirty strokes, the Sub-Prefect bade his servants stop.

"Get rid of this woman at once," he said. "Let her marry whom she pleases. I am not going to have her here to ruin my family."

Young Master Li could not bear this. He knelt down before his parents and cried: "I would rather die than give up this woman."

Then the Sub-Prefect ordered his servants to shut up the young man in a room at the back of the house. He was put in chains, for his father meant him to die there.

"My lord," the Sub-Prefect's wife said to him, "you are of official rank, and you are more than fifty years of age. You have only this one son. It is not right that you should let him die for the sake of this woman. When you are old and retired, who will care for you?"

"No," the Sub-Prefect said, "so long as he is here, I shall have everybody insulting me."

"Then send them away to Zhengdingfu, where our home is, if you won't have them here," his wife said.

The Sub-Prefect agreed. The young man was brought out again and told that he would have to take his wife and leave for his native place within three days.

When Chen Jingji and Chen An left Yanzhou, they removed their luggage from the temple and went back to the inn where they had left Yang.

"Yang told me he had received a letter from you saying you were not coming back," the host said. "He has taken everything and gone."

Jingji could not believe this. He went to the river to look for the boat, but it was not to be seen. "What an outrageous scoundrel!" he said then. "Why did he go away without waiting for me?" He had just come out of prison and had no money. So he and Chen An got on a boat and pawned their clothes to pay the passage money. They looked like a pair of stray dogs, like fish wriggling out of the net. All the way along, they asked for news of Yang the Elder, but heard nothing. It was now the end of autumn. The leaves were withered in the woods, and the West wind drove fiercely. It was sad and cold.

> Sadly, the lotus withers
> Leaf after leaf, the *Wutong* fades
> The crickets chirp in the rotted grass
> The wild goose rests on the barren sand
> A fine rain drenches the dark forest
> A heavy frost chills the air.
> He who is not a wayfarer
> Will never know what Autumn is.

At last Chen Jingji reached home. Chen Ding was standing at the door. Jingji's face as black as lacquer and his clothes were nothing but rags. The servant was shocked. He took his master in and asked him where the boat was.

For a long time the young man could not speak. Then he told the servant what had happened to him in Yanzhou. "Fortunately," he said, "the Prefect set me free or my life would have been in danger. Then that heaven-destroying rascal Yang stole my merchandise, and I have no idea where he has gone." He told Chen Ding to go to Yang's house to find out if he had returned. Chen Ding was told that Yang the Elder had not yet come home. Then Jingji himself went to Yang's house, but could get no information. He was very much upset and went to his wife's room. He found her quarreling with Feng Jinbao. Indeed the two women had spent all their time quarreling while he had been away.

His wife said that Feng Jinbao had given a great sum of money to the old procuress and that the old woman came every day, stole things away, and brought food and wine that she ate with her daughter. She herself could get nothing to eat. Feng Jinbao used to sleep until noon and would not give her a penny to buy anything with.

Feng Jinbao said that Ximen Dajie did not do a stroke of work. She would not even stoop down to pick up a piece of straw. She stole rice and changed it for buns. She stole the preserved meats and ate them with her maid.

Chen Jingji believed what Feng Jinbao said and cursed his wife. "You whore!" he cried. "Are you starving that you must steal rice and change it for buns? And you and your maid have been stealing meat."

He beat the maid and kicked his wife. This annoyed her so much that she went and beat her head against her enemy's. "You whore!" she cried. "It was you who stole the things and gave them to the old whore. Yet you lie to my husband and say I stole them. That is like the thief arresting the policeman. You told my husband to kick me. Well, I will live no longer and you shall die with me."

"How dare you, you little strumpet," Jingji cried. "You are not worth one of her little toes."

With one hand he seized his wife's hair and beat her with the other. He kicked her, too. She bled from nose and mouth and was unconscious for a long time. Jingji went to the other room with the singing girl.

Alone in her room, Ximen Dajie sobbed bitterly. Her maid went to sleep in another room. At midnight, Ximen Qing's daughter tied a rope around the beam and hanged herself. She was only twenty-four years old.

The next morning, when her maid got up and tried to open the door, she could not. Jingji and Feng Jinbao were still in bed. Feng Jinbao told her maid to go to Ximen Dajie and ask for a bowl so that she could wash her feet. But the maid could not open the door.

"What!" Jingji cried. "Is she still in bed? It is not early now. I will go and open the strumpet's door and pull her hair for her."

The maid looked through the window. "She is up there," she said; "I can see her swinging. She looks as if she were trying to be one of the dolls in a puppet play."

Then Ximen Dajie's maid looked through the window. "Father," she cried, "Mother has hanged herself."

Chen Jingji was much disturbed at this. He and Feng Jinbao got up. They forced open the door and cut Ximen Dajie down. But she had been dead a long time, and nobody knew the hour at which she had died.

When Chen Ding heard of his mistress's death, he was afraid he might be involved in the matter and went to tell Wu Yueniang. So she heard that her daughter had hanged herself and her son-in-law had taken up with a singing girl. The hatred between herself and Jingji was like ice three feet thick, not the result of one night's frost. She went with servants, maids, and women, seven or eight of them, and came to Jingji's door. There she roundly declared that her daughter had hanged herself, and made a great to-do. She seized Jingji and beat him and even stuck awls into him. The singing girl, Feng Jinbao, hid under a bed, but was dragged out and beaten until she was half dead. They smashed the doors and windows and took away the bed and curtains and furniture that had belonged to Ximen Dajie.

Then Yueniang went home and sent for Uncle Wu the Elder and Uncle Wu the Second.

"Sister," Uncle Wu the Elder said, "we must take this opportunity and bring him before the courts, or he will make things very unpleasant in the future. He is sure to come and demand his property, and, if we don't look a long way ahead, we shall have trouble. We had better go to law at once and have the thing settled once and for all."

"Brother, you are right," Yueniang said.

They drew up an accusation and, the next day, Yueniang herself went to the magistrate. When she went to the Town Hall, her accusation was sent in.

The new magistrate was called Huo Dali. He was a graduate and a native of Huanggang, an upright and conscientious man. When he was told about the suicide, he went to the hall and took the accusation. It said:

The accuser is the Lady Wu, thirty-four years of age, widow of the late Ximen Qing, Captain. She accuses her evil son-in-law as a deceiver and oppressor. He believed the words of a strumpet and forced his wife to hang herself. The Lady Wu implores you to investigate this matter and save her life.

This son-in-law is Chen Jingji. He came to her when he was in trouble and lived in her house for many years. He was fond of wine and caused trouble. He was undutiful and created disturbances within and without the household. Being a law-abiding woman, she got rid of him. Ever since that time he has hated her and treated his wife badly. He beat her and ill-used her, but she bore it for a long time.

Then he brought home a strumpet from Linqing, a certain Feng Jinbao. This woman occupied the room that should have been the Lady Wu's daughter's. He believed whatever she said to him, and ill-used his wife in every way. He pulled her hair and kicked her till her body was covered with bruises, and she could bear it no longer.

Then, at the third night watch on the twenty-third day of the eighth month of this year, she hanged herself.

This Chen Jingji obstinately seeks to oppress the Lady Wu, and threatens that he will kill her also. This is intolerable, and she implores your Lordship to arrest and try him for being the cause of her daughter's death.

So may evil doers know the law, and the good live in peace. So will the dead be avenged.

With this accusation, the Lady Wu accuses this man. To the Magistrate of the District, whose justice is that of the Blue Heavens.

The magistrate looked at Yueniang. She was wearing white. She was, he remembered, the widow of an officer of the fifth class. She was dignified in manner and refined in appearance. He rose and said: "Lady, stand up. I believe you are the widow of an officer. I understand. Go home and leave a servant to take your place here. I will have the man arrested at once."

Yueniang thanked him and went home in a sedan chair, leaving Laizhao behind. The magistrate ordered two runners to take the white badge to their office and arrest Chen Jingji and Feng Jinbao, and order the attendance of the watchman in that neighborhood.

Jingji was very busy making preparations for the funeral when he heard that runners had been sent to arrest him at the request of his mother-in-law. He was almost distracted. Feng Jinbao, who was in bed after the beating she had received at Yueniang's hands, was so terrified when she heard that she was under arrest, that she hardly knew whether she was alive or dead. Without stopping to think, Jingji tried to bribe the runners, but the runners bound them with one cord and hauled them to the Town Hall. The neighbors and the local watchman went to the Town Hall with them.

When the magistrate heard that they had come, he went again to the hall. Laizhao knelt down on the left, Chen Jingji, Feng Jinbao and the others on the steps.

"You wicked man," the magistrate said to Jingji, "why did you listen to this singing girl and cause your wife's death? Have you anything to say?"

"My lord," Jingji said, "I did not beat her. It is all because of a partner I had who went away with me to do business. He stole my money, and when I came home I was in a very bad temper. I asked her for some food and she would not listen to me. I did kick her that time. Then, in the night, she hanged herself and so died."

"You had that strumpet," the Magistrate said angrily. "Why should you ask your wife to get you food? It was unreasonable. According to the accusation that has been brought against you, you beat your wife and she killed herself. Is that true or not?"

"The Lady Wu hates me," Jingji said, "and she has made up the whole of this story. I implore you, my lord, to go most carefully into the matter."

"Her daughter is dead," the Magistrate said. "Do you imagine you are going to get out of it?" He told his attendants to give Jingji twenty strokes with the rod.

Then Feng Jinbao was called forward, and thumbscrews were put on her. The magistrate gave orders that they should be thrown into jail and told one of his underlings to go with the neighbors and police to examine the body. They found bruises all over the body and the mark of the rope around Ximen Dajie's neck. They wrote down this report: "After Chen

Jingji had severely handled her, she hanged herself, unable to bear his ill usage any longer."

When this report was brought to the magistrate, he was very angry. He ordered ten more strokes to be given to Chen Jingji and ten to Feng Jinbao also. He declared that Jingji was guilty of his wife's death, and sentenced him to strangulation. Feng Jinbao was sentenced to a hundred strokes with a rod, and afterwards to serve as the public whore.

Jingji was in a terrible state. He sent a note to Chen Ding and told him to take every penny there was in the shop and his wife's ornaments, a hundred taels in all, and secretly take them to the magistrate. So, during the night, the magistrate altered the sentence and made it appear that he had been found guilty of having been the cause of his wife's death in the less criminal sense, imprisoning him for five years with permission to purchase his freedom.

Yueniang continually pressed the magistrate for justice.

At last he sent for her. "Lady," he said, "we have discovered the marks of the rope on your daughter's neck, so it is clear that she was not murdered. I do not wish to be unjust to anyone and, if you are afraid that he will make trouble with you in the future, I will arrange matters in such a way that he will never come near you again." He sent for Jingji and said to him: "I have been very lenient with you. You must amend your evil ways and begin to lead a new life. I forbid you ever to go and cause a disturbance at this lady's house. If you come before me again, I shall not forgive you. Go home and buy a coffin and bury your wife and then come back and report to me. I shall send an account of this matter to those in authority over me."

Jingji paid the fine that gave him back his freedom, and went home. He put his wife's body into a coffin, but kept it at home only seven days. Then the religious service was held and the body taken outside the city and buried. He returned to the Town Hall, and there spent much money. Feng Jinbao had gone; he had lost all his property; his things were sold and his house disposed of. Only his life was left to him. He dared not mention his mother-in-law's name.

CHAPTER 93

Chen Jingji Becomes a Monk

He stands on the steps and his tears fall silently
In the crowd his heart is full of discontent.
He breathes the air about him in a daze
And knows not his own feelings.

A warm breeze comes to the merry feast.
The sun shines brightly on the pollen of the flowers.
Yet even here his sorrow deepens.
He lives a life apart and only longs
To see the Springtide pass.

Chen Jingji had saved only his life. He sold his house and he had spent all his capital. His wife's ornaments were all gone, and there was no furniture left. He suspected that Chen Ding had made money at his expense, and dismissed him. Now he led a miserable existence without a penny to spend. He went several times to Yang's place to find out if Yang had come back with the goods.

One day, he went and shouted: "Is Yang the Elder at home?"

Now Yang had stolen Jingji's things and sold them. He hid himself in one place and another until he heard that Jingji's wife was dead and that the young man had been sent to prison for sometime on his mother-in-law's accusation. Then he came home. When he heard Chen Jingji's voice outside asking for the return of his property, he told his younger brother to go out and see him.

"You took my brother away on some of your business," Yang the Second said. "We have not heard a word from him for months, and, for all we know, you may have thrown him into the river and murdered him. Now, here you are, daring to come and ask about your merchandise. Do you think your merchandise is more important than my brother's life?"

This Yang the Second was a very bad man, a terrible fellow to meet in the gambling den. The purple muscles stood out on his arms and there was a mop of yellow hair on his chest. He was a villain pure and simple. He caught hold of Chen Jingji and demanded his brother. Jingji was frightened, struggled, and tried to get away. Yang the Second picked up a broken tile with three edges and deliberately gashed his own head so that the blood ran down. Then he ran after Jingji.

"I'll shove my spade in your mother's eye," he said. "What do we know about your money that you come farting around our house? Come here, and taste my fist."

Jingji ran for his life. When he got home, he fastened the door as tight as the lid of an iron pail. Outside it, Yang the Second cursed Chen Jingji, his father and his mother. Then he took some stones to smash open the door and Jingji held his breath. He had just come out of jail and had to put up with it. He was like a man who has once been bitten by a snake, afraid even of a piece of rope that he sees in a dream.

Some days later, he sold his house and got seventy taels of silver for it. He rented a small house in a very quiet road and went to live there. He sold the maid he had bought for Feng Jinbao and kept Ximen Dajie's maid to sleep with him. In less than a month, he sold the small house and went to live in a lodging house. Chen Ding no longer served him, and the maid died. He was alone in the world. He sold what furniture he had and was as poor as an old suit of clothes. Then he could not pay his rent and had to go and live at the Beggars' Rest.

The beggars knew he had been a rich man, and he was a good-looking fellow, so they gave him the stove bed to lie on and cakes to eat, and recommended him to the watchman as a bell ringer.

In the twelfth month, towards the end of winter, it was snowing heavily and the wind was very cold. Jingji came back from beating the alarm for the watchman. Then he went around the streets again with his bell. There were wind and snow together, and he had to tramp over the icy ground. It was so cold that he hunched his shoulders and bent his back and shivered all the time. About the fifth night watch, he saw a beggar ill and collapsed against a wall. The policeman thought the beggar was going to die and told Jingji to get some straw to warm him. Jingji went to sleep there, after doing all he could for the beggar. He had a dream. He dreamed he was back again in Ximen Qing's house, enjoying luxury and wealth, playing and joking with Pan Jinlian. Then he cried and woke up. Some of the other beggars came and asked him why he was crying. "Ah, Brothers," he said, "you do not know what I have had to bear." Every night, Jingji went to the Beggars' Rest, and every day went out to beg for food.

> Long years he has suffered hardship
> Bewailing his wife's death
> Without clothes to cover his body
> And food to put in his mouth.

His horse is dead
His servant run away
His house is sold.
Now, all alone, he wanders through the land
Standing, in the morning, outside the shops
To beg a scrap of bread
And, in the evening, lodges beside a ruined wall
Away from human habitation.
One hope alone is left to him
To go the watchman's round in the cold night.

In the city of Qinghe there lived an old man called Wang Xuan, whose other name was Ting Yong. He was more than sixty years old and very wealthy. He was a kind-hearted man who spent his money trying to help others. He always gave alms to the poor and assisted those in distress, and was very kind and very devout. His two sons were both married. One, Wang Qian, had inherited his grandfather's position at the royal mews and held the rank of Captain; the other, Wang Zhen, was a student at the Academy of Learning. The old gentleman had a small pawnshop. He had all the food he needed and all the clothes he could wear, and nothing to do but go to temples and monasteries to hear the preachings of the monks. He used to distribute medicine to the people, count his beads, and study the teachings of Buddha. He had two apricot trees in his garden, and took as his name in religion the Hermit of the Apricot Trees.

One day this old gentleman, wearing a monastic habit and a double-brimmed hat, was standing outside his door when Chen Jingji came along. The young man knelt down and kowtowed to him. The old man made a reverence in return.

"Brother," he said, "who are you? My sight is so bad I can't recognize you."

Jingji stood shivering. "Sir," he said, "I am Chen Hong's son."

The old man thought over this for a long time. "So you are Chen's son," he said at last. "My good nephew, how do you come to be in such a state? How are your father and mother?"

"My father died at the Eastern Capital," Jingji said, "and my mother is dead too."

"I believe you have been living with your father-in-law," the old man said.

"Yes," Jingji said, "but when he died, my mother-in-law would not have me any longer. Her daughter died, and we had a lawsuit. I had to sell my house, and I was cheated out of the little money I had. I have no work to do, and there is no way in which I can make a living."

"Where are you living now, my good nephew?" the old man said.

Jingji hesitated a long time, and at last said, "I will tell you the truth. It is like this. . . ."

"Dear, oh dear!" the old man said. "So you are now a beggar. And yet, if I remember rightly, you come of a very respectable stock. Your father was a great friend of mine. But you were a little boy then, and had your hair dressed in a knot, and were going to school. Can it be possible you have come down to this? I am very sorry for you. Have you no relative who can help you?"

"There is my Uncle Zhang," Jingji said, "but he has not come to me, and I don't feel I can go to him."

The old man took Jingji into his house. He told his boys to bring food and cakes and bade Jingji eat as much as he could. Then he saw how poor and thin the young man's clothes were, and found for him a long black cloth gown, a felt hat, and a pair of strong winter shoes and socks. He gave Jingji a tael of silver and five hundred coppers.

"Good nephew," he said, "these clothes and shoes are for you to wear and this money is for you to spend. Rent a little room and start yourself in business with this tael of silver. You will at least be able to make something to eat that way, and it seems to me better than staying at the Beggars' Rest, where you are bound to go downhill. When you have found a room, come and tell me what the rent is and I will pay it for you."

Jingji knelt down on the floor and thanked the old gentleman. He promised to do what he was told and went away with the money. But he did not go to look for a room, nor did he start a business. He spent the coppers in a wineshop, and changed the tael of silver into base money and spent it in the street. Then the police arrested him as a common thief and, when he was taken to the police station, he was well beaten. He came away with nothing but the torn flesh on his back.

In a couple of days he had gambled his clothes away, and even taken off his socks to change them for food. Then he went back to begging on the street.

One day he again went past old Wang's door, and the old gentleman was standing outside. Jingji came and kowtowed to him. The old man looked at him and saw that the clothes and socks had gone. He had only the hat on his head and the boots on his bare feet. He was shivering with cold.

"Master Chen," the old man said, "how is your business getting on? I suppose you have come for the rent for your room."

Jingji could not think what answer to make. At last, when the old gentleman pressed him, he said what had happened and how everything the old man had given him was gone.

"Ah, my good nephew," the old man said. "That is no way to make a living. You are no use for manual labor; you must get some sort of little business. It is much better than this begging. If you become a beggar, people will look down on you, and you will bring disgrace upon your father and grandfather. I wonder why you did not do what I told you."

Again the old man took Jingji into his house and ordered a boy to bring him food. When he had finished eating, the old man gave him a pair of trousers and a white cloth gown, a pair of socks, a string of coins, and some rice.

"Take this," he said, "and do start some business. Even if you sell firewood or charcoal or beans or melons, you can at least make a living, and it is surely better than begging."

Jingji promised and took the money and the rice away. In a few days he had spent all the money on food and meat and noodles that he shared with the beggars in the Beggars' Rest. Then he went gambling and sold the white cloth gown.

It was the beginning of the year, and, clasping his shoulders with his hands, he went wandering about the streets. He felt very shy about approaching the old man again, but nonetheless went to the old man's place and stood in the sun beside the wall. The old man saw him, but looked at him with cold eyes and said nothing. The young man came up hesitatingly, knelt down, and kowtowed. Then the old man found out again how Chen Jingji had spent his money.

"Good nephew," he said, "you are off the track altogether. Our bellies are as deep as the sea, and time flies as quickly as a weaver's shuttle. Nobody can help you to fill a bottomless pit. Come in. Now, let me tell you. I know of a quiet and peaceful place. It would be the very best place for you, but I fear you will not wish to go there."

Jingji, kneeling before him, wept and said: "Uncle, if you will only take pity on me once more, I will go, no matter where you send me, and stay in peace there."

"Not far from the Linqing wharf," the old man said, "there is a temple called the Yangong temple. It is a place that produces rice and fish, and much business is done there. The Abbot is a good friend of mine. He has only two or three novices at present and, if I take you to him with some presents, I think he may accept you. It will be very good for you to learn how to read the sacred books and perform sacred music. Then you will be able to offer divine worship for people."

"Uncle, I am very grateful to you. It is an excellent idea."

"If you are willing," the old man said, "come here early tomorrow morning. It is a good day, and I will go with you to the temple."

Jingji went away. The old man sent at once for the tailor and told him to make a religious habit, a hat, shoes, and socks for Chen Jingji.

The next day, Jingji came to the old man's house. He was sent into an empty room to take a bath. Then he combed his hair and put on the new hat, and dressed himself in a whole suit of new clothes. The old man took fruits, a jar of wine, a roll of silk, and five taels of silver. He mounted a horse and gave Jingji a donkey to ride. Two boys went with them and carried the presents. They went outside the city and came to the river, about seventy *li* away. The sun was setting when they came to the temple. Old Wang dismounted and went in. The pine trees were very luxuriant, and the dark cypress trees were massed closely together. The walls were shaped like the character *pa*. On the north side were three rooms. It was a very handsome temple.

The young monks at the gate saw them coming and went to tell the Abbot. He came out to receive them dressed in his robes. The old man told Jingji to stay with the presents outside, and went in with the Abbot. When they came to the Abbot's apartments, the priest said: "My lord Wang, why have you been so long without coming to see me? Why am I favored today?"

"I have been very busy, or I should have come to see you before," the old man said.

They sat down and young monks brought tea.

"It is late," the Abbot said, "and you will not be able to go away this evening." He gave orders that the old man's horse should be taken to the stable.

"I have come to this most venerable temple to ask a favor of you," old man Wang said. "I can only hope that you will grant it."

"Give me your orders," the Abbot said, "and I shall not fail to obey."

"I have brought with me a young man, the son of an old friend. His name is Chen Jingji, and he is twenty-four years old. He is very handsome and not lacking in intelligence. But his parents died while he was still young and his upbringing has been neglected. His family is a very estimable and noble one. At one time they were rich, but they were unfortunately compelled to go to law, and now the young man is homeless. Because of the old friendship between his father and myself, I have suggested that he should come and become a monk in your temple."

"Since that is your wish, how dare I refuse?" the Abbot said. "Unhappily, though I have two or three novices here, none of them has any intelligence and they give me a great deal of trouble. All I should like to know is that this young man is honest."

"I can assure you, Sir, that he is most well-behaved. He is painstaking and clever in all things. I am sure he will make an excellent novice."

"When will you bring the young man?" the Abbot said.

"He is waiting outside at this moment. I have also brought a few humble presents that I ask you to accept with a smile."

"My lord," the Abbot said, "why did you not say so before?" He gave orders that the young man should be brought in. The servants carried in the presents. The Abbot looked at the card: 'Your humble disciple Wang Xuan respectfully offers a roll of coarse silk, a jar of wine, a pair of pig's trotters, two roast ducks, two boxes of fruits, and five taels of silver.'

The Abbot quickly made a reverence to the old man. "Why do you give me such a valuable present?" he said: "it would be rude for me to refuse, and it embarrasses me to accept."

He looked at Jingji, who was wearing a Daoist hat, gown, and shoes, and a girdle about his waist. He had beautiful eyebrows and bright eyes. His teeth were bright, his lips red, and his face as white as though it were powdered. He stepped forward and kowtowed four times to the Abbot.

The Abbot asked how old he was.

"My animal is the Horse," Jingji said, "and I am twenty-four."

The Abbot realized that Jingji was indeed intelligent. He gave him the name Chen Zongmei. The other novices were called, one Jin Zongming, and the other, Xu Zongshun. Old Wang asked the Abbot to introduce Jingji to the others. The Abbot accepted the presents; boys brought a light and the table was set. There was plenty of food on the table, and, needless to remark, chickens, ducks, fish and meat. Old man Wang could not drink very much and, though the Abbot tried to persuade him, he soon refused any more and, asking leave to retire, went to bed.

The next morning, boys brought him water and, when he had dressed, the Abbot came to offer him tea. Then they had breakfast and, after it, the old man drank two cups of wine. His horse was well fed, and the Abbot gave a present to each of the two boys.

Before the old man went away, he sent for Jingji. "Work hard," he said, "at learning the Sacred Scriptures, and obey the orders your Teacher gives you. I will come and see you again, and bring clothes, shoes and socks for you at every season."

"If he does not obey you," he said to the Abbot, "punish him. I shall not blame you."

Then he took Jingji aside. "You must cleanse your mind and change your ways," he said. "Learn. If you still remain as bad as you have been, I shall cease to trouble about you."

Jingji promised, and the old man went home. So Jingji was established at the temple, and became a novice.

The Abbot was elderly and red-nosed. He was tall and had a loud and resonant voice. His beard was long; he was a good talker and a good drinker. He spent all his time receiving visitors. The business of the temple was managed by the novice, Jin Zongming. At that time, the government had just completed the canal and built two sluices at Linqing to control the water. So all boats, whether those of officials or people, had to stop there, and it was customary for those who traveled upon them to visit the temple. Some said prayers, some offered gifts, some came in quest of miracles, some came to do works of charity. They gave cloth and money and rice, oil, paper and candles. Some gave poles and mats.

With the money that he could not spend, the Abbot had set up a money-changing shop and a rice store on the river, and put his novices in charge of them, taking the profit for himself.

Jin Zongming was not a good young man. He was about thirty years old, and spent much of his time in the bawdy house. He was a great fellow for wine and women. He had some younger novices of his own, very smart, good-looking boys, and spent the night with them. When Chen Jingji came, Zongming saw how handsome he was, how white his teeth and how red his lips. He seemed so intelligent that he could make his eyes speak for him in place of his mouth. So he asked the young man to come and sleep in his room. In the evening they drank and, when Jingji was drunk, they went to bed together. At first, one had his head at one end of the bed and the other at the other end. But Jin Zongming complained that Jingji's feet smelled, and asked him to come over the other way. Then he complained that Jingji's breath was bad, and asked him to turn his face around. Jingji pressed his back against the other monk's stomach and said nothing, feigning sleep. Then Jin Zongming's penis became firm and erect like a spear. He smeared it with spittle and plunged in. When Jingji had been living among the beggars, two of his companions had misused his bottom and stretched it, so the monk's path was now easy. Jingji still said nothing. "This fellow will fall into my hands," he thought. "He doesn't know who I am and he can't do me much harm. I will let him have a taste and then I will get hold of his money."

He suddenly cried out. Jin Zongming was afraid the Abbot might hear, and covered the young man's mouth with his hand.

"Brother," he said, "don't make a noise. Tell me anything you want and you shall have it."

"I will not tell anybody," Jingji said, "if you will promise me three things."

"Good Brother," Zongming said, "do you say three things? I am ready to promise ten."

"Very well," Jingji said. "If you want me, you must leave the other boys alone. You must let me have the keys of all the rooms. And, if I go anywhere, do not ask me where I have been. If you like to promise these three things, you can do whatever you wish."

"I will do everything you say," Zongming said. They spent half the night in their wild pursuits. Jingji had been a dissolute young wastrel and knew all the tricks of the trade. He used these tricks for the benefit of Jin Zongming, who was perfectly delighted. The next day, he gave all the keys to Chen Jingji. He kept his promise that he would sleep no more with the boys.

Days passed and Jin Zongming was always singing the praises of Jingji to the Abbot. The Abbot believed him and bought a priest's diploma for Jingji. He was not suspicious, and the young man frequently took money and went to the town. There, one day, he met a certain Chen the Third who told him that Feng Jinbao's mother was dead. The girl herself had been sold to Zheng's bawdy house and given a new name. She was now frequenting the wine houses in the street. Chen the Third asked Jingji if he would like to see her. Jingji had not forgotten his old love for the girl. He took his money and went to a large wineshop. He had been happy enough before, but now it was as though he met her whom he had loved for five hundred years.

> Do not spare your clothes of silk and gold
> Do not let your youth be wasted.
> When you see a flower that is ripe for gathering,
> Gather it.
> Wait not till all the flowers are faded
> For then only bare branches will remain
> For you to gather.

The wineshop to which they went was the finest in Linqing. It was known as Xie's wineshop, and had more than a hundred rooms. There were green balconies with, at the back, a little hill and, at the front, the river. It was in a very busy position, and all the boats called there.

> The sun shines on the carven eaves
> The painted columns shimmer in the air.
> There are low green rails under the great windows
> And long green curtains hanging there.
> Young noblemen play the flute and the *sheng*
> Singing girls and dancing maidens serve the wine
> And bear the wine jars.

The drinkers feast their eyes on the blue sky
And the cloud-covered mountains.
Water and mist, like snow of good omen,
Take away the breath.
The wild birds sing in the green willows
And horses in gay trappings
Are tethered to the willow beside the door.

Chen the Third took Jingji in, and they went into a small room. He bade the waiter bring wine and food and send them a singing girl from downstairs. They heard footsteps coming up the stairs, and Feng Jinbao came into the room. She was carrying a little gong. She made a reverence to Chen Jingji. When the two lovers met, they could not prevent their tears from falling.

Jingji asked her to sit down with them. "Where have you been since I last saw you?" he asked her.

Feng Jinbao dried her tears. "After I came out of prison," she said, "my mother died. The shock had been too much for her. Then I was sold to Madam Zheng the Fifth. But lately, few people have come to see me, and I have had to go to the street to pick up business. Yesterday Master Chen told me that you had a money-changing shop here. I was anxious to see you, and at last my wish has been fulfilled. I have thought of you all the time." She began to weep again.

Jingji took out his handkerchief and dried her tears. "Sister," he said, "do not worry any more. I am all right again now. When I came out of prison, I had to spend all my money. Then I went to the Yangong monastery and became a priest. The Abbot trusts me absolutely, and I shall be able to come and see you as often as I like. Where are you living?"

"I am at Liu the Second's place," Feng Jinbao said. "It is west of the bridge. He has more than a hundred houses, all occupied by singing girls. Most of them come to the wine houses during the day."

They sat side by side and drank together. While the wine was being warmed, Chen the Third gave her a lute and she sang for them.

Tears fall in pairs
Tears fall in pairs
Three cups of wine at parting
Three cups of wine at parting
The phoenix and his mate are together no more
The phoenix and his mate are together no more.
Over the mountaintop

The slanting sun sinks gradually to rest.
Beyond the mountain the sun sets.
Now the sky is dark and the earth is gloomy
They do not wish to part
They do not wish to part.

When they had had wine enough, Jingji and Feng Jinbao went into a small room and did the work of love. It was a long time since Jingji had touched a woman, and he was very eager. Now that he had found Feng Jinbao, he put forth all his strength. They wished that they might never make an end, but at last they did so, and put on their clothes again.

It was late. Jingji left Feng Jinbao. He gave her a tael of silver, and three hundred coppers to Chen the Third. "Sister," he said to the girl, "we will meet here again. Whenever you want me, ask Chen the Third to tell me." He paid three *qian* of silver for the wine and then started back for the temple. Feng Jinbao went with him and left him at the bridge.

CHAPTER 94

Sun Xue'e Is Sold to a Brothel

Those of her kin are dead, and all is lost
Unwillingly she must become again
A light of love.
Her tears fall like great drops of jade
She leaves her home and with her dainty feet
Walks to the brothel.

Before the mirror she sighs
Laments the fate of her most perfect beauty
And before men begins to play the whore.
Rain and dew in springtime are like the waters of the sea.
She mates with Master Liu
Whom she finds better than Master Yuan.

Chen Jingji and Feng Jinbao met at the wine house every two or three days. If he failed to come, the girl would send him a message by Chen the Third. And every time he came he gave her a tael of silver or five *qian*. He also gave her rice and firewood, and paid her rent. When he went back to the temple, his face was always red. The Abbot would ask him where he had been drinking, and Jingji would say that he had drunk two or three cups with customers at the rice shop because he was so tired and worn out. Jin Zongming supported him in everything he said, to make sure of his companionship during the night. So things went on for a long time, and Jingji robbed the Abbot of nearly half his takings.

Liu the Second of the wine house was a famous tiger in this neighborhood. He was the younger brother of the wife of that Zhang Sheng who was the trusted servant of Major Zhou. He set up a number of houses for singing girls, foregathered with rich and powerful people, and oppressed the weak. He lent money to the singing girls, taking from them interest at three times the ordinary rate. If they did not pay, he altered the contracts, adding the interest to the loan and so making it more and more. He was fond of wine, and very quarrelsome in his cups; no one dared to cross him in any way. He was indeed a leader of those who beat singing girls and a captain of wineshop bullies.

He had observed Chen Jingji, a handsome young fellow and a novice of Abbot Ren, spending a great deal of time at the large wine house with the girl Feng Jinbao. One day, when he was drunk, he came to the wine house his two fists the size of rice bowls, and demanded Feng Jinbao. The host, Xie, bowed and said: "Uncle Liu, she is upstairs in Number Two." The man bounded upstairs with great strides. Jingji was drinking wine with Feng Jinbao behind a closed door with the lattice pulled down. Liu pulled aside the lattice and demanded that Feng Jinbao should come to him at once. Jingji was so terrified that he held his breath. Liu kicked open the door, and the girl had to come out.

"Uncle Liu," she said, "what can I do for you?"

"You whore!" Liu cried, "you haven't paid me any rent for three months and now you are trying to get away from me."

"Uncle," Feng Jinbao said, smiling, "go home and I will tell mother to send you the money."

Liu struck her in the chest and felled her to the ground with one blow. Her head hit the stairs, and blood streamed over the floor.

"You whore," Liu cried, "I'm not going to wait. I want my money now."

Then he saw Chen Jingji. He went forward, took hold of the table and smashed everything that was on it.

"Who are you," Jingji cried, "to come here and behave in this mad fashion?"

"I'll pound your mother's rice for her, you priest," Liu cried. He dragged Jingji by the hair, knocked him down, kicked him, and struck him. Meanwhile, the people in the wine house stood and watched him as if they were silly. The host could see that Liu was drunk and did not dare to interfere, but when he saw that matters were really getting serious he screwed up courage enough to come and say: "Uncle Liu, don't be annoyed with him. He doesn't know your honorable name, or he would never have done anything to upset you. Please forgive him and let him go, for my sake."

Liu paid no attention and went on beating Jingji until he was half dead. Then he sent for the police and told them to arrest both the girl and the young man and take them before the court. He had, in fact, a commission from Major Zhou to direct the police and keep watch for thieves and bandits on the river.

The Abbot did not know that Jingji had been arrested. He thought the young man had stayed at the rice shop for the night.

The next day the police took the young man to the court. They handed their charge to Zhang Sheng and Li An. This declared that Chen

Zongmei, a priest of the Yangong monastery, had picked a quarrel with Liu the Second, and that the girl was a harlot.

The people at the court asked Jingji for money. "We are the executioners here," they said, "and there are twelve of us. We leave it to you. And there are the two officers who must not be overlooked."

"I had some money," Jingji said, "but it was stolen when I was having the trouble with Liu. He tore my clothes to rags. Now I have no money, only this silver pin, and that I must give to these two gentlemen."

The men took the pin to Zhang Sheng and Li An. "The fellow has no money," they said, "he only offers this pin, and it is of very inferior silver."

"Bring him in, and I'll see what he has to say," Zhang Sheng said.

They brought in the young man and he knelt down before Zhang Sheng.

"When did you become a disciple of Abbot Ren?" Zhang Sheng said. "What is your civil name? I don't remember having seen you before."

"My name is Chen Jingji," the young man said, "and I am of good family. I have only recently become a priest."

"Since you are a priest," Zhang Sheng said, "it is your duty to study the Sacred Scriptures; not to come out from your monastery, associate with whores, and make trouble with others. You seem to think my position here is not very important and that it is not necessary to give me anything. Why! if I throw this pin into the water, it won't even cause a ripple on the surface."

He ordered the attendants to take the man away to await the pleasure of his superior officer. "This doggish pair is very stingy," he said. "The only thing these priests care about is their money. Now this is an official matter, and when people come here to a dinner party, the least they can do is to bring a handsome handkerchief to wipe their mouths. When you beat him," he said to the others, "see you do it well."

Then he sent for the girl. She brought a man with her who gave three or four taels to the officers.

"You are a singing girl," Zhang Sheng said to her, "and of course you go to any place where it is busy to make a living. You did nothing wrong. It will all depend on whether my chief is in a good temper or not. If he is in a bad temper, you may get a beating; if not, he may let you go."

After a while they heard the signal, and Major Zhou entered the hall. The officers stood in ranks on either side.

In the eighth month of the year before this happened Chunmei had given birth to a son. The baby was now six months old. His face was like a piece of jade and his lips were as red as rouge. Zhou looked upon this child as the most precious thing in all the world. His first wife had died, and he had put Chunmei in her place. She lived in the upper rooms and had two nurses to look after the child, one called Yutang; the other, Jinkui. She also had two maids, Cuihua and Lanhua. She had two favorite singing girls, both sixteen years old, called Haitang and Yuegui. All these girls were devoted to the service of Chunmei alone. The Major's second wife had only one maid, Hehua.

Very often, Zhang Sheng would take the baby outside the court to amuse him and, when the magistrate was hearing a case, he would stand there with the baby in his arms and look on.

Today, when Zhou entered the court, a number of people were brought before him, but he decided to begin with Chen Jingji. So the young man and Feng Jinbao were brought forward. Zhou read the charge. "You are a priest," he said. "What do you mean by breaking your rule, frequenting whores, drinking, and disturbing the public peace? It is disgusting."

He ordered Jingji to be given twenty strokes of the rod, and canceled his priest's diploma. He put thumbscrews on Feng Jinbao, ordered her to be given a milder punishment, and sent back to the bawdy house. The attendants bound Jingji, took off his clothes, raised their rods and shouted. They were just about to begin their beating when the baby, who was with Zhang Sheng outside the hall, stretched out his arms to the young man and wanted to go to him. Zhang Sheng could hardly hold him. He was afraid that the Major might see the child and hurriedly took him away. The baby cried, and did not even stop crying when he was in his mother's arms again. Chunmei asked what was the matter with him.

"My master was in the hall trying cases," Zhang Sheng said, "and he was just about to have a priest beaten, a man named Chen, when the baby began to struggle and try to get to the man. I had to bring him away and then he began to cry."

When she heard the name Chen, Chunmei gathered up her skirts and went softly to the hall. There she peeped through a screen. She could hear the voice of the man who was being beaten and it sounded like that of Chen Jingji. But she could not understand how Jingji could have become a priest. She called Zhang Sheng to her.

"Do you know the man's name?" she asked him.

"He told me that his name as a layman was Chen Jingji," Zhang Sheng told her.

"It is he," Chunmei said to herself. Then she said to Zhang Sheng: "Go and ask my husband to come and see me."

Major Zhou was watching the punishment being administered to the young man. Jingji had had ten strokes when the Major was told that his wife wished to speak to him. He ordered the officials to stop, and left the hall.

"The priest you are punishing is my cousin," Chunmei said to him. "Please forgive him, for my sake."

"Why didn't you tell me before, my dear?" the Major said. "I have already given him ten strokes, and I can't take them back."

He went back to the hall and told the attendants to release both the man and the girl. Then he told Zhang Sheng to go after the priest and also to find out whether Chunmei wished to see him. This was just what Chunmei did wish, but she hesitated. After thinking for a long time, she said to Zhang Sheng: "Let him go. I will send for him another time."

So the Major allowed Jingji to go after no more than ten stripes. He went back to the temple.

The Abbot heard that his novice, Chen Zongmei, had been carrying on with a singing girl at the wine house, that he had got into trouble with Tiger Liu, and been beaten nearly to death. He heard, too, all that had happened afterwards. Now the Abbot was an old man and fat. He was very much upset. He opened his boxes only to find that many of his most treasured possessions had disappeared. Then he collapsed on the floor. The monks came and sent at once for the doctor. They poured medicine down his throat, but without effect. At midnight, the Abbot breathed his last. He was sixty-three years old.

The next day, as Jingji was approaching the temple, some of the people who lived near by said to him: "Do you still think of going to the temple? Because of you, your Teacher died last night!"

Jingji rushed back to Qinghe like a stray dog.

When Chunmei had told Zhang Sheng to let Jingji go away, she went back to her room. She took off her headdress and her long gown and went to bed. She groaned, pressed her hands to her bosom, and said she felt a pain. The whole house was upset. The Major's second wife came and said: "Lady, you have been very well until now, what is the matter?"

"Leave me alone and don't ask questions" was the only answer Chunmei would give to anybody.

Then the Major came from the hall. When he found his wife lying on the bed, groaning, he too became alarmed.

"How do you feel?" he said, taking her hand.

There was no answer.

"Has anyone been annoying you?"

There was still no answer.

"Perhaps it was I, when I punished your cousin."

Chunmei would not say a word.

The Major did not know what to do. He went out to Zhang Sheng and Li An. "You knew that man was your mistress's cousin," he said. "Why didn't you tell me instead of allowing me to punish him and upset my wife? I told you to stop him and let your mistress see him. Why did you let him go? You are a pair of fools."

"I told the mistress," Zhang Sheng said, "but she said she didn't wish to see him. That's why I let him go."

Zhang Sheng went weeping to Chunmei.

"Lady," he said, "please say a word to master for us, or we shall be beaten."

Chunmei opened her eyes wide and raised her eyebrows. She sent for the Major. "I am not well," she said, "but these two men are not to blame. As for that immoral priest, it is better he should suffer a little. I do not wish to see him now."

Zhou said no more to Zhang Sheng and Li An, but told Zhang Sheng to go and fetch a doctor for Chunmei. She was still in pain.

When the doctor had felt her pulse, he said: "It is anger that has upset this lady." He gave her some medicine, but she would not take it. The maids did not dare to try and persuade her, and they sent again for Major Zhou. He begged her to take the medicine. She took one mouthful and no more. Then he went away.

"Lady, do take some of it," the maid Yuegui said, taking up the cup. Chunmei took it and threw it in the maid's face. "You thievish slave," she cried angrily, "why do you try to make me drink this bitter stuff? What is there in my stomach now?" She told the maid to kneel down.

Then the Major's second wife came and asked why Yuegui was kneeling there. The other maid said: "Because she gave our mistress the medicine."

"But she had had nothing to eat," the Second Lady said. How could she take medicine?"

"Lady," said the second wife, "you have had nothing to eat today, but Yuegui did not know. Won't you forgive her?" She told Haitang to go to the kitchen and get some gruel for her mistress.

Chunmei told Yuegui to get up. Haitang went to the kitchen and very carefully prepared some gruel and four small dishes. She took them to Chunmei, all steaming hot. Chunmei lay on the bed, her face turned to the wall, so that the maid dared not disturb her, but had to wait until she turned over. Then she said: "I have brought you some gruel. Will you have a little?"

Chunmei did not open her eyes, and made no reply.

Haitang said: "Please, Lady, do get up and take some gruel. It will be cold soon."

"Lady, you have had nothing at all," the second wife said. "You must be better now you have had a sleep. Do get up and eat something."

Then Chunmei got up and told the nurse to give her a light. She took a mouthful of gruel and threw the bowl away. Fortunately, the nurse caught it and it did not break.

"You told me to have some porridge," Chunmei shouted to the second wife. "What sort of gruel do you call this? I am not having a baby. Why do you give me slops like this?"

Then she said to the nurse: "Box that slave's ears four times for me." The nurse did so.

Then the second wife said: "Lady, if you don't care for the gruel, have something else. You must not starve yourself."

"It is all very well for you to talk," Chunmei said. "My stomach is too weak." After a while, she said to Lanhua: "I will have some chicken soup. Go to the kitchen and tell that whore there to make me some chicken soup. She must be sure to wash her hands first, and put some pickled bamboo shoots into it. I want it very hot and very sour."

"Lady," the second wife said, "since you fancy it, it will be as good as medicine for you."

Lanhua went to the kitchen. "Mistress wants some chicken soup," she said to Sun Xue'e. "Make it at once: she wants it now."

Chicken soup is made of the wing, cut into very small pieces. Xue'e washed her hands, killed two chickens, plucked them, then cut the meat into very fine pieces with a sharp knife. She took onions and pepper, pickled bamboo shoots and sauce, and the soup was made. She filled two bowls, put them on a red lacquer tray, and Lanhua took them, very hot, to Chunmei.

Chunmei examined the soup under the lamp and tasted it. "Go and ask that whore what she calls this," she shouted. "It is nothing but plain water. It has no taste at all. You talk about my eating something and this is the sort of stuff you bring me."

Lanhua was afraid of being punished. She hurried to the kitchen and told Xue'e that her mistress complained that the soup had no taste. Xue'e did not say a word. She swallowed her anger and humiliation, washed out the pan, and made some more soup. This time she put more pepper into it. It had a delicious smell. Lanhua took it to her mistress.

Chunmei complained that it was too salty, took up the bowl and threw the soup on the floor. If Lanhua had not moved aside, the soup would have caught her.

"Go and tell that slave I know she hates cooking anything for me, but if she doesn't make good soup next time, she will know what to expect."

Then Xue'e made a great mistake. "You have not always been so high up in the world," she muttered, "but what airs you give yourself."

Lanhua heard this and told Chunmei. The woman opened her eyes wide and raised her eyebrows. She clenched her teeth, and her pale face flushed. "Bring that whore here," she cried.

Three or four women dragged Xue'e into the room. Chunmei tore at her hair and threw her headdress to the floor.

"You whore!" she cried, "how dare you say I have not long been so high up in the world? Well, I don't owe my position to Ximen Qing. I bought you so that you should do what I told you, but I find you are too proud. I told you to make some soup for me, and you make it either with no taste at all or with too much. Then you tell my maid that I nave not always been what I am now, and that I only wish to insult you. Why should I keep you here?"

She sent someone for her husband. Xue'e was taken to the courtyard and made to kneel down. Then Chunmei sent for Zhang Sheng and Li An and told them to strip the woman of her clothes and give her thirty strokes with a rod. The servants took lanterns and torches, and Zhang Sheng and Li An each had a big stick. Xue'e refused to take off her clothes. The Major, who was afraid of his wife, did not say a word.

"Lady," the second wife said. "Let her be beaten, but don't make her take off her clothes with all these men and servants about. I know she was in the wrong, but do forgive her this time."

Chunmei would not listen. She insisted that the woman's clothes should be stripped from her.

"Let anyone try to stop me, and I will kill my child first and then hang myself," she cried. "Then I shall be dead and you can have this strumpet in my place."

She did not give the word to beat Xue'e, but fell on the ground in a faint. Zhou was excited, picked her up, and said: "Tell them to beat her, and don't let yourself get upset like this."

Xue'e was thrown to the ground. Her clothes were stripped off and she was given thirty strokes, till the skin and flesh were torn from her bones. Then they sent for old woman Xue, who was to take her away immediately and sell her. Chunmei took old woman Xue aside. "I want eight taels of silver for her," she said, "and not a penny more. But I insist that she must be sold to a brothel. If you let her go anywhere else and I find out, you will never see me again. Otherwise, you can make what profit you like out of her."

"How can I do other than obey you?" old woman Xue said.

She took Xue'e away. The woman cried all night and Xue tried to console her. "Don't cry," she said. "It was your unhappy fate that brought you back to your old enemy. Your master was fair enough, but unfortunately there was an old hatred between you and her. She treated you badly, and the master could do nothing for you. Now she has borne him this son, he does absolutely everything she asks. Even his second wife must always give way. It is like an old bandit becoming governor of a granary; we have to put up with it. Don't cry."

Xue'e dried her tears and thanked old woman Xue. "I only hope," she said, "that I may come to some place where I shall get food enough to live."

"She told me repeatedly that I must sell you to a brothel," Xue said, "but I have children of my own, and I must think of what is right. I will find a husband for you, some merchant in a small way, and he will treat you as his wife and let you have all you need."

Xue'e thanked her gratefully.

A day or two later, one of the neighbors, Madam Zhang, came to see old woman Xue. "Sister Xue," she said, "who was it I heard crying so bitterly the other night?"

"Come in," old woman Xue said. "It was this lady. She comes from a very exalted family but she had a quarrel with her mistress and was sent away. Now she is here, hoping to find another husband. She doesn't want any more trouble and would like a single man."

"There is a guest from Shandong staying with me," Madam Zhang said, "a dealer in cotton wool. His name is Pan, and he is the fifth in his family. He has large stocks of cotton wool and keeps them at my place. He is thirty-seven years old. Only a day or two ago he told me that he has an old mother, an invalid of about seventy. His wife died six months ago, and he can't find anybody to look after his mother. He asked me, if I could, to find somebody for him to marry. I have looked about, but so far I haven't been able to find anybody suitable. This lady would do for him very well, I think."

"She has belonged to a very good family," old woman Xue said. "She can make clothes, both plain and fancy; she can sew well, and she is an excellent cook. She is thirty-five years old. There ought to be no difficulty, since they are only asking thirty taels of silver for her."

"Has she any boxes?" Madam Zhang said.

"No, she has only the clothes and ornaments she stands up in."

"I will go and tell him. Then he can come and see her for himself," Madam Zhang said. She had tea and went away. That night she told the man all about Xue'e and, the following afternoon, took him to see her. He thought her beautiful and still young, and immediately offered twenty-five taels for her with an extra one for the old woman herself. Old woman Xue did not attempt to bargain. She took what he offered and settled the matter. That evening, he took Xue'e away, saying that he was returning home next day.

Old woman Xue altered the contract and took eight taels to Chunmei, telling her that she had sold the woman to a brothel.

Pan slept that night with Xue'e at Madam Zhang's place. Before dawn next day, he thanked Madam Zhang and set off for Linqing. It was now the sixth month and the days were at their longest. When they came to the wharf, it was about the time when the sun turned to the west. They went to a wine house. There were many wine houses at Linqing, all occupied by singing girls from everywhere around. Xue'e was taken to a small one. She went into a little room with a bed in it. An old lady about sixty years old was sitting there. There was a maid too, about seventeen or eighteen. Her hair was dressed in several knots, her face powdered, and her lips red. She wore a silken dress, and played a lute as she sat on the bed. Then Xue'e cried out, for then she knew that this man, Pan the Fifth, was a woman-dealer, and he had bought her for a harlot.

The man proposed to send Xue'e to the wine houses to make herself agreeable to the customers and so make money. Without a word, he gave her a severe beating, then sent her to bed and kept her there for two days. In those two days, he gave her nothing but two bowls of rice to eat. Then he told her to learn a few songs and taught her how to play, and, when she did not succeed very well, he beat her again. When she was sufficiently trained, he dressed her up in pretty clothes and bade her stand outside the door and smile at the passersby.

Then Heaven took pity on her. One day, Zhang Sheng came to the river to buy ten measures of yeast for his master who wished to make some wine. When Tiger Liu saw his brother, he cleared a room in his wine house, and offered Zhang Sheng a feast. The waiter heated the wine and said: "Uncle, there are several singing girls here. Would you like one? Liu mentioned four names and the waiter went to fetch the girls. Soon laughing voices were heard and, one after the other, the four singing girls came into the room. They seemed as beautiful as flowers and were all dressed in light, soft silken clothes. They came and made reverences to the two men. Zhang Sheng looked at them. It seemed to him that one of them was very like Xue'e, whom his master had dismissed. But he could not understand how she could have become a singing girl. Xue'e recognized Zhang Sheng, but neither of them spoke.

"Brother-in-law," Zhang Sheng said, "who is this girl?"

The Tiger pointed them all out.

"This one, who you say is from Pan the Fifth's house, seems very familiar to me somehow," Zhang Sheng said. He called her forward. "Are you not Xue'e?" he whispered. "What are you doing here?"

Xue'e began to cry. "It is a long story," she told him. "Old woman Xue sold me for twenty-four taels, and here I am. I come to make myself pleasant to the guests, and sing for their entertainment."

Zhang Sheng had long been attracted by her beauty. Now, Xue'e entertained him so pleasantly and talked so agreeably that he was very pleased with her. She and one of the other girls took up their lutes and sang for him. Then they passed the wine and Zhang Sheng was more and more delighted. As the proverb says: Money, girls and wine houses are three things that no man can resist. That night, he asked Xue'e to stay with him. She let him appreciate her skill upon the bed, and he was perfectly satisfied.

The next day, when they got up and dressed, Tiger Liu had prepared an excellent breakfast for his brother-in-law. There was as much as they could eat. Zhang Sheng packed his luggage and fed his horses. When they were laden with the yeast, he started off with the other servants. He gave Xue'e three taels of silver and asked Tiger Liu to look after her and give her his special protection. Ever afterwards, when Zhang Sheng came to the river, he went to the wine house to meet Xue'e. They remained attached to one another, and, every month, he gave a few taels to Pan the Fifth so that he might reserve Xue'e for himself and she should not be forced to go out and receive all comers. Liu, who wished to please his brother-in-law, would not let him pay for the room. He took money from others and paid for the room with that. He also kept Xue'e supplied with rice and firewood.

CHAPTER 95

Ping'an Meets His Deserts

> Only a few monks live in the ancient temple
> Few travelers cross the ruined bridge.
> When a house is poor, the slaves deceive their master
> When one in authority is weak, his underlings will serve him ill.
> Where the water is shallow, the fish will not stay
> Where the wood has few trees, the birds will not sing.
> So it is with the affairs of men.
> We can only sigh and be sorry for it.

After the death of Ximen Dajie and the lawsuit with Chen Jingji, Wu Yueniang's servant, Laizhao, died. His wife took her son, Little Iron Rod, and married again. Laixing was given charge of the gate. Xiuchun became a nun with Nun Wang.

After the death of Laixing's wife, he did not marry again. The nurse, Ruyi'er, often used to take Xiaoge and play with him. Laixing gave her wine and, in course of time, their relations became very friendly. Yueniang noticed that Ruyi'er often came back to the inner court with a very red face, and so found out what was happening. She reproached Ruyi'er, but did not make very much fuss about the matter. She gave the nurse a dress and four pins, chose a day of good omen, and married her to Laixing. In the daytime the nurse came to the kitchen and looked after the baby, and at night she went to Laixing.

The fifteenth day of the eighth month was Yueniang's birthday. Her two sisters-in-law and the three nuns came to congratulate her, and she gave them wine in the inner court. In the evening they listened to the nuns reading their texts in the room that had once belonged to Yulou. About the second night watch, Zhongqiu was sent to the kitchen to make some tea. Yueniang called her several times but got no answer. Then she herself went to her room to try to find the maid. She did not find her, but discovered Daian and Xiaoyu on the bed amusing themselves to their own very great satisfaction. When Yueniang came in, they were so taken aback they did not know what to do with themselves.

"You young scamp, what are you doing here? Why don't you go and make tea?" was all Yueniang said.

"I told Zhongqiu to go," Xiaoyu said. She hung her head and went to the back. Daian went through the second door to the other part of the house. Two days later, when the nuns and the two Aunts Wu had gone, Yueniang told Laixing to go to the rooms that Laizhao had had, since he was now the gatekeeper, and gave Laixing's old rooms to Daian. She fitted out Daian with two sets of bedclothes, a new suit, a hat, shoes, and socks. To Xiaoyu she gave a hairnet, some gold and silver ornaments, four pins of silver with gold heads, rings, and two silk dresses. Then she selected an auspicious day and married Daian to Xiaoyu. Xiaoyu spent her days waiting upon Yueniang and at night went to Daian. The girl was always taking away dainties for her husband, but Yueniang pretended not to see. As the proverb says: If you are in love, you never see your lover's faults. Another proverb tells us: A greedy man will never be satisfied. When food and wine are distributed unequally, there will be trouble in the household, and when the mistress is unfair, maids and women will complain.

Ping'an saw that Yueniang had married Xiaoyu to Daian, and that he was given better clothes than the rest. He himself was two years older than Daian—he was twenty-two—but Yueniang had never thought of finding a wife for him.

One day he was in the pawnshop when somebody pawned a set of gold ornaments and two gilded hooks for thirty taels of silver. They were to redeem the things in a month with interest. Clerk Fu and Daian took them and put them in the large press in the shop. Ping'an stole them and took them to Long-footed Wu's place in Nanwazi. There were two receivers of stolen property there, one called Xue Cun and the other Pan Er.

Ping'an stayed there two nights. The man of the bawdy house noticed that he was spending money freely, and also saw that he had some gold ornaments in a box. He pretended to go out with a silver pot to buy some wine, but actually went to the police and told them what he had seen. The police came and found the young man there. They beat him about the head and then arrested him.

It happened that Wu Dian'en, who had recently been made an Inspector, rode down the street, with his tablet of office carried before him. He asked who this man was whom the police had arrested. The police knelt down and said: "This fellow stole some things and came here to spend the money in the bawdy house. We had reason to be suspicious and took him into custody."

"Take him to my court," the Inspector said. They all went to the Inspector's court. When Wu Dian'en had taken his seat, his underlings standing on either side, Ping'an was brought in. He recognized Wu Dian'en, who had once been one of Ximen Qing's friends, and thought he would certainly be set free.

"I am Ximen's servant," he said, "and my name is Ping'an."

"If you are a servant in Ximen's household," Wu Dian'en said, "why did you take these things and go to the brothel?"

"My mistress had lent them to one of her relatives and sent me to fetch them," Ping'an said. "I got back very late and the city gates were closed. I went to the brothel to pass the night. There, unfortunately, the police arrested me."

"Nonsense!" Wu Dian'en said angrily. "Have Ximen's people so much gold and silver that they even let you, a slave, look after gold ornaments like these and take them to the brothel? I believe you stole them. Tell me the truth and you shall not be beaten."

"Really," Ping'an said, "my Mistress's relative borrowed these things, and I was sent to bring them back. I am telling the truth."

Wu Dian'en was angry. "You slave," he cried, "you are a regular thief. I know you will never tell me the truth unless you are beaten. Give him a beating and put the thumbscrews on him."

The boy made a noise like a pig being killed. "Please stop," he cried, "and I will tell the truth."

"Tell me the truth and then I will stop," Wu Dian'en said.

"I stole the ornaments and the hooks from the pawnshop," Ping'an said.

"Why did you do it?"

"I am now twenty-three years old," Ping'an said, "and my mistress promised that she would see about getting a wife for me. She never did so. She has another servant, Daian, who is only twenty, but she has married him to one of her maids. I stole the things because I was jealous."

"Perhaps Daian has had some dealings with your mistress, and that is why she gave him her maid," Wu Dian'en said. "If that is what you say, I will forgive you."

"But I can't say that," Ping'an said.

"If you don't, I must put the rack on you again."

The attendants applied the rack again. Ping'an was so terrified that he cried: "Don't do it. I will tell you."

"Tell me and I will let you go," Wu Dian'en said. He told his attendants to put the rack away.

"Yes," Ping'an said, "my mistress secretly slept with Daian, and Daian also misconducted himself with Xiaoyu, the maid. My mistress found out what was going on between Daian and the maid, but she never said a word. She gave them clothes and ornaments and allowed them to marry."

Wu Dian'en ordered his clerk to write down what Ping'an had said.

Then he kept the boy at his office and issued a warrant for the arrest of Yueniang, Daian, and Xiaoyu.

When Clerk Fu discovered the loss of the ornaments, he was very much upset. He asked Daian what he knew about the matter.

"I have been having my dinner in the medicine shop," Daian said. "I know nothing about it."

"I put the box into this cabinet, and it has disappeared," Clerk Fu said.

Then they looked for Ping'an. He had disappeared. Clerk Fu was in a terrible state. He swore all sorts of terrible oaths. When the owner of the things came to claim them, Fu could only say that he had not yet brought them from the house. The man came several times, but still the things were not forthcoming. Then the man stood outside the shop and shouted: "I pawned my things for a month only, I have paid for them and the interest too. Why don't you let me have them? They are worth seventy or eighty taels of silver."

In the evening, Clerk Fu could still see no sign of Ping'an, and realized that the young man had stolen the things. He sent people in every direction to try and find him. The owner of the things came again and kept shouting outside the door. Fu suggested that they should give the man fifty taels, but he would not accept it. He said the ornaments were worth sixty taels, and the hooks and jewels on the ornaments another ten, seventy in all. Clerk Fu offered ten taels more, but the man still refused. While they were disputing and arguing, a man came and said to Clerk Fu: "Your Ping'an has stolen the things and taken them to the bawdy house in Nanwazi. Now Inspector Wu has had him arrested. You had better send somebody to identify them."

Wu Yueniang knew that Wu Dian'en had once been a clerk in her husband's business. She sent for Uncle Wu. Together they made a statement and sent it by Clerk Fu to Wu Dian'en. She thought that the matter would be settled as soon as he received it. Fu took the paper to the office, quite sure that his old friend Wu Dian'en would give him the things at once. To his surprise, he was called an old dog. Indeed Wu Dian'en ordered his attendants to take off Fu's clothes and flog him.

Meanwhile, the Inspector said: "Your boy is here. He tells me that Mistress Ximen has been carrying on an intrigue with Daian. I am sending a report to the authorities, and later I shall send and examine Mistress Ximen herself. I am surprised that you, you old dog, dare to come here and claim these things."

Clerk Fu was sent away, with many shouts of "Old dog!" to pursue him. He hurried home as fast as he could and told Yueniang everything that had happened. She was so frightened that she felt as though her skull had been broken open and icy water poured into it. She was hardly able to move her feet and hands. Then the man who owned the ornaments came again and made a great to-do outside the door.

"You have lost my property," he shouted, "and now you will neither return it to me nor pay me what it is worth. You keep on telling me to come here and go there. Today, you say, you will go to the office and claim the things; and tomorrow, you will tell me to wait a little longer. Where are they? This won't do at all."

Clerk Fu went to the man and pacified him. "Give us one more day or perhaps two," he said, "and you shall have your things without fail. If we do not get them for you, you shall have double what they are worth."

"I will go and see what my master has to say," the man said, and went away.

Yueniang, what with one trouble and what with another, wore a continual frown. She sent a boy to ask her brother, Uncle Wu, to come and talk the matter over. "You must go to Wu Dian'en," she said, "and get this matter settled before things get any worse."

"I don't imagine he will do anything for us unless he gets well paid for it," Uncle Wu said.

"Remember that he owes his position entirely to us," Yueniang said. "And he still owes us a hundred taels of silver. My husband never asked him for any note, yet he repays our kindness by hatred."

"Ah, sister," Uncle Wu said, "there are only too many people who do that."

"Brother," Yueniang said, "I am counting on you to settle this. I will give you some money, and you can get back the ornaments and so end the wretched business."

When Uncle Wu had had something to eat, Yueniang took him to the gate. By chance, old woman Xue went past with a young maid. She was carrying her box.

"Where are you going, old woman?" Yueniang said. "I haven't seen you for a very long time."

"No, indeed, Lady," Xue said. "I have been very busy lately. Yesterday the young lady sent for me several times, but I could not go."

"Old woman, you are crazy," Yueniang said. "What do you mean by this young lady of yours?"

"Well, she is not a young lady any longer," old woman Xue said. "She is the mistress of the household now."

"How did she get into that position?" Yueniang said.

"It was just her good luck," the old woman said. "First, she had a baby. Then the Great Lady died, and the Major made her his first wife. His second wife has to do what she tells her. She has two nurses and four maids to wait on her, and two of them are very good singers. Though the Major has slept with both of them, if the lady takes it into her head to punish them, he never says a word to stop her. And still he is always anxious lest she should have something to complain about. The other day, for some reason or other, she punished Xue'e and pulled her hair out. She was sent away one night and sold for eight taels of silver. This morning, even before I was up, she sent for me twice. I was told to go at once and take two sets of green ornaments and one set of nine phoenix ornaments. They gave me five taels of silver. I have spent the silver, and they haven't seen the ornaments yet. Certainly I shall get a terrible scolding when she sees me."

"Come in and let me see what the ornaments are like," Yueniang said.

She took Madam Xue into the hall of the inner court. The old woman opened the box and took out the ornaments. They were indeed exquisitely made, with a beautiful blending of gold and green, and the backs gilded. Each ornament had a phoenix, and each phoenix held a string of little pearls in its beak.

"This set," the old woman said, "is worth three taels and five *qian*. The other, one tael and five *qian*. I have made no profit at all out of them."

As they were talking, Daian came and said: "The man has come again for those things that were pawned with us. He wants to know how much longer he will have to wait. He says if we don't get the things by tomorrow there will be trouble for Uncle Fu. He will go with Uncle Fu to a certain place. Uncle Fu is not well and has gone home. The man has gone too."

"What is it all about?" old woman Xue said.

Yueniang sighed. "Ping'an stole a set of gold ornaments and a pair or hooks from the pawnshop. He went to the bawdy house outside the city and there Inspector Wu arrested him. Now he is in jail and the man keeps coming for his things and shouts outside the door. Inspector Wu deliberately refuses to give the things up. He beat Clerk Fu. I don't know what to do. Ever since my husband died, I have had nothing but one trouble after another. It is very hard for me to have to put up with all these insults." She began to cry.

"My good lady," old woman Xue said, "there is one way out that you have not thought of. Let me go to the young lady, and ask her to send a card to the Inspector. Then you would get ten sets of ornaments if there were so many."

"Major Zhou is a military officer," Yueniang said. "What can he do with the Inspector?"

"Lady," the old woman said, "don't you know that he has special powers. He has many functions that a military officer usually does not have.

He has something to do with the river and the taxes and the soldiers and all sorts of things. He seems to be able to settle any sort of question. And it is his business to see to the capture of robbers who go to the river. This is the very thing for him."

"Well," Yueniang said, "will you go to the young lady for me and ask her to speak to the Major on my behalf? If I get those ornaments back, you shall have five taels of silver."

"Money is not everything, my good lady," old woman Xue said. "I should not think of taking money for helping you out of such a sad predicament. Ask someone to write a note for you and I will take it to the young lady at once. If I do this business for you, just give me anything you think fit."

Yueniang asked Xiaoyu to give Madam Xue some tea.

"If you don't mind, I won't have any tea," the old woman said. "Tell a boy to write the note. I am rather busy."

"You must have something to eat. You have been out half a day."

Xiaoyu brought them tea and cakes, and the old woman ate something with Yueniang. She gave two cakes to the girl who was with her.

"How old is she?" Yueniang asked.

"She is twelve."

Daian finished the note and brought it in. Xue drank her tea and put the paper in her sleeve. She picked up her box and went away.

When she came to the Major's house, Chunmei was still in bed. Yuegui told her that Madam Xue had come. Chunmei told Haitang to open the windows and let in the bright sunshine.

"What, Lady," the old woman said, when she came in, "are you not up yet?" She set down her box and kowtowed to Chunmei.

"There is no need for ceremony between us," Chunmei said. "Stand up. I am not very well. That is why I didn't get up before this. Have you brought my ornaments?"

"Yes," the old woman said, "and I had a very hard business getting them. I did not get them, in fact, until last night. This morning, I was just going to bring them to you when your servant came for me."

She took the ornaments from the box and gave them to Chunmei. Chunmei did not care very much for one of the sets, but she put them in the box and gave the box to Yuegui. When the old woman had had some tea, she called forward the little girl who had come with her and told her to kowtow to Chunmei.

"Who is this?" Chunmei asked.

"The Second Lady has several times told me that her maid is only useful for cooking," old woman Xue said. "She wants a young girl to do needlework for her, and I have brought this one for her to see. She is a country girl and twelve years old. I think she will turn out well."

"You should have got her a town girl," Chunmei said. "Town girls are more intelligent. Indeed, I never think a country girl has any brains at all. How much does she cost?"

"Only four taels," old woman Xue said. "Her father is going to the army and needs the money."

"Take this girl to the Second Lady," Chunmei said to one of her maids. "We will pay for her tomorrow." Then she said to the other maid: "There is some Jinhua wine in the jar. Heat some for Madam Xue and bring her some cakes. If we don't give her cakes, she will say that we only give her wine to drink in the mornings and nothing to eat with it."

"Sister," the old woman said to the maid, "don't heat any wine for me. I have something to say to your mistress. I had some wine before I came."

"Where did you have some wine?" Chunmei asked her.

"I have just come from the Great Lady," old woman Xue said, "and she gave me something to eat. She is in great trouble and she cried to me. Her boy, Ping'an, stole a set of gold ornaments and a pair of gilt hooks from the pawnshop and went after some whore. Then he was arrested. Meanwhile, the owner of the things keeps coming and shouting and demanding his property. Inspector Wu was once a clerk in her family, and when Ximen Qing was alive he was very kind to Wu. But now the Inspector has forgotten all about that, and looks the other way. He had her servant beaten and refuses to give up the things. He insulted Clerk Fu and beat him. Fu got such a fright that he had to go home, ill. The Great Lady told me to bring you her love and ask you to take pity on her. She has no relatives of her own to help her, and she said I was to ask you if you would speak to the Major, so that she can get back the ornaments and give them to their owner. If you are good enough to do this for her, she will call to thank you.

"Have you brought any paper with you?" Chunmei said. "My husband is away on duty, but when he comes back this evening, I will tell him."

"I have the paper here," the old woman said. She took it from her sleeve. Chunmei read it and put it on the windowsill.

Then Yuegui brought four dishes on a tray. She filled a large silver cup with wine and offered it to the old woman.

"Lady," Xue said, "why do you give me so large a thing?"

Chunmei laughed. "It is not so large a thing as your husband's," she said. "If you can put up with that, you can drink this. If you won't drink it of your own accord, I shall tell Yuegui to hold your nose and pour it down your throat."

"Well, give me some cakes first so that I have something to make a foundation for it," the old woman said.

"You are an old liar," Chunmei said. "A moment ago you said you had just had something. Now you say you want something to make a foundation."

"I only had two cakes," old woman Xue said, "and they won't last forever."

"Mother Xue," Yuegui said, "drink the wine and then you shall have the cakes. If you won't, it will mean another beating for me. My mistress always says I am no use."

Old woman Xue could not help herself. She drank the wine and immediately felt as if a young deer were careering about inside her. Chunmei made a sign to Haitang, and the maid gave her another cup. The old woman put it aside.

"Mother," Haitang said, "you took the wine Yuegui offered you. You can't refuse mine. If you do, my mistress will give me a beating."

Old woman Xue knelt down.

"Well," Chunmei said, "give her some cakes to eat with it."

"Mother Xue," Yuegui said, "nobody is so kind to you as I am. I have kept these rose cakes especially for you."

She brought out a large plate of rose cakes, but the old woman ate only one.

"Take the others away and let your old turtle have them," Chunmei said.

When Madam Xue had had some wine, she wrapped up in paper some dried meat, buns and goose, and put the paper into her sleeves. Haitang pressed her to drink another half cup. Then she saw that the old woman was on the verge of being sick, so she cleared the table and urged her no more. Chunmei told her to come the following day and paid her for the ornaments. When Xue was going, she said: "Now, old woman, don't pretend to be deaf and dumb. One of these sets of ornaments is no good. I shall expect a better set tomorrow."

"Very well, Lady," the old woman said. "Will you send a maid out with me? I am afraid of the dog biting my leg."

"My dogs know what they're about," Chunmei said. "They will stop when they get to the bone." But she told Yuegui to take the old woman to the gate.

It was sunset when Major Zhou came back from his office. He went to the great hall. The maids took his hat and clothes. He went to see Chunmei and his little son, and was very happy with them. When he had sat down, the maids brought tea to him and he told Chunmei about the work he had done that day. Then the table was set and they had dinner together. Afterwards, candles were brought and they drank wine. He asked if anything special had happened in the household, and Chunmei gave him the paper that old woman Xue had brought.

"Mistress Ximen's boy, Ping'an, stole some ornaments," she said. "Then he was arrested. Inspector Wu refused the people who went to claim the things and beat the boy severely to make him declare that Mistress Ximen had behaved improperly. He says he is going to send the case to a higher authority."

"But this is my business," Major Zhou said. "What does he mean by talking about sending the matter further? He is a most unreasonable fellow. I will send for him tomorrow and see how he likes a beating himself. I believe he used to be one of Ximen Qing's men. When Ximen went to the Eastern Capital with presents for the Imperial Tutor, it was he who got this appointment for Wu. Now he is trying to do all the harm he can to Ximen's family."

"That is just what I was going to say," Chunmei said. "You must look into the matter tomorrow."

The next day, Major Zhou told Yueniang to send an accusation to him. In his great hall, the Major wrote out an instruction and put it in an envelope. "The Major's office wishes to investigate a certain case of theft," it said. "The thief and the stolen property are to be sent to this office immediately. This instruction will be delivered by officers Zhang Sheng and Li An."

Zhang Sheng and Li An took the document. First they called to see Wu Yueniang. She entertained them with food and wine and gave each of them a tael of silver with which to buy shoes. Clerk Fu was still in bed, so Uncle Wu went with the two men to the Inspector's office.

Wu Dian'en remarked the fact that although Ping'an had been in prison for two days, nobody from Ximen's household had been to see him. He was preparing a document to send to his superiors. Then the two officers from Major Zhou's office came in and handed him an envelope. He read the superscription and opened it. Inside was an accusation from Yueniang. He was alarmed and made himself most agreeable. He gave two taels of silver each to Zhang Sheng and Li An. He wrote a document in reply, sent those concerned to the Major's office, and went with them himself.

After a long time, Zhou came to the great hall, and his underlings stood on either side. They went in and the Inspector handed his document to the Major. The Major read it. "This business belongs to my office," he said. "Why did you deliberately delay handing the matter over to me? You must have had some evil purpose."

"I was just preparing the document when your instructions arrived," Wu said.

"You doggish officer," Major Zhou shouted. "What is your rank that you should dare to go contrary to the law and disregard your superiors? By his Majesty's command, it is my duty to protect this district, control the soldiers here and the river too. You know what my duties are, yet you dare to arrest people, and do not send them to me. You abuse your authority and even punish people yourself. Then you accuse the innocent. Certainly you are actuated by some evil motive."

Inspector Wu took off his hat and kowtowed to the Major.

"I ought to punish you, you doggish officer," Zhou cried, "but this time I will forgive you. If anything of the sort happens again, I shall certainly deal with you as the law requires."

He called Ping'an before him. "You slave," he said, "you stole these things and lied most disgracefully about your mistress. If all servants were like you, no one would dare to employ one." He ordered that Ping'an should be given thirty severe stripes, and sealed up the stolen property until the owner should claim it. Then he called for Uncle Wu, who gave him a receipt for the things.

Then he sent Zhang Sheng with his card to Yueniang. Yueniang gave the man wine and another tael of silver. When he returned, he told the Major and Chunmei what she had said. So Inspector Wu gained nothing by arresting Ping'an, but lost a few taels of silver. Yueniang returned the ornaments and hooks to their owner, who examined them, recognized them as his own, and took them away without a word.

Clerk Fu was very ill and, after seven days, he died. He had taken medicine, but it did him no good. After this trouble in the pawnshop, Yueniang decided to let people redeem their pledges, but would not accept any new ones. She put her younger brother and Daian to look after the medicine shop, and this brought in sufficient to pay the household expenses.

When the business was settled, Yueniang sent for old woman Xue and gave her three taels of silver. The old woman refused to take the money, saying that if she did so, her young lady would be annoyed.

"But I am very much indebted to you," Yueniang said, "and Heaven does not employ people without assuring them of their reward. You need not say anything about it to her."

Then she got ready four dishes, a pig, a jar of wine and a roll of silk, and asked Xue to take them to Chunmei as a mark of her gratitude. Daian, dressed in black clothes, took the list of presents. The old woman took him to the hall in the inner court and there Chunmei came to see him. She was wearing a golden arched headdress, an embroidered coat and a silken skirt, and her women and maids came with her. Daian knelt down and kowtowed. Chunmei told the maids to give him something to eat.

"I have done nothing," she said. "Why does your mistress trouble to send me these presents? I don't think my husband will allow me to accept them."

"My mistress told me to say that she is very grateful for all the trouble you have taken over Ping'an," Daian said. "She has nothing worthy to offer you, but sends these trifles in the hope that you and his Lordship will condescend to give them to your servants."

"It embarrasses me to accept them," Chunmei said.

"If you do not take them, Lady," old woman Xue said, "I am sure the Lady Ximen will blame me."

Then Chunmei asked her husband to come, and asked him what he thought about it. They decided to accept the pig, the wine, and the prepared food, but not the roll of silk. Chunmei gave Daian a handkerchief and three *qian* of silver, and two *qian* of silver to the porter.

"How is your young master?" she asked Daian.

"He is very merry and plays all the time," Daian said.

"When did you first dress your hair as a man's, and when did you marry Xiaoyu?"

"I married her in the eighth month," Daian said.

"Thank your mistress for me and say how glad I should be if she would come and see me. The Major will be away on duty and, in the first month next year, when it is your young master's birthday, I will pay a visit to your mistress."

"Lady," Daian said, "I will tell my mistress as soon as I get home and say that she must expect you."

Then Daian was dismissed.

"Young man," old woman Xue said to him, "you go home. I have something to say to the lady and I will stay."

Daian took the empty boxes and went away. When he got home, he said to Yueniang: "Sister Chunmei took me to the hall in the inner court and entertained me with tea and cakes. She inquired after the young master and asked many questions about this household. She gave me a handkerchief and five *qian* of silver. She also gave two *qian* to the porter. She told me to thank you. For a long time she would not accept the present, but old woman Xue and I urged her, and at last she took the food, the pig and the wine, but made me bring back the roll of silk. She says she would like to send you an invitation, but she cannot do so now as her husband is going away on duty. She is going to come and see us on the young master's birthday. She occupies the upper apartments now, five rooms. She was wearing an embroidered gown and a silk skirt. Her headdress has a gold crown. She is taller and fatter than she used to be and has a great many maids and servants to wait upon her."

"Did she really say she was coming to see us?" the Moon Lady said.

"Yes," Daian said.

"We must certainly send someone to receive her," Yueniang said. "Why hasn't old woman Xue come back with you?"

"When I left, she was still talking to the lady," Daian said. "She told me to come back first."

After this, there was close friendship between the two households.

CHAPTER 96

Chunmei Revisits Her Old Home

It was the twenty-first day of the first month. Chunmei spoke to her husband and prepared a table of food, four kinds of fruits, and a jar of wine, and sent the servant Zhou Ren with them to Wu Yueniang. It was now two years since Ximen Qing had died, and this was the anniversary of his death; it was also Xiaoge's birthday.

Yueniang accepted the presents and gave the messenger a handkerchief and three *qian* of silver. Then she told Daian to put on his black gown and take a card to Chunmei. On the card was written this message: "To the most virtuous Lady Zhou. Heartfelt thanks for your most precious gifts. Now I have made ready wine and await the honor of your presence. I hope for the coming of your exalted carriage and shall be grateful for the honor of your visit. Wu, the widow of the late Ximen, kowtows."

It was about midday when Chunmei came to see Yueniang. She was wearing many pearls, and her ornaments were those of the golden phoenix. Her gown was broad-sleeved with a unicorn embroidered on it, and her skirt had the design of the hundred flowers. There was a golden buckle on her girdle. Her sedan chair was carried by four men. It had a black silk cover with golden ornaments. Before it soldiers with staves marched to clear the way, and servants carrying dressing cases came after it. There were two small sedan chairs immediately behind for her maids.

Yueniang had invited Aunt Wu. She had also sent for two singing girls. When Chunmei arrived, Yueniang, dressed in mourning, and Aunt Wu went to receive the guest in the outer hall. Yueniang was wearing a five-arched hat and very few ornaments. Her gown was of white silk, and her skirt of light blue. The sedan chair was carried to the second door, and there Chunmei got out and the crowd of servants followed her. When they went into the hall, Chunmei hastily knelt down and kowtowed to Yueniang. Yueniang made reverence in return.

"Lately," she said, "I have given you much trouble. Yet you would not accept the silk and, today, you have sent me valuable presents. I find it hard to express my gratitude."

"I am only sorry that my husband has nothing better than these trifles to offer," Chunmei said. "I have been intending to send you an invitation for some time, but I have not been able to do so because my husband is so often away on duty."

"Sister," Yueniang said, "when is your birthday? I hope to come and see you with a few presents."

"It is the twenty-fifth of the fourth month," Chunmei said.

"I will come to see you on that day," Yueniang said.

Then Chunmei made a reverence to Aunt Wu, and Aunt Wu returned it formally.

"Aunt Wu," Chunmei said, "you should not do that. You should stand and allow me to make reverence to you." But Aunt Wu would not agree, and finally they contented themselves with half the usual ceremonial. Then they sat down. Yueniang and Aunt Wu sat together in the host's place. Then the maids, the nurse, and the serving woman came to see Chunmei. Ruyi'er was carrying Xiaoge.

"My son," Yueniang said, "this is your sister. She has come to wish you many happy returns of the day."

Xiaoge seemed inclined to get down and bow to Chunmei. "You are a good boy!" Yueniang said to him, "bowing like that instead of kowtowing as you should."

Chunmei took a silk handkerchief and a set of gold ornaments from her sleeve and put them on the child's cap. "Sister," Yueniang said, "why should you give him such presents?"

Then Xiaoyu and the nurse kowtowed to Chunmei. She gave Xiaoyu a pair of pins with gold heads, and Ruyi'er a pair of silver flowers.

"Sister," Yueniang said, "I don't believe you know that Ruyi'er is now married to Laixing. His first wife died."

"She is a good woman," Chunmei said, "since she is ready to stay in this household always."

A maid brought tea. After it Yueniang said: "Sister, shall we go to the back room? It is cold here." Then Chunmei went to the room where Ximen Qing's tablet was. There were candles lighted before it. Food was set out, and Chunmei offered it. Then she burned paper offerings and shed a few tears. A screen was brought in and coal put on the fire. A large square table was set, and tea was brought with delicious cakes and rare fruits. The tea was of the scarcest kind. After tea, they asked Chunmei to go and change her clothes in the upper room. She took off her long cloak: her woman opened the box and put on her a dress of embroidered silk with a skirt the color of a purple clove. Then they all sat down in Yueniang's room.

"How is your baby?" Yueniang said. "Why didn't you bring him?"

"I should have brought him to kowtow to you," Chunmei said, "but his father said it was too cold and the boy might get a chill. He has gone to the great hall because he doesn't care for the rooms. I don't know what is the matter with him, but he has been crying a great deal the last few days."

"When you go out, does he often want you?"

"Yes, but there are two nurses to look after him."

"His Lordship is not a young man now, and he must be pleased you have borne him a son. He is your lucky star. I understand the Second Lady has a girl. How old is she?"

"The Second Lady's child is four years old," Chunmei said. "She is called Yujie, and my boy is called Jin'ge."

"I understand that his Lordship has two girls," Yueniang said.

"Two of our maids are learning music," Chunmei said. "They are both seventeen years old and very troublesome."

"Does his Lordship go to them very often?"

"He has hardly any time at home," Chunmei said. "He is nearly always on duty. There are so many thieves and bandits about nowadays. By his Majesty's command, he has to occupy himself with all sorts of matters. He is responsible for the charge of the district; he has to keep watch upon the river; to search out the bandits, and to keep the troops well disciplined. Yes, he has to spend a great deal of his time away."

Xiaoyu brought more tea. Chunmei said to Yueniang: "Lady, will you take me to the garden, where my mistress used to live?"

"Sister," Yueniang said, "you can hardly call it a garden now. Since my husband's death, nobody has bothered about it. It has gone to rack and ruin. The artificial mound has fallen in; the trees have died. I seldom go there now."

"Never mind," Chunmei said. "I only want to see the place where my mistress lived."

Yueniang could not refuse. She told Xiaoyu to find the garden key. Then she and Aunt Wu took Chunmei there. Chunmei went first to the Sixth Lady's room. There were a number of broken tables and chairs upstairs. Downstairs, all the rooms were locked. Grass was growing on the floors. Then she came to the place that had been Pan Jinlian's. The store for medicine and incense was still upstairs. In the room that Jinlian herself had occupied, there were only two cabinets, no bed.

"Where is my mother's bed?" Chunmei said. "I don't see it."

"The Third Lady took it away with her when she married," Xiaoyu said.

"When my husband was alive," Yueniang said, "he gave Meng Yulou's bed to my daughter, so when she remarried, I gave her your mistress's bed."

"But didn't you get the bed back when your daughter died?" Chunmei said.

"I sold it for eight taels of silver and gave the money to the officials at the Town Hall."

Chunmei nodded. Tears fell from her bright eyes. She remembered how, when Jinlian was alive, she always tried to have something that others did not have. "She asked my father to buy her that bed," she said to herself, "and I should have liked to have it to remember her by. Now somebody else has taken it." She was very sad.

"What has happened to the mother-of-pearl bed the Sixth Lady used to have?" she said to Yueniang.

"It is a long story. Ever since your master died, I have been spending money all the time, but no money comes in. As the proverb says: If we cannot make both ends meet, it is no good having gold lying about. I was pressed for money and I sold that bed."

"How much did you get for it?"

"I only got thirty-five taels," Yueniang said.

"What a pity. I remember Father saying it was worth sixty. If I had known you wished to sell it, I would have given forty myself."

"But it never occurred to me that you would like to have it," Yueniang said. They both sighed.

Then a servant came and said to Chunmei: "His Lordship asks you to go back early as the young master is crying for you."

Chunmei went back at once to the inner court, and Yueniang ordered Xiaoyu to lock the garden gate. When they returned to the upper room, they set the screen in position, pulled down the blinds, and wine and food were brought. The singing girls began to play the lute and sing. Yueniang offered wine and asked Chunmei to take the place of honor. Chunmei would only do so on condition that Aunt Wu sat with her. The two ladies sat down, and Yueniang took the host's place. After the wine had been offered, more food was brought in. Chunmei told her servant, Zhou Ren, to give the cook three *qian* of silver. It was an excellent meal, and they encouraged one another to drink.

About sunset, Major Zhou sent servants with lanterns to escort his wife home. Yueniang would not let her go but ordered the two singing girls to sing again. "You must sing your very best songs for Lady Zhou," she said. Then she ordered Xiaoyu to fill a large cup with wine and set it before Chunmei.

"Sister," she said, "bid the singers sing your favorite song and then drink this wine."

"Indeed, I cannot drink any more," Chunmei said, "and I am anxious about my baby."

"You have nurses to look after him, and it is still quite early," Yueniang said. "Besides, I know that you can drink."

Chunmei asked the singing girls their names and where they came from. They knelt down. One said she was Han Yuchuan, the younger sister of Han Jinchuan, and the other that she was Zheng Jiao'er, Zheng Aixiang's niece. Chunmei asked them if they could sing "Languidly I Paint My Brows." Yuchuan said they knew it. Yueniang offered wine to Chunmei before they began. Then the two singing girls, one with a lute, the other with a zither, sang.

> When shall I cease to love you?
> Spring is gone and Autumn is here
> Who knows my heart?
> Heaven sends me sadness. I grow thin.
> I wept when I had news of you
> The past is always in my mind
> I never thought you would so cruelly desert me.

Chunmei drank her wine, and Yueniang told Zheng Jiao'er to pour another cup for her.

"Lady," Chunmei said, "you must drink with me." Their cups were filled, and the singers began another song.

> For you, my lover, I cast happiness aside.
> Now the magpies chatter in the courtyard
> Their voice is sad, and yet they have no cause.
> It must be that Heaven
> Has made me love you always.
> You have gone away, but I never forget.
> I never thought you would so cruelly desert me.

"Lady," Chunmei said, "you must ask Aunt Wu to drink a cup."

"Aunt Wu is not a great drinker," Yueniang said. "I will give her a small cup." She told Xiaoyu to set a small cup before Aunt Wu. Then the two singers went on with their song.

> For you, my lover, I am become so sorrowful.
> I think of you by night and day,
> Sitting and walking,
> My dainty skin is wasted, my softness become hard.
> I am so lonely that my tears fall always.
> Yet once we lived together and loved.
> I never thought you would so cruelly desert me.

Xiaoyu was standing beside Chunmei, and Chunmei gave her a cup of wine.

"Sister," Yueniang said, "she cannot drink."

"Oh, she can drink one or two cups," Chunmei said. "When I lived here, I often drank with her." She gave the cup to the maid. The two singers continued their song.

> For you, my lover, I have suffered griefs
> I have been ill and lain for long upon my bed
> The sadness in my heart has knit my brows.
> You have forgotten me but I still think of you
> The thought makes tears stream down my cheeks.
> We said that we would be together forever.
> I never thought that, after but one year,
> You would so cruelly desert me.

Chunmei asked the singing girls to sing this song because she was thinking of Chen Jingji. She could not meet him, but he was always in her mind. For her, the songs expressed a secret sorrow. She was pleased that the singing girls addressed her as "Lady" and told Zhou Ren to give them each two *qian* of silver. The two girls put down their instruments and kowtowed to her.

Then she rose. Yueniang could not persuade her to stay longer and ordered a servant with a lantern to take her to the gate. Chunmei got into her sedan chair, and her maids into the smaller chairs. Before them and behind were four great lanterns, and an escort of soldiers followed.

Chunmei was anxious about Jingji. She did not know where he was. When she reached home, she went to bed at once in a bad mood. Her husband saw this, and decided she must be worrying because she did not know what had happened to her cousin. He sent for Zhang Sheng and Li An and said to them; "I have already told you to find my lady's cousin. Why haven't you done so?"

"We have looked," they said, "but we have not been able to find him. We told the lady so."

"I will give you five days," Major Zhou said. "If you have not found him by that time, you know what to expect."

The two men went all over the place, poking their noses everywhere, questioning people, and their faces became more and more gloomy.

When Jingji left the Major's court, he had intended to go back to the temple. But, when he was told of the Abbot's death, he did not dare. Neither did he dare to go and see old man Wang. So again he wandered about the streets by day and slept at night in the Beggars' Rest. One day when he was standing about the street, he saw Yang the Elder. Yang was wearing a new hat and a white silk gown. He rode on a donkey with a silver-mounted saddle, and a small boy followed him. They were coming down the middle of the street. Jingji recognized Yang at once. He went out and grasped the donkey's bridle.

"Brother Yang," he said, "I haven't seen you for a long time. After you stole my property at the river I went in quite a friendly way to ask at your place. But your brother, Yang the Second, broke his own head and ran after me all the way to my house. Now I am poor, and you are having a fine time."

Yang the Elder could see that Chen Jingji had become a beggar. He smiled haughtily. "This must be an unlucky day for me, that I should come to the street and meet a pestilential fellow like you. You are a beggar. Where could you get the money to buy goods? Do you say I stole your things? Keep your hands off my donkey, or I will use the whip on you."

"I am poor and you are rich," Jingji said. "I only ask you to give me something. If you don't, I shall take you to the proper place and the matter shall be thrashed out there."

Seeing that Jingji still held the donkey's bridle, Yang the Elder jumped off and thrashed Jingji with his whip. "Drive this beggar away," he cried to the small boy. The boy pushed at Jingji with all his might and the young man fell to the ground. Yang kicked him, and Jingji made as much noise as if he had been a devil. A crowd assembled. Among them was a man wearing a high black hat, a kerchief, a purple gown and a white vest. He had bare legs, and a pair of straw sandals on his feet. His eyes were sunken and his eyebrows broad and thick. His mouth seemed to curl upwards and he had three wisps of beard. His face was strong and red and the muscles stood out upon his arms. He had had wine to drink, and this had made his eyes seem fierce.

"Brother," he said to Yang the Elder, shaking his clenched fist, "you are unreasonable. Why should you beat a man so young and poor? You know the saying that a clenched fist should never smite a smiling face. This young man did nothing to provoke you. If you have any money, treat him as friend and give him some. Why are you beating him? I don't think it is right, and I shall be on his side."

"You know nothing about it," Yang the Elder said. "He says I stole his property. How could a beggar like him have any property worth stealing?"

"I believe he was rich once," the man said. "He doesn't look to me as if he came from a poor family. And as for you, I very much doubt if you have been rich all your life. Now listen to me. If you have any money with you, let him have some."

Yang brought out a handkerchief in which was a piece of silver worth about four or five qian. He gave it to Jingji and raised his hand in salute to the man. Then he mounted his donkey again and rode proudly away. Jingji got up. He saw that his savior was no other than a man he had known in the Beggars' Rest, a fellow called Flying Ghost. He was now acting as foreman to a gang of fifty men who were working at a temple south of the city, building some new rooms. This man took Jingji by the hand. "Brother," he said, "if I had not used strong language to that man, you would not have that silver. He knows when it is time to give way. If he had not done so, I should have let him taste my fists. Come with me and have some wine."

They went to a small wine house, sat down, and ordered two pots of wine and four dishes. The waiter set out the dishes and two pots of olive wine that, at that time, was greatly liked. They drank this wine in large bowls instead of small cups.

"Brother," the man said, "which will you have, noodles or rice?"

"Our noodles are freshly washed and our rice the finest white rice," the waiter said.

"I will have noodles," Jingji said, and noodles were brought. Jingji had two bowls and his friend one.

"Brother," the man said, "come with me to my place today, and tomorrow I will take you to see the Abbot of the temple where I am working. We are building some rooms and cottages there, and I have fifty men working under me. I will give you a very light job. You will only have to carry earth, and for that you shall have five *fen* a day. Then I will get a room and we will sleep there together. We can cook our own food and lock our door, and I will let you have all you need. That will be better than the Beggars' Rest, and going around with the watchman. It will be much pleasanter for us to live together."

"You are very kind," Jingji said. "May I know if this work will last for long?"

"We only started a month ago, and I think we shall finish in the tenth month, but I am not sure."

They drank as they talked and finished two large pots of wine. The waiter brought them the bill. It was for one *qian* and three and a half *fen*. Jingji was going to pay, but Flying Ghost pushed his money aside.

"Do you think I would let you pay, you silly fellow?" he said. "I have money of my own." He brought out a handkerchief and gave the waiter one *qian* and five *fen*, taking back the change. Then he put his arm around Jingji and they went back to his place. That night they slept together. They were both drunk and behaved in an unseemly manner. Indeed they did so all night. Jingji called the man his brother, his sweetheart, his husband, and other attractive names. In the morning they went together to the temple. Here Flying Ghost, whose name was Hou Lin, rented a room with a fire and bought cups and bowls and other things that were necessary.

The workmen saw that Jingji was only about twenty-four or twenty-five. They noticed his white face and handsome appearance and realized that he was Hou's man. They made many jokes about him.

"Young man," one said, "what is your name?"

"I am called Chen Jingji."

"Well, Chen Jingji, you certainly live up to your name."[1]

And another said: "You are very young. How can you do such strenuous work? Are you sure that pole isn't too much for you?"

Then Hou came up. "You beggars," he said, "what do you mean by making fun of him?" He gave spades and shovels and baskets to the workmen, and they went to their tasks. Some carried earth, some mixed the mortar, some worked on the foundations.

One of the monks in the temple was called Ye. The Abbot had given him instructions to cook for all the workers. Ye was about fifty years old. He had only one eye. He wore a long black gown, and his feet were bare. There was a ragged girdle around his waist. He could not read the sacred scriptures, but he was very attentive to his devotions. He was a skillful fortune-teller.

One day, when the work was done and the workers had had their meal, they were all gathered together, some lying down, some squatting on their haunches. Ye looked hard at Chen Jingji.

"This young man is a newcomer," one of the men said to Ye, "why not tell his fortune?"

"In my opinion, he is half one thing and half another," one of them said.

The priest asked Jingji to go to him. "Too handsome and woman-like," he said. "A charming voice and a tender body are unpardonable. When an old man is like this, he will come upon hardship. When a young man is like it, he will not be stout and strong. You suffer from that smooth face of yours. All your life, you will be a woman's man. Eight, eighteen, and twenty-eight. With eight years, eighteen, and twenty-eight, from the root of your nose to the top of your hair, whether you have any means of livelihood or not, you get less at both ends, and at thirty you cannot have a blackness between your brows. Your eyes are very handsome, and your mind is clever. Even if you cannot read, you have charm enough without. Whatever you do, people like you. When you play a trick, it is taken for the truth. Forgive me for saying so, but you are very cunning and get much sport from women. How old are you?"

1. There is a pun, of an ambiguous nature, on the word *ji*.

"I am twenty-four," Jingji said.

"I am surprised that you got past the year before last," the monk said. "Your brows are narrow, and your son and your wife both die. The hanging jade is very dark, and your family will be ruined. Your lips do not cover your teeth and you will have many troubles in your life. Your nostrils are like the hob of a furnace, and you will not be able to keep your property. Have you experienced any such misfortunes?"

"I have had them all," Jingji said.

"One thing I must tell you," the monk said, "that your nose is detached is not a good sign. As the great teacher Ma says, he whose mountain root is broken will waste all his substance in his youth. He will bring ruin to the property he has inherited from his ancestors, and no matter how much his father left to him, he will spend it all. Your upper half is short and the lower half long. This is a sign that you are sometimes successful and sometimes fail. You spend your money, and money comes to you again. But, in the end, you will not leave a family behind you; you will be as when the hot sun shines on the hoar frost. But there is one sign of luck for you in the future. You are to be married three times. Have you ever been married and, if so, is your wife dead?"

"Yes, she is dead," Jingji said.

"Well, three marriages are indicated for you," the monk said. "But there is trouble also. "When you are about thirty, you will suffer from the machinations of others. You must not visit the flowers and the willows."

Then one of the workmen said: "Father Ye, you have made a mistake. He is a wife himself at this very time. How can you say that he will have three wives?"

All the workers laughed. Then the Abbot gave the signal, and they all took their tools and went to work again.

Jingji stayed for about a month and worked there. One day, in the middle of the third month, Jingji, who had been carrying earth, leaned against the temple wall and searched his body for vermin in the sun. A man who wore a swastika in his hat, a black gown with a purple lining, a girdle, and a pair of sandals, rode up on a brown horse. He was carrying a basket of fresh flowers. When he saw Jingji, he jumped off his horse at once and bowed low.

"Uncle Chen," he said, "I have been looking everywhere for you, and here you are."

Jingji, astonished, returned the greeting.

"Brother," he said, "who are you?"

"I am Zhang Sheng, the servant of Major Zhou," the man said. "Since you left the court, my mistress has been ill all the time. My master ordered me to find you, but it never occurred to me that you would be here. And even now I should not have seen you if my mistress had not told me to go to the country for these flowers. It is really a stroke of good luck for me. Don't waste a moment. Take my horse and go to my master's place."

The workmen stood and gazed. They did not speak. Jingji gave the keys to his friend Hou, mounted the horse, and rode quickly away.

CHAPTER 97
Chunmei Finds a Wife
for Chen Jingji

When they came to Major Zhou's place, Chen Jingji dismounted and Zhang Sheng went in to tell Chunmei. She ordered him to take Jingji to a room where he could have a bath, and told a woman to take him fresh clothes, boots and hat. The Major was still in the great hall, and Chunmei gave orders for the young man to be taken to the hall in the inner court. There she waited for him, beautifully dressed. Jingji came in and made a reverence to her as though she were his cousin. They sat down facing each other and talked of the things that had happened since they last met. Tears were in their eyes.

Chunmei expected the Major to come at any moment. She looked meaningfully at Jingji and said softly: "If he asks you any questions, say that you are my cousin and that I am a year older than you. I am twenty-five and was born at noon on the twenty-fifth day of the fourth month."

"I will remember," Jingji said.

The maid brought tea and Chunmei asked him how he became a priest. "My husband did not know that we had anything to do with one another," she said, "or he would not have punished you. He is sorry now. At that time I could not ask you to stay here, though I should have liked to, because Xue'e was here. That was why I let you go away. I got rid of her as soon as I could and told Zhang Sheng to look for you. I never imagined that things would come to such a pass that you would become a workman outside the city."

"It is a long story," Jingji said. "After we saw each other last, I made up my mind to marry Pan Jinlian. Then my father died at the Eastern Capital, and I came back too late. Wu Song had killed her. I heard that through your kindness she had been buried at the Temple of Eternal Felicity. I went there and burned paper offerings for her. Then my mother died. When I had buried her, my money was stolen. I came home and my wife died. That strumpet, my mother-in-law, took me to law and made off with all my wife's things. To settle the law case I had to sell my house and then I was as poor as if I had been cleaned completely out. Fortunately, I met an old friend of my father who took me to the Yangong temple to be a monk. Then some rascal gave me a beating. I was arrested and taken to the court. When I got away from there, I had no relative or friend to give me a helping hand, so I went to the temple and joined the workmen there. It was good of you, Sister, to tell Zhang Sheng to find me. I feel I am a new man now that I see you again." They both shed tears.

Major Zhou came from the hall. A servant pulled aside the lattice and he went into the room. Jingji stepped forward and knelt down before him. The Major hastily returned his greeting.

"I had no idea," he said, "that you were my good cousin. I was misled, or I should never have treated you so unbecomingly. I must apologize."

"It was my fault," Jingji said. "I have not been to see you. I trust you will forgive me." He again knelt down before the officer. Major Zhou helped him up and begged him to take the place of honor. Jingji was too clever to do this, and sat on a chair in the lower place. When they had all sat down together, tea was brought.

"Good cousin," Major Zhou said, "how old are you? I haven't seen you since we met that day. How did you come to go to the temple?"

"I am twenty-four years old," Jingji said, "a year younger than my cousin here. Her birthday is on the twenty-fifth of the fourth month. I went to the Yangong temple because my parents are dead and my family ruined. I did not know that my cousin had married you. If I had known, I should certainly have called to see you."

"Your cousin has been so worried about you all this time that she has never been at ease," Major Zhou said. "I sent out people to look for you, but they could never find you. It is a piece of good luck that I see you here today."

Major Zhou had been a friend of Ximen Qing. It was therefore to be expected that he would have made the acquaintance of Chen Jingji. But though Zhou was a friend of Ximen, he was an honest man and had never pried into his friend's domestic affairs. Always, when he had been at Ximen's house, Jing and Xia and other officers had been with him and he had never met Jingji. Besides, the young man had been a priest, and it never occurred to Zhou that he was Ximen Qing's son-in-law. So he was deceived by his wife and Jingji and believed that they were cousins.

Zhou ordered the servants to prepare dinner, and it was soon upon the table. The wine pots were of silver and the cups of jade. Wine was poured in a golden stream, and they feasted until the evening. Then the Major bade Zhou Ren prepare a room in the west court. Chunmei found two sets of bedclothes, and a boy called Xi'er was told to wait on him.

The time passed very quickly, the sun and moon racing like a weaver's shuttles.

When the old year drew near its end,
We saw the plum blossom.
Now, suddenly, New Year's Day is here
Dainty flowers appear upon the branches.
Fresh lotus leaves come out
Upon the surface of the water.

Jingji had been at Major Zhou's house for more than a month. It was Chunmei's birthday. Wu Yueniang sent Daian with a plate of longevity noodles, two geese, four chickens, two plates of fruit and a jar of wine. Major Zhou was sitting in the hall when a servant told him that Daian had come. He ordered the presents to be taken in. Daian brought the present list and came in and kowtowed.

"Tell your mistress it is very kind of her to send us these things," Zhou said to Daian. Then he handed the present list to a boy and told him to take it to his uncle. He said that Daian should be given a handkerchief and three *qian* of silver, and the porter a hundred coppers. Then he put on his ceremonial dress and went out. Daian stood at the door of the hall to wait for the return card. He saw a young man wearing a hat with a ribbed rim, a black gown, summer shoes, and light socks come through a corner door and give money to a boy. Then the man went back again. Daian thought he looked very like Chen Jingji, but he could not make out how Jingji could possibly be there. The boy gave Daian the handkerchief and the money, and he went home. He gave the return card to Yueniang.

"Did you see your sister?" Yueniang said.

"No, but I saw brother-in-law," Daian said.

"What do you mean, you young rascal?" Yueniang said, laughing. "What brother-in-law are you talking about? Do you have the audacity to speak of the Major as your brother-in-law, a man of his years?"

"I don't mean the Major," Daian said. "It was Chen Jingji I saw. When I got there, Major Zhou was in the great hall. I gave him my list and kowtowed. He said I was to thank you, and gave me some tea. Then he said to a boy: 'Take this card to your uncle and ask him for a handkerchief and three *qian* of silver for this man and a hundred coppers for the porter.' He dressed then and went out. I saw Master Chen coming by the corner door, and it was he who gave the return card to the boy. Then he went back, and I picked up my box and came away. I am sure it was he."

"I don't believe it, you scamp," Yueniang said. "I am sure that that young lamb must be wandering in other pastures now. He has probably died of starvation by this time. How could he be in that house? Would the Major have him there? Why, Chunmei herself would not have him."

"Lady, will you have a wager with me?" Daian said. "I am sure it was Master Chen I saw. I should know him even if he had been burned to ashes."

"What was he wearing?" Yueniang said.

"A new hat with a ribbed rim and a gold pin," Daian said. "He had a black gown, summer shoes, and white socks. He was looking very well."

"I can't believe you," Yueniang said.

Jingji went to the inner court where Chunmei was adorning herself in front of a mirror. He showed Yueniang's card to her. "Why is this woman sending you presents?" he said.

Chunmei told him that she had met Yueniang at the Temple of Eternal Felicity at the Festival of Spring, and that Ping'an had stolen ornaments from the pawnshop that Major Zhou had recovered for her. "She sent presents to thank my husband," Chunmei said, "and on the baby's birthday I went to see her. Now we are excellent friends, and she promised to send me birthday presents."

Jingji looked very hard at Chunmei. "Sister," he said, "you must have a very short memory. Have you forgotten how that whore treated you? She separated us and she is responsible for Jinlian's death. I only hope I may never set eyes on her again, and here you are actually befriending her. Why did you prevent Wu Dian'en from beating the boy? Then that woman would have been arrested and exposed. It was no business of ours. And, besides, if she has not been carrying on with Daian, why did she marry him to Xiaoyu? If I had been here then, I certainly would not have allowed you to do that. She is our enemy, and I can't understand why you let her come here. Friendship does not seem to mean anything to you."

Chunmei said nothing for a long time. Then she said: "Why not let bygones be bygones? I have a soft heart, and I do not like nursing a grievance."

"In these days," Jingji said, "if you have a soft heart you will suffer for it."

"Well, she has sent me these presents. I can't accept them without doing something in return. She is expecting me to send her an invitation."

"Have no more to do with her," Jingji said. "Why should you invite her again?"

"I shall feel very awkward if I don't," Chunmei said. "I will send her a card, and whether she comes or not will depend upon her. If she comes, you go to the other court and keep out of sight. Afterwards, I will break off relations with her."

Jingji was angry and went off without a word. He went to the front and wrote a card, and Chunmei sent a servant with it to Yueniang.

Yueniang dressed and, with Ruyi'er carrying Xiaoge, went to call upon Chunmei. Daian went with them. Chunmei and the Second Lady both came to welcome them. They went to the inner court and there greeted one another. Ruyi'er, with the baby, made a reverence. Jingji, who was in the other courtyard, kept out of the way.

Tea and wine were set out in the inner court and two singing girls played and sang. Daian was entertained in a small room at the front. He saw a boy, carrying a tray of food and cakes, going to the corner door on the west side. Daian stopped him and asked him where he was taking the tray.

"To my uncle," the boy said.

"What is your uncle's name?" Daian asked.

"Chen," the boy said.

Daian quietly followed the boy and went into the small courtyard on the west side. The boy pulled aside a lattice and went in. Daian peeped through the window. There was no doubt about it. Jingji was lying on a bed, and, when the food was brought in, he got up and began to eat. Daian went back to the front. In the evening people with lanterns came to take Yueniang back. Daian told her what he had seen. From that time onwards, Jingji dissuaded Chunmei from having any more to do with Yueniang, and their relations were broken off.

Jingji, unknown to everyone in Major Zhou's house, associated secretly with Chunmei. When Zhou was out, they had meals and drank wine together, and sometimes played chess and other games. When he was at home, Chunmei sent a maid with food to the young man and sometimes went to him herself, even in the daytime. She used to stay in his rooms for hours at a time. So they came and went one to the other and grew more and more attached.

One day, when Major Zhou was out with some of his men upon a tour of inspection, it was the Summer Festival. Chunmei arranged to have a feast in a summerhouse in the west courtyard. She and the Second Lady and Jingji drank together to celebrate the festival. Their maids and women were all there to wait, and Chunmei bade Haitang and Yuegui sing for them. They drank till the sun turned to the west and a very fine rain came to bring coolness to the day. Chunmei took a great gold cup, shaped like a lotus blossom, and urged the others to drink more. The Second Lady could not, and went to her own room to sleep. Jingji and Chunmei were left alone in the summerhouse. They guessed fingers, played games, and drank together. After a while, the maid brought lanterns and the nurse took away the baby to put him to bed. Jingji lost the game, went to the study, and refused to come back. First, Chunmei sent Haitang for him, but he would not come. Then she sent Yuegui. "You must drag him here, if necessary," she said. "If you fail, I shall box your ears ten times."

Yuegui went to the young man's room. When she opened the door, she saw him lying on the bed, snoring.

"My Lady says I must bring you back with me," she said. "If I do not, she promises to punish me."

"It doesn't matter to me whether you get punished or not," Jingji murmured. "I have had as much wine as I can drink, and I don't want any more."

Yuegui pulled him up. "I have to take you to my mistress," she said, "and if I can't drag you to her somehow, I shall own myself a feeble creature."

Jingji pretended to be more drunk than he was. He put his arms around Yuegui and kissed her. Yuegui made a fuss. "I came to take you away from here, not to behave like this," she said.

"My child," Jingji said, "do what I want of you and I will not treat you as a servant." He kissed her again, and they went together to the summerhouse.

"I have brought uncle," Yuegui said, "so you will not have to punish me."

Chunmei told Haitang to fill the large cups, and they played chess together. They played one game after another until the maids were sleepy and went away, all except Haitang and Yuegui, and Chunmei packed them off to get some tea. Then Chunmei and Jingji were alone together in the summerhouse. They kissed each other.

When they had been very happy together, Haitang returned with the tea. She asked Chunmei to go to the inner court because the baby was crying. Chunmei drank two more cups of wine with Jingji, then they rinsed their mouths with tea and she went to the inner court. The maid cleared the table and Jingji, with the assistance of his boy, went to his study and to sleep.

One day there came an Imperial Edict that instructed the Major to take his soldiers and join Zhang Shuye, magistrate of Jizhou, in an attack upon the bandits in Liangshan, who were led by Song Jiang. Before he set out on this expedition, he said to Chunmei: "Watch carefully over the baby, and send a go-between to arrange a marriage for your cousin. Then I will take him to the field with me. If he has good fortune and does his duty to his Emperor, he will get official rank, and that will be pleasant for you."

Chunmei promised to do this. In two or three months, Zhou joined his troops and went away. He took Zhou Ren with him and left Zhang Sheng and Li An at home.

One day Chunmei sent for old woman Xue. "When he went away," she said, "he told me to see about a marriage for my cousin. Go and see if you can find a suitable girl for him, someone about sixteen or seventeen. She must be beautiful and intelligent, because he has not the best of tempers."

"I know him," old woman Xue said. "You need not go into details. I remember that Ximen's daughter did not satisfy him."

"If you don't find a good girl for him, I shall box your ears," Chunmei said. "She must be pretty, because she and I will be living here as sisters. You must take the matter seriously."

She told a maid to give the old woman some tea. Then Jingji came in for something to eat. "Brother-in-law," the old woman said, "I haven't seen you for a very long time. Where have you been? I find I must congratulate you. I have just been told to find a pretty wife for you. What will you give me as a reward?"

Jingji scowled and said nothing.

"Why don't you speak, you old beggar?" the old woman said.

"You mustn't call him brother-in-law," Chunmei said. "That is all over and done with. You must call him Uncle Chen now."

"I ought to be punished," old woman Xue said. "My doggish mouth gave him the wrong title. In the future, I will remember to call him Uncle."

Jingji could not help laughing. "I am glad to hear it," he said.

The old woman put on a great air of gaiety. She went up to him and gave him a little tap. "You old beggar," she said. "I am not your sweetheart. What do you mean by saying you are glad to hear it?"

Chunmei laughed. After a while, Yuegui brought cakes and tea for the old woman.

"I shall take the very greatest pains to find a suitable girl for you," Xue said, "and as soon as I find one I will come and tell you."

"We will see about clothes, ornaments, and all that sort of thing," Chunmei said. "All we care is that she should be a decent girl. This is not an ordinary family."

"I realize that," the old woman said, "and I am sure I shall be able to satisfy you."

Sometime later, Jingji finished his meal and went to the outer court.

"When did he come here?" old woman Xue asked.

Chunmei told her how he had become a priest. "I want to treat him as one of my relatives," she said.

"Excellent!" the old woman said. "You know your way about. I hear Mistress Ximen came here on your birthday."

"Yes," Chunmei said, "she sent me some presents, and I sent her an invitation in return. She was here quite a long time."

"I was very busy that day," the old woman said. "I very much wished to come, but I could not get away. Tell me, did Uncle Chen see Mistress Ximen?"

"He did not, indeed," Chunmei said. "He scolded me terribly because I invited her. He was very angry because I helped her and said I have no memory. Wu Dian'en, he says, should have punished the boy and dragged Mistress Ximen into the case. He says we ought to have left them alone and not bothered about them, because she treated us badly."

"I can understand his feelings," old woman Xue said, "but I don't think we ought to remember the things of the past forever."

"I had accepted her presents, and I could do no less than invite her," Chunmei said. "I have no wish to return evil for evil."

"No," old woman Xue said, "and that is why you have got on so well. You have a good heart."

They talked for some time, then old woman Xue picked up her box and went away. Two days later she came again. One of Master Zhu's daughters, a girl about fifteen, wished to marry as she had no mother. Chunmei considered the girl too young and would not agree. Then the old woman came again and suggested Ying Bojue's second daughter, who was twenty-two years old. But Chunmei would not have this either. Bojue was now dead; his daughter's marriage would have to be arranged by her uncle and she was not likely to have any dowry worth mentioning. So she returned their papers. A few days later, old woman Xue came again with some artificial flowers. She brought with her a proposal of marriage. On it was written: 'The eldest daughter of the silk merchant Ge Yuanwai. Her animal is the Cock. She was born at the hour of the Rat, on the fifteenth day of the eleventh month.'

"Her name is Ge Cuiping," the old woman said. "She is as beautiful as a picture. She is not tall, and her face is shaped like a watermelon seed. She is gentle, well-mannered and clever with her needle. Her parents are both alive and in good circumstances. Her father keeps a silk shop in the High Street and does business in Suzhou, Hangzhou, and Nanjing. We are not likely to find anyone more suitable. Besides, the furniture her father is sending with her is all of the Nanjing make."

"Let us settle this," Chunmei said. She told the old woman to take word to the other party at once. When she came to Ge's place, the silk merchant found that she came from Zhou's house and sent for another go-between, called Zhang, to go back with old woman Xue. Chunmei got ready two packets of tea leaves, dainties, and fruits, and asked the Second Lady to go to Ge's place and see the girl. The Second Lady, when she came back, said that the girl was really very pretty. She looked like a flower, she said, and the family seemed to be a good one. Chunmei found a day of good omen for the betrothal. She sent the girl sixteen different kinds of fruit and food, two sets of ornaments, two sets of flowers and pearls, four wine sets, two sheep, a hairnet, and a complete outfit of gold and silver pins and rings. She sent two silk gowns and dresses for all the year round, with silk and cloth and twenty taels of silver. This was for the betrothal day.

The Master of the Yin Yang selected the eighth day of the sixth month for the wedding. Chunmei asked old woman Xue if the girl had a maid. "No," the old woman said, "her father will supply her with all her furniture, but no maid."

"Then we must buy a girl about thirteen or fourteen years old for her," Chunmei said.

The old woman promised to bring a girl the next day and did so. She was thirteen years old and came from the household of Huang the Fourth, the merchant. Huang and Li the Third had got into trouble over the official finances; they were arrested and thrown into prison and stayed there for more than a year. Li the Third died in jail, and his son was taken in his place. Their property was all sold. Laibao's son had run away and become a groom for some stranger. Laibao, Chunmei discovered, had changed his name to Tang Bao. He was mixed up in this affair.

"How much do they ask for the girl?" Chunmei said.

"Four taels and a half," the old woman said. "They want the money very badly so that they can pay off the authorities."

"Four and a half is too much," Chunmei said. "Give them three and a half, and I will have the girl." She gave the old woman the money and so the matter was settled. She called the girl Jinqian.

On the eighth day of the sixth month, Chunmei put on a pearl headdress, a crimson gown with broad sleeves, a girdle with gold ornaments and jade buckle, and went to meet the bride. She was carried by four men in a large sedan chair and a band of musicians and lantern bearers went with her. Chen Jingji rode on a white horse with a silver-mounted saddle. Soldiers marched before him. He wore a scholar's hat and a black silk gown, a pair of black boots with white soles and a pair of golden flowers in his hair. He seemed like the rain that visits the land after a long drought, or like a man who meets an old friend in a foreign land. Indeed, the happiest day in a man's life is that on which he marries, or passes his examination.

The bride's sedan chair came to Major Zhou's place. She was veiled in a veil of scarlet embroidery and carried a vase. When she had entered the great gateway, the Master of the Yin Yang took her to the hall. When the ceremonies were over, she was taken to her own room. Chunmei watched and then came away. When the Master of the Yin Yang had finished what he had to do, the bride and bridegroom sat together for a while. Then Jingji mounted a horse and paid a call upon his father-in-law to thank him for giving him his daughter. When he came back he was drunk. That night this very lively young man and the beautiful maiden enjoyed the first pleasures of their marriage. They were as happy as two lovebirds and as merry as fishes in the water.

On the third day after the wedding, Chunmei gave a feast in the hall of the inner court. Musicians were engaged and friends and kinsmen were invited.

Every day, Chunmei asked the young couple to take their meals with her. She called the bride her sister. They were so much together that the maids and serving women looked upon the new bride with respect. Chunmei gave them three rooms in the west courtyard and the rooms were papered till they looked like a cave of snow. New curtains and blinds were fitted. Jingji's study was outside the courtyard. There he kept a bed, tables, and some old books, and there he attended to Major Zhou's correspondence. There, too, Chunmei came to him, not always for conversation only.

CHAPTER 98
Wang Liu'er's Return

In the house of pleasure
The girls adorn themselves with powder and rouge.
When they are idle, they sit down
Looking at the flowers.
When they hear the old melody, they are sad,
But when they would go back to the old country
Where is now their home?

Before the mirror her cloudy hair is but half dressed;
Her tears flow and her silken gown is wet.
Today, once more, she met Pai Ssū-ma before the wine cups
And told her sorrow, playing the lute.

One day Major Zhou and Zhang Shuye, the magistrate of Jinan, took their forces and attacked the bandits of Liangshan. The thirty-six leaders of the bandits and more than ten thousand of their men were captured and order was restored. The victory was reported to his Majesty. The Emperor was pleased and promoted Zhang to be Censor and Commissioner in Shandong. Zhou was promoted to be general in Jinan to command all the forces there, guard the river, and pursue bandits and thieves wherever they might be. All Zhou's officers were advanced one degree in rank. Chen Jingji's name was put on the list, and he was appointed Counselor. Every month he was to draw two measures of rice. Now he was able to wear ceremonial hat and girdle, much to his delight.

In the middle of the tenth month, the new general was permitted by the Emperor to bring back his soldiers. He sent runners in advance to bring the news to Chunmei. She was delighted. She sent Jingji, Li An and Zhang Sheng to meet her husband outside the city. At the same time she prepared a banquet in the great hall to do honor to her husband. A number of officers came with presents.

When Zhou reached home, he went to the hall in the inner court and there his two wives welcomed him. Jingji, dressed in scarlet ceremonial gown, with hat, boots, and girdle, came with his wife. Zhou admired the bride and gave her a dress with ten taels of silver so that she might have some ornaments made. In the evening, Chunmei and her husband talked over the business of the household.

"My cousin's wedding, I am afraid, has cost you a great deal of money," Chunmei said.

"He is your cousin," Zhou said, "and since he has come to make his home with us, we could hardly leave him without a wife. We have spent some money, it is true, but he is not a stranger."

"Now you have secured this honor for him, it is indeed all that he can ask," Chunmei said.

"His Majesty has commanded me to go to Jinanfu to take up my new appointment," the General said, "but I shall not take you with me. We will give your cousin some money to set him up in business with someone. He need only go to look at the accounts every three or five days. If he makes any profit, it will be something for him to live on."

"That is an excellent idea," Chunmei said. They were very happy together and went to bed.

The General only spent ten days at home. Then he started for Jinan to take up his new appointment. It was the beginning of the eleventh month. He took Zhang Sheng and Li An with him and left Zhou Ren and Zhou Yi to look after his house. Jingji went as far as the Temple of Eternal Felicity to speed the General on his way.

One day Chunmei said to the young man: "My husband thinks you should go into business with a partner. If you make any money, it will be yours."

Jingji was delighted. He went out to find a suitable partner and, by chance, met his old friend Lu Bingyi on the street.

"Brother, I haven't seen you for a very long time," Lu said, bowing.

"My wife died, and I had a lawsuit," Jingji said. "Then Yang the Elder stole all my property and I was completely cleaned out. Now things are better again. My cousin married Major Zhou. I went to her, and she found a wife for me. Now I am a counselor and have the right to wear ceremonial robes and hat. I am looking for someone to go into partnership with me, but I haven't found anybody yet."

"After Yang the Elder stole your things," Lu told him, "he started a wineshop at Linqing. He is a partner of Xie. Besides owning that wineshop, he is acting as a moneylender and doing very well. He lends to the people of Linqing and especially the singing girls. He wears smart clothes and eats good food. Every few days he gets on a donkey and goes to the wine house to collect his share of the takings. He doesn't care for his old friends any more. His younger brother has turned his place into a gambling den. He still keeps dogs and goes in for cock-fighting, and nobody dares to interfere with him."

"I saw him last year," Jingji said. "Instead of showing me the least kind-ness, he struck me. Fortunately a friend saved me from him. I hate that man as though my very marrow were imbued with hatred."

He took Lu to a wine house on the street, and they talked of finding a way by which Jingji could get his revenge.

"There is an old saying," Lu said, "that if a gentleman hates at all, he hates well. A great man must have a hand that can deal out ruin. When you come to deal with him, you must remember that unless you see a man's coffin, you do not weep for him. I have an idea. Brother, all you need do is to make out an accusation, send it to the court, and demand the money and goods that Yang stole from you. We can get his wine house. Then we need only add a little capital and carry on the place as a business ourselves. I will go and help Xie to manage it, and you can come every few days to go through the accounts. I am sure you would make more than a hundred taels a month. I can think of nothing else that would pay so well."

"Brother, you are right," Jingji said. "I will go and speak to my cousin and her husband about it. If we can get hold of that business, I will let you and Xie manage it."

They drank their wine, went downstairs and paid the reckoning. Jingji impressed upon his companion the necessity for keeping the matter secret, and they parted. When he got home, he mentioned the matter to Chun-mei. "The General is not at home," he said. "What can we do about it?"

Zhang Sheng was there. He said: "Uncle, all you need do is to write out your accusation and say how much was stolen. Then seal it up with the General's card and I will send it to the magistrates. They will certainly or-der Yang's arrest and, when he has been punished, we shall get the money."

Jingji wrote out an accusation at once. He put the General's card with it and gave it to Zhou Zhong to take to the courts. When Zhou Zhong came in, the two magistrates were in the hall hearing a case, but when they heard that Zhou had sent them a letter they called Zhou Zhong before them at once. They asked him about his master's new appointment, then opened the envelope and took out the card and the accusation. They were only too anxious to do anything for the General and issued a warrant for Yang's arrest at once. Then they gave Zhou Zhong a return card, and said: "Give our respects to your mistress and tell her that we will send you word when we get the money out of Yang." Zhou Zhong took the card and went home.

"The magistrates ordered Yang's arrest," he told Chunmei. "They say we have only to wait, and they will get the money back for us." Jingji looked at the card. It bore the words: "He Yongshou and Zhang Maode kowtow." He was very pleased. Two days later, the Yang brothers were arrested and the magistrates tried them upon the accusation Jingji had brought against them. They beat them and cast them into prison. Then the two Yangs gave up three hundred and fifty taels of silver, a hundred rolls of cloth, and the wineshop was valued at fifty taels. The total sum that Chen Jingji had mentioned was nine hundred taels, so they were still three hundred and fifty taels short. Yang sold his house for fifty, and was utterly ruined. Thus Jingji came into possession of the great wine house and went into partnership with Xie. Chunmei gave him five hundred taels more, so that he had a thousand taels in all. He made Lu Bingyi his manager. They redecorated the whole place, painted the walls, and brightened up the balconies. Everything was made to look new, even the tables.

It was about the middle of the first month when Jingji started this business, and every day they took thirty or fifty taels. Xie and Lu managed everything between them, and Jingji only came every few days. He used to ride there on horseback with a boy in attendance, and Lu and Xie always had an especially beautiful room prepared for him upstairs. They gave him wine and food and picked out the most beautiful singing girls for his benefit. Chen the Third was a waiter there.

One day in the third month, the Spring was bright and beautiful and everything sweet and fragrant. The willows and the locust trees on the banks of the river were wonderfully green, and the pink apricot and peach flowers seemed like embroidery. Jingji, leaning on the railing of his balcony, admired the exquisite scene.

> The breeze blows softly
> The mist enwraps the embroidered earth like a mantle.
> In this season of peace the days grow longer
> The hero's spirit grows lighter
> And the beautiful maidens are gay once more.
> The willows on the river's bank lengthen their branches
> A pole is set beside the apricot tree.
> The young man has not done all he would
> Yet now he can enjoy the singing
> And make his way into the world of dreams
> To which wine leads.

As Jingji was looking down, he saw two small boats draw to the wharf. They were weighed down by boxes and furniture. Four or five men began to carry these things to the rooms downstairs. On the boat were two women, one middle-aged, tall, and dark-complexioned; the other young and very fair, her face powdered. She seemed about twenty years old. They entered the wine house.

"Who are they?" Jingji said to Xie. "Why did they walk in so haughtily instead of asking leave?"

"They have come from the Eastern Capital to visit a kinsman," Xie told him. "They cannot find a house, so they asked our neighbor Fan to give them a room. They are only going to stay two or three days. I was going to tell you about them when you asked me."

Jingji felt annoyed, but the younger of the two women came and made a reverence to him. "Sir," she said, "please do not be angry. It is not your manager's fault, but mine. We need a room so much that we came without giving you notice. I am very sorry. We shall stay only for a few days. Then we will pay for our rooms and go away."

Jingji listened to these soothing words and looked at the young woman from head to foot. She gazed at him with star-like eyes. Jingji thought: "I have seen this woman before." Then he looked at the other woman, and she looked hard at him.

"Are you not Ximen Qing's son-in-law?" she said to him.

Jingji was taken aback. "How did you know?" he said.

"I am Han Daoguo's wife," the older woman said, "and this is my daughter Han Aijie."

"But you and your husband live in the Eastern Capital," Jingji said. "What are you doing here? Where is your husband?"

"My husband is on the boat seeing to the furniture," the woman said.

Jingji ordered a waiter to go and bring Han. After a while he came. His hair was now white.

"Chen Dong," he said, "of the Imperial Academy, brought an accusation against six of the highest ministers of the Court. They were Cai, the Imperial Tutor; Tong, the Grand Marshal; Li, the Minister of the Right; Grand Marshal Zhu, Grand Marshal Gao, and Grand Chamberlain Li. The Censors supported this indictment, and the Emperor accepted it. They were all arrested, brought before the Supreme Court, and sentenced to banishment for life. Cai Yu, the Imperial Tutor's son, has been executed and his property confiscated. We three ran for our lives. We went first to Qinghe to find my brother, but he has sold my house and disappeared. Then we took a boat and came here. I am very glad to meet you. Are you still in Ximen's household?"

"No," Jingji said, "I left there. Now I am a counselor in General Zhou's department. I have two partners here and keep this wine house for a living. Now that I have met you, I shan't let you go. You must stay here and make this place your own."

Han Daoguo and the women kowtowed to Jingji. They went on

moving their things into the wine house. Jingji found things going too slowly, and ordered Chen the Third and a boy to help them. Wang Liu'er thanked him again.

"You really must not thank me," Jingji said. "We belong, as it were, to the same family."

It was late and Jingji began to think of going home. He told his manager to give Han everything he needed to eat and drink. Then he mounted his horse and went home with his boy. All night through, he could do nothing but think of Han Aijie.

Two days later he again dressed himself in his best clothes and went to the wine house with his boy. He attended to his business and then Han Daoguo asked him to take tea. As a matter of fact, he was thinking of going to them when the invitation was brought to him. He went to them. Han Aijie came smiling towards him and made a reverence. Then she asked him to go into their room. Wang Liu'er and Han Daoguo were both there. After tea they talked over past days. Jingji looked at Han Aijie and Aijie looked at him. They soon came to an understanding.

Before very long, Han Daoguo went out. Aijie asked Jingji how old he was, and he asked her. "We are both the same age," she said, smiling. "And we were both members of Ximen's household. Now we meet again here. It would really seem as though Destiny had brought us together over so many miles."

Wang Liu'er saw that they seemed to be on very good terms with one another. She made some excuse and left them. They now sat face to face, alone. Aijie spoke to him with sweet words that he could not fail to understand, for he had been used to the society of women ever since he was a child. He smiled at her.

Both Han Aijie and her mother, on their journey from the Eastern Capital, had done some traffic in their bodies. Now that the girl met Jingji she felt that Heaven had sent him to her. They seemed to understand and love each other without need for words. She came closer and sat beside him.

"Will you show me that gold pin in your hair?" she said. "I should like to look at it." But before he could take it out for her she had taken it out for herself. "Come upstairs," she said, smiling, "and I will tell you something." She led the way and Jingji, who was only waiting for such an opportunity, followed her immediately.

"Sister, what is it you wish to say to me," he asked when they were upstairs.

"You and I have come together today," Aijie said, "and to me it seems that Heaven has ordained our meeting. I am ready to enjoy with you the pleasures of the bed."

"I am grateful to you, Sister," Jingji said, "but aren't you afraid some-one may find out?"

She put forth all her powers of fascination. She threw her arms around him and, with her dainty fingers, took down his trousers. Then they gave rein to their passion till they lost all control of themselves. She took off her clothes and gave herself to him.

Jingji asked what place she held in the family. "I was born on the Summer Day," she told him, "and they called me the Fifth Maid, but my name is Aijie."

When they had taken their fill of pleasure, they sat down again to-gether. She put the gold pin back into his hair. "My parents and I came from the Eastern Capital to visit our kinsman," she said. "We are very poor, and, if you have any money with you, I will ask you to give my fa-ther five taels and I will pay it back to you with interest."

"I will lend it to him without interest, since you ask," Jingji said.

He gave her the five taels and sat with her for a long time. But he did not wish anyone else to know what was happening, so he would only take a cup of tea with her, and when she asked him to stay and have something to eat, he declined. "I can't stay now," he said, "I have some business to attend to. I will bring you some more money."

"This afternoon, I shall prepare a poor cup of wine for you," the girl said. "That you cannot refuse. You must come." Jingji took his dinner in the wine house and then went to the street for a stroll. In the street he met Jin Zongming, the monk of Yangong Temple. They talked about the things that had happened there.

"I didn't know you had settled down in the General's household and had set up this wineshop, or I would have come to see you," the monk said. "Tomorrow I will send a boy with some tea. I hope you will come to the temple when you have leisure."

Then the monk went his way, and Jingji went back to the wine house.

"Our guest Han has been asking for you," Lu said. "He is anxious to offer you some wine. But we could not find you."

As they spoke, a messenger came from Han Daoguo asking them, the two managers and Jingji, to go. They went. Wine and food were set out on the table. Jingji took the place of honor and Han Daoguo the host's place. The two managers, Lu and Xie, sat facing Wang Liu'er and Han Aijie. Han's servant heated the wine for them. After it had been around several times, the two managers began to see light. "You stay," they said to Jingji, "we must go and attend to business."

Jingji had not a steady head, but, when the two managers had gone, he drank without restraint. After a few cups he began to feel tipsy.

"I suppose you won't go home today," Han Aijie said to him.

"No," Jingji said, "it is late. I will stay until tomorrow."

Wang Liu'er and Han Daoguo went downstairs. Jingji gave five taels of silver to Han Aijie, and she went to give the money to her mother. Then she came back, and they went on drinking. They did not stop before sunset. Aijie took off her long coat and asked Jingji to stay with her. They spoke hot words of love together, and her voice was as sweet as an oriole's. They enjoyed every manner of love's delight.

When Han Aijie had lived in the Eastern Capital as Zhai's concubine, she had often visited the Imperial Tutor's mother. She had learned how to read and write, how to play various instruments, and sing. She had become accomplished and attractive, and Jingji found her equal in charm to Pan Jinlian herself. He sported with her all the night. It was late the next day when he rose, and Wang Liu'er prepared a meal for him. Then he and the girl drank a few cups of warm wine.

The managers invited the young man to have dinner with them. He dressed and went. Afterwards, he came back to say good-bye to Han Aijie. She hated to see him go away, and shed tears.

"Never mind," he said, "I will come and see you again in a few days." Then he mounted his horse and, with his boy following, went back to the city. On the way, he warned the boy that he must not mention the Hans to anyone at home. The boy assured him that he did not need to be told.

When they reached home, Jingji told them that he had had so much to do that he had not been able to come back the night before and had spent the night at the wine house. He gave Chunmei the money he had brought back with him, about thirty taels. His wife, Cuiping, suspected that he had been with another woman and had left her alone at home. Now she clung to him for seven or eight days and would not allow him to go to the wine house. The boy was sent to fetch the week's money.

Han Daoguo was in such need of money that he had to tell his wife to get some other man, a merchant or one of those who came to take tea or to drink in the wine house. He had found before that he was well able to live upon his wife's earnings. It was true that she was growing older, but there was Han Aijie to take her place, and no reason why the business should come to an end. They even followed it openly.

When Chen Jingji did not come back, the waiter Chen the Third found them a merchant from Huzhou. His name was He. He was about fifty years old and had silk goods with him worth a thousand taels. He was very anxious to have Han Aijie, but she was thinking of Jingji and made the excuse that she was unwell. Several times she refused to come down and see the merchant. Han Daoguo was greatly annoyed.

This merchant He saw that Wang Liu'er was tall and dark. Her hair was dressed in long braids and her starlike eyes were extremely seductive. Her lips were painted very red. He thought it undoubtful that she must be skilled in the arts of love, so he gave her a tael of silver and spent the night with her. Han Daoguo went to sleep somewhere else. Han Aijie did not come down. He enjoyed himself immensely. He became so attracted to Wang Liu'er that they were almost inseparable. Every two or three days he came to her and spent the night, and Han Daoguo was very well paid for his self-denial.

Han Aijie missed Jingji. She thought of him so much that one day seemed like three autumns and one night as long as half a summer. She was, in fact, utterly lovesick. At last she sent their old servant to the city to try to get news of her lover. He went to the General's house and secretly questioned the boy.

"Why does your master not come to the wine house any more?" he said.

"My master has not been very well," the boy said. "He has not been out at all."

The old man came back and told Han Aijie. She spoke to her mother, and they decided to buy a pair of pig's trotters, two roast ducks, two live fish, and a box of cakes. Han Aijie made some ink and wrote a card. They gave the things to the old man and told him to take them to Jingji. "When you get to the city," Han Aijie told him, "you must take the things to Master Chen yourself and get a return card from him."

The old man tucked the card away and took the things to General Zhou's. He sat down on a large block of stone. After a while the boy came out.

"What are you doing here again?" the boy asked him.

The old man bowed to him and took him aside.

"I have come to see your master and brought him some presents. Go and tell him I am waiting here to see him."

The boy went into the house, and very soon Jingji came gaily out. It was the fifth month and very hot. He was wearing the lightest of clothes, a brimmed hat, summer shoes, and white socks. The old man bowed to him.

"Master," he said, "are you better? Han Aijie has sent me with these things. Here is her card."

Jingji took it. "How is she?" he said.

"She is not very well, now that you have been so long away from her," the old man said. "She told me to say that you must go."

Jingji looked at the card.

To my lover Chen [it said]. Ever since you left me, I have been thinking of you all the time. You promised me you would come back, and I have stood at the door and waited for you, yet you have never deigned to visit this poor place. Yesterday I sent our old servant for news of you, but he came back without seeing you. He heard only that you were not well. That word made me so sad that I cannot sit or lie down in peace. I wish I had wings that I might fly to you. You are at your own home, where you have a delightful lady to give you pleasure, and you think of me no more. I am like the kernel of a fruit that you have spat from your mouth. I send you some cakes and food to show my love for you. Please accept them with an indulgent smile, for my love knows no bounds. Your unworthy Han Aijie greets you.

Then came the words:

I am sending you an embroidered red bag with a lock of my hair to show how much I love you. The twentieth day of the second month of summer. Han Aijie again makes reverence to you.

Jingji read the letter and looked at the little bag. There was a lock of black hair in it, and, attached to it, a small label with the words "To my lover, Chen." He folded everything up as it had been before and put it in his sleeve.

Not far from the house there was a small wineshop. He told the boy to take the old man there and give him something to drink. "I am going to write a letter," he said. "Take in the presents and, if your mother asks whom they are from, tell her that my manager Xie at the wine house has sent them."

The boy took in the boxes. Jingji went to his study and secretly wrote a letter. Then he took five taels of silver and went to the wineshop.

"Have you had some wine?" he said to the old man.

"Yes, Master! Thank you very much. I can't drink any more because I must be going back."

Jingji gave the letter and the silver to the old man. "Tell Han Aijie," he said, "that she is to spend this money. I will come and see her in two or three days."

The old man took the letter and the silver and went away. When Jingji went home again, his wife asked him who had sent the presents.

"Xie, my manager at the wine house, heard that I was ill and he sent them."

His wife believed him. They gave one of the roast ducks, one fish, and one pig's trotter to Chunmei and told her that they had come from the manager of the wine house. Chunmei suspected nothing.

The sun had set when the old man came back to the wine house. He gave the silver and the letter to Han Aijie. She read it in the light of the lamp.

> Younger Brother Jingji [it said] kowtows to his beloved Han the Fifth. I thank you for your letter and the delightful gifts that came with it. I, too, feel the desire for clouds and rain, and have not forgotten the joys of the bed I tasted with you. I have thought all the time of coming to you, but I have been ill and you have been disappointed. It was good of you to send someone to see me and to give me such charming dishes and that exquisitely made embroidered bag. I thank you with all my heart. I am offering you five taels of silver and a silk handkerchief, as a token of my love's sincerity. I trust you will appreciate my gift. Jingji kowtows.

There was a short poem written on the handkerchief.

Han Aijie read the poem and gave the silver to her mother. So both women were pleased. They waited eagerly for Jingji's coming.

CHAPTER 99
The Murder of Chen Jingji

There is a white cloud over the mountain
The leaves are red upon the trees.
They have seen the rise and fall of many things
Yet this world is as it has been always.
Many times the evening sun has passed over the fragrant grass
Many times the tide has ebbed and flowed
They have seen the generations come and go.

The way of Yuan
The road of Yang
They turn and twist like the guts of a sheep
And the wheels of the carriages go astray.
Where the horses neigh near the dreary bushes,
The strains of the recorder and the silver zither
Once were heard
And the sound of singing through the night.

Two days later, it was Chunmei's birthday, the twenty-fifth day of the fifth month. There was a feast in the hall of the inner court and the household kept holiday. The next morning, Jingji said: "I haven't been to the wine house for a very long time. Today I have nothing else to do, so I will go there. It will give me an opportunity to get away from this stifling heat, and I can go through the accounts with my managers,"

"You must take a sedan chair and not tire yourself," Chunmei said. She ordered two men to take him in a chair. He set off with his boy and came to the wine house about noon. When he got out of his chair, the two managers welcomed him and asked if he were better. He thanked them, but he was really thinking about Han Aijie. He had hardly sat down before he was up again.

"Get your accounts ready," he said to the managers, "and I will go through them with you when I come back."

He went to the back of the house. There the Hans' old man saw him and hurried in to tell his people. Han Aijie was upstairs on the balcony, composing a poem. Gathering up her skirts, she ran swiftly downstairs.

Mother and daughter smiled. "Sir," they said, "it is seldom that we are allowed the pleasure of seeing you. What good wind has blown you here?"

Jingji bowed to them, and they went together into the room and sat down. Wang Liu'er made tea. When they had drunk it, Han Aijie took the young man to her room. They were so delighted in each other's company that they were as merry as the fishes in the water, and they spoke the tenderest words to one another.

Under the ink slab there was a piece of colored paper. Jingji took it and looked at it. "That is the poem I have been writing," Han Aijie told him. "I was thinking of you when I wrote it, but I fear you will find it very bad." Jingji read it.

> I rest upon the embroidered bed
> And am too weary to move.
> Alone, I pull down the silken curtain and bend my head.
> My treasure has gone
> And I have no message from him.
> I think of him throughout the day.

Jingji told her the poem was delightful. Then Wang Liu'er brought them wine and food. She took away the mirror and set out the food on the toilet table. They sat down together and Aijie offered him a cup of wine with both hands. She made a reverence and said: "Since you went away, I have been thinking of you all the time. The other day our old man brought the money you sent, and my parents and I are grateful to you."

Jingji took the cup and bowed to her in return. "It was only because I was ill that I did not come to see you," he said. "I am sorry." He drank the wine and gave the cup back to her. Then they sat down again and drank together. Wang Liu'er and Han Daoguo came up and had some wine with them, but they went away again almost at once. They knew that the young couple would rather get on with their lovemaking.

When they had drunk wine enough, their blood was stirred. They did not only what they had done before, but many things that were new, and their love seemed limitless. Then they dressed again, washed their hands and went on drinking. After a few more cups their eyes sparkled, and they felt that still they were unsatisfied.

The young man had been very ill-content at home. He had been thinking of Han Aijie all the time and had not touched his wife. Now that he again met the girl he loved, he could not be satisfied with one encounter. Their love seemed to have been maturing for five hundred years. He was fascinated by her. Soon his passions were roused again and he set to. Then he felt weary and could do no more. Indeed, he did not even take any food, but simply lay down on the bed and went to sleep.

That day the silk merchant He came to the house. Wang Liu'er drank with him, and her husband went to the street to buy fresh vegetables and fruit. While he was out, the merchant and Wang Liu'er took their pleasure together. When he came back, all three drank together.

About sunset, Tiger Liu rushed into the wine house. He was drunk and his unbuttoned clothes revealed his purple flesh. His hands were clenched. "Where is that Southerner He?" he cried.

The two managers were alarmed. They knew that Jingji was asleep upstairs and did not wish him to be disturbed. "Brother Liu," they said to the Tiger, "he is not here." Liu would not believe them. He strode to Han Daoguo's room, tore the lattice aside, and went in. The merchant was sitting beside Wang Liu'er, drinking.

"Ha, you doggish pair!" he cried. "I have been looking for you everywhere and at last I've found you. You had two girls in my wineshop and you haven't paid them. You haven't paid your rent either, and here you are with another woman."

He stood up at once. "Don't be angry, my friend," he said. "I am just going."

"Going, are you, you dog?" Tiger Liu said, in a furious temper. He drove his fist into the merchant's face, so that it swelled up immediately. He did not trouble about his face; he was only anxious to get to the door and run away. Liu kicked over the table and smashed all the plates. Wang Liu'er cursed him.

"Who are you, you thief? How dare you come farting here? You won't bully me."

Liu went to her and knocked her down. "Who are you, strumpet?" he said. "What do you mean by coming here and practicing your trade in secret without asking my leave? I do not permit you to stay here. Clear out at once, or you will taste my fist."

"Rogue, who are you?" Wang Liu'er said. "I suppose you think I have no one here to defend me. Well, I won't live any longer." She banged her head on the floor and sobbed loudly.

"Woman, you don't frighten me," the Tiger said. "I shall smash your belly in."

There was so much shouting and quarreling that all the neighbors came to look on. One of them said to her: "Mistress Han, you have only just come here, or you would know that this is the famous Tiger Liu, the brother-in-law of Master Zhang of the General's office. He lives at a wine house, and singing girls are his specialty. It is he who controls all the wine drinkers in these parts. You must let him have his way. You don't know how powerful he is. Nobody here ever dares to offend him."

"There must be somebody over him," Wang Liu'er said. "Why should I do what he tells me?"

Lu, seeing the Tiger in a fury, at last succeeded in getting him away. Jingji had heard the noise downstairs. He saw that the sun was setting and got up to ask what all the noise was about. Han Daoguo had disappeared, but Wang Liu'er, her hair in disorder and her face dirty, ran upstairs and told him.

"I don't know who he is," she said. "I only know they call him Tiger. They say he is the brother-in-law of Zhang at the General's office. He came here to see one of the guests and struck and insulted me. He upset the table and smashed all the plates." She cried loudly.

Jingji sent for the two managers and questioned them. They could only tell him the truth. Liu the Second, they said, had come to look for the merchant He. He saw the man he sought in Han Daoguo's room, went in, pulled up the lattice, and struck him. He ran away, and then Liu quarreled with Mistress Han. He knocked her down and people came out of the street to see.

Then Jingji remembered that this Liu was the man who had beaten him in the days when he was a priest. He knew that Liu was too much for him to deal with, so he said no more at that time, except to ask where Liu was then. "We got him out," the managers said. Jingji tried to console Wang Liu'er. "Don't worry," he said. "I am here, and I will protect you. You stay where you are. I am going home, and I shall know how to deal with him." He took the money from his managers, got into his sedan chair, and went home. It was quite dark when he arrived. He was very angry. He gave all the money to Chunmei and went to bed. The next day, he was several times on the point of telling her about Wang Liu'er, but, whenever he thought about it, he decided to say nothing. "I will wait and see if Zhang Sheng does not do something wrong," he said to himself. "Then I will tell Chunmei, and the General will put an end to him. I have never sought trouble with that fellow, but he has bullied me several times. It is his fault, not mine."

One day, Jingji went again to the wine house. He saw the mother and daughter, and they talked about the quarrel.

"Has Liu the Second been here again?" Jingji asked.

"No," Wang Liu'er said, "not since that day."

Then he asked Han Aijie if the merchant He had been to see them again, and she said he had not.

Jingji had his dinner, examined the accounts, and went upstairs to amuse himself with Han Aijie. Then he sent for the waiter, Chen the

Third, and asked him if he knew anything that could be held against either Zhang Sheng or Tiger Liu. The waiter told him how Zhang Sheng was keeping Xue'e, who was now a singing girl at the wine house. He told him, too, how Liu lent money to people at a very high rate of interest, and indeed brought much discredit upon the General's administration. Jingji listened very carefully to all this. He got his money from the managers, gave Han Aijie three taels, and took the rest away. Then he rode home. He never forgot the trouble between Liu and himself, and the hatred between them was so strong that it seemed certain that, if they met, trouble was inevitable.

About this time, Huizong, the Son of Heaven, heard at the Eastern Capital that the army of Jin had attacked the frontier and even plundered places on this side. The situation was serious. The Emperor held a conference with his ministers, and it was decided that an envoy should be sent to them to declare that the Emperor was ready to pay several millions of money every year for the sake of peace. At the same time, he abdicated in favor of his son. Thus the seventh year of Xuanhe became the first year of Jinkang, and the new Emperor took the title of Qinzong. The old Emperor called himself the Supreme Daoist Emperor and retired to the Palace of Dragon Virtue. The new Emperor placed Li Gang, the Minister of War, in command of the whole imperial army, and Chong Shidao was appointed Marshal and Generalissimo.

One day an order came to Jinanfu appointing Zhou to the command of all the troops in Shandong, and instructing him to take ten thousand men to garrison Dongchangfu. There he was to join the Censor, Zhang Shuye, and check the advance of the Jin army.

When Zhou received this order, he sent at once for Zhang Sheng and Li An, placed them in charge of his treasure, and sent them home with it. He had been in Shandong for nearly a year and had amassed a considerable amount of wealth. Everything was carefully packed and the men were instructed to take the utmost care of the valuables entrusted to them. The General told them that he would set out for his new appointment from Qinghe.

When the two men reached home, they handed over the treasure to Chunmei. Jingji saw that Zhang Sheng was back again, and heard from him of the General's new appointment, and that he would be home very shortly. He decided to tell Chunmei about Zhang Sheng, so that they could both tell the same tale to Zhou when he arrived.

One day his wife, Cuiping, went to see her mother, and he was asleep in the study when Chunmei suddenly came in. There was nobody about, and they undressed and took their pleasure of one another. At that moment, Zhang Sheng was making the rounds of the house with a bell. When he came to the door in the courtyard by the study, he heard the sound of a woman's laughter. He stopped ringing his bell and went quietly to the window; so he discovered what Chunmei and Jingji were about. He heard Jingji say how he hated Zhang Sheng, and how badly Zhang Sheng had treated him. He heard him say that Zhang Sheng had ordered his brother-in-law, Tiger Liu, to go to the wine house and drive away his customers. The Tiger, with Zhang Sheng behind him, was lending money to people. Zhang Sheng was also sleeping with Xue'e, and keeping the matter dark. "I kept the matter to myself," he said, "because I didn't wish to worry you. But now the General is coming back, and so I tell you. If I don't, I shall never be able to go to the wine house to attend to my business."

"What a scoundrel the fellow is," Chunmei cried. "I sold Xue'e. How dare he sleep with her?"

"He ill-treats me and he has no respect for you," Jingji said.

"Wait till my husband comes," Chunmei said, "and we'll get rid of him for good and all."

The pair never suspected that Zhang Sheng was outside the window and could hear every word they said.

"If I don't finish them, they will finish me," Zhang Sheng said to himself. He put down his bell and went to his room. There he took a dagger and sharpened it on a whetstone. Then he went to the study.

Fortunately, Heaven saved Chunmei's life. One of her maids called her away. The baby had fallen, she said, and asked her mistress to go and see him. She had just left the room when Zhang Sheng, with his dagger, entered it. Jingji was still in bed.

"What do you want?" Jingji said.

"Uncle, I have come to kill you. I was not seeking trouble, but you dared to tell that strumpet that I must die. The proverb says: Black-headed vermin should not be spared; they eat human flesh. Don't try to escape. My knife is waiting for you. A year from today will be your year's mind."

Jingji had not a stitch of clothing on him. He could not get away, but he gripped the bedclothes tightly. Zhang Sheng pulled them off. He drove the dagger into Jingji's side and the blood gushed forth. As the young man still struggled, Zhang Sheng drove his dagger into his breast. That was the end. Zhang Sheng grasped him by the hair and cut off his head. Jingji was only twenty-seven years old when he came to this miserable end.

Zhang Sheng, still grasping his dagger, went behind the bed to look for Chunmei, but she was not there. Then he rushed to the inner court. But when he came to the second door, Li An, who was also going the rounds, saw him coming like the god of wrath, dashing towards him with the dagger raised. He asked Zhang Sheng where he was going but got no answer. Then he stopped Zhang Sheng. Zhang Sheng pointed the dagger at him. Li An laughed. "My Uncle," he said, "is Li Gui the famous Demon of Shandong. You shall know what I can do." He lifted his right leg and kicked the dagger out of Zhang Sheng's hand. It fell with a clang on the floor. Zhang Sheng fought desperately, but Li An got him down and bound him with his girdle.

Chunmei heard the noise. Li An told her that he had secured Zhang Sheng. Chunmei, who had just finished seeing to the baby, was so frightened that she changed color. She rushed to the study and saw that Jingji had been killed. Blood was still running over the floor. She screamed. Then she told servants to go for Cuiping. The young wife came. When she saw that her husband had been murdered, she shrieked and then fainted. Chunmei helped her to her feet, sent to buy a coffin, and put the young man into it. Then she gave orders that Zhang Sheng should be thrown into prison for her husband to deal with.

When General Zhou returned, Chunmei told him of the murder of Jingji. Li An put the dagger before his master and told him what he knew of the story. The General was very angry. He went at once to the hall and called for Zhang Sheng to be brought before him. Without asking a single question, he ordered the attendants to give the man a hundred stripes. So Zhang Sheng was beaten to death. Then he sent to arrest the Tiger. When Liu was taken, Xue'e feared that she too might be arrested. She went to her own room and hanged herself. When Liu was brought before the General, he too was ordered a hundred stripes, and so he died. The news created a great stir in Qinghe and tremendous excitement in Linqing.

> Man should avoid deceit
> For above his head, God waits.
> If they who do all manner of evil
> Received not their reward
> Then all the ruffians in the world
> Would devour each other.

By this execution, the General rid the district of two devils. He bade Li An go to the wine house and give it back to its original owner, bringing back the things that belonged to him. He told Chunmei to hold a service for Jingji, and afterwards the young man was buried at the Temple of Eternal Felicity outside the city. Then he gave orders that Li An and Zhou Yi should remain at home to look after the place, while he took with him Zhou Ren and Zhou Zhong.

In the evening, Chunmei and the Second Lady offered him wine before he left. They shed tears and said: "You are going away and we have no notion when you will come back. You must take care of yourself when you are in the battle. The barbarians are very strong, and you must not regard them lightly."

And the General said to them: "You who stay at home must be always prudent. Take care of my son. Don't trouble about me. I take the Emperor's pay, and I must render loyal service to my country. Whether I live or die is on the knees of Heaven."

The next day the troops assembled outside the city. The General took his place at their head, and they marched off. When, one day, they came to Dongchangfu, he ordered a soldier carrying a blue flag to go first into the city. This was a notification to the Commissioner Zhang Shuye that General Zhou's army had arrived. He came out with the Prefect of the place to receive the General, and they went together to their headquarters. There they discussed the military situation and sent out scouts to get news of the enemy. The next day the army set forth to defend the city.

When Han Aijie heard of Jingji's death, she cried day and night and would not take anything to eat. The only thing she could think of was going to the General's place to see the young man's body. She thought that if she could only do that she would be content. Her parents tried to console her, but still she insisted that she must go. Han Daoguo sent his old servant to get what news he could. The old man came back and told them that Jingji had already been buried at the Temple of Eternal Felicity. Then Han Aijie determined to go to the temple to burn some paper offerings for her lover. She would bewail him at his grave.

Her parents could do nothing to dissuade her, so they hired a sedan chair and took her to the temple. There they asked a monk where Jingji was buried, and the monk sent a boy to take them to the grave, behind the temple. Han Aijie got out of her sedan chair and burned some paper money. She made a reverence before the grave and said: "Oh, dearest brother, I had hoped that I might live with you always. Never did I think that you would die so young." She gave a great cry and fell fainting to the ground. Her parents were frightened and came to help her up. They called her, but she made no answer and they became more frightened still.

It was the third day after Jingji's funeral. Chunmei and Cuiping, in two sedan chairs with their servants following, came to burn papers and offer food to the dead. When they came near the grave, they saw a young woman dressed in mourning, lying on the ground, and a man and woman of middle age trying to revive her. But when she got up, she collapsed again in a faint. They were astonished and asked the man who the girl was.

Han Daoguo and his wife made reverence to them, and told them how they had known Chen Jingji, and that the girl was their daughter Han Aijie. Then Chunmei remembered her from the days in Ximen's house and recognized Wang Liu'er also. Han Daoguo told her how they had come to leave the Eastern Capital.

"My daughter was a friend of Master Chen," he said. "Now he is dead, she came to burn paper money for him. But she cried so bitterly that she fainted."

They went back to their daughter and again tried to bring her around. After a while Han Aijie spat out a little water and revived. She still sobbed, but not so loud as before. She kowtowed four times to Chunmei and Cuiping.

"Though I was only his mistress," she said, "we loved each other truly. I had hoped that I might always belong to him, but Heaven would have it otherwise and decreed his death. Now I am all alone in the world. When he was alive, he gave me a handkerchief on which he had written a poem. I knew he was married, but I was willing to serve only for his amusement. If you doubt me, look at this handkerchief." She showed it to them and they both read the poem.

"I gave him a little embroidered bag too," Han Aijie said, "and he always carried it about with him. It had double lotus blossoms on both sides, and on each of the petals I wrote a word. 'I offer this to Chen my lover,' I wrote."

Chunmei asked Cuiping if she knew of this little bag. "It was under his clothes," Cuiping said, "and I put it into the coffin with him."

When they had made their offerings at the grave, they took Han Aijie and her mother into the temple to have tea with them. It was late and Wang Liu'er wished to go home. Her daughter would not hear of it. She knelt down before Chunmei and Cuiping and wept. "I do not wish to go back with my parents," she said to them. "I wish to live with you. Then I can see his tablet every day. We were lovers, and I should like people to say that I had been his wife." Her tears fell like the water from a spring.

"Sister," Chunmei said, "I am afraid you are very young to live such a life. You will be wasting the best of your years."

"No, Lady," Han Aijie said. "For his sake, I would cut out my eyes and break my nose. I shall never marry anyone else."

"You go home, old people," she said to her parents. "I am going with these ladies."

"We have been hoping that you would support us in our old age," Wang Liu'er said, with tears. "We have only just brought you from the Dragon's Pool and then you leave us."

"I will not go back with you," Han Aijie declared, "and if you try to make me, I will kill myself."

Then Han Daoguo saw that his daughter had made up her mind. He and Wang Liu'er cried and went back to the wine house. Han Aijie got into a sedan chair with Chunmei and Cuiping and went to the city with them. Wang Liu'er thought of her daughter and wept all the time. Han Daoguo saw that it was late, so he hired two animals to take them back.

> The horses are slow and the heart is eager
> It is a hard road that they travel
> They are like the weed that floats on the pond
> The climbing plant that creeps along the wall.
> The moon over the royal palace looks down
> Upon their parting
> The parting of those who go to the east
> From those who go to the west.

CHAPTER 100

The End of Ximen's House

The wealth and splendor of the past
Are now as nothing.
The silver screens and golden halls
Are now the stuff of dreams.
The setting sun shines on the ruined walls
And the withered rushes.
A cold mist shrouds the ancient palace
And the green moss.
In the passage below the ground
The lamp is nearly out.
The phoenix mirror in the tiring room
Is locked and sealed away.
To whom shall I speak of ruin or prosperity?
The slow moving cloud is a priest's gown
And the wind fills its sleeves.

Han Daoguo and Wang Liu'er went back to the wine house. Their daughter had left them and they had no way of making a living. They sent Chen the Third for the merchant He. Now that Tiger Liu was no more, He had nothing to be afraid of. He came back again to Wang Liu'er. He said to Han Daoguo: "Your daughter has gone and she will not come back. I suggest that, when I have sold all my merchandise and got the money, you had better come back to Huzhou with me. It is better than carrying on this business here."

Han Daoguo thanked him and agreed. That same day the merchant sold all his goods, collected the money, hired a boat and started back with Han Daoguo and Wang Liu'er for Huzhou.

At the General's house, Han Aijie wore mourning with Cuiping. They called each other "Sister" and were very great friends. They spent their days with Chunmei. The General's little son was now six years old, and his daughter ten. The women had nothing to do but look after these children.

But the General was away on duty, and Jingji was dead. Though Chunmei had the choicest food to eat and the finest clothes to wear, though she had golden ornaments and jewels and pearls, everything that she might desire, yet at night she was lonely and she could not bear it. The fires of passion consumed her. She saw that Li An was a man full of vigor. After Zhang Sheng's death, he kept watch over the house and did his duty faithfully.

One winter day, when Li An was on duty in the office, he heard a knocking at the door and asked who was there. Whoever it was, no answer was given: he was simply bidden to open the door. He opened the door. Somebody rushed in and turned with her back to the light. Li An looked closely and saw that it was the nurse.

"Nurse," he said, "what are you doing here so late?"

"I have not come on my own account," she told him. "My lady has sent me."

"Why did she send you?"

"Don't you understand?" the nurse said, smiling. "She told me to come and see if you had gone to sleep. I was to give you these." She took some clothes from over her shoulder. They were women's clothes. "They are for your mother. The other day you had much trouble, bringing back all our master's things. And you saved my lady's life. If you had not been there that day, Zhang Sheng would have killed her."

She put down the clothes and went to the door. But she had hardly taken two steps before she turned around again. "There is something else for you," she said. From her sleeve she took a piece of silver worth about fifty taels, threw it to him, and went off. Li An could not understand what all this meant.

The next morning he took the clothes to his mother. She asked him where he had got them, and he told her what had happened the night before. His mother cried bitterly.

"Zhang Sheng," she said, "did wrong and he was killed. Now she gives you these things. What does it mean? I am more than sixty years old. Your father is dead, and you are my only hope. If anything happens to you, what will become of me? Don't go to that place again."

"If I don't go back, they will only send for me," Li An said. "What shall I do?"

"I will tell them you have a bad cold," his mother said.

"We can't tell them that story always," Li An said. "And my master will be angry with me."

"Go and spend a few months with your Uncle Li Gui," his mother said, "and then we will think what we can do."

Li An was a dutiful son. He did what his mother told him, packed up his luggage and went to Qingzhou to his uncle's place. When Chunmei found that the man did not come to her, she sent a boy for him several times. At first the old woman said her son was ill. Then people came and demanded to search the house, so she told them that he had gone to his native place to get some money. Chunmei was very disappointed.

The days passed quickly. The cold season came to an end, and the days grew warmer. In the first ten days of the first month the General, who was with eleven thousand men in Dongchangfu, sent Zhou Zhong with a letter to Chunmei. It directed his two ladies and their two children to go to him. Zhou Zhong was to stay at home to look after the place and the General's younger brother would look after the estate. This brother, Zhou Xuan, lived on the estate. Zhou Zhong and Cuiping were to remain with him. Zhou Ren with an escort of soldiers took the ladies to Dongchangfu.

At last the party arrived safely. The General was very pleased. He found a place for them at the back of his headquarters. Zhou Ren told his master that Zhou Xuan had gone to live at the house and that he and Zhou Zhong were taking care of it. Zhou Zhong was Zhou Ren's father.

"Where is Li An?" the General asked.

"You do well to mention Li An," Chunmei said. "I was very kind to him. 1 gave him clothes for his mother, thinking how he had secured Zhang Sheng that night. But one night, when he was supposed to be on guard, he came to the inner court and stole fifty taels of silver. The money, which was on the table, had come from your brother. I sent several times for him and answer came back that he was ill. Then I sent for him again, but he had run off to Qingzhou, his native place."

"I would never have believed it of him," the General said. "Later, I will see about his arrest."

Chunmei said nothing to the General about Han Aijie.

The days passed. General Zhou devoted all his energies to the duties of his office. So careful and diligent was he that he hardly took a minute for dinner in the middle of the day. He had no time at all for lovemaking.

Chunmei came to the conclusion that Zhou Yi, the second son of Zhou Zhong, was a fine, handsome lad. He was nineteen. She made her eyes and eyebrows carry a message to him and soon began an intrigue. Morning and night, they sat together, playing chess and drinking wine. The only man who did not know what was going on was the General himself.

The King of the Jin country had conquered the kingdom of Liao in the north. Then he gathered a great force and invaded China from two directions, at the very time of the new Emperor's coronation. General Nian Muhe with a hundred thousand men came down by way of Taiyuanfu in Shanxi to attack the Eastern Capital. The second general, Gan Libu, came down from Tanzhou and made a raid upon Gaoyangguan. The troops on the frontier gave way, and the Minister of War and the Commander-in-Chief sent desperate orders to the six generals of Shandong, Shanxi, Henan, Hebei, Guandong and Shaanxi, to place their troops in the road of the invading forces and protect the cities. These generals were Liu Tingqing of Shaanxi, who was in command of the Yan Sui army; Wang Bing of Guandong, who commanded the Fen Jiang army; Wang Huan of Hebei, in command of the Wei Bo army; Xin Xingzong of Ho-nan, of the Zhang De army; Yang Weizong of Shanxi with the Ze Lu army, and Zhou Xiu of Shandong with the armies of Qing and Yan.

When General Zhou realized that the barbarians were massing on the frontier in such strength, and when letters so urgent came from the Ministry of War, he at once marshaled the army and advanced with forced marches. But when his advance guard came to Gaoyangguan, the enemy had already captured that city and there had been a great slaughter there. It was the beginning of the fifth month, and the wind suddenly raised such a sandstorm that the men could not open their eyes. The General was still advancing, when suddenly the enemy attacked. An arrow struck him in the neck and pierced his throat. He fell from his horse dead. The barbarians with hooks and cords tried to secure the body, but the General's own men recovered it and brought it back on a horse. That day many soldiers were wounded. General Zhou was only forty-seven.

When Zhang Shuye, the Commissioner, saw that the general was killed on the field of battle, he immediately ordered the gongs to be sounded as a signal for retirement. The roll was called; he found how many soldiers had been killed or wounded, and took the remainder of his forces back to Dongchang. From there he sent a report to his Majesty.

The killed were brought back by the army. Chunmei and those of her household cried so loudly that the sound shook the skies. They put the general into a coffin and returned his seal of office. Then Chunmei and Zhou Ren took the coffin and went back to Qinghe.

After Chunmei had gone away, Cuiping and Han Aijie ate only the simplest of food. They kept their word and lived as widows. One day, at the beginning of summer, when everything was fresh and bright and the days were lengthening, they took a walk and came to the summerhouse in the west courtyard. There the flowers were blooming, the orioles singing, and the swallows chattering. The beauty of the scene saddened them. Cuiping was not so much depressed, but Aijie, who was thinking of Jingji, was greatly stirred. Frequently, a familiar scene will produce this effect. She wept.

While they were in this sad state, Zhou Xuan came to them. "Sisters," he said, "you must not be so melancholy. You must try to be cheerful. I myself have had several bad dreams these last few nights. I dreamed that a bow was hanging from a flagpole and that the flag was torn in half. I don't know whether the omen should be taken as good or evil."

"It may mean something about the master," Han Aijie said.

They were trying to make up their minds when Zhou Ren came to them in mourning dress. He was in a great hurry.

"Evil news," he said. "Our master died on the field of battle on the seventh day of the fifth month. The mistress and the Second Lady are bringing his coffin."

Zhou Xuan hastily made arrangements to clear the outer hall. The coffin was brought in and set down there. They made offerings to the dead general, and all the members of the household cried and lamented. Then vegetarian food was prepared, and Daoist and Buddhist priests were summoned to hold a funeral service. The two children were dressed in mourning. A host of people called to offer their condolences. Finally, a suitable day was chosen, and they buried the General in the tomb of his ancestors.

Zhou Xuan, acting for his little nephew, sent a memorial to the Emperor asking that royal homage might be offered to the dead general and that some title might be conferred upon the child. The Emperor sent a document to the Ministry of War, and the Minister of War sent it on.

> This dead General, Zhou Xiu, forgot his own life in the service of his country [the document said]. His loyalty and courage are worthy of the highest praise. His Majesty therefore appoints an officer to offer food to the dead and confers upon him the title of Marshal. His son shall receive a pension and, when he is of age, shall inherit his father's rank and position.

Chunmei had nothing to live for now but pleasure, and her passions seemed stronger than ever. She often made Zhou Yi spend the whole day with her. He came to her in the morning and did not go away till evening. They enjoyed themselves without the slightest restraint. Then Chunmei began to suffer from a wasting sickness. She took medicine, but her appetite fell off. Her spirits were depressed, and her body became very thin. Still, she never gave up the joys she most loved.

It was the sixth month, and her birthday was past. The weather was hot. She did not rise early but stayed in bed with Zhou Yi. They were doing the work of love, when suddenly, her breath grew cold. Water came from her cunt, and she died with Zhou Yi still upon her body. She was twenty-nine years old.

The young man was alarmed. He opened Chunmei's boxes and stole gold and silver and all the jewels he could lay his hands on. Then he fled.

The maids went to tell Zhou Xuan. The old man, Zhou Zhong, was put in chains and they went to find his son, Zhou Yi. He was arrested as he was going to his aunt's house. Zhou Xuan knew this, but he was afraid that all the dirty business would come out and that, if it became public property, it would be very unpleasant for his young nephew when he came of age. So he asked Zhou Yi no questions but simply ordered him to be given forty stripes. So Zhou Yi died. Jin'ge and the Second Lady were both present.

Chunmei's funeral was hastily arranged, and she was buried with the General. Zhou Xuan dismissed the two nurses and sent away the two girls, Haitang and Yuegui. Only Cuiping and Han Aijie still remained. Han Aijie refused to go.

Then the army of the Jin people captured the Eastern Capital. Both the reigning emperor, and his father were taken and sent to the north. So China was without an emperor and the empire was completely disrupted. Soldiers and war were everywhere, and men and women wandered over the face of the land. The common people cried as though they were drowning in mud, as if they were hung up by their legs. Then the barbarians invaded Shandong, and the people ran away in such a flurry that husband and wife often went in different directions. Fathers and sons lost each other. Devils cried, and Gods screamed.

Cuiping's mother took her away, and they fled for their lives. Han Aijie was left alone. She dressed herself simply, packed a few things, and set off for Linqing to find her parents. But, when she got to the wine house, the place was closed and the managers had fled. Fortunately, she met Chen the Third. He told her that her parents had gone to Huzhou with the merchant He. She went on. She had taken a moon guitar with her, and on the way she sang songs for the people. Day and night she traveled, like a stray dog escaping from confinement or a fish slipping out of the net. Her feet were very small and the journey was hard for her. After several days she came to Xuzhou. It was very late when she came to a lonely village. There she went to an old lady about seventy years old who was standing before a fire cooking rice. Han Aijie went to her and made a reverence.

"I am a native of Qinghe," she said to the old woman, "and I am on my way to find my parents because the country in the north is in such a disturbed state. It is late and I should like to spend the night with you. I must set off again early tomorrow. I will pay you."

The old woman realized that this was no poor girl. Her manner was too gentle and her face too beautiful. She asked the girl to come in and sit down. "I must get on with the cooking of this rice because the men want it," she said.

The old woman put more fuel on the fire. She prepared rice and beans, chopped up some vegetables, and put them with salt on two plates. Then a few men came in, all barelegged and rough-haired. They were wearing short trousers covered with mud. As they came in, they set down their shovels.

"Now, Mother," they said, "is dinner ready?"

"Come in and help yourselves," the old woman said to them. Each took his own food and vegetables and ate it by himself.

There was one man who seemed about forty-five or forty-six. He had a very red face and his hair was light. "Who is that sitting on the bed?" he said to the old woman.

"It is a lady from Qinghe. She is going south of the river to find her parents. It is very late, and she came and asked me if she might spend the night here."

The man asked her name.

"My name is Han," the girl said. "My father is called Han Daoguo."

The man went over to her and took her hand. "Are you not my niece, Han Aijie?" he asked her.

"You must be my uncle," Han Aijie cried.

They threw their arms around each other and wept. He asked where her parents were and why they had come back from the Eastern Capital, and how she had come to be there. Han Aijie told her uncle the whole story. "I married a man at General Zhou's place," she said. "Then my husband died and I did not marry again. Father and mother went to Huzhou with a merchant called He, and I am going to them. But the country where I have come from is in such an unsettled state that I could find no one who would take me there. So I came alone, and I have been singing on my way to get the necessaries of life. Then I met you."

"After your parents went to the Eastern Capital," Han said, "my business went to bits, so I sold the house and came here as a worker on the river. Every day, I earn just about enough to keep me. I will go with you to Huzhou."

"That will be splendid," Han Aijie said.

Her uncle gave her a bowl of rice, but it was such coarse stuff she could only swallow a mouthful. Finally, she succeeded in finishing half a bowl.

The next day, when all the other men had gone to their work, Han the Second paid the old woman and set out with Han Aijie. She was delicate and her feet were very small. The only property she had was a few pins and ornaments, and she sold these to pay for things on the journey. When they got to Huai An, they took a boat and came to Huzhou by river.

So, after a very long journey, they found Han Daoguo and his wife at Merchant He's place. He had died and left no wife, so Wang Liu'er was looking after his daughter, who was now six years old. He had left a few acres of rice fields. A year after the merchant's death, Han Daoguo died too. Wang Liu'er had been intimate with her brother-in-law before. Now they married regularly and worked in the fields to keep themselves alive.

Several of the rich young men of Huzhou wished to marry Han Aijie, when they saw how beautiful and clever she was. Her uncle urged her to marry one of them, but she cut off her hair, went to a temple, and became a nun. In her thirty-first year she fell ill and died.

The Jin army plundered Dongchangfu and came on to Qinghe. When they came there, the officers had fled and the city gates were closed, even by day. The people fled in all directions and fathers and sons lost each other. There was dust and mist everywhere, and yellow sand obscured the sun. The wild pigs and the great snakes attacked and devoured one another. Dragons and tigers fought for supremacy. Black banners and red flags appeared in the outskirts: men cried, women sobbed. There was tumult in every house. Valiant soldiers and heroic generals swarmed like ants and bees. Short daggers and long spears were as a thick bamboo forest. Here were corpses; there, decaying bones scattered on the ground. Broken swords and broken daggers lay about. People gathered their babies in their arms, bolted their doors, and shuttered their windows. They fled like rats. Nowhere was any trace of Music or the Rites.

Wu Yueniang learned that the barbarians had arrived and that people were fleeing. She took such valuables as she could and set off to Jinan with Uncle Wu the Second, Daian, Xiaoyu, and Xiaoge, who was now fifteen years old. She proposed to take refuge with Yun Lishou. Uncle Wu was dead. She locked all the doors of the house. She went to Yun Lishou; not only to escape the barbarians, but because she wished Xiaoge to marry there. On the way everybody she saw seemed terribly excited and afraid. The poor Yueniang, dressed in her plainest clothes, followed with the crowd. There were five of them altogether. They struggled and got out of the city. Then they hastened onward. At last they came to a crossroads. There stood a monk wearing a purple gown, a staff with nine rings in his hand. He had straw sandals and, on his shoulders he carried a cloth bag that contained his sacred books. He strode up to Yueniang and made a reverence to her.

"Lady," he said, "'where are you going? You must give my disciple to me now."

Yueniang was frightened and changed color.

"Father," she said, "what disciple do you mean?"

"Lady, don't pretend you do not know," the monk said. "Many years ago, when you were being pursued by Ying Tianxi at Taishan, you came to my cave and spent the night there. I am the old monk of that snow cave and my name is Pujing. You promised that I should have your baby for my disciple. Why have you not given him to me?"

"Master," Uncle Wu the Second said, "you are a priest, and you must not be so unreasonable. These are troublous times, and we are fleeing for our lives. She wants her son to continue the family. How can she let you have him?"

"Are you sure you will not give him to me?" the monk said.

"Don't talk like this, Master," Uncle Wu said. "We must be going on our way. The soldiers are behind us. Time is precious."

"It is late," the monk said. "You can go no farther now. If you will not give me the boy, come to my temple and go on your way tomorrow. Even if the Jin soldiers are coming, they will not be here yet."

"Where is your temple, Master?" Yueniang said.

The monk pointed to the other side of the road. "There is my temple," he said, and showed them the Temple of Eternal Felicity.

Yueniang had been there before and recognized the place. When they reached it, they found that the superiors had gone and there were only a few monks sitting in the hall at the back. A great glass lamp was still burning before the image of Buddha, and incense was burning too. It was nearly sunset.

Yueniang, Uncle Wu, Daian, Xiaoyu and Xiaoge spent the night in the temple. One or two of the young monks knew them and set out food for them. The old monk sat down in the hall and began to beat a wooden fish and recite the sacred books.

Yueniang, Xiaoyu, and Xiaoge slept in the same bed. Uncle Wu and Daian slept together in some other room. They were all very tired and, except for Xiaoyu, went straight to sleep. She got up and went to the room where the old monk was. Through a crack in the door she peeped in. He was still reading there.

It was the third night watch. The west wind was melancholy and the moon very dim. It was quiet everywhere. There was not a sound to be heard. The light before the statue of Buddha was very low.

Seeing the disturbed state of the Empire and the pitiful condition of the people, of whom so many had perished, the old monk was sorry. With all his heart he prayed to Buddha that their sad spirits might be purified and that hatred might cease among men. He wished to clear the path so that all might come to paradise. A hundred times he recited the same text, which was for bringing peace to the minds of men.

After a while, the cold wind came sadly. Several scores of ghosts appeared. Their heads were burned, their cheeks torn, their hair was tousled and their faces dirty. Some had broken arms and legs, some had their bellies ripped open so that their bowels protruded. Some had no heads and some no limbs. Some had died by hanging and some had chains and cangues about their necks. They all came to the old monk and stood on either side of him while he prayed for them.

"You are men who have always repaid evil by evil," the old man said to them. "You have never had a thought of reconciliation in your hearts. I ask you: when shall this hatred cease? Listen to me, and I will send you to the place of your desire."

> I exhort you
> Hate not one another
> For hate deep rooted in the heart
> Can never be done away.
> Hatred may arise in a single day
> But in ten thousand days it will still exist.
> If you use hate to combat hate
> It is as though you cast water upon snow.
> If you return hatred for hatred
> It is as though a wolf meets a scorpion.
> Of men that quarrel, none, I know
> Escapes the bitterness of hate.
> This is a year of gloom
> I wish to make you understand.
> Regard your own true nature
> Then hatred and ill will will melt away to nothing.
> I look deep into the sacred texts
> To find salvation for all evildoers.
> Go now to be born again
> And forgo hate forevermore.

The ghosts all bowed to the old monk and vanished.

Xiaoyu looked at them carefully but could not recognize any of them. After a time, there entered a tall man, seven feet high. There was an arrow in his breast. This was General Zhou. After his death on the field of battle against the barbarians, he came to the Teacher to receive his blessing. Then he went to the Eastern Capital to be born again there as Cheng Shoushan, the son of Cheng Zhen.

The General had only just gone when there came a man in beautiful clothes. He said he was a wealthy citizen of Qinghe and his name was Ximen Qing. He had died from a trouble of the blood. He received the Teacher's blessing and went to the Eastern Capital to be born again as

Cheng Yue, the son of Cheng Dong.

When Xiaoyu recognized Ximen Qing, she was afraid, and dared not make a sound.

Then came a young man with his head in his hands and his body all covered with blood. He said he was Chen Jingji and that he had been killed by Zhang Sheng. He received the Teacher's blessing and went to the Eastern Capital to become the son of a certain Wang.

When he had gone, there came a woman. She, too, held her head in her hands and her bosom was covered with blood. She said she was the wife of Wu Da and Ximen Qing's concubine, Pan Jinlian. Wu Song, her enemy, had killed her. She received the Teacher's blessing and went to the Eastern Capital to be born as the daughter of a certain Li.

Then came a short man with a purple face. He said his name was Wu and that he had been poisoned by Jinlian with the connivance of old woman Wang. He thanked the Teacher for his blessing and went to Xuzhou to be born as the son of a countryman named Fan.

He was followed by a woman, whose face was pale and thin. Water and blood issued from her body. She said she was Li Ping'er, the wife of Hua Zixu and a concubine of Ximen Qing. She received the Teacher's blessing and went to the Eastern capital to be daughter of General Yuan.

Another man followed who said he was Hua Zixu. He had died, he said, as a result of his wife's misdeeds. He received the Teacher's blessing and went to the Eastern Capital as the son of Captain Zheng.

Then came a woman whose face was pale and thin. She said she was Chunmei, the wife of General Zhou, and that she had died from overindulgence in the pleasures of love. She received the Teacher's blessing and went to the Eastern Capital to be the daughter of a wealthy man.

Then a woman whose head was bound with the wrappings of a woman's foot. She said she was the wife of Ximen Qing's servant, Laiwang. She had hanged herself. The Teacher's blessing was granted to her, and she went to the Eastern Capital to become the child of a certain Zhu.

Then came a man, naked, and with his hair all in disorder. His body was covered with bruises. His name, he said, was Zhang Sheng and he had been beaten to death. He received the Teacher's blessing and went to the Eastern Capital to be the son of a poor man named Gao.

He was followed by another woman who had a long white cloth wound around her neck. She said she was Sun Xue'e, a concubine of Ximen Qing. She had hanged herself. Now she received the Teacher's blessing and went outside the Eastern Capital to be the daughter of a poor man called Yao.

Then came a young woman who said she was Ximen's daughter and Chen Jingji's wife. She had foot ribbons about her neck. She had hanged herself. Now she received the Teacher's blessing and went outside the Eastern Capital to be the daughter of Zhong Gui, who was servant to a foreigner.

She was followed by a young man who said he was Zhou Yi. He had been beaten to death. He received the Teacher's blessing and went to the Eastern Capital to be the son of a certain Gao. He was going to be called Gao Liuzhu. Then he vanished.

Xiaoyu was terrified and shivering. She realized that this monk could indeed speak to the ghosts. She wished to tell Yueniang what she had seen, but Yueniang was fast asleep and dreaming. She dreamed that she and those with her had with them a hundred large pearls and a ring of great value. They were going to Jinanfu to see Yun Lishou. They reached the city and asked for Yun's place. Then people told Yun, and he knew that she had come about their children's marriage. They greeted one another as old friends. Mistress Yun had recently died and Yun sent for his neighbor, old woman Wang, to entertain Yueniang. She was taken to the inner court and given a great feast. Uncle Wu the Second and Daian were entertained elsewhere.

Then Yueniang talked about the marriage of their children and the troubles in the country. She offered the hundred pearls and the precious ring. Yun Lishou took them but said nothing about the marriage. In the evening, he told old woman Wang to sleep with Yueniang. He wished her to talk to Yueniang and find out what she thought.

The old woman said to Yueniang that, although Yun Lishou was only a military officer, he was an educated gentleman. Since they had arranged the marriage between their children, he had taken a great fancy to her. Now his wife was dead and he had not remarried. Though his position was not very high, he rode on horseback and had soldiers under his command. When he dismounted, he attended to public business. He had powers of life and death.

"Lady," the old woman said, "unless you think he is too far beneath you, he would ask you to marry him and it will be to the advantage of you both. Your son can marry too and he can go home when peace returns."

When Yueniang heard this, she was amazed. For a long time she could not speak. Then the old woman went to Yun Lishou and told him. The next evening, Yun Lishou prepared a great feast in the hall and invited Yueniang. She believed it was to celebrate the wedding of their children and went gladly. When she sat down, he said: "Sister, this is but a poor city, but I have a number of soldiers under my command. I have gold, property, clothes, and jewels in plenty. But I have no wife to manage my home for me. I have been thinking of you all this time, and now I feel like a man dying of thirst who craves for water to drink, or as one who seeks coolness in the broiling heat. You have come here, Lady, for your son's marriage. It is surely the will of Heaven that we should arrange not one but two marriages. If we marry, we shall be happy all our lives here. And I see no reason why we should not."

Yueniang was very angry. "I did not realize," she said, "that beneath a human form you hid the carcass of a dog. My husband always treated you well, yet now you speak to me in the language of dogs and horses."

Yun Lishou smiled and went closer to her. He put his arms about her and pleaded.

"Lady," he said, "why did you come here? You came and, why I cannot tell, my spirit seemed to become wholly yours the moment I saw you. I cannot help it, and we must marry."

He offered wine to her.

"Send for my brother," Yueniang said.

"Your brother!" Yun Lishou said, laughing. "I have killed both him and Daian." He ordered a servant to bring proof of what he said. Two heads, blood still dripping from them, were brought in. Yueniang looked at them in the candlelight and her face became as pale as yellow earth. She cried and fell to the floor. Yun Lishou raised her up.

"Lady," he said, "you must not be sad. Your brother is dead, but I am asking you to marry me. I am not unworthy of you. I am a military officer of high rank."

"This man," Yueniang thought, "has murdered my brother and my servant. If I do not yield, he will kill me too." She began to smile.

"You must do what I wish," she said, "and then I will marry you."

"I will do anything you ask, no matter what it is," Yun Lishou said.

"First let your daughter marry my boy, and then I will marry you."

"Good!" Yun Lishou said. He sent for his daughter and pushed her over to Xiaoge. They drank wine together, exchanged the knotted heart, and so were married. Then Yun Lishou pulled Yueniang to him, and wished to make love to her, but she struggled with him. He was furious.

"You whore!" he cried, "you have deceived me. You got me to marry my daughter to your son. Do you think I am afraid to kill your son?" He drew his sword, and with one blow struck off the boy's head. The blood spurted for yards.

When her child was killed, Yueniang shrieked.

Then she woke up. It was a dream. She was so terrified that her body was drenched with sweat. "Strange! Strange!" she murmured.

"Lady, why are you crying?" Xiaoyu said to her.

"I have had a terrible nightmare," Yueniang said, and told her everything she had dreamed.

"A little while ago," Xiaoyu said, "I found I could not sleep. I went to watch the old monk. He was speaking to the ghosts. I saw him talking to my master, the Fifth Lady, Chen Jingji, Sun Xue'e, General Zhou, Lai-wang's wife and your daughter. Then they all disappeared."

"Some of them were buried outside this temple," Yueniang said, "but they died such miserable deaths that they come to the monk. It is so quiet too."

The two women talked until the fifth night watch. The cocks began to crow. Yueniang washed her face and dressed her hair. Then she went to the sanctuary and burned incense before the statue of Buddha. The old monk was there, sitting on a low stool. "Lady," he said in a loud voice, "I think you know now what I mean."

Yueniang knelt down. "Holy Master," she said, "with my fleshly eyes and human body, I did not know that you were Buddha himself. Now, since I have had that dream, I know everything."

"You understand," the old monk said, "so now there is no need for you to go to that man. If you do go, you will find that things happen exactly as they did in your dream. You will all die. It is fortunate for your son that you have met me. It is a reward for your good heart. Had it not been for this, you and your son must soon have parted. You remember what a bad man your husband Ximen Qing was. Your son is your husband. He would spend all your money, ruin your estate, and die by having his head cut off. Now I bless him, and take him as my disciple. You know the proverb that says when a son becomes a monk there is salvation for nine generations. If he becomes a monk, your husband's misdeeds will be forgiven. If you do not believe me, come and see."

He rose and went quickly to the other room where Xiaoge was asleep. The old monk lifted his staff and gently touched the boy's head. He turned around suddenly, and Yueniang saw that it was Ximen Qing. Upon his neck was a heavy cangue and there were chains about his waist. The old monk touched him again with his staff, and again Xiaoge lay upon the bed.

Yueniang cried. She realized that Xiaoge was another incarnation of Ximen Qing. After a while the boy woke up.

"You are going to stay here," his mother said to him, "and become the disciple of this holy teacher. He will cut off your hair and give you orders in the name of Buddha."

Yueniang took the lad in her arms and cried bitterly. She felt that she had brought him up in vain. He was fifteen years old, and she had hoped that he would inherit the property and continue the family. Now the old monk was taking him. Uncle Wu the Second, Xiaoyu, and Daian were all sad. The old monk took the boy and called him Mingwu [Bright Enlightenment].

When Yueniang was going away, the old monk said to her: "You need go no farther. The Jin army is going to retreat. Then land will be divided between two dynasties and we shall have an Emperor again. In ten days all the soldiers will withdraw and peace will be restored. Go home then and spend the rest of your days in peace."

"Master," Yueniang said, "you have blessed my child. When shall I see him again?" She clasped the boy in her arms and cried aloud.

"Lady, don't cry," the old monk said. "Look, there is a Holy Master coming."

They all turned their heads to look, but when they turned around again, the old monk had vanished and become a pure vapor. He took Xiaoge with him.

Yueniang, her brother, and the others stayed ten days more at the temple. Then indeed the Jin people made Zhang Bangchang Emperor at the Eastern Capital, and set up a new administration, both civil and military. The two emperors, Huizong and Qinzong, were taken to the north. Then Prince Kang crossed the river on a clay horse and established himself as Emperor Gaozong at Jiankang. He appointed Zong Ze as his commander-in-chief and took back Shandong and Hebei. Thus the empire was divided into two parts. Soon peace was restored, and people returned to their old occupations. Yueniang went home. She opened all the doors and windows. Nothing had been disturbed.

She gave the name Ximen An to Daian who, in due course, came into the property. People called him Master Ximen. He lived with Yueniang. When she was seventy years old, Yueniang died. Her end was peaceful, a fitting reward for her kindness and virtue.

> The record of this house must make us sad.
> Who can deny that Heaven's principle
> Goes on unceasingly?
> Ximen was mighty and a lawless man
> He could not maintain the issue of his house.
> Jingji was wild and dissolute
> And met a violent death in consequence.
> Yueniang and Yulou lived long
> And ended their days in peace.
> Chunmei and Ping'er were wanton
> And soon made their way to Hell.
> It is not strange, therefore,

That Jinlian reaped the reward of evil,
Leaving a foul reputation to be spoken of
A thousand years.

THE END

"Books to Span the East and West"

Tuttle Publishing was founded in 1832 in the small New England town of Rutland, Vermont [USA]. Our core values remain as strong today as they were then—to publish best-in-class books which bring people together one page at a time. In 1948, we established a publishing outpost in Japan—and Tuttle is now a leader in publishing English-language books about the arts, languages and cultures of Asia. The world has become a much smaller place today and Asia's economic and cultural influence has grown. Yet the need for meaningful dialogue and information about this diverse region has never been greater. Over the past seven decades, Tuttle has published thousands of books on subjects ranging from martial arts and paper crafts to language learning and literature—and our talented authors, illustrators, designers and photographers have won many prestigious awards. We welcome you to explore the wealth of information available on Asia at **www.tuttlepublishing.com**.